D1648520

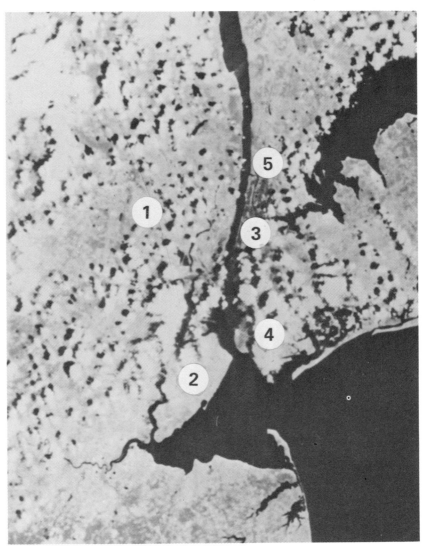

As seen from space: New Jersey (1); Staten Island (2); Manhattan Island (3); Long Island (4); Westchester (5). Courtesy, National Aeronautics and Space Administration.

CAMPAIGN OF CHAOS ...1776

In the Jaws of the Juggernaut an Eaglet Held the Stars

PETER HENDERSON

1975

ARCHIVES INK, LTD., Publisher

Box 1776

Haworth, New Jersey   07641

First Limited Edition, 1975

Library of Congress Cataloging in Publication Data

Henderson, Peter, 1908–
     Campaign of chaos — 1776

     Bibliography: p.
     Includes index.
     1.   United States—History—Revolution—Campaigns
and battles—Fiction.   I. Title.
PZ4.H5114Cam   [PS3558.E493]   813'.5'4   75-9231
ISBN 0-915528-01-0

PRINTED IN THE UNITED STATES OF AMERICA

COMPOSED, PRINTED AND BOUND BY
LithoCrafters, Inc.
Ann Arbor, Michigan

To

Elisabeth Murphy Henderson,
My Wife, My Critic, My Rock
and My Love

CAMPAIGN OF CHAOS — 1776 . . .

In the Jaws of the Juggernaut An Eaglet Held the Stars

[A Documentary of the Revolutionary
War's New York-New Jersey Campaign
of 1776]

By Peter Henderson
A.B., University of North Carolina
M.A., Montclair State, New Jersey
Ed.D., New York University

An Historical Novel

Campaign of Chaos — 1776 *is a carefully documented account of the historically slighted episodes in the crises hours of America's birth. Into these events is woven an Eighteenth Century romance with a number of fictional characters whose lives are blended into the historical narration. These "people of the period" are clearly distinguished from the historical figures in this story of a nation born out of colonies.*

Each of the thirty-five chapters in the book centers on a day, a date of historical significance, in the campaign's perilous 181 days following the American nation's conception on July 4. Considerable focus is placed on the much-ignored military contribution of the Palisades along the Hudson. Around the Palisades and the river develops the unfolding drama, taking the reader through the critical hours and principal battles. The work closes following the tragic march through the Jerseys, ending with the climactic Battle of Princeton, Friday, January 3, 1777.

Contents

Part III Disaster

Part IV Hope

Maps and Illustrations

Some of the maps, illustrations and research data used in this work have been extracted from the author's original treatise, *Shadow On the River*, copyright, 1959. In that mimeographed study, data, maps and illustrations, though not all used, were courteously provided for the author's assistance by, among others: The British Museum, London; The War Records Branch, National Archives and Records Service, Washington, D.C.; The Library of Congress, Washington, D.C.; The William Clements Library, Ann Arbor, Michigan; The New York City Public Library; The New York Historical Society, New York City; The New Jersey Historical Society, Newark, New Jersey; The Bergen County Historical Society, Hackensack, New Jersey; The U.S. Military Academy, West Point, New York; The Pierpont Morgan Library, New York City; Colonial Williamsburg, Virginia; Princeton University Library, Princeton, New Jersey; The Valley Forge Park Commission, Valley Forge, Pennsylvania; and numerous regional libraries, librarians and their assistants in both the United States and England.

Regretfully, many of these maps and illustrations and others, since provided the author by the above and other sources, cannot be used owing to space limitations. However, those used herein will be properly credited to the best of the author's knowledge as of the date of publication. For any errors and omissions the author humbly apologizes.

Preface

In the pages of this work the reader will be taken back to the last six months of Seventeen Hundred and Seventy-six. It was that half-year, during a period of one hundred and eighty-one days following the signing of the Declaration of Independence, that the union of the independent states of America teetered daily and precariously on the precipice of failure. One misstep would send it hurtling into treason, disgrace and death. One misstep would bind it forever, a dependency under the reins of a monarchy.

All eyes of the Eighteenth Century world were focused upon the tragic drama which in England acquired the name of "The New York Campaign of 1776." It was the aftermath of the Crown's adamant decision that the colonies of North America must bend under the rule of the United Kingdom of Great Britain.

Thus the New York Campaign became the crash campaign to crush the American Rebellion. But its initial momentum under the British commander slowly wound itself down in the face of unanticipated defiance. It therefore dragged out into unexpected days, weeks and months—months, owing to that defiance, which would become years. At the end of the 1776 crisis year, it became evident, despite the many more crises to come, that eventually the war's outcome would bring failure to the British Empire.

It is the salient days of this 1776 crisis period which this work attempts to relive and re-enact, particularly those days and events which history has glossed over or ignored. Each will be envisioned, as much as possible, viewed from the American center of the campaign's principal intelligence seat—the high rock on the bluff promontory of the giant Palisades of the Hudson River.

For it was there that once was located the very heart and pulse of the American army's central department under the American Commander-in-Chief.

The Northern Department under Major General Philip Schuyler was occupied defending the Canada border; and the southern division, to which Major General Charles Lee was assigned to counterattack General Sir Henry Clinton's move in South Carolina, was defending Charleston. Neither of these movements is examined in this work.

The principal emphasis here is on the frightfully awesome and tragic struggle of the American forces in New York and New Jersey against the greatest army and armada in all Europe.

Campaign of Chaos — 1776

The Palisadean Bluff Rock site has been chosen, not only owing to its military location, but because the author has visualized in it, the laughter, love, tragedy, death and despair—and finally the hope—prevalent in every American colonial village in those crucial days. And from here he imaginatively visualizes the new nation physically rising from out of the womb in which it was conceived July 4 to begin its extraordinary trek into world destiny.

Although the work is carefully documented with largely primary source references in respect to the military movements and occurrences relative to the entire campaign of those momentous months, the author has introduced a number of fictional characters and events pertaining to it.

Many of these figures are drawn from the lives of people who actually did exist at that time. Some have been taken from Eighteenth Century tales and folk stories, handed down through generations. And in the process their actual existences have been colored by imagination, exaggeration and additions—most of which could be true.

Note:

Author's Friendly Suggestion to Readers

To enjoy *Campaign of Chaos — 1776* the author suggests that the reader ignore the numerical references until after having read through the chapters of the work. The numerical references to sources found scattered through the pages of the book are principally the works or authorities consulted in documenting the history.

These "Notes" will mainly interest historians and scholars desiring to examine the author's treatment of the Eighteenth Century Revolutionary War literature. It is hoped that they will provide dispute leading to further research into this important epoch in the American nation's genesis, for there is much of the great campaign that is yet to be treated and substantiated.

However, the interruption of the reader's travels through this era of America's past by stopping to delve into "Notes" will rob him of full enjoyment of these historic moments. They will frankly dull his journey through the book's many landmarks that lie largely buried under today's "megalopolis."

Therefore the author recommends that if maximum reading pleasure is desired the reference notes of the work be disregarded until after a first leisurely reading.

Peter Henderson

Part I

Defense

1

Friday, July 12. . .

The Invading Fleet Bares Its Fangs

Where Sailed the *Half-Moon*

S uddenly, seemingly out of nowhere, the dark storm-laden clouds swiftly gather ominously and directly over the smoothly sailing little pettiauger, *Hope*, and its three occupants. The small but solid little river sloop had bucked the tide after leaving the Bull's Ferry landing, the only stop on its long way downriver to New York town.

Slowly under the Palisades the little craft glides in midstream, well off from Wehawk and the Hoboken ferry dock south of it. It is bound for the Cortlandt Street landing pier on Manhattan Island's west side, north of the American rebel army's river batteries.

Papa Pete Baummeister knows old Hendrick Hudson's river and its ways. He knows the waters as well as he knows the grim Palisadean walls, rising above them out of the deep river's bottom to three and almost four hundred feet in places.

"Kom aft back here und take der till, Ellie," he calls to his daughter in the bow.

And she does so quickly. For 18-year-old Elaine Baummeister can handle a sloop as well as any man on the river.

"Paully," he orders his timid, nine-year-old son, "git forw'd und hold dot shib line, vile I da mains'l reef. Zen push doz boxes mit berries und tings up forw'd out da vay! Quick!"

The boy promptly obeys. Paul is opposite from his somewhat tomboyish sister and her unpredictable ways. Both of Baummeister's children are by nature studious. Paul has ever hungrily sought something to read ever since his tutorial-minded sister first taught him how.

Strangely, however, his terrible fear of drowning always draws him hauntingly toward all tales of the sea and man's terminal battles with the conquering forces of water in nature's unrelenting dominion. But death or dying in any other form summons up no fears whatsoever in his mind. This is the reward of youth. Only the thought of drowning terrifies him.

So the scholarly youngster has never displayed much interest in water. In fact he has never shown an attachment for anything which is not well secured to Mother Earth. So Paul particularly dislikes getting caught in one of the river's violent squalls. The boy has heard many hair-rising stories that have instilled in him a deep-seated fear of what many still call the North River. To the Baummeisters, and to many others, it is the Dutch discoverer's river. It is Hudson's river. But to Paul it is water. And water, except in books, is frightening.

There are many who describe in their own fashion the explorer's ancient ascent up the waters. Some tell of the Lenni Lenape's welcome to the rich lands and of the generosity which provided the white men all the food and supplies needed. Settlers still show where, on the Manhattan Island side, the *Half-moon* anchored. Paul knows all that, yet it does not change his opinion of the river on which he lives.

Both Paul and Elaine are good swimmers. Their father has always insisted on that. Those living by waters must know how to walk on them, he has told his children.

However, river squalls are something to be feared even by good swimmers. Baummeister had not expected to encounter storms today. Right now, as he glances overhead and then downriver, something else seems to be bothering him.

It is the masts and sails in the far distant outer bay, some of which seem to be unfurling canvas. Probably they are headed out to sea. But what if they are headed north upriver in his direction? He decides to keep his observation to himself.

Throughout the long months on the cliff's side, Elaine and Paul have looked forward to the summer trip which the ferrymaster makes to New York town. Always he and his wife, Marie Louise, load their sloop, *Hope*, with presents for the Baummeister's city

relatives. That is if the ferry business, run and owned by old
Stephen Bourdette,[1] has had a profitable year.

This is the first of the year's four seasonal trips which Marie
Louise has missed. In fact she had opposed the children's going
after having been overruled by her husband in urging it be canceled.

The British ships, numbering in the hundreds and standing at
anchor off Staten Island, have not only given Marie Louise something to fear, they have put all of New York and New Jersey as
well as the Continental Congress, in a state of alarm.

Refusing to be intimidated by a show of strength, only Old
Stephen, and Papa Pete, two very stubborn, self-willed Dutchmen,
give little indication of apprehension over the English fleet
assembled below The Narrows, that swiftly flowing river-pass
between Brooklyn and Staten Island separating the upper from the
lower New York Bay.

Mention of the British and their threatening might, merely
causes both men to momentarily take their clay pipes out of their
mouths and insolently spit upon the ground. It is because they
recognize each other's stubborn headstrong natures and fully
respect the other's accepted peculiarities, that the two elderly men
get along so well together.

So no British ship in the outer lower bay is big enough, or so
Baummeister thinks, to stop him and his children from their
routine pilgrimage to New York town. However, Paul would have
much rather spent the day on the great Bluff Rock above the ferry
where his schoolmarmish sister often takes him and other youngsters of the river's edge to give them some schooling.

Certainly he would prefer to be there now instead of out on the
churning river under a threatening summer squall. And as if that
were not enough to worry a terrified landlubber, the whole of the
King of England's navy is gathered just 12 miles below New York,
ready at any moment to pounce upon the port city with thousands
of British and Hessian soldiers.

Then out of the darkening sky, one lightning bolt after the
other streaks through the warm air. Each seems to be accompanied
by ear-splitting explosions from the heavens that now open up
with a cloudburst of rain, hail and wind.

Transformed from bright sunlight into a twilight darkness in
only minutes, the early afternoon seems to have been suddenly
swallowed up by the wild white-capping river waves, angrily
thrown in all directions by the black clouds' whistling winds.

Like the poundings of a giant anvil, the blasts of thunder crash against the Palisadean walls of igneous rock and echo back and forth across the violently seething waters. In the semi-darkness, the gusting winds with ferocious spurts, slam their sprayed beads into the faces of all three busy hands. They drench the little vessel and its oilskin-covered occupants.

Wind, rain and hail seem intent upon combining all of nature's elements for the sole purpose of destroying *Hope*. Yet on she streaks beside the furious wind. But she carries far too much sail for safety. That Pete realizes as he struggles to haul the mainsail down.

To be caught in the very eye of a violent squall is something that 50-year-old Baummeister would ordinarily enjoy. But not this time. His children are his life. He is not one to take chances with them. He knows now that he has delayed too long in heading for the nearest Jersey or New York shore.

Seeking a scapegoat for his mistake, since by nature he is a man reluctant to admit error, he blames the British ships in the distance. He had been sure that his observation was correct and the frigates were headed for the upper bay. He had not wanted to arouse the children's fear and, therefore, had said nothing.

Sighting the British ships had put an entirely new complexion on the proposed New York visit. The armed frigates excited his concern and monopolized his attention. Unconsciously, he ignored the gathering clouds overhead.

Absorbed by the vessels in the distance, he silently weighed their intentions. Then, drawn back to the increasing threat overhead, he pondered whether to make for shore, or attempt to reach the Cortlandt Street wharf before the storm broke and before the warships ascended the water way if, indeed, that was their aim.

Obstinacy, defiance and determination overruled sound judgment. Baummeister set a course for New York town. Then the storm struck.

A wild blast of wind suddenly tears the sail from his hands. Much like a horse that has broken its tether, the little boat spins around in the severe blow. A gust blasts itself against her open canvas and her beam, careening *Hope* until her mast is almost parallel with the frothing seas.

For a few seconds the pettiauger appears doomed. Instinctively reacting in accordance with their knowledge of boat handling, both Elaine and Paul, along with their father, immediately throw their weight to the starboard side when the gust strikes.

All three know the *Hope's* idiosyncrasies. No Baummeister has to be told how to act under emergencies. Not a second too soon the shifted weight slowly pulls the keel back and steadily it drops into the river righting the little craft.

Baummeister, an old veteran of the sea and its battles, recovers the mainsail lines, hauls them taut and manages finally to reef the canvas. His pipe still in his mouth is as wet and dripping as his wind-blown face.

Ahead of them now is the biggest task of the struggle. To keep the wildcat craft close into the storm's head. To ride it out without running aground on the reefs that lie along the New York shore.

Elaine holds the bow close into the wind while her brother bails with all the strength he can summon. He takes time out only to push the crates of berries and garden produce up under the bow's bulkhead.

Now the sturdy old sloop begins literally to fly with the wind over the brining, foaming cresting waves, criss-crossing with the strong current against the incoming tide. Attempting to tighten his stays and, at the same time control the boom, Baummeister, hatless as are his son and daughter, stands framed, pointing with his finger to the course he wants Elaine to follow. She struggles to keep the vessel pointed in the direction indicated by her father's ghost-like finger, seen through the mist of the rain-swept bow.

Her brother, frightened by the thoughts of drowning, prompted by the tales he has heard of capsized boats in storm-tossed waters, looks up for encouragement at the calm, serious face of his sister behind the tiller. Paul feels he is facing a reality he has acknowledged but one he has not had any desire to experience. From his sister he has always received a boost in confidence whenever he needs it. Now he needs it.

Staying low and working himself aft along the gunwale toward Elaine at the helm, Paul reaches her. He has succeeded in concealing his fear of water from his father—a thing the sea-loving man would never understand in *his* son.

So, in a low voice but loud enough for his understanding sister to hear over the roar of the wind and the flying sheets of hail and rain, he asks, as though she had omnipotent knowledge of earth, sea and air, "Are we go'n drown, Ellie? We are. Ain't we?"

His words are definite. His wide eyes, wet with tears and rain drops, reflect resignation.

Though strained under the tension of her task in edging the

leaning, speeding pettiauger just so close and no farther into the violent wind, she speaks, in answer, without taking her eyes off the bow and her father's occasionally pointing finger.

"Not *ain't*, Paul. You know better. "*Aren't*," she replies, totally ignoring his fright and revealing her schoolmarm side for her young brother's benefit, as usual.

Pausing as her father brings the boom around and as she adjusts the tiller, Elaine finally answers Paul, though not once taking her eyes off the bouncing bowsprit.

"No! No we *ain't*. We *are not* going to drown! How many times have you heard Papa say: 'When everything else is lost, then you still have God. And in God is hope.' . . . Now get you back there! And you just bail, pray and hope! Quickly now!"

"But where's God now when we needs him?" Paul queries hopelessly. "He ain't seemin' to watch none while all this water is a'comin' in!"

"I meant, 'isn't,' Ellie!" he hollers back over the noise of the howling wind.

But he obeys his sister. He has had his reassurance from Heaven's principal earthly plenipotentiary, insofar as he is concerned.

Paul is now fully satisfied that "the Other World," which the Preacher Domine Remlin talks about, is not, as he had thought back there for a few moments, just over *Hope's* bowspirt. Obediently back to his task he goes with restored vigor.

Never has the old pettiauger moved so swiftly. Elaine, keyed high with the thrill of danger which is in radical contrast with her routine life on the water's edge under The Mountain, is certain that the rugged little river boat is speeding faster than it has ever gone before. On it ploughs at a frightening clip, riding out the storm.

For twenty minutes that seem like an eternity, Baummeister wrestles with the loosening stays, the flapping canvas and the violently straining boom fighting to be set free. The boy bails furiously with both hands, calling upon every ounce of his strength. He stops intermittently only long enough to push the shifting berry boxes back up under the bow, while his sister, like a veteran mariner, keeps the craft exactly on her father's pointed finger course.

She is sure now, as the mist rises and the shrouded grayish curtain lifts revealing the spectral-like outline of the Jersey shore, that Papa has purposely been heading them for the Paulus Hook

ferry and the army post beside it. She does not question him. She
never has and never would. But she knows his reason. She, too,
had seen the towering masts of the British square-riggers far in the
distance, full-blown in the wind.

One glimpse of them and she knew her father's thoughts.

Men-of-War Port of Bow

Despite the whistling gale of the cloudburst and its pelting rain
and hail, Elaine knew her father's pointed-finger course was not
directed to Manhattan Island's tip. Her long auburn tresses stream
behind her less wildly now as the lightning and thunder let up and
the wind and rain slowly subside, causing the vessel to slacken
speed and slowly thump less regularly over the pounding waves.
The keeling craft straightens slightly, lifting the port beam higher
off the seas' churning surface.

Then, almost as abruptly as it had closed in upon them, the
severity of the storm dissipates over the vessel, leaving its occupants sodden wet and looking half-drowned. Their battered ship, in
disarray, seems, however, to be proudly holding up her bow in
successful defiance to the retreating forces of nature.

Dispersed as though by a rescuing angel, the angry elements
withdraw and the sun peeps through again. Reluctantly the winds
give in, receding upriver with their black cloud mantle.

Suddenly, lifting out from behind the distant spectral curtain,
the shores of the river appear, bathed in bright warm sunlight. The
calming sea, the earth and air around it on either side look as
though no raindrop or hail pellet had ever fallen. The blue sky
turns into its heaven once again.

But definitely, way downriver, far off in the distance, approach
two mighty British ships of war and their tenders. Clearly they can
be seen catching the westerly breeze. They are unquestionably
headed for the upper bay into Manhattan's tip.

Baummeister now knows that he has made a wise decision in
changing his course during the storm from the Cortlandt dock to
Jersey's Paulus Hook. There is their only refuge. The Paulus Hook
Post and the Van Vorst's ferry on the Jersey side make a safe haven.

Constantly clenching the perpetually held clay pipe between his
teeth—a seemingly physically attached extension of his profile—
Baummeister relieves his daughter at the helm. The girl knows her
duties without being told. She automatically goes forward and
unreefs the mainsail.

There is plenty of time to get out of the midstream and clear of the King's armored frigates. The men-of-war are still a long way off from Manhattan's southernmost battery. Both Elaine and Paul gaze in awe upon the distant sight.

Before them is war in the making. Never have they seen so many ships' masts as now rise up with their countless spars from the surface of the outer bay off Staten Island. They had heard the river men talk of the "sea of masts" in the bay. There it is before their eyes.

Now off the pettiauger's starboard bow looms the welcome refuge, Paulus Hook. The fort's flag can be seen flying high over the main six-gun parapet. Vaguely visible behind the tall stockaded abatis, and northeast of the main works, is the lengthy oblong redoubt.[2]

The entire post is an island, approached by a bridge from the northwest. There, the Causeway, which comes down from the heights, passing Prior's mill and through the salt marshes past Van Vorst's place, runs to the east of the work's moat and on to the ferry landing.

It is a pleasing sight to Baummeister who had, for the past few moments, experienced more trepidation than his customary bold front would allow him to reveal. He breathes much easier, finds some dry tobacco and, tries unsuccessfully, to light his pipe.

Then, suddenly, trouble!

Within 300 feet of the ferry cove's haven, *Hope's* rudder snaps. Either loosened during the storm, or struck by some submerged jetsam on the ferry approach, it now refuses to respond.

Uncontrolled, the helpless sloop, her boom spanking back and forth as the pettiauger bobs around with the wind, falls to the mercy of the outgoing tide. Immediately, Elaine, calling her brother to her aid, hauls down the mainsail and lowers the jib, while her irate father tries to discover the rudder's breakdown.

His profanity, which often borders on blasphemy, is safely couched in Dutch and French terms and whatever other languages and expressions he has acquired from his early life as a seaman. His children have learned to disregard his rare tirades. They, like his beloved Marie Louise, know they amount to little and merely give vent to his anger, which occasionally slips away from his usual calm gentle manner.

Then he and Elaine, with an oar on either side, attempt to paddle the loaded craft shoreward while Paul, using a canoe paddle in the stern, attempts to steer it toward the ferry landing.

. .All had heard of the "sea of masts" in the bay . . Archibald Robertson painting, Spencer Collection, The New York Public Library (View of the Narrows with Lord Howe coming in, July 12, 1776).

But all is in vain. The vessel drifts with the strongly flowing current farther and farther away from the wharf.

Before the storm, soldiers had gathered along the rampart's earthworks behind the parapet to observe the frigates moving northward in the distant outer bay. And the ferry passengers, irate over the cancellation of the early afternoon ferry on orders of Colonel John Durkee,[3] had gathered along the Causeway near the ferry tavern and the stagecoach stables. They complained that the ferry could have crossed safely before the frigates would have come anywhere near it. Then the storm drove them to cover, but not before a few had pointed out the sole river boat, a pettiauger, making its way downriver toward the Cortlandt landing.

Throughout the violent squall, all wondered how the little sailing vessel was faring in the blow. Their concern for the major drama, the warships, all of a sudden took second place. The side show became the main attraction.

Usually a dull uneventful place since the horse races were discontinued owing to the war, Paulus Hook, or Powles Hook and Powleshook, as some natives still call it, is suddenly alive with the excitement of two dramatic events taking place around it.

A few had witnessed, through the gray misty light of the storm, the valiant struggle of the sailing craft. Others now come, hearing that a little pettiauger is headed straight into the path of an approaching British man-of-war.

The stranded ferry passengers now forget their irritation with the post's commander. They are resigned to the fact that Durkee will keep the ferry closed until it can be ascertained what the enemy ships are up to.

Durkee also demanded that all those civilians and others, not under the jurisdiction of the fort, stay inland and away from the water-front in fear of a possible surprise bombardment by the approaching enemy ships. Thus far, few have bothered to obey the orders, preferring to watch the sloop which has changed its course, after coming through the squall, and is now headed for the post.

Besides, except for a few lonesome sentries, Colonel Durkee and his men are on the island across the moat and are busy preparing for a possible brush. Furthermore, no guns have ever been fired in any battle hereabouts. Why should the British begin now? So only the obedient and timid move back inland.

Then, when it is only a hundred yards or so from the dock, the sloop spins suddenly in a crazy gyration. It is evident that something has happened to throw it out of control and send it cavorting in circles. Then all her sails are quickly hauled. Ignoring the pending war drama in the distance, those on shore fasten their eyes on the pettiauger's latest predicament.

Realizing the current is too strong to buck, Baummeister throws over his anchor. Ignorant of *Hope's* problem, those on shore watch the figure of a man on the port side and a woman on the starboard attempt to paddle as the youngster in the stern struggles to steer. They cannot understand the boat's strange action until the anchor is thrown overboard. Then the cause of the trouble is realized.

Five of the waiting ferry passengers who arrived behind the stage in an army wagon from Newark, are on the way to the New York encampment. All five are army personnel with varying assignments and missions.

One, newly commissioned Lieutenant John Gray, a tall, lanky Philadelphian, is on his way to report to the Continental Army's artillery commander, Colonel Henry Knox. Another is Captain Charles Craig, who heads a special company of scouts and is traveling with his Indian sergeant, Andrew Abbott, a tall, straight figure who, most of the time has been occupied in trying to hold up the heavily inebriated captain. Both members of the scouts have been inspecting horses for army purchase and are returning from the West Jersey province.

The fourth and fifth are a freed Negro and his son. Private Tom Graves, known as "Big Tom," owing to his height, bulk and strength, is attached to an artillery battery on Manhattan. With him is his son, Jocko, who goes wherever his widower father is assigned. The boy carries his own weight with the American army. Big Tom is returning from Amboy where he had delivered two wagons and teams to General Hugh Mercer, commander of the Jersey post opposite Staten Island.

All five are attached, or to be attached, to General Nathanael Greene's command on Manhattan Island. All five have traveled together from Newark where they all met and found their destinations the same. Least communicative have been the drunken captain and the taciturn Indian sergeant.

All seemingly have found a strange relaxation and friendly comradeship through each other's company in the back of the ammunition carrying six-team wagon. Many have been the stops at inns and taverns along the way.

Despite the critical glances they have received by eyes which have silently revealed their qualms about mixing whites, blacks,

Indians and a drunken captain, they have all held firmly together
in an inexplicable loyalty that has presented a formidable front,
unchallenged at two taverns and now at Michael Cornelisen's.[4]

Few of the ferry passengers, in the short time the five men have
been on the Hook, have dared to even as much as raise an
eyebrow. And this respect comes as much from the rough and
tumble, motley mixture of men of the fort, supposedly the hard
core of the Flying Camp, as it does from the citizenry.

So, drawn outside the tavern after the storm, the five travelers
join the curious on-lookers along the north side of the ferry slip.
Puzzled at first, they know that sooner or later someone will have
to do something about the little ship's erratic behavior.

To most, it is evident the craft is in need of help. And fast! If
the anchor drags, as anchors do in these waters, and the pettiauger
is seriously disabled, it could be thrown to the swift tide and the
stiffening late afternoon breeze. It might then drift out helplessly
into the bay and into the path of the oncoming men-of-war.

And certainly, if the enemy frigates decide to shell the Hook's
works, the crippled sloop would be in the ships' direct line of fire.

Wearing light buckskins, Indian moccasins and a band holding in
his long black hair, Sergeant Andrew Abbott has held himself
silently, slightly apart from his companions. He stands beside Craig
who is in a half stupor leaning his back against one of the wharf's
pilings. Busy preventing the captain from indulging in further
libations, Abbott has not paid much attention to the pettiauger
and its problem off to the northeast.

His eyes finally focus upon it along with everyone else's on the
Causeway and the dock. The Indian squints and brings his hand
over his eyes.

Like a hunter who has suddenly espied his quarry, he straightens
and then looks more sharply at the small river boat tugging at its
anchor and bobbing like a cork. The scout drops his cupped hand
from over his eyes and swiftly runs to the far end of the dock for a
closer look.

In a minute he is back, trying to arouse Craig who now has
gently drifted from the hands of Bacchus into the all-encompassing arms of Morpheus. In short he is, Abbott realizes, dead
drunk.

In disgust, the Indian sergeant looks down at the well-known
and well-informed white man army captain of the wilderness scouts
whose tracking knowledge and acquaintance with the Pennsylvania,
Jersey and New York colonial lands, forests streams and highways,

has made him, despite his drunkenness, indispensable to the Continental Army in New York.

Abbott had wanted to enlist Craig's help. But he knows it is hopeless to count on the captain at such times as this. Sober, he is another man entirely. Craig is one army officer with an undisputed captaincy, despite his sprees. It is all owing to his knowledges of the woods, the terrain and the enemy.

Leaving the sleeping captain, Abbott runs again out to the end of the pier. Gray who has watched the Indian sergeant with curiosity ever since his first indication of sharpened interest follows Abbott to the end of the wharf.

Just then Baummeister's deep voice rings out over the water from the craft's bow, making it clear that the vessel is in need of help.

"Ahoy, dere!" he shouts. "Vee need a line! Haff ye got a boad for to breeng to us der shore?"

All the small craft were taken up the inlet and into the far end of the cove on Horsimus Bay on the north side of Paulus Hook as soon as the British ships were sighted under sail. Those were Colonel Durkee's orders, but Van Vorst had not waited for orders before getting his two ferry barges out of danger. They had led the little fleet of Durham boats, whaleboats and sloops, leaving no craft immediately available to send out to tow in Baummeister.

Seeing the plight of the pettiauger, Colonel Durkee orders a squad of men to bring back one of the Durham boats and tow the unsteerable sloop out of its imperilled position. A bellowing post sergeant shouts out that help will come and Baummeister relaxes.

However, owing to the cove's distance from the blockhouse, it could take between fifteen and thirty minutes, precious time, before such assistance might reach the vessel. This, Baummeister does not know.

But Abbott does. His home is atop the Palisadean mountain, a few miles south of the Bourdette ferry landing. Abbott had recognized the Baummeister sloop, *Hope*. He had spotted the father and his two children and knew that they were his friends and close neighbors on The Mountain.

Andrew Abbott and his parents, the last of the great Lenni Lenape tribe of the area, are highly respected on The Mountain and among the people of the river's edge. Except for the Loyalists among them, all were proud when Andy Abbott was asked to serve with the American scouts.

It was immediately evident to Gray that Abbott was seeking

Craig's help and that he intends to go to the assistance of the anchored sloop. He knows that the uncommunicative Indian will not ask for others' help.

Watching Abbott throw off his light jacket and outer buckskin trousers, Gray approaches him and begins to knot the two ends of hemp lines which he sees that the sergeant intends to take out to the stranded craft.

The Indian says nothing as he ties one end of the line around the waistline of his browned body.

"If you can swim it, Sergeant, with the weight of that line," Gray assures him, "I will see that all of us pull her in, once you get aboard and make it fast."

" 'Tis well!" is the only response Abbott makes.

Educated at sea and in the home of his mentor, the late Swedish Captain Arnold Nordstrom, Abbott makes little display of his formal education, gained under Nordstrom and his wife.

The childless couple, who had lived on the river's edge under The Mountain, had treated him like a son. They had sponsored him through a year of schooling in England. Both had died before Abbott returned as a seaman on a British merchantman.

Without saying another word, the strapping army scout dives from the dock and strikes out with beautiful, long, rapid strokes for the sloop 300 feet away.

Gray calls to those gathered on the dockside and along the Causeway to give him a hand. Even before his words are out, there are plenty of hands surrounding him. Up in front are Big Tom Graves and Jocko. The powerful Graves quickly fastens the rope's end to one of the ferry cleats while Gray slowly lets out the line tied to Abbott's waist.

Small of stature but wiry and strong for his fifteen years, Jocko rapidly unsnarls the line before it reaches Gray who carefully portions it out no faster than the swimmer moves in order to reduce the burdensome sagging weight.

When Abbott reaches the pettiauger, all three on board immediately recognize him. They greet him with unrestrained surprise and joy, but Paul's "Hurrah! It's Andy!" can be heard back on dock.

Never had they thought it would be one of their own mountain people. And Andy Abbott at that! It was months ago that he had left the cliffs. The American army staff had sought him out and asked him to serve owing to his vast knowledge of the area.

Holding the anchor line with one hand, he passes the hemp from around his waist to Baummeister who hauls the muddy, sopping, seaweed covered rope on deck. Elaine and Paul give Abbott their father's oilskin and a heavy linen drying cloth.

Baummeister tugs the line up and is about to make its end fast to the bowsprit cleat when the craft suddenly lurches in a gust of wind. The slippery hawser squirms like an eel and slides as rapidly as one out of Pete's grasp. It sinks with a heavy plop back into the river and disappears. Abbott, realizing what has happened, swiftly dives over in an attempt to recover it. He dives once and fails, comes up for air and dives again without success.

Baummeister has never in his life become so annoyed that he could not say at least a single blasphemous word, until now. He is embarrassed and furiously angry with himself. These two things in combination have never before happened to him.

On the shore all eyes sweep back to the two British frigates off the banks of Long Island's Brooklyn country. The big warships' square-rigged sails are full-blown in a spanking wind. But the armed vessels are staying a respectful distance away from the guns trained on them at Red Hook. And certainly the New York artillery battery at Manhattan's tip is ready and waiting.

But the men-of-war are staying out of range. It is believed that Howe intends only to pierce the American defenses and stride up Hudson's river in a display of contempt for the rebel army.

Colonel Durkee at the Paulus Hook post is taking no chances. A captain of artillery on the main redoubt shouts commands as preparations are speeded. The entire post is active as a beehive. But the plight of the pettiauger is not forgotten. Another officer is heard to call out to the detail up the cove to make more haste in bringing around the Durham boat.

Gray, watching every move on the anchored craft, sees what has happened on board. He feels the sudden slack on his line and watches Abbott dive twice in attempting its rescue. Knowing recovery is impossible, Gray, with Big Tom and Jocko behind him, hauls in the line.

The lieutenant throws off his outer clothes, ties the soaking, muddy end around his waist, giving Big Tom and Jocko instructions to let it out slowly behind him. He dives and makes slow steady progress toward the unfortunate sloop.

A cheer goes up from the gathering on the dock as the army officer reaches the Baummeisters and hands the line up to the Indian sergeant on deck. Abbott passes it over to the self-reproaching Baummeister whose gritted teeth press hard upon his unlighted pipe as he makes the tow rope fast upon the bowsprit cleat. He had said nothing before. He says nothing now.

Gray had not previously paid much attention to the occupants of the boat. He had been concentrating entirely on the sergeant's every move. Now, as he reaches up to pull himself over the sloop's gunnel, he looks squarely into the eyes of the thankfully smiling young girl, handing him a linen cloth towel and her own oilskin coat.

Both are taken by surprise in the electrifying moment when their eyes meet. Both stare deep into the far-reaching, unexplored recesses, where the unfathomable minds and souls of humankind may touch but once in a mysterious, prismatic sanctity. It is for seconds only.

To each of them those unforgettable seconds will seem as unending as eternity itself. Fulfilling as the physical coalescence of mankind may be, it never reaches the everlasting permanence of the single melding of two beings' impenetrable minds and souls into a solitary spirit. And in this inexplicable fusion, suddenly the time is up and Elaine withdraws blushing, though she cannot understand why. Blushing is not one of her weaknesses.

Courteously she smiles and, leaving the cloth and the oilskin for the lieutenant's use, she helps Baummeister and Abbott with the anchor and the lines. Paul, eying and sizing up Gray, while, at the same time, stowing away the oars and paddle, asks one question after the other about the Paulus Hook fort, the Americans in New York and the British vessels.

Faithful to Abbott, whom he admires above most of the men he knows, Paul reminds Gray that, though the lieutenant did make a good swim out to the boat, Sergeant Andy "was a might faster in doing it."

Gray completely agrees with him, admitting the sergeant is a much better swimmer, and adding that practice can help to make any good swimmer a much better one. Paul nods his head in sad agreement as those on shore get the signal and begin pulling *Hope* into the ferry's slip.

Discharging Elaine and her brother on the landing, Baummeister, with Abbott and Gray's assistance and that of the army detail and their Durham boat (The post's men and their Durham reached the scene just as the *Hope* arrived at the landing.) moves the vessel up the inlet. He leaves it at Van Vorst's drydock with instructions for its immediate repair.

Accompanied by Gray and Abbott, who is brought abreast of all the latest news from The Mountain by the garrulous ferrymaster, Baummeister joins his son and daughter, as well as others, who have flocked to the high grounds behind the Van Vorst house to watch the British ships.

Both the rescued and the rescuers seek a drink from the deep, cool well on the ferry proprietor's grounds. Leaving Baummeister with a clenching, warm welcome from his old friend, the pleasant, jocular Paulus Hook ferry owner, Cornelius Van Vorst,[5] Gray walks over to the well sweep, fills one of Madam Van Vorst's dippers from the well bucket and hands it to Elaine.

All eyes now focus across the river. All Paulus Hook seems to be tremulously awaiting the enemy's action as the two frigates and their tenders are seen less than half a mile off the Manhattan Island battery.

Gray, showing far less interest now in the British ships than he displayed before, finds, however, that words fail him. Standing beside Elaine, who like the rest, is apparently—but only apparently—absorbed in the river scene, he is convinced that he has been suddenly and swiftly swept into an uncontrollable infatuation with the river skipper's daughter, this vibrant, charming, though plain young girl from upriver.

And she? Does she, he wonders, think the same about him?

It has all happened so fast! Never has he felt this way before. It began that moment when he came alongside of the *Hope*, looked up and directly into those smiling eyes. And she, as intently, had looked deep into his.

Though neither Gray nor Elaine was aware of it, Papa Pete, Paul and Andy Abbott had seen it, each with a glance. Abbott slightly noticed it. A spark of a smile crossed Baummeister's face as he saw it. And Paul, viewing it through the eyes of a brother-protector of an older sister, thought it silly and stupid. One of those strange boy-girl looks that he never could quite figure out!

But, in that moment, John Gray and Elaine Baummeister were oblivious to everything around them.

Gray's searching, analytical mind always looks for causes and effects. He asks himself what it is that attracts him to this girl. True, she is from this great Palisadean mountain that he has read, heard and thought so much about. Always he had hoped someday to see those Palisades. And now he stands upon a piece of that great, volcanic wonder.

Between looking at the distant canvas of the square-riggers and then north at the ascending rock wall rising out of the river, he steals a glance at the young woman standing close to her worried father.

Could it be, he ponders, that his long entrancement with the 40-mile long rock mass has something supernatural to do with his affinity for her?

Could it be that this towering, monolithic phenomenon of nature which had belched itself out of the earth's bowels ages upon ages ago, wielded some occult power over mortals, undreamed of by man? Who knows? Stranger things have happened. Regardless, he likes her. Logic, reason, causes and effects be hanged!

What annoys him is that here is a girl, her father and brother who have lived their lives on this awe-inspiring geological wonder and think nothing of it. And Indian Abbott had lived his life on it yet never mentioned it!

To John Gray, who had lived his life, the scholarly son of a tanner and cobbler in the closeted city of Philadelphia, it seemed sacreligious that an inhabitant of the so-called "Mountain" could take his existence there almost for granted.

A strange fellow, this Indian, Gray says to himself. He had said few words to anyone, even though it was clear to Gray and to the perceptive Graves and his son that Abbott was well educated.

Jocko has found a high knoll just behind the Van Vorst house. It is an excellent vantage ground for observing the river. It looks down into the Paulus Hook fort, over the ugly abatis of oblately spiked and cunningly interwoven trunks and limbs of trees,[6] and in upon the works and block-houses.

Gray, Graves and Abbott, turn at Jocko's shrill whistle. All three join him. It appears to all now that the British ships have no intention of shelling. They seem to be bound upriver.

The lull and silence on the hillside causes Gray's mind to become momentarily distracted by the odd mixture of Americans he sees around him. They are of Dutch, English, French, Irish, Indian, African, Polish, Swedish and Welsh blood. He is sure that below, spread out before his eyes, soldiers and civilians, there must be some whose origins could be traced to almost every foreign land.

All of them now absorb his attention. He conjectures that they all remind him of the once hot molten lava of the Palisades. That is in a strange imaginative sort of way. For they, like the volcanic revolt of the earth in ages past, are on the brink of creating a new world in a violently explosive revolution.

But some of those non-military travelers and inhabitants of the area are, he is sure, strongly opposed to the cause and to the recent signing of the Declaration. There are some, for he has overheard part of their conversations, who feel the struggle is a wild fantasy. It is they who are loudly demanding that the Americans throw down their arms and get some concessions from the King. Surely, they say, there is not a chance in a hundred for the insurrection to succeed.

Ah, he thinks, to look into the far distant future of their lives and those of their descendants! To look across time with such ease as now he looks across the river and the bay at the men-of-war! What a sight, he thinks, would it behold!

As the magnet draws the needle, the cliffs of the Palisades draw his eyes to the north. The giant stretch of stone flashes his mind back to his long discussions at the college in Prince Town with the institution's president, Doctor John Wetherspoon[7] and Professor Ezra Clynes. How often and how late at night had he and others listened to learned men debate the possibility that the North, or Hudson River's precipice walls of igneous rock were once a volcanic opening in the earth.

The crack extended, in Doctor Ezra's opinion, all the way from the Tappan Zee, across the Jerseys to Trenton on the Delaware. Smaller and smaller the crack, or aperture, in the earth became, he believed, until it vanished, perhaps at the Delaware. But of this he had no proof. It was a theory, one of many, he would give his students to think about, investigate and test.

John Gray had been smitten by the erudite scholar's description of the earth's phenomenal beginning and the wondrous formation along Hudson's river on the great American continent's eastern edge. "The wonder of the Western Hemisphere," Clynes had called it.

And so it was that the science-minded youth with a sensitive bent for the beautiful in nature and in man, fell in love with a geological formation. And very possibly, also, now with one of its inhabitants.

Gray's eyes drift toward her, holding her brother's hand as they both stand beside their father who, in turn, stands beside his old friend, "Fatty" Van Vorst, as the pleasant, well-to-do ferry-owner is known.

Gray contrasts her lithe little figure in her blue bonnet and her homespun blue gingham with that of the heavy-set buxom wife of the ferry's proprietor, who stands beside Van Vorst. At the same time, as though she felt the eyes of someone upon her, Elaine's also drift away from the New York scene. Her head turns to the right and her eyes meet again those of the tall, gangling officer with a red cockade in his blue tricorn hat. Again they both smile. Again she turns slowly and reluctantly away.

Gray and Abbott have both been thanked and commended for their rescue-swims. Not only by the Baummeisters but by those who had watched the episode. However, both are reticent men who shun accolades and the center stage. Both had steered themselves to the rear of the assemblage.

"Sir Sees All"

The black boy, who had been named "John" by his mother but whose early attachment and love of horses as well as his riding skill, earned him, somehow along the way, the name of "Jocko," has stayed close by the lieutenant. Though a devoted son, he has somewhat neglected the side of his father for that of the young officer.

Both Jocko and Big Tom are strongly independent personalities. And each respects the other's rights. For freedom, or *independence*, has a very special, sacred meaning all its own to them. As it does indeed to all freed men.

Out of the corner of his big, bright, brown eyes, whose sharp vision acuity has caused his father often to dub him jestingly with the title, "Sir Sees All," Jocko catches the young couple's exchange of smiling glances. Reveling in his secret espionage, he lifts his head up toward the officer, saying with a whisper meant only for Gray's ears, "Lordy, Lootenan! Dat dere boat-lady shor has 'n eye for youse!"

Taken completely off guard, Gray looks down at the smiling, mischievously exuberant, lovable little black face. It is shaded by an over-sized old gray tricorn hat. Gray's quick glance takes in the clean but ragged, torn and over-mended clothes and the shoeless feet. The officer's raised eyebrows drop from surprise into a laugh.

"Yes, but you, Jocko, have an eye for everything, methinks!" he replies.

Just then the roar of cannons fills the air. As one thunders out its bark and rolls its boom over the river, echoing against the solid rock walls of the Palisades, another and then more follow. The air is shattered by the frigates, *Phoenix* and *Rose*, leveling their broadsides violently on New York town.

It is not a total bombardment. Only a few of the *Phoenix's* 40[8] guns and one of the *Rose's* 20[9] are brought into play. And the fire is concentrated upon the American battery on Manhattan's tip. The frigates drift slowly within range of the rebel artillery. Then the Americans open up. The warships' three tenders stay out of range and in the river's midstream.

The duel is brief. Little damage seems to have been done to the enemy vessels. However, six Americans lie dead around their guns at the Grand Battery and others lie screaming from wounds and injuries.

Only two of the dead were killed by the enemy. The others are the casualties of a mis-managed 32-pounder which exploded, sending a cloud of smoke over the American battery. The black pall spreads like a mantle of gloom over the city.

Balls and grape from the enemy broadsides strike several houses, going right through two homes between Reverend Shewkirk's Moravian Church and Greenwich Street. One man suffers a broken leg from falling timbers.[10]

Both warships head away from the New York guns, joining their sloop and tenders in midstream. There they begin their defiant ascent up Hudson's river. Ignoring the Paulus Hook post's batteries on the Jersey side, they nevertheless momentarily come within range of Durkee's artillerymen. Each rebel cannoneer itches for the command to fire. Behind them on the hillock the gathered onlookers watch breathlessly.

At the exact moment, Durkee gives the command. With an earth-shaking deafening roar, the Hook's guns bark, covering the post in a thick cloud of smoke, but the enemy ships seemingly are untouched and veer eastward out of range into the safety of the upper river and beyond reach of either shore.

Every observer on both banks along the waterway knows that Admiral Howe's objective is to cut the supplies and communications routes between Jersey and New York. Beyond that immediate aim is his intention to sever all communications between New England and the south, west of Hudson's river. So, unmolested, they sail jauntily up toward Mount Washington headed for the Tappan Zee.

The American Commander-in-Chief had foreseen this, though he had not looked for it quite this early. He had expected that the cross-fire from Manhattan and the Paulus Hook batteries would deter the break-through. Certainly he had hoped that Howe would have had to pay more heavily for it.

Since early this morning The General and his chief engineer, Colonel Rufus Putnam, with a large party of officers and a company of men from Fort Washington, have been surveying the area on The Mountain above Bourdette's ferry landing. The site is at about the very center of the high natural wall fortress, an excellent location for the post he badly needs on the Jersey side.

The General's Choice For A Sister Fort

Long an admirer of the rebel Chieftain, a staunch patriot and a devout Whig member of the separatist, religious Coetus Party of the Hackensack Valley, Stephen Bourdette personally guided The General after his landing at the ferry. Making their way up the gorge road, the party followed the rocky, rugged path east of the gorge on to the great, 300-foot long table rock that rests atop the sheer precipice cliff.

Here the cliff rises from the water a height almost equal to its table-top length. And here the American Leader walks out along the massive Bluff Rock, as it is called, and decides that it is here the cannon emplacements must go.

Before his eyes, there spreads out beyond him a breath-taking panoramic view of the aged river hundreds of feet below, of the entire island of Manhattan, of Westchester and Long Island Sound far off to the northeast, and, to the south, the upper and lower bays emptying into the distant ocean.

Between the bays he sees the Narrows, the wide channel that joins the bays with Long Island's Brooklyn on the east and Staten Island on the west. He can spot only the eastern tip of Staten Island where is clustered the British fleet some 20 miles away.

This indeed is the site for establishing his Jersey fortress. Its position, directly opposite the Mount Washington post named in his honor, will enable the twin forts to command the river. For from point to point here is the narrowest breadth of the Hudson until many miles upstream.

Certainly the two forts and their batteries, in conjunction, could surely inflict severe damage upon any vessel that might attempt to run through their fire. The rebel's Leader was sure Howe would soon ascend the river. He did not expect it would be today.

Through a field glass an aide points out that several of the vessels appear to be getting under way. Since others are seen arriving in the outer bay, it cannot be ascertained what, if anything, is actually taking place. One intelligence report from Perth

Amboy yesterday stated that Lord Howe was due to arrive sometime this day. This could account for the activity.

The General briefly discusses with Putnam the position battery
emplacements on the Bluff Rock should be given. He advises Major
General Thomas Mifflin, army quartermaster and commandant of
Fort Washington of what will be needed. He stresses the urgency
of immediate construction of the Bluff Rock batteries and redoubts,
pointing out that a field fort should be located on the main mountain up the west side of the gorge road. This could come later.

Proceeding over the gorge road which separates the Bluff
Rock—a geological fault—from the main, mountainous ridge, the
party inspects the Bourdette and Baummeister pasture lands on the
summit for future use. Observing that the vast forest area will
provide the lumber needed for huts and firewood, The General and
his aides make their way back to the road. They observe that the
gorge road up from the ferry, turns west over the mountain's
summit and winds its way down into the valley on the west slope.
It is the road, they are told, that connects with the south-to-north
King's highway from Bergen Point, opposite Staten Island, to
Tappan and thence to Albany. The slope road also winds across
the valley to the town of Hackensack.

The party is now fully satisfied with the preliminary report that
Captain Charles Craig presented. He, with his Indian sergeant and
their scouts, had covered the area over a week ago, confirming its
exceptional advantages as a post for defense and communications
purposes.

After lunching with the Bourdettes in the large river-side homestead and inn, not far from the Baummeister house to the rear and
up the slope a way, the military party began an inspection of the
water-side for river battery emplacements. But suddenly they were
caught in the storm that had enveloped the *Hope*, a glimpse of
which an aide before lunch had seen well down the river.

It was the confirmed observation of the two British men-of-war
far down in the outer bay which made the rebel Commander
decide to get back to New York town as quickly as possible.

As soon as the storm blew over, he thanked the Bourdettes for
their hospitality, paying, however, in full from his own pocket for
the expenses entailed. He then made the crossing safely over to
Jeffrey's Hook under Mount Washington's Point Redoubt. Mifflin,
Putnam and the Fort Washington men separated, leaving The
General and his staff to their long fifteen-mile ride down the island
to the city.

Almost at the same time they began their journey they could hear the cannonading from the *Phoenix* and the *Rose*, answered poorly, it seemed, by the New York artillery. And about twenty minutes later they saw the two enemy frigates ascending the river on their right.

Reining in their horses, they stopped to watch the enemy cruisers pass Mount Washington just where the American party had crossed less than a half-hour before. But the King's ships, aware of the Fort Washington emplacements and redoubts above the shore, hugged the New Jersey side. Neither the vessels nor the shore batteries fired. The British mission upriver now seemed merely intent upon piercing the American defenses.

The two frigates will safely anchor off Haverstraw in the Tappan Zee. In the morning they will be recruiting Loyalists from among Orange County's Hudson Valley inhabitants.[11]

A few hours later, the American Commander and his staff, as well as all the ferry passengers on Van Vorst's Cortlandt Street run, had set foot in the panicky town, suffering from its first strike in the conflict. It has suddenly been transformed from a gay, lively little seaport, first into a military post and now, after an attack by only two of the Crown's numerous battleships, into a city of frightened, trembling people.

The faces of the inhabitants show it. Many are already preparing to move out. The populace borders on panic. New York has been hit and the far-off war is now on its doorstep.

So Fatty Van Vorst and his wife had little difficulty persuading Baummeister not to complete his visit to New York. Only Elaine was disappointed. She had hoped they would follow the ferry across, the ferry John Gray had boarded with a casual wave to those still lining the wharf and Causeway. It was a wave she knew was meant for her and so returned it.

Baummeister accepted his friend's hospitality for the night and decided to catch the morning tide on his return upriver early in the morning. Van Vorst, accepting a goodly share of the berries and produce for himself, promised to deliver the rest to the Baummeisters' New York relatives tomorrow on an early ferry crossing.

A good distance below the upper New York Bay and The Narrows and to the west, off Staten Island's southside, a series of cannon shots, carefully timed, is heard. It is the British fleet's gun salute to the arrival in the lower bay of Admiral Lord Richard "Black Dick" Howe, commander of the King's Navy. He stands in full uniform, an impressive, almost regal figure on the poop deck of the flagship, *Eagle*.

The war has at last and indeed come to the Americans' major seaport. The New York - New Jersey Campaign of 1776, which is to spread through part of Long Island, then up the island of Manhattan, into Westchester County and finally across and through the Jerseys, has begun.

It will end three days after the year, 1776, has closed its pages. It will end some 80 miles away on Friday, January 3, 1777, on the college grounds of Prince Town.

Ahead now lie 175 perilous days of crises for the American dream. To most of the strange mixture of humanity, calling themselves "Americans," such as those Lieutenant John Gray scrutinized on the tailish part of the monstrous Palisades at Paulus Hook, it is truly an unimaginable "dream."

The idealistic Gray had heard that so-called "dream" read aloud in Carpenter's Hall, Philadelphia, the very day he was appointed a commissioned officer by authority of the Continental Congress. That was only eight days ago.

How well he remembered now his proud father standing beside him. And his sister on his other side, enthralled by the simple scene before them. He recalled how deeply, inwardly he was moved when he heard the words of the Declaration of Independence read aloud, yet almost indifferently, almost as the town crier would read an announcement by the Lord Mayor.

He would never forget the impression the words—not their reading—made upon him. He knew then he had done the right thing in postponing his final college year at Princeton until the great issue was resolved, one way or the other.

Gray also recalled the memorable day of June 7. On that day he decided to enter the army. He had come home from the college and on that Friday walked over to Carpenter's Hall.

On that day he heard Richard Henry Lee, the Virginian, submit his resolution to the Second Continental Congress. It called for a committee of the Congress to draft a declaration of independence from England. Actually, therefore, he had seen it in its inception.

It was, he thought, as though this "dream," this idea, which was planted in Carpenter's Hall, was there and then conceived in America's womb. He fantasied that it was as though the "dream" was in reality the union of America with the world of peoples from all nations. America and her distant origins united in an unbelievable union.

Certainly, he thought, it is far less treacherous a union, a far less illicit coition, than the coupling of America with Holland, Spain or England. It was more, he thought, like the idealistic hopes nourished in the dreams of unity by Tristram and Isolde. But, he hoped, without their tragic ending.

A Paper-writin' Thingumajig

So John Gray had listened attentively, and with good reason, to all the talk and misunderstandings bandied around about over the Declaration. Some he has disliked. Some admired. Some he has found amusing in their ignorance.

It was at Cornelisen's tavern at Paulus Hook that he had overheard an army postrider, drunk with grog, boasting that he had brought the "paper-writing' thingumajig" from the Continental Congress to the American Commander-in-Chief. In fact, it was last Monday, the 8th, at dusk, the rider told his tavern friend, that the Paulus Hook ferryman took him across to the Abraham Messier[12] wharf at Cortlandt Street. It was, he explained, the last leg of his long ride from Carpenter's Hall in Philadelphia with "dat 'portant paper."

He told his friendly listener that he was stopped at headquarters by the sentry who knew him and queried, "I doan 'spose 'tis some good money dem thar Con'rassmen is sendin' this time, eh, Buckskin?"

" 'Wish 'twas. No, 'tain't!' I says," continued the messenger as he proudly recounted his important mission to his drinking companion. Draining down hefty swigs of liquor in between accounts, the postrider continued with, " 'The Gen'l could use money more 'n he can them thar papers,' says I."

" 'So could I!' says he. 'Deckla-ation! Whata we need dat fer?' says he. ' 'Tis money, wimmin, food, grog and clothes we needs, not a lot a paper-writin'.' "

The messenger, all in earshot of Gray, who had sought shelter in the ferry tavern with the others when the storm was at its height, then went on to tell his companion how very important that paper really was. All the officers, he said, had been wagering on which of the Congressmen would never sign it and which would.

It was so important, he declared, that the Chief ordered it to be read word for word on the Bowling Green Tuesday, the 9th,[13] to all the troops on parade. And then it caused such a big hullabaloo, he went on, among the soldiers that they ended up that night knocking down the heroic, equestrian statue of King George (Rex III) on the Green.[14]

He did not recount that The General reprimanded all those who took part in the statue-toppling. However many knew their Chief was later happy to hear that the statue's two tons of lead were to make 42,088 musket balls when melted down.[15]

That was one of Gray's early glimpses into the character of some of the troops occupying New York town. It was his first inkling as to the spirit of the men whom he would soon be leading as an artillery officer under General Henry Knox's command.

Upon stepping off the Van Vorst ferry pettiauger, Gray turned, took a long breathless look at the lengthy distant Palisades across the river to the north. His eyes had been fastened on the sight much of the way over.

Then he took a last long look at the Paulus Hook fort and ferry landing to see if the Baummeister vessel was on its way. It wasn't. And he knew it wouldn't be. His heart fell a little.

He saw no sign of the *Hope* and wondered now if he would ever again see the young woman who had so completely captured him.

Now turning to the city and seeing the frightened faces he is reminded of Dante's *Inferno*. Amazed at the extent of the damage Gray now acquires greater respect for British broadsides. The stench of gunpowder in the streets still hangs heavy in the late afternoon air.

Alone now, after parting with his traveling companions, Gray makes his way toward the headquarters of American Artillery Commander Colonel Henry Knox in the Kennedy house on the west side of Broadway.

For the young newly commissioned Lieutenant the War For Independence has just begun.

2

Sunday, July 14. . .

"To Conquer or Die"

Search For Dignity

T he death of four of his men, the ineffectiveness of his mis-
managed battery and the passage of the ships through his barriers unscathed, all contributed to the heavily built, gruff-voiced
artillery commander's irascible humor. So Gray's arrival Friday was a
welcome interlude for Colonel Henry Knox.

Gray had studied all about artillery in Philadelphia upon arriving
home from Princeton. At the college he read everything available
on military tactics. Much was in translated Prussian literature.
Gray, therefore, was immediately assigned a battery command
under Colonel Daniel Hitchcock on the city's west side along
Hudson's river.

Enemy vessels slipping past the island's southernmost batteries
are to be his target. That is providing they come within range. If
not, they are to be handled by Paulus Hook's guns on the Jersey
shore. Thus, the British ships will be made to run the gauntlet of
the batteries next time, it is hoped.

Gray was given a free hand in the selection of new recruits to
make up his complement. So when Big Tom Graves asked to join
Gray's unit, the answer was an immediate welcome. The black
freedman had been serving under an artillery lieutenant who had
an overlording white supremacy attitude. The officer's manner had

30

even been distasteful to some of the troops from the southern colonial states.

The New York born and bred Negro-hating officer and the North Carolina born and bred black freedman and his son had clashed too often. And too often Graves was on the edge of insubordination as the freed black man's fervor of resentment over the officer's goading infringements of his rights to military recognition as a soldier, daily increased.

The situation had become dangerously flammable. All knew it. Then the wise Colonel Hitchcock temporarily separated the bigoted second lieutenant from the Graveses. He simply assigned Big Tom and Jocko to the wagon train transfer to Amboy.

It was only a temporary solution to a ticklish situation pending the possible reassignment of Graves to one of the three forming all-black regiments, an assignment which Graves did not wish, yet knew he could not oppose. So Lieutenant Gray's immediate acceptance of the black man and his son to his battery swiftly solved a rough problem for Hitchcock and, at the same time, put Gray in good standing with the high command.

"The Lieutenant," as his men began calling him from their first meeting, gave Graves and Jocko complete charge of the battery's cannon carriages. This included the wagon and its team of horses, a responsibility which delighted the horse-loving Jocko. Big Tom was to be a swabber and a loader on one of the 24-pounders.

In a short time, the big black man's pleasant, affable, open manner and his insistence on cleanliness and order earned him the deep and admiring respect of the men.

Jocko has always been rapidly accepted as a popular, likeable mascot with the outfits with which his father has served in the six months he has been in the army. And swiftly now he industriously carries out his duties and responsibilities to become a respected part of the battery's operations.

It does not take long for the entire battery to see that Jocko is obviously one of The Lieutenant's biggest admirers. And it is similarly obvious that if the officer has any particular favorite among his command, Jocko is that one.

Had he asked for a preferred assignment and location, Gray would probably have chosen the one he has been given, particularly in view of its location. Opposite him, across the river, is his much admired mountain.

Before attending Sunday services this morning, he went down to the water's edge with his copy of John Locke's "Essay On Human

...A Prehistoric Monolithic Lizard. . . .

Understanding" under his arm. His swim and bath in the river's water as well as Locke's essay, lost his interest as he became absorbed in the volcanic cliffs on the opposite shore. They rise up from the river brightened by the rising sun and back-dropped by the blue morning heavens.

It was a welcome respite after his first, long, hard day at his new assignment. He could see miles upriver where in the distance lies the Bourdette ferry and the Baummeister home where lives that girl, Elaine.

He had heard that their pettiauger had not attempted a crossing to New York. It was just as well. Since the ferrymaster-skipper of the *Hope* had told him he intended to go back the next day, Gray was sure that the sailing sloop he had seen in the distance, close to the Jersey shore yesterday morning, was the repaired Baummeister craft.

What, he wondered, was she doing now? Was it possible that she liked him? Him with his pale, emaciated, almost ugly, pock-marked face, smallpoxed in childhood. Or was her smile merely one of courteous thanks?

He asks himself, what does it matter? Probably he will never see her again. His thoughts shift. He looks at the high Palisadean walls, tapering off south into the bays and disappearing into the depths of the Atlantic. To the north he sees the mountain's back rise higher and higher beyond his sight as though he were looking up from the tail of a long, prehistoric, monolithic lizard.

His mind flashes back to Dr. Ezra's description of the creation of the Palisades, the islands and the rivers surrounding it. He remembers, almost word for word, much of that awesomely fascinating picture the scholarly teacher conjured out of his limitless vocabulary that moonlit night on the college president's wide veranda:

"In the flaming, fiery genesis of the world . . . centuries upon centuries ago . . . up from the earth's innermost bowels in a great volcanic inferno rose the lava-dripping Palisadean wall . . . later over the once-smoldering canyon came the great glacier, covering all and eventually leaving a great sea above the land . . . and soon the waters receded and only rivers were left flowing down around the great mountainous range of igneous rock whose sheer cliffs rose up from the deep river's bottom . . . But there, in the mountain's center, a great flat-top bluff of hot lava rock was thrown violently out and away from the main mountain ridge . . . And so it stands today, a sentinel, hundreds of feet high . . . It is like an overlord of the great land of America's eastern edge, looking down upon the islands east across the river that it made, looking down upon its river flowing southward to the ocean . . . And then came green vegetation to the land and life itself—the hadrosaurus, the laelaps and the dinosaur . . . And here came to live and hunt the gray wolf, the panther, fox, and eagle . . . And all killed, but killed to live, not in hate, jealousy and treachery."

They were not the exact words, but Gray remembered that here the kindly man, whose patriotism and love of country so easily transferred itself to his students, would talk lengthily about the beauty of the red man and the cruelty of the white man.

"And so came the Wapenachki, the Lenni Lenape," he would continue. "Their name means the 'Original People.' They hunted, not to kill, but to eat, obeying the laws of nature. Soon came the Dutchman and his *Half-Moon* whom the trusting Original People welcomed and fed. Then came the Spaniard, the Frenchman, the Englishman. With them came the good and the bad of the Old World. And all was mournfully watched from the high Bluff Rock of the Palisades, which gazes down upon man, his inhumanity and greed, his avarice and wars, all in his suicide."

Perhaps, Gray thinks, as he contemplates the elderly scholar's wisdom and nature's untrammeled beauty, kaleidoscopically fanning out before him, perhaps Doctor Clynes, in his aging, has lost his faith in man. Perhaps the war, the independence, the freedom, the rights man seeks and needs, will bring the better world.

He looks again across the river at the long, towering wall. At last it stands, a reality, before him! It is no longer something imagined, a mystic figment.

How often he had dreamed about it! Visualized it! Wanted to climb and touch it as one would like to touch and see the great beginning of creation.

What next, he thinks, will that distant, giant Bluff Rock look down upon? And behind it—behind the massive, mountain ridge—westward lies the expanse of America. Behind its western slope nestle the valleys and the streams along which the Dutch and French Huguenot settlers built their tidy, sandstone homes he has heard so much about.

And all of that is guarded, hidden from the view of Manhattan Islanders who can see only the reposing menacing monolith. 'Tis no wonder, he tells himself, that the long-dead, Indian chief, Mannahatta, is said to have drawn his line and never crossed to the west side of the river.

Gray sees the Palisades, a protective shield for the valley people on its far side like a massive curtain, screening the coming, dreaded scenes of war from the beautiful lands and distant wilderness country over The Mountain.

That thought turns his mind downriver. His eyes sweep along the Jersey river bank, picking up the points he had seen on the map in Hitchcock's headquarters: Bull's ferry, Wehawk, Horsimus Cove, Van Vorst's ferry, Paulus Hook's battery. And up on the diminishing southern ridge tail of the Palisades: Bergen's village, Communipaw, Bergen Point, the Kill van Kull, Staten Island, the bays, The Narrows and the distant ocean to the far south.

He sees in the massing fleet of British ships with their countless towering masts and spars the overture of war. He sees it as the answer to the conception at Philadelphia. Someone had told him that there were 400 British vessels including 52 warships, 10,000 of the King's sailors, and 32,000 British and Hessian soldiers,[1] all based on Staten Island, all said to be pillaging the inhabitants in preparation for an invasion of New York. And supervising the tremendous operations are, it is said, six British and Hessian generals, determined to abort the American "dream" that he watched conceived in Carpenter's Hall.

The size of the enemy force was first impressed upon him when he landed at the Cortlandt Street dock. An excited officer with a field glass, still unnerved from the enemy cannonading, allowed Gray use of the instrument to see the arrival of six enemy warships, escorting 28 transports, said to be carrying 2,600 guardsmen and 8,000 German mercenaries. It was the arrival of British Commodore Hotham.

Surely, Gray thought to himself, it is an armada twice as big as that amassed by the Spaniards against the British 188 years ago. And, at headquarters, one officer told another he heard it was costing the Crown over £850,000.[2]

Viewing that warlike panorama to the south, Gray reminds himself that it is a far way from Princeton. "I am, methinks, unquestionably in the middle of the rebellion. 'Tis best I look a last time at Dr. Ezra's mountain until more peaceful times."

Tucking his book under his arm, he ascends the path back up the embankment to the battery and makes his way from there to the Sunday church services.

War Council At Black Sam's

The American Commander and his staff will, today, after church services, inadvertently affect the destiny of the Philadelphian, John Gray. In the Long Room of Black Sam Fraunces' Queen's Head Tavern[3] on Broad and Pearl Street, the Council of War will, among other things, unanimously approve The General's plans for the construction of a defense post above Bourdette's Landing.

However, since a few of the Council had remarked about its "rattle snakes," its "questionable advantage" and were disinclined to approve another post ten miles upriver and on the Jersey side, he and his aides argue that:

1. The colonial states' chief seaport, New York, is the enemy's immediate objective.[4] It is a prize that the Crown must try to take.

2. A fort on the Jersey side, opposite Fort Washington, will act in concert to prevent the enemy from gaining control of the river. Fort Washington alone could not long be defended under attack by British ships, shelling it from the west side near the Jersey shore, out of range from the American cannon.

3. The Congress has ordered the Commander-in-Chief "by every art and whatever expense to obstruct effectively the navigation of the river."[5]

4. Though every precaution has been taken for the defense of Brooklyn across the East River south of the New York City batteries, and Generals Greene and Stirling are hurrying its defenses, it is believed the enemy may move up the North River, invading Manhattan at several points simultaneously. Formidable works on the Jersey side would help to offset such maneuvers.

5. Since the Northern Department, or army, under Major General Philip Schuyler on the Canada border, looks to the Central Department, under the American Commander-in-Chief, for strength and morale, as does the Southern Department, or army, presently under General Charles Lee, the decision to meet the enemy's invasion cannot be altered and full defense preparations must be made.

6. From the standpoint of civilian morale, it is imperative that the army face the enemy in defense of Manhattan Island. Not to do so will undermine the morale of all the colonial states, the militia as well as the regulars of the Continental regiments. Not to do so will weaken the Congress, strengthen the spirits of the numerous Tories, particularly the many Loyalist strongholds in New York and the Jerseys, and weaken the resistance efforts of the Whigs and patriots.

7. Finally, since all efforts must be made to prevent the enemy from severing communications between the New York army and the New England states and its Northern Army Department, a major supply and communications post must be established on the Jersey side of the river north of Paulus Hook.

No further questions or objections are heard. The plan for the construction of the new post is approved unanimously.

The General orders that all regiments prepare to send over work companies, engineers and carpenters to prepare the grounds for an artillery emplacement.

As usual, Black Sam Fraunces, always the perfect host, walks out of the big, mansion-like tavern house alongside of the American Leader. He is one of The General's devoted admirers. A strong supporter of the cause, it is believed by some members of the Council that Fraunces has often provided the Chief with valuable information. A few are almost certain that the Queen's Head is a secret meeting place for a number of Whigs. And there are many of these patriots who eagerly seek an opportunity to undermine British plans, Tory sympathizers, and plotting Loyalists.

The wide-shouldered, deep-chested, rebel Leader stands an erect six feet four inches and more beside his favorite gray. His arms and legs are long and in good proportion to his frame. When standing beside the mare, Old Magnolia, Fraunces thinks that his erectness of posture would make a ramrod humble. He decides to remember that and tell it to Phoebe.

What worries Fraunces is that the big man never smiles. Always though, he looks straight, full and unflinchingly into the eyes of those with whom he converses. It is this that Black Sam particularly likes about the 44-year-old former surveyor, frontiersman and veteran of the French and Indian War as he mounts with the agility of a much younger man. Straight and upright in his saddle he sits, and the tavern keeper is now convinced he is every bit as majestic on Old Magnolia as beside her.

In his customary courteous manner, The General thanks and commends Fraunces for his hospitality. The big man looks down from his mount with his piercing blue eyes below his powdered brown hair, hair that rounds out beneath his cocked hat and, in a few well-chosen words warns Fraunces to stay neutral for his own safety.

The Queen's Head proprietor thanks him and notices the firm, well-chiseled features, the straight, slightly heavy nose. They give him, Fraunces thinks, an appearance of strength and dignity which men find so seldom among their own kind.

The West Indies-born tavern owner of French extraction has often described The General's appearance to newcomers to the Queen's Head, always adding something more but ever emphasizing his deliberate, and engaging manner. Never does he mention those pock-marks on his face. The General had contracted smallpox while visiting the Barbados in 1751.

And neither does Fraunces ever mention the General and Chief's slightly heavy rump, for in Fraunces' view of this man whom he all but worships, nothing is to mar his perfection. So his descriptions are always in glowing terms, including invariably, of course, his excellence as a horseman.

Even as the big man mounts, Fraunces notices the large, size 13 shoe, the spotless Sunday blue coat with its golden epaulets and the buff-colored breeches. The all-observing Black Sam particularly noticed today, the rebel Chieftain's sad, solemn countenance, the heavy set of his mouth and the tightly pressed lips, owing, Fraunces knew, primarily to his troublesome teeth.

Invariably, however, the tavern proprietor always looks for and hopes that he will see what he has never seen—a slight indication, even the slightest indication, of a smile on the stern, grave features. It never comes.

Fraunces' daughter, Phoebe, who is the American Commander's housekeeper at the Mortier[6] house headquarters, joins her father on the steps of the Queen's Head Tavern. He unburdens his concern over the perilous state of the city and the multitude of problems facing The General.

Among other things, he tells her that he had heard the American Commander, only the other day, had sent a long letter to the Continental Congress strongly urging that it approve his recommendation for defenses at Bergen Neck and other locations along the Jersey shore opposite Staten Island.

"His arguments fall on deaf ears, " Fraunces tells his 21-year-old daughter. She is her father's close confidante as well as his right arm in the tavern business.

"The Jerseyans," he continues, "are set against providing any help in the protection of New York. There are many in each of the new states who still think provincially. Some say they refuse to fight beyond their own borders. The Jersey Flying Camp men have made that clear to everyone."

Samuel Fraunces further tells her that the only reason Congress has insisted that the Hudson must be blockaded and defended at all costs is because the wealthy Hudson Valley landowners have demanded protection. They have shouted so loud, he tells her, that their bellowing can be heard "clear down to Philadelphia."

"There is not enough strength in his army to do what he has to do," the highly respected business man laments, "without having to take care of every one of their crying demands."

He sadly informs her that he has good reason to believe the British will be occupying New York town in less than a month. That, he tells her, they must think about.

Phoebe Fraunces, like her father, has come to an almost idolizing appraisal of the rebel Leader, despite his rapidly descending star of popularity in contrast with a year ago. She has heard the widely circulated rumors that he is no longer admired and revered by the Congress and the country as he was fourteen months ago. The miracles they had expected were not in his power to perform.

Rumblings Of Discord

Furthermore, many of his former supporters, particularly in the Congress and the army, have shifted their previously strong sentiments in the direction of General Charles Lee. They are now putting him on a pedestal, extolling his reported deeds in the South.

Of course the American Chief still has devoted supporters in the Congress, the army and throughout the colonial states. But there are an increasing number who criticize him unjustly. Consequently these undermining rumblings of discord within the high echelons of the supposedly uniting territories seep down and infect the military ranks.

It is manifested most in clashes between "Yankees"—a name that has been somewhat derogatively pinned on all Northerners in the army—and the "Buck-skins"—a similarly somewhat belittling title tacked on all Southerners. In the barracks and around the campfires, the sectional differences give rise to dissensions and boiling point antagonisms which often pour over into heated brawls. This is particularly so when the troops are busy only with the construction of fortifications and have no enemy upon whom to vent their anger.

Fraunces notes that the Commander-in-Chief's decision to hold, or retreat from New York, is his alone to make. The effect, he tells Phoebe, will be felt as much by Schuyler's Northern Department at Ticonderoga as it will by Lee's Southern army in Charleston, South Carolina.

Phoebe remembers Lee who came to New York to prepare its defenses in the past winter. It was Lee who had strongly contended the city could not be successfully defended against the British might.

So The General's momentous decision, Fraunces points out, will seriously affect the American morale no matter whether he holds or withdraws. Aside from the military strategy and its effects, the tavern's proprietor declares that the swaying sentiments of the people must also be weighed. For no army can be recruited, especially one built upon such short-term enlistments as The General's, if the people and their government lose confidence in it.

"Here in New York," he says, "is the vulnerable center of America. Here are the ports to across the seas—the doorway for the country's imports. Here are the junctions of the highways, reached by ferries, it is true, but junctions and intersections where the colonial states find access to each other. What will happen to the cause once New York is taken?"

At his headquarters in the Mortier house on Richmond Hill, the rebel Leader reminds his aide to note, for later insertion in his "Accounts Of Expenses" the words, "To my own and party's expenses. laying out (The Fort) on the Jersey side of North River, £8.15,0."[7]

There is little hope in the Commander's mind that New York can be held by a small band of soldiers who have had little if any warfare training. How, and the world is asking the same question, can such an army pit its strength against the world's mightiest military machine and expect to achieve victory?

So the selection of the Bluff Rock site atop The Mountain will not only be for offensive use against the enemy's shipping, it will be—as he foresees it—a possible escape hatch. If all Manhattan should fall to the enemy, and there are many who feel that only a miracle can prevent it, a crossing of the army into Jersey would be inevitable. The Bluff Rock then would be an important part of that movement. For The General perceives that withdrawal may be his only strategy, retreat his only ally.

To give an inkling of this to those around him could be disastrous. Were the army, the rank and file, under the impression that flight from the advancing enemy was expected and planned for, the morale of the troops could be destroyed overnight. Defense and defiance, a show of strength, must be made.

Interrupting his thoughts, he walks over to the south window of the headquarters. At the same time he dictates to an aide the general orders for the coming day:

"The Gen'l flatters himself that every Man's mind and Arms are now prepared for the Glorious Contest, upon which so much depends. The time is too precious, nor does the Gen'l think it necessary to Spend it in Exhorting his brave Countrymen and fellow soldiers to behave like Men fighting for everything that can be dear to freedom. We must resolve to conquer or Die."[8]

After completing the customary Sunday routines and correspondence with his aides, the Continental Army Commander again walks to the west window and looks out upon the hot, sullen July afternoon. He watches a few of the newly arrived militia and the regulars attending and instructing them.

They are, he observes, a heterogeneous mixture of men. Some young, some old. They come from every walk of America's colonial life and from almost all corners of the thirteen territories. They are on the whole, men with high principles, he has discovered, men ruled by the cardinal virtues.

There are those who do not attend church services. That he knows is something to be expected. Even so, his orders are that the Sabbath be observed as a day of worhsip and rest throughout the army when military procedures permit it. And most of his troops, he is sure, approve.

Reflecting on their appearance on the parade grounds last Tuesday when the Declaration was read aloud to all regiments, he remembers now what thoughts ran through his mind. One in particular was: "If the Crown, Lord North and the Howe brothers were to see them—few decently clothed, some without shoes and in tattered dress, many under-nourished and ill—all of Great Britain and its agents in America would relax in confidence, well assured that the rebellion was all but over."

Nevertheless, his mind is primarily occupied with preparations and with probing for an answer to: Where will the Howes strike?

The state of the troops, particularly the militia, and their questionable ability to stand up under shot and shell, worries him. Excepting for the Continentals who were with him in Boston, most have never been near a battle.

Only the well-outfitted Delaware and Maryland troops are thoroughly and completely equipped. Only they are dressed to look like soldiers. They alone have full and proper uniforms.

As for the complaints he has heard of factions and fracases within the ranks, he has told his staff that, in view of the nature of the geographical cross-section of the country and the varied characteristics of its peoples, harmony must be sought out of discord. It is to be expected that in such a body of men, representing thirteen separate cultures, there will be many with differing moral and ethical scruples.

The increasing number of court martials for theft, rape, pillaging and desertion, attest to that. And many of them, honest men included, will be driven, as in any war, to extremes for self-survival. In times of need, when want and hunger strike, they will acquire the necessities of life as quickly as they have been acquiring the local farmers' chickens, a stray calf, or heifer.

He insists the people must be reimbursed but reluctantly reminds his staff that court martials will not cure hunger.

All these thoughts, which run through his mind, are suddenly interrupted by an aide who brings him word from Colonel Reed. Reed's messenger delivers the news that an enemy barge, under a flag, has anchored off Brooklyn about four miles below the city.[9] The rider states that Colonels Reed and Knox will go out in a row-galley and determine the purpose of the flag, unless The General wishes otherwise.

The General directs the messenger to inform Reed and Knox to proceed as properly as they deem wise and to keep him fully informed and as swiftly as possible. Then, taking his field glasses, he observes the white flag of the enemy boat far down the bay and, periodically, keeps his eye on the distant visit from the enemy's emissaries.

The Unknown "Mister"

Colonel Paterson, the British Officer on the barge, bears a letter from the Howe brothers stating that General Howe has come to America with the express wish of His Majesty that a peaceful settlement may be reached ending the insurrection.

It is with regrets, he declares, that he is late, a reference assumably to the fact that he would have preferably made his overture prior to the signing of the Declaration. However, the letter emphasizes that Howe has been invested by His Majesty "with very great powers to pardon."[10]

Howe's letter will not be read by the Americans today. It will not even be accepted. In fact, Colonel Paterson, distressed and disappointed, will carry it unopened back to Howe, since as Colonels Reed and Knox courteously inform him, there is no one they know under the name of "Mr. Washington" or "George Washington, Esq." And that is the way the letter is addressed.

However, eight days from now, under a second British flag, and bearing a letter properly addressed to the American Commander-in-Chief, Colonel Paterson will have to return to his commander with The General's courteous reply. It will state that General Howe has "come to the wrong place," implying that his letter should be addressed to the Continental Congress; and, secondly, that the Americans had not offended, therefore they needed no pardon."[1][1]

Today, however, Colonel Paterson only succeeded in getting as far as Colonel Reed and Colonel Knox, who politely sent Paterson, his staff and the British barge back to Staten Island with an undelivered communique.

Reed had wisely ordered the well-outfitted, well-dressed Delaware and Maryland troops to be drawn up in parade formation along the shore. And it was observed that Paterson and his party took particular notice of the sight. The British officer had expected to see rags and tatters.

It is after midnight when Colonel Knox gets around to penning a letter home to his wife, Lucy, detailing an account of the day's outstanding event. He writes, in part:

"July 15, 1776
". . . Lord Howe yesterday sent a flag of truce up to the city. They came within about four miles of the city and were met by some of Colonel Tupper's people, who detained them until his Excellency's pleasure should be known. Accordingly, Colonel Reed and myself went down in the barge to receive the message. When we came to them, the officer, who was, I believe, captain of the Eagle man-of-war, rose up and bowed, keeping his hat off:
" 'I have a letter, sir, from Lord Howe to Mr. Washington.'
" 'Sir,' says Colonel Reed, 'we have no person in our army with that address.'
" 'Sir,' says the officer, 'will you look at the address?' He took out of his pocket a letter which was thus addressed:
'George Washington, Esq., New York

'Howe.'
" 'No, sir,' says Colonel Reed, 'I cannot receive that letter.'
" 'I am very sorry,' says the officer, 'and so will be Lord Howe, that any error in the superscription should prevent the letter being received by *General Washington*.'
" 'Why, sir,' says Colonel Reed, 'I must obey orders.'

" 'Oh, yes, sir, you must obey orders, to be sure.'

"Then, after giving him a letter from Colonel Campbell to General Howe, and some other letters from prisoners to their friends, we stood off, having saluted and bowed to each other. After we had got a little way, the officer put about his barge and stood for us and asked by what particular title he chose to be addressed.

"Colonel Reed said, 'You are sensible, sir, of the rank of General Washington in our army?'

" 'Yes, sir, we are, I am sure my Lord Howe will lament exceedingly this affair, as the letter is quite of a civil nature, and not a military one. He laments exceedingly he was not here a little sooner'; which we suppose to allude to the Declaration of Independence; upon which we bowed and parted in the most genteel terms imaginable."[12]

Meanwhile, ten miles above the town, at Fort Washington's headquarters on Mount Washington, General Thomas Mifflin, quartermaster of the army, is completing some routine correspondence. His major task, assigned to him by the Commander-in-Chief a few days ago, is to speed up the preparations on the Jersey Bluff Rock just above Bourdette's ferry landing.

Mifflin's inefficiencies in the office of quartermaster will prompt him to resign from the army in February 1779. His resignation will be accepted by the Congress without hesitation.[13] But now he is commendably carrying out orders to rush the task to completion. The insolent passage of the frigates, *Phoenix* and *Rose* past Fort Washington's works Friday has resulted in a furious acceleration of the work on the Jersey side.

With word in hand that The General's Council of War has unanimously approved the plans for the mountain fortification and that a report of progress is urgent, Mifflin writes his chief:

"The party opposite us on the Jersey side are at work on the mountain and will soon have the ground prepared for cannon."[14]

All through the Continental Army there is a restless itching for action. It is, in part, the constant urge in man to test himself and measure his worth against his opponents. But among the American forces, generally, it is the determination to repel the invasion of their lands.

Little is the American army's strength in contrast with His Majesty's forces, but against Britannia's renowned naval superiority, the rebels have nothing. That is unless row-gallies, Durham boats, whaleboats, pettiaugers, yawls and fishing smacks can be considered the nucleus for a navy.

Therefore the river batteries must suffice. Fort Washington, and the new works opposite it, will have to take the place of a navy if the enemy is to be prevented from passage upriver. Certainly they will make the foe much less contemptuous and cause the British admiralty to think twice before attempting to break through again.

Something else is also being considered. It is no longer a secret that the Chief has liked General Israel Putnam's plan to construct a blockade of sunken, stone-laden, ships' hulls from bank to bank across the river. If that is done under the heights on which are mounted the heavy cannon of the two sister forts, Bourdette's on The Mountain and Fort Washington on the opposite bank, the artillery gunners on both sides will have some standing targets in their sights. Or at least some very slow moving ones when the enemy vessels approach the barrier.

The Hudson Valley Trembles

And so the preparation for battle, ever a feverishly exciting, macabre thing, proceeds now at a grueling pace. It is the battle itself which becomes fearfully appalling. And this all soon will discover.

The upriver Hudson valley landholders are frightened and are loud about it. They want. no part of the battleground and they form a powerful bloc when all their pressure is exerted upon the Philadelphia Congress. But Congress tactfully shifts the pressure to the American Commander-in-Chief. Consequently the flaunting manner in which the enemy vessels passed under Fort Washington and roamed the river from The Narrows to Nyack, has made the whole Hudson Valley tremble, the Congress irritable and The General responsible.

The upriver valley people, like the descendants of the Dutch, Huguenot and English settlers in the Hackensack and Passaic River valleys in Jersey across the river, are torn apart by the war in their allegiances. Whigs, Tories, dissenters and neutralists in New York's Westchester and The Highlands, as in the East Jersey valleys, are constantly haranguing and harassing one another.

The peoples of all the river regions, as well as the inhabitants of New York town, know that the stronger side will draw in the weakest among the wavering partisans. Once the aurora of victory, is in the air, loyalties for and against the cause will split and sever families and friends.

Both Whigs and Tories know the adage of the victor and the

spoils. And, still much closer to their homes and lives than sentiment, is the fear of being stripped of livestock, property and
possessions. The Tory partisans await a British victory; the Whig
and Patriot partisans await an American miracle.

So, with only geography and chance, and a small, poorly
equipped army of recruits, volunteers and militia, all holding only
short-term enlistment papers, the American Commander must make
every possible effort to keep the Congress and the people confident.

To do so, he has concluded that he must meet the British
invasion with the best efforts he and his army can muster. For,
though wisdom dictates withdrawal, politics dictates a show of
strength.

To protect the Hudson Valley and his communications with
New England he must:

(1) Commit a strong force to Westchester which will act as a
secondary line of defense north of Manhattan and help to counteract any possible wedge the enemy may attempt to drive from east
to west;

(2) Establish a defense along the Palisades on the Jersey shore,
protecting the routes from Paulus Hook, Newark and Hackensack
and the highways to Philadelphia and the South.

And, (3) acknowledging that the Hudson Valley could be the
key to New England for Sir William, he must, without any
semblance of a navy, blockade the river and prevent British shipping from penetrating Westchester, thus cutting off his communications with, not only New England, but the Northern Department
(army) above Albany.

All of this must be done without knowing when or where the
Howe brothers will strike and invade. But The General is certain
his enemy will attempt to sever the American supply lines at the
earliest opportunity.

It is a quiet summer day in the sleepy valleys lying west over
the Palisadean mountain in Jersey. Only the working parties from
Mount Washington ignore the Sunday rule of rest. They have been
steadily busy on the Bluff Rock above Bourdette's ferry landing.

And there at the long dock, Pete Baummeister, ignoring the
continuous movement of army personnel and equipment from
across the river and up the gorge road to the Bluff Rock, repairs
the *Hope*'s mainsail which had been ripped in the wind.

Beside him on the dock, Elaine helps, holding the torn canvas
exactly as he wants it. She watches every boat coming over from
the Fort Washington post as though she were expecting someone.

Then, looking downriver, she says to her father, "Do you think, Papa, that we will ever see him again?"

The pipe hardly moves in his mouth, as he continues sewing the stiff canvas and answering her at the same time without looking up from his work, "Yah, praps so! Praps so! Yah."

Unlike the frightened, tension-stressed faces in the quiet valleys, on the boats in the rivers and in the army encampments, Papa Baummeister and his daughter seem not too concerned about the coming war. They have learned to accept things as they are, as they come. Besides, they have other problems and worries.

3

Monday, August 12. . .

Soft as the Eaglet's Shell

Unpopular Aborigines

Daily the work on the Bluff Rock emplacements proceeds without letup. Every week a new party of about 150 men arrives usually under a field officer, three captains, six sergeants and six corporals.[1] The relief party always marches ashore with its own drums and fifes, while the relieved work party moves out accompanied by its own happy-faced drum and fife corps.

And for a month now, Elaine has thought, and even dreamed about the *Hope's* adventure to Paulus Hook, particularly about the rescue deed of Lieutenant Gray. So each Monday she has watched the new arrivals from New York's city. But last week she finally concluded it was ridiculous. For the girl is by nature a practical young woman, and so decided to forget all about her first "imaginary" romance.

As the high flat table-top Bluff Rock above the ferry is now the American army's province and can no longer serve as Elaine's outdoor school classroom, the school has been discontinued, at least until she can use the Baummeister parlor. The cliffside children and Elaine's brother, Paul, have enjoyed her daily lessons, which have the pleasing side advantage of enabling them to escape, even for a little while, the countless chores that are daily awaiting the river's edge young people.

47

Nevertheless, she and the children still frequently climb the rocky cliff path which, at places, is almost level with the Bluff Rock's top. And, besides their observations of nature's work, they become engrossed also with the army men and their difficult task of positioning the heavy cannon.

Unlike the natives of The Mountain area, the soldiers have a loathing fear of the sun-bathing rattlesnakes and copperheads. The rocky clefts, where eagles, hawks and sea gulls rest and nest, is the refuge of the reptiles. They prey upon the big birds' eggs as the latter do upon the fish, fowl and smaller beasts below.

However, the natives have a respect and admiration for the aborigines and stay in respectful distance. For the cliff people have learned from the gentle Lenni Lenape to kill and destroy only for the need of food.

Unfortunately, their "live and let live" motto is not adopted by the snake-frightened Continentals. The soldiers' slaughter and destruction of the wild life when carried on beyond necessity, brings strong criticism from The Mountain's guardian-like people.

It is the fear of snakes that puts happy faces on those working parties returning to New York town after a tour of duty on The Rock. And always the newest recruits arrive with wide, scare-stricken eyes, for the older hands take a devilish delight in frightening the uninitiated with exaggerated stories about the size and ferocity of the Bluff Rock's reptiles.

Still many of the older men have had a turn on the Bluff without as much as having seen the signs of a snake of any kind. Nevertheless, the customary jocularity and jesting about the "squirmers" make for conversation which, in turn, helps time pass more rapidly.

Thus, when a doctor from General Horatio Gates' Northern Army, comes through on his way to Philadelphia, all the men and officers perk up their ears around the evening campfire when he begins to tell the story of a soldier's rattlesnake bite at Ticonderoga. Until then they had paid only courteous passing attention to his report of the deplorable state of affairs with the American army in the North.

The Northern Department's hardships, the soldiers' sufferings, the extent of small-pox and the deaths it has caused with many men dying from attempted self-inoculations, the lack of supplies, provisions and stores, and the exhausted state of the American troops under Major General Horatio Gates, fighting off the British forces coming down from Canada into Lake Champlain—all these accounts were impressionless in contrast with his mention of the Ticonderoga rattlesnakes.

When he declared that the Northern Army was "in a state but little short of desperation"[2] they politely disregarded the doctor's account except for the mentioned soldier who was bitten by the snake. So the physician acquiesces and obliges with a detailed description.

He explains how a worker on the Ticonderoga fortification, in a display of bravery before his astounded comrades, imprudently seized a rattlesnake by its tail. Disgusted with man's stupidity, the doctor sarcastically recounts, the intelligent rattler threw its head back and generously imbedded its fangs in the young soldier's hand.

Quickly dropped, the reptile slithered off, leaving the brave, stupid soldier, as the doctor described him, with a new-found respect for snakes, if not all beasts, but with "a hand-made problem."

Since the loquacious surgeon has found the key to his audience's attention, he continues even more vividly than before. And as the young men around him listen wide-eyed, he tells how another doctor found the soldier a few minutes later with immense swelling and severe pain.

"Within a half hour his whole arm up to his shoulder was swollen," the physician said. "Soon his arm was twice its natural size with the skin turning a deep orange color."[3]

"Then," continues the story-teller, "the soldier's body began swelling followed by nausea, pain and shock. Two other doctors also came to his aid. For several hours all three directed the man to swallow large and repeated doses of olive oil until he had drunk a quart. At the same time they rubbed the affected limb with a very large quantity of mercurial ointment.

"In about two hours the remedy took effect," concludes the entertaining medic. "The swelling went down. The pain went away. In two days he was back with his company as good as new."[4]

There will be more than one of the doctor's young listeners who will decide to stay up and near the campfire's, snake-repelling light tonight.

The works on the Bluff Rock are daily nearing completion under General Mifflin's direction despite the working parties' reptilisphobia and nature's silent objections.

However, the place still has no name. Since its beginning just a month ago, it has been called "The Mountain," Burdett's Ferry,"

"Burdett's Landing," "Moor's Landing," "The Works Opposite Fort Washington," and "The Mountain Opposite Jeffery's Hook."

The latest rumor has it that it will be named, "Mount," or "Fort Constitution." Everyone knows this will be confusing for there already is a "Fort Constitution" which lies upriver in the highlands between Peekskill and Newburgh.

The writing of a "constitution" for the newly formed nation is a big topic of conversation. Consequently the name, Fort Constitution, is proper for one such post. Not for two, even though some are saying, "It takes a good *constitution* to climb to the Bluff Rock and a bigger *constitution* to prevail over its aboriginal inhabitants."

Despite their bold front, Bourdette, Baummeister and their families have much to fear in the event of a river battle under the Bluff Rock. General Mifflin, reflecting his Commander-in-Chief's concern for the Bourdettes and the river people, has 30 pieces of cannon mounted on the Fort Washington side. He is attempting to balance this with the same number on the Jersey side. Including the barbette and redoubts on The Rock, the defenses will consist of seven or eight batteries along the shore to protect the ferry and the homes adjacent to it.

The Bourdette house-inn, barns, stable and stagecoach station are west of the long Bourdette ferry dock. Behind the Bourdettes' place and southwest near the gorge road, is the big, two-story Baummeister homestead.

Between the two houses runs the brook after streaming down the mountainside under the bridge over the gorge road. It pours down The Mountain from its over-flowing pond at the summit. A cowpath runs up the rocky gully to the mountain's crest and on to a cattle-grazing field. Not far from the pond is the hamlet's burial ground.

It is to the north of the Bourdette ferry, on the east side of the deep gorge road that runs along the shore up from the ferry and through the ravine, that rises the great sentinel Bluff Rock. It is as though a colossal knife had cut it off and away from the main, mother ridge, leaving the gulch between them to provide the ascent from the river to the giant mountain's summit.

The gulch, or gorge, road carries the traveler from the wharf up over the mountain, down the west slope joining the King's highway north or south through the valley, or west to Hackensack. However, there is also a river road, often impassable in places, which runs from Paulus Hook north to the Wehawk landing, then on to the Bull's ferry dock and from there to Bourdette's where it runs into the gorge road.

Birth Of the Blockade

So The Mountain and its cliff dwellers beneath it have suddenly become the center of the war's focus. And Bourdette, in whose household the American Commander-in-Chief feels comfortably at ease, should be more concerned than he appears.

The outspoken patriot has enjoyed antagonizing the Tory elements, regardless of whether they are passing through, or are local inhabitants. It is, of course, fully realized that the Tories and Loyalists merely await their turn to assist the Crown. Meanwhile strife and tensions mount.

There is no doubt that an enemy vessel hugging the west bank could destroy the little hamlet by the waterside with only a few broadsides. For this reason alone, The General insisted that a battery redoubt be placed at the ferry road but in from the river bank. Such defenses are not too difficult to acquire through the New York Secret Committee which is making every effort to build the defenses at the twin posts. Such efforts, it is hoped, will prove effective in protecting New York's upper Hudson River Valley inhabitants.

William Duer, appointed to the Secret Committee at a convention of the New York representatives, had strongly urged the construction of emplacements on both banks, saying:

> "If proper batteries are erected near the water at Mount Washington and on the opposite side mounted with guns of 18, 24, and 32-pounders, it will not be practicable for any vessel to be so near as to prevent our working under the cover of these works upon the proposed constructions."[5]

Consequently, the river batteries were the first to be constructed by General Mifflin. Mifflin, among others, knows that gun emplacements, redoubts and shore batteries may not be enough to stop enemy shipping from gaining command of the Hudson.

Thus, it is with optimism that the patriot inhabitants and the military look upon General Israel Putnam's plan for blockading the river with rock-laden, submerged ships' hulls.

Putnam, writing to General Gates today, explained his proposed naval stratagen—a blockade construction, or "chevaux de frise." He states that it will consist of sunken logs and barges, all tightly chained together. They are to be stretched across the river at a point underneath the northernmost section of the Bluff Rock to Jeffery's Hook. This is about the narrowest part of the river, he tells Gates, adding that he has ordered four vessels sunk close by Fort Washington "for this purpose."[6]

If the news circulating around the campfires tonight concerning the state of affairs of the Northern Department is sad and disheartening, it is not so of the dispatches arriving from the Southern Army under General Charles Lee. Word has come from Philadelphia that Lee has written Congress telling how he has twice repulsed the enemy at Charleston and that he has inflicted great losses upon them.[7]

Meanwhile, in the American Army encampment in New York, waiting and wondering when and where Howe will strike his blow, Colonel Daniel Hitchcock reads over his orders for the day. It is he who is assigned with his men to man the newly completed artillery batteries at The Mountain above Bourdette's ferry landing.

He received his directions several days ago and immediately notified his command from which he met some grumbling reactions. The soldiery would much rather meet Howe's 35,000 troops than the Bluff Rock's guardian serpents.

As though he were being exiled and feared his end were close, Hitchcock writes a revealing letter to his friend, Colonel Little, stationed on Long Island under General Greene, that he regrets Little is not going along with him. Hitchcock adds:

"I hope we shall be able to defend ourselves against rattlesnakes without you which I am told are very plenty there."[8]

Hitchock, who has taken an immediate liking for the newly arrived Lieutenant Gray, offered to assign the officer to the east sector battery on Manhattan, commanded by the disliked and openly bigoted Lieutenant John Duychinck. It was from Duychinck's battery that Gray had acquired Big Tom and Jocko Graves at their request. And Duychinck, although a Middlesex New Jerseyan and a part of the Middlesex Second Regiment, has less desire than Hitchcock in going over to The Mountain.

Call Of the "River Lady"

Consequently, when Gray insists upon staying with his battery and going across under Hitchcock, he unintentionally acquires the appreciation of, not only Hitchcock, but also "Old Two-Faced" Duychinck, as the men of Duychinck's company call him behind his back.

Gray's insistence upon going across is certainly not motivated from a charitable interest in Duychinck's welfare. And most everyone knows of Gray's intense interest in "The Rock" across the river. And a few, including Jocko and Big Tom Graves, suspect that the young "river lady" is part of the attraction to the Jersey shore.

Gray has not mentioned the Baummeisters to anyone since he left them and their pettiauger a month ago at Paulus Hook. However he has impressed everyone with his knowledge of the Palisades, although he seldom volunteers any information unless someone shows interest in the "wonder range."

So, amidst the grumblings of the men in Gray's battery, only The Lieutenant himself—though outwardly showing no emotions—was thrilled as the barges pushed off from the Cortlandt Street wharf, bound with this morning's early tide for Bourdette's landing. Loaded into barges, Durhams and flatboats, Hitchcock's regiment sorrowfully look back upon the New York seaport town and dejectedly look forward to the mountainous wilderness in the distance.

To the sound of their drums and fifes they marched to the New York dock, harassed by the jests of returned working parties who, in no gentle terms, assured them they would have plenty of food—"roasted rattlesnake meat!"

But Hitchcock's men are a rugged mixture, a cross-section of Continentals from many of the colonial states. Most of them disdainfully ignored the working militia companies entirely, while others sneered at their would-be annoyers, recognizing them only with a swift spit from out of the side of their mouths.

Of the few who got a piece of mail at the wharf, mail that had come with yesterday's post, The Lieutenant was one. It is a copy of the July 15 issue of *The Pennsylvania Packet*. Gray's father had promised he would see that *The Packet* was sent him as regularly as possible. The Lieutenant stuffed the newspaper in his side pocket and went about the business of embarking.

It was mid-afternoon before Hitchcock's forces were fully disembarked and still later before they were marched again to the sound of their drums and fifes to the clearing on The Mountain's summit and to the Bluff Rock site emplacements where the artillery battery was assigned. Gray, on the landing pier, supervised the disembarking of his unit while his subordinate officers took charge of the unloading on the Bluff.

Jocko's horses had come across well. With the army wagons left

at Bourdette's he made trip after trip up the gorge road, emptying
supplies and baggage. On his last return, Colonel Hitchcock tells
him to inform Gray at the dock that Hitchcock welcomes him to
share his tent on the summit clearing tonight if The Lieutenant so
desires.

But there is no Gray in sight on the landing pier as Jocko
prepares to make his last ascent up to the Bluff Rock battery. He
sees the two houses, the Bourdette house and beyond it to the
southwest another house which the Bourdette ferryman and handy-
man, Honest Sam, tells him is the direction the officer took after
the last barge was unloaded.

"That is," he assures Jocko, "Mista Pete's house, and it is likely
they "is a milkin' their cows now and Missy Ellie is a doin' the
milkin' as she most allus does."

Jocko tethers the team and walks over toward the barn behind
the Baummeister home. For almost at the same moment he had
started, Jocko saw Gray going toward the partly closed barn doors.

Inside, milking one of the cows, which her brother pats on the
head, Elaine, on her milking stool, goes about her job on the teats
of the bovine's plump udders with the dexterity of a farmer.

Gray, meanwhile, was met on the Baummeister stoop by Papa
Pete who gave him welcome and directed him to Elaine in the
barn.

As he opens the barn door, Paul, who faces the door to which
Elaine has her back, exclaims, "Oh, look, Ellie! There's that Lieutenant Gray who swimmed us a tow!"

"Paully!" Elaine says angrily without lifting her bonneted, perspiring head from the cow's belly, "if you tease me any more
about that man, I'll tell Papa! Now, Paul, I mean it! I've had
enough of you and him!"

Then from the doorway not many feet behind her, comes the
deep voice of the man she had heard and seen but once and had
dreamed of for a month, "Paul is right, Miss Elaine. I am the
fellow who swam a line. And I only wanted to say hello."

As soon as he spoke, she straightened up on the stool, lost her
balance and fell over backwards to Paul's amusement.

Her face, already dirty from her chores, was now a match for
her soiled apron over the milk-splashed, printed calico. Elaine
could not have looked much worse and she knew it.

At the instant she toppled, Gray sprang to her side, picking her
up quickly.

"Well, Lieutenant," she says calmly brushing herself off, "he has been teasing me and now you know. It is true I am glad to see you again, but not this way that I am. Truth is I never thought we would meet again'"

"Nor I you, Miss Elaine," Gray replies. "Yet 'tis here on the battery above that I am now assigned."

"It is welcome then that you are to visit us here," she retorts. "Come! Come to the house for a cooling drink. Papa will be glad to see you again."

"I have already seen him," says Gray. "He directed me here."

"I should have known that! It is just like him, knowing as he did, how terribly I look. Well come and meet Mama anyway!"

But Jocko's voice now breaks in. He had appeared unnoticed in the doorway. Interrupting, he tells Gray of Hitchcock's invitation and reminds him that he has the wagon and team ready to ascend the gorge.

Gray thanks Elaine, whose eyes are suddenly bright and lively as they have not been for many weeks. He promises to return after supper on the morrow at which time he will, he assures her, look forward to meeting Mama Baummeister.

Bright Are the Lights In Nassau Hall

Gray remains with his men around the campfire on the Bluff rock after supper, planning to join Hitchcock later and take advantage of his large tent for the night's lodging. Suddenly, feeling something in his pocket, he pulls from out of his coat the newspaper he had stuffed inside early that morning.

Several of the men along with Jocko urge him to read something from the newspaper to them. The first story that meets his eye is dated July 15, 1776. It is an account from "Prince Town," so Gray obliges and reads:

> "Last night Nassau Hall was grandly illuminated, and INDEPENDENCE proclaimed under a triple volley of musketry and universal acclamation for the prosperity of the UNITED STATES. The ceremony was conducted with the greatest decorum."

"Lootenant, ain't that where you schooled at, Prince Town?" questions Corporal Mike Monahan. "Ain't it?"

Gray nods his head in agreement and continues, but the account is difficult for them to follow. They are more interested in how rapidly news had traveled. That happened only 25 days ago and was reaching them way in the wilds of East Jersey. This was the remarkable thing!

To The Lieutenant, who started back across the gulch to the main mountain's summit and Hitchcock's tent, the importance of the item had far greater meaning. He stopped and picked up the broken shell of an eaglet's egg dropped from a high towering pine tree. Then, crushing the pieces of shell in his hand, he counted silently and concluded that the United States of America was, on this day, just 39 days old—a little over a month "in the womb of liberty," as he put it.

Glancing up at the large eagles hovering over their nest in which rested another eaglet embryo in its shell, possibly only about 39 days also, he thought, "How soft the eaglet's shell! God grant they both can survive!"

4

Sunday, August 18. . .

Battling for the Hudson

Monarchs Versus Fire Rafts

For 37 days the British frigates, *Phoenix* and *Rose*, have lain at anchor in Haverstraw Bay. There off the town they ended their haughty ascent of the river July 12 after skirting out from under the Fort Washington batteries, 24 miles south.

At Haverstraw they have recruited men for the British Army with the active assistance of the many Tory partisans. For the Tories have frightened the "neutrals" with wild rumors, threats and merciless raids upon livestock and property. So neutrals as well as patriots and Whigs have suffered severe losses since the plundering acts discourage many borderline patriots from any further defiances of the Crown.[1]

The mischief these warships have caused with their guns constantly pointed at the town and its inhabitants, has created angry opposition among the local New York State militia. With the help of Continentals of the Line, the militia have been more than busy in a quiet way.

Constructing large rafts, the local patriots and militia have concealed their strange craft, secluding them in marshes and carrying on their clandestine enterprise with the utmost secrecy, waiting patiently for a favorable night, wind and tide to carry out their spectacular and ingenious, fiery, plan.

57

" 'Long as we ain't got no navy to fight 'em with," says one of the leaders, "we'll fight 'em with everything we got."

The surprise plan was a simple one, relying mostly upon nature. At the right nocturnal hour the rafts were to be set afire and guided into the helpless, floating hulls of the frigates.

Since the schooner and tenders were placed as guardian outposts for the larger ships, they had to be the first objects in the attack plan.

Late last night the weather, wind and tide began cooperating with the rebel patriots' scheme, and early this morning, in the dark hours after midnight, the Americans hauled out their rafts.

Each has been prepared and readied for ignition. Kindling wood and tinder are heaped high. The sky is overcast, hiding a waning moon. A light breeze from the east blows along with the incoming current, enabling the rafts to be towed out from the marshy cove and sent directly into the sides of the schooner and the tenders.

Over the calm water, gently and quietly moving with the tide, the oarsmen quietly tow the three, still unlighted fireboats up to the anchor lines of the guardian vessels. Two more are readied for the big frigates.

Suddenly the hidden torches blossom with yellow flames. In seconds they are engulfed in the center of the fiery rafts[2] which quickly ignite the sides of the schooner and one of the tenders.

The third raft misses its mark and drifts in toward the big black hulk of the *Phoenix*. Deck sentinels shout out their ear-piercing alarms from their posts on all the British vessels, and, within minutes, the crews are battling the flames with water-buckets while some in row-gallies attempt to pole the fireboats away from the ships' hulls.

Only the windless night and the quick assistance received from the crews of the other vessels save the valuable schooner from a fiery end. But it is several hours before the destructive fire is controlled and finally extinguished.

One of the tenders suffers considerable damage. The second and the two men-of-war escape, owing largely to the fury of the bright flames. So much light is cast upon the water that the two burning fireboat torches are left to float around the bay unguided. They and the one that headed for the *Phoenix* are successfully staved off by the alerted crews until they burn themselves out, causing mischief but no damage.

In the eerie light, amid the wild confusion of shouting sailors, men overboard, and row-gallies and barges battling flames and directing the fiery rafts off from the vessels' sides, the American oarsmen easily return to shore. There they watch their mischief at work. By dawn they scatter, disappearing into the woodlands. For them the night's work was a blazing success.

Not only was it a success, it also has far-reaching after-effects. His Majesty's ships, officers and crews are now threatened with a new type of nocturnal, marine ambush for which they have no defense. Never before has the King's Navy been called upon to fight this type of river warfare. No longer do officers and men feel secure and in control. Another such mysterious attack might find His Majesty's frigates mere hulks, burned to the waterline by such tactics if the wind stiffens.

Captain Parker[3] on the *Phoenix* immediately orders all hands to prepare for returning downriver on the tide. Temporary repairs are hastily made to both the schooner and the tender.

By mid-morning the British ships head back south, favored by an easterly breeze. Into their sights now come the twin forts and the blockade. Only Fort Washington had confronted them when they ascended the stream a little over five weeks ago.

Now before them are batteries on both banks of the water. In addition, a formidable looking barrier, the Americans' new Chevaux de Frise, stands directly in their path. But the most menacing sight to Captain Parker and his little flotilla is the threatening looking Barbette Battery and redoubts high on the great, towering Bluff Rock on the *Phoenix's* starboard side.

Though he sees little with his spyglass other than the outlines of the precipice-top batteries, he knows the rebel gunners are waiting for him. His main thought is to crash full force through the river blockade and get out from under the two forts' flanking fires.

Facing Captain Parker and his already severely wounded five-vessel flotilla, there is no alternative. One escape course might be possible through the Spuyten Duyvil, the opening at Manhattan's northern end, separating New York island from Westchester. This leads into the Harlem River and then into the East river, but surely along both banks there the Americans have artillery emplacements far more numerous than along the much wider Hudson.

From Fort Washington across to the new fortress on The Mountain between which the blockade stretches is less than 4,000 feet. And the deepest navigable channel lies closest to the towering Bluff Rock's side. So the dauntless Captain Parker and his men steel themselves as they head directly into the center of the Chevaux de Frise.

It is a little past noon. All hands at all the redoubts and batteries on both sides of the river are at their posts. They have been waiting ever since the British ships were first sighted and the alarms rang the air above both fortresses with the call to stations.

The lieutenant who left his studies at the college in Prince Town to enlist in the American cause, is in command of the big Barbette Battery, as it is called, high on the prominence of the great rock. He has been hastily summoned from the Baummeister house at the foot of the gorge road, for he is almost a daily luncheon guest at Papa Pete's amply supplied dining table.

So, when the breathless, excited Jocko Graves rides down on one of his horses and commands, "Lootenan! Come quick! Da big ships is a comin' down the ribber! Quick!," Gray takes the old nag's reins and, with Jocko behind him, makes for his post in record time.

Jocko, who is now thoroughly adopted by Gray's Barbette Battery, is the only member of the company who, it seems, can give orders to the officer, outside of his military superiors, and have them immediately obeyed.

Since all of Gray's free time is spent with the Baummeister family, Jocko always knows where to find him. For within the short period of a week, Baummeister has virtually adopted the artillery officer as wholeheartedly as the battery has attached itself to Jocko.

Everyone knows that The Lieutenant's main interest is the 18-year-old, five-foot five beloved favorite of the Baummeister family and the neighboring Bourdette household as well. And everyone knows that her thoughts have, for some time, been transferred from her adored ferry-master father to the safety and welfare of the Pennsylvanian for whose 21st birthday, ten days hence, she is spinning from flax, two initialed handkerchiefs.

For Elaine Baummeister, in contrast with most women folk of this century, makes no pretense at concealing her emotions and affections. She has always been openly honest and sincere with others. Her likes and dislikes are seldom secret. Most people soon know where she stands, and she, in turn, expects the same sincerity from others.

So, within minutes after the panting, 15-year-old black boy reaches Mama Baummeister's garden fence-gate, interrupting the conversing lovers, the young officer is back up on the Bluff Rock. He now levels his field glasses on the approaching gliding targets headed for the blockade under his guns. Yet, as he gives last-minute instructions to his cannoneers, loaders and wipers, he feels a sense of wickedness in destroying such beautiful ships and taking the lives of those within them.

His sensitivity and love of man now suddenly jolt him. But his guilt falls rapidly away from his thoughts as he sees the enemy cannon pointing for, and sighting on his battery over 3,000 feet above the flotilla. For he knows that the absence of guilt is the basic axiom of war.

The work on the Chevaux de Frise was begun on the east bank not much more than a fortnight ago.[4] It is still in progress.

A large craft of any kind coming down from north, upriver, riding with a stiff wind and the tide, could, with not too much difficulty, break through the obstructions. And two of them striking the blockade in unison, might easily snap the links of the chain holding the sunken logs and hulls together. Especially since the tightening and strengthening work has not been completed.

This intelligence Captain Parker learned days ago from the upriver Tory informers. And the artillerymen know that vessels stilled and entrapped, make easy targets. Once stalled by the Chevaux de Frise, it is expected that any enemy vessel will not survive very long, sitting in an unmovable position under the constant poundings from shore batteries on both sides of the river.

Secure behind the high parapet, The Lieutenant peering through his telescope, distinguishes the names on the bows of the frigates, *Phoenix* and *Rose*—the same two armed frigates he had seen in warring anger that memorable day at "Powlershook," as the Dutchman Van Vorst and others call it.

That was six weeks ago. Now the two magnificent but awesome monarchs of the sea, swept by their following wind, appear like full-blown birds as they skim silently over the water, their tenders and the schooner between and behind them.

It is evident that Captain Parker, Captain Wallace, and Lieutenant Brown who commands the schooner, *Tryal,*[5] plan to strike the blockade with such force that they may, without stalling, be carried through and across it.

It is a long chance and a risky one but their only possible course of action. With all the canvas they can spread they push their vessels to six, seven and more knots toward the partially submerged barrier.

Restlessly impatient, every gunner at his post on both sides of the river awaits the command to destroy and kill. All fort commanders join the artillery emplacements. Each carefully observes

"Forcing the Hudson River Passage," Painting By Doninque Serres.
Courtesy U.S. Naval Academy Museum.

the approaching vessels, biding his time before issuing the order to fire.

To the Americans it is like watching a fleeing animal running toward a wall with the slim hope of finding a hole through which to escape, or possibly hurdling it with a do or die leap. However, in this case, the animal is armed.

A deathly silence hangs over the forts along the Jersey and New York shores as the enemy ships noiselessly bear down into range.[6] Then, as all eyes watch breathlessly the *Phoenix* and then the *Rose* strike the chains between the half sunken barges with the full force of their heavily plated bows.

Jolted by the terrific impact, the vessels' timbers shudder violently, though the thuds are hardly audible up on The Rock. But the shroud lines of the frigates' masts can be seen shivering as though in frenzied wrath from the collision. The sails of both the warships momentarily flap loosely in the wind as the *Tyral* and the tenders come up from behind and toward the frigates' sterns.

Under Cross Fire

As though the impact were the signal, the stillness of the early afternoon is suddenly shattered by the angry, roaring thunder of the battleships' broadsides. They pour their heaviest fire east and west at the rebels' forts. Parker has no means of judging the amount of American power that can be returned. All he can do is hope that his show of defiance and confidence will tend to discourage, if not disperse, the American artillerymen.

In this expectation Captain Parker is sorely disappointed. For almost immediately the British barrage is answered by all the artillery emplacements within range from both sides of Hudson's river. And then, for a few brief moments, the excited feverish activity of the British seamen, carrying out in perfect order their assigned tasks on the vessels' decks, is clearly seen from the Bluff's heights.

Now the warships, protectingly flanking their slowed auxiliary craft, are clustered briefly in mid-river. Their guns bark out incessantly at both shores like stags at bay, turning to fight their pursuers. The battling vessels are soon hidden under the pall of smoke raised by their thirty constantly firing broadsides.

The *Phoenix* with its forty guns is closest to Fort Washington's east shore upon which it trains twenty cannon, all on the larboard side. Captain Wallace's *Rose*, which is the smaller of the two frigates carries only twenty guns. It is closest to The Mountain, the Bluff Rock and its shore batteries. The *Rose* has ten cannon trained on the river's west bank.

Unable to observe the results of their firing, the Americans hammer away with all the gunnery they command. They use all weapons that cover the range. The noise is now almost beyond description. The blasts echo back and forth over the water while the stench rises and drifts westward over the Palisades and the valley beyond, frightening the inhabitants and sending wild life fleeing frantically in every direction.

The balls from the American redoubts at the mountain fort and from Fort Washington fall through the canopy of white gunpowder smoke over the faltering British sails. Havoc seems to prevail all over the battle scene.

The Erroneous Assessment

To the Americans' dismay the vessels stall only momentarily under the mantle of smoke from their own barrage. To the British seamen, showered on both sides by canister shot, grape and shell from above their pall of smoke the moment of pausing uncertainty is like an eternity.

The big question—have the ships' bows broken apart the chains and opened a passage through the barrier?—is answered when the frigates' sails recapture the wind and, slowly at first, glide through the snapped chains of the Chevaux de Frise.

Ringing the air with their exultant cheers, the seamen come out from under the smoke still showered heavily by the continuous American bombardment on all five vessels. But the strong northeast wind fills all canvas as the flotilla breaks out toward midstream in the widening river, hurriedly straining for distance and escape from the range of the forts' artillery. The first battle for control of the upper Hudson is over.

The first test of the Chevaux de Frise is, in the opinion of the American commanders and their artillerymen, a disappointment. To the inhabitants who observed the spectacle along the river's banks, the enemy ships appear to have sailed through the barricade as though there were none. As they saw it, the American fire from the twin forts seemed to have produced little effect if any upon the warships, their schooner and the tenders. They survey the damage on shore done by the British broadsides and they gather the King's cannon shot for the army's use.

It is discouraging news to General Israel Putnam, especially upon hearing of the American casualties suffered from the enemy barrage and receiving no reports of damage done to the flotilla. General Putnam and his distant relative, Chief Engineer of the American Army Colonel Rufus Putnam, are certain that had the chains and sunken barges been tightened and more firmly placed, the ships would never have broken through.

Three American privates who were manning the shore batteries at Bourdette's lie severely wounded. Four artillerymen at Fort Washington are casualties. All are to be sent to the General Hospital on Chambers Street in New York under the surgeon, Dr. Solomon Drowne.

It is the pessimistic judgment of the American staff officers that the British ships escaped without sustaining any damage. The staff's conclusion spreads throughout the American posts, among the inhabitants on both sides of the river, throughout the valleys and the New York American encampments. They throw a cloak of gloom over the artillerymen and the soldiers who had worked so hard upon the construction.

Only the Tory partisans and Loyalists are exuberant over the rumors and reports. They, too, have yet to learn the real extent of damage the flotilla has suffered, not only in Haverstraw Bay, but in the reckless running of the American blockade.

Elaine, who had stood off to the south gorge road with her family, the Bourdettes and the local inhabitants of the cliffs, had watched the action safely away from the firing. When it was all over, her first concern was for the young artillery officer on the Bluff Rock.

All hurriedly go back to their homes to assess what damage was done. Fortunately, the only damage counted is a pillar on the Bourdette house which took a cannon ball. The missile lodged itself in the timber. Bourdette decides to leave it there as a memento to the inaccuracy of the British gunners.

Elaine, her father, mother and brother make a quick reconnaissance of the homestead, cattle and grounds. She then picks up the luncheon basket she had earlier prepared for Gray and heads up the gorge road for the Barbette Battery. At her heels, Paul has trouble keeping up with her.

The girl recovers her composure as she passes the sentry and sees John in the distance discussing with his men the good and bad points of their actions during the battle. In a glance she is relieved to see no observable casualties, but she notices Gray holds his left arm, burned slightly from a hot breech during the fight.

Since she brings the first news from the water's edge, all of Gray's men crowd around as she reports on the action, casualties and damage encountered by the shore batteries near the landing. It is The Lieutenant's burned arm that primarily concerns her. She excuses herself and goes back to where she left the lunch basket and there, with her back to the battery, she tears a long strip of cloth from her blue petticoat.

Then, returning to Gray, she begins bandaging the arm, first coating it with butter taken from her lunch basket. The artillery crew are all ears as she talks and simultaneously dresses the officer's injury, the only one sustained by his entire battery.

All listen attentively as she tells how Colonel Ward's men at the ferry landing redoubts suffered three severe casualties from the British shelling. All the wounded moved over in a barge to Fort Washington as soon as the enemy vessels were out of sight. But her most exciting story is her account of the attempted desertion of the American carpenter, Nails Hardenbrook.[7]

Hardenbrook, she tells them, worked for her father before joining in the construction task at The Mountain's works, but always displayed a strong affection for the Crown. Then she described his drowning a few hours ago.

When the British warships struck the blockade and stopped, Elaine relates, the carpenter dashed away from the men watching the battle. No one knew what he was up to. Suddenly, he ran down the cliffside and plunged into the river from the ferry dock.

With all his strength he began swimming out toward the tender, staying away from the *Rose's* guns nearest the Jersey shore. Some thought the tender was having trouble, but the cloud of smoke over the ships made it impossible to be sure.

Then, halfway between the tender, which seemed to have been hit in its rigging, and the shore, Nails went down, Elaine recounted.

"His arms went flailing in all directions like this," she says, gesticulating in imitation of the carpenter's last moments. "Then under he went, came up gulping and then finally disappeared entirely."

Most of the men of the Barbette Battery had known Nails Hardenbrook. There were many whom he tried to influence with his arguments for abandoning the revolt against the Empire. There were some who had even suspected that he was only working on the fortification in order to pass on whatever information he could to his Loyalist friends.

Since it is easy to sense a man's views and learn his true thoughts in such close living quarters as those on The Mountain, few soldiers or inhabitants had placed much trust in the Crown-admiring carpenter. Actually, Hardenbrook was finding it quite difficult to get along with anyone at Bourdette's Ferry for the past several weeks.

Colonel Ward,[8] it was believed, had not only suspected him but had sufficient information, lacking just a few facts, to charge him with consorting with the enemy. This, it was believed, was behind Hardenbrook's attempt to escape.

So the once popular carpenter was forced to weigh the values and allegiances of insurrection, revolution and war and die with his convictions. Little mourned by one side, he succumbed loyal to the other. And the other was unlikely ever to know of his existence.

Thus, little remorse is felt for Nails Hardenbrook. It is the Americans' own wounded and dying comrades on whom the rebels' thoughts are now focused.

When Elaine leaves and joins her father on the lower end of the gorge road, the men of the Barbette Battery begin their clean-up and preparations for the enemy's next attempt. It could come at any time, for the control of the river is one of the British army's main objectives in the conquest of Manhattan Island. So it is late this afternoon when the critique is called to assess the morning's action.

Many of the artillerymen swear they scored direct hits and are sure that extensive damage was the price the British paid. Others, mostly among the officers, think otherwise. The staff commanders finally decide that no one will probably ever know for certain since Howe is noted for concealing his losses from his enemy's intelligence when possible.

However, casualties, damages and losses cannot always be kept secret. Sooner or later the truth comes out as, for example, when the late afternoon post packet brings a newspaper from New York for one of the Barbette Battery's privates.

In it is an extract from a letter dated July 23, from Fort Montgomery. Somehow the extract found its way into the August 5 copy of the *New York Gazette and Weekly Mercury*. But the only things the private can read in the paper his optimistic mother has sent him are the cartoons.

The account puts an entirely different light on the American marksmanship and skill in the brief duel between the British ships and the Grand Battery at New York's tip July 12.

When one of the private's friends makes a stumbling attempt to read the letter, the young soldier snaps it away from him and asks The Lieutenant to read it to them all.

Always courteous and helpful, Gray often reads soldiers' mail aloud to them including that of Davey Pollock. Private Pollock's widowed mother carries on her deceased husband's candle-making business on South Street in New York town.

Unable to read English herself, she takes it for granted that her only son can. So she has one of her customers send him the popular *Weekly Mercury*. Pollock frequently asks others to read it to him. Jocko is a similar scholar who picks up reading in the same way.

Around the evening campfire, Gray takes the newspaper and first reminds the attentive audience that the American intelligence

reported the British ships were unscathed by the New York batteries in the July 12 exchange off the Paulus Hook post and the
Fort Washington artillery. For the benefit of the new men he
explains how the people of New York city ran in panic, fearing for
their lives[9] and how the American Commander-in-Chief has been
ordered by the Congress to defend the city.[10]

In answer to one question, inquiring why the enemy ships want
to go upriver, The Lieutenant echoes the thinking of the rebel
army's chieftain.[11] With a pointed stick he sketches a rough map
on the ground, diagramming the island of Manhattan, its position
in relation to the command of the North River, and how the
enemy could cut the communications between the Northern and
Southern Departments as well as disrupt the flow of supplies
among the colonial states themselves.

"We know all that maccaroni, Lieutenan'! Read the damned
letter!" It is the impatient Sergeant MacNamara interrupting as
usual. "Them's that don't know it best go back to drill school!"

The sergeant gets a good laugh from the men who voice their
agreement. And the young officer laughs along with his men, nods
and reads, reminding the soldiers that it is dated almost a month
ago:

> "The ships of war in the North River are now at Haverstraw. 'Tis evident
> their designs are frustrated, not expecting we were so well prepared to
> receive them.
> "Last Thursday a man made his escape from on board the *Rose*, by
> swimming. He is well known here by officers and men from Boston in the
> train. He was taken last summer by the *Rose* in going to the West Indies.
> "He says that the most damage they received was in passing the Battery
> at Powles Hook and the Blue Bell. The cook of the ship had a leg shot off,
> some others wounded, a 12-pounder lodged in their foremast, one came
> through her quarter galley into the cabin, and that her shrouds and rigging
> suffered much.
> "The *Phoenix's* damage he could not tell, only that she had received a
> shot in her bowsprit. What he saw he declared. As he was a prisoner, 'tis
> not likely they would let him know their disasters."[12]

Shouts of joy and cheers go up. Now every man in the battery
is positive that certain shots they fired struck their targets despite
the disillusionment of the command post. Now they are all convinced that they achieved more success today than any of their
officers realize.

Only the Eagle Knows

The cannoneers all are convinced that if they had had their weapons mounted for defense and ready on Friday, July 12, and if the blockade had been completed, the *Rose* and the *Phoenix* would have been destroyed. And they add that alongside of them at the bottom of the river would be the auxiliaries.

Only the Bluff Rock eagles' piercing eyes, only those dauntless British seamen aboard the beleaguered ships and only the British Admiralty will know the exact extent of today's damages until long after the war.

It will be then that the American cannoneers' confidence in themselves will be upheld. For the ships that today came under their fire are now in the lower bay off Staten Island licking wounds. The severity of those wounds will convince both the Howes that the conquest of the Hudson will be far from easy.

Among the casualties sustained by the flotilla are seven dead.[13] The Barbette's guns hulled the *Rose* once. Mount Washington's batteries hulled the *Phoenix* three times.[14] One tender was struck badly. It was therefore no wonder that neither the tender's crew nor the seamen from the other ships could extend a hand to the drowning carpenter, Hardenbrook. None could have attempted his rescue even had they had time to do so.

Future records will show that the flotilla was in constant peril this morning. So only the British and the eagles know the truth. History will learn it many decades from now. However the Americans will learn tomorrow that the action today cost them six lives from among their ranks.[15]

So on The Rock this evening there is no better morale-builder for the men of the Barbette Battery than that packet that bore the *New York Gazette and Weekly Mercury*. For in its pages was the uplifting news—routed by way of the far north post at Fort Montgomery and all around the British ships in Haverstraw Bay— telling the Barbette Battery at Bourdette's Landing of the uncredited success of their own batteries in New York town almost six weeks ago.

However, The Lieutenant's biggest morale-builder tonight is a lengthy blue bandage, wrapped around a slight burn on his left arm.

Bandage? Not exactly. It is more than that. Far more than that! It is a stripping from Elaine's blue, linen petticoat, a far more therapeutic device than a simple bandage.

5

Thursday, August 22. . .

Defiance Meets the Threat of Force

The Hovering, Darkening Cloud

It is four days since Captain Parker's ships returned limping into the haven of Staten Island's bay. Parker's expedition has convinced the Howes that naval strategy cannot alone sever the New York-New England communications. Only a full scale campaign, only an invasion is the answer to the rebels' defiance. For certainly the Crown's tremendous show of force has not intimidated the Americans' stubborn determination to continue with their rebellious resistance.

For two months the King's ships have poured into outer New York harbor. Thousands of British and Hessian troops have landed on Staten Island. It is a threatening display of might intended to force the thirteen colonies and their rebel army to sue for peace. The colonists know that peace is far from likely now and that unless it can be miraculously restored, attack and invasion are inevitable.

Under this frightening cloud people's tensions in New York town, in the valleys westward and along the upper Hudson and throughout the colonial states, are as strained as those of the soldiers. Tempers flare at the slightest provocation. And provocations are many.

One traveler, Simon Becker, a seller of wares, was in just such a

70

flaring mood when he came through the sentry post last night with a pass through the Bourdette Ferry. He was on his way to do business with the commissary at Fort Washington. Angry at the rough treatment he received yesterday at the Three Pidgeons[1] tavern south down the valley, he was ready to vent his spleen on the ferry landing sentinel. And he did!

In consequence of Becker's curt manner with the guard, both the post's duty officer and Lieutenant Gray, who was on post picket duty, quizzed Becker extensively.

"It's a bed of brazen Tories," the itinerant peddler told them, referring to the popular tavern in the Bergen Woods. "I tried my best to keep my tongue still. A few who I knew were of us said the Tories seem to know something big is going to happen. Something very big! Every danged one of them is all out sured the war is coming to an end. They swear the rebels will all be crushed."

There was nothing new that Becker added to what was common knowledge. Sir William and his brother have a force of upwards of 30,000 troops poised and ready. And their next move is everyone's guess. But before today's sun is high, it will also be common knowledge what that "something very big" is.

For even now, at 8 o'clock in the morning, there are 75 flatboats filled with the King's soldiers, all fully equipped for battle, lying in lower New York bay and about to cross it. Behind them are eleven gun-carrying batteaux. And, scooting in and out among the craft are a number of supervisory galleys, cheering the men and assisting the boat officers in maintaining strict discipline and order.

Northward from this massing naval arena, several armed frigates lie strategically near Denyse Point in the Narrows off Long Island. A number of others are anchored in Gravesend Bay. All are supported by bomb ketches. And all have one main service to perform: to cover the British landing operation on the shores of Gravesend Bay.[2]

Observers on the Jersey shore opposite Staten Island, have variously described the scene, calling it "A forest of masts," "A sea of 90 sails," or "Troops and more troops in 150 warships of the line." Similar verbal pictures, painted by those in New York town who can get a glimpse of the sight from rooftops or at the Grand Battery, spread fear and anxiety from mouth to mouth and from province to province.

The rebels have no defenses on Staten Island, no redoubts or batteries south of Red Hook on the New York side, or south of

Bergen Point and Paulus Hook on the Jersey side. So the British forces have taken over the island without meeting any opposition. Thus far, only the Americans' river defense batteries northward have barked out their defiance of the King's navy.

It is a build-up of strength that began with General Sir William Howe's arrival June 25 in his flagship, *Greyhound*, and two other men-of-war in the vanguard. Four days later 45 vessels joined the armada and two days after that came 82 more. In the following two months Staten Island and its surrounding bays, harbors and wharfs have become a veritable naval fortress, sheltering the most formidable army and navy ever assembled by Great Britain beyond the limits of her own shores.

Admiral Richard "Black Dick" Howe, whose arrival July 12 was celebrated with the bold ascent up the river of the Captain Parker flotilla, came directly across from England. Sir William, of course, had only to come down the coast, having evacuated Boston, leaving it to the American Commander's northern forces. Boston is too much of a patriot hotbed. New York, the Howes have been told, is a hotbed of Tories.

If peace cannot be restored, Howe plans to take Manhattan from the rebels instead of continuing his hopeless siege against the stubborn patriots of New England. However, the giant Palisades and the rivers around the New York Island now look far more formidable than they did on paper up in Halifax.

On Staten Island, once used by the Lenni Lenape Indians for their summer camping grounds, thousands of British tents have been erected in regimental order. Drums roll continuously. Parades, drills and military maneuvers have turned the former Indian summer playground into a vast British military and naval battle-training and staging area.

In and under this overwhelming massive display of force, the Howes—said to be the grandsons of George I and carrying, allegedly, the traditional Howe Family sympathy for the American cause[3]—had concocted a peace proposal. With it they had hoped to effect the end of the insurrection and return the Colonies safely to the Crown. For a peace settlement is the Howe Brothers' principal aim. War is not. But war it will be if peace cannot be negotiated. And Great Britain's reasons for restoring peace are numerous.

However, the brothers have found, much to their surprise, all their overtures thus far courteously rejected. The admiral had played chess with Benjamin Franklin when the Philadelphian philosopher was in London representing the Colonies. But when

Admiral Howe sent Franklin a letter in a attempt to feel out his sentiments toward a peace proposal, the wise old statesman of the Congress politely, but stiffly, sent back a noncommittal reply.

And Sir William also has made an effort. He had tried through a white flag to reach the American Commander-in-Chief. However, he had made the mistake of erroneously omitting "General" and addressing the rebel Leader as "Mister," adding, "Esq., etc. etc. etc."[4]

The Howe Brothers' Dilemma

Such negotiations, the brothers were told, are up to the Congress. But since the Congress is, in the eyes of the Crown, not a legitimate body and, consequently, its Declaration of Independence is not a legitimate act, the Howes have found themselves at a loss as to what agent or agents they might address themselves in an effort to negotiate a peace.

Since the emissaries whom the British General and the British Admiral have sent out on their missions return with reports of having met great courtesy and gentility from the so-called "rebels," the Howes are convinced they certainly are not dealing with ordinary, backwoods insurrectionists. If the brothers had felt that all that the rebels were waiting for was assurance that they would be pardoned for their insurgence, William and Richard now know better.

In order to emphasize that a peaceful negotiation is his primary concern, Admiral Howe has gone to the trouble of christening many of his ships with titles of good will. On the sterns of some of the vessels lying at anchor, are such names as: *Good Intent, Friendship, Amity's Admonition,* and *Felicity.*[5] It is Lord Howe's way of saying that peace should be restored and war should be avoided.

The Howe family in Great Britain is far from alone in its sympathetic leanings for the American cause. Edmund Burke's stentorian echoes on conciliation with the colonies still ring through the House of Commons. They have sown many seeds for thought throughout the British Isles. The seamen and the soldiers often are found discussing and arguing over the debates.

Similarly, in America the present Governor of the Virginia Commonwealth, Patrick Henry, has spread the concept of "liberty" around the world with his orations. His choice of "Liberty or Death" in his speech last year still resounds from his seat in the First General Congress at Philadelphia.

Thus it is that throughout the Empire and its colonies there is, in this Eighteenth Century, a surging wave toward democracy. It has fired even the most devoted adherents of monarchy with its insurgence for change. Now finally has arrived the new epoch which has slowly been cast from out of Absolute Monarchy into an era sprouting in the sunlight of the great Magna Charta of Runnymede 561 years ago, and the Bill of Rights, now 87 years of age.

It is today an England nursed on John Locke's recently widely accepted arguments for civil rights, religious liberty, and greater human considerations and understanding.

In the recorded history of the governing of mankind, democracy appears to many, to be the utopia of ideologies. And it is this "many" who now sing the praises of Athens' "Golden Age" of Democracy, pointing to the similarity of the American search for the "Golden Fleece of Independence, Rights and Liberties."

In the tragic cycle of government by democracy, this so-called "search" now in progress in America, is but the first phase of the circle. After it, some say, will come, unless carefully controlled, the second phase, the "reach"—the reach for greed and, in its wake uncontrolled crime and corruption.

For control, it is said, ever struggles to hold the reins of freedom, liberty and license but always succumbs to excessive permissiveness which destroys moderation, reason and wisdom in its rampaging path.

And, after "reach," in the tragic cycle of uncontrolled democracy, comes deterioration and decadence—the third and final phase, "decay." Then through its self-inflicted decay, there comes its suicide, thus completing the tragic cycle.

So, as though presaging this, the Howe brothers strive for a last-minute restoration of the peace. For, regardless of the new America's possible future, the rebellious war today in Britain's colonies in North America cannot be, and is not a popular one with the British people. Within their breasts also are felt the rumblings of the surging wave.

Hessian Hireling Pawns

Were it a popular war in England, the Crown would likely not now be seeking mercenary soldiers from outside the isles to conduct it. Volunteers could not be recruited from Ireland since it was a good potato year there and little need for Irish youth to

spread their wings. Few recruits came out of the Scottish High-
lands to offer their services and not many more from Mother
England herself. Thus the word went out among the heads of
Europe that George III was in the market for mercenaries.

At first only German-born Catherine II, Empress of Russia,
showed an interest in providing the British Crown with a foreign
army for a goodly sum. And this interest is surprising since she has
acclaimed herself the "most enlightened monarch in Europe."

Too, has she not often expressed her admiration for the free-
thought loving, anti-violent Francois Marie Arouet, Voltaire?

Despite the attractive and inviting monetary award, however, it
is a neighbor's antipathy for such "sordid business" which finally
influences her reluctantly to decline the offer. For that neighbor,
Frederick The Great, Frederick II of Prussia, is one she needs to
please, not offend.

Therefore it is with reluctance that George III has turned to the
Teutonic principalities, training grounds for the sternly disciplined
soldiery, for his military hirelings. It is there that the princes,
dukes and underlings of the independent German states, who are
always living beyond their means, sign treaties (business contracts)
with foreign governments desiring to make use of their especially
trained armies. The biggest dealer of all the Teutonic states in the
business of mercenaries is Landgrave of Hesse-Cassel and his son,
William, Count of Hesse-Hanau.[6]

Not all of the mercenaries come from Hesse. Some of the
30,000 hired are from other parts of Germany. Of them, about
10,000 will relieve British units in such outposts as Gibraltar,
enabling the Gibraltar-based British soldiers to join the main army
in America.

And so it is that there are, on those ships headed this morning
for Gravesend Bay off Long Island, many young men with no
interest at all in preserving America for the Crown. Most of the
German soldiers do not even know where they are. And few of
these unfortunates, coming as they do from Brunswick-Luneberg,
Anspach-Bayreuth, Waldeck, or Anhalt-Zerbst, speak or understand
a word of English. Yet many of them may find some of their own
distant kin over here, cousins, friends of their family and even
uncles and aunts who now are unable to speak a word of German.

It was only ten days ago that the last large contingent of ships
and men arrived in the bay. It was the final addition to the
flourishing show of might and power. Under Commodore Hotham
six warships that morning escorted 28 transports into Staten

Island's harbors. The vessels unloaded 2,600 more guardsmen and 8,000 more German mercenaries. Since the majority of these hirelings are from the principality of Hesse, they have been given the name of "Hessians."

Never in Great Britain's history has such a host of military, naval and amphibious might been assembled. Observers from Jersey and New York have counted 427 vessels in all. Of these, 52 are warships.

About nine of the men-of-war have come up from Charleston, but they seem to show very little damage which General Charles Lee has recently told Congress he inflicted upon them. Lee has not been at all modest in claiming full credit for the victory in the Charleston, South Carolina, battle.

Twice the Size of Spain's Armada

However, in South Carolina, full credit for the Charleston Bay defeat of Britain's Major General Henry Clinton and his fleet under Commodore Sir Peter Parker, is given to their own militia under Major General William Moultrie. Consequently, while Moultrie is being honored in Charleston and the fort there renamed in his honor, Lee, on his way back to New York, is "bowing right and left, airily accepting ceremonial swords and testimonial scrolls, a hero."[7]

Despite American encouragement from the reported defeat of Sir Peter Parker's fleet, the ships now appear none the worse as they sail into New York Bay and join the mass assemblage of the enemy's forces around Staten Island. In all, the Americans estimate their enemy strength at 10,000 sailors and 32,000 able-bodied troops.[8]

In contrast, the Americans have, on paper, possibly 23,000 at most, but many of these cannot be classified as "able-bodied." Against Britain's naval strength of 427 ships, the Continentals can display nothing but barges, flatboats, sloops, batteaux and pettiaugers, most of which are privately owned, or recently commandeered and paid for by the army. However, the Americans have Colonel Glover and his Massachusetts fishermen and seamen to man the American rowboats and sailing craft.

In its effort to force a swift end to the American rebellion, mainly through a show of overwhelming force, the British Crown has brought to the insurrectionists' shores—all in battle array this morning off Staten Island—more ships, men and equipment than the Americans will ever again see. In total tonnage it truly is twice the size of the Spanish Armada. In cost it represents almost a million pounds,[9] an expense the Crown can ill afford at this time.

And now Long Island, New York and the Hudson valley people tremble as a part of that war machine begins its long-dreaded, and long-expected redcoat invasion.

The answer to "Where will it be?" is seen on the beach at Gravesend Bay. Howe's objective seems clear. He will strike through Long Island by getting control of Brooklyn Heights just across the East River from the Americans' main encampment and defenses in New York town.

There is no opposition at Gravesend. The vanguard there is meeting only farmers who wish to sell the soldiers produce. But from the American-held fortress on Brooklyn Heights, seven miles north of the British beachhead, General Nathanael Greene's reconnaissance keeps its eyes on the enemy's vast movements. Transports discharge waves of redcoats in glittering armor upon the sand-swept shores of the great elongated island.

On the Bluff Rock above Hudson's river new inexperienced recruits today replace the Barbette Battery and the artillerymen in charge of the redoubts and the riverside emplacements.

Lieutenant Gray is frequently seen carrying a book. His few leisure moments are generally spent reading when he is not down at the Baummeister house. His treasured possession is a copy of John Locke's *Essay On Human Understanding* which he tucks in his pocket because a more important paper comes into his hands. It is the new orders, transferring him and his company to the defenses at Brooklyn Heights.

Leading his company along with other units down the gorge road toward the ferry, Gray's mind centers on one thing. He must say a farewell to Elaine.

The hold will be long at the ferry since the regiment is already backed up waiting for the slow transport across to Jeffery's Hook below Mount Washington. During the fall-out at the clearing near the Bourdette landing the men rest on their knapsacks. Some pick berries. Some grumble and complain. Others snooze. Gray walks southward toward the Baummeister house.

He hurdles the fence where both the Bourdette's and Baummeister's cattle often graze. The blue petticoat neckerchief he wears around his throat is his telltale sign.

As he makes his way around the south side of the big frame homestead, his men who know his objective lose sight of him.

Swiftly he rounds the corner of the old house and hurries into the arms of the half crying, half smiling Elaine.

Those inside, behind the multi-paned windows shaded from the morning sun by the wide over-hanging eaves, stay indoors. Marie Louise, or Mama Baummeister as all know her, has discreetly drawn the blue muslin curtains with their Dutch windmill imprints, closing out Paul's peeking view of his sister and her beau.

It is a brief goodbye. John Gray replaces the cockade in his hat, takes his treasured copy of Locke's book from his pocket, and, pulling up her downcast chin, says,

"Keep this for me, Elaine, until I come back. We'll read more of it together then."

But John Locke's essay on human understanding falls to the ground as they embrace. He breaks away, turns once, waves a final farewell and then disappears around the corner of the house. Elaine picks up the book, presses it close to her bosom and wipes the tears from her eyes as the household come out to console her. All walk toward the shore and wave to the men boarding the vessels.

The Lieutenant's Barbette Battery boards the flatboats and batteaux and begin their crossing. It will be followed by the long march down Manhattan's post road along the river's shoreline to New York town. Gradually the little fleet of sails and row-galleys become little specks across the river and are barely visible as they reach the New York side.

Jocko, in the stern of the last boatload, quietly nudges the straight-faced officer in front of him, whispering in his ear, "Lootenan, Missy E is yonder dare on da landin' awavin' ta ya back dare. Ain't cha gonna wave her back?"

Gray returns the whisper to the boy's ear, "You wave to her for me, Jocko."

On Dreams the Living Build Their Lives

Gray, gliding peacefully under the darkening shadows of the arrogant Palisades, knows that the coming conflict will spare him no time to read essays on human understanding. In fact he doubts whether there ever can be such a thing among peoples and nations with so many variables in their make-up.

Right now he knows—as does every man in the Continental Army—that he will count himself fortunate if he gets through the war with his life. And then, he ponders with a brief glimpse at the precious future.

Surely someday when it is all over—as certainly someday it must be—he, Elaine and perhaps their child, or children, will be fishing there. Together they will find with him peace and pleasure in these now troubled waters.

They are waters that will reflect stronger and stronger in the dark nights ahead, the ever-increasing fiery glow of Mars, tinging the river red as the turbulent river thrashes angrily on and over the little sloop, *Hope*.

6

Tuesday, August 27. . .

Battle of Long Island

A Sigh Of Relief At Fort Defiance

Roaring cannons, splitting the air over New York Bay, waked many late sleepers in Jersey, New York town and on Long Island early this morning. It was the warship, *Roebuck*, signalling the beginning of the British invasion of Long Island with a barrage attack on Fort Defiance, the American outpost at Red Hook.

The Red Hook battery lies several miles southwest of the American defenses and garrison stationed at Brooklyn Heights. Today the wind is right and the enemy broadsides can be heard and seen even from far up along the Hudson's Palisades.

True to her name, the little Fort Defiance outpost sends out its own thundering reply to the enemy frigate as the vessel begins bucking a northeast wind. This was not expected.

The *Roebuck* struggles to get between the Red Hook and the Governor's Island guns. It is bent upon ascending the East River.

If the *Roebuck's* Captain Hammond,[1] leading the squadron, can break through up the East River, he will steal behind the main American entrenchments on Brooklyn Heights, cut off the American defenders on Long Island from the army in New York and put a wedge between the Continentals.

It is a smart piece of stratagem, a part of a plan by Commodore Hotham and the Howes. But the wind is dead against this phase of the strategy, and now the *Roebuck's* sister-ship, *Repulse*, falls back with the rest of the squadron and its tenders.

Outdone by the adverse wind and harassed by the Fort Defiance and Governor's Island redoubts, Hammond finally gives up as he sees the remainder of his squadron forced to desert him. He comes about and rapidly returns into the outer bay.

The Americans watch and breathe a long sigh of relief.

British Military Map Depicting the Fleet's Invasion At Gravesend Bay and the Movement of the Troops In the Battle of Long Island, by William Faden, 1776. British Archives and Clinton Collection, Ann Arbor, Michigan.

On the Bluff Rock and on the summit of The Mountain where the open field and cow pasture looks off southward at almost the whole of Manhattan Island, the people of the hamlet gather to try and see the action off Brooklyn. The distant sound of cannonading is like an alarm. Word of it wherever it resounds spreads like fire through the valleys.

Exercising seniority rights, the homesteaders, old and young, pay little attention to the post's young militia guards. The natives move around wherever they desire despite some blocking efforts by over-zealous pickets. The edge of the high rocks, which most know as well as they know their own hearthsides, is their popular vantage point.

Least bothered by the encroaching military garrison as it spreads from the Bluff Rock site over to the top of the main mountain itself, are the Bourdettes and the Baummeisters. Another with similar prestige, one who demands and gets respect by out-shouting the loudest corporal or sergeant of the post, is Madam Carrie Kearney, or "Ma" Kearney, as she is known by almost everyone within miles of Bourdette's Landing.

Ma's life has been a difficult one since her fisherman husband acquired the wanderlust years ago, leaving her to fish the river, sell her wares and rear their only child, Edmund.

Yound Edmund, spoiled by an indulgent mother, has joined the Bergen County militia. And his proud parent tells everyone how invaluable her son is to the Grand Army as a private in Captain Board's regiment, now stationed at Bergen Neck on Newark Bay.

So Ma Kearney joins Elaine, Paul, the Baummeisters, Bourdettes and others on their perches along the precipice. Some line up in front of the Barbette abatis, straining to see an occasional flash from the men-of-war, or the American battery at Fort Defiance.

It is a worried, solemn-faced gathering. Soldiers and civilians alike gravely reflect the seriousness of the critical situation at last unfolding far in New York's Upper and Lower Bays. As one soldier puts it," There's Old George's grand push! It's on!"

Everyone, even the American Commander-in-Chief himself, expects the main attack will be upon New York town.

Many believe Howe's forces landing at Gravesend are nothing but an enemy feint. Generally it is conceded that the Gravesend landings are an attempt to draw the Americans out of New York's city, leaving it vulnerable to an invasion strike by the British fleet of transports, all standing in the bay ready for action.

Howe Shows His Hand

So until Saturday last, the American Commander-in-Chief was convinced that Howe was using about 8,000 of his men, landing on Gravesend Bay's beaches, to effect a diversionary movement, a sham,[2] in an effort to draw the main body of Americans out of Manhattan and over to Long Island in support of Brooklyn's defense. Since such strategy would leave Manhattan easy prey for a British main assault, the rebel Leader has been hesitant in sending the best of his Continentals after a will-o'-the-wisp. He has, therefore, committed only raw and inexperienced troops to Brooklyn. But, since Saturday, he has changed his mind. The reason is clear.

Despite their careful covering and their attempt to keep their numbers secret, the enemy force, the American command learns, has now clearly exceeded an 8,000-troop build-up. The invasion strength is far greater than that needed to effect a sham movement or a diversionary tactic.

For almost a week the invasion corps have been building up their might, assembling what first looked like a scouting expedition. It now takes on the appearance of an invincible military machine. Heavy British land guns accompany an army of over 24,000 thoroughly disciplined, excellently trained and equipped British and Hessian troops. In their support, lurking in the bay behind them, is a fleet of enemy ships of every description.

Facing this rising, thundering crescendo of naval and military might are 10,514 American effectives. They are so lacking in numbers, discipline, support, experience and weaponry that, man for man, their military power, or effect ratio, stands at one to the enemy's fifteen against them.[3] In addition, Howe's strategy has forced the American Commander to divide his forces if he intends to stand up against the King's men on Long Island and still maintain defenses on Manhattan.

The American defense pattern for New York's city has always been a difficult one but various requests, suggested defense posts, controversy and Congressional pressures have left the plans nebulous, to say the least.

The first attempt to give Manhattan protective defenses began early last spring when General Charles Lee was in command of New York. Quite correctly he told the Continental Congress that New York could only be used as a battleground.[4]

Lee informed Congress that the city could not be defended against an all-out British sea and land attack. And this now was exactly what the American forces were up against, an all-out enemy assault. Nevertheless, the Congress, over 100 miles away in Philadelphia, has insisted that the American Commander-in-Chief make every effort to hold Manhattan against the massive British Juggernaut. The Congressional decision, under pressure from the upriver, Hudson Valley, patriot land-holders, has slowly become a strong "order" from the nation's lawmakers.

The wavering determinations and decisions as to what pattern of defense, if any, should be designed for the big port city, began when General Charles Lee and a body of 2,000 men began building its defenses in March. Lee had made it clear that New York town could not be held against the Crown's great superiority, but proceeded, as instructed, fortifying both sides of the East River and the North, or Hudson, River.

When Lee was reassigned to the Southern Department to aid in the defense of Charleston, General Lord William Stirling continued the work. In the pattern, Brooklyn Heights, across the East River from the city, was to be a formidable defense post. For the enemy who successfully stormed those heights could throw the defenders into the East River and then bombard New York town at will.

Consequently, the American Leader has heavily occupied that post and has, within the past three days, ordered it more strongly reinforced owing to the unexpected enemy build-up on the Long Island shores. Howe's clever strategy, therefore, has forced the Continentals to divide their forces between Brooklyn Heights on the east bank of the East River and New York on the west bank.

Below, or south of the Brooklyn entrenchments, lies the plains. In some places it is a wooded, rugged and marshy area which stretches on the west toward the Gowanus Creek, New York Bay and the enemy's invasive army assembled at Gravesend. On the east the so-called "plains" stretch to the ocean.

Sir William Howe's army began its invasion last Thursday, the 22nd, and continued disembarking thousands of troops, first the Hessians under General Von Heister and then the British Black Watch Highlanders. This force was sent north, taking a position in the center of the British west-to-east line across the southernmost part of Long Island's Brooklyn.

A second division of Scots under Major General Sir James Grant forms the western sector of the line, making up the left flank. It has proceeded westward along the Narrows Road toward Gowanus Bay. And the third division, comprising the main British army force under General Henry Clinton, forms the eastern sector of the line, making up the right flank. It has proceeded somewhat eastward, fanning out toward Flatland. Its objective is to secure the Flatbush and Bedford Passes.

It is clear that Sir William plans to close his right and left wings around the Brooklyn Heights post and its entrenchments. Then, combining the east and west assaults with a frontal push, he will try to drive the Americans back into the East River, forcing them to surrender unconditionally.

Unopposed, the jaws of the British Juggernaut close in and around the villages of Utrecht and Flatbush. Slowly the enemy's encirclement strategy moves toward a position at which the barrage will be laid down, supported by the men-of-war on the rebels' backs.

Behind the American lines, General John Sullivan first took over command following Greene's return to the New York encampment. For seven days Greene, suffering from the fever, has been confined to bed, but on Saturday, Major General Israel "Old Put" Putnam relieved Sullivan.

However, no staff officer knows the terrain as well as does Nathanael Greene, excepting possibly General Stirling. Greene is recognized as one of the Continentals' outstanding field officers. Nevertheless, Stirling has had a long acquaintance with the topography through his task in preparing Manhattan's defenses.

Uncertainty in detecting Howe's plan has resulted in a weakened American defense system. Little if any American intelligence and communications methods have been devised. And since the British movements could not be effectively observed from the Heights, the enemy's maneuvers were not discerned as early as they should have been.

Looking south from the Heights, on the west side of the plains, Putnam has given Brigadier General William Lord Stirling command of the American right wing. Stirling's brigade forms a spur extending into the Gowanus Bay sector toward which British General Grant is moving.

Realizing these two forces will clash, Putnam sends the well-equipped, properly uniformed and disciplined Marylanders and Delawarean regiments to support Stirling whose brigade had comprised only one rifle, one musketry regiment and three corps of Pennsylvania militia. Though 1,600 strong they are now in trouble and do not know it.

For, in coming face to face with Grant's troops, a far superior force, Stirling, instead of ordering a slow withdrawal, stands and contests the ground. Grant has orders to feint an assault and then wait for a signal—two cannon shots—before smashing through. The British left flank attack is to be synchronized with that of Von Heister's center and Clinton's right flank.

Grant's feint is intentionally a weak one, giving Stirling and his men false confidence in their position and in Grant's potential. But, unknown to Stirling, Grant has 5,000 Scots and has sent back requesting Howe to send him reinforcements. Meanwhile, Stirling, with his 1,600 against Grant's 5,000 and more on their way, decides not to budge.

Behind Stirling, Admiral Howe's five men-of-war, struggling against the same headwind that earlier drove the *Roebuck* and Captain Hammond's squadron back down the bay, attempt to get into Buttermilk Channel. Once in the channel, behind Stirling, the warships can easily lay down a barrage preventing Stirling's escape from Grant's Scots and the rebels' withdrawal into the safety of the Brooklyn Heights entrenchments.

In reply to Stirling's three-pounders, the enemy howitzers answer with periodic shelling. Under Colonel Edward Hand, the 200 Pennsylvanians of the First Pennsylvania Regiment let go a continuous fusillade of musketry and Grant's men answer in kind. There is no advance movement on either side. No ground is asked. None is given. Stirling is puzzled. And Grant impatiently waits for the two blasts of the cannon signaling the opening of a synchronized attack on all sectors.

Meanwhile Von Heister's Hessians and Highlanders have moved above Flatbush toward the Flatbush Pass in the center sector. The Americans' center, facing Von Heister, is under General Sullivan. His spur, out from the Heights' fortifications, is ordered to attempt to defend the vitally important Flatbush and Bedford Passes. Sullivan's Continentals now are showered with much pointless cannonading from the Hessians who move forward occasionally in pretense of attack. For they, too, are waiting the two-cannon-shot-signal.

Sullivan personally leads his troops and takes over command of the Flatbush and Bedford posts, comprising Captain Tom Knowlton's Connecticut Continentals, part of Colonel Daniel Hitchcock's Rhode Islanders, and Colonel Moses Little's Massachusetts Continentals. But the Americans' line, from west to east, is scattered and thinned by a pitiful lack of strength.

Beginning on the west with Stirling's right wing spur, the American line flows east into Colonel Atlee's Pennsylvanians, then, on their left, Colonel Huntington's Connecticut Continentals. These, in turn, are flanked on their left by Sullivan's command which tapers off eastward with virtually no defense at the extreme American left—the vulnerable Jamaica Pass.

Militarily, the American line is a classic example of a left flank dangling "up in the air." For actually only five young mounted militia officers guard this important pass which lies three miles east from the Bedford Pass. And it is this, the Jamaica Pass, that now is Howe's secret objective as his right wing pincers steadily grind in that direction.

Unknown to the Americans, the British column with General Clinton leading, has moved quietly through the night and pre-dawn hours. Undetected, it has swept eastward in a circling movement, headed for the vital pass. Clinton has thus far executed an exceptionally stealthy piece of maneuvering.

Clinton's van, a detachment of infantry under Captain Evelyn, is sent forward to reconnoiter the area. Evelyn discovers that the pass is guarded by only five horsemen. Sweeping in upon them, the redcoat officer captures all five without resistance. He learns, to his surprise, that the outpost has no other defense, and, therefore, no immediate barrier faces the King's troops just beyond the now safely cleared narrow way.

Westward, beyond the pass, Sullivan's thin, long strung-out central sector tapers on its left flank eastward with sparse, widely scattered contingents. They comprise Colonels Sam Wylly's and Solomon Wills' Connecticut Continentals and the Connecticut State Regiment and Colonel Samuel Miles' Pennsylvanians.

At 7 A.M. this morning, without benefit of orders, Miles decides to take his 400 Pennsylvania riflemen through the woods and head south toward the poorly protected Jamaica Pass. By separating his force from Wylly's and Wills', he further imperils the already dangerously thin American left wing.

There is as yet no suitable intelligence and communication system worthy of the name. Tar barrel fires have helped in signalling, but even a mounted detachment of dispatch riders, as offered by some Connecticut farmers with their old mares, has been unwisely rejected. Some of the American officers laugh at the idea.

However, such a service could now help maintain communications among the strung-out units of the rebel forces. For the British main column, after pushing through unopposed at the Jamaica Pass, has stopped for breakfast. It is a column of 10,000 troops two miles long. Well ahead of it, its vanguard continues circling and reconnoitering.

In doing so, the redcoat scouts move eastward, while Colonel Miles' rebels moving westward on a higher plateau through the woods, miss Evelyn's British van entirely. Miles, instead, runs head-on into the enemy's rear and its well-protected baggage train.

With Captain Evelyn and his redcoats at his rear and the British rearguard battalions confronting him, the rebel colonel is trapped. Escape is entirely cut off.

The Pennsylvanians put up a short hopeless fight. After several brief encounters, the American colonel and half his men surrender.

Running under close pursuit the rest of Miles' detachment flee through the deep woods, crawling over crevices and floundering through swamps. They eventually bring the surprising news of Clinton's encirclement maneuver to General Putnam.

Putnam immediately notifies Sullivan and Stirling that there is still time for them to withdraw safely to the entrenchments on the Heights. Unfortunately he does not order it.

Signal To Attack

Meanwhile the entire British main army, all pausing for breakfast, comprises on its right wing General Clinton's forces, supported in his rear by Generals Cornwallis, Percy and Howe, in that order.

At 9 A.M., from the village of Bedford, two heavy cannon blasts thunder the air. With it the redcoats and Hessians launch their attack on all sectors. To the young raw recruits in the American militia it seems as though all Hades' devils have been unloosed on Long Island.

Errors and tragedies strike thoughout the American line. Sullivan's forces are suddenly entrapped. Beside the major general stands his Colonel Philip Johnston of West Jersey's Hunterdon County. And just as Sullivan turns to speak to Johnston, the colonel drops dead with a ball through his chest. This morning the Hunterdon county officer celebrated his 35th birthday.

Concentrating on their own front, the Sullivan forces have failed to detect Clinton's clever maneuver. For the British general has, undetected, stolen behind Sullivan's line. Clinton has placed his forces between Sullivan and the distant Heights to which the rebel general should have withdrawn earlier. Now Clinton closes in upon Sullivan's rear, forcing him into the bayonets of the unending regimented lines of Hessian regulars charging in upon his front.

Back and forth between the two closing claws the hard fighting Continentals waver, hopelessly outnumbered, completely entrapped. Remnants of Miles', Wylly's and Will's forces are cornered in with them. Often the hotly pressed Continentals get off no more than a single shot before the bayoneted muskets of the Grenadiers are at their breasts.

Amazingly they fight on against their enemy both behind and in front until the overwhelming King's men force them to break, run and, if they can, escape.

Dodging bullets, rifle clubbings and bayonets, many are able to make it safely into the woods, down the slopes, across marshes and creeks and into the fields leading to the fortified camp behind the entrenchments on the Heights.

Many do not make it. Some lie deathly wounded, screaming in agony. Others—some of the enemy included—lie silently shocked by the gravity of their gaping, bleeding wounds. They stare blankly, awaiting death. Hundreds are taken prisoner. Among them General Sullivan.

Sullivan's Sector Falls

It is 11 A.M. In two hours of hand-to-hand fighting, Sullivan's central sector has fallen. Clinton's army has swept the ridge and established itself two miles in front of the formidable looking, Brooklyn Heights fortifications. The captured American troops, including a general, are marched to the rear of the enemy's lines. It is a severe blow to the rebel forces, but worse is yet to come.

To the west, where General Grant's corps forms the British left wing, that redcoat commander has delayed his attack upon Stirling's line which now has its back on Buttermilk Channel. Grant disregarded the two-gun signal for a simultaneous attack, pending the arrival of his reinforcements. With their arrival—2,000 British Marines—Grant's corps is swelled to 7,000 men. Itching for action they impatiently wait to charge their enemy rebels.

Informed that his opponent is Major General Sir James Grant, Lord Stirling recalls his special visit to England some years ago. Seeking the rights to his British title, the pro-American Englishman, had attended a session of the House of Lords at which Sir James, addressing Parliament boasted: "Give me five thousand troops and I'll march from one end of the colonies to the other!"[5]

Lord Stirling knows that the arrogant, rotund British aristocrat in the field before him has a low opinion of American soldiers. For

Grant had served in the French and Indian War and was not impressed with the independence and lack of regimental discipline characteristic of the backwoodsmen whom he was called upon to command. Therefore he was quite positive in telling Parliament how he would handle the American uprising and its rebel followers.

Stirling's Sector Falls

Regardless of how he felt standing before Parliament when the American insurrection had become the House of Lords' Number One topic, Sir James now feels more secure in launching his attack with 7,000 troops rather than 5,000 against Stirling's pitiful 1,600. Stirling has been imbued, as have all the rebel officers, with the concept that, wherever possible, a stand must be made in defiance of the enemy's might. Precipitous flight on the battlefield, they believe, will swiftly curdle the American morale throughout the thirteen free and independent united states of America.

Stirling's position of defiance is his undoing.

With their rears backed against the marshes bordering on Gowanus Creek, the stubborn 1,600 stand and fight Grant's oncoming divisions. The only support on Stirling's left, to the east, is Colonel Samuel Holden Parson's Connecticut and Massachusetts regiments. However they are too far distant to be brought to Stirling's aid and are encountering their own difficulties with the enemy pressing in on them. Parsons has successfully repulsed several brief assaults and will need everything he can muster when the British decide to move on him in strength.

For hours Stirling's men maintain periodic fire and for hours they take the same from the redcoats. Then Grant begins moving in. He forces the spirited rebels to give ground. Grant drives hard, crowding in for hand-to-hand combat until he pushes the Americans ever closer toward the creek.

Despite the critical situation in which every moment becomes more hopeless, the battered, bleeding Continentals—the dead and wounded from both sides falling around them—hold their line. Screaming men drop and are trampled upon.

Five times Stirling attempts to break through the blocked Gowanus Road, his only escape route. And five times he fails. The fighting Americans seem determined to hold out against the inevitable.

On both sides the casualty horrors mount. Outnumbered but not outclassed, the rebel force struggles to the edge of the swamps where now the enemy warships unleash a barrage of broadsides on their heads.

The escaping Continentals scatter in all directions.

Some flee safely through the mucky marshlands. Soaked in mud up to their necks some try to disentangle themselves from decades of thick reeds enmeshed around their legs. Others drown among the high cattails. Some fall from exhaustion, some from musket balls, or from the showers of grape hurled by the bombarding warships in the channel. Their last cries of pain and prayers for help are unheard, unanswered in the calamitous din of battle.

Stirling, who survivors later will report, fought "like a wolf," is rushed upon, surrounded and captured. Then Brigadier General Udell[6] is caught in the net of sweeping redcoats and Hessians, making the enemy's catch of three generals a calamitous loss for the Continental Army.

Badly whipped but still defiant the remainder of the Continental Army line now slowly withdraws toward the Brooklyn Heights fortifications. The rifle companies' best marksmen force the on-coming enemy waves to pay for every yard they gain.

Those Americans not shot or bayoneted down, not captured, or drowned in the marshes, pour back into the temporary safety of the entrenchments and redoubts which bear such names as Fort Putnam, Fort Greene and Fort Box. Sweat pouring from their bodies, some nursing serious wounds, the Continentals drop exhausted behind their works.

Rushing over at the outbreak of the hostilities from his New York headquarters, the American Commander-in-Chief watches the action and sends out orders from his Heights observation post. He tries to conceal his personal feelings. However, careful observers discern the emotional distress that is tearing at his insides.[7]

Behind his retreating troops, their Hessian pursuers trail them to within musket-shot distance of the American redoubts leading to the Heights.

It is noon. The tragic battle is over. Only the big push, the final drive, the assault-attack upon the American fortification remains to be executed. The rebels now are backed against the East River. All that now faces them is Howe's coup de grace and The General's surrender and with it the war's end.

Though exhausted the Americans spend the afternoon digging in. They grab a handful of sea bread made of canel and peas-meal. Eating, digging, working and wondering, they look up occasionally to see their enemy in the distance. The Hessian and British troops can be clearly observed at times cooking around their campfires. Others appear to be making preparations for the assault.

Some of the American militia who have seen no action help the wounded Continentals down to the East River's shore to be transported over to the New York hospital.

A blanket of gloom lies heavily over the tired, despondent rebel army assembled on the Heights, waiting, it appears, to be annihilated at will by the jaws of the British Juggernaut. Hopelessly the rebels know that at any moment the enemy cannon can open up on them, showering them with death and softening them up for a massive British and Hessian bayonet attack.

In the Fort Box redoubt, Lieutenant John Gray and his artillerymen successfully repulsed a Hessian advance picket force which surprised the battery during the early morning assault attempt.

In the brief encounter, while Big Tom Graves was loading the three-pounder, a ball from an enemy musket pierced his arm below his left shoulder.

Gray's clothes are still red with the blood that gushed out of the wound, almost draining the life out of the big strapping freeman. The Lieutenant's hurried answer to young Jocko's plea for help for his wounded father and the officer's swift action in applying a tourniquet, dressing the wound and rushing Graves down to a boat along with other wounded, headed for the New York hospital, saved Big Tom's life.

Gray ordered Jocko to stay with his father and release the tourniquet periodically until he is safely in the hands of a hospital surgeon. The officer, four days ago, had all but ordered Jocko to stay on Manhattan away from the battlegrounds without success. He feels relieved now that the black boy is away from the action that is momentarily expected on the Heights.

Before all eyes, but especially before those of the young recruits who have never seen war until today, the sick, wounded and dying, lying in the sun waiting for transportation back to New York, present a frightening spectacle. Some in shock have lost consciousness. Some, moaning with pain, lie with broken arms, legs, or gaping, bleeding head and body wounds. Some are the results of bayonet thrusts. Almost all are wrapped with dirty cloths owing to the scarcity of bandages.

The cries and death throes can be heard lifted above the stink of battle on both sides as the stench of flesh, sweat, fire, filth and burned powder saturates the heavy, hot summer afternoon air over the two armies. Both forces rest to regroup and take an accounting of their losses. In addition, Howe must count his bag of prisoners.

In the Americans' favor now, nature has smiled and brought a strong warm and intensifying wind. Changing from north to northeast, it prevents the British warships, all heavily armed, from ascending above Red Hook into the East River.

Sir William's Costliest Error

If they had been able to do so earlier, they would have cut Stirling's corps to pieces with their broadsides. What they were able to do from a distance was bad enough.

And had they ascended the East River, as was the Howe Brothers' plan, they would have positioned themselves between the city and Brooklyn Heights, severing the rebels' communications and connecting link with New York town.

Then, by a bombardment from behind the Heights' entrenchments, Clinton's artillery would pound them from their front until they struck their colors. Howe's objective: complete surrender, might have been inevitable.[8]

It is still the British commander's plan once the wind shifts. Howe believes it is senseless to take needless risks. Time is on his side. An endless sea of masts and sails are at his command, and he has countless reinforcements on Staten Island hoping to get in the fray.

Overhead storm clouds mass and promise rain as night and darkness approach ending a day that will not be forgotten by those who have lived through it. Since the outbreak of the war over a year ago, there has never been a large scale open field military battle such as this. It is the first time that American and British forces have met in this type of formal warfare. And it has ended in the first great defeat for the rebel army.

In the future the Battle of Long Island will be fought and re-fought by many who will place blame and responsibility for the American disaster on everyone from the Congress to The General, from the troops to the apathy of the people in the colonial states. Arguments will become heated over the causes of the failures, over the strategy used and over the decision to hold as against the advice to evacuate Long Island and New York town itself.

No post-battle arguments will erase the extent of casualties on the American side. The Continental Army lost 1,012 men of which 200 were killed and the remainder captured and wounded. British losses number 392 killed, wounded and taken prisoner, although no one knows for sure since both sides try to hide their figures from the enemy.

Tomorrow is feared. Yet tomorrow must come. So tonight the guards and pickets along the breastworks are doubled.

Up on the towering Bluff Rock and on the high cliff of The Mountain's summit, the inhabitants have gathered at various times all day long, attempting to watch, if nothing else, the flashing of the guns in the distant battle. Then as the rain clouds gathered and night began to fall, slowly all wandered dejectedly back to their homes, their faces haggard and sad.

The last to leave are Elaine, Carrie Kearney, Baummeister and Paul. They do not speak as they watch and wonder. And it will be long, probably very long, before they know . . . know for sure.

7

Thursday, August 29. . .

The Cul-de-sac

Blurred Is the View

For two days the heavy rains have poured down upon the two opposing armies, bringing the Juggernaut's smashing victory Tuesday to a water-logged halt on the plain in front of the American works on Brooklyn Heights. Howe's plans for a follow-through attack on the rebel fortifications yesterday bogged down with the wet weather.

And for two days the inhabitants around Bourdette's Ferry as well as the militia troops stationed at Fort Constitution, strain their eyes in an attempt to discover what is taking place downriver. Young recruits at the slowly expanding works are learning to handle the big guns on the Bluff Rock Barbette Battery. Others are being trained and drilled for replacements on Long Island.

Presently under the command of General Hugh Mercer, the fort on The Mountain has added a hut to the hospital tent for treating the convalescents, the injured and the many daily reporting on sick call. Doctors are scarce, and Mercer, himself a surgeon, has asked the local inhabitants for help in making bandages and assisting the visiting surgeon who comes over from Hackensack. Elaine and Ma Kearney have both offered their services. Consequently they have been given privileges not usually accorded non-military personnel.

One privilege is access to the ledge that runs below the Barbette on the Bluff Rock. Only Elaine and her brother are passed through to observe downriver toward the site of the Long Island action almost any time of day.

So daily, usually at noon, Elaine ascends the gorge road with Paul. Generally it is shortly after she dismisses her class of local youngsters, her brother included. She teaches them in the big Baummeister parlor if the weather is too inclement to hold school outdoors.

Though little can be seen at such a distance, except sometimes the firing of the heavy guns, she stands on the ledge and watches in silence. It is the same ledge on which she and John so often sat and read to each other from his collection.

Elaine has not been her usual self since The Lieutenant left. All have noticed that her gay laughter is gone. She smiles generously at everyone but seldom stops and talks with the neighborhood people as she used to do.

Often the girl climbs the cliffs with Ma Kearney who also stares off into space as though the view before her eyes entranced her into silence, an attribute for which Madame Kearney is not noted.

Ma never smiles. However, her gruff voice and rough demeanor belie a soft heart. Those of the old command post who had once called her "Crabby Carrie"—and not because she is the fisher-woman of the river—soon regretted their sarcasm.

Many of the artillerymen have tasted the bread and cookies she regularly brings to the sentries. And she virtually gives her fish away to the soldiers, seldom charging them even half the price she asks of the natives.

Today the heavy rains have prevented any visibility from the ledge rock where both Elaine and Ma ascended only briefly before returning down the cliff. For life goes on among the river people, the cliff dwellers and the mountain folk, unmoved for long by sorrow, tragedy, war and death. Life goes on as it has for decades, struggling, bleeding, crying.

The rain which has brought curses from the militia manning the works on Fort Constitution and especially from those wallowing in the muddy redoubts north on the Bluff and along the shore, is heaven-sent to the men clustered in the American fortification on Brooklyn Heights. So 25 miles south of Fort Constitution the deluge and stiff northeaster are doing their best to save the Continental army balancing in the winds of chance on Long Island.

After the battle Tuesday and the rebel withdrawal behind their entrenchments on the Heights, Howe, deciding not to follow through with his advantage, encamped on the plains and woodlands below the Continentals' outer works and waited for the rains to stop. Some of the King's men were within musket-shot distance of the rebel redoubts.

So all through the heavy drenchings yesterday the jittery American officers kept up a perpetual vigil. And today, despite the continued bad weather, the fear of a bayonet attack has doubled that vigilance.

Gloating over the taste of their first victory, the Hessian troops were all for pursuing their enemy right into their redoubts. Howe had prevented this, ordering a halt below the rebel works.

He wants no more casualties than absolutely necessary, and a hand-to-hand combat with the enemy behind the security of their own entrenchments could prove costly, if not disastrous. Tired soldiers, he feels, are not effective ones against misguided soldiers fanatically defending their homelands.

Sir William believes that an easy victory with minimum cost to the Crown in lives and materiel is easily within his reach. Once Brother Richard gets his men-of-war behind the entire rebel army closeted on the Heights their jig will be up.

After Tuesday's battle the British commander came to the conclusion that the entire American works can be had "at a very cheap rate through regular approaches."[1]

However, the two armies are today in the exact positions they were two days ago. Only occasional barrages from both sides and a few brushes between scouting pickets foraging for food and supplies have broken the silence and disturbed the unexpected lull.

While the main cause may be rain, mud and their adverse conditions for warfare, another stronger reason is Admiral Howe's inability to get upriver. The northeaster offers too much risk for square-riggers in the East River's narrow passage. The weather must improve. Sir William does not intend to move his army until Captain Hammond and his *Roebuck* throw their broadsides from the river's middle into the rebels' rear.

Meanwhile the American Commander has demanded incessant vigilance. With his enemy entrenched only 150 rods away from the Fort Putnam works and redoubt, every man is on constant alert. Many of the troops are without tents or blankets. Most were lost or left behind to lighten loads in the heat of battle and the urgency of flight.

As for food, there is little to be had which accounts for the numerous nightly foraging parties. Sea bread[2] and pickled pork is about all there is to eat. And most of the pork must be eaten raw since fires do not easily stay lit under the downpours, and those that do are in great demand.

The American camp is ankle-deep in water and muck. Men shiver in their soaked clothing. In some entrenchments soldiers sometimes stumble waist-deep in muddy water filled with debris and filth. Muskets are useless. The flintlocks, priming pans and touchholes are drenched as is most of the ammunition.[3]

Every American defender is tired, hungry and wretched from lack of sleep and from the mental anguish that fear and uncertainty bring. The one man who knows the debilitating effect that these strains have upon the spirit, the physical endurance and the morale of his enemy, is General Howe. And so Sir William feels no need to rush the coup de grace.

Also, the British commander-in-chief has nursed a healthy respect for American marksmanship. He acquired it, and the lesson that went with it, last year on Breed's Hill. He has not forgotten the accurate, deathly rebel fire that poured down from behind their breastworks, slaughtering his troops that day. So Sir William does not intend to underestimate his enemy's potential as he did in Boston.

It is the rebel General who is quietly planning the next move— the only one he can make: an escape from the cul-de-sac. A last resort, he knows its chances of success are poor.

Nevertheless early this morning he sent orders to General William Heath at Kingsbridge and to Hugh Hughes, Assistant Quartermaster General in New York. He directed them to gather up every kind of boat that can be used for transporting troops and to hold them on the New York side of the East River.

To conceal his plan and avoid the impression of a withdrawal, The General makes it clear for the ears of his enemy that the crafts are to be used for transporting reinforcements from the New York encampment to Brooklyn's defenses. To support this deception the Manhattan guards are marched out of their encampment through New York's streets toward the river in a continuous line as though preparing for a crossing to the beleaguered Long Island Heights.

Then later this morning he summons his generals for a council of war. In strict secrecy he submits the plan. All unanimously approve its execution in darkness tonight.[4]

A Benevolent Deception

Eight good reasons are listed to get the council's sanction. Each is sufficiently valid in itself. It is agreed that until the maneuver is clearly evident to all none of the troops know what is taking place. The generals are aware of the panic that would follow such advance information were the 9,000, half-starved, suffering, dispirited soldiers to know beforehand.

The least disciplined—volunteers and militia—would madly scramble for the first boat across if they knew a retreat were in progress. The enemy would get the word as soon as the rebels.

Consequently, the Commander's general orders are intentionally deceptive. They announce that the troops from the Flying Camp[5] at Amboy are coming in later today and room must be made for accommodating them. Accordingly, reads the orders, since the sick are presently an encumbrance, they are to be removed to New York so that proper provisions may be made for the new troops.

Fortunately the deception works. In war, that art can become a soldier's best ally, or on the other hand, his worst enemy. But on Brooklyn Heights tonight it becomes the defenders' benefactor.

Carrying on the deception, the orders further read that regimental officers are to prepare the sick for removal. And further, officers are advised that the Commander-in-Chief proposes to: "relieve a proportionate number of regiments and make a change in the situation of them."[6]

And still further, they instruct the field commanders to parade their men with all their arms, accoutrements, and knapsacks at 7 o'clock this evening at the head of their encampments where they are to "wait for orders."

A separate order goes out to the highly prized Continental troops to man the forward lines. Among those assigned to this secret task are Colonel John Haslet's Delaware regiment, Colonel John Shee's Third Pennsylvania Battalion, Colonel Robert Magaw's Fifth Pennsylvania Battalion, Colonel John Chester's Connecticut Battalion and what is now left of Colonel Alexander Smallwood's Marylanders.

These are a part of the cream of the Continentals. Though they are unaware of the role they will be playing in covering the retreat, most sense that something far more than "a change in situation" is taking place. All are placed under the command of Major General Thomas Mifflin.

Over the entire American army's spirits has spread a mass depression which is abetted by the miserable weather.

It was not long before the rebel rank and file, assisted by wild and exaggerated rumors, realized the full extent of the army's tragic defeat. The loss of three generals—and Lord Stirling among them—has not helped to quell rising fears and excite curiosity as to what The Chief will, or can, do now.

Curiosity is aroused still more and rumors spread when General John Glover's amphibious regiments, the Marblehead fisherman and sailors,[7] are withdrawn from their perilous post only 250 yards from the enemy.

It is they who are the first to learn about the operation of which they will play a vital role. This time their task is incredible: to move undetected, an entire army across a river in the black of night. Under daylight such a maneuver is a mammoth undertaking.

The Delawareans and Marylanders now step into their front line, mud-hole positions. Theirs is the dangerously exposed left flank. In the event of an attack they cannot be supported.

They are destined to soon learn how precarious is their situation. For one by one the units will pull out, leaving their comrades isolated and alone. As each branch marches off into the night, every passing moment will find the Continentals' rear guard more vulnerable.

Adding to the troops' hovering gloom are a slowly diminishing rain and an increasingly heavier mist. Together they spread a covering veil over the entire movement.

At twilight Glover's men and Hutchinson's amphibious regiment from Salem began taking over the boats as they begin arriving. All oars are muffled. The regiments on parade are drawn off and marched one at a time down the Heights.

Volunteers and militia, the least experienced and most likely to be lacking in discipline, are loaded aboard first. With baggage and equipment they laboriously grope their way to the ferry landing.

Strict silence is imposed. Quietly they board the waiting boats. In amazing soundlessness the vessels disappear over the river's Stygian darkness, headed for the South Street dock and the haven of Manhattan's shores.

Any noise that would tip off the mass movement to the King's men is carefully avoided. To keep the enemy in ignorance as long as possible, General Mifflin's sole guardians of the rapidly emptying American lines are directed to provide the usual nocturnal noises attendant around any encampment.

Meanwhile, the Hessians' camp sounds—the clashing of cooking utensils, the thud of a pick-axe striking into hard ground and stones—are all clearly audible behind the British forward breast-works. The two armies are so close that even above the rain and racket voices can often be heard. The Americans can hear their enemy's English, broken English and German speech.

It is estimated that Mifflin's men, only about 700 strong at most, are facing about 25,000 of the enemy. And those are excellently trained and equipped redcoats supported by blue and green coated mercenaries. All are well refreshed, well fed and thoroughly rested from two nights of sleep under dry tents and bedding.

American staff commanders are surprised at how successfully the evacuation proceeds. Just as busy as his officers, the American Leader is seen, first at one end of the columns of the silently moving men and then, minutes later, at the other.

He and his gray charger, Old Magnolia, seem to be everywhere. Sometimes he is at the ferry, directing officers and assisting them in the embarkation of the troops. A few minutes later he is on the Heights, helping to get the formations started.

The General, as always, sets the example for his staff, becalming the frightened, encouraging the weak and consoling the sick and wounded. He steps far out of his character at times and exchanges a rare jest with the men in order to disguise the extreme dangers they face in the hazardous crisis.

His life guards struggle to keep up with him. One is a young sergeant from Knowlton's Rangers. Steeped with pride in his honored assignment, he stays close to Old Magnolia's flanks, alert at all times to everything around him.

The sharp-eyed Ranger replaced the late Sergeant Tom Hickey who was hanged for high treason Friday, June 28, for his part in the Tory-instigated conspiracy, one step of which, it is rumored, was to assassinate The General with poisoned peas. And the rumor has it that it was Phoebe Fraunces who helped to discover Hickey's treachery and saved the American Commander's life.[8]

Though the Commander-in-Chief's bodyguards are all highly trusted young men, there is the constant fear of Tory attempts upon his life since the Hickey complot was uncovered. However such fears among the guards do not surface owing to the under-mining distrust of each other they might incite.

The General always seems unruffled. He gives no outward evidence of concern over possible conspiracies. What generally sits uneasily on his mind are the weaknesses and inefficiencies of his militia and many of his officers, to say nothing of the manner the

Continental Congress drags its feet when it comes to military matters.

Now the perilous operations of crossing his army over the rough, river waters in the darkest hours of the night is his immediate objective. Just as everything seems to be going smoothly, an alarming mass commotion and confusion occurs near the head of the column moving out of the fortifications.

Within moments, flanked by his guards, he is there, discovering, to his dismay, that a simple, an almost impossible misinterpretation and discharge of an order, perilously threatens to upset the success of the secretly conducted, extremely dangerous and vulnerable expedition. Only history will know how much the unborn eaglet's future momentarily rests on pure chance.

It was a few moments after 2 A.M. in the very height of the smoothly operating maneuver that Major Alexander Scammell, adjutant to the General and Chief, informed Mifflin that the boats were ready to take off his men. In the darkness and owing to inadequate intra-regimental communications, Scammell miscalculated the length of the long lines making their way slowly down to the beach into the vessels.

Actually, Mifflin and his covering party, which will be the last to withdraw, must hold their dangerous front-line positions for several more hours. Upon their ruse and success in preventing enemy picket observations from getting the slightest inkling of a withdrawal hinges the outcome of the whole enterprise. The abandonment of the front-line and the last defense post with several thousand men yet uncrossed could mean horror for all.

Consequently, Mifflin, believing the order is premature, questions Scammell and the advisability of completely evacuating the entrenchments and redoubts until the columns of men leading to the ferry are fully embarked. But Scammell insists there is no mistake in the order. Reassured, Mifflin orders his men out of their works and into formation in the assembly area on the Heights' summit. His sentinels and advance guards are ordered to bring up the rear.

The front-line evacuation, despite its quiet conduct, now spreads great concern throughout the long ranks of men. Stores and ammunition are hauled to the waiting vessels.

One detachment of artillery is still spiking heavy cannon, particularly the oldest and most worn which cannot be moved with ease. Gun carriages are wrapped in rags, muffling the sound. One of these artillery officers is Lieutenant John Gray.

Everyone knows the tall, lanky youth, mostly through the reputation he has acquired through his so-called "good luck" scarf always around his neck.

"Gray?" someone will pause and question when inquiry regarding him is made. "Oh, yes!" will come the reply. "The lieutenant with a stripping of a woman's blue petticoat for a scarf."

It is difficult to see very far through the pitch blackness of the night. Only a few campfires are kept burning. They are shielded in order to reflect the light toward the enemy and conceal the hosts of shadowy figures behind them. From the enemy's viewpoint, Brooklyn Heights is apparently fully garrisoned and, if anything, the rebels are bringing in reinforcements but attempting to conceal their action.

Over the pre-dawn darkness the heavy rains have now tapered off into a drizzle.

The Lieutenant, noticing the defense lines diminishing and the men quietly and orderly abandoning the fortification and moving out, spurs his own command to complete their work, spiking the big pounders soon to be an undesired gift for the enemy. Gray repeatedly cautions his men to keep noise at a minimum.

It is at about this moment that the Commander-in-Chief gets word, senses and feels the confusion and commotion taking place in the rear of the long lines, marching two abreast. Abruptly swinging his mare around he dashes up to the scene on the Heights. He heads for Mifflin.

In the Nick Of Time

Fury fills his steel blue eyes as he passes Mifflin's Continentals, withdrawing in large numbers from the frontal breastworks. Astounded by the unbelievable sight he gallops up beside the brigadier's old black stallion and charges Mifflin with possibly ruining the entire operation.[9]

His anger erupting but controlled, the Commander immediately orders that the Continentals return to their forward defense posts without delay. Mifflin's anger also rises though controlled. He explains that he was carrying out the Commander's orders as received through his aide-de-camp.

The General, perplexed that this could be, then tells Mifflin that detection of the maneuver is imminent. He warns that there is increasing confusion among the men, particularly those approaching the landing docks and that any more could prove catastrophic.

In countermanding Scammell's order, the American Leader tells Mifflin that unless his men are speedily returned to their posts— deserted now for over an hour—before the enemy realizes they have been abandoned, "the most disagreeable consequences would follow."[10]

Then without balking, the Continentals—the flower troops of the American army—fully aware now of their role and the dangers and responsibility incumbent upon them, unhesitatingly about face. Though they whisper muttering complaints about the stupidity and inefficiency of officers in general, they return to their posts, taking their risky places within earshot of the enemy's advance pickets and forward observation sentinels.

When it is done, every officer on the Heights who is aware of what was happening, breathes a sigh of relief. And the evacuation continues as muffled oars ply their loaded boats from shore to shore.

For the handful of American soldiers standing between their retreating comrades and 25,000 of Europe's finest troops this night seems to have no ending. In the dark stillness muscles are tensed by the slightest sound. Often it is nothing more than a night-prowling animal, but with every noise, hands tighten around rifle and musket butts, always in expectation of the worst.

At dawn—now vaguely lighting the eastern heavens—the entire movement will surely be detected by the British observers. And now that the rain has stopped and the wind is shifting, Admiral Black Dick's men-of-war will soon be ascending the bay and heading for the East River.

There they will begin their bombardment of the Heights, cutting off all escape for those caught in the cul-de-sac. Few of the men marching down the slope and hopefully into a place on an embarking boat, visualize much hope for their survival when they see the masts and sails of the enemy's frigates.

While the fading cover of darkness holds the operation's key to success, there is a new hidden threat about to menace the nocturnal expedition. Only the smiles of Chance have so far kept the escape operation's head above the water. Now the maneuver faces Tory trouble.

Nicht Verstehen Sie

A strong Loyalist woman, whose home near the river bank commands a fairly good view of the ferry landing below the Heights, has secretly observed the American movement. Convinced that it is an attempt to escape across the river, she finally sends her black servant through the woods to inform the British commander-in-chief.

The servant's back road avoids the American lines. He has been told to tell Howe, or the first British officer he meets, that the rebel army is escaping by water. After considerable difficulty he makes his way through the night to a forward Hessian sentry post.

Speaking only German, the sergeant's guard and the young second lieutenant in command are unable to understand a word the servant says. They question him in German.

Uncomprehending, the black speaks on in English until they are convinced he is one of the American slaves they have heard so much about who has run away and become lost. Since no one can understand what he is trying to tell them they order him to sit aside and wait. He does so until dawn.

Back and forth throughout the long night and into the dawning hour the hundreds of boats cross the chopping river waters. By dawn the skilled seamen and fishermen from Marblehead and Salem have rowed and sailed very nearly the entire American army to the safety of the New York shore.

Except for those troops waiting to board who have caught brief cat naps, few have slept in the past forty-eight hours. Despite the thousands of soldiers, baggage, field guns, horses, stores and provisions they have crossed since darkness set in last night, the hardy seamen remarkably show little sign of strain and fatigue.

At dawn Mifflin's men quietly move out behind the last of the withdrawing army in the final step out of the cul-de-sac. In their usual, well-disciplined order the guardians of the massive evacuation march proudly toward the wharf. Suddenly a heavy fog begins dropping an opaque curtain over the Heights and the river. Soon it is impossible to distinguish figures more than 20 feet away.

As the morning mist drifts in with the first rays of dawn over the emptied encampment, a lone, probing, British picket becomes curious at the unchallenged advance he is making on the American breastworks. Farther and farther he probes, pushing himself up almost to the rebels' outer abatis and fascines on the fortification's eastern fléche.

The inquisitive scout smells the burning wood of the campfires that have been sparking throughout the night. But there are now no noises, no signs of sentinels nor pickets. Suddenly he realizes there are not only no voices, sounds, or any entrenching tool noises but not even the snorts of heavy sleepers.

The picket is joined by others. Together they hurl rocks over the abatis through the densing fog and get no returning cursing. Since they dare not fire their musket, they report the oddity to their superiors. Finally the report reaches the non-English speaking Hessian lieutenant, the same duty officer who had ordered the Tory woman's black messenger to sit aside and wait last night.

The lieutenant now excitedly orders a volley of shots be sent into the American works which brings other Hessian officers on the run. The firing wakes up the dozing black man, who now ambles on through the British lines toward the staff headquarters unmolested.

Immediately the alarm spreads through the entire Hessian and British encampment, calling every man to arms. Among the red-coats the Negro servant is clearly understood. His message sets off activity in the British sector where, at the same time, Howe's headquarters learns the Hessians have walked into the deserted American fort.

Minutes later the attackers swarm up the heights and over the works' defenses which the eager Hessians had wanted to scale three days ago. They are dry, well fed and refreshed from two days of rest and sleep. However the dense fog forces them to tread slowly and carefully.

Each step into the white enveloping mist confirms the embarrassing realization that their enemy has tricked them. Spiked cannon, campfires burning brightly, reflecting toward the British-held positions, emptied storage houses and magazines and not a rebel straggler in sight.

Through the soupy-like haze, their officers, believing there may be still time to entrap their escaping foe at the river, order their ranks to fan out and proceed with drawn bayonets to the docks. Unable to keep abreast and in line through the haze—in fact unable to see where they are going—the Hessian spearhead, supported in the rear by the redcoats, comes to a halt. Stymied by the Continentals' blessed fog, the enemy is forced to move slowly and is robbed of scoring even a minor victory.

In addition, not a single British ship is able to move through the becalmed, mist-enshrouded bay. But the American Marbleheaders and Salemites, experienced from their grueling all-night performance in criss-crossing the mile-wide river, find the fog no obstacle. For them it is a comforting security as they cross the remaining rear guards.

A contest now develops among the boats' helmsmen. Each wants his to be the last vessel out of the embarkation wharf. Every crewman hopes his craft will be the lucky one to take over the last man. For they surmise the last man will be The Gen'l himself.

Therefore Colonel Benjamin Tallmadge of the Connecticut brigade, friend and classmate of the fiery patriot, young Captain Nathan Hale, is unexpectedly surprised when a helmsman is so willing to carry him back across to get his horse. Upon securing his men safely on the Manhattan shore Tallmadge finds his boatmen waiting for him and eager to retrieve the animal, still tethered to a tree. For the seamen, this is a last chance that their boat may get the "honor" of convoying the Chief.

Unfortunately for the accommodating helmsman and his crew, their big barge is not the last. It has. a capacity load with Tallmadge's horse, men and baggage. And still left to go are The General, his horse, some guards, an aide and two of his staff. Two other transports, the last, move in to finish the great, supposedly "impossible" task.

As they do, the banks above the shore resound from an increasing staccato of small arms firing from the unseen enemy's forward pickets still a good distance away. Every now and then a cannon shot splits the air.

The disappointed helmsman sadly observes that one of the two vessels—the one directly behind him and not the last—takes on The General. It is the remaining guards and Old Magnolia that make up the final evacuation load, comprising the last of the 9,500-man army, horses, baggage and impedimenta in the miraculous escape from Howe's sack.

Tallmadge's helmsman pulls his barge out and in front of the landing. He backs into The General's vessel, throwing a safety line into its bow. The General's craft in turn casts a line to the last transport. All three in unison quickly pull out into the stream when Glover himself gives the order and steps in alongside of the American Commander.

Connected by their stern lines, the three vessels are not far into the stream before rifle fire spits through the fog-engulfed shore. The shots blast the air over the embarkation dock. They are not yet close enough to be effective, but there is no time to lose. The oarsman increase their tempo.

Tallmadge, among other officers in the bow of the cursing helmsman's "unlucky craft," eyes the American Chief for whom he has always held a devoted admiration. He had observed him directing the very last movement of his enterprise until the moment of his unmounting.

Some had said The General had not been out of the saddle during the past 48 hours. Tallmadge believed it as he watched the big man stretch and shake his feet, then walk calmly over to the nearest clump of trees and urinate. The greater the man, thought the colonel, the less chance he has of privacy.

Tallmadge had noticed the American Leader's concern for Old Magnolia. She was boarded carefully, tightly tethered, her feet bound and head hooded. Unable to imagine what was going on, she turned her head wonderingly toward her master's scent in the forward boat.

Tallmadge observed that her master's head, just before boarding, had turned toward the abandoned fort. For a brief moment The General stood and stared rigidly in the direction of the enemy that had taken so many of his men and three of his most promising generals.

Well out in mid-stream now, there is little chance of any pursuit for some time to come. The Americans have not left a single craft that can float anywhere along the banks. If the silence order were not still in effect, almost every man aboard the three boats would let out boisterous hurrahs. All are close to exhaustion but none so close as certainly should be the gallant Marblehead and Salem seamen.

Through the lifting fog, which seems not to have blanketed New York town with the severity it covered Brooklyn, the Connecticut colonel again glimpses the army's "Grand Old Man" in the boat behind. He sees him lift off his sopping wet, tricorn hat and reach up to his brow, wiping away the sweat.

"In all," Tallmadge says to the young officer beside him, "I'd say he," (and Tallmadge nods in the direction of The General) "has slept not a single wink in three days."

Lieutenant John Gray lifts his dozing head up from the gunnel on which it was resting and peers into the boat at his vessel's stern. Actually Gray's mind had been preoccupied with thoughts of someone far up Hudson's river. That, and the sudden realization that the 28th day of August and his 21st birthday, had somehow, passed by unnoticed, bring thoughts of marriage to his tired brain, seeking escape to happier things. Tallmadge's words brought him abruptly back to reality. He looks at The General wiping his brow.

"Colonel," replies Gray, "I'd say he never sleeps. Up on the works while we were spiking, there he was. Then on the lines, when you'd never expect him, there he was. All along the march he'd suddenly appear, seldom saying anything, just watching. Once in awhile he spoke, giving the men a word of cheer."

Tallmadge turns to Gray as he speaks. The colonel looks at the younger officer's dirty cloth stripping around The Lieutenant's neck and smiles.

"You speak well, rather like a Yankee who attended Yale," Tallmadge says, almost completely disregarding the substance of Gray's answer.

"No, Sir! A Pennsylvanian who attends Princeton," comes the quick reply.

"I meant it as a compliment," Tallmadge retorts, somewhat apologetically.

"And I took it as one, Sir. I consider it so," returns Gray. My apologies if I led you to think otherwise, for I know of you and that you are of the excellent Yale school."

"I, too, have heard of you, Lieutenant," Tallmadge says. "I must admit it is through your unusual neckerchief rather than your schooling. I have heard, too, of the good fortune it is said to bring you."

Then Tallmadge adds, "I am surprised The General has not asked of you what brigade it represents."

Gray smiles, making no reply. But the Lieutenant's uninhibited Corporal Mike Monahan, sitting in the bottom of the boat nearby, has overheard part of the conversation and laughingly interjects,

"Ah, 'tis 'rong ye air, Kerrnel, 'causing' Oi wez thar meself when Tha Ald Mon, God bless 'im, tarked to Tha Lootenan and sez, sez he, 'Boi the why, Lootenan', Oi trusts yer Lidy will knit ye a marr appropreeate neckerchief before winter!' "

All those within hearing distance of the loud-mouthed cannoneer, in addition to Tallmadge and Gray, who takes the jibe in his usual unperturbed manner, break out with laughter. The healthy outlet is an open vent, for suddenly the long, pent-up tension of the men and the crew huddled in the boat disperses as does now the fog.

Tallmadge, realizing an opportunity to return what he still feels was Gray's barb at Yale says,

"He, too, speaks well," referring to Monahan, "like a southerner who attended Princeton."

"If you mean The General," replies Gray, knowing he didn't, "you are quite wrong. Great figures, I fear are seldom cut out of formal schooling. He is a product only of the field schools of Virginia."

"Touché!" retorts the colonel. And both men laugh.

Two bursts of the enemy's cannon on the Heights end the conversation. Another barrage opens up from the British-captured shore. The fieldpieces drown out the increasing musket fire.

The nearest to a hit is the heavy plunk of a ball in the steaming-like water far off to the vessels' starboard sides. The British cannoneers have found the range but not the location.

Soon the three transports approach the dock at the foot of South Street. Like the thrilling sight of a landfall to a storm-tossed mariner, before their eyes appear the outlines of the port city.

Weather-beaten little shacks dot the shore in front of the larger shops, homes and buildings of the city. Behind them, reaching northward up Manhattan are spread out the large farms and landed estates. In the dawning light the picturesque church steeples rise up out of the mist like overlords of the village, its stores, shops and the more pretentious business establishments.

It is as though New York town were gradually growing up from out of the white ground cover and from behind the rising curtain of the morning's disappearing mist. The edges of the dense fog that had so heavily closed over the river and the Heights have, oddly enough, barely reached the little city.

Like a fairy land, undisturbed by the duel-to-the-death drama which has flared across the river only a cannon-shot or two away, the mile-square port of entry into Eighteenth Century America awakes as it does every morning. It appears to have no relevance with the war.

In fact the city, like its many Tory inhabitants, appears to want no contact with the filthy, smelling, ever-hungry, boisterous rebels, nor with the moaning cries of the wounded, maimed and dying. Both the war and its harvest are cast upon the island's doorstep. And so with the last arrivals—whether welcome or not—a great cheer goes up from the soldiers marching along the shore toward the New York encampment when the three last transports touch the dock.

The dawning is Friday, August 30, and the East's red fire ball throws sharply brightening shadows on New York's river-front. Its rays single out the town's slums, occupied by day laborers, dock-hands, fishermen and free Negroes. Its beams ferret out the river's upstream shores where, in contrast, stand the stately homes and mansions of the wealthier merchants in the era's fading glory of Colonial wealth.

Between the two extremes, and figuratively in behalf of both, are spread out the supposedly strongest wing, the central department, of the American Army, or rather the remaining 9,500 of them.

Though it cannot be foreseen, it is, nevertheless, the prelude to the most miserable, disheartening, military misfortune and the most remarkable and astounding retreat ever recorded in the wasted, horrendous annals of warfare. And, though it cannot be envisioned, this is the beginning of a nation's giant grasp for individual, societal, national and international freedom and independence.

It is, though predictively unbelievable, the historical genesis of the free and independent united colonial states of North America.

To accelerate the speed of the present American retreat will be calamitous. This The General knows. Withdrawals, rather than a massive retreat, may save the army's dwindling morale, preserve the flickering hopes of the peoples in the thirteen varied and separate sections of the loosely united country, and stave off Tory partisans.

It is the Tories' constant, internal mischief that always must be considered. For the Tories and fellow Loyalists ever seek a quick return to government under the Crown.

On the other hand, to slow down or halt the retreat could end it conclusively. That is the catastrophe which the British high command aims and hopes to achieve. It can be done in one battle if the rebels will only stand and fight.

On the New York shore Gray snatches one of the papers a dispatch rider from Philadelphia had in his saddlebag. It is a copy of the *Pennsylvania Journal And Weekly Advertiser* dated August 28. His birthday! Therefore he considers it a birthday gift—a suitable one for an avid reader and for one hungry for news from home.

The one account that gets his full and immediate attention is the report of an address by Dr. Ebenezer Elmer before the Committee of Inspection for the County of Cumberland in the State of New Jersey. Elmer, a surgeon of the Second Regiment of the New Jersey Continentals, is one of The Lieutenant's idols and a close friend. The doctor had been instrumental in Gray's decision to enlist last May.

The Philadelphian, whose men have broken ranks waiting for their orders to march to the Bowery, finds an empty keg to sit on. Chewing on sea biscuits, distributed in large quantities to all the men, Gray begins reading.

Tired, hungry and exhausted from the past few grueling days, it is Gray's first moment of respite. He knows it will not last long.

Philadelphia! Over a hundred miles away! And here in his hands is news from his home city—news only two days old! To Gray it seems impossible, amazing—a fantastic thing!—to hear about things so recently occurring so far away. Over again, he reads Elmer's speech, mainly one part in which the surgeon says:

> "... No people under Heaven, were ever favored with a fairer opportunity, of laying a sure foundation for future grandeur and happiness than we. The plan of government established in most states and kingdoms of the world, has been the effect of chance or necessity, ours of sober reason and cool deliberation, our future happiness or misery therefore, as a people, will depend entirely upon ourselves.
>
> "If actuated by principles of virtue and genuine patriotism, we make the welfare of our country the sole aim of all our actions; If we entrust none but persons of abilities and integrity, with the management of our public affairs; If we are steady and zealous in putting the laws in strict execution; the spirit and principles of our new constitution, which we have just now heard read, may be preserved for a long time; but if faction and party spirit, the destruction of popular governments, take place, anarchy and confusion will soon ensue, and we shall either fall an easy prey to a foreign enemy, or some factious and aspiring *Demogogue*, possessed of popular talents and shining qualities, a *Julius Caesar*, or an *Oliver Cromwell*, will spring up among ourselves, who taking advantage of our political animosities, will lay violent hands on the government, and sacrifice the liberties of his country to his own ambitious and domineering humor. ..."[11]

"Just like Dr. Elmer! Just like him!" The Lieutenant thought. "But how true he speaks! How right he is!"

Gray then wonders whether this was a thing to be read to the men of his battery. Except from the more intensely committed among them, he knew what fun they would have with that!

He had tried patriotic speeches on them before. With them deeds counted. "The better the deed, the better the patriot," they would say to him in so many words. And he could not help but agree.

One thing he decides he will do, and must do, before he sleeps tonight—if he can stay awake—is to write Elaine. Since he expects they will send Big Tom to Orange Town or Hackensack over The Mountain, Jocko, who will go along with his father, could take it to her after they pass the river at Bourdette's.

A World's Destiny In His Hands

The consequences of this day and the days of the year yet to come, will gradually mold the future lives of the thirteen newly created states. They will design the lives of unborn generations. They will shape the future of millions yet to come across the seas. They will dictate the thinking and the fortunes of countless millions who will never see the America which, in a variety of ways, will control their destiny. The consequences are stupendous and completely unimaginable to the contestants.

Strangely and frighteningly those consequences are virtually, in the hands of only one man and the powers within that one man's mind.

The General's prestige, which had climbed so high a year ago, is now tottering. The wavering image of the soldiers' "Grand Old Man," is common talk in the Congress and the States.

Back on the high Bluff Rock a new day has arisen. The rain, which had given Elaine time to finish two handkerchiefs, bearing the crocheted initials, "J.G." and the date, "August 28, 1776," has at last stopped.

Yet throughout The Mountain and along the cliffs and within the homes close to the river Hudson's banks, wonder, fear and trepidations rise as swiftly as does the heat of the fading summer's hot and rising sun.

8

Tuesday, September 3. . .

In the Womb of Little Hope

After-effects Of Long Island

Only "catastrophic" fits the colonists', the Congress's, and the army's reaction to the state of the new nation in the wake of the tragedy of Long Island. Nothing in the two years of dissension and war has so dimmed the prospects for the American Revolution as has the Battle of Long Island.

News of the Brooklyn tragedy far overshadows the army's miraculous escape. Up on The Mountain at Fort Constitution, where Colonel Ward[1] had been drilling the new recruits for replacements, garbled accounts of the battle and its progress are all that can be learned from dispatch riders, travelers and the wounded now arriving. Ward, on the basis of the official information Mercer received, informed his men last Saturday of the Long Island action.

There is no way to interpret the results except as an overwhelming British victory no matter how it is reported. Suddenly all those who had but one interest days ago—to "get into the action"—now are disheartened. These newly recruited militia only last week had been hungry for the excitement of battle and impatient to be at war.

Therefore any accounts, passed on to the garrison by travelers or post riders, are voraciously devoured. The naive youngsters, fresh

114

from the inlands, are torn between believing stories told by the pro-British Tories, or those accounts given by the pro-American Whigs.

An example of this took place Saturday when two staunch patriots, an associate preacher named Dereck Remlin and his cousin Garry Ledbecker, crossed from New York on a ferry passage with a strongly suspected Tory named Nicausie Klep. Klep kept to himself all the way over.

After refreshing himself from the mountain spring water trough near the stage stop Klep began talking. His loud explanation of the battle on Long Island soon attracted a gathering of residents. In earshot of the shore's sentry post, his voice soon attracted the soldiers' attention as well. Klep had been the first to get through the guard's examination of passengers.

When his pass was found in order, he secured the attention of a few eager ears at the trough. With that hungry audience he was encouraged to undermine as many as possible with his biased and imaginary accounts.

The news-hungry inhabitants and soldiers swallowed whole the personally concocted tales with their lurid descriptions of Americans slaughtered by the thousands, the American Chief of the Army believed mortally wounded, almost all the American generals killed or captured, and thousands of the rebel army drowned in the swamps in their effort to escape.

Klep gave every indication of knowing what he was talking about. His audience stood aghast.

Coming down the gorge road after their morning visit to the hospital tents, Elaine and Ma Kearney walked directly into the gathered bystanders. Elaine was petrified in silence by what she heard. Both women, along with all the rest, could not help but accept such a report as valid.

Ma Kearney is not a woman reputed to be very gullible. Her first thought was Elaine. Immediately she comfortingly encircled her arm around the girl's shoulders.

Then, like the burst of a howitzer that almost caused Paul to jump out of his deer-hide moccasins, Ma Kearney hurled her booming voice at the astonished Klep who was by then complimenting himself on his undisputed success in deception on behalf of his King.

Shaking her fist, she bellowed at him on vocal cords that would make a mountain lion envious. Ma added a few choice epithets that made at least one hausfrau, Polly Onderdonk, blushingly run back to the sanctity of her own kitchen.

"Git out, you! Git out, you . . . you damned liar!" shouted Ma at the top of her voice which could easily be heard at the top of the gorge road. "Git out and on yer goddamned way! Ye air nothin' but a lyin', bastardly good-fer-nothin' scoundrel! And ye know it! Now git!"

And Klep did 'git" as fast as he could into the waiting stage. Never had man or woman ever talked to him like that before. Few people of either sex had ever tangled with Ma Kearney and emerged the victor. As for her weapon, a loud mouth and a frightening vocabulary, she always later apologized. Yet everyone knew there would always be another bombardment when her feathers were ruffled.

As for atonement, Ma would wait for the hard-pressed, young itinerant Catholic priest, Father Bulger, to make his rounds to The Mountain. And with one fell swoop, as always, she would unload her confessions upon the lap of the kindly cleric whose worried countenance and shaking head presaged great concern for the woman's status in the world hereafter.

Noticing the Assistant Preacher Remlin had come up to the gathering from behind with Garry Ledbecker, Ma blushed and made a note to apologize later to the Dutch Reformed clergyman. Actually, both the young preacher and his cousin had heard enough of Klep's inflamatory remarks to become as furiously enraged as the fisherwoman.

In fact the preacher's ire was so great at what he did hear Klep say that he secretly wished he had been able to author Ma's rebuke. Nothing could have pleased Remlin more than to see the badly whipped, Tory-minded Klep run to the coach like a beaten dog.

The Coetus-Conferentie Conflict

Both the assistant Domine and his cousin are pillars of the Coetus Party in the splintering rift that has long smouldered and frequently flared among the congregations of the many Dutch churches throughout the valleys.[2]

The opposing faction in the church-split is called the "Conferenties." That party is led by Garry Ledbecker's Loyalist cousin who is a domine in the valley church, also named Garrett Ledbecker. And Nicausie Klep is a devoted follower of that clergyman, having no use whatsoever for the Coetus Party.

Klep and the Tory Ledbeckers are residents of the valley to the west, over The Mountain, they live at opposite ends of the area known as English Neighbourhood, or Neighborhood, as some call it.

In the Dutch churches throughout the lowlands and along the mountainous Palisadean peninsula, the politics of religion has caused a down-the-middle cleavage in the congregations. And over The Mountain and along its western slope there is as sharp a division in the thinking as there is to the west in the Schraalenburgh and the Hackensack areas.

On the one side, the Conferenties hold to the traditional ties, doctrines and tenets of the homeland church. However the Coetus Party prefers independence from all foreign ties. Therefore, it has followed rather logically, that the Conferenties have sided with the Tory or Loyalists' political concepts in the present rebellion. Similarly, the Coetus Party has aligned itself with the Whigs, or "Patriots."

Klep had a few pro-Crown sympathizers and as many neutrals still believing him when Ma intervened and when the angry young patriot Domine, with Garry at his heels, followed the inciter to the stage. Morally supported by his handful of sympathizers, Klep sneered through the open window with his nose high in the air as Remlin and Ledbecker shook their fingers and fists in his face, branding him, "Liar! Liar!"

Emotions now ran high among the crowd. Just when it looked as though fists would soon be flying along with whatever could be picked up and thrown, Pete Baummeister strode slowly but defiantly through the confusion of voices. At the ferry landing he had very soon learned of Klep's words and the excitement they stirred, but his concern was for his daughter and the distress it would cause her.

His big, powerful frame always demanded respect, and his thunderous, broken-English voice was a match for even Ma at her best.

"Ve vill alls shtop dese noish aund pushin'," Baummeister demanded in his firm, deep voice. "Und ve will hear vot dere goot, Reverend Preacher Remlin haas to say. He vas down dere, too, und vot dot man shpoke vas not vot dere goot Reverend heard."

Remlin, whose finger was shaking very close to Klep's face, straightened up. He, too, is a highly reputable figure in the area. Tories have feared him. Whigs have admired him. Though only an assistant he is much respected for his frank and honest approach in dealing with all issues.

His account of the battle was acquired from the most reliable sources in New York, for he had visited both the Seaman and Townsend families and talked with troops who had been in the battle. The Seamans and Townsends are neutrals in appearance only. In truth they are the nucleus of the American army's developing intelligence corps.

Remlin acknowledged the defeat and the possible loss of many lives on both sides,

"But," he asked, "do you know that the whole army escaped with baggage and all supplies safely across the river at night without the British knowing it until every man was safely across?"

After that question was given to the assemblage, it was easy to determine who in the group were the Whigs, who the Tories. For the Whigs cheered the statement and the Tories glanced toward Klep who drew back from the window and hunched back on the stagecoach seat. He had not counted on the necessity of matching the credibility of Preacher Remlin.

Were it not that at that moment the stagecoach driver got into his seat, wiped his mouth from a heavy draft of grog he always helps himself to from the Bourdette wine cellar, and pulled out and up the gorge road with a yell to his four-horse team, Klep might have been pulled out of the coach and severely pommeled. And Klep knew it, breathing easier as the coach and four ascended the steep incline and made its way over The Mountain and down into the King's Highway, then into the valley.

The enthusiastic clergyman, once started in his delivery, unraveled all he knew for the audience when Klep's stage departed. He might have been rehearsing his sermon for his Sunday service the following day.

He told of the heroic actions of Stirling and his men. He described various incidents that he and Garry had heard recounted. In detail he explained how "Providence intervened" with a fog that covered the escape and a northeaster which had stilled the enemy's fleet.

Calling upon his pulpit training, Remlin emphasized "Providence's intervention on the side of righteousness and justice," noting that, "The sun rose brilliantly on the American side of the East River Friday morning, but not so brilliantly on the Redcoats' shore."

In concluding his impromptu address, Remlin declared, "One half hour after that fog lifted, every man was safe on the south docks and could see swarms of the enemy troops along the opposite shore and in the ramparts on Brooklyn Heights. How," he asked, "can it be doubted that we have the Divinity on our side?"

By this time, Klep's supporters had melted away. There was not one who decided to force a dispute under the very noses of the now unfriendly detachment of American troops, especially when their spokesman had left them so precipitously.

As Klep passed through, he had not missed observing the large number of troops arriving and departing from the landing. And he had taken in everything he saw on The Mountain's summit where, it is clear to any passer-by that preparations are under way to build a major encampment on the main mountain ridge. Nicausie Klep told himself he would have much to tell his pro-British cronies when next he meets them at the Three Pidgeons Inn just off the highway on the road through Bergen Woods.

Elaine had not cried though she was visibly upset as her father had surmised. Seeing this, the young preacher, immediately after closing his talk, went to her side, consoling her and assuring her that he was sure "everything will turn out all right." Pressing his hand in appreciation, Elaine thanked Remlin. Standing between Ma and her father, she waved a goodbye as Remlin and Ledbecker mounted and rode off.

The near fist-fight at the ferry reflects the boiling point tempers of the people generally. Every move the enemy makes is magnified by the Crown's civilian sympathizers.

Simultaneously with the attack on Brooklyn Heights a week ago yesterday, the British turned their cannon on the town of Elizabeth in Jersey, firing across the Kill van Kull from their emplacements on Staten Island.

Though the Jersey militia returned the fire and reported no damage, the Tories there for miles around spread highly exaggerated tales that the inhabitants were abandoning their homes in the wake of the advancing British army.

It is hard to believe that there was the country and those were the people who were, many years ago, described as "the most Easie and Happy People of any Collony in North America."[3]

And the Tories fed further fears into the hearts of the Jerseyans when they magnified the American withdrawal from the vulnerable post at Red Hook last Friday after the escape of the Continentals into New York.

It was true that the post's defenders made a narrow escape across the bay into the safety of the Paulus Hook fortifications[4] in the cumbersome Durham boats. It was true they abandoned quantities of stores and all their cannon.

Pursued by the swift British frigates, *Phoenix*, under Captain Parker, the *Rose*, under Captain Wallace, and the *Greyhound*, under Captain Dickson,[5] the fleeing Continental Army garrison's over-loaded awkward little boats, designed for river, not rough bay usage, barely made it to the protecting cover of Colonel Durkee's heavily armed Paulus Hook batteries.

However, throughout Jersey and New York, the Tories circulated stories of great American losses and destruction of all the boats and men. British sympathizers declared loudly that none of the Red Hook post rebels were able to escape to Paulus Hook and the safety of the Jersey Shore.

In the winter of 1775, the American Commander-in-Chief had proposed to Congress a series of defenses that were to have centered around Staten Island. Only now, much too late, does his proposal of last winter seem to make good sense to some of the plan's erstwhile "Doubting Thomases."

The General had developed the plan when Major General Charles Lee presented his report on the state of New York, Manhattan Island, its environs and defenses. That was last January 5, in Cambridge, Massachusetts.

It was at that time that the crystallization of the present New York campaign began to take shape. It was about then that the American rebel Leader heard that General Howe was outfitting his fleet in Halifax for what was certainly to be an invasion of New York and New Jersey, in the opinion of the American Commander.

The British Halifax preparations plus the acute political situation in New York town, where 40% of the population were strongly pro-British in their sentiments, convinced the American Chieftain that New York and New Jersey were to be Sir William's next objective.

But owing to Congressional dissensions and governmental interventions from the colonial representatives, demanding their own colony's security, the American Commander-in-Chief's plan never did reach the stages of defense he had long proposed. Paulus Hook was but one of the intended vital defense posts, each of which was to be a dependent link in the over all defense plan.

The Hook is now the only defense post on the west side of the Hudson's mouth. And only the American Grand Battery at Manhattan's southern tip challenges the enemy shipping at the mouth of the Hudson's east shore.

Together Paulus Hook and the Grand Battery are to prevent passage of enemy shipping which, if successful, must then run through the twin forts at Bourdette's and Jeffery's Hook.

The General had wanted Staten Island fortified to ward off any invasion. However, New Jersey, which claims the island, had put the matter of proposed defenses into the hands of its Committee of Safety.[6] The committee procrastinated and the plans that could have thwarted an enemy fleet moving in upon the two key states through New York's outer bays, were never carried through.

It was not simply a matter of procrastination. It was also largely the characteristic parochial viewpoint rampant among all the thirteen colonies that was responsible. The New Jersey committee's "East Jersey First" concept was merely a twig of the tree acting with the customary independence of its thirteen branches.

So despite Brigadier General Lord Stirling's arguments which he advanced on behalf of his Chief last spring, the New Jersey Committee of Safety dallied over proposals for defenses on Staten Island, defenses designed to prevent the enemy's easy ascent up the Hudson to New York's front door.

The Committee of Safety insisted on fortifying Elizabeth Town Point, Amboy, the Kill van Kull, Bergen Neck and Paulus Hook[7] --all along the Jersey side. However, the committee members held that New York town was a Loyalist Party stronghold and saw no point in protecting a "Tory nest."

Though letters went back and forth and days went by with many appeals, nothing was done. Staten Island, which the Commander of the Continentals had so strongly urged be fortified, was entirely undefended.

As a result of this and the disinclination to support The General's defense plan, entrenchments, which were begun elsewhere throughout the system including those on Lower Manhattan, were half-hearted, unconvincing and indefensible. Not one of the forts was under way until too late. Thus everything hinged limply around Fort Putnam, Fort Greene, Red Hook, Governor's Island, Paulus Hook and the Grand Battery on Manhattan.

Paulus Hook: The Only Operable Post

The serious state of the city internally was realized as far back as June 10. On that date Colonel Knox reported that he was unable to get crews in New York to man his ten guns. To the colonel, commander of the army's artillery, this was a sure indication of the port city's disinterest in the American cause.

So inverted and altered by political whims was The General's original defense plan that before the battle, "only four percent of the entire gun-power of the American army was installed where it was originally planned to have been erected."[8]

Paulus Hook was the only post outlined eight months ago in the original project which was in actual operation by June 10. It was designed as a link in The General's proposed chain of posts. Alone it is ineffective even firing in conjunction with the Grand Battery opposite on the New York side. Certainly, albeit jointly with the Manhattan battery, it cannot repel Great Britain's armada.

Consequently the inviting campgrounds of Staten Island, and the inadequate defenses surrounding its bays and The Narrows separating it from Long Island were made to order for General Howe and his admiral brother. And they have so far made the most of it.

Now the combat has evolved into a deathly game of chess and chance. Undoubtedly the enemy's next objective must be New York. Within that "Tory nest" Howe knows he will have much assistance. On the other hand the American Commander believes there are enough patriots in the city to counteract the Loyalist elements.

In New York the franchise is restricted to property owners who alone control the city's politics. And in New York, Tories are said to own two-thirds of the town's property. So it is no wonder Sir William is determined to acquire the city and, with it, political control.

The British command knows that the New York Tories through their influence on Manhattan have been notoriously successful in corrupting the American soldiers and in fattening their own pockets by overcharging the Continentals. And Howe is happy to hear that New York's Loyalists have their primary interest to save the city so it can become the future British capital of Britain's American Colony.

All this seriously disturbs the worried Continental Congress which too late has seen its errors. One great mistake was to allow The General's opponents in the Congress last May to select their own Military Committee, permitting it to direct the defense strategy for the then impending conflict in New York.[9] That action sapped the American Army's strength for weeks by ordering the building of entrenchments in the city, entrenchments which may never be defended or used at all.

So it is that the people are torn by the dissensions around them. They are hesitant to trust the new Second Continental Congress and its weakly united government tied together only by a declaration of independence. And they are becoming skeptical as to the ability of the American Commander-in-Chief to succeed.

After all, has he not already lost Long Island, some of his best generals and an undisclosed number of troops, armament and supplies?

The people of the newly created united colonial states actually find there is little left for them to be optimistic about. Few realize that the task of conducting a war with a *weak central government*—a government ever fearful of antagonizing any one territory, committee, or any one of the thirteen constitutent governments—is not only next to impossible but tantamount to governmental suicide.

Even more discouraging was the news Saturday that Howe has circulated the story that Long Island inhabitants are saying they were "forced into the rebellion." The British commander also has spread word that everyone on Long Island had submitted to the King's forces and all are ready to take the oath of allegiance to the Crown.[10]

This news strikes fear particularly among the "neutrals." Before long every inhabitant of the valleys and in the Juggernaut's path will be offered one option: to take the oath of allegiance to the Crown.

What neutral, in fact what patriot, will refuse when he knows he will otherwise face ruin, the loss of all he owns, and possibly death?

It is a terrifying and discouraging hour, not only for the populace who juggle one question alongside of the next, seeking answers no one can give, but for the army straining to hold its morale intact. Only the stalwart Continentals display the stamina that gives hope to the cause.

Even among them dissension is as rife as it is among the militia of the Northern and Southern states. They seldom see eye to eye. Militia in companies, and regulars whose enlistments have expired, pack up frequently and leave for home in large numbers. There is nothing holding them. The Congress has provided an army which has no staves to bind it together. Desertions and court martials are daily occurrences. And the Congress seemingly cannot realize that its own existence is now dependent upon its military strength.

The General's opponents have increased within the year. The Loyalists have taken full advantage of this whenever possible. The Battle of Long Island's losses, not the successful escape, has provided ammunition for Loyalists and for The General's opponents.

Consequently, Howe, still seeking the coup de gras he bungled on the Brooklyn Heights, will aim to get it on Manhattan Island. And the American Commander knows that another all-out enemy attack is imminent and with it his enemy's success could spell the end.

Therefore, the commander has concluded that the army's only possible salvation lies in a slow withdrawal up Manhattan, across the Harlem River at King's Bridge, with possibly a holding force at Fort Washington. After that, he foresees a race with the British frigates across Hudson's river into Jersey. It would follow that the army would then make its way south to protect the Congress in Philadelphia.

Speculation is high among the officers and troops. Some feel that a full scale retreat will be ordered. Others contend that The General holds an ace in his hand.

Some have little faith in the Leader. One of these is Colonel John Haslet of the Delaware regiment who wrote to a friend on Saturday: "Would to Heaven General Lee (Charles Lee) were here is the language of the officers and men."[11]

Those that argue against the possibility of a full scale retreat out of Manhattan point out, and quite accurately, the disastrous effect it would have on the country. Nothing, they say, will destroy the morale of the new nation as much as would a wild scramble for safety.

A rout at this hour would bring defeat and ruin. And this the American Leader knows from his experiences in the French and Indian War.

Needed: A Secret Weapon

Such an action, with little or no show of defense, with no semblance of defiance, would calamitously overnight, destroy all public support. It would isolate the patriots, those many loyal Whigs who have placed their trust and their lives in the cause. It would so embolden the Tories that they would unhesitatingly wreak vengeance immediately upon all who supported the Revolution and on the neutrals as well. It would bring about the collapse of the army's already dwindling morale, scatter the Congress in all directions and crush the rebellion through one single precipitated action.

So the American Commander-in-Chief, as does any military leader who finds his predicament precarious, is not averse to listening to the story of an inventor who, supposedly, has a new secret weapon.

The General and his staff, after a council of war, have determined that defiance must be maintained, but the rebel Leader is convinced that meeting the enemy in formal, open-field warfare will not again be attempted.

However, he agrees that there is no reason why a Mr. David Bushnell's so-called submarine should not be inspected, especially if it can do the things the inventor says it can. Therefore The General orders General Putnam to investigate the contraption.

Putnam arranges a date and place for Bushnell secretly to demonstrate his underwater craft which the inventor calls, *The American Turtle*. According to its designer, the engineer who operates it should be able to get under a British man-of-war, bore a hole in its hull, deposit a delayed powder fuse to a keg of powder and blow a big enough hole in its hull to sink it.

Putnam suggests Bushnell proceed to prepare a demonstration in the seldom-traveled upper reaches of the East River.

Among those few who know about it, there is enthusiasm and hope. The American Commander, though interested, is wary. He does not expect miracles to rescue him and his army. His main hope—his main weapon—lies, he knows, in the spirit of the soldiers and the people of the country in his hands.

He still has the support of most of the officers and men under his command. Those who escaped from Long Island still applaud their Chief for the remarkable maneuver that out-foxed Howe and probably saved their lives. To them he can do no wrong.

Among his staunch disciples is certainly Colonel Ben Tallmadge who wrote home to Connecticut from his headquarters Saturday, saying what had been on his mind:

"In the history of warfare I do not recollect a more fortunate retreat. After all, the providential appearance of the fog saved a part of our army from being captured, and certainly myself, among others who formed the rear guard.

"The General has never received the credit which was due to him for this wise and most fortunate measure."[1][2]

At the same hour Tallmadge was writing home from his headquarters in New York town, a whaleboat, filled with soldiers, was heading for the Bourdette ferry landing under the precipice and the Bluff Rock at Fort Constitution.

Sinister behind its abatis and unnatural attire of redoubts, cannon and men under arms, The Rock looks awesomely out over the great, ever-changing, man-encroaching expanse below it. To the men in the whaleboat it is a comforting sight.

From its high point of Bluff the sentry saw the dark figure of a man in the bow and, by his side, a young boy, waving wildly and shouting loudly, seemingly in an attempt to get someone's attention on the shore. The youth held tightly to the gunnel with one hand. The other excitedly fanned the air as the soldiers and crew of the heavily loaded boat watched amusedly.

The Sentry noticed that no one returned the greeting. Among the figures visible below him along the shore, only Pete Baummeister and his daughter were on the ferry landing dock. The ferry-master was repairing a few of the landing pier boards while his daughter, at his side, held the spikes, handing them over as he needed them.

Neither paid any attention to the adjoining military dock where soldiers were constantly landing and leaving. One more boat of soldiers amid the noise of raised voices, the shouting of orders and the general confusion surrounding any military wharf was nothing new, even when one of the boats—still some 100 rods off shore— had a waving, shouting youth in its bow.

So neither Papa Pete nor Elaine, could hear the happy voice of the black youngster in the whaleboat, furiously attempting to get their attention. The splash of the oars, the laughter of the boat's occupants, the shouting and confusion on the military wharf, plus Baummeister's incessant hammering, were too much competition for Jocko's lungs.

The sentry, "Sharp Sighted Stash," as he is called by his comrades, like most of the army post's rank and file, knew of the ferry-master's long sheltered life under the cliffs, of his devoted love for his children and of his affection for his favorite, the young vivacious apple of his eye who, it is said, is in love with a lieutenant with the army in Long Island. But he had not been told of Jocko.

Every man on the Barbette Battery knows of the old company that manned the guns on the Bluff and of their officer who courted the Baummeister girl. Without ever having to be told, or cautioned in advance, they hold the Baummeisters, the Bourdettes and particularly Elaine in the utmost respect. This is true of the entire rank and file, for it comes, unexpressed but strongly implied, from the post's commander himself.

The sentinel, casting his eyes down on the figures of the girl and her father far below him, was reminded of his own father and sister, Mary Maureen, back home in Brunswick.

Baummeister, too, seemed to shower his daughter with that extra bit of fatherly attention, though not consciously. And the lonely sentinel, in his reverie, likened himself to Paul, a sort of runner-up. And, as in the case of his own sister, thought the sentinel, Elaine seemed to eye her father as the epitome of all that is good in man.

To the young soldier on his observation post, this somewhat blind, but frequently found filial love of a daughter for her father seems the right thing—the thing he hoped he, as a father someday might earn from his own daughter.

He had seen Elaine helping her father in the numerous chores that must be done to keep the home, the farm and the business of the ferry going. And he had noticed that always she was beside him when the preacher held the Sabbath Day services.

But the soldier-guard then became concerned about the approaching boat with the wildly waving boy whom he then discovered to be a Negro youth, gesticulating toward the ferry dock and the two Baummeisters.

What could it be about? Was the youngster warning them? Could they be in danger from something not visible from the Bluff's height?

The sentry was in for a surprising shock. Though the soldier's insight into the lives of Elaine and Papa Pete was quite correct, he had not seen much beyond the surface. Actually Baummeister is not a possessive-type father. He had happily watched his daughter's first infatuation grow into deep love for Gray.

What is still even more comforting to the ferry-master is that he liked the officer from the very first. On that occasion when they looked into each other's eyes, the older man felt immediately attracted to the wholesome frankness of the youth. Unconsciously he seemed to know that this was the man for his only daughter.

As time went on the wise father took The Lieutenant's side or none at all rather than lean toward the prejudice that drew him naturally toward his daughter's defense in little discussions, spats and lovers' quarrels.

The departure of The Lieutenant from the post in the mobilization of the troops against the invasion, the ensuing battle in the distance, the lack of any letter in the days since and the gloom and despondency that had overcome his child, all had affected him almost as severely as the events had sickened her.

Baummeister had exhausted all the devices he could think of in an effort to cheer Elaine, or a least keep her mind busy with other things. Nothing had worked. Every post, every express was eagerly met with hope for a letter.

Casually Elaine lifted her head from watching her father's steady, accurate hammer strokes. As any number of times before, her eyes were drawn to the approaching boat. She had long given up hope of suddenly seeing John appear in one of the military vessels that constantly cross loaded with soldiers.

Then her attention focused on the small figure in the bow of the approaching, but still distant, whaleboat. He appeared to be frantically waving a paper of some kind in her direction. She was certain that he called her, as only one person she had ever known called her, "Missy E." She cupped her hand over her eyes and listened more attentively. The boat sped rapidly now toward the military wharf.

"Missy E!" cried the youngster. "Missy E! It's me! It's me, Jocko!"

With an excited scream that startled everyone in the vicinity of the two landing docks and bewildered the already perplexed sentinel on the high Point of Bluff, Elaine ran down the ferry dock, then on to the shore and out on the military wharf just as the whaleboat docked. Jocko, followed closely by his wounded father, jumped ashore.

Gaping in astonishment, the soldiers in the boat and on the pier—and particularly the guard up on The Rock—were not sure they could believe their eyes. All except those of the old cadre on the landing. They knew of The Lieutenant's ever-present shadow, Jocko Graves, and the close relationship that had developed among the trio.

For Elaine, although not much taller than the boy, grabbed and hugged him "as though," one private later told another, "he was her lost brother." She then embraced Big Tom, his right arm bound in a sling, but her eyes searched eagerly in vain for Gray.

Jocko, his face reflecting the disappointing news he carried that Gray was not coming held out the letter. The gesture, Elaine realized, meant exactly that.

Her questions momentarily turned to Big Tom's arm, wrapped tightly from the shoulder down and held in a make-shift cloth sling. And then, as though she feared the worst with an unopened letter in her hand, she held Jocko's two arms in her hands, asking:

"Is he all right? Jocko, tell me! Tell me he is all right!"

"Ise tellin' yo he is, Missy E!" Jocko insisted. "Ise tellin' yo he is! Whatcha think dat dere lettah am oll 'bout? Da Lootenan don gabe me dat lettah to gib to yo. Only yo, he sez. Ise tellin' yo heez oll right!"

"Thar's right, Missy," Big Tom assured her. "Da boy am right. Yor Lootenan's full fit. Ah reckon dat lettah sgonna tell yo oll yo wants to know. Weez here am jus some ob dose who ain't hurt so bad an' needs a little fixin'. Ya see dese fellas oll can walk mostly. Da Lootenan' he ain't hurt none a'tall so heez still sabe down dere wid da bat'rey."

It was true that none of the men in that load were severely wounded. Big Tom's was about the worst. Others had fingers, hands, head and leg wounds enabling them to cross over to Jersey and be treated at the Hackensack hospital.

And now Elaine went from one to the other, consoling each man as he came off the boat on the dock. A tear of gratitude was in her eyes as she thanked her God that John was well and safe. Seeing all were in good hands under the company charged with transferring them to a military wagon, she clasped her letter tightly and moved away to the privacy of her room in the river homestead.

On the old walnut bed she fell, sprawling herself over the down quilt and read John's letter. Not once but a dozen times.

Baummeister who stopped hammering and watched his daughter, soon understood what was going on. He saw Jocko and Big Tom with his bandaged arm and realized Gray was not with them.

The ferry-master hurriedly made his way toward the military pier as Elaine, with a letter in her hand, sped up the path to the house. Baummeister embraced Jocko and his father and was told that Gray was safe in New York.

He asked about Big Tom's wound and inquired of the officer in charge what if anything he could do for the boy and his father. Assured that they would be well taken care of in Hackensack, Baummeister saw them into the wagon and up the gorge road to the post headquarters from which they moved over the ridge into the valley.

As one of the soldiers put it in a later description, "I knew of the story that a black freed man once owned all that is now Fort Constitution and Bourdette's Ferry, having been willed it many, many years ago. When we saw the ferry-master and his daughter lovingly hugging and embracing the young black boy and his father, we thought certainly the descendants of the ancient Negro owner had come back to reclaim the military post and all that went with it."

Most of the soldiers, particularly those in Jocko's boat and up beside him in the bow, applauded the welcome given to the Graves. Some even cheered as though it were the final act of a drama when Jocko handed Elaine John's letter. For Jocko had previously informed his boat companions of his own important part in the love affair of "The Lootenan and his lady."

If anyone was acquainted with the love affair, it was Jocko. Surely it was no secret! And much less by the time the whaleboat reached Bourdette's.

Jocko's account, steeped with his evident affection for The Lieutenant and Missy E, took up a good part of the river voyage from New York. Big Tom looked on, disapproving but not curtailing his son's exuberant enthusiasm in exposing The Lieutenant's private life.

Tom has a tinge of guilt whenever he is compelled to restrict, or control Jocko for anything. In the black man's mind, his son has little enough joy and pleasures from life. And Graves long ago decided he would not be the one to restrict those simple pleasures. Besides, he tells himself, no father could have been blessed with a finer, more loving son than he.

Therefore, those who did not know of the "Blue Petticoat Scarf Lieutenant" on the Fort Constitution-bound whaleboat, soon had first-hand information. So it was they who cheered.

It is now a week since the Battle of Long Island with its ever-mounting consequences. A strange foreboding quiet seems to have settled over The Rock's near and distant landscape, if not over the entire country.

Only the almost constant marching of troops far down the island, across in the sister fort, below the Bluff Rock's Barbette Battery and along the clove road at the ferry, break the silence. The shouts of commands, or the sounds of fife and drum, only disrupt the monotonous tread of feet and the stomping hoof beats of straining horses and their creaking wagons.

The strained and nervous inhabitants take the woe-laden atmosphere somewhat for granted now. The merchants and travelers passing through Fort Constitution stare in wonder at the ragged soldiers, few of whom wear decent uniforms.[13]

By 9 o'clock in the morning of this warm first Tuesday in September, clusters of people gather by the stagecoach-stop up from the Bourdette landing to exchange the latest hearsay. It is a customary procedure. Tuesdays the venders come through to sell their wares and the farmers from the valley come up The Mountain with their produce, most of which is sold to the army or transported downriver to New York town.

Today the gossip is spiked with rumors which distract more and more eavesdroppers from their duties in order to listen to "first-hand reports from down at the Grand Battery."

One river boatman has it that General Howe and his brother, the Lord and admiral, are giving the Americans their last chance to surrender. That is why, he tells his eager listeners, there has been no action down below since the fight last week.

In answer to one strategist who contends that the guns on the Paulus Hook post and those on the Grand Battery will keep the enemy from going any farther, a ship-builder, arguing a rebuttal from his wagon seat, asks:

"How long do ye expect the Chief can hold New York oncet those British ships move in with all them devil Hessians on Long Island behind them?"

Even the American Commander-in-Chief was wondering the same thing at his temporary headquarters in the Franklin Mansion at Franklin Square.

Bad Tidings

The General's dispatch to the Congress yesterday will not please those who urge that New York be held. For the Commander's message includes this discouraging inclusion for the states' representatives:

". . . Till of late I had no doubt in my mind of defending the place (New York), nor should I have yet, if the men would do their duty."[14]

It is only part of the long, three and a half page letter of bad tidings. But it will be devoured word by word in Philadelphia since it contains a report and account of the tragic battle and the depressing effect that it has had upon the army.

And the Congress, particularly those who have never fully supported The General, now seeks a scapegoat for its own weaknesses in not having approved the American Commander's earlier proposed defense plans for New York. After all, had not the Chief months ago said, "It is the Place (New York) that we must use every Endeavor to keep from them (the enemy)"?[15]

Those who now decry his change of mind are those who most

actively blocked his plans for defenses along the shores and on Staten Island. They are now conveniently oblivious to their earlier apathy when the American Commander-in-Chief had wanted to construct formidable defense positions under Stirling, previously started by Charles Lee.

Lee had always held that New York could not be indefinitely defended but believed that the King's men could be made to pay a high price for its possession.[16] It was then that The General had hoped for strong Congressional support for the proposed fortifications on Staten and Long Islands. Congressional indecision, the politics of the two states and the strength of the Tory Party's opposition in and around Manhattan were factors he had not anticipated.

However, he had always recognized the strength of those who had opposed or questioned his appointment in 1775. He knew the power that could be massed against him and the Congressional strings that could make a states-supported militia, mostly of volunteers, ineffective.

Even so, the enthusiasm that had spread from Liberty Pole to Liberty Pole over the country, the enthusiasm that the uniting of the colonies seemed to generate and the culminating patriotic fervor from which had sprung the powerful document for independence, all had assured him that a powerful army would be at his command.

And now, today, deserters abandon their posts in large numbers. Many whose enlistments have expired are going home, disgusted and despondent. These are not from the Continentals' ranks, the regulars. They are from the militia, headed by some of the self-seeking, inexperienced, politically appointed officers who, with their temperamental attitudes, are a grave concern for the high command.

Despite this worrisome problem, among others, more recruits are coming in. And, if anything is heartening along the gloomy horizon, it is the reports that the back roads are filling up with men from the distant countrysides and villages from all parts of the land. It is true that they are young, inexperienced and as yet untrained for battle, but it is a hopeful sign that brings encouragement to the populace as well as the troops.

Offsetting this favorable note is the disappointing realization that the Congress's promises of rations and uniforms have not been kept. Few of the troops have seen any of those assurances fulfilled.

Yet by Congressional order the troops were to have been given:

1 lb. of beef, or 3/4 lb. of pork, or 1 lb. salt fish; 1 lb bread, or flour, daily; 1 pint of milk and 1 quart of spruce beer, or cider, per day; weekly allowances of peas, beans, or other vegetables, rice or Indian meal, candles and soap.

Instead they have existed, at times, on far less and whatever they can scrounge. On Long Island some of the soldiers had nothing more than acorns, sea biscuits and roasted Indian corn for days.[17]

As for Congress's promises of good firelocks with bayonets and brown uniforms with varied regimental facings, little has come of them so far. Only the Delaware and Maryland regiments actually look the part of soldiers in their properly outfitted dress.

In addition, muskets are not standardized. This was also promised. Therefore it is impossible to supply the proper ammunition most of the time. As for bayonets, the men jestingly say that they are as scarce as tea in Boston.

Supplying the men with food is one of the biggest problems. Many complaints were heard of the meagerly distributed battle rations last week. The curses were particularly loud from those who tried to hold out for days on sea bread of canel and peasmeal. Each man had to grab his share and extras if he could as he walked by the kegs placed along the line of march. The biggest hands made the biggest hauls.

"Hard enough for musket flints" was the way one young soldier described the hardtack, adding: "Had we not foraged for our own food on the island, some of us might not have eaten at all."[18]

The pay is always a major complaint among the disgruntled. While most of the Continentals seldom complain too much about anything, seemingly basing their hopes upon the founding of a new and better world, not all are so idealistic.

It is those, whether regulars or militia, who howl loudest for pay days that seldom come that break away with their shillings for the nearest harlot[19] once they get paid.

The Congress, which has proven long on promises and short on deeds, now encourages enlistments. Their latest pronouncement is that soldiers are to receive a bounty of twenty dollars allowance of rations and a hundred acres of land for their services during the war, all in addition to wages. Officers will receive land in proportion to their respective ranks from two hundred to five hundred acres.

The monthly wages now, in the wobbling Continental currency, are:

colonel, $75; lieutenant colonel, $60; major, $50; chaplain, $33.33; surgeon, $33.33; surgeon's mate, $18; adjutant, $40; quarter-master, $27.50; regimental pay-master, $26.67; captain, $40; lieutenant, $27; ensign, $20; sergeant-major, $9; quarter-master sergeant, $9; drum-major, $8, fife-major, $8.33; sergeant, $8; corporal, $7.33; drummer and fifer, $7.33; privates, $6.67.[20]

So not a little of the soldiers' money on pay days—when and if they come—finds its way into the pocketbooks of the prostitutes[21] who follow closely upon the heels of every army encampment. In New York's city what the prostitutes do not reap the callous and cheating Tory merchants will.

Following along with their army husbands, always in the wake of the marching men, are many loyal and devoted wives who set up their camps close by. They stoically take the bad with the good. Struggling as best they can, they accept fortune or mis-fortune as falls their lot.

So, in "Camptown," as it is called, the poorest dressed, it seems, are always the wives, striving hopefully to keep their children and their families together. The best dressed, and most prosperous looking, are the prostitutes, the residents of Camptown's so-called "Holy Ground."

It is in this setting that the Commander-in-Chief finds himself unknowingly in agreement with the ship-builder, sitting in his wagon seat under the Bluff Rock this morning. Howe's inactivity could mean many things but least of all a change in strategy. For right now Sir William holds almost all the cards.

Howe's Plan: Sever, Capture, Conquer

The American Commander knows that the Howe brothers see the Hudson as the dividing line between the "colonies," as General Howe still persists in calling them. By controlling Hudson's river, the British commander believes he can easily separate the northern American army from the southern forces and break the ties of communication between the two sections of the thirteen states.

Once he has done this, Sir William believes it will be easy for him with his superior forces to leisurely move on Philadelphia and take the rebels' capital itself.

That, however, is not the way the rebels' General sees it. He is committed to a slow and cautious withdrawal, though he recognizes, as does most everyone else, his vulnerability on the tip of Manhattan. And for five days now this has been everybody's concern.

For years to come The General's strategy in this campaign will be argued pro and con by historians and militarists. His decisions made in conjunction with his Council of War and the resulting difficulties to be encountered, will be loudly praised by some and as loudly ridiculed by others.

Writers, historians and strategists will label his conduct of this campaign with varying descriptive terms for centuries to come.[22] Some, in the Nineteenth Century era, preferring to avoid even the implication of American susceptibility to "retreat" or "defeat" will choose to gloss over the entire New York-New Jersey Campaign of 1776, jumping rapidly from the successful East River crossing to the surprising American victory at Trenton.

For the American General: Distrust, Disgrace and Doubt

For before this campaign of crises is brought fully to its closing, the most crucial low in morale of the war will have been reached. The American Commander himself will almost have been replaced by General Charles Lee. In this campaign the rebels' military Leader will come closest to a permanent return to the farms at Mount Vernon until at last his eventual arrival there in 1783.

Reflecting the attitude that is not now uncommon among the regimental officers, tomorrow, September 4, Colonel John Haslet of the Delaware Regiment, who wishes Lee were with the army, will send off a letter to his friend, Caesar Rodney, saying:

> "The Gen'l I revere, his Character for Disinterestedness, Patience and fortitude will be had in Everlasting Remembrance, but the Vast Burthen appears to be too much his own. Beardless youth and Inexperience Regimentated are too much about him . . ."[23]

Also quill pen in hand on this day is General Howe. Well satisfied with his victory and the certainty that the uprising will shortly be over, Sir William is drafting his report of the battle for Lord George Germaine and Parliament.

In his temporary headquarters at the Newtown encampment on Long Island, the British commander entitles his message, "A Detail of the Battle at Long Island." Included will be the list of casualties and captives. The list of prisoners taken alone will be enough to impress Parliament and the King:

> ". . . Three Generals . . . Three Colonels . . . Four Lieutenant Colonels

... Three Majors ... Eighteen Captains ... Forty-three Lieutenants ...
Eleven Ensigns ... (one) Adjutant ... (three) Surgeons ... (two) Volunteers ... (1,097) Privates ... Nine officers and fifty-eight privates, of the
above, wounded ..."[24]

The British general's report will estimate the American "killed,
wounded, prisoners and drowned" at 3,300. It will enumerate the
five field pieces and one howitzer taken, the brass and iron
ordnance, shot, shells, arms, pikes, ammunition carts and many
articles captured but not yet listed.

For General Howe: The Order Of the Bath

For his victory, the King will confer The Order of the Bath[25]
upon General Howe. And Britain's commander-in-chief will receive,
as well, the praises and admiration of his countrymen. For all of
England is now hoping for a prompt end to a disagreeable misun-
derstanding within the United Kingdom. Certainly General Howe
and Admiral Howe, with this outstanding success, should soon
bring that end about before many more days have passed.

And today, after a long inexplicable lull, Howe has, at last,
begun to move again. He and his brother have sent the 32-gun
frigate, *Rose*, up the East River, towing thirty flatboats.

When she pulled into Wallabout Bay, just north of New York
town and dropped her hooks, the American batteries on the East
River's west bank opened up. They inflicted so much damage that
the warship with its flatboats still in tow, pulled out and made for
the safety of Newtown Creek.[26]

This action and a few earlier hostile displays by the enemy's
navy are the only indications of coming events. Howe is set on
getting New York for his winter bivouac even if the war should
end earlier as is expected in some quarters.

In the event the uprising is not completely crushed by then,
New York will be the seat and springboard for further military or
political steps.

The American Commander-in-Chief's mind, contemplating the
varied steps of withdrawal, foresees Howe taking over Manhattan,
possibly with the exception of Fort Washington at the northern
tip.

He considers the possible funneling of his forces up Manhattan
and across King's Bridge into Westchester. Another outlet would be
through Fort Washington, possibly abandoning it under heavy
pressure, and then assembling his army in force on the high

mountainous precipices around Fort Constitution. This could be the ideal winter quarters since main enemy movements on Manhattan and in its surrounding waters could be observed from the Bluff Rock.

Looking still farther ahead, The General conjectures that if the enemy pursued him across the river, he would pull back his forces through the Jerseys for a defense of Philadelphia. He knows from the bitter lesson of experience learned in Brooklyn that Indian-type warfare, rather than regimented, open-field, strictly formal battling, will be his principal strategy. And he knows that the wilderness to the west would prove a difficult if not an impossible terrain for the British and Hessian troops, inexperienced as they are in tree-to-tree warfare.

So The General today writes General Hugh Mercer, his close confidant and commander of the Flying Camp at Perth Amboy, detailing his wish to expand the camp at Fort Constitution and develop a post, entrenchments and works west of, and in from, the Bluff Rock and its battery:

". . . a strong encampment on the Jersey side . . ."

"It appears to me of the utmost consequence that the most salutary consequence may result, from our having a strong encampment at the post on the Jersey side of the North River opposite to Mount Washington on this island."[27]

In this same communique, which his aides will send off in tomorrow's dispatch, the Commander will order Mercer to send a body of troops from Amboy with a skillful engineer to "lay out such additional works."

Mercer's prompt reply will assure The Chief that the engineers are ready for the assignment. It will move the appreciative Leader to respond courteously on Thursday, September 5, saying:

"When I wrote for troops to be sent to the post opposite Mount Washington, I did not imagine you would have so many to spare. About a thousand under General Ewing in addition to those already at the post, I think, will be fully competent to do its defenses and such works as may be necessary to erect and will also be sufficient to carry them on."[28]

On that same Thursday, when his Council of War is debating whether New York should be put to the torch when it is evacuated, The General visualizes the likely possibility that the army will winter over at Fort Constitution. And so he will write General Philip Schuyler at Albany, where Schuyler has succeeded

Horatio Gates as commander of the Northern Department, asking for "a quantity of boards for barracks."

All too soon the present beautiful fall weather will suddenly turn into winter snows. The men must have barracks. Such preparations clearly indicate that there is no thought in the American Leader's mind of the capitulation which Sir William believes is quite near.

So General Biddle replies, informing his Chief that the 300 wagons he requisitioned will soon be on their way to the new encampment site[29] at Fort Constitution.

Wagons are not yet scarce in the valleys west of The Mountain. In fact they are busier than ever carrying the farmers' abundant produce to the ferries. At the docks the larger pettiaugers, those flat-bottomed, two-masted, schooner-like vessels, are loaded with as much as ten or twelve tons of cargo.[30] They transport the produce and wares to the New York town merchants.

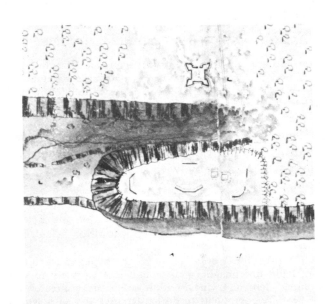

The above Library of Congress 1778 unfinished American Military Map delineates the exact positions of the batteries on the Bluff Rock and indicates with the standard military symbol the main field fort's location. The draft also shows the location of the water-front redoubts. The map is in the Library of Congress, Geography and Map Division.

The Dutch settlers have long preferred the sturdy little vessels, of which Baummeister's *Hope* is a small copy. They meet exactly the needs of the river-ferrying business just as do the Dutch settlers' well built, solidly constructed farm wagons and their similarly well built, comfortable sandstone block-constructed homes, meet exactly their safe, practical needs for work and pleasureful living.

It is some of those British-sympathizing Dutch farmers' wagons which Biddle is procuring. Few of the Tory-minded settlers are ever satisfied with the price the army offers, especially when it is only "promised" money.

It is in one of the first of these wagons to arrive from the Hackensack valley and come to a stop at Fort Constitution, that Tom Graves and his son are returned with others from the temporary field hospital in the Hackensack village. Big Tom's arm is still in a sling.

Much to Jocko's delight, his father will be temporarily assigned to Fort Constitution's quartermaster. Therefore the Graves will be in charge of the horses, the stables and sheds on the top of The Mountain.

Nothing could please Jocko more. A warm bed of straw at night, and horses, his greatest love, to brush down, groom, feed and ride. He thinks that he might again, as once before, hear The General himself ask him to take care of "Old Magnolia."

Best of all, by just going over to the gorge road, past the sentry and up the well-beaten trail to The Rock, he would in a jiffy be with his friends, the men of the Barbette Battery. Even though only a few now were of the old comapny, most of them know Jocko.

Someday his father will be reassigned there. He is sure of that, for Jocko lets everyone know that Pappy is among the best artillerymen anywhere. Who knows but what soon even The Lootenan' will be back.

Then too, Missy E lives only just down the clove road, and he can now keep an eye on her for The Lootenan's sake. It will be good to visit the Baummeister home, the barn and Dame Baummeister's flower and herb garden she tends so carefully—all snuggled there just in from the ferry landing, always warmly basking in the flickering light of the late afternoon's setting sun.

As he watches below, he sees Dame Baummeister slowly making her way down to the landing where her husband stands solemnly looking out over the river, puffing his pipe quietly and gently.

It is good, Jocko thinks to himself, to be home again.

A Quiet Hour In An Eaglet's Struggle To Be Born

It is the end of another long day, a day of fears mixed with hopes for Baummeister as he waits, leaning on the rail beside the dock for Marie Louise, to come up from behind to join him. The wisps of smoke from his pipe rise up over his head as he looks toward the east where the rising moon soon will peek over the horizon and cast a silvery reflection like a sparkling ribbon over the river's waters.

It is his customary contemplation time under the great Bluff Rock. Tonight he thinks how meaningless are man's wars, man's hates—his conquests, his toils—when measured alongside of the beauty to be found in just one couple's love for one another.

And now Marie Louise, his mate, companion and his beloved these many years, steals up beside him. She slips her hand in his as she so often does as they seek this quiet hour when the moonlight streams. This is the place the aging couple frequently end their day together, reflecting in the river's quietly moving tide upon their lives, past, present and future.

Seldom in the past has there been so little happiness and so much fear and tragedy seemingly riding on the moonlight's beams. It is hard to imagine that all around, a newly conceived nation's fetus struggles to be born out of a mountain of decisions into a trembling cradle of dreams.

9

Saturday, September 7. . .

Secret Weapon:
The Turtle Submarine

To Burn Or Leave Untorched

Whether to evacuate New York's city and to put it to the torch, or to attempt to hold it against the enemy's might, this morning becomes the principal debate at the American staff's Council of War.[1] Insisting that it is not only necessary to evacuate the city, General Greene argues that it must also be burned. Nothing should be left for the enemy Greene insists.

While it is generally believed that the field commander is echoing The General's sentiments, it is the American Commander himself who reminds the Council that he had informed the Congress on Tuesday last of the possibility of withdrawing from the city. He further tells his staff officers that he had also asked the Congress's position regarding setting the entire port city afire rather than leave it intact for Howe to comfortably set up his winter quarters.[2] However, the Congress promptly replied, New York was not to be burned.

That did not settle the matter for Greene who Thursday wrote his Chief a lengthy letter from his quarters at King's Bridge. In it he set forth numerous reasons why it was militarily sound for New York to be put to the torch.

Persuaded by the Congressional directive, the council majority opposes further discussion on torching the city. Green, neverthe-

141

less, argues that the Congress should be told more about the
military aspects and urged to retract its disapproval.

"Two-thirds of the property in the city of New York and the
suburbs belongs to the Tories,"[3] Greene argues. He can see no
reason why such Tory strongholds should be given any considerations.

Contending that a "general and speedy retreat is absolutely
necessary, and that honor and interest of America require it,"
Greene insists that it is unsound to hold New York's city.

"We have no object on this side of King's Bridge," he tells the
council. "The city and island of New York are no objects for us."[4]

Convinced he cannot get approval for the torching of New York,
the Rhode Islander decides to concentrate on getting the council
to agree on evacuating the city. And this, he is sure is The
General's wish, but, like all major decisions, it should have the war
council's approval.

The officers are divided on the question of evacuation. Some
construe Congress's disapproval of the burning of the city to mean
that the national body in Philadelphia want New York held despite
the enemy's overwhelming strength.

However, next week when The General informs the Congress of
this understanding by his staff officers, the legislators will hurry to
deny that implication, stating that holding, or withdrawing, is to
be the military judgment of the Commander-in-Chief.[5]

So on this Saturday morning the Council of War officers,
thirteen in all, find it difficult to arrive at a firm decision on
evacuating the city. They all agree that it is vulnerable to the
enemy's will. And they listen attentively to their Chief's argument
that the enemy might "enclose us . . . by taking post in our rear
. . . and oblige us to fight them on their own terms, or surrender at
discretion."[6]

They all hear him out on the inadvisability of a hasty retreat
from the city. He warns of the dangers of a "speedy" withdrawal.
He emphasizes the weakening effect it would have on the soldiers
and the country at large.

"It would dispirit the Troops and enfeeble our Cause,"[7] The
General tells his officers.

The divided thinking results in a council vote against withdrawal.
Instead they compromise and recommend that The General have
Putnam's 5,000-man division remain in defense of the island's
southern section, practically all of the city.

The council further suggests that Heath's 9,000-man division be assigned to hold the ground from Harlem to the northernmost point of Manhattan's island at King's Bridge. And they advise that Greene and his five brigades, mostly militia troops, should be posted along the East River, guarding Kip's and Turtle Bay.[8]

The vote is not unanimous. Those who are aligned with Greene declare the recommendations are unsound. The American forces, Greene states, will be in a dangerous position. Then with few words the Commander-in-Chief tells his council that the divided decision is not acceptable and not binding upon him. He asks that they further explore their recommendations.

The Persistent Quaker's Son

Nathanael Greene, who was born into a Quaker family the son of a prosperous iron foundryman, was a merchant until he entered the army as a musket-carrying private. He is not one who gives up easily. His earlier rheumatic illness left him with a slight limp and a stronger will to overcome adversities whether they be on the battlefield or at the conference table.

So Greene persists in his argument until after midnight. For at that hour the staff assembles at the Grand Battery to witness the operation of a secret weapon, a so-called under-water boat, or submarine.

The Whigs throughout Manhattan have heard about the "secret invention." No one knows what it is, but hearsay and gossip have stirred up speculation. So wild are the rumors that the Tory camps and Loyalist gatherings are not resting comfortably.

The encouraging idle chatter spreads optimism under the Palisadean cliffs, or "klips," as the Dutch settlers insist on calling them. And from under the "klips," rumors travel rapidly among the patriots. Each story-teller adds gross exaggerations, always building on ignorance.

So 34-year-old Inventor David Bushnell of Connecticut, a graduate of Yale College, has started rumors and caused hopes to rise with his secret device, the underwater craft called *The Turtle*.

Under the cover of secrecy, Bushnell this morning explained the privy workings of his contraption to another member of the Yale alumni, Colonel Ben Tallmadge. Tallmadge included his newly acquired friend, Lieutenant John Gray, in the private explanation, introducing Gray as "a fellow scholar from that New Jersey college at Prince Town."

Bushnell's biggest problem has been in getting an engineer to operate the underwater vessel. His brother, who is skilled in the manipulation of the machinery, became ill several days ago.

In his place, Bushnell has secured Sergeant Ezra Lee of Lynne, Connecticut. Lee has not had much time to become acquainted with its intricate functions. He maneuvered it successfully on the one and only trial run he attempted. That was a secret trip up the East River out of sight from the curious.

The peculiar looking rig actually does resemble a giant turtle. It is constructed of huge oak timbers, scooped out and fitted together in the shape of a clam. The timbers are bound together by iron strips. All seams have been caulked and then tarred to make the vessel watertight.

Seven hundred pounds of lead are stored in its bottom, keeping it from turning over on its beam. Two foot-operated pumps enable the one-man pilot, who can stand up inside if he so desires, to dive and ascend. In order to move forward or backward there is a hand crank which turns a two-bladed, wooden screw-propellor.

At the back of the submarine, attached by a screw, is an egg-shaped magazine containing 130 pounds of gunpowder. The object is to dive the ship under an enemy vessel's keel. A drill, protruding from the top of the vessel and operated by hand from inside, is then used to make a hole in the unfortunate ship's hull near the keel. A fitting is attached and the egg-shaped, powder-loaded magazine is affixed and set for ignition by a one-hour time fuse.[9]

The ingeniously designed vessel holds enough air for the operator for a period of 30 minutes. An aperture at the bottom admits water into the craft so that by its added weight the vessel submerges to the depth desired. Contrariwise, pumping out this water enables the ship to ascend.

Glass windows admit light. At night the craft can be steered by a compass which is placed near some decayed, phosphorescent fibers called foxwood. This decaying matter emits an awesome eerie light, especially in darkness under water which, nevertheless, permits fair vision.

After midnight this will be Sergeant Ezra Lee's guiding light to the underwater planks of the hull of the British fleet's flagship.

The Turtle Makes For Its Victim

Shortly after sunset, a whaleboat towed the submarine to the foot of Whitehall Street at the Grand Battery where the General and his staff assembled a little later.

General Putnam, who is largely responsible for promoting this first test of American ingenuity, is the one who convinced the American Commander-in-Chief and the Congress to financially support Bushnell's invention. He stands next to the Commander.

Greene, who was reared breathing in the heat of iron forges and molten metal, has seen many ingenious devices turned out in his father's foundry. He is familiar with the hopes of the inventors and creators of iron, wrought into a multitude of shapes on the anvil. Being a practical man, he has little hope for the success of a virtually untested, untried "secret weapon."

Greene's interest in the submarine experiment is, therefore, secondary. His primary concern is winning over the staff officers who have opposed the withdrawal of the army from New York. He is undismayed by the vote taken at the council session this morning. Another session can always be called.

Greene corners one officer after the other as he almost totally ignores the shadowy underwater craft, making its lonesome way boldly toward the mighty British naval vessels, drifting at anchor in the dark distant waters of upper New York Bay.

Listening to Greene with one ear and watching *The Turtle* with both eyes pressed into their field glasses, the officers are generally of the opinion Bushnell's experiment will work. If it does, certainly it will create havoc among Admiral Howe's seamen as well as General Howe's overconfident soldiery. Evacuation of New York might be unnecessary.

If successful it would put a different perspective on the status of things. A surprising bold strike frequently helps in throwing the enemy off balance. And this is what is needed.

The General is certain, regardless of the outcome of the submarine experiment, that New York must be abandoned. As he looks through the night's darkness at the many silhouetted, towering masts of enemy ships and realizes the tremendous power they can hurl against him, he knows that he must inform the Congress that New York will be evacuated. For he holds little hope that some miraculous "secret weapon" will be at his command.

So tomorrow the American Leader will write the law-makers explaining the wisdom of abandoning New York, saying, in reference to his decision:

> ". . . nor am I insensible of the contrary effects, if a brilliant stroke could be made with any Probability of success, especially after our loss upon Long Island."[10]

In *The Turtle*, Sergeant Lee goes over in his mind the instructions Bushnell has given, and the little undersea vessel paddles away on the surface of the tide, a seemingly harmless speck on the dark waters of the bay. Its important mission is to destroy Admiral Howe's flagship, *Eagle*, and return safely to the Grand Battery.

It is a perfect moonless night for the operation. *The Turtle's* path is obscured from the enemy battery on Governor's island which lies just south of the New York's Grand Battery. Sergeant Lee's target lies to the west since the *Eagle* lies moored off Staten Island.

On board the flagship Captain Reeve is in command. And Commodore Hotham is asleep in his quarters on the British navy's proud man-of-war.

When Lee feels he is close enough to escape detection by the warship's watch and is within proper distance for submerging, he puts the craft into its dive sinking beneath the dark choppy bay waters.

Finally submerged under the enemy vessel, Lee begins drilling. But the British flagship is a sturdily constructed, well re-enforced battleship with iron under-plates near the rudder where the sergeant unfortunately has chosen to drill. The heavy plates were something Bushnell had not counted upon. Lee's drill buckles and fails to make a penetration.

Again and again he tries, rising under the cover of the warship's stern end occasionally to replenish his air supply.

Inexperienced in the over-all operation, the sergeant fails to bore a hole for the attachment of the magazine and, in addition, now faces an increasingly stronger tidal current which brings more difficulty in replenishing his air supply. Time is rapidly running out. Dawn could break over the horizon at any moment.

Reluctantly, Sergeant Lee gives up the attempt and begins propelling his craft back across the bay toward the Grand Battery, making his way slowly on the crest of the choppy waters.

Before long dawn outlines him clearly in view of the sentries on Governor's Island. There the British pickets are uncertain of what they see. They order a patrol boat launched to investigate the strange looking craft, but the boatsmen, fearing it might be "a Yankee trick," go out only a short way, then turn about and head for shore.

Meanwhile, Lee, who has observed the British patrol through his window, expects at any moment to be apprehended. And since the towing of the powder-filled magazine impedes his progress, he sets its timer and disengages it from *The Turtle*, hoping it will drift into the path of the approaching British barge.

The Underwater Weapon Leaves An Explosive Impression

The powder-keg, pre-set for an explosion, is carried in the opposite direction by the tide, swirling up the East River. Then, in view of all the British sentries on Governor's Island and on Brooklyn's Woody Heights, the magazine explodes with a thunderous crack. Its wooden pieces are hurled high in the air, splintering the early morning's calm with its roaring blast.

The explosion brings hundreds of people to their windows, some out upon the streets and some rushing to the embankments on both sides of the waterway. It throws the King's men on Governor's Island, as well as the other British posts on Long Island's shore and at Brooklyn Heights, into confusion. The curious vainly seek an explanation.

Other than that, *The Turtle* makes no great dent on the British fleet and the redcoats and does not visibly raise any of the Howe Brothers' eyebrows. Yet at the Grand Battery, as Sergeant Lee climbs out of his safely landed craft, shouts of cheering hurrahs go up from the onlooking soldiers in recognition of the non-commissioned officer's daring deed.

Though the mission was not accomplished as planned, congratulations are freely passed around and Bushnell, among others, is convinced that the undersea ship has proven itself and its possibilities. The confident inventor, certain of its future, is determined to continue working on its perfection.

To most of the onlookers, impressed by the thunderous explosion under the nose of the British garrison occupying Brooklyn Heights, there is no doubt that Bushnell's submarine has succeeded in throwing a scare into the enemy.

One British officer's letter will tend to bear that out, for in referring to the explosion, he will write that "the ingenuity of these people is singular in their secret modes of mischief."[11]

When it is evident that *The Turtle* is returning without having accomplished its objective, the staff officers disband. Greene, however, still persists in arguing with one colleague after the other over the necessity of abandoning New York.

All members of the council, including the Commander-in-Chief himself, are disappointed in Bushnell's experiment and, temporarily at least, are resigned to turn their minds away from possible secret weapons as the means for overcoming their dilemma. And so now they listen to Greene.

With his head bowed in contemplation, The General makes his way over to Old Magnolia and Black Billy who rides beside him. Followed by his aides and guards, he and his party make their way back up Manhattan Island to the Commander's new headquarters. It is the vacated home of the Tory English refugee, Colonel Roger Morris.

Most of his aides are aware that Roger Morris has married Mary Phillipse. And almost everyone knows that Mary Phillipse was once very much admired by the American Commander-in-Chief in his younger days.[12]

The men speculate that the "Grand Old Man" still nurses a spark for the former Mary Phillipse. But Colonel Morris and his household have long since left Manhattan Island, planning to return when the British take New York away from its rebel occupants.

Some of his aides wonder what their Leader's thoughts are as he climbs the stairs to his room in the Roger Morris house long after midnight at the end of this long day.

With The General's party, riding off from the Grand Battery earlier tonight, were Greene and Adjutant General Joseph Reed. Only for Nathanael Greene has the night been a complete success. He and his persistence have succeeded in winning over five other officers to his side.

Reed, who thinks as Greene on the matter of abandoning the city, is not, unfortunately, a member of the Council. However, Greene now has a block of six votes for withdrawal to countermand the Council of War's decision of this morning. Now the problem is to reconvene the Council.

"Between Hawk and Buzzard"

Greene and Reed are comforted in their assurance that the Chief agrees with them about holding New York. Both men know that The General is convinced that withdrawal is the American army's only recourse. This was made clear at the conference table this morning when The General politely rejected the council's compromise recommendations. With or without the council's approval The General will evacuate the city. That is assured.

Reed, reiterating the thoughts he expressed in a letter to his wife yesterday, describing the American position, tells Greene, "We cannot stay and yet we do not know how to go, so that we may properly [be] said to be between hawk and buzzard."[13]

After leaving the officers who had gathered at the Grand Battery to watch Bushnell's contraption, Lieutenant John Gray made his way past the sentries to his hut adjoining his post and battery on Hudson's bank. Gray had declined an invitation much earlier to join some of the young subaltern officers when it was evident *The Turtle's* mission had failed. Most of them headed for the Dutch Tippling House. He, with his thoughts on Elaine, headed for his barracks.

As on any, and especially this Saturday night, the young officers will begin at the Tippling House and eventually end up north of the city. There in Camptown are the squatters' huts, tent houses and the town's loosest women and lustiest men. On a Saturday night the place, like a magnet, attracts the soldiery, particularly after pay days.

Gray made for his own hut and cot. But he did not fall asleep until he had read and reread under his flickering candlelight, the five-page letter brought from Bourdette's Ferry by yesterday's post.

Sunday morning's early light poured through the roughly fashioned glass window of the hut and spread itself upon the youth's gaunt, tired face. The five pages of Elaine's letter had slipped to the sand floor when his weary eyes finally closed, leaving his hand dangling the last page that would not leave his clenched fingers.

The tell-tale, worn, dirty blue petticoat scarf is around his neck. Some say he never takes it off. And a few of his fellow-officers declare, "It looks it!" The candle is burned out.

For 17 days Gray has counted each sunset. For 17 days he has spent countless moments wondering what Elaine "is doing now." And for 17 nights he has dreamed of her touch and looked into her wide trusting blue eyes—eyes that melted into the smoke of battle, the stench of gunpowder, blood and death.

He has devoured every word in the girl's long letter as a starving man would hungrily devour each morsel within his grasp. And now he smiles in sleep as do restless souls who find their peace in blessed slumber.

Letters, with their messages, gossip and rumors are—except for their assurances of devotion, outspoken or implied—of little consequence to lovers. One sheet of the letter, facing upward in the early morning's light, reads in part:

"Papa says there is much going on over the top of the gorge road and that this soon will become a big, big place. There is some talk of an armistice that may bring an end of the war and peace at last. I hope so for us and for you, my Beloved John. But me, all I do, it seems, is worry, worry, worry and hope, hope, hope.

"Did you know that many in the valley are afraid New York will be put to the torch? Some say it is so. They would then have no place to sell their produce. Do you believe it could be so?

"Mama talks to herself, her flowers in the garden and the dog and cat who never leave her side. The other day I heard her say, 'I think, Dear God, that you made a big mistake. After you made flowers and animals, you should have stopped and never made man because he hates for the sake of vengeance and he kills for the sake of killing.'

"You must be careful. You must for me, and for Jocko, who is here with the army helping Big Tom get well. I think you know how much he thinks of you. He thinks you are much greater than The General. With him, My Love, I do agree. . . ."

And so to the timeless Bluff Rock which has heard the love call of the prehistoric wild beasts, of the gray wolf, of the eagle, of the earliest man and of the Lenni Lenape Indian, the love call of a lonely soldier and his betrothed is nothing new. To the Bluff Rock, this is a perpetual thing, unmoving, unexciting but changing, ever changing.

To both Elaine and John The Rock has become their own symbol of enduring strength. There they courted and melded their lives. There they vowed to hold their loves until death, making the great Bluff Rock an infinitesimal part of their devotion. Their own high secluded ledge is a flat, protruding piece of the precipice stone. It extends out from the climbing path to the face of the summit. And it commands a breath-taking view of a part of the world from which they hope to mold their lives.

". . . Justa wondren."

It is there that Elaine and John have sat so often. It is there that he has read to her of "human understanding."

Now, as the Sunday morning sun floods the face of the great rock precipice, only a lonesome sea gull rests momentarily on the lovers' ledge, undecided, it seems, where to spread its wings and fish this day. The hungry, graceful bird knows that if he waits long enough the girl will bring and toss him some bread as she and her young brother frequently do.

Instead the gull detects other footsteps along the ascending path.

Frightened, the beautiful, sharp-eared creature rises quickly and is off. He relinquishes the spot to another lonely little figure, the boy, Jocko Graves. Often now he also comes as though to guard the spot and send his searching, bright brown eyes to the distant southeast.

It is down there somewhere that his friend, The Lootenan', must be. But where? And what big cannon is he bossing?

It is there, way down there on that distant island's shore where only a fortnight ago his young eyes saw, for the first time, the horrifying specter of man in hate, of man at war, of man at kill, of man at his violent worst.

As the white bird hovers high, looking almost as blue as the clouds behind him, and rises far above the river's waters, Jocko wonders with his ever questioning mind. He looks up at the heavens, asking aloud:

"Ise jus't wond'ren, Massa Gen'l Lawd God, a'ways ub dare. Whad makes dis peoples ob yors so a'fillin' full ob hates? Ise doan blame yo, Massah Gen'l Lawd, 'ceptin fer som ob da tings yo's shor messed ub on in pourin' in da fillins. Yose jus wuz a'gettin' tie'ed, 'n wuz'in lookin', lak Ise do fer a spell som'times. Bud how's dat yo made so many ob dem so spy'tin mean 'n cruels? Eben ta demselbs dey is! Why's dat, Lawd? Wuz ya jus not a'lookin'?

"Why's dey ain't ahll good lak a horse's good? Why's dey ain't good lak yo tells 'em in yor book? . . . Why's dey ain't lak dat dare burd a'flyin' and a'peekin' down at me? Dare ain't no hatin' in enny ob dem. Why's dey ain't ahll lak mah pappy? Or lak mah Mammy ub dare wid yo? Or lak Missy E 'n Da Lootenan? Why's dat, Massah Gen'l Lawd God? . . . Ise ain't in no hurryin' fer yor xspenashun, Lawd. Ise know how busy yo'all is ub dare wid som ob dese critters yo makdt. So Lawd Bossman, taks yer time, cauzin' Ise wuz jus wond'ren."

10

Wednesday, September 11. . .

Down Goes the Olive Branch

A Rising Son

If the letter that arrived with the post on the ferry this morning for Ma Kearney were from the Commander-in-Chief himself, the fisherwoman could not have been any happier. Jubilantly she abandons her horse and wagon in the middle of the roadway. The smelly, rickety, old cart is filled with fish nets to be repaired and stored for next spring's shad runs . . . when she "gits 'round ta' it."

The untethered horse, dragging his cart behind him, finds delightful grazing beside the Baummeister house. There the Hudson's only woman fisherman has hurriedly entered to get that "smart one," Marie Louise or her daughter to read the letter from her soldier son.

The deep rough voice of the rugged, rapidly aging 45-year-old woman has brought Elaine running down from her upstairs room. For the girl is eager to tell Ma about the letter she has received from John.

But the illiterate Ma Kearney clutches the paper from Edmund. And nothing else matters.

As Marie Louise reads, the fisherwoman's kindly, weather-beaten face lights up with every sentence, each word of which she wants repeated over and over again. Her son, almost illegibly, writes that Captain Board has made him a "sargin" in the militia company.

"Just think!" she says, interrupting Marie Louise's reading, "A reg'a'la surg'ent! My Eddie!"

Under the circumstances, Elaine realizes she has no hope of getting Ma to listen to her letter from John. She stuffs it quietly into her bosom and concentrates on her mother's reading of Edmund's new experience in the militia.

Elaine, who has grown up with Edmund, knows him probably better than his mother. Being over a month and a half older, she had—as is the custom of juveniles—adopted the "older sister" attitude toward young Kearney.

It is an attitude he had accepted in early youth but which he now resents. For in their childhood, Edmund had been treated as the younger child, the one most in need of protection and direction.

Not only did it naturally fall into Elaine's province to take on this responsibility, but others similarly adopted a patronal attitude toward the fatherless boy which, in his approach to manhood, he not only came to dislike but has come to resent bitterly.

Knowing Edmund's strengths and weaknesses, particularly his deceptive tendencies and his increasingly braggadocio mannerisms which hide his frailties, Elaine is sure that he is not a sergeant. Corporal perhaps. But not sergeant. She is sure of it, but says nothing.

Elaine does not wish to make Ma Kearney's rough life any more unhappy than it is. In the opinion of all the Baummeisters, Ma, who is constantly considering others with little regard for herself, is entitled to every possible ray of sunshine that can enter her life.

Elated by the happy news, the fisherwoman is bubbling with joy. She cannot wait to tell "my boys," as she calls the young soldiers up at the Barbette Battery on The Rock, "this news 'bout my Eddie!"

Then, holding the letter tightly in one hand and taking the reins of her old nag, Gen'l Sweeney, in the other, she stands up in the cart, blissfully driving up the gorge road to the battery, singing "Yankee Doodle" in her usually loud, fish-vending voice.

Once a week she makes a donation of fish and biscuits to her favorites in the encampment, the men in charge of the park of artillery on the Bluff Rock.

No question about it! She has big news for them today, especially some of the new ones who might have doubted all the big things she has told them about her Edmund.

So engrossed is her mind on Eddie's promotion, Ma Kearney

entirely obliterates one interesting thing in his letter which both Marie Louise and Elaine immediately grasp.

As they recall it, the youth had written that he will be in a picket guard to be sent to Perth Amboy on the eleventh—this very day!—for a special assignment that is supposed to be all hush, hush. Edmund heard that the pickets were part of a company assigned to guard three members of Congress on their way from Philadelphia to Staten Island, the enemy's stronghold.

"We is bout to gard 3 mans frum Kongrass," Kearney writes. "Them are frum Fildelfia an is bout to vizit the enimy Admul lord How at hiz qauartrs in Billeps big manson hous as 1 of them is ole Ben Franklan who we is to gard."

All that means nothing to Ma. The big news is that Eddie is a sergeant. To the choice morsel, the big tidbit of news, Ma pays no mind. It has electrified both Elaine and her mother. It will do the same for others, giving rise to false hopes for peace.

Both mother and daughter ask each other: What are Benjamin Franklin and other members of the Congress doing at Howe's headquarters in Staten Island? Is the Congress suing for peace? Does the failure of the American "secret weapon" on Saturday night mean there is no hope for American independence?

Before long the rumor will spread from Moor's Landing to Bull's Ferry[1] and across The Mountain and into the Valley. It will be embellished a hundredfold by ears and tongues from Perth Amboy to Philadelphia, through the highway of grapevines out of Hackensack, Elizabeth Town, Newark, Bergen and up the King's highway to Tappan Town and the Hudson Valley.

It evokes in Elaine a rushing surge of joy. For a few brief moments she is carried away, buoyantly, gloriously happy. Then suddenly she feels overwhelmed with a sense of shame. For, if true, then all the dreams so many have so long talked about would be forever lost. Were they to be exchanged for that happiness she seeks for John and herself?

Questioning the realizations that taunt her mind, she asks herself: Are not John's hopes, yea, even his dreams, far too wrapped up in the great cause? Is he not too much the patriot, the idealist—as are so many others—to surrender the cause? Would he, or any of them, ever really entirely succumb? Impractical people don't, she tells herself. And John is impractical, not like her.

Perhaps, she reflects thoughtfully, there are too many of them like that.

"I cannot," she says, tossing it all around in her mind, "I cannot be that way. Perhaps I should. But, oh, dear God, I cannot. I know I am not, though I should be for his sake. Yet for his sake I cannot be, as long as I think of him behind those cannons."

As she looks out of the upper half of the open door, overlooking the river and the Fort Washington fortifications along the river's opposite shore and on the mount, she weakens at the thought and sights of war. Her eyes drift back again to the ferry landing and the adjoining military wharf. There she sees her father at the landing, helping another barge load of soldiers disembark.

Behind Edmund's report and the wildfire rumor of a possible peace, are the Howe Brothers, resting for two weeks now on virtually complete inactivity after their success on Long Island. General Howe believes he has his own so-called "secret weapon" in General Sullivan.

Both Major General Sullivan and Major General Stirling have been Howe's prisoners for the past fifteen days. Last week Sir William, after having been unable to get anywhere with Lord Stirling, convinced Sullivan, who is an attorney in civilian life, to accept the role of a flag-bearer in exchange for part of his parole. Sullivan, much to Stirling's dismay, agreed to take Howe's message and his suggestion for a peace conference direct to the Congress in Philadelphia.[2]

Stirling, branding the action a breach of military protocol, would have no part in it and remained imprisoned, choosing to wait out his release, pending a proper prisoner exchange. However, Sullivan accepted the proposal after both Sir William and Admiral Howe convinced Sullivan that the Howes were primarily interested in achieving an end to the uprising.

Accordingly, Sullivan was released and, keeping his word, went before the Congress, explaining to the representatives the extensive peace-seeking powers which the Crown has extended to the British commander. Sullivan, as directed, emphasized that the Howes could not treat directly with Congress in arriving at terms, but that Admiral Howe would like to meet with some of the "members as private gentlemen."[3]

In Carpenter's Hall, Sullivan's presentation was met with a few snorts and much sniffing of the snuffboxes. The members agreed that it must never be said that they were not "ever desirous of establishing peace on reasonable terms."[4]

Condescending to send a committee, the Congress carefully decided exactly what such a committee's mission shall be, directing that it determine "whether his lordship had any authority to treat with persons authorized by Congress for this purpose, and what that authority was, and to hear such propositions as he should think proper to make respecting the same."[5]

Dr. Benjamin Franklin, John Adams, Esq., and Edward Rutledge, Esq. were appointed as a committee of three.[6] They left Philadelphia Monday, arriving at Perth Amboy yesterday. Adams rode on horseback. Franklin and Rutledge in chairs.[7]

All three Congressmen had heard of the despairing rate of desertions from the army, of the expiring enlistments, and of the present apathy and disinterest in re-enlisting. It has been said that companies, and even regiments were walking home when their service-time expired.

Along their route from Philadelphia the three Congressmen were heartened by what they saw. Instead of soldiers walking away from New York and the battleground, they find troops by the hundreds marching east. Pleased and encouraged at discovering the roads jammed with new recruits, the representatives from Congress were informed that they were mostly militia on their way to take part in the New York Campaign.

On the Raritan River landing, the emissaries this morning were met by a British barge under a white flag. Its sole passenger was a redcoat officer who left his oarsmen, came ashore, greeted the three Congressman and offered himself as a hostage, insuring the safe return of the representatives.

All three members of the committee laugh at the thought and unanimously refuse. In fact, Franklin insists he accompany them across to Staten Island.

Three Trusting Gentlemen From The Continental Congress

Holding its distance, the American picket guard stands at attention as the British officer makes his overtures. The Continental officer is visibly annoyed at Franklin for his display of trust of the enemy. Besides, he and his militiamen had looked forward to entertaining an officer of the King's army as their hostage.

The British captain, meanwhile, is nonplused by the committee's demonstration of politeness on the part of "rebels." Their consideration and action were as unexpected as it was for him to find American soldiers with a military manner and to come upon gentlemen, well-dressed, courtly and intelligent. He had expected to see crude, buckskin backwoodsmen for he had heard horrible stories of the ragged ruffians who man the post north at Paulus Hook.

So, since the Congressmen insist, and there is no effort or desire to retain him on shore as hostage, he gladly joins them in his own barge as they direct.

On the beach at Staten Island the party is met by Admiral Howe. This is an unexpected surprise—an almost unbelievable one—for the Congressmen. Of the three emissaries only Franklin had met either one of the Howe Brothers. In London a year ago the Doctor had been introduced to Sir William, but not even Franklin had imagined the Lord Admiral would be on the beach, waiting to greet them.

After exchanging courtesies, the party makes its way up through the two columns of military guards toward the stately Billop house mansion. The palacial home has been turned over to the naval commander for his headquarters during the campaign. The impressive stone residence overlooks the beautiful bay south and gazes out upon the distant ocean.

On both sides of their ascent to the conference house, Hessian Grenadiers line the way at arms rest. Their brightly polished brass buckles and steel swords shine brilliantly in the late morning sun. They look like stone statues until they come to attention in paying respect to the visiting dignitaries. Every move, every order is performed rigidly in strict conformance with the proper military etiquette reserved for such occasions.

To the Congressional representatives, who are accustomed to the sight—more often than not—of half-starved, dirty, smelling, poorly garbed buckskin and Yankee Continentals, the appearance, in contrast, provides an almost welcome, if not comic, atmospheric relief.

Apologizing for his brother's inability to be present, the Admiral explains to his guests how difficult are the pressures and duties which keep Sir William rather confined and tied down on Long Island.

"That," says Franklin, "is indeed understandable."

The Admiral refrains from discussing any business relative to the principal purpose of the conference until after lunch. The dining room conversation, though sparked by courteous, bright but guarded exchanges of repartee, is almost typical of one that might be overheard in a manor house outside of London.

Over American mutton, tongue, cold ham, bread—all touched off by a fine vintage of claret—Howe and his very observant, and somewhat baffled guests, talk mainly about American and British foods. The Admiral explains the sharp difference that characterizes the American foodstuffs which, he says, do not possess the fine variety of delicacies afford the people of England.

Though Lord Howe appears to be indicating his homesickness for Mother England's produce, the Congressmen believe they are reading into his thoughts the losses which war and separation will bring to America if it does not behave.

Offered tea by their host, all three visitors courteously and tactfully decline. Only the colonel of the regiment, assigned to the Billop house naval headquarters by the military command, and Lord Howe's personal secretary, who make up the luncheon party of six, join the Admiral in his beverage.

The Case For The Crown

The offer of tea—the Congress's most highly boycotted import—is the lord's most pointed, intentional, etiquette faux pas. The three Philadelphia delegates stay with the claret.

After the colonel properly excuses himself as planned, leaving the Admiral, his secretary and the Congressional representatives alone, Howe opens and monopolizes the conversation.

Every sentence is molded, almost memorized as though pre-designed in accordance with the London orders his lordship and his brother have been given. Howe's cousin, King George III, and the Crown's advisors, have all tied the hands of both the British Admiral and Britain's military commander-in-chief with restrictions.

Polite and appreciative of the fine things the colonists have heretofore done, Black Dick makes it clear how deeply grieved he is over the rebellion. He tells the emissaries how tragic it will be for America and its people if the colonial empire were to fall apart.

To this, Franklin, avoiding the word "colonies," responds that the *Americans* will exert their utmost endeavors to "save your lordship that mortification."[8]

Limited by the curtailments that have been placed upon him by London, unable to make any commitments on his own, and forced to hide the unrealistic demands which Lord North and the British Crown would impose upon the rebels in exchange for peace, Richard Howe, basically an honest and forthright man becomes vague and ambiguous. He has said all he is permitted to say.

The realization that he must make no mention of those distasteful impositions preys upon his mind. His restricted thoughts, forced into concealment, now conflict with those high principles upon which his code of ethics is based. His own rules of conduct run head on into those surreptitious requirements so mandatory in deceptive diplomacy—a role he was not made to play.

Richard Howe looks across the table at John Adams. Adams returns the look. The two men hold each other's gaze intensely. Adams' irises are unflinching, sharp and piercing.

Unconsciously the admiral estimates the measurement of Adams' collar width. For in those secret orders, he knows that there are certain exceptions for the granting of amnesty. One of those exceptions is John Adams.

So the somewhat disturbed naval commander finds that he cannot erase the thought that comes to mind, for Adams, by order of the Crown, is to be one of those destined to hang. His gibbet, Howe tells himself, may possibly be the yardarm of the admiral's own flagship, *The Eagle*.

More and more garbled, it seems to the guests, becomes the lord's monologue. Under questioning, it is difficult for him to answer any inquiries. He can make no promises. No guarantees. He cannot mention that those secret orders demand that the "Colonies" give guarantees of their future good behavior; that they must guarantee this sort of thing must never happen again, et cetera.

And, furthermore, he cannot tell them that the orders demand that, before reconciliation, both the colonies of Rhode Island and Connecticut must give up their charters. These are liberal charters in operation for almost two hundred years. To Rhode Island and Connecticut it would be like asking the people of England to renounce their own Magna Charta.

Black Dick is fearful that his own wandering tongue will be trapped by the quietly bubbling, twinkling, penetrating eyes sitting in front of the mind of Dr. Franklin. He is sure that Franklin, if not Rutledge and Adams as well, are aware of his unskillful efforts to play the game of deception in the courtyard of diplomacy.

When he sounds conciliatory and yet can make no offer, no promise, his lordship fumbles for words.

The representatives of the newly united colonial states then assure him that Great Britain has everything to gain from good, profitable relations with its now independent, thirteen provinces. But that it has everything to lose by attempting to keep those states dependent and crushed under the heel of supreme domination.

They assure him that never again can the old matriarchal relationship exist. They impress upon him that independence is now in America and in America it is destined to stay, and that America is now in thirteen united "states," no longer "colonies."

At the very word "independence," the admiral seems to flinch. He shakes his head as though he were about to scold officers under his command. He strives at every opportunity to get his visitors to ask for, or inquire into, the granting of "pardon." Always around that word he attempts to incite interest. Always around that word there is none.

Franklin, Adams, then Rutledge, each in turn, indicate the unanimity of the committee in their thinking. Courteously each assures the Lord Admiral that there is no possibility of discussing details until the "independence" of the former colonies is fully recognized and conceded by the Crown. And therein lies the stalemate.

Sassafras For An Olive Branch

Again Howe winces at the word "independence." He sadly shakes his head and then politely agrees that there is no point in continuing the conference.

All rise. All bow respectfully in taking leave. And all bring to a close the fruitless three-hour attempt to avoid five more costly and useless years of war. Only the colonel accompanies them to the dock.

On his way to the launch, Franklin stops and picks a large sprig from a sassafras tree. He gives a piece of the branch to each of his colleagues.

"Chew on it," he tells Adams and Rutledge. "It will settle your stomachs on the ride across. It is the closest, Gentlemen, we will ever get to tasting an olive branch. Man, as you must know, is not as yet an animal communicably well enough endowed to save itself from extinction."

In a few minutes the oarsmen and the captain who accompanied them over, carefully assist the three Congressmen into the admiral's barge. They all turn and look backward at the rapidly disappearing conference house behind them as the oarsmen pick up speed.

The house, Franklin tells Adams and Rutledge, is the home of the devout Loyalist, British Colonel Christopher Billop, who was instrumental in paving the way for the British fleet and its safe anchorage off Staten Island last June.

Far off to the east they are able to see momentarily only a small tip of Long Island's southernmost beaches at the inlet to Jamaica Bay. Failing to see Manhattan Island, the wise old doctor explains to Rutledge and Adams the reason with a brief lesson in the area's geography.

Regardless, Adams and Rutledge look to the northeast hoping to get a glimpse of New York. They strain Franklin's geography lesson and their eyes in vain. For in all of their minds there is the haunting question now of whether the Congress did the right thing last week when they ordered that the Commander-in-Chief was not to burn New York town were it evacuated. All three had voted with the majority.

Now, as they see the massive armada which the King's men have brought against the city and the American defenders, as they see men-of-war, transports, flatboats, tenders, schooners and sloops— the "sea of masts" they have heard so much about—they wonder, each to himself, if their 'yea' vote strengthened the Tories' hand and weakened the Commander's.

A Frightening Rumor Runs Wild

Far to the Congressmen's north—about 31 miles as the crow flies—a big encampment is springing up just behind the big, guardian Bluff Rock and its batteries. And, up from the valley west of The Mountain's top, and up from the gorge road from the ferry to The Rock and on to The Mountain's summit, men and supplies are rapidly moving in.

While one rumor persists that something is taking place far down below at Staten Island, another spreads, frightening and angering the valley people. It is the hearsay that New York is to be put to the torch. The gossip has two versions, Whig and Tory.

The Whigs say that the British are planning to burn New York to force the Americans out. The Tories contend that the rebels plan to burn it so that Howe will find it unlivable should he attempt to make it his winter quarters.

The rumors have spread into the headquarters of the British command on Long Island and have worried General Howe and his staff.

One British officer, Captain Frederick Mackenzie of the Royal Welsh Fusilliers, in writing home the day before yesterday, expressed the fears of the Crown's military, declaring:

"... It is in our power at any time to drive them from New York and take possession of it, but if we attacked them there, they might set fire to it and once more slip out of our hands. It is of very material consequence to prevent them from burning the town, which will no doubt afford quarters to a considerable part of our army during the ensuing winter, and be made the principal depot of stores, and harbour for our shipping."[9]

In New York, long dissatisfied with the Council of War's September 7 decision "to defend and not to destroy and evacuate the city," General Greene, with the American Commander-in-Chief in full agreement, today petitioned for "another council of war to re-consider the question."[10]

Part II

Defiance

11

Sunday, September 15. . .

Kip's Bay: Flight from the City

Under Fire the Men-of-War Ascend the River

Louder and heavier the dueling cannons roar against each other eleven miles downriver at Paulus Hook. On the observation heights, sentries at the Bluff's Barbette train their field glasses upon the British men-of-war forcing their way past the Paulus Hook works.[1] The early Sunday morning cannonading drowns out the church bells for miles around.

When the three enemy frigates—bent on running through the cross fire from Colonel John Durkee's breastwork guns at the Hook and Colonel Knox's batteries on Manhattan's tip—came out of the bay and began ascending Hudson's river, the Hook's Captain Dana ordered the barrage to open. At the same time, Knox began firing from the New York side. Then suddenly and violently, all three of the battleships returned fire in a hot exchange. Despite the American guns the vessels broke through and anchored upriver out of the shore batteries' range.

It was brief and thunderous, causing damages on both sides. The short raging contest of the broadsides against the American artillery's heaviest pounders brought most of the inhabitants along the river out to the water's edge or scrambling up the precipices of the Palisades to see what was going on.

It was not until much later in the day that river travelers

**Admiral Howe's Fleet prepares for the Invasion of Manhattan—From Charles C.
Coffin's** *A History of the Battles of the Revolution, 1876.*

informed the Bourdettes and the Baummeisters that the Paulus
Hook fort had been raked and the American artillerymen had, in
turn, scored some damaging hits on the enemy ships. The three
frigates and the schooner they were escorting can be seen by the
Bluff Rock sentries, safely moored off the Hobuck[2] ferry landing.

One of the travelers, a blacksmith from Bergen Village on his
way to visit relatives in Tappan Town where he will join the
Orange County militia, knows the Paulus Hook men and their
works. He tells his listeners not to worry about the enemy ships.

"Be sure," he chortles, "ye can count on it! Those boys an'
their colonel—that Durkee feller comanding' 'em thar at Powles
Hook—ain't gonna let those redcoat boats stand thar long. They'll
have some mischief 'for 'em b'for ye can say 'Yankee Doodle
Doo.' Watch an' see!"

The smith is a well of information and hearsay about Bergen
Point and all lower Bergen. He glibly recounts the fears of the
inhabitants there, a stone's throw across the Kill von Kull to the
British and Hessian troops occupying Staten Island. He tells the

news-hungry stagecoach passengers at Bourdette's inn stories of
depredations he has heard the enemy committed on both Staten
Island and Long Island.

In fact, he tells them, it is the rape of his own cousin on Long
Island that has made him decide to join his relatives in Orangetown
and the militia company there.

Declaring he was a neutral until the King's men began their
mischief-making, he describes "the fair nymphs of Long Island" as
being in a "turbulation." One of these, the blacksmith tells his
listeners, was his cousin, Ashbella, who was "forced by seven
men."

Shocked by this, one of his stagecoach audience asked solicitously for her welfare, adding how awful it must have been for
her.

"Oh, she did not complain of that!" he answered. "She despised
that! But she complained about their takin' from her her ole
prayer book since 'twas one for which she had a partic'lar affection."[3]

Jocko had been brushing down his horses when all the commotion began. From his favorite perch, the ledge rock on the
Bluff—the same spot Elaine and her brother frequent where she
and John had found seclusion together—the youth sees Elaine on
the precipice path below. Her four school children tag along at her
side.

He climbs up the path through a side entry into the Barbette
Battery and down the back path to join her. As he runs, his
thoughts ramble: She has asked him to come to her school at the
Baummeister house. Helping his father whose arm is still in a sling
is more important. ... Building cover for the animals in the camp
is more important ... No, he has not wanted to stay away from
her school. ... The young ones are all his new-found friends,
particularly Katie May ...

". . . Surely it would be nice to get some writin' and' readin' . . .
Surely it would be fun ... play a little ... fish a little ... In the
army there is no time for those things ... All of his friends like
him, he tells himself as he hurries out of the post and past the
sentry who recognizes him and nods ... All of his friends look to
him ... They have heard from the soldiers—not from him—how
Jocko Graves, mascot of the gun battery at Fort Putnam, survived
the 'big battle' ... And that 'Da Lootenan' is his close friend ...

". . . The youngest 'man' in the American army is what the
soldiers call him, and their grapevine travels like a musket ball!"

It is not from Jocko that anyone hears such tales. Never given to boasting and unimpressed by braggarts are characteristics he unconsciously shares with his friend, "Da Lootenan'." The youth, more mature than his fifteen and one-half years, still feels the shocking horrors of war.

They were ground ineffaceably into his memory 20 days ago. He does not even like to recall the nightmarish scenes of those horror-filled hours though they still vividly appear in his sleep. He remembers it—the shot that ripped through his father's shoulder, tearing through flesh and bone—the quick-thinking on the part of The Lieutenant in getting the wound bound and his father to safety, saving his life.

And so Jocko's thoughts continue buzzing as he speeds toward Elaine and the youngsters:

". . . If only his new friends would forget about it too, and stop asking him questions . . . It is enough to wake up at night without having to think of it in the day . . . But then he asks himself, why is it he comes to see the river battle? . . . Maybe it is mostly just to see Missy E and his friends. . . .

"First there is his secret attraction, pretty Katie May, the 12-year-old daughter of the bound couple owned by Jeffery Gartleck.[4] The Gartleck house is a little over a mile south of Moor's landing . . . And her brother, Ben, is 16 . . . he can read and write . . . But that Mister Jeffery is always arguing against the Americans and wants them to surrender to the King. . . .

". . . Besides, that Mister Jeffery is always after Ben, making him do all the hard chores. And he does not look too kindly on Missy E for 'attrackin'' Ben and Katie May away to the school even though it's off from chore-time."

The Widower Gartleck is not alone in opposing schooling for blacks. There are others like him. However his deceased wife, Sarah, who had been devoted to Elaine since the girl was born, was opposite to her husband and silently opposed his thoughts on many things.

So Sarah had become one of Elaine's strongest admirers. And Elaine has spread her father's word that schooling must be given to all people since all people benefit when all people can read, write and understand one another. Sarah agreed. Jeffery did not, saying this was a Thomas Jefferson dream.

Then, continuing his run toward Elaine, Jocko reviews in his mind some things about each of his school friends:

". . . There is that chubby little white boy, 10-year-old Hans

Onderdonk.[5] He comes from over the ridge a way and can speak Dutch a little and considers Jocko a hero—a hero almost as important as Hans's soldier uncle, Corporal Abraham Onderdonk ... His Uncle Abe is in Captain James Smith's company of Orange County militia under General Putnam. It amazes young Hans to think that Jocko has seen General "Old Put" Putnam. And even more than that! Jocko has seen the American chief "The Big Man," "The Gen'l" himself—and very close up!

"And there is Joseph, the West Indian boy. The same age as Katie May, Joseph can speak Spanish words. Joseph tells everyone how his father, Philip Reales, the wagon master, knew and talked to the Gen'l when he visited the Bahama Islands 25 years ago.[6] But, Joseph always adds, that was before he was The Gen'l ... And of course there's Paul, Missy E's little brother who is always at her side ...

"... Yes, they are his good friends, he tells himself. Oh, certainly they have chores to do. Many of them. Not as many as he has. ... He misses one old friend most, 'Da Lootenan'.'

"... Not once all week has he seen Missy E ... Not since she made him promise he would someday come to the class ... Missy E is worried about The Lieutenant, too ... He could help cheer her up, he thinks to himself ... This afternoon he will pick her some wild grapes. Then maybe she will give him another loaf of her mother's hot baked bread for Pappy. He needs good food now. And he likes that bread ... The army rations! Certainly not what they were before Long Island! ..."

The thought of Long Island sends a chill down his spine. His thoughts then jump to The Lieutenant:

"... Won't he be surprised! ... The changes that have taken place on The Mountain ... How big it is now! And all the Flying Camp soldiers that are here from Amboy ... And with them the new camp adjutant, Thomas Paine ... and this great man is only five feet and ten inches tall ... With his hair cued and curled and so well dressed all the time, just like those Englishmen ... Wish I was tall like my Pappy and could dress like that ... And the way that fellow Paine looks right through you and smiles gently underneath his roundish face and heavily shaped nose ...[7] And the most famous writer in the country now! ... But why wasn't the Lieutenant made the adjutant here? He's smarter than all of them ... And he can write well 'cause Missy E reads me some of them things he wrote her. ..."

Jocko's running reverie abruptly ends as he reaches the lower precipice path and its ledge where Elaine is explaining to her four school pupils the meaning of fall and the discoloring of the leaves. Elaine, whose eyes had earlier been drawn, as they always are, to the upper ledge rock, had seen Jocko up there meditating on his usual perch and knew he would soon be scrambling down to join them.

Elaine is aware that the upper ledge which she and John—and also Jocko—had virtually taken full possession of in the short time John had commanded the Barbette Battery, has jokingly been dubbed "Lovers' Ledge." Unembarrassed by the reference, Elaine looks upon it as a compliment from the men of John's battery.

They had made quite a point of it without disrespect. In fact they had displayed a sort of admiration as though they had a part ownership in The Lieutenant's love affair.

It had started when one of the sentinels had peered over the parapet one late Sunday afternoon and, to his amazement, saw The Lieutenant reading a book to his lady love on the ledge below.

Later, some swore by all that was holy that they had seen The Lieutenant kissing his sweetheart. But they quickly promised a bayonet through the chest for anyone who dared to repeat what they had said.

From then on, the men of Gray's battery called the upper ledge rock, "Lovers' Ledge" and, seemingly in agreement, gave no one any explanation.

Elaine's greeting of Jocko, who was a little out of breath from his flight down from the heights, was harsh: Jocko knew that it would be.

"Why," she questioned, "didn't you come at least once? Tom told me you could have been here Tuesday. The others are learning to read and write and you, Jocko, are not!"

Jocko, thinking Elaine sounds more like a schoolmarm than ever before is about to answer her when the church bells ring out their summons calling Whig and Tory alike to the pulpit of their choice, coetus or conferentie.

It was clearly evident to Jocko that Missy E had been doing a little silent crying. The earlier cannonading of British broadsides against American batteries had assured her that there is no peace in the wind down below as some had hoped and prayed.

The clear, clarion call of the church bells almost simultaneously is muffled by the roar of cannon from another section far to the east. The incessant pounding and rumbling echoes against The Rock.

It appears to be about three or four miles above New York town in the direction of the East River. In a few minutes, clouds of smoke and occasional yellowish flashes pinpoint the rolling cannonade.

They are the British frigates' broadsides pouring into the American entrenchments along the New York East River shore just south of Kip's Bay.[8] The barrage has been ordered by Sir Henry Clinton. His troops, loaded in flatboats from the transports, are poised and ready for invasion when the covering curtain of fire is lifted.

At the clarion call of the church bells the children had made a hurried departure. Each headed homeward, leaving only Paul and Jocko by Elaine's side. The three now strain to see through the distant haze over which puffs of smoke rise by the hundreds like angry Dutchmen smoking their clay pipes.

They peer from their shielded eyes, each thinking he sees something beyond the scattered, rolling woods and rock-strewn terrain which form a belt-like forest around Manhattan's island at its center.

The Sassafras Sinks and the Howes Strike

Now the entire battery of inexperienced militiamen line the parapets above Elaine, her brother and Jocko. Puzzled, the officers grope unsuccessfully for a reason behind these two Sunday morning attacks—one on New York town's west shoulder at Paulus Hook on the North River, opposite New York tip's Grand Battery, the other north of the town on its east shoulder south of Blackwell's Island in the pocket of Kip's Bay. What does it mean?

Before long the villagers are again scrambling around the precipice path, seeking a spot to view they know not what. Even Elaine's school pupils, Joseph and Hans, who had started toward home, come running back on the path again.

Far south, just to the west of The Narrows at the southern tip of Staten Island, the sassafras branch which Dr. Benjamin Franklin plucked from the Billop House grounds on his way to board the admiral's launch four days ago, now thoroughly water-soaked, is settled at the bottom of the bay.

Admiral Lord Viscount Richard Earl Howe and his brother, Sir William, did indeed offer the olive branch. Both had viewed their assignments to America as missioners of peace. Rejected, they feel they now must proceed to quell the rebellion.

Seen from their perspective, New York must be taken for the army's winter quarters. Snowy weather is not the time for waging war. And if they can occupy Manhattan, British raiding parties could fan out from time to time destroying any pockets of resistance once the King's navy ascends the Hudson.

The Howes hope to link their forces with the northern British army under General John, "Gentleman Johnny," Burgoyne. Once this were accomplished, the Crown's forces could seal up the Hudson River and proceed to cut the colonies in two.

Thus, without any communications with the American army around New York, and robbed of all defensive strength, the Continentals and their rebel Leader could be brought to their knees.[9]

That is the way the Howe Brothers see it except that they may have to march on Philadelphia if the Congress does not capitulate and return America to His Majesty.

So, in this overall objective, the first step is to have Admiral Howe acquire control of the Hudson by ascending it with enough shipping to enable him to cut off any American retreat and block the rebels' cross-river supply lines.

At the same time, General Howe will invade just north of New York town at Kip's Bay on the East River. The men-of-war will lay down the covering barrage as the redcoats move ashore. It is these two cannonades that puzzle the Bluff Battery artillerymen high on the Palisades.

Sir William plans to cut across Manhattan's east to west belt line, and, with his overwhelming might and some good fortune, divide and drive the split American forces, now holding the city, into surrender or the bay.

Then, with the British men-of-war pounding the Americans both from the East and North Rivers, blocking their escape across the Hudson and so preventing them from securing re-enforcements from Jersey or upriver, the end could be in sight. So think the Howe Brothers this Sunday morning.[10]

Seen from the American Commander's perspective, New York City is no longer tenable. It is less so in view of his inadequate army. In addition, the Tory-dominated populace is more than a thorn in the American side.[11]

The rebels' front has only two guardians, standing virtually alone to ward off the enemy's vast armada and its mighty machine. Those lonesome guardians are Paulus Hook on the Jersey side and the Grand Battery and their flanking redoubts on Manhattan's tip.

Paulus Hook without the Grand Battery's assistance is incapable in itself of restricting enemy shipping, even though that shipping is perilously under sail and at the whim of the winds and the tidal Hudson. And the Grand Battery without the Brooklyn Heights' artillery is incapable of obstructing shipping up the East River. Without Paulus Hook the Grand Battery cannot prevent the enemy from ascending the Hudson.

Both the Red Hook and Governor's Island batteries were abandoned by the American defenders after the escape from Brooklyn. They are now in the enemy's hands as is, of course, Staten Island—the one place which The General had wanted well fortified.

Had that recommendation been followed Howe's men and armada would not now be so restfully settled upon it. Without firing a shot the King's forces, unopposed, safely nestled all over the island enjoying all the comforts of a home base without the discomforts of contesting opposition.

And so it was that three days ago the Commander-in-Chief's Council of War agreed—but only through General Greene's insistence—that the city of New York must be evacuated.

Reconsidering their September 7 decision at Greene's especially called Council of War meeting last Thursday, the officers overrode their earlier recommendations and by ten to three voted to evacuate New York. After much discussion the following decided to re-consider and withdraw: Generals Beall, Scott, Fellows, Wadsworth, Nixon, McDougall, Parsons, Mifflin, Greene and Putnam.

Voting "to adhere and defend" were: Generals Spencer, George Clinton, and Heath.

Also considered was the question: "What number of men are necessary to be left for the defence of *Mount Washington* and its dependencies?" Eight thousand[12] it was agreed.

However, evacuation has been too slow. And now it is almost too late. It was decided that the army would withdraw to the northern tip of the island—to Mount Washington on the east side of the Hudson and to Fort Constitution opposite on the Jersey side of the river.

Tentatively it was planned that Fort Constitution would become the American army's winter quarters, and Fort Washington would be manned with eight thousand troops. The council hoped that the two river fortresses would block Howe's passage upstream.

Meanwhile, it was decided that the Northern Division must block Burgoyne's efforts to move south down from Canada, through Lake Champlain, Crown Point, Lake George, Saratoga,

Albany and Stony Point in the Hudson Valley.[13] For if Burgoyne could accomplish that, it would be easy for him to join forces with the Howe brothers and cut the Americans' communications with New England.

A week ago today the American Commander had informed the President of Congress of his decision to abandon New York, despite the Council of War's earlier decision. He had wisely anticipated his officers would have a change of mind. And they did.

In his communication to the Congress he regretted withdrawing, owing to the work and labor spent upon defenses. Secondly, he noted the dispiriting effect retreat would have on the troops and the country in general. And, in conclusion, he lamented the necessity of evacuating, since, he stated, New York is considered "the Key to the Northern Country."[14]

The General, in explaining his plans to the Congress, wrote:

> "... I am fully of opinion that by Establishing strong posts at Mount Washington on the upper part of this island and on the Jersey side opposite to it, with the Assistance of the Obstructions already made and which may be improved in the Water, that not only the navigation of Hudson's River but an easier and better communication, may be effectually secured between the Northern and Southern States."[15]

Pointing out to the Congress that a retreating army is "incircled with difficulties," and that any military commander "declining an engagement" will be reproached, he anticipated censure and criticism.

However, the Continental Army Leader declared that the "fate of America" must be put foremost. He revealed what is to be his strategy in these words:

> "... to avoid a general Action, or put anything to the Risque, unless compelled by necessity, into which we ought never to be drawn ... (preferring that) ... on our Side the War should be defensive. ... (since) ... it has been called a War of Posts ..."

His letter made it clear that he no longer would attempt to defend even "strong Posts, at all hazards."

"The honor of making a brave defence," he told Congress, "does not seem to be a sufficient stimulus, when the success is very doubtful, and the falling into the Enemy's hands probable."

His observations of the enemy ships anchored off New Town Creek opposite Kip's Bay and the intelligence he had received, made him conclude his letter with the prediction that Howe would strike at his rear. However, he expressed the belief that the strike would be made at King's Bridge or on the Harlem River's west shore.

"They mean to enclose us on New York island,"[16] he informed the states' representatives, explaining how the enemy's ships could easily secure his front, Manhattan Island's tip.

The General made it clear that in such an entrapment the Americans would be cut to pieces and lose their arms and stores— material and supplies which cannot soon be replaced. And he also told Congress he was not pleased with the resolution forbidding the American army from destroying New York.

The Commander-in-Chief recalls the British withdrawal from Charlestown after the battles at Bunker and Breed's Hill on June 17, 1775, over a year ago. It was the enemy then who without compunction set fire to the city of Charlestown in order to clear it of snipers. And it was from across the Charles River on that day that General John Burgoyne watched the conflagration and later wrote his nephew in England:

> ". . . Howe sent us word by a boat and desired us to set fire to the town, which was immediately done . . . now ensued one of the greatest scenes of war that can be conceived . . . a large and noble town in one great blaze. The church steeples being of timber were great pyramids of fire above the rest. . . ."[17]

So now, among the American officers, the question is raised: Why should it not be done to New York, a powerful Tory stronghold?

The Continental Army staff commanders, some of whom have opposed evacuating the city, are generally in agreement that it should not be handed over to the enemy, comfortably prepared and ready for their occupation as was Staten Island.

Why should it be left neatly intact? Why should the enemy enjoy the city for their winter quarters while patriots run from it to escape with their lives?

Thus, despite the Congress's opposition to torching New York and the Congressmen's "interference" with military operation—an "interference" over which many officers take umbrage—General Greene has written a lengthy letter to his Chief recommending New York be burned.[18] Greene has presented a valid argument, citing his reasons for the recommendation.

So on this warm September Sunday morning such matters spin within the minds of the American Commander-in-Chief and his staff. These thoughts provide the perspective from The General's viewpoint as he first hears Colonel John Durkee's barking cannons at Paulus Hook dueling with the three frigates, armed with 114 guns.

And they are still his perspective at a quarter of eleven this morning when he hears the opening barrage from the five men-of-war in the East River, hammering at the American entrenchments facing Kip's Bay.

The Grand Prize: Hudson's River

The warships are leveling 180 cannon on their targets. Their small arms rake the shoreline with grape, pinning the dust-covered defenders to the ground. Some have already been buried under the earth and wreckage.

Both of the opposing high commands know that the grand prize in the battle for New York is not the city itself. It is not the importance of its seaport. It is not Manhattan, Long Island, or Connecticut. It is the Hudson, the North River.

The enemy's principal objective now is to gain its control. This is a feat that only England's massive and powerful navy and army can accomplish. In conjunction with General Burgoyne's expected conquering of Lake Champlain, it will enable Howe to close off all intercourse by land and water between the New England colonies and those to the south and west of the Hudson.

The responsibility is Burgoyne's in Lake Champlain. It is Sir William Howe's and the admiral's in the Hudson River valleys.

Certainly the political results will be as advantageous as the military from the enemy's standpoint. For at this early stage of the war, the spirit of independence is far more prevalent and fanatic in the New England states than it is in the predominately Dutch-settled valleys and villages of New York and New Jersey. Isolate the fanatic spirit of New England and the center and the south will soon fall, Howe believes.

"Perhaps nowhere, except in South Carolina, does independence burn more glowingly than in New England. Therefore, politically and militarily, Howe must cut off New England."[19]

Two years from now, the American Commander will again struggle to hold these same communications intact, attesting to their importance in such correspondence as the following with Admiral D'Estaing of the French Navy:

"... A candid view of our affairs," he will write, "which I am going to exhibit, will make you a judge of the difficulties under which we labor. Almost all our supplies of flour and no inconsiderable part of our meat are drawn from the States westward of Hudson's River. This renders a secure communication across that river indispensably necessary ...

"The enemy being masters of that navigation, would interrupt this essential intercourse between the States. They have been sensible of these advantages ... If they could by any demonstration in another part draw our attention and strength from this important point, and by anticipating our return, possess themselves of it, the consequences would be fatal. Our dispositions must therefore have equal regard to co-operating with you (at Boston) in a defensive plan, and securing the North River, which the remoteness of the two objects from each other renders peculiarly difficult."[20]

(Within the year, the British command will send General Burgoyne from Canada to force his way by Lake Champlain to the Hudson. At the same time, General Sir Henry Clinton will move north from New York with 3,000 troops. Upon reaching West Point, Clinton will send part of his force up the river by boat to within 40 miles of Albany.

There the British officers will hear the discouraging news of Burgoyne's surrender at Saratoga. Greatly disheartened, Clinton's corps will, under orders from Howe, return unsuccessfully to New York.

In later years, Howe will regret his failure to commit his larger force to the operation which might have severed the communication links between New England and the states south and west of it.

But greater still will be General Howe's remorse in those later years of reflection for having made the mistake of committing his nation's sea power in the autumn of 1777, to transport the larger force of his army, some 14,000 men, from New York to the head of the Chesapeake Bay in order to attack Philadelphia from the rear. Unwisely he will be lured into chasing "The Fox" rather than cutting off his sustenance.

That move, a year from now, will be a success insofar as its political objective, Philadelphia, is concerned. But, militarily, the conquest of Philadelphia, seat of the Continental Congress, will prove to be unsound. Finally it will be abandoned.

The dispersion of the British forces will be costly, particularly in the loss of intra-unit mutual support owing to the widely scattered expanse of territory Howe will attempt to control. It will cost the British commander-in-chief the control of the Hudson which he

*had at first so forcibly sought, but which he will lose in his
pursuit of the Philadelphia Congress.*

*So in later years of reflection, General Howe will regret that he
did not throw his 14,000-man army up in support of Burgoyne's
7,000 troops instead of seizing Penn's City. Thus, he might have
completely overrun and sealed off the head waters of the Hudson,
maintaining 8,000 of his finely equipped, superior troops to defend
New York's island with support of the King's navy.*

Might he then, in 1776-1777, have succeeded in ending the war?

*That thought will be on his mind when, in February 1778, he
resigns his command and sails back to England, destroyed by
adversity.)*[21]

What the eyes on the Bluff Rock and those peering off from the
heights of Harlem are now seeing, and what the villagers all around
are now hearing, is the end of peace talks. It is the drowning of
the olive branch. It is the beginning of the second phase, the first
and greatest of the crises periods, in the long, bitter, deathly duel.

Its end is five years away, waiting the cessation of the senselessness of man's wills, his hates, his deaths, his mutilations, his fire,
his destructions, his famines—all in the "art" of warfare. Waiting
there—five years away in a remote Virginia fishing village on the
York River, opposite Gloucester's Point, just west of the
Chesapeake Bay—is Peace. For it takes years and years for
"civilized" man to reach decisions by waging wars—decisions that
could be reached by intelligence in a few days, a few hours, or a
few minutes at a conference table, were he properly intellectually
disposed and not too proud to make concessions.

The American Commander had feared, yet doubted, a Sabbath-
day attack when he wrote Congress prophetically last night:

> "... We are now taking every Method in our Power to remove the
> Stores & ca. in which we find almost insuperable difficulties. They are so
> great and so numerous, that I fear we shall not effect the whole before we
> shall meet with some Interruption. ..."[22]

Sick, Wounded and Dying Are Crossed To Paulus Hook

At the same time, The General, anticipating the "Interruption,"
ordered that "the sick" be sent to Newark by way of ferriage
through the Paulus Hook garrison on the Jersey shore.

Therefore, that order was carried out last night under the cover
of darkness. But, owing to their poor condition, most of the

feeble, sick and wounded, could get no farther than Paulus Hook. Some were lodged overnight at Hoebuck.[23]

Most of the "sick" are suffering from wounds received in the Battle of Long Island. They had been safely taken off the battlefield and ferried over to New York on the crossing night seventeen days ago. Since there is only one house near the Paulus Hook post and only one for their accommodation at Hoebuck, many were obliged "to lie in the open air until this morning."[24]

The Paulus Hook commander, Colonel John Durkee, ordered everything be done for them, particularly for the dying. Those were to be given every comfort possible. Durkee arranged that they be sent on today to the post at Bergen and thence to the Newark hospital.

The sight of these victims of war this morning moved the post's chaplain to write in his journal:

"... When I walked out at daybreak (their distress) gave me a livelier idea of the horror of war than any thing I ever met with before. ..."[25]

Their pitiful state was worsened when at seven o'clock this morning the British frigates, hugging the Jersey side to avoid the guns of New York's Grand Battery and its shore works, opened fire on Paulus Hook.[26] Ironically—though the British could not know it—the New York batteries were preparing for evacuation. Much of the heavy armament was being dismantled and most of the cannon were inoperable.

Emptying their fury on Paulus Hook's works, the 50-gun *Renown* under Captain Banks, the 32-gun *Pearl* under Captain Wilkinson, and the 32-gun *Repulse* under Captain Davis, all under full sail, forced their way upriver. Their mission was to pierce through the river's lower defenses between the Hook and the Grand Battery. And with no opposition from the New York side, they did so; not, however, without encountering Durkee's heavy fire from the Jersey shore.

It was a month ago that the *Repulse* became the first ship to fetch northward far enough to fire upon the American batteries at Red Hook. This action eventually resulted in the abandonment of the Red Hook and Governor's Island batteries as useless in the face of British naval power. Now, with those works evacuated and Manhattan Island's tip defenses dismantled, the only sentinel guarding the New York Bay and the lower Hudson River, is Paulus Hook.

So it is the Jersey post's 20th Continental Regiment that, early

The Paulus Hook Post, Painting by Edward L. Henry—From
The Enterprise Against Powles Hook, **New Jersey Title**
Guarantee and Trust Company, Jersey City, 1930.

this morning, returns in kind the broadsides from the three men-of-war.[27] Only one-half of the warships' 100 guns are brought into play against the Paulus Hook works. Their grapeshot barrage rakes the whole length of the Hook, but the Continental artillerymen remain at their guns striking back with the full weaponry of the garrison.

Under the escort of the men-of-war is the *Asia*, an armed, troop-carrying schooner. Staying safely out of range, the *Asia* tacks away and heads upstream followed by her escorts which end their brief but heavy exchange and make their way into the clear. All four vessels ascend the stream, dropping anchor about three miles upriver off the Jersey shore.[28]

Paulus Hook: A Doomed Guardian

Paulus Hook is doomed as a defense post. But only its defenders refuse to think so.

Captain Dana's artillery company of the train had expected that the enemy would come down upon them. They became convinced that a landing attempt was planned and that only their return fire caused the British officers to change their minds.

The post, fortunately, sustained only one casualty. Killed in action was "Old Mug," the garrison's faithful and beloved wagon horse. Long a popular racer on the Hook's once-famous track,[29] Old Mug had thought himself retired among old friends.

The men of the post are angered by Old Mug's death. That and their desire for a scrap caused the post's chaplain, the Reverend Benjamin Boardman of Middle Haddam, Connecticut, to write in his diary:

> "... They (the men of the garrison) were evidently animated by the whistling of the enemy's shot, which often struck so near as to cover them with dust."[30]

It is these men, rough, crude, adventurous, who squintingly eye every traveler who crosses at the post's ferry landing. Few of them would hesitate to pillage, and few would think twice before pilfering a neighboring villager's goat, heifer, or hog. Many of them would not hesitate to desert at the slightest provocation if they were so moved. Few things faze them.

One English merchant, Nicholas Cresswell, a strongly suspected Tory spy, trembles whenever he passes through Paulus Hook on his way back and forth from Newark to New York. Upon returning to Newark last Sunday, Cresswell wrote in his diary:

> "... While we waited for the stage, (we) viewed the *Sleber* fortifications here (Paulus Hook). They are made of earth, but what number of guns or what size I cannot tell. No admittance into the fort. The troops stationed here are Yankee men, the nastiest devils in creation. It would be impossible for any human creature whose organs of smelling was more delicate than that of a hog to live one day under the lee of this camp, such a complication of stinks. Saw a Yankee put a pint of molasses into about a gallon of mutton broth. The army here is numerous, but ragged, dirty, sickly and ill-disciplined. If my countrymen are beaten by these ragamuffins I shall be much surprized ..."[31]

These are the men who will find great glee in executing certain secret plans which Colonel Durkee and Captain Dana have prepared as an especial surprise for the enemy ships once they are quietly resting at anchor some midnight. It will be in the darkness of early morning when they send the ships a few blazing, floating fire boats, allowing the flaming rafts to drift into the helpless frigates. But it will be at an hour the enemy least expects rebel mischief.

It is the British officers' intention to use their men-of-war to block passage of any large-scale escape by the American army out of Manhattan to the Jersey shore. The frigates are to prevent the rebels, when forced out of New York, from crossing to Paulus Hook, Hoebuck landing, or Bull's Ferry after Howe launches his invasion of Manhattan. So it is off Bull's Ferry where Captains Banks, Wilkinson and Davis have dropped their hooks, waiting to catch any Americans attempting to flee to Jersey.

Howe's activities on the East River had been watched for the past twelve days with great curiosity by the American forces. The rebel Commander, lately pressing all hands into the business of evacuating the city, knew the enemy invasion was imminent but has been unable to pinpoint the site.

Under command of British Captain Wallace, the 32-gun *Rose* towing 30 flatboats up from lower New York Bay, safely ascended the East River on Tuesday, September 3. She had safely defied the New York Grand Battery and anchored off New Town Creek. But annoyed and molested by the American batteries near the Kip's Bay shore, the *Rose* weighed anchor and pulled out of range, mooring up the creek where it has swung with the tide in the midst of bustling redcoat activities.

Then, on Friday last, four more frigates, escorting two transports loaded with soldiers, joined the *Rose*. They, too, had successfully run past the New York East River rebel batteries which, to their surprise, had let them pass with unexpectedly light fire from the shore.[32] For these ships' officers also were unaware that the Americans and their armament were moving out of the city.

The rebels on Manhattan's shore were, in turn, amazed that the ascending ships did not once return the small arms fire as they passed. Yet they were heavily armed men-of-war!

These were the 44-gun *Roebuck* under Captain Sir Andrew Snape Hamond in the lead, the 32-gun *Orpheus* behind her, the 28-gun *Carysfort* next, and the 44-gun *Phoenix* following in their wake. All were under orders to hold their fire unless the American cannonade was heavy and threatening which the disassembled rebel heavy artillery prevented.

Concerned with the need to preserve the city[33] for their quarters and their take-over, the British high command had especially emphasized the "Hold Fire" orders. So not one of the navy's four frigates and their 148 guns barked back at the Americans' shore-sniping. This left the perplexed Continentals amazed and heightened their confusion.

It was General Howe's hope that by making the rebel forces in New York feel secure behind their posts, and by instilling a false sense of safety within his enemy's ranks, he could better save the city from destruction. His invasion-attack was to be executed in surprise, swiftly and decisively.

Sir William purposely sought to deceive the American Commander into believing the strike would come at the northern tip of the island, opposite Astoria. And there he made his feint.

So with the British *Renown, Pearl, Repulse* and *Asia* riding at attention and virtually in command of the lower Hudson River, and the *Roebuck, Orpheus, Phoenix, Carysfort* and the *Rose* with its 30 flatboats in command of the East River, the second cannonade of the Sabbath morning rends the air again. This time over Kip's Bay.

The men-of-war off Bull's Ferry had no sooner dropped their anchors when the East River warships began their barrage. So shocking and so deafening is the violent thundering of the enemy cannons that startled church-goers stop their carriages to listen to the roaring broadsides. Some rush on to the expected security of their houses of worship. Others hastily return home.

It is after 11 o'clock in the morning before the barrage is lifted and some 84 flatboats, filled with redcoats and Hessians, are carried to the East River's western banks at Kip's Bay. Boat after boat is emptied, returning continuously to be reloaded from the transports.

These are the men of the four divisions which were secretly assembled yesterday on the opposite Long Island shore for the invasion operation. Throughout the night they moved into the transports and later, while 85 of the warships' 170-gun total raked the American entrenchments 200 yards away, they moved into the flatboats and bateaux in readiness for the shore attack.

They head for the sector where for two days and nights an American brigade of Connecticut militia under Captain William Douglas[34] has attempted to dig in along the high rocky bank. The site was one of several the Commander-in-Chief ordered to be posted.

Owing to its location, the spot was judged a likely enemy landing place "because it was easily navigable and from its shore rises a large, open, V-shaped meadow, an excellent beachhead and assembly area."[35]

The so-called defense line is "nothing more than a ditch dug along the bank with the dirt thrown out towards the water."

South, below the cove, is James Wadsworth's brigade. Still farther south on the bank are Sam Holden Parson's men. Captain Scott's brigade is at Corlear's Hook.

As each defense position last night passed along the watchword, "All's well!," two of the American sentinels were astonished to discover one enemy frigate so close to the shore its watch overheard the Americans' "All's well!," and replied loud and clear, "We will alter your tune before tomorrow night!"[36]

And so they have. For by 11:15 o'clock the terrific enemy cannonade has pounded the works and collapsed what little trenches had been dug.

Some of the rebel defenders will later describe the opening attack as "such a fire as nothing could withstand ... so terrible and so incessant a Roar of Guns few even in the Army & Navy had ever heard before."[37]

Meanwhile on the Hudson side of Manhattan the American defenders prepare for what certainly will be a secondary, a west-side, attack and invasion from the *Renown, Pearl, Repulse* and *Asia*, lying in midstream all too quiet now after raking Paulus Hook.

The Howe Brothers have succeeded in puzzling the city's defenders and forcing them to split their attention and forces between Manhattan's east and west sides.

A glimpse at the British high command's military operational map with its overlay of black markings almost resembles a gigantic, open-jawed, prehistoric monster, rising out of New York Bay. As though lying on its right side, it seems to have its lower jaw reaching up the Hudson while its upper one stretches toward the East River. It appears to be gobbling up Manhattan Island and the American army within it.

Gnawed by hunger through the night, Continental Soldier Private Joseph Plumb Martin awoke shortly after daybreak this morning. It was long before either one of the cannonades when he wandered away from the line of trenches and stumbled into an empty old warehouse looking for food.

Finding molasses and Indian corn, he made a fire and roasted his cobs, washing them down with molasses water. The scattered papers on the warehouse floor provided him reading material. All was pleasant until the distant firing on the Hudson disturbed the peace.

Owing to its remoteness he settled back and read and ate some more until he was "jolted by such a peal of thunder from the British shipping that I thought my head would go with the sound."[38]

Dropping everything but his corn cob, he ran back toward the entrenchments and sought cover with his comrades. Later he would describe the sight of the British flatboats as "like a large clover field in full bloom."[39]

Covering his head along with the soldiers of his regiment, Martin waits and trembles until the cannonading abruptly ends. Then the "clover field" moves in.

In waves the enemy troops disembark from the flatboats and, at a signal, began to ascend the rocky bank. Charging in with bayonets drawn, the howling redcoats drive down upon the rebel defenders in their battered entrenchments.

Frightened, inexperienced, the young American officers are so overcome and bewildered they fail to issue firing orders. The irritable, hungry men, who have had no food rations for over 24 hours owing to supply line difficulties, become angrily perplexed by their leaders' inability to command.

Like Martin, most of the troops have had nothing to eat but acorns since yesterday. And then they were all in competition with squirrels. Such soldiers, even were they headed by competent officers, are far from ready to hold their ground and fight.

No superior officers are within the lines to take over command and issue orders. Seeing this disastrous state of affairs in face of the powerful British lines of bayonet-flashing infantrymen pouring in upon him, Captain Douglas—certain now that there is no alternative—gives the order for all lines to pull back from the entrenchments just as the enemy's bayonets push closer toward them.

A mad scramble, instead of an orderly withdrawal, now takes place. The lines of militia and some chagrined Continentals break. They run in two directions. Some head south, alerting the lower lines. Others fly west and north toward the second line entrenchments, adding others in their headlong dash for safety.

As they scatter, stumbling sometimes over one another and dropping their muskets and knapsacks in their haste, the enemy's grapeshot and langrege fly about their heads. One after the other falls, wounded or killed, as the battle-shocked recruits take to the distant woods in an attempt to get out of range.[40]

In no time it becomes a full-blown, American rout. Like a flood tide it spreads all the way down through the rebel lines. Slowly, steadily, and in carefully drawn regimental formations, the British and Hessian troops move inland. They pursue the fleeing defenders like some sort of mechanically operated giant caterpillar bent upon crushing everything in its way.

The American Commander-in-Chief guessed erroneously that his enemy would attack at the King's Bridge. Therefore, he has amassed a large part of his army, excepting those still evacuating the city, on the rocky plateau inland and north of Kip's Bay on the Harlem Heights.

The Harlem plains and its heights have good possibilities for maintaining a strong defense but only if the army can be fully assembled there in time. However, one half are still in the city and part of this division is manning lines on both the Hudson and East Rivers. It is the East River's five defense brigades, mostly new, raw recruits, whose flight before the enemy is now in full swing.[41]

Victory Within the Lion's Grasp

Under this division of the American forces the British can now easily cut across Manhattan Island's middle below the Harlem plains and split the Continental army in half.

Two main roads run irregularly up the length of Manhattan from its southern tip at the Grand Battery all the way to King's Bridge at the northernmost point. One of these roads, the Post Road, makes its way to Boston.

It skirts Sunfish Pond west of Kip's Bay and then climbs a broad hill called Incleberg where it passes the Murray House. From the Murray House it turns east toward the East River then swings westward again toward the center of the island. At about the center it runs northwestward via Mc Gowan's Pass through Harlem Heights to King's Bridge.[42]

The other highway, the Bloomingdale Road, is less traveled and far more rugged. It winds north along the west side of the island, paralleling Hudson's river. This rough road is intersected by old trails and unmarked crossroads which make it difficult to follow.

Both of these south-to-north highways up the island are intersected by a cross-island road. It is an east-to-west link across Manhattan's midriff which runs from the Post Road through the Incleberg near the Murray House. There it veers westward until it forms a junction with the Bloomingdale Road, not far from the Hudson's east shore.

Two things now occur simultaneously. First, at Mahattan's tip at the Grand Battery Major General Putnam and his troops are interrupted in the throes of evacuation by the second and long-sustained severity of the East River cannonading.

Secondly, the American Commander-in-Chief, concerned and puzzled by the early brush between the frigates and the Paulus Hook post and by the ships' ascent up the Hudson, continues his inspection of Fort Washington but brings it abruptly to a close with the sound of the bombardment at Kip's Bay.

Under Putnam's supervision at Manhattan's foot Colonel Knox pushes his men harder. They struggle to get already loaded equipment and heavy arms off in small boats and across to the Jersey post at Paulus Hook. With one eye on the stilled enemy vessels upriver and the other on the smoke hovering over Kip's Bay, they continue their task under increasing pressures. The heavy cannon that must be left for the enemy are to be spiked to prevent any further use.

Putnam had the East River shore lines manned north beyond Kip's Bay. He now orders the defense posts along the Hudson to be on the alert for any action on the part of the four warships off Bull's Ferry. On both sides of him the enemy presses.

Not anticipating a Sabbath morning strike, Old Put had planned to move his approximately 4,000-man force out of New York under cover of darkness tonight along the Post Road. The brigades manning all the shore defenses on the west and east sides were to have fallen, one by one, into the line of march northward out of the city, joining The General at Harlem Heights. However the cannonading changed the American plan that might have left Howe holding another empty bag. Another sprung trap!

At the sound of the distant cannon off Kip's Bay, Putnam spurs his horse toward the East River defenses. He and his staff gallop directly into Wadsworth's and Scott's brigades. All are widely scattered and in full flight entirely beyond control.

It takes Putnam but a few minutes to realize no stand can now be made.[43]

Ordering Wadsworth and Scott to reorganize as best they can to bring about an orderly withdrawal and then join the main force moving out of the city, Putnam swings his horse around. He whips his sweating steed back to save Sullivan's brigade, Knox's artillery, the militia units and the men manning redoubts, dismantling cannon and assembling stores at the city's tip. He has no alternative but to lead them out on the poorly marked, rugged and circuitous Bloomingdale Road along the Hudson's west side, instead of along the preferred Post Road as originally planned.

The sounding of the American alarm following the furious cannonading brings all troops into assembly under orders to march under arms. They pour into the assembly area at the Bowling Green from out of Broad Way, Greenwich Street, the batteries at the Exchange, the Ship Yards, Jones's Hill, Starr Fort, the easternmost Round Redoubt as well as the Grand Battery. Much equipment, baggage and impedimenta must be left behind.

One last perilous mission, the spiking of the guns that cannot be taken, is to be left to one company of artillerymen. Knox asks for and gets volunteers. The Blue Petticoat Scarf Lieutenant and his battery of artillerymen step forward and remain behind to carry out the task. They face an extremely high chance of death or capture and each one knows it.

Stragglers from the broken East River lines trickle in, joining the Putnam assembly as do the more orderly retreating units. Frightened, thirsty and exhausted, they are given aid and fall into the regimental formations which have already begun the long and precarious trek out of New York town and up Manhattan's island.

The Bloomingdale Road is the most difficult of the two roads north. It is crossed by pathways leading in many directions. But its alternative route, the Post Road on the east side is now bulging with the mobilizing enemy units still coming ashore.

It is streaming with the redcoated British and blue-coated Hessian jagers—a frightening sight with their brightly shining steel bayonets, long, heavy muskets and brass-hilted swords. With their high hats and their high-heeled boots the thoroughly disciplined and well-trained Hessian chasseurs appear much taller and far more fearsome than the redcoated Britishers.

As the two enemy arms land, they branch out both left and right, north and south along the shore defenses and the Post Road. Fleeing before them like scared rabbits flushed out of a field, the American raw militia recruits, already battle-shocked by the heavy barrage, run wildly south toward the city or northward toward Harlem's heights.

So for Major General Israel Putnam there is only one escape route, a poor one, but his only hope of avoiding the enemy's jaws.

Only one man, a New Jersey-born young captain, who has lived in New York town and knows the pathways and wagon roads through Manhattan, can lead the army out. He is Putnam's own aide de camp, Captain Aaron Burr,[44] a Princeton law graduate with the Class of '72. Burr, who is an abrupt, outspoken man, has often been sharply and unreasonably critical of The General and his conduct of the war.

Under the mid-September, sweltering sun, the American troops follow behind Burr. More in anger and disgust than in fear the hardy Continentals, unlike the young, raw, militia recruits, begrudge every inch of withdrawal, cursing the King, his army and his navy. They are the rugged backbone of the American army, and Putnam is determined to save them from the enemy and their own brazen audacity.

Racing his sweating horse up and down the long lines of men, he encourages the bravado grumblers, assuring them they will soon enough get their turn. He jests with those who seem frightened. He shouts orders to subalterns. Occasionally he laughs with the bolder ones. To the sick and weak he extends a helping hand and orders places for the fallen on the over-loaded wagons which often sink deep in mire and muck.

For twelve long miles he keeps up his straining pace hour after hour without rest. For momentarily he expects to hear that the enemy is in sight. Hour after hour passes as the unending lines gradually plod their way up along the Bloomingdale's trails, roads and pathways, paralleling, for the most part, the waters of Hudson's river. Yet there is no word or sight of the enemy.

To Israel Putnam, to Henry Knox, whose men trudge along slowly under the burden of the heavy artillery that was rescued, and to Aaron Burr, the failure of Howe to have at least sent a probing advance force across the island is incredible. And thus far none of Howe's left flank have appeared in the Americans' rear. Yet from east to west across lower Manhattan is less than two miles. So now Putnam's large bulk of the American army are winding their way upriver, widening hourly the expanse between the Bloomingdale and the east side Post Road.

Only stragglers from the overrun East River defenses and the guards make up the army's rear. Some of the sick, wounded and a number of frantic patriot townspeople are left behind, fighting for ferry passage from the Cortland, Barclay, Murray and Chambers Street docks. All small craft have been commandeered into a frenzied ferrying of arms, supplies, children, women and old men across to the Jersey post at Paulus Hook.

All watch with fear the distantly anchored British frigates off the Jersey shore at Bull's Ferry. Momentarily they expect intervention but the warships await a mass exodus in a large scale flight. They have little interest in what appears to be merely the escape of Whigs and neutrals in view of the impending battle.

It is the beleaguered American army which they hope will appear along the river bank seeking crafts of all kinds in which to flee to Jersey. No such running army appears on the Hudson's shore. Old Put's escaping division, bound north, is invisible on the treacherous Bloomingdale Road.

The second thing the cannonading has done is to force the American Commander to abandon his inspection trip and speed back to headquarters, ordering an alarm and all regiments ready for battle.

He meets briefly with his staff at headquarters. It is the home of

British Colonel Roger Morris, an ardent Loyalist whose wife The General once courted.

Outside, following the brief conference and confirmation that the enemy has made his move at Kip's Bay, an aide hands the Commander his field glasses and points toward the ships as they end their barrage of the American shore defenses.

It takes the rebel Leader only a minute to sum up the action. He mounts Old Magnolia and with General Mifflin and others of the staff, races off toward the Post Road.

Soon the hard-riding officers are running headlong into the fleeing, panic-stricken raw recruits and their equally terrified young officers. Mostly militia, only a few have ever smelled the smoke of battle before. All are in rout, pursued up the Post Road by the British right wing, fanning northward up the highway in the direction of the Harlem plains.

Empty-bellied, hot, thirst-driven, bewildered and drenched in their own sweat—some in their own blood—about 400 in number, they have just glimpsed the sparkling sunlight glittering on the bright steel bayonets of no more than 60 probing British pickets in the enemy van.

In Panicked Flight Before the Juggernaut's Jaws

Moving cautiously but steadily onward, like two rows of scarlet automatons, the British van can be seen far in the distance down the road.

Shocked by the cannonading, overawed by the size and momentum of the enemy invaders, and with no officers to lead them, the scattering American brigades, without firing a shot, break and run before the enemy's advance. All beeline it for the high ground and the temporary security behind Harlem's defenses. From across corn fields, from out of the woods and along the road they scramble, emptying into the highway directly in the path of the Commander-in-Chief and his party.

In vain The General, Mifflin and their aides along with others in the party, try to stop the rout, urging the soldiers to stand their ground and fight. But the battle-shocked recruits pay no heed in face of the mass confusion. They bolt away in every direction but the enemy's, bent only upon getting safely behind the army's defenses on the heights.

Enraged by what he deems to be cowardice of the first order, the American Commander flails with his riding crop at his own frantically scurrying men, upbraiding them and their officers alike. Feverishly he and Mifflin attempt to restore order, employing every device they can think of.

The rebel Leader in desperation whips out his pistol, aiming it over the heads of his men and pulls the tirgger. The long unused firing piece fails to discharge[45] and the wild stampede, though now slowed by the presence of the army's Chief, continues.

"Take to the walls!" orders the exasperated Commander-in-Chief. "Take to the fields!"[46] he shouts, pointing to the stone wall fences and overgrown hay fields where the forces could be regrouped for making a stand and an orderly retreat.

No voice, not even his, is able to bring them back into a line of defense. In their mad haste before the oncoming enemy they discard knapsacks, hats, coats, gear of all kinds. Even muskets are thrown aside in order to speed flight. All have heard stories—some much exaggerated in their repeated telling—of how American rebel prisoners are treated by the enemy. The roads, forests and fields are strewn with equipment, much is tenting that will be sorely needed during the coming winter weather, yet the enemy's small vanguard is hardly in sight.

Grabbing his hat and hurling it angrily down upon the ground, the Leader of the new nation's wobbling army exclaims in undisguised disgust, "Good God! Have I got such troops as those!" And then, turning to Mifflin, he questions without anticipating an answer, "Are these the men with whom I am to defend America?"[47]

Only in the eyes of Chaplain Benjamin Trumbull of the First Connecticut Regiment will the men of the panicked regiments be exonerated for their disorder. He will write:

> "I imagine the fault was principally in the general officers, and it is probable many lives were saved, and much loss to the army prevented in their coming off as they did, tho' it was not honourable. It is admirable that so few men are lost."[48]

Almost dumfounded by what he sees, the American Commander sits astride Old Magnolia, defiantly facing the oncoming scarlet uniforms as his terrified, flight-bent militia—men, officers, the rank and file—scramble for preservation behind the lines on the heights.

The General sits squarely in the path of the approaching enemy. His face is firm. His angry eyes flash above tightly closed jaws and clenched teeth. To the British picket officers and men who glimpse the statue-like horseman, tall and formidable in the saddle, it is an impressive sight and one which makes them halt in fear of an ambush.

The General's aides now close protectingly around him. One, with General Mifflin's assistance, brings the two horses' heads and reins gently together. They cleverly turn Old Magnolia's head northward out of danger without their Leader becoming too aware of being led. All slowly begin to withdraw to the Point of Rocks[49] out of range of enemy marksmen.

Members of the General's party credit the intervention of the Chief's bodyguards, his aides, Mifflin and the officers nearby for saving their Leader from almost certain death.

There on the Point of Rocks where the plains before Harlem rise up to begin the heights, the men of the post who have been pressed into digging new entrenchments, stop momentarily and gaze on an amazing sight below to the south.

Up from lower Manhattan, making their way silently northward along the Bloomingdale road beside Hudson's river, is the vanguard of General Putnam's corps—the other half of the American force joining the main army on the heights.[50] The sight is a relief, for some had believed the entire corps had been swallowed up by Howe's left flank forces. It had been a long time since word of their whereabouts had been received.

From the Point of Rocks, The General and his staff watch through their field glasses as "Old Put" and his marchers, with Burr in the van, wind through a maze of bypaths over rocky forests and fields.

Owing to the rolling contour of upper Manhattan the American marchers are hidden from their enemy who are now in full command of the east side of lower Manhattan and the Post Road approach to Harlem. Under Burr's guidance, Putnam's corps is headed for the intersecting path—the roadway which joins the Bloomingdale and Post Roads. It is slightly south of Harlem's plains.

The gathering observers congregating on the heights suddenly glimpse a large body of British troops marching up the east side north on the Post Road. They are just behind the pickets that sent the American militia flying. The long train is headed toward Incleberg,[51] commonly called Murray Hill.

The enemy force is the bulk of the British army's first division. Under Generals Howe, Clinton, Cornwallis, Vaughan and Matthews, the Juggernaut suddenly halts. Howe wants his second division closer in support before advancing farther. Since he is waiting to hear they have safely crossed East River and made the Kip's Bay beachhead without difficulty, he holds up his advance until that news is received.

The first British division comprises, in addition to the main battalions, Leslie's light infantry which swung to the right flank on landing and Von Donop's Hessian grenadiers who took the left southward toward the city. Von Donop met and engaged Wadsworth's retreating force of New York militia, capturing some 300[52] and scattering the rest who fled toward the city and joined Putnam's retreat march.

On the Point Of Rocks They Watch In Fear

It is Howe's force, moving north up the east side, and Putnam's troops, advancing north along the west side toward Morningside heights, that have gripped all eyes nervously watching on the Point of Rocks. Neither of the opposing forces is aware of how close they are to one another.

As the two roads verge into one and inland, away from the rivers, the opposing armies advance, paralleling each other in a strange deathly stillness completely unaware of what is happening. At times only a few square blocks of rocky, heavily wooded terrain separate Putnam's Continentals from Howe's Redcoats.

Then, just when it appears that the British vanguard is about to ascend the hilly area over which they would see to the west the sweating Americans struggling along to reach the Harlem plains, the British division comes to its complete and surprising halt.

Sir William and his officers have halted—and very conveniently so—close to the home of Robert Murray, a staunch Quaker. The hospitable Madame Murray, a motherly woman who has reared twelve children, welcomes the British commander-in-chief and staff.

Dame Murray feeds her guests cake and wine. She smiles unperturbed when some of the officers jokingly twit her over hearsay that she has Whig and patriot leanings. Joining in and partaking of the refreshments is British Governor of New York, William Tryon. The Governor has come along with Howe in preparation for taking over the city.

In days to come much will be made of this very costly pause for refreshments.[53] Some will even contend that Dame Murray manipulated the stop-over in order to delay the King's men while the Americans made their way safely into Harlem's heights. They will contend that had it not been for Dame Murray and her cake and wine, the American army, or certainly Putnam's corps of it, would have been wiped out.

The Redcoats Take New York Town

It is now five in the afternoon. Black, ominous, rain clouds hover over the entire island. The enemy's second division in numerous waves of flatboats has landed 9,000 troops on the East River's shore in support of Howe's first division. This second division's latest contingents include five brigades and two regiments of British regulars, one brigade of Hessians and the divisions's heavy artillery.

One newly arrived British brigade immediately takes off to the south in support of Von Donop's Hessian command. Houses, barns and buildings of every kind are commandeered by the invading troops who will be billeted all along the Post Road into the city itself before the night is over.

Unseen by their enemy who is almost sitting on top of them, Putnam and Knox, simililary yet unaware of their foe's proximity, drive their 4,000-man train safely into the Harlem plains, Burr at the spearhead.

The phenomenal inability of the advance scouts of both opposing armies in their lines of march to observe some part of the movement of the other, will never be satisfactorily explained. The only plausible explanations will be the scouts'—both British and American—unfamiliarity with upper Manhattan's terrain and their inadequacy for the task.

It is Burr the Americans have to thank. But it is Old Put whom they have to cheer. His horse, frothing at the mouth and constantly in sweat from the straining ordeal, has traveled twice the distance of the corps. For Putnam, without once letting up, raced constantly up and down the lines like a nervous sheepherder fearing an attack by wolves upon his flock. Whenever and wherever needed he was there.

Certainly Dame Murray's cake and wine were helpful ingredients in the rebel army's evacuation of New York, but without Israel Putnam's vast energy, will and the incessant drive he demanded—and without Aaron Burr's exceptional knowledge of the terrain—"it is probable the entire corps would have been cut to pieces."[54]

After their pause for Dame Murray's refreshments, Howe and his staff lead the main British column northward to McGowan's Pass. And there they spend the night.

Meanwhile some of the units in the British southern flank begin entering the city in large numbers. Some find comfortable billets through the help of the city's elated Tories.

Relentlessly the port city's Loyalists join Von Donop's guards and pickets in the hunt-down of stragglers. Some Tories run alongside the British regulars who begin a useless pursuit of the American rearguard units. The redcoats are under orders not only to search out rebels but also rebel sympathizers.

Only one American company remains behind the guards disappearing up the Bloomingdale road. It is the battery under The Blue Petticoat Scarf Lieutenant, John Gray. In very good time they complete the spiking of the cannon left behind and the burning and destroying of some of the supplies and equipment not able to be carried away. Now dragging some equipment and a howitzer, they suddenly find themselves entrapped at the Rector Street landing with no craft to cross them to the safety of the Jersey post at Paulus Hook.

An express rider, escaping in a flatboat along with others, has seen their plight and yells over the water from the stern, assuring them he will send help from the Jersey side. He does.

Prepared for such an emergency, Colonel Durkee at Paulus Hook hears the express rider's relayed message before the flatboat has docked. He swiftly dispatches two parties and an officer with three whaleboats and two flatboats to attempt the rescue.[55]

A refreshing rain begins falling over the river. Invigorated by its cooling coating over their perspiring faces, the oarsmen speed up the synchronized timing of their heaving oars. Fortunately a rising mist helps to accelerate and conceal their mission.

They meet a few sloops and whaleboats carrying refugee patriots and their meager belongings out of the city and over to Jersey. Some of these try to give the appearance of fishing boats, fearing the Paulus Hook boat crewmen may be British.

Approaching the Rector Street wharf the captain in charge at last sees the rear guard party he is to rescue. A few can be seen carefully hauling the heavy howitzer to the landing at the foot of Rector Street.

In answer to the captain's request for two volunteers among the oarsmen to provide a picket guard and coverage while the detail of men and their gear are loaded, Privates Jesse Squire[56] of Norwich and Paul "Frenchy" Durie of Haverstraw quickly offer their services.

Squire and Durie are a fearsome twosome, always itching for

action—a fight of any kind. It is their task, the officer informs them, to move only a little way inland and watch for any sign of the enemy. In short, they are to cover the maneuver until the last of the three vessels is ready to embark.

A driving rain now empties over the land and water.

"It is a godsend," The Lieutenant on the loading dock tells his men, the dirty, wet stripping of a blue petticoat flying loosely from around his neck.

For John Gray knows that the advance British patrols are not far behind him and the rain will slow them down. And now, with help in sight, they may get those extra minutes needed to escape.

With a grateful smile on his rain-splashed face, Gray welcomes his rescuers. Immediately the small company of artillerymen, who could look no more drowned had they been just fished out of the tide, begin loading aided by the oarsmen.

Carrying only bayoneted muskets which cannot fire when wet, Squire and Durie take their left and right picket points about 20 rods off the shore. Their captain tries to warn them to shorten the distance. But his voice is drowned under the cloudburst.

On the dock, the drenched soldiers load two brass howitzers and over two tons of valuable military stores[57] into the five boats.

One additional member has been acquired by Gray and his company since their gun-spiking and flight from the Grand Battery. The addition is a young officer, a second lieutenant, who a few hours ago in the east side debacle, had escaped capture by feigning death.

A searing wound from a Hessian ball had burned his right side and left him bloody from the flesh wound. For the missile had only slashed skin, missing penetration by fractions of an inch. The young officer had succeeded in patching himself up. Then, stealing through the woods, he made his way toward the Grand Battery.

Now his tireless energy in helping the loading of the river craft brings admiration from the entire unit. For 19-year-old Second Lieutenant Asher Levy is thankful to his God that his life has been spared, or that he is not one of the unfortunate prisoners taken and marched to the rear of Von Donop's troops.

When the New York-born youth stumbled into the gun-spiking company just outside of the Grand Battery post, it was not the first time John Gray and Asher Levy had met. A year ago Levy had visited Princeton inquiring cautiously into the possibilities and opportunities for a Jew to secure admission as a student of medicine. It was Gray with whom he struck up a conversation and who was helpful and encouraging in making preparations for the entrance examinations.

But the war had interrupted those plans. And Levy, securing a commission as a second lieutenant, was assigned to a company of the 12th New Jersey Infantry attached to Wadsworth's battalion.

Levy is one of many who narrowly escaped the enemy round-up of some three to four hundred prisoners now in the hands of the Hessians. His concerns are divided between his comrades and the American patriots of the city, presently at the mercy of gloating Tories. One of these is his friend and patron, Haym Salomon.[58] Levy describes Salomon to Gray as they work side by side on the dock. He informs Gray that he fears his friend has been too outspoken in the city where his past sentiments may get him the gallows.

Gray advises Levy that there is nothing to be gained by going back in the city in an effort to help Salomon. Gray convinces the younger officer to remain with the retreating forces.

"After all," he warns Levy, "we are all still in the trap and may never get across, but it is the only chance we have. You can do more for your friends and the cause in the service than in a dungeon."

Dissuaded from becoming a fugitive in the captured town, Levy stays with Gray and his men.

Loaded to the gunwales, the five boats prepare to pull out, one behind the other each in tow. The last vessel to cast off is held waiting for the two pickets, Squire and Durie.

The two guards have—with devilish delight—spotted a patrolling party of the enemy which landed earlier under cover of barrage "near Mr. Stuyvesant's house in the Bowery."[59] They are the first enemy soldiers Squire and Durie have ever seen and both are determined to have a shot at them. It will be something to tell their comrades back at the Paulus Hook post.

Shouting above the drenching rain, the American captain calls out repeatedly. The oarsmen join in. But the two pickets, either unable to hear or too engrossed in the redcoats, do not move from their posts, one behind an old barn, the other at the corner of a warehouse building. Both believe they have kept their firing pans and powder dry and that a few pot shots will send the enemy scurrying.

The captain then sees the redcoated pursuers. He again yells at the guards. Shouting for them to run for the boat, he curses when they do not move. But Squire and Durie are determined to get off at least one shot.

Then the advancing party sees the two men holding up their rifles in firing position and the three boats, one still at the wharf.

Their commanding officer orders a charge. As they do so Squire and Durie trigger their muskets. Neither fires. The flintlocks are too moist to spark. In no time they are surrounded.

Realizing he can do nothing for them, the captain orders all boats to clear the wharf and make for the Jersey side. The security lines, from vessel to vessel, aid the oarsmen in the navigation of the tidal river.

Minutes later the British patrol reaches the shore. A few raise their muskets, but, like those of the unwise and unfortunate prisoners, the triggers click harmlessly.

There is no further pursuit. Gray, Levy, the rescuing captain and the men of the artillery battery along with the oarsmen, relax. The strain and pressure is lifted. They slump tired and weary under the lightening rain drops and the steady dipping of the oars and flapping sails. But the loss of two men hangs heavily over all.

Down Goes the Rebel Banner: Up Goes the Royal Colors

No one mentions the lost men, but all fear their fate. Though they are prisoners at least they have their lives. That is their comrades' only consolation as they stow aside their oars.

And so, along with the other captives, two over-daring Paulus Hook fighting men are now destined for the enemy's prison ship. It is the price paid for the valuable arms and stores so difficult to replace.

As the rescue vessels reach the Hook's landing, the rain lets up. Each man has spent his reverie. Gray's was a longing look far upstream toward the great Bluff Rock at Fort Constitution. Levy's was at New York town toward the house of Haym Salomon.

Now all eyes turn toward the conquered city. To the south, at Manhattan's tip, where so much hope had been held for the Grand Battery's power to repel the enemy, there will be a new works called "Fort George."

As the men on the vessels look in that direction and the eyes of the sentinels on the ramparts of Paulus Hook's redoubts are drawn to the same site by the blast of a British cannon, they see the American banner hurled down from the New York City post's flagstaff.[60]

In a few minutes, in its place are raised the King's colors. They fly high now under a clearing sky on this late Sunday afternoon of September 15. The Americans' flight from the city is ended.

12

Monday, September 16. . .

Harlem Heights: The Turnabout

Baked Bread and Sausages For the Wounded

Many boats carry the wounded and dying from the Kip's Bay rout across the Hudson on the long journey from Mount Washington to Fort Constitution and then to the Hackensack hospital. Some will go on to the one at Newark. Others will eventually be transported to Philadelphia.

It is a busy, pitiful scene that greets the eyes of the inhabitants this morning under the Bluff Rock and on The Mountain. Soldiers and inhabitants sadly watch the horrible sights as the bleeding, wounded, mangled bodies of the maimed and dying arrive on the military landing at Bourdette's Ferry.

All the youngsters in Elaine's school have insisted that school be called off so they can watch the wounded arriving. And it was today that Elaine had hoped to initiate the use of a large slate board which her father had acquired from the nearby cliffs. He had set it up between two empty wine kegs in the Baummeister parlor much to Marie Louise's silent disapproval.

Mama Baummeister approved Elaine's idea of giving the young children some of the schooling Elaine herself had acquired. She did not, however, like turning her parlor into a schoolhouse. Nevertheless, she silently went along with it, conceding, as she has always done, to the wishes of her husband and her children.

Marie Louise's "parlor" is one of the cliff woman's few luxuries.

So everyone knows what a big concession she has made in turning it over a few days each week to Elaine for her school. The nearest schoolmaster is over The Mountain in the valley. It is there that mostly the older children go by horseback or wagon. But horses and rides over The Mountain are not easy to come by these days.

And since Elaine's mind is on yesterday's unknown events—for everyone along the cliff is talking about the distant cannonading— she dismisses the youngsters. However, she orders they all help fill the buckets and casks for the soldiers as they pass through on the way to the Jersey hospitals.[1]

The less seriously wounded gather on the shore waiting for wagons to transport them. They give varied accounts of yesterday's invasion. As the helpless ones are borne to the wagons, Elaine hesitates to look or ask questions, fearing that among them she may see the one face her mind constantly dwells upon. She tells herself repeatedly that John is safe but insures her thoughts with prayer.

In preparation for such heartbreaking occasions, the women of the cliff have bandages ready, cut up from linen and wool cloths— all of anything that can be gathered. Elaine takes hers and her mother's contribution, as well as the baked bread and pork sausages they have prepared. She places them on the supply wagon with those of the other women.

As her father and Bourdette watch the tragic scene from the Bourdette landing, puffing slowly and silently on their pipes, Baummeister sees his daughter deposit the food and bandages on the army carrier. When she about faces and runs back to the house, he knows and understands what she feels. For the ferry master, too, fears what he at any moment might see. But John Gray is not among the wounded.

Above the misery-shrouded, waterside scene—the seldom noticed or remembered aftermath of battle—up on the high ramparts before the Barbette Battery, Colonel Daniel Hitchcock[2] trains his field glasses across the river.

With difficulty he is able to distinguish some military action taking place north of Bloomingdale on the Harlem Heights and on the plains south. Something is happening for occasionally he can see the rapid movement of troops. Often he is able to glimpse men, apparently from both forces, circulating through the intervening open spaces of the distant, densely thicketed woods of upper Manhattan.

Hitchcock's binoculars first begin a sweep left, northward up the river, glistening like silver in the early morning sunlight. Northeast he picks up the defenses at the King's Bridge on Manhattan's northern tip. It is there he barely makes out the point where the Harlem River turns itself westward to cut Manhattan off from Westchester and make its way through the Spuyten Duyvil into the Hudson. All there seems quiet.

Steadying his glasses on one of the great igneous rocks beside him, Hitchcock focuses southward from Spuyten Duyvil down along the Hudson's east shore to Jeffery's Hook, directly opposite him under the Fort Washington redoubt and its heavy cannon. He sees the small boats carrying the disabled from Mount Washington to Bourdette's below him.

Then his glasses span the length of Mount Washington opposite his own battery on the Palisades' defenses of Fort Constitution. He holds his scope on the highest summit of Mount Washington. There he sees more than the usual amount of activity from one end to the other.

Now he sweeps his sightings southward down toward the Harlem heights south of Mount Washington and then on to the Harlem plains. In his scope he is able roughly to delineate the forward lines of the two opposing armies. He can with difficulty make out the positions of the two forces as they are aligned on either side of the upper middle belt line roadway across Manhattan's island.

They have held these positions since the close of yesterday's disastrous battle. Only three miles separate the two armies' forward lines at their widest points.

Each army occupies a relatively high plateau. In between these two plateaus runs the so-called Hollow Way. This deep depression in the terrain is from about one quarter to three quarters of a mile wide. It is a part of the belt-like roadway which stretches across Manhattan from the village of Harlem on the east westward, passing through the Hollow Way to the heavily wooded area south of the heights.

And it is south, behind that wooded area, where the main British army has spent a restful night after celebrating a successful day and a victorious invasion. The King's troops are obscured in their bivouac behind their front line. American observers on the north plateau and on the heights of Harlem, are unable to determine their enemy's strength or movements within the forested area.

The Howe forces, paralleling the rebel defense line along the heights, are stretched out two miles east to west from Horn's Hook on the East River to Bloomingdale village on Hudson's river.

In toward Bloomingdale the vital McGowan's Pass winds its way at the west end of the British-held plateau. Through that pass which Putnam's corps safely cleared yesterday with a great sigh of relief in their withdrawal from the city, is the only route on the west side that leads from Harlem's plains to the lower part of Manhattan and New York town.

The most forward of the British picket guards are at times less than two miles distant from the Americans' forward entrenchments.

About a mile behind in support of the British van are the enemy army's front line brigades, the guards.[3] About three miles south of the American front line defenses, these British guards hold the high enemy plateau grounds. They protect Sir William Howe's main encampment located behind the heavily wooded area.

From the Barbette on the Bluff Rock, about three or four miles distant, crow-flight, Colonel Hitchcock can only speculate on what is taking place around the Hollow Way. There, on and below the Harlem heights, the two armies have had a good breakfast. The American supply wagons have at last caught up with the troops in their long withdrawal up the island.

The rebel regiments which flew before the British drive are the least rested. Most of them have had an uncomfortable, wet, tentless night on ground, layered with leaves and warmed by their camp fires. Many of them escaped only with their lives. In their stampede to evade the redcoats' riflemen and bayonets they discarded knapsacks, bedding, tenting, canteens and even muskets.[4]

Kip's Bay Losses Mount

Late yesterday afternoon and well into the night, the British detachments were rounding up prisoners. Some are unscathed, some wounded and dying. Individually and in squads they were overtaken before they could get behind the American lines.

The Continental Army's losses yesterday are estimated at 17 officers and 350 enlisted men.[5] Very few have been reported killed. But capture and imprisonment by the enemy is considered by some worse than death.

So great are the American losses of ammunition, stores and weapons that an accurate count is impossible. Much was left behind in the army's haste to evacuate the city. Quantities of valuable gear lie strewn along the roads and in the fields.

Between 50 and 60 heavy cannon, part of the American defense installations ringing New York town, are now in enemy hands. These constitute a tremendous loss to the artillery commander, the youthful, 26-year-old, Bostonian book-seller, Colonel Knox, whose deep, bass voice and massive stature have caused some of his men to dub him "The Little Giant."

Many of the heavy guns were spiked by the retreating army. Rear guard units, such as Lieutenant John Gray's, destroyed much that the conquering enemy will never use—at least not until it is melted down.

Word has reached Knox's staff that Gray's sabotage company have all been rescued by Colonel Durkee's men from Paulus Hook. Durkee's messenger informs the artillery commander's headquarters on the heights of Harlem that several brass howitzers and some small pounders on carriages, as well as several hundred pounds of stores, were safely taken off. But the report notes that it was at the cost of two of Durkee's finest men.

Owing to the need for every fieldpiece possible for the defense of the American forces now gathered on upper Manhattan, the artillery staff command orders that Gray come across at Bourdette's.

At the very moment headquarters in Harlem was learning of Gray's safety, The Lieutenant and his command were finishing breakfast inside of Colonel Durkee's Paulus Hook battery with, as Gray will write his father and sister, "the roughest assortment of Yankees I have yet to see."

It is they, he will write, who saved him and his company from certain death or capture. And it is they who have generously shared their food with the rescued artillerymen.

It is characteristic of the Paulus Hook rank and file to admire bravery. So, in the opinion of these coarse, hardened rebels, The Lieutenant, despite the officer's petticoat neckerchief, which they do not quite understand, has—along with his men—proved to be of the metal they admire.

It was these excitement-loving men of Paulus Hook who last night stole up the river with their fire-ships, set and ready to be torched. Then, awaiting the early morning tide and the wind, they guided the harmless looking but highly inflammable, flotsam-appearing craft toward the British frigates. At the right moment they ignited the destructive projectiles, released them to the wind and tide from their towlines and speedily rowed themselves safely ashore.[6]

Within seconds the flames from the fiery rafts lit up the early morning darkness for miles around. Each of the enemy's ships became clearly silhouetted before and behind curtains of fire. Alarms rang out over the water from the watches on each of the endangered British vessels as the ships' crews, abruptly awakened, raced on deck.

Frantically the officers and crews dashed about on the decks. Some carried water-filled buckets. Others in feverish desperation attempted to pole away the flaming rafts. But pushing them out and away served only to have them drift back again at some other point along the vessels' hulls.

Some of the fire-ships which jammed into the frigates' sides ignited the hulls. One of the warships seriously damaged was the *Renown*. Also suffering badly was the troop-laden *Asia*.[7] All hands were summoned on deck to fight the creeping, flaming destruction. Just as they were getting the fires under control, a brazen party of Paulus Hook's rebels broke the *Renown's* mooring and grappled[8] the warship from their whaleboats in an attempt to cause it to drift toward shore and go aground.

For a short time it looked as if several of the British vessels were headed for destruction. Only the super-human efforts of His Majesty's crews and a sudden change of wind saved two of them from meeting a fiery end in the shoals off Bull's Ferry.

So brilliant and eerily mysterious was the sight as viewed by the sentry on the Bluff Rock that in a few minutes after the flames leaped into the night sky, Hitchcock and his staff were watching from the ramparts. No one was certain what was going on, but Hitchcock, who is well acquainted with Durkee's battery and their exploits, was sure it was one of the post's "Durkee-planned mischief-makers" specially designed for the ships that ran through his pounders.

Through the excitement of the night's terrifying attack, The Lieutenant and his company slept comfortably in the emptied barracks. The Sunday which had dawned so peacefully yesterday morning turned out to be twelve of the most harrowing hours of their lives. Sound undisturbed sleep was their reward.

It was not until morning, and after Gray and his company had enjoyed a hearty breakfast, when the men of the "emptied barracks" returned from their night's mischief-making. It was then that Gray and his command learned of the important "side activities" which Durkee's post employs to harass the King's men and local Loyalist sympathizers.

Never again would they jest about the "easy, do nothing" life of the troops on Paulus Hook, the last remaining guardians of Hudson's mouth.

Even though Gray had been earlier informed of the planned fire-ship attack, he could not have kept his eyes open to see the distant action if he had wanted to.

It was a comfortable, restful feeling for the Pennsylvanian to be back on Jersey's pleasant, home-like earth. There was something delightfully thrilling in again standing on the long tail of the Palisades, back on the same soil and ridge of rock as his Elaine. And just 15 miles from her door!

Fortunately, he tells himself, he will not be expected to cross at Bull's Ferry. All the ground on Manhattan's west side, Durkee has informed him, is now in the enemy's hands or is likely to be. Howe is reported in control of Manhattan Island, west to east as far north as the Morningside Heights.

Therefore Gray is happily resigned to make his return crossing at Fort Constitution's ferry. And at last he will see Elaine again!

He tells himself this time he will ask what he should have asked and proposed before. His dream last night convinced him that this is not the time for bashfulness. And he can count on Papa Pete's approval and support. He knows that.

Colonel Durkee has assigned two guides to lead the officer and his command out and on their way up the river's west bank through its rugged pathways. Two of the scarce wagon teams, reluctantly released by the Hook's quartermaster, are now filled with the stores and the lighter artillery that was rescued.

Gray places the wagons and their contents in charge of Second Lieutenant Levy after the escorting guides say a goodbye at a point just beyond the British ships. The damaged vessels lie licking their wounds off to the east of Bull's Ferry in the midstream.

Wisely and cautiously the Paulus Hook scouts have led their charges in close to the Palisadean cliffs, carefully avoiding observation by the ships' crow's-nest lookouts. A broadside driven into the cliffs above their heads could touch off an avalanche that would bury them within minutes. Once safely beyond the range of the enemy men-of-war, the guides leave them on their own.

Actually the British seamen have too much to do without looking for more trouble. Cleaning up after last night's wild attack has been continuous since the last of the fiery rafts was extinguished or sunk. The near catastrophe has kept all hands busy repairing the damages.

For the exhausted naval officers and men of the four

jeopardized vessels it has been a night of nightmares. Decks, masts, shrouds and canvas silently testify to it.

The Frigates Flee Durkee's Prometheans

Suddenly in astonishment, Gray and his men turn their heads and pause briefly as they see the four ships raise their canvas into the brisk northwest wind. First the *Asia* lifts her hooks and gently heads toward the Manhattan side. Then follows the *Pearl, Repulse* and *Renown*.

All stay east of the midstream and tack carefully back west, but not again in range of Durkee's Paulus Hook artillery. They are all in a much bigger hurry running back south than they were yesterday running up north.[9]

The ships' close hugging of the New York shore is conclusive proof to Gray and Levy that the warships' commanders know New York is in Howe's hands. Whatever their purpose, Gray tells Levy, whether to feint a landing, assist their army's left flank up Manhattan island, or block escaping parties which never made it across, their plans definitely changed.

"And," says Levy, "Colonel Durkee and his Prometheans have scored a victory that few will ever know about."

Gray smiles, replying, "You have learned your Greek well, Asher. Prometheus would be touched by your analogy. I trust Zeus will not exact the Promethean penalty upon our good Colonel Durkee."

As the little band continues its way, winding along the old animal and Indian paths that have become in places a "road" in name only, paralleling the river's bank, they hear two broadsides explode the air between the Grand Battery and Paulus Hook. It is the *Repulse* obviously sending a parting gift or two toward the Jersey battery as a vengeful effort for last night's insult.

Levy tells Gray to notice how much the enemy vessel keeps its distance from the "Hook's fiery firemen." It is clear to both the young American officers that the strikes hit nothing but the open water, well forward of the battery and its ramparts.

"Durkee is not even going to give them the courtesy of a reply," Gray says after waiting to see whether the British broadsides would be answered.

While the detachment is making its way up the shore road toward the Bull's Ferry landing, Colonel Hitchcock on the Barbette sweeps his binoculars toward the scene of last night's fire-ship attack. He had watched excitedly after realizing that the Hook's men were responsible for the flaming boats dodging in and out among the enemy's frigates.

Now all that he is able to see is the *Asia* making her way hurriedly down the New York side of the river, the *Renown* evidencing a slight career to port,[10] and the *Pearl* taking the lead. He too sees and hears the *Repulse's* two broadsides as it brings up the rear, well clear of the Hook's guns.

The two yellow flashes of the *Repulse's* starboard guns and the projectiles' steaming hot geyser-like splashes into the bay waters fronting Paulus Hook, seem to be the closing curtain in the two-day drama. Hitchcock watches and listens in vain for an answer from Durkee's works. There is none.

With no sign of further action downstream Hitchcock points his field glasses back and across at Manhattan's midriff where the two armies are drawn up facing each other. All appears quiet. So assured, the colonel withdraws to his quarters about ten rods north of the Barbette Battery on the Bluff Rock.

The officer's field glasses have not caught an evolving drama taking place on the Harlem heights, the plains and in the Hollow Way. A large party of unobserved American Rangers is stealthily making its way up toward the forested area on the enemy plateau.

For days the rebel Chief has spent every waking hour attempting to outguess Howe's next move. He feels it imperative that some effort be made to determine what the British commander intends to do and the exact strength of the forces he plans to do it with.

Yesterday his disgust with his troops reached an unprecedented high. He had not expected, even from new recruits, such an undisciplined display.

He conceded that they were inexperienced in battle, as are most of the poorly trained and inadequately equipped militia now coming in as reinforcements.

He had not believed it possible, however, that men and officers would resort to flight without making at least the pretense of a stand. A show of defiance would have enabled an orderly withdrawal and forced the enemy's respect, thus hampering the invaders' thrust. Consequently The General's anger is reflected in the report he sends off to the Congress this morning in between strategy discussions with his officers. He writes:

"We are now Encamped with the Main body of the Army on the Heights of Harlem where I should hope the Enemy would meet with a defeat in case of an Attack, if the generality of our Troops would behave with tolerable resolution. But, experience, to my Extreme affliction, has convinced me that this is rather to be wished for than expected."[11]

The General's "affliction," as he puts it, is not so much with the troops as it is with the Congress itself. However his words are guarded. Far more so than they were almost two weeks ago when he spoke out boldly against the military system the Continental Congress has imposed upon the American Army.

On September 4, The General had written to the President of the Congress, "We are now, as it were, upon the eve of another dissolution of our army."

His reference then was to the expiration of the Congress-approved, short-term enlistment periods. Most of the soldiers under him had enlisted for terms which would expire at the year's end. Some before. Consequently he devoted most of the lengthy letter to the evils of the Congressional military system.

His anger was far from veiled. In fact his opinion was unusually blunt. He argued that both men and officers needed better pay and more inviting inducements. Some enlistments, he contended, should be for the entire duration of the war. Referring to officers, he said in part:

> "It becomes evident to me then, that, as this contest is not likely to be the work of a day, as the war must be carried on systematically, and to do it you must have good officers, there are in my judgment no other possible means to obtain them but by establishing your army upon a permanent footing and giving your officers good pay. This will induce gentlemen and men of character to engage; and, till the bulk of your officers is composed of such persons as are actuated by principles of honor and a spirit of enterprise, you have little to expect of them."[12]

In the past month he has seen happen what he predicted: a militia impatient to return home, "going off" in large numbers, even whole regiments at a time; a spreading, disheartening morale affecting the regulars, the Continentals, and the State armies; and the diffusion of a dispiriting infection throughout the country that is instilling panic.

The Congress' dread of "standing armies"[13]—a fear born out of their costs, misuse and needless bloodshed by Europe's monarchs— has prevented, until now, any change or improvement in the system. But today a more frightened Congress, reeling from the Battle of Long Island, is slowly revising its thinking and its dread of "standing armies."

This morning as the American Commander's latest message is

traveling by courier express from Harlem to Philadelphia, the Congress will be resolving that 88 battalions be enlisted "as soon as possible to serve during the present war."[14] So, though now unaware of it, the Commander-in-Chief is winning a partial victory over the nation's representatives in his quiet, patient battle with the lawmakers.

The General Takes the Offensive

The American Commander's opponent, surrounded by his vast military machine somewhere in the forests over the Hollow Way down below the plains of Harlem, has him puzzled. In an attempt to look into Sir William's plotting brain, The General has ordered a probing reconnaissance.

In the Continental Army there is a highly respected, fearless band of scouts known as The Rangers. Led by Colonel Knowlton, they are a part of the Connecticut regiments. It is Colonel Knowlton and 120 of his men who volunteer for The General's special reconnaissance mission.

It is their stealthy, probing movement toward the Hollow Way and in toward the enemy's forest-clad positions which Hitchcock on the Bluff Rock is unable to see. Even the British pickets have not as yet observed them.

It was before dawn that Knowlton and his corps set out from the American lines. They moved southward across the Hollow Way and slowly stole up toward the woods on the enemy's plateau. Beyond those woods is Howe's left flank and the main British army in the distance.

The young, erect, cool, courageous six-footer, Lieutenant Colonel Tom Knowlton, is idolized by his men. Courteous and affable, Knowlton has never been known to raise his voice or lose his temper. One of his ardent patriot officers is Captain Nathan Hale.

Hale, it is rumored throughout the camp, recently volunteered for a special espionage assignment which it is believed he is even now carrying out behind the enemy lines in Long Island.[15]

Knowlton's men, who will blindly follow him into almost any situation, move perilously close within their enemy's territory. An empty stone house on their way seems to be a good point to halt and reconnoiter. But just as they approach the building the advance picket guards of Major General Alexander Leslie's light infantry battalions spy them and sound the alarm. Within minutes some 400 of Leslie's infantry start closing in.

Leading his men to cover behind the farm's stone wall, Knowlton, whose corps is but one quarter the strength of the British force, orders his men to open fire from their protected positions. So devastating is the Americans' fusillade that the light infantry stops and slowly pulls back.

At this point Knowlton observes a large body of enemy troops emerging from the forest and moving around their left, intent upon outflanking them. The circling body is the 42nd Highlanders, the Black Watch Regiment.[16]

Meanwhile the sharp cracking exchange of musket fire alerts both encampments high on their zealously guarded plateaus. There on the northern rise the American Commander and his staff hear, though cannot see, what is taking place. But they know that Knowlton has advanced too far and been spotted. The General immediately orders all regiments under arms.

The Continentals are eager to wipe out yesterday's disgrace. A do or die spirit rises among the troops for action in battle.

It is that strange, natural stimulus of man that now works to erase his humiliation at whatever the cost. And the Kip's Bay debacle on top of the defeat on Long Island and the expulsion from the city stings the Continentals to the quick.

Knowlton, seeing the inadvisability of making a further stand and having now lost ten of his comand in the brush with the light infantry, orders his corps to fall back. They do so in good order, getting off an incessant blanket of musketry as they withdraw. Leslie's battalions follow but come to an abrupt halt at the edge of their plateau as though sweeping off some annoying insects.

A Fur-raising Bugle Call

From all appearances the British disinterest in further pursuit seems to have closed the action completely. Then suddenly, as though mocking the flight of the American Rangers in their retreat to their defense lines, the British bugler blows the bugle-horn notes which are customarily used, as everyone knows, to sign the end of a fox-hunt.[17]

Among the American Continentals there are many former fox-hunters including the Chief himself. Nothing now could be more insulting than this in heaping one humiliating disgrace upon the other.

Throughout the American camp anger boils. This time the King's men have gone entirely too far in adding scorn to scourge. Not even some of the tales of atrocities, allegedly committed by both sides, could have provoked and incited more anger than the insulting bugler's horn on the ears of the Continentals. To them it meant the enemy pictured them as frightened, fleeing foxes, slinking back into their holes.

Though all in earshot of the firing are certain that some American unit has been attacked, chased and or captured, and that the insulting bugle call is the enemy's proclamation of another victory, only The General and the staff command know of Knowlton's scouting probe.

The firing assured them that something is revolving about the colonel and his Rangers. And so, at the first sound of rifle fire, Adjutant General Joseph Reed was ordered to ride down and determine the source of the exchange and the status of Knowlton's corps.

Galloping back to the Commander in order to urge that immediate reinforcements be sent to Knowlton's aid, Reed comes up to the side of his superior just as the insulting bugle call sounds. And at this precise moment the Redcoats come into view on their plateau. The sight and the sound stiffens The General as well as the officers under him. His eyes suddenly become beady and cold.

When Reed recounts the events of the day in his letter to his wife tomorrow, he will say: "By the time I got to him (The General), the enemy appeared in open view and in the most insulting manner sounded their bugle horns as is usual after a fox chase. I never felt such a sensation before; it seemed to crown our disgrace (the rout from Kip's Bay)."[18]

Almost flying, Old Magnolia races down through the center of the three lines of entrenchments and fortifications guarding the American heights from the high ground on the East River to the similar rocky shelves on the Hudson. The General comes up behind Knowlton's corps, withdrawing in good order and carrying their dead and wounded up on the American plateau.

Commending Knowlton and his Rangers, The General immediately decides upon a stratagem which could take the enemy off guard. It also could help to parry the bugler's blow and possibly somewhat counteract yesterday's indignity to the Continental Army.

He orders Brigadier General John Nixon to take 150 volunteers from his brigade and feint a frontal attack under the command of Lieutenant Colonel Archibald Crary of Rhode Island. Crary is to draw the British light infantry down to the open ground of the Hollow Way.

If the feint succeeds, a larger force is to sweep around on the east and encircle the British light infantry's right flank. Then, through a fierce, lightning, two-prong attack from the front and rear, the enemy battalions are to be cut off and surrounded before their reinforcements can be summoned. It is a daring plan with as much chance of failure as it has of success.

For the main flanking movement, The General turns over its execution to Knowlton and his Rangers who were almost similarly entrapped earlier by the identical British light infantry maneuver. The Rangers are given the support of three companies of riflemen from General George Weedon's Third Regiment of Virginians under the command of Major Andrew Leitch.

Leitch, who has just recently come up from the South to join the main army, will lead a 230-man party. In all the full flanking force will comprise 350 troops. They will attempt to maneuver behind some 400 of the King's light infantry under Leslie.

Exactly as planned the feint works.[19]

Crary's volunteers boldly advance into the Hollow Way as though in retaliation for the attempt to encircle the Rangers. Their move invites Leslie's Redcoats who take the bait and march to the encounter.

Running down the hill from off their plateau, the advancing British infantrymen throw their fire from behind fences, stone walls and bushes. But their distance from the American frontal force is too great for accuracy.

Then, according to instructions, Crary's troops pull back. Firing as they retreat they suck the Redcoats into further pursuit down into the American pocket.

In order to give greater credence to the Crary deception, The General orders the 800 reserves of Nixon's brigade in Crary's support. This invites the light infantry to disregard its flanks under the belief the Americans are concentrating upon a frontal action.

The semblance of an open field, regimented conflict, so disastrous for the rebel army on Long Island, is well maintained for over an hour. During this time the unobserved, stealthily moving Rangers and their supporting riflemen, maneuver behind and almost encircle the British corps in the cup of the Hollow Way.

Guided by Colonel Reed, Knowlton and Leitch arc around Leslie's right. They manage to make their way successfully, first eastward through the woods. And then, doubling back, they slip westward behind the redcoat light infantrymen who are headed straight into the rebels' pocket.

For the Americans all is going well. Only two or three hundred yards more must be covered to put them atop the enemy's plateau, a ledge of rocks. Once there they need only to sweep behind and around to the redcoats' left and tie the knot.

It is a tense moment. Ten more minutes are needed and The General's carefully conceived maneuver will net death or surrender for a big bag of the Crown's finest fighting force.

The Battle

Some of the inexperienced, over-anxious young rebel officers disobey the orders to hold fire until signaled. Their ardor outweighs discipline and reasoning. Prematurely they give the order to fire.

Though boiling with rage at the sound of the shots and the disregard for orders so firmly agreed upon earlier, Reed, Knowlton and Leitch realize they must make the best of it. Warned by the unexpected firing, the alarmed Leslie sees the encircling attempt on his right and rear.

Immediately the major general orders his men to withdraw to an open field some 200 yards west, safely slipping out of the noose. Crary's men and the flanking corps follow in close pursuit.

While the encircling maneuver has failed, the Americans enjoy the chase in their pursuit of Leslie and his fleeing battalions. It is the first time the rebels have ever had a chance to see their enemy's backs. They are determined to make the most of it.

Breaking out of the open buckwheat field the harried redcoats continue their retreat before the advancing American force. Leslie sends for reinforcements as he leads his men to the top ridge of the enemy's high plateau. There they form a line behind a stone fence and again resume their fire.[20]

The fighting becomes intense and the exchange of musketry and rifle shot is heavy and continuous. Reed's horse takes a ball behind his fore shoulder and bolts almost throwing the adjutant general.[21]

Out in front, leading Captains Thornton, West and Ashby's rifle companies and forming a perfect target, Major Leitch reels as one, and then two more balls pierce his body.[22] He is taken with the wounded to the rear. Death soon ends his courageous, short career.

A few minutes later Colonel Knowlton drops to the ground, mortally wounded. Reed dismounts and attempts to comfort him. Before his death he asks Reed if the enemy has been driven off. Reed assures him they have. On each side of the ridge lie the wounded and dying.

Despite the loss of two of their most daring leaders, there is no confusion within the American ranks. In good order the subaltern officers commendably take over command of the Continentals.

It is in direct contrast with yesterday's disorder and panic displayed by the predominantly militia units. As though seeking revenge in quantity for the ignominies heaped upon them, the rebels push on in further pursuit.

From the American heights, the Commander-in-Chief watches the affair grow from a skirmish into a full blown battle. He sends down nine companies of Genèral Reazin Beall's Maryland State troops, then Colonel Paul Dudley Sargent's brigade from Connecticut and Massachusetts.

But most surprising—and of great importance—in with the reinforcements he orders the remnants of Douglas's regiment which hightailed it out of Kip's Bay yesterday. It is purely a morale-builder intended to restore not only the regiment's morale but the army's as well.[2][3]

On the battlefield arrive Generals Putnam, Greene and George Clinton. And in support of the forces, several field guns are put into action. The fierce intensity of the fight increases hourly as the agonizing cries of the fallen rise even above the din of battle.

Leslie's Redcoats, although reinforced by additional light infantry and the Black Watch regiment, fall back before the vigorous American pressure. The British major general looks for support from the frigates which had ascended the river Sunday morning. He is unaware that they moved back downriver. The British field commander calls for more reserves as the rebels bear down upon him.

From their posts three miles in the rear of the British lines, up come the British grenadiers, the 33rd Regiment, a battalion of Hessian grenadiers and a company of jagers hauling two field pieces. In all the enemy have now committed 5,000 troops to repel some 2,000 Americans.

For two hours—from noon to around two o'clock—the fighting rages. In a vain effort to stop the rebel drive the British pour sixty rounds of ammunition into the American ranks. So intense is the enemy fusillade that the Hessians, and then the Scotsmen run low on ammunition. Both units, compelled to retreat, find the rebel pursuers closing in behind them.

Through fields ripe with wheat, through underbrush and forest patches, around rocky slopes and across fences, the Continentals persistently harass the withdrawing King's men.

A general battlefield engagement is what the American Leader knows he must avoid. Difficult though it is for him to stop the hypnotic enthusiasm induced by insults and stimulated by victory, he directs his aide, Tench Tilghman, to order full field withdrawal. And besides, the proximity of the American vanguard to the main British reserves is getting perilously close.

Gloating with success, the American troops sound out in unison a clamorous "Hurra!"[24] It vibrates and echoes through the forests and fields and is picked up and shouted repeatedly down the American lines. With it the entire military action grinds to a halt. In the distance the British troops slowly disappear into the forest areas behind their lines.

The Battle's Toll

When the American costs are counted, 30 are recorded as killed and less than 100 wounded or missing. General Howe will report that his losses totaled 14 killed and 78 wounded. However his figures will differ from those of Hessian Major Baurmeister who will place the British losses at 70 killed and 200 wounded.

Severest loss for the Americans is the death of two popular valiant officers. Knowlton's death will be particularly lamented by his men. Many of them served under him during his heroic stand at Breed's Hill.

The American success after such a long series of defeats and setbacks gives the rebel army a glowing sense of confidence and a renewal of the dignity they had carried from Boston. The news will spread hope throughout the country. For, among other things, the battle has proved that the American Yankee from the North and the American Buckskin from the South can stand side by side with the American woodsmen from the West and fight back in unity when the hour calls for it.

Until today there was much concern, if not downright fear, that the peoples of the country's extremes would not, in time of need, be united in mutual defense. There are many who still are not convinced.

However among those who are is The General himself.

As for the King's men, they have learned again that they can be defeated, and they have learned again that the ragged army is determined to be respected.

Since the news of victory travels rapidly, Lieutenant John Gray over on the Jersey side with his detachment now arriving at

Bourdette's Ferry, hears accounts of the Harlem Heights affair from the ferrymen.

He and his party have made their way up the river's west bank to the foot of the trail to the gorge road. There at the spring pouring down from the mountainside, he stops. It is an ideal spot to break for a rest before ascending the climbing gorge road to the fort's headquarters.

And besides it is right near the Baummeister house!

Leaving his second lieutenant to carry on, he informs Levy and his men that he will meet them on The Mountain. Every man of the detachment knows where the Blue Petticoat Scarf Lieutenant is going. The dust is thick upon his clothes and his face is black with dirt over his tan. Slowly he walks toward the Baummeister homestead.

With weighted steps he rounds the back of the home and approaches the same old Dutch door. At the very moment he does, a piercing shriek—the joyous scream of a woman in love—electrifies the air and echoes through the cove up to The Mountain's top. Its vibrations echo like the soldiers's elated "Hurra!" on the plains of Harlem.

13

Friday, September 20. . .

City on Fire

Bethrothal News At Bourdette's Ferry

Anyone for miles around Fort Constitution who is not aware that Elaine Baummeister is soon to marry The Lieutenant of the blue petticoat neckerchief is either very hard of hearing or does not listen to Ma Kearney's gossip.

When Gray and his battery arrived on The Mountain post last Monday, delightfully surprising all those who knew and had been concerned about them, Jocko Graves was almost as happy over Gray's appearance as Elaine. The boy's close relationship with the two lovers has given him, he feels, a perfect right to share significantly in circulating the betrothal news. One of his biggest pleasures was announcing the event to The Lieutenant's artillerymen on The Rock.

The joyous news has also been widely spread by the ferrymaster himself. In fact Papa Pete is known to have a standing wager with his superior and close friend, Bourdette, the ferry owner. The first to become a grandfather will be the winner. And thus far Old Stephen's only married son is still childless.

Jestingly, Bourdette, in whose river home the Commander-in-Chief has twice been a guest this past summer and wherein American generals are frequently dined, advises Baummeister that The General will keep The Lieutenant busy across at Fort Washington day and night until the war is over. "And," he laughingly assures his friend, "I'll have The General see to it!"

Pete, despite his friends' humor, realizes that Gray and his men, along with the handsome young Jewish officer they acquired in New York, may be permanently assigned to Fort Washington. For there is where they were bound Tuesday morning after leaving Fort Constitution.

And, upon arriving at the Harlem headquarters, the armament, supplies and their successful gun-spiking mission won for the whole company high commendation. This Baummeister learned from a courier yesterday.

To have a future son-in-law like that is something Pete feels he can legitimately brag about. So, in reply to Stephen's jesting, the ferrymaster merely picks his teeth with a twig, spits with perfect accuracy at a jetsamed crate within his usual ten-foot range, and smiles.

Both men now, however, have more important things to do. The Commander's orders today call for General Greene to appoint "a careful officer" at the ferry "to examine passengers and see that none come over but such as have proper passes."[1]

And besides, the commander is due to come across at any hour on his way, reportedly, to inspect the posts at Paulus Hook and Bergen.[2] Things must be neat and orderly whenever he passes through. That is Bourdette's standing rule.

Thirty-one year old General Nathanael Greene, whose arthritic leg causes him to limp—at times more noticeably than at others—has been in command of Fort Constitution only three days.[3] The post's rapid expansion west behind the Bluff Rock fortress has been pushed hard by General James Ewing[4] who preceded Greene

A Century Later—News at the Landing as of Days of Old—Copy of an old print attributed to H. G. Williamson.

as fort commandant. Ewing is to remain and continue in his task, commanding the construction of works and barracks and the expansion of the camp's accommodations.

Brigadier General John Nixon's brigade came across yesterday, feeling exuberant after their successful fight with Leslie's crack infantry troops Monday. Other units are coming in from West Jersey as well as from Manhattan. Some are speculating that all of Manhattan's island may soon be evacuated with the exception of only Fort Washington.

Before the month is over Greene's command at Fort Constitution will comprise, in addition to Nixon's men, Brigadier General James Clinton's brigade, Brigadier General William Irvine's brigade, Colonel Dey's and Bradley's regiments and some fresh militia and state raw recruits from Jersey and Pennsylvania. The post's full complement will number 3,521 troops, rank and file fit for duty, before the end of September.[5]

Consequently the need for tightening security is becoming greater. And Bourdette has assured headquarters that he will do his part in cooperating with the American command.

Down from the main mountain encampment now come riding Greene, Paine, Ewing and their aides. Also, with the staff are Captain Charles Craig and Sergeant Andrew Abbott, the two inseparables whose combined scouting knowledges are almost legend in the army.

But Abbott's woodsmanship, knowledges and ability have been legend with The Mountain people of the Palisades since the twenty-seven year old descendant of the Great Chief Oratam of the Lenni Lenape Haqninsaq, or Achensacky, Tribe was a youth roaming through The Mountain's crags and along the river's bank.

No one living, it is said, knows so well every foot of land in the valleys to the west and the animal and man-made pathways to the distant "open frontier"[6] as does Andy Abbott. As for Captain Craig, there is no question as to his ability . . . when he is sober.

All are carefully groomed in preparation for meeting the American Commander and his party. Bringing up the rear is Tom Graves, who has been told by the post's surgeon that he may never have full use of his arm again. In the wagon-seat beside Graves is his father-worshipping son.

Both are in the camp's headquarters' wagon. Jocko handles the reins. Three saddled horses are tethered to the backboard in the event The General and his aides do not bring across their own.

The welcoming party dismounts before the sentry's house where

Bourdette and Baummeister, whose arm caressingly lops over his daughter's shoulder, engage Greene in conversation. In the midstream they see the Commander-in-Chief's boats approaching.

Greene informs Bourdette of the officers assigned to examine the ferry passengers. Then turning to Elaine and her father, he says, "My best wishes to you, Mademoiselle. It would be difficult here on The Mountain not to have heard the news that your good father is acquiring one of our finest officers for a son-in-law."

Elaine's wide blue eyes sparkle happily in the glint of the early morning sun. They seem to reflect the streams of sunlight from the water and the cloudless azure heavens as she replies in her usual, frank, unruffled manner, "Thank you, Sir, but we have no idea when that will be."

"Humbug!" interjects the Ferrymaster. Then, casting a mischievous glance at his friend and employer, Baummeister declares, "Der shooner der bester. Der shad runs der river here only vunce der year."

"Papa!" scolds Elaine. "Stop it!"

And Pete obediently stops. The middle-aged ferrymaster's weather-roughened face twitches. His lips pucker impishly into a wry smile beneath the graying locks hanging out from under his Dutch cap. His eyes twinkle in devilish delight as puffs of smoke slowly rise up from out the glowing bowl of his inseparable pipe.

Turning from her father and toward Greene, Elaine tells the post's commander, "Your spy system is remarkable, General. I only knew myself on Monday. And I know only the few who knew."

It is the fort's adjutant, Tom Paine, who now joins in the conversation saying, "You forget, Mademoiselle, that the Commandant and the American battery have Jocko Graves assisting in espionage."

Greene smilingly nods his head as Elaine replies, suddenly fully enlightened, "Ah, yes! Now I understand!"

Baummeister and even Bourdette laugh as all join in. All except Elaine whose eyes turn up the sloping roadway to Jocko.

Holding the reins of his three horses, but keeping his eye on the group in their conversation, Jocko intuitively felt the discussion had turned to him when eyes glanced in his direction. So hesitatingly and sheepishly he waved to Elaine who waves smilingly in return.

Greene closes the conversation as The General's boats move into the landing, saying to Elaine, "Whenever it is, you must let me know. If it takes a whole regiment to get your lieutenant to the nuptials, which I am sure it will not, I'll see to it he gets there."

Then with a twinkle in his eye he adds, ". . . And that he gets a full half-day leave for the occasion."

Bourdette and Baummeister leave the group to supervise the docking of the boats and to greet the Continental Army Leader. Craig and Abbott also move in on the wharf. Both have acted as escorts and guides for The General on his previous inspections through the valley.

Born Out Of Opposite Poles

The Craig-Abbott comradeship is an unfathomable enigma to the men and officers who know them. When sober, Craig is a flawless woodsmen, a dauntless and beloved leader for whom his men have unbounding faith and respect. That is when it comes to making their way through uncharted forests, over mountains and across rivers, night or day. When drunk he is unrecognizable.

Were it not for Abbott's strange, sympathetic covering of Craig's irresponsibilities when he is drowned in firewater, the scout company's captain would have long ago probably lost his command despite his valuable talents.

Abbott whose people suffered, died and eventually disintegrated years ago largely owing to the white man's alcohol, has come to like Craig. The two men of different worlds share a mutual trust for one another. The captain does not stand on custom and protocol. It was he who demanded that Abbott be given the non-commissioned officership in the scouting company. And it is Abbott who, as the last of the great Chief Oratam's descendants, knows the strangle-holding addiction horrors of the White Man's Curse even upon the white man himself.

There are two things Craig and Abbott have in common. One is their admiration for the American Commander. The other is a deep, instinctive love for nature—the outdoor life—for the land and its bounteous gifts to man and for the untouched wildernesses yet untrammeled and unraped. These two bonds cement the friendship of the silent twosome.

For both Craig and Abbott are men of few words. Far better are they at imitating the cry of the eagle, the roar of the mountain lion and the eerie nocturnal noises of the primeval forests than they are at conversing with their own kind.

Thus, the bonds between them are deeply rooted in the earth

from out of which they sprang and from out of which, they believe spring all things, good and bad. So, enduringly strong are the ties that bind these two men, born out of opposite poles.

On the dock Paul joins his sister. Others too have heard of the arrival of "some important persons." Whenever that announcement goes through the cliffside and along the edge waters, hausfraus, children, servants and soldiers alike become curious.

And customarily they congregate near the cliff trail where the waters of the mountain spring trickle down the rocky precipice, then gushingly fall to the foot of the ravine. There by the horse-trough, where the stage coaches generally discharge their ferry-going passengers and where Ma Kearney and Klep clashed, has been the gathering place for gossipers, speech makers and for the reading of proclamations and announcements for many years.

Monday's victory on the heights of Harlem imbued the spirits of civilians and soldiers with renewed hope. The fear that all Manhattan may be lost is still uppermost in the minds of the inhabitants. A number of them derive their livelihood from the river, or from their farms over The Mountain. Some exist from their commerce with the island and the city at its foot.

The concentration of so many troops at Fort Constitution has, however, offset much of their dependence upon trade across the river. Loyalists and neutrals are as fearful about the fort's development and expansion as the patriots are happy over its presence and expansion, especially since, in the immediate vicinity, Tory sympathizers are silent and stay out of sight and out of mischief.

This is particularly so since Monday when Gray's men stumbled by chance on a cache of weapons and ammunition in a deserted farmhouse on their way up the river trail. It was at a spot north of Paulus Hook. They had paused at midday to eat before continuing on their way to Bourdette's.

A few of Gray's men, scouting for fruits and berries, saw a figure dismount at an old, abandoned house. When they approached the building, he suspiciously got back on his horse. However, the soldiers closed in around him and held the animal's reins.

His actions and stammering increased their curiosity especially in view of the fact that enemy vessels were anchored off Bull's Ferry. A few minutes later they discovered a "large quantity of lead, musket balls and buck shot"[7] which he denied knowing anything about.

The Lieutenant promptly dispatched one of his own men with

an express to Colonel Durkee, crowning the suspect's embarrassment by having the messenger use the captured man's horse.

Giving his name as Nicausie Klep, the prisoner and the stores were held until a detachment from Paulus Hook arrived. Confiscating the find, the Hook's men took the stores and the suspect back to the post. The Lieutenant, though offered the opportunity to keep the horse, refused and sent the animal along with Klep back to Durkee.

At the Paulus Hook post, Klep disclaimed all knowledge of the cache, declaring he had stumbled upon it and believed Gray's men were Tory raiders. Klep, producing a string of Whig names in the area of English Neighborhood and Liberty Pole, was permitted to go on his way.

That discovery of arms and the British frigates off the shore caused all posts from Bergen Point north to Fort Constitution to be on the alert for raiders and mischief.

Howe's Undercover Work Threatens Bergen Neck

The American Commander's inspection of the south end of the long Bergen peninsula and the valley will determine how long Paulus Hook, Bergen Village and Bergen Point can be held. Increasing Tory activity up the Bergen Neck, opposite Staten Island and north, and the outstretching tentacles of the British army make it questionable whether further maintenance of those posts is advisable.

In collusion with General Howe's undercover machinations, the Tory activities are becoming difficult for the scattered American outposts to cope with despite the heartening morale effect the stations have upon Whig sympathizers and neutrals leaning toward the cause.

Only yesterday the Howe brothers issued a proclamation urging all Americans "to return to their allegiance, accept the blessing of peace, and to be secured in a free enjoyment of their liberty and properties."[8]

Since the failure of Admiral Howe to reach the Congress through the conference at the Billup House, there is left no recourse except to appeal directly to the populace. The proclamation is a veiled threat which Tories will use, intimidating, raiding and pillaging those who do not defect and are too remote from American posts to enjoy their protection.

So the rebel Leader must come to some decision regarding the lower neck and its far-flung outposts. At the landing Bourdette heartily greets his friend, The General. And briefly and courteously the Continental Army's Chief accepts the greetings of the reception party.

Slyly Jocko brings the Commander-in-Chief's horse close to Elaine in order that she and the children gathered around her will be able to see The General close-up. The soldiers, guards and the reception committee have already tightened around him so that the youngsters cannot see. Jocko's considerate act assures them of a view for now the American Chief must come to the horse. And so he does.

Baummeister rejoins his daughter by the carriage stone where the children, Jocko and The General's horse await him. Greene and Paine whisper something to the big man who has previously recognized and spoken to the Ferrymaster. The General frowns slightly as though not fully comprehending Greene's message, then smiles and courteously addresses Elaine.

"Milady," he says in a cool, unemotional voice as he is about to mount the horse whose reins Jocko holds, "I have difficulty choosing officers as you must know. You, from what I hear, have exhibited good wisdom and excellent discretion in doing the same thing. I wish you happiness. And I must add that I indeed trust he will launder his neckerchief in time for the nuptial."

For the first time that her father can remember, he sees Elaine blush. For once in her life she seems speechless. She had not expected the army's Chief would notice her. But to speak to her! And with accurate knowledge of her betrothal! She is taken completely by surprise.

Neither blushes nor reticence have ever been part of her character, yet now her only response is a polite curtsy.

Jocko smiles broadly in amazement at Elaine's embarrassment as he looks up at The General who recognizes him from other visits and from Long Island's battle.

"I thank you, Jocko," he says. "How fares your father and his wound?"

Almost as embarrassed and amazed as Elaine, Jocko now is struck dumb and nods, looks and points to his father standing by the wagon to the Chief's rear. As the rebel Leader's head turns, Big Tom replies.

"Jus middlin', Gen'l Suh," Big Tom answers as he pats his sling-held arm with his good hand. "Jus middlin', thankus, Gen'l."

As the American Supreme Commander nods with an understanding shake of his head, Jocko, finding his voice, says:

"Tain't even dat good, Suh!"

"You take care of him, Jocko," commands The General. "You are a man now."

"Yas, Suh," the boy replies.

With a brisk wave of his hand the Commander and his party ride off and up the gorge road.

In the past when The General's personal servant, Billy and his horse, Blueskin, have not come across with The General and his mare, Old Magnolia, the Continentals' Commander has enlisted Big Tom Graves. And on short trips Jocko has often tagged along.

Unaware of this, Elaine's pupils look in awe at Jocko. The General had actually talked to him! He had held his horse! To them suddenly Jocko's small stature has risen higher than General Greene's.

Elaine has told the youngsters of Jocko's experiences alongside of his father in the Brooklyn battle. That was some time ago and made only a passing impression on the children. Now they have seen Jocko speak to The General and hold his horse. This made their eyes open and the Graves youth their hero.

After overcoming their awe Elaine takes advantage of an academic opportunity and asks each one to give his impressions of the American Leader. All have learned about "Liberty Poles," and now before them has stood the chief figure, the nation's symbol in the fight against European control of America's destiny. None of them had ever been so close to him before.

"Ise didn't know he was so big and stood so straight. Jus' like Indian Andy," says Joseph.

"*Sergeant* Andy Abbott!" Elaine snaps, sternly correcting the West India-born youth, as though she could prevent youngsters from using their own identifications of adults they know and talk about.

"And he has such nice eyes!" adds Katie May.

"Did ya see his scars, Missy?" inquires Katie May's brother, Ben. "Did ya sees his scars? Ise never knowed he had them. Ise never knowed *he* had the pox."

"It isn't important what we look like, Ben," Elaine philosophically injects, echoing the homespun maxims of her parents. "Isn't it what we are inside and what we do outside that counts?"

Ben looks quizzically at her for a brief second before replying, "P'haps maybe youse right, Missy." he answers. "P'haps. But times is when Ise feels youse wrong, Missy."

And so they go on describing the man they had heard so much

about. Few of them had ever seen him before, even from a distance.

Ten-year old Hans thinks he looks too stern and strict, but likes the way he dresses, his blue coat and "pretty gold things on his shoulders." Soon the youngsters are learning new military words such as "epaulettes," "cockade" and "surcoat." Hans also talks about The General's powdered hair and especially the beautiful small sword and pistol at his side.

Back in Marie Louise's parlor-desecrated classroom the subject for the morning is pre-determined. Besides reading and writing, the big subject of the day will be the American Rebellion, the thirteen new united states' fight for freedom and all they can find out about the Continental Army's Chief.

And today Graves urges his son to attend Elaine's class. It did not take much persuading on his father's part, once the team was unhitched, for Jocko, smelling very much like a horse, to beeline it back down the clove path to join Elaine's school.

On the Bluff Rock the American Commander holds his field glasses on the Harlem plains. His favorite observation spot[9] has always been a high ledge piece just in front of the Barbette Battery.

Directly across the river, above Jeffery's Hook, he sees troop detachments manning Fort Washington and the post's outlying entrenchments. Above and to the northeast he focuses upon King's Bridge and then trains his sights southward down Manhattan's island to the British-held city, the bay south of its tip and the enemy's ships in the Narrows and off Staten Island. Owing to the concave curvature of the Palisadean precipices he can see only the eastern tip of the isolated and lonesome Paulus Hook post.

Seeing nothing warranting a change of his plans to visit the endangered outlying garrisons, he and his party make their way down the western slope of the Palisades with Craig, Abbott and the scouts well in the lead. At the King's Highway in English Neighborhood, the party turns left toward the Three Pidgeons Tavern[10] in Bergen Woods.

There they stop to rest and eat before making their way to the Bergen Post. Farther on they pause at the Tuers house before leaving for the furthermost works at Bergen Point. From there they double back, taking the road out of Bergen Village to the Van Vorst homestead and then on to the causeway to Paulus Hook[11] where they are greeted by Colonel Durkee.

It is now past ten o'clock in the night. On The Rock a busy day is ending, and also it is the end of another hard 24 hours on the square bastioned, rapidly expanding fortress with its construction of protecting earthworks on The Mountain's summit.

The new, big field fort is west of the Barbette Battery on the Bluff Rock and across the deep ravine, or gorge, which separates it. Soon it will become the central communications center for the American army. And its easterly guardian will be the Bluff Rock's works hundreds of feet above the river.

Lieutenant Joseph Hodgkins of the Massachusetts line is on night duty on The Rock's Barbette Battery. His eyes are heavy. All day he has, along with others, been helping build some of the hundreds of log huts which the men are erecting around the main fortification and encampment site. The work is rushed, for each day more units are brought over to the fortress on top of Jersey's Palisadean wall.

Hodgkins had slept only on the ground since the Battle of Long Island. He is proud of his own log hut which will have a chimney, an inside fireplace and a cot off the ground.

The dwelling will be shared with four to six or more men throughout the coming cold winter. For certainly this campaign is rapidly coming to an end until next spring. Everyone is just about convinced of that! And certainly these grounds on The Mountain provide the ideal place to drop 24-pounders on the Crown's ships should they dare to run the blockade below in the coming winter months.

Besides, who is so foolish as to believe that Howe will attempt to by-pass Fort Washington and Fort Constitution and launch an invasion of the Jerseys this late in the year?

So, to pass the time, Hodgkins, under the candlelight of the sentry house, begins writing his wife in Ipswich. But he will be interrupted, and another ten days will pass before he finally finishes his letter. It reads in part:

> "We are on the Jersey hills. . . . and I hope we shall stay here this campaign as I have been at the trouble of building a log house with a stone chimney. I got it fit to live in three days ago, before which I had not lodged on anything but the ground since we left Long Island . . ."[1][2]

In the Distance, A Fiery Glow

Breaking in upon him, a sentry informs the officer that a fiery glow like that of a great fire can be seen on the foot of York island. The excited sentry tells the lieutenant that it is of such intensity he should see it for himself.

Grumbling, through the brisk, chilling wind that blows hard against his face as he climbs the parapet, with only the sound of barking dogs breaking the silence along the river's edge, Hodgkins is jarred by the sight in his field glasses. Training his binoculars on the glowing spectacle fifteen miles south, the duty officer is almost hypnotized by the unbelievable spectacle. New York city in flames!

Even as he watches to make certain that the distant inferno is really what it appears to be before informing his commander, Hodgkins sees the massive yellow sheets of flame rising wildly and spreading out on a northwestward course up the town's west side.

Since Greene is at Fort Washington on an inspection tour and will spend the night there, Hodgkins' superior is General Ewing. It is up to Ewing to decide whether to inform the Commander-in-Chief who rode in late this evening and is bedding the night at Bourdette's house.[13]

Across the river the dim outlines of Fort Washington's bastions are barely distinguishable under the starlit darkness of the cold September night. Flickering campfires dot the outlying encampments and sentry posts along the American Entrenchments and breastworks.

The eerie campfire lights cast long, ominous shadows which make the forward pickets uneasy as the lengthening shapes triple the size of the figures, occasionally moving in front of the flames. Similarly the size of the parapets extend themselves like elongated walls over the barren grounds.

Frequently a hoot owl breaks the dark silence. He is answered by the howls of loose dogs. To the fidgety, young militia pickets, whose farm or mountain cultures have left them bound in Stygian fears and superstitions, it is a night for warlocks and witches.

Upsetting their imaginative adventures into unearthly hallucinations with ghosts and evil spirits, the banging of pots and frying pans, falling to the earth from an overturned table at the hands of a family of exploring raccoons, jars the youthful sentries back to earth.

With it rises the excited voices of the women in the encampment on the outskirts of the Harlem bivouac located east and away from headquarters.

Even at this late hour the camp women carry on their arduous drudgery, cleaning, baking, washing clothes and cooking utensils while trying to put their children to sleep, or rock the little ones with a lullaby, some sweet and low and other lyrics scary enough to cause the more obstreperous tots to quickly rush into dreamland before "the Big Banshee" can catch them.

An Irish-born mother's voice, orchestrated by a baying hound, sings melodiously awesome through the outstretched arms of the shadowy trees:

". . . If you don't go to sleep, the Banshee will come, And far, far far a . . way he'll take you. . . . He'll bury you in a bog so deep, and nev . . er more will you see yer home or yer friends or the ones you love . . . so hush, my little one, hush . . . 'less you want to be a carried a . . way by the Big Banshee. . . ."

The faithful women follow close in the wake of their husbands, loved ones and fathers, many of whom have been drawn into the rebel army by the assurance of pay, food and clothing as well as an intense desire to repel the invaders and fight for their country's independence.

And off by themselves in a separate area of the camp followers' bivouac, are the cruelly shunned, disfranchised and isolated derelicts of the American colonial social structure, the harlots, the widowed common law wives and mistresses.

From all walks of life they have come, lured, fallen, or forced into a huddled mass of humanity, seeking a livelihood—bread and lodging—or daily dreaming of a chance at wealth and station, rapidly evaporating beyond their aging reach. Now many look forward only to the troops' next pay day.

In the darkness on the heights of Harlem along the vast lines of entrenchments, it is difficult to realize thousands of soldiers are nestled close to the gound on beds of leaves for another long and restless night, concealed behind ravelins, redans and redoubts.

On picket duty tonight on the heights are John Gray and Asher Levy. Both are assigned the pre-midnight vigil.

Gray's popular scarf, carefully laundered, mended and pressed three days ago at the Baummeister house, waves around The Lieutenant's neck as he stands on the northwest forward redoubt alongside of Levy. It is the first time in days they have found time for one of their occasional talks about war, peace and the budding America.

They are the topics that they enjoy discussing in addition to Gray's favorite, philosophic subject, "Man's Inhumanity to Man."

And so, high on the parapet, they carry on: The slaves of ancient Egypt . . . Slavery in Eighteenth Century America . . . The persecution of the Jews, the Christians, the Catholics and the Huguenots and others . . . Biases and prejudices and their roots in the wars over religious issues . . .

On and on they go, two hungry scholars clamoring for knowledge and truth.

"But neither you nor I, John," says Levy solemnly, "can do more than drop a grain upon the shore."

"Aye," replies Gray as he takes note of one of his sentries coming down toward him from a prominence to the west. "I agree with you, Asher. "But persecution, born of hate, in turn born of vengeance, and in turn born of prejudices, is tyranny of the worst kind.

"Only when man can see himself in the mirrors of retrospect will your grains of sand hopefully bury man's abominable traits and with them the tyrannies and tyrants they nest and nurse."

Both now take notice of the sentry making his way rapidly toward them. Both assume he wants relief, probably owing to an attack of the "Green Apple Fox Trot."

Changing the subject abruptly as he gestures toward New York town, Levy says, "I have told you how much I owe to Haym Salomon[14] down there. I wish only that you could have met him while we were in the city. He is a loyal friend and a staunch supporter of our cause. So much so that I fear for his life. He is outspoken against the Crown and bitterly denounces the Tories. 'Tis too much so for his own good. His love of liberty may, I feel, earn him a set of chains and possibly the gallows."

The excitedly puffing sentry interrupts, pointing to the city, gasping out, "Lieutenant, look! . . . Look from the parapet wall! The city! It is afire . . . in flames!"

Both Gray and Levy dash to the parapet. Gray squints, reaches for his field glasses and trains them southward. He stands suddenly erect and exclaims, "My God! It's true! He's right!"

Levy's face whitens as he focuses his eyes southward, taking the binoculars offered him by Gray and directing them at the island's tip. Sickened by the mushrooming yellow flames which now rise ever higher, no longer requiring field glasses, Levy shakes his head, saying almost under his breath, "God help poor Haym now!"

Noting that the yellowish light spreads like a fiery, cylindrical roller up from the tip of the west shore toward the heart of the city, Gray immediately orders Levy to notify their superior duty officer, Captain Alexander Hamilton.[15]

"Alert Captain Hamilton that the city is afire to the best of our knowledge .,. . It is what Nat Greene wanted, but I hope, not ordered," Gray tells Levy.

Into Focus: Wanton Destruction

Levy, throwing his canteen strap around his shoulder, looks at Gray, exclaiming angrily, "Wanton destruction! Each side awaits its turn! . . . May God help them down there!"

From the Whitehall Slip, through the Exchange, up Broad Street, the fire rages amid the sounds of rolling wagons, shouting soldiers, and the agonized cries of men, women and children.

Whipped by the strong southeast wind, the towering flames and flying embers appear in the night sky like myriads of flaming witches' brooms, showering sparks that dance wildly over the house-tops. One by one, building after building is ignited and in moments submits itself to the diabolical fury like sacrificial offerings to some ancient god's great funeral pyre.

Frantic excitement fills the air as New York's terror-stricken rush from street to street and house to house, warning families to abandon their homes in the path of the spreading conflagration. Bewilderment turns to fear and fear, confusion as finally panic reigns in terror throughout the famous port city's gruesomely lighted, roasting streets in the cold night wind.

Thatched roofs, easily and quickly ignited by flying sparks, go up like tinder, consumed in minutes. Left exposed are the burning, blackened timbers, adding their stenching, acrid odor to the smoke-laden night air. Soon into the torrid, smoldering ruins the giant timbers crash and crumble with crackling, explosive thuds upon the ground, showering their broken pieces on the streets and walkways.

In the rapidly crawling fire's relentless wake are only smoking, charred remains of houses and buildings constructed a hundred years ago. In moments a century and a half of Dutch and English, hand-hewn settlements, forged out of a wilderness, lie disintegrated as though before some ancient Roman altar honoring the prophecies of the God of Fire, Vulcan himself.

It is as though the massive, hand-hewn beams were determined to close their centuries of life in a final burst of glory. Their dying sparks spent, gracefully they break apart and fall almost gently into a swan-like dive, crashing mightily, back at last, into the dust from out of which they rose. Thousands of these laboriously constructed joists and braces rain down on the once immaculately clean cobblestone streets.

Still better tasting to the flame's hungry tongues are the hand-made shingles. Most of the homes and many of the barns and other buildings are covered by the cedar shingle roofing. Dried out from the hot sun the day before, they catch the slightest spark. The houses on Stone and Beaver Streets, now only burning embers, are testimony to the fire's consummate taste for cedar roofing.

Fiendishly the unchecked flames jump and hurdle through the black sky up the horrendously brilliant, fire-engulfed city's west side. Now the sweeping, yellow peril reaches the King's College grounds. Its tentacles, like golden arms with flaming fingers, creep on, devouring everything inflammable in its path as it crawls toward the Broad Way.

The townspeople, Loyalists and Patriots alike—although few outspoken Whigs now remain in the city—join with the British soldiers and sailors in their futile attempts to fight the fury with water buckets. Two regiments of the Fifth British Brigade have been called in to try to curb the spread.

Its Origin

It started a few hours ago, beginning with an unexplained blaze that originated in the back of The Fighting Cock Tavern. Often called "The Harlots' Nest," the place was located on the wharf near Whitehall. The flames fanned out wildly when no effort was made to control them, leaving the tavern burned to the ground. But the showering sparks danced rapidly in the air, igniting, warehouses, wharf buildings and private homes within minutes.

After that there was no controlling the wind-blown fires and their torching, red hot dancers. It was not long then before blocks of blazing property, stores and wares were enveloped in the holocaust that now threatens all New York City.

Church bells, used to announce fires in the town, summoning firemen and inhabitants, young and old, to help could not be rung. The American troops had taken all the church bells with them. Therefore no alarm alerted the city at the outset when the flames might have been controlled.

In addition the fire companies are undermanned and disorganized. Fire engines and pumps are out of order. And, on top of all this, there is a scarcity of water and a disastrous shortage of fire buckets.

Many of the ships's seamen are enlisted to aid the soldiers in destroying buildings that could furnish connecting fire lanes with other structures. They now work frantically amid crackling timbers, crumbling, charred burning homes and the frequent cries of youth and age seeking loved ones.

All carry, or pull, small carts filled with whatever of their household possessions they can carry. Crazed and confused voices rise up with the smoke, stench and flying sparks, mixed with the ground-rumbling of a hundred wagons brought in by the army.[16]

Dazed and horror-stricken men and women, trailed by wide-eyed, gaping children, carrying in their over-filled arms some pet or cherished toy, give the gruesome night of terror the ugly, frightening appearance of some horrible scene from Dante's *Inferno*.

Every available wagon is piled high with whatever can be loaded quickly of the accumulated furnishings of a lifetime.

"Odd it is," says one British officer to his companion, "to see what one will save in the final choice of things. Those of sentiment often win over those of value."

Wagon after wagon is rapidly driven to The Commons and there emptied on the ground in order to return without delay for another load.

In frenzied bedlam each family tries to find its own salvaged possessions among the scattered piles dumped upon the green. All night long the rumbling army wagons, soldiers, sailors and townsmen go back and forth attempting to empty houses and buildings directly in the path of the unchecked raging destruction. Often the brave, daring young British and Hessian soldiers and sailors barely escape with their lives as the enveloping flames close in around them.

Some families no sooner move out of their doomed homes into a neighbor's or relative's, believed to be safe when that, too, is abandoned as it ignites under a cedar spark. And the exodus repeats itself.

The Reverend Mr. Shewkirk[17] has opened his house on the north end of the city on the corner of Broad Way to all who come by.

Mrs. Sykes is one of those trudging along toward the Shewkirk's haven. Her two children struggle along behind her with their arms carrying as much of their possessions as each can bear. Not a hundred feet from the preacher's home the woman collapses with exhaustion.

On the ladder of his house Shewkirk, who is trying to wet down his roofing, sees the woman fall. Descending rapidly to the ground he carries her inside. The children limp in behind. It is one of many heart-rending scenes simultaneously taking place all over the town.

When the corner house on Shewkirk's street catches fire, the preacher orders all ladders fetched from the burying grounds. Others are borrowed from neighboring cemeteries. Then all of Shewkirk's friends, relatives and his newly acquired congregation form a human chain, carrying buckets of water to the men on the ladders. They in turn hand them to the men on the roof.

Through this cooperation it is not long before the many laborious dips into the well so thoroughly saturate the shingles that the flaking embers resting on them ineffectively struggle and die, or are easily extinguished. And so The Reverend's home is among the fortunate ones saved.

Fortunately the southeast wind has thus far confined the disastrous devastation between Hudson's river and the Broad Way. Credit also goes to the efforts of Howe's men and the hundreds of townsmen who have successfully kept the conflagration to the west of the Broad Way.

A New Kind Of Terror Rises

Under orders from Howe, other British units have been directed to round up every person who looks suspicious. A growing wave of anger is surging through the populace and among the members of the armed forces as well. Rumor is widespread that the fire is the work of Rebels and Whigs or both.

Yet, though only softly whispered, there is hearsay that it is all the fault of the King's men in their pillaging and sacking search for rebels and patriots. So the Whigs guardedly say it is the Crown's raiding parties who started the fires by igniting a known Rebel sympathizer's home without realizing what the wind would do.

Nevertheless, it is generally agreed that the city has been willfully torched. And in the British-held port city it is the Americans who are most suspect in the bearing of the blame.

Newly ignited fires break out in places too far remote from the hotly burning areas to have been started by their sparks.[18] It is this that gives rise to accusations that it is the work of rebel arsonists, continuing their mischief.

Certainly, it is argued, the American army would not be unhappy if the city that General Howe has taken over, is found destroyed and unsuitable for the winter quarters Sir William has counted upon for himself and his troops. And certainly the American Commander would not shed tears over the burning of the vital port city that has nested so many Loyalists and Tory inhabitants.

Hearsay has it that "villains" were left behind by the Rebel army and were concealed by patriot sympathizers until tonight. Then, according to the rumors, at a given hour they came out of hiding and began their "dastardly" work. And so, as the rumors spread, the witch hunts begin.

Now a wild search is under way for anyone who even looks like a rebel. Some poor wretches who were said to have had matches and combustibles hidden in their clothes, or in their houses, are taken. Some, it is said, were caught setting fires inside empty buildings, a good distance from the main conflagration. For some this provides an excellent opportunity to get rid of an objectionable neighbor.

It takes little to convince the maddened mobs and the infuriated soldiers and sailors of guilt. Many of the British soldiers have been assigned to quarters in a number of the homes now burned to the ground.

Reason and sanity suddenly seem to be swept away with the flames and devoured by the smoke-laden wind in the violent darkness of the harrowing night.

One sailor has collared a man who reportedly abused a woman as she was carrying water to the fire engines. Amid shouts he was accused of cutting the handles of her buckets. How else, she yells excitedly, could they have so easily come apart?

No time is wasted. The seamen and soldiers on the spot string up the unfortunate man by his heels.

Suddenly the wind seems to be shifting. It begins with gusts from the west. For the first time the billowing smoke and fiery fragments begin to blow across the Broad Way. Now the entire east side of town is alerted. Frantically the eastsiders dip into their drying wells in a mad rush to wet down their roofs and sidings.

It is there on The Commons where the remaining possessions of the homeless have been strewn, presumably safe from the incendiarism. Now a wild scramble begins. What was simply a massive center of confusion in an effort to locate one's belongings, becomes turmoil as those who have found their things and their families try to move them again out of the flaming path.

Fear, bordering on panic, soon grips the entire east side of the city. It is heightened by a new and dreadful sight—the creeping serpentine-like flames, encircling and gorging upon the beautiful, shingled spire of old Trinity Church.

Rapidly, like giant red and gold fingers, lifting from out the fiery depths of hell's furnaces, the crawling horror slithers upward from the spiral tower's base. Then, in a final gulp, synchronized with the shifting, stiffening wind, the graceful steeple is engulfed in a blanket of fury.

Flames Engulf Trinity's Steeple

Thousands of hours by devout parishioners in their thankful and obeisant dedication to their God go down within the edifice, entombed beneath the pyre. Despite the many hands, the countless hours, the love, the efforts and the sacrifices that have gone into its magnificent construction, in a few brief moments the shingled-covered conical spire becomes a gigantic flaming yellow torch.

Like a lofty pyramid, enveloped in blazing waves of fire, the spectacle is visible for miles. It presents a scene majestically but sickeningly grotesque. The sight will never be erased from the minds of those who now stop in horror and look up in the eerie light of the night's unforgettable drama.

All of the wild-eyed inhabitants have heard its great, bronze bell toll out across the island, the rivers and the bay, summoning the Sunday worshippers. And many are those who welcomed its sound in the fog-bound waters.

Soon every shingle is burned away. Only the skeletal frame of the flaming structure is silhouetted against the black sky. Every separate timber severs its way apart and falls in a fiery death into the churchyard below, spewing embers over the headstone-marked graves of the long-deceased builders, founders and forgotten parishioners. It is like a parting gesture to the peace that once was here.

Now only the basic columnar beams remain ablaze, standing like the burning remnants of some ancient, treasured and noble prehistoric monster. Then, as though by a given signal, the towering spiritual elegance of a waning era—the former, simple semblance of man's eternal reach for righteousness and heaven—topples and crumbles in the appalling holocaust.

No pity is spared for the wretched suspects caught in the wild "witch-hunting" net. Loyalists who were hounded by Whigs and Patriots when the Americans were in the city, now seek revenge. Former tormenters, neutrals, or just long-standing enemies, become the tormented. The Tories become the accusers, judge and jury. The soldiers the executioners.

No more than hearsay evidence is necessary. One or two are charged with carrying fire brands in their hands. Bodily the sus-

pects are lifted and thrown screaming for mercy into the roaring
fires. Some are spitted on bayonets and hanged. Others, more
fortunate, are bludgeoned to death on the spot while a few are
only bayoneted. These are left to die, engulfed in flames. Those
slightly suspect are carted off to prison.

Then, almost as rapidly as it rose, the brisk west wind subsides.
And as it does the tongues of flame curl back, withdrawing into
the charred ruins beneath them. For awhile all fear to believe their
eyes. As the sickening stench of charred wood, burning debris,
mixed with the acrid smell of scorched fats, beef hides and vats of
molasses, settles nauseatingly down upon the blackened city in a
shawl of putrid mist, cheers go up in a rising crescendo.

It is realized at last under the pre-dawn darkness that the worst
is over, and the city east of the Broad Way is saved from the
disaster that has consumed the west side.

Throughout the early hours of the morning, as throughout the
whole night, and long into the sunlight of the coming day, the
crackling fires will persist, slowly expiring, starved to death by
their own gluttony.

The British soldiers and seamen are credited by the populace for
preventing greater destruction and tragedy than has occurred. It
was as much their valor as that of the inhabitants that prevented
the blaze from spreading deep across the Broad Way. And it was
largely due to some of these units that control was finally achieved
over the debacle.

As it is, one quarter of New York lies in smoking ruins fourteen
hours after the first flames broke out.[19] The oldest and the largest
of the English churches is no more. The old Lutheran church is
destroyed. St. Paul's at the upper end of Broad Way narrowly
escaped the fate of Old Trinity. All of Pearl Street is a blackened
wasteland. And no one will ever know how many lives have been
sacrificed this night to Vulcan's fury.

Four hundred and ninety-three houses[20] and possibly a total of
one thousand buildings will be counted among the ashes by eleven
o'clock tomorrow morning, September 21. And by then the last
of the embers will be burning out.

Many of the city's homeless inhabitants have walked dazed
throughout the streets all night. Many of them will now be
reduced to beggary.

It is said Sis Kilburn lost two houses. Pell lost three. Jacobsen
one. The Widow Zoeller lost her home. Lepper lost his. Eastman,
among many others, lost his. The list is long and tragic.

The responsibility for the conflagration will never be pinpointed. Many will suffer punishments, justly or unjustly no one will ever know for sure. No firm proof of guilt, or evidence that would warrant conviction, will be found. Actual responsibility is never to be accurately determined.

In the years to come, Whigs will blame Tories. Tories will accuse Whigs. The Continental Army will blame the British armed forces. And the King's men will charge the rebels with full responsibility. For this is the way of war.

Howe Angrily Charges Incendiarism

Suspicions will fall heavily upon the Whigs and Patriots owing to their earlier, widely circulated boast, "We'll set fire to our own houses before we will let them be occupied by the King's troops."

Though it was considered only an empty threat of bravado at a time when the Americans were in full control of the city, it is now one of General Howe's convincing arguments. The boast is proof for Howe that some of the inhabitants conspired with the rebel army in carrying out the incendiary act. Now the "empty threat" has come back to imperil all those even slightly sympathetic toward the American cause.

Further inciting Howe's wrath is word from his intelligence arm, reinforced by enraged Tories, that the American troops holding the post at Paulus Hook happily enjoyed the sight of the British-held Loyalist stronghold going up in smoke. It is said that the Paulus Hook garrison had a long-standing grievance with the Tory-dominated church congregation at Old Trinity. All of the parishoners there had sent up prayers for the British, it was claimed, but none ever were said for the American cause.[21]

Religious men of the Protestant faith, the Howe Brothers' anger rises when they hear that the Hook garrison sent up a loud and mighty cheer, heard across the water when the Trinity Church spire fell.

Sir William's anger has almost reached the point of infuriation. New York's destruction is for him a major disaster. He had counted heavily upon making full use of the homes to accommodate much of his army throughout the winter, for the city will be his headquarters. He must not only find additional barracks and warehouses for his men and supplies but, in addition, housing for the Loyalists who have lost their homes.

Then, too, he must assign a large number of his forces to the task of cleaning up the ruins and preventing the spread of disease. Adding to his problems is the sudden influx of Loyalists, drawn to the city by the security offered under its British occupation. Many of them fled the port after the Continental Army began moving into it.

Now Howe's newly acquired domestic problem is to see that New York's Loyalists, in addition to his army, are properly sheltered and that the civilian as well as the military population is suitably provided for.

It is a worrisome obligation tacked on to his major objectives: The destruction of the Rebel army, the crushing of the rebellion, and the return of the colonies to the Crown.

General Howe is in no mood for leniency to anyone in any matters pertaining to the American cause. He has done with overtures. The time has come for avenging, for justified retribution.

After all his cautious maneuvering in an effort to save the city from the torch, Howe stands in a sense, defeated.

He knew that New York's burning was a likely possibility for he had heard of Greene's recommendation to the American Commander. He had heard of the Congress's refusal to approve New York's fiery destruction. Erroneously he concluded that its torching would therefore not happen.

Actually he somewhat blames himself for letting down his guard and for misjuding the degree of hate motivating his antagonists. There before him lie the ruins. So he is indeed an angry man.

While the Tory-minded New York press will call the act an "atrocious deed" and charge that the "New England people are at the bottom of this plot," Howe will write Lord George Germaine saying, "the wretches succeeded too well."

At the same time he will order a scrutinous search for any and all of the incendiaries.[22] For there is no doubt in Sir William's mind, nor that of his brother, that the conflagration was a willful act.

Thus the days ahead will not be easy for the patriot sympathizers still in New York. In fear of their lives they will stay inside their homes or places of business as much as possible, often behind closed doors and shutters.

At the height of the fire, up on the heights of Harlem, Greene, Knox and Colonel Magaw kept their glasses glued upon the burning city, writhing in the scorching death throes of its funeral pyre. None of them spoke a word. From all appearances each seemed to be as surprised as the other.

Unlike their staff superiors, the headquarters officers and subalterns chatted in groups scattered widely along Fort Washington's high earthworks. Most of the enlisted men, awakened by the commotion were either not impressed enough to leave their bedding or took one look and returned to it.

One grumbling veteran, still half asleep, queried aloud: "What's so spittin' bad 'bout a fire in York; 'Taint near's bad as was Long Island."

Another, a youth hardly out of his teens and suffering from the agonies of the "French Disease," growls from his bed upon hearing of the flaming city, "Good! I hope every damned whore goes up in fire with it!"

At the forward watch Gray and Levy are still on duty. Levy watched motionless and dazed, his mind almost bordering on shock. He had loved the city—so much so that he kept telling himself, "It cannot be! It cannot be!"

John Gray has come to like and respect the scholarly Jewish youth in the short few days of their acquaintance. He sees much in the second lieutenant's make-up that closely remembles his own interests, leanings, philosophy and ambitions. Therefore he believed he knew what his friend was thinking. But Gray also knew there was nothing he could say or do to soothe Levy's troubled thoughts.

Many of Levy's friends, and Haym Salomon in particular, were down there. Levy thought of them not only as friends but as extensions of himself. And now they were not only embroiled in the striving of the political, ideological forces of a government in overthrow, but also with a physical repercussion of its violence.

The beautiful dream that bloomed from ideas now fights to survive in the scorched earth of the catastrophic war it has spawned. It is the price that ideological dreams must pay to earn their birthright.

So in his friends' hours of distress—at a time they needed him most—Levy suffered the pangs of blameless guilt. He had deserted them, he thought. And a dismal, unwarranted spirit of self-condemnation overcame him as he stood on the parapet, powerless.

Straining to assure himself that his countrymen were not to blame, Gray became chagrined by the fear that they were. Slowly he raised his arm and quietly, commiseratingly, he said with that wordless gesture—a pat of his hand on Levy's shoulder—all that can be said to a grieving friend by a colleague in arms. It is the same mute voice and tapping that centuries of warriors all know no human words can say as well.

Also, Gray's pockmarked cheeks have long since taught him that the tongue is often far more deceptive than the touch. Two eyes, he once said to Elaine, that meet and linger long within each other's depths, speak truthfully, and, like the firm handshake of friendship, say more than one can ever verbally express.

The stocky, solidly built Asher turned. Through eyes that seemed to be fighting to hold back welling emotions, he looked up directly at his slightly taller and older friend. A smile broke faintly across both their faces.

Levy, attempting to steer his thoughts elsewhere, broke the silence, saying, "My transfer to the artillery was approved today. Captain Hamilton informed me when I reported the fire."

"Welcome, then!" Gray replies. "I knew it would be so but it is happy I am to hear it confirmed."

And at the height of the fire up on the great Bluff Rock, some time after Lieutenant Hodgkins assured himself that the mysterious, brilliant light spreading a fan-like glow over New York's tip was indeed the port city in flames, General Ewing and his staff came down The Mountain and across the gorge to The Rock's Barbette. Hodgkins' excited messenger left the sleepy-eyed Ewing no choice.

Having torn himself from a sound sleep, the fort's acting commander only expected to see a speck of fire in the distance. He felt it was his duty to look for himself at whatever it was. The general was soon wide awake, agreeing with his staff and Hodgkins' opinion that they were looking at New York city's burning.

Ewing immediately dispatched a message to the Bourdette House, for it was there that the American Commander was spending the night. Late though it was, the Chief was still in council with Colonel John Glover and the army's engineer, Colonel Rufus Putnam, concerning the recently completed military maps which lay spread out over the Bourdette's large dining room table.

As usual at such times, the Bourdette family in respectful courtesy turned over most of the house and inn to The General and his aides.

Stephen, up in his bedroom could hear the guard's challenge, the messenger's countersign, the commotion following the messenger's entrance and the sudden departure of The General and his officers. The old man guessed that something was up but knew that he would hear all about it in the morning.

Carefully crawling in under the down quilt beside his heavily snoring Rachel, the ferry owner reached out to snuff out the candle, first placing his pipe gently on the night table. In a few minutes his breathing vibrations were sonorously blended with those of his spouse.

Training his binoculars on the distant fiery red blotch which became continuously brighter under the yellowish canopy it threw up into the night sky, the Continental Army's Commander abruptly lowered the field glasses from his eyes.

Turning to Glover who stood staring in amazement at the scene which appeared all the more horrendous without the benefit of an eyepiece, The General calmly looked at the Massachusetts seaman, saying, "Well, I am sure it is so."

Though he registered no definite emotion one way or the other, it was clear to those around him that there was more regret in his voice than any feeling of exultation.

All imagined what he must be thinking. And most knew that the sight surely recalled to his mind—as it did to the memories of those who were with him when the British burned Charlestown June 17 of last year—the scenes of the Charlestown fire. That holocaust was indelibly recalled to all their minds as they watched from the great Bluff Rock, the famous old port city writhing in flaming agony.

Yet as they watched no one mentioned Charlestown. Nevertheless each one of them who was there recalled how the enemy had ordered that city be put to the torch in order to clear it of snipers.

Through their minds ran the common theme of men, armies and people at war: Retaliation, Retribution, Avenging Swords—an eye for an eye.

All those who were in Charlestown that tragic night could not escape remembering far more than what Howe and General Johnny Burgoyne had seen, for the men watching New York in flames were *in* the fire at Charlestown. So British General Johnny Burgoyne's view of the Charlestown burning was not the same as theirs.

Burgoyne watched the Charlestown incendiarism from across the Charles River on that tragic Saturday night in June of Seventy-five. And then he wrote his nephew in England:

"... They (his British regiments) were ... exceedingly hurt by musketry from Charlestown ... Howe sent us word by a boat and desired us to set fire to the town, which was immediately done ...

"Now ensued one of the greatest scenes of war that can be conceived. If we look to the height, Howe's corps ascending the hill in the face of the entrenchments and ... much engaged. To the left the enemy pouring in fresh troops . . . and in the arm of the sea our ships and floating batteries cannonading them. Straight before us, a large and noble town in one great blaze. The church steeples being of timber were great pyramids of fire above the rest . . ."[23]

"Providence, or some good honest fellow . . ."

Again the American Commander lifted his glasses after pulling his wind-blown cape tighter around his throat. For several minutes he held it steady.

Blowing harder now than before, the sharp southeast wind whistled briskly against the Bluff Rock. All of the men, taking a cue from their Chief, pull their cloaks close around them.

They watch as finally the big man drops the field glasses at his side and steps down off the parapet. He again turns to Glover, for whom he has great admiration particularly since the escape from Long Island. Unemotionally and stern of face, the American Leader addresses the ruddy-faced New Englander:

"Providence, or some good honest fellow has done more for us than we were disposed to do for ourselves."[24]

Again down at the landing before going back into the Bourdette House, The General and his party stopped to observe the scene downriver from sea level.

As Glover watched the Continental Army's Commander lifting the binoculars to his face, the New Englander noticed how strongly firm the big man's jaws were set, how flexed were the muscles of his scar-marked features and how his eyes, particularly in the torch-light held by the guards, gave off the glint of a priceless foreign saber. Glover quickly reminded himself that he was prejudiced yet, like Knox, he thinks The General looks good to him under any circumstances.

The Massachusetts colonel was impressed by the seemingly untiring coldness of those eyes—eyes that reflected, he thought, great reservoirs of indefatigability. That glimpse of the American General would be one the Massachusetts colonel would long remember.

Meanwhile the American officers engaged in muffled conversations scattered as they were in small groups.

Then from downriver a messenger from Colonel Durkee's post sped his canoe up on the bank, bringing word confirming that York was burning to the ground.

Now one unanswered question puzzled all: How did it start?

Then the wind changed. The distant southeast sky suddenly began losing its radiance, changing into what might have been compared with a beautiful, spectacular miniature sunset.

There, in reality, a reputedly "sinful" old city in terms of the new world's conceptions, was partly dying. It had fought to the death its enemy, the unfriendly wind. And on the wind rode the chill of fall stalking into the morning of September 21. With its dawn the great conflagration turned one more page of the new nation's fiery search for birth.

When General Howe's very busy and angry hours of the next few days are behind him, he will have time to write and report to Lord Germaine.

It will not be until this long nightmarish weekend is over. It will not be until, on top of all of his other problems, he will execute a young man without a trial and remember that impulsive decision for the rest of his life.

General Howe's Report

On Monday, the 23rd, he will give this account of the New York fire to his superiors in London:

"Between the 20th and 21st instant, at midnight, a most horrid attempt was made by a number of wretches to burn the town of New York, in which they succeeded too well, having set it on fire in several places with matches and combustibles that had been prepared with great art and ingenuity. Many were detected in the fact, and some killed upon the spot by the enraged troops in garrison, and had it not been for the exertions of Major General Robertson, the officers under his command in the town, and the brigade of guards detached from the camp, the whole must infallibly have been consumed, as the night was extremely windy.

"The destruction is computed to be about one quarter of the town; and we have reason to suspect there are villains still lurking there, ready to finish the work they have begun; one person escaping the pursuit of a sentinel the following night, having declared, that he would again set fire to the town the first opportunity. The strictest search is making after these incendiaries, and the most effectual measures taken to guard against the perpetration of their villainous and wicked designs . . ."[25]

And so from out of the ruins, in a few days a new New York City will begin rising on the town's west side—a new city under the rule of His Majesty, King George III of England.

14

Sunday, September 22. . .

"Apprehended Last Night. . .
This Day Executed "

Clay Pipe Smoke Signals

No longer do the Baummeisters attend the English Neighborhood church over The Mountain south of the Little Ferry in the valley. But when the Domine Dereck Remlin visits the encampment and conducts Sunday services for the troops, the Baummeisters always attend.

And even Greene and his adjutant, Tom Paine, are often seen standing in the rear of the assemblage for the Domine seldom preaches without berating the local Tories, the Crown, the Howes and the Hessians. However, though both Greene and Paine are the offspring of Quakers, it is known that neither is a Quaker. In fact there are those who spread the rumor that Paine is agnostic, if not atheistic. However few know him well.

Following the services this morning, the ferry-master talked lengthily with the Domine Remlin. When they finished it was clear that Pete had made a satisfactory agreement with the patriot preacher in arrangements for his daughter's marriage when the time comes.

Always when Baummeister concludes a successful business deal—usually after laying down demands, making concessions and much haggling—the puffs of smoke from his pipe are seen rising gently and well spaced. They calmly waft away on the breeze.

And that is the way they rise this morning. If matters were not settled to his complete satisfaction, everyone would know it by the ascension of small, rapidly discharged, cloud-like balls—a sure sign of his displeasure with the negotiations.

It is a bright sunny morning. Throughout the countryside, particularly among the military, the cheering news that the Americans forced the British and Hessians to turn on their heels and run at Harlem has suddenly disrobed the enemy of their frightening aura of invincibility. It has inspired the strong patriots, assembling as they do around their Liberty Poles to discuss and debate each day's events and take a fresh look at the supposedly unconquerable invaders.

As devastating as the New York fire was, despite cause or origin, the effect has also served to boost the American morale. Both Harlem and the fire have served as a temporary elixir in reviving the spirits, people and troops, throughout the colonial states.

While the Whigs and Patriots pass the catastrophic fire off with a "Well, that's war!" flippancy, the Tories and the Loyalists decry it as a wicked, inhuman act perpetrated by villains. On the other hand the Puritanicals contend it was the will of Providence like Sodom and Gomorrah. And the practical, materialistic shop keepers allege it was unwarranted perfidy, carried out in a spirit of unnecessary vengeance.

The Charlestown destruction, they say, was a military necessity. New York's destruction was not. Charlestown's burning, they argue, unlike New York's, did not affect business and pocketbooks on such a large scale.

Only a selected few of the "cliff dwellers," as the Palisadean natives are called by the soldiers, have free access to the post. The Baummeisters, Bourdettes and Ma Kearney are on that "approved" list. It is a politically expedient list for the fort commander, since each one on it conducts a business on which the post is somewhat dependent.

Consequently those on the "approved" list are also on the unwritten "preferred" list from which they derive some extra benefits of protection. This makes them much despised by the Tories, one such known Loyalist sympathizer being the Domine Garrett Ledbecker of the English Neighborhood church in the valley.

Ledbecker, whose namesake cousin is as strong a patriot as the Preacher Ledbecker is a Loyalist, has lately raised his voice even louder against the American cause. His church, which his patriot cousin, Garry, of Liberty Pole village shuns and calls a stronghold of Tory dogs, draws many neutrals into its fold but few Whigs. The Patriot Party of the valley, most of whom are members of the coetus group of the Dutch Reformed Church's coetus-conferentie conflict within the congregations, boycott the Domine Ledbecker and his preaching.

As the Baummeisters walk down the gorge road back home following the services, they are impressed by the large number of men now stationed on the mountain-top encampment. Even the Bluff Battery has had a measurable increase in its personnel complement. Roughly estimated, it is said that over 3,000 troops, plus some wives, children and friends bivouacked in the surrounding outskirts of the fort, now occupy the once forested, rock-strewn mountain summit.

Where only wild game had roamed over the primeval setting but two months ago, now a virtual city has sprung up in its stead. But for the "cliff dwellers," the fort is security, giving them new hope.

And in Elaine's heart there is a new deeply comforting warmth and an overwhelming joy of living that radiates, particularly in youth. It rises from a strangely ignited glow that two sparks from the unfathomable depths of a man's and a woman's soul can, in unison, create. More simply, it is love.

War or no war the young girl's effervescent nature is doubly vivacious as now she envisions the culmination of all her girlhood dreams appearing at last over the horizon.

It is indeed a bright morning. Just as her parents have anticipated, Elaine and her brother, as usual, leave the older folks on the downhill gorge road and forge up the Bluff Rock walk toward the path skirting along the precipice under the Barbctte Battery's outer ramparts. They make their way to Elaine's favorite look-out ledge.

High above the Hudson that flows hundreds of feet below them, brother and sister stand and breathe in the salt-tinged air. But most important to Elaine are the distant heights of Harlem.

It is there that she focuses her eyes and her attention. Somewhere within the American lines she knows he and his battery are stationed. Somewhere there she sends over her brief prayer for his safety.

Far south of the American lines at Fort Washington and Harlem's heights, far south of the no man's land lying between the British and American entrenchments, are Howe's headquarters in the James Beekman house.[2] The hour is a little before eleven on this bright and pleasant—from all outside appearances—Sabbath morning.

Inside the headquarters compound the scene is quite the opposite. It is gruesome. For walking boldly erect out of the Beekman's greenhouse where he has been confined all night, an American spy, the Continental Army Ranger's captain, Nathan Hale, is being escorted to the gallows six rods away and especially erected for the occasion.

Inside the mansion house at his table desk in the large parlor room used for his office, Sir William angrily assesses the damages done to his recently conquered city. Over one quarter of it destroyed!

Extremely disgusted with the discouraging turn of events, Howe wonders where he is now going to find housing for his troops. From the Beekman parlor window he sees his ruined city lying far in the distance at Manhattan's southern tip.

It is the handsome, muscular youth, walking between two British guards across the grounds to the hastily constructed gibbet, upon whom Sir Williams's eyes rest as he glances out the window from his chair.

The sight of the young rebel soldier makes him momentarily recall his own youth in 1750 when he was twenty-one. Swiftly he erases the thought from his mind, assuring himself he is right in ordering the execution.

To Sir William Howe, the man, the rebel youth is a spy who deserves what is in store for him. To General Howe, Hale is a symbol of everything that has gone wrong since the beginning of this campaign, a campaign now in its third month. And the British forces have not as yet gotten a foothold on the mainland.

A Lesson For the Rebels

Captured last night, the unfortunate Yale College graduate, walking fearlessly to his death, spells not only "espionage" to Sir William but also "sabotage," "incendiarism" and an excellent means for dealing out swift retribution as a lesson to all those rebelling against the Crown.

After all, he is self-confessed! He is an admitted secret agent on whose person were found the incriminating sketches. Has he not brazenly and insolently admitted his entire spying mission?

So Howe has ignored the ethical codes prescribed in war—codes which he usually pursues with infinite attention and courtesy. Why should he not disregard the customary court martial and order the youth hanged?[3] Is it not his prerogative? Is not this insurrection? Rebellion against the King? Against the Empire?

Sir William signed the execution papers swiftly but with concealed anger last night. He then turned the prisoner over to the custody of William Cunningham, provost marshal of the British army.[4]

A cold, unemotional, unscrupulous disciplinarian, Cunningham always carries out his prescribed tasks with an undisguised sinister delight. He is the right man to eliminate a troublous icon that is annoying his chief, for William Cunningham is the perfect example of a brutally hardened soldier who enjoys cruelty.

The last few days have been hard on Howe. So have the past few months. One disappointment has followed the other. Nothing has gone according to his expectations. Even Long Island, though a successful, military, field engagement, was a failure. Then and there the insurrection should have ended. Instead on it goes.

Howe's meditations vex him even more. Certainly, barring a miracle, the rebellion cannot be suppressed this year though he still must strive for that objective. He recalls the many factors that have gone against him and his admiral brother.

Before Sir William's mind flashes rapidly one event after the other:

"... So many unexpected obstacles rose up to plague them ... so many errors, not his alone, ... so many disappointments have steered the course of events away from victory—the victory—he has promised His Majesty ... so many things the Crown, Lord North, Lord Germaine and Parliament could have— Nay! Should have!—done differently ..."

Then looking again at the scene outside and listening to the steady morbid, beat of the drums, he muses, "Ah, had we all but one half the foresight powers given to us in our hindsight, what a better world we'd have!"

It is his hindsight, in his brief seconds of recall, that now controls his thoughts:

"... First there is that damnable, elusive rebel Fox he opposes. The fellow is not fighting a conventional war. Certainly not in accord with proper, battlefield procedures! He hits and runs. He invites action and then retreats from it. These Americans have learned too much from the Indians ... They must and will be crushed! Yet here it is the seventeenth month of the rebellion and the third month in New York ... In June it seemed certain that the insurrection would be put down by this time ...

"... Secondly is that bastardly declaration the colonists have

*been duped into signing ... Had the military command in the
field been given the powers to compromise before July 4th all
thirteen of the colonies might now be safely back under
England's rule ... Where was Parliament's foresight? Why had
his government been so adamant? Why had it insisted on
grinding the rebels down under its heels with the humiliating
demand for unconditional surrender? Why had not his government listened to and heeded the warnings behind those many
soundly sensible conciliatory speeches? ... And now the tremendous costs and expenses rise each day heavily burdening the
Crown's coffers ...*

"*... And thirdly are the false assumptions that the rebel
nucleus is centered almost entirely in New England and that
only a small band of Whigs are backing the army in New York
and New Jersey. To date it is true that there is a strong body of
Tories and Loyalists in York and the Jerseys. Yet they are, more
often than not, cowered until the King's men are directly behind
them, or in front of them ...*

"*... No, York, the Jerseys and Westchester are not the great
Loyalist centers they were said to be. Even New York city
harbors far more rebel sympathizers than the British command
were led to believe ... Many hundreds of those who sign the
King's "Oath of Allegiance" today have no intention of holding
to it tomorrow. It depends upon the wind that blows. Allegiance
to some means only who is occupying the town and who will
today threaten to 'take our cattle, confiscate our livestock and
empty our barns'...*

"*... Finally, despite their vast differences, these Americans
are like separately fighting cocks that mass together in one unit
when something comes at them from outside their barnyard ...
They have their internal differences in religions, in customs and
even in their languages. Southerners argue with Northerners.
New Englanders with Pennsylvanians. Yankees with Buckskins.
The blacks mistrust the whites; the whites mistrust the blacks;
and the browns mistrust them all. Nevertheless, generally, most
of them come unanimously together in their individual and
collective quests for liberty, freedom, rights, and the franchise
... 'Tis when they find a common cause that they unite and
fight to the death side by side, these people from almost every
part of the world."*

Sir William's mind struggles to keep his thoughts away from the
scene outside his window. He prefers instead to recall the countless

logistic, strategical and technical problems he had only recently reviewed with Brother Richard who has yet to make a successful advance up Hudson's river.

"Countless" seems to best describe the host of matters that requires Howe's attention. Of less importance is the minor hanging of a spy. The problems parade through his mind, each seeking a category of either immediate or later action. Some must be noted and included in his next report to Germaine and Parliament. So, quickly they flash in review:

". . . Uprooting the vast army from its bases on Staten Island and the smaller islands and relocating them on Manhattan . . . Providing a continuous supply of food for soldiers and seamen, some 35,000 in all, to say nothing of shelter and weaponry . . . Resolving the problem of a fleet that cannot maneuver up rivers as simply as it can cross oceans; frigates must drop anchor when winds subside and thus become the prey of river fire-ships, for night and tide make them helpless. This is so even if they break through blockades and elude the fire of enemy batteries on both sides the river . . . Deciding how and when to move, for a move too fast can rupture his taut lines of supplies while a move too slow will enable his flexible enemy to pull back and out of the trap before it closes . . .

". . . And how to avoid the mistakes of the past—the unexpected and the unanticipated—as when no favorable wind on August 29th, but rather a northeaster, rain and fog, enabled the Americans to escape across the East River . . . As when he errored and delayed in following through with an attack on the cornered Americans crowded vulnerably on Brooklyn's heights. There, certainly, should have been delivered the coup de grace! . . . As when, instead of pausing after the invasion at Kip's Bay, he should have struck across Manhattan, cut off Putnam and Knox and then swallowed up half the Ameircan army.

". . . Had he done so Putnam and his rebels would never have reached Harlem's heights . . . And why did he not send a battalion of dragoons immediately into New York town when they came ashore at Kip's Bay? They would have cornered every suspect and might have easily protected the city and saved it from the torch. And too, had he not thought the fire, when first noticed, was merely an American ruse, he would have at the outset ordered troops from the mid-Manhattan lines to control it . . . And in that battle on Harlem's heights, why were his officers so blind, so over-confident as not to see the American Rangers' trick which almost became a catastrophe?"

From a swift review of errors of commission, Howe's thoughts now leap around the people, the North American Colonists themselves, the undermining forces behind the insurrection, the international complexities the rebellion poses. He asks himself:

"... Are these people really British subjects? Can they ever be? These immigrants from all over the world, this mixture! ... Are they not clamoring for privileges they already enjoy in the Bill of Rights, guaranteed by Britain's Parliament for 87 years? Privileges granted to them as much as to anyone else in the Empire by the Magna Charta 561 years ago? ... Do they not know how well they are protected under those documents? Do they not know what they are letting themselves in for by opening up this box of dangerous liberties? ... They denounce to the high heavens the injustices inflicted upon them yet they enslave their African immigrants and deceive and defraud the Indian natives with as much ungodliness as they pour out upon each other ... Are they not hypocrites who only wish to rule each other? ...

". . . Then there is the mounting encouragement the Americans' rebellion is gathering from other countries. Particularly sympathetic to their cause are, of course, all of Great Britain's adversaries. This is ominous. Unless the insurrection is soon crushed, aid—already trickling in from France with her own benefits in mind—will come across the sea instead of mere sympathy. First will come the liberty-seeking fanatics, then money, ships and troops will follow ...

". . . This wave of 'fanatical thinking' is as much encouraged from abroad as it is engendered from inside. It is caused as much by England's 'Sensational School' as it is by the 'Great Awakening.' It is as much the echoes of Galileo and Newton as it is those of Plato and Socrates. It is as much the voices of the Cromwellian era as it is those of the 'Bourgeois Revolution.' It is as much Thomas More as it is Erasmus's humanism. It is as much Rousseau as it is Locke. It is Saint Thomas Aquinas and René Descartes as much as it is 'The Rise of Liberalism' and the 'Scientific Revolution.' It is no more to be blamed upon Edmund Burke and his adherents in Parliament than it is to be attributed solely or collectively to John Adams, Benjamin Franklin, Thomas Jefferson, Patrick Henry and the other voices of Congress ...

". . . Neither is it the Puritans who founded New England, the English who settled in New Jersey and the mountains of Virginia

*and the Carolinas, the French Huguenots and Holland Dutch
who colonized the Hudson Valley, the Swedes and Norwegians
who founded New Sweden on the Delaware; nor is it the Irish,
Scots and Welsh who settled the southlands. And it is not the
Germans, Poles, Italians, Russians and Asiatics, for there are not
as yet enough of them ... But it is the encouragement they are
all getting ...*

*"... The impotency of the British commander-in-chief and
the admiral, unable as they are to negotiate a peace settlement,
makes it impossible now with the declaration signed to expect a
solution other than on the battlefield ... And London, 3,000
miles away with time and distance slowing communications,
demands nothing less than unconditional surrender! ...*

*"... Unquestionably the Howes by now, despite their sym-
pathetic leaning toward the rebel cause, could have effected a
wise settlement and a profitable one for England if they had
been permitted to do so. ... Surely the United Kingdom must
realize that colonial control is only possible in proportion to the
degree of contentment maintained by the mother country! For
control can be stretched to the breaking point when it is
restricted by, or removed from, inadequate communications ...*

*"... What better example is there than in the army's ranks?
The mercenaries from Germany's Hesse-Cassel and Hesse-Hanau
are far distant from their strict Prussian-trained owners. They
arrive doctrinated. Soon they no longer believe they will be cut
up, stewed and eaten if captured by the wild American
cannibals. And not only the Hessians but also the British are
deserting in numbers and escaping inland beyond the
frontier ..."*

The phenomenal powers of the mind to speedily fly the past
before one's mental vision, covering, sorting and categorizing
thousands of bits of data in the fraction of a second, do not strike
Howe with any more surprise than they do most of mankind.

So his problems, significant and insignificant ones—trivial and
major errors and occurrences—all flash hurriedly in review without
amazing him with their remarkable brain-dance. But they do add
to his woes.

They all seem to point to one certainty: the seeds of peace are
no longer fertile. It is time for the business of war to the death—
war and all the villainies and evils that it spawns. His mind centers
on the lines opposing him on Harlem's heights and on that
damned, so-called "impregnable" Fort Washington on Mount

Washington's heights. That and its still higher sister fortress, Fort Constitution, on the Jersey side of the river now crowd into his thoughts:

"... *The officers on the* Eagle *say, half in jest, that the towering menace on the high Palisades should be called 'The Crow's Nest' or 'The Eagle's View' since it looks down on everything that goes on along the river or throughout the island ... Its great height provides the enemy rebels an expansive, scenic picture of every move the British army and navy make below the lofty rock fort. It is a constant threat, not so much to the King's men physically, but to their morale ... Its guns, along with those of Fort Washington and the blockade stretching across the river between the two forts, have taken their toll of British seamen and showered His Majesty's frigates with destruction ... Undoubtedly the Americans are counting heavily on making Fort Constitution their winter quarters ... That menace must go! ...*

"... *What is to be the next move? ... Both armies face each other across Manhattan as though astride a huge seesaw ... The rebels on the heights are in a position easy to defend from a frontal attack ... Attacking it is too risky while the Americans sit safely and invulnerably on the island's and Jersey's highest pinnacles ...*

"... *And downriver, opposite the city, they cling to the Paulus Hook fort on the Jersey side ... Then, behind that to the west, they still man the posts at Bergen and Bergen Point—grounds which are no longer of great importance but garrisons the Crown must take ...*

"... *And had it not been for the dastardly torching of New York town the Paulus Hook post would now be in his possession ... Sunday around eight in the morning has always been a propitious hour to surprise his enemy and he had planned to attack Paulus Hook this very day[5] ... All arrangements had been made; all was set. Then came the fire and such excessive pressure was placed upon soldiers and sailors alike that the attack order had to be canceled ... On top of everything else came the capture of this spy! ...*"

There is little hope in Sir William's mind that the war can be brought to a successful conclusion this year. Even now the long-range military strategy is still in the formative stage. Yet some of his staff are of a different mind, convinced that the rebels can be forced to capitulate before the year ends. General Sir Henry Clinton is one of those.

Since Tuesday last Clinton has been constantly pressuring Sir William to consider making a "double envelopment." This strategy, Sir Henry points out, was successfully effective in Long Island.

Clinton's plan would call for the seizure of King's Bridge[6] with one corps while a second corps would drive simultaneously and frontally at Harlem's heights. Then a third division would move out of King's and advance to New Rochelle by the coast road, thus avoiding the dangerous necessity of using the navy's windjammers in a passage through the treacherous waters of Hell Gate. From New Rochelle the third force would sweep back and behind the American lines, crossing the Hudson if necessary to include in the envelopment the rebels' Fort Constitution and its works.

But General Howe prefers to employ his brothers's navy in the operation, moving up into Westchester in a secretive maneuver by water. The combined land and sea brother act appeals to him in preference to Clinton's plan.

Howe sees the navy playing a more significant role in the operation than it would in Clinton's proposal. He envisions the possibility of cutting across Westchester in the Americans' rear. And then, aided by the men of war ascending the Hudson and breaking through the Harlem after taking King's Bridge, Howe would cross his main corps to the Hudson's west bank into Jersey.

Meanwhile, with his other two divisions keeping the rebels occupied on Harlem's heights and simultaneously pincering them from behind at King's Bridge, the British commander-in-chief would steal behind Fort Constitution. The while laying siege to it, he would send an advance body on a forced march through the Jerseys to strike at undefended Philadelphia.

His prize would be the capture of the Continental Congress. This is what Sir William believes is his only solution. It is his only chance for quashing the American uprising before the end of the year. Of that he gradually becomes convinced.

Outside the Window the Spy's Fate Dangles

All day the British commander's mind has been laboring over these problems. They are his major concerns. Not the spy in the courtyard. Then suddenly the spy and the suspicious fire—and Howe feels that in some way they must be connected—dwarf everything else.

The British commander rises from his desk and goes to the window. He watches the young spy—the symbol of all the ills and frustrations that the rebels and their insurrection have caused him. He is amazed to see no faltering in the rebel captain's step, nor any sign of fear as the American youth marches defiantly toward the big, heavily set mulatto known only as "Richmond." The brown-skinned giant has long been the British army's official hangman.

American intelligence of the British movements has never been very satisfactory. No efficient espionage system has yet been devised. The American General has few reliable contacts. And his great need early this month was to know where Howe would move next after his victory on Long Island. This was before the invasion at Kip's Bay.

So it was that The General sought a good officer for a special secret mission and approached Lieutenant Colonel Thomas Knowlton before his death in the Harlem battle. He asked Knowlton if he would seek from among his Rangers "a volunteer for a dangerous mission."

It was the end of a difficult search by the American Commander when a young athlete, then one of Knowlton's finest young officers, Captain Nathan Hale, stepped forward. A graduate of Yale with the Class of 1773, Hale was a schoolmaster in Haddam, Connecticut, before the war.

An ardent patriot, the youthful captain volunteered without hesitation. Impelled by a strong desire to do something helpful for the cause he firmly believed in, Hale would not listen when his close friend, Captain William Hull, a Yale classmate, urged him to change his mind.

Hale and Hull served in Webb's regiment when they first entered the army. Later Hale transferred to the Rangers, attracted by their reputation for fearlessness and the name they have earned for bold and daring exploits.

Hull's efforts to dissuade his friend from participating in the "disgraceful profession of espionage" were fruitless. He argued long and forcefully, but Hale was determined to carry out the mission regardless of its character or dangers.

Answering Hull's entreaties, Hale replied, "Every kind of service necessary to the public good becomes honorable by being necessary."[7]

It was just three days before the British invasion at Kip's Bay that the twenty-one year old Ranger captain left the heights of Harlem. In full uniform, accompanied by Sergeant Stephen Hempstead, Hale carried a suit of plain clothes and a general order, enabling him to pass to any place he designated on any American vessel. Also, in his pocket, he carried his Yale diploma, a vital necessity for a supposedly unemployed schoolmaster seeking a position in September.

When the two men reached Norwalk, the Captain sought Captain Charles Pond and his sloop, *Schuyler*, and was conveyed across to Long Island at Huntington. There the Ranger officer changed into his civilian garb and gave all the appearances of a schoolmaster with the exception of his pair of silver shoebuckles.

Such finery was certainly not befitting a traveling pedagogue seeking to teach 1776's wartime children the joys of the work ethnic, plain living and humility. So Hale wisely removed the silver buckles and turned them over to his sergeant who made his way back to the Harlem post.

What happened to the ill-fated Hale after leaving Hempstead no one really knows. Actually the inexperienced spy had very little protective insulation.

First, almost every man in the Rangers outfit knew he was going on a "dangerous mission." Most of them realized this meant espionage on Long Island. Why else would he be sent there carrying civilian clothes?

Secondly, since Hull, who is not a Ranger, knew about the mission, it is only logical to suppose that others from other units also knew about it. If any attempt was made to keep his mission a secret, Hale's table waiter at Harlem was an Asher Wright, and certainly he would inquire, along with others, where the captain disappeared to.

Thirdly, Captain Hale was easy to identify in the event that word reached the British lines of a Ranger spy in their midst. Hale's face was rather badly scarred by a gunpowder blast. This was a telltale mark. Furthermore, he was well known among New Englanders. His features and erect stature were easy to remember and identify.

And finally, it could not be to his benefit that his cousin, Samuel Hale, an avowed Loyalist, is the British Army's deputy commissary of prisoners. And Samuel was stationed on Long Island when Hale began his mission.

It is not known whether the captain was given any money. Certainly he would have needed it. He had no contact points or assists that he could depend upon in the field. Being a novice in the business of spying on the enemy, Hale probably had no planned, assigned "covers" for seeking asylum or protection when the hour warranted them. And he was given none of the newly invented, disappearing, or "sympathetic," ink.

Therefore the sketches and drawings of the enemy works, fortifications, lay-outs—the strengths and the positions of troops and weapons—were clear, legible, easily identified and totally incriminating. Codes in espionage work are not yet developed by the Americans. The art is still in its infancy.

Any secret British agent within the American ranks might very easily have put together the loose pieces and discovered what the missing Ranger captain was up to and where he likely could be found.

While the Rangers' loyalties are not to be questioned, wagging tongues are another thing entirely. For it is possible that Hale, by some oversight, may not have been given suitable instructions on keeping his silence. And it may be that he was, but violated such advice. Certainly Hull could have learned from other sources but most likely Hale informed him, probably with the enthusiasm of a man with a new, reckless assignment to be filled.

It is also questionable whether there were any carefully planned efforts made at the American headquarters to cloak the mission with any secrecy at all. Little seems to be known about any of the details, the preparations and the adventure itself. Certainly there are many questions left unanswered.

Nevertheless, Hale did make his way within the enemy's lines. He noted everything that had any military significance relative to the British preparations for attack. He sketched emplacements and indicated landmarks around and within the British-held works on Long Island.

When he had finished he began working his way back to Manhattan Island. He aimed for New York City. In doing so he encountered difficulties since the British were already attacking and invading at Kip's Bay.

It was not until after the Americans had evacuated New York and in the midst of the city's fire and confusion that he was able to get across and mingle with the panic-stricken inhabitants. Chaos reigned, but every stranger became suspect.

Though only conjecture, it is believed Hale may have easily escaped detection as he pushed northward until he reached the British lines facing the American's defenses on the heights of Harlem. There he may have observed and sketched much more vital information since now, with the Americans chased out of the city and the British established in it, all the Long Island intelligence he had gathered was useless.

Of great value to The General would be whatever observations he could collect on the King's men and their works on Manhattan. Whether he observed and sketched Lord Percy's troops and positions, Sir Henry Clinton's, Lord Cornwallis's, or brazenly bold and recklessly defiant, Sir William Howe's headquarters itself, no one will ever be sure. But this information was indeed what the American Commander-in-Chief was thirsting for.

It is known that at the appointed day and hour, pre-arranged between Hale and Hempstead before they parted, the sergeant waited well north of the military zone at Norwalk. There on a signal from the Long Island shore, Hempstead was to have sent over a boat for his captain. But hours and days went by without any sign from the Ranger.

Then the military situation changed drastically with the Kip's Bay attack and the American evacuation of the city. Thereafter the danger of executing the initially planned rescue increased, making it necessary to abandon a further watch at Norwalk. So Hale was, and had to be, on his own.

During the excitement attending the burning of the city it was easy in such confusion to make a crossing at the lower end of Manhattan. And it is likely that is what Hale safely did.

Between Flames and Hysteria

Yesterday will never be forgotten by New York's inhabitants, especially those homeless ones whose dwellings and possessions lie in ashes. The laborious work of cleaning up and rebuilding has only just begun.

The angry populace, Howe, his army, his brother and the seamen are all in a dismal and antagonistic mood, leaving no room today for sympathy for anyone. Certainly not for the rebel spy apprehended, questioned and incarcerated after being captured somewhere between the city's outskirts and the British forward lines last night.

Some say he was taken because he mistook a boat from an armed British frigate for an American-manned craft. Some say he was betrayed by a Tory who recognized him at Mother Chich's—the Widow Chichester's—Tavern where he reportedly spent one night.

And some say that the Tory informer was no other than his own Cousin Samuel. No one knows for sure.

However, seized he was before midnight. And now shortly after dawn of this beautiful Sunday morning, the papers which were found upon him lie strewn over the British commander-in-chief's desk. Hale's own confession was enough to convict him. The documents he carried placed the noose firmly around his neck.

Seldom has a captured spy been so rapidly disposed of. There are few of the enemy in Hale's brief, hostile imprisonment who are touched at all by the youth's tragic misfortune. However there is one, Captain John Montresor, Chief Engineer of the British Army in North America.

Montresor has witnessed almost every step that has taken place since Hale was brought into Artillery Park and swiftly condemned to death in Howe's headquarters. For Montresor's marquee is on the edge of the parade grounds and commands a good view of the Beekman mansion and the bivouac areas adjacent to it.[8]

This morning the entire British encampment was informed about the spy's capture, the damaging evidence found in his possession and his own admittance of guilt. Some of the men who have spent long hours in the fire-fighting brigades are convinced the captured man certainly must have been the arch incendiarist, judging from the swiftness with which the high command has condemned him.

They and an irate crowd, many of whose homes are today nothing more than fire-gutted, charred timbers, have gathered to acclaim the hanging.

Sir William looks out on the procession moving toward the gallows. The deathly slow, rhythmic roll of the dooming drums is the only sound that pounds upon his ears. It brings him wrestling closely with his conscience:

". . . Had the boy pleaded innocence, certainly he would have granted him a court martial! . . . But he confessed his guilt! . . . It would be a needless waste of time and effort to convene a court . . ."

Sir William convinces himself of the propriety of his action. It was a quick and firm decision. No protracted, agonizing delays. To have done otherwise under the circumstances, he tells himself, would be inhumane.

But as he watches the procession and observes its rather lengthy halt, he wonders:

" . . . Why is there delay at the gallows? . . . Why has the march stopped so suddenly? . . . Are the damned preparations not complete? . . . And now why is Montresor escorting the fellow into his tent? . . . True, it is not yet eleven . . . The orders were for eleven o'clock . . . The Provost Marshal is a precise man. If it calls for eleven, it will be done at eleven. Not before and not after . . ."

A Callous Provost Marshal

It is now five minutes before the hour. From out of the marquee Cunningham and two guards escort the amazingly calm, rebel captain onward to the morbid looking structure with its menacing upright frame and crossbeam.

Behind them follows Captain Montresor. The army's chief engineer is visibly moved. He is obviously one of few among the witnesses who effuses sympathy for the condemned soldier and horror at the callous methods civilized man employs in his demands for retribution.

There is one more pause. A few words are exchanged. A surprised look crosses Hale's defiant features as he faces the sneering Cunningham, staring directly into the snarling provost marshal's lowering eyes. The words, whatever they were, were brief. But seemingly they have upset the doomed Ranger more than the execution itself.

Even as Richmond places the noose tightly around his neck, Hale does not take his eyes off those furiously burning out of Cunningham's maddened face.

The fact that at no time did this rebel enemy cower before his fate, beg for his life, or lose his erect posture and calm manner, has infuriated the British army's custodian of prisoners. It is this attitude that Montresor, among others, despises in Cunningham, but it is an attitude army protocol condones in its military police work.

General Howe turned back toward his desk when the rolling beat of the drums ceased. As he sat back down in his chair behind his desk, piled high with papers and maps, he heard the thumping, whip-like noise, the sound of ahs and hurrahs from the appeased and the unappeased onlookers, and then the resumption of the rolling drums. They sound more jubilant now than they did before.

To Montresor the groaning ahs, ohs, and hurrahs are like the primitive voices of aborigines—mere expletives and exclamations of contempt, satisfaction, requited vengeance and possibly of some horror, sympathy and regrets. He cringes at their sound as they rise above the courtyard and adjoining Artillery Park on this pretty Sabbath September morning dropping down on a burned out city.

Howe's aide enters the commander's headquarters suite, having respectfully left his chief alone in the room until after the execution. He hands him the completed orders of the day.

Sir William reads them quickly. He pauses and goes back, reading again the first subject on the parchment scroll. He inserts a correction, adding the phrase, "by his own full Confession" to the item which now reads in full:

> "Head Qrs New york Island, Sept 1776 ... A Spy fm the Enemy (by his own full Confession) Apprehended Last night, was this day Executed at 11oClock in front of the Atilery Park--."[9]

Montresor will within the week secure permission from Howe to approach the American camp under a flag of truce. There he will be taken under a flag to Captains William Hull and Alexander Hamilton of the artillery. With respect and courtesy he will explain the circumstances surrounding the death of the Ranger officer.

Montresor will tell of the youthful captain's highly commendable behavior which British Captain Frederick Mackenzie described as of

> "great composure and resolution," adding that Hale had said that he thought it "the duty of every good officer to obey any orders given him by his Commander-in-Chief, and that he desired the spectators to be at all times prepared to meet death in whatever shape it might appear."[10]

In recounting the Connecticut Ranger's last hours, Montresor will reveal what he can of his capture, his stated object in coming within the British lines and his admissions of guilt. The British captain will inform Hull and Hamilton that Cunningham is "a refugee and hardened to human suffering and to every softening sentiment of the heart."

He will say of Hale that, "He was calm and bore himself with gentle dignity."[11]

But what will be most surprising to the American officers will be the British engineer's open admission of his complete disrespect for Cunningham, and particularly his attitude and actions throughout the proceedings. One such inexcusable action, Montresor will say, was Cunningham's refusal to grant the condemned man his request for a Bible or a clergyman.

The British officer will explain how, during the delay in the procession, he persuaded the provost marshal to allow the prisoner to make use of his tent. And how, at Hale's request, Montresor provided him with paper and ink on which the American captain wrote his last letters to relatives. One was to his brother, the Reverend Enoch Hale.

Unknown to Montresor, the Ranger officer's last letters will never get beyond Provost Cunningham. American Major John Palsgrave Wyllys,[12] who was taken prisoner by the British on

September 15, will be shown both letters as well as Hale's Yale diploma. And it will be the depraved Cunningham who will gloatingly display them before Wyllys' eyes.

When the major is exchanged many months from now, he will tell Enoch Hale how Cunningham approached him with his customary contempt for American prisoners, making his usual threats against them—many of which he carried out.

It was on one such occasion, the American major will tell Reverend Hale, that the British custodian of prisoners diabolically showed him the ill-fated Ranger's undelivered letters and his college diploma, confiscated by the demoniacal provost marshal.

Death For A Purpose

But going back again into today's scene at Artillery Park, the Sabbath seems profanely defiled by the lifeless corpse swinging hour after hour from the gallows since eleven o'clock this morning. For this is the practice, and has been the custom of civilized war long before the medievalism of the Middle Ages, long before the Medicis and the Spanish Inquisition.

Dangling grotesquely above the ground until sundown, it is now intended to give those who would do likewise a message. It is the warning method and far more refined than carrying a severed head upon a pointed spear.

It marks the end of a promising youth's career. It marks the end of Ranger Captain Nathan Hale, Yale College graduate of Connecticut. But it is the costly, tragic impetus the new nation badly needs to rekindle the somewhat dimming fires of patriotism.

Captain Nathan Hale has done much more than uselessly sketch and note the British emplacements and division strengths. For, inadvertently, Howe and Cunningham have unknowingly played into a dead man's hands. Both have helped to erect his statue.

Down in York city arrests are being made by the hundreds. In some cases only the word of a Tory is sufficient evidence for apprehension. Loyalists, just now returning to the homes abandoned when the Americans were in control, are among the loudest accusers.

Two British guards in a party of ten under a Redcoat captain break open doors when no one answers their knock. But at a small house just off the Broad Way, the door is opened before the officer reaches it.

"Are you Haym Salomon?" inquires the stern, strait-laced

captain of the rather dark, thinnish looking man, about thirty odd years of age, who appears at the door.

"I am," is the reply. "How can I be of help to you?"

"Simply by coming with me," replies the officer. "'You are under arrest for collusion with enemies of the Crown."

Salomon, who recently sent a package by a secret express to his friend, Asher Levy, surmises that the charge stems from that act.

"Is it collusion," he asks, "to send a bolt of cloth to a friend?"

The officer does not answer. And Salomon, despite the cries and wails of his family now clustering behind him, is marched away to a British gaol. Salomon and his family know that to be imprisoned in one of His Majesty's gaols in these times is often tantamount to a death sentence.

And so Haym Salomon, among others, is incarcerated and placed under the custodianship of Provost Marshal William Cunningham.

By Ferry: A Bolt Of Irish Linen

It is late in the afternoon under the Palisades' Bluff Rock. The first leaves of fall are tumbling down from some of the numerous dogwood trees on the heights.

Inside the Baummeister House, the ferrymaster has just handed his daughter a large package which came over by ferry from the Harlem camp a few hours ago. A package of any kind is rarely delivered to anyone in the undercliff hamlet. Few ever receive letters, particularly now with the war at their doors.

Surrounded by every member of the family, Elaine excitedly opens the well wrapped, carefully sealed box. With a rapturous shout of joy she lifts out from inside a bolt of beautiful white Irish linen. Beneath it she finds a scribbled note and reads it aloud:

"Enough to make him a new scarf and you a wedding gown to match, I do hope. . . . . . Asher Levy."

15

Monday, September 23. . .

Avenging Broadsides Take the Hook

A Bustling Mountain-top

Hundreds of hands pounding hundreds of hammers tap and rap the brisk Monday morning September air with their irregular staccato beats, nailing away at the newly constructed huts and buildings on Fort Constitution's mountain-top encampment. Their constant drumming is interrupted and often drowned out by the shouts of men and the whinnying of straining horses. The sweating animals tug and pull, forcing their bulging muscles to move their burdensome, overloaded wagons.

Never before has this wilderness, once the quiet home of the bear, wolf, fox, eagle and rattlesnake, been so quickly and so ruthlessly destroyed by man. Cursing, swearing wagonmasters, whose country wagons and Philadelphia teams have bogged down in mired ruts, or stalled with broken wheels and axles, add their blasphemies to the noise and confusion.

But often the blasphemers are overheard and angrily upbraided by some newly added chaplain, conscientiously executing his ordained business. For the new clergymen are determined to keep the men on the righteous road, particularly since the paths to hell-fire and damnation are made all too readily convenient by the presence of the God of War.

Most of the clergy scoff at any suggestion that their heavy salvation tactics have anything to do with a recent sweep of

Quaker-like tranquility felt throughout the camp since its new commander, General Nathanael Greene,[1] and his adjutant, Thomas Paine, have assumed charge. For the young clergymen know that the Quakers have long since disassociated themselves from both the men and their military pursuits.

In both those leaders—each a force in his own field—there is that strain of imperturbability acquired from childhood training. It is a calming manner, permeating the atmosphere around them. It strikingly affects all who come within the aura of their minds.

The fort and its construction are not short of assistance. Inhabitants along the road skirting the encampment's west slope, as well as the few residents along the edge of the river, offer all kinds of help in the post's development. For them, there is a new-found pleasure in this sudden transformation from near-wilderness into a bustling community—a protecting fort, manned by soldiers and weapons, the Continental Army itself! And more arrive each day.

Most of the natives, as well as the troops stationed at the garrison and massing under the security of the ageless rock, think the war is across the river. Not here. The fear of invasion, at least this year, is too remote to arouse anxiety.

Yet all know that Howe is closing in on Manhattan's American-held posts, one by one. And they realize that Brother Richard, admiral of the fleet, is bearing down on every river fort. For the Admiral's principal job is to wrest control of Hudson's river from the enemy while Sir William's is to drive the rebels out of Manhattan and break their power to resist. Certainly, if backed against the Palisadean wall, they might soon disband and sue for peace.

If he follows his step-by-step procedure, Howe can see the finish not far distant from the end of his sights.

In the Baummeister kitchen, reeking with a delectably inviting mixture of appetizing odors in which the aroma of herbs, burning hickory wood and oven-baked bread predominate, the bolt of Irish linen, spread out over the large Windsor rocker, is the center of attention. Even Granny Bourdette and her ever-present consort, Black Jennie, who have come over from the Bourdette house to see it, gasp in astonishment. A heavy bar of gold could not have brought half so much pleasure to the eyes of the women of The Mountain.

It is laughing, robust Jennie with her inimitable knack for slyly changing dreams into reality—and always with that maddening look of feigned, naive ignorance—who exclaims realistically, "Oh, Lawdy! How many bandages would dat make?"

The elderly mammy's seemingly innocent exclamation strikes Elaine, Marie Louise and Granny Rachel like a streak of lightning. Each is suddenly speechless. They know that the beautiful bolt of cloth may, at any moment, have to be turned into badly needed bandages. A wedding dress it may, or may not become, and if it does, it will not be one for long. And certainly it never will be a family heirloom.

Jennie, as is usual with the former bound black woman, has used a few subtle words to say a lot of things their happy minds had momentarily tried to block out. The city-like wedding of their feminine dreams suddenly bounced back into the real world—the wilderness and the war around them. Before their eyes appears the new mountain-top hospital filled with the sick, wounded and dying.

It is that thought which crowds their minds. Each looks at the other. Each knows Jennie—sensible, practical, common sense Jennie—is right again!

Elaine breaks the momentary silence which, like a blast of arctic wind, chilled the kitchen air. She smiles, places her arm around the black woman's wide waist. Her words speak the thoughts of the others.

"God bless you, Jennie! You always save us from ourselves. I don't know how many it will make. But now is the time to find out. . . . except for one piece. Of that I will make a new neckerchief for John. 'Tis a bandage, you know, in a way, for when he should . . . God help he doesn't! I have orders to launder his other. This will do better."

Marie Louise, a tear in her eye, nods in wisdom's silence and agreement. But Granny Rachel, in her usual loud and determined voice, pokes a jibe at Jennie, who she readily admits always bests her "in mighty near ever'thin'."

"That one," she says, nodding her head with a pixie-like glint in her eye toward the amused servant, "is allus sayin' or doin' somthin' to spoil my fun! Acours'n she's lashin's right, though! 'Ceptin' Irish lin'n ain't good for a'makin' bandage. Shirts, yes. Not bandagin'. Tis cheese cloth they need up there most'n. But, never you mind, Elainey," she adds, patting the younger woman's hand warmly, "You're gonna wear my white silk brocade, 'n the hoops is in it. 'Twas my weddin' one when Stephen married me. Just as good as new, too. An' my veil, 'tis in silver, French lace trim . . . Well, so, whut if 'tis a little out of fashin'! Who'll know't 'round here?"

All laugh at the sensible, logical solution as Elaine replies, "Thank you, Granny dear. It sounds fine. Why not, if you don't mind?"

At that moment Elaine's father breaks into the room through the outside kitchen door. His weather-beaten face has that long, scowling countenance with its ever protruding pipe emitting short puffs clearly indicating the ferry-master is upset, if not downright angry. His voice booms out loudly.

"Zey haf ketched dot Connekshucut fella dot here across comed jost a fortnight ago. Dot Capt'n Hale! Ellie, you 'member him, no?"

Elaine nods her head, anxiously waiting for her father to go on. His face is flushed with the red blood of anger pressuring into his veins as he says, with a quick snap of his fingers:

"Zey hanged him jost like zis! A spy da redcoats sez he vas! Liars!"

Elaine and Marie Louise, knowing the ferrymaster's frequent angry explosions always end with his gasping for breath while his heart pounds like a hammer, force him to sit and calm down.

It was just about two weeks ago that Colonel Benjamin Tall-madge and his party of Rangers, headed by Lieutenant Colonel Tom Knowlton and the impressionable young Captain Hale, came across the ferry. They were on a surveillance mission south to Bergen's point and north to the Ramapo Pass. It was a secret assignment ordered by the War Council to determine "the lay of the land."[2]

Guided by Captain Craig and Sergeant Abbott, the party returned to the mountain post two days later. The following day they recrossed to Fort Washington.

All had paused at the Baummeister spring that morning while waiting for their ferriage. Both Bourdette and Baummeister had talked with the three Connecticut youths at great length.

Two Out Of Three Lie Dead

Hearing the children inside the Baummeister house counting and reciting, Hale asked Baummeister if he might look in at the parlor-converted schoolroom in the river-side home. The ferry-master acquiesced.

Inside, the former schoolmaster introduced himself to Elaine, calling her "Marm" in respectful deference to her assumed school-marm role. Elaine courteously introduced him to the six children,

for even Jocko had joined the class that day. "This is Paul ...
Joseph ... Ben ... Katie May ... Hans ... and Jocko."

So the shocking rumor of the reported hanging could not have
hit anyone harder than it does Baummeister and his daughter. Both
had enjoyed the three jesting, likeable Connecticut officers who
had brought them news about John's battery—at least as much as
they knew. Now only Tallmadge of the three friends is still alive.

Elaine hears her father's words, and tears well into her eyes. For
a moment she says nothing and then, almost under her breath,
exclaims "God save us!"

Hurriedly she leaves the kitchen and enters the parlor school
classroom, praying the rumor is false.

A few of the children are already in their make-shift seats,
writing on small slabs of slate rock they have gathered from under
the cliff. Elaine decides not to mention the news, which of course
is as yet only hearsay. For the children had that day enjoyed their
visitors. All three officers had been particularly nice to them.

It was the ex-schoolmaster they liked the most. He had asked
them questions they could answer, and he knew so much about
their work. No, Elaine would say nothing. At least not now.

While Baummeister has only rumor to go on, such rumors are
most often true. This one spreads rapidly. Each repetition gathers
imaginative, macaber-like additions, slapped on by revengeful
Tories or irate Loyalists.

Before any official word is received, even the company and their
park of artillery on the Barbette Battery, as well as the soldiers
and civilians in and around the main field fort, are buzzing with
the news. An American captain in Knowlton's Rangers captured
and hanged!

Though unsubstantiated, the news has suddenly tended to unite
the men. Even the northerners and the southerners momentarily
forget their differences as accounts trickle in about the rebel
officer's tragic death. With each account animosity for the enemy's
tactics increases.

When he has somewhat subsided, Pete is urged toward the door
by Marie Louise who tells him to quiet down, that he can do
nothing about the inevitable destinies of men, and to "tend his
chores and see the hands be kept' busy." Quietly she nudges him
outside, hushing him from disturbing Elaine's school children.

Bourdette, who is talking at the water trough to a stagecoach
driver, just arrived from Paulus Hook, sees his ferry-master coming
toward him. Old Stephen can tell the extent of Pete's anger by just

counting the smoke puffs furiously rising over Baummeister's head. The ferry owner knows something bad has taken place and listens with his puffs as Pete tells him about Hale.

Bourdette, in turn, gives Baummeister the Paulus Hook news direct from the stagecoach driver's limitless well of information, revealing that the Hook may even now have been evacuated by the Americans.

Both the clay pipes pour forth and upward their little clouds of anger, concern and fear. Nothing could better reveal how deep the Lion's teeth are tearing into the Americans' minds than the character of the curling smoke from the ferrymens' tobacco.

As the stagecoach driver aptly told them, "Dem redcoats, shur as floodging's, could larn a heap of thinkin' from dem sig'nls ye two fellas sends up!"

The three men carry on their exchanges of news while the coach horses drink lustily from the water trough. But the cascading spring from the high rocky precipices of the Palisades quickly replenishes the supply.

After the three men finish lengthily discussing the vicissitudes of the war, and the sun has ascended directly over their heads, they part.

Then within an hour the distant rumbling of heavy cannon brings everyone running up the gorge road to the ledge rocks, or along the shore where the embankment river batteries suddenly are alerted. All strain their eyes downriver at the distant cannonading.

Men, women and children scramble for choice positions, paying little attention to the pickets' falling rock warnings. Guards at the military outworks stop all who attempt to pass through the sentry lines.

There is no doubt that the guns are from the men-of-war in New York bay sending their broadsides into the Hook. Without a sign of letting up, the enemy vessels lay down an incessant withering barrage, yet no returning fire seems to come out of the American works.

Cannonade Downriver

It is the convex curvature of the Palisadean ridge which recedes west, back inland at the southern extremity where the Paulus Hook works were erected, that prevents a clear observation of the post. Only the British warships, firing repeatedly in rapid succession, can be seen from the cliffs as they move ever more boldly in upon the post from which no opposing fire comes.

Every adult in Fort Constitution easily distinguishes cannon fire from natural thunder. Along the shore-front the men of the half-dozen riverside redoubts, as well as the inhabitants, quickly take cover at the sound of thunder. For thunder storms and lightning are their Nemesis. All too often the frequent rock slides are triggered by a single bolt of lightning, or by a sudden cloudburst.

Cannon fire, on the other hand, brings soldiers and civilians rushing toward a high perch, preferably the Bluff Rock parapets if they can get by a sentry post whose eyes are glued on something else, or who just kindly looks the other way. If not they seek the foot trails, or the ideal open grounds just below the new fort field's southern earthworks.

For it is there where often The General himself has been seen standing with his field glasses trained on the site's commanding view of Manhattan Island. From there can be seen Long Island in the distance. But this location, unlike the Bluff Rock, which blocks the main fort from a view of Fort Washington across the river, or from a northward view upriver, is only ideal for a southern observation of the river and the island.

However, even the Bluff Rock's vista upriver is limited to just north of Spuyten Duyvil[3] owing to the irregular projections of the Palisades out from the shore. And owing also to the river's north-westward winding course beyond the Spuyten Duyvil.

As though on a given signal the warships' cannonading suddenly ceases. The distant barrage has brought every man, not assigned some vital task out on the open field south of the main fort.

It was once the old Bourdette hill-top cow pasture. Even now part of it is still used for grazing. At its northwestern extremity is the burial grounds used by all the nearby inhabitants.

It is within a large area of these old fields and pasture lands where rough streets have been laid out and soldiers' huts, each with a chimney, are under rapid construction. Everyone is watching as the enemy frigates and tenders, their guns now silent, move into the Jersey shore almost twelve miles below The Mountain.

As they make for land to empty their small boats filled with troops on the Paulus Hook garrison for the infantry assault, they disappear from the curious, wide-eyed observers on Fort Constitutions's crest. And only conjecture and assumptions are left to vivid imaginations.

"Nothin' a'needin' fer ta worryin' 'bout"

Jocko, leaving his father in charge of the stables shortly after the rumblings began, made his way directly for the ledge rock. He knew he would find Elaine, Paul, Hans and Joseph already there.

As all strain their eyes downriver toward the frigates leveling their broadsides on the river mouth's guardian post, Jocko assures Elaine that Gray is safe with the troops on Harlem Heights.

There is "nothin' a'needin' fer ta worryin' 'bout, Missy E," he nonchalantly keeps reminding her in an effort to console the girl's troubled mind, "nothin', Missy E, fer ya ta worryin' 'bout."

Elaine, prompted by what she has heard from John and others as well, places great trust in Jocko's uncanny ability to make sound judgments, particularly where the military is concerned. For he is a careful listener who has learned from necessity, but unwittingly, the art of eavesdropping with discretion, analyzing with caution and reasoning with wisdom.

Short though his life has been, it has sharpened his wits and taught him to temper his conclusions with restraint. But his love of people, of mankind generally, is the strongest fiber in his rare, unusual and magnetically lovable character. It is his most vulnerable spot in the opinion of those who know him. They fear his trust of all men is a trust which all men have not as yet earned.

It is his implicit faith in man that Elaine and John have admired in their discussions of Jocko between themselves. It is this simple belief in others that they fear someday will be strikingly shaken.

Elaine finds in Jocko a strong desire to better himself and improve upon his own self-image as the son of a freed black. She has seen ambition in his eyes, ambition stemming out of an intense urge for respect built upon his own deeds.

It is when the subject of liberty, freedom and the rights of all men are discussed with the children in her class that Elaine sees the black youth smiling at the idealistic aims of the rebellion that seethe around them.

Though he says nothing, Elaine knows that Jocko, like all bound, indentured and freed men fighting with the army, has little faith in all the beautiful words behind the rebellion.

It is not, she feels, the cause and the immediate visions it promises that they fight to defend and to which they give of their lives. It is the deeply buried hope that over and beyond the elusive horizon, they too, or their descendants, will find realized, the dreams so nobly espoused within the verbal framework of the Declaration.

So Elaine has grasped the youth's thinking very much as he has similarly gripped her mind and John's. It is upon this intangible, almost spiritual plateau, totally divorced from matter, color, race and creed, and purely bred from mind, that Elaine, John and Jocko and lately Asher Levy, have found a strange unity of affection, admiration, respect and love.

However, none of them see themselves in this light. All they know is that each is in some mysterious way drawn to the other. In Elaine's mind she sees in Asher Levy a web of thinking similar to that which clouds Jocko's thoughts.

For she has felt the Jewish officer's similar inward doubt when talks have turned to The Cause. Asher, Elaine believes, is ever questioning the new nation's true dedication, its sincerity.

And it is certainly logical, she has told herself, for many of the non-Anglicans, the non-English descendants—her father, mother, brother and herself included—to skeptically question the American outcome.

But her mind now, high on the precipice ledge, turns and dwells upon her betrothed. Jocko's consoling words have immeasurably helped to relieve her fears.

The cessation of the blasting cannons emptying their weapons on Paulus Hook, last guardian of York's harbor, causes her to look eastward. There somewhere on the heights above Harlem across the river she sends her thoughts and prayers to John Gray.

Throughout the ramparts of those heights there has buzzed angrily all day the word that one of Knowlton's proud Rangers has been hanged by the enemy. Only the cannonading in the bay and the sight of Lord Howe's men-of-war attacking the Hook on the Jersey side takes precedence over all else.

Training their field glasses on the distant action southward and west toward the bay, Gray and Levy are among the many, including the American Commander and his staff, silently watching the fall of the last outpost on the river.

With each enemy broadside leveled on the isolated Jersey garrison a burst of smoke rises. Yet still no American guns return the fire, causing a pall of gloom to spread among the observers. They are concerned for fear the post has not been safely evacuated and that the shelling has wiped out the American defenders.

The action, instead of disheartening the troops combines with the courage displayed by an executed Ranger and now they jointly instill a new-found determination. So together the two isolated events inject the sagging morale of an army with one more badly needed transfusion.

Gray's eyes turn away from the Paulus Hook attack. He had heard that the garrison had been ordered to pull out most of their supplies, equipment, armament and personnel. And having met Post Commander Colonel John Durkee and glimpsed his mode of operations, Gray is sure the Lord Admiral wasted shot.

Having shared with Levy their own rear-guard mission through the Paulus Hook post a week ago, Gray is convinced that there is nothing within the Hook's barricaded abatis and its log stockade to greet the invaders except empty barracks, magazines and weaponless ramparts on the lonesome, ghostly, former fortress. For both Gray and Levy had been impressed with the efficiency of Durkee's garrison in that one glorious night of sanctuary in their breathtaking escape from the Juggernaut's jaws. Both are sure that the enemy will have nothing to rejoice over once they land.

Gray's mind shifts suddenly to Elaine across the river as though answering a summons. His eyes are inexplicably drawn westward over the Hudson's calm waters. And there they focus on the distant Bluff Rock site.

Levy, almost instantly aware of his comrade's thoughts, turns in the same direction. Smilingly, he speaks,

"There is every indication we will be bivouacking over there before another fortnight. Is it not so?"

"Ay," Gray responds. " 'Tis right. we may. But, ah! For how long?"

"Methinks," replies Levy calculatingly, "about as long as it takes you to have a parson tie you to Elaine 'until death do ye part'."

Levy's eyes twinkle under his raised eyebrows.

"Elaine would have it so," Gray answers wryly smiling, his hand unconsciously reaching up, throwing the end of his petticoat neckerchief back behind his throat.

His smile fades as he adds, "It makes not good sense to mix matrimony and war. Look at those poor souls yonder in the field tents behind the works! Sweethearts and wives some were not many days ago. Widows are they now . . . and with them the orphans of the battlefields . . . And so many more to be so!"

"I had not told you," interjects Levy, paying little thought to Gray's remarks, "but that package the merchant brought me from Salomon Saturday?"

"Ay, I recall it."

" 'Twas a bolt of cloth, of Irish linen," Levy continues. "I sent it to your lady over there."

Gray, surprised, abruptly turns his eyes away from the

Palisadean ridge and looks directly at his friend with a questioning half-smile on his lips, inquiring, "But why?"

"Can you not guess?" asks Levy. " 'Tis little enough for all I owe you, her and her family as well for the hospitality they gave a stranger as we came through there."

"A gracious thing for ye to do!" Gray says. "I thank thee, Asher!"

Disregarding Gray's thanks, Levy continues, "I asked Salomon by the same merchant, who of course is one of us, to see she got the best that could be got these days of scarcity. 'Twill make her a gown if," he adds with a chuckle, "she should ever marry ... Oh, and possibly you a new neckerchief!"

Gray, pleasantly surprised, is momentarily speechless. He breaks out with a grin, uttering almost inaudibly, "I thank thee, Asher!"

Their conversation is suddenly interrupted by Colonel Tallmadge who gallops toward them up from the field and over the earthworks. The colonel dismounts near the group of staff officers atop the western scarp, observing the silent vessels off the Hook. He speaks briefly with Hamilton and Burr, then hurriedly walks over to Gray and Levy.

Both men know, as do all the staff officers, how hard Tallmadge has taken the execution of this close friend and Yale classmate, Nathan Hale. It is suspected that Tallmadge has always wanted to work with the Commander-in-Chief in the army's poor, undeveloped area of enemy intelligence. Now he is more eager to do so than ever.

There is a perfunctory salute as Tallmadge addresses Levy, saying, "I regret to inform you, Lieutenant, but I have learned that your friend down below, Mr. Salomon, a fine patriot it is said, has been imprisoned among many others by the enemy. I thought you would want to know immediately. What, if anything, I hear I shall see that you are fully informed. My regrets, Sir! I know he is a close friend."

Aghast at the sudden impact of the distressing news, Levy stands momentarily in shock, staring unbelievingly at Tallmadge. Recovering his composure quickly, he inquires, "Have you any knowledge as to why, Colonel? On what charge?"

Even the mention of enemy prisons strikes terror in the hearts of those who have heard of the British military gaols. Tallmadge, knowing this, answers sympathetically, "I know not. Yet it is said that Salomon is much respected by the enemy's command and that he is well treated. It is said that the enemy immediately made use of his speaking knowledges of many languages in the translation and interrogation work of the foreign-speaking prisoners and natives."

Gray, upon hearing the news, immediately feels for his friend. The Pennsylvanian's mouth firms. His facial sinews tighten as he shares with Levy the crushing blow.

Levy, whose face and body had slumped at Tallmadge's announcement, takes hold of himself as the colonel tells of the enemy's respect for Salomon's language knowledges. Summoning his fortitude, Levy straightens and with dissembling coolness hastily says, "Thank you, Colonel! I shall be deeply indebted for any further news you may receive."

Levy turns and walks away, leaving Gray and Tallmadge standing alone. The Lieutenant, taking advantage of the first opportunity he has had to speak to Tallmadge since word of Hale's death reached the post, extends his sympathy to Tallmadge over the death of his friend.

Tallmadge* accepts his condolences and, changing the subject, looks toward York's bay where the war vessels can be seen at anchor off Paulus Hook, nine miles southwest.

End Of A Noble Guardian

"There, Lieutenant," says the colonel, pointing in the direction of the besieged post on the Hook, "is the end of a noble guardian. Many a stage left there for Philadelphia. Your home is Philadelphia, is it not, Sir?"

"You have a memory that would do credit to a Prince Town man, Colonel," retorts Gray, mischievously reminding him of their conversation on the memorable river crossing night last month.

"Touché! Touché, Sir Knight of the Blue Petticoat Scarf!" replies Tallmadge.

Then, with a wave of his riding crop, the colonel makes for his horse, sending back over his shoulder to Gray the comment, "Should you be interested, there are excellent laundresses at Yale, especially adept in finishing neckerchiefs."

Gray smiles faintly as he succumbs to the colonel's parting repartee. But he is impressed with the alarming rapidity with which men at war can usher death and catastrophe to the recesses of

*Colonel Tallmadge in 1780 was to befriend the ill-fated British officer, John Andre, following his capture as a spy, and was to accompany him through his execution by hanging at Tappan, New York, October 2, 1780.

their brains and resort to the cover of humor. ... Humor, the tragic jester's raiment of laughter, cloaking misfortune in forgetfulness!

Again Gray's mind and eyes sweep over the Paulus Hook scene, sadly aware that these are the last minutes of the post's existence under The Grand Union's Continental Army flag with its strikingly beautiful red and white stripes.

He recalls the banner's inspiring and welcoming sight during the nightmarish escape from New York to Paulus Hook only a week ago. The great, lumbering windjammers, bristling with their giant guns, now appear to Gray like mammoth sea monsters whose claw-like tentacles seem to close in and around their helpless victim before finally gobbling it down.

The Lieutenant's mind flashes briefly to his memorable hours listening to Doctor Ezra in those seemingly far-off days at Prince Town. He recalls the learned man's explanation for the prehistoric animals' inability to survive owing to their inability to adapt.

Now Gray, looking at the flapping sails of the British men-of-war—so out of place on the wind-starved river, far from their home on the broad seas—anachronistically sees a strange imaginary resemblance to the pterodactyl and the dinosaur, starving to extinction on the food-less glacial tundras of the Pleistocene Epoch.

Could it be that the great, white-winged British pterodactyls, boldly flying the colors of St. George and his dragon, are likewise destined eventually to flounder on a monarchy-opposing tundra, the unionized states of North America?

Gray's eyes move northward up the Jersey shore along the ever-rising, Palisadean ridge. They stop and pierce the haze, coming to rest on the heights of the great Bluff Rock. He has the peculiar feeling that on that ledge of theirs Elaine is standing. Probably around her are the youngsters of her school and, of course, Jocko. All probably looking eastward. She, he knows, is looking as hungrily in his direction as he, this moment, in hers.

He thinks of the children there that he has come to know. A few months ago their names, their personalities, meant nothing to him. Now each seems to be a part of his life. He quickly corrects himself—his and Elaine's life!

"Children, children!" he cogitates. "How carefree! How loving, trusting and believing they are!"

He suddenly realizes that he had never given much thought to any children before.

"It seems the Creator must have made a mistake," he tells himself, "to have them grow up and change from happy little things, wrapped in childhood innocence and love, to growling, awesome creatures, swathed in adulthood's selfishness, greed, distrust, and surrounded by their hates and prejudices . . ."

Asking himself why the omnipotent Creator did not turn it all around and have good grow out of bad, rather than bad out of good, he thinks, pleased with the idea, "Why not have children's joyous souls grow out of adulthood's ugly weeds?"

His wandering, worrisome reverie makes him think of Shakespeare's *Hamlet*. He paraphrases the soliloquoy on death while his thoughts play on the coming plans for marriage, "To marry or not to marry . . ."

Then, amused, but with a feeling of sudden self-reproach, Gray abruptly breaks off his train of thought and returns to headquarters and his duties. His mind switches to concern for Asher and his imprisoned friend, Salomon.

And from that to the court martial on which he must sit at four o'clock. He dreads it. Three wretches accused of murdering a companion over the division of plunder and their desertion.

All, he knows, will surely go before a firing squad. And he, he must cast his ballot! He must share in the taking of another American's life!

Close-up On Paulus Hook

The fall of Paulus Hook was long expected. It has amazed the American high command that the attack was postponed to this late date. Orders were actually given early yesterday morning "to remove the artillery, stores and baggage and hold (the post) in readiness to retreat."[4] And, actually, before nightfall Colonel Durkee had carried out most of the order.

Before night had fallen yesterday evening all that was left on the Paulus Hook post were some large quantities of artillery stores along with the garrison's complement of troops. The gun carriages and ammunition had been held back to defend the fort in the event the enemy attacked before withdrawal was completed.

The extremely rapid steps toward evacuation were initiated Saturday night when an American seaman from Providence, Rhode Island, who was captured by the British and had been forced to serve as a deck hand on the *Roebuck*, jumped overboard and swam to the Hook.[5]

Almost dead from exhaustion when he was pulled out of the bay after his long swim across the swift tide at the river's mouth, the seaman revealed to Durkee and his staff that an enemy attack was imminent. He stated that a large body of redcoats were assembling on the island's west shore at Greenwich Street dock, two miles north from Manhattan's tip.[6] A number of armed vessels, he declared, were all in readiness for striking the Hook in the enemy's initial invasion of the Jerseys.

The enemy troops were being prepared to "endeavour to cut off any American retreat,"[7] according to the seaman's knowledge.

Armed with this intelligence, Colonel Durkee immediately appealed to his commander, Brigadier General Hugh Mercer, for reinforcements to defend the post. The American command, deciding Paulus Hook could not be defended against the enemy's might, ordered Durkee to hurriedly begin its evacuation.[8]

Since the seaman added that the British attack was to have been executed "this morning (Saturday, September 21) but the fire (New York's burning) prevented it,"[9] the feverish evacuation activity was in full swing at the Hook Sunday morning when something else happened.

At 9 o'clock yesterday morning with the sound of the Sabbath church bells ringing clearly across the water, the American sentries and observers reported a concentrated enemy movement. Durkee immediately put the post on alert. Since there were still much impedimenta, heavy armament, ammunition and supplies to be taken out of the post, Durkee ordered operations to proceed but all troops to prepare to repel an expected enemy attack.

He had good reason. As the seamen had predicted, the redcoats marched in large numbers along the shore and began boarding some thirty flatboats and tenders. Meanwhile, four men-of-war in the upper bay hoisted sail south of the Hook's fort and silently headed for the river guardian post. There was no question but that the attack was about to begin.

Suddenly, however, with no plausible explanation, the warships dropped their sails and came to anchor well off from the rebel fortress toward which they had headed. And then, adding to the amazement of the rebel sentries and the troops manning their few remaining artillery pieces as well as those lining the Hook parapets, the troop-laden enemy river boats surprisingly came about and headed back for Manhattan's shore. Not a shot on either side had desecrated the Sunday Sabbath.

Later, the Reverend Benjamin Boardman, the Jersey post's chaplain, would say:

"Had they came at this time, we must either have retired and left them large quantities of artillery stores, or fought their army and navy at the same time with our small detachment, and that under every disadvantage, but they thought fit to retire to get more strength, as appeared afterwards, though they could not be ignorant of our weakness, the men being paraded every day in full view of them."[10]

Whether it was "to get more strength," or whether the enemy high command suspected some kind of American "trick," will be debated by American officers for some time to come. Tactics discussing Continental commanders believe that Howe suspected that York's fire and Hale's espionage were behind some rebel ruse in the making. It was for that reason, according to the strategy-thinkers, that the Paulus Hook attack was abruptly called off Sunday morning.

Regardless, the postponement enabled Durkee to complete his withdrawal and proved to be a costly delay for General Howe. The extensive British preparations and the elaborate planning, with army and navy units acting in concert, achieved nothing for the Crown except the accelerated capture of a vacant fort. It was a fort which had served its purpose and lost its value and strength when its sister battery on lower Manhattan fell with the British occupation of New York town.

Paulus Hook, like Fort Constitution, was of vital importance only in joint operation with the military batteries on the opposite banks. Paulus Hook and York's Grand Battery were inter-dependent as are Fort Constitution and Fort Washington, one upon the other.

Together the sister posts could, and have, harassed enemy shipping under sail attempting to navigate upriver between hostile batteries on either side of the narrow waterway. Direct hits on masts, spars and sails could, and did, greatly disable sailing vessels daring to make a run for it.

So, though delayed too long to achieve any kind of victory, the attack on the Hook's works began at one o'clock this Monday afternoon. By that time Colonel Durkee and his battalion had removed everything of value.

A Rolling Barrage Blasts A Deserted Post

All personnel were safely out the stockade's gates well before the *Roebuck* sent her first round into the post's 250-foot long main redoubt. Then the broadsides leveled in on the second mound, the emplacement which had, until yesterday, six guns. Next the enemy cannon fired into the block-house while fusillades of small arms fire raked, in blankets of wasted wrath, the entire grounds.

Not a single rebel weapon answered the enemy's deafening barrage, leaving the puzzled British officers wondering if their fire was so remarkably effective as to have silenced the rebels with their first few strikes.

Owing to the cloud of dust, smoke and fire raised by the shelling, British observers could not see the well-withdrawn American battalions moving safely and slowly about one mile west into the breastworks on the heights above Prior's mill.[11] Halting only long enough to occasionally look back and observe the enemy's rain of devastation on their former home, Durkee's men were immediately put to work throwing up entrenchments.

The only disorder came as a few of the raw militia recruits broke ranks when the roar of the Admiral's guns pounded into their ears. Overcome with fear they hightailed it in all directions shortly after the bombardment opened.

Their display of fear and cowardice with the enemy so far in their rear infuriated General Mercer[12] who had joined Durkee in leading the garrison out of the works. It particularly angered and embarrassed the men of the Continental line, the rough and tumble fellows who were all for staying and fighting it out with the British attackers.

Mercer told Durkee that The General is sure to make much of it when he hears of "that caper." It is sure, Mercer stated, to be on the end of the Commander-in-Chief's quill when he reports to Congress.

"'Twill add powder in his horn," Mercer said as he watched the terrified youngsters who had never before seen gun fire no less cannon shot, scatter as several of the bursts came close upon their heels. "The Gen'l will have more ammunition to tell Congress how much we need trained and disciplined men."

Like Mercer, most of the American high command, share The General's lack of faith in militia troops. This very day Major General Henry Knox at his quarters on Harlem's heights is writing his brother a letter highly critical of the state of the army owing to the poor quality of its officers and enlisted men.

"As the army now stands," writes Knox, "it is only a receptacle for ragamuffins."[13] And tomorrow, as Mercer seems to know in advance, the American Commander-in-Chief will send a report from the end of his quill to John Hancock and the Continental Congress from his Harlem headquarters at the Colonel Morris House. In it he will have much to say bout "the dissolution of our Army." He will write:

> " . . . As the War must be carried on systematically, you must have good officers . . . by establishing your army on a permanent footing . . . With respect to the Men, nothing but a good bounty can obtain them upon a permanent establishment; and for no shorter time than the continuance of the War, ought they to be engaged . . . To place any dependence upon Militia, is, assuredly, resting upon a broken staff . . ."[14]

The General's letter then goes on to recount the difficulties encountered with the weaknesses in the "Rules and Regulations," the inadequate pay, poor food, lack of clothing and insufficient shelter, the problems arising from the soldiers' enforced plundering to stay alive, from desertion, mutiny and other criminal acts.

Were they asked to add other difficulties, most of the rank and file would include: petty jealousies between Continental line men and State troops, between both of those and the militia, between the south's "Buckskin" men and the north's "Yankees." They would also undoubtedly add the countless arguments and brawls arising constantly over food, clothing and tenting. Wranglings that wear down and strain to the core the moral fiber of the army, particularly so now as winter approaches.

Mercer's Command Withdraws To Bergen's Heights

Up on the Bergen ridge heights above Prior's Mill, the ousted Paulus Hook battalions soon reached the security of the breastworks, started some time ago in preparation for this contingency. This was Durkee's first step in Mercer's withdrawal plan.

Area Commander Mercer had ordered some four thousand troops from the Bergen Neck posts to join Durkee's men on the escarpments to give the enemy a fight if they pursued the American forces inland.

The long Bergen ridge is one of the last of the rocky precipices at the southern end of the Palisades' long tail reaching southward toward the sea. The ridge works are a natural fortress, a part of the igneous rock's final tapering off before it descends and finally disappears at Bergen Point, sinking into the bays off Staten Island.

And now the expelled battalion, reinforced by the 4,000 men from Bergen's defenses, dig in, watch and wait. The high grounds offer a commanding view of Paulus Hook, the fort inside and out, the surrounding lowlands and salt marshes and the invading enemy's amphibious attack on an empty, deserted objective. The redcoats' maneuver gives all the appearance of a simulated operation—a rehearsal or drill—in preparation for the real thing.

Across the bay the Americans can see the island of Manhattan and New York town spread out in the distance. It is certain that the high grounds can offer only temporary sanctuary.

Sooner or later the whole Bergen ridge, its garrisons from the southern tip at Bergen Point up the peninsula, at least as far north as their position above Prior's mill, will be overrun by the superiority of the King's men. That they know.

Here the dispossessed troops of the old fort watch as the 40-gun *Roebuck*, the 40-gun *Phoenix*, and the 20-gun *Tartar*, all standing off in the bay, carry on their senseless 100-gun barrage. Billowing smoke and dust and sporadic flashes of flames from the fires ignited by the shelling, hide their eyes from the fort's interior.

Then suddenly the smoke dissipates and the works reappear within view while the British gunners pause to let their red-hot gun barrels cool. In those moments the little fort's outlines again take shape causing the men of the former garrison to send up wild hurrahs.

To those who worked so hard on its construction, manned its guns and cheered its hits upon the enemy's frigates during the past few months, it is as though the unmanned fort was insisting upon defying its attackers.

Though not even a stray chicken was left within the stockade, the enemy's light weapons began raking the post from one end to the other with not a single living target within their range.

It was about then that a few of the frightened militia who were, a little while before, head and shoulders in front of their galloping feet, came scrambling out of the marshes and lowlands.

They were seen from the ridge, again hightailing it as though someone were spurring their flying legs. But this time they were charging toward the amused old Continentals of the line and up toward the safety of the entrenchments on the heights.

It was their first sniff of gunpowder and most of the old veterans sympathized with them, fully understanding what the power of modern weaponry, particularly artillery can do to the fellow holding a rusty musket—a musket which all too often misfires and is useless in wet weather.

The veteran troops of Paulus Hook, though they had a deep

loyalty toward the old works on which they spent so much time, know, as do most military men, that none of the lower river and bay fortifications were built to withstand the Crown's combined army and navy assault capability. Few of the posts were even started before it was too late to turn them into strong defense works.

From Bergen Point up through to Paulus Hook, in New York town and on Long Island, as well as on the off-shore islands fronting Manhattan, the long-delayed, weak, inadequately manned outposts were all considered "death traps" by the troops called upon to defend them.[15]

- The Commander-in-Chief's original plan had called for a system far superior to the one Congress belatedly approved. So there are many old veterans who do not blame raw recruits who run for their lives from certain death. Even Mercer and Durkee will overlook the young soldiers' actions in this instance.

Despite the depressing sight before them as the empty stockade succumbed to the pointlessly ridiculous onslaught, the Continental veterans of many previous encounters with Sir William's men, found humor and a good laugh at what they saw. Howls of rebel laughter rose up shortly after the thirty barges loaded with infantrymen and marines swarmed ashore immediately after the barrage was lifted.

With fixed bayonets a wave of 500[16] redcoats, reorganized in attack columns after disembarking, slowly to the steady beat of drums cautiously stole toward the fort's outer abatis. Unchecked by any sign of opposition, the columns of marching men—evidently expecting some surprise action from behind the stockaded walls and earthworks—rolled up a gun carriage mounting a 20-pounder and blasted open the main west gates.

Simultaneously the redcoats charged through the opening while others from the east, racing up from the shore and landing docks, stormed through the cunningly woven outer trunks and limbs of trees. They valiantly broke through the ugly abatis with its oblately spiked spears and clambered over the log stockade certain that at any moment the "tricky rebels" would spring their surprise. The surprise that never came.

Instead they found themselves facing each other while far up on the heights to the west they could hear what sounded like a roar of laughter. This was synchronized with a far off bugle call sounding out of the distant Bergen ridge.

A bugler, who had remembered hearing of the British bugler's blowing the end of the "fox chase" a week ago on Harlem's heights, now sounded out the same notes in a mocking jest to signal the Crown's capture of the foxless foxhole.

Despite their fun at the enemy's expense, the Americans who had held Paulus Hook since the outset of the campaign are far more deeply hurt by its easy take-over than appears on the surface. For them it is an unfortunate loss with a fortunate escape, touched off by an unexpected laugh, and an enemy victory that should not have been permitted at such a cheap price.

To the King's men it has been nothing more than an excellent drill, a fine exhibition of their amphibious tactics sans the interference of opposition. That it was not defended is somewhat of a disappointment and rather embarrassing.

Its conquest eliminates a thorn in the side of the Admiral's fleet. For now the frigates without annoyance, can ascend the river, at least within a healthy distance of Fort Constitution and Fort Washington.

Those two river forts and their submerged blockade ten miles upstream are still waiting any further attempts by Lord Howe to run their gantlet. And the obliteration of that "gantlet" is gradually becoming an obsession in the combined minds of the Howe Brothers.

Post Chaplain Reverend Ben Boardman sarcastically described the British attack in these words:

> ". . . a great number of boats and floating batteries came down from just above New-York, the latter ran up into the cove, opposite the causeway that leads to Bergen. After taking a considerable time to see that there was nobody to hurt them, they began a most furious cannonade on our empty works, which continued until they had wearied themselves. In a word, they dared to come much nearer, and displayed the boasted British valour in much brighter colours than ever they had while there remained a single man to oppose them.
>
> "Meanwhile our little battalion retreated, with drums beating and colours flying, to Bergen, and before night, the brave Britons stormed on shore, and took possession of our evacuated works, where they have taken every precaution to prevent our formidable detachment from returning and driving them from a post which, with so great a dispaly of heroism, they have got possession of."[17]

Colonel Durkee and his men, who had been for months somewhat isolated out on the fringe of the marshland neck where the Paulus Hook river post had stuck itself boldly out into the river, had only a few neighbors.

It was these that they now worried about with the post in enemy hands, for all three—the Elsworths, Van Vorsts and the Priors—had been good neighbors and seemingly staunch patriots who had been helpful to the post and borne up well through the trials of having it and its problems almost under their noses.

Cornelius Van Vorst is the owner of the Hook and the ferry which he operates at the terminus of the stagecoach lines' land route to New York town. Verdine Elsworth's farm provides a good supply of produce and is well plenished with livestock which makes it a kind of general store, while Jacob Prior, who operates his mill on the mill road leading up to the high ridge is a vital dispenser of the army's—and the nation's—basic food staple, flour.

Their future is not only worrying Durkee but it is upsetting the thinking of all those who are inhabitants of the Hook. The commandant of the former American battery fears that the loss of each American outpost rapidly undermines the civilian morale, turning good patriots overnight into sworn Loyalists. And along with them speedily follow the "neutrals."

Durkee has one consoling thought: that the Paulus Hook inhabitants, especially the ferryman, miller, farmer and their families, will have little to fear. For upon them the enemy garrison will have to depend extensively for ferriage, produce, bread and meat.

As the dispossessed rebel garrison, comprising a strange heterogeneous cross-section of Eighteenth Century America, looked down on their fallen fort, a few only realized how little the land view before their eyes has changed in the past 143 years.

But those few southerners and northerners—Jerseyans, Pennsylvanians and New Englanders—some of whom are members of General Mercer's "Flying Camp,"[18] have been told about the long-forgotten Indian post.

They have repeatedly heard at fireside hearths how Michael Paulus, or Paulusen, in 1633 built his Indian trading post hut on the shore front and set up his business with the friendly Lenni Lenape on some 65 acres. They are the same acres which spread out under a rising cloud of battle smoke below their eyes.

It was from that beginning that the area acquired the name of Paulus's Hoeck, Paulus Hook, and Powles Hook after the Dutch Anglicized it. Then the English in their attempts to derive a suitable Dutch-English spelling concession, called it variously, Paulaz, Paulusen, Powles, and finally Paulus Hook.

But before its Dutch beginnings, the tract was known as the peninsula of Aressick and was described by early explorers as a neck of land west of Ahasimus. Soon the area's sand hills became a popular place for the growing of tobacco.[19]

The young soldiers, who had so often listened to travelers' tales at hearthsides throughout the land, had heard of how the early Van Vorst family acquired the hook opposite York's town back in 1669. They had made it an early terminus for ferries from the city port across the river and for the "Flying Coach" and other stages from Philadelphia.

And they had listened excitedly to the stories of the races run on Cornelius Van Vorst's 1769 horse racing track and of the earliest American fox hunts held just west of it, up in the Bergen woods. These stories thrilled them with the far away thought of someday seeing the big city port on Manhattan's great island and the place of the ferry that would carry them there.

Most of them had heard of Van Vorst's biggest horse race. It was in 1771, just five years ago. As youngsters, they had heard tell of it. It was the race between the stallions, Booby, Mug and Quicksilver. Twice around the track they sped, for a great purse of thirty dollars was the winner's prize.

And some of the ejected garrison troops remember the winner. In his later days he became known as "Old Mug," the Hook's favorite animal. And never will they forgive the enemy whose attack on the fort just eight days ago brought death to the post's pet.[20]

Killed by an enemy cannon ball, the warrior stallion was accorded a soldier's burial by the Hook's garrison.

Then, befitting his past achievements, they had, with proper pomp and ceremony accompanied by the roll of drums and the mournful sound of fifes and pipes, buried their beloved animal just off the race track.

It was there, they felt, that he had made a name for himself in those far, far more peaceful days. It was there, they believed, between the track and his military post, that he would be most content after giving his life for his country.

The Link Of A Chain Never Forged

Colonel Durkee's mind was not on the post's history nor on the death and burial of Old Mug. His thoughts and those of General Mercer were concentrating upon its brief history and its loss.

It was January 5, 1776, that the Paulus Hook post was born on paper. It was a part of the plan called, "The Defences of the

Liberties of America." That plan was a chain of fortifications which were to have been constructed from Staten Island to Fort Constitution as primary strongholds guarding the Hudson and Manhattan. In that chain, the "Powles Hook" fortification was a most important link.

Mercer reminds Durkee as they recall its beginnings, that not one of those important links was begun until it was too late to avoid the foreseen invasion and attack on Long Island.

As early as May 21, Mercer recounts as staff aides gather beside him and The Hook's commandant—helplessly watching the British troops move into the distant stockade far beyond and below them—"The Gen'l wrote Chief Engineer Rufus Putnam, who planned and designed the works, 'I would have that (work) at Powles Hook set about immediately as I consider it of importance.' "

Other staff members recall that it was the same day he inspected Amboy and Staten Island, finding to his disgust that no spade had been struck in the ground at either place by the local arms of the vacillating New Jersey Safety Committee.

Durkee recalls that it was at the Hook, shortly afterward, that Rufus Putnam requisitioned and received a captured enemy prize which he used in beginning construction on the works.

It was the 300-ton ship, *Cork*, taken by the Americans under the enemy's nose. The vessel was loaded with sand-bags and intrenching tools, just the thing to start the fort's emplacements. And by June 19 the fortifications were partly completed.[21]

Mercer, assuring his staff officers that he feels the British have no immediate plans to pursue the Continentals, puts down his field glasses and listens as Durkee and others—through open charges and innuendoes—attribute the loss to Congressional ignorance.

They note that it was on June 10 that the Commander-in-Chief's original plan had been so completely inverted by intervening Congressional orders that only four percent of the gun-power of the army was installed where it was originally planned.

They add, with a great deal of respect and admiration for their former command, that the only fort named in the prime project which was erected, or under construction, as first proposed, was Paulus Hook. It was noted also that by the middle of June it was housing both Colonel Bailey's and Colonel Reed's regiments.[22]

One of the aides reminds them that General Knox reported on June 10 that the armament allotment for the post included:

"Two—twelve-pounder guns with traveling carriages; three—thirty-twos, garrison carriages; and two—three-pounders, iron field pieces."

Beside Connecticut-born John Durkee, despondent and wearied from the pressure of the past few days and the loss of his command, stands Reverend Abiel Leonard, former pastor of the First Church of Woodstock, acting chaplain for Durkee's own Twentieth Regiment of the Continental Army from Connecticut. Durkee had been relieved of his regimental responsibilities when Mercer gave him command of the post. One of its main operations, outside of its strategic defense duties, had been to operate much of Mercer's Flying Camp processing owing to the post's strategic location since the Battle of Long Island.

As night slowly falls over the rocky heights of north Bergen and the tired Continentals, the men dig in and prepare the first good meal they have had all day. Over the light of the campfires they can gaze down on their former domain. They listen to their own sentinels sounding off along the rocky ridge instead of at their former, familiar sentry posts on the ramparts of the old fort. Waves of angry, bitter resentment periodically sweep over them.

They say little as they look longingly down upon it with mixed thoughts. . . . The strong, solidly built stockade, its cannon-blasted, fallen gates.

In the lowering twilight they can see the outlines of the 16-rod long oblong redoubt ten rods in width . . . How proud they were of that! . . . And the big redoubt with its big 32-pounders that turned the *Roebuck* and its sister vessels back . . . How busy were the gunners racing around its parapet that day! . . . So many, many days and hours of work, day in and day out, had they given to it all! . . .

Then, there, the barracks which have taken the British broadsides' direct hits . . . What stories and tales they have heard told over and over again through lonesome nights! . . .

One tough old gunner, Tony Talo, a veteran of the siege of Boston, says, looking down at the distant redcoat figures moving like little ants throughout the old works, "Tis a compliment to our Old Man that George Rex's men take over it with narry a single complaint to the landlord."

A few of the men at his side let go with a sickly laugh as he continues, "But one of these days we'll oust their damned hides fer not sayin' a thank ye and payin' us rent!"

His companion, the over-cautious Swede, Orlof Swenson, forces a laugh. But his sigh registers serious doubt as he says, "Yah, yah! You haf goot hopes. But Oi tank you hopes wrong."

Nevertheless, the old gunner is not far wrong from an accurate, chance prediction. For actually it will be two years, ten months and 19 days in the future morning of August 19, 1779, that the British-held Paulus Hook garrison will be attacked and overrun by American raiders.[2][3]

Major Henry "Lighthorse Harry" Lee will on that day make amends for this one. He will storm the surprised redcoat garrison in a lightning stroke, overcome its British defenders, and then, with the loss of only three of his own men, the brilliant young officer will safely return with his legion to the American lines. Before him he will herd some 150 British prisoners in one of the most remarkable, secret American strokes of military acumen in the entire war.

Under The Mountain, War Is Far Away

Back northward now this night, some twelve miles up the spiny, rocky back of the Palisades, darkness is also falling over the great Bluff Rock and the Continentals on Fort Constitution.

Below The Rock a few sails make for the safety of the shore before darkness settles over them. Each is loaded with its catch of fish. And along the water's edge black and white men, following the instructions they have been getting from their friendly master woodsman, Sergeant Andy, throw their nets out into the river.

Except for the many campfires and the varied mixture of sad and jolly songs of the soldiers above and below, few would believe that a war is raging in temporary silence around them.

Stars overlaid on French Ministry Map (Paris, France, circa 1777) show American posts held along the Hudson until Battle of Kip's Bay and the Fall of Paulus Hook: (1) Bergen Neck; (2) Paulus Hook; (3) New York City; (4) Bulls Ferry; (5) Fort Lee; (6) Fort Washington; (7) Sneden's Landing. Arrows indicate the British drive out of Staten Island, through Brooklyn on Long Island, up the East River into Kip's Bay. Map is from The New York Public Library Map Room.

16

Sunday, October 6. . .

In the Interlude Comes Love

A Lull That Hides the Attacks Within

The long lull in any major British activity has dangerously circulated the feeling throughout the region that the campaign for
this 1776 year is over. That Howe is bedding down for the winter
seems to many inhabitants a certainty. Outside of possibly a few
nuisance raids and occasional brushes with the enemy they foresee
a gradual letting up of the war's pressure until next spring.

Some say that the city's terrible fire sixteen days ago consumed
so much of the homes and buildings which the Crown's men were
to have used for their winter quarters, that re-building before the
snows set in has become Howe's main concern. Certainly the
positions of the two opposing armies have remained static since
then, with little noticeable activity since the loss of Paulus Hook.

As for Admiral Howe and his navy, they have likewise been
quiet, consolidating themselves on the conquered Paulus Hook
post. That is until this morning when Black Dick sent three armed
frigates upriver in another apparent attempt to run the blockade.
Finding the American gunners on Forts Constitution and Washington too accurate for their comfort, all three vessels came about and
returned downstream.

Like the two sister forts on the river's opposite banks holding
off the Lord Admiral, the American defenses on and below Mount
Washington along Harlem's heights, likewise present a too

formidable front for Sir William to risk a frontal assault. Besides, the high grounds there, and on the even higher Bluff Rock site across the river, give his rebel opponents an almost unobstructed view of every move he makes.

General Howe, despite his reverses insofar as peace overtures are concerned, still retains strong pro-Whig sentiments which he hopes to use in swaying the "colonists" and avoiding further bloodshed.

His latest move is to attempt destruction of the rebel army from within. To effect this he has offered inviting terms to any American leaders who desert the rebel cause.

Employing all the presses at his command, Howe is circulating handbills which attack the Continental Congress and threaten those who continue to support it and the rebellion. They offer enticing inducements and protection to those who accept the King's amnesty and give their pledge of allegiance to the Crown.

Behind Sir William is the strong, pro-British New York press.[1] It has already reached and successfully influenced many American troops in Orange County as well as large numbers of so-called "neutral" Dutch and French descendants—farmers of the valleys.

Particularly successful in persuading the vacillating landowners has been Rivington's *Gazette*. It is constantly offering attractive inducements to the fence-straddlers and to some of the more easily swayed militia who, Tom Paine tells Greene, are only "sunshine soldiers" who are useless to the cause anyway.

Up on the Palisadean wall and all around it there are few neutrals, few who feel the American cause is hopeless and few who are interested in Howe's offers. For most of the local inhabitants are convinced Fort Constitution and Fort Washington will be the impregnable guardians of upper Manhattan and the surrounding area at least until next spring.

They are certain Fort Constitution will be the army's winter quarters. Also there is something comforting about the name, "Fort Constitution," and the fact that it now is "one of the principal military works in the country."[2]

Under General Greene's command for the past 19 days, Fort Constitution, besides being the pivotal point of the American midriff army, also serves as the launching site for forays, military and civilian express runs south to Philadelphia and north to Albany, and also for reconnoitring missions. Often such missions are coupled with inspection tours on which The General, coming over from headquarters on Harlem's heights, rides southward into Bergen's remaining posts and northward to Tappan town and Sneden's ferry. Frequently he is accompanied by Greene.

Neither the Commander-in-Chief nor Greene share the popular belief that Howe is finished for the season. Both are certain that the silent guns are merely cooling while the Howe Brothers plan their strategy. Both know, as does Sir William, that attempts to undermine the sound foundations of the rebel cause with inviting platters of amnesty will never succeed in reversing the deeply imbedded American determination for independence.

However, only the Howe brothers and their staffs know in what direction the campaign soon will be moving. And thus far the King's men have successfully concealed the operations they have made from the prying American eyes high on Mount Washington and higher still on the great Bluff Rock.

One thing that enables their clandestine movements along Manhattan's east side is that the Howes have made extensive use of the East River since landing at Kip's Bay. So much redcoat activity has gone on there on both sides of the waterway that any additional operations can be carried on without arousing rebel suspicions. Consequently British plans and preparations in that sector are not likely soon to be detected.

When the concentration of troops and transports finally appears to be increasing daily, the American command begins to suspect that Howe may be planning to come behind the American's Harlem post with an attack at its northernmost point, King's Bridge. This concern and General Howe's handbills, inviting Americans to defect, are two things weighing heavily on The General's mind this Sunday morning.

Boring From Within Brings Its Dividends

Greene has reported that militia officers are complaining of a decided drop in enlistments as a result of Howe's handbills and their demoralizing effect. Fewer and fewer men are interested in joining militia units, preferring to stay on their farms and remain close to their families.

One such officer, Colonel A. Hawks Hay of Orange County complained to the New York Committee of Safety and appealed for help saying that most of his men were now refusing "to attend the service, though repeatedly summoned."[3]

The handbill campaign has not only touched some of the indecisive among the militia, it has also had some pernicious effects upon scattered segments of the people throughout the new colonial states.

Some feel that the Congress should give in to the British offers of reconciliation. In most cases these groups are reflecting the thinking of some staunch British sympathizer, such as Nicausie Klep on The Mountain, or Loyalists who pose as neutrals and get the ear of the unwary.

Klep is typical of a few of the King's "underminers." Unsuccessfully Baummeister has tried to expose him. The avid Tory seems always to come within a fraction of an inch of arrest every time. It was just three weeks ago that Gray sent him back under suspicion to Durkee when he was taken beside the mysterious cache of arms above Bull's ferry.

Like others of his ilk, Klep has latched on to the peaceful, neutral farmers' rationale that: "If we leave our farms, our families will starve. If we defy the King's men, the conquering enemy will take all we have ever acquired if not our lives as well. If we sign the oath of allegiance, we stand well before the conquering enemy and may be spared our lands, our properties and surely our lives. All we desire is peace, liberty and safety. If we can secure that, we will be content. General Howe has promised us peace, liberty and safety and that is all we want."[4]

So it is this rationale which Klep and his cohorts promote and expand, stirring up not only civilian inhabitants throughout the land but infiltrating the militia with seeds for desertion and defection. The resultant spread of fear and discontent accomplishes much that the Howe Brothers have not been able to do with their army and navy.

Although the slow, insidious poisoning does not have any significant effect upon the backbone of the army—the hard corc, freedom-loving Continentals—or the Bourdettes, the Baummeisters and the Dereck Remlin type of patriots, its proportions soon seriously disturb Nathanael Greene.

Greene's Solution Shunned

In a letter to his Chief, Greene, referring to the militia problem, asks The General: "What is to be done with them (The militia who are refusing to obey their officers)? This spirit and temper should be checked in its infancy."[5]

Greene suggests sending 50 Continentals from Fort Constitution to bring back the recalcitrants to the Palisadean post and put them to work "and service here at Fort Constitution."

But the Commander-in-Chief advises his junior officer that he could not agree with, or approve, such an action.

So the war of revolution, now smoldering in a strange silence all around Hudson's river, is on this Sunday morning merely pausing in order to sharpen its pointed pitch-forks of hate, vengeance and death. Like the briefly dormant volcano that once rose here out of the earth's bowels, the needless, unnecessary war slackens before erupting once again.

In the countless caves of the Palisadean mountain, rising up majestically as though held on high by the river's waters, the wolf, bear and panther sleep. On the summits of the lofty precipices, the tree-tops drip down their tired, falling, multi-colored leaves.

On the topmost limb of one old, dying pine, hanging perilously over the cliff's side, a bald eagle and her mate watch their fledgling about to leave them forever.

Then suddenly, with a screeching thank-you, he dives gracefully into the air, rises and soars away. With no backward glance at his once-doting parents and the nest that was so long his home, he sets himself free to seek his mate and a tree-top of his own.

And below his strong and graceful figure where his shadow swiftly sweeps over the shore toward the river, the rattler, the copperhead and the weasel look up hungrily at the ascending flocks of south-bound birds.

The winged creatures fly with their instincts. Strangely, intuitively they have been forewarned of the coming of winter's rains that turn to ice and snow.

Only they now have the power of escape from the bitter cold that blessedly dulls the senses and stills the pangs of hunger through the long nights and dreaded days of near-starvation. Only they can mass together and flee, leaving the wintry land to the more rugged, to the old, to the crippled.

Though most of the thousands of living things, which have by birth, or choice, selected the great queen-like, Palisadean mountain range as their home, must now think of their individual survival, some few think also of their mates.

As the eaglet disappears southward over the river's trail to the sea, the male flies up and comes to rest close to his partner upon the long pine limb. Both now seem to peer downward where a large bass jumps just off the Bourdette Ferry dock.

And there, where Marie Louise has come from the house to join her husband, leaning on the ferry's guard rail, the jumping fish has caught Pete's attention. His wife silently slips her hand into his, and he takes it, not the least surprised, but rather as though he had expected her.

Without looking away from the jumping bass, he says, as she expected he would say, "Dot's a big vun! Too bod 'tis Shunday! Oddervise ve'd ketchem! ..."

Then, after pausing briefly, he turns and looks at Marie Louise, adding, "Dey kom bak today, no? ... I miss my Ellie, Liebchen ... I miss her ... But he is a goot man. A goot man."

Marie Louise nods her head acquiescingly. She squeezes her husband's hand tightly in silence.

Also among those on The Mountain who think less of themselves and more of their mates are the bride and bridegroom. Cozily together they walk this day arm in arm on the ancient castle grounds of the long-dead Indian Chieftain, Oratam.[6]

There on the western slope of the Palisades several miles south of Fort Constitution, Elaine and John Gray, man and wife for a week and a day, prepare to return to the seemingly far distant post. The couple stand now where once the great chief, the senior Sagamore and Sachem of the Haqninsak[7] tribe of the Unami Division of the Lenni Lenape Nation, looked down upon his people and his valley, now the valley of the Hackensack.

It was a week ago yesterday morning that Baummeister, holding back a tear, gave his daughter's hand in marriage to the Blue Petticoat Scarf Lieutenant. And it is the one and only day The Lieutenant has not worn that scarf.

The order was a strict one from Elaine, "No petticoat scarf!"

Besides, it made the easily embarrassed Domine Dereck Remlin much more comfortable performing the ceremony ... And many others also found its removal less affrontive to the moral and virtuous sensitivities of womanhood.

So the Lieutenant reluctantly complied.

The large, military Long House is used only for some few chapel services, councils of war and court martials. But General Greene with, it was said, the Commander-in-Chief's permission, had turned over the building for civilian use just this once. Particularly since it was in order to solemnize the marriage of Pete Baummeister's daughter.

It was, Elaine openly admitted, the biggest event of her life. In fact it was also the biggest event that ever took place among the wilderness families all around The Mountain.

It was also the biggest social event in the short history of Fort Constitution. It brought soldiers who did not know the couple in addition to Gray's own men who pushed through the doors to see their "officer and his lady spliced."

Oratam, Senior Sagamore and Sachem of
the Hackensack Indians—Bust photograph
and Oratam's symbol are from Francis C.
Koehler's *Three Hundred Years*, Chester,
New Jersey, 1940.

It became an event not soon to be forgotten. The Lieutenant's
battery made that certain with whooping as the wide-eyed, unsuspecting Preacher Remlin pronounced the couple man and wife.

With no home of their own—they will reside with the Baummeisters—there was no place for the soldier bridegroom to steal
away alone with his new wife, so both Elaine and John had readily
accepted Sergeant Abbott's offer of his mountain-top hut. Little
did they know what it was like then. Now they are much wiser.

Believed to be the last direct descendant of the great Oratam, Abbott's offer of his now seldom used sylvan home is an unheard of gesture toward white men. His log hut, hewn out of forest timber, adjoins that of his aging parents. The two abodes rest on the edge of the western crest of the mountain that overlooks the beautiful valley below it and the Ramapo and Minisink Mountains which run westward into the very far distant Shawangunk ranges.

And so there, through the scattered rising chimneys of the brown, sandstone homes and villages of the early settlers, were once the vast lands of the Lenni Lenape, branch of the Algonkians and known by the white man as the Delawares. For indeed their lands reached far and beyond the river Delaware, some 60 miles southwest as the crow files.

Once The Lands Of The Lenni Lenape

From afar Andrew Abbott has long admired Elaine and long has he befriended, and been befriended by her father. Often he has asked advice from both Bourdette and Baummeister in his long efforts with his parents, Perawae and Minnie Abbott, to hold as tenaciously as they can the last holdings of his ancient tribe—an isolated level of the rocky summit where once stood Oratam's home, built from the rocks of the cliffs themselves.

With the passage of years and the coming of the white man the tribe diminished as white man's illnesses and white man's liquor brought about their dissolution and retreat, farther and farther into the interior.

Soon only a handful of Indians clung to the cliff's grounds, the last remnants of a village. And soon the white man called the stone structure in the wilderness, "Oratam's Castle."

Little now of that remains. Only the Abbotts' well-built, bark and thatch-covered huts, the lean-to stable, corn field and vegetable garden grace the long-lost highlight of the kindly Lenni Lenape's forgotten culture.

A winding, circuitous trail leads to the surprising hideaway. At its summit the trail levels, coming onto a fertile plateau which, like an amazing Garden of Eden, appears to be cut carefully and purposely out of the wilderness around it. At its very center on the precipice edge are the stone ruins of the so-called "castle."

High brush and tangled vines climb over the abandoned structure. They lie, sadly reminiscent of a missing page in the treasured annals of some long-buried empire. Not far distant are the two well-built, neatly kept, thatched-roof Indian abodes.

Each hut shows definite influences of the Eighteenth Century American settlers, particularly their local Dutch-English architecture. Each home holds basically to its builders' tribal traditions.

Each has its earthern floors, rugs of bear-skin, wolf and deer. These blend in properly with the furnishings made by careful loving hands from the trees and growths of the forests.

All seem to reflect the union of the so-called "Original People" with their earth-given surroundings—with the natural gifts and wonders of nature that they were known to have respected and worshiped. For the Lenni Lenape live close to the earth and the sky and the wonders they perform.

It was to the dwelling, not too far distant from that of his parents, where Abbott had brought his young squaw three years before. He had built the home especially for her, his Little Bear Princess.

But after only six moons he bore her in his arms to get help from the white man, the only friend he knew. Through the snows he carried her on his horse along the cliff above the Baummeisters. There he dismounted, carefully holding the bundled, wasting little body in his arms down the rocky slope to the Baummeister's. All Minnie's remedies had failed. It was a last resort.

Shortly after, Abbott's beloved Andrea, Mahtocheega, died with child in the sixteenth winter of her young life.

And Andrew Abbott never forgot the efforts Marie Louise and Pete Baummeister made—the long sleepless nights they all gave—in an unsuccessful effort to save the life of the frail, coughing, young Indian girl and her child six months in the womb.

Soon after Andrea's death there was much talk and speculation that Andrew would accede to the seldom expressed desires of Perawae and Minnie who had long wanted to follow the tracks of their people northward and westward into the setting sun. But the young Indian youth's attachments to the white people of The Mountain, the coming of the war and the army's request for his services, changed, at least temporarily, any plans he nurtured for joining his receding, vanishing Lenni Lenape nation.

The Mountain people knew how deeply Andy Abbott loved his child princess. Granny Bourdette looked upon the match between the direct descendant of Oratam and the almost certain daughter of the King of the Delawares, as a last hope—Indian Abbott's dream she called it—for the perpetuation of the Unamis and the Lenni Lenape Nation in the changing new American world. But whatever dreams and hopes he had for his people were dashed into oblivion the morning Andrea died.

All the people of The Mountain remember and still talk about how straight he stood, how silent his lips and how emotionless he seemed, as though shocked into a terrifying stupor by a paralyzing bolt from the sky when the last gasp of breath from the choking, collapsing little lungs faded with the morning's cold and freezing February dawn.

All remember how grateful were The Mountain and the cliff's people—all excepting Nicausie Klep and his close friend, Jeffery Gartleck—when Abbott consented to the burial of his young bride and unborn child in the white man's burial grounds. It was as though Oratam's last descendant were succumbing at last to the white man's ways and rituals.

So it was that Indian Abbott never forgot. And he never forgot how Elaine, then only fifteen—a year younger than Andrea—tried to console him, though he paid little attention to anyone for many months.

And he has, with eyes that seemingly are at the back of his head, known and seen how the Baummeister girl has often picked handfuls of flowers, climbed the trail up to the mountain-top fields and its burial grounds on the northern fringe. And there she has placed them on the stone-marked grave of the Indian princess just north of the still water lake.

No one knew for sure that Andrea was the lost daughter of Teedyuscung, King of the Delawares. But the Norwegian sea captain, Arnold Nordstrom, and his wife, Ina, believed she may have been.

The captain had found the warmly wrapped papoose hanging from a tree near the river, Delaware, some distance from the burned out, completely deserted and still smoldering Indian village. She was the sole survivor of the twelve inhabitants about whom no trace has ever been found.

Nordstrom and his wife adopted the child, reared her as their own in their home on Hudson's river up on the cliffs above Bull's Ferry. Then Ina Nordstrom died and the grieving captain soon followed her to the grave, leaving most of his worldly goods to Andrew and Andrea.

His house he left to his long-faithful, half-breed housekeeper, Nellie, with the provision that Andrea was to be given its shelter as long as she was unmarried.

The Abbott family was one of the very few Indian families left in the area. It was inevitable that Andrew's protective interest, as charged to him by his benefactor prior to his death, would soon become more than that, especially under Perawae and Minnie's subtle urgings.

So the romance blossomed not long after Andrew, sent to England by the captain to learn more about the white man's ways, returned to The Mountain.

Abbott had learned much from his trip to England. Upon his return he found even greater respect and friendship from white men whom, like all Indians, he had never fully trusted nor completely believed. His reading and writing of the English language put him in a class by himself insofar as the white man's respect and opinion were concerned.

In the years before the war started Abbott was almost constantly seen with the young Indian maiden by his side as well as, occasionally, with other Indian youngsters, learning from him the ways of the river and the woods.

It was known that the captain had named her Andrea out of his liking for the Indian youth he had earlier come so strongly to admire. And it was possible that the old sea dog had quietly maneuvered the Andrew and Andrea courtship.

Regardless, The Mountain people looked upon and liked the developing love affair which ended in the tribal nuptials on Oratam's castle grounds to which no white man was invited and which no white man saw. That was in August 1773 when, upon the rising of the new moon, the orphaned, Indian girl of the Delaware became Andrea Abbott, as The Mountain people preferred to call her.

But to the slightly British-educated Oratam descendant, the Indian girl bride was always Mahtocheega, Little Bear Princess. His respect and reverence for his people and their culture became second only to his affection and devotion for Mahtocheega.

So everyone knew that Andy would give his life if necessary to defend those burial grounds. At times the developing army post came close to desecrating the graveyard with its expansion activities. But always any accidental encroachments were apologetically corrected. An angry look from the army's Indian scout was sometimes more effective than a complaint from an inhabitant or even the Preacher Remlin himself.

Consequently all around the quaint little cemetery with its slightly raised mounds of earth, most of which are topped by rounded sandstone markers, the encampment expanded carefully revering the spot. Not far northwest of it the post's own burial grounds were begun.

All of these memories flash through Elaine's mind as she walks with her husband for the last time around the ancient village grounds. She knows that soon they will stop and drink berry juice with their host and hostess, Old Chief Perawae and his squaw, Minnie. For Abbott's parents have treated them as though they were some visiting king and queen. For the past eight days, a drink of berry juice at this time of day has been a part of their kindly host's gracious ritual.

Elaine's eyes wander across the level field coming to rest on the old couple, laboriously husking corn in front of their forest home. She takes in the humble but immaculate abode, noting how many were the improvements Andy had made in the construction of his hut over the home of his parents.

Her arm tightens around her husband's waist and his responds as she visualizes that some day just such a little place—their first home—might be hers and John's. Elaine drinks in the scene around her, suddenly realizing how much she has learned from Abbott's people—how much she liked of it all, and how much she would do differently in a home of her own.

A Last Glimpse Of "Paradise"

Literally and figuratively John and Elaine have left the war, destruction and death behind them for just this one beautiful week of their lives. It was as though, Elaine thinks to herself, the kindly, thoughtful, loveable Andy had tried to show them a glimpse of the paradise that was once his people's—the paradise that the white man has gradually destroyed.

For certainly Abbott has guided them to a world apart which neither she nor John had dreamed existed so few miles from the most important military center in the country. Regretfully she reminds herself that very shortly now, Andy will arrive to guide them back to Fort Constitution, to home, to her loved ones . . . a married woman.

In their last ambling together over the high plateau, Elaine and John slowly approach the large flat rock jutting off from the plateau's edge. It overlooks miles upon miles of valley and rolling hills that spread out westward below them, reaching off into the distant mountain ranges and the setting sun.

Often have they come here during this week. For here they could in silence, yet in union, reminisce upon man, his past, present and the future. And here together their eyes struggle to see their own hopes in a future questionably stretched out before them like the shadows of the clouds in the landscape below.

Putting together all that they have seen and the little that they have heard, the young couple sense the history of the massive stone table, visualizing that it was here that Abbott's ancestor, the great Oratam, stood in silent contemplation. That it was from here that he looked protectingly down upon his peace-loving people in the Indian village of Achenkesacky.

From here he watched the squaws and young ones tend their gardens and their fields of corn. From here he watched the old hunters teach the young braves the ways of the animals, the ways of the forest, and the ways of the streams and rivers. From here he watched them launch their heavy vessels, dug out from great trees, and their birch bark canoes that dotted the rivers and the bays as far as he could see. From here he watched them smoking the meat of their hunt, skinning the arrow-pierced carcasses, and tanning the hides that would make winter clothing for their bodies and warm rugs for their lean-tos and dwellings.

And from here he frowned with fear as he watched with ever more and more trepidation, the encroaching white man's increasing greed. From here he saw the disappearing hope for the redman's dream of peace.

"It is like seeing the other side of man, Elaine," John says, breaking their silent contemplations. "Our rock over on the east side of The Mountain under the Barbette Battery looks out upon the approaching enemy, out over war and death. And this looks out upon . . . well, upon the opposite, upon hope . . . upon . . ."

"Upon, as Domine Remlin would say, man's better face," Elaine interjects. "Is that not what you mean, John-G?"

"True!" replies her husband. "For what could be more peaceful looking than that quiet, hidden valley yonder? Its little villages spotted there in the distance with their church spires and the rising puffs of smoke from the farmhouse chimneys make me wonder how 'tis possible there is war about us."

"Think you, John, 'tis any different inside those homes than in the houses of your Philadelphia?" Elaine queries. "'Tis not all so peaceful within as it seems. I know those people and of the silly, stupid arguments they have over worship, politics, The Cause, dress and habits. I know!"

"Yea, I know, Elaine." John replies. "But it looks so . . ."

"Peaceful," Elaine says, completing his thought for him. "Like, you are about to say, like paradise," she adds half jesting. "And I do not want to hear one word or quotation from your John Milton and his paradise. I have had enough of him all week. Rest his poor soul! This is our time to be alone together. And little now there is left of it for us!"

As she smiles up at him he grasps her in his arms, hugs and kisses her intensely in a deep and long embrace.

Then suddenly he stiffens, grasps her hand tightly, commanding in a hushed whisper, "Don't move! 'Tis a giant rattler . . . Behind ye, to my right . . . but only six feet away on the edge of the rock . . ."

Despite his warning she slowly turns away and toward the serpent and says, scolding him, "John Gray! Serpents want none of us. He'll harm you not less you harm him."

Facing the puzzled reptile, one of many she has known and put up with on the rocks of The Mountain, she, unflinchingly, addresses the snake in a calm, low voice, "Get you gone, Wiggler! Be off about your business . . . Sis . . . sis, sis, sis . . ."

Promptly obeying her hisses, the creature disappears down the slope. Any avenue of escape, he seems to feel, is better than a confrontation with the peculiar looking creatures that are gradually invading his world.

Turning then to her open-mouthed husband, she declares in her best schoolmarmish tone of voice, "My father says, 'Fear not the serpent who loves living as well as doth thee, but must willingly and bravely die, as do all things living, to assure the continuance of his progeny and his kind.' "

"Mayhap your father knows his reptiles well, *Madame Eve*," replies Gray with a relieved touch of laughter in his voice, "but I have also heard him say, 'Watch out for the woman who has forked tongue like serpent!' "

"1, 2, 3" In Any Language

"Enough of that!" snaps back Elaine, smiling at her husband's sense of humor.

Then, noticing some figures chiseled into the rock which had not before caught either of their eyes, she asks, pointing to them, "What do they mean? Look, you there under the sign of Oratam![8] See! Is it not a one, two and there a three? What make you of that?"

"I know not," John replies, pushing the dirt and leaves away. "One hundred and twenty-three, I suppose."

3

Oratam's Symbol

He chuckles at the logic of his answer, adding, "Truly I had not noticed them until ye did."

"Tis not one hundred and twenty-three," Elaine replies, correcting him. "Were it so, each number would be on line adjoining the other."

Their discussion is interrupted by the approach of Old Chief Perawae, or Matthew Abbott, coming up from behind them. The great, great, great, great grandson of the ancient Chief Oratam smiles broadly as he calls them with his, "Pachgandhatteu! Pachgandhatteu!"[9]

Addressing them in his kindly, courteous manner, he says, "Squaw Minnie has water of the berry for you and much food cooked for eat before you go. Andy now in low trail. Soon he be here. You come! Pachgandhatteu!"

Both Elaine and John know the meaning of Old Chief's "Pachgandhatteu!," or "Come eat!" Both thank him.

John asks the meaning of the "1, 2, 3" carved in the rock below the sign and symbol of Oratam. Perawae had shown them Oratam's sign when they first arrived on the castle grounds.

The question causes the old man to draw back a little as though it were something he did not wish to speak about. But his hesitation is momentary.

Elaine notices that his whole facial expression suddenly changes from one of a smiling pleasant host to an old man deeply beset by some tragic memory. A faint trace of moisture seems to come over his vision as the tired, aging, yet unwavering, piercing brown eyes look intently and sadly at the three numerals etched in the rock.

His voice, though usually deep and firm, now becomes obviously slower and significantly more hesitating.

"Andy learn much writing and numbers from the sea captain and from when Captain Nord send him to land of Englishman,"

Perawae begins, slowly weighing his words. "Andy and Andrea look at, read all Captain Nord's books and learn white man's writin' and numbers.

"Andy bring her here much. Minnie she like her much. I like her much. At night they come here, watch Moon God sail cross sky. He teach her many numbers, one, two, three, four, five and more to count like white man quick. Then she no like learn no more and only want look at him.

"So he say she only must learn one, two, three. He say that must be their sign. He say, one is stand for Andrew, him. Three is stand for Andrea to be squaw—he say bride—of Andrew. And he say two is stand for the bark, the great spirit that binds together the branches of the trees and makes them hold together. He say two is what white man call love but he call spirit of the earth, rain, snow, sun and sky.

"So always they have sign together only for them. They call their sign, '1, 2, 3'. Next day after marry her, he write with her there on rock with iron stick their sign, so '1,2,3'!

"He tell her in white man's talk it say, 'I, Andrew, love you, Andrea, but in Lenni Lenape people talk, it say two spirits tie together like one, like bark tie together two trunks of tree and soon come from them little spirits like little acorns.'"

Now the old man's voice drifts off and almost fades as he tells his attentive listeners how Andrea stood up on the high flat stone and whistled like a bird three sharp, thrilling notes—notes which, Perawae said, he later often heard her sing out and which Andy answered wherever he was in a replying trilogy that echoed through the forest and out over the valley below.

"Too soon—much too soon—Great Spirit call Mahtocheega," continued the Old Chief, "and Mahtocheega take with her little papoose who never see light from Sun God. So Young Eagle—Andy called Young Eagle 'cause was grandson of Chief Big Eagle—much sad, much alone."

Elaine and John have taken in every word the old man has said. They have known Andy's Lenape name is Young Eagle but that he has shunned its use in his desired leaning toward an amalgamation with the white man's ways—a course the Indian sergeant thinks is inevitable for the welfare of the few remaining people of the Lenni Lenape Nation.

It was old Captain Arnold and his wife, Ina, who had let it be understood that the youth wanted to be known as Andrew and not by his tribal name. So rarely has anyone ever mentioned his Lenape title.

"Now Perawae no have grandchild," continues Old Chief, recovering his composure and smiling faintly. "So gone too, once great village of Achenkesacky and all great Oratam's people soon all go way, soon all die ... Now you come! Come! Pachgandhatteu!"

Though John has listened attentively and is moved by the old man's story, it is Elaine who has been most impressed. The account has struck her with a shockingly new enlightenment.

It is, she feels, as though she has, for much of her life, seen Abbott and his people without seeing individual human beings. It is, she tells herself, the same way she has seen Jocko, Big Tom, Katie May, Ben and even little Joseph Reales and Asher Levy—all as people apart from The Mountain ... as people of differences where no differences exist, other than as human beings like herself.

Who, she suddenly wonders, looks upon her, her people, The Mountain people, the cliff people, the Baummeisters, the Bourdettes, as people—people with unreconcilable differences from their own—rather than as people with differences to be shared? Certainly some do. Certainly some must.

Now, all very suddenly, John's "sermons," as she calls them, about man's inhumanities, about John Locke and his rights of man, about Milton's imperfectability of man, crashingly strike the conscience-bothered chord of humanism in her mind.

Somehow all of those thoughts and lessons he implanted no longer seem to apply to some vague, abstract race of people, to isolated sects or creeds. Instead, now they all seem to be pointing the finger of shame at the people of her country, at so many of the injustices that this new nation must correct.

What right, she asks herself, as she looks over the hidden valley, had her people to invade the lands of the Lenni Lenape, to totally banish and destroy "The Original People"?[10]

Does not the Bible say, "An eye for an eye"? Is this war upon us then a war of retribution? Should it not be so that those who wantonly kill and destroy be wantonly killed and destroyed? Else where is the ever-elusive, beautiful tomorrow?

John's "peaceful" valley before her eyes looks much less peaceful than it did before. The farms, the villages, the silver-white sails of the Dutch pettiaugers and the flatboats on the rivers—the Hackensack and its Overpeck Creek, and the Passaic winding distantly down from the Ramapo Mountains in the background—suddenly overcome her with a sense of groundless and unjustified personal guilt.

Like an avalanche, all the antagonistic thoughts she has heard
spoken by some people about the Indians—all the horrible and
vicious things she has heard some say bout "the inhuman, uncivilized slaves and savages" about the Negro and the Red Man, the
bitterness expressed against opposing religious sects and creeds, or
against the Jewish people, German, French, Irish, English and the
Asiatics, or about the inferiorities of the redemptioners, the bound,
the indentured and the unbound—crash in upon her thoughts.

To herself she confesses, "John is right. We are all savage
usurpers of one another, yet we are all reaching out for a human
paradise on earth—like that hidden valley below us only appears to
be—but among us are those whose selfishness, inhuman greed,
evilness, hate and bigotry ever pull the best that is in us, farther
back from the beautiful goal, the finest dream of civilized man for
all mankind. John is so right . . . How much I do love him!"

Swiftly through her mind flows Perawae's tragic tale of
Mahtocheega. She feels a depressive chill of both guilt and sympathy sweep over her. Her sympathy goes out now, far more than
before, for Andrew.

Somehow, she tells herself, it seems all so different. Could it be,
she ponders, that she, who had always thought herself so understanding of others, so open-minded, had not realized that an Indian
was capable of real love such as hers for John? If that is so, it is
she who should be reproached for her own inhumanity to man.

Throughout her self-condemning contemplations, her hand has
tightly held that of her husband's. At times she has pressed it hard
with the trend of her changing thoughts. She takes one more last
look westward, remembering—as John had previously pointed
out—that far in the distance beyond, Newark, New Brunswick,
Prince Town where he was in college, Trenton, the great river,
Delaware, there lay his home in the big city of Philadelphia.

Will she some day, she wonders, go there with him in one of
those fancy new "Flying Machine" stagecoaches to meet his
widower father and his sister? She has heard much of John Gray
Senior and "Sister Marion," whom she already feels she knows,
and the leather shop the Grays run in Penn's city.

And what, she thinks fearfully, if they do not like her? After
all, they are English. The Baummeisters, German and French!
There, once again, crop up before her thoughts the frightening
specters of differences.

Then, quickly she recovers, telling herself that it is no time for
sad thoughts. Her fingers grasp her husband's strong hand, but

carefully she avoids touching the tender, healing wound burned by the gun's hot breech weeks ago.

Both of them, hand in hand, stand briefly looking down at the simple numerals, "1, 2, 3," etched into the flat rock's surface.

This time there is no curiosity in her eyes, but rather a deeply respectful, devout look of sharing in silent reverence.

Elaine feels her husband's firm pressure tighten around her hand. He squeezes tightly once, relaxes, and then gently squeezes the little fingers a second time. Again he relaxes and then again gently squeezes the understanding hand of his bride.

In Wordless God-like Splendor

Neither one utters a syllable. Both have learned together that the deepest and sincerest of human emotions are, like the stars, most beautifully uplifting in soundless, wordless, God-like splendor.

Quietly it dawns upon Elaine that Andrew and Andrea have inadvertently passed on to them their lost and buried unfulfilled dreams, or so she chooses to imagine. It was, she thinks, the Indian couple's own love sign of the spirits, "bound like the bark into one." Quickly she returns her husband's message, squeezing softly, but firmly gentle, three times around the fingers of his scarred hand.

Then silently they follow Old Chief off and down from Oratam's ancient stone, still bearing his sign chiseled into the rock's side. It is the unmistakable, lightning-like emblem of the Senior Sagamore and Sachem of the long-dispersed, widely scattered tribe. It is the sign of "The Good and Affable One," as is translated the name of "Oratam."

Elaine and John trail behind Perawae as all three make their way to the Abbott's Long House where, at the entrance, stands the patiently waiting Minnie. Beside her, with one arm draped gently around the shoulders of the Lenape woman, stands her son. From out the bowl of fresh, clear spring water she has just handed him, he drinks in deep gulps with his free hand.

His back is toward his father, Elaine and John. All three greet him joyfully as he turns. Andrew courteously returns their greetings with a few words, a shake of his head, acknowledging their pleasure and thanks for his and his parents' kindnesses, and then tethers the two extra horses he has brought along to a tree.

Chinqueka roams freely but never far from her master on whom the animal's eyes are turned while she eats away at some field hay outside the corral.

It has always amazed Elaine how animals are attracted to Andy. She had often watched in wonder at the readiness with which horses, dogs and cats attach themselves to him without any visible inducement. And now she observes that attraction as the sergeant's mare watches his every move.

Elaine looks at the tree to which the two army horses are tied. They are the same fillies that had carried her and John up to the Indian hideaway just a week ago. And now they are the ones, she sadly realizes, that will soon carry them away—perhaps forever— from their peaceful retreat, the closest, she feels, that she and John ... that man can ever come to paradise on earth.

It is in the Long House where Minnie prepares her foods and where all the meals are eaten. And there, squatting on the animal rug flooring, the four eat heartily of Minnie's many delectable concoctions after emptying their earthernware bowls full of Perawae's favorite berry juice. Each then fills his crockery cup with soup, for soup warms continuously in the giant pot over the smoldering fire.

In wooden trays the Indian woman serves each a generous portion of Indian maize, mixed with squash and dried fish, clams, oysters and venison.

No one speaks. It seems eating is not a time for talking. John and Elaine found that out when they first came and were told so by Minnie.

Through the Long House's open entrance, Elaine looks into the adjoining old couple's log hut. It is a vast improvement over the wickham where first they lived which still stands nearby. But the wickham is used now only for storage owing to its somewhat dilapidated condition.

She sees and counts the many chores Minnie has under way— chestnuts roasting on the fire, grape leaves and corn husks waiting to be wrapped around the baking meal, sweet bear fat ready for swabbing before storing the smoked fish, and the waiting work on the animal hides Old Chief has brought in.

On a rough-hewn table made of sturdy birch branches lie coats of skin, their stitching and braiding yet unfinished. Those they do not use themselves they will sell or trade to the people of The Mountain.

By the pine stool are several pairs of deerskin moccasins in the making. With them Minnie has established quite a reputation and, because of her excellent workmanship, quite a demand. Perawae never has any difficulty trading or selling any of "Minnie's

Moccasins" as the villagers call them or, for that matter, any of her leather crafts.

John Gray's knowledge of the tanning and treating of hides and his familiarity with the art of leather craft, acquired working with his father in the Gray family's tannery, had immediately put The Lieutenant in a favorable light with both Perawae and Minnie. Especially Minnie with whom John had talked at length about her work, praising it as far better than he had seen done by white men.

Now, as Elaine watches the cooking fire's hot burning embers, she thinks of the many joys and simple pleasures they have had together and shared with the old couple during the past few fleeting days.

As she unconsciously counts the deer meat droppings plop, plopping into the pointed-bottom pot sunk deep in the rocks around the fire's base, and then glances back into the old couple's room and the wolf, bear and raccoon skin pelts neatly placed on the sides and ends of the big, hard board beds, thickly covered with straw and soft grass matting, Elaine realizes her touch of paradise is over.

How very much, she tells herself, has she learned in this short week. Never again, she thinks, will she feel the same about herself, her life and her own people's ways of living.

Meanwhile, Andy and John, having finished eating, move outside to ready the horses and harness the baggage to the saddles. This is the opportunity Gray has sought to ask the sergeant for the latest news of the post and the war.

In answer to the officer's questions, Abbott replies with his customary brevity, relating the salient events of the week including:

. . . That General Knox is being quoted all around for saying that Manhattan Island could have been saved had the Americans held the Jamaica Pass[11] . . . That General Sullivan, who was captured on Long Island, is back, having been exchanged for General Richard Prescott who had commanded the British "at Chamble"[12] . . . That Colonel Biddle has been at Fort Constitution bringing in many supplies and forwarding much of them over to the army in Manhattan[13] . . . That a count on September 29 showed there are a total of 3,531 troops now on the muster rolls of Fort Constitution.[14]

Gray is more than a little surprised at Abbott's thorough acquaintance with the state of things generally and at the post. In these times when so many of the northern Indian tribes are leaning heavily toward the invitations of the Crown to protect them from the "land-hungry Colonials"[15] and are therefore throwing their support to the British, Abbott's pro-Americanism is somewhat puzzling to Gray.

But since Abbott's loyalty is not to be questioned, and since it is known that he has no love for the British-supporting Iroquois and Joseph,[16] the Indian chief who is aiding General Howe, Gray wonders if the army scout is not much more than just another soldier in the Continental Army.

Could it be, Gray wonders, that the wise Lenni Lenape and his cohort superior, Captain Craig, are more than scouts and guides? Could it be they and Tallmadge, whom they know so well, are part of The General's developing secret service or intelligence corps?

Likely not, Gray concludes, but Abbott's knowledges and background could, The Lieutenant feels, certainly be put to good use in that direction. His officers know that the Commander-in-Chief keeps closely tuned to the Indians of the country with whom he had, in the past, tried to maintain good relations.

Gray continues his countless questions and continues to receive Abbott's short replies with no elaborations:

... That Nixon's, Clinton's and Irvine's brigades have come over to join with Greene's command at Fort Constitution and that Bradley's and Dey's regiments also have been added[17] ... That, except for an observation guard, all the troops stationed on the narrow neck of land in Bergen from Bergen Point north, yesterday began evacuating the posts there and are today moving into Fort Constitution.[18]

Elaine, who has joined her husband and is listening attentively to the sergeant's report of affairs, now interrupts. She inquires of Abbott whether Ma Kearney's son, "Sergeant" Edmund Kearney, is among the contingent from the Bergen Post now at Fort Constitution.

Abbott has known Edmund almost as long as he has known Elaine. Often he had watched the two when, in their childhood, they played together along the edge of the waters where Abbott and his father fished. After fouling the fish nets with their homemade rafts, the youngsters soon learned from the Abbotts the Indian methods for catching bass, shad and sturgeon.

But, no, he replies to Elaine's inquiry. He does not know whether young Kearney is among the new troops on The Mountain. However, he assures her that Young Kearney must be

among the militia that has come up. Almost abruptly he goes back
to answering Gray's questions.

As for the enemy's most recent movements, Abbott informs
him:

... *That Howe's forces, facing the Americans' Harlem defenses*
on the heights, are reportedly getting ready for some move but
that a frontal attack is not expected ... *That, since many of the*
King's ships are gathering in the East River, some rumors have it
that Howe is planning to circumvent the Continentals holding
Manhattan's northern tip ... *That in order to discourage Admiral*
Howe from further attempts to force the blockade between Forts
Constitution and Washington, the Chevaux de Frise has been
greatly strengthened by Colonel Rufus Putnam's men who work on
it daily.

Then, in the same calm voice, Abbott adds almost in a matter-
of-fact manner, that this morning three British frigates attempted
to break through the barrier again but were repulsed when the lack
of wind and the American cannonading from both sides the river
forced them to come about and return back downstream.

Amazed that Abbott had not told him about this at the outset,
since Gray's own battery—his own command given to him by Knox
with Greene's approval—was certainly involved, The Lieutenant,
painfully and with evident annoyance, almost angrily asks Abbott,
"Why did you not tell me this first? 'Twas my own battery in the
brush."

Looking straight into Gray's eyes across the burning embers of
the outdoor fireplace over which Minnie boils her water and bakes
her clay pottery, Abbott, somewhat momentarily stunned, hesitates
before replying. Then, in a surprising shift in his English manner of
speaking, thinking and expressing himself, Abbott summons from
his ancestral background the jargon and wisdom of his people and
analogously answers The Lieutenant.

"Could you fly like the eagle to your perch you would find the
nest safe; for the hawk cannot mend its wings before two, maybe
three, suns. Why race with tomahawk swinging for enemy that is
not there?"

Elaine, with a trace of a smile, enters the conversation though
obviously not to her husband's liking. "You see, John," she
admonishes him, "Andy means only that you can do nothing
about what has happened. Besides, the men-of-war may not come
back for days. If they cannot get through there, they will try other
tricks."

John disregards her remarks although he realizes she and Abbott were right and that his impatience with the sergeant was unjust.

Andy explains how the *Phoenix, Roebuck* and *Tartar* were driven back. He tersely describes the brief encounter, adding that when the wind died, the frigates were at the mercy of the American batteries on both sides. Much damage was believed to have been suffered by the British ships before they were able to come around and make their way back, struggling to take advantage of every breath of wind on the river. But, Abbott notes emphatically, no damage or injuries were suffered by the Bluff Rock's batteries.

Old Chief meanwhile has brought the horses before the door of his son's hut which the bridal couple have called their home for a week.

Parting Is A Silent Understanding

Elaine, looking longingly for the last time upon the little dwelling walks over to Minnie, hugs her shoulders and then those of the slowly stooping Old Chief who holds her horse while she mounts. No words are spoken.

No words are necessary although it is known now that she may never see the elderly couple again since Andrew has persuaded them to join the Lenni Lenape people who have moved south and west to the pine barrens of West Jersey. Some have already moved farther westward than that.

It was Perawae who explained to her and John that Abbott intends to help get them there and join them when his work with the army is completed.

Attaching her small satchel more securely to the pommel of her saddle, Elaine urges her horse forward following Andrew on Chinqueka. It was Mahtocheega who four years ago, had named the mare after the goldfinch owing to a streak of gold that runs up her muzzle and down her crest and withers. But the name also applies to an old Indian legend.

John, bringing up the rear, follows on his filly after saying a word of thanks and parting to both of Abbott's wistfully sad-eyed parents. Both he and Elaine turn in their saddles and wave a last goodbye. Soon they disappear from the elderly couple's sight and slowly make their way down the mountainside toward the middle range.

It is well past the noon hour. The low-riding, rapidly weakening

October sun, though still ten weeks from the winter solstice, drops its rays into long shadows over the fall's colorful, leaf-strewn landscape. Every leaf that still holds to its last, fast fading, living spur with earth, throws off a violent hue, distinctive in its own right as if in its final glorious demise it wishes to repay its God and nature for the joys of its earthly visit.

The forests, closing in around the three returning travelers, hungrily reach up and catch every downward burst of sunlight. At times the earth's mantle of fallen leaves seems to be aflame with glowing embers. Almost every varigated spectrum of the rainbow seems to spout from out the forest's floor and deepest recesses.

To Elaine, the thrilling splendor of this magic-like brush stroke of nature's phenomenal fusion with all that is good and beautiful, is wonderously awesome. It is, she senses, as though there were some swift and urgent need to cover the war-torn world and earth. It is as though the earth were in search of nature's finest blast of beauty in order to bury forever the careless, soulless, heartless errors of mankind.

The young bride sees the cloak upon the earth as a massive, quilted blanket, rich with many splendored colors. Her eyes lift upward toward the cumulus white clouds scattered far and wide under the azure canopy of the distantly suspended blue heaven.

It is, she thinks to herself, as though someone were trying to say without words that the way of man must be peaceful, that the way of man must be through a truce with nature, his mother. That the ways of man must be one with the ways of nature. That when the trees are no more, the leaves, like mankind, will be no more. That greed festers into hate and hate into murderous wars. All this nature rejects and man in opposition to nature, promotes.

"Were the Christ who sought peace throughout the earth," she asks herself, "to see this bloodletting world today, would he, as others now do, despair for all mankind?"

Her mind shifts to thoughts for her husband and their future. But the unfolding landscape from the middle ridge's precipice walls on the path now grasps her attention.

The trail, which is not much more than a seldom used footpath, winds from south to north along the middle ridge of the Palisades' western slope. It is approximately half way between the valley at its base and the summit of the mountain range. And silently the three horses and their riders wind their way northward to the high grounds of the English Neighborhood.

Every so often they emerge from dense forest into open areas that lie along the ridge's rock walls. Occasionally they come out upon one of the many elongated rock ledges which overlook the breath-taking expanse of valley lands that lie spread out far below them.

Like an expansive, richly decorated massive rug thrown over the distant landscape, the valley appears to be sprinkled with radiant shades of yellow, orange, green, red and brown clusters of colorings.

It is as though the cloak of autumn has fallen gently over the rolling land for as far and as wide as the eye can see. The striking greens of the stately, persistently uniform pines blend quietly into the multi-colored garment, contrasting vividly with the reds and yellows of the earthly covering.

The scene spreads itself from the great bay near Newark, far southward, north upward through the pine forest, meadow lands and marshes to the finger-like rivers and streams. These winding waterways sparkle like spiraling, silver threads as they flow circuitously from the north and westward mountains southward into Newark's bay which gathers them up for their journey around Staten Island to the distant ocean.

From the far-off mountains' summits the rivers, Passaic and Hackensack, make their way through the little hamlets and the sparsely settled farms. The waters curl aound the scrawling hills, or bergs, along the "Schraalenburgh," as the Dutch descendants still call their gravelly, hilly ridges. The last traces of the glacial waters, the winding rivers push through the forests and open fields, ever quietly drawn implacably toward their origin, the sea.

Now only the plodding rhythmic hoof-beats of the horses disturb the sylvan silence along the mountain's middle ridge. Occasionally the staccato beats are broken by the animals' stumbling and slipping over the countless rolling stones, also remnants of the prehistoric glacial era.

The Forest: A Universal Contest For Survival

Far ahead in the path frequently can be heard the excited rustling of leaves and the crushing of brush. Often it is the swift exit of a frightened doe and her fawn. Sometimes it is the panther in pursuit. More than once it is a fox who, in her hunger-driven dash to feed her young, pounces ferociously upon the hopeless fleeing rabbit.

And overhead, a hawk, its vise-like beak clamped around a

screeching eaglet, strains in vain for altitude. Then suddenly the enraged, bald-headed eagle mother viciously dives down from its hovering flight. Quickly the hawk drops its catch and skirts low and fast through the forest's tree-top branches, preferring life over hunger.

It is, Elaine thinks, the under-canopy of Creation's cruel carnival. It is the universal contest for survival. It is the universal instinct to preserve each species' progeny and to perpetuate its existence, always in the face of nature's sharp and leveling shears trimming out the excess, the weak and those incapable of competing and surviving.

"Man," she reflects, "also trims his species although he does it in defiance of nature's laws. For does he not use hate, vengeance and war to trim his kind, destroying not the weak and incapable but the strongest and ablest of his race? . . . Yet perhaps man will learn from this war. Perhaps it will be his last, and he will see the need to live, not opposing his God and nature—not attempting to harness his God and nature as we do these poor fillies—but rather in harmony with his God and nature and the quest for peace for all mankind."

Suddenly overawed by a strange, flooding tide of spiritual reverence, by the seemingly nearness of her God, as well as by the trust and security from the love of her husband behind her, Elaine senses a lightning-like surge which vibrates physically through her body. It is a mysterious, uncanny feeling.

With it she is simultaneously aware of an almost uncontrollable wave of deep inexplicable attachment and devotion for her lover. The feeling seems now to encompass her entire being at the same time blending into her mind and spirit. Unable to explain it to herself, she believes she feels as though her soul were reaching to enthrall, as into one, her closeness to what Minnie called "Earth-mother." She is, she feels, drawn closer to her God and even closer in commune with her husband.

The strange feeling goes away as rapidly as it came. And, with a shrug of her shoulders, she is herself again. However its effect remains.

Now she turns slowly in her saddle and looks appreciatively at John. Though they are some twenty-five feet apart, their eyes meet. The brief glance brings them together almost as though they were alongside of each other.

Returning her eyes to the trail, Elaine folds the little finger of her right hand under the thumb, closing them closely into the palm. She lifts her arm above her shoulder displaying three fingers.

For a moment or two her husband is not sure of what is meant by the lifted right arm. Bringing his horse closer he sees and quickly understands the three-digit sign. It could not mean anything else.

He responds with a gentle but distinct bird call, whistling three sharp notes, following it shortly after with three more. At that Elaine brings her hand down and back on the horse's reins.

Up forward, Abbott abruptly turns his head upon hearing the repeated trilogy. Knowing it was The Lieutenant and ascertaining quickly that it was not a warning, or signal to stop, the sergeant scout returns his eyes to the trail.

They are sad eyes that have suddenly recalled a sacred memory. They now search straight ahead. For him, the one, two, three voice of the past is forever stilled.

What matters if the white man and his mate have discovered it and carry it on? Is that not what one disappearing people should, intentionally or not, bequeath to the next—all that is good, permanent and sacred?

In the far distance can be seen the rising smoke from the chimneys of a few homesteads. The three travelers recognize them as the dwellings that lie along the road leading up to the summit of The Mountain and the encampment at Fort Constitution.

The lowering sun seems to enhance the multi-colored, earthern garment over the valley as the trio, riding slowly over three rods apart from one another, reach the last open space still high above the valley floor. The sight before her eyes, and her own ebullient emotions cause Elaine to think of a family verse she had once learned.

As a child, she had frequently heard her grandmother sing it of a Sunday afternoon as the matriarch deftly struck out the hymn-like melody on the priceless family harp that had come from England almost a century before.

For, according to the story, the eulogistic tribute was composed by Elaine's grandfather for his wife during their courtship days. However, his spouse soon changed the "girl" to "man." Then on her harp she put it to music as in turn, a tribute to her husband.

He had called it after her middle name, "Elisabeth," the Biblical spelling which he contended meant "God's Oath." But she called it, "For So Much Of Thee."

After the old man died no one ever heard his widow sing again.

Often, throughout her childhood, Elaine did hear her mother humming the tune and singing the verse which Elaine understood to be an expression of admiration for her husband.

Gradually the tune and lyrics return to Elaine's memory. Quietly to herself Elaine hums the music which the beautiful old stringed instument had so melodiously reverberated through her grandmother's parlor many years ago. Then, keeping her voice below the audible range of Abbott up in front and her husband in the rear, she sings almost under her breath, the old folk's forgotten song.

Not too proud of her own ability to carry a tune, Elaine is certain she wants neither of her companions to hear her attempt at a vocal rendition. Her grandparents' memory is a beautiful thing, she feels. Therefore her voice is not lifted, largely owing to her reverence for the past.

Besides, she remembers, there are those—mostly among the clergy—who believed the liturgical song had a personal, private twist that was questionably sacreligious. And this opinion they held to despite the fact that her grandfather had written several hymns in his day.

To Elaine the words have now more meaning than they ever had before. So she assures herself that the primeval-like setting around her is well-fitting and more than proper for recalling "God's Oath" as the forest's stillness provides her orchestration.

. . . For So Much Of Thee

"Thank Thee for this world of Thine,
For the stars, for the moon, for the bright sunshine.
Thank Thee for the morning tide,
For the waves' deep voice on the mountainside,
For the wind in our sails as we homeward glide.
And thank Thee for the open sea,
For the call of the shore and its rest for me.
Thank Thee for so much of Thee.

Thank Thee for the hills on high,
For the forests, the plains and the endless sky.
Thank Thee for the heavens' hue,
For the rising sun 'til it sleeps in blue.
And thank Thee for this voice to sing,
For the flowers, the trees and the birds they bring,
For winter, summer, for fall and spring.
Thank Thee so for everything.

But thank Thee most for that man of mine,
For his heart, for his love through Thy fields of time,
For the moments, the hours, for the days and years,
Through joy and laughter, through grief and tears.
And thank Thee for Thy hand so kind
When darkness that love and our lives unbind.

So thank Thee for this beauteous grace,
That through his voice I found Thy embrace,
And through his eyes I have seen Thy face.[19]

17

Wednesday, October 9. . .

The Piercing of the Chevaux de Frise

The Central Hub

A strange feeling of suspense coupled with a stepped-up tempo of activity mark the atmosphere surrounding Fort Constitution. In the hamlets adjacent to the post this same suspense amid nervous bustling is evident in the daily lives of the inhabitants, particularly this morning.

Over a month ago, the new works, the fort field, was first begun on The Mountain west of the Gorge Road. Rising on the east side of the gorge are the older of the two works, the batteries on the Bluff Rock. Together they make up the central hub for the American army.

It is generally thought that here at Fort Constitution, The General intends to winter unless the Howes decide to make a last-minute crossing into Jersey.

Most people are convinced that only minor clashes will be taking place with the enemy until spring. Besides, Howe enjoys his luxuries. It is, they laughingly agree, ridiculous to believe that Sir William will extend himself very far in America's cold climate as long as he can enjoy the comforts of New York.

The General and his second in command, Nathanael Greene, are not convinced of Howe's intentions to relax, however. Nevertheless, they concede that, barring an enemy river crossing, Fort Constitution will be the preferable winter quarters for the army in this sector.

322

The Continental Commander's second choice, depending upon Howe's possible penetration into Jersey, would be in the foothills of the Watchungs, in the vicinity of Lord Stirling's manorial plantation near Morristown.

And so the blockade of the river, the "Chevaux de Frise," becomes the center of attention and the principal subject of conversation.

Can the enemy shipping break through it? Can it and the sister forts, Constitution and Washington, successfully block Admiral Black Dick Howe's men-of-war? These are the Continental Command's unanswered questions.

The Crown warships' unsuccessful attempt to run through the barrier Sunday last, October 6, was not a real test for the device. The wind that morning was against the vessels. Ever since, the British seamen have been awaiting the wind and itching for orders to hoist sail and leave their anchorage downriver off Bloomingdale. And on both sides of the water everyone waits in suspense.

General Israel Putnam's river blockade "scheme" was an idea which "Old Put" had nourished for some time. When The General approved its construction, the task of executing the plan fell to the Continental Army's Chief Engineer, Colonel Rufus Putnam, "Old Put's" distant relative.

The unique blockade suggestion was the best offered to thwart enemy marine passage upriver. For, once unchecked access up and down the waterway is established by the enemy, full control of Hudson's river, the entire Hudson valley and the land routes to and from New England are Howe's.

The forces on Mount Washington would be cut off, isolated and starved out unless evacuated. Alone, Fort Constitution would be a valueless river guardian. New England's and the Northern army's communications with the central and southern states would be severed almost overnight.

This is Howe's aim. However, occasionally he envisions the capture of the Continental Congress in Philadelphia and at those times the control of the Hudson and severing of the New England communications drop to second place in his thinking.

So the mechanically-minded General Putnam sees his river blockade as a major deterrent to the British commander-in-chief's hopes for a quick severing of American communications and a rapid end to the war. Almost three months ago he wrote to his friend, Major General Horatio Gates, describing the plan he had in mind. He explained the "scheme"[1] called for two ships' sterns to be laid toward each other about 70 feet apart.

In that letter, on July 26, he wrote Gates:

"Three large logs, which reach from ship to ship, are fastened to them. The two ships and logs stop the river two hundred and eighty feet. The ships are to be sunk, and when hauled down on one side, the pricks will be raised to a proper height, and then must stop the river, if the enemy will let us sink them."[2]

Early in August the blockade construction began.

On the night of August 4, "four ships, chained and boomed, with a number of amazing large chevaux de frise, were carefully sunk close by the fort under command of General Mifflin, which fort mounts 30 pieces of heavy cannon."[3]

The rows of spiked and jagged logs, intended to halt or slow down frigates under sail, acquired the name "chevaux de frise" from the French military term for such constructions.

In French military parlance the words refer to the spiked and jagged trees used in the erection of such barriers.

The term, "chevaux de frise" was coined by the Netherlanders who had no horses (chevaux) to stop the Spanish horsemen at Friesland (Frise) in the Dutch Netherland Revolt almost 200 years ago. Instead they made use of trees which they fashioned into lengthy spikes with jagged sides, calling them "the horses of Friesland." In French military jargon they became known as "chevaux de frise."

Under the guns of the sister forts, Constitution and Washington, therefore, a 200-year-old world idea called "The Horses of Friesland" has become a modern, 18th Century underwater construction to blockade the river, called "The Chevaux de Frise."

Putnam's fear last July that the enemy would stop the construction of the blockade is still one of Colonel Tench Tilghman's major concerns as he undertakes to direct additional work on the barrier. In his capacity as one of the Commander-in-Chief's principal aides, Tilghman, writing six days ago from the Harlem Heights headquarters to General Heath at King's Bridge, advised Heath to be on his guard in the event the British launched an attack on the men working on the river project.

Referring to the frantic preparations for sinking two additional boat hulks at the Chevaux de Frise, Tilghman pointed out that the ships were being loaded on the shore south of Dobbs Ferry before being towed down and sunk into place beneath the blockade's chains. He wrote Heath further, stating:

"You will therefore be pleased to order Captain Benson to be as expeditious as possible in getting the new ships afloat and ballasted."

Noting the location of the enemy's frigates, Tilghman declared that a hundred men had been ordered upriver to assist a detachment of artillery in covering the workmen. Excited haste was everywhere in the air.

In closing the letter, the colonel said,

"While I was writing the above by His Excellency's direction, he went to bed. I thought it a pity to disturb him to sign it. I therefore have the honour to subscribe myself your most obedient servant . . ."[4]

As of today the two additional rock-laden ships' hulls have not arrived at the Chevaux de Frise. In the prevailing air of suspense and anticipation pervading throughout the forts there is a depressing feeling that the two new hulks with their spiked logs will not arrive before the enemy.

The Bluff Rock observers have already reported unusual and extensive action among the seamen on the decks of the British men-of-war anchored downstream. In addition, a brisk southeast wind is blowing up in their favor as the first streaks of dawn rise over the eastern horizon.

As the morning brightens it is clear to the observing American sentinels that the decks of the *Phoenix, Roebuck* and *Tartar* are alive with activity at Bloomingdale's offshore cove. Duty officers Gray and Levy are immediately notified.

Both men have been assigned by General Greene to the main Barbette Battery. It is Gray's old command post, and one which is now an ideal assignment for the "Blue Petticoat Scarf Lieutenant."

Despite the fact that he is now a man eleven days in wedlock, Gray still wears his good luck piece, the tell-tale blue neckerchief of his courtship days. Its principal difference now is that it is more frequently laundered.

When not on duty he merely hurries down the precipice trail to the gorge road, bolts the back fence to the Baummeister house and he's home. The addition of a soldier son-in-law has made Baummeister the most envied father-in-law among the cliff dwellers. No soldier could ask for more.

When Jocko's duties at the stable are not pressing, the youth is generally not far behind The Lieutenant. For, when off duty, Jocko too has become almost a part of the Baummeister household, performing chores in exchange for all the goodies he and his father can eat from out of Marie Louise's kitchen, a welcome change from the army's hodgepodge messes.

For the present, Jocko is not pushed to attend Missy E's school all the time. For most of the youngsters have for a fortnight been going over to the village school in English Neighborhood on their own horses.

The scarcity of horses is severe owing to the frequent military demands for any nag that can walk when supplies, baggage and troops must be hurriedly moved. But when the action lets up, the animals are generally turned back to their owners to be cared for, and Greene tries to make sure the owners are fairly reimbursed.

A lucky scholar might have use of the family horse. Frequently two ride down over the hill from the fort on the back of one steed, allowing the animals to make their own way back to their barns. All invariably do without any great loss of time. The walk home from the English Neighborhood school is a longer process unless the children can hitch a ride with a farm or army wagon on its way up The Mountain.

Even if he had time, Jocko has made it clear to his father that he would not run through "the schoolmaster's Chevaux de Frise" as he calls the male teacher's attitude toward Negroes, including freed slaves and their rights to schooling. Everyone knows the village schoolmaster's likes and dislikes. He considers all blacks and Indians "servants," which, for him, is another word for "slaves."

Jocko has much work to do. His father's slowly healing wound still requires care. In addition he has been helping Elaine and the neighborhood wives assist the surgeons in the new hospital hut. Since the evacuation of the lower Bergen posts more sick and wounded are coming in from below and from across the river.

In the three weeks and two days that Greene has commanded Fort Constitution, so named shortly after his arrival, the personnel complement has doubled. Under Greene the new works are growing systematically but with intensifying haste and pressure.

Stone and log huts are under construction in preparation for a long, cold winter on The Mountain, the enemy permitting, of course. The buildings should help restore the spirit of the men who have slept mostly on the ground for over six weeks.[5]

Exact construction directions for building barracks were issued in Greene's General Orders yesterday, under date, "October 8, 1776, Fort Constitution." The orders came just before the post commander issued his alarming edict which ordered the clearing of all inhabitants from the waterside in anticipation of a river battle.

The barrack-construction command gives the subaltern officers specific orders:

> "Cap. Olney of Col Hitchcock's Regiment and Cap. Warner of Col. Little's are appointed to assist in overseeing the fortifications and are to be excused from duty.
>
> "Commanding officers of regiments are requested to fix upon proper places for barracks, none to be nearer the fort than 50 rods. The general desires commanding officers to divide the regiments into messes of 8 men. The men must build timber huts, as boards are not to be had. Boards are to be had only for the roof. The huts are to be 12 feet long by 9 wide, to have stone chimneys and to be ranged in proper streets."[6]

So the encampment constructions are spread out south and southwest of the main fort. A line has been drawn 50 rods from the outworks where streets are laid out and named.

Anticipating the order the Continental Army veterans of the campaign's summer days on Manhattan are nostalgically naming the streets after the ones they lived on or recall from some of their experiences in New York City before the Battle of Long Island. On the corners and intersections of the rows of tents, gradually replaced by log huts in various stages of construction, are numerous street signs duplicating the titles of those in the port city.

Painted in crudely scribbled letters on the flat boards atop the posts are such names as Broad Street, The Broad Way, Pearl Street, Pine Street, Wall Street, Greenwich, Cortlandt, Whitehall, Beekman, Dock and Great Dock Street.

One tent bears a placard, "Queen's Head Tavern," so dubbed by the occupants or some friendly jesters. It is a reminder to many of the old veterans of hours spent in the tavern run by Black Sam Fraunces.

On the same post outside the tent, one collector of memorabilia has tacked a parchment sign he "borrowed" from some inn along the way. It reads, in silent, sarcastic disaffection with the rigid character of the military encampment:

"Rules Of this Tavern
4 pence a night for bed
6 pence with potluck
2 pence for horsekeeping
No more than five to sleep in a bed
No razor grinders or tinkers will be taken in
Organ grinders to sleep in the wash house"[7]

West of the earthworks where daily the Philadelphia teams and country wagons have been carting away loads of earth and rock, are the lean-to stables. To the southeast, down The Mountain's slope and over the gorge road, but up from the water's edge, are the Baummeister and Bourdette homesteads.

Bourdette's is closest to the river and lies in front of the Baummeister home which is higher on the slope and nearest to the thoroughfare. The road, after descending from The Mountain and separating the Bluff Rock as it winds down, continues past the Baummeister place along the bank on a rough and untraveled shore route to Bull's Ferry.

Unceasingly the mountain stream pours down from the summit and under the rough planks of the gorge road bridge above the Baummeister's. Beyond the bridge it cuts slightly north at the coach stop where it partly channels into the horse trough. The stream's source is a spring in a large pond atop The Mountain, a good 20 rods southwest of Bourdette's cow pasture.

A blockade of sunken ships' hulls called the Chevaux de Frise was stretched across Hudson's river beneath the batteries of the two towering forts at approximately where today is seen the shadow of the George Washington Bridge.

The army's commissary tent stands in a part of the ferry owner's cow pasture. Near it are the slaughter-house and the baking ovens. About 400 feet to the southwest is the deep well-hole lying above the brook to its north. Not far to the east of the well is General Greene's Long House, used mostly for council meetings, court martials and for quartering special guests. It is now known as the place of the wedding of The Lieutenant and his lady.

North and northwest of Greene's Long House are two temporary tents set up for the care of the sick and wounded. Called "Flying Hospitals," the facilities and provisions for ministering to the sick are poor and unsanitary.

In most cases of illnesses each regiment takes care of its own invalids. But the so-called regimental hospitals, as they are called, are little more than isolation tents. They are only a slight improvement over the regimental quick help stations.

However, a log hut is under construction for expanding the post's hospital facilities. Most of the serious cases, the patients who cannot walk, are transferred to the Hackensack Hospital. And some are sent on down to Philadelphia.

In the center of the Palisadean summit-top encampment is the rapidly shaping square-bastioned inner fort. It is surrounded by, though well separated from, the tents, buildings, huts and log-constructed service buildings and magazines. Preparations are speedily under way for housing at least 3,500 men.

The four bastions, two on the east and two on the west, are under construction and will extend out from the main interior works. They will be surrounded by an exterior rampart. About 800 feet beyond the outer ramparts, to the south and southwest, are the barracks areas. Now daily growing in size the encampment area there resembles a little city.

In between the two flanks of the southern curtain of the fort, which looks out on the lower, southern flow of Hudson's river and the southern half of Manhattan Island, are the parade grounds. And in between the two flanks of the western curtain is the main gate. It leads out westward down the Palisade's west slope into the valley.

The two flanks of the northern curtain command the road which leads up The Mountain from the King's Highway through English Neighborhood. The Fort Road, as it is called, passes by the scattered homesteads built by the early settlers and still used by their descendants. It continues eastward over The Mountain, joining the gorge road to the river's bank.

The gorge road separates the Bluff from the main mountain and the fort on its summit. The main fort's eastern curtain spreads out between the northern and southern bastions and commands the gorge road leading up from the shore and its ferry landing.

Menacing Batteries Above and Below

Owing to the Bluff Rock looming up in front of the main eastern curtain, observers on The Mountain cannot see the river north of the ferry landing and little of the landing area itself. Such observations and all observations of the northern tip of Manhattan Island above Harlem's heights must be made from the Bluff Rock and its Barbette Battery post.

The Bluff Rock batteries on the east side of the gorge road, above the cut, or ravine, are now part of a triple threat which includes the guns on Fort Washington and the blockade strung between. Only in combination with its sister fort and the river barrier can the Bluff Rock's works successfully shower devastating blows upon enemy shipping attempting to run through.

Any vessel under sail trying to do so must cut the barrier with its bow. At the same time it must fight off dual barrages from the high redoubts concentrating upon it from both sides of the river. If it is blocked, or forced to pause too long, it becomes a highly vulnerable stationary target from the overhead artillery.

The 3,000-foot long Bluff Rock is like a massive flat table, narrowing at the southern "Point of Bluff" end. It widens its table-top appearance to over 300 feet at the northern end. There it is attached to the main mountain by a gentle declivity which is now hedged by an impenetrable abatis of felled trees with pointed ends facing into the path of any possible attackers from the west.

At the Point of Bluff a large redoubt and gun emplacement, or redan, towers over the ferry, guarding the approach to the shore. In this task it is well supported by a number of shore batteries lining the river's bank.

The redan and observation post look down upon the wide river and out upon the whole of Manhattan Island. Few major movements on the New York side can escape observation from this scenic spot.

Several hundred feet north of this redan on the table rock, at about the center of The Rock, is the main battery called "The Barbette." It commands the east face of the precipice and the river below it. Behind The Barbette, to the west, is an infantry entrenchment which guards the ascent to the Bluff Rock from the gorge road in the event of an enemy landing at the ferry. The entrenchment is protected by an extension of the abatis at the northern end.

At the ascent trail from the gorge road in front of the entrenchments, is a sentry's shelter. In, east from the entrenchments, are the barracks and The Rock's headquarters post, the powder house and magazine. They lie several hundred feet north of the entrenchments and the guardhouse.

At the far north end of the table rock, in front (east) of the abatis, is a second long infantry entrenchment. To its east, commanding the Chevaux de Frise at the foot of the precipice, is the Bluff Rock's northernmost redoubt. The cannon of this emplacement menaces any shipping coming south down the river, especially if it approaches too close to the Hudson's west shore.

In anticipation of the coming river battle General Greene yesterday ordered a strong reinforcement of the shore batteries protecting the ferry landing. In that order he directed that the residents along the river's edge be evacuated and warned them to remain out of the area pending a determination of the enemy's intentions.[8]

A captain with 40 of Colonel John Glover's Marblehead seamen has been assigned to the ferryboats, the landing and shore guard duty. Most of these skilled fishermen and sailors are veterans of the remarkable crossing of the East River six weeks ago.

Though much criticism has been leveled by the American Commander-in-Chief at the quality of the officers[9] in the Continental Army, none of it has ever been directed at the "Marbleheaders." But, as pronounced in letter after letter in his reports to the Congress and in his correspondence with his generals, the American Leader has deplored the character, the weakness and the incompetence of the American army's officers generally.

Most of the subaltern officers are politically chosen. Sometimes they are appointed through the pressures of the federal or state governments. Particularly is this so in the appointment of the leaders in the various state militias.

Held up as examples by The General of what should be models for the new army which Congress has at last approved, at least in "parchment promises," are the officers and men from such units as the Delaware, Maryland and Massachusetts Continental regiments.[10] It is the hope not the expectation of The General and his staff that the new army will soon be financed and enlisted.

For now of much concern to the rebels' Commander and his generals is the constant possibility of the present divisions' dissolving almost "overnight." Forthcoming expiration dates for enlistments will enable men and officers to walk away at will when their terms end.

Increasing illnesses among the rank and file as winter approaches present another constant threat to the army's stability. Colonel Tallmadge's "Return Of Officers" report last Friday showed, instead of the usual three or four, 26 officers in Chester's and Prescott's regiments reporting ill.

Then there are the countless daily desertions and their subsequent court martials, depleting the army's ever-waning strength. Persistent reports of lack of discipline among the men, often leading to criminal actions for everything from minor to heinous regulation infractions, plague the generals. They attribute the large number of such crimes and their necessary court martials to the inefficiencies of subaltern officers.[11]

In addition to these discouraging conditions the Congress persists in delaying proper steps to remedy the situation. Its paper promises to improve recruitment methods are of little encouragement to the high command. The august body in Philadelphia has yet to provide suffcent funds for pay, clothing, equipment and stores.

Of great concern also is the lack of proper facilities to provide for the increasing number of incapacitated. Diseases, wounds, injuries and the general illnesses that ordinarily haunt any body of troops present increasing problems with which the military alone cannot cope. Added to this is a dire shortage of hospital supplies and doctors, compounded by the charges and complaints that regimental surgeons abuse their trust and embezzle "the publick stores committed to their care."[12]

In describing these conditions to the Congress, Greene writes:

> "The sick of the army, who are under the care of the regimental surgeon, are in a most wretched situation, the Surgeon being without the least article of medicine. . . . There is no circumstance that strikes a greater damp upon the spirits of the men, who are yet well, than the miserable condition the sick are in. They exhibit a spectacle shocking to human feelings, and as the knowledge of their distress spreads through the country, will prove an insurmountable obstacle to the recruiting of the new army.
>
> "Good policy as well as humanity, in my humble opinion, demands the immediate attention of Congress upon this subject, that the evil may be sought out and the grievance redressed. The sick in the army are too numerous to be all accommodated on the contracted plan of the General Hospital . . ."[13]

Deserters too are a constant worry to the regimental commanders. As morale drops and discontent rises, particularly among the militia, the number of desertions increase proportionately. Together, sickness and desertions are rapidly depleting the roster of men fit and able for duty.

The Pennsylvania newspapers carry regular announcements of reported army deserters. Even in today's issue *The Pennsylvania Gazette* announces the desertion of James Mellone from Captain Matthew Smith's company on its way from Princeton to King's Bridge.[14] And *The Pennsylvania Packet* reports the desertion of Michael Wane from Colonel Moore's regiment of the Flying Camp. It adds that Wane "seldom looks a man in the face."[15]

Added to the woes of the military are the problems within the civilian ranks. The "disaffected"—those wavering Whig and neutral inhabitants who bend a willing ear to Howe's propaganda—are sometimes as much a threat to the cause as the Tories themselves.

The uneasiness they cause is best expressed by the New York Committee of Safety which recounts its fears in a letter to Generals Schuyler and Clinton concerning the "disaffected in this State (New York) . . . on the east side of Hudson's river."[16]

While many of these "disaffected" have been discovered, according to the committee's letter, and "sent to the westward," many more remain undiscovered.

"Should the enemy and the disaffected be able to concert measures," the generals are warned, "so as to form a junction of the latter with a party from on board the ships in the river, the Committee of Safety are apprehensive of the want of a very speedy assistance. . . ."[17]

These are some of the things concerning the high command and Greene's staff on this chilly October morning. However, the major immediate problem facing Fort Constitution is the coming attack heralded by the approach of the frigates under Captain Parker in the *Phoenix*.

Enemy In Sight

Their broadsides pointing upward, the men-of-war, bearing down toward the river barrier, have sent the area's inhabitants scurrying north and south along the shore. Every man at both the sister forts is at his post. Every weapon is loaded and ready. For it cannot be determined at this point if the ships are carrying infantry troops intending to invade.

On the twin forts' high redoubts the artillerists have loaded and sighted their cannon on the channel approach to the Chevaux de. Frise. An ominous silence settles over Fort Washington's heights on the Bluff Rock batteries and those lining the river's shores on both sides of the water.

All that is moving anywhere in sight are the ships in Parker's flotilla. The squadron's sails are full with the southeast wind's favoring blow. And the wide-spread canvases carry nature's powers down into the rapidly plowing bows of the speeding square-riggers. Like sharp knives the vessels' prows cut through the river water spurred by the incoming tide. They leave ever-widening ripples in their wake that spread out V-shaped behind them resembling giant arrows extending to the shores. It is evident that the ships will ram the blockade and that invasion is not their present intention.

Since the break of dawn all hands on the Bluff Rock's Barbette, like those manning all the redans and works along the shore, have patiently awaited the approaching moment.

Lieutenant Gray, summoned from slumber at the Baummeister home, upon arriving at his post, found that Second Lieutenant Levy had already figured out the trajectory. The officer carefully took into account both the wind and the estimated knots of the approaching vessels. A skillful mathematician, Levy has proved to be a superior artillery officer, far more suited for the artillery than most of the other subaltern officers Gray has encountered.

Gray knows from previous firings that Levy's trajectory computations are uncannily accurate. Despite the rapidity of his subaltern's calculations, he has proved exceptionally accurate in practice firing. His alignments have impressed others as well as Gray.

In Levy's company, Jocko, who has had to adjust to Gray's new domestic interests, has found a suitable substitute. And from Levy, who has succumbed to the youth's magnetic personality, Jocko feels he learns something new every day. Things, he tells himself, he can use "more'n schoolin'."

So Gray finds the youth closely watching Levy and assisting in whatever way he can. But Jocko has no intention of staying once the firing starts. Since Long Island he has acquired a bitter hatred for the bloodshed and disaster of war.

Big Tom also has returned to the Bluff's works for light duty under Gray's strict orders. Though handicapped by his slowly healing arm, Graves is still considered a first-rate gunner. The officer has assigned both father and son to minor duties at the magazines across the gorge on the main mountain when enemy action begins.

Relegated to message-carrying, Jocko, who with his father, is permanently assigned to the horses, wagons and stable, can use a mount for delivering messages. His horsemanship, he feels, at last has been recognized. Few can handle a horse on the rocky sloping paths as well as Jocko. With this skill and his knowledge of the terrain there is no one better for message-carrying from the main fort on The Mountain to the Bluff Rock's batteries and those below it along the shore.

Almost exactly at 8 A.M. the *Roebuck* and the *Tartar*, in the lead of the flotilla, open up with their heaviest cannon. The *Roebuck* on the west sends its barrage against Fort Constitution. The *Tartar's* guns bark out at Fort Washington as it approaches Jeffery's Hook the eastern terminus of the Chevaux de Frise.

Behind the two leading frigates, close under their cover and between them, attempting to hold close to the center of the channel, is Captain Parker's *Phoenix*. Parker's vessel guards a small, armed sloop and three supply-carrying tenders[18] which run before the *Phoenix*.

Headed under full sail into the Chevaux de Frise the little British squadron gambles everything on a break-through. Confronting them on the other side of the blockade and well north of it, Parker sees four armed American galleys in the middle of the river facing them and presumably ready to pound them if they should succeed in running by the obstacle. On one galley is mounted a 32-pounder on a swivel. The others are each equipped with two nine-pounders and two four-pounders.

Suddenly, in answer to the fusillade, the Bluff cannons split the air, sending up clouds of smoke to fuse with that of their enemy's high above the water. Then from the opposite side, Fort Washington's artillery lets loose a thunderous barrage. In reply, Captain Parker's frigates answer with a continuous broadside barraging of both sides of the river.

The two leading men-of-war, firing incessantly, drive into the river's barricade. Both bounce back from the impact, shuddering from crow's-nest to keel.

For an eternity, in the minds of the seamen, the vessels hesitate. For several catastrophic moments they lie still, seemingly stunned from stem to stern. Mainsails whip dangerously loose on their spars. The spankers flap wildly on their booms.

Break-through

But the *Phoenix's* powerful bow thrust is too much for the weakened blockade. The heavy chain breaks off from its fastenings to the half-submerged, rock-laden hull and its pointed stakes, opening a passage for the vessels through the narrowed channel. For here is the Hudson's shortest distance from shore to shore, from the Tappan Zee south to the bay. Meanwhile, the twin forts' batteries lay down a shower of raining death on the vessels.

Then the wind fills the *Roebuck's*, the *Tartar's* and the *Phoenix's* sails as their gunners, under the heaviest fire they have ever felt or seen, fire back through the massing white clouds of smoke. All seven of the lumbering ships break through. One after another they stretch their wings out of range from the fort's destructive armament.

Now they are annoyed by the American galleys which had peppered them from a distance during the crashing of the barrier and now, in vain, fire a few last rounds at the frigates bearing down upon them. The galleys then hurriedly make for the safety of the shore.

During the battle most of the inhabitants had taken refuge over the crest of The Mountain. None were permitted within the confines of the main fort itself. Flooded for days with a Tory-promoted rumor of an imminent invasion comprising an overwhelming force of British and Hessian soldiers, the farm people clustered in groups along the Fort Road that leads down into Day's place at English Neighborhood.

Few saw any part of the battle. Most had to be content with listening to its thunder and hearing about it from soldiers moving up from the riverside or down from the Bluff Rock. For west of the clove there is no clear view of the river for those moving over The Mountain and down into the valley.

Elaine, her mother, Granny Bourdette and Ma Kearney, among others, have tried to calm the more frightened inhabitants. Many of them have assembled at the Widow Lemater's house on the Covenhoven farm.[19]

Among these is little Hans Onderdonk, whose home adjoins the Lemater house. Hans is never frightened by the heavy exchange of cannon fire. After all it has taken place before, and besides it is far off, way down on the other side of The Mountain, out in the river. Hans is more concerned with showing off and introducing around his favorite uncle, young Abe Onderdonk of the "up valley militia."

The 19-year-old, pleasantly smiling soldier is on a short furlough from Captain James Smith's Orange County Militia company.[20] Onderdonk's striking personality, his courteous respect and attention to the frightened elderly and his deep, calm voice radiating confidence, soon make him the center of attention and interest. His nephew's praises promote his rapid acceptance by The Mountain people.

Among those impressed are Elaine and Ma Kearney. Both would like to get back to the fort. The younger to hear about her husband. The older to hear about her son. Elaine's mind is on John at the Barbette. Ma's is on her Eddie who has been assigned to the shore battery under Captain Board. But the minds of both are also on the welfare of the sick at the fort whom they have been attending.

The two women were annoyed with General Greene's order last night which barred them from making their evening visit to the hospital tent. Along with the rest of the hamlet, Elaine and Ma remained in their own homes until persuaded to leave for the mountain-top ground at 7 o'clock this morning.

The Bourdettes, Baummeisters and Ma Kearney always get favorable treatment from the post and its command. It almost took an order, however, to get them away from the waterside this morning.

Though Greene bends way over to be lenient with the long-established Palisadean settlers, his concern for their protection is uppermost. He held steadfastly to his refusal last night and this morning to grant them permission to visit the hospital until the blockade battle was over.

Convinced that a visit from a smiling soldier from upriver would be beneficial for their hospital patients' morale, Elaine and Ma successfully contrived to use Private Onderdonk and his military pass, as well as their own acquaintance with the sentries, to get by the inner guards. There the busy sentinels were too preoccupied with Onderdonk and his flashy new uniform to notice the two women, their arms loaded with cloth bandages, pass through on the far side of one of the supply wagons.

Then at the precise moment the women passed through the gate on the far side of the wagon, the main barrage and counter barrage resounded up from the Chevaux de Frise and from the bombarding shore batteries on and below the cliffs.

From the Bluff Rock's heights, Greene, with Colonels Ward and Hitchcock watched the scene from the beginning to what they judged a disappointing end. They had expected the entire flotilla would be taken, for if the blockade had held there would have been no alternative for Captain Parker but to hoist a white flag. This was what the American staff wanted, not the destruction of a small British flotilla necessarily.

So Greene quietly, hopefully, watched his artillery open up from both sides the river as if on a given signal. He concealed his anxiety as the Barbette's fusillade thundered out with explosive sound waves that sent their vibrations up and down the mighty stone walls of the Palisades.

Unconsciously he counted the flashes of fire from each discharge. A few of the enemy's crashed close to the Barbette, bouncing off the precipice rock like raindrops. Some plummeted down on the main encampment grounds. Others raked the shore in a futile attempt to still the batteries along the river's edge.

The forts' commander tensed as he saw the big vessels crash into the barrier which had not been completed and reinforced as planned. There were tons of rock and several hulks lying upriver which had not yet been added to the sunken obstructions.

Why? Why had this not been done?

The two big men-of-war speared into the blocking chains under full canvas. They struck hard, shivered and bounced back in a momentary halt. Greene's face reflected a subdued satisfaction for a few brief seconds as the ships almost closed in upon each other. All now were motionless targets for the artillerists and they made the most of it as smoke from guns on all sides enveloped the vessels.

Then their canvas caught the wind's power once again midst a merciless and devastating exchange of shot and shell. One by one the squadron moved on through the opening, cleanly pierced by the men-of-war. The ships had won.

Greene's jaws clenched in anger and disgust. The blockade had failed its crucial test. The Chevaux-de-Frise was punctured.

What had gone wrong? Was he at fault? These thoughts raced through Greene's mind as the vessels broke out into the open.

But what about damages and casualties? Were there none on the ships?

Smoke over the masts and decks obscured any accurate vision of the seamen. Over the frantic shouts, the raised voice-commands of officers and the excited yells of the participants, the deafening cannonading absorbed all human sounds. Even were there agonizing cries of wounded and dying aboard the vessels, they could not have been heard or seen.

As soon as Greene saw the frigates bounce back from the shocking drive of their prows into the massive chains and heard them tear out the bolts from the half-submerged hulk's frame, he knew the battle was lost. His body slumped despairingly as first the *Roebuck*, then the *Tartar*, followed by the sloop, tenders and the *Phoenix* sped away free into the open waters. Only Parker and his men know the serious extent of their casualties and damages to their riggings, canvas, masts, spars and decks.

Without speaking to either Ward, Hitchock, or Paine, who had joined them, Greene turned, mounted his horse and, followed by his staff, made for the gorge road and its ascent pathway to the main camp's headquarters.

Admiral Black Dick Howe had proved His Majesty's ships could pierce the rebels' river blockade. And Green now had to admit it.

Parker, however, was convinced the blockade was too formidable to tackle again. And Admiral Howe would soon be ready to admit it.

Also disappointed were the American gunners whose firing ceased once the British flotilla had passed out of range. The shouts of glee and hooplas from the infantry troops, stationed back from the shore in the event of an invasion, and the victorious yells of the artillerymen at every strike made, soon turned to groans and curses.

Unlike Greene, who wished only to see a raised flag of surrender, the infantrymen and artillerymen wanted the entire squadron sunk and added to the blockade's river barrier.

Stags At Bay

Seeming to gloat with new-found defiance, the enemy sloop breaks out of the squadron and heads for the two escaping American row-galleys.[21] No match for the men-of-war, or the smaller gun-mounted vessel bearing down upon them in the distance, the galleys cease their drifting and firing. Under full canvas they head for the shore near Dobbs Ferry as the *Roebuck* penetrates the barrier. Meanwhile, the two American schooners set sail for Phillip's Mills and its safety from pursuers within the militia-guarded inlet.

Like wounded birds, fighting the snagging ropes of a trap and hounded by distantly barking dogs waiting for the kill, the enemy vessels had endured the galleys' few minor strikes and numerous near misses while floundering at the chain. It is now the King's turn, and the single-masted, armed, cutter-like craft with its shell-punctured canvas flying crazily, swiftly makes for the American oarsmen and their hand-made men-of-war.

The galleys are now the stags at bay. Impeded by the weight of their armament, they find the *Roebuck* and its guns as well as those of the sloop, both firing as they take up the chase. Precariously the American galleys struggle in the path of the entire trap-escaped flotilla.

All artillerymen and oarsmen are part of Captain Tinker's Connecticut State's seamen,[22] especially enlisted for this service. Now they prove it. Almost as fast as the slightly damaged sloop, they force their little craft through the river's waters as the oarsmen tug ever more furiously at their oarlocks. Every shot of the enemy plops short of them into the stream at their stern.

The rowing galleys head into the shallow waters near Dobbs Ferry. Though closely pursued, the Americans escape and scramble ashore. The enemy sloop which draws more water than the galleys wisely comes about before running aground as it now could in the uncharted shoal. However, it lowers its tender with armed seamen aboard who head inland in pursuit.

Both the American galleys run aground, forcing all hands aboard to swim and wade ashore after abandoning their vessels. However, the British sloop's captain has ordered his seamen to carry the day's action to its bitter end.

The British seamen from the sloop's tender, joined by a tender of musket-carrying seamen from the *Roebuck*, capture the crewless row-galleys which are confiscated by the captain of the *Phoenix*. Then the enemy seamen storm ashore in pursuit of the escaped rebels.

Coming upon the Dobbs Ferry general store, they rush in only to find it deserted. The patriot storekeeper, who had seen them coming, loses no time in following the rebel seamen into the woods north of the village.

There, undetected by the King's men, the storekeeper watches with the Connecticut men as the irate enemy raiders plunder his shop, stave in his casks and set fire to the building and the wares they cannot carry back to the ship.[23]

The *Tartar*'s brief attempt to pursue the escaped American schooners soon proves fruitless. But both the *Tartar* and the *Roebuck*, still stinging from their skirmish with the artillerymen on the mountain-tops and their narrow escape through the Cheavaux de Frise, seek some retaliation for their wounds. The victims are a

schooner   and   sloop   anchored   offshore,   north   of   Dobbs
Ferry.[24]

Raiding parties from both the frigates take the schooner with its
full load of rum, sugar and wine while the British men-of-war train
their guns on the merchant vessel in the event it resists.

The sloop also is surrounded until a British boarding party takes
it over. On board the vessel is David Bushnell's underwater
machine, *The Turtle*.[25]

Death Of *The Turtle*

Puzzled at first by the strange contraption they find aboard the
rebel sloop, the redcoats soon discover its purpose, its intentions
and its value. Captain Parker is personally summoned to look over
the extraordinary prize.

In from the shore, well out of sight, the abandoned craft's
American crewmen and Inventor David Bushnell himself, watch
helplessly as the fate of the sloop and the ill-fated *Turtle*
submarine is pondered by the King's men. The British officers
carefully examine the device which was to have blown the bottoms
out of the vessels that have captured it.

It is soon evident to the Americans what their sloop's fate will
be. The vessel is stripped but the heavy sumbarine is left on deck
undisturbed. Then from his tender Parker gives the signal and the
condemned bark with Bushnell's extraordinary invention fastened
to its deck is scuttled at its mooring.

As the craft slowly sinks to the bottom of the river carrying
with it the rebels' much talked about "secret weapon," Bushnell
turns away from the company of men and walks dejectedly alone
into the forest to recover in solitude from his sickening sight.

It is clear to the Dobbs Ferry villagers that the British frigates
can prowl the Tappan Zee waters of the upper Hudson fully in
control of the waterway. True they must get up there and run the
Chevaux de Frise blockade first. Today that did not seem too
difficult. However, Admiral Howe must determine whether his
control of the upper waters of Hudson's river is worth the risk that
was taken this morning under the guns of the sister forts.

Gloom hangs over the military and patriot inhabitants of the
twin posts and their surrounding areas. One old artilleryman
summed it up by declaring, "Ole Put's fence across der river diden'
stop Ole George's lion from a'jumpin' it."

Generally it is believed that the enemy ships breezed through without any significant damage. Most inhabitants feel that the flotilla was hardly impeded at all by the barricade. Despite the artillerymen's arguments to the contrary, many rank and file contend that the seven ships were virtually untouched.

The disappointment is widespread and threatens further erosion of the army's and the people's already weakening morale. There is no way of knowing the effectiveness of the Chevaux de Frise. In fact no one within the Continental Army will know until long after the war is over. Only then will the severity and the costliness of the battles of the blockade to Admiral Howe and his navy be told in full.

Those later revelations will support the arguments of the cannoneers but will in no way detract from the bravery of Captain Parker and his British seamen. They will, in fact, add to their heroism and to Parker's skillful and daring navigation through the obstacle under intense American fire.

For the astute Parker and his lead ships, though under ripping cross fire and through clouds of dense smoke had, despite the confusion of battle, somehow struck the blockade's "weakest link." And under the double striking force of the two frigates' heavily reinforced copper-plated bow, the chain's section snapped.

Though their ships were then subjected to the heaviest fire of the battle and the wounded, dead and dying were falling on the decks, the seamen did not budge from their stations nor swerve from the execution of their duties. It was during those tense moments that Parker led his squadron through the gap and out from under the American barrage.

It is said by the rebel troops that the British are much like the Indians in one respect. They know how to conceal their casualties and damages from their enemies.

Certainly the Americans, making use of every available field glass could not ascertain any extensive damage upon the enemy except on some riggings. From the standpoint of the shore observers, the heavy American barrage had inflicted minor damage. In fact those few who were able to get any glimpses of activity aboard the vessels and beneath the hovering cover of billowing smoke, reported no damage or casualties and were not complimentary about the accuracy and effectiveness of Colonel Knox's artillerymen.

The general impression of the battle from the Continental Army's viewpoint will be summed up by Colonel Thomas Ewing. However, history will prove his report next Sunday to the Maryland Council of Safety erroneous. Ewing will write the Safety Council his impression of the battle, saying:

"About four days ago there was three men-of-war, frigates, went up North River past all our forts. One gentleman walked the second deck, seemingly in command as if nothing was the matter, and seven forts keeping a constant fire at the ship. What damage was done is uncertain, but believed to be very trifling. . . ."[26]

The American Commander is also deceived as to the extent of damages sustained by the flotilla. He had witnessed the battle from the heights of Fort Washington. Like Ewing and others he judged it to be another American failure to stop the British Juggernaut.

Tomorrow The General will write Schuyler from his headquarters on Harlem Heights. He will inform his commander of the Northern Department, stating:

"We are again deprived of the navigation of this river by three ships of war, two of forty-four and the other of twenty guns, with three or four tenders, passing our chevaux-de-frise yesterday morning, and all our batteries, without any kind of damage or interruption, notwithstanding a heavy fire was kept up from both sides of the river. I have given directions to complete the obstructions as fast as possible, and I flatter myself if they allow us a little time more, that the passage will become extremely difficult, if not entirely insecure. Their views I imagine are chiefly to cut off our supplies and probably to gain recruits . . ."[27]

The discouraging news will travel fast. William Ellery, a friend of Rhode Island's governor, will write to Governor Cooke from Philadelphia on Friday informing him that The General notified Congress of the passing of the chevaux-de-frise "without interruption or damage."

Ellery will add this questioning and significant statement:

"How the chevaux-de-frise came to be insufficient, I know not; but I am afraid that the enemy's ships will cut off the communication by the North River. . . ."[28]

And tonight in the gloom-shrouded headquarters at Harlem Heights, Tench Tilghman, writing to the New York Committee Of Safety for the American Commander, will echo the disappointment of the entire American army command. He will say:

". . . and (the ships) stood on with an easy southerly breeze towards our chevaux-de-frise, which we hoped would have given them some interruption, while our batteries played upon them. But to our surprise and mortification, they all came through without the least difficulty, and without receiving any apparent damage from our forts, which kept playing on them from both sides of the river. . . ."[29]

Though far from satisfied with the battle's results after having anticipated so much from the blockade, General Greene will, in his Friday letter to Governor Cooke in Rhode Island, reflect a considerably higher degree of optimism in an attempt to buoy all spirits. After all his command must bear the responsibility for success or failure. So Greene, at first ignoring the blockade battle, will write Cook:

> "If the different States complete the establishment agreeable to the resolves of Congress, and the troops come well officered, (for on that the whole depends) I have not the least doubt in my mind, but that in a few months we shall be able to seek the enemy instead of they us. I know our men are more than equal to theirs, and were our officers equal to our men, we should have nothing to fear from the best troops in the world. I do not mean to derogate from the worth and merit of all the officers in the army. We have many that are in the service deserving the highest applause, and has served with reputation and honour to themselves and the State that sent them . . ."[30]

Greene, in an effort to reassure the Rhode Island governor who, Greene has been told, has been flooded with pessimistic reports that could dangerously undermine New England's morale, adds in his letter to his home state's chief executive a few words to offset the discouraging news about the run-through. After admitting that the enemy ships passed through the obstruction "and went up to Tapan-Bay," Greene writes:

> "Our army are so strongly fortified, and so much out of the command of the shipping, we have little more to fear this campaign . . ."

Greene's Quaker background with its focus upon humanitarianism, from which can largely be attributed his deep concern for the sick, comes out in this same letter. In the hope that Cooke and others will take his cue and press for better hospitals, more doctors and medical provisions, Greene states in referring to the great increase of respiratory ailments:

> "The troops have been and still are exceedingly sickly. The same disorder rages in the enemy's camp as it does in ours, but is much more mortal. . . ."[31]

Were the Truth Known

Were the results of the river battle today fully known by the Continental Army and its commanders, they would be far less able to criticize the American cannonry, "Ole Put's fence" and to feel any sense of "mortification," as The General put it. Rather, they would now be extolling the artillerymen for their marksmanship and praising the Chevaux de Frise for stopping the small fleet momentarily, but long enough to enable the rebel gunners to score disastrous hits.

For Captain Parker's report to Admiral Howe following the battle will make it very clear to the British high command what it really did cost to run the American blockade this morning. Parker's report will convince the Howes that breaking through the obstruction with fire pouring down from both sides of the river is too risky and far too costly.

Parker's account will make it clear that such an enterprise should not be attempted too often. At least not with both the twin forts in the enemy's hands, for the cross fire alone could surely destroy a flotilla.

Both the Howes conclude the sister fortresses and their Chevaux de Frise are a far greater hazard than they had estimated. And, oddly enough, they have no idea that the Americans now believe the blockade an ineffective, useless failure. Consequently the Howes will decide to concentrate upon ground troops and strategy to eliminate their menace on the river. Their enemy, on the other hand, in ignorance of the effectiveness of their forts and barricade, will prepare for more assaults by the King's ships.

Both Admiral Howe and Sir William, in concealing their losses, have executed an excellent piece of deception which any Indian war party would be proud of. It will be confidentially revealed to the Admiralty Office in London next month when the Admiral will report:

"... By the accounts I have a few days since received from Captain Parker, I find the ships had suffered much in their masts and rigging; the loss of men, as in the inclosed return, was less considerable. ..."[32]

And the "inclosed return" which Admiral Howe will prepare on board his flagship, the *Eagle*, November 23, will arrive in London on December 30, reading:

"Return of the killed and wounded on board his Majesty's ships passing the batteries, the 9th of October, 1776.
"*Phoenix*. 1 Midshipman, 2 seamen, 1 servant killed;
"1 boatswain, 1 carpenter, 8 seamen, 1 servant, 1 negro man, 1 private marine, wounded.
"*Roebuck*. 1 Lieutenant, 1 midshipman, 2 seamen, 1 corporal of marines, wounded.
"*Tartar*. 1 Midshipman killed; 1 Lieutenant of Marines, wounded.
"Total. 9 killed; 18 wounded."[33]

Howe will imply that the damage to the ships was greater than that to the men. For he will say, "the ships suffered much in their masts and rigging," giving no other details; yet, of the casualties suffered, he will declare, in reference to the "9 killed; 18 wounded," "the loss of men was less considerable."

And of all this the Americans will be ignorant until long after the war.

Surely such damages and casualties are not, as the American officers disparagingly described them, "very trifling," of "no apparent damage," or "without any kind of damage." But it will be a century and more before the Bluff Rock artillerymen and their comrades on the shore and on Mount Washington are vindicated and properly credited for their work today.

If the American military's Council of War nurtures any indecision over rebuilding and reinforcing the Chevaux de Frise, their indecision will soon be dispelled. For on Friday, October 11, the Continental Congress will pass a resolution "to incur any possible expense to obstruct the river."[34]

The Howes will reap one profit from their costly running of the blockade. The effect of British men-of-war carrying well-armed troops aboard, right into the backyard of the upper Hudson valley's landowners, is far from comforting to the upriver inhabitants.

Civilian morale in the area has already suffered considerably. And now, as is to be expected, the disaffected, deserters and Tories will be seeking council with the officers of the frigates. The New York Committee of Safety's pressure on Congress will consequently soon be vociferously increased.

At the twin forts the men of the works silently, sluggishly and despondently go about the business of cleaning up after the battle. Over the Barbette and all the artillery stations lurks the acrid smell of gunpowder. The odor, mixed with the stench of human sweat, pervades the atmosphere, rising slowly with the dust stirred up from around the emplacements.

All that they know of their results following the long grueling hours of the morning is what the officers have reported. And none had given them good news of their cannonading. Told again and again that the pigeons were right under their noses and escaped, the artillerymen on both the river posts are a depressed lot.

And all the bad things that could be said about a blockade that has not successfully blocked are now being said about the Chevaux de Frise. After months of work and preparations, a failure!

"But May God Damn This War"

Lieutenant Gray has never been so despondent. Even Jocko has not dared to speak to him, knowing that The Lieutenant is not in a mood for talking about anything. It is Levy who quietly tells Gray that Elaine is at the sentry gate waiting for him, wanting to be assured by him personally that he is all right.

Tired almost to the point of exhaustion, the bedraggled Gray, his dirt-covered, blue petticoat scarf dangling from his neck and over his shoulder, gives a few final orders. Turning, he walks toward the sentry's gate and accompanies his wife up the steep, Palisadean path in the direction of Fort Constitution's headquarters where he must report.

Gray's thoughts dwell on the discouraging reports of the observers and weigh, on the other hand, the sworn certainty of so many of the gunners that they had perfect strikes.

He questions the accuracy of the unfavorable reports. After all how could the observing command officers make accurate observations through so much smoke and firing?

Gray has not heard a word of Elaine's tale. But as she holds onto his arm while ascending the rocky path, she talks continuously, telling him of the horrible state of things at the hospital, the scarcity of medicines, of the visitor from the Orange County Militia, Abe Onderdonk, Hans' uncle, and of how she and Ma Kearney succeeded in getting into the fort and completing their morning chores at the hospital tent in the very midst of the battle.

Suddenly she realizes that her husband's mind is preoccupied with thoughts far afield of her conversation. She stops and says, mildly rebuking him, "Well, do not talk to me, then! All morning I have tried to keep busy so as to keep from thinking of you there at that cannon. All I know is that I am glad you are all right. For if anything ever happens to you. . . ."

Gray, stopped by her outburst, recovers his thoughts. He turns, faces her, smiling apologetically, and puts his large hands on each of her small shoulders.

"You would what?" he scoffingly asks her. "Jump off the Bluff Rock? How flattering! That, Dear One, has been done before. Is there not something more novel you could do?"

Ignoring his ridiculing amusement, she replies very stiffly, "John, do not do this to me! You make me very angry."

Gray's face loses its smile and turns serious. He bends over, kisses her gently and affectionately. Then tenderly and deliberately he speaks.

"Ye are my adored, Elaine. Ye must never forget that. Ye must never forget how deep is the well of my love for thee. . . . But may God damn this war!"

He holds her tight to him for a brief second. Neither one has heard the approaching footsteps from around the bend of the rugged uphill path.

Tom Paine had not intended to eavesdrop. But even if he had tried to avoid hearing any part of Gray's statement, he could not have done so.

"Pardonnez-moi, Madame Gray," Paine says as he politely excuses himself and passes the couple, moving ahead of them on the narrow footpath.

Carefully choosing his steps up the path, Paine stops slightly beyond Elaine and John. He turns and addresses himself to Gray.

"I could not help but overhear you say, Lieutenant, 'May God damn this war!' I would agree. But should He not have time to damn the whole thing, perhaps we could prevail upon Him to dam the river at the Chevaux de Frise a little more than 'twas today."

Gray, slightly surprised at the adjutant's greeting and his rather unusual attempt at humor replies quickly, "As an officer, Sir, I find it always advisable to ask for far more than one has the slightest chance of acquiring, especially when dealing with head-quarters at the top echelon."

Paine, moving on up the path, chuckles at the reply as he disappears.

During the heat of battle Paine got around. He seldom missed anything that was going on. He would be seen on the Bluff Rock ramparts and minutes later alongside of the cannoneers at the shore batteries.

The adjutant has scoffed at the British belief that they can cut off "the communication between the Eastern and Southern States by means of the North River." He calls it visionary, declaring that "no ship can lay long at anchor in any river within reach of the shore."

Later he will support his argument by reference to one of the enemy's attempts to pass the sister forts. He will say, in pointing out that "a single gun would drive a first-rate vessel from anchor," and he will add:

> "This was proved last October at (Forts Washington and Constitution), where one gun only, on each side of the river, obliged two frigates to cut and be towed off in an hour's time."[35]

And so at least one voice, the adjutant general's, silent though it now must be, is as convinced as the enemy of the efficacy of the Chevaux de Frise and its two towering forts. Though not openly disagreeing with the American high command's assessment of the battle, Paine unknowingly has for once agreed with the Howes on something.

18

Saturday, October 12. . .

Circumvention Via Westchester

Objective For the Nonce

Though it has been almost four weeks since the Battle of Harlem, the run-through of the blockade on Wednesday last seems to indicate that the Howes are far from calling an end to the campaign before bedding down for the winter. Warm, pleasant days have made this an unusually mild fall. But the nights are gradually becoming damper and colder.

Such changeable weather has been conducive to respiratory ailments which have accounted for numerous feverish, bedridden patients. These illnesses have led to widely spreading dysentery and contagion which, for want of any accurate medical understanding are merely termed, "The Ague" or "The Fever." The malady is running rampant throughout both armies.

Regardless of widespread sickness in both armies the weather is ideal for carrying on war. And the Howe brothers plan to make the most of it.

If running through the Chevaux de Frise's gantlet at great cost to Admiral Black Dick's ships and personnel accomplished anything, it acted as an excellent diversionary tactic for what Sir William has been hoping to carry out today. For below the British lines that stretch across Manhattan and face the American entrenchments on Harlem's heights, 80 or more enemy vessels of all kinds and an initial wave of 4,000 men are now ready on the East

River to advance into Westchester. Their objective: Invasion of Westchester and circumvention of the American army which holds the northern end of Manhattan Island.

To reach that objective Sir William has chosen Throg's Neck[1] for his next move in the game of military chess. It will prove to be one more costly error for the British commander-in-chief.

Ordinarily Sir William is a careful planner, known and respected for his sagacity in military scheming. However, he requires ample weight and force on his side of the fence when the action begins. He has found the American lines on Harlem and Mount Washington entirely too strong in their defenses to risk a frontal attack. He must be assured of his success before the attack. In his own words, which he will later pen in a report to Lord George Germaine, General Howe will explain his strategy and intent as follows:

> "The very strong position the enemy had taken on this island (Manhattan), and fortified with incredible labour, determined me to get upon their principal communication with Connecticut, with a view of forcing them to quit the strongholds in the neighbourhood of King's-Bridge, and if possible, to bring them to action."[2]

The British chief has concluded that the least costly strategy is circumvention of the rebel army, a move which now offers him the best chance of success. By an amphibious assault he will strike at the rear of the American flank. While his left wing is piercing behind the rebel fortifications on Manhattan at Mount Washington and Harlem from King's Bridge, his right will cut off all communications with New England. In his maneuver the Admiral's men-of-war in Tappan Bay can play a major role.

Once the King's Bridge garrison is taken, Admiral Howe will easily sever all communications coming from the north down Hudson's river. Fort Washington then will be isolated except possibly from limited contact across the river with Fort Constitution and from what provisions can be sent precariously across the stream through Bourdette's Ferry.

In consequence, the British high command expects the rebels' Harlem lines, south of Mount Washington, will be forced to join Fort Washington's garrison in a full evacuation of Manhattan owing to their loss of ties and lifelines of communication with the northern outposts and with the central hub, Fort Constitution on the Jersey side. Howe's plan appears to be flawless.

The British commander-in-chief is sure he has planned for every possible contingency. Lord Percy is to remain with three brigades, two of redcoats and one of Hessians,[3] manning the British lines below the American defenses at Harlem. Percy is to make occastonal feints, pending the signal for a frontal and rear assault in the pincer movement.

Thus, Howe foresees his two divisions forming a giant set of jaws. The northernmost will crush down upon King's Bridge, sweeping into the rear of Mount Washington and Harlem's defenses. The southernmost, under Percy, will press simultaneously into the beleaguered Harlem Heights' works. Meanwhile, Lord Howe's ships will again smash at the Chevaux de Frise and again snap it. This time he will concentrate the vessels' broadsides on Mount Washington in conjunction with the army's artillery barrage on Mount Washington.

If the rebels can be forced to stand and fight at King's Bridge, at Harlem and at Fort Washington on open ground rather than retreat and escape across the Hudson to Fort Constitution, Howe is convinced he can at least break the backbone of the Continental Army. And the most that can be expected is complete surrender.

Slowly, the secret operation begins. As in most great enterprises that meet failure, it is the small overlooked factor such as a buckle on a horse's saddle strap, which often dooms the venture. For Sir William, today that upsetting little item is an island that should have been a part of the mainland. The little cog which will jam the Jaggernaut's wheels is a bridge joining Throg's Neck Point to the mainland.

If Howe knew Throg's Neck was an island, he did not know some rebels, taking unusually precautionary measures last night, chopped down the bridge's structure. It made good campfires through the chilly dawn.

On the East River Admiral Howe and Commodore Hotham prepare the expedition which early this morning began moving upriver toward Hell Gate and Long Island Sound. Even before daybreak the ships were hoisting anchor and setting sail from Montressor's Island.

The spotty early morning fog has been to their advantage thus far. The enemy observers have either not seen the ship's movements or have not been alarmed by them.

Far from dissipating, the fog now has thickened as the fleet of the King's navy heads through the dangerous Hell Gate waters.

Swept rapidly by the powerful, swirling Hell Gate tide, the ships' crews valiantly struggle to keep their vessels on course. The task becomes greater with each periodic blanket of fog that rises before them in dense white clouds obscuring all vision. There is no possibility of calling off the expedition or of returning to the safety of Montressor's Island. The flotilla must proceed.

Some of the craft are blanketed completely for long moments in the fog banks which, fortunately for the seamen, are carried away to dissipate in the light and occasionally brisk east wind. Some of the vessels narrowly escape ramming one another as they appear to fly over the surface of the choppy waters which become incredibly swift in the narrowing channel.

Only the superior seamanship of the British sailors prevents the expedition from suffering a major catastrophe.[4] All have heard of the treacherous Hell Gate waters. All are aware that many proud ships have sunk in this channel.

One of the heavily loaded artillery boats is in serious trouble. It carries three six-pounders in addition to a full crew of seven. The captain at the helm strains to hold his vessel's bow firmly into the rapidly flowing current of the churning, eddy-filled seas surrounding it.

The heroic efforts of the hopelessly struggling crewmen appear doomed. They lower their little ship's mainsail, casting their lot upon their skill with the oars. Valiantly they pit their strength against the East River's ocean-pushed tide. But the waters now collide with the sweeping turbulence of Long Island's swelling seas in the very center of Hell Gate's narrows.

In the battle, nature's elements do not easily succumb and very seldom relent. They suddenly summon from out of the depths the seemingly incalculable forces of ten thousand sea monsters, waiting to pounce when man relaxes and loses his controls, even for a fraction of a second.

In the fog-shrouded early morning mist, a captain of one of the large frigates sees the predicament of the distressed vessel which veers broadside and bounces around like a cork. The crew on the fast-moving man-of-war throws one line after another off in the bobbing artillery craft's direction. All are too short and are lost in the encircling mist.

Just as it appears the crew may have regained control of the vessel one of the starboard six-pounders breaks from its stays, rolls across the starboard deck and collides with the ship's portside gunnel. It rocks back and forth a few inches as though awaiting the proper moment of impetus, gravity and a sufficient lurch of the vessel before charging back at the irons that had held it.

A seaman gunner, its master, rushes to grasp the runaway's

dragging chain and hook it firmly to the claw of its iron block. A few yards out of its reach, he slips on the wet deck as the artillery-carrying craft suddenly dips its beam into the violent foam.

As though waiting for that signal and the desired angle of descent across the sloping deck, the loosened cannon again starts its rampage. It hurtles down upon the screaming seaman-gunner struggling to get back on his feet.

The rolling fieldpiece's muzzle strikes its horrified victim fully in the chest, crushing him into the starboard gunnel through which the heavy cannon crashes. The smashed gunwale opens like paper, and the heavy iron weapon carries its "master" to the bottom of the Sound.

The waters rush through the gaping hole in the bulwark causing the battered ship to list perilously. Two crewmen jump overboard and grasp the dangling lines thrown by the crew of a sister craft. Another less fortunate seaman fails to catch the line. He is swept away by the swirling current and disappears below the surface of Hell Gate's waters.

Hell Gate Exacts Its Toll

Two more of the crew desert the careening, sinking vessel. They swim with the current until they catch the stern lines of one of the smaller boats. Each ship in the squadron attempts to hold its own against the treacherous current. Impenetrable clouds of fog, periodically passing, compound the flotilla crewmen's difficulties in the viciously swirling waters.

Only the captain of the sinking vessel remains with it. Staying at the helm he attempts to run it ashore hoping to save his charge from total destruction. He soon realizes his vessel is doomed. He has waited too long.

Unable to swim and hoping the ship will strike a shoal, he desperately clings to one of the two remaining six-pounders. The weapon's barrel is raised high in the air on the portside of the dangerously listing craft. Unless the ship strikes a shallow or a sand bar, the vessel threatens momentarily to overturn. The captain's only hope now is to jump for a line from the first boat-crew that sweeps by.

At last one of the larger sloops closes in. The crew speedily throws a line to the stranded man. Then, without warning, the heavy iron monster which the captain straddles, holding one hand on the gunnel rail, rises high in the air with the listing ship.

The 900-pound cannon strains against its creaking, stretching chains as its tremendous weight dangles over the rising surface of the angry seas. The ship's entire portside rises vertically from the surging, billowing waves.

Then a loud, whip-like crack splits the air. One chain breaks under the weight of the six-pounder. The other slowly tears away a section of the gunnel as the ship's officer and the loosened fieldpiece dangle for a brief second before man and weapon are torn from the gunwale and dropped into the foaming waters.

Drawn under the surface by the powerful suction of the plummeting weapon, the captain rises once. His arms flail desperately for a grip on the ship's half submerged deck. Seconds later he disappears again. And within minutes his craft follows him beneath the surface,[5] adding more victims to the countless tombstones in Hell Gate's graveyard.

One artillery boat, three six-pounders and several seamen are not present as the frigate, *Carysfort*,[6] covers the invasion at the so-called "Throg's Neck Point" at 9 A.M. this morning. Hell Gate has exacted its toll.

To some of the British seamen the beginning hours of the invasion have started off with an ominous note. Not so for General Howe. With his predilection for overwhelming might and force, Sir William has just enjoyed an added boost.

As he had expected, "a number of transports with troops, among which are Bourgoyne's Sixteenth Regiment of British Light Dragoons, have arrived in New York."[7] The additional force gives him more of that essential "might and weight" he likes to have.

The additions spur confidence among the British command staff. The new regiments will help offset the ranks so badly depleted by recent illnesses.

Certainly now a powerful set of jaws can be readied to break the rebels' backs. A clean sweep from Throg's Neck Point across to King's Bridge, matched by a strong arm of light dragoons pressing down on Harlem will do it. The operation gives all the indications of a successful enterprise.

But the commander-in-chief of the King's army has made an unfortunate mistake in choosing Throg's Neck Point rather than Pell's Point, as his stepping stone to the mainland in his plan for the circumvention of the rebel army. The difference is that Throg's Neck Point is actually an island—a fact probably not fully realized by the King's surveyors until too late. Or, if they were aware of its terrain, they had not counted on a bridge that could be destroyed before their van reached it. And neither had they weighed the difficulties of fording a tidal marshland that lies south of it.

The bridge and the causeway on the mainland are at the lower end of Throg's Neck Point. A fording at low tide is possible, though precarious. The fording point is at the opposite side of the island from the bridge. The bridge and ford are the only connecting links to the mainland, and both are guarded by American outposts under Heath's command.

However, the Pell's Point location, three miles to the east of Throg's Neck, is a part of the mainland. An invasion there would not be obstructed by bridge crossings. Nor would the British there have to be concerned with fording tidal, marshland creeks. Of most importance, Pell's Point is unguarded since Heath's forces are not ample enough to allow for unlimited picket posts at every possible point of invasion.

So Howe's army lands on an island at Throg's Neck Point, faced with crossing a guarded bridge, a bridge which could easily be destroyed. And then the only alternative would be to ford the guarded creek and its almost impenetrable morass, all under the well-concealed guns of the rebel defenders on the mainland.

General William Heath's rebel headquarters are at King's Bridge. His responsibility is to cover the mainland north in Westchester, supporting and defending Colonel Magaws's defenses at Fort Washington. Heath's forces are largely concentrated on the north bank of the Harlem River near its emptying point into the Hudson River at the Spuyten Duyvil. Located about nine miles south of Dobb's Ferry, Heath commands the northern wing and outpost for Mount Washington's defenses.

Harlem Heights' southernmost defense outposts and the works above it on Mount Washington are the last remaining footholds the Americans possess on Manhattan Island. General Greene's command, across Hudson's river on Fort Constitution, is the lifeline of communcations and supplies upon which the Harlem and Mount Washington defenders are almost entirely dependent.

Greene and his Fort Constitution complement are the communications center, the principal commissary, and the main reinforcement post for all three American forces now concentrated on the east bank of Hudson's river.

The American officers generally agree that Howe—if he does not go into winter quarters—will do one of two things. Either he will attempt a frontal attack on Harlem and Mount Washington, or invade the mainland at Westchester with an amphibious force pouring in through Long Island Sound. The combination is such a likelihood that General Heath has kept pickets stretched eastward from King's Bridge north and then up to the bridge and causeway from Throg's Neck.

For this could be the British back-door leading the redcoats into the American flank, guarding Fort Washington. And the Council of War's unanimous decision last month was that Fort Washington is to be defended and held if possible against the enemy's assaults.[8]

Fears, Defeats, Desertions and A Creeping Hopelessness

The American Commander only last night sent the President of the Congress his reaffirmation that the enemy may soon strike again. The activities in the East River prompted it.

So, writing from his Harlem headquarters, The General makes note of the apprehensions expressed to him by the New York Committee of Safety over the way the "disaffected" in the state are joining Howe's Loyalists and taking up arms in behalf of the enemy.

After noting that he has sent part of the Massachusetts militia under General Lincoln to offset some of the Tories' mischief and to prevent consequences from their conspiracies, the rebel General informed the Congress of his judgment regarding the native Loyalists' intentions stating:

"I am persuaded that they are upon the eve of breaking out, and that they will leave nothing unessayed that will distress us and favour the designs of the enemy, as soon as their schemes are ripe for it."[9]

Tench Tilghman wrote to William Duer last Tuesday, the 8th, from The General's staff headquarters at Harlem, noting how American preparations were being made in expectation for some enemy penetration:

"A bridge of boats is to be thrown over Harlem River, just at this place, which will form a fine, easy communication between, should the attack be made either one side or the other."[10]

Long inactivity within the American lines, illnesses, enemy propaganda, weaknesses in the leadership of the subaltern officers promoting a lack of confidence by the troops in their commanders, inadequate pay, inadequate food and clothing and tenting shortages have all combined to undermine the rapidly corroding morale of some segments of the American army. Only the stout-hearted Continentals seem to stand firm and unwavering as the Juggernaut moves in.

Sleepless nights without shelter on the slowly freezing ground make endurance in the army of rebellion ever more difficult. Many of the state militia beeline home to their firesides immediately upon the expiration of their enlistment periods. Others, refusing to put up with the agonizing conditions, desert, often in large numbers, depleting entire companies within a few nights. It is the regulars, the Continental troops generally, in whom the Commander-in-Chief and his staff must place the bulk of their reliance.

Even today, almost at this precarious hour, Deputy Adjutant General Samuel Griffin at his headquarters in Perth Amboy, is dismissing Colonel Allison's battalion of Pennsylvania "Associators." They are members of the Flying Camp for which so much hope had been held. Griffin, writing today, October 12, and reminded by one of his staff that it is the anniversary date of the discovery of the new world 284 years ago, at which he shrugs his shoulders, orders:

> "Colonel Allison's battalion ... having done their duty while in camp as good and orderly soldiers, and furnished their full complement for the flying Camp, are hereby dismissed from the service of the States, and permitted to return home."[11]

The pressures to return home, the expiration of enlistments, the coming of winter and the feeling that the New York Campaign is about over until the spring, all promote a creeping hopelessness in the American Cause. For causes, such as the Continental Congress has declared are just, need victories.

But defeats and retreats have left no victories for The Cause to feed upon. Howe's "might and force," augmented by Tories, Loyalists, the "disaffected," internal strife within the Congress and the creeping American wave of hopelessness give Sir William the upper hand.

Though General Howe's advantages are many and though he would like to end the conflict and return to England, he does not seem to be able to push the war to a quick end. The Americans have not been driven into suing for peace. There is still time to bring his enemy to their knees before winter, but Sir William now must consider winter preparations.

In those preparations the British commander, who can more easily do without his necessities than his luxuries, plans to include his dazzling blonde mistress, "The Sultana" as an adjunct to his winter quarters in New York.[12] This is small enough compensation for the annoyances the rebel band has created which he may have to endure until spring. These are among Howe's main concerns as winter approaches.

The Americans' problems are more acute. Both civilian and military are infected with the jitters and the growing uncertainty that the united colonial states can endure at all. The "jitters" surface everywhere. Tensions are rife, particularly among the pickets and the sentinels, who sometimes jump and fire without thinking.

This was brought to mind with a shock yesterday afternoon. A nervous artillery officer and his men on Fort Washington's high breastworks mistakenly opened his artillery fire on the American Commander-in-Chief's own launch.[13]

The General's barge had made it up the river well before the blockade battle. Then yesterday, the seamen aboard took advantage of a fresh breeze. With its topsail flying, the vessel came back down passing through the channel waters under the guns of Mount Washington.

The General Escapes Death From the Cannon On His Namesake

Warned to be wary of any redcoat "tricks" and believing that the barge was from Captain Parker's British squadron in Tappan Bay, the nervous battery commander ordered his artillerists to open fire. The crack gunners aimed for her midship. Perfectly the twelve-pounder struck its mark.

The young artillery officer had not known about The General's launch which, for safety measures, is kept as secret as possible. He was certain, therefore, that this was an enemy craft on some nefarious mission, possibly aimed at blowing a hole in the Chevaux de Frise through which Parker's squadron might escape back downriver. He was sure his hit now would bring him his long-awaited promotion.

But not so. The strike ripped through the barge's gunnel, killing three of the American crewmen on deck and wounding its captain. Fortunately the American Commander-in-Chief was not on board. The General had spent most of yesterday at his Harlem head-quarters.[14] Small as it is, the American "navy" (if it can be so called) has started off learning much about land-sea communications, but at a costly price. Jittery landsmen can be as dangerous as the enemy.

Farther up in Westchester the army will soon be as bad as they are along the Hudson. General Heath has posted Colonel Edward Hand and his First Pennsylvania rifle regiment at the bridge and causeway leading to Throg's Neck Point. Far from being jittery, Colonel Hand and his regulars are—and always have been—itching for action.

They are so remote from King's Bridge where they believe the brush will come that many have expressed open disgust at being sent so far north. One old soldier summed it up by saying, "We's all mights' well be wit Schuyler 'nd da North 'in Dep'artmen' as way off up here!"

But the "Old Soldier" soon changed his mind. The first report of possible enemy activity last night stirred up an excited wave of relief mixed with joy among Hand's spirited troops. Most of them have scores to settle from Long Island and New York town. When it was rumored enemy scouts had landed on the Neck, Hand immediately sent word to Heath at King's Bridge and began an investigation.

Then this morning Hand's pickets reported that waves of British and Hessians were pouring on shore at the Point. The wily rebel colonel, convinced that the vanguard landing last night was not simply a stray foraging party or part of a feint, orders the strengthening of his entrenchments and the destruction of the few remaining plank boards of the bridge across the creek.

Hand positions his men under the cover of a long stretch of piled cordwood at the western end of the Neck on the mainland side where the bridge had stood. This secluded entrenchment will be his forward defense line.

And there the crack Pennsylvanians wait patiently for the British and Hessian grenadiers to make their appearance. Unknown to the enemy, Lieutenant William Smith and his corporal's guard have now completed the bridge-demolishing job they started last night and which kept the campfires burning. Their work leaves General Howe and his Juggernaut virtually stranded on an island.[15]

Hand has assigned several companies of his regiment to guard the ford, the only other route the redcoats can take to the mainland. The colonel anticipated that the British, if repulsed at the bridge, would next make an effort to ford the stream and marshlands at the lower end. So there, also, stands a well prepared ambush waiting for Howe's forces.

When the British van reaches the bridge, the little band of riflemen open up.[16] The King's men had not expected to

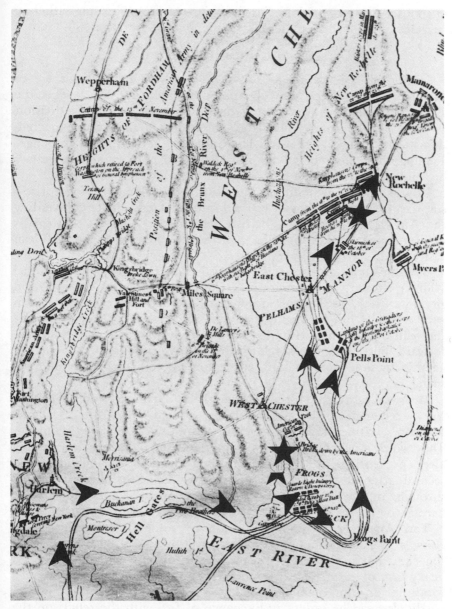

Overlaid on this "Plan of the Operations of the King's Army" (Map 600RtC.)
Sauthier-Faden, 1777 drawing, are the arrows showing the British attempt to
land on Throg's Neck, the repulse and the later move into Pell Point, then up
into New Rochelle—original in the Clinton Collection, W. L. Clements Library,
Ann Arbor, Michigan.

encounter any opposition. Thrown into confusion by the withering fusillade, the invaders pull back to the nearest elevation.

The Juggernaut Is Stopped

Instead of attempting a second effort, realizing that passage to the mainland is impossible at that point without the bridge, the British commanders swerve their operation back and send a division to cross at the ford. There too, they meet a similar unexpected, devastating blanket of fire. The invaders keep up an exchange. Finding that the rebels hold the advantage plus an accuracy they had not anticipated, the redcoats pull back.

Howe's entire expedition has lost every element of surprise— surprise that was to have been a principal factor in circumventing the American forces. The British commander-in-chief's strategy is now an open book which the American General and his staff can easily read.

By the time the scattered British vanguards regroup, Colonel William Prescott's Massachusetts Continentals and Captain David Bryant's crew, by Heath's order, are up with their six-pounder in support of Hand. So the British invasion comes to a dead halt at the causeway where Hand's 25 Pennsylvania riflemen hold the forward line behind a stock-pile of cordwood. They prevent the enemy division from making any effort to temporarily rebuild the span.

Meanwhile, at the ford, Captain John Graham, leading a New York regiment of Continentals, is joined by Captain Daniel Jackson's artillerymen with their six-pounder on the mainland. They come up behind Hand's right flank detachment, now resting after preventing the enemy's fording over to the mainland. A second attempt by the Crown's men is then sent staggering back through the marshes under the heavy artillery and small arms barrage.

The American defenders now have some 1,800 men facing Howe's grenadiers and jagers who total around 4,000, comprising the first wave of enemy troops. Howe, always reluctant to send heavy lists of casualties to London, is soon convinced that forcing a foothold on the mainland at Throg's Neck is certain to be too costly. Instead he orders an exchange of fire with the rebels on the mainland side of the creek.

So throughout the day the American riflemen and the King's jagers keep up "a scattered popping at each other across the marsh."[17]

By late afternoon the rest of Howe's force committed to the circumvention are loaded from more transports onto the Neck. The force comprises the bulk of the British army, all now assembled on Throg's Neck Point[18] and all literally pinned down by less than 2,000 American Continentals, a few fieldpieces, and a spirit not yet infected with the "creeping hopelessness."

Embarrassingly stranded on an island by two relatively minor details, a destroyed bridge and a tidal, swampy ford, Sir William and his staff hold a conference.

Convinced that the creek and the marshes cannot be crossed without sustaining forbidding losses, and aware that the operation has lost every element of surprise it had so strongly depended upon, Howe and his command settle down. They must now await their baggage and supplies on the way up from New York and, at the same time, determine an alternative strategy.

Lieutenant William Smith and his little corporal's guard, by turning a bridge into firewood, have halted and stymied the King's Juggernaut.

For the next five days the mighty British machine will be stalled on Throg's Point. Informants, and those who had earlier recommended other invasion points, convince the Crown's command that Pell's Point is the alternative. Pell's Point is an integral part of the mainland and offers no bridge to cross or fording obstructions to bar the redcoats' way.

Throg's Neck Triggers the Rebels' Alarm

Since surprise is no longer a factor on his side, and since some rebel troops will undoubtedly be posted at every possible invasion point, Howe takes his time and revises his plans.

Pell's Point is a solid part of the mainland. It offers no natural barriers to an invasion force, and the Americans there will have no natural obstacles to make use of in their defenses. Furthermore, the defenders at Pell's Point have no narrow-way at which they might stem the overwhelming tide of the King's men.[19]

Pell's Point will be Howe's steppingstone to the American continent. Frustrated in Massachusetts, he is determined that Westchester will give him the footing enabling his encirclement of the rebel army and a severing of its links with both the north and south.

Before nightfall news of the American defense today at Throg's Neck reaches every American post and garrison along the Hudson

River and every inhabitant in the Hudson Valley. Heath dispatched the surprising news to the Commander-in-Chief at Harlem before noon. There all troops were ordered under arms and prepared to move out on notice.

General McDougall's brigade, joined by Colonel Smallwood and some independent companies are immediately marched out of Harlem to King's Bridge, reinforcing Heath. Colonel Thomas Ewing and his Marylanders under Major Eden and Captains Posey, Young, Lowe, Hanson, Magruder, Tillard, Bowie, Forrest and Brooks are given orders to instruct their troops to "cook three days' provisions, and to hold themselves in readiness for an immediate march."[20]

Colonel Tom Ewing, who never fails to keep his Maryland Council of Safety informed of events, prepares to inform his home state council that:

> "in the last return, I had two hundred and thirty-seven privates sick, besides officers, owing to our lying on the cold ground without straw or plank, which is not to be had, and medicine very scarce. Great numbers of the soldiers are badly off for clothing. ... Numbers of the soldiers are without blankets. Several never received any, and some of the first three companies lost theirs in leaving New-York (city),"[21]

So the colonel and his Marylanders are not happily looking forward to an "immediate march" with "three days' provisions," pre-cooked.

At Fort Constitution, General Greene, alarmed by the news of the British action, immediately orders his command on full alert. Admiral Howe has ample vessels to make another attempt at ascending the North River. It might be timed with General Howe's land action off Long Island Sound. It could be diversionary or the real thing. Greene knows that the post and its sister fort on Mount Washington must now be ready for anything.

At five o'clock this afternoon, Greene, from his quarters at Fort Constitution, writes The General. He tells him that he has "three brigades in readiness to reinforce you," and adds:

> "General Clinton's brigade will march first; General Nixon's next, and then the troops under the command of General Roberdeau. I don't apprehend any danger from this quarter at present. If the force on your side are insufficient I hope these three brigades may be ordered over, and I with them and leave General (Brigadier General James) Ewing's brigade to guard the post."[22]

Recognizing Greene's many problems, and having the permission of his immediate commander, Gray makes an appeal to the post's Adjutant General Paine, requesting that Corporal Edmund Kearney be excused from duty.

The youth's mother lies seriously ill with the ague in the Kearney's cabin near the river. At times the fisherwoman is delirious with the fever.

Elaine sent word to Edmund by Paul. Still bitterly resenting his failure to be promoted to sergeant as he had undeservedly expected, Kearney walked away from his post without leave to go to his mother's side.

Gray's quiet intercession in behalf of the excited, self-willed Kearney was made without Edmund's knowledge at Elaine's bidding. The permission was granted, saving the youth from another one of his frequent infractions of the rules. Soon he is by his mother's side in the ramshackle old house just north of the Chevaux de Frise.

Ma Kearney's almost daily care of the sick, wounded and dying at the tent hospitals with Elaine has proved too much for the fisherwoman, if not also for Elaine who is also showing strain.

On top of her chores and her fishing business, the good-hearted woman has paid little if any attention to her own heavy cough and severe chest pains. Even her strong, fighting Irish constitution has not helped her this time.

Gray, as well as everyone else, is aware of the fisherwoman's proud affection for her son. His attachment for his mother developed firmly through the years after the youth's father, ever a wanderer, left them to fend for themselves ten years ago. Ma's life since then has been centered around her only child.

Aside from his close attachment to his mother, Edmund Kearney's only other feminine interest is that which he has and secretly held for his childhood playmate, Elaine. Yet not even Elaine has suspected that Edmund's interest in her was anything more than hers for him—a close friendship, bordering on a brotherly-sisterly relationship.

But Edmund, passing into his late teens as is Elaine, had grown to look upon her no longer as a childhood playmate, but rather as his future wife. Thus, the news of her marriage to John Gray was a shocking announcement that took the fisherwoman's son completely by surprise.

Elaine, if she is cognizant of this change in Edmund's attitude, has not admitted it to herself. But Gray has sensed it and has recognized an undercurrent of antagonism the young corporal harbors for him as Elaine's husband. It is the male's natural instinct enabling him to detect another suitor's threat to his mating union.

It had first been detected by Gray when Kearney was stationed at the Bergen post and had written letters home to his mother and Elaine. From what Elaine told him of those letters Gray derived his first suspicions.

Therefore, The Lieutenant's mission on Kearney's behalf is an exceptional gesture, considerate and confidential insofar as he and Elaine are concerned.

The corporal will learn of it in due time, for Tom Paine, who is ever conscious of man's oft-latent humanity, assured Gray that the soldier would be granted a furlough. Furthermore, Paine declared he would see that the corporal whose enlistment period is shortly expiring, was transferred to the Bluff Rock battery in order to be closer to his mother's residence under The Rock. That, Gray had not wanted.

So Corporal Kearney, whose mother had been deceived into promoting him to "sergeant," reaches her sickbed far more disgruntled with the army than he is chagrined with his deception. It is a deception, he feels, not of his own making. It is the army's fault.

Upon returning to The Mountain, assigned with his company to an outpost on the western slope, the corporal had visited his mother once and allowed her to assume he was a militia sergeant saying as little as possible about the matter. And Edmund did not now intend to tell her otherwise.

The fisherwoman's condition has rapidly worsened. Her voice has become hoarse and her mind wanders. She speaks incoherently and breathes with difficulty. The special Indian poultices and herbs that Minnie and Perawae Abbott have brought down from their mountain home have failed to cure their friend. Even the post's surgeon visited her and, deciding that bleeding would not help, prescribed a concoction of molasses, vinegar and butter.

Elaine tries to hold her head while the sick fisherwoman attempts to swallow. Unable to do so, she becomes distressed and convulsed at every effort. Discarding the surgeon's concoction, Elaine then takes from Minnie's patiently waiting hands the Indian woman's special herb drink.

Little by little Ma Kearney downs it. The muscles of her throat lose their tenseness. A relieved smile comes over her face. She relaxes and dozes, holding Elaine's hand on one side of the bed and her son's on the other.

The bride's drawn and tired features have greatly concerned her husband. He has begged her repeatedly to let the surgeons of the post take care of the hospital ill. Obstinately she has refused to do so, but Ma's illness now has frightened her and her husband as well.

In the past Elaine and Ma Kearney together have enlisted housewives from everywhere in the vicinity of the fort to help take care of the increasing number of hospital cases. The two women have been the main supports of the hospital sick for weeks. They have also solicited and received help from the freed, the bound and the indentured—blacks, whites, male and female. Among them are the widower Gartlick's servants, who Ma Kearney has angrily charged are Gartlick's mistreated "slaves," not servants.

The late Sarah Gartlick was as staunch a patriot as her husband was a Loyalist. She was as thoughtful of others and as considerate of the sick in the hamlet as her husband was unmindful of them. She had encouraged her black servants' independence which often led them to visit and assist others in need of help. Her death put an end to all that. Gartlick has little interest in helping his neighbors, most of whom he dislikes.

So reluctantly Gartlick occasionally permits Ishiah and her daughter, Katie May, to spend some time helping out Elaine and Ma at the hospital. It is an easy way for Gartlick to find out what is going on in the rebels' camp. However he seldom allows Immanuel and Ben to go off the place, always keeping them busy at repairing nets, if nothing else.

Elaine, assured that the help so badly needed in the hospital tents will be there, has promised her husband that as soon as Ma Kearney is comfortable for the night she will go home and to bed. The knowledge that Edmund is by his mother's side and that Minnie and Perawae will remain with her relieves Elaine's concern for the sick woman through the night's long vigil.

Cheery News For General Lee's Admirers

For some there is one encouraging piece of news spreading throughout the post and The Mountain as night falls. Word has been received that the hero of Charleston is on his way to Fort Constitution. Only six days ago he was given a great ovation by Congress in Philadelphia after arriving there from his victory in the south.[23] One dispatch rider stated that Lee left Philadelphia Wednesday and is now inspecting the Perth Amboy works.

Some are not impressed with General Charles Lee and quietly question his vaunted leadership. To those "doubters" now is added one more, Sergeant Abbott.

In a corner of the Bergen Woods tavern this evening several garrulous post riders, all in their cups, find a letter which has fallen from an envelope in one of their packets. In an attempt to ascertain to whom it is going and from whom it has come, one of the riders—far more literate than the others—reads part of it aloud before the lost envelope is finally found and replaced.

It is yesterday's letter slowly wandering from William Ellery to Governor Nicholas Cooke of Rhode Island bearing the date October 11.

The post rider's loud reading voice in the North Bergen Three Pidgeons Tavern is easily overheard as Abbott and Craig are eating at a nearby table. The letter in part tells of Lee's arrival and departure from Philadelphia. It is that part the rider reads aloud:

> "He (Lee) brings the good news, that the Carolinians had utterly defeated the Cherokee tribe of Indians, had burnt their towns, killed two hundred and fifty of their warriors, got seventy-five scalps, and that the remainder of that tribe had fled to the Mississippi. This expedition, the sickliness of the troops, and the strong garrison at Augustine had prevented an attempt upon East-Florida."[24]

If Abbott had had no opinion at all about General Charles Lee, he has one now. This so-called "good news" carried from Lee to Ellery is not to Abbott's liking. Both the army scouts, though annoyed at the post riders' act, have no intention of interfering. They look up from their plates at each other as they listen without comment to Ellery's letter.

Lee's Popularity Travels Ahead Of Him

The suddenly popular post rider whose literacy had never counted much or drawn him friends among his associates before, is now urged to read on by his overly-imbibed, inquisitive colleagues. He declines, declaring all the rest is only about:

> "The garrison at Augustine consisted of eighteen hundred German and one thousand British troops ... the *Sphinix* and *Raven* (British men-of-war) were at Georgia and that the *Scorpion*, *Falcon*, and *Cruiser* (also British men-of-war) are at Cape Fear."[25]

So Lee's popularity, gathering friends and admirers for his deeds credited him at Charleston and for his astute observations of the state of things in the South, is traveling ahead of him—in one way or the other. Everyone of those who now herald him as "The Knight of The Flaming Sword" is convinced that great things will come of his arrival in the North.

Today his presence in Perth Amboy has uplifted the sinking spirits of the troops there. At the Amboy post no knowledge has yet been received of Howe's landing and attempted invasion of Westchester at Throg's Neck Point.

If General Mercer, commanding the post, had received the news, he would have immediately informed his important visitor, General Lee. And Lee, had he known, would not have written from that post today, the impulsive letter he pens to the President of the Continental Congress in Philadelphia.

The letter, or "advice" as it might more suitably be called, is another one of Lee's frequent communications he will have cause to regret. It is another example of his actions, prompted by vanity and yet, in some degrees, founded upon a superior knowledge of military strategy.

In his lengthy admonishing counsel to the august body in Philadelphia, among which gathering his admirers are increasing, Lee presents an extremely unwise prognostication. Had he waited one more day, he would not now make the mistake of telling the Congress that Howe will drive for the Delaware and head for Philadelphia, when the King's men are, on the contrary, invading Westchester—a movement Lee does not even consider in his communication.

Consequently, Lee's pompous letter to the Continental Congress, dated today at "Amboy, October 12, 1776," makes him out to be a poor prognosticator of Sir William's plans and intentions.

On Monday the Congress will hear from the American Commander that Howe's forces are stranded on an island in an unsuccessful attempt to effect a surprise invasion of Westchester. It will also be hearing General Lee's prophecy, forecasting that Howe would move in a direction directly opposite from that which he did.

And so there will be snickers heard in Carpenter's Hall. Raised eyebrows will be observed as well as many faces marked with chagrin as the secretary reads Lee's impulsive and erroneous counsel, part of which says:

> "The Hessians who were encamped on Staten Island opposite this post, last night disappeared and there is the greatest reason to think that they have quitted the island entirely, which announces some great manoeuvre to be in agitation.

"I am confident they will not attack General Washington's lines; such a measure is too absurd for a man of Mr. Howe's genius; and unless they have received flattering accounts from Burgoyne that he will be able to effectuate a junction, (which I conceive they have not) they will no longer remain kicking their heels at New-York."

Lee does not use conditional terms such as "might," "may" or "probably" very often. The overconfident, high ranking commander is self-assured and, in making his prognostications, generally uses "will" as though he had a direct line of communication with the highest ethereal authorities. Referring to the British forces in New York town, he continues:

"They will put the place (New York City) in a respectable state of defence, which with their command of the waters may be easily done, leave four or five thousand men, and direct their operations to a more decisive object."

If Lee had ended his letter at this point, every member of the Continental Congress would probably have been impressed with his military acuity and hungered for more of his wisdom. But Lee is a man who has always been impressed with his own brilliance. This self-image was a major factor in his earlier decision to discontinue his services to the British army which he believed had not recognized his worth, and thereby so gain from the Congress the American army rank he was certain befitted his stature.

So the opinionated "Hero of Charleston" gives further of his advice to the American nation's representatives, making himself out to be a poor analyzer of Howe's stratagems.

Erroneously the major general predicts:

"They will infallibly proceed either immediately up the river Delaware with their whole troops, or what is more probable, land somewhere about South Amboy or Shrewsbury, and march straight to Trenton or Burlington.
"We must suppose every case. On the supposition that this will be the case, what are we to do? What force have we? What means have we to prevent their possessing themselves of Philadelphia?
"General Washington's army cannot possibly keep pace with them. The length of his route is not only infinitely greater, but his obstructions almost insuperable; in short, before he could cross Hudson river, they might be lodged and strongly fortified on both banks of the Delaware."

Many of the members of the Continental Congress Monday, upon hearing this, will imagine what heights the representatives' fears and anxieties would have reached that day had they not had

word from the American Leader that Howe and his army were
bogged down on Throg's Neck Point.

So, fortunately, they will listen to Lee's counsel with respect
but not with any immediate, frightened concern.

In concluding, Lee writes:

> "I shall make no apologies to Congress for thus so freely offering my
> opinion; the importance of the matter is a sufficient apology. For Heaven's
> sake, rouse yourselves; for Heaven's sake, let ten thousand men be immedi-
> ately assembled and stationed somewhere about Trenton.
>
> "In my opinion your whole depends upon it. I set out immediately for
> Head-Quarters, where I shall communicate my apprehension that such will
> be the next operation of the enemy, and urge the expediency of sparing a
> part of his army (if he has any to spare) for this object . . ."[26]

And so Lee set out for Fort Constitution and Fort Washington,
happy with himself but ignorant of his grand faux pas.

Undoubtedly, Lee's "prophecy" and his interpretation of what
should have been Howe's action is a good indication of the
American major general's ability as a military strategist. Lee's
assumption of what Howe should have done is a far better military
maneuver than that executed by the British commander today. But
there are sound arguments on both sides.

While it may be that Lee desired to impress the Congress with
his genius, it is likewise possible that had Howe executed the
operation Lee outlined, the British army might have met far
greater success tomorrow, headed for the Delaware, than they met
today on Throg's Neck. Certainly the move would have put the
American army on a forced march to Pennsylvania.

There is no question about the fact that Sir William, despite the
vast help that he has received from his admiral brothers's armada,
is now bogged down on a small offset little island. Separated from
the rebel-defended mainland by marshlands, streams and tidal
waters at one end and a destroyed bridge at the other, the British
forces have lost control. Howe's 4,000 troops face certain failure,
or extremely high costs in casualties if a crossing is attempted
anywhere along the morass.

In New York town, Mrs. Joshua Loring, the so-called "Sultana"
since General Howe made her his mistress back in Boston, waits for
her lover to finish his war. In payment, her cuckold husband soon
will be given the sinecure post of Commissary of Prisoners. Loring
will consider this satisfactory compensation for the Sultana's
services to Sir William and the Crown.[27]

No Soldier Gave More . . .

Under the night-darkened shadows of the Bluff Rock, the chilling October wind blows the fiery embers out of the house chimneys in spiraling shapes toward the starlit skies. Up on The Mountain and along the Bluff the army's campfires send up their glowing sparks to join the dance and quickly die within it.

In the little shack by the river's edge, snugly settled below the towering precipice walls, a life is rapidly ebbing away. Ma Kearney looks vacantly up at those around her as Elaine gently rubs her roughened fevered brow. For Elaine, despite her husband's wishes, has remained at the bedside.

The young itinerant Catholic priest, Father Bulger, who has come in answer to her son's call, is giving the unconscious woman the last rites. Lingering between brief periods of consciousness, Ma at times tries to speak but her words are inaudible.

Jennie, who earlier this evening left Granny Bourdette to fend for herself and came to help the dying woman, lifts the caldron of stew off the hanging rod and on to the hearth. But Jennie's eyes are concernedly upon Elaine. She moves behind the tired girl and gently mops her perspiring forehead.

A worried look comes across the Negro servant's face as her hand touches Elaine's feverish head. Her eyes flashing fear, the older woman knows that the girl's brow is not merely perspiring from the warmth of the room.

Edmund, carrying in a load of cordwood, drops it by the fireside and nervously moves over to the opposite side of his mother's bed. In her intermittent delirium, Ma Kearney strains to speak. Her words are hoarse, sometimes clear, sometimes mumbled. But all listen.

Her half sentences and seldom distinguishable words occasionally break through Father Bulger's liturgical supplication: "... Me Eddie ... a surge'nt! Tha fish! ... in the net ... Catch him! ... E's a big 'un! ...

Edmund can hold himself back no longer. He drops sobbing on his knees beside his mother, crying, "Ma youse iz gonna be aw' right. Ya can't leave me, Ma! Ya can't!"

She does not hear him. Her wavering mind is elsewhere.

Edmund's voice rises in hysterical sobbing as the priest lifts him to his feet and escorts him outside into the open air.

For a moment the woman seems to come out of her delirium. She looks up at Elaine and says in a hoarse whisper, her breathing irregular and difficult, "Write me Eddie, Elaine, we'll win ... We'll win . . . Eddie mus' stay wee Tha Gen'l . . . Stay wee tha land . . . With Tha Gen'l . . . We'll win. . . ."

It is Ma Kearney's last breath. Her mouth falls open, her eyes become glassy and stare glazedly upward at the rough beams of the ceiling.

Father Bulger returns to her side and draws the quilt over her head. Solemnly he says almost to himself, "No saljer air gave mahr fer The Kars than did this 'un. She goos ta tha Lawd tonight fer a deservin' rest. En' now God be wee ye, Carrie Kearney."

19

Friday, October 18. . .

"Knight of the Flaming Sword" To the Rescue

The Hungry Hunt For A Hero

It is less than a month since Howe executed the popular American Ranger captain for espionage. Building up in its wake there had arisen an angry fighting spirit within the military which has spread as well among the people throughout the colonial states. The callous insensitive manner of the act has provided a cause celebre which has given a needed boost to the American morale. Even a ballad has been written about young Nathan Hale.[1]

The youth, whose brief manhood was imbued with the highest ideals of the revolutionary movement in its inviting basket of freedoms, has, in his death, enabled his compatriots to indict Britain further for allegedly conducting an immoral war. Some argue vociferously in behalf of moral wars as others argue in behalf of human bondage.

But the anger, the fighting spirit, the boost in morale are somewhat tapering off under the succession of retreats and disillusionments. Behind the drooping American army morale are the many poorly officered troops, expiring recruitments, desertions, cowardice, plundering, court martials, mutiny, thefts, illnesses, lack of provisions, diminishing supplies—clothing, shelter, tenting, ammunition, food and the staple commodities an army must depend upon.

An incompetent militia, for the most part, compounds the countless difficulties, but more than anything else militarily is the need for greater support from the Congress and its States. And what all are now personally seeking above everything else, is an iron-handed, upright, self-sacrificing leader who will put his country's welfare above his own.

A great hero is needed to satisfy the people's age-old call for a physical and spiritual "leader of the pack." The newly formed country has the sound, devoted, self-denying political leaders it needs for its Congressional body in Philadelphia, but all of them combined do not answer the people's demand for strength and force on the battlefield.

Defeats and retreats do not satisfy the public hunger for victories and success. As in all creature-packs the clarity possible through rationalism is obscured. It matters not by what magic or means the powerful leader accomplishes—sometimes the humanly impossible—act of instilling and inspiring confidence through deeds of daring and boldness resulting in success, as long as he produces "the impossible." Reasoning, analysis and rational thinking seldom enter "the pack" mentality searching for leadership and direction.

So now the dissatisfied among the people and their army not only yearn for a new dynamic leader, they demand one. That demand and hunger, gnawing at the public spirit, seem to have found an answer. For there are many now who are sure that the "Knight Of The Flaming Sword" is heaven-sent to carry a newly inspired army confidently to an overwhelming victory over the enemy.

In General Charles Lee, hero of Charleston, whom the Congress has recently welcomed back from the South and extolled, many of the people and the military are certain the new, united, independent states of America have, in truth, found their idol. Charles Lee's star is indeed in the ascendency.

Ever since the Long Island debacle, which came on the heels of Lee's victorious triumph over the British at Charleston, the persistent echo has been, "Would to Heaven General Lee were here!"[2] As commander of the American army in Charleston, Lee was given the entire credit and held it.

But in reality, much of the success was due to the work of his subordinates, particularly Colonel Moultrie's men,[3] to the Fort Sullivan garrison, and to the people of Charleston as well as to the flow of reinforcements from Virginia and North Carolina.

But, since General Lee has not made any mention of them little if any of their contribution is known northward 700 miles from

Charleston, South Carolina. And it is very unlikely that Lee will allow any credit to be lifted from his escutcheon.

He is certainly now second in command to the American Commander-in-Chief. His chances of being named to replace the Chief are far too good to risk by any courteously deserved distribution of accolades.

It was primarily a British naval defeat in the Charleston harbor. The port's waters played as much a part in the defeat as did Captain James Barron's earlier capture of a British vessel in the Chesapeake Bay. The captain of the captured vessel carried the secret papers which revealed the British plans in advance.[4]

It was a humiliating catastrophe for British Commodore Sir Peter Parker. His losses were severe. And Sir Henry Clinton's 3,000 troops were never able to get a foothold on the mainland.

Lee became the hero back in Philadelphia. But in Charleston, Moultrie and his daring men were credited with the victory. Among other things, their fine marksmanship carried away the seat of Sir Peter's breeches leaving an imbedded splinter that prevented him from sitting down for several days.[5]

Total British casualties exceeded 225 men. Several of the best vessels in Parker's squadron were lost. And for this Lee received full credit, earning from his Northern admirers the title "Knight Of The Flaming Sword."

Naturally those admirers welcomed him back triumphantly from the South. His praises rang out at the same time the country was hearing about the defeat on Long Island.

Nothing was said of how Parker had been pitted mainly against Moultrie, and that it was owing to Moultrie largely that General Clinton was unable to get his troops on the mainland.

Last month such officers as Colonel William Malcolm were singing Lee's praises to all who would listen, assuring them that in Lee was at last to be found the true American leader. Writing at that time from New York to John McKesson, Malcolm said:

"General Lee is hourly expected as if from heaven with a legion of flaming swordsmen."[6]

Oddly enough, the American Commander seems unperturbed by the upsurging wave in behalf of his second in comand. The rebel General has always held "a high opinion of Lee."[7] He has admired and respected the former British commander for his military ability and for his accomplishments as an army officer. Immediately upon Lee's return north the American Leader ordered that Lee be given command of the troops north of King's Bridge.[8]

However, that assignment had been expected. Tilghman, who reflects the Chief's thinking and handles much of his correspondence, indicated this was likely in his letter to William Duer October 8. Writing from Harlem Heights, Tilghman stated:

". . . Our troops have evacuated Bergen and the places adjacent and will form an entire body, under General Greene in Jersey, opposite this post. When Lee arrives, I think we may form a fine disposition: Greene in Jersey, The General on this side of Harlem, in the center, and Lee on the other side."[9]

By "the other side" Tilghman refers to the north and east side of Harlem River, or generally the area north of King's Bridge.

But yesterday, after Lee had been with the troops for only three days, Tilghman's next letter to Duer on the state of things did not voluntarily mention Lee and almost reflected a disinterested attitude, if not a loss of enthusiasm for Charles Lee. For Tilghman wrote Duer:

". . . You ask if General Lee is in health, and if our people feel bold? I answer both in the affirmative. His appearance among us has not contributed a little to the latter."[10]

It is undeniable that Lee's presence has provoked much talk and controversy. There are those who feel that he has "an enormously exaggerated opinion of his own shrewdness and abilities."[11] Some suspect Greene to be among these and certainly not one to be counted among Lee's admirers.

Some point to the fact that Greene pointedly left Fort Constitution on Sunday last for Perth Amboy with the excuse that he would participate with General Mercer in an attack on the Staten Island Hessian garrison post there.[12] But there seems to have been no valid reason for Greene's presence in Amboy except that Lee was due to arrive at Fort Constitution that day.

And so it was that the Charleston hero rode up to the gates of Fort Constitution with his party Sunday only to find himself greeted humiliatingly by the post's subordinate officers rather than the post commander personally.

This cannot be construed as anything else but an affront to a man as pompous as Charles Lee. Especially is this so when—and it is no longer a secret—this very post is to be renamed "Fort Lee" in his honor. Many know that this change of name from Fort Constitution to Fort Lee is much to Greene's disapproval.

Lee knows that this gesture and his assignment to "the troops above King's Bridge, now the largest part of the American army,"[13] are Congressional attempts to placate him for not being given the Continental Army's command. That is what he feels he is owed. And that is what he expected to get after Long Island and New York fell in the wake of his own "outstanding success" at Charleston.

The Mountain Bows To The Flaming Swordsman

As for the American Commander-in-Chief's absence from Fort Constitution upon his arrival, Lee was satisfied that the Continental Army Leader was justified in carrying out a reconnaissance mission.[14] Lee had been informed of the Throg's Neck Point landing by the enemy and accepted the necessity of The General's presence in Westchester as reason enough for his absence.

But this, in Lee's opinion, did not excuse Greene. Furthermore, it had been understood that Lee was to meet the Chief in Harlem Monday morning, so his presence at Fort Constitution was expected. Greene's absence and visit to Amboy was, in Lee's opinion, an attempt to avoid him.

Consequently, though sorely annoyed, Lee accepted the hospitality of Fort Constitution offered him by its Acting Commander General James Ewing. Ewing, carrying out the orders of his superior, provided Lee with all the courtesies available at the post. And, as a most distinguished guest, Ewing housed Lee and his adjutant in General Greene's quarters in the Long House.

Upon hearing of Howe's move into Westchester, Lee had not bothered to reproach himself for having written the Congress six days ago that Howe would head for Philadelphia. His blunder in erroneously advising the Congress had only slightly upset his equilibrium. For Charles Lee is ever the first to overlook his own mistakes. His possible annoyance with them, even though they be errors of his own commission, is not directed at himself. Always he seeks a scapegoat.

So it was that in this mood last Sunday afternoon, upon arriving at Fort Constitution, he wrote his friend, General Horatio Gates, Commander of the Northern Department at Ticonderoga.[15] And to Gates, Lee unraveled his disgust with Congress, a bold act which others often would like the audacity to commit.

"My dear Gates," he began, "I write this scroll in a hurry. Colonel Wood will describe the position of our army, which in my own breast I do not approve. *Inter nos*, the Congress seem to stumble every step. I do not mean one or two of the cattle, but the whole stable.

"I have been very free in delivering my opinion to 'em. In my opinion, General Washington is much to blame in not menacing 'em with resignation, unless they refrain from unhinging the army by their absurd interference.

"Keep us *Ticonderoga*; much depends upon it. We ought to have an army on the Delaware, I have roared it in the ears of Congress, but *carent auribus*. Adieu, my dear friend; if we do meet again, why we shall smile.
"Yours,   C. Lee."[16]

General Lee's two dogs, natives of Pomerania, seldom leave his side. The two animals, appearing more like little white bears than dogs, eat their meals at his table.

They are as much a part of him as is his copy of Thucydides' history of the Peloponnesian War which Lee carries with him constantly, reading the work in its original Greek. For among the languages with which he has considerable proficiency, in addition to his mastery of profanity, Charles Lee can read and quote Latin and Greek.

His correspondence completed, much to his dogs' delight, Lee took the sharply yelping animals out for their late morning stroll. Besides, he was curious to know about the voices and the digging going on in the carefully manicured little graveyard not far from the Long House at the western end of the fort's field.

The cliff people's cemetery skirts the outer works of Fort Lee and overlooks the gently flowing river hundreds of feet below and Manhattan's rocky crested forests in the distance. Off in the northwest corner of the burial grounds, Lee saw the gravedigger struggling with the hard earth.

Carmen Luciano had almost completed the task he demanded to do by himself. It was the debt he felt he owed Ma Kearney. Two of the Bluff Rock Battery's men stood by, ready and willing to give help, but the stubborn Italian threatened them with the butt end of his shovel if they interfered. They didn't.

Hatless, slovenly dressed and out of uniform, Charles Lee, with his dogs at his side, stood silently watching as the digger finished his job and jumped out of the grave. Lee was unrecognized. And he wanted it that way.

He soon learned from merely watching and listening that Luciano had been nursed back to health by the woman who was soon to be buried there. Little did Carmen or his companions know, or care, who was watching them.

The idle stand-by diggers made it clear to a third soldier newly arrived on the scene, that Luciano had been a seaman on a Portuguese vessel. Determined to adopt the new land, he had dived overboard and barely made his escape in the choppy waters after injuring himself in the plunge. It was Ma Kearney who had doctored him and saved his life.

Now a volunteer in Hitchcock's regiment, the "Eyetalyen," as he is referred to by the Bluff Rock Battery men, felt that digging the fisherwoman's grave was the one way he could repay her for her kindness to him.

And so General Lee, his two dogs sniffing at the fallen leaves around him but staying close by their master, watched the distantly approaching funeral procession. His slightly stooped figure only appears tall, outlined against the barren trees on the rise just west of the graveyard.

Despite the solemnity and the serious business of the occasion, there was unintentional humor around the excavation. Each of the other diggers had felt he owed Ma Kearney something for the many generous things she had done for all and for the numerous gifts of food she little could afford to give away.

But every attempt to move a spade of dirt or a rock was rebuffed with an angry threatening look. For Carmen's very limited knowledge of the English language gave him a decided advantage with a spade in his hand.

As the burial party came up the old cowpath that ascends The Mountain from the river's edge the gathering of mourners grew. A funeral on The Mountain is, among the hamlet's people, a major event and Ma Kearney's was special, not average.

Some were strangers, drawn through curiosity; some were soldiers; some were officers. The assembled soon surrounded the little burial place.

Off to the side, close by the grave of his beloved Mahtocheega, was Abbott standing where he had stood twenty moons ago when his Little Bear Princess was lowered through the cold February snows in the white man's custom.

Now his eyes were on the figure standing on the distant knoll. He alone had spotted the stranger and identified him, knowing that the troops were to be paraded before the "great general" tomorrow.

As yet few cliff dwellers have heard of his arrival on The Mountain, for he came in without fanfare pending a proper salute tomorrow. But Abbott and Craig had been sent down to Bergen to meet his party and guide them to the fort last night.

Abbott now has a better chance of sizing up the man for whom he had acquired a dislike in the Three Pidgeons tavern long before meeting him. Lee looks the part of a scholar, gangling and almost ugly owing to his Cyrano de Bergerac-like nose.

The sharp-eyed descendant of Oratam had observed Lee closely last night when the 45-year-old major general's party was met near Bergen Woods by Craig's scouts. Then it was that Abbott, drawing upon his own memory and observations while in England, saw Lee as more of a Londoner than a New Yorker.

Abbott had heard of his generosity insofar as his friends are concerned. He had heard also that he was an officer who considered his soldiers' welfare and was concerned about them. In England and in America it was known that Charles Lee had a remarkable ability for making friends of important people, but Abbott had also heard of his eccentricities, his critics' complaints about his poor manners and his extensive ability with profanity.

Recalling having last night noticed Lee's gray, mocking eyes, set close together besides the walls of his long nose, Abbott particularly observed his come-and-go smile which he can quickly wipe from his face as though he suddenly smells something bad.

Abbott had often heard that the general frequently allows his tongue and his pen to run a little wild. Putting the American Commander's good and bad features all together, Andy concluded this was not the man to replace the rebel army's Commander-in-Chief.

He knew others—many others—were of the same opinion. But, torn between his traditional ties and the white man's new world which has swallowed not only him and his people but his thinking as well, Abbott tells himself to let the white man settle his own problems. For were not they of his own making?

It was at about that moment in Abbott's musings that Lee followed by his dogs, turned from the burial scene and disappeared over the far side of the knoll. And it was at about that time that Father Bulger completed the graveside ritual, turned and placed his arm around the weeping Edmund and escorted him back in the empty hearse driven by Jocko.

The hearse was Carrie Kearney's own fishing wagon pulled by her old nag, Gen'l Sweeney. Faithful to the last, the tired animal seemed willing and ready to follow his mistress and friend into the land of rest and quiet.

Gray, a worried look upon his face, Levy, Bourdette and Baummeister had been the pallbearers after the wagon had reached the cemetery. Big Tom Graves had stood by, his arm still in a sling. Now all disbanded, making their way separately down The Mountain.

To the people of the Palisades, the men, women and children, and to the soldiers of Fort Constitution, the death of Ma Kearney was a loss as great as though a massive chunk of the Palisades had fallen and crashed into the depths of the river below. The Mountain had known and loved her.

Fort Constitution had awakened in the early morning hours to her call of "Fresh fish for a penny!" And the echoes of her voice and her deeds would be remembered even in the newly renamed Fort Lee, despite the changes, the tensions and the fears that soon will fill the air.

Abbott alone still stood in the burial ground beside the grave of Mahtocheega after all had left and the diggers had piled the earth above the fisherwoman's remains. He watched in silence as Charles Lee reappeared farther in the distance and made his way back to the Long House.

As the young Indian watched, he could not know that exactly two months from that day, Lee's now glorious name is destined to be buried as deeply in disgrace as the beloved memory of Ma Kearney is now buried deeply in the hearts of The Mountain people.

His eyes fell back upon Mahtocheega's grave. A small bunch of withering black-eyed yellow daisies rested near the headstone where Elaine had placed them several days before. Abbott knows this has long been one of Elaine's quiet practices and one of which she never speaks.

He picked up a few of the faded dried flowers, crumbled them gently and affectionately in his large brown hand and cast their dust and seeds softly over the mound of earth.

The British action at Throg's Neck had been the principal topic on most every soldier's tongue. But on the minds and tongues of the inhabitants of the water's edge and the sick under the hospital tents, as well as the men of Lieutenant Gray's battery, was a worried concern for Elaine Gray. Her fond attachment for Ma Kearney was well known, but Elaine was not among the mourners in the procession.

Elaine Baummeister Gray is not beautiful. No one, however, could have made a bigger dent in the hearts of the people and the soldiers of The Mountain than has the slightly pugnosed, almost plain-faced, but neatly trim, kindly and humanity-loving young bride.

So when Rachel Baummeister, Granny Bourdette and Jennie also failed to attend the burial services, it was not long before the entire community knew how deathly ill was the delirious young girl. Even while Ma was being lowered into her grave, there was in the minds of the nursing women by Elaine's side, the frightening possibility that the young bride of John Gray would be next.

In her deliriums Elaine kept repeating, "My baby! My baby! Don't hurt my baby!" Then, minutes later would follow, "John! John! Our baby! . . . Who will take care of our baby?"

"She's just bad dellairus," said Granny Bourdette. "She just has imaginins she's gonna have a baby. Ah doan seen no signs 'a it."

"Youse doan havta see no signs 'a it," Jennie snapped back at her elderly charge.

This was just a common sampling of the repartee that has gone on between the two women for years. It is purely a sham that conceals a strange love and admiration each has for the other in which color and class differences have not the slightest place.

"Youse doan havta see no signs ta knows dey's dare," Jennie continues. "Basides dat, she ought ta knows better'n youse!"

That was five days ago. Elaine has since come through the crisis, though she is far from fully recovered. And if there are "any signs" of pregnancy, no one knows of them.

Elaine has no recollection of any of her delirious ramblings. She laughs, though somewhat forcedly, at what she had said. Her thoughts have now all been sadly centered around the death of her friend and comforter.

The October 16th Council of War

Throughout the camp today—five days after The Mountain's catastrophic Sunday, the thirteenth—the news that Howe has at last pulled out of his calamitous mistake on Throg's Neck Point, spreads wildly among the troops. Howe is reportedly marching his men on board their ships and emptying them into Pell's Point.

The Pell's Point landing site is about three miles above Throg's Neck. It offers all the advantages for an invasion of Westchester which Throg's Neck lacked. Pell's Point, unlike Throg's Neck, is not defensible in view of the might that General Howe and his forces can throw against it.

It is no wonder, say the wagging tongues, that the American Commander called an important council of war on Wednesday last, shortly after General Lee arrived at Headquarters in Harlem. Lee had already been handed full command of the troops north of King's Bridge.

Now, in the opinion of Lee's supporters, the highly exalted commander will provide the army with the "flaming sword" necessary to end the American defeats and retreats.

Had not the American Chief himself said of Lee, "He is the first officer in military knowledge and experience we have in the whole army. He is zealously attached to the cause, honest and well-meaning..."?

This was indeed true. The General had written these words and more to his brother following Lee's appointment by the Congress. And "the more" of the letter included this additon:

> "...but rather fickle and violent, I fear, in his temper. However, as he possesses an uncommon share of good sense and spirit, I congratulate my countrymen upon his appointment to that Department."[17]

The General Orders this morning make it clear why the Council of War Wednesday was held at Lee's new headquarters just above King's Bridge.[18] Among other things, including the measures to be taken against Howe in his landing at Pell's Point, the announcement was given that Fort Constitution was to be changed to Fort Lee.

The General had counted on Greene's presence at the Council's meeting. For this was a golden opportunity to inspire all officers in the service with an encomium properly citing General Lee for his victorious accomplishments. And, in addition, it was another critical hour needing all the inspiration that could be garnered for the enemy was then poised in Westchester and ready to pounce.

But Ewing at Fort Constitution informed his Chief that Greene had departed for Amboy to assist Mercer in a minor raid on a small Hessian rear-guard post on Staten Island. That was the day Lee arrived at Fort Constitution.

The General, perplexed if not amused, ordered Greene to return immediately to Harlem, expressing the desire of his presence at the Wednesday Council of War at Lee's quarters. The order for some reason did not reach Mercer's post until 11 o'clock Wednesday morning, the very day and hour of the Council's session.

This is understandable since Amboy is over 40 miles distant from Harlem Heights with the unbridged Hudson River to cross. So when the Council of War took place the day before yesterday, the others of the American staff command bestowed their congratulations upon Lee sans Greene.

Lee's addition to the Council of War is, for the most part, a welcome one. And his command of the King's Bridge sector, where the pot now is said to be boiling, is where the staff command spent the full day reconnoitering the enemy's movements and devising strategy.

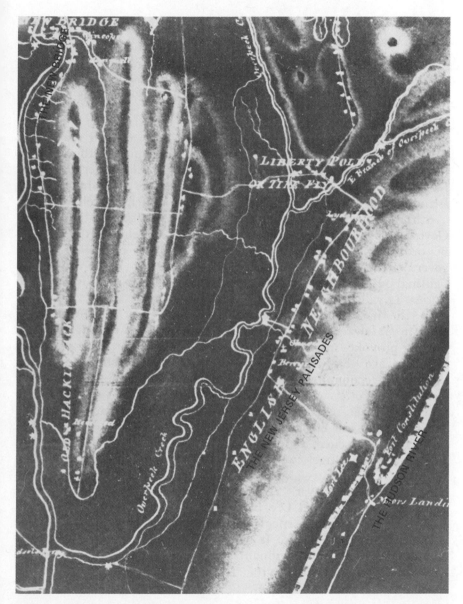

This John Hill (British Military) map, 1781, indicates the King's chorographers still had difficulty mapping the terrain behind the Palisades. Tine Fly is the same as, or south of rather than north of Liberty Pole. The New Bridge should be much farther northwest than shown. The map shows two names for the American post: Fort Lee is the field fort on the summit; Fort Constitution (with works indicated) is the Bluff Rock batteries—Original in Clinton Collection, Clements Library, Ann Arbor, Mich.

Those present at the Council of War and strategy planning session Wednesday included:

> "... His Excellency General Washington. Major-Generals Lee, Putnam, Heath, Spencer, Sullivan. Brigadier-Generals Lord Stirling, Mifflin, McDougall, Parsons, Nixon, Wadsworth, Scott, Fellows, Clinton, Lincoln. Colonel Knox, commanding Artillery ..."[19]

Although the Council was undertaking some critical matters, it was, nevertheless, the first opportunity for some of the staff to meet Lee. It was also General Lord (William Alexander) Stirling's first reunion with his fellow-officers since his capture on Long Island. Though a war council it had a social touch as well.

Stirling was recently exchanged by the British for their Royal Governor Brown of the Bahama Islands. The rebel lord had been no ordinary prize nor an easy one to take. His price was high, a governor for a general. The enemy's interest in a bit of royalty fighting on the rebels' side was of more than passing interest to Tories, Loyalists and the King's army in general.

In the now Tory-controlled New York paper, the *New York Gazette and Weekly* of October 14, was proof of the high interest Stirling provokes among the periodical's readers, for one item notes in bold face that Stirling was observed by British pickets "the other day reconnoitring in front of the Rebel Lines."[20] If there were some Tories who doubted he would return to the American army now that it was so close to destruction, the announcement was proof of their error.

Stirling's presence, especially in view of his noble lineage, and Lee's added prestige—two former Britains serving the American cause—give needed weight and dignity to the American high command's Council of War. Yet no two personalities could be more unlike than Stirling and Lee.

But it was Lee's presence that dominated the scene around the council table Wednesday. It was Lee to whom they all quietly listened. It was Lee's arguments which not only sounded logical and sound, but in reality were.

To Hold and Fight Or Fight and Run

"Our forces," he told them, pointing to the roughly sketched map of Westchester, "must be taken from hence (Throg's Neck) and extended toward the east and west center to outflank them."[21]

He insisted that this should be the strategy and then he "vehemently urged a retreat (be made by all American lines) to safer positions."[22]

It was then that he was respectfully advised that this recommendation was in conflict with the Continental Congress's resolution exactly one week ago. In that resolution the country's spokesmen had informed the Commander-in-Chief that it was the Congress's desire that:

> "if it be practicable, by every art and whatever expence (he was) to obstruct effectually the navigation of the North (Hudson) River, between Fort Washington and Mount Constitution."[23]

This restraint upon the military by a non-military body is what accounts largely for Lee's impatience and irritation with the Continental Congress. But, in contrast with his nature, he held his tongue before the Council of War. Discreetly he concealed those feelings he had allowed to roll from his quill in his *"Inter nos"* letter to Gates three days before.

Then began the arguments for or against retreating to safer grounds and evacuating Fort Washington. But Charles Lee was tactful. For he is skillful in making friends among those in high places. In the end the minutes of the meeting were read for approval.

If anything reflects the state of mental anguish—the pressures, the distress and the uncertainties that go with long-debated, heterogeneous, group decision-making—the confused phraseology of those October 16 minutes does so.

The minutes, or *Proceedings Of A Council Of General Officers At A Council Of War held at the Head-Quarters of General Lee, October 16, 1776,* read:

> "After much consideration and debate the following question was 'stated: Whether (It having appeared that the obstructions in the North River have proved insufficient, and that the enemy's whole force is now in our rear on Frog Point) it is now deemed possible in our situation to prevent the enemy cutting off the communication with the country and compelling us to fight them at all disadvantages, or surrender prisoners at discretion?"

This statement of the proceedings was prefaced with other matters taken up by the council including:

> "...sundry letters from the Convention ... turbulence of the disaffected in the upper parts of this State (New York) ... sundry accounts of deserters showing that the enemy's intention is to surround us ..."

But, in answer to the principal question as stated above, the minutes continue:

> "Agreed, with but one dissenting voice, (viz: General Clinton) that it is not possible to prevent the communication, and that one of the consequences mentioned in the question must certainly follow.
> "Agreed, that Fort Washington be retained as long as possible."[24]

So only General James Clinton, a native of the State of New York, voted, and forcibly so, to oppose Howe with all the might the Continentals could muster. This is the action which his constituents, the frightened Hudson Valley landowners, are demanding. And they are a powerful force in the Congress and in the country.

Two Symbols High Against the Rising Tide

The astute General Lee knows this. The fact rests quietly on a niche in the back of his mind. In the critical days to come he will use this factor as a partial excuse to remain with his forces secluded in the Hudson Valley, rather than lead them in support of the main army escaping toward the Delaware. Defiance, spawned by ambition, then will become a device in his self-seeking reach for personal power and glory.

But Wednesday, in the dispute over holding or evacuating Fort Washington—the Americans' last stronghold on Manhattan Island—Lee argued well and wisely against continuing its defenses. He knew that the respect the general officers held for the Mount Washington post was largely owing to its title.

So Lee spoke carefully and logically, gaining even The General's tacit agreement. For the Commander-in-Chief, like many others on his staff, is convinced that the sister forts and their Chevaux de Frise have not obstructed the British shipping.

Well aware of the sensitive note its defenses strike among the officers, in the Congress and among the landowners, Lee, having made his point, agreed with the staff to hold Fort Washington "as long as possible."

For this stand, in which it appeared that military logic, common sense and impersonal objectivity were wisely counseling, Lee would later be compensated for whatever error he had made in predicting Howe's strategy to the Congress.

For Lee to have done otherwise over the wishes of the Congress would be, in the least, most impolitic. Particularly inasmuch as the fort opposite was to bear his own name. After all, he had made his point and the words "as long as possible" were inserted largely owing to his arguments.

Besides, now more than ever it would be injudicious to urge further evacuation of Fort (George) Washington while Fort (Charles) Lee stood strong and impregnable on the opposite bank.

And after all, are not these two mountain-top forts, Fort Lee on the west bank, Fort Washington on the east bank, symbolic of the two military forces holding back the tide of the King's army and navy? Are not these two namesakes, bearing the titles of the new nation's two highest ranking military commanders, symbols of the strength and courage of the army's leadership?

Certainly Lee's supporters, if not Lee himself, think so. So Lee graciously agreed with the staff officers but with reservations.

After Wednesday's Council of War the American forces spent the next 36 hours preparing for certain battle. Fortunately for the rebels, Howe has lost his hopes for a flashing surprise movement. As early as last Sunday the Americans were alerted. It was then that The General ordered a massive evacuation of his forces out of Harlem and northward into Westchester to meet the invaders.

The rebel countermove has been marked with haste, pressure and great excitement. At times the strain upon the moving army borders on frenzy. For there are great scarcities in wagons, horses, food, clothing, ammunition and materiel of all kinds.

New orders are issued upon old ones. Complete personnel changes are made, sweeping away all old assignments in order to facilitate the gigantic operation. From Harlem Headquarters last Sunday came the order that required:

> "all the men have four days provisions ready, dressed at all times; for which purpose the Commissaries or the Deputies are to keep the butchers constantly killing till such supply is had."[25]

General Orders also announce the distribution of supplies. They give details on marching procedures and repeat the instructions for striking tents and properly maintaining them, forbidding "covering the bottom of the tents with earth, as in a few days, that situation must render them totally unfit for service."

In an effort to inspire the troops the General Orders of the 13th read in part:

> ". . . As the enemy seem now to be endeavouring to strike some stroke before the close of the campaign, The General most earnestly conjures both officers and men, if they have any love for their country, and concern for

its liberties, regard to the safety to their parents, wives, children and countrymen, that they will act with bravery and spirit, becoming the cause in which they are engaged . . ."[26]

The orders that day concluded with:

". . . so that if we do not conquer, it must be our own faults. How much better will it be to die honourably fighting in the field, than to return home covered with shame and disgrace, even if the cruelty of the enemy should allow you to return! A brave and gallant behaviour for a few days, and patience under some little hardships, may save our country, and enable us to go into winter quarters with safety and honour."[27]

Most of the troops, particularly the officers, are certain the words of the orders are those from Tench Tilghman's quill. They have become used to his vocabulary and are well acquainted with his sincere dedication to the cause of liberty.

The movement of some of the troops on Sunday to King's Bridge and the main body northward into Westchester has resulted in a great deduction of the forces on Harlem's heights. Now only 600 forward pickets man that post. They face Lord Percy's rear guard picket which protect Percy's three brigades, left behind by Howe to defend the lines across Manhattan.

On Monday, Colonel Bailey's regiment joined General Clinton's forces under Colonel Glover near Pell's Point. Colonel Lippet was ordered to join General McDougall's brigade. Lippet's orders directed that his men "take their tents and cooking utensils and lose no time." And the two Connecticut regiments under the command of Colonel Storms and Major Greaves, previously on Manhattan, were ordered "to be in readiness to march into West-Chester at a moment's warning."[28]

Remaining on the island of Manhattan, in accordance with the Monday orders, are all the rest of the brigades which have been formed into two divisions. These comprise Heard's, Beall's and Weedon's. They are all under Major General Putnam and make up the first division. The second division consists of Lord Stirling's, Wadsworth's and Fellow's regiments under the command of Major General Spencer.

Putnam has orders to defend the lines in front of Harlem's heights and extending across the island east to west. His assignment also includes the defense of the works on Mount Washington and its fortress as well as the Chevaux de Frise's eastern end.[29]

Over 200 men are still working constantly on the river blockade. They load old ships' hulls with heavy stone, chain and submerge them in preparation for the next enemy attempt to run through the barrier.

On Tuesday Colonel Joseph Reed's regiment joined McDougall's brigade. Colonel Hutchinson's joined General Clinton's, having been pulled from under Colonel Glover's command. And Colonel Sargent took over command of a brigade comprising his own regiment and Ward's, Chester's and Colonel Storrs.' Then Storrs was assigned to take over Major Greaves' battalion with orders "to march immediately into West-Chester."

Greaves was then assigned to join the regiments commanded by Colonels Douglass and Ely, all of which were formed into a brigade under the command of General Saltonstall. The two remaining Connecticut regiments which are encamped on the Harlem River opposite Headquarters have been added to General Parson's brigade.[30]

In summary, the American divisions stand as follows: *one on Manhattan Island under Putnam; a second under Major General Charles Lee at King's Bridge includes Nixon's, McDougall's and Colonel Glover's forces; a third under Major General Heath in Westchester comprises Parsons', Scott's and Clinton's brigades; a fourth under Major General Sullivan, comprises Saltonstall's, Sargent's and Hand's; and a fifth under Major General Lincoln comprises the Massachusetts militia.*

The same orders that today aligned the American forces also brought the exhortation to all officers that they were:

"to inform their men of what is expected of them and that The General wishes to avoid the rise of any confusion in case we should be suddenly called to action, which there is no kind of doubt, is near at hand; and he hopes that the only contention will be who shall render the most acceptable service to his country and his posterity."[31]

Again the Juggernaut Moves

Howe's shift from his unsuccessful attempt to break out of Throg's Neck to a try at Pell's Point, three miles east, and his landing at Pell's Point this morning were no surprise to the rebel forces. Uncertain as to exactly what the British commander-in-chief now had in mind, the American staff commanders have spread out their brigades "in detached camps every where from Valentine's Hill to the White Plains."[32]

Arising early this morning after a brief and restless sleep at his Harlem Headquarters, The General, at the suggestion of his aide,

Robert H. Harrison, looks over the night's incoming dispatches. He allows his fried eggs, dry toast and tea, freshly made from the boiling water out of the Roger Morris samovar, to get cold. For one message has grasped his attention.

It is a lengthy report from General Benedict Arnold from his quarters at Crown Point. In it the adroit and daring major general tells of his naval battle there and asks for ammunition and "a dozen batteaus, well-manned . . . to tow up the vessels in case of a southerly wind."[33]

The rapid hoof beats of a galloping horse and great commotion at the outside sentry post cause all aides in the large dining room to stop and look from the window. But the breathless courier has already unmounted and been passed by the door guard. He hands Harrison a dispatch from General Heath that the enemy troops are renewing their movement against the defenses at Throg's Point.

The American Leader quietly orders Harrison to forward Arnold's dispatch to Congress with a copy to Gates. He further directs his aide to write Major General Schuyler in Albany that the

"Stockbridge Indians might render material service here as scouting parties, if the situation of affairs in the Northern army do not require their continuance."[34]

In short time he and members of his staff are galloping their horses on the road to King's Bridge, about five and a half miles north. After a brief pause there, the party completes the next five and a half miles through Westchester, drawing up behind Heath's lines before the Throg's Neck causeway and the ford just below it.

General Heath advises his Chief that a change in wind has enabled the additional British ships which had been anchored off Hell Gate, to make for Pell's Point, but that Howe has renewed his attack on the American defense lines at Throg's Point. The General immediately orders a thorough reconnaissance of both the enemy movements.

It is soon learned that Howe is shamming an attack at Throg's Neck while loading regiment after regiment on his men-of-war and disembarking them three miles east on Pell's. The Rebels' Commander directs Heath to move his division southwestward in order to block a possible enemy invasion at Morrisania.

Thus, the American Commander begins a giant swing of the American forces which have had their front facing south, looking down Manhattan's island. Now it begins to move with its former left front swerving around to the east facing Howe in his attempt to get behind the American left flank. Heath's division begins to form the American right flank in Westchester. It will extend south to Morrisania on the east bank of the Harlem becoming a flexible line that will enable the bulk of the Continental Army to move behind it north or south, depending upon the enemy's strategy.

Though one express rider has come with the news to Heath that "the whole British army (are) in motion,"[35] the American command staff has successfully uncovered Howe's feint, recognizing Sir William is disembarking his troops in massive numbers on Pell's Point.

Heath now sets up his defense lines west of Pell's Point. He has stationed Shepard's, Reed's, Baldwin's and Glover's regiments in a frontal position. All now steel themselves against the coming enemy thrust into Westchester.

Farther to the west of these vanguard forces, the Americans are strung out in a long series of posts that stretch from the Valentine's Hill fort all the way along the Bronx River's west bank. It is behind this line that the main Continental Army can move with its supplies and maintain its communications as far north, if necessary, as the White Plains.

Every employable wagon, mule and horse is pressed into duty in order to maintain the long supply lines. Each wagon, repeatedly loaded, makes its run from Harlem and King's Bridge, unloads in Westchester south of the White Plains and returns for another. It is a mammoth operation to swing an entire army's left flank fully around from south to north, but this one's success depends upon the speed with which it can be executed.

The General Orders of the day carry the parole for the next 24 hours as "Stamford" and the countersign, "France." But they also indicate the seriousness of the problem facing the army in its communications owing to the south to north dispersion of over some 30 miles of rough terrain. In part the orders read:

> "As the brigades of the army now move at such distance from each other, that a punctual attendance at Head-Quarters (Harlem Heights) for orders cannot be expected, one Brigade Major from each Major-General's division, is to attend as early in the day as he can. The several Brigade—Majors, or Adjutants, who act as such, are to attend him at a stated hour, and then distribute the orders through the several brigades and regiments, as fast as possible."[36]

Preceded by the Grenadiers, the British "Light Infantry and other Corps of the First Embarkation"[37] begin their move down the Pell's Point peninsula. Their bayonets and buckles sparkle

brilliantly in the bright October morning, pre-noon sun, for they
have had encampment inactivity, except for spit and polish, for
over a week.

At last has come the order that has happily broken the
boredom of marching, drilling and dress parades. But after having
gone only two miles down the peninsula and having arrived slightly
northeast of the isthmus, they come to an abrupt halt.

Before them an American brigade blocks their passage with a
force of about 750 men and three field pieces.[38]

The redcoats prime and load. With their muskets cocked, the
vanguard, slowly and orderly in line, moves forward with the even,
steady beat of the drums and to the tune of bagpipes and fifes.
They know that behind the innocent-looking stone walls the rebels
wait. The Americans, holding their fire until ordered, include the
troops under Colonel John Glover, Joseph Reed, William Shepard
and Loammi Baldwin.

The British van under Captain Evelyn's order comes to a halt.
They aim and fire with a fusillade that rings through the clumps of
trees and sends a volume of smoke up over the brown, frost-
touched fields.

The Americans take it without a single casualty. They return a
blistering fusillade that drops four of the redcoats at the 50-yard
distance.

Round after round is exchanged. And when the air clears, two
Americans lie dead, several lie wounded. Struck by a ball in his
throat, the American Colonel Shepard is among the fallen.

Defiantly and boldly moving forward, despite heavy losses but
constantly replaced with reinforcements from the rear, the British
advance within 30 yards of Glover's defense line. Glover orders his
men to fall back. They do so reluctantly and orderly. Reed and his
troops take concealment behind another stone fence, well beyond
the first.

The enemy now charges, shouting at the top of their lungs.
When they come within 30 yards of Colonel Reed, he gives his
men the order. The entire regiment rises up in unison, sending a
vicious round of fire into Captain Evelyn's Grenadiers.

The American's whole charge is emptied into the British ranks,
striking them with momentary panic and confusion. Captain
Evelyn drops. An officer, coming from the rear to replace the
fallen captain, orders the men to fall back. They do so, taking
some of their dead and wounded with them. Stunned, the
Grenadiers now wait until the main army comes up behind them.[39]

Mourned Tonight, Tomorrow Forgotten

Left behind, dead on the field, is Britain's Captain W. G. Evelyn.[40] Seeing the lifeless body of the British captain not far distant from him on the other side of the wall, an American soldier swiftly hurdles the stone wall and seizes the dead officer's hat and the desirable canteen of water lying at his side. He hurdles back over the wall with his precious booty as rapidly as he departed.[41] For, as in all the wars of man, survival is the one rule subordinate to victory.

Evelyn, like Shepard, has been a friend to his men, likeable and popular. Both officers, though fighting on opposite sides, were soldiers and youths with great promise. In both armies tragic casualties will be lamented and mourned tonight.

For an hour and a half the Crown's men stand stalemated before their enemy's blocking lines. Each side keeps up an occasional popping back and forth. Soon almost 4,000 of the King's army are drawn up in support behind the grenadiers.

Then seven heavy fieldpieces are dragged forward by the artillery and placed in position behind the British van. But as they are brought closer to the stone wall and not more than 50 yards distant, Glover gives the order to fire.

As one, the American muskets bark when the riflemen stand up from behind their defenses and let go their entire charge. In reply the British light infantry and chasseurs, under the command of Lieutenant Colonel Musgrave of the First Battalion, and the troops formerly commanded by Evelyn, unleash a constant fire of artillery and musketry.[42]

Then, under their own curtain of gunpowder smoke, the redcoats again advance to within a short distance of the rebels crouched behind their stone walls. Again the Americans rise and fire in alternate companies. Each in turn dropping down and disappearing, priming, reloading and firing again.

The exchange continues until the Continentals have discharged seven rounds. At this point Glover calls for and gets an orderly withdrawal of his men. Having personally taken over the command of the stricken Shepherd, Glover maneuvers his own troops to the rear and to the left of Shepherd's regiment.

Shepherd's men are well secured behind a double stone wall. Toward them the British light infantry slowly make their approach without a shot coming from the rebels' lines. Shouting and pushing close behind each other, the British move in with fixed bayonets to within a few hundred feet of the concealed Shepherd regiment.

When the redcoats reach within desired range, the Americans rise up and fire by platoons keeping up a constant discharge through seventeen full rounds of ammunition. Time after time the devastating fire drives the British infantrymen back. And repeatedly they reform and move closer in upon the rebel lines.

Glover is soon convinced of the overwhelming superiority his enemy has brought against him. He has held his own skeleton force of amphibious Marbleheaders from his Massachusetts regiment to man the lines behind the forward troops. Now he orders the front lines to retreat behind the action-loving Marbleheaders.

Serving as a rear guard the fishermen keep up a steady fire on the approaching redcoats while the rest of Glover's brigade pulls back. Slowly they withdraw out of the field of battle and disappear into the wooded slopes with the British artillery playing upon them and the Americans replying from the distance until nightfall. Neither side is affected by the useless exchange and waste of shot and shell.[43]

Though they have had no food nor water all day, Glover's troops wearily march through the long night along the road to Dobbs Ferry. In his own words Glover will later recall the march under the cover of night with these words:

> ". . . The heavens over us and the earth under us, which was all we had, having left our baggage at the old encampment we left in the morning."[44]

On the morrow he will march his tired hungry contingent back to the regimental base at Miles Square. Despite the Continentals' stand against the mighty Juggernaut, Sir William Howe has his feet firmly on the mainland in Westchester.

Glover reports to Heath on the action, giving his losses. Heath in turn forwards the account to the newly appointed commander of the front, General Lee. Heath's report reads in part:

> ". . . between thirty and forty men killed and wounded; among the latter Colonel Shepard in the throat, not mortally, although the ball came well-nigh effecting instant death . . ."[45]

General Howe reports his losses to be:

> "Lieutenant Colonel Musgrave and Captain Evelyn wounded, the latter mortally; three soldiers killed, twenty wounded."

The American camp rumor disagrees. The account in the Continentals' headquarters is based upon:

"authorized intelligence of their (the British) losing 500 killed and wounded."[46]

Since according to the rebel army's accounts, "the chief (part) of the attacking force were Hessians, and their losses were not always included in the British official reports," the Americans are certain that the Hessian losses were very heavy.[47]

Howe's entire plan had hinged largely on a successful surprise movement. It had been Sir William's intention to march his army clear across Westchester from a point of invasion on Long Island's Sound to Hudson River.

But the surprise is lost. The rebels' counter action almost instantly aborted his plans at Throg's Neck. However, it was to the Marbleheader, Colonel Glover and his troops, to whom General Howe owed most if not all of his troubles today.

Though he is only a colonel, John Glover had been given a heavy responsibility this morning when he found himself commanding an entire brigade. Added to his own Fourteenth Regiment Continental Infantry of Massachusetts, were Colonel Reed's Thirteenth of Massachusetts and Colonel Shepard's Fourth, also of the Massachusetts Continental Line. Glover has never before commanded so large a force.

The "Fish Dealer" Versus The King's Best

A short laconic figure—"a tough little terrier of a man"[48]— Glover is limited in his military knowledge and experience. But limited or not he is determined to succeed as a military officer.

Glover, along with all the American army officers, is aware how the American officers' civilian professions tickle the British high command in their discussions as to the make-up of the rebel army. "Civilians In Officers' Dress" are what the enemy staff call the Yankee and Buckskin leaders.

The Marbleheader knows that he is called, "Glover, The Fish Dealer"; that it is "Greene, The Blacksmith"; "Washington, The Farmer"; and "Knox, The Stationer," and so on. Consequently, the weight of his responsibility had hung heavily upon him since he was given it yesterday. A cautious man, he had carefully examined the area's terrain and taken every precaution in view of all possibilities—a factor that resulted in his success and Howe's unexpected setback today.

For Glover had found little sleep last night. At the first glow of dawn this morning he ascended a hill near his encampment at East

Chester with his trusty mariner's spyglass in his hand. That glass had more than once identified troublesome situations in the seas off Marblehead. To his amazement it suddenly brought before his eyes the sight of more than 200 enemy sail "manned and formed in four grand divisions."[49]

The mariner colonel quickly sent his own adjutant, a Major Lee, to inform his superior commander, General Lee (unrelated to the adjutant messenger) three miles away. But without waiting for orders Glover immediately led his brigade from East Chester to the Pell's Point isthmus.

Glover knew that his instructions were only to delay the enemy, not to stop them. And he did so. But not without many anxious moments. Wishing all the time that he might have General Lee, or some experienced officer to approve his actions, he later recalled his thoughts.

Relating his thinking at that time, he wrote:

> "The lives of 750 men are immediately at hazard, and under God their preservation entirely depends upon their being well disposed of . . ."[50]

Glover's deep concern and anxieties for the lives of the men under him are as sincere as those of a humane ship captain for the lives of his crew and passengers. The responsibility filled him with great trepidation, for he and his Marbleheaders are not basically warriors. They are seamen. Adept in boat handling and in river navigation logistics, they can hurl men, equipment and supplies across a river as well if not better than the enemy and their far superior resources.

But a militarist Glover is not. And the rugged self-disciplined army colonel knows his own strengths and weaknesses and is bent upon improving himself for his country's cause. Though the duty before him was not to his liking, Glover executed it with the same efficiency he seems to be able to summon for any task.

He will later recall the event and the thoughts that went through his mind. He will later remember how he had weighed the lives of the 750 men under his command in the face of the might of four grand divisions of the enemy disembarking from their 200 ships and marching straight for him and his little brigade. He will write:

> Besides this, my country, my honour, my own life and everything that (is) dear . . . appears to be at stake."[51]

And so it was that this morning the so-called "Fish Dealer"

summoned from that fathomless and mysterious human reservoir, the skill, knowledge and judgment to thwart the plans of one of the world's most eminent military leaders.

But Charles Lee is Glover's commander and Lee cannot take much credit for something he did not order. In fact General Lee has not fully assumed his new command. For this or some unknown reason the action on the isthmus is not widely heralded. After all the big battle is certainly ahead.

If gambler he is, now is certainly the time for Howe to gamble. He can do one of two things, either strike across Westchester to the Hudson as originally intended or direct his forces fully against the American army's concentration at King's Bridge while Percy simultaneously hammers at Harlem from the south.

With the withdrawal of Glover's needle from his side, Howe, whether he knows it or not, is actually "in the rear of the (American) army."[52] Certainly there is a good chance of a successful strike across Westchester where he could cut through the string of rebel posts which stretch sparsely from Morrisania to the White Plains.

With the might that the King's commanders can call upon, there is no point along the scattered, weak, poorly equipped American defense line which he could not breach with little difficulty. True, the bulk of the rebel force is still centered around King's Bridge where an all-out attack might prove fatal to the American cause. But that too is a gamble.

However, even the news that Lieutenant General Knyphausen has today arrived in New York with the second division of Hessians and a regiment of Waldeckers[53] does not inspire Sir William with sufficient confidence to make a direct assault around the concentrated American wing at King's Bridge. And neither does he feel it wise to attempt a severing of the American lines with a dash toward the Hudson.

Such a move, he feels, is too risky and could entrap him. Howe prefers to be sure of his chances and decides, instead, to move his right and center two miles northward of New Rochelle on the road to the White Plains.

Fearing he has insufficient strength to conduct a Westchester campaign in view of the rebels' turn-about and his loss of the elusive element of surprise, Howe calls upon Lieutenant Colonel Harcourt[54] to bring up with him from New York his Sixteenth and Seventeenth Regiments of Light Dragoons.

In 56 days Harcourt and his men are destined to topple Charles

Lee's career. On December 13 they will capture America's second in command in a humiliating episode in the little village of Basking Ridge. It will be the beginning of the end of Lee's star, so high in ascendancy today.

Counting on Harcourt's additional forces, the British command's plans now call for Lieutenant General Heister with his two brigades of Hessians and one of British, to occupy New Rochelle. And Lieutenant Colonel Rogers, who commands a corps of about 500 Tories called "The Queen's Rangers,"[55] is to take possession of Mamaroneck. Rogers' band and their renegade attacks on the Westchester patriots are hated and feared throughout the county.

In reserve for any action that might be necessary in sustaining the Mamaroneck post, will be Brigadier General Agnew and his Sixth Brigade. Knyphausen and his troops, it is decided, are to remain at Myers Point, southeast of New Rochelle, in order to cover the disembarkation of the stores and provisions.

A careful cautious military planner, the British commander judges it "expedient to move to White Plains, and endeavor to bring them (the American army) to action."[56] Faced with a selection of objectives, he now chooses to circle northward and force an open field confrontation in which his superior might would undoubtedly have the upper hand.

Glover, his men and their successful restraining effect upon the King's army and its Juggernaut this morning, have seemingly had an intimidating effect upon Sir William. Their bold spirited fight and Howe's loss of surprise have certainly, temporarily at least, forced Britain's commander-in-chief to abandon his original plan of operation.[57]

There is no doubt in the minds of the American command staff that General Howe plans to drive directly across Westchester. For such a drive with all the powers he has behind him will be aimed at cutting American communications with New England. Since the British admiral's men-of-war are anchored in the Hudson's Haverstraw Bay under Captain Parker's command, there can be no doubt that Sir William intends to link his army with his navy in their objective.

Yet Howe is not apparently doing what is expected of him. No enemy movement has been directed at Morrisania where Heath was ordered by the American Leader to expect a brush.

Heath has one brigade posted on the high ground north of Morrisania and south of Valentine's Hill. It is ready to move quickly to the east, if necessary, joining the lines facing Throg's

Neck, or it can pull back northwest to King's Bridge. And on short notice it can withdraw north to Valentine's if the occasion demands. But the occasion does not so demand.

News of the Pell's Point landing and action convinced many of the American staff officers that the enemy would head toward King's Bridge. This was reflected in Heath's own report of the day in which he stated:

> "It now becomes necessary immediately to quit the position in the neighbourhood of King's Bridge, the British being in the rear of the left of our army."[58]

The puzzlement of the entire rebel staff command is reflected in Heath's next statement in which he declares:

> ". . . and it is not a little unaccountable that they did not attempt to stretch themselves across to the Hudson, which might have been done with great ease. They only moved higher up on the other side of the little rivulet Brunx which was generally fordable."[59]

So, in view of the tensions within the Americans' strung out lines, all encampments have doubled their picket guards tonight. Some wonder who among their comrades with Glover's oppressed brigade will never be seen again.

In his field encampment tonight outside the little village of West Chester, General Charles Lee is less impressed with Glover's men and their intrepid accomplishment and escape than in today's General Orders. For in those orders it is proclaimed that Fort Constitution will henceforth be known as Fort Lee.

This is a proud accomplishment for the gentry-born son of John and Isabella Lee of Dernhall, Cheshire, England. Is it not a great honor that he, an Englishman, should have the principal fort on the rim of the Palisadean mainland of America named for him? Yet does he not deserve it? Has he not left his native land and gambled his life and fortune on a country he was the first to describe as "Liberty's last and only asylum"?[60]

So today has been an important day in Charles Lee's life. For him it has been a day in which his contributions to America have been, in part, recognized. It is the first day that the fort on the Hudson's west bank atop the great precipices of the Palisades—the true edge of the American mainland—has borne his name. Though he may have his eyes on something more, he nevertheless savors the taste of its equal rank with the sister fort across the river.

At Fort Lee it has been a sign-changing day. But that business has been shared with rumors and confused, contradictory reports of the army moving through Westchester in preparation for a certain battle of decision with the King's men. The width of the river and the tendency for travelers to go to Manhattan rather than to Westchester have made the great expanse of lands north of Manhattan Island almost as remote as Connecticut and upper New England.

Apparently not overly impressed with his command post's change in title, General Greene yesterday displayed more interest in a horse. He wrote the New York Convention from "Fort Constitution" asking for permission to purchase a steed that was confiscated from a Tory who deserted to the British on Long Island.

Explaining how William Bradford, Colonel Hitchcock's adjutant, had acquired the animal from a Jacob Wicoff, a Tory deserter, at great risk, Greene wrote the Convention:

"I think it my duty to acquaint you that I have the horse in my possession, and shall be delivered to your order, either to the Adjutant as a reward for his bravery, or to be sold for the benefit of the State, as you may think proper. If the horse is to be sold, I should be glad of an opportunity to purchase him as I am in want of a horse, mine being worn out in the service."[61]

Greene's letter carried the place and dateline, "Fort Constitution, October 17, 1776."[62] It stands as the last known piece of correspondence from the camp under that name. For tomorrow, Saturday, October 19, a letter will be dated from the camp, describing today's affair under Colonel Glover's command in Westchester, and that letter will read:

"Extract Of A Letter From Fort Lee (Late Fort Constitution, But Now Altered By General Orders,) Dated October 19, 1776."[63]

But it will be some time before the villagers in and around The Mountain post will get used to the newly acquired name. Even now it is a subject that provokes extremes from jest to anger.

At the Baummeister house late this afternoon, Big Tom Graves, using only his one good arm, Jocko, Asher Levy and John Gray have been sawing and chopping wood for the Baummeister's winter pile. It has been a busy morning and afternoon at the post for all.

Dark and Re-occurring Is the Specter

The rapidly diminishing hours of sunlight have made the days increasingly busy, particularly for the inhabitants of the homes under the cliffs where darkness comes long before it settles on The Mountain's summit. All know and must prepare for the coming cold winds, ice storms and blanketing snows.

From the second floor window, Elaine, still recuperating from her close call with death and now feeling more like her own self again, gazes down at the men below as she occasionally looks up from her loom.

Weaving the flaxen thread, exactly as she, her mother and her mother's mother have been taught, the bride periodically lifts her eyes and looks down, watching each move her soldier husband makes. Adoring him from afar, she occasionally stops to note how well his axe strokes cleave the logs apart.

As she sees his sinewy muscles bulge with each swing, she seems to derive from her vision an ever-increasing sense of security, interrupted only now and then by ominous passing clouds that grimly shade over the scene.

Strangely they fill her heart with momentary terror, then pass on and away. It is like the dark re-occurring specter of war and its demon attendants flying wildly over the world and here and there striking down like lightning upon some hearth, then swiftly disappearing leaving it scarred with death and steeped in mourning.

So it is that in her mind flashes the constant torturous realization that he is a soldier, one of many in a war that feeds on death and misfortune. This fear, this sword over her head, she tells herself, like that of Damocles, must be her secret.

It is not the custom of the women of The Mountain to reveal their feelings. Often Elaine has shocked the hamlet's people in the past by a display of emotions, merely to show her independence and be defiantly different. But now she has succumbed and must be one of them.

She alone knows how much it burrowed into the heart of Ma Kearney to keep her feelings to herself. And if Ma could keep up a strong front, Elaine is sure that she can do so too. For that, she tells herself, Ma would say, as she so often did, "Ye dee ye self proud, me Lass!"

The men now have piled the last cord of wood and all cluster around Papa Pete, repairing a damaged rudder. His pipe puffs evenly and regularly. Therefore each one among them knows his work is going smoothly.

They all watch Baummeister's skilled hands finish his carpentry job expecting any moment to hear Marie Louise's call to supper. It will be a big one tonight for it has been a hard day and there is lots to talk about.

Only Jocko and his father must return to the post with the wagon and team, carrying a special meal Marie Louise has carefully prepared for them alone. It is packed in her favorite Indian basket which Minnie gave her years ago.

An apple for each of the horses, which now impatiently await them is, she tells Jocko, to be given "after they eat their oats." And, she adds, that the loaf of hot baked bread is to last them at least until Monday.

Gray and Asher accompany the ferry-master into the house at Marie Louise's call. He grumbles his usual complaint that he never gets the news first any more from the army messengers like he does "from the reg'lar pass'agers dat haff not gots sooch tight mouffs." But the conversation soon turns from Westchester, about which they have little information, to the renaming of the fort.

Just then Jennie walks up from the Bourdette path carrying a giant pumpkin for Marie Louise as they all approach the big Dutch doors of the Baummeister house. It is Jennie who gets the last word in after hearing the discussion of the name "Fort Lee."

"Ise doan know 'bout dat man so much, but Ise just doan thinks Ah laks 'im!"

Part III

Disaster

20

Sunday, October 27. . .

Revised Objective:
White Plains, Then the Hudson

Behind Are Left the Trembling Families

For two frightening weeks the Whig and neutral inhabitants from Bergen Point, opposite Richmond port in Staten Island, all the way north through Bergen Village into Hackensack and up into the Hudson's valley, have trembled. They suffer in fear and sympathy with the Whig and neutral home-owners of Westchester County in New York.

In Westchester the more brazen of the Tory renegades who have long raided and plundered their former neighbors, have joined General Howe's army. This has struck fear into the lives of the ardent patriots who live along the Palisades and in the valleys lying under their western slopes. When such forces become part of the enemy's army in Westchester, it is time for those across the Hudson in Jersey and in the upper New York Hudson valley to the north, to shudder.

The Hackensack valley people feel that it is only a matter of time before they too will fall prey to the British army's Jersey Tories. The fearful thought that newly named Fort Lee may have to be evacuated preys heavily upon their minds. For if that happens both The Mountain and the valley people will be isolated in enemy territory. The thought haunts Whig and neutral alike.

All that is holding the Jersey Tories in check and preventing them from breaking out in force are Fort Lee and its outposts. The northern, or left flank outpost is above Ma Sneden's Landing,[1] often called Dobbs Ferry since from here the Sneden's ferry runs across the river to Dobbs Ferry. The southern or right flank outpost is at Bull's Ferry.

Under the long, sweeping, gable-roofed homes of the earliest Dutch and Huguenot pioneers and beneath the beautifully sloping hand-hewn cedar shingles of the gambrel roofs, firmed on thick, brown sandstone block-constructed houses, built by the late-comers, fear is a new word. More so now, than before the Bergen and Paulus Hook posts fell into British hands.

It has been three weeks since the American garrisons withdrew from Bergen and the Hook. In their place and now controlling Bergen Point, Bergen Village and Paulus Hook under the Crown's aegis is one of the erstwhile Hackensack valley community leaders, Abe Van Buskirk. At the war's outbreak, he was one of the first chief American militia officers on the Bergen peninsula. Now Abraham Van Buskirk, the surgeon from Saddle River, is a lieutenant colonel in the King's Volunteers.[2]

Van Buskirk has turned his back on the patriot committees with which the doctor first aligned himself. For a surgeon's rank is considered rather low in the militia hierarchy of the Hackensack valley area.

Gathering other supporters of the King with him, Van Buskirk deserted his neighbors who, like him, are descendants of the earliest Dutch and French Huguenot settlers. But unlike them, most of whom are staunch American patriots, Van Buskirk has thrown in with Howe. As a reward he is now enjoying rank and reputation as he recruits others for the British army.

Van Buskirk has established his headquarters in Bergen Neck which post he has renamed Fort De Lancey in honor of Oliver De Lancey,[3] a Westchester Tory who has also joined the British army.

In the months ahead the very mention of the name, "Van Buskirk," will infuriate Bergen County's villagers and farmers. Even those of his kin who bear his name but not his sentiments will come to despise him.

Though Van Buskirk needs no model to follow in leveling his wrath upon his former neighbors, Major Robert Rogers and his Westchester Tories under the name of "The Queen's American Rangers," is Van Buskirk's archetype on the New York side of the river.

Rogers had acquired a notorious reputation as a bold but ruthless officer in the French and Indian War. He now upholds that reputation as an arm of Howe's army in Westchester County and the Hudson Valley where his ruffian renegades are especially detested by the American troops as well as by the frightened inhabitants.[4]

However in East Jersey Van Buskirk and his King's Volunteers must bide their time. Fort Lee and its outposts are all that hold his anger and violence in check. His plans for plundering and attacking unsuspecting Whigs and neutrals have been confined by the very presence of the Continentals.

The rebel evacuation of the Hook and more recently of Bergen has placed the Jersey Tory chieftain virtually in command of that area. From there he can launch his raids unmolested, although he must constantly be wary of Mercer's forces at Perth Amboy and Greene's at Fort Lee.

Consequently there is not a Whig, a patriot or a neutral who is not trembling over what each morrow might bring to his lands, his home and his family. Most frightened now are the inhabitants of the Bergen Neck area.

The abandonment of the posts there and the evacuation of the militia, as explained by one soldier in a letter published October 9 in *The Pennsylvania Journal and Weekly Advertiser*, give the soldier's point of view. The letter does not, however, allay the fears or raise the hopes of the unfortunate inhabitants. Writes the militiaman:

> "For my own part, I am sorry that the enemy should possess another inch of ground, but prudence requires a further sacrifice. The reasons of leaving this place (The Bergen Neck area), I take to be these: Bergen is a narrow neck of land, accessible on three sides by water, and exposed to a variety of attacks in different places at one and the same time.
> "A large body of the enemy might infallibly take possession of the place whenever they pleased, unless we kept a stronger force than our numbers will allow. The spot itself is not an object of their arms; if they attacked, it would be to cut off those who defended it, and secure the grain and military stores. These have been removed . . . a naked spot is all they will find.
> "No other damage will follow, except a depression of some people's spirits, who unacquainted with places, circumstances and the secret reasons of such relinquishments, are apt to despond as if everything was lost . . ."[5]

By abandoning the ground the Americans are forced to leave the inhabitants at the mercy of the enemy. Were "the enemy" solely the British army, the natives might more easily accept the loss of livestock, grain and stores. For these are understandable military confiscations in wartime. But when "the enemy" are former neighbors out to wreak vengeance, whether Tory over Whig or Whig over Tory, hatreds burn and spread with an emotional fury far worse than the devastations of the militarily-controlled death and destructions on the battlefield.

Fanned by long-smoldering personal grudges, the attacks of the renegade raiders—all natives of the area—become bestial. In their wake are left the ravages of rapine, arson and murder.

People On A Seesaw

So it is that many families stand stoically in front of their homes, livestock and all their earthly goods which represent their life's savings. They wave weakly with smiles that hide their hopelessness as the disappearing militia guards withdraw.

They try to conceal their dread fears for the days to come. All know that soon will follow the raids that lawlessness invites.

Teetering like a seesaw, the people of the once-quiet, hidden valley of the Hackensack will waver back and forth under the occupying forces of the two opposing armies. In the years ahead the long Bergen Neck and its northward stretching peninsula will be invaded and overrun by first one side and then the other, by renegade attackers and by counteracting regulars and militia.

In the atmosphere created by the American troop withdrawals, therefore, are soon sown the seeds of crime. Even the enemy soldiers fight among themselves. British redcoats angrily protest that the Hessian hirelings are permitted to plunder[6] with impunity while the King's own men are punished for the slightest evidence of personal pillage.

The Continental Army as well as the British punishes atrocity crimes. Court martials in the American ranks are regularly called to hear charges of plunder, rape and murder. But efforts by both armies to prevent atrocities are not too successful.

From out of all this there is now growing on the fringes of the two military machines two rival marauding factions. One counterattacks the other. They will eventually comprise the "irregulars" of both the opposing forces. The Tory marauders will be called "Cowboys" and the American guerrillas will be named "Skinners."[7]

In the years to come they will slaughter cattle by the thousands. They will wantonly burn, plunder and kill under the psychotic hypnosis of war and hate in man's eternally maniacal reach for his mesmeric and tragic tendency to revert to ancestral behavior.

And so, in time, some countryside areas above New York town from King's Bridge to beyond Tarrytown and in a radius of 30 miles around the city will become known as "no-man's-land." Though that is destined for the long war years ahead the ground is now harrowed.

In that future the war-weary inhabitants, owing to seeds now being sown, will become momentary "Loyalists" when the British forces ride through, "Patriots" when the Americans take over.

In between, Tories will steel themselves against raiding Whigs, and raiding Tories will fall upon unwary Whigs. And there will be neutrals who persist in trying to remain so, only to find there is no such thing as neutrality when one attempts to stand between two warring nations.

Illustrating the extent of the problem and its rapidly developing repercussions are such letters as those of Eben Hazard, the American, and Lewis Morris, Jr., the Tory.

Hazard, in a letter to Major General Gates earlier this month, wrote how permissive pillaging has divided the King's army, saying:

"The Hessians and British troops disagree and are kept entirely separate. The latter do not like the former's being allowed to plunder while they are prohibited from doing it.[8] Those rascals plunder all indiscriminately; if they see anything they like, they say:

" 'Rebel, (this is) good for Heese-mans!' and seize it for their own use. They have no idea between the distinctions of Whig and Tory. I have been credibly informed that a Tory complained to General Howe of his having been plundered by the Hessians and that the General replied, 'There is no avoiding it. It is their manner of fighting.' "[9]

And indicating that despite restricting orders, criminal acts are perpetrated as much by one side as by the other, since seldom can war—itself a crime—control crime, Lewis Morris Jr. wrote his father from New York September 6.

In his correspondence he stated that the American troops under Colonel Hand had:

"plundered every body in Westchester County indiscriminately, even yourself (referring to his father's lands) have not escaped. Montrasseurs Island they plundered and committed the most unwarrantable destruction upon it; fifty dozen of bottles were broken in the cellar, the paper tore from the rooms and every pane of glass broke to pieces."[10]

Howe Demands the Signing Of the Oath

More feared than the act of plundering are the horrible atrocities that frequently accompany the raids by the renegade bands. Often rape, arson and murder follow in the wake. And sometimes openly declared patriots and Whig sympathizers are, on false charges, dragged off and imprisoned in the British Sugar House Prison or on a prison ship. The Americans—soldiers and civilians alike—fear these notorious, so-called "hell holes of death" more than they fear a musket ball.

The Honorable Sir William Howe Knight of the Bath & Commander in Chief of his Majesty's Forces in America— unidentified engraver, 1777....Anne S. K. Brown Military Collection, Brown Universtiy Library, Courtesy National Portrait Gallery, Smithsonian Institution.

Few Whigs and neutrals in the vast valleys of the Hudson can hold out against the overwhelming pressures Howe's forces can bring against them when British soldiers, Hessians and Tories move into a void vacated by the hard-pressed rebel army. Caught between the choice of losing their homes, lands, possessions and possibly their lives, few hesitate to transfer their allegiance from The Cause to King George III.

For, to many of them there is no other logical recourse, particularly since the country's defenders continually draw back, leaving the inhabitants on their own. And when "on their own" they are at the mercy of the attacking and infiltrating enemy.

Therefore it is comparatively easy for Howe's propaganda machine, spread out as it is by both his army and naval recruitment officers and by widely distributed handbills, to get the neutral inhabitants—and many of the patriot Whigs—to sign his oath of allegiance to the Crown. It is a simple document. The clerk fills in the blank spaces as he reads, with the frightened oath-taker—in most cases—repeating after him as best he can:

"I do hereby Certify, That _____ _____ of (County or location) has, in my Presence, voluntarily taken an Oath, to bear Faith and true Allegiance to His Majesty King George the Third; and to defend to the utmost of his Power, His sacred Person, Crown and Government, against all Persons whatsoever.

"Given under my Hand at New-York, this ____ Day of ____ in the Seventeenth Year of His Majesty's Reign, Anno. Dom. 177– . . ."[11]

Those in New York town who do not sign the oath are likely to find a large "R" written on their doors, according to one New York Tory's letter to a friend in London. Fully in favor of General Howe's methods, the jubilant Tory last Sunday, October 20, wrote this description of the British occupation after stating that the King's troops had entered the city to the great satisfaction of the loyal residents:

> "The inhabitants have for a long time past suffered every hardship from a set of tyrants that is impossible to be conceived; however, they are now rewarded for having withstood the traitors and remained firm to their King . . ."

He goes on to point out that the Howes do all that is possible to alleviate the sufferings of a persecuted people, "who rather than turn Rebels, have despised death and ruin."

As for those who are identified as "patriots" or "rebels," he says:

> "There is a broad "R" put upon every door in New York that is disaffected to Government, and examples will be made of its inhabitants; on the other hand, every person that is well affected to Government, finds protection."[1][2]

The Tory writer's closing of his letter to his London friend illustrates how the British Juggernaut's slow but methodical beating back of the American army has bolstered the Loyalists' morale:

> "They fly before our victorious army on every onset; and I don't doubt but in a very little time this daring rebellion will be crushed. It would before now have been the case, had not the Americans been fed with hopes from the Court of France.
> "But now let France or any other Power dare to assist them, we are prepared, and don't at all fear but that we shall be able to give you an account of an end being put to a Government that have dared call themselves the Independent States of America."[1][3]

And in Westchester the increasing arrogance of the Loyalists is fired by the emboldened Major Rogers who is now firmly supported by the landing of General Howe and his army. Encouraged beyond his expectations by the invasion, the Westchester Tory Rangers' leader has redoubled his efforts toward bending the recalcitrant inhabitants back into the King's fold.

But in addition to his strikes upon the people and instilling fear in the hearts of the landowners, Rogers has made some highly successful hit and run raids upon the American Westchester militia. He has marched off with large quantities of the rebel army's stores and provisions. His bold and daring acts have made him the American militia's most sought-after prize of war.

The Rebel Raid On Rogers' Rangers

Last Tuesday morning, October 22, General Stirling decided it was time to clip Rogers' wings. "The Old Indian Fighter," as the Tory leader is often called, was to be given a blow that would not only discredit him but that would put him, at least temporarily, out of commission. Colonel Haslet's Delaware regiment was chosen by the brigade's General to execute the job.

Haslet's audacious veteran Continentals have little respect for the average American militiamen, calling them, along with some of their own Continentals, "The Long-faced People" owing to the sad facial expression they seem to convey wherever they go.[14] So the Delawareans, who have been reinforced since the Battle of Long Island by southern troops from Maryland, Virginia and North Carolina, derive a certain amount of pleasure out of a chance to save face for the militiamen Rogers' has raided.

On Monday night Rogers' 500-man corps[15] had lain encamped about two miles above or northeast of Mamaroneck. The Tory major and his men had formed the farthermost outpost of the British invasion force's right wing. But, as Stirling had soon discovered, they were detached from the main body. Thus Haslet was commanded to move upon them in a night attack.

Moving out of their encampment at White Plains, Haslet's regiment noiselessly covered the approximate five miles during the early pre and post midnight hours. It was after midnight when they stole quietly up to the outskirts of the Queen's Ranger's post.

Fortunately Stirling had secured good intelligence beforehand regarding the encampment. Haslet was supplied with a rough plan of the camp and knew that at one point only there was a single sentinel guarding the way into the Tory raiders' bivouac. But Haslet did not have an exact layout of the entire post.[16]

The success of the Americans' operation depended upon surprise, and surprise upon silence. Since Howe had recently moved his main army's right and center two miles north toward White Plains from his New Rochelle encampment,[17] the Americans could hear the enemy's right wing pickets changing guard in the distance. These were Brigadier General Agnew's British Sixth Brigade.

Stealthily Haslet's van moved in and seized the Tory camp's single sentry on the southern approach. The way now should have been clear into the main area, but the ever-cautious, astute old Indian fighter had just the day before decided his post was insufficently guarded. Between the lone sentinel and the main body Rogers had posted Captain Eagles with a body of 60 riflemen.[18]

Of this Haslet had no knowledge. The rebel colonel and his regiment are known for their fearless fighting spirit. It is a reputation earned on Long Island and one which has followed them into Westchester. His contingent of 750 men is often called upon for conducting dangerous enterprises. And now in the darkness, the American van found itself stumbling over Eagles' 60 sleeping riflemen wrapped in their blankets.

Within seconds the surprised Queen's Rangers were jumping up and shouting at the tops of their voices to spread the alarm. Reaching for their rifles they ran off in all directions in order to find a safe place to prime and load.

The commotion sent Haslet's supporting force rushing up into the dark shadows of trees where disordered men ran in wild turmoil amid a confusion of voices and commands. The uproaring free-for-all in the night's darkness and the popping of firearms now alerted Rogers' entire encampment.

The wily Rogers had taught his Rangers tricks in the art of military deception, all learned from his Indian fighting days. And now in the darkness they used them. One was to assume the role of the enemy. All were well acquainted with each other and could easily distinguish one of their own from an American rebel.

Carrying out their subterfuge, the Tory Rangers began yelling loudly, "Surrender, you Tory dogs! Surrender!"[19]

Hearing these shouts, Haslet's fighters, believing the voices were coming from their own men's lips, would praise the men who so bravely shouted, turn away and find themselves struck on the back of the head with the butt of the true "Tory dog's" rifle. In this wild confusion the Americans were never sure who was who. It was a clever trick that worked. Haslet had not expected to encounter Indian fighting in British units.[20]

In the wild melee Tories and Continentals grappled with each other. During the height of the tumult, Captain Eagles escaped with about a third of his men to the bivouac and the fully alerted Tory leader. The remainder were left subdued or captured.

Haslet and several of his companies swiftly took off after Eagles and poured into the empty Tory camp followed by the regiment's main force. Warned by the brush with Eagles' outpost, Rogers had made a hurried exit, leaving a rear guard to exchange fire with the rebels before disappearing into the thicket.

The rebel raiders then withdrew not wishing to risk returning to the main road in the light of day. Contenting themselves with partial success, they counted 36 prisoners, a pair of colors, 60 muskets and 60 highly prized blankets. Haslet lost three of his men killed in the fighting. Twelve were wounded.[21]

Tench Tilghman, writing William Duer the day after the attack, Wednesday last, October 23, stated in his communique from White Plains in referring to the episode:

"Every man of thirty-six taken at Mamaroneck are natives of this Government. If I was superstitious, I should call it a judgment."[22]

Two of the prisoners have been found to be spies. One is charged with desertion from the army.[23]

General Howe has attributed Haslet's success to "the carelessness of his (Rogers') sentinels (who) exposed him to a surprise from a large body of the enemy . . ."[24]

It is General Howe's customary practice to report only the British redcoats killed, wounded or imprisoned. This keeps his casualties low and pleases Parliament. Hessian losses for the most part are overlooked in reports. So also are losses suffered by irregulars such as Rogers' Queen's Rangers. Such a corps is considered a detached unit. Therefore in his dispatch to Lord Germaine, Sir William can state:

> ". . . He (Rogers) lost a few men killed or taken; nevertheless, by a spirited exertion, he obliged them (Haslet's men) to retreat, leaving behind them some prisoners, and several killed and wounded . . ."[25]

The one distant observer of the Mamaroneck action had been General William Heath who had brought his division from King's Bridge to Chatterton's Hill just south of the White Plains in a forced 12-hour march Tuesday morning.[26]

It was 4 A.M. when Heath ascended the hill to survey the terrain. His attention was drawn to distant flashes of fire in the southeast. The general immediately sent out scouts and learned later in the day that what he had seen was the exchange of fire from Haslet's attack on the Tory Rangers' bivouac.

The sound counsel Heath had received in his instructions from The General, preparatory to moving his troops the long 13 rugged miles from King's Bridge to Chatterton Hill, had enabled the major general to move into a defensive position without detection or incident. For Heath, en route, had to pass through Valentine Hill Monday where the Continentals' Commander was spending the night in General Lincoln's quarters.

There Heath received his instructions from his Chief who advised him to watch the road coming from Ward's Bridge. The enemy, he was warned, could easily attack his right flank at that critical point if his movements were detected.

The General directed that he move under the cover of darkness in order to conceal the operation from the British observers. The advice and the division's strong foothold on the hill above the plains, ruin Howe's plan to get in behind the American army's rear.

Also amazing to Heath was that no part of his line of march

encountered any of the enemy. His men had steeled themselves throughout the long night expecting an ambush from Rogers' outposts against their long line.

But Rogers disappointed them. To most of the veteran Continentals this was more surprising than the absence of Howe's pickets.

The tales the older men enjoyed telling the new recruits were always—when it came to Rogers' Queen's Rangers—magnified into hair-raising accounts that frightened some young replacements out of their wits. Wide-eyed and open-mouthed, they had listened to the exaggerated stories concocted by the hardy, veteran pranksters around the campfires at King's Bridge. Indeed, true accounts were frightening enough without the embellishments of pranksters.

Certainly many a raw recruit in Heath's long marching lines through the darkness Monday night and Tuesday morning would have marched less jittery through the tall black leafless trees of the forests had he known for sure that Colonel Haslet's regiment was at that very hour surprising the Tory chief.

If the attack on Rogers' encampment gave Sir William a message besides convincing him he was not as deep in the enemy's rear as he had thought, the American Commander's ruse the next day, Wednesday, gave him something else to think about. For The General on the 23rd baited the Hessians out of their hole into a pocket, proving he too had learned some tricks from the Indians.

The incident occurred after Howe moved north out of New Rochelle Monday, leaving Hessian Lieutenant General Heister to occupy the grounds with two brigades of Hessians and one of British.[27] At Heister's southernmost outpost, a large Hessian detachment occupied an abandoned farmhouse. The forward pickets extended well in advance of the post.

Grasping a golden opportunity to singe the Lion's tail, the rebel Commander-in-Chief ordered several small detached American parties to probe and advance as far as possible into the Hessian's outpost. They were to annoy the enemy detachment with small arms fire until the Hessians pursued them. Meanwhile, Colonel Hand was to stand concealed in the attacking parties' support with 200 riflemen.

Then, as expected, the probing parties lured the unwary Hessians down into Hand's cross fire. The trap, the second blow for Howe in two days, slowed down the entire British Juggernaut.

Man-of-War Off Dobbs Ferry

The ambush ended in a rout with the Americans pursuing the fleeing Hessians out of their farmhouse outpost, sending them reeling back to Heister's encampment. Ten of the enemy were counted by Hand's forces which brought in three prisoners, one of whom was mortally wounded and "a parcel of shirts which had been left to wash."[28] The American colonel reported two men lost in the action.

In General Howe's report next month to Lord Germaine, the British commander will ignore the incident.[29] Fortunately none of the King's redcoats were involved.

All this time the men-of-war, which have lain restlessly upriver in the Tarrytown-Haverstraw Bay area well north of Dobbs Ferry, are still waiting for Sir William's breakthrough across Westchester to Hudson's river. No sign of the British army has been sighted. The ships alone can do nothing but intimidate the inhabitants, encourage enlistments and wait.

But Wednesday one of the southernmost vessels heaved anchor, leaving her mooring off Tarrytown and sailed down to Dobbs Ferry.[30] To all intents and purposes the frigate, accompanied by two transports, was ordered to interrupt communications between the American posts on the New York side near the ferry and the American's left flank outpost for Fort Lee, Sneden's Ferry Landing. The ferry landing is eight miles north of Greene's post.

For one full day the enemy ship and the transports lay threatening any traffic attempting to cross from Dobbs on the east bank to Sneden's on the west. Even Ma Sneden and her Tory-sympathizing sons found the blockade damaging to their ferriage business. But the Snedens are suspected of strongly favoring the Loyalist Party in spite of the rebel outpost above their heads.

A man-of-war at such a spot on the river indicated Howe might be planning to strike out for Dobbs Ferry.

Or might it be one of the Howe brothers' tricks to conceal some other intention?

General Greene at Fort Lee could take no chances. Upon hearing from his northernmost outpost at Sneden's, Greene immediately ordered an alert along the river-front. Among the precautions "The Petticoat Scarf" Lieutenant Gray, with a detachment of volunteers, was assigned the task of carting an 18-pounder to support the Sneden's Landing pickets. His mission was to help thwart—or at least annoy—a possible enemy party incursion.

First to volunteer to drive the wagon was Jocko Graves. But, to the surprise of many, among the rifle company volunteers was Corporal Edmund Kearney. His enlistment in the militia was shortly expiring and his attitude of disinterest in his fellow-man and The Cause has become far more noticeable since he failed to become a sergeant.

To his comrades the corporal's volunteering seemed to reflect a change in attitude. Perhaps they should not longer call him "Long-faced" Kearney, an expression even militiamen adopt and use against disgruntled soldiers.

But his volunteering now concerned Jocko Graves. Intuitively Jocko suspected something more sinister in Kearney's act than simply "a change in attitude." That was "a change" he knew could not be, particularly since he had overheard Elaine and Kearney in a heated argument at the Baummeister's well-sweep three days before.

Jocko had no intention of eavesdropping when he stood between his two horses watering at the spring-fed trough above the Baummeister house. Edmund Kearney's angry voice could have been heard by anyone nearby.

Furiously he stood accusing Elaine of not waiting to marry him and, instead, of "rushin' an' weddin' da likes of dat 'Tinks 'e Knows It All' Filladellfin." He raved on in a release of pent-up anger telling his former childhood playmate she had fallen for the first sight of a "brass buttoned officer."

Jocko, glancing under the neck of one of the horses, saw Elaine's amazed expression and then heard her let go a tirade, denouncing and upbraiding Edmund as she would one of the children in her school.

"You know, Edmund Kearney," she scolded, "that's not so! And you certainly should know that there never could have been anything but friendship between us! You are stupid, Edmund! What would your dear mother—Bless her heart and rest her dear soul!—think of you? And you don't really care. You never really loved her as she deserved. I know you, Edmund! But I have always been your friend, and I hope John and I always will be. That's the way it is! Now you go on and get back there to your company and do something good for your country and stop feeling sorry for yourself and always putting *you* first."

Jocko, taking in every word, said to himself, "Thass right, Missy E! Give 'im it good! . . . Just lak a schoolmarm!"

With that, Jocko recalled, Kearney wheeled around and continued his way up the clove road to the military barracks.

The fisherwoman's son returns only once in a while to the now unoccupied Kearney homestead, sleeping mostly with his rifle company at the fort. There he points out to all who will listen to him that he will soon be out of the army and making real money in New York with the wealthy merchants of the port.

After all no one there will know he was ever a rebel militiaman. He has his plans, he tells them.

Thus, Edmund's volunteering for a mission only surprised his comrades but it worried Jocko. Puzzled for an answer, the youth decided it was not really any of his business and decided to say nothing about his eavesdropping to anyone.

Later that same night John Gray listened in astonishment when Elaine told him of Edmund's jealous outburst at the well. Between the young married couple there are no secrets.

That was one of the promises each had sworn to uphold on that memorable night under what he had called "The Great Creator's heavenly canopy of eternal infinity." That was their unforgettable night. Their night alone in the dark peaceful quietude of love and silence.

Though it had been only three weeks ago since they returned to the hate-enveloping world of man, John remembered those priceless hours now as he listened to Elaine and thought how far away seemed that world of serene beauty, that world surrounding Oratam's castle of peace, that world so sadly fading into the distant past.

John had long sensed Edmund's affection for Elaine was more than brotherly. He had soon recognized that its depth of attachment was deeper than the Platonic magnetism of childhood. But he expected the younger man to become reconciled. He even hoped, for Elaine sake, that he and Edmund could become friends.

So despite the incident earlier in the week, Kearney's volunteering Wednesday was construed by Gray to be that the youth had undergone a change of attitude and become penitent under the effects of Elaine's scorching oratory. Gray has himself felt the sting of some of his bride's "righteous" lectures. He knew their potency.

Unknown to the artillery lieutenant, the chasm of rank which normally separates commissioned from non-commissioned officers deepened viciously within those few days. Between Kearney and Gray there could never be an adjustment of emotions.

Released within Kearney were those inexplicable human emotions. In their emergence, temperance and reason were swallowed up in fanatical fantasies and devious thoughts motivated by human desires. The virtues which once controlled the capricious vagaries of the mind were suddenly drowned, victims of the ageless green-eyed monster.

Packed like the venom of a cobra, jealousy, the offspring of warping emotional drives, evilly lurked in the recesses of Edmund Kearney's unstable brain Wednesday. And, as in such human triangles, a wildly maniacal mind, its emotional outlets infected, surreptitiously prepared to do violence.

All through the long ten-mile trip from Fort Lee to Sneden's Landing outpost, the worst of Kearney's character began to show itself. Each man among the rifle company soon realized that the snickering corporal with his snide remarks was aiming all his spears at The Lieutenant and his ever-attached blue petticoat necker-chief.

Though disgusted and angry at Kearney's actions, Jocko said nothing. While he cared little for what Jocko thought, Kearney was careful to be out of Gray's hearing distance when delivering his barbs.

His undermining work first began with subtle remarks, never loud enough to be overheard by Sergeant MacNamara or other superiors. He would refer to Gray as "Dat ugly Yankee Dood from Filladellfa," expecting a laugh but seldom getting a look of any kind.

In appearances, the rather good looking corporal far outclassed the gangling pock-marked John Gray. The almost homely appearing, plain featured Gray is a surprisingly sad contrast with the medium-built and sharply chiseled features of the sulking-faced Kearney.

Next, the corporal's searing temper would ridicule some of the artillery officer's decisions, past and present. Then, glancing ahead and catching a glimpse of the blue petticoat scarf around Gray's throat, the vindictive youth would redouble his efforts with bitter remarks reflecting his anger and hatred.

If Gray were unaware of Kearney's perfidy, he was alone in such ignorance. If he were aware of it, he gave no indication. Calmly he carried on his communications through MacNamara to Kearney or directly with Kearney at times.

It was this unruffled attitude for which The Lieutenant is known and respected that incited Kearney into deeper resentment.

It was a minor thing. Gray ordered the corporal to see to it that the right rear and forward left axles be immediately greased. In quiet defiance, largely intended to show he could disobey Gray's commands if he wished, Kearney ignored the order.

Gray, realizing that Kearney was intent upon seeking a confrontation on any grounds, overlooked the corporal's action. Instead he gave the same order to McNamara who handed Kearney the greasing rod and advised him that he, rather than one of the privates, was more skillful at the swabbing job.

MacNamara, who few men ever defy, has a special genius for turning tense moments into humorous situations. But the humor of the men furiously fanned Edmund Kearney's glowing embers now fully fired with hate.

By the time the company and its cannon arrived at Sneden's Landing everyone in the unit felt the rising tensions between the two men. Yet only The Lieutenant appeared oblivious of the powder keg. And outside of Jocko, no one except the officer himself had the slightest idea of what was behind the friction.

By the time The Lieutenant had his 18-pounder set up in support of the post's smaller cannon, the American weaponry from the opposite side of the river opened up when a rebel militia patrol which had been probing out a small Hessian advance began firing upon the frigate and the transports lying at anchor in mid-river. The vessels were closer to the Hudson's east bank and consequently within better range of the opposite bank's rebel militiamen who were, however, only equipped with small arms. Under what little wind they could muster and the power of their oars, the two transports took off and headed upstream.

Taking his cue from the Dobbs post firing, Sneden's outpost commander, Colonel Durkee, ordered all cannon into play. The man-of-war, her broadsides facing up and down the river instead of at either bank owing to the change of tide, found its bow and stern dangerously exposed to the annoying rebel shore batteries.

Close Of the River Engagement

Rolling up two light weapons, one at the bow and one at the stern, the British gunners began answering the cross fire. Hoisting anchor and unfurling sail, the crew meanwhile struggled in vain to get the vessel under way. But only a breath of wind stirred over the becalmed frigate.

Launching their longboats over the side under the Americans' fire, all oarsmen went to work tugging at the oarlocks of the four longboats with frenzied efforts.[31]

After being hulled 11 out of 15 times by the American cannoneers,[32] the damaged, impotent ocean-going Goliath slowly disappeared upriver out of range. Humiliatingly towed to safety by over 25 British tars and their four longboats, the great vessel sulked back with its flotilla. The Americans could only guess casualties and damages.

While this action was taking place on the river several more brigades of the rebel army were rapidly moving into position at the White Plains. And more were coming. The bulk of the American Commander's entire New York army is now encamped there.[33]

But today on the west side of the river, opposite Dobbs Ferry, the Sneden's Landing rebel post men are congratulating themselves on a job well done last Friday. Certainly forcing a man-of-war and its two transports to flee back upstream was a feather in their cap even though they had help from Fort Lee and the militia units on the east bank.

The artillery officer with the blue petticoat scarf and his men from the main fort left the landing area in the rain yesterday morning. They departed with one man injured in a fall down the embankment. However that "accident" had much more behind it than the post commander or any of his men could possibly imagine.

Though not having anything to do with the incident, one man had been added to Gray's company in Orange County as the military detachment moved through Tappan. There they had picked up the young and likeable Private Abraham Onderdonk who, Gray remembered, had so impressed Elaine at the fort two weeks ago. His furlough ended, the Tappan youth was on his way to join his company of Orange County militia under Captain James Smith, encamped with the American left wing at White Plains.

Onderdonk, who had visited the Fort Lee hospital tent accompanied by Elaine and Ma Kearney October 9, was shocked to hear from Gray that she had died with the fever. Onderdonk recalled how she had talked of her "Eddie" with the Bergen County militia under Captain Board. And now Onderdonk was meeting him for the first time.

Attempting to offer his consolences to the glumly staring corporal the Orange County militiaman was met with a gruff rebuff. The puzzled private was somewhat flabbergasted. This certainly was not the same person the motherly woman had described.

As the party proceeded on towards the Sneden outpost

Sunday, October 27 . . . 425

Onderdonk made a quick and accurate appraisal of the angry corporal. The private was sure that Kearney was more interested in damaging the reputation of his superior officer than he was interested in hearing words of praise about the corporal's deceased mother. So the Tappan youth soon closed the door on any further efforts to do so.

Soon after the shelling of the frigate and the clearing of the river, Onderdonk said his goodbyes with a broad wave from the ferry's bow and crossed with one of the Sneden brothers to the Dobbs Landing. For the river was now again open to traffic for the first time in 48 hours.

There was something about the youth that Jocko liked. It was what most people saw.

Onderdonk seemed to Jocko to lack hate and distrust. He appeared to be the direct opposite of Edmund Kearney. There was something about Kearney that Jocko despised. And so through Jocko's mind there flashed his re-occurring impression of all mankind. Man, unlike horses has two faces, two selves. Even he himself finds he is two people, one at peace with his father. The other not so at peace with the world and man.

The Lieutenant ordered the return march to the fort early yesterday, Saturday morning. If everything went well the unit could be back Saturday night.

The roughest stretch in the entire line of march was up the embankment over the rock-strewn, precipice road from the Sneden's Landing post to the crest of the Palisades. Even with plenty of help from the outpost's men it was a difficult climb with cannon, equipment and supplies.

At this point of the long Palisadean ridge, the mountain tapers down to only a few hundred feet above the river. But the old wagon road had been washed away during a heavy storm and had not been reconstructed. Both of the company's wagons had therefore been unloaded near the top of the crest and had remained there.

Supervising the movement of the train from below, Gray saw that the two wagons, with Jocko's in the lead, were loading without incident. Kearney was in the middle position directing the men and supplies up the precipice path.

Every man was doing his job in the hauling of the two field-pieces up to the wagons' level. With the help of the post's small garrison the task was all but completed.

Gray, now alone, brought up the rear. Twice he struggled to

hold his footing under the weight of an overlooked bundle of tenting that had been inadvertently left behind. Lugging it along with his own gear and his own weight instead of ordering one of his men to do it, presented an uncommon sight. Most officers would have ordered a special detail to recover it later on. Not John Gray.

The act brought silent approval from, not only the men of the Fort Lee post but from those of the Sneden's Landing garrison.

However the sight again stoked Edmund Kearney's warped emotions with hate. The burning anger that has been slowly storing up within him now consumed his twisted, jealousy-driven brain wildly seeking an outlet.

It was for this moment he had waited. It was for this moment he had volunteered. Now, at last, was the opportunity to destroy. It was the moment for which he had intensely hungered during the past two miserable days.

There below him was the object of his hatred, *First Lieutenant* John Gray!

"Lieutenant be damned!" he said to himself. Beside him, about an arm's length away, Kearney saw the exact type of boulder he was looking for. Once he set it free by a quick and powerful thrust of his foot, it would certainly take two and then other larger ones in their hurtling stampede down the gully's precipice path into the officer's body.

No one could ever prove it was anything but an accident. He was sure of that! This was the chance he had hoped for. And likely no one could see him do it. The heavy overcast sky and threatening storm were in his favor. The brush was thick except in the gully that in rainy seasons funnels the waters down the mountain into the river. At this time of the year it can be used as a short dangerous cut to the summit.

Kearney knows the ways of loose boulders on the Palisades. He has grown up with them. He has made avalanches happen and enjoyed in his childhood watching the building momentum and terrific forces that the glacial rocks generated in their long-delayed final dash into the depths of the great river.

But even if he were observed from above, he had a right to ascend to the top. And in ascending how could he be blamed for slipping and striking the key rock that would give John Gray his comeuppance.

Now was the moment! Facing up the mountain the corporal steadied his left foot against the large boulder which rested delicately held on the slope by smaller rocks.

To himself he said, "Now, Pock-face, see if you can get out of this!"

With that he powerfully thrust his leg muscles and drove the wobbling boulder out of its cushion. Instead of breaking loose it only rocked perilously and returned, seated back in its pocket.

Angrily now, Kearney struck it again, certain that the men above could not observe his action.

Kearney could not know that Jocko, high on the seat of the wagon on the roadway, had a clear view of every step he took. The suspicious youth did not trust the corporal in a ravine of rocks with The Lootenan behind him.

The black boy had also watched every step his officer friend took as Gray struggled up the incline. Then Jocko saw that Kearney was deliberately forcing the rock to plummet down the slope. Through his mind immediately flashed the danger that now faced the man who had once saved his father's life.

On the embittered corporal's third and finally successful effort, Jocko, realizing what Kearney was up to, yelled, "Lootenan! Lootenan! Watch out! Jump! Jump!"

His voice rang out through the forested ravine alerting every man in earshot scattered along the trail and on the road above the gully.

Gray quickly recognized Jock's warning voice from days past. He knew that tone of voice meant trouble and swiftly lifted his eyes to see the slowly tumbling, momentum-gaining boulder just pressed away from Kearney's foot.

Gray's vision grasped its rapidly increasing speed as it struck another and set that too on its way. Rapidly the officer's reflexes responded to his brain's frantic demands and swung his agile body, rolling it parallel with the gulch's run but up on the high grade out of the path of a tumbling avalanche of death.

It was a narrow escape. The tenting and his own knapsack, dislodged in his sudden movement, lay flattened in the dried-out stream bed when the escapade of the boulders came to a stop. Gray unharmed raised his head from out his crossed arms in front of him.

But as he looked up at Kearney's position where it seemed the source of the avalanche began, the corporal was in serious trouble.

The last angrily-powered thrust of Kearney's foot was too much for the youth's weight. The severe force of his drive against the boulder and its immediate release caused the corporal to lose his hold. Gradually he slipped out of his own control behind the bouncing boulders.

Then suddenly one rolling rock struck his leg against a tree stump as he continued falling. Half dazed and severely injured he tumbled on. When his body came to a stop, he lay semi-conscious above Gray in the hollow of the ravine.

The Lieutenant, looking up, grasped the situation in a glance but waited for the last of the gravity-pulled stones and rubble to end their crazily careening journey before rising to his feet.

Strangely, as he waited, he thought little of the peril of the situation. His mind instead momentarily focused on the passing, wildly loosened, rumbling rocks, freed once again after millions of years of imprisonment.

Not unlike man himself, he thought, they never lose the mad impulses that continue their drive after centuries upon centuries— from the very beginning of time—to rush back insanely to the bottom-most depths from which once they were so majestically launched. Not unlike man, Gray tells himself, they rise, falter, stumble and totter to fall cyclically back, as do all things, to the sea's and the earth's deep pits from which they came.

Amazed at his own thoughts at this time, Gray banishes them quickly and rolls back into the stream's bed, rises unhurt, and makes his way up to the corporal's limp form. Within moments the men of the short-cut detail were at the officer's side helping him. Rigging a lift, four men brought the unconscious, injured soldier safely up the precipice path.

After assisting the men with their make-shift carrier and getting the casualty started safely up the slope, Gray brushed himself off, counted a few minor scratches and then looked up at the wagon. He glanced toward Jocko who was now standing up on its seat.

The youth's eyes suddenly changed from fear to joy. When he saw the officer standing and apparently uninjured, a smile as broad and as happy as a Cheshire cat's spread across his face.

However, the relieved expression concealed his anger. But he welcomed The Lieutenant's signal, the hand limply reached upward toward his face across which came a faint smile of acknowledgment and appreciation, was all Jocko needed. However the half-waved hand was in itself a salute of thanks.

In a few minutes the men brought the unconscious Kearney to the roadway. Jocko's wagon was first in their path. The second wagon was in the lead now. Both had been turned around in the positions they had upon arrival.

"Put 'im in dat odder wagon," Jocko sourly ordered, as the men attempted to deposit Kearney's limp, bleeding form on the tenting under the 24-pounder's barrel. "Dere ain't no room in dis 'un."

Even though a wagonmaster is, in a sense, "the captain of his ship," the men were on the verge of disregarding Jock's imperious order until it was evident that the other wagon did have more blankets and cushioning and offered more comfort for the injured man.

Before the detachment moved out, Gray climbed into the back of the vehicle, gave the now conscious Kearney a large swig of rum, bandaged his gaping thigh wound and told him to rest as best he could until they reached a doctor in Tappan town.

Kearney said nothing. Neither man was sure of what the other man was thinking. The corporal had no way of knowing that anyone knew his act to have been a deliberate one. And Gray had no way of knowing that the avalanche was not purely accidental.

As for Jocko, there was no doubt in his mind that Kearney deliberately started the avalanche, but he kept the conviction entirely to himself. All others of the company and of the Sneden's Landing garrison judged it accidental. But had Gray been the injured one there would have been no doubt in their minds of the corporal's villainy.

Kearney's guilt-ridden eyes avoided the officer's piercing gaze as The Lieutenant bent over him and dressed his leg. But soon the injured soldier convinced himself that no one knew the truth. After all was not he the one who was hurt?

Leaving the injured man with a partially filled jug of rum by his side, Gray jumped into the rear vehicle's wagon-seat alongside of Jocko as the return march began. Then, in a half-reprimanding half-humorous tone, the officer turned to his driver, saying "Lot's of room left in this wagon, wouldn't ye say, Jocko?"

"No, ut 'taint!" The youngster quickly replied with a rapid negative shake of his head. Then switching the subject to the offense he asked, "Lootenan, who ya supposin' started all dem rocks a'fallin' anyways? An what ya supposin' maked'ted me tell ya ta jump?"

Now Gray was on the defensive, replying, "I dunno. But I sure might have been a bloody mess right now if ye hadn't. And I thank ye, me lad. We make now for Tappan town. If this storm breaks we won't make the fort tonight."

Jocko knows Gray well enough to realize that no more was to be said of the incident. A report would have to be made and in it Jocko knew the incident would be an "accident." And now the whole company headed for Tappan as a misty rain beat steadily upon their faces. They knew this Saturday night would not be spent at Fort Lee.

On the Barbette Battery today the Sunday morning sun was just beginning to come up over the storm-clearing horizon. Second Lieutenant Levy was somewhat nervously completing his third day in full command of the artillery post taken over when Gray set out on his mission to Sneden's Landing over twelve miles of rough road away. A courier from upriver had reported "the cannon company" would be back Saturday night. To Levy this Sunday, October 27, is a welcome one. For The Barbette, to Asher's relief, had seen no action during Gray's absence. Gray would soon return to command.

Sunday Callers Are Men-of-War

This morning another messenger arrived directly from Gray's outfit informing the post commander of the expedition's success on the river, the accidental fall of Corporal Kearney and the injuries he sustained, the severity of the storm and the difficulty encountered near Tappan with a wagon axle, and finally the necessity that the company spend the night in bivouac at Tappan. Gray's message informed the commander that the company would be back at the post late Sunday afternoon.

Sunday is always the customary time for General Howe to initiate some mischief but his presence over in Westchester confronting The General and his Continentals puts him out of mind but leaves his brother, the admiral, a likely possibility. The admiral's ships are always one of the chief concerns of the Fort Lee and Fort Washington commands. But Second Lieutenant Levy is hoping the King's navy will postpone further blockade-crashing below him until The Lieutenant's return.

Judging from the number of men now working on the river barrier—some 200 are daily strengthening it[34]—Levy and the artillerymen of The Barbette are becoming confident that Black Dick is not likely to soon try again. Vessels running through the obstacle, flanked as it is by the heavy cannon on both sides of the Hudson, daily make such an attempt more risky.

The early risers in the vicinity of the mountain-top fort waked with the dawn this quiet Sunday morning, wondering with trepidation what the coming week will bring. Such fears for each coming week face them every Sunday morning before the church bells sound. But this dawn ushers in the first week of the cold bleak days of November. And Elaine Gray is one of those early risers who, like the others, is becoming ever more gravely concerned about the future.

From out of her second floor window Elaine can look across the tranquil, softly flowing, beautifully clear stream. In the sky, flocks of birds are hovering in circles above the river and the precipices. Some have just arrived for their single day's migratory stopover in the autumnally robed forests of the great Palisades during their nocturnal journey to the south lands.

In the distance the pale-faced bride, still recuperating from her fight against the fever, sees the last flickering lights of some of the Fort Washington campfires and the rising smoke of others preparing breakfasts for the garrison troops. But her thoughts are elsewhere.

Where is John? What was the accident that happened to Edmund? And why had not the courier brought a better explanation of the delay at Tappan?

Ever since she had heard that Edmund was to be one of the company sent under John to Sneden's, Elaine felt qualmish. She had good reason to, she believes, after what had taken place at the well-sweep.

And during the past three nights she had awakened twice from frightening dreams. Then, on Friday, she recalled having had a strange premoniton that something was wrong. Now, sure enough, the courier's message confirmed it. Everything that her mother and father had said in an effort to reassure her, fell on deaf ears.

Now, as she glances southward downstream, she sees through the rising mist over the river, the unmistakable outlines of two British men-of-war.[35] Their sails catching a light wind out of the east, the frigates are boldly ascending the Hudson. One hugs the east bank, the other the west.

Almost at that very moment the post's alarm bell rings out through the fortress compounds of the mountain above the Baummeister house. On the Bluff Rock The Barbette's southernly redoubt cannon barks out a loud earth-splitting blast. It cracks the air with a thunderous clash, waking every inhabitant for miles around with an alacrity early Sunday morning church bells never do.

Elaine is suddenly wide awake. Her mind pictures the furious activity, the stench of sweat in the heat and commotion of battle that is going on above her head. She knows the exhaustion that weighs upon the artillerymen carrying heavy loads of ammunition. She knows that harrowing feeling each man must face alone in the ever-present dance of death within the battery itself. And always there is the frightening accuracy of the enemy's marksmanship.

"At last, and at least for this one time," she tells herself, John is not there and in the center of it! Thank God!"

But her sympathy now goes out for Asher. She is aware of his hatred for war. It is even greater, she believes, than her husband's. John is more fired by The Cause than by the repulsiveness of war and the destruction of life. Yet she knows that in both men there is, innately buried, a hatred for violence and the resorting to arms for resolving man's problems. These thoughts now obsess her thinking.

She dresses hurriedly, focusing her mind on thoughts of youth in war. They include the British tars out there manning the approaching enemy ships. All have been brought, she has heard, from peaceful ways on farms, in businesses and from schools which have served them nought.

But Princeton College Still Calls Her Flock

"How long," she asks herself, fearing an answer, "will it be before all are returned home or at least those who live through it all? How long will it be before many of them are found lying crumbled and ——?"

She stops short of saying "dead"—the word that constantly strikes fear in her heart. Instead, she rapidly tightens the stays of her corset. In so doing she glances down on the desk and at her husband's papers and books. On top is a lately arrived notice from Prince Town, sent on to him by his father in Philadelphia.

Since it is open, Elaine knows John has seen it. Though he has not made any comment about it, she is certain he has read it over and over again. And so has she. Dated from "Princeton," and published in the *Pennsylvania Journal and Weekly Advertiser* on October 22, 1776, it reads:

> "The students of the College of New-Jersey, and all who intend to enter there this fall, are desired to take notice, that the vacation will be up and College Orders begin to take place on Monday, the 4th of November.
> "They are also desired to remember, that on Wednesday the 6th the Chambers will be fixed and assigned, so that those who do not appear that day will lose all claim from their former possession, unless they have leave of absence previously asked and obtained.
> "The grammar School will begin at the same time, where boys are taught the Languages, Writing and Arithmetic with the utmost care."[36]

Asher Levy has lived most of his life horrified at the thought civilized man must war with his fellow beings, and perplexed by his strong homicidal tendencies. He has lived repulsed by the thought of taking another's life. He has lived hating war as intently as he has abhorred the infringement of all men's birth rights and freedoms. And, paradoxically, these were the reasons why he entered the service and supported The Cause.

His convictions, he believed, were as strong as any staunch Quaker in this respect. And, Quaker-like, he had hoped to avoid direct participation in actual combat. But it had not worked out that way.

Now, in the sight of the approaching men-of-war, Levy's new perspective dominates his thinking. He sees the armed vessels as encroachers, trespassers, as attackers of his country's proper destiny. Instead of only cannon projecting out from below the ships' gunnels, instead of individual seaman, each with a God-given spark of life, a brain, a body all his own waiting for the next command, Levy sees them as evil configurations rising to destroy him.

All the debates and discussions over war, death, peace, pestilence, poverty and politics which Levy has had with Gray, rush in visional review before his mind. In summarizing all of those discussions, he remembers that there is always the same prevailing theme which both agree upon: a better world in a better tomorrow. Each of them firmly contends that in America's victory lies the hope of all mankind.

Now the frigates come within range. His gunners, silent and tense, await his command. Then suddenly his voice rings out. For the first time he is confident that his command to fire is unquestionably in behalf of a reach for peace. For the first time now he feels the order to rain down destruction from the great Bluff Rock upon the enemy below is for the sake of a world yet to come. For a world that he may never know. For a posterity and its generations upon generations yet unborn throughout perhaps many other lands that will never know of him.

For the first time he feels that he, the battery, the Continental Army is fighting for the obliteration of a present wherein hope no longer exists. It is a present wherein fear is far too prevalent to make existence longer endurable.

To Asher Levy, all at once, death, if it should come, seems honorable, almost a noble thing. For suddenly he feels that the end of earthly living should be invited if it will for certain assure that those unknown, unborn will find here a better life on earth tomorrow.

The forward of the two vessels, making its way upriver west of midstream, cuts sharply eastward as The Barbette's 32-pounder roars out, sending its shot a good 100 rods in front of the frigate's bow. Veering away from Bourdette's ferry dock and the death-dealing Barbette above it, the man-of-war glides closer to its sister ship heading up just to the east of midstream.

Men-of-War In A Perplexing Baulk

Earlier General Greene, now riding along the shore road and examining the batteries there, had given orders to all artillery officers on the post to fire at will. All inhabitants were ordered to evacuate the river-side area when the enemy craft were first sighted. Therefore immediately after Levy's artillery opened up the shore batteries joined in.

As though this were the pre-arranged signal, the Fort Washington southernmost redoubts on the eastern shore now bark out with resounding cracks that echo against the Palisadean walls like heavy claps of thunder.

The British ships, still well out of range, hold their fire and plow on. The Barbette and all redoubts steel themselves against the expected heavy barrage the British gunners will let loose immediately before attempting to crash through the Chevaux de Frise.

Then, to the surprise of all, the two square-riggers reef in their sails and drop anchor a good distance south of the ferry landing and well in the middle of the stream, a safe distance from all the American batteries and redoubts.[37]

General Greene at Fort Lee and Colonel Magaw, commanding at Fort Washington, are puzzled. Why did they not attempt to run the blockade? That was what most artillerymen on both sides the river were hoping for.

Instead the ships begin an exchange of fire with the annoying rebel batteries on their flanks. One broadside drops its ball into the fort field atop The Mountain. Several others pound the shore areas. One barely grazes Stephen Bourdette's chimney. And what few fires they start extinguish themselves owing to the wet terrain, still drenched from last night's soaking rains.

Soon, despite the distance, the heavy artillery from the two forts find their angles. One after another the shots strike closer and closer to the frigates' masts and spars.

Finally a ball from Levy's Barbette hulls the nearest vessel broadside as the ship swings around with the incoming tide bringing it exactly within range of The Barbette's cannoneers. The strike brings forth a tremendous roar from the excited observers on both sides of the river.

That proves to be enough for the British captain of the expedition. Both ships rapidly weigh anchor, come about with full sail and return downriver, majestically proud and virtually unscathed. But if the intention of the men-of-war was to sever the American communications across the river or destroy the Chevaux de Frise, the mission failed.

The sight of the King's ships repulsed brings a roaring cheer from the viewers along the river's shores. Soldiers and onlookers alike join in the hoorays.

Those inhabitants who were hurriedly cleared from the riverside before seven o'clock this morning,[38] followed the Baummeisters and the Bourdettes over the crest on the west side of the clove road. All sought a vantage place to watch what they were sure was to be an attempt to break through Colonel Putnam's new strongly reinforced Chevaux de Frise. The sight of the vessels' retreat downstream, while provoking their heartiest of yells was a disappointment.

By nine o'clock all the riverside people were back in their homes, readying themselves for Sunday church services. Owing to the unusually rapid cadence of the belfry bells, which had not ceased to sound throughout the cannonade, the inhabitants of The Mountain and its environs were aware of the Domine Dereck Remlin's anger at the "carrying on of war on the Sunday Sabbath."

One or two of the few biased among them were all for blaming that "Jewish lieutenant of Gray's Barbette for starting it."

"Who else, except the Howe brothers," they ask angrily, "would begin the shooting on a Sunday?"

With the "day of rest" recovering itself and the post gradually returning to order, Greene and his staff find themselves disagreeing as to what the Howes are up to. It appears certain to some that the ships' objective was to disrupt cross-river communications. Certainly their attempt to anchor off the ferry was very similar to their upriver sister ships' attempt to do the same thing off Dobbs Ferry last Thursday.

To others on Greene's staff the expedition this morning was a clever feint. Possibly the Howes were attempting to divert attention in preparation for something bigger.

Some are convinced that Black Dick will not risk running the blockade again. He surely knows that now, more so than on October 9, it would be suicide to risk an expensive armed vessel on such a perilous mission.

The admiral's ships, they argue, suffered severe damage before. And now Colonel Putnam has vowed they will not be able to get through again.

Still others rebut that argument, declaring the vessels can crash the blockade at will and that the admiral fears it not at all. The Howes, they contend, control the river and will strike when it pleases them.

General Howe would like to think that way but knows better than his enemy the extent of his brother's losses in the previous attempts to cut the river's communications. The Howe brother's respect for the blockade and its two guardian posts is probably much greater than is imagined by the Continental Army high command. Sir William has very wisely kept his losses and damages concealed, thus making his opponents resort to guesswork in their assessment of British-incurred costs.

In his report to Lord Germaine at the end of the coming month, Howe will write that General Knyphausen established himself on the "York side of King's Bridge, within cannon shot of Fort Washington, which was covered by very strong ground, and exceeding difficult of access . . ."

Then, in an explanation of his further strategy, he will add a backhanded compliment to the Chevaux de Frise which the American Commander-in-Chief and his staff will never know about. Howe will say:

> ". . . but the importance of this post (Fort Washington), which with Fort-Lee on the opposite shore of Jersey, kept the enemy in command of the navigation of the North River, while it barred the communication with York by land, made the possession of it (Fort Washington) absolutely necessary . . ."[39]

It is clear only to Sir William Howe that Fort Washington now must be taken and its threat to British control of Hudson's river and all of Manhattan's island be ended. It is clear only to Sir William that his hope for an early end to the rebellion depends upon forcing his elusive enemy to stand ground and fight to the death in an open field battle before winter closes in.

The Continental Army Chief's misinformation regarding the blockade and its defenders' successes was made clear in his letter to Governor Trumbull of October 9, the day of the enemy piercing of the Chevaux de Frise.

In that communication The General wrote the Connecticut governor that the British ships had passed up the North River "without meeting any interruption from the chevaux-de-frise, or receiving any material damage from our batteries."[40]

And on the same day Tilghman, writing at The General's direction to the New York Committee of Safety in the same vein, said:

> ". . . but to our surprise and mortification, they (the British ships on October 9th) all came through without the least difficulty and without receiving any apparent damage from our forts . . ."[41]

These erroneous assessments, largely attributable to Howe's clever concealment of his damages, circulated through the States and their representatives in little time, accounting for such communications as Ellery's "wandering," mishandled letter to Governor Cooke of October 11.[42] His "disappointment" was soon passed on to others in an unfounded wave of pessimism and disenchantment with the twin forts and their blockade.

Consequently it is no wonder that the army staff officers on the heights of Fort Lee are very much bewildered this Sunday afternoon. All have their own opinions. And most are split in their conjectures as to what exactly are General Howe's and his brother's objectives on Hudson's river.

Does Sir William intend to make a direct attack upon the American forces, daily augmenting in number above the White Plains? Or will he drive a wedge between the lines, along with a thrust through King's Bridge and unite with Brother Richard's ships which are now impatiently riding at anchor off Tarrytown?

A slice through Westchester, isolating the American troops in White Plains and cutting off their communications with King's Bridge and Fort Washington, could scatter the rebel left. For that wing is strung out in disunited detachments along the west bank of the Bronx River all the way to the White Plains encampments.

Splitting the Continental Army in two, such a maneuver would enable Howe to leave the clean-up task to the Hessian regiments and Rogers' Rangers while the British commander led the bulk of his troops across the Hudson and into Jersey.

Then, cutting off Fort Lee, he could drive down into Philadelphia and there capture the Continental Congress. It is an elaborate but plausible possibility.

Once both Fort Washington and Fort Lee were surrounded and besieged, it would only be a matter of time before they would be

starved out and forced to surrender. This would leave a clear path
open for the British garrisons on Manhattan and in Westchester to
unite with Sir Guy Carleton's divisions, presently opposing Gates'
Northern Department at Ticonderoga above Albany.

New England would be severed from its communications with
the central and southern states. The backbone of the American
Rebellion would be broken.

These are the thoughts and fears that beset the American high
command and the staff officers on Fort Lee Bluff this afternoon.
But many questions are left still unanswered by the puzzled
Continental officers.

Were the Dobbs Ferry and Bourdette's Ferry incidents actually
bonafide attempts to sever communications in advance of a
planned crossing by General Howe? Were they purely feints? Were
they intended to distract, confuse or cover up some other enterprise? Or could they have been nothing more than probes to test
the river defenses?

But now, with few surprise packages left in his bag of tricks,
what will be the British commander-in-chief's next move?

The sad lack of sound military intelligence in both opposing
camps leaves the American command operating under the false
assumption that the British have control of the Hudson and its
navigation. It leaves the King's forces operating under the
erroneous belief that the Americans know they have control of the
river.

Previously there were few Continental command officers who
doubted that Howe had planned to cut through the American left
and center and invade New Jersey. All agree now that, after the
Throg's Neck fiasco, he completely lost the surprise advantage that
had been on his side and was forced to revise his plan.

So, many feel that he may make a feint at crossing through
Westchester and instead force an engagement at the White Plains.
And in this conjecture they are correct.

Chess With Breathing Men

Sir William is certain that in a field fight he can destroy the
rebel army and bring the New York Campaign to an end. If not
that, he is certain that he can scatter the culprits and close the
jaws of his machine around Fort Washington. That will give him
all of New York's Manhattan Island, an important immediate
goal.

Overlaid on British Sauthier-Faden Map are shown the movements of the
opposing armies toward the White Plains. Americans on left, or west, moving
out of Harlem Heights and British on right, or east, moving out of New
Rochelle.

And, of most importance, it will end the menacing control which the two forts in conjunction with one another, have over him and his brother's shipping. Howe knows that Fort Lee alone is a powerless guardian of the river and without Fort Washington, a useless post for the Continentals, except from the standpoint of an observatory.

Many think the rebel forces are close to the end of their rope. Looking through their field glasses at the White Plains and the American encampments, not a few of the British and Hessian officers believe they see in tomorrow the final battle of the war.

If not tomorrow, soon, for the end should not be far away. And what better Christmas gift could the King's men give the Crown than a return of the colonies to Mother England?

Therefore General Howe and his staff tonight prepare for the total destruction of the American army and the wresting away of control over Hudson's river. So it is now that the minds of two men are closely pitted one against the other. Both of them have suffered setbacks which sting with the gnawing frustrations of defeat.

It is like a colossal chess game with living, breathing men obediently performing in the awesome, ancient contest that decides the ideologies under which nations and their peoples are to exist and be ruled.

But always out of each setback arises an ever greater desire to resist and to conquer. For the mind of civilized man is strangely endowed with determination born of defeat. So it is with the two military minds which now must carry out the determinations of their rulers and their peoples.

Thus, in the massive game of nations, it is of minor consequence that Gray and his battery of tired men and one injured corporal move slowly through the outpost guards up into the fort's grounds at twilight this Sunday night. Their mission has been accomplished. That is all, except that Corporal Kearney, moaning loudly, is rushed to the hospital compound. Shortly after, Elaine brushes past her husband and into the tent to help care for the youth's wound.

Angry and annoyed, Jocko turns upon his favorite officer, scoldingly asking, "Ain' cha gonna tells 'er, Lootenan?"

Gray replies sharply, "No, Jocko! and neither shall you! Hear?"

The black boy clenches his teeth, shakes his head and walks away.

So it is that this last Sunday in October slowly sinks away. As peacefully as it came up, it quietly and beautifully fades into the reddened west's closing night on the horizon beyond The Mountain.

Soon it will sail off into oblivion, relinquishing its hold to the starlit heavens and they in turn to the dawning sun of October 28, 1776.

And all along the eastern shores of the new world, especially on the white plains of Westchester, it will only appear to be a peaceful day.

21

Monday, October 28. . .

Battle of the White Plains: Operation One

Howe's Well Planned Step Toward Victory

Like a hatchet cutting a towline in two, the British command can envision the slicing of the Hudson when both army and naval forces will sever the colonies and their north-to-south communications. First must come a major confrontation with the rebels' forces entrenched at White Plains.

Having briefed his officers last night for the attack he will launch this morning, General Howe emphasizes the absolute necessity of bringing the Americans out in the open. This he sees as the initial step preceding a crossing of the river. And the crossing of the river and its control he sees as the necessary step preceding a linking with Carleton's army moving down from Canada. And that is dependent upon Carleton's certain success in breaking the back of General Gates' obstinate rebels defending Ticonderoga.

A junction with General Sir Guy Carleton's army, slicing the American lines straight through Hudson's river, will isolate New England from New York and the south. But command of the river requires he destroy the rebel army now waiting entrenched before him.

His plan in Westchester is to cut off the Americans' two principal routes leading into New England by land. One road goes through Rye, the other is by way of Bedford. Both funnel through the White Plains making that quiet little village a crucial area in the chess game.

Before dawn the main Juggernaut began moving out of its encampment nine miles north of New Rochelle in two columns. The left column is under the command of General Philip von Heister, and the main, or right column, is headed by Lieutenant General Henry Clinton.

It is planned that the enemy's advance parties are to be driven back behind their works by the British light infantry and chasseurs, once the army has been formed with its right on the Mamaroneck-White Plains road about a mile in front of the rebels' center. The left will be extended along the "Brunx" River, placing this end of the redcoats' line about a mile from the forward American entrenchments which have been thrown up north and northwestward on the other side of the plains.[1]

Before the marching King's men the Whig families flee, more in fear of what the emboldened Tory inhabitants will do to them than from fear of the enemy troops. Unprotected they scurry away, carrying whatever few possessions they can take along with them.

While the main force of the Crown's men will strike at White Plains, the Hessian division under Lieutenant General Wilhelm von Knyphausen, which has lain behind the British Juggernaut at New Rochelle since last Tuesday, the 22nd, will become the giant left arm of the entire movement. It will swing off westward across Westchester and act as a principal diversionary movement.

Knyphausen and his six battalions of Hessians are already on the move. Headed for King's Bridge they are sweeping back the American outposts before them.

The Hessian commander has left one regiment of Waldecks behind in New Rochelle. They will temporarily hold the New Rochelle post and will follow Knyphausen on a more northerly route November 4.[2]

Westchester inhabitants and militia have expected Howe's army would make for the Hudson. And those around the King's Bridge area believe the brass-bedecked high-hats with their shining belt-buckles and sparkling bayonets pointing high in the air, are surely the belated main push of the Juggernaut on its way to the North River.

Knyphausen's troops will drive westward through the rebel posts at Miles Square and Valentine's Hill, scattering the detachments and terrifying the populace. As expected, their diversionary action will look like the real thing, the main stampede.

Its alarming news will spread like reverberating echoes along the river's banks from Philipsburg to Jeffery's Hook and from Orange Town to Schraalenburgh. It will spread alarms and rumors, upsetting Whigs, bolstering Tory morale and cheering the seamen on the King's ships in the Hudson.

It is Knyphausen's purpose to force the Americans holding the heights of Fordham back south under the protection of Fort Washington. And within four days the Hessian commander will have cut through the weakly held and widely scattered detached camps along the Bronx River.

They will have dispersed the thin rear guard line of rebel troops, chasing them either back into Fort Washington, or north toward the American corps in the White Plains. By November 2, General Knyphausen will be encamped on Fordham's high grounds north of King's Bridge. But the post will have then been almost totally destroyed by the evacuated troops.[3]

On this chilly fall morning the Continental Army staff officers are sure Sir William's long rest has ended. It is 15 days since the British commander landed at Throg's Neck. It is nine days since the affray at Pell's Point.

Everyone seems convinced that Howe and his brother no longer believe reconciliation with the colonies is possible without further bloodshed. Many are sure that both are ready to jump again before winter. But until this morning no one in the American camp was certain where and when.

One Recourse Left For the Rebel Chief

Flexibility of movement, in the opinion of the American Commander, is the only strategy left open to the weak, out-numbered and ill equipped Continental Army in face of the enemy's superiority. Therefore The General knows that to avoid the crushing power of the Lion's jaws upon the American cause there is only one recourse. He must entice the enemy into combat and then adroitly pull back until their supply lines are over-extended, and vulnerable to small, hit and run attacks. This will necessitate retreats, and unfortunately the people clamor for offensive tactics and victories, not retreats.

Poring over his maps at his White Plains headquarters behind the American lines just south of the heights of North Castle, the Continental Army Commander with his staff officers last night took stock of his untenable situation. Meanwhile his main divisions continue arriving from below—a steady stream flowing out of Manhattan and Fordham, safely along the west bank of the Bronx River.

Behind him lies the district of North Castle and the Croton River. To the west the Hudson River and the Haverstraw Bay spread out beyond his right flank. From his present position he could pull back east into Connecticut, or he could—as a last resort—draw back into the distant, western wilderness. There he could always regroup and strike at the heels of his enemy's long, over-extended lines, worrying him if nothing else.

Far upriver the Northern Department under Gates could still make a link with the New York-New Jersey rebel defenders along the upper Hudson if necessary. For Gates' army is still standing up under Sir Guy Carleton's poundings.

General Arnold, the mainstay of that department, is to be thanked for that. His intrepid stand and naval action on October 11, 12 and 13, though considered a British victory will in the long run prove to be a British setback of dire military consequences.

Although Arnold's little fleet of row-galleys, gondolas and small sloops was, after great difficulty by Carleton's forces, utterly defeated, the delay operation caused the British command to forego an attack on Fort Ticonderoga.

For Carleton this will become a regrettable victory since he used up valuable time building a fleet to meet Arnold's threat. And, following his victory, the British officer disastrously postponed his follow-through attack on Ticonderoga.

The gallantry of General Arnold and his men ultimately will bring about what some will call "the greatest American victories in the war."[4] They will be credited to the desperate fight of Arnold's command and to the closely connected sequence of events which will follow. But the Northern Department is far distant from New York and the contest in the Hudson's valleys.

So the American Commander and his staff cannot count on the Northern Department's aid in Westchester, and they entertain no high expectations of defeating the King's powerful Juggernaut on the White Plains. However, the new American states must be assured that their defenses are resisting and fighting for their preservation. This is part of the Continental Army's obligation.

Nevertheless, The General has no intention of further pleasing General Howe by parading his small army before The Empire's mighty lion in the open field as he erroneously did on Long Island.

Throughout the past week the Continental Army's strategy has been to march parallel with the invading forces as they advanced out of Pell's Point. This was so until this morning when the redcoats split their forces, one branching left toward the King's Bridge, the other right toward White Plains. The Americans have moved northward on a line with their enemy but protected by the Bronx River whose west bank provides a natural barrier.

As the Americans have proceeded toward their main position at the White Plains, they have constructed a series of entrenchments along the little river's embankments in the course of their advance. Though a source of annoyance to the British, these works have protected the long lines of rebel wagons, artillery and supply trains moving into White Plains up from the lower garrisons at Harlem Heights, Fort Washington and King's Bridge.

The word "plains" in "White Plains" is misleading, except to the natives. The very word is a source for much amusement among the American troops as they find themselves clambering up cluster after cluster of rugged little hills in the so-called "white plains"—in a land where they had expected to find *white plains*.

So, to the Continentals, the name, "White Plains," is a misnomer as they struggle up and down the slopes and dig their entrenching tools hard and noisily into the deep sub-surface volcanic rocks, which have been lying undisturbed since they were hurled there several billion years ago. And there they now give comfort to the rebels and await the enemy.

The glacial boulders and rocks of all sizes, kinds and shapes—the deposits of the prehistoric Pleistocene Epoch—and their own hard digging make the Continental soldiers' task a difficult one. But, for their enemy the resulting defensive walls present formidably repelling obstacles.

Looking south eastward from the crest of these hills, which roughly form a kind of concave semi-circle around the little village, can be seen early almost every morning a white mist. It rises over the marshy flatlands at the base of the hills. To observers on the summits it is as though one were looking down from the rim of a half-section of a giant cup and into the bowl of that cup spread outward and southward before them.

Like a long irregular fissure in the base of the bowl, is the Bronx River. Appearing like a twisting crack in the cup's base, it flows down from the north and south through the flat bottom-lands, a winding, ever-bending waterway. It is a natural defense barrier for the American defenders.

Actually the early morning mist over the village on the "plains," or lowland, is nothing more than the haze from the river rising into the warmth of the morning sun. In that almost daily occurrence there always rises first out and up from the ghostlike mist the spire of the village church. It appears each morning like a specter on a tranquil sea.

The early Indian inhabitants called the lowlands, "Quaroppas," meaning "big white marshes." The settlers adopted the idea and named the site "White Plains." Its vast boggy grounds and swamps, half circled by its hills and interlaced by the circuitous river flowing along their base, now make the site an exceptionally good one for defensive tactics. And the American Chief knows it.

If he must meet Howe in battle—and he knows that he must—this is the ideal place. And he and his Continentals here intend to make the best of it.

Lord Stirling's corps was the first to arrive in the Continental Army's move into White Plains. That was 9 A.M. the 21st, exactly a week ago.

Stirling's men immediately began occupying the several hills which form the semi-circle northeast of the village. Here they began constructing a line of fortifications at strategic points along the Bronx River's west bank.

Today Church Bells and Drums

So now from the steeple, lifting up above the white mist, the customary pealing tones of the tolling church bells strike out their awakening notes to the frightened villagers. Today none are secure, peaceful and quietly content as once they were with the world around them.

Today all tremble excepting the Loyalists among the inhabitants. For on the outskirts the vanguard of the British Juggernaut is approaching. The redcoats step briskly to the sound of fife, bag-pipe and the steady, ominous rolling of the drums.

What General Howe and his staff officers see as they arrive on the outskirts of White Plains village is not to their liking.

As they look northeastward from the southern edge of the town, the King's men, arriving on the York Road from New Rochelle and Scarsdale, see before them a half-circle ring of hills, instead of "plains."

Almost directly northeast and at the center is Purdy's Hill. At its base is the Jacob Purdy house and its adjoining 132 acres of rich farmland. It roughly makes up the northern limits of the little village. The Purdy house is the American Commander-in-Chief's temporary headquarters.

Looking to the southwest of Purdy's Hill, the redcoat observers see the American defenders entrenched on Chatterton Hill. It rises up out of the west bank of the Bronx River. On its serpentine course south from its origin in the distant upper highlands, the river separates Purdy's Hill from Chatterton.

The British officers know that their every movement can be observed from the heights of Chatterton. Clearly visible, therefore, to the Americans, the Crown's troops emerge from the forest road into the heart of the lowlands. The rugged terrain appearing before the British soldiers' eyes does not present the vista they had hoped to see.

From their vantage point—a hillock at the southern end of the village on the Post Road—the British command officers can see another hill called Travis, lying north of Chatterton and rising up on the west side of the river.

All of this becomes clear and more easily distinguishable as the mist ascends and dissipates with the rising sun.

Now the British officers can make out Michael Chatterton's house on the river's west bank at the northeastern base of the hill. It stands at the intersection of the east-to-west road to the Hudson at Dobbs Ferry, a winding six miles away. The Dobbs Ferry highway eastward passes through the village of White Plains. And there it veers northeast to Bedford in Connecticut, thus connecting New England with New York and the south. Consequently the highway is a vital communications artery linking the states.

Called the Bedford Road after passing through White Plains, the highway winds between two other hills on its way to New England. Those are Merritt on the south side of the road and Hatfield Hill on the roadway's north rise.

Both these "little mountains" are on the northern outskirts of the village. Between them lies Horton's Pond. At its southern end is Horton's gristmill on the immediate outskirts of the village.

Beyond Lie the Hills Of North Castle

These two hills, Merritt and Hatfield on the south and north sides of the Bedford-bound road, will become the Continental

Army's extreme and flexible left flank. They will eventually enable the wing to back up and if necessary withdraw to a more distant cluster of hills to the northwest. These farthest rises are known as the North Castle hills since they lie in that hamlet.

Therefore the American General has his escape hatch planned in advance. For North Castle will be the army's last line of defense and a good one. But after that, if the chase continues, must come a withdrawal beyond the upper Croton River and across the Hudson.

The hills of North Castle lie north, or behind, Purdy's Hill at the far northern outskirts of White Plains village. There is one that looms up in the middle of the main road out of White Plains which sits in command of the road. It is a natural fortress-like rocky and precipitous hill rising up from a cove on its western side. In that cove, under the hill, is the home of the late Elijah Miller. Consequently the hill bears his name.

The top of Miller's Hill not only commands the road below but the road into North Castle from White Plains' northern end and the valley to the west. Up and out of that little vale rises the previously mentioned Travis Hill, lying on the opposite side of the Bronx River. To attack Miller's Hill frontally would be nothing less than suicide. Its front is a high vertical wall of rock.

To the east of Miller's Hill is Mount Misery, a formidable monolith which, like a guardian tower, stands in command of the secondary roads leading northward out of White Plains.

Just to the east of Mount Misery on the other side of the passes, lies Fisher Hill. It is clearly visible from Miller and is located about midway between Misery and Hatfield, the extreme American left flank.

Fisher Hill's great value lies in the protective cover it affords against any attacker attempting an assault on either Miller or Mount Misery. That protective cover for the defenders comprises tons of mammoth boulders strewn all over Fisher Hill which make an assault upon its defenses—which defenses in turn protect the Miller and Misery works—almost out of the question.

These then are the hills—a far cry from what both rebels and redcoats expect from the white "plains"—which the British command sees and which the American command have occupied. And these are the hills from out of which the American Commander-in-Chief has planned and formed his primary and secondary defenses.

And now as the church bells softly fade into stillness and the

British drums quietly roll into silence, General Howe lifts his field glasses and begins to assess the difficult situation his enemy has enticed him to taste. Before him lie a cluster of damnable hills. "Howe's Hell Hills" is the way one well-entrenched Yankee soldier calls them in a passing remark to a friend.

The British commander-in-chief prefers open battlefield fighting. In fact, not a few of his own men had half-way believed that the aspect of a battle on the plains—exactly to Sir William's taste—was what had been so inviting about meeting the rebels at and on the White Plains, or at least it was a possible enticement in addition to the village's critical position on the ancient crossroads.

Sir William is known to be a cautious planner. So some wonder if he blundered nine days ago in not sending "his light infantry, grenadiers, and jagers, 4,000 strong across by the straight road to Kingsbridge, only six miles away, in a swift attack upon the long, straggling" American line.[5]

It was then that he could have struck confusion in the rebels' movement. Instead he had lain three days at New Rochelle, his original plan ruined. And then he next moved only three miles to Mamaroneck. There he remained inactive for four more days. To some, Howe's reluctance to pursue his foe more vigorously arouses suspicions.

Does he indeed seek a victory on the battlefield? Or are Sir William and Lord Richard—both originally designated as missioners of peace—still striving for reconciliation with the colonies?

Certainly—as some see it—the "General and the Admiral" have not displayed an energetic propensity for carrying through their successes. This has given many the impression that the Howes do not want to "whip" the colonists into submission if there is the barest possibility they can make peace.

This morning's arrival at White Plains represents a British advance of seventeen miles in ten days. Not a very remarkable achievement for a military commander bent upon destroying his foe!

To the casual observer, Howe's well-planned flanking stratagem was bungled by a rebel-destroyed bridge. And that has since provided some spicy tea-time conversations.

From his headquarters at Purdy's Hill, the American Commander on Old Magnolia watches behind the center of the Continental Army's lines while the enemy corps arrives in the distance. As he faces south, he sees General Putnam's right wing, which stands ready and well-entrenched, extending westward over the Bronx

River bridge and along the stream's west bank on the opposite side. Old Put's lines reach up into a commanding position on the 180-foot high crest defenses of Chatterton's Hill.

As the General looks to the east he observes General Heath's left wing extending out eastward from the center line and along the Bedford Road to Connecticut. Heath's wing swerves somewhat northeastward to the Hatfield Hill. This line from Chatterton to Hatfield through Purdy's Hill comprises the Americans' primary defense works.

Behind the primary line, a secondary defense system, still under construction, provides the Continentals with a strong back-up protection. This secondary system makes excellent use of Travis Hill on the west, protecting Putnam; and Miller's Hill, Mount Misery and Fisher Hill on the east and northeast, protecting Heath.

Hatfield Hill commands the west side of the vital Bedford highway leading to Connecticut. Just south of it on the east side of the Connecticut road is the other lofty highway guardian, Merritt Hill where Heath has stationed his extreme left arm outpost.

So the "damned hills," as some redcoats call them, are not inviting to the Crown's men. Into them the ever-elusive foe can all too easily disperse and disappear.

This was proven early this morning with the British van's first clash with some American pickets. In that brush the rebels gave the precision-marching Hessian regiment a sampling of the rebels' new strike, disperse and disappear tactics.

It occurred when the British army's two Hessian and British columns approached along the Post Road from Scarsdale. General Heister was on the left, Clinton's column on the right. Suddenly, about two miles south of the rebels' primary defense lines, Heister's Hessians stopped short, surprised by an ambush pouring a heavy fusillade down upon them from behind stone walls. The Hessians panicked and broke.

The Opening Skirmish

The fusillade was from General Joseph Spencer's six regiments, a part of Charles Lee's division. About 1,500 strong, the rebel contingent was sent out to meet and harass the approaching enemy.[6] Waiting in ambush until the Hessian vanguard was within 100 feet of them, the Continentals rose up suddenly from behind a fieldstone wall and let go a devastating volley into the fierce looking grenadiers, scattering them in all directions.[7]

Heister quickly ordered Colonel Rall and his Hessian regiment up from the rear to disperse the attackers while the panicked troops were reorganizing. Then just as Rall was about to turn the rebels' left, the wily Spencer adroitly pulled back behind a second wall.

Again Rall came on through a fierce exchange of fire, and again the American battalion under Major Austin in the forward position, withdrew behind still a third stone wall. There Spencer and Austin carried on a heated fight, holding their posts until Rall had almost outflanked them.

The Hessian colonel summoned reinforcements which Spencer quickly realized would be too much to face. Ordering his troops to retreat cautiously to the west bank of the Bronx River, Spencer ended the skirmish, withdrawing his regiment into Chatterton's Hill and safely behind the breastworks under construction by Colonel Rufus Putnam and his engineers.[8]

The ambush slowed the British lines but cost the Americans 12 lives. Twenty-three wounded were taken from the field and two are reported missing. It is estimated that the enemy casualties are much greater, but since they are Hessian mercenaries, Howe may not mention the brush or his losses for some time.

However now the British high command knows it must prepare for Indian warfare, for tactics at which they are not adept.

The action has brought both of Howe's columns to a dead halt. Reorganizing and regrouping is still going on. It has left the British commander far more concerned abut the nature of the terrain and the formidable positions which the so-called "tatterdemalion"[9] army has established than before. He had not expected this type of greeting.

Young Abe Onderdonk has over-extended his furlough but not entirely of his own accord. No one knew two weeks ago that his unit would be in White Plains today. The difficulty of getting through the tightened security of the lines around Dobbs Ferry, the frightened and suspicious attitude of the inhabitants—Whigs, Tories and neutrals, all of whom hesitate to give any stranger a wagon ride—and his unexpectedly long stay with the Hart family at Hart's corners, have contributed to his delay.

The Harts are his mother's old friends. And Mother Onderdonk made her son promise he would go by and at least spend one night. He had spent two. In return for his lodging and food, the young soldier helped with the countless chores.

Also of great attraction was their 17-year-old granddaughter,

Etiennee Lassalle. When Etiennee's mother died her distraught father, a Canadian-born Huguenot, joined the Northern Department's army and left his daughter in the care of her grandparents, storekeepers at Hart's Corners.

News that the British were on the move reached Onderdonk's ears from a highway traveler just as he was thinking of the pretty Etiennee Lassalle back at the Hart's. In fact, since leaving there, he had thought of little else until he found himself cutting across fields and through farmers' lands on his hurried way along backwoods short-cut trails southwest of Chatterton Hill toward the Bronx River road.

In the distance the youth heard the exchange of fire, not knowing it was Spencer's troops skirmishing with Heister up on the Scarsdale road.

He could see nothing but was told the redcoats were advancing through Scarsdale headed for the White Plains village. The conscientious Onderdonk had hoped by noon to rejoin his unit under Captain Jim Smith in General Heath's division, posted far to the east on the other side of the village. He wished now they were closer on Chatterton Hill.

With his knapsack heavy on his back but not burdened by any arms, Onderdonk sprints for awhile and then slows down to a rapid walk. His main concern is to reach his unit before he runs into an enemy picket.

Like others in his company, the Orange County private has heard stories of the ferocious-looking Hessians and their total indifference to bayoneting to death any Yankee who runs across their path. So there is something terrifying in the knowledge that these horrible, war-hungry "monsters" are likely to jump up before him at any moment. He would much prefer that when that moment comes, he is in or near an American encampment and not alone on some remote short-cut off the highway.

The spic and span, carefully laundered uniform that Mother Onderdonk made for him and meticulously brushed off before he left home, is now soiled and dust-covered. He is in need of a good washdown.

The strong October sun indicating it is still long before noon, a beckoning sparkling pool of the Bronx River, the silencing of the distant guns and the proximity of his position to the American lines on Chatterton Hill, induce him to stop and clean himself up.

It is not unusual to find soldiers, travelers and villagers washing and filling buckets at the stream's edge. But now no one is anywhere around. The youth feels sure that he can take a quick ducking, cold though the water is, clean up his uniform for his mother' sake and make a better appearance when he ascends Chatterton and reports to the nearest post. The bend here in the river, a safe distance from the military's sentinels which lie yet well ahead, seems the ideal place to pause.

Private Abe undresses rapidly. He places each garment over the thick bushes after first shaking it out vigorously. Last off are the heavy woolens his mother had made for him. Now naked, he draws from his knapsack his precious bar of lye soap, one of many he made for his mother in the peace and quiet of Tappan Town last spring.

At this moment he is surprised to see another youth even younger than he but just as naked making his way down the river's bank directly opposite him on the east side of the stream. Each one of them is startled as their eyes meet.

Their wide-eyed alarm at the strange unexpected sight of another foolhardy early morning bather leaves each of them quickly when they simultaneously burst out laughing and swiftly dunk themselves in the waist-deep pool of the gushing river. It is too cold to talk or ask questions. Both want but one thing, to get in and get out fast.

Onderdonk, after soaping himself, passes the heavy bar over to his bathing companion who makes use of it in the same way. Only "O-o-o's" and lip-quivering "Ah-ah-ah's" can be heard rising up above the river's noisy rock-splashing dash over the short falls below the pool. The sun on its way to the hour before noon streaks down through the trees playing upon the shivering young men.

Both duck under the water once and then each starts toward his own shore and embankment, but suddenly Onderdonk is stopped by a tap on his shoulder from behind. The blond-haired youth from the east bank hands Onderdonk back his soap and with a broad smile breaking out across his teeth-clicking mouth, he profusely repeats, "Danke! Danke! Danke!"

Then tapping Onderdonk appreciatively on the shoulder, the youth darts with an exceptional burst of speed out of the water and up the bank. Onderdonk makes the same speed in the opposite direction.

The expression, "Danke!" makes no impression on the American militiaman who is of Dutch ancestry. It is not uncommon in the Dutch and Huguenot valleys to hear French, German and Dutch sprinkled in with English and vice versa.

But when the blond boy turns midway up the east bank and smilingly shouts a happy, "Auf Wiedersehn!" the pleasant, ever-congenial rebel private wonders if the fellow he bathed with is really another young Dutch descendant like himself. He has known many a lad like the blond youth in the farmlands around Tappan Town. But what is it about him that is less Dutch than his own neighbors back home?

Surely, Onderdonk muses, he cannot be but a youngster. His chest was virtually hairless. Then there was that paucity of puberty hair around his genitals. And that ludicrous attempt to grow a mustache! Certainly the boy cannot be more than 16 years old!

Onderdonk is puzzled and curious. As he dresses he keeps his eyes glued on the youth dressing on the opposite bank. It is difficult to make out the garments piled on the grounds but there definitely he sees a soldier's knapsack. Could it be the young boy is a soldier?

Onderdonk doubts that. He watches intently as the fellow dresses himself.

The woolens are somewhat like his own. Now he pulls on a pair of flaming red breeches. Then the American private observes his river-bathing friend draw up a pair of black, high-heeled boots. This causes Onderdonk to wonder if it were possible that he, Private Abraham Onderdonk of the Militia, had been bathing with an enemy soldier, possibly a fifer or a drummer.

Now it seems the youth, much to the American soldier's astonishment, rises up over six feet high after having rubbed off the dust of his boots, revealing a brilliantly polished shine. Naked in the pool, Onderdonk had judged the youth was several inches shorter than he. And he is five feet ten.

More entranced than worried, the rebel militiaman watches attire make a man. For the tall figure now puts on his black, knee-high gaiters and then carefully takes up a queue of artificial hair, pasted with flour. Gently he places it just so on his head, allowing the braid to hang down his back. It gives an added touch of respect, if not an air of maturity and fearlessness to his rapidly growing stature.

When the youth, who Onderdonk now is certain is a Hessian mercenary—though he can hardly believe it—lifts the blue coat from the ground and proudly puts it on, fastening a series of shining brass buttons down the front, Onderdonk gulps in amazement. On his belt the boy soldier attaches a brass-hilted sword and scabbard.

Finally, from a nearby bush he removes the towering Hessian hat which now almost completes the transformation of a farmer-like youngster into a fearsome looking warrior who could well enact the role of an ogre.

Completing the ensemble, except for knapsack, water and rum canteens around the waist, is his very long weighty musket to which is affixed a lengthy heavy bayonet.

And so there in the distance before his eyes Onderdonk sees at last, his first real live breathing Hessian soldier.

In time, "Danke," as Abe Onderdonk has decided to name him, will be able to grow a curled mustache which he will blacken to add to his "ferocity," thus emulating his older comrades.

Invisible to the soldier on the opposite bank, Onderdonk watches as the mercenary from Hesse-Hanau strides off to rejoin his outfit, rejoicing that he got a refreshing bath without getting caught by the American rebels who, he has been told, "eat the prisoners they catch."

"So that," the rebel private thinks to himself, "is the frightening Hessian I have heard so much about!"

Then, looking at his own plain, dirty uniform and his dusty surcoat of much lighter weight than the Hessian's, he makes his way toward the distant American post near the foot of Chatterton's Hill.

He meets no difficulty as he passes through the guards and reaches the vicinity where Spencer's troops withdrew from their skirmish with Heister's men earlier this morning. A few of the wounded are still there, lying in agony and waiting patiently with their more fortunate comrades for assistance northward to the hospital tent behind the lines.

For the first time in his life the farm youth from Tappan town sees the battlefield's wounded, dead and dying. In the distance he can see Colonel Rall's Hessians regrouping as they retire to the British lines, stationed on the Post Road high ground south of the White Plains village with its towering church spire.

For the first time in his life Abe Onderdonk is seeing war. But now he sadly sees it from the banks of a river's sparkling pool bathed in nature's laughter and morning's golden sunlight.

He concludes that the participants on battlefields are really not at all what they seem to be in the eyes of those who are commanded to destroy them, or be destroyed by them.

As the militiaman ambles up the busy Chatterton Hill to the post's summit headquarters he glances back and down at the scene below. Masses of enemy troops such as he has never seen before are forming in battle array.

He wonders where in that multitude of men, guns and heavy armament being dragged up to the front of the British lines is that golden-haired boy with whom he bathed, so free, naked and jovially this morning. Where within that awesome horde of men, horses, sabers, rifles, milling around in various formation does his friend "Danke" now stand six feet tall? Far into the rear the lines of troops extend, melding into the baggage and supply trains.

While dodging out of the way of the passing men in and out of their companies, horses and wagons with supplies and ammunition and gun carriages being steadied in their positions, the furlough-ending soldier is entranced by the activity of his own army's busy troops around him.

Who will ever believe his story about the Hessian soldier this morning?

Onderdonk decides it best not to tell anyone, at least not for the time being. One thing he knows is certain and that is that "Danke" surely destroyed his fierce image of the Hessian soldier.

"And another thing," he jestingly tells himself, "Both armies have two clean infantrymen. That should please all the chiefs of staff!"

Private Onderdonk has had cleanliness drilled into him, not only by the militia officers of the army but also from the cradle by his Dutch forebears. Therefore a discarded copy of the General Orders for last Thursday, dated "Head-Quarters, White Plains, October 24, 1776," which he picks up from the ground gives him a chuckle as he ascends the trail up Chatterton's slope. It reads:

> "Commanding officers of regiments are immediately to have necessaries dug, decently covered, at a small distance from their encampments. They are every day to be covered over with fresh earth, and once a week to be filled up and new ones dug.
> "All bones, meat and other dirt of the camp, to be carefully gathered up every day . . . If officers would reflect how much cleanliness would conduce to their own health, and that of their men, they would want no inducement to attend to it particularly."[10]

Onderdonk simultaneously walking and devouring every word on the scribbled, mud-spattered piece of paper, makes his way gingerly through the orderly moving platoons of men.

Shouting commands fill the air as squads of riflemen break off and take their prearranged places in the newly constructed entrenchments along Chatterton's crests.

In and around the numerous companies of troops getting last-minute firing instructions from infantry and artillery officers and jumping over hastily thrown up barriers, Onderdonk plods on. At the same time he tries to read the last few sentences of the wet, soiled orders.

That last sentence worries him:

"... Any man who is found half a mile from the camp, not on command, will be punished very severely."

The militiaman compliments himself on his good fortune so far, but he has his pass through the lines that Captain Smith gave him over two weeks ago. He now double-checks it to make sure.

Realizing that it would be inadvisable to report to the Chatterton Hill headquarters in view of the excitement that now grips the hill, the Orange County rifleman decides instead to go on through. He will make his way down the north side of the hill, cross the river and head for Heath's division northeast of the town.

In all his nineteen and one half years, the Tappan town farmer's son has never seen so much human activity. The nearest to it was up at the Jersey mountain post earlier in the month. Here now there is an awesomeness in the excitement and tension of running, sweating men, of neighing, whinnying horses straining under wagon loads of heavy ammunition and of angry reprimands and commands ringing through the forest-clad summits of Chatterton Hill.

The Spellbinding Scene Below

The crests of the high hill-top command an expansive view of the lowlands and the quaint little village almost centered below. The scene reminds the young militiaman of his own Orange County hills and their villages nestled beneath them. He looks spellbound down on the enemy army massing far off on the flat lands but clearly in his view.

Though knowing he should be on his way, Onderdonk is fascinated by what he sees. The youth finds himself unable to take his eyes off the tremendous difficulties which he finds men go through in a determined effort to destroy, maim and kill their own kind.

General Howe's forces in the southeast look no larger than ants, all clothed in colorful dress as they prepare for battle with a precision such as the youth has never before seen. Suddenly they remind Onderdonk of the little wooden men on his father's chess-board.

He sees 150 fieldpieces being hauled up into positions on the forward rim of the lowland's plain where the enemy have seemingly established their front. It is not far from the river's east bank and entirely too close for comfort, Onderdonk thinks. Some of this heavy artillery looks, to the militiaman, as though it were pointed directly at him and the hillcrest works. And some of it is.

The Americans have made no move. Not a shot has yet been fired by either side.

Westward, Onderdonk sees where approximately behind the distant ranges must be his own Tappan Town. His thoughts go home and drift into the future. There are things he must do for his mother and his aging father when the war is over . . . many things! And maybe, he thinks, projecting himself farther into the future, he will go back to Hart's Corners and court that pretty little maiden, Etiennee.

After all she did seem to like him. She did say, "You must come back soon and see us, Master Abraham." And she did tell him, "Tomorrow will surely be a better day because of soldiers like you and my father."

Now he turns from his brief momentary reverie and notices a Continental colonel whom he hears addressed as "Colonel Haslet," and other staff officers pointing to and discussing the enemy's movements on the so-called plain below. He notices that Haslet's field glasses are trained on the spectacle unfolding down there on the opposite side of the little river—the river in whose clear pool of sparkling water he enjoyed a bath with "Danke" this morning. The lowlands are spread out like a grand theatrical arena beneath him.

In his excited state, Onderdonk had forgotten his hunger. Seeing the Delaware and Maryland troops dipping into the battle rations' casks, he is reminded that he has eaten the last of Madam Hart's package of victuals. Etiennee had stuffed it in his knapsack when the Harts bade him good bye. That was at sunrise this morning.

When an opportunity presents itself and no one is near, Onderdonk dips in and takes some sea bread, stuffs a roasted ear of burned-black, Indian corn in his surcoat pocket and fills his cup from the cider barrel.

He had noticed how John Haslet's Delaware and Maryland troops were indeed (as he had been told) the best uniformed troops in the army. Others in contrast look like rags. His, thanks to his mother, is far better than the average. With the unusual distinction of wearing a good looking outfit he hopes no one will challenge him. And no one does.

Slowly the gnawing hunger pains vanish as the Tappan farmer boy munches sea biscuits. Then, feeling better, he debates whether to take one more look at the enemy spectacle from the cliff before traveling on.

The call to duty loses and self-reproachfully the youth makes his way through men, wagons, horses, ammunition carriers, across the entrenchments under construction, and stands once again entranced by the scene beneath him.

The entire British army seems assembled down there in a wheat field,[11] while about them and behind them toward the rising bowl of the imaginary giant cup, the bright autumnal sun pours down upon the brilliantly falling leaves for it is a beautiful fall day.

Each tree, though sparse within the bowl holds or gently drops its multi-colored rainbow plumage. Each leaf sparkles brightly in its mingling with its sisters to enact a festival-like dance above and below the horizon.

Like terpsichorean muses the leaves flutter from their summer lodges and return unregretfully to the earth from which they sprang. And there amidst nature's proud raiment in its most spectacular dress, hordes of marching soldiers offer striking competition.

Dressed in varied radiant colors, their arms, buckles of brass and their bayonets of steel sparkle vividly in the sun's bright light. They appear like puppets, gruesomely attempting to compete in earth's roundup for a place in the colorful exhibition which God's autumn only has mastered.

It has been clear to the observers on the hills that the British staff officers were holding a council of war. It had been going on for some time. And when it ended, it appeared as though the enemy's first move would be directed against the fortifications north behind the village at the American center on Purdy's hill.

Surprisingly that attempt or feint comes to a sudden halt. Now, while the lines of British soldiers stand at rest in their positions, their leaders can be seen holding an important field conference.

General Heath, viewing the sight from the heights of Purdy's Hill, will later describe the scene in these words:

> "The sun shone bright; their arms glittered, and perhaps troops never were shown to more advantage than these now appeared. They now halted and for several minutes the troops set down in positions in which they stood, no one appearing to move out of his place . . ."[12]

Were it not that the deathly seriousness of the circumstances is indelibly impressed upon the minds of everyone, everywhere within view of this arena of war at a critical hour in the birth of a new nation, the drama in progress on the wheat field "stage" would be almost comical.

It had looked as though the British attack would be directed at General Heath's division to the northeast. The Crown's right column on the Mamaroneck-White Plains road under General Clinton appeared poised for it.

Then Clinton suddenly opened with a brisk cannonade, answered just as briskly by Heath's artillery. When it subsided the redcoat general sent a corps of sword-brandishing light horsemen at full gallop along the road leading to the Court House directly in front of Heath's forward lines. The dragoons leapt a wheat field fence in their wild dash toward Heath's ranks, the van of which lay over a hillock. Unaware that on the other side of the ridge, obscured from their vision, Colonel Malcolm's regiment of Continentals was waiting for them, the shouting horsemen sped on.

A burst from Lieutenant France's rebel fieldpiece struck squarely in the midst of the fence-hurdling dragoons as they came over the rise, pitching one of them off his frightened steed and leaving him crumpled on the ground. The surprised cavalrymen wheeled around and galloped back off the field as fast as they had come.

Reorganizing themselves behind a little hill in the road, the dragoons clustered in conference for a few moments. Heath's men could just see the tops of their caps. Then, a few minutes later, the hats disappeared as the cavalrymen made their way swiftly back to the main column.[13]

It was after this action that Clinton's column halted and the conference took place in the big wheat field. If it were a feint, it did not draw off any troops from Chatterton as Howe may have hoped.

Council Of War In The Wheat Field

While the council of war in the wheat field was in progress, the Americans found amusement in looking down upon a vast enemy army, close to 15,000 fully equipped, well fed, handsomely clothed, perfectly disciplined King's men sitting down in their positions.[14] And, while they are so arranged, their leaders in a huddle, all mounted, attempt to arrive at some momentous decision. In the interim not a single redcoat breaks away from his squatting ranks.

Then, to the surprise of the Americans, after the conference the British left column begins swinging around, facing west directly into Chatterton Hill instead of north at Heath's lines.

Howe, it would appear, has decided that Chatterton on his left is an obstacle menacing his entire corps, particularly inasmuch as Clinton has found Heath's division on the right much stronger than expected. Or else he had planned it all the time.

On a plateau on the river's east bank the British artillery begin hauling up 20 fieldpieces directly under the nose of the Chatterton Hill defenders. It is obvious they will lay down a barrage covering a British infantry attack coming across the stream to storm the hill's defenses.

And the only possible crossing is where the Americans have destroyed the bridge. Therefore, they must either build a bridge or slosh their way over at one of the fording places far to the south.

The call of duty is still strongly beckoning Private Onderdonk but the sight below him and the heated activity along the hill's slopes keep him glued to his secluded and partly concealed observatory rock on the cliff.

Not far from the procrastinating militiaman, who looks more like an off-duty army messenger than an infantry soldier, a young artillery captain gives his cannoneers some final firing instructions. Onderdonk overhears the men refer to him as "Hamilton."

Watching the officer and noting how well he seems to know his business, Onderdonk is sure that this must be the youthful, Nevis Island-born patriot, Alexander Hamilton, of whom he has heard good things.

All around officers excitedly issue last minute instructions and order all men to their posts. Just then the alarm sounds and Onderdonk realizes that he must move on. But now in a thunderous blast the enemy cannonade begins with an earth shaking barrage.

One artilleryman shouts out, "Ah! The ball is open!" And so it is.

Shot after shot whizzes overhead. Some of them crash into trees in Onderdonk's rear as he hurriedly scrambles back on the path. This time he definitely intends to be on his way. But torn between fright and curiosity and overwhelmed by a spectacle exceeding anything he has ever imagined, the private, unwisely ignoring the warnings of others, shouting for him to "Get back! Get back!"

looks over his shoulder once more on the dramatic spectacle below.

It is his last. There is now no "getting back" for the Tappan town farm boy. A six-pounder strikes through his neck, decapitating the young militiaman cleanly below the chin.

The tousled-haired auburn locks on the young head that only a few hours ago wore the face of youthful eagerness, are with lightning swiftness detached from his shoulders. Head and locks fly off with almost the same rapidity that the spark of life he had held so closely for 19 years, speeds into that mysterious, far less worrisome world beyond mortality. The headless body now lies estranged and stilled.

Incessantly the British artillery hammers at the hill's defenders. The thunder echoes across the valleys, bouncing from hill to hill as though these were the terrifying crescendos in the final overture to end the American insurrection.

Haslet's men waver under the terrible barrage. The shocking sight of Onderdonk's death and then that of one of Colonel Putnam's young militia engineers in addition to the crashing and exploding enemy balls and canister shot, against which they have little defense, put the Delaware and Maryland militia troops on the edge of panic. Particularly frightened are the new raw recruits.[15] Haslet, knowing that waves of light horse, jagers, chasseurs and crack riflemen will storm the hill when the barrage lets up, tries to reassure his men.

Foreseeing the difficulty that was certain to beset Haslet when the enemy troops turned on Chatterton, the American Commander earlier ordered the First New York Regiment under General Alexander McDougall, the Third New York under Lieutenant Colonel Rudolphus Ritzema, Lieutenant Colonel William Smallwood's regiment of Marylanders, Major John Brooks Massachusetts and Colonel Samuel Webb's Connecticut regiments to reinforce Haslet.

With the reinforcements coming up behind them the Delaware and Maryland militia regain their composure and hold their ground. Haslet's old, hard-fighting Continental veterans of the Long Island, Kip's Bay and Harlem Heights battles boldly stand up under the steady barrage. They do more to restore the wavering spirits of the new recruits than even Haslet himself and the arriving reinforcements.

General McDougall, coming up with his Third New Yorkers, is senior officer on the hill and therefore becomes the lines' commander. His troop strength numbers 1,600.

"This Liberty Is Going To Seem Easy . . ."

In advance of the arriving reinforcements, Hamilton brings his fieldpiece up on the rock ledge. McDougall, sizing up the situation, agrees with Haslet that the system's only two fieldpieces should be quickly brought into alternate firing action. The commanding general orders that the other gun, an old and badly damaged piece, be hauled up and placed in play with Hamilton's weapon. The Delawarean doctor colonel personally assists in dragging the heavy piece up behind the regiment in the ascent to the summit.[16]

Then, while Haslet is standing at McDougall's side on the hill's crest, a detail carrying the dead and wounded passes them on the way to the rear. They both pause briefly as they see the severed body members of what only a few hours ago was a young farmer boy turned soldier, now a corpse, a life wasted in his country's service.

McDougall, stemming his own horror at the sight, notices a roasted, burned-black ear of Indian corn falling out of the new, blood-stained, loosely draped surcoat covering the body. He does not see in death a waste. Turning to Haslet, he says quietly and calmly, "It is true, John, as The General says, 'This liberty is going to seem easy when men no longer have to die for it.' "[17]

Haslet says nothing. He is chiefly concerned with getting the old fieldpiece in place. He leaves McDougall's side to give orders for positioning the weapon. Just as Haslet and his cannoneers are forcing the heavy gun into its stops, a British ball whines and whizzes with a blasting roar into the center of the gun carriage. Shot and powder are scattered from the impact, igniting a blazing tow in the pounder's center.

The strike throws the cannoneers to the ground. Fortunately, however, not a man is injured by the hit. Having been almost unfit for use before, the weapon now is worse from the impact[18] but still operable.

There is much uncertainty among the American command whether Howe is serious in his apparent intentions to assault Chatterton. Every move that is made below on the lowlands is carefully analyzed.

The American Commander watches the move toward Chatterton's slopes from his center lines at Purdy's place. The action could still be a feint, intended to draw more strength from the center and left wing lines, thus easing a British attack through the American center or left. Yet every passing moment serves to dispel any doubts.

To the American command an assault on Chatterton seems illogical. Of what value can the hill be to the British? Has General Howe been misled into believing it threatens him to that extent?

A frontal attack directed at the American Commander-in-Chief's center is certainly the logical operation. But Sir William is a man determined never to carry out the expectations of his enemy.

Soon it is realized Howe is deadly serious. The American right flank—Chatterton Hill—is his objective. One after the other, the British platoons turn off from their apparent march toward the rebels' center. They move left (westward) toward the river and Chatterton above it.

The redcoats' 20-gun bombardment covers the Hessian and British engineers as they attempt to rebuild the bridge directly beneath Hamilton's weapon. The young artillery captain and his battery unload a barrage so accurate and so intense that the enemy's engineers are sent scurrying for safety. The bridge reconstruction is soon abandoned.[19]

Sir William's assault plan comprises two simultaneous actions. General Leslie with his English and Hessian brigade is to make the frontal. Colonel Rall meanwhile is to circle left and ascend the hill's south slope with his all-Hessian regiment in a surprise encirclement maneuver.

Without the bridge Leslie is forced to move downriver to one of the fording places Rall has already crossed. Then, sweeping through and dispersing the scattering outpost rebel guards, Leslie's forces hug the side of the hill, staying out of view and range of the Americans entrenched on the slopes.

In face of a continuous American fusillade, the British and Hessian troops begin storming the hill immediately upon the lifting of their own covering cannonade. Clambering up the steep hillside with heavy muskets and full packs, the King's troops slow down to reorganize, firing only periodically at the defenders in order to rest between charges.

On the heights some of the over-optimistic American officers interpret the lull as a certainty that the enemy is worsted. They erroneously order the slopes' defenders to hold their fire. The crackling of small arms on the lower slopes they believe to be the shots of their own riflemen in the forward entrenchments popping away at the retreaters.

Soon the subaltern officers' mistake spreads throughout the hill's entire defenses causing all but the most forward regiments to let down their guard.

Unknown to the men manning the upper lines and the company officers along the higher slopes, the crackling is from the advance units of Leslie's brigade coming upon the first line rebel entrenchments. And there Colonel Smallwood's Maryland regiment and Colonel Ritzema's New Yorkers now rise up from their positions and confront the bayonet-attacking enemy at the very foot of the mountain-like hill.

With no cover from above, owing to the officers' communications error, the first line American defenders are soon repulsed by overwhelming enemy numbers. They slowly give ground, withdrawing up the slopes in face of the oncoming enemy.

The sight of the retreating American front line scrambling toward the hill's summit pursued by bayonet-fixed Hessians and British redcoats, sends a wave of terror through the militia recruits. They begin breaking all along the hill's right wing flank and head for the rear.

At the same time Rall and his Hessian regiment have stealthily completed their encirclement. They begin a charge up the south slope in an attempt to unite with Leslie's frontal-assault forces. Despite the flight of the raw militia recruits to the rear, McDougall and his regulars fiercely contest the Hessians' advance as the Americans swing the hill's center to the right, while still struggling to hold back Leslie's forward units. Blood flows as Hessian, redcoat and rebel clash and fall, crumpled under foot.

Rall's force, with strength and weaponry on its side, overcomes Spencer's right wing but meets defiant resistance from Brooks' and Graham's Massachusetts and New York militia regiments. Forced to swing around, changing their front from east to south, the Massachusetts and New York regiments come between the cross fire of Leslie's and Rall's men.

In addition to the merciless cross fire, the Americans attempting to hold the right wing, see in the distance, charging up the slope on a gallop, some 250 mounted light dragoons. Howe, deciding to take no chances, has ordered Birch's British cavalry to come up behind Rall to end the fray.

The charging dragoons, their sabers flailing and flashing in the air, strike terror in the hearts of the green militiamen. Never before have they seen cavalry in action.[20]

Besieged on all sides, the American troops on the hill's south and southeastern brow break and flee in great disorder. Their pursuing attackers circle to cut off retreat into the rear lines. Before they can reach the safety of the main secondary entrenchments, the enemy horsemen fall upon the scattered groups killing and wounding as many as come in the range of their sabers.

Then a hundred of the south slopes' defenders angrily turn, rally and try in vain to resist the onslaught. But the overwhelming odds are against them. Some surrender. Some escape into the woods and eventually find their way back into the American lines.[21]

The successful enemy assault has uncovered McDougall's right flank, leaving Haslet and his Delaware regiment alone, standing unsupported in the forested area on the right of center. Seeing that he could shortly be encircled, Haslet attempts to draw his men back to the north. But Rall, with the total force of his command, falls upon him.

Under the hard-driving Hessian attack, three Delaware companies break and are driven from the field. The fighting Haslet holds the rest of his men together despite the withering fire of his enemy. Backing up slowly, Haslet lines up his men behind a stone fence and "twice repulses the Light Troops and Horse of the enemy."[22]

Meanwhile, a battle rages between McDougall's stubborn defenders opposing Leslie's superior infantry forces in their frontal attack. Both the New York and Maryland troops under McDougall have been driven back, but Smallwood's men still fight on.

Smallwood has been wounded twice but stays with his men. Ritzema's New Yorkers, though holding up gallantly, are rapidly weakening under Leslie's continuous attack waves. It is now apparent to all the rebel staff officers that further resistance is hopeless.

Despite word from the Commander-in-Chief that he is sending General Putnam and his division, already on their way, McDougall orders the New York and Maryland troops to withdraw to the Dobbs Ferry Road[23] which, eastward, crosses the river into the American center lines along Purdy's Hill.

The British dragoons, emboldened after their pursuit of the retreating rebel forces across the hilltop fields toward the main encampment, try to reform for an attack on Haslet's lone Delawareans attempting to take the same route. But before they can do so, the Delaware troops, defiantly taking their time behind their fence, and uncovered in their withdrawal through the open field, send a fusillade ripping through the cavalry and scattering the horsemen before they can launch their charge.

Though dangerously exposed to the enemy, the Delawares stop repeatedly, load, aim and fire alternately by companies. Their perfect order and their seeming determination not to break and run under any circumstances, cause both the Hessian commander and the light horsemen to exercise caution.

Defiantly, Haslet's troops pull back toward the retreating American lines on the Dobbs road and the New York and Maryland troops ordered to cover them. So unhurried are they that they haul behind them the last remaining Continental cannon.[24]

In their slow, sullen retirement from the field on which an all-out attack by the enemy's power easily could wipe them out, Haslet and his men meet a detachment sent back by McDougall to support him. Then reforming his own lines, Haslet, politely allows the supposedly supporting force to precede him and marches his proudly defiant troops behind McDougall's withdrawing regiments.

The last to leave the field and the Chatterton Hill defenses, the Delawareans are greeted with a loud hurrah from the assembled Continentals before the entire, exhausted, hungry, badly mauled but still highly spirited force withdraws with its wounded and dead down toward the Bronx River bridge.

Into the gully and across the edge of the lowlands[25] they make their way to ascend the westerly slope of Dusenbury Hill. There they join the main army under The General on Purdy's Hill. And there McDougall makes his battle report to his Chief.

Howe Has His Hill But Fails To Follow Through

Under Leslie, the redcoats and Rall's Hessians take over the hill, now cleared by Birch's mounted dragoons. By the thousands the King's men assemble on the summit, rounding up their prisoners, attending their dead and wounded but making no attempt to pursue the Americans in their withdrawal. On the hilltop and along its crest the troops form and dress their lines. Chatterton Hill is Howe's.

Its advantage—and its only apparent advantage insofar as the Americans can see it—is that Howe can peer down upon the rebels' works and easily observe their movements up to the eastern end of Purdy's Hill very much the same as the rebels on Fort Lee have been eyeing him on Manhattan. Except at night.

The American losses are estimated to be from 100 killed and wounded to a possible 400 including prisoners. Since a number of the frightened raw militia recruits disappeared into the woods down the western slopes, many of them are believed to have continued, turning their retreat into desertions.

British losses are said to be 28 killed including five officers and 126 wounded, counting officers. Hessian casualties are put at 77.[26]

Howe's new position alters the rebel Chief's defense plans. It is not yet clear to the American command whether the defiant Chatterton resistance has checked Howe or merely whet his appetite.

Earlier this morning the rebel Leader sent his sick, wounded and much of the army's baggage to the rear lines. In addition, he ordered his headquarters removed from the Purdy house to the Miller house at Miller Hill on the edge of the range that fronts North Castle.

For the American Commander has decided that Sir William will not stop at Chatterton Hill. More than likely he will try again, pursuing his advantage by combining a frontal assault with a strike from Chatterton on the now exposed American right.

Hours go by and still there is no sign of a British follow-through. The American lines settle down to a long tense, sleepless night. Every rebel position is strengthened as the troops work continuously in the dark to fortify their positions. Sleep is out of the question. By morning the American lines will look so formidable that General Howe will be forced to think twice before attacking.

And by early morning they do. So much so that Howe will now order reinforcements up from New York before continuing his drive.[27] The "hills" and the intensity of his opposition are more than he had anticipated.

Throughout this long day on the Palisadean Bluff Rock and its adjacent ledges, soldiers and civilians have gathered to see the source for the distant thundering guns. A few have said they saw flashes above Westchester near the White Plains where it is known the main army is bivouacked. All expect it will be there, where New England links with New York, that the two armies will clash.

Elaine, on her way home from the hospital tent, stops by the Barbette Battery to return with her husband to the Baummeister house. Asher Levy greets her near the sentry's box, passing a few remarks about yesterday's river battle and about the cannon firing in Westchester about which she nervously inquires.

But suddenly she excuses herself and runs to her husband when he appears on the path. He places his arm around her shoulder, bends down to gently bestow a kiss upon her cheek before they both move down the gorge road. It has been his first day back on duty with his Bluff Rock Barbette battery.

"How fares Kearney?" he asks her on the way.

"Poorly," she replies, explaining that he has had a high fever, is part of the time out of his wits, but when clear of mind will say nothing to her or anyone else.

"Levy believes he suffers a great loss in his mother," Gray tells her. "The loss of one dear to him could be part of his trouble."

Gray has said nothing to anyone other than what he recounted in describing the "accident" that befell Kearney. He is sure that Jocko will say nothing. But now, having been told by Elaine of the incident between her and Kearney at the well sweep, he follows up on Levy's thoughts and questions Elaine.

"Would, then, two great losses in one's life, and on top of them, an accident, even worsen his mind's condition?" he asks Elaine.

Elaine does not reply. Her husband, as though hurriedly explaining that this was not his thought alone, says, "Asher seems to think so."

"John," Elaine asks, "what does Asher know? . . . I mean how much can he know about Edmund? He has seen him so little. He knows him not well."

Gray, looking down at her, replies, "He seems to know that Edmund was a suitor for your hand, or else he surmises so."

"He was never that!" Elaine angrily insists.

"Regardless, Elaine," John comes back, "he was so more than you thought. And that is what Asher surmises is part of Edmund's upset state of mind. Asher reads every medicine book of every kind he can find, for to be a surgeon is his ambition. He says that two great losses for one like Edmund Kearney are more than one of his ilk can endure. I believe Asher may be right."

"I like not to talk more about it," Elaine answers huffily. "Now tell me, will they send you to the fray in Westchester?"

Gray, knowing his wife, realizes there is to be no more discussion of Kearney, at least for the time being. He is aware the topic of conversation is to be changed. And so he succumbs reluctantly and answers, "I know not that!"

And they enter the backdoor to the Baummeister's kitchen.

To John's uneasiness and Elaine's as well, Marie Louise greets them with news that Minnie and Perawae, who were selling their wares at the ferry today, planned to stop by the hospital tent to see Edmund. The motherly wife of the ferry-master believes Minnie can do more for Edmund than a doctor and says so.

She also supplies the couple with the shocking news that the elderly Abbotts are soon to give up their castle grounds home and that Andrew is preparing to take them to join the Lenni Lenape, now settled far south in West Jersey.

It was this sorrowful announcement that spread a gloomy mantle over the Baummeister household, but particularly over the recently married pair whose happy hours with Minnie and Old Chief Perawae on their lofty Indian retreat in the mountain forest are still indelibly impressed upon the Grays' treasured memories.

In Elaine's worried and somewhat confused mind it seems as though the whole world she knew—the old world she had so loved—was gradually crumbling around her. A deep fear of the future and a strong dislike for the present fill her mind and obscure her dreams that lie disturbed and unsettled beyond the present.

Several times today General Greene has walked from his quarters in the Long House through the field fort grounds and down over the gorge, then up to the Barbette Battery. His inspections of the works have been cursorily inadequate. And he knows it. The artificers' shops, the slaughter house, hospital tents, the soldiers huts on their New York-named streets, the magazine dungeons, the prisoners' stockade and compound, the baking ovens and the drilling troops—all such inspections today have been more perfunctory than usual.

Greene's main thoughts are for his Chief at whose side he would like to be. The sedentary task of commanding a safe and isolated field fort where only an occasional river battle breaks the monotony, is not for him. He prefers to be on the battlefield in Westchester standing alongside the Leader he so deeply admires.

General Greene's ears also have picked up the distant rumblings of heavy cannon, a sound that makes him suddenly feel useless. His field glasses have caught glimpses of flashes and rising clouds of smoke. As yet no dispatch has come to give him news of the distant action.

The battle yesterday on the river below the sister forts has left the post's commandant with many things to do personally, in the absence of his adjutant, Tom Paine. He sent Paine and several staff officers this morning over to Fort Washington on a routine examination of Colonel Magaw's post. It is a follow-up on yesterday's brush with the enemy frigates.

On an old table-desk a native had donated to the headquarters when it was still called Fort Constitution (a name he silently wishes it still were) Greene sets aside his other paper work. The sun has long set. The noisy rattling of skillets and pans by the shouting, boisterous cooks and bakers now has quieted down.

There is little control anyone has over cooks and bakers. And these days more than ever they tap themselves proudly on the back after every meal, admiring their own ability to scrounge out another menu for the large contingent of men, mostly raw recruits—young, hungry militiamen—in the midst of diminishing supplies.

The Long House's log fire comfortably warms the large room where the Adjutant Paine spends so much .of his time writing. If not military matters, he writes about the military's affairs.

Twelve slender candles are the only light, now that the autumn sun has dropped behind the western horizon. The smell of burning wood, especially the apple logs, fills the room as it pours up from and out of the numerous campfires and chimneys of the soldiers' huts. The pleasant odor spreads over the leaf-covered mountain-top and its now almost silent encampment.

Only the periodic sounds of a sentry's challenge disturb the silence. Or the changing of the guard. Or occasionally it is the swiftly running feet of a soldier, hoping against hope that he can subdue nature long enough to reach the delightful paradise of the latrine before the Green Apple Fox Trot takes over his controls.

Some distance away from the Long House, and not too far away from the well—the deep well that some of the men call "The Gen'l's Well" owing to the Continental Army Commander's frequent indulgence from its delightfully tasting, cool water—stands Greene's courier and horse.

The animal is saddled and waiting while his master warms his hands over an outside trash fire around which several men are seen roasting ears of Indian corn. They quietly pass a small jug of rum around from one to the other.

Told to wait and prepare for carrying off some urgent dispatch, the rider glances impatiently at the Long House door and the sentry outside of it.

Inside, Greene, frequently rubbing his ever-bothersome, rheumatism-pestered leg, reads again the letter he has just finished writing to the President of the Continental Congress:

"General Washington and General Howe are very near Neighbors"

"Fort Lee, New Jersey, October 28, 1776
    "Sir:
    "This being a critical hour wherein the hopes and fears of the country are continually alarm'd; and yesterday there being a considerable heavy cannonade most part of the day, I have thought it advisable to forward an (message) with the account of the action of the day.

"The community between this and the grand Division of the Army is in a great measure cut off. Therefore it will be sometime before you will have any account from his Excellency General Washington.

"A ship moved up the River early in the morning above our lower lines right opposite to Fort 1 near to Head Quarters at Morrie's. She began a brisk cannonade upon the Shore. Colonel Magaw who commands at Fort Washington got down an Eighteen pounder and fired Sixty rounds at her; twenty six went through her. The confusion and distress that appeared onboard the Ship exceeds all description. She was towed off by four boats, sent from the other ships to her assistance. She cut her cable and left her anchor.

"Had the tide run flood one hour longer, we should have sunk her. At the same time the fire from the ships began. The enemy brought up their field pieces and made a disposition to attack the lines, but Colonel Magaw had so happily disposed and arranged his men, as to put them out of contact on that Manoever.

"A cannonade and fire with small arms continued almost all day without much intermission. We lost one man only. Several of the Enemy were kild; two or three of our people got brought off the field and several more were left there. The firing ceased last Evening and has not been renew'd this morning.

"General Washington and General Howe are very near Neighbors. Some decisive stroke is hourly expected, God grant it may be a happy one. The troops are in good spirits, and in every engagement since the retreat from New York has given the Enemy a drubing.

"I have the honor to be your most obedient humble servant

Nathanael Greene"[28]

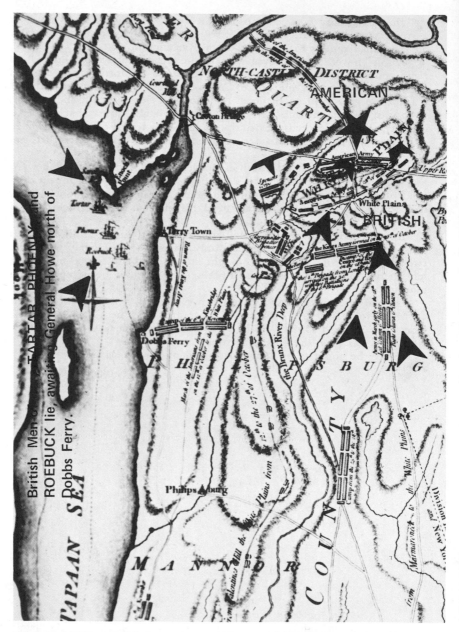

Overlaid on Map #603 Operations of the King's Army, are the lines drawn in the Battle of the White Plains. This British Sauthier Faden map shows the British men-of-war in lower Haverstraw Bay awaiting Howe's orders—Original Map in the Clinton Collection, Clements Library.

22

Friday, November 1. . .

Duels in the Hills
North of White Plains:
Operation Two

The Rebels Pivot And Disappear

Through the sky's overcast and haze last Tuesday morning, just
three days ago, General Howe and his staff officers awoke to see
across the lowlands through the town and all along the slopes of
Purdy's Hill, an obviously reinforced and greatly strengthened
system of American defenses. At least it seemed that way.

All night long the rebel army had worked in shifts to entrench
solidly—or to make itself look so—behind its strategic fortifications. The works appeared to scowl down upon the Crown's
men, whose left flank spreads eastward across the Bronx River. For
it now includes Chatterton Hill, enabling the British wing to reach
out and around to threaten an envelopment of the rebels' Purdy
Hill grounds.

To the British high command, the rebels' posture now appeared,
however, like a menacing wall entirely too imposing for a frontal
assault unless Sir William could secure more adequate encircling
power. So General Howe sent word to General Lord Percy, manning the Manhattan defenses, to spare him two brigades. And Percy
reluctantly prepared to send him one.

To the American high command, the positions of their lines
through the town and along the brow of the hill, were not to their

liking despite the all-night stiffening of the works. The Continental Commander and his staff were convinced that their fortifications and defenses were untenable in view of what their enemy could throw against them.

The General therefore, immediately ordered a massive secret operation. He would drop the entire army back north on the distant secondary line of hills and defenses previously established.

The entire movement was to be silent and mostly nocturnal. Its success would be largely dependent upon whether Howe made his attack before it could be completed. It was a long chance. And on Wednesday, when there was still no sign of any enemy activity in the air, the movement of supplies, baggage, the sick and the wounded quietly began. And so did the storm.

Wednesday's intermittent rains helped to conceal the preliminary movements of the American operation. But the activity under the wet, cold and depressing weather conditions, has not been an easy one. The Chief's headquarters were among the first to go out in the transferring operation. The new headquarters have been set up in the Miller House on the Broad Way at the foot of the western slope of Miller Hill.

Through Miller Hill, which rises like a towering sentinel on its southern reaches, will run the key works of the present defense system. The new lines extend through the rugged, rocky hillsides along the northern tip of the White Plains village outskirts and the southern edge of North Castle.

The towering, perpendicular, rocky escarpment at Miller Hill's southern edges commands the vital road north out of White Plains. The new Continental Army headquarters at Miller's is about two miles north and to the rear of Purdy's Hill.

But in addition to the rain clouds that were emptying on the American operation at its outset, came the gloomy news that Howe was being reinforced with a New York corps, already arrived in Westchester. This could only mean one thing, Howe was planning a major, all-out blow. And that blow was more than likely to come the next day, yesterday, Thursday.

Howe was indeed ready and fully set for that all-out attack yesterday. Percy's Fourth Brigade and two battalions of the Sixth Brigade[1] began pouring into the British encampment late Wednesday. Though rain-soaked and weary from their voyage on the transports and their long march from Pell's Point to the White Plains, the redcoats were eager for action.

Pressed for time the Continentals, despite the intensity of the late fall rainstorm, increased the tempo of their operation Thursday. Supplies, baggage, ammunition could not be moved until the sick, the wounded and the dying were moved to new tent quarters behind the lines.

Troops assisted engineers in preparing the supporting entrenchments fronting the main earthworks, which also had to be started in advance of the infantry arrivals. Stealthily the men transferred baggage, artillery, ammunition, stores and weapons over the rough, two-mile road, all without the enemy's knowledge of what was taking place.

Finally, straw men were to be left in the evacuated entrenchments along with logs, imitating cannons. These were partially covered giving the impression they were strong camouflaged fortifications.

Much of all this could be carried out during daylight. But the big task of transferring equipment, magazines, and the enormous impedimenta of an army at war, as well as thousands of troops over two miles and more of rough terrain—all under a constant downpour without the enemy's knowledge—had to be executed at night. And the only night left to the American army was last night.

The certainty that Howe would strike Thursday would mean that skeleton forces would have to man the evacuated works while the main force withdrew. And consequently, if the attack came on Thursday as seemed certain, much of the equipment and armanent as well as supplies would have to be left to the enemy.

But to the British command's disappointment and to the American command's relief the rain continued with no sign of letting up. And in view of the storm Howe postponed the attack until today.

Therefore what the Americans could accomplish clandestinely in daylight Thursday in their transfer operation was done under drenching rains. There was no let up.

All through the night they continued under the deluge, lighter at times and heavier at others. There were few even among the exhausted who found any sleep.

Every soldier and officer strained along with overloaded horses and wagons. And it was almost all carried out in ankle-deep mud through stygian blackness in a miserably cold, wet introduction to November.

For the rebel army, time had now become a nocturnal race through hell before this morning's brilliantly dawning sun.

Those who could go on no longer without warmth and rest, sought temporary relief in barns or under hastily and roughly constructed lean-tos placed along the way. Ever ingenious, whether regular or raw recruit, the Yankees and Buckskins all seem to have acquired that uncanny ability to work with nature or annoy it with some trick to combat its forces of destruction.

For those among them who survive this campaign, last night will be remembered as "the most miserable one of their lives."[2] But with this morning's sun they lie hungry and exhausted safely within the partly completed entrenchments of their new lines.

And as yet General Howe is unaware of it.

Contrary to a rumor spreading around Manhattan and seeping into the American lines, General Sir William is far from wounded or dead, as some have erroneously reported.[3] The false account probably stems from the mortal wounds received by one of the enemy, "a high ranking British officer" killed on Chatterton Hill Monday.

It was actually Lieutenant Colonel Carr who suffered wounds from which he died the next day. But the description was such as to lead many to believe it was the British commander-in-chief.

Very much alive, however, General Howe this morning looks over at the defiant-looking American lines stretching through the village and across Purdy's Hill. After 24 hours of steady rain his troops are ready for the long-planned attack and encirclement.

Up In Flames Go Life-long Efforts

During the night commotion stirred when British pickets reported a number of barns in the village were in flames. The fires initially excited the King's men, but owing to the weather it was assumed the scattered conflagrations were started accidentally by rebels attempting to keep campfires going all night in barns and sheds.

Far from accidental, the torched buildings were ignited by the rebel rear guard under orders to destroy all unremovable stores and forage in the last hours of the evacuation. So in the night's rainy darkness the torched structures sent flames high in the air while their hapless owners watched in tears from a distance. For most inhabitants have fled the coming battlefield, seeking sanctuary with friends and relatives on the outskirts. From far off they saw their barns and outbuildings ablaze—their livelihood, representing the efforts of a lifetime, go up in smoke.

Early this morning the British sent out waves of reconnaissance troops to probe for weak spots in the American front. Sir William also wanted to know more about the burning of the villagers' barns.

The British commander's curiosity about fires in villages has been sharpened by the burning of New York City. There is always the possibility of a ruse or trap.

Every precaution must be taken in conducting this frontal attack for it must be skillfully maneuvered with a combined left and right wing drive if the American Fox is to be ensnared. The rebel Leader has thus far played an "entrench and fight with the spade and mattock"[4] game, a strategy Howe dislikes but now must face.

Sir William's unhappy experiences at Breed's Hill have made the British commander over-cautious when it comes to attacking the Americans entrenched behind their own lines. Those old experiences have provided him with lessons reflected in his strategy. And his strategy is clothed in caution.

Suddenly the redcoat probers are seen proceeding entirely too near the rebel defenses yet no shots ring out against them. Tension rises within the British command staff as first squads, then platoons and companies of the King's men go through the believedly impenetrable American fortifications. They knock over with their hands semi-concealed, heavy-looking artillery pieces, mere logs designed to look like cannon.

One van of pickets far extends itself to the house where yesterday in the rain 100 of them had sought shelter and were set upon by 30 American Rangers of General George Clinton's rebel command. They rush toward the place with vengeance only on their minds.

In yesterday's brush the British pickets lost one man, but the American Rangers lost their Captain Van Wick, only recently appointed to the Ranger command. Van Wick had stopped to reload his piece when a ball pierced his head, killing him instantly. Then the lieutenant under him, in turn shot and killed his captain's slayer. The British unit, taking their dead with them, quickly withdrew.

So now they return to the site, eager to renew the fight. However there are no rebels anywhere along the lines they so securely held yesterday.

Howe and his staff at first doubt the accuracy of their own scouts. They disbelieve the physical possibility of the surprising evacuation. The astounding withdrawal of an entire army on such a night without detection is a humiliating blow to the British soldiery from the commander-in-chief on down. Howe orders the deserted camouflaged lines overrun and the enemy pursued, assuming the Americans are in retreat and still within his grasp.

Just beyond the lines the British van espies the last of the rebel rear guard. It is General Clinton's covering force. They cautiously head for the safety of their new lines. The rebel unit is a good distance ahead of the redcoats who bring their artillery into play and blast Clinton's rear with a heavy cannonade. One man is killed by the barrage, but the Continentals escape to the new defenses with no other losses.

Sir William's carefully devised plan to draw a semi-circle around his foe in their fortifications through the village and Purdy's Hill, is now a scrap of waste paper. General Howe is not a happy man.

He is not inclined to improvise without carefully contemplated planning. But now he decides to lead his own reconnaissance across the Broad Way and prepares to attack the American left flank on Hatfield and Merritt Hills.

Sir William Seeks A Weak Spot

Aware that the rebels are not in retreat and that he has been out-foxed, Howe judges the sister Hatfield-Merritt hills—the American Chief's left wing—to be the most vulnerable spot in his enemy's defenses. Their penetration, he thinks, is the easiest way to begin an encirclement of the new rebel fortifications.

However, General Heath in command of the American left wing is a clever military strategist and one with many surprises tucked under his tricorn. Heath is an astute chance-taker.

Leaving his left and center in occupation of Purdy's hill, Howe leads a strong cavalry corps, one artillery regiment and several columns of infantry toward the narrowing lines into the pass between the two sister hills.

It is through that pass through which the road[5] out of White Plains village runs over the Broad Way into the distant towns of Rye and Bedford, Connecticut.

Were it not for the deep swamps south of the hills, Howe could make a wide flanking movement. The marshes force him to compress his lines via the Broad Way approach, narrowing them into the pass between the hills.

Through their field glasses the British officers see Heath's formidable looking breastworks, a threat to the columns if they proceed too far. The works above the redcoats prominently line the tops of both hills.

In between them runs the pass or hollow through which the highway winds. Hatfield is on the road's left (west). Merritt on the east as the enemy approaches. The sight causes Howe to stop and ponder his next move. Behind those stalwart-looking breastworks Heath has some surprises. Of that Sir William is sure.

After last night and this morning's discovery of logs for cannon, the British leader feels his enemy is capable of any kind of deception.

Reconnaissance parties have probed all the Americans' old defenses for four days. They are sure they know the works under Heath's left wing command on Hatfield and Merritt. And they now know that Heath's forces are the pivot around which the Americans have swung around their army northward and backward to Miller Hill.

Overnight in his backward wheel, the American Commander pushed his right wing back leaving it held by a weak string of small picket and artillery detachments on Travis Hill, rising up on the west side of the Bronx River.

Travis lies north of the British-held Chatterton which is Howe's left wing. Chatterton and Travis are now the opposing armies' extreme western defense lines.

From Travis the new American defenses stretch eastward across the Bronx River, fordable at this point depending upon the rains. After crossing the river they run into the vale and up the slopes of Miller Hill, the American center and main headquarters.

From Miller, the formidable, mountain-like defenses stretch northeast to adjacent Mount Misery. Between Miller and Mount Misery runs the main highway north which, like the Bedford Road, winds upward into New England.

From Mount Misery the new lines extend in an arc southeast through part of Foster and then through Fisher Hill, the latter lying south of Foster. Across another vale, east of Fisher, the lines continue, running over an old roadway and up the slopes of Hatfield.

Opposite Hatfield, on the southeast, is Merritt which, with Hatfield, in combined defenses, guards the main Bedford Road to New England. And there Heath's forces man the left wing, the pivot which has remained intact in the northwest swing-around.

It is on this pivot which Sir William has fastened his eyes. If he can hammer his way through the enemy's left here, breaking it, he could encircle and ensnare the entire rebel army in its new lair.

Heath and his men look down from Hatfield's summit upon the British columns slowly coming to a halt before the pass. Heath had expected Howe would strike at the Continental left even before it pivoted.

Does it not command the main artery to New England? Once it folded Howe could send his cavalry and infantry spearing through the Americans' rear while the British left similarly charged the rebel right and diverted the Continental Army's center.

All the Americans' works could collapse under such a maneuver, if successful. And with Howe's strength his chances of success are high. So Heath has spent four days planning and waiting for the British commander-in-chief's appearance at the pass. And there before Horton's Pond and grist mill the redcoats halt to await orders.

Recognizing his enemy's superiority and the inequality of his poorly disciplined raw recruits and militia supporting the bulk of his more reliable veteran Continentals, the ingenious, 39-year-old, rapidly promoted major general from Roxbury, Massachusetts now pits his wits against the commander of the most powerful army in the world. And in doing so he makes use of whatever help the surrounding terrain offers him.

On the summits of Hatfield and Merritt Hills the wily Heath earlier in the week put his men to work preparing the outlines of imposing looking redoubts. Menacingly they look down upon the pass ready to destroy the enemy attempting to break through it. They give Howe some Homeric sober second thoughts.

From the fields, Heath's troops had ripped up and gathered lengthy cornstalks which they used to construct formidable and impregnable appearing redoubts, three on each hill.[6] Each is located and designed, apparently supporting the other.

Heath and Howe Like Hare and Hound

The cornstalks were pulled out of the earth carefully enough to retain a large clod of soil on each. These were placed slanting outwards in front of the false-front works. Soil then was heaped up around the outside base which gave each redoubt a realistic and impressive appearance. When finished, at a distance they could not be distinguished from stoutly constructed defenses with an excellently built network of fascines guarding strong and very threatening earthworks.

It is these formidable looking works on the hills' summits that have brought the British caravan of infantry, cavalry and artillery to an abrupt halt. They pause at the bridge south of Horton's Pond under Hatfield Hill's dangerous looking fortifications above them. And there Howe and his officers hold a council of war.

They have already narrowed their columns in order to enter the confined hollow-way. To pass farther through, they will have to draw in even more, exposing themselves to a murderous cross fire fusillade from the impressive redoubts atop the sister hills.

In addition to Heath's deceptive bastions, the left wing commander has cleverly concealed from view two large fieldpieces on the slopes, genuine in every way. He has put Captain Bryant and his artillery battery in charge of one. Lieutenant Jaxson and his cannoneers control the other.[7]

Across the ravine on his sister hill Heath placed Colonel Malcolm and his regiment. They occupy the "cornstalk" works on Merritt. Handling the heavy weaponry for Malcolm are Lieutenant Fenno and his artillery battery. Fenno also has concealed his weapons.

And so the hare makes ready for the hound.

It is not yet mid-morning, and it is an hour since Howe overran Purdy's Hill and headed for the Bedford Pass. All this time the American General has been kept informed of the enemy's movements, observing most of them from the summit of Miller Hill. When Heath's pickets brought him word that Howe was headed toward him, Heath immediately sent the news to the rebel Commander.

Carefully watching the British officers in conference, Heath soon realizes that they plan to outflank Malcolm's force on the east brow of Merritt Hill. He judges it will be a simultaneous attack up the hollow-way's west slope in a design to encircle the American lines' extreme left defenders. Therefore Heath orders their withdrawal. He sends one of his aides, Major Keith, to make the perilous dash across the ravine.

Keith is well on his way when his commander foresees a more preferable course of action and changes his mind. He orders a countermand, sending another aide, Major Pollard, to cancel the directions to Malcolm "to come off immediately with Lieutenant Fenno's artillery."[8]

Under the opening barrage both Keith and Pollard complete their missions at great peril. But, coming up behind Keith, Pollard countermands the order and informs Malcolm to hold out for support.[9]

Heath's revised decision is attributed to a lengthy stone wall that curves around the base of Merritt Hill at the head of the hollow. For now he sees in that wall an ideal means for thwarting Howe's strategy.

He sends several regiments down out of view from the foe, to man the fence. He sends another body to positions directly opposite on the Hatfield hillside. This enables both parties to shower the trespassers with oblique angle fire. Quietly and undetected, despite the first few cracks from the enemy's cannon, the Continental riflemen move down through the brush and take their places. They patiently await their firing orders.

Howe gradually increases his cannonade on the American breastworks.[10] Heath's main hilltop batteries above the straw redoubts respond. Frighteningly and threateningly the barrage continues for some time before the British lift their fire.

Galloping through the lines after receiving Heath's dispatch, the American Commander and his staff reach Gilbert Hatfield's farm when they hear the cannonade in the distance. Roweling their horses harder they race through the farmer's lands, ascend Hatfield's north brow and finally rein up at Heath's side on the hill's summit.

Quickly assessing the situation through his field glasses, The General expresses concern for the entire division's safety. Assured by Heath that, "They are all in order," the American Leader, seeing Malcolm's forces isolated on Merritt Hill, turns to Heath, saying:

"If you do not call them off immediately, you may lose them if the enemy push a column up the hollow."[11]

Heath replies that a strong rifle regiment has been lying concealed at the head of the hollow behind the long circling stone wall, and that another is ready to provide oblique fire from the Hatfield side enabling Malcolm to retreat if necessary.

Heath looks directly into the strained blue eyes of his Chief who shows the effects of sleepless nights throughout the past few weeks. Never, he thinks, has he seen The General's aging face so drawn.

Yet his spirits seem high, reflecting as always that ebullience of confidence and optimism which, in a strange manner, infects men who are drawn magnetically to him, infusing hope and inner strength when both are waning, a rare ingredient in the twisting bends of man's character that destines only a few to supereminence of being.

Again focusing his field glasses on the opposite hill, the big man addresses Heath in regard to Malcolm's apparent untenable position.

"Take care," he warns, "that you do not lose him."[1][2]

"Be assured, Your Excellency," Heath answers, "we shall not lose him."

From the high summit where on a clear day can be seen Long Island to the east and the distant Palisades, including Fort Lee, in the southwest, the staff officers issue commands and study the enemy's fire power in the artillery duel—the prelude to Sir William's assault. It is a rare opportunity for the Americans to see the enemy from above and examine so clearly Howe's strategy revealing itself under a hilltop perspective.

With the lifting of the British barrage, Dunlop's Hessian Grenadiers slowly advance up the hollow way in two columns. In support behind them appear a battalion of Hessians and a party of light horse cavalry dragoons.

All that seems to be barring the enemy's way is some suspiciously light, periodic ineffective shelling from the rebel cannon on the hilltops. Unharmed, the emboldened grenadiers move forward now with increasing confidence and rapidity.

Suddenly, when less than 30 rods away from the stone wall, the surprised Hessians see a company of Continentals rising from behind the barrier. The rising rebels send one volley into the startled enemy troops and quickly drop down, disappearing, while another company rises up, fires and disappears. Then another, and another. Alternating, company after company, the rebel small arms fire pours down upon the luckless Hessians from behind the full length of what was supposedly a farmer's harmless-looking stone fence.

The alternate firing and loading is timed with a surprising American cannonade from Captain Bryant's and Lieutenant Jaxson's concealed artillery pieces on the slopes of Hatfield Hill. The oblique cross fire from Lieutenant Fenno's battery on Merritt and the continuous fusillade from behind the stone wall stagger the entire British force trapped in the hollow way. The Hessians break and run in panic, forcing the entire body with its cavalrymen to fall back and seek cover.

Caught in marching formation in the open and under a continuous deadly fusillade with oblique cannon fire over their heads, the enemy force had no alternative but to break and run. Confusion and panic spread wildly through the forward Hessian battalions. Howe, seeing his troops on the brink of a rout, orders their retreat. The enemy forces hurriedly collect their dead and wounded. Retiring from the field, they return behind the lines of their army on the other side of the bridge.

It is a stunned Sir William who now levels his field glasses on the American works. What surprisingly impresses him are the forbidding looking breastworks and the rugged slopes leading up both the sister hills.

On Merritt Hill he notices the smoke rising out of the concealed rebel battery manned by Fenno and his men. He had no knowledge of it, or of the other concealed weaponry prior to his attack.

How much more could be secluded and concealed beyond and along the distant slopes?

And behind the stone wall are accurate marksmen. Certainly behind and above them are still more manning the hills' redoubts. More, far more than he had counted upon.

To storm those defenses as he is fully capable of doing would be far costlier than Howe desires to pay in casualties, already high. The rebel Fox would surely take a heavier toll and then possibly draw back before he could be encircled.

The hollow way road is a vitally important link in the American supply lines from New England, and Howe's plans call for cutting the artery that links New England to the Hudson and also runs down into Manhattan. This is the main objective, and if the rebels have built such strong defenses on their left, there is a good possibility they have drained their right and center to do so.

Perhaps the American right flank is the place to strike, and strike fast. It could be the key for getting in the Americans' rear. For surely the right and center, to which the rebels moved only last night, are not as established and entrenched as their Hatfield-Merritt left wing. That wing has had a week to emplace itself.

Calling off any further attempt to storm Hatfield and Merritt, Howe wheels his army around. Much to the surprise of the American defenders of the sister hills, he about-faces and heads back toward the Broad Way. Though the sun is still high, the Americans decide Sir William has called it a day.

Instead he leads his army north along the Broad Way, down the cemetery road, across the Bronx River and continues north along the river's west bank to the outskirts below Travis Hill. There the British commander is now determined to make a reckless assault on the Americans' right flank.

Fox Outfoxing Fox

Eastward across the Bronx River from Travis Hill, over the small valley and marshes lies Miller Hill. It is a larger and steeper piece of nature's work. Its summit is well protected by the rocky precipice-like walls that rise up on its southern and western slopes. It looks down upon Travis and southward out upon the village of White Plains. Its towering south nose commands the village's road to North Castle.

Only nine months younger than the American General, Colonel John Glover, who with his 14th Massachusetts Regiment of Marbleheaders has superintended much of the main army's transportation tasks since Long Island, watches the British movement from Miller's summit. His men are poised atop the crest of the post's formidable breastworks.

Glover, upon seeing the strong redcoat force bearing down on his men holding his far right flank on the Travis slope, calls them off. Howe, unopposed, moves into the vacuum. Meanwhile British pickets move forward to probe the American center under Glover's nose.

The Marbleheader, believing his enemy knows that not even a feint would be a wise move under Miller's cannon above the roadway where now the probing redcoats move in, orders his men to hold fire. Glover seeks bigger game.

Looking southwestward, the rebel colonel watches as the main British army attack force advances along the Travis slope. The crafty Glover holds all fire and lulls the Juggernaut's advance into a false sense of security.

The silence is ominous. American weaponry and defense systems have been excellently concealed. But Howe, exercising his usual caution, doubts his enemy has withdrawn again and his scouts assure him of it. He has been outfoxed once today. It is his turn to do the outfoxing.

Short but solid in stature, roughened by the winds and weather from the hauls off Nantucket and Cape Cod, swift in reaching decisions and laconic in his manner of speaking, Colonel Glover warily keeps one eye on the reconnoitring British infantrymen below him and another on the attempting enemy spearhead through the American right wing.

He mentally concentrates on Howe to move faster and farther in. Almost as though they read his mind, the mounted Queen's Light Dragoons dash up the Travis slope from which the rebel pickets only departed a short time before.

The British command is pleased with what it finds. They believe the suddenly withdrawn rebel pickets from Travis were the rear guard of the withdrawing army of rebels.

The total lack of any enemy fire and the inability to discern signs of enemy defenses convince the British commander and his staff that their decision to strike here was a proper one. General Howe is certain that only lightly scattered rebel infantry troops are guarding Miller Hill.

This is what he had thought would be so. If there are artillery batteries to cope with, they will probably be light and easily handled since Howe only intends to make a feint upon the post.

Sir William's maneuver from the Americans' far left over to their far right has been intentionally a swift one. And it has been very well executed in view of the massive logistics problems involved. His plan is a flexible one. If it works, much may happen of great moment to the Empire in the next few hours.

By feinting a west side and frontal attack on Miller, Howe believes he can draw the American command and most of their strength off the Hatfield-Merritt wing, causing them to turn about and concentrate upon Hatfield's northwestern brow and Fisher Hill's east slope. This would be the American command's most logical and sensible strategy to meet a British assault upon the rebels' center on Miller Hill.

Howe, leaving a token force to continue the feint and keep the American main army occupied in protecting Miller Hill, will take the bulk of his division in a swing behind Miller, sweep over to the main road north through North Castle and close it. He will continue his enveloping move around Mount Misery, send a strong force behind Foster Hill and extend his circle northeast of Hatfield. There he can cut off the Bedford and Rye roads to New England.

Percy meanwhile will bring his division up through the Hatfield and Merritt hollow way—the Bedford and Rye roads—from which the main defense had been withdrawn, and join Howe behind Foster and Fisher Hills, thus completing the encirclement. The supporting division left in White Plains would squeeze in with the British feint on Miller, tying a knot around the redcoats' sack with the rebel Fox within it.

It is a big bag around which to pull the cord and the British command staff is ready to execute it. But that ominous silence makes Howe suspicious even though his Queen's dragoons reflect a spirit of confidence and success as they sweep through the slopes of Travis Hill.[13]

The same ominous silence greets the reconnoitring infantrymen as their van moves closer into the undercliffs of the Miller nose without the greeting of a spark from the supposed defenders on the summit. They have advanced close to the famous "Indian Treaty Oak Tree" at the intersection of the Broad Way and the road leading under Miller Hill westward.[14]

The redcoats approach no farther as they see before them the towering, menacing precipice under Miller's southernmost summit. To their right rises Mount Misery, separated from Miller by the road north through their defile. And Fisher lies behind them to the southeast.

All were supposedly well defended, or at least believed posted with strong, though scattered, detachments of the rebel army. But where were they? Some of the redcoats begin to think that this may be the easiest feint the King's men have ever attempted.

Meanwhile to their west, their comrades in the British main division, led by the dragoons, a Hessian infantry battalion, and an artillery company hauling several heavy fieldpieces, push on under Travis Hill. While it is planned that this van will distract any defenders appearing on or along Miller's west slope, the main force will pass through north and eastward behind Miller and execute the enveloping movement.

Colonel Glover, in the opinion of some of his men, has let the enemy go too far. But the colonel is not to be hurried. Under his command are a brass howitzer, a three-pounder, a six-pounder, three iron twelve-pounders and a twenty-four pounder.[15]

All of Glover's weaponry as well as his troops, the 14th Massachusetts Infantry Regiment, lie in hushed concealment. Every weapon and redoubt has been thoroughly camouflaged. Every piece of artillery and every musket is loaded and primed awaiting the command to fire. Strategically placed behind the seclusion of felled trees and all covered by fallen leaves, wet from the previous day's heavy rains, the armament is completely hidden from the enemy's view.

Slowly the British van moves into the narrowing defile. Each redcoat's eyes turn eastward, peering up at the glowering sheer wall of rock rising not too far above him on the right. The scouts and the leading picket van had passed through safely. There should be no trouble. At most, it should be only light arms fire from the withdrawing rear guards. But even this has not come.

Word now arrives from the frontal attack van of pickets under Miller's nose. They have dared to go as far as the Indian Treaty

Tree where they send back word that no shot has been fired and report no sign of the enemy.

General Howe is a puzzled chief. He calls a halt to the entire formation and summons his officers for a council. He is almost certain something is wrong when none of the forward scouts who scaled the west wall of Miller Hill come back· or send word. Suddenly surprised and overtaken from the rear, they are now prisoners in the rebel encampment behind the lines.

The British commander is on the verge of pulling his forces back and waiting definite confirmation about the terrain above and before him and the whereabouts of his enemy. He weighs that last thought alongside the rapid progress of his division and concludes, too late, that he has gone too far. He considers pulling back but decides instead to probe farther and await word from his scouting pickets.

From Here Above the Plains Amid the Hills, Suddenly a Rain of Deadly Fire.

Suddenly A Rain Of Deadly Fire

As for John Glover, the exact moment has come. He watches some British cannoneers struggling to get their two weapons up an incline and probably into action.

Glover waits no longer. The command rings through the entire crest of Miller Hill. The defenders let go with a devastating bombardment. It rains down on the British division on the west and the pickets on the south front with a withering effectiveness. Pounders of all sizes, howitzer and small arms fire, shower the panicking troops.

From behind hidden redoubts the rebels pour down a fusillade with an accompanying cannonade that scatters the terror-stricken cavalry and infantry. But in amazingly good order the well-disciplined soldiery reorganize after withdrawing some distance. Then one redcoat battery wheels its cannon into a forward position and commences a return barrage on the Miller defenses.

Again the American batteries let loose. But the British and Hessian troops, compelled to look up and unable to clearly discern their targets are at a disadvantage while they themselves are clearly in their enemy's sights.

On the west side of the Bronx River, the British forces, nearest to and in clear view of Glover's men, are in the most hazardous position. With no protection for themselves, they can provide none for the main column if it should continue its advance.

Four times they ineffectively try cannonading the Americans' hill. However the trajectory of the rebel fire is destructively accurate, pinning down the entire British van.

Sir William, for the second time today, is forced to order a withdrawal. Slowly all columns about-face and pull back as November's first long afternoon shadows begin falling with the setting sun.

The Americans, though affecting a cold facade, individually watch with those unexpressed, human-for-human emotions, the tragic sight of their enemy taking up their dead and wounded.

No gun is fired. No attempt is made to interfere in the customary post-battle ritual—the farcical effort of contemporary man to manifest civility in primitive exhibitionism.

Only a dragoon, killed and left under the corpse of his faithful fallen horse, is left on the battleground behind the withdrawn army.

When all have cleared the field, Glover himself fires the last cannon. It is not aimed. It has no violent intent.

Its ball rises high and drops harmlessly into the deserted field of battle, for it is intended to express the philosophic will of defiance rather than the maniacal will of destruction. But others see it differently.

To General Sir William Howe it signals the end of a daringly bold but fruitless effort to put an end to the American Rebellion and hastily restore "The Colonies" to the Crown. For General Howe it is a sound that summons the depressing realization that his enterprise in Westchester has been a dismal failure.

The Fish Vendor Tops the Famous Viscount

Though he does not know it, Colonel Glover has fired the last shot in the five-day, misleadingly named "Battle Of the White *Plains*." As he does so, he fails to see the scowls that pass across the faces of the American Commander-in-Chief and General Heath.

Both, on word from Glover, had ridden fast to the Miller Hill summit shortly after the cannonade opened. Neither The General nor Heath, a farmer by profession, smile on needless waste.

But there is no time for such concerns. The problem facing the American Commander is what will Howe do tomorrow. The Americans, their hidden defenses revealed by the uncovering of the camouflage, now look out at the distant British troops settling down in their bivouac. Later Heath will say in his memoirs, recalling this night:

> "The two armies lay looking at each other and within a long cannon shot. In the night time, the British lighted up a vast number of fires, the weather growing pretty cold. These fires, some at the foot of the hills, and at all distance to their brows, some of which were lofty, seemed to the eye to mix with the stars and at different magnitudes. The American side doubtless exhibited to them a similar appearance."[16]

And so thinks William Heath tonight as he looks out on the scene beyond and below John Glover's surprisingly effective defenses, defenses "that 'the fish vendor' helped to design and to man in order to thwart 'the viscount' and his hopeful plan."

The cold star-lit darkness closes in upon the men of both armies. Each man sleeps with his hunger despite the extra supper rations. Soon the dying embers of the flickering campfires dotting the darkened hillsides gradually expire. Not a man on either side is aware that Glover's last shot has temporarily ended the Westchester hostilities.

Sir William's unsuccessful attempt to bring the American

Commander into an open field battle, added to the frustrated efforts he has met in hilly terrain with which he is not prepared to cope, assure Howe and his staff that the alternative is to strike across Hudson's river. Many King's officers have expressed the feeling, in quarters behind closed doors, that that is what should have been done in the first place.

Still another factor, a new and astounding one, is dictating a change in plans.

Contact has been made with the British high command from a person of reportedly high rank within Fort Washington's staff who, for a sum and other considerations, is willing to defect to the Crown with military intelligence of great value to His Majesty's army. This is secret intelligence few know outside of Howe.

Suddenly, the British commander and his closest confidants give indications of a plan to withdraw entirely from White Plains, proceed along the Dobbs Ferry road, turn south down the river and meet with General Knyphausen's forces at King's Bridge.

Certainly, if the Hudson River is to be spanned, it should be at Dobbs Ferry. Definitely no farther downriver where the Palisades are a barrier to an inland Jersey movement.

Therefore, there arises among the Crown's headquarters staff the question: If Howe plans to cross the Hudson, why should he choose to move south to King's Bridge and join Knyphausen?

Whether or not their commander is being seduced into leaving White Plains by a choice morsel of intelligence rich in possibilities, or by the sudden realization that his army is unprepared for rocky, almost mountainous, combat, becomes a matter of much officer speculation.

The intelligence Howe has received is alone sufficient justification for him to withdraw from the scene. But he rationalizes that the Westchester operation is not a total loss. It has produced some beneficial results.

One such result, in the opinion of the British command, is that the Loyalists and their desire to hold true to the Crown are bolstered by the strong show of force in this Whig-dominated countryside. The redcoats' presence alone has done much to encourage Tory leaders like Colonel Rogers and James Delancey.

Both men and their followers have felt the sting of the Patriots' scorn and anger. Now they have been able to retaliate in kind.

As a result of the Westchester campaign, the local inhabitants will be subdued and far more willing to cooperate with the King's men. More of the inhabitants will surely see the errors of their ways, and more—among the neutrals particularly—will sign the Oath Of Allegiance and enlist in His Majesty's army.

Though allowing Colonel Rogers and his Rangers to do much as they like in handling the inhabitants, Howe's British redcoats have been ordered to make friends rather than enemies with the West-chester people. And to some extent they have succeeded.

With consolation thoughts such as these, Howe tomorrow, Saturday, November 2, will pull his army back into the village. Sunday he will issue new marching orders. Monday his entire camp will hum with such activity that the Americans will begin digging their heels in, certain, from the noise and wildly flying rumors that a new attack is pending.

On Tuesday morning,[17] the fifth day of the month, a month that will be long remembered in the hatching of the American eaglet, Howe, much to the amazement of a suspicious rebel army will head his Juggernaut cross-country and leave White Plains.

He will go from Dobbs Ferry down the Hudson's east bank toward New York, not west across Hudson's river, but south to join Knyphausen on Wednesday, November 13, at King's Bridge.

Later, in explaining his withdrawal from the White Plains, General Howe will write Lord George Germaine from New York on November 30, 1776:

> "All these motions (Referring to the American withdrawal to the North Castle Heights) plainly indicating the enemy's design to avoid coming to action, I did not think the driving of their rear back an object of the least consequence."[18]

Between darkness tonight and the departure of the last redcoat over the brow of Chatterton Hill, the American lines will be in constant alert. Entrenchments will be strengthened. Picket guards will be doubled. Officers and men will strain their imaginations in futile efforts to perceive what is going on in Sir William's mind. No one imagines that he will pull out, especially in view of the amount of trouble he has gone to in order to get where he is.

As for the Continentals, they know that their backs are to the wilderness. Behind them is the Croton River. If they are pursued across it and then split into smaller units, Howe could maneuver his forces to chew them up piece by piece. For there is no support possible for them to the immediate north.

However there is one thing to their advantage. Howe dislikes wilderness fighting. Besides, he has shown himself in Westchester not to be too adept at it.

So between now and Tuesday, tensions within the Continental Army will be severely strained. Three more days of wondering and waiting will not add to their already anxious minds.

The humming activity on Monday throughout the enemy encampment will only serve to heighten fears. It will be particularly difficult for the already frightened Whig families and the Patriot Party throughout all of Westchester.

When the rear guard of the great Juggernaut fades out of sight over Chatterton Hill's road westward toward Dobbs Ferry, jubilation will sweep through the American army like a wave of chattering locusts. Tar barrel signals will carry the message from hill to hill.

The false feeling of having achieved a great victory will spread wild glee through the American lines. Some of it will spill over and beyond to sweep some repercussions of encouragement through the thirteen "colonies."

It will be only a few of the most rabid Tory-minded occupants of the White Plains who will take up their possessions and follow the British army. Others of them will resign themselves to the sudden, unexpected change of status. And they will, as happens every time that a new sweep-through occurs, swear they were forced into defections.

So it will be that the Tory strongholds in the town, and a number of these have popped up during the enemy's occupation, will become the objects of vengeance by both soldier and patriot civilian. A look ahead to Tuesday night will prove it.

After that day of celebrating Howe's withdrawal, night will fall to find little rum or cider available in camp for those still imbibing. Among those heavy drinkers will be Major John Austin of Massacusetts.[19]

Austin and his men are credited for having successfully slowed down the British van in the skirmish on the outskirts last Monday. He and his troops are still angry over the losses of a number of their comrades in that fray.

A part of Lee's division and under Spencer's command Monday, Austin's battalion did well in the fight, which took place not far from the Wayside Inn on the outskirts of Scarsdale Village.

The Austin ambush not only gave the Continentals precious time to prepare fortifications through the village, but it also enabled the more vociferous patriot inhabitants along the way to vacate the area before the Tories of the region moved in.

What was not known at that time was that Lee's division with which Spencer and Austin were marching toward the American lines narrowly escaped a British ambush earlier that morning enroute to White Plains.[20] Had it occurred, and it was good fortune only that prevented it, much of the rear guard in the Lee division lines, wagons and supplies could have been lost and become a major disaster.

The Austin men were among others who were certain that Tory informers at the Wayside Inn on the Post Road out of Scarsdale had tipped off the British resulting in the unsuccessful ambush. More than that, Austin and his men were convinced that Tory informers from the same inn warned the British that morning that Austin's party was somewhere in the ravine.

The rumor spread among the Hessian and British troops whose officers were alerted but took the news lightly. Austin therefore attributed his losses that day to Tory informers upon whom he is now determined to wreak vengeance.

Consequently when darkness covers the British-evacuated village Tuesday night, Austin and a party of his men will be there. Each will be drunk. All will be harboring a deeply ingested hatred for Loyalists, Tories, the enemy in general, and particularly for those unknown Tory informers.

Orgy Of Destruction: Retribution and Rum

Fired by the avenging spirits of retribution and rum, the party will arrive in town with a blind determination to burn "the whole damned Tory stronghold" to the ground.

With hate and vengeance blindly consuming their liquor-addled brains, Austin and his men will become totally oblivious of the fact that most of the town's inhabitants are staunch Whigs and patriots. Disregarding the lives and properties of the innocent, the obsessed drunks will turn into demonic arsonists. Running through the village with their torches, they will set fire to one building after the other in their orgy.

First the County Court House will go up in a blaze of flying embers. Then the Oakley Tavern. And the Hatfield Tavern, followed by the Presbyterian Church. Smoke and flames will engulf houses, barns and other buildings throughout the village. In giant leaps into the night air, the long tongues of fire and flaming sparks will light the sky for miles around in a holocaust of stench and smoke.

The burning village's spectral, sky-lighting consummation in the night's darkness will be seen for miles around. It will create new, wild rumors and outlandish imaginative fantasies, all fed through the trembling brains of a terror-stricken people in a frightened and wobbling new nation.

In the crazed fury of the night, men, women and children will wander through the burning village dazed and homeless. Seeking shelter, some will spend the night wherever they can find a roof. Others will spend it searching for the remnants of lost precious possessions, hopefully lying unharmed among the smoldering ruins.

The shameful act will hurt the American cause, particularly locally. The responsible Whig elders of the town will raise irate voices against the entire Continental Army. They will broadly condemn the whole military system and the Congress as well for allowing it. Few will realize that the majority of the military are as horrified by such acts as are the inhabitants.

Though the calamity will add fuel to Tory arguments, many will have their faith restored to the cause when the American soldiers move in and render aid the next day. The army's volunteer help will serve to reduce the aroused animosity for all Continental soldiers.

Whether Tory-instigated or not, there will be heard the cry throughout Westchester that the King's army does not wantonly burn men, women and children out of their homes. They will be words of great comfort to the Crown's men. And they will help to promote the Tory argument that it was unquestionably the rebels who torched New York town.

Tories will shout that the burning of White Plains village is proof of that. And their arguments will gain much credibility throughout Manhattan and Westchester.

Angered far beyond his usual facade of imperturbability, the American Commander will immediately order Austin's arrest. The major will be court-martialed and charged with "wanton, cruel, barbarous treatment of women and children, unworthy the character of an officer and inhuman to a degree."[2][1] Major Austin will be found guilty and discharged from the service.

Those events are yet to come. But tonight the two armies sleep almost within each other's arms.

Over the field of battle below Miller Hill tonight, just a few hours after it was a raging hell of gun fire and death, the acrid odor of smoke and powder from Colonel Glover's cannon has long since dissipated in the cold north wind.

All that occasionally disturbs the darkened quietude through which can be seen the smoldering campfires of both armies, are a sentinel's voice and the eerie hooting of a distant owl. As though answering the owl's lament, a lone wolf sends up his mournful howl directed to his wandering mate.

Fewer become the lights of the campfires. Less do the nostrils catch the sweet odor of burning apple tree logs. In both camps of the opposing armies there arises from within that ever-present sound of guards changing their watch. Each man among those not on duty—redcoat, Hessian, rebel alike—now seeks the one common ally all fall to at day's end. Sleep, which releases the child briefly from his play, releases the soldier briefly from his war.

In each man's silent vision through and over the soundless, bloodstained, battlefield of death, Lady Sleep comes and lifts him softly in her arms to take him gently back in time. Then in her chariot of dreams she swiftly carries him away and, through the night's fairyland of stars, back home.

There by the gate, or humble kitchen door, she reins in her snorting steeds and smilingly points him on his way.

Through doors, through walls, beside his dog, his toys of yesteryear, over his loved ones—mother, father, sister, brother, wife—he hovers, enwrapped in the inexplicable phenomena of the subconscious, reliving hours, days and months in brief mysteriously protracted seconds of unfathomed time. And there, within his room, his bed awaits him once again. . . .

The midnight-riding radiant, ebony steeds feel dawn and paw the earth to call him back. Reluctantly he goes, and in Sleep's soft restful arms speeds back. And now before the light of dawn, she halts her chariot above reality. Then sadly she turns him back to restless slumber, promising his uncertain life no assurance of her pleasant return. . . . in life, in dreams, or in the still uncharted seas beyond, where fallen comrades walk alone tonight.

Work, Not Sleep, In the House Of the Widow Miller

Among those not visited too often by sleep, no less dreams, is the American Commander. In the Miller House headquarters to which he returned after Glover's last shot, the Widow Anne Miller has given over her home to The General and his aides.

She had done so on condition that she may return from her brother's house each morning to see that all her rules are met and to make sure The General gets a good breakfast of hot porridge, eggs, sausage and toast. To this The General's aides and life guards finally agreed, though reluctantly, even under the Widow Miller's pressure.

It has been a long, hard day for the rebel Chief who must use most of the night disposing of the many dispatches that his aides have opened, and he has had no time to consider personally. Furthermore, he must give some time and thought to what General Howe's next step will be.

A week has past, a week as replete with strain and anxieties as any of the past few months, since he wrote Congress. What he had suggested then, the formation of two armies, seems even more reasonable now after the past week, than it did then.

The American Leader, aware of the Congress's fear that Howe plans a march on Philadelphia, had left General Greene at Fort Lee to keep his eye on any enemy move by land in that direction. But Greene, who has had to undertake a host of other responsibilities, has not a sufficient fighting force at his command to oppose a strong enemy push down through the Jerseys.

Letter Of the 25th

With slim hopes of getting it, but feeling obligated to putting it in the record, The General on October 25 had advised Congress:

> "that two distinct armies should be formed, one to act particularly in the states which lay on the east, (of Hudson's river) the other in those that are on the south of the river."[22]

His staff officers had endorsed the recommendation.

Admiral Howe's river attacks against the twin posts guarding the Hudson and the enemy's attacks by Knyphausen upon the Fort Washington outposts, the King's Bridge garrison and Fort Independence, north of the Spuyten Duyvil, all bear out the wisdom of The General's recommendation. And General Greene's correspondence of the 29th, reporting on the enemy's activities in his area, timed, it seems, with Howe's assault in the White Plains certainly further support the soundness of the "two-army" theory.

Though two armies as recommended were not possible, Greene in Fort Lee and the Commander-in-Chief in Westchester represent what The General has in mind. They provide the protection of, at least, two commands, or operations.

While The General has been busy with General Howe in the White Plains, Greene has completed a difficult and trying two weeks with Lord Percy's remaining forces below Harlem, General

Knyphausen's division in King's Bridge and Admiral Howe's ships on the Hudson. The Rhode Island brigadier general now is beginning to realize why his Chief disregarded his offer to join him at White Plains.

First there was the Sunday, October 27th attempt to run the blockade, then the skirmish following a probe by the enemy into Magaw's force at Fort Washington, and finally Knyphausen's drive into the Fort Independence outpost north of Magaw's post. And, in addition to enemy movements, Greene has been carrying out his superior's orders to set up a series of wayside military supply posts from Fort Lee to Philadelphia.

The American Commander's order to evacuate some of Fort Lee's supplies and establish a string of "Fort Lee to Philadelphia depots" is not an order Greene favors. Greene, unlike The General, does not foresee the necessity. He does not believe a retreat through the Jerseys will have to be made. Certainly not before spring. And besides, Fort Washington's impregnable defenses are too strong for the enemy to risk attacking.

Regardless of his personal opinion, Greene carries out his Chief's command, establishing magazines and supply bases along the route, south on the other side of the Passaic River. And he does so while keeping up a bold front before Percy's Manhattan detachments, Knyphausen's raiding parties against Mount Washington's outposts and Admiral Black Dick Howe's frigates.

In addition he keeps recruits, wagons and supplies flowing over to White Plains. And from his Fort Lee pivotal center of the army he processes through the wounded from Westchester. It is one more of his many other responsibilities in this vital linking post. Just keeping the communication lines open through his outpost at Sneden's Landing and across the river has been a difficult but an indispensable task.

On Thursday, October 24, Greene wrote from Fort Lee, informing his Commander at the White Plains that he was sending over "the cartridges, 90,000 and more and also all the wagons that could be collected."

The New England commandant of the Hudson's sister forts also reported on his progress in establishing the wayside magazines along "the back road to Philadelphia," saying:

> "We have collected all the wagons within our power, and sent over. Our people have had extreme hard duty. The common guards, common fatigue, and the extraordinary guards, and extraordinary fatigue, for the removal of the stores and forwarding the provisions, has kept every man on duty . . .

"I have directed the Commissary and Quartermaster-General of this department to lay in provision and provender, upon the back road to Philadelphia, for twenty thousand men for three months. The principal magazine will be at Equacanack (Acquanonk). I shall fortify it as soon as possible, and secure that post and the pass to the bridge which is now repaired and fit for an army to pass over with the baggage and artillery. . . ."[23]

Letter Of the 29th: Loss Of Fort Independence

The same day the Continentals battled the British and Hessian forces on Chatterton Hill, Howe's large left wing division under the Hessian commander, General Knyphausen, was forcing Greene's Fordham Heights garrison to evacuate. And the next day the commander of the sister forts and its environs sent a dispatch dated October 29, describing that withdrawal.

The American Commander-in-Chief now reads again that dispatch sent him from Fort Lee three days ago. He brings the three-spiked candlestick closer to him on the table-desk in the big second floor bedroom of the Miller House.

This time he peruses it to study the contents for clues to Howe's possible intentions. He particularly reads of the burning of barracks and the loss of Fort Independence of which Greene states:

> "Colonel Lasher (commander of the rebels' Fordham Heights post) burnt the barracks yesterday morning, three o'clock; he left all the cannon in the fort (Fort Independence). I went out to examine the ground, and found between two and three hundred stand of small-arms that were out of repair about two miles beyond King's Bridge, a great number of spears, shot, shells &c., too numerous to mention.
>
> "I directed all the wagons on the other side to be employed in getting the stores away; and expect to get it completed this morning. I forgot to mention five tons of bar iron. I am sorry the barracks were not left standing a few days longer; it would have given us an opportunity to have got off some of the boards.
>
> "I think Fort Independence might have kept the enemy at bay for several days, but the troops here and on the other side are so fatigued that it must have been a work of time . . ."

Implying again that he was ready to join the army at White Plains if needed there, the Rhode Islander closed with, "I hope to be commanded wherever I can be the most useful."[24]

Letter Of the 31st: The Blockade Holds

A third report from Fort Lee gives the Continental Commander pleasure. Greene wrote the message yesterday. It arrived this morning but did not come to The General's attention until this evening. His aides, Tilghman and Harrison, had read the letter, noting that Greene had reported the Chevaux de Frise was still holding fast.

This had been a matter of great concern for the entire American command staff. For if the blockade is run through there may be little chance for the Americans to escape across the river. Certainly, the destruction of the Chevaux de Frise would not make their crossing any easier.

Now, after poking up the fire on the hearth's burning embers, the rebel Leader goes back to his chair and reads the Fort Lee commander's last dispatch, which was written by Greene's adjutant, Tom Paine. He finds it easy to read Paine's writing as contrasted with the self-taught post commander's style and penmanship. For the Fort Lee adjutant general has an ability all his own. It reads:

"Fort Lee, October 31, 1776

"Dear Sir:

"The enemy have possession of Fort Independence on the heights above King's Bridge. They made their appearance the night before last. We had got every thing of value away. The bridges are cut down, and I gave Colonel Magaw orders to stop the road between the mountains.

"I should be glad to know your Excellency's mind about holding all the ground from King's Bridge to the lower lines. If we attempt to hold the ground, the garrison must still be reinforced, but if the garrison is to draw into Mount Washington and only keep that, the number of troops on the island is too large.

"We are not able to determine with any certainty whether those troops that have taken post above King's Bridge are the same troops, or not, that were in and about Harlem several days past. They disappeared from below all at once; and some little time after, about fifty boats full of men, were seen going up towards Hunt's Point, and that evening the enemy were discovered at Fort Independence. We suspect them to be the same troops that were engaged in the Sunday skirmish.

"Six officers belonging to (American) privateers that were taken by the enemy, made their escape last night. They inform me that they were taken by the last fleet that came in. They had about six thousand foreign troops on board, one quarter of which had the black scurvy, and died very fast.

"Seventy sail of transports and ships fell down to Red Hook. They were bound for Rhode-Island; had on board about three thousand troops. They also inform that after the Sunday action, an officer of distinction was brought into the city badly wounded.

"The ships have come up the river to their station again, a little below their lines. Several deserters from Powle's Hook have come over. They all report that General Howe is wounded, as did those from the fleet. It appears to be a prevailing opinion in the land and sea service.

"I forwarded your Excellency a return of the troops at this post, and a copy of a plan for establishing magazines. I could wish to know your pleasure as to the magazines as soon as possible.

"I shall reinforce Colonel Magaw with Colonel Ralling's regiment, until I hear from your Excellency respecting the matter.

"The motions of the grand army will best determine the propriety of endeavoring to hold all the ground from King's Bridge to the lower lines. I shall be as much on the Island of York as possible so as not to neglect the duties of my own department.

"I can learn no satisfactory accounts of the action of the other day (Battle on Chatterton Hill, presumably).

"I am, with great respect, your Excellency's obedient servant,

Nathanael Greene.

"To His Excellency, General Washington,
at Camp at the White-Plains"[2 5]

Greene's letter is reassuring in that it brings the comforting news that Admiral Howe has not penetrated the Chevaux de Frise. The Commander-in-Chief has felt strongly that the enemy ships would drive through the barricade before this. That they have not pleasantly puzzles him.

At least, as of yesterday, they have not. And, at least, as of yesterday the garrisons at Fort Lee and Fort Washington are holding. This news and the fact that he has temporarily held Howe off make him thankful for the moment.

Certainly if Admiral Howe intended to try for control of the Hudson, the time to have done so was the past week.

Does the barrier across the river strike more fear in him than would appear to be the case?

Surely it must be evident to the admiral that the two posts have been greatly weakened by the drawing off of the American army into the White Plains.

It is a matter for much conjecture. Perhaps it should be weighed in council with his generals. Tomorrow he will do it.

The Continental Army's Chief has never disguised his liking for Greene. And neither has the brigadier general hesitated privately or publicly to show his devotion to the rebel Leader. There is a close bond between the two men. And tonight his much-respected junior officer has pleased him by ending his day with some good news.

As The General comes to the last paragraph of the report, his eyes can remain open no longer. He gets up from the table-desk, stretches, peers out the window into the post-midnight darkness. He smothers the coals of the fire and undresses.

Then, like all the rest, the Continental Army's Chief also at last rides off with Sleep. . . .

. . . Over the Roanoke and Rappahannock the swift steeds fly. But it is on the Potomac's shores where Sleep reins in her dark, intriguing chariot, gleaming in midnight black's invitingly soft unconsciousness.

. . . And there she gently drops him off and stands beside her prancers to await his soon return. She watches as he wanders, and, like some ghostly apparition, he ascends the walk, enveloped under Virginia's comforting stars from Heaven, to pass at last below the great veranda, through the closed door, disappearing appreciatively happy, within the sturdy and beloved walls of Mount Vernon . . . He is home . . . Home until there comes the sadly beckoning, pawing hoofs of dawn.

23

Saturday, November 2. . .

The Army Has Its Disillusioned

A Muddled Brain Rambles In Fever

Hope for Edmund Kearney's recovery from his infected wound had been waning until Minnie Abbott took over with her Indian remedies several days ago. Close to death, he had lain in one of the small hospital tents with his severely gashed leg gradually worsening and his fevered mind deliriously carrying him through a strangely assorted, kaleidoscopic review of his life. Never before has he seen his own dual personalities appear before the closed windows of his eyes.

And now his muddled brain is uncomprehending as his alternating egos reveal themselves in surprising revelations that flash before his mind and pour from out his lips.

Again and again he has let out a scream, either calling for his deceased mother, angrily scolding her, in his hallucinations, or damning the army surgeon in absentia, for advising him that it might be necessary to amputate his leg. His agonizing days and nights have been divided into periods of consciousness and delirium.

Those who had caught various bits of his ravings had at times listened to him reveal deep affection for his mother and then heard him turn his incoherent mental wanderings into a vitriolic condemnation of her. But he always periodically slashed out at a father who had deserted him in childhood.

Elaine and the other women, Jennie, Granny Bourdette and Minnie who have been caring for him since he was brought back to the Kearney house, slipped furtive side glances at one another as he raved about his childhood attraction for the ferry-master's daughter. And they heard enough to know he had of late bitterly resented his unrequited love and her marriage to John Gray.

Then his mind would jump, clearly disclosing that he had found a sadistic pleasure in the outlet which the insurrection provided him through enlisting. His meandering brain little by little revealed his intense hatred for the army.

For him this war was a revolution of a different kind. This was a revolution enabling him to escape from drab realism, from youthful frustrations and pressures he could no longer stand. It was to have been a vent for his emotions.

Army life has not provided Edmund Kearney with a vent. It seldom therapeutically does so.

Instead, his failure to be. promoted in accordance with what he felt he deserved, provoked a hatred for the military. And in one of Kearney's more rational moments in the hospital tent, the non-church going, agnostic-thinking youth told his mother's former priest this and more in an outburst of anger against his army, God and country.

But when Kearney called for the man of God again later in what Elaine hoped was to be a change for the better, the much respected cleric was on the other side of the valley and could not be reached.

Quietly, unobtrusively, Father Bulger has held masses and heard confessions from his few and widely scattered constituents throughout the region. Even among some of the strongest bigots within the predominating Huguenot, Dutch Reformed, Presbyterian and Anglican inhabitants in the valleys, there range varying degrees of tolerance, respect and admiration for the itinerant Catholic priest. However, among the few, extreme unwavering intolerants there is no compromise with the Catholic Church. Obsessed with a fear of the papacy and its representatives, these bigots carry their antipathies over to the Irish Catholics in particular. But they extend their antagonisms toward all denominations and sects which espouse doctrines contrary to their own.

Strangely, though, these prejudices are not generally found in the thinking of the river and The Mountain people. Though there are some bigots always to be found among them, there is more tolerance along the river than in the valleys. They are usually bound together more by the strings of weather, wind, tide and all the orderly arranged forces of nature than by the conflicting doctrines of mankind.

Abounding bigotry has made the Irish Catholics, among others, suspicious of the strongly biased in the valleys of the rivers. And much of that bias has been seeded by the persecution of the French Huguenots under Louis XIV which along with other prejudices have resown themselves in countless ways.

So it is not unusual in the valleys to find those with dissenting views and philosophies often mistreated, shunned and persecuted by a small but vociferous core of bigots.

The young Catholic priest was sharply reminded of it last winter. As he was walking through the snow from Tappan town to Hackensack, a couple stopped their buggy and gave him a ride. But upon learning their guest was wearing the robes of a Catholic priest, the angry couple stopped their carriage and instructed him to get out and walk.[1]

Father Bulger, accustomed to such affronts by narrow-minded extremists of whom he repeatedly says, "You must forgive them, for they know not what they do," thanked the couple and blessed them as he got out, prodded by their insistence.

Torn by their own self-perpetuating persecution complex they whip their horse to a gallop as though attempting to escape from their guilty consciences.

Left behind in the deepening snow, the priest tightened his coat around him and walked on through the storm. It was a long eight-mile walk that night for Father Bulger from the Indian-named Hohokus hamlet, which the Lenni Lenape had called the "land of the kindly sheltering red cedar," to the village of Hackensack.

The incident is one example of the many ways in which bigotry and persecution fiendishly rebound together in the valleys of the rivers.

Another is found in the warped thinking of Edmund Kearney, both inside and outside his rational hours. Thoroughly convinced that the army, the hamlet people and Elaine have deceived and persecuted him, he seeks escape in whatever manner is easiest for him. Therefore to avoid the trials of persecution which the priest and others endure for their religious beliefs, Kearney, for some time now, has quietly renounced all his mother's teachings. Included are the Catholicism under which he has been reared, and his God as well.

Burning with a waning fever, Edmund, though past the crisis

danger, called for Father Bulger. This gave Elaine the momentary hope that he might be shedding his bitter antagonisms. Since the priest was on the other side of The Mountain and was not asked for again after that, no one would ever know whether young Kearney was in a confessional mood.

Attempting to explain Edmund's bitterness and seek an excuse for his irrational reasoning, Elaine believes its roots are imbedded in that small core of religious and political bigots who hurl their poisoned darts of prejudice at Catholic, Jew, gentile, race, creed, and at their own sects or internal factions, wherever and whenever teachings, doctrines and pigment differ with their own.

Elaine has seen that it is the few extremely narrow-minded who often dominate the thinking of others. It is they, she feels, who will unhesitatingly, unprovoked, resort to the commission of villainous acts upon those they oppose.

Thus violence, uncontrolled, begets violence. And thus the Baummeisters see within America's war of rebellion the added torments of these internal conflicts flaring up throughout the valleys. They, like insidious little forest fires, are the disastrous personal "holy wars" of hatred and blind intolerance.

Reflecting the thinking of her parents, Elaine sees the prejudices of these few dominating, intolerant white people around her, similarly extending to the red man and the black man. She sees them fostering the same fears of violence which they find boiling up within their own ranks.

As these thoughts flash through Elaine's mind, she silently blames her society for all of Edmund's woes. The older of the two, the young woman has through her childhood with Edmund watched over him like an older sister, protecting and defending him.

This pattern continues to hold, for she has seen Edmund's boyhood disrupted by father-desertion and poverty. She has pitied him and sympathized with his attempts to hurdle the confusing doctrines, tenets and philosophies of the complex world around him. It is a world with which he has been unable to cope, especially in view of his limited ability to think rationally.

Reinforced by her father's teachings, Elaine has realized that only the very strong, the very wise and the very determined survive. This is vividly impressed upon her mind by the tragedy that has overtaken the Africans and now the Lenni Lenape and the other Indian tribes. For the Indians are constantly haunted by the fear the white man's few hard core of vicious exploiters of the weaker beings among all races of man, will attempt to enslave them as they have their own black African brothers.[2] It is the fear of human bondage which has haunted all mankind down through the ages.

Elaine and the other women at Edmund's bedside were silently and sadly surprised by the corporal's delirious outbursts, revealed during the height of his fever. Jennie, Minnie, Old Granny and Marie Louise listened to his ramblings. Like Elaine, they, too, were forced to look critically at their society's morality values, supposedly based upon godliness.

Chief Perawae and Minnie have often fished with Ma Kearney and her son. In the past, whenever they came down from their mountain-top home, they occupied the loft of the old, partly burned Kearney barn which Ma had used only for hay and storage.

And when Elaine heard of the surgeon's fear that Edmund's leg would have to be amputated, and Kearney's violent reaction upon hearing of it, she insisted he be removed to the unoccupied Kearney homestead. There the Abbotts, in the midst of preparing to join the last of the Lenni Lenape tribe in West Jersey, moved in temporarily to care for the youth and his infected wound.

Sentries and picket posts along the water front all know the "Old Chief" as he is affectionately called. He and his squaw, Minnie, and their antequated dug-out canoe, the one thing he hates to leave behind him in his destined move south, have unmolested right of way along the west bank of Hudson's river. The old couple, under their son, Andy's instructions, had come up on the tide last Tuesday with all the possessions they could carry.

The Last Visit Of the Last Unamis

For the last time, the "Old Chief" in his usual ritual at the ferry landing, unloaded Minnie's hand-made baskets for sale and trade at the water-front. All the handicraft, pelts and hides must go. Andy had made it clear, for there would be no room in the two canoes and later on the pack horses for any extras. So, in his old familiar spot at the trading place near the stage stop by the ferry, the aging descendant of Oratam quietly sat by his wares smoking his long-stemmed pipe and taking whatever pennies or trinkets he could get for his products.

The old man's jovial smile, sprightly step and proud bearing, like that of his squaw and his son, have given him singular respect and prestige in the community. Of most interest to the youngsters who often crowd around him are his unique blue head-band and the identifying marks of a Unami chieftain on his forehead, chest and arms.

It is the tortoise-shaped pendulum hanging on shell beads around his neck, and the matching beads on his moccasins and deer-hide breeches, that sadly recount the silent story of the disappearing glory that was once the great Lenni Lenape Nation.

His friends know that Andy Abbott had feared for his parents' welfare alone on the old Castle grounds, particularly since Abbott was certain that the entire peninsula would soon be overrun by the British and Hessian forces. Most of the inhabitants who know the Abbotts felt they were losing a part of their hamlet when they heard the Indian scout was taking a furlough to escort his parents south downriver and across the country to join the last of his Unami people at Edgepillock, the Brotherton Reservation in Burlington County.[3]

So for the past few days the old man has been saying his good-byes, selling his wares and preparing the birchen canoes for the long first leg of their journey. Their first stop will be Amboy on their trek across the Jerseys, which Perawae still calls, "Sago-ri-gi'-vi-yogs-tha"—the Lenni Lenape name for New Jersey, meaning, "place where justice is done."

Meanwhile, Minnie, whose early beauty has gently followed her into what she calls her winter moons of life, immediately upon arriving at the ferry landing took her richly decorated hickory splint basket of herbs and victuals into the barn behind the Kearney house. Included were berries, dried roots and nuts. She knew what she would need for Ma Kearney's son and set them aside.

When the canoes were unloaded and beached, she hastily joined the other women on their way up to the hospital tent. She and Granny Bourdette had delivered Edmund almost eighteen years ago the last day of December.

Since the youth has been returned to his home from the hospital tent, Minnie has devoted most of her time to nursing him back to health. Through the benefits of her mysterious concoctions of herbs, poultices and liquids, not only has the corporal's fever been dissipated, but he has almost fully recovered. Owing to a severed muscle, however, he has been told he will always have to limp and can never expect the full use of his leg.

That news has made him more sullen and disagreeable than usual. However, it has brought him the good news that he had not expected for another month, word that he can be discharged from further military duty. That fact has speeded his recovery.

Now his mind, no longer in fever, is concerned with how much everyone knows about the "accident." He has not succeeded in learning anything from Elaine.

By her eyes and manner, Edmund suspects Elaine knows something as well as perhaps does the whole camp. But he questions himself. How could anyone? There is no evidence.

The Kearney house, like most of the river-side fishermen's little frame homes, has two bedrooms, a big kitchen and a high loft. Edmund occupies his own bedroom. The Abbotts, at everyone's insistence, have occupied Ma Kearney's room instead of the barn loft as in the past.

In such cramped quarters ordinary conversations in the kitchen are audible to anyone in the bedroom with the door ajar. And to keep the rooms warm, doors are seldom closed.

So late this afternoon, and not without good reason, Elaine has brought along Paul, Katie May and Hans, who as yet knows nothing about his Uncle Abe's tragic death.

All three children are more interested in visiting with Minnie than paying any attention to the recuperating Edmund. They have always been attracted to Minnie, especially since she is such a good teller of tales. And intentionally Elaine prods the kindly Indian woman to tell the children again the legend of Chinqueka.[4] The ferry-master's daughter knows that the telling will be in Edmund's earshot.

In her own broken English words, which the youngsters have no trouble understanding and which she sometimes mixes with Dutch and Huguenot expressions, Minnie recounts the sad Indian love story of Chinqueka, princess of the Naraticongs from the Delaware clan of the Lenni Lenape. They listen spellbound as she tells how the visiting prince of the neighboring Manhataes fell in love with Chinqueka and she with him.

Minnie recounts how the Prince stayed on after his fellow tribesmen returned home. Soon he became the suitor favored even by Chinqueka's father, Chief of the Naraticongs.

Then the jealous Manasamitt burned with anger. For the Naraticong brave had been the leading suitor for Chinqueka's hand until the Prince came to the village. Secretly he stalked the two devoted lovers until one afternoon he came upon them sitting high on top the great chimney rock not far from the bounding brook. And, Minnie added, "it is a place far distant from here toward where sleeps the sun."

After a fierce fight the enraged Manasamitt slew the Prince and hurled his body over the great precipice as Chinqueka ran as fast as the doe back to the village to get help. But, ah, too late!

Then, grieving for her lost lover day after day, poor Chinqueka would eat no food. Alone she would go to the high chimney rock and mourn her lover. Then finally she heard her Prince call out to her from off in the space beyond the great rock. She poised briefly on the brink and listened.

The children now sit motionless on the hearthstone, their eyes wide open in wonder as the dramatic tale unfolds before their minds. Outside the tapering rain lightly taps the hand-hewn cedar roofing shingles. In the adjoining room Edmund's eyes dart back and forth, compelled by interest and isolation to listen as anger and shame silently overcome him.

Often he and Elaine as children had acted out the Chinqueka story on the Bluff Rock. But Edmund had always been the Prince and a rock was used to play the role of Manasamitt who always lost the fight in their childhood production. In that way Edmund, the Prince, always succeeded in throwing a rock, Manasamitt, over the precipice. And now he listens and twitches with discomfort as Minnie concludes. He has no choice.

Then, continues Minnie, the grieving Princess was sure she heard her lover cry out, "Come to me, my Chinqueka! Here we will be happy and in peace never more to part! I have found the great happy hunting ground! Come, my beloved!"

Convinced it was her lover's voice calling her, Chinqueka paused momentarily on the cliff's edge, Minnie tells her breathless listeners. Then, stretching out her arms, she leaped out over the great rock and was carried high and far by her lover into the west wind, for there was never any sign of either one of their remains found below the big chimney-like rock.

However, Minnie told her young audience, that was not all. The Prince's tribe swore vengeance for his death and soon there followed the long, bitter, bloody war between the Manhattae and the Naraticong. The great war, the old Indian woman tells them, lasted until the first white men came to the lands of the Lenape which lay between the two great waters.

Here Perawae's squaw points to the river out the door, calling it "Mahicanittuck" and then waves westward, calling the river far toward the setting sun, "Delaware."

" 'Tis where the fork of the Delaware is that Perawae and Minnie must now go to join our people," Minnie says sadly in ending her tale.

All the lands between the two great rivers, she tells the children who ask one question after the other, once belonged to her people, the first people. This and more they already know yet still would hear again.

Suddenly from up toward the ferry landing is heard the clear, trilling, whippoorwill-like whistle which Elaine and the children all quickly recognize as John Gray's. It is his own unusual, distinctive call. Always, the youngsters note, it is repeated thrice. And this to them seems an unnecessary waste. But not so to Elaine.

As the three youngsters are about to leave, each courteously shouts a "fare-thee-well" into Edmund's room. Edmund disregards their courtesy, calling out that he wants to see Elaine. Telling the children she will catch up with them, she walks up to the side of Edmund's bed and looks into his shifting, sheepish eyes. He turns his gaze away from her censure.

"Why did you do it, Edmund? Why?" Elaine asks. "I heard how it all happened. And, though they all say it was an accident, I don't believe it! You may have fooled the others. But you have not fooled me. When we parted at the well sweep, I feared you would do something stupid. But why?"

"Den yous is da only one dat tinks I did it ta hurt 'im?" Kearney replies. And, getting no answers, continues, "Supposin' it wuzen an akceedden'. Supposin' I only meant ta scare 'im becaus'n he kum 'tween us like he done?"

Elaine's eyes now flashed with anger causing Edmund to pull back as she scolded, "Did you not know I love my husband as I do my life? I have tried to help you and like you as a sister would a brother. And that is all, Edmund! There was never any 'sweetheart' love for you from me, and I never, for the life of me, even dreamed you had any such attraction for me. Now that is the way it is, and that is the way it is always going to be! Do you hear me, Edmund? . . ."

Seeing the youth is too cowered to reply, Elaine, staring steadily at him, continues, "I feel as though you may not have intended to, but you might have killed John or yourself. Yet I blame you less than I blame this war, this useless fighting. It has turned men into murderers. I suppose you know you are to be discharged if you wish. The papers await you. I think you should sign them before you kill yourself trying to kill others."

Searching for something to say, Edmund answers, "I diden' mean it. I mean I diden' mean ta hurt 'im. I wuz just mad at 'im and yous too! . . . and I knows ya put Minnie up ta tellin' dat story to da kids . . . Ya memba, Ellie, I wuz allus the Prince? So I wouldn't hurt 'im . . . jus scaren 'im a little. Dat's all I wuz gonna do. Would I go a'hurtin' 'im?''

"You were a child then, Edmund." Elaine replies. "You are a man now. And the army has filled you with hate and meanness. Find yourself a craft and stay away from bad company. Now I must go. I will not breathe what I know, so you may rest at ease about that."

"Den I say gud-bye ta ya now, 'causn I ain't a'stayin' 'round here. I'm a goin' across river. So I ain't gonna be here fer ya birtday party . . ."

"What birthday party?" Elaine asked astounded.

"I takes credit fer it, 'causin' I told da Irish actor an da Engless songs writer up on da Barbette when ya birtday wuz," Edmund replies. "Dey says dey wuz gonna gib ya a party up dere nex' Sater'da."

"Well, you just tell them I want none of it!" Elaine retorts brusquely. "And you did me no favor by telling them. Rubbish! I want none of it! I want this fools' war over and my husband in one piece."

Her eyes flashing, she says, "Enough of this! It is raining hard. My husband awaits me at the wharf. He has had a long tour of duty and there is much preparation going on up above. You do as Minnie tells you."

Then, turning back towards him as she goes through the door, she says, "You take that discharge, Edmund. Your mother would want it that way . . . now . . . And go somewhere away from this horrible war where you can try to forget and ask forgiveness."

She strides rapidly across the big kitchen room and out into the rain through the center door which fails to close behind her. Hurriedly the worried and confused bride hastens to catch up with the children, headed toward John and the wharf-house sentry post. As she does so, her clouded mind clears enough to realize she had not said goodbye to Minnie.

The Indian woman could not help but hear the conversation that had gone on between Elaine and Edmund. Quietly Perawae's squaw had continued stirring the soup in the huge iron cauldron swung out from over the fire on its long cast-iron hanging rod. Knowing how upset the young bride was upon leaving, Minnie said nothing. She got up from Ma Kearney's old favorite four-legged stool after swinging the cauldron back over the fire's logs and closed the door with a sad shake of her head.

Elaine is unable to erase from her mind the tragic realization of what happens to the mind of a male child such as Edmund when the physical stresses of his harnessed adolescence destroy his powers of sanity and reasoning. In Edmund, lying in his bed cowering from her angry upbraiding of his actions, she feels she has seen an entirely different person from—the boy—the child she knew.

The phenomenon disturbs her as she accelerates her steps through the mud and drizzling rain. It is something she is certain has its causes rooted in the war. Everything that is constantly upsetting and crumbling the world around her, she thinks, stems from the rebellion against the King.

Assured that no one really knows what Edmund had truly tried to do, Elaine decides the entire matter is one she must keep entirely to herself. Certainly she cannot discuss it with John. And surely she owes something to Ma Kearney and to the dead woman's once so beloved only child. Elaine convinces herself that the least she can do is to protect Ma Kearney's memory by silence and forgetting.

Elaine, with the children running beside her, dashes toward her husband and falls into his arms. She knows it will be difficult if not impossible for her to forget how close to death she has inadvertently brought him.

Getting up and out of bed with a great deal more ease than he has displayed when anyone was around, Edmund ambles over to the window, watching Elaine as she leaves. In the pre-dusk of the evening with the wet gray skies darkening behind the cliff's west side, he sees his childhood playmate rush into the arms of his hated adversary.

Kearney's eyes narrow. His teeth clench when the married lovers embrace. His anger builds and the passion of his fury explodes. He strikes his fist down violently upon the washstand beneath the window. The force of his blow shakes the water pitcher off the stand and sends it crashing to the wide-boarded floor where it breaks into pieces.

The sound brings Minnie hurrying curiously into the room. She sees what has happened, but says nothing. Kearney, his eyes betraying his guilt, grunts with a shrug of his shoulders, "Akceedden' . . . 'Jus falled. 'Couldn'den help it."

Minnie, turning around and returning to her cauldron of soup, says nothing. She does not even bother to pick up the broken crockery. On his cane, Kearney soon follows her into the kitchen.

Knowing he can collect his pay and get his discharge, thus ridding himself of the military forever, the frustrated soldier reaches his decision. For the youth is haunted by the fear that if Elaine knows or suspects what he has tried to do, so possibly does the entire encampment. He is certain that he can never be sure. So, perturbed by the embarrassing stigma that everyone will suspect, though will never be able to prove that he had attempted to murder an army officer, the corporal decides he must flee the area.

Determined that he must get out and as far away as soon as he can the disillusioned corporal enters the kitchen just as Perawae comes through the outside door with his arms loaded with fire logs. Abruptly Edmund announces to the attentive Indian couple that he is leaving at dawn.

Neither one attempts to dissuade him. Both merely nod their heads. Were it not the couple's usual custom for treating almost any white man's announcement, Edmund would be certain that they too knew his dark secret.

Kearney's greatest fear in putting off his flight from The Mountain and the cliffs any longer is that he may meet Gray or the black boy, Jocko, face to face. That fearful possibility of encountering either one of them causes the corporal to break out in a cold sweat.

He nurses a sneaking suspicion that both Gray and Jocko saw his entire action on the cliff. In fact he suspects that possibly one or the other of them reported it all to Elaine.

His pay and severance papers can be secured at Headquarters. But when that is done, unless it is very early in the morning or late at night, every man who musters out is first lectured as to the country's welfare. By clearing out at dawn he believes he can avoid all that "blarney, rigmarole of duty, liberty and patriotism." Of that, he mumbles, he has had enough!

Kearney asks the old couple to keep his leaving a secret since, he tells them, he does not care to say a lot of Godspeeds. Then, scribbling a note for the duty officer at Headquarters that he intends to pick up his discharge and severance pay at daybreak tomorrow, Edmund sends the obliging Old Chief up the gorge road with it. He asks Minnie to prepare him some victuals for a long trip and to have Perawae get his mother's old horse, "Gen'l Sweeney," from the Bourdette barn and hitch him to the old wagon before sun-up.

Generously Kearney advises Minnie that both she and Perawae are to stay on at the Kearney house just as long as they wish.

Minnie shakes her head in appreciation but tells him that they must go south when Andy comes for them.

More out of respect for Ma Kearney's memory than for her son, the Old Chief and his squaw do as they are bid. They do not question or interfere with the white man's strange ways. They do not even care to understand the perplexing and deceptive machinations behind the white man's thinking.

But the kindly Minnie does warn Edmund to stay off his feet and rest as much as possible until the wound is entirely healed.

Still solicitous about the babe that she once helped to bring into the world, the Lenni Lenape woman dresses his leg injury at bedtime and gives him an already prepared package of bandages, Indian healing potions and herbs for poultices to take with him.

In the morning the old couple will watch him set off up the shore road toward the gorge pass. On its summit he will make two stops. The first at his mother's grave just as the sun begins to glow in the east.

There, overlooking the great river hundreds of feet below and the vast island of Manhattan distantly coming into another light of day, he will stand, head bowed. And he will momentarily be brought back to the days of his prayers.

The cold November morning wind will be at his back. Only a few rustling brown leaves, escapees from the night's rains, will break the serene stillness of the burial grounds.

The next and final stop will be at Headquarters, his big moment. The moment before freedom and escape. And much to his surprise, his pay and severance paper will be waiting for him. For at John Gray's request, the surgeon will have speeded the discharge paper in anticipation of Kearney's decision to accept it. After all, there are a number of wearied, hungry, homesick soldiers, among the militia in particular, who would jump at a discharge for any reason. And there are many who even now fretfully await the approaching termination of their enlistments.

The post's sleepy-eyed duty officer will be shivering and yawning and in no mood to give any departing soldiers one of the customary lectures on what the country expects of him, an ex-soldier.

And Kearney, troubled by a guilty conscience, will avoid looking the duty officer or anyone else in the eye. He will suspect that everyone he meets will be looking at him as "that non-commissioned officer who attempted to murder a lieutenant."

If it had been any other officer except John Gray, the "enlisted man's friend," Kearney knows he might have had some sympathizers. But Edmund knows John Gray's popularity and that he, The Lieutenent's would-be executioner, stands isolated and alone with his hatred.

So tomorrow Kearney will sign a paper that the officer at Headquarters will thrust in front of him. With one hand the bleary-eyed second lieutenant will dash the quill's wet ink with sand from his sandbox shaker, and with the other he will cover his yawns and rub his half-closed eyes. There will not even be an exchange of farewells since Edmund Kearney, civilian, will lose no time in getting out and on his way.

As he hurriedly limps off on his hickory stick cane toward his wagon and begins awkwardly climbing up on the seat, he will see the men of the post falling out for formation with their companies. At the same time a relief picket will be noticed taking over the guard post commanding the fort road west into the valley.

Edmund will not use that road and travel via the Sneden Ferry to Dobbs since very often the black boy, Jocko Graves, brings his horses up through the Fort road and down into the valley at daybreak for pasturing.

And among the relief pickets, Edmund could also meet up with Gray and men from that outfit. The thought of running into any of them, uncertain as he is as to what they all may know, will frighten him, for a face-to-face confrontation is the last thing the conscience-stricken soldier wants.

The corporal will see one sure way out of his quandary. It will be the Bourdette ferry that will take him across to Mount Washington. From there he will make his way into Westchester.

That early morning ferry always has a flat-boat tow, just the one on which he can take his horse and cart unless an army wagon or a stage is waiting to cross. Swiftly then the newly made civilian will wheel his horse and cart around and drive down back the gorge road and on to the empty flat-boat waiting it will seem, almost as though it were just for him.

Only the old ferryman will be puzzled. He has known Edmund Kearney since he was a child. The old waterside hand had often watched the young boy helping his mother with her fishing business for Edmund was never one for school and when he did attend, he seldom stayed the day.

Kearney will tell the old man only that he has received a discharge owing to a battle wound and that he is going over to Westchester to work with friends as a carpenter ... perhaps on army constructions ... in the upper valley ... anything!

And the ferryman in an effort to help will tell him that carpenters are needed at Fort Washington's works. And this will give Kearney an idea for some thought.

Only a few military personnel, some army supplies and a dispatch rider will make up the passengers and cargo of the ferry sloop and the flat-boat it will tow.

When the craft pulls into Fort Washington Point under Jeffery's Hook, the corporal will decide to take the road up to the main works and consider the ferryman's advice. Perhaps he may be able to get civilian work there. But at that point he will rejoice that he is out of Fort Lee, out of Jersey, on his own, and thankfully, unknown. And then at last, Edmund Kearney will breathe easier than he has for days.

His paper will clear him through the sentries and get him safely by the Fort Washington Headquarters Post. But just as he will be passing through the sentry gate on to the Long Hill Road, he will hear a guard behind him shout, "Halt!"

The unnerved youth will think his heart has jumped up into his throat. And then, fearing the worst, he will rein up old "Gen'l Sweeney" with a tug that will almost bring the old horse up off his fores.

Then the guard will come up to Kearney and his cart and will tell him that the post adjutant wants to talk to him. The frightened corporal will almost be tempted to whip his horse into a gallop and run like the wind.

Through his mind will rush all kinds of fears as he will turn to see a short corpulent robust figure approaching from behind and evidently from out the guardhouse.

Trembling at the thought he has at last been caught and must now pay for his misdeeds, Kearney will be almost ready for any kind of a confession in order to rid himself forever of his pursuing and tormenting guilt complex. When the guard asks him if the adjutant can hitch a ride with him down to the "Neutral Grounds," Kearney will find his heart restored from out his mouth but not his voice and with a deep sigh will merely nod his head in relieved agreement.

The thing that will most impress the shaking corporal about the man will be the manner in which he so tightly will cling to the two, heavy leather pouches which he will hold pressed to his side. Only the surcoat which the so-called "adjutant" wears gives him a military identification. That and his tricorn hat.

But the coat will be one similar to Kearney's and to those often worn these days by civilians who have served with the Continental Army.

Then, speaking unnecessarily loud, the fat little man will say—as though primarily for the benefit of the guards—"I see by your papers, Corporal, you have just been discharged. Since I have important business to conduct in the forward lines near the neutral ground and since you may have difficulty on that road with our pickets, jittery as they are, I trusted you would like a passenger. And I am willing to pay you for your trouble."

Kearney will be so relieved from his temporary shock and so overcome by the fortunate turn of things that he will reply cheerfully, "Git right in, A'ju'ten! Youse is right as da roe in da upribber shad! I shor kud use a 'hextra shillin' er so! Git yeself up chere!"

After a rather long silence Edmund will ask timidly, "Ain't youse one of dem ad da top along wid da Kernel of Mount Wash'enten?"

"Yes," will come the adjutant's abrupt reply. And then, after a pause, he will add, "but still only an ensign!"

Then reflecting a few more seconds, the little fat man will say, soberly and cynically with the trace of a self-satisfied sneer on his lips, "*Ensign* William Demont, Adjutant to Colonel Robert Magaw, Commandant of that great, noble, unconquerable place you see up there called Fort Washington on Mount Washington!"

Impressed but thinking he has detected a note of angry dissatisfaction and sarcasm compounded into alleged injustices very much like his own, Kearney will look with considerable curiosity at his new-found friend.

But the free and happy Edmund will have no idea that he is looking at a man who is about to commit an act of treason of such calamitous magnitude that it will be destined to condemn thousands of human beings to death.

Most will die from starvation, inhumane treatment and disease in the dark, underground, unheated cold dungeons of ancient gaols or in the rat-infested holes of prison ships.

24

Saturday, November 9. . .

The Great Juggernaut
Grinds to an Ominous Halt

Companions In Discontent

Within the past week Edmund Kearney has acquired a close companion. And within the past few days he has made his companion, William Demont, former adjutant general of Fort Washington, into a demigod.

Kearney's hero worshipping began shortly after the discharged corporal drove Demont through the American lines, carrying him in Ma Kearney's old fish cart, pulled by faithful Gen'l Sweeney through the neutral grounds and straight into the British Headquarters below Harlem.

And within the week, William Demont has succeeded in betraying the American cause. For in his tightly held leather pouches, Colonel Magaw's adjutant had carried, and has now turned over to the enemy, the detailed plans of all approaches and works on and around Fort Washington.

Of this, Magaw and his staff at the fort know nothing. They know that the adjutant is away on leave.

Therefore the chance meeting of the quietly fleeing Demont with the happily escaping Kearney was almost made to order for the American army ensign in the perpetration of his plot. And for the slightly dull witted Edmund, hungering to place his trust with someone, it seemed a heaven-sent opportunity to climb in importance by casting his lot with someone of such high rank and prestige as the adjutant at Fort Washington.

Demont's smooth tongue easily convinced the credulous Kearney that the packet of papers the adjutant carried and clutched so tightly to his person would bring a quick and a just end to the war. But the first step was to deliver them safely and personally into General Howe's hands.

Thus, within the past week, the former Continental Army soldier has become a disciple of Demont's thinking and a convert to his treachery. Whether wittingly or not, the former militia corporal is now an accomplice in Adjutant William Demont's plot to bring about the fall of his country's sole remaining military post on Manhattan Island.

After all, reasoned Kearney, reflecting the thinking that Demont had convincingly instilled in his mind, the American rebellion has little chance of success. It has been doomed from the beginning. Everyone should now know that!

Further exploring his actions, he asked himself: Was it not Elaine's greatest hope? Had she not told him, "I want this war over!"?

It was not long before the disloyal ensign had Edmund believing that he too would be sharing in the fame and glory that the King and the colonists would heap upon them both.

The ensign informed his young friend that plans of the post and all the defenses on the entire Mount would enable the King's men to take the fortress by surprise. This, Demont told Kearney, would stop the bloodshed and bring a quick end to the war.

And so, within the past week, Kearney has followed the former rebel adjutant around like one of the numerous, homeless, faithful dogs that chase after the soldiers.

The youth, limping on his cane, was close behind the deserting American officer when the traitor entered Lord Percy's headquarters at Harlem and announced his desire to give General Howe some vital information on behalf of the British Empire. Later Edmund was at the ensign's heels after the pair arrived at Howe's camp at White Plains. And it was there that Demont was escorted before Sir William last Sunday night, November 3.

Convinced by his staff and by area-wide Tories of the authenticity of Demont's story and the plans he carried with him, Howe assured the American adjutant safety within the British lines.

And so the rebel betrayer returned to his obsequious accomplice, certain that he would soon be basking in the light of international fame. The secretive, self-seeking Demont gave no indication to Kearney or to anyone else what Howe promised as compensation.

For General Howe, still nursing his wounds from the unsuccessful White Plains operation Friday, Demont's defection opened up a whole new avenue of possibilities. By Monday morning, November 4, he ordered the Juggernaut on the move out of White Plains.

His marching orders, issued Monday morning for execution the following day, were intentionally puzzling. Few of his staff had the slightest knowledge of what was about to take place. Most thought, as also would soon the American staff command, that Sir William was headed for Hudson's river and planned to make a crossing into Jersey.

British General Grant was ordered to move out with his Sixth Brigade to De Lancey's mill on the Bronx River at West Farms. The Fourth British Regiment was to move to Miles Square in the same town.

The Hessian Waldeck Regiment, which had been earlier left behind by General Knyphausen to act as a support and as a holding force at New Rochelle, was ordered to the bridge three miles above De Lancey's mill on the same river. The Waldecks were eventually to rejoin Knyphausen who on Saturday, November 2, was encamped on New York's Manhattan Island at King's Bridge.

Knyphausen's push into King's Bridge sent the American defenders scurrying back behind the safety of the rebel works at Fort Washington. From the American viewpoint, Knyphausen's operations seemed to belie any immediate intention by the British Juggernaut to cross the Hudson and invade New Jersey. However, the Hessian maneuver could be a feint.

The lull in White Plains Saturday and Sunday, November 2 and 3, was looked upon by the rebels as a temporary respite, giving them extra time to dig in and prepare for Howe's follow-up attack. The Continentals, pondering the enemy's next move, expected action Monday. It didn't come.

They were sure, from the activities going on within the British encampment Monday night and Tuesday morning that something was happening. But they never expected Sir William and his Juggernaut would about-face and head westward, entirely abandoning their encampments.

At first, however, all that the American Commander and his staff could ascertain was that a great movement was in progress. The hills suddenly reverberated with the sounds of men on the march, the rumbling of gun carriages, wagons and heavy artillery. Howe's entire army was on the move through the white, fog-covering mist over the village of White Plains.

When the fog lifted over the town Tuesday morning, November 5, it was evident that the British commander-in-chief and his entire army were leaving. Bewildered, the forward American pickets watched unbelievingly. They excitedly reported their surprising observations until they watched the British rear guard troops fade out of sight over Chatterton Hill on the Dobbs Ferry road, leaving White Plains and the rebels to fathom the mystery.

The Fort's Secrets Lie In Howe's Hands

The astute commander of His Majesty's military forces in America, who fourteen years ago was cited as "one of the most brilliant of the junior officers of the British army," knows what is going through his enemy's mind. The movement will be interpreted by the rebels to mean that either the British leader will cross over the Hudson into Jersey or return to New York down the river's east bank.

Howe knows that if the Americans anticipate a British crossing, they will pull back across the Croton and then ferry the river farther north to keep the Juggernaut in sight. And if they anticipate a return of the King's forces to Manhattan, they will march parallel with the British lines but along the Hudson's west bank. Either way, Howe thinks, he will entice the Americans across Hudson's river and be able to execute a swift, devastating assault upon Fort Washington.

Somewhere within the great marching Juggernaut Tuesday morning rode Sir William. And with him the priceless plans that detail every defense construction including even the smallest redoubts on the sister post opposite Fort Lee.

Those plans give all the military information an assaulting enemy would want regarding location, size and nature of the earthworks and entrenchments that have been under construction for six months. Such information along with the complete layout of the inner fortress makes an attack on the so-called "impregnable mountain" practicable and feasible.

Accurately Howe quickly assessed the inestimable value of Demont's stolen plans. It would have been impossible to seek out from deserters and Tory informants the invaluable data now in his possession.

So with this priceless intelligence in his hands, Howe decides to employ every artifice at his command to deceive the American command and throw it off balance.

By heading for Dobbs Ferry and Hudson's river, Howe intentionally misled the American command into believing an invasion of Jersey was imminent. The British maneuver also eliminated the likelihood that the rebels would come down upon Howe's back and bite at his heels. For the Continentals, Sir William assumed, would be too busy getting themselves back on the Hudson's west bank. Howe knew that if he moved back through New Rochelle the rebel army would be constantly snapping at his tail.

To some of the Continentals holding the hills of White Plains, the withdrawal of their enemy signified a rebel victory. Even some of the Tories interpreted it as a British defeat, fleeing along with the redcoats.

When the uncalled for torching of the village brilliantly lighted up the Tuesday night sky, November 5, Howe at Dobbs Ferry was not the only one who assailed the incendiarism. So did the American Commander-in-Chief. However, to many, unfortunately, the town's torching seemed to be a celebration.

Now the rebel Leader is primarily concerned with his enemy's intentions. He was doubtful at first that Sir William was headed westward. He had ordered both Clinton and Scott to reconnoiter the evacuated grounds with great caution. And all posts were directed to remain on full alert under arms.

It was not until Tuesday afternoon that The General was thoroughly convinced that the King's men were en route to Dobbs. Then only was the alarm lifted.

With word from his scouts that Knyphausen had made a thrust at King's Bridge, The General and his staff, when informed Howe was bound for the Hudson River, were sure of one thing. The Juggernaut was definitely not returning to New York town.

By 2 P.M. the American Colonel Malcolm and 50 men moved into the evacuated enemy lines and took over the White Plains Court House and its grounds. The honorary assignment went to Malcolm and his riflemen owing to their previous perilous position on Merritt Hill when the little band was but a musket shot's distance from the British and a good mile away from their own lines.

As the British command had hoped, the American Leader and his staff, totally unaware that Fort Washington's innermost secrets were now lain bare, concluded that Howe was definitely planning to cross the Hudson—a logical military maneuver under the circumstances.

Certainly a bold strike by the British across the river, down through the Jerseys and then on to Philadelphia was the thing for Howe to do. It was a course of action which Howe's critics will later say he should have taken.

Another conjecture in the American camp is that Admiral Lord Howe may attempt to block the river while his brother's army surrounds Fort Lee.

A blockade by the Admiral, supported by the redcoat army, could isolate the American forces from their vital communications north with New England. It would sever the supply routes with the west, with the Jersey militia and the Pennsylvanians, and it could result in an effective encirclement of The General's army.

As for the possibility that Sir William in conjunction with Black Dick's men-of-war might lay siege to Mount Washington, the rebel officers are sure such an offensive would be too costly for Howe to risk. The British commander has a distasteful memory of his battle losses in the direct assault which he tragically ordered against astoundingly accurate American marksmanship on Breed's Hill in 1775.

So, in anticipating Howe's likely plan to cross Hudson's river, The General decided to counteract by moving his army north. He would cross Pines Bridge at Yorktown and proceed along the Westchester Crompond Road to Verplanck's Point. And there he would cross the Hudson by the King's Ferry.

But this called for a council of war. He summoned it for the following day, Wednesday, November 6.

On the 6th, just three days ago, the Council's officers patiently listened to each man's opinions, Colonel Reed, in reporting the proceedings, wrote on the same day:

> "Opinions here are various; some think they (the British) are falling down on Mount Washington; others that they mean to take shipping up North river and fall upon our rear; others, and a great majority, think that finding our army too strongly posted they have changed their whole plan, and are bending southward, intending to penetrate the Jerseys, and so move on to Philadelphia."[1]

General Lee, who had not forgotten his October 12 erroneous prediction to Congress regarding Howe's intentions, reported it to the army's Chieftain a short time later. And on Wednesday he repeated it to the council:

Howe would leave a strong force behind to hold New York and possibly effect a junction with Burgoyne in the north. . . . With his main army he would move on down to Trenton and then press on to take Philadelphia and the Continental Congress.

Lee's reputation and his weight at the Council of War persuaded the council that Howe would cross the river and storm through the Jerseys.

When all members of the council had their say, it was unanimously decided to throw a body of troops into Jersey. A force of 3,000 would be placed at Peekskill, 20 miles northwest of White Plains. They will guard The Highlands. General Lee was to be left behind with his 7,000 troops at North Castle to protect New England.

Howe should be happy with the American Council of War decision November 6.

Howe's Reason For Leaving White Plains: "A Political One"

It seemed so unlikely to the Continental Army's war council Wednesday that the enemy would attempt to fall upon Fort Washington, that little thought was given to the possibility. Neither Fort Washington and its surrounding posts nor their defenses are mentioned in the council's proceedings.[2]

However, The General had indicated his concern over the post's safety in a letter written that day. In a memorandum the rebel Chief wrote the Pennsylvania committee that "all communication with Mount Washington has now been cut off for two weeks."[3]

This interruption of American communications is understandable in light of the British army's far-reaching controls. For Howe's surveillance now extends widely over Westchester. It reaches from Knyphausen's lines north and west into the main divisions. And the British network has the support of its frigates and sloops roving off Dobbs Ferry and in Haverstraw Bay.

On that same day The General also wrote John Hancock, President of the Congress, explaining General Howe's movements:

"The design of this manoeuvre (Howe's withdrawal and march out of the White Plains) is a matter of much conjecture and speculation, and cannot be accounted for with any degree of certainty."[4]

Sir William, in his later report to London, will explain his reason for withdrawing from the White Plains without attempting a follow-up against the rebels as "a political one."[5] And a "political one" cannot, Howe thinks, be diplomatically or delicately put in writing. For the treasonable act of an American defector, ensign and adjutant of the supposedly largest and most impregnable fortress standing in the path of the King's troops, was not a matter to be routinely reported, if indeed at all.

Certainly to storm successfully such well-defended works as Mount Washington without inside help would be a remarkable, if not an impossible, military achievement for even the most powerful army in the world. To accomplish the act inside help was imperative. And Sir William now secretly holds all the inside help he will ever need for the task.

When the long war is finally over, William Demont, the traitor adjutant of Fort Washington, having fled in ignominy to England will appeal to the Crown for compensation. He will ask that it be granted to him for betraying his country and forced into exile.

He will request of the King 1,800 pounds for having "brought in with me the plans of Fort Washington, by which plans that fortress was taken by his Majesty's troops the 16th instant."

In his letter to the Reverend Dr. Peters, clergyman of the Church of England, Demont will make his indirect request to the Crown, writing:

"Rev, Sir:
"Permit me to Trouble you with a Short recital of my Services in America which I Presume may be deem'd among the most Singular of any that will go to Upper Canada. On the 2d of Nov'r 1776 I Sacrificed all I was Worth in the World to the Service of my King & Country and joined the then Lord Percy, brought in with me the Plans of Fort Washington, by which Plans that Fortress was taken by his Majesty's Troops the 16 instant, Together with 2,700 Prisoners and Stores & Ammunition to the amount of 1800 Pound. At the same time, I may with Justice affirm, from my knowledge of the Works, I saved the Lives of many of His Majestys Subjects,—these Sir are facts well-known to every General Officer which was there—and I may with Truth Declare from that time I Studied the Interest of my Country and neglected my own—or in the Language of Cardinal Woolsey had I have Served my God as I have done my King he would not Thus have Forsaken me.

"The folliwing is a Just Account due me from Government which I have never been able to bring forward for want of Sr. William Erskine who once when in Town assured me he'd Look into it but have never done it, otherways I should not have been in Debt.

"This Sir though it may not be in your Power to Get me may Justify my being so much in Debt, & in Expectation of this Act being Paid, together with another Dividend, from the Express words of the Act where it Says all under Ten Thousand pound Should be Paid without Deduction, I have received only £464 which I Justified before the Commissioners:

"Due for Baw, Batt. & Forrage	£110.7.0
"For Engaging Guides Getting Intelligence &c	45.9.7
"For doing duty as Commissary of Prisoners at Philadelphia Paying Clerks Stationery, &c	16.13.8
	£182.10.3

"The last Two Articles was Cash Paid out of my Pocket which was Promised to be Refunded by Sirs Wm Howe and Erskine.

"I most Humbly Beg Pardon for the Length of this Letter & Shall Conclude without making Some Masonac Remarks as at first Intended, and Remain

Rev'd Sir with Dutiful Respect
Your most obedient and Most Hum'l Serv't.
William Demont.

"London
Jany 16th
1792
"P.S. the Inclosed is a true account of my Debts taken from the different bills received."[6]

The British government will recognize the American turncoat's services in bringing about the overthrow of Fort Washington but will only allow him less than a third of his asking price. The Crown will grant Demont £60 and close the account.

Dissatisfied with his meager reward, the former American adjutant, unhappy with his lot, will die in England, an outcast of the new nation across the sea.

All Signs Point To A British Crossing

So on Thursday, November 7, the Continental Army Commander prepared for Howe's crossing of the Hudson while his British counterpart prepared to disappoint him by laying out a battle plan for besieging the last American stronghold on Manhattan Island.

Eleven days ago His Majesty's two men-of-war stole through the Chevaux de Frise and now lie upstream. That running of the American blockade has given the Continental Army staff officers further reasons to think the Howes have a massive amphibious move in mind. The false assumption contributes to Howe's deception.

And on Thursday, while the Americans were preparing for the crossing, a minor river action gave more credence to the certainty that an amphibious operation was in the making.

On that day, just two days ago, General Greene at Fort Lee loaded several pettiaugers with flour at the river's edge landing. They were destined for the main army in Westchester. However, the crews' major problem was to get by the enemy frigates lying at anchor in the Tappan Zee bay off Dobbs Ferry. And, as the crews feared, it was there that the tenders spotted the little American vessels.

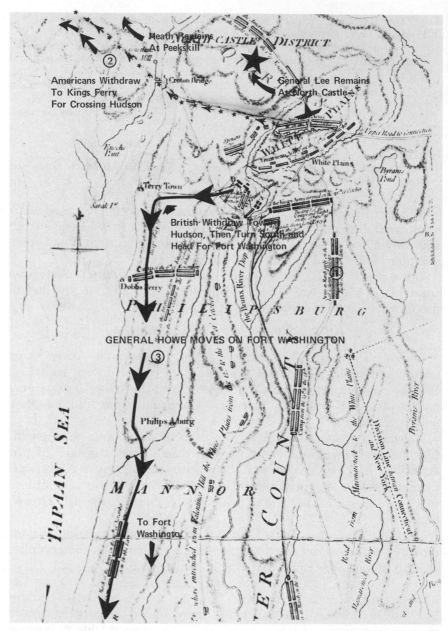

On this Overlay of the British Operations Map (600 upRt), Howe's Feint toward Hudson is shown with his turn south on Fort Washington after withdrawing from White Plains. The American withdrawal to Kings Ferry is shown at top.

Immediately two of the enemy boats, a row-galley and several barges, set out after the rebels' pettiaugers in an effort to seize them and their cargoes.[7]

"Our people," Greene reported to his Chief, "ran the pettiaugers ashore and landed and defended them."[8]

Despite repeated attempts by the British tars to land on the shallow flats, the attackers were forced to retire under the American fire. The rebels' defiance and skillful maneuvering enabled them to save themselves, vessels and cargoes. The admiral's sailors were up against men who knew their waters and its shores.

And also on Thursday morning the American Commander-in-Chief showed concern over Howe's lingering at Dobbs Ferry. From his White Plains headquarters, The General penned a warning to the Jersey Committee of Safety in Essex County stating that:

> ". . . General Howe, with the army under his command had retreated from that place (White Plains) with an intention, as (he) supposed, of sending a detachment of his troops into the Jerseys."[9]

This alarming warning rapidly spread havoc through the lands and caused the safety committee to notify the inhabitants, announcing:

> "The General therefore advises all those who live near the water, to be ready to move their stock, grain, carriages and other effects back into the country. He adds, if it is not done the calamities we must suffer will be beyond all description, and the advantages the enemy will receive will be immensely great.
>
> "They (the British) have treated all here without discrimination, the distinction of Whig and Tory has been lost in one general scene of ravage and desolation. The article of forage is of great importance to them; not a blade, he says, should be left; what cannot with convenience be removed, must be consumed without the least hesitation.
>
> "They have further intelligence, by a letter of this day from General Mercer, at Fort Lee, per express that General Green had just received advice from General Washington, that he was now fully convinced the enemy intended to cross the North River (Hudson River), and make an incursion into this State, desiring we may be prepared in the best manner possible to defeat the design of their coming."[10]

Consequently, General Howe's feint was working even more effectively than he had expected. Greene, looking down from his high perch on top of the Palisades, has not been convinced that Howe will cross. At least not at this time.

A fortnight ago, in complying with General Putnam's request

from Mount Washington for reinforcements, the commandant sent
over about 300 troops from Colonel Durkee's regiment. This act,
the reinforcing of Fort Washington, Greene more wholeheartedly
favored over the intended crossing of too many men from Westchester into Jersey.

Thus he took an opposite view from that of General Lee and
the Council of War. He was convinced that Howe's open movement
toward Mount Washington was not a feint as it appeared to be.[11]

Therefore the Fort Lee commander, in a letter to his Chief
tomorrow, November 10, will say that he doubts the enemy really
intends to invade New Jersey. He will write the American

**Major General Nathanael Greene—Portrait by C. W. Peale,
1783, Courtesy of Independence National Historical Park
Collection, Philadelphia, Pennsylvania.**

Commander that the British high command would not have given such a clear indication of its intentions were they preparing to invade. Nevertheless he will assure his superior that he will take the exact same precautions he would have taken had he expected Howe to fall down upon him in Jersey

Greene will write in part:

> "I am taking every measure in my power to oppose the enemy's landing, if they attempt crossing the river into the Jerseys, I have about five hundred men posted at the different passes in the mountains fortifying. About five hundred more are marching from Amboy directly for Dobbs Ferry (Sneden's Landing on the Hudson's west bank).[12]
>
> "I have directed the Quartermaster General to have everything moved out of the enemy's way, particularly cattle, carriages, hay and grain. The flour at Dobb's Ferry (Sneden's Landing side of river) is all moved from that place; and I have directed wagons to transport it to Clarke's (Tappan) and Orange Towns.
>
> "I am sure the enemy cannot land at Dobb's Ferry (Sneden's Landing), it will be so hedged up by night. The flats run off a great distance; they can't get near the shore with their ships. If the enemy intends to effect a landing at all, they'll attempt it at Naiac's (Nyack) or Haverstraw Bay."[13]

Greene's communique will be in reply to The General's warning yesterday, the 8th, in which the American Leader advised his Fort Lee post commander:

> ". . . and so far as can be collected from the best sources of intelligence, they (the British) must design a penetration into Jersey and fall down upon your post (Fort Lee)."[14]

Though going along with his Council of War, the American Commander-in-Chief also suspects Howe is staging a feint. He is certainly not as convinced as many of his staff that a crossing will be the sole British operation. His concerns for the safety of Fort Washington were also very much on his mind Thursday. And so he further unburdened his mind to Nathanael Greene, writing him from his headquarters at Peekskill:

The General Recommends Fort Washington's Evacuation

> "We conceive that Fort Washington will be an object for part of his (Howe's) forces, while New Jersey may claim the attention of the other part. To guard against the evils arising from the first, I must recommend you to pay every attention in your power, and give every assistance you can to the garrison opposite. (Fort Washington, opposite Greene's Fort Lee post is also under Greene's command).

"If you have not sent my boxes, with camp tables, and chairs, be so good as to let them remain with you, as I do not know but I shall move with the troops designed for the Jerseys, persuaded as I am of their (The British) having turned their views that way."[15]

The American Chief sent that message to Greene the day before yesterday as he was preparing the withdrawal of his main army from Westchester.

At that time, Thursday, almost all the troops had been pulled out of White Plains. Only a rear guard detachment and General Lee's 7,000-man force were left behind. Stationed with his large division, the largest of the soon-to-be divided corps, Lee will occupy the heights of North Castle protecting the passes to New England. He will try to maintain overland communications between New England and the lower states.

In the pre-dawn darkness Thursday, two British supply ships under a brisk southeast wind successfully stole under Fort Washington Point's batteries.[16] Cloaked by a light rain and a starless sky, they gingerly made their way through a small passage between the eastern terminus of the blockade and the shore.

Hearing of this yesterday, Friday, The General's growing lack of faith in the Chevaux de Frise made him doubt the wisdom for continuing to hold Fort Washington. It caused him to write Greene again. This time he advised, but did not command, that Greene consider the evacuation of all troops and equipment from the entire Mount Washington-Fort Washington defense systems.

The Commander-in-Chief tempered his recommendation to Greene by saying:

"The late passage of the 3 vessels up the north River ... is so plain a proof of the inefficacy of all the Obstructions we have thrown into it, that I cannot but think, it will Justify a Change in the disposition which has been made. If we cannot prevent Vessels passing up, and the Enemy are possessed of the surrounding Country, what valuable purpose can it answer to attempt to hold a post from which the expected Benefit cannot be had? I am therefore inclined to think it will not be prudent to hazard the men and stores at Mount Washington, but as you are on the spot leave it to you to give such orders as to evacuating Mount Washington as you Judge best, and so far revoking the order given to Colonel Magaw to defend it to the last."[17]

The General realizes that Greene is one among many of his loyal officers who nurses an attachment for Fort Washington symbolic to the affection he holds for his Chief, and that this admiration unwisely extends itself to defending the post "to the last."

Through this communication the rebel Leader has, he believes, released Greene from considering sentiment in his decision-making and freed his mind to make a sound military judgment.

But Greene, as well as all the staff officers, knows that the evacuation of Fort Washington and its mountain works will further undermine American morale, both civilian and military.

Never in his life will the 31-year-old Nathanael Greene be faced with a graver decision. Never in his career will the 44 year-old American Commander-in-Chief more regret the granting to his subordinates a major role in primary military decision-making than now in deciding the destiny of Fort Washington.

Despite his great affection for Green and the staff officers, The General is soon to wish he had not delegated primary military decision-making to others. He will be forced to conclude that the weights of responsibility and judgments in military matters must rest squarely and completely upon the head of only one decision-maker. The most that others can do, he will decide, is to recommend. But it will be a costly lesson.

Since the Continental Congress has by demand had to listen attentively to the voices of its constituent 13 States, and since the new nation's foundations rest upon decision-reaching through the will of the majority, the Congress has lauded The General's Council of War procedure for arriving at conclusions.

But the Congress of civilians is oblivious to any distinction in decision-forming between the steering of the eaglet country and the running of the eaglet country's new army in time of war. From the Congressional viewpoint, "Council of War" decision-making is preferable, giving, as it does, high officers from all 13 States a voice in field military matters.

From the military viewpoint: it becomes costly in delaying decisions; it is unwise from the standpoint of efficiency; and finally, it plays into the hands of the extremely capable and astute *enemy* commander whose decisions can be final because of arbitrary, unilateral powers, powers possibly equally susceptible to error as the multiple-mind judgments. And this the American Commander-in-Chief knows, and the American Congress is shortly to discover.

Given the power to decide whether to hold or withdraw from Mount Washington, a decison for which the Commander-in-Chief himself must in the end bear full responsibility, Greene is unwisely swayed despite his superior's advice, by sentiment rather than by objective military analysis.

Like many others within the American high command, Greene regards The General in that strangely magnetic light that is so often woven by hero-worshipping youth around some idol. Greene, even more silently than the others, is a devoted admirer of the Virginian, 13 years his senior.

In Greene's opinion there is little that the American Leader can do wrong. Greene ranks among the many officers who refuse to listen to The General's critics—critics who will soon harshly condemn the American Commander in the tremulous days ahead.

For the limping Fort Lee commandant from Rhode Island, it is a signal honor to have been named commandant of the sister forts on Hudson's river. It is particularly rewarding for Greene to have the responsibility for Fort Washington and the mount's works, since he is, in a sense, guardian of The General's namesake, the most important post and outworks in the nation.

Greene's interest in Fort Lee is purely military in contrast with his deeper attachment for Mount Washington. Fort Lee is just another army post, a post from out of which oozes no sentiment, particularly since it was renamed.

How could he now, when the fort appears so impregnable, issue an order to abandon it to the enemy?

After receiving his Chief's message yesterday, Greene crossed the river from The Mountain and remained on the east bank inspecting the Fort Washington defenses and counseling with its commander, Colonel Magaw until late last night[18]

It is the last American-held post on Manhattan. It does, in Greene's much unshared opinion, help with Fort Lee to protect the Hudson from Howe's shipping. Its defenses could not be stormed successfully without great and prohibitive loss to the enemy, *unless*, of course, *the enemy were in complete knowledge of its works and their lines of communication*. It is undoubtedly a symbol of America's military strength as well as that of its Commander-in-Chief, a morale-building symbol to the nation as long as it stands in defiance of the enemy.

Colonel Magaw, informing Greene that his adjutant, Ensign William Demont, is apparently taking an extended leave of absence, assured his superior that Fort Washington, additionally bulwarked by the stout surrounding defenses of Mount Washington, is virtually impregnable.

Nothing in that long day of inspecting and decision-making served better to boost Greene's confidence and spirits than Magaw's words. They, as much as his own encouraging observations of the works and the men's morale, helped him to reach his decision.

And so this morning, November 9, the Rhode Island commander of the twin forts penned his Chief these words:

> "Upon the whole I cannot help thinking the garrison (Fort Washington) is an advantage; and I cannot conceive the garrison to be in any great danger. The men can be brought off at any time, but the stores may not so easily be removed, yet I think they can be got off in spite of them, if matters grow desperate. This post (Fort Lee) is of no consequence only in conjunction with Mount Washington. I was over there last evening; the enemy seem to be disposing matters to beseige the place; but Colonel Magaw thinks it will take them till December expires before they can carry it."[19]

Greene has erred. Though he may have hoped to have put his Commander-in-Chief's mind at rest concerning the safety of Mount Washington, the Rhode Islander is to make his greatest mistake.

All night long he wrestled with the pros and cons of that decision, foreseeing only what might happen to the morale of the country if Fort Washington were evacuated.

Then, looking on the other side, he would visualize the bloody battle if the enemy should attempt to storm the well-defended slopes. He foresaw the forbidding costs by shot, shell and bayonet if Howe chose to pay the price, and he believed he saw an escape route if the siege were to stretch into days and weeks.

By morning his eyes were heavy from loss of sleep. And hesitating no longer, he wrote his Chief. Greene had made his decision.

How could he know that it would be such a costly error? How could he know that he was being duped by a traitor into setting the stage for one of the most disastrous tragedies of the entire war?

The catastrophic military lesson will eventually make of the "Blacksmith from Rhode Island," not simply a general with average military ability, but an exceptional army commander. For hereafter Greene's judgments will be made with extreme caution, based upon carefully weighed, analytical reasoning.

This growth from out a tragic experience, coupled with his natural ability to execute matters with dispatch and efficiency, will bring Greene wide repute. It will cause him to be rated second only to the American Commander-in-Chief as a military leader in the hierarchy of the Continental Army. But his decision this morning will become that ever-present thorn, spurring him toward expiation by achievement.

In contrast with some mortals who fall apart when difficulty
confronts them Greene will find, much as his Commander-in-Chief
has found, the will to overcome the severest of adversities.

It is that omnipotent resurgence of being—a force that only
mankind's chosen few can summon—which man's indomitable will
alone produces. And by producing, sows the seeds of success in the
barren holes of failure. This, then will become the key to Greene's
future services to his country.

Among the many factors influencing the commandant's thinking
in arriving at his unfortunate decision is the nature of the winters
in the northeast. Greene is a New Englander who watches the sky.
He knows the depth which the snows can reach almost any day now.

The unusually mild fall with its occasional heavy rains has been
an exception. And no army, not even the most powerful one in
the world, puts much hope in becoming victorious on the battlefield in the wintertime. This is the season for war-makers to seek
their winter quarters.

While the yet clement weather may induce Howe to expect its
continuation, Greene knows that the shorter days, the increasingly
colder nights, the approaching ice storms and the blinding, unpredictable blizzards momentarily could drive both armies stampeding
into their quarters until spring. And Howe's winter quarters are in
New York town.

It is there, as everyone knows, that "The Sultana" impatiently
awaits Sir William. And the British army's commander-in-chief
likewise looks forward to seeing her. Rumor has it that he awaits
her more eagerly than she awaits him.

Greene thinks that a British crossing into Jersey so late in the
fall is unlikely. His judgment is also based upon the present
placement of the enemy's scattered brigades.

As for an attack upon Mount Washington, the commander of
the sister forts is certain that Howe, cautious as he is, will not take
the risk. A siege possibly but not an assault.

The Rhode Island blacksmith, standing on the great Bluff Rock
at Fort Lee this morning during his inspection of The Mountain's
works, concedes that Howe could be planning to encircle and
isolate the Fort Washington garrison. But, he reminds himself, Magaw
has assured him that the post can hold out until the first of the year
if necessary. That would leave plenty of time, under the cover of
winter and darkness, to get off the troops, armament and supplies
with the aid of the Fort Lee batteries and the Chevaux de Frise.

And then, shortly after noon today, came the encouraging dispatch from Colonel Magaw that his men had come upon an advance Hessian company close to the Mount Washington defenses and had overwhelmed them. The colonel reported that his defenders had "killed thirteen Hessians and an officer, and stripped them."[20]

When that report reaches Howe, Greene is convinced that it will certainly impress the British high command with the cost of a direct attack and its inadvisableness. The enemy probe is further proof, in the post commander's mind, that Howe is planning a long siege against the works. Greene is now leaning toward the certainty that Howe will try to starve the Continentals out.

Another dispatch arrived this morning from upriver at Sneden's Landing. It reported Stirling and his van came across the river from Peekskill, landing at Haverstraw. Greene learns from this intelligence that Stirling is moving down through the valley on his way to Hackensack.

The dispatch further informs the Fort Lee commander that Howe is still at Dobbs Ferry opposite Sneden's, and that the rest of the Continentals have evacuated White Plains and will follow in Stirling's path. Stirling, according to the messenger, crossed the river into a gap called "The Cove" in Haverstraw Bay which Stirling's advance scouts located and where the remaining brigades will also land.

Greene concludes that the Commander-in-Chief will cross with the last division since according to the dispatch the American Commander was recently reported with his staff reconnoitering The Highlands below the Mohegan Indians' territory. The Fort Lee commandant, recalling that The General had asked to use Craig and Abbott for scouting, now realizes why. No one knows the Mohegans and their trails better than does Indian Abbott.

However, Greene now begins to experience uneasiness. It has suddenly dawned upon him that the bulk of the American army is moving across the river and down into Jersey. This withdrawal movement will leave only Charles Lee and his corps of about 7,000 troops in northern Westchester and General Heath with a 3,000-man force in Peekskill.

These then, and less than 2,500 fighting men under Magaw's command at Fort Washington will now comprise the only—and widely scattered at that—deterrent rebel forces confronting Howe's 35,000 troops in lower New York State.

Greene wavers between grave concern and puzzled curiosity,

especially inasmuch as Howe's Juggernaut has seemingly come to a strangely ominous halt.

There is reason for concern since Heath, farthest north, will be guarding The Highlands from his Peekskill headquarters, and Lee, 11 miles southeast, will be watching over the passes to New England. The combined forces of fewer than 10,000 men fit for duty can be of little emergency assistance to Mount Washington over 30 miles away.

The uncertainty of what to expect next is as much a topic of conversation among the frightened inhabitants of the valleys and The Mountain as it is among the troops themselves. All kinds of stories have seeped down to Philadelphia, up to Boston and over to Ticonderoga.

On top of wonder and fear and all the other problems attendant with an army constantly on the defensive and a civilian populace, fearful that they are about to lose all they own, is the increasing number of sick added to the hospitals' overload of wounded and dying.

And lately to Fort Lee from Bergen has come General Mercer with many of his Flying Camp troops in the wake of the Paulus Hook evacuation. They have reinforced Greene's complement but not without adding to his commissarial and billeting problems—and also to his overcrowded hospital tents. Some of the hospital's new patients are victims of brawls frequently caused by jittery troops seeking an outlet when the enemy is quiet and uncertainty fills the air.

Many such fights stem from the soldiers' own regional loyalties and their particular likes and dislikes, the Yankees for their North, the Buckskins for their South.

And the Jersey Flying Camp men, who once swore they would never cross Hudson's river to fight in defense of New York, nurse a bitter anti-New York animosity that promotes arguments among the other troops, many of whom are from New York, the Carolinas, Virginia, Pennsylvania and New England.

Those from New York as well as those from the other States who were quartered last summer in the city, take pride in seeing the lanes between the barracks and huts at Fort Lee named, not after Jersey's towns and roads, but after New York's streets and avenues. Thus, it is the New York Staters in particular who poke fun at the Jersey Flying Camp men when they walk along "Broadway," "Wall Street," "Cortland," "Pearl" and the "Bowery."

Goaded into a fight by jests and reminded of their sworn oath "never to fight in defense of New York," the Flying Camp Jerseyans soon find themselves on Fort Lee's "New York streets" in a wild melee with the Yorkers. And, when the rum flows heavier, others join in, taking one side or the other.

In the end it is the surgeon who complains of bandaging the heads of disorderly soldiers when he has more than he can handle among the legitimate sick and wounded.

Both Mercer and Greene have complained of the inadequacy of medical facilities in the Continental Army. It is one more thing the two men have in common, the first and foremost of which is their admiration for the American Commander-in-Chief.

It was a week ago that Mercer left his headquarters at Amboy in order to turn over part of his Flying Camp personnel to Greene. With them came 75 sick, 9 wounded, and 19 distressed. All had been treated and recorded by Dr. Shippen.[21] These are in addition to the sick, wounded and dying in the hospital hut and tents at the post.

Their condition causes both Greene and Mercer to express their alarm at the total figure, now reaching 152.[22] But both men agree they should take up their quills to complain about the army's inability to give the sick humane attention. Greene notes that he had sent a letter to the President of the Congress October 10, just a month ago but has as yet received no reply.

"In Bod Need Of A Mir'acle"

Sitting in on the conversation, Greene's adjutant, Tom Paine, produces a copy of the letter and, with his superior's approval, turns it over to Mercer to peruse. He does so, agreeing with its contents which in part reads:

> "The sick of the army who are under the care of the regimental surgeon(s) are in a most wretched situation, the surgeons being without the least article of medicine to assist nature in her efforts for the recovery of health. There is no circumstance that strikes a greatest (sic) damp upon the spirits of the men who are yet well than the miserable condition the sick are in. They exhibit a spectable shocking to human feelings, and as the knowledge of their distress spreads through the country will prove an insurmountable obstacle to the recruiting army."[23]

"Whut con a mon do morr?" asks the Scottish-born Mercer, himself a physician, looking up from the copy of the letter." 'Tis them la'rds een Fil'adelfia who'll be a'wishin' they tark betta karr of their sik in the month a'comin'. Fer 'tis, I ken, thot morr thon

2,000 'nlistments 'twill by thon be expir'ren 'nd 'tis ev'rry mon, ible-bodies er not, will be a'usin', less by thon they'll ahll be a'gon 'nd deserr'ted."

Greene, evidencing some difficulty in understanding Mercer's rolling R's, nods his head in agreement.

Paine looks upon the backs of the two men as they stand engaged in conversation. He is hesitant to interrupt them in their continuing discussion while they look out through the south window of the Long House, peering over the Palisadean cliffs and across the river down upon the once peacefully quiet island in the distance. Before their eyes there stretches, Mercer reminds Greene, the ancient hunting grounds of the long-forgotten Indian chieftain, Mannahata.

"Methinks, Friend Nathanael, we ar're in bod need of a mir'racle such as pohrr Mannahata warrs eeen want of," the 51-year-old former surgeon's mate veteran of the Battle of Culloden under the Army of the Young Pretender, says, shaking his head pessimistically from side to side.

A great respecter of his older comrade who is 17 years his senior, Greene replies, "I learned much from one, Ezra Stiles, Sir, and believe it is not the army's weakness we face, but rather that of the people."

The 39-year-old Paine listens attentively as Greene pours out to Mercer some of his opinions about the people of the colonial States in general. Admitting that it was not Ezra Stiles' thoughts, but his own, the erstwhile Quaker, son of an ironmaster, lashes out critically by finally quoting John Adams' pointed remark about "the men who are raising themselves upon the ruin of this country."

An army, unlike a civilian society, unlike the people of a nation, Greene contends, has an avowed commitment to succeed and survive regardless of the cost in order to defend and protect the society or the nation, whose banner it carries. To succeed, he states, the army must destroy its undermining causes at the first exposure of destructiveness.

Mercer listens, agreeing generally but with some reservations, as the youthful Fort Lee commandant, who only three years ago was expelled from a Quaker meeting for attending a military parade, says:

"I think, Sir, that when any band of people—whether it be an army, a society of men or a ship of state—fails to destroy the shipworms that would bore into the timbers of its foundations, the army, the society, or the nation, crumbles and is eaten away in proportion to its own weakness of will to survive.

"It is through such loss of control and self-discipline, through the disdain for moral standards and behavior, through a toleration—if not an admiration—for criminal acts and corruption, and through the disrespect and defiance of God's, nature's and man's laws for the preservation of the best in all mankind, that the great republics of the past have committed suicide.

"They died," Greene continues," as John Adams says democracy can, by self-destruction. They died no longer capable of survival. They died losing the will to survive. And 'twas owing to their own weaknesses, owing to their own permissiveness, under the guise of 'Freedom.' For they permitted the destruction of their foundations—the institutional pillars of their societies—to be eaten away, to be decayed from within.

"This, Sir, I think is our greatest danger. It is, I believe, far more to be feared than that our army will fall apart."

Greene, turning aside to include his adjutant, adds, "I know that the quill of our talented adjutant says all this better than I. Methinks they are probably his words I have turned. For you, Thomas, have written these thoughts. Is it not you who say, 'Those who expect to reap the blessings of freedom must, like men, undergo the fatigue of supporting it.'? That is close. Is it not?"

Paine, who had wanted to remind Greene of something and had hesitated to interrupt, now finds his opportunity. He ignores the invitation to participate in the discussion. Instead he shifts it to the business of the day and reminds his superior officer that some days ago he had given permission to the men of the Barbette Battery to stage a little fun on the Bluff Rock honoring the birthday of the wife of thier commanding officer, Lieutenant John Gray.

"Ay, is it thot one they call 'The Blue Petterr'coat Scarrf Looten'nant?" Mercer questioningly breaks in, recognizing Gray's name as an officer from his former State of residence, Pennsylvania.

"Yes," replies Greene. "The same. A fine officer. We could not ask for better. And that wife of his, a native of this mountain, has proved almost as good as a bona fide physician for our sick. Give them what help you can, Thomas. 'Tis well we do something for the ferry-master's daughter. Well she deserves it."

During the past few weeks Greene has driven his men harder

each passing day. The mounting crisis has created severe tensions and cross tempers. Excitement has permeated the air already heavily burdened with fear.

The troops have been hard pressed under the mounting responsibilities placed upon the garrison. Fort Lee has become the main pivot of the campaign. The post has served as the chief source for supplying the forces across the river with armament, ammunition, grain, foodstuffs and the constantly demanded accouterments of war.

It has maintained a 24-hour vigil along the river. It has provided the army with a center for its communications through its observatory eyes over the enemy on Manhattan Island.

In addition Fort Lee has secretly become a key distribution center for the gathering and disseminating of intelligence. Early in July the Commander-in-Chief had initiated General Mercer into the role of a central intelligence officer. But Mercer "had failed then to get an agent to Staten Island"[24] from his command post at Amboy in order to be of help in the battle on Long Island.

However he has since succeeded in getting some of his spies scattered through the Jerseys, in New York and around Philadelphia. The intelligence system has begun, and its center is Fort Lee.

An Afternoon's Diversion

Thus the terrific working pace has given the exhausted Fort Lee garrison little time to dwell on tomorrow. The Saturday night respite is the one time during the week the troops can find relaxation. But since Sir William has made Sunday one of his most popular days for springing some action, even Saturday has lost its former lure for letting go.

So Greene has welcomed the Barbette Battery's request for a last day of the week afternoon diversion. He knows that most of the post's soldiery will find their Saturday night avenues of interest in far more harmful channels. Brawling with one another or drinking themselves under the table in the taverns of the valley are not uncommon occurrences among some of the troops on a week's end.

But the Barbette Battery men are a distinct breed all their own. They are not the Saturday night run of the mill brawlers and carousers.

Some are talented entertainers. Their pranks, songs, skits and fancy dances—all handed down from their widely differing heritages—have in the past given both the soldiers of the post and the inhabitants of The Mountain and the river's edge, a refreshing change from the tiresome monotony of the ever-present fifers and drummers. And behind their clever entertaining programs is one man, one dynamic personality, Corporal Lawrie MacNamara.

The Barbette Battery's men are isolated on the high Bluff Rock, remote from the main mountain encampment. As a result of this separation they are closer to one another than all the others of the fort's personnel.

Independent, carefree and self-willed, these artillerymen of The Barbette have earned a singular reputation. Highly rated artillerists, they are from varied walks of life. But they have found in Gray and Levy the only officers who, they think, understand them and their idiosyncrasies. It is only due to their respect for the two lieutenants that they, less reluctantly than for others, carry out some assignments.

Then too the entire battery has acquired a deep respect and admiration for the "Blue Petticoat Scarf Lieutenant's" petite bride. The delightfully friendly and cheerful wife of their officer has almost become an integral part of The Barbette.

Elaine dresses their wounds, helps them through their depressions and listens to their complaints with sympathetic understanding. For they have little faith in regimental surgeons and not much more in the profession's competency to heal. And unhesitatingly they say so.

But Elaine has not only attended them when ill. She has also willingly listened to their problems, their woes and the latest news about their sweethearts whom they hope some day to marry.

The shake-up and redistribution of the troops manning the Fort Lee garrisons that occurred on the eve of the Westchester campaign, have placed John Gary's and Asher Levy's Bluff Rock park of artillery and its command under Major Blodget. Over Blodget is Colonel Bedford who lodges with General Greene. All are part of Brigadier General James Irvine's regiments, the last of Greene's original troop command to remain with the commandant.

For when Nixon's and Clinton's regiments were transferred to Mount Washington, General Roberdeau's troops moved in to replace them. Then, when Bradley's and Dey's command went across, McAllister's and Clotz's regiments took their places.[25]

Colonel Bedford and Major Blodget, who is described by one soldier in his letter home as "quite fat and laughs all day," leave the running of the battery on The Rock and most of its directives in the hands of Captain John Gooch and Lieutenant John Gray and his friend, the Jewish second lieutenant.

Colonel Bedford and Major Blodget have wisely taken Adjutant Tom Paine's advice as gospel. Paine had told them, "They are all for one. 'Union' is seemingly their countersign. You best be resigned. It is doubtful anyone else but Gray and Levy can handle them."

A great admirer of his adjutant's talents with a pen, Greene respectfully, and with no derision intended told Colonel Bedford and Major Blodget, "Mr. 'Common Sense'[26] is right. 'Twould be best we give them rein within regulations and limits, certainly!"

It was the jocund Major Blodget who then laughingly proposed, fully aware of Jocko Graves' popularity with the men of the battery and his influence with Lieutenant Gray, "Gentlemen, I suggest we make Jocko, the senior commander up there. I gather from all accounts 'tis he who gives the orders to the officers of the battery anyway."

Even the straight-faced Paine and the serious-minded Greene allowed themselves a chuckle. Like most of the garrison they are aware of the friendship that has developed since before Long Island between the sharp-thinking black youth and the college-educated officer.

Even among those who cannot understand and some who cannot tolerate equal-footing, interracial friendships and affiliations, there is a growing respect for the Gray, Levy and Graves relationship.

It is as though there were hanging over it a "Don't Disturb!" sign. And with it a warning that anyone who dared to do so would have to answer to the whole Bluff Rock Barbette Battery. The artillerists' protective interest for each other does not invite "disturbers."

So on the great Bluff Rock this late fall, sunny afternoon, there is a festive mood of laughter and joy, and for a brief interlude the war will be forgotten. The surprise birthday party for the ferry-master's daughter has suddenly lifted the tensions of the soldiers and the inhabitants of The Mountain and the river's edge. For all have been invited.

Always by mid-afternoon on Saturday the army work details slow to a close for the week's end. Only the routine duty assignments go on. For the past few weeks the instigators of the affair have secretly found time to work up their little entertainment from an idea that was promoted by Sergeants Lawrie MacNamara, Denis Benson Kidd and Corporal Mike Monahan.

Monahan, who boasts that he once performed before Royalty on London's stages, is the only one with a professional background in histrionics. As a result of this rare experience he became the unchallenged director, songwriter, actor and organizer of the entertainment. His magnetic personality, coupled with his talents and his powers of persuasion, automatically made him "chief in charge."

And without the knowledge of The Lootenant but with the full cooperation of Second Lieutenant Levy and Headquarters, Monahan has made good use of his powers. He has engaged almost all the men of the battery in some way, making use of the talents that Jocko Graves, Carmen Luciano, Tony Talo, Swede Swenson and wagon-masters Tom Graves and Philip Reales never knew they had.

How they have succeeded in conducting their secret practices and preparations without the Grays knowing it, is more than Levy can understand. But the second lieutenant himself has been the one most responsible for keeping the Grays uninformed.

However, the acquisition of a pianoforte, which is closeted away in the magazine storehouse, has been bothersomely preying upon Gray's mind for some time. It was seized by a picket company on patrol out of the post some weeks ago. And for some strange reason it was approved by Headquarters for storage in, as Gray puts it, "The Barbette Battery's magazine depot."

Gray was assured by Paine that it was not illegal plunder when the Barbette's officer angrily complained of its storage on "Our Rock." The wagon, it was explained, when taken with its cargo, was carting the instrument and supplies from Philadelphia to New York under the protection of a band of disguised Tories.

As the Tory band headed through Bergen Neck on their way to Paulus Hook, Gray was told how the post's pickets jumped them. The surprise attack caused the Loyalist to scatter and disappear in the woods, leaving horse, wagon, pianoforte and the supplies behind.

In answer to The Lieutenant's inquiry why it had to be stored on the Bluff Rock, Gray was told by Blodget, who with Levy was in on the party-planners' scheming, that the Post Commandant heard that only one man in the garrison could play such an instrument. And that man was Sergeant Kidd.

It was Kidd who had appealed to Levy to arrange for the piano's storage in the Barbette's magazine shed. And it was Levy who enlisted Blodget's help and then told Gray he had approved the storage.

Then Gray reluctantly agreed.

In this devious way the Barbette men got their instrument. And with such a keyboard they could spin their program around music and song and practice during off hours without being heard or disturbed.

Gray could not help but think how nice the pianoforte would look in the Baummeister parlor with Elaine at the keys. How much better it would be than the ancient harpsichord which the late Captain Nordstrom of Bull's Ferry had given to Papa Pete. And what, Gray wondered to himself, can the army do with a pianoforte?

Perhaps, he thought, there may later be a way by which he could buy it for Elaine.

So the piano, secluded in the magazine shed, secretly carried out MacNamara and the cast's complot. The clandestine rehearsals not only proved highly successful, they also caused the battery's artillerymen to speed up their daily chores in order to get back to preparations. For MacNamara is a careful planner as well as a clever producer. And all are excitedly waiting now for this afternoon's surprise performance.

It has been arranged for Jocko to bring Elaine by some ruse, up to the couple's favorite ledge rock on the cliffside trail just under and out of sight of The Barbette's grounds. Since the entire Baummeister and Bourdette families are in on the plot, this should be easy.

Adjutant Tom Paine has agreed to detain The Lieutenant at Post Headquarters until the signal is given for him to come over. On his way he will be told Elaine is on the cliffside trail and wants to see him.

It is planned that by then the music, singing and commotion on The Rock's platform will cause both John and Elaine hurriedly to make their way up to see what all the noise is about. Unless the invited inhabitants of the water's edge and The Mountain—not more than 20 to 25 all told—give the secret away, The Lieutenant and his bride should certainly be surprised.

And so it happens. All around the flat Barbette Battery's Bluff Rock the men of the company gather along with the inhabitants the selected friends of the post and the artillerymen.

Behind them are the sentinels, the unlucky ones who drew picket duty for the day, and along with them, the observation guards. Watchfully they keep their attention focused on the movements below and across the river, occasionally glancing surreptitiously at the unusual festive celebration.

Every soldier is dressed in his finest. And in most cases the attire is a worn, dirt-stained, ragged hunting shirt, sometimes of leather or black brocade, covered by shabby surcoats, some of which, including breeches and shirts, may have once been worn by enemies.

Some have shoes or boots. Some have wrappings around their feet, saving their footwear for marching. Some wear beaver hats, some tricorns, cocked to the side and befeathered. And some are hatless.

Their descriptions do not much belie that of an English officer who wrote in his diary last Tuesday, November 5:

> "Many of the Rebels who were killed in the late affairs, were without shoes or Stockings & Several were observed to have only linen drawers on, with a Rifle or Hunting shirt, without any proper short or Waistcoat. They are also in great want of blankets."[2 7]

Another British officer, John Andre, will describe the Continentals later in these words:

> "I believe no nation ever saw such a set of tatterdemalions, few coats and what there were out at the elbows. In a whole regiment there is scarcely a pair of breeches."

But it cannot be said that the inhabitants of the post's environs, standing and sitting beside them, are dressed much better. Most of The Mountain and the river's edge people have given extensively of their own effects to assist the men of the fort and provide for their needs.

And now, John and Elaine, with Jocko bringing up the rear, make their way up the cliffside trail to ascertain the source of the commotion on The Rock. Without hesitating they pass a smiling sentry at the guardhouse and rush up the path.

Beyond the sentrybox they stop short, surprised and amazed by a happy, laughing crowd of soldiers, friends and relatives. All greet them with boisterous jubilation.

The Lieutenant looks from one to another as though searching for an answer. He sees his second lieutenant in the background beside a sentinel, but Levy, embarrassed, turns his head and looks over the parapet.

Elaine, in astonishment, stands with her hands covering her mouth almost on the verge of tears. Then MacNamara strides over to the pianoforte, positioned in a clear area before the center of the gathering on what is supposed to be the stage. He stands before the group but addresses Elaine, saying:

"Milady Gray, this music box is from us—all of us blighters on this post—ferr ye. But ferst Sergeant Kidd is 'bout to play some songs on't. Then we will give ye a little bit of enterteinement we 'ave fixed up jest ferr yer barthday. So 'tis happy, as happy at best we ahll kin be, ferr ye 'nd yer foine 'usband on this, yerr barthday."

With that, there rises up from The Rock a loud shout of "Hurrah for Elaine!" It echoes across the gorge road and over on the main encampment. Then MacNamara, asking all to settle back, says:

"Ahll of us know whut Milady Gray 'as done ferr the sik. 'Nd therr is nort a mon among us thot does nort know therr's nort a batterry nowherre thot 'as a looten-nant as sharp as is our Looten-nant. If ye ahll dinna ken 'ow sharp thot is, I'll tell ye. 'E wuz sharp 'eenuff to marry the Lidy Gray! Thot's 'ow sharp 'e wuz!"

When the laughter dies down, MacNamara tells the audience that the "sel'bratin'" is for both of them, but especially for Elaine on 'er nineteenth barthday." The corporal announces that Sergeant Kidd " 'as been a'makin' up songs jest ferr today." Then the soldier-entertainers begin their repertoire.

Elaine, her hands still clenched and pressed closely together with her thumbs between her teeth, is stricken silent, overwhelmed by the shock. Kearney's forgotten warning comes back all too late. John, by her side, realizes that the surprise has unduly upset her. He keeps his arm protectingly around hers.

Few pay much attention to the couple as MacNamara introduces Jocko with the first number on the program, identifying the black boy as "the youngest soldier in the battle of Long Island."

Jocko's number is a take-off, as everyone realizes, on Granny Rachel and Old Stephen Bourdette. The standard joke throughout the encampment and The Mountain is that every time the ferry owner wants to do something, his wife invariably says "No!" And every time Granny Rachel says, "No!" there is no appeal. And, vice versa, there is likewise no appeal for him if he says, "No!" when she says, "Yes!"

With Kidd at the pianoforte, Jocko starts off the program with loud laughter from his audience as he goes into his well known swinging dance step, singing:

"WHEN MAMMY SAYS 'NO!'"

"When Mammy says, 'No!,' it's, 'No! No! No!'
And when Mammy says, 'Yes!,' it's 'Yes!'
But when Pappy says, 'No!,' it's 'Yes! Yes! Yes!'
And when Pappy says, 'Yes!,' it's 'No!'
'Cause when Mammy says, 'Yes!,' it's gotta be 'Yes!'
And poor Pappy, he can't say, 'No!'
So, if Pappy says, 'Yes!,' and Mammy says, 'No!'
You can bet both your boots it's . . . (Whoa! . . . Ise bet ya alls know!)"[28]

Amid the laughter, the trace of a smile appears on Elaine's face. For she can just hear Granny Bourdette's scathing tirade tomorrow morning when the irate ferry owner's wife fully realizes that she was the target of the barb. And she can hear Jennie twitting her elderly charge up to that delicate brink of anger where the black servant laughingly and wisely stops short.

But right now the matriarchal septuagenarian looks puzzled. She has no idea that the skit is a take-off of her and her "Stevey." It has made an impression on the entire audience, but not on "Old Granny" whom it was jestingly intended to describe.

Not so Old Stephen. He immediately got the point. And his long, clay pipe revealed it. Quick, short puffs of smoke belched up over the rock on which he sat. However soft spurts from short inhales are an indication that, while he may be disapproving, there is a certain amount of humor in what he has heard or seen.

For Stephen Bourdette is not thin-skinned. He can abosrb the brunt of ridicule from most anyone except Pete Baummeister even though it strikes home with more impact than when it is aimed at others.

What annoys Old Stephen is Baummeister's happily contented smirk as the ferry-master sits on a rock opposite him.

His pipe pours out long, gentle, evenly spaced whiffs of smoke, denoting complete approval. And, in addition, across Baummeister's face is spread that wry little smile which always aggravates the one or the other, depending upon which one has been somehow bested by the other.

Gray, like all the rest, thought it good fun and laughed for the first time. However, he is concerned for Elaine, knowing the affair has upset her more than it has him. He holds his wife's arm comfortingly in his.

He had withheld his mirth, but Jocko's performance, though not by any means a finished product—the black youth's singing voice leaves ample room for improvement—was a treat for Jocko's closest friends, John and Elaine.

One number now rapidly follows the other with many of the men of the battery taking some little part in their escape from war. A few of the planned skits are so poorly executed that their hilarious enactment provokes more fun and laughter than if they were performed with errorless perfection.

While there were others who performed minor roles, it was MacNamara, Kidd, Monahan, the Graveses, Reales, Luciano, Swenson and Talo who kept the audience in a jovial mood as the performers forgot lines, missed cues and sang through their noses, sounding like husky-voiced, discorded songbirds.

There were many highlights. Among them was Monahan's rendition of "Tom Bolynn." Several of The Mountain's most prudent ladies registered deep shock when Monahan came to the chorus parts, singing gayly:

"TOM BOLYNN"

"Tom Bolynn had no breeches to wear
So he bought him a sheepskin to make him a pair.
'With the fleecy side out and the furry side in,
They'll be nice, light and warm,' said Tom Bolynn.

Tom and his wife and his wife's mother
All got into one bed together.
The weather was cold; the sheets were thin.
'I'll sleep in the middle,' Said Tom Bolynn.

But his wife's mother said the very next day,
'You'll have to get another place to stay.
I can't lie awake and hear you snore.
You can't stay in my house any more.'

Tom got into a hollow tree,
And very contented he seemed to be.
The wind did blow and the rain beat in.
'This is better than home,' said Tom Bolynn."[29]

When Swede Swenson begins the British drinking song, "How Stands the Glass Around," Reales and Talo as planned come out and hit him on the head. But Talo hits Swenson too hard and a fight almost ensues.

MacNamara and Monahan quickly separate the two. They then all together sing "Yankee Doodle." Kidd, at the pianoforte, tries nobly to accompany the mixture of voices which pour forth with:

"YANKEE DOODLE"

"Father and I went down to camp
Along with Captain Goodin,
And there we saw the men and boys
As thick as hasty puddin'.

Yankee Doodle keep it up,
Yankee Doodle dandy,
Mind the music and the step
And with the girls be handy.

And there we saw a thousand men
As rich as Squire David;
And what they wasted every day,
I wish it could be save'd.

And there was Captain Washington
Upon a Slapping stallion,
A'giving orders to his men.
I guess there was a million.

And then the feathers on his hat,
They looked so 'tarnal fine, ah!
I wanted peskily to get
To give to my Jemima."

At the close MacNamara solos the last stanza, adding:

"Yankee Doodle is the line
That we all delight in.
It suits for feasts' it suits for fun'in
And just as well for fightin'."[30]

Following this several of the men join in with Monahan singing "The Liberty Song." Monahan announces that it is a new tune recently written by John Dickinson:

"THE LIBERTY SONG"

"Come join hand in hand brave Americans all,
And rouse your bold hearts at fair Liberty's call.
No tyrannous acts shall suppress your just claim,
Or Stain with the dishonour America's name.
In Freedom we're born and in Freedom we'll live.
Our purposes are ready. Steady, Friends, Steady!
Not as slaves but as free men our money we'll give.
Then join hand in hand, brave Americans all
By uniting we stand; by dividing we fall.
For Heaven approves of each generous deed.
...... In Freedom we're born ... etc. ...."[31]

Kidd then announced that his next song is dedicated to The Mountain, the post and to all those present. The pianist sergeant accompanies Monahan whose Irish tenor voice is refereshing and surprising. But any change from his "Yankee Doodle," which Monahan sings well, though tiresomely often around camp, is welcome.

After a few tries, they begin, giving the title:

"MADE IN U.S.A."

"We were never very sure before that the Thingumajig would work.
It would shudder, quake and shimmy like a dancing harem Turk.
But you now can sure be certain when you hear the fellow say,
' 'Tis the greatest thing on earth, good Friend, 'cause it's Made In U.S.A.!'

We were never very sure before that the plowshare wouldn't break.
And when—By George!—it came apart, we knew we'd got a fake.
But you now can sure be certain when you hear the merchant say,
'This plowshare is the best there is, 'cause it's Made In U.S.A.!'

We were never very sure before that Rex's tax was any good.
It made us struggle, scowl and crawl, till we sat instead of stood.
But you now can sure be certain when the collector you must pay,
That the tax tastes somewhat sweeter, 'cause it's Made In U.S.A.!

And a lass was never sure before that the swain she loved would stay.
Though she'd dress and primp and shy and cry, yet still he'd get away.
But she now can sure be certain when she hears her father say,
'I guess he's true, for his new tattoo reads: Made In U.S.A.!'

Nor was a soldier sure before that his love would wait for him.
Though he'd hope and scheme and sadly dream, yet off with a Sam she'd skim.
But you can now be certain sure when you go back home to stay,
That the lassies who are waitin' are those Made In U.S.A.!"[32]

Again the hurrahs and laughter fill the air. It is little Paul sitting by his mother whose question is clearly audible to some around them as the uproar dies down.

"Mama," he asks Marie Louise, "where's that? Where's that place?"

Many of the audience who overhear him, laugh. But Marie Louise, merely smiles quietly and explains to her son that those are the initials for the new "Free and Independent United States of America."

Some among the adult gathering do not themselves, at first, know the meaning of the song's "U.S.A." title. No one wishes to display his ignorance. Marie Louise had taught them something.

The Baummeisters, man and wife, admirers of Thomas Paine, have often heard the revolutionist writer mention the "new

American nation" and the "United, Free and Independent States of America." For the post's adjutant is credited with being the first to have used the term, "Free and Independent States of America" and "the American nation,"[33] if not the title, *United States of America*, as well, a term Kidd has contracted to "U.S.A." for his song.

By this time the rapidly disappearing contents of a cider barrel have made the spirits of the men merry, but few have over-indulged. Most, including all of the women, have stayed with the dipper in the well water barrel.

However, the festivity and the gay mood of the gathering have tended to make all oblivious to the war that rages around them, now thankfully in silence.

Only the Bluff Rock's heavy armament, its military look of watchful preparedness, its big guns, the 32 and 24-pounders of The Barbette and the redoubts with their heavy cast iron cannon balls, missiles of death and destruction, stand darkly outlined in instant readiness. They are the realistic reminders of the surrounding perilous crisis. But these now are the exiled and foreboding shadows of the future, temporary outcasts of tired, frightened, diversion-seeking minds.

The somewhat aloof and strangely reserved attitude of The Lieutenant, and especially of his lady, has been evident to some of those who know the couple well. Both Elaine and John have smiled, but not over-joyously. Both have accepted the remarks, the harmless jests and the good wishes of soldiers, friends and neighbors with pleasant, affectionate, yet not very happy smiles on their faces. But neither has showed the enthusiasm that had been expected of them.

It is the keenly observant Jennie, standing by Old Stephen and Granny Rachel who first notices the Grays' less than happy attitude. Knowing Elaine and her moods since the ferry-master's daughter was first brought into the world, and knowing her almost, if not as well as her own mother, the astute black servant says, "Oh, oh! Look at her! Missy Elly doan like awl dis chere stuffin's."

The performance goes on. John and Elaine quietly move back behind the others. They sit on the Barbette's swivel platform on which is mounted the 32-pounder the men of The Barbette have nicknamed "Old Constitution" in remembrance of the fort's former appellation.

As a result of the cannon's nicknaming some will erroneously call the big weapon "Fort Constitution." This reference, intended to be for the cannon on the Bluff Rock, will often be applied to the Bluff Rock batteries themselves.

It will cause British spies and Tory informers to forward British chorographers the misleading information that the Bluff Rock's works are called "Fort Constitution," and the main works or encampment on The Mountain, "Fort Lee." At least one enemy map-maker will so label his drawings.[34]

Among those missing on The Rock now is Asher Levy. The battery's second lieutenant has heard the performance time and again in its frequent rehearsals. And he has helped the men in many ways to put it all together. Levy has quietly retired to his barracks to observe, as he generally does, his Sabbath in rest and solitude.

Many now suspect that the two recently married lovers are not enjoying the event which has brought Paine, Bedford, Gooch and the laughing Blodget to the entrance gate to look in on the affair. They are not there long before a messenger hands Paine a note and all three men hurriedly leave, making their way back to Headquarters.

Slowly the sun begins its rapid drop behind the mountain tree tops. It lengthens the growing shadows over the expansive view to the east—a view with which the gathered inhabitants have long lived and which for some no longer is impressive. Down and beyond the precipice rocky cliffs, the gaunt shadows crawl slowly across the majestic river.

Brief gusts of the forerunners of winter's winds rustle through both the young and the old of the stately oaks and cedars. The sudden bursts whip the multi-colored leaves from the deciduous trees, loosening their grip on life and their hold upon spring and summer's past glories.

Now, resigned, they soar off, torn away at last from their tree of life and its umbilical cord. Then, as though glad of their release, they fly high, set free to climb and dance with the wind they had so hard and so long fought. And soon each leaf in its final, lonesome, free-fall homeward gives itself up to once again replenish Mother Earth.

This sight, more than the songs and laughter of the younger people, grips the minds of the old ferry owner and his close friend and companion. It is the distant setting sun which they and all the elderly ones feel and see more clearly than the mundane things in the world of youth around them. Each day for them becomes more precious than the one before it.

Then Monahan and Kidd, becoming suddenly more serious and in a most respectful manner, bring their audience to silence, stating that they wish to close with a final piece that was written just for their guest of honor.

All the onlookers have patiently awaited the finale. All are wondering what Elaine will say. The thought of a priceless pianoforte here in the rough wilderness, despite the comfortably furnished Baummeister homestead by the river's edge, is almost ludicrous.

Both Kidd and Monahan preceded their final selection with a number the two had worked on, entitled "Everyone Has a Birthday, Even the U.S.A." It had brought a good response from the audience but left them noisy and fidgety under the disappearing sun and colder breezes.

With all quiet, Kidd announces simply and seriously that the last number is entitled "Elaine, The Lieutenant's Lady." He then tells them that all the men thank her for all she has done, and all of this is just to let her know it.

With Kidd at the piano, Monahan sings:

"ELAiNE, THE LIEUTENANT'S LADY"

"Oh, I think you'll like Elaine.
And I'm sure you'll remember her name.
Whether high on this mountain.
Or under the main,
In winter, in summer, in snow or in rain,
Oh, I'm sure you will like an Elaine.

She may be tiny and neat, tall or petite.
She may be winsome and witty, or clever and pretty.
She may be bashful, or bold, hot or cold, young or old—
Whatever, whatever, whatever you're told.
She may be a perfect figure eight,
Or just a lass who didn't rate
The ribbon of blue except from you,
Or you, or you, or you, or you.

But when you look on her features
And gaze on her face, and see there a woman
You just can't erase,
That's the Dame, that's the Jane, that's Elaine.
When you hold her hand and dwell in her eyes
And all of a sudden your hypnotized,
That's your Dame, that's your Jane, that's Elaine.

But if you don't hound her
Once you have found her,
You'll end in pain on memory lane,
Where you'll find desire
Can burn like a fire
And Heavens will thunder her name.
In winter, in summer, in snow or in rain
You'll be a dreamer, not a lover, of Elaine."[35]

The bubbling reaction of the assemblage and the cheers which follow the Kidd and Monahan number leave everyone but John and Elaine in high spirits. The couple stand impressed but stunned, Elaine more so than her husband.

The corporal clears his throat and goes over to the water barrel to quench his thirst and cool his much overworked larynx, while Sergeant Kidd stands and makes the presentation speech. Kidd declares that he is speaking in behalf of the entire garrison, saying:

"I know you all call The Lieutenant's lady, Missy Elaine, but I have to say, Madam Gray, for I speak for the soldiers of the fort who know her as that. I speak for all those who have come and gone from here who have been helped by her healing powers and kindness.

"We reckon that you all know how much we all think of our Lieutenant John Gray's lady and . . . well, Milady Gray, we just want you to have this fancy music instrument . . . and the song we made up and sang for you goes with it . . . from all of us on The Rock and on The Mountain."

Everyone waits in silence for Elaine to speak. Those who know her well are sure that she will say something. But more than that, those who know Elaine very well are never quite sure just what she will do.

They have always been able to count on the Baummeisters' daughter for doing one thing—the unexpected. They have always known her to do generally just the opposite of what she is expected to do.

Letting her arm free from his, Gray helps her up the ramp onto "Old Constitution's" platform. And then, in front of the big gun's breech end, Elaine responds.

She addresses them as soldiers, friends, neighbors and relatives, mentioning all of the performers by name, very much as she would her school children whose intentions might have been good but whose acts were impetuous. There are tears still in her eyes as she says:

"I, and I know my husband, admire and love you all for all this. You must know that we do. This surprising day and all the things that all you have done just for me, make me feel very happy, but at the same time, very sad.

"This is not the time for any of us to be laughing and festive-making. Not when we have men killing and maiming each other. Not when we have our people dying, leaving wives, children and sweethearts to pay the worst of the sacrifices and many costs of war. Not when we have so many of our people's loved ones suffering and dying right here at this post on The Mountain ... Just there over the gorge is our own hospital hut and the tents filled with the cries of the sick and the dying.

"How can I appreciate all this that you have tried to do for me today when I pray God each night to end this war—to end it no matter how!"

At this, a gasp goes up from among the assemblage. The air suddenly becomes tense. Those who were sitting now get up on their feet. All strain to hear every word. John Gray looks up at his wife. A worried look comes over his face.

"Yes," she continues, "no matter how! I see how surprised you are, but I say it again. For today I became a neutral. And until this moment, my husband did not know of it. Why? I will tell you why!

"Almost everyone I know is here today. Almost everyone except one little boy. Yet none of you have missed him. But this morning, through her tears, his mother asked that I break the news to Hans Onderdonk of how his favorite uncle, Corporal Abraham Onderdonk, died. I told him as gently but as little as I could.

"It is when you look into the eyes of a little boy or girl and say a brother, father, mother, sister, cousin or uncle has given his life to satisfy hate and vengeance and things that little ones cannot understand or care about. It makes me wonder if the King and all of us too, have not lost our minds.

"I cannot longer see any cause that is not able to be settled around a table. Why can this not be?"

Then, from the back of the gathering a man's angry voice shouts, "Can you, Elaine, talk with tyrants at a table unless you have a weapon in your hand? How would you win Liberty? How would you win Freedom from monsters? From oppressors?"

Shouts of, "True! True! True!" fill the air, but Elaine boldly goes on, ignoring the interruption:

"As for the pianoforte, Sergeant Kidd, surely you all know that

it must belong to someone who loves it. Someone who may play it
so beautifully one day and who the next may be found lying torn
and rotting in his own pool of blood when the smoke of battle
rises. I could never accept it thinking such thoughts. Certainly,
whoever is its rightful owner, needs it more than I. I would that it
go back to your enemies and that it play for the return of peace.

"So I thank you deeply for all you have tried to do for me and
my husband who has no part of these thoughts of mine. For his
mind and his life are his. And though I may lose you and even my
kith and kin—yes, even my husband—for saying all this, I must be
truthful with you and condemn the cause on both sides. For I am
no longer Whig, Patriot, Tory, or Loyalist. I am a neutral . . . I am
for peace . . ."

At this point Elaine breaks into tears. Sobbing almost hysterically, she turns to John who helps her down from the gun
platform.

A path is opened for them through the mumbling, whispering
crowd as voices rise and lower, some with angry epithets hurled in
Elaine's direction.

Standing straight, his head held high, Gray appears unperturbed
as he considerately escorts his weeping wife down the trail on to
the gorge road toward the Baummeister house. Not far behind,
trail the Baummeister family and the Bourdettes.

Hailing the distressed young woman and her husband from
behind, and hurriedly stepping to catch up with them Colonel
James Baxter, who arrived yesterday on his way through to a
command across the river, finally stops the pair.

A dashing young officer of the rough and tumble school, but
scholarly in knowledge, the colonel introduces himself as "Baxter,"
a commander of 200 Bucks County militiamen.[36] He and Gray
had met earlier in the day and chatted lengthily with each other.
In that discussion the two philosophy-minded men had found each
other's company mutually interesting.

Baxter and his unit have been alerted by Greene for transfer in
the morning to Mount Washington. The colonel, a lover of life and
of people generally, detests war and the settling of disputes by
force.

He had heard about the birthday affair and had watched it with
amusement from the parapet in the rear. Though a peace-lover, the
officer considers defense of a noble cause war's only justification
when all else fails.

Elaine's surprising lecture, excoriating the well-intentioned promoters of the affair, struck the colonel's chords of admiration. They also supported the arguments he has made so often in officers' gatherings. His theory has always been that women, not men, control the destinies of man.

As a general rule, according to Baxter, women are gifted with calmer and consequently more sensible reasoning powers than men. He contends that the great majority at the height of their early maturity are able to see the wisdom and the advantages of peaceful debate as the intelligent way to settle disputes.

It is Baxter's belief that man, his society, his nations and eventually his entire civilization will either rise or fall depending upon the strength or weakness of the character behind the women of a nation.

It is women, he points out, whose thinking and ideals filter into the receptive minds of men, moving them to actions for either good or evil.

It is women, he holds, who control the key to family adhesiveness, to the morality of man and to man's respect for himself, for nature and for his God. And, in defense of his reasoning, Baxter invariably cites the fall of Greece, Pompeii and Rome, tracing their disintegration to the fall of the women of those nations. Women, he will say, not men drag down the moral fibers of mankind or, on the other hand, uphold them.

When the colonel gets into the topic of the superiority of women over men in office discussions, the sparks fly like angrily disturbed embers. Then it is that reasonable discussion and debate turn into bitter haranguing which explodes fiercely into swearing denunciations of the colonel's theories. And it is heatedly so when Baxter declares that "man is instinctively a ruthless killer who destroys life wantonly, impelled by hate and greed."

However, his contentions—though they leave him usually alone, unsupported and isolated in his thinking—deposit lasting impressions on the male minds. For Baxter often cleverly makes those who debate with him agree that, among other things, women's intuition is greater than man's, that women's reasoning often is generally more beneficial for the society as a whole than man's, and that women's perception, instincts and earlier physical and mental maturity provide the female with countless advantages over her counterpart.

So Colonel Baxter introduces himself and tells Elaine that he was impressed with what she said and that he wanted to commend her for being so bravely outspoken. The war, he stated, is a tragic way for man to have to throw off the yoke of tyranny.

Attempting to point out that when tyranny, like fire, begins wildly to engulf all that stands in its path, Baxter declares there is a point where no man can longer stand by and be neutral. Noting that he had struggled against taking sides and then decided he must bear arms for The Cause, Baxter told her, "This is more than a cause. Give it all your thought before you are sure that the neutral's way is the right way."

And then he added:

"You, as I, may some day come to the conclusion that this is a war to raise man above the level of the animal kingdom. And if it is to be done, you, the women of this new nation, must take a part in it greater than you dare imagine. Not only in sacrifice but in intelligently leading the sadly confused men of this country to saner solutions than the force of arms.

"But, for saying what you did up there this afternoon, you should be thanked, Madam, not scorned. Be proud of it, Milady, even though you may be alone. I, too, have been alone with my beliefs. I know your feeling well. I admire you. . . . Now, farewell to you both. I cross over tomorrow to settle my troops for the winter on the Mount Washington slopes."

Between her sobs, Elaine thanked him. Then, leaning heavily on her husband's arm, she continued down the gorge road. Baxter, taking the opposite direction, ascended the path toward the main encampment.

In a few moments the Grays reached the white, weather-beaten Baummeister homestead. In silence they closed the Dutch door behind them and went upstairs to their room. Out of the window, arm in arm, they looked speechlessly across the smoothly flowing river under twilight's darkening autumn shadows.

Jocko, who at the finale had occupied his usual perch on the parapet, joined his father as the gathering dispersed in a mumbling mood. Elaine's tirade fell upon the previously happy crowd like a cloudburst upon the dancing embers of a campfire.

Jocko asked his father what it would mean for Missy E being "neutral like she sez."

The wise Big Tom responded, "Whutsit mean? It means she's gonna be alone. Dat's whuts it gonna mean. Peoples jest ain't made ta be in betwixt even dough dey's assayin' 'zactly what awll da odders on bode sides ain't got somick ta say. Ev'body's scairt ta be alone, Jocko . . . Ev'body!"

"Youse is allus alone, Pappy," Jocko reminds the kindly, gentle black man.

"No, no, Boy!" Tom quickly corrects his son, "Ise ain't. Ise got chu. An' when Ise ain't got chu, Ise got cha Mammy up dere ta talks ta. An' when she doan ans'r no more from a 'gettin' tir'd from a 'flyin' 'round all day, Ise got Him up dere ta talks ta. Who's youse awl thinks don fix'ted mah arm up so Ise can raise it now? Who's ya think? . . . Da Gen'l? . . . No, Sir'ee! He's ain't dat good!"

At Headquarters, Paine, Bedford and Blodget, who Greene notices is for once not smiling, are busy interrogating a British deserter named Broderick. The young redcoat had run off from Lord Percy's forces below the Harlem heights in a rainstorm last night.

Making his way to Captain Graydon who was on guard at the Point of Rocks, Broderick was examined by Colonel Magaw shortly after. He was then sent over to Greene at Headquarters after he had insisted, swearing he was telling the truth, that the Americans had best prepare for a British attack.

Howe's Next Attack: Could It Be November 16?

Magaw's message informed Greene that, according to Broderick:

"We might expect to be attacked in six or eight days at furtherest, as some time had been employed in transporting heavy artillery to the other side of the Harlem, and as the preparations for the assault were nearly completed."[37]

Confronted by Greene and his staff, the deserter tells the same story. If he is telling the truth, the attack will come between the 15th and 17th.

Could it possibly be that the Americans have pinpointed the exact date of Howe's next attack? Could it be November 16?

Greene, Bedford, Blodget and Paine pose the question among themselves. But no one of them really thinks so.

25

Friday, November 15. . .

Hour of the Ultimatum

Marchers From Out the White Plains Raise the Inhabitants' Fears

Six days ago, Saturday, November 9, thousands of raggedly dressed Continentals under General Lord Stirling began the American evacuation of the White Plains. They poured into Peekskill[1] where they began the slow, tedious crossing of the Hudson.

Loading into pettiaugers, flatboats, bateaux, Durham boats, barges, even in whaleboats and sloops, in any vessel that Glover's men, patriots and Whigs on both sides of the river could commandeer, Stirling's advance brigades led the way in the massive movement. Instead of ferrying directly over, they took advantage of the tide and headed south downriver, landing in the cove off Haverstraw's bay.

From there they began their long march down through the Hudson's highlands toward the Hackensack valley, moving in from the river along the old King's highway south under the western slope of the Palisades. Their sudden presence in large numbers, their poor equipment and appearance immediately spread fear among the inhabitants.

Awe-stricken, the frightened farmers could only assume that it was an army marching in defeat from Westchester. And certainly the enemy must be following close behind.

These fears were heightened owing to the night crossing of the brigades to avoid detection by the British scouts. Stirling's force cleared the way for the main body of Continentals under the Commander-in-Chief himself. And by Tuesday, the 12th, all of the army that were to cross had been transported without mishap to the west bank.

The Hudson waters at Peekskill are at the narrowing part of the river. Peekskill lies upriver 19 miles north of Dobbs Ferry where Howe has located his temporary headquarters. So, taking advantage of the southern flowing river and the outgoing nocturnal tides, Stirling and Glover ordered their little transports to hug the river's western shore in order to bring them down into Haverstraw Bay.

They stealthily passed under Thunder Hill where Tories have been known to gather and on past Stony Point and its small rebel garrison. Without stopping they quietly head into the cove off from Haverstraw's village three miles south of Stony Point. The site had been chosen for the army's disembarkation spot by the scouts, Craig and Abbott.

If the British were aware of Stirling's crossing, and later that of the army under The General, they made no effort to interfere with the operation. The Americans drew the conclusion that the night-conducted maneuver succeeded without their enemy's detection. However, surely now, with such a large rebel force moving through an area sprinkled with Loyalists and informers, Howe would soon be aware of his adversary's location. This the Continentals knew.

The older veterans of The General's campaigns were sure that the "Old Fox" was out-guessing Sir William again. Some wagered their rum that Howe planned to cross from Dobbs and land at Sneden's. But "The Gen'l," they declared loudly, "will be there a'waitin'."

Under the Continentals' fire, say the old soldiers, the redcoats will be unable to land and will either have to hightail it back under a fierce American barrage or drown in an overturned boat, unable to get ashore. It was idle boasting prompted by the falsely assumed victory they believed they had scored over the redcoats at White Plains. But it did bolster the waning spirits of those younger comrades who believed themselves to be in retreat as much as did the trembling civilians.

Those Who Cannot Speak the Language Are the Least Informed

However, none of this braggadocio made any of the Dutch, English, or French Huguenot farmers, the craftsmen, journeymen, fishermen civilians and the raw recruits among the militia, any happier. Stirring the populace fears even more is the army's secret message-sending system, the tar barrel smoke signals that rise in billowing black clouds from mountain to mountain. Ignorance as to what enemy-action news they convey simply gives rise to dreadful interpretations setting off frightening rumors.

There are no newspapers to bring these people accounts of the war which they feel is surely now coming to their doors. Few among the elders can read or speak English very well, if at all.

Only on Sunday after attending church services, conducted mostly in Dutch, do they hear about the war and its progress. And most of what they hear is unreliable hearsay. Or else they must depend upon the explanation and interpretation of all events as the pastor, or dominie, of the church sees them.

For the dominie is generally accepted as an authority in all things. He is the principal source for information. What the valley knows or thinks about the war news sometimes largely depends upon who the dominie is and how he slants his hearsay.

If the dominie is a Loyalist and an advocate of the Conferentie Party within the Dutch Church, the news will have a pro-British angle interpretation. If he is a patriot and an advocate of the Coetus Party within the church, the news will have a strong pro-American, a rebel slant. And many of the dominies are itinerant visiting preachers. Their traveling status gives them prestige and respect.

It is quite different farther south in West Jersey. For below the Watchung mountains and beyond the shorter hills leading into Morristown, Brunswick and Trenton along the roads to Philadelphia, the settlers are predominantly English.

There they can more easily come by copies of the gazettes, or of *The Pennsylvania Packet*, *The Pennsylvania Evening Post*, *The Pennsylvania Evening Journal*, and even *The New York Gazette and Weekly Mercury*, pro-Tory though it now is under enemy occupation.

Those Who Can Speak the Language Find Ways To Keep Informed

Furthermore the West Jerseyans predominantly of English backgrounds, speak and read the English language fluently just as do the inhabitants of some of the English-speaking sections of East Jersey. One such example of an area with high English language fluency in East Jersey is the English Neighborhood.

Also contributing to West Jerseyans' greater solidarity is their stronger religious and political unity. Less divided in their beliefs, the West Jerseyans are as a rule more solidly behind the patriotic cause. Consequently they have made better home defense preparations in anticipation of an enemy invasion.

This is evidenced in the Morristown area. For there, when the militia defenders wish to give warnings to the inhabitants, they use a novel, sophisticated method. Instead of waiting until church time on Sunday to advise the inhabitants that enemy troops—or even rebel parties—are moving in upon them, they use a cannon shot.

When the cannon booms they hide their best heifers, horses, sows, silver, foodstuffs and order the women indoors. The shot also is the signal to put the rum, cider and milk safely under a secluded hay stack unless the cold cellar provides a suitable hiding place. Many do have secret "parson's cupboards"[2] concealed from the eyes of plunderers.

In the short hills, the militia's thunderous cannon is called "Old Sow," so-named because its booming signal sounds more like the grunting noise of an old porker than it does like an artillery piece. But it provides the inhabitants for miles around with a comforting cloak of security in addition to alerting the militia, or by the number-signal method summoning them for assembly. It is a type of warning not employed by the independent East Jerseyans.

So the Hackensack valley and Hudson highland dwellers watch in fear as the thousands of marching rebel troops pour down from the Hudson's valley areas, moving as though fleeing southward toward Clarks, Fort Lee and Hackensack. They could use a signal system such as "Old Sow" to warn of friendly or unfriendly troop movements.

Stirling and his corps' rear guard made their way up from the shore of Haverstraw Bay early last Monday morning, the 11th, through rain, mud and across the Miniscongo Creek. Here, just south of the thunder hills, or "Dunderbergs,"[3] as the natives living around the village of Haverstraw call them, the van found the hollow way which Craig recommended into Clarks, or Tappan town.

Through the hollow way, an ancient pass once carved by glacial ice and its melting waters, the division slowly made its way. The marchers trudged on along the roughly hewn stage coach road, winding southward down under the western slope of the Palisades which rise above it on the east. The long circuitous highway extends south all the way through the lengthy peninsula to its southernmost tip at Bergen Point on the Kill van Kull opposite Staten Island, 40 miles away.

Known as the King's Highway the road leads out of Haverstraw. Twelve miles south it crosses the New Jersey-New York State line near Orange Town and Tappan. Out of Haverstraw, on its way south through the valley, it passes De Noelle's place, Van Houten's, Onderdonk's Mills, Kakiat Court House, New City, Rider's Hook, Caspar's, Mabie's and Blauvelt's, arriving at Orange Town and Tappan.

It is there to the east of Tappan town where the first and only sea-level opening, or gap, in the long Palisadean ridge occurs. It is the hollow way, the pass, that the scouts advised. From the southernmost point of the Palisades where the mountainous range begins rising from out of the sea at Bergen point, all the way north some 40 miles along the peninsula to Tappan town, which is inland west from the Tappan Zee, there is no other break-through, or cut, in the Palisades.

The first and only break is this pass, or hollow way and its creek, known as "The Sloat." The Sloat's sluggish waters empty into the wide Tappan Zee, or bay, where the Hudson stretches four miles across from shore to shore.

Three miles upriver from the Sloat is the village of Nyack. And three miles downriver lies the Sneden's Landing outpost under the Palisades' cliffs on the water's edge. The garrison there has somehow been misnamed, acquiring the misnomer, "The Dobbs Ferry Garrison," or "Dobbs Ferry Outpost," instead of, properly, the "Sneden's Landing Outpost" above which dock it is located.

The Dobbs' home and ferry lie across the river on the east bank. Sneden's Landing is the ferry's west terminal.

So, it was at the Sneden's Landing road off the valley highway which leads to the outpost, that the Continental Army halted. There Stirling, with his staff and guides, left his brigades to climb the Palisades' west slope and make his way to the American garrison on the river.

On the opposite bank, upon which he trained his field glasses, the British-born lord could discern little activity along the river's east shore. But in and around Dobbs Ferry village he was certain that much enemy movement was taking place.

In Lord Stirling's opinion, as well as that of his officers, the nature of the activity they saw was not a preparation for a river crossing.

The stream here is two miles across. Why pick such a wide part of the river for such a massive crossing operation? And also it appeared strange to the observers that all that was visible on the water were the frigates and tenders that had broken through the blockade. Where were the transports so necessary for an amphibious invasion if one were to be made any time soon?

But, in the opinion of the American officers, there seemed to be no doubt that Howe, quartered somewhere over there near Dobbs Ferry and its village, was preparing for a major operation. And it did not appear to be a river crossing. Certainly not at the Dobbs Ferry-Sneden's Landing area.

Ready Are the Outposts Surrounding Fort Lee

Colonel Durkee is in charge of the Sneden's Landing outpost. Durkee, former commander of the Paulus Hook garrison, greeted Stirling Saturday afternoon.

The command post, which is Greene's left wing, northernmost guard along the river, comprises in addition to Durkee, one major, six captains, seven lieutenants, eight second lieutenants, eight ensigns, thirty-one sergeants, fourteen drums and fife, and three hundred and twenty-seven privates.[4]

They are all furnished from Greene's command at Fort Lee. And all on the post were brought out in a dress parade to greet "one of the outstanding heroes of Long Island." Stirling is also introduced as one of the generals who was captured, held and finally exchanged for a British officer.

Greene has kept all of his outposts well strengthened. Besides the Sneden's guard, which is about 12 miles north of Fort Lee, there is the Bull's Ferry outpost, the right wing guardian for the Palisadean fort. Bull's Ferry lies about five miles below, or south of the mother fortress on The Mountain.

In addition Greene has other outlying picket and observation garrisons, one at Bergen north of the now British-held Powles Hook and still another at Hoebuck. A fifth is located across the river north of Fort Washington at the Spuyten Duyvil.

All of these outlying guardians are in addition to Fort Lee's supporting forces which are located in Hackensack and in addition to Fort Washington and its outposts opposite Fort Lee.

From Fort Lee one soldier writing home last Sunday morning summarized the status of the two armies in this way:

> "The enemy have not decamped as was reported but are still at Dobb's Ferry (east bank of Hudson near Dobbs village). Part of our Army have come this side of the river. ... Deserters confirm the suspicions of the enemy's designs to pay us a visit in the Jerseys; but the attempt is so dangerous and so long delayed that I can scarcely believe it is seriously in agitation."[5]

Last Sunday, November 10, brought a welcome change from the rains and the ever colder nights. Dawn came up with a warming sun, and the day stayed pleasant in spite of approaching winter. The recent cold rains which have harassed the wearied, poorly clad foot soldiers had, it was thought, put an end to "the finest weather for the season ever known, and such a fall as no man can recollect."[6]

Despite the beautiful day, the Sunday Hackensack valley church-goers were brought face to face with the war as well as with their neighbors holding opposite religious views.

On their way to the church and the minister of their choice they snub all those in the opposing sectarian party of the split Dutch Church congregations, even to the point of blocking their horses and carriages in passing. But they also pass by hundreds of marching Continentals.

One historian will describe Sunday, November 10, 1776, this way:

> "Dominie Dirck Romeyn preached to a full church at Schraalenburgh, baptizing our children when the service was over; Warmoldus Kuypers preached at Hackensack; Garret Leydecker at English Neighborhood; Domine VerBryck at Tappan, and Dominie Van der Linde at Paramus, but it was hardly a serene Sunday. Everyone in the county knew that the heights of the Palisades were a hive of military activity; Schraalenburgh church-goers from Closter and Tenafly passed hundreds of marching troops on the County Road as they came to the morning service."[7]

And early that Sunday morning last, the American Commander-in-Chief over at White Plains was completing a conference with General Lee. Lee, it had been decided, was to remain with his command at North Castle.

At 11 A.M. the rebels' Chief, preceded by 5,000 Continentals under his personal command left the White Plains and headed for Peekskill.[8]

For him it was the end of two long weeks in which his small army had successfully thwarted Howe's carefully planned objective to bring the war to a close in Westchester. Or so it certainly seemed.

While The General's brigades were ferrying across—the bulk under the cover of darkness late Sunday and Monday nights, the 10th and 11th—the Continental Army's Leader reconnoitered the highlands. His party, aside from his guards and guides, included his chief engineer, Colonel Rufus Putnam.

After an inspection of the works at Fort Independence and Fort Montgomery in the hunting grounds of the Mohegans, The General returned to Peekskill. There he took leave of Colonel Putnam with instructions that he "ascertain the geography of the country with the road and passes through the high lands."[9]

Then, on Tuesday last, the 12th, the American General crossed over the Hudson in the rain under Colonel Glover's personal direction disembarking at Stony Point. The Marblehead seamen under Glover's command were carrying out the final episode of their long, arduous task of moving the main body of the American army to the west bank of Hudson's river in four nights and three days.

The entire operation had been executed under the assumption that General Howe was surely planning a crossing, possibly from Dobbs village across to Sneden's Landing with intentions to pierce through the Jerseys.

But Sir William had tricked his adversary. The British commander-in-chief had other plans.

From the promontory at Stony Point, the American Commander and his officers trained their field glasses on the southern end of Haverstraw Bay and the Hudson's eastern shore some four miles down stream. Shivering in their wet, mud-soaked clothing, The General's troops, assembled and waiting for marching orders, warmed themselves over their campfires on the landing area at the cove near Haverstraw.

Would this, they thought, be their last day and night before their likely rendezvous tomorrow with the King's Army in the Hackensack valley six or eight miles away?

From the heights of Stony Point's small militia post which The General believes should be expanded, could be seen dimly outlined in the distance, the British men-of-war riding at anchor off Dobbs Ferry village.

In the morning's light Wednesday, Colonel Glover, from the hills above the army's bivouac at the Haverstraw cove, identified the vessels as the Tartar, Phoenix and Roebuck.[10] Also riding at their moorings were their supply ships and bateaux. All had squeezed undetected under the nose of Fort Washington's batteries, through the narrow passageway between the eastern blockade barge of the Chevaux de Frise and Jeffery's Hook six nights ago, Thursday, November 7.

The enemy's ships had avoided going through or over the blockade that night. They had learned earlier that this was too dangerous and almost an impossibility. Instead, on Thursday last they cleverly made their way around the sunken hulks.

This was easy owing to a blunder that occurred when one of the barges was being linked into the chain-blockade. The stone-laden hull was to have been sunk in the opening between the last submerged barge and the shore. But the loaded vessel bilged too soon and went down far from its intended position.[11]

The costly American error left a wide passageway. Through this the intrepid Captain Parker of the Phoenix, aided by a rain-shrouded night, led his little flotilla safely into the widening river's deep channel.

All the efforts of the rebels to totally bottle up the enemy fleet below the Chevaux de Frise seemed to have proved futile with that skillful enemy accomplishment.

The sight of the British vessels defiantly riding at anchor below Haverstraw Bay convinced the American Commander that he was on firm ground when he wrote Greene four days ago asking, "What valuable purpose can it answer to attempt to hold a post from which the expected benefit cannot be had?"[12]

Yet The General had left it up to Greene's discretion to hold or to evacuate Fort Washington as he saw fit. And Greene, an intelligent officer, is apparently intent upon defending the fort.

Yet why hold a mountain river post under which the enemy's men of war can pass unharmed almost at will?

So there now The General saw the British ships calmly lying at anchor and showing no signs indicating an army crossing of the river.

This and Howe's lingering at his De Lancey's Mills headquarters near Dobbs Ferry village combined to puzzle the American Commander-in-Chief. What else except the investiture of Fort Washington is on the enemy's mind?

Certainly Colonel Magaw's report of a brush with enemy pickets last Saturday on Mount Washington's perimeter added to the aggravating mystery.[13]

Was that an indication of things to come? Was that an enemy probe of the fort's defenses? Was that the opening move against the last American stronghold on Manhattan Island?

Moving ahead of his troops with his staff Wednesday morning, The General, followed in Stirling's path making his way to the Sneden's Landing heights, the so-called "Dobbs Ferry Post," and its garrison.

Again Colonel Durkee had his men fall out, this time to welcome their Commander-in-Chief, an event which called for even more cleaning and polishing than before.

The Open-Mouthed Juggernaut
Solves the British East Bank Question

Durkee's report to The General repeated what he had told Stirling: No signs of any enemy troop movements that indicate a river crossing from Dobbs.

But had The General's field glasses, wet from the chilling November rain, been able to penetrate behind and over the hilly ridge across the Hudson and on to the road from Dobbs, south to Philipsburg, Wepperham, Yonker's Mill, the heights of Fordham and to King's Bridge, he would have seen a far more ominous sight.

For there in the distance the British commander and his main army were on the march. Howe's objective was a junction with General Knyphausen's Hessian forces at King's Bridge 12 miles south of Dobbs.[14]

The great Juggernaut was opening its jaws once again. And this time its eyes were on Fort Washington.

As early as last Tuesday the rebels' Chief feared Sir William had out-foxed him and executed one of the most successful feints of the campaign, if not of the entire war. The Howes, it seemed, were definitely not in any hurry to cross Hudson's river. Furthermore, they were in no hurry to seek winter quarters.

The only logical answer to the British east bank puzzle, therefore, was that Howe intended to take advantage of the favorable stretch of weather, rainy cold spells notwithstanding, and lay siege to Fort Washington.

But the rebels' formidable Manhattan Island fortress is considered impregnable. Few Continental officers believe their enemy will attempt a frontal assault on the works.

A long siege of the fortress?—Yes. That they can see as a possibility. But not a frontal attack, not on Fort Washington!

Both sides recognize that a successful attack on Fort Washington, though extremely risky in view of the fort's repellent powers, would end all American occupation on New York's island.

It would seriously depress the Congress and the country and lower still the already drooping morale of the military. Also it would immediately reduce to nought Fort Lee's use as a defensive or offensive post. And it would virtually eliminate the wisdom of its further occupation.

Of what value would it be to maintain an impotent military works and its outposts on a peninsula the enemy could surround or skirt around at will?

It is also realized that a successful Fort Washington assault would give the British army and navy mastery over the Hudson and this could open the gateway to Albany, New England and the British army's northern corps under General John Burgoyne. For Burgoyne with a little help then could seal the fate of the American Northern Department fighting under Gates and Arnold.

It is all this that the American command fears will follow in the wake of the fall of the sister forts on Hudson's river. This was the great dilemma that confronted and annoyed the rebel Leader as he rode away from Colonel Durkee's post above the ferry landing operated by Ma Sneden and her sons.

The Snedens, however, are not found among the strong supporters of the American Chief. Ma Sneden has openly expressed her objections to the American cause, and her sons usually agree with the hard working, rugged, pioneer widow from the upper Palisades. The Loyalist-leaning, river-loving matriarch sees no reason to fight for independence from a King 3,000 miles across the sea. Ma Sneden should know, if anyone does, what Sir William Howe's next move will be. But this time neither she nor her sons have gathered anything more than the usual number of groundless rumors.

In the Cyclical Course Of All Things . . .

After bivouacking near Tappan, The General Wednesday headed his cold, rain-drenched 5,000-man army[15] south into the Hackensack valley toward Liberty Pole. His command comprised New Jersey, Pennsylvania, Maryland, Virginia and Carolina troops. To them, the upper valley's Dutch, English and French Huguenots, coming out in rain to watch, appeared to be a frightened people, lonesomely isolated on their wide-spread farms and rock-walled fields.

Seeking some news, any bit of information that would enlighten them as to what was going on, they offered food and water to the passing brigades. But little information was forthcoming from soldiers who themselves had no idea where their enemy was, or what was next in store.

The line of marchers slowly passed by the brownstone home-steads, each with its immaculately maintained house and barn from out of which came farmers and their hausfraus with their hands full of foodstuffs, quickly grabbed up by the tired, hungry troops. There was plenty at the De Baun's house, the Major Joun Mauritius Goetschius house, the Demarest's, Westervelt's, Major Hammond's, the Bogert's and Lozier's.

Skirting Tienevly, or what the British call "Tine Fly,"[16] the army's route carried them past the school house and then finally to the Liberty Pole at the crossroads inn.

From here the Commander-in-Chief's brigades moved westward across the valley to the Hackensack River's New Bridge and into Hackensack village for their encampment on the village green. There they joined Stirling's brigade and the Hackensack garrison, mostly of militia, bivouacking off the village green in support of Greene's command at Fort Lee, eight miles east.

Never have the valley people seen such a military force. Never thus far has the war of the revolution come so close. Never have they felt before the violent and oppressing threat of force.

And, once again, in the omnipresent cyclical path that all things take, the valley inhabitants feel it is they who now wear the trembling moccasins of "The Original People," the Lenni Lenape.

At the Liberty Pole The General took leave of his troops, delegating his subaltern officers to lead them into Hackensack. He and his aides struck out for Fort Lee, galloping by the Lydeckers' house, Van Horn's and then reining in at the English Neighborhood crossroads.

Passing the outlying pickets, they turned left up the Palisades' western slope on the fort road. At the lower guardhouse Greene and his officers greeted the party. It had been a long time since last the two men had seen each other. Riding alongside of his Commander, Greene gave The General news of the latest intelligence.

It was only Tuesday, November 12, Greene told his Chief, that he himself became convinced of Howe's intentions to attack Fort Washington. The post commander added that he had so written President John Hancock and the Continental Congress. The major general repeated what he had written Hancock to whom he had stated, in part:

"I expect General Howe will attempt to possess himself of Mount Washington, but very much doubt whether he will succeed in the attempt. Our troops are much fatigued with the amazing duty, but are generally in good spirits."[17]

It was after noon Wednesday before the Commander-in-Chief rode into Fort Lee with Greene and then reviewed the troops. The rousing reception by the rank and file was unlike anything ever before seen or heard on the mountain's top. The entire garrison had apparently turned out for the event. Seemingly every fife and drum of the camp was brought into competition.

When the troops were dismissed, The General repaired to his favorite quarters, the Bourdette homestead. Often the Bourdettes have been his hosts beginning with his first visit four months ago.

During his many visits he has always made it a point to praise Madam Granny Bourdette for her famous Indian corn cakes and also for her breakfasts of flapjacks.[18] Even Black Jennie admitted that she herself could not turn out corncakes and flapjacks like Missy Rachel's.

But, alone with Granny, Jennie, half jesting, half serious, accuses her elderly mistress of being a fraud. Laughingly she charges that Granny had "gawn 'n took Minnie Abbott's recipes."

This always touches off a Granny-Jennie skirmish ending up with Old Granny reluctantly conceding, under Jennie's gibing taunts, that Minnie may have helped her some with the "ferst cookin' of 'em . . . But only helped . . . 'nd dat's awll!"

Upon the Commander's arrival at the Bourdette house, the matriarch of the household, Jennie at her side, stood at the door of the ferry owner's home. Both women peered out over the lower half of the Dutch door, awaiting The General's ascent up the stairs and across the threshold of the big house. Dressed in her republican costume, a red coat with gold buttons, white satin hooped skirt over her linsey-woolsey petticoat, Rachel stood heavy, formidable and slightly bent in her stout leather shoes. For both of the women it was another big day in their lives.

Seventy-four-year-old Rachel Bourdette, as a rule, fears no one. The exception is, and has been, the American Continental Army's Commander. This has been so ever since he first appeared at the wide open Bourdette house Dutch doors.

However, with the matriarch it is not fear; it is a deep admiring respect. The elderly grandmother readily admits that she would jump into the river if The Gen'l told her to. And her husband does not for a moment doubt it.

Standing on her tiptoes behind her charge, Jennie gazed wide-eyed over the shorter and older woman's shoulders. She had left her cooking, as she said, "go hang" for the time being. Most important now for the black woman was to be one of the first among the riverside women, as she usually is, to welcome "Dat Beeg Mahn."

On the second floor observation porch which provides an expansive view across the river and to its south, "Old Honest Sam"[19] looked excitedly down upon the arrival scene. Honest Sam, or "Old Sam," as some call the Bourdette's aging hired man, had never been known by any other title. But Sam claims his first name is "Honest" and his surname is "Sam." He had come in from cutting wood in the farmyard "jest spec'll fer ta see Der Gen'l."

Before the rambling river house, which also occasionally serves as an inn for travelers unable to continue farther on their way at night, waited Old Stephen. Standing by the massive carriage stepping-stone, the old man had been proudly telling everyone he was there to greet "My Friend," as he has called the American Commander since he first escorted him up to the Bluff Rock.

And, of course, among the welcomers who crowded around, were Papa Pete and Marie Louise Baummeister, her arm endearingly encircling the shoulders of her son, Paul. Elaine Gray had dismissed her school children before noon. And, as she does each day, she left immediately to attend the sick in the hospital compound.

Other than those two daily responsibilities, Elaine has paid little attention to anything, or anyone else for the past four days. Her avoidance of all her friends and their embarrassed avoidance of her, have put a pall of gloom over the Baummeister house if not the entire river's edge.

So among the missing in the little welcoming gathering was Elaine. Her husband was, of course, still on duty at the Barbette Battery to which he had returned his men after the parade.

Inside the Bourdette house, Jennie and Rachel, who knows she is called "Old Granny" behind her back—and still doesn't like it—had prepared a big dinner for The General and his party which includes his servant, "Billy," two aides and two guards.

When one of the guards carelessly slipped and referred to Rachel as "Old Granny" within her earshot, the insulted matriarch nearly stared the young soldier out of his past few years of growth. Tremulously stuttering, he almost fell over himself apologizing.

If he did not learn his lesson then, he was to learn it later and at breakfast flapjack-time when he was the last to be served with the least.

Jennie's son, Caesar,[20] had caught several striped bass in his nets that Wednesday morning, so tea, baked striped bass and Rachel's Indian corn cakes made up the menu.

The guarded Indian recipe is one of Rachel Bourdette's best kept secrets. However, once before when the rebel army Chieftain came by and praised her for her tasty cakes, Rachel insisted he send the recipe back to Virginia[21] to Lady Washington.

The American Commander replied he would never think of trusting such a valuable piece of "intelligence" to the post. He promised, however, that instead he would keep it and personally take it back to Mount Vernon with him when he returned home. Nothing could have pleased Rachel more. From that time on everything he touched in the Bourdette household immediately became sacred.

Filled with a fruit concoction flavored with peach brandy, The General's favorite punchbowl stood on the top of the beautifully polished cherry-wood buffet. At the head of the carefully set dining room table, also made of cherry-wood matching the buffet piece, was the honored guest's favorite arm-chair.[22]

Everything had been arranged for his comfort based upon his likes and dislikes which the Bourdettes have come to know, from his frequent visits. Rachel keeps the chair only for an ornament until The General comes. Even Stephen is chased out of it.

Despite the affection shown for him by soldiers and inhabitants of The Mountain and the river's side, it is the youngsters[23] of the area who stare with admiring wonder upon America's now famous military Leader. Most of the youth of the vicinity for miles around come running when the news of his appearance is spread about as it always rapidly is.

In awe the children gathered around Paul who had broken away from his mother and run to the side of Old Magnolia as The General sprang from his saddle. The Chief, leaving his horse in the hands of his faithful valet, Billy, had, upon dismounting, affectionately patted Paul on the head. This, to the other children, was akin to having knighted Paul with the King's sceptre.

Crowding around the young "knight" who had been touched by the "king," the children now looked upon young Baummeister as someone special. However, all soon diverted their interest to Billy who led Old Magnolia and his own horse, Blueskin, over to the watering trough.

The somewhat haughty black man, who is said to be the only one who can dictate to The General, generously answers all the youngsters' questions before finally taking the two horses into Bourdette's pasture. Billy is a ready and willing conversationalist when it comes to The General.

In the American Leader, the youngsters, all too young to become even army drummer boys, have found a hero. In him is the spirit of revolt which surges through the soul of the home-tied child, ever-straining to pull out from under the protecting wing of the mother bird as she clings desperately to her offspring until his final escaping flight. For now like the eaglet, he must soon soar alone.

In their "hero" they see the other worlds—the beckoning lands beyond the horizon, the alluring vistas over the misoneism of the day-in, day-out routines of The Mountain and the ever-flowing river below it.

Each envisions himself similarly a great and respected leader of men, fighting and defending some noble cause far removed from kith and kin.

Each young mind sees itself unbound and freed, flung enchantingly away from the routines of farming and distantly carried far from the boring chores of homelife. Each seeks the vibrating, changing pulses of man-made adventures. Each seeks to shed nature's boring cloak of simplicity, serenity and sameness.

To youth, The General is an inspiration for dreams, dreams in which fame, fortune and success are envisioned. And they are visions which dwell constantly within their fertile minds, always with the hope that someday they will materialize.

And so now around one man is sown the mysteriously strange seed of apotheosis. Only defeat of great magnitude will destroy the phenomena of its indestructible growth throughout centuries.

From their high stadium seat in the Palisades' natural colosseum the artillerymen of the Bluff Rock's Barbette Battery had looked down on The General's welcoming scene far below them in front of the Bourdette house. They pushed and crowded around each other in order to get a glimpse of the reception committee and their famous guest. They shoved each other as though it were the first time they had ever seen their Commander-in-Chief, even though he had reviewed them only a few minutes before.

But at that time he had seemed less interested in the park of artillery on The Rock than he was at looking down from the east precipice at the Chevaux de Frise. It was that construction and the works across the river at Mount Washington that had drawn his attention and a lengthy sighting with his field glasses.

No one knew his thoughts though all could guess. For he had made no comment to Greene, the officers around him, or to his aides, until he had completed his observation.

Then, turning to Greene and Irvine, he asked several questions, causing all three to train their glasses again on the distant heights. And that was all.

In a few minutes he and his party, leaving the post's command and their staff officers to repair to the main fort, moved down the trail road from The Rock and then down the gorge road. They passed the water-side redoubts where every man of each station stood at attention as the horsemen rode slowly by toward the Bourdette place.

The Juggernaut Moves; the Rebels Speculate

While the American Commander-in-Chief was being welcomed at Fort Lee Wednesday, Howe was settling his forces on the high ground along the Westchester side of the Harlem River. The site is hidden from the Bluff Rock since it drops from view behind Mount Washington on the fortress's high northeastern slopes.

On Wednesday Howe's army stretched from the Hudson, with his right flank resting largely on the Bronx River, southeast through Westchester back to his base, the left flank which still holds the grounds below the American-held Harlem Heights—Mount Washington's outer defense system. Unchanged since the Harlem Heights battle, these redcoat southern lines extend south of Harlem across Manhattan Island to Hudson's river at Bloomingdale.[24]

American observers argue that the upper Westchester British lines have not appreciably altered for weeks. The only exceptions, possibly, are the Hessian extension of the right wing under Knyphausen up onto the Fordham heights and recently the concentration of large numbers of redcoats on the Harlem's northern banks.

Otherwise the enemy looks as though they are making their way back down behind their own Harlem Heights lines. Or, and it has been so argued, they are awaiting transports to cross them over the Harlem for an assault on Mount Washington's eastern slopes.

Then there are some who have contended that Howe has no present plan to cross the Hudson, has no designs against Fort Washington but is preparing to retire with his army into New York for winter quartering.

If the American General was annoyed Wednesday that his advice to his younger protégé suggesting the evacuation of Fort Washington was not heeded, he did not show it. And he has since made no further demand upon Greene to do so.

Despite the worrisome signs and the now total isolation of the Fort Washington garrison on Manhattan, Colonel Magaw and his men behind the Mount Washington defenses seem to be in a defiant, unworried mood. So, too, does General Greene.

Yet, in gradual steps the enemy has approached closer to the supposedly impregnable fortress and proportionately farther away from a Hudson crossing.

In places the steep rocky escarpments around the sister fortress on Hudson's east bank rise almost perpendicularly out of the Harlem and the Hudson rivers. They help to present a frightening obstacle for any enemy attackers even though the storming assaulters may stand well shielded behind the fire-snorting nostrils and massive jaws of the great British Juggernaut.

Fort Washington and its mount lie in a place that is like a beautiful ornament of nature on a wonderland of deep forests, hills and dales leading onto rocky slopes that reach down to the sandy streams emptying into the mount's encircling rivers.

One historian will someday describe it, saying:

"In the northern part of the island of Manhattan is a narrow, high, rocky, wooded region of singular natural beauty; unique as a feature in modern cities, and precisely such a spot as in an ancient Greek city would have been chosen for its Acropolis.

"Separated from the rest of the island by the plains of Harlem on the south, and extending thence to Kingsbridge on the north, a distance of about four miles, its average width is only about three-fourths of a mile.

"Bordered on the east by the narrow winding, umbrageous Harlem, and on the west by the magnificent Hudson, the two united by the historic inlet of Spuyten Duyvel, it rises from these rivers in sudden, rocky, forest clad precipices, nearly a hundred feet in height, which for well nigh three-fourths of its circumference are almost inaccessible.

"These natural buttresses support an irregular plain, the surface of which rises toward the centre to an eminence on the side of the Hudson two hundred feet above its waters, and to another on the side of the Harlem of almost equal height, between which lies the most level part of the entire region. This towards its northern end sinks into a narrow valley or gorge, through which runs the road to Kingsbridge.

"Besides the Kingsbridge, which connected the island with the mainland of Westchester, there was another bridge, a short distance south east of it, called Dyckman's bridge. Opposite these bridges the rocky bluffs recede to the west for nearly a mile, leaving between them and the Harlem river a small plain, on which rise two or three low hills.

"At the southern end of this plain was a little branch of the Harlem called Sherman's Creek, still in existence, directly above and south of which rises the high eminence on the Harlem above-mentioned, then termed 'Laurel Hill,' and since, and now, 'Fort George.' "[25]

So yesterday, the 14th, when minds were much on Fort Washington and an unexplained departure of British ships from Sandy Hook, Lord Stirling came over to Fort Lee from Hackensack in a final meeting with the Chief and Greene before moving with his brigade south to Brunswick.

Advising Stirling that there was still much fear that Howe may attempt an invasion of Jersey with strikes at Brunswick, Princeton and Trenton, the American Leader warned that his Lordship should be wary of that possibility.

In view of some recent enemy excursions out of Staten Island, The General stated, it cannot be certain that such maneuvers are only feints intended by Howe to mislead the American command.

General Stirling, whose manor home and farm lie outside of Basking Ridge, 16 miles from Brunswick, knows West Jersey. No Continental Army officer is better able to maneuver through the short hills than Stirling should the British move from Amboy into Jersey.

So, after dining with The General and Greene last night, Lord Stirling early this morning, Friday, November 15, led his brigade out of Hackensack destined for New Brunswick.

A bright dawn fell over the land the same hour and at Fort Lee Colonel Moor of the post found time to write his friend, Henry Hill in Philadelphia, giving Hill a reflection of the mood of the American officers and some of the late news.

Wrote Moor:

"... It is some time since we arrived at this place where we live in the Woods in Tents, there is a constant expectation of an action opposite to us at Fort Washington, which make no doubt will be in a short time; Yesterday past by this place Lord Stirling's Brigade on their way to Brunswick; it is thought the Enemy is on the way to the Southward . . ."[26]

Poor and inadequate observations and intelligence are now more than ever contributing to the American staff's bewildered uncertainty. Indicative of this is the American Chief's letter to the President of the Congress which he penned yesterday, Thursday, the 14th, from "General Greene's Head-quarters."

In this report he told John Hancock, among other things, that:

"It seems to be generally believed on all hands that the investing of Fort Washington is one object they (The British) have in view . . ."

. . . And Inefficiencies Plague The General

The General's dissatisfaction with the army's supply and transportation services is still much on his mind. In this same letter he criticizes what he calls "the miserable state of disarrangement of the Quartermaster General's department," blaming the inefficiency of the department for the army's inability to maneuver rapidly owing to inadequate transportation facilities when badly needed.

And, whether or not he now foresees it, he will soon be seeking greater and far more extensive transportation services than ever before.

He closed the communique, stating:

> "I propose to stay in this neighborhood a few days, in which time I expect the designs of the enemy will become disclosed, and their incursions be made in this quarter or their investiture of Fort Washington, if they are intended."[27]

One thing the long lines of straggling, weary rebel soldiers have done in addition to heightening the fears of the populace in the valleys, is to embolden the Tories. The Loyalist raiders are sure they are witnessing a great retreat march as thousands of American troops pass, rumbling by with their supply trains, gun carriages and some of their sick and wounded in the back of the Philadelphia wagons. Some of these are crowded in on top of magazines and gun powder kegs, while behind are tied the cattle following in the wake of the long caravans. Certainly the sight does not give the appearance of an army victoriously marching back into battle.

The Loyalists throughout the entire Hudson valleys have been somewhat quelled by the American strategy in Westchester and by the strong garrisons on Mount Washington and at Fort Lee with its many outposts. They are sure that what they are seeing is the whole rebel army marching in defeat, a retreat march through the highlands and the valleys southward.

Thus the Tories begin coming out from behind their enforced seclusion. Gradually they now renew their annoying tactics, venting their spleen against all inhabitants who have shown patriot leanings.

To offset these increasing raids and the mounting activity among the Tories, the Fort Lee post has included "Tory Hunting" as routine assignments for night duty pickets. In this way General Greene, reacting to the frightened demands of the valley inhabitants, is attempting to counteract the sudden increase in attacks upon the villages' and hamlets' outlying farmers.

The effectiveness of these enemy promoted raids is a constant source of concern to the American command, undermining as it does the morale of the populace.

One officer who had been on a "Tory Hunting Party" to Clinton Point[28] opposite the Spuyten Duyvil last Tuesday night wrote of his experience to a friend posted with the militia in Philadelphia. Dating his letter, "Fort Lee, November 13, 1776," he declared:

> "Last night I went tory hunting with a party of 50 men, but the birds had flown before we arrived; however, we were repaid by a sight of the enemy's encampment (across the river) whose fires being very numerous, and greatly extended, exhibited a delightful appearance."

He then spoke of Lord Stirling's brigade and Colonel Hand's forces and their preparation to march to Brunswick, adding:

> "They will be ready to prevent any attempts on the Amboy shore, and give you assistance if the enemy should be so mad as to think of Philadelphia.
> "I was just now interrupted by the sergeant of the guard we left at the river side opposite to the ships. He informs me, they have taken a *red hot tory* coming from the enemy's vessels, so our expedition was not entirely fruitless."[29]

But Tory-snapping at the Americans' heels is a minor matter to the Continental Army's staff command in comparison to the anxiety that Howe's mysterious maneuvering has created. The uncertainty of what next to expect from Sir William has been greatly augmented by the sudden departure of 100 of Admiral Howe's ships Wednesday, the 13th.

The vessels in a surprising move, weighed anchor with the morning tide, set their sails and breezed out of Sandy Hook, steering a course straight for the open sea.

Frustrated by a dearth of military intelligence as to their foe's actual designs, the American command's momentary hope that an enemy Hessian deserter who had come over to the rebel side, would give some clues as to the ships' destination and Howe's intentions, was shattered by the German soldier's broken English.

He was more concerned over whether he was going to be eaten or hanged by the American rebels. That alone seemed to be the Hessian mercenary's prime motive for fighting to the death, as one soldier at Fort Lee's garrisons yesterday saw it, in writing of the event. But of other things the deserter knew nothing.

Dating his letter from the Fort Lee post, November 14, 1776, the American soldier's account reads, in part:

"The enemy at Kingsbridge have been reinforced with only one regiment, who are encamped near Fort Independence. This morning a Hessian soldier deserted to Fort Washington, the very first that has done so. He encourages us to hope that many of his countrymen will follow his example, as soon as they are *assured* the Americans will not hang them for meddling in the present war; a notion that has been so industriously planted, and is firmly rooted, that it will be difficult to eradicate it . . .

"On Wednesday last 100 sail of vessels, left Sandy Hook, and put to sea, but whether they have troops on board is uncertain. Various are the conjectures of their destination, but the prevailing opinion is that they are empty transports, and are bound to Ireland for provisions, for the British troops . . ."[30]

One of the conjectures, and the most worrisome one of all, is that the ships have been loaded with troops and are headed for the Bay of Delaware with designs on Philadelphia. It was this possibility that caused the American Commander earlier to order Stirling into West Jersey. So Lord Stirling moved out this morning considerably ahead of schedule.

On paper the American army appears to be ready for its enemy regardless of where the strike, or strikes, are made. But never have the rebel forces been so precariously scattered and, consequently, weakened. For the dispersed, over-extended and widely separated brigades can alone do little offensively to impede Howe's powerful Juggernaut once it opens its jaws.

The American Commander, reaching desperately for a revelation accurately assuring him of his adversary's next move has attempted to prepare for all possible contingencies. By deploying his divisions to the probable attack points, he hopes to meet Sir William's strike and stall for time while he moves supporting forces up for counter-offensive operations.

The General has covered the passes to New England with General Lee's troops, quartered in Westchester at New Castle. Mount Washington on Manhattan is defended by Colonel Magaw who has informed Greene he can hold off the enemy from the formidable fortress, certainly until late December. Its twin post, Fort Lee, is manned by General Greene's remaining regiments.

General Lord Stirling's brigade is on its way to Brunswick. The Commander-in-Chief's own command of Continentals is bivouacked in Hackensack. And General Heath's 5,000 troops are at this very hour crossing from Peekskill over to the Hudson's west bank.

Heath is under orders to guard the high lands of the upper Hudson from the river west to the Minisink and Shawangunk mountains with special orders to keep open the vital Ramapo Pass.

It is Howe's puzzling feints and inexplicable maneuvering that have brought about the wide dispersion of rebel troops. Only 18 days ago most of the now scattered divisions were a united army, solidly concentrated within the hills of the White Plains, a strong, repelling defensive force that had held back the Juggernaut.

Heath's withdrawal to the west side of the Hudson leaves Lee alone in Westchester, except for a token picket post and headquarters staff in Peekskill. Forming a wide semicircle from the Hudson to the mountain passes west, Heath, the 39 year-old major general from Roxbury, Massachusetts, is stationing his 3,500 troops, not all of whom are fit for duty, in strategic positions in defense of the Hudson's high lands.

Under Heath's command are four brigades, including Connecticut and New York troops under Generals Samuel Parsons, James Clinton, George Clinton and John Morin Scott. At the vital Sidman's Bridge, Heath has placed Colonel Huntington with two regiments. And yesterday, the 14th, he posted a brigade at the King's Ferry landing. Still others of his command have been assigned to posts in and around Haverstraw, Nyack and Tappan.

General James Clinton's troops are garrisoned at Forts Clinton and Montgomery. All of Heath's troops are under orders to begin the construction of huts for winter quarters.[31]

The disposition of Heath's men, largely on the Hudson's west shore, does not sit well with General Lee, virtually isolated with his roughly estimated 7,000 troops on the east side of the river.

Only the 2,800 men on Mount Washington under Colonel Magaw, and Lee's brigades in North Castle, remain on the Hudson's eastern shores. Together they comprise the last of the over 20,000-man American army which began assembling last summer to defend Manhattan and the vital port city.

Lee's bitterness toward his chief is reflected in a letter to his friend, General Horatio Gates. The day before yesterday, the 13th, Lee penned these words to Gates in Albany:

"Entre nous, a certain great man is most damnably deficient. He has thrown me into a situation where I have my choice of difficulties. If I stay in this Province, I risk myself and army; and if I do not stay, the Province is lost forever . . . our counsels have been weak to the last degree."[32]

Lee remembers how he predicted at the last Council of War that

Howe would cross into Jersey and attempt a junction with Burgoyne in the north. And neither does he forget that he declared a strong force, his own, was needed to thwart that attempt.[33] So Charles Lee's memory haunts him as he writes Gates and pets and feeds his two dogs at his feet.

Ambitious, and preferring to be where he can exercise that predominating drive in his character, Lee's present isolation at North Castle is, despite his rationalization, largely his own recommendation. This he tries to ignore as he does the plaguing thought that he predicted to the Congress on October 12 that Howe was headed for Philadelphia when actually he was marching to Westchester.

The former British army officer is not one who listens to others' advice, unless it furthers his ambitions. He is an independent man, a good general, liked by his troops but imbrued with two violent drives: inordinate ambition and an extreme tendency to act impulsively.

It is the latter which makes for a troublesome weakness, leading him to perform irrationally on the footlighted stage in the peak of his career.

And both of his faults are now rapidly carrying him on an unretractable collision course with an ill-omened destiny, waiting sadly in the wings.

Wilkinson and Malloy In Rainy Darkness Clear the Blockade

Following the heavy rains last night, Thursday, the 14th, the twin forts lay this morning shrouded under a cold mist. The chilling fall night left a gray morning with a brisk east wind biting from out the Atlantic.

Last night's weather was exactly like that which a week ago favored British Captain Parker and his successful run through the blockade. And it was exactly the kind of a night, with the wind east northeast, which Captains Wilkinson and Malloy of His Majesty's Navy had been patiently waiting for.

If Parker was able to negotiate the tricky passageway between the sunken hulk and the shore under Fort Washington Point in larger vessels last week, certainly, thought Wilkinson and Malloy, could they. They had only two sloops of war but were under orders to tow fifteen empty, flat-bottomed troop barges behind them through the perilous course at night from Bloomingdale to Harlem Creek.

Upon the delivery of those barges to Howe's army on the east
bank of the Harlem River depended the time and crossing of the
British forces for their attack on Fort Washington. Other barges
from the East River would furnish the transportation for the
troops at the southern end of Harlem Creek. Howe was ready to
show his hand.

So the task before the daring British sea captains last night was
both difficult and vital. The job facing Wilkinson and Malloy was
to get those barges through the blockade, safely up the Spuyten
Duyvil and then down the Harlem to the creek's east bank
opposite Mount Washington.

And last night Wilkinson and Malloy, to the consternation of the
Fort Lee and Fort Washington batteries, successfully executed their
dangerous mission. Undetected, the sloops and their flat-bottomed
tows made it without so much as a cannon bark from the rebel
batteries.[34] At dawn today they rode safely at their moorings.

However, the rain which had so generously aided the British
vessels in penetrating the Chevaux de Frise continued into today,
causing the British commander to call off his attack, scheduled for
this morning.

Nevertheless, Howe has his transportation ready and all preparations set for assaulting the American stronghold. His plans call for
a storming of the north, east and south slopes and their forbidding
looking precipices.

Unaware of his enemy's operations and of how close the fort
that bears his name is to the impending siege, the American
Commander early this morning, with Billy at his side, moved out
with his staff for the village of Hackensack. Making their way
down into the valley and then south toward the little ferry and
across the Hackensack River, the party arrived at the American
Chief's headquarters in the Peter Zabriskie house[35] by 10 A.M.

The beautiful, rambling, Zabriskie mansion home, built only 25
years ago, faces the village green. Zabriskie, gloating with pride
that the Continental Army commander has accepted his offer of
hospitality, does everything possible to make his famous guest's
stay comfortable.

In A Mansion House 65 Miles From the White Plains

Here before the brick hearth in the spacious living room of the
"big house," which is called a "mansion" in these rural and
predominantly Dutch villages and farmlands, the Virginia Leader
and his aides warm themselves.

The Mansion House on the Green
shown before being razed in the early
Twentieth Century—From Francis C.
Koehler's *Three Hundred Years*, 1940.

They hold their hands out, rubbing them briskly together to
catch the heat from the fireplace as it rises up toward the long
beautiful mantel shelf over the Holland-made blue tiles. The hand-
made, three by four-inch, ornamental glazed clay pieces sparkle
from the flickering fire's light to give their elaborate designs of
windmills, dykes and miniature Dutch figures of the homeland's men
and women a comfortable feeling of Amsterdam, Holland, from
which many of the early settlers came.

For the Continental Army's headquarters staff and for the
soldiers encamped on the green outside, here now ends the long,
wet, cold, circuitous, forced 65-mile march out of the White Plains.

The enemy's control of all the territory below, or south of
Peekskill to Fort Washington had made it necessary to move north

for a safe crossing. And this is what The General will now tell Congress as he and his aides begin attending to their long overdue reports and correspondence.

The General will write Congress:

> "I hastened over on this side with about five thousand men by a roundabout march (which we were obliged to take on account of the shipping opposing the passage at all the lower ferries) of near sixty-five miles."[36]

After lunching with his host, the Continental Army Chief completes his routine correspondence and, with his staff, begins a reassessment of "The Grand Army's" present predicament. Most of the staff are becoming convinced that Mount Washington will be put under siege. The question now is what to do about it and how long can the garrison hold out?

General Putnam, going along with the optimists' point of view, displays "an overweening confidence in the impregnability of Fort Washington."[37]

In the minds of the optimists is the assurance from Colonel Magaw that he and his men can hold Fort Washington against Howe's forces until December if necessary. And has not Magaw said that should matters grow desperate, he could carry off his garrison and the stores to the New Jersey side?[38]

Putnam's characteristic optimism, Magaw's extreme confidence, and the impregnable reputation of Fort Washington and the mount's defenses around it, contribute much to allay the fears of the American command for the fortress's safety.

Since no one has the slightest suspicion of any treachery afoot, the consensus of opinion within the staff command is that Fort Washington can successfully repel the enemy. Furthermore it is believed that though the British may attempt to lay a long siege against the works, such an operation coming in the very face of winter would most likely meet with similar failure.

So, a matter of secondary concern, the wide disbursement of The Grand Army troops, becomes the next problem in the grand dilemma.

General Howe has not only successfully deluded the Americans' "Old Fox" this time, but the "Old Hunter" has also, unwittingly or not, dispersed the rebel Leader's entire army. Howe knows that the American General still believes that the Juggernaut may even yet strike out for Philadelphia. Else why has he sent Stirling and his brigades toward Amboy and New Brunswick?

So while the American staff command ponders its present predicament with such a scattered army, Sir William, whose Tory informants are proving to be his best source of intelligence, is apprised of the almost unbelievable disposition of the rebel forces.

The knowledge that his enemy's army is so widely dispersed is more than Howe had counted upon in his enterprise against the Manhattan post.

He carefully examines the reports from his scouts and his informers. The Americans' far-flung troop positions convince him that the time for striking could not augur for a more propitious hour. Always a cautious planner, Howe once again looks over the surprising information his aides lay before him:

●*Stirling's eight regiments, estimated at 1,200 men,[39] on their way to New Brunswick, about 50 miles away;*

●*The American Commander's brigades, estimated at 5,000 troops, encamped at Hackensack, about 12 miles and over the Hudson and Hackensack rivers from Fort Washington;*

●*General Greene, commander of the twin forts, with about 4,800 men[40] of which about 2,800 are reportedly holding Mount Washington while the remaining 2,000 plus are across the river at Fort Lee and its outposts—the nearest supporting force Fort Washington can call upon;*

●*General Heath's four brigades, estimated at much less than 5,400[41] effectives, guarding the Hudson's high lands on the west side of the river, about 30 miles away to the northwest;*

●*General Lee's brigades, estimated at about 7,000[42] but not all fit for duty, lying isolated at North Castle, about 20 miles north.*

With an army of over 35,000 fighting men, Lord Howe's naval vessels, and the detailed plans of Fort Washington disclosing its most vulnerable attack points in his hands, General Howe foresees an easy victory within his reach.

The intelligence report, revealing as it does the rebels' weakened forces of less than 24,000 troops in all, thinly spread over a wide arc from North Castle to New Brunswick for a distance of almost 100 miles, is all that Howe needs to reassure him, settling any lingering doubts he may have nursed.

Never, in the eyes of the British high command, would the Fort Washington apple be any riper for plucking than right now. As for those of General Howe's staff who had strongly recommended crossing the Hudson, linking with the northern British army and striking out for the Continental Congress in Philadelphia, a Fort Washington victory would vindicate the viscount commander-in-chief's decision.

The island of Manhattan must be cleared and the effectiveness of the defiant twin forts must be destroyed. This is the next step in Sir William's opinion. This must be done before the rounding up of the remaining rebels and the winding up of the war in Jersey or Pennsylvania.

Howe's estimates of Greene's strength at Fort Lee notwithstanding, Greene's return of troops yesterday showed:

> "2,667 rank and file fit for duty, of which 508 (under Colonel Durkee and Major Clarke) were at Sneden's Landing (Dobbs Ferry); 145 were detached to Bergen (town), Hoboken, Bull's Ferry, Hackensack and Clinton Point, opposite Spuyten Duyvil; 1,510 were detached to New York island (Fort Washington)."[43]

And in today's orders from the American Commander in Hackensack came a directive to the Fort Lee post commandant to stop two brigades that were to pass through and hold them at the mountain-top encampment to strengthen that garrison.

The General's order, as he later explained it, stated that he had:

> "stopped General Beall's and General Heard's Brigades (at the fort) to preserve the post and stores here, which with other troops I hope we shall be able to effect."[44]

Today's returns, reporting on General Greene's total military complement, give a figure of 4,682 rank and file under his command at both Fort Lee and Mount Washington, its fort and all outposts.[45]

The total number of Continental Army effectives is far less than Howe's intelligence estimate of less than 24,000. Actually the number fit for duty is closer to 17,800.

And their wide dispersion reduces their potential as a combat force, particularly up against an enemy twice their strength and far more adequately equipped. Actually, under the Commander-in-Chief and his younger commandant at Fort Lee, there is a total of only about 7,200 troops fit for duty.

Of that number, only about 2,800 are holding Mount Washington and its fortress. And they stand alone, across a wide river from their supporting forces on the Jersey mount.

However, on the side of the Americans' last post on Manhattan Island is its reputation as the strongest American defense post in the thirteen states. Its commander has reinforced its entrenchments and redoubts. And there is not a doubt in Magaw's mind that the fort will repel the siege.

Among Howe's Helpers: Over-confidence and Delusion

The "siege concept" in Magaw's mind is best explained by Captain Graydon. Graydon, who is under Magaw's command, contends that his colonel has "heard of sieges being protracted for months and even years" and since the place he has to defend is called "a fort and has a cannon in it, he thinks the deuce is in it if he cannot hold out for a few weeks."[46]

Therefore, working surreptitiously within the American military minds on behalf of His Majesty's army, are those two ageless dethroners of kings and the erodents of men and armies—Over-confidence and Delusion. They add two more pieces of armament to Howe's forces as the re-scheduled assault hour approaches.

Bowing to adverse weather, Howe has set the attack for 10 A.M. tomorrow, Saturday, November 16. It will be a good day for such a surprise. His foe will be barracks-building in the high lands, at Croton-Bridge, Peekskill and at North Castle, digging in under the false belief that they will remain there "for their winter habitations."[47]

One of the main British attack sectors is the redcoats' right wing under the command of Lieutenant General Baron Wilhelm von Knyphausen who heads the entire Hessian division. Knyphausen has "for some days established his post on the York side of King's Bridge, within cannon shot of Fort-Washington which was covered by very strong ground and exceeding difficult of access,"[48] as Howe will later tell Lord Germaine.

Knyphausen's task is the most difficult one of the enterprise. On it, the scaling of the northern precipice, depends the successful execution of the entire operation.

The obliteration of Fort Washington and its defenses on the mount is not only for General Howe an immediate military objective, with him now it has almost become an obsession. However, he will stress the military reason for destroying the American post when he reports to London on the battle later. In that account he will state:

> "But the importance of this post (Fort Washington), which with Fort-Lee on the opposite shore of Jersey, keeps the enemy in command of the

navigation of the North-River while it bars the communication with York by land, makes the possession of it absolutely necessary."[49]

Though certain of victory, Sir William desires to avoid bloodshed if he possibly can. Reminding himself of his former sympathies for the American cause and his and his brother's initial desires to act as missioners of peace, the British commander-in-chief assigns his adjutant general, Colonel Patterson, the honor of delivering the ultimatum.

Riding up to the outer gates of the fort below the mount's summit under a white flag of truce at noon today,[50] Patterson is met at the bastion's entrance by the commandant's acting adjutant general, Colonel Swoope. Patterson turns over a written ultimatum addressed to Magaw but signed by Patterson, ordering the surrender of the entire Mount Washington garrison with a warning of the consequences that "must attend a general attack."[51] The ultimatum is delivered by order of General Howe.

While Patterson and his aides wait beside their horses, Swoope carries the paper back into the fort and turns it over to the colonel. The fort adjutant informs Magaw that the British general wants a reply within two hours.

The wording of the ultimatum, clothed in strict military parlance, is translated by Magaw and his staff to mean: "to surrender at discretion or suffer the consequences of a storm"; and this, in turn, under military law means that failure to comply and capitulate will expose the garrison to the liability of being put to the sword if taken.[52]

Swoope, under Magaw's directions, informs the British adjutant that he will receive his reply in due time, whereupon the flag-carrying party returns down the slope, escorted by the American guide. Beyond the outer works' boundary they make their way to Knyphausen's camp and to Howe, waiting alongside of the Hessian general.

In the absence of Magaw's adjutant, Ensign William Demont, who seemingly has taken French leave and has not been heard from in almost a week, Colonel Swoope, acting as adjutant, helps Magaw and the fort's staff officers pen a reply to Howe's ultimatum.

All are of the same mind. All are agreed to defend the post. Before the two hours are up, Magaw's answer is on its way to the British adjutant, to whom it is addressed, and indirectly to the commander-in-chief of His Majesty's Army. It reads:

"To the Adjutant General of the British Army.—Sir, If I rightly understand the purport of your message from General Howe, communicated to
Colonel Swoope, this post is to be immediately surrendered, or the garrison
put to the sword.

"I rather think it is a mistake than a settled resolution in General Howe,
to act a part so unworthy of himself and the British Nation. But give me
leave to assure his excellency that actuated by the most glorious cause that
mankind ever fought in, I am determined to defend this post to the very
last extremity.

Rob't Magaw, Colonel Commanding"[53]

Magaw immediately sends a courier with the news to Greene at
Fort Lee. At 4 P.M. Greene sends a dispatch rider over to the
Commander-in-Chief in Hackensack. The General in the midst of
receiving the remaining rear guard troops from out of the White
Plains, has just returned to his Zabriskie Mansion House head-
quarters.

Soldiers, inhabitants and, particularly the Hackensack
youngsters, on and around the wet, sloppy Green south of the
headquarters, are drawn to the sight of the mud-splattered dispatch
rider and horse galloping toward the guards posted beyond the
green. At full rein he passes the sentries who know him.

Then, before the guard at the Zabriskie house, he roughly draws
rein and brings his sweating, frothing steed to a sudden stop. He
leaps off the animal and rushes through the door, passing the
amazed sentry without a nod and dashes into the living room
headquarters of the Continental Army's General and Chief. There
the Commander's aides receive him and summon their Chief.

Outside and all through the village spreads the word of the
galloping messenger. Soon the curious onlookers spread the news
that they saw The General and his aides ride off and cross the
Hackensack by way of the Little Ferry. Everyone is sure something
is in the making, either at Fort Lee or across the North River at
Fort Washington. Just what is anybody's guess. And everybody
guesses.

There is no halting this time for The General, as he customarily
does at the ferryman's home three miles from the Village Green.
The ferry owner of the so-called "Little Ferry," Captain Josiah
Banks, has carved out of the wilderness here a picturesque spot for
his home and farm. He has cleared only 80 acres of his 500-acre
riverside plantation, most of which provides him with:

"... timothy grass and clover and bears good crops of rye,
Indian corn, oats and other grains; on the other part of the meadow may

be cut two hundred tons of good fresh grass. All the produce of the farm may be transported to New York, Hackensack or elsewhere. The boats from Hackensack daily pass by. It affords excellent pasture in the spring and summer seasons, and is very commodious for raising cattle. There is on it a good house, kitchen and barn, placed so advantageously on an eminence as to command a view of the whole farm."[54]

Captain Banks, recognizing the American Commander's request for speed hurries his ferrymen in polling the rebel party across. Behind them the sun sets with outstretched wings of red glowing flames that reach the length of the horizon's distant mountain range. Slowly the great ball slips below the range to leave the day in darkness.

Greene sent his Chief Magaw's message, the ultimatum and reply, adding in Magaw's own words: "We are determined to defend the post or die."

The seriousness of the situation, in the Commander's opinion, offered no alternative but an immediate personal assessment of all conditions. Besides, Greene's comment in the dispatch carried a note of bravado which seemed to hide concern and the hope for an immediate conference, and, most of all, The General's encouragement.

In the Mid-stream Of the River's Darkness

It read merely: "The contents will require your Excellency's attention."[55]

Upon arriving at Fort Lee the rebel Leader finds Greene has crossed to the New York side to confer with Magaw. By the sentries' "All's well!" it is now 9 P.M.

The night is cold as Bourdette and Baummeister help get three boats ready for the Chief and his party's emergency crossing.

In the river's tranquil darkness The General and his bodyguards, under the care of four of Glover's boatsmen, begin crossing unaware that at the same time, Greene and Putnam are returning from the New York side. In the middle of the channel, just to the south of the Chevaux de Frise, the two parties meet.

Bringing the vessels alongside of each other, the boatsmen hold their craft under the lee of the blockade barges while the three generals confer. In the course of reporting on the state of the works and garrison, both Greene and Putnam assure their Leader that the troops are in high spirits and will make a good defense.[56]

The American Commander later will say, in recalling this conference:

". . . and I had partly crossed the North River, when I met General Putnam and General Greene, who were just returning from thence (Fort Washington), and (they) informed me that the troops were in high spirits and would make a good defence; and it being late at night I returned."[57]

Setting out with his party by the long New Bridge route back to Hackensack, The General, seeing a light still burning in the window of the Liberty Pole Tavern at the crossroads in the valley reins in Old Magnolia. To the pleasant surprise of the Whig innkeeper The General and his riders stop for refreshments before continuing to Hackensack.

As he has throughout the ride to Fort Lee, and now on his way back to Hackensack, and over his glass of wine at the inn, the Virginian Leader of the Continentals turns the decision as to evacuating Fort Washington over in his mind. Even now, he tells himself, there may be time to get the entire garrison and most of its stores off Mount Washington and safely on the Jersey shore.

The North River, so long his ally, now becomes an impediment. The crossing of almost 3,000 men, closely pursued on land by the enemy's military might and on the river by their naval vessels, offers a problem but not an insurmountable one.

However, the Congress wants Fort Washington held. His staff wants to hold it and believes it can.

Yet, is not the evacuation of the post the wisest step to take? What matters if its forfeiture to the enemy does dampen the Americans' spirit of defiance? Are they not already depressed in heart? Should not the assured safety of the garrison now be of primary consideration?

Three years from now, in recalling this night, the Continental Army Commander will write to Joseph Reed that Greene's opinion, the wishes of Congress, and various other conflicting considerations "caused *that warfare in my mind,* and hesitation which ended in the loss of the garrison."[58]

It has been a harrowing day for all in and around the fort on The Mountain and the works on the Bluff Rock. Just as tensions seemed to be subsiding, the vague news reports this afternoon from across the river that the British were up to something rekindled new fears.

Whispering voices among the riverside people soon reach the inhabitants over The Mountain. From there they are carried like a sputtering fuse into the valleys and across the rivers, always gathering more fire and bringing more fear to the gullible uninformed.

It was late before John Gray returned to Elaine in their room at the Baummeister's. He, along with many headquarters officers, was called from his bed upon the Chief's sudden arrival owing to Greene's absence. And for what reason no one would know exactly, until tomorrow.

Earlier this evening after supper, in the big upstairs bedroom of the old house, Elaine and John had reached an impasse in a long, almost wordless argument that began with an ominous silence between the two after the evening meal. It became the first major altercation in their short married life together.

It all began when Elaine stated the army was to blame for Edmund Kearney's injury and should do something to help him if he needs it.

When John disagreed and contended that Edmund had no reason to leave and go "running off to the other side of the river," one thought winged its words to another. Then, unintentionally, John allowed his tongue to slip.

It was when the discussion branched into military and political areas. Without realizing that his words and tongue had not cleared themselves with his brain, John declared that no one should be discharged until the war was over unless incapacitated . . . and that *no one* can afford to be neutral in this war.

It was the last sentence which John wished he could retract. The word, "neutral," has not been mentioned in the Baummeister household since the episode on The Rock last Saturday.

No one has even mentioned the event in the presence of the married couple. And not even in the privacy of their own room have Elaine or John referred to the disastrous birthday party.

John has suffered silently for the past week. During the night he has often been awakened by Elaine's muffled sobs. But he knows that his wife prefers not to talk about it.

To do so with Elaine would only tend to compound the fears that churn within her—fears which he knows are centered around her love and concern for him and their future. It is that future which she so zealously wishes to protect.

It is this, he knows, and nothing else that has turned her suddenly from a patriot to a neutral and that would, to protect him, turn her into a Tory if such were necessary to save their future.

It is this kind of love for him, deep and strange as it is, that John Gray knows exceeds the boundaries of causes whether they be political or religious. It is this kind of love that worries him, knowing as do all the men in the Continental Army, that there is no war that guarantees its participants a passage of safety. There is no war that assures the corporeal form of man immunity across the battlefield to the valleys of peace.

So both Elaine and John, wrenched in silence, have suffered each alone in silence. But their usual conversations, which bar the Saturday night affair, and the family's customary discussions at the dinner table had not changed. Not until tonight.

The young officer's explosive mention of the word, "neutral," struck the dinner table like a lightning bolt. Marie Louise dropped her serving spoon. Papa Pete gulped and looked unbelievingly at his son-in-law. John closed his eyes and clenched his teeth as though he were suddenly stabbed with a knife.

Elaine straightened for a brief moment. Her face showed no reaction. Wiping her mouth slowly with her linen table napkin, she appeared to completely ignore her husband's last sentence. Then telling her mother that the shad roe was deliciously flavored by the addition of the new herbs, she excused herself and retired to the kitchen to help, she said, Honest Sam with the pot cleaning.

Only Paul showed no interest in the adults' conversation. He had thought Elaine made a good speech but should have kept the pianoforte. As for her talk about being a "neutral," he did not think that was so bad for women to be anyway just as long as they "keep standin' up fer the Continental soldiers." So Paul merely held out his plate for some more fish when John finished speaking.

The couple have never aired even their smallest differences before the family, or before anyone else. And never do they raise their voices in disputes which, if they hold at all, are under the couple's agreed rules always within the walls of their own room. Though both were over-tired tonight from the strains of a long, hard week with its heightening tensions, they carried on an innocuous conversation upstairs in their quarters after all had retired.

Finally, John said, "Elaine, let us not talk more about shoes, clothes and the wash tomorrow. Let us talk about what is on our mind. Ourselves."

"John, you said tonight that no one should be neutral," replied Elaine. "This means you think I should not be . . . that I was wrong to say what I did Saturday last."

"I said that not, Elaine," John interrupted.

"But 'tis what you feel, John. Am I not right?"

"Yes, 'tis what I feel and think," frankly answered her husband.

"I cannot say, nay. For each must his own mind hold; each must his own thoughts keep."

". . . So I wish to be neutral. I hate this war and both its sides!" she retorted testily. "I cannot help it as long as it holds you. Look what war has done to us here! Look what it does to people! When I see what it has done to men, to women and to children, I want it not. What matters really what the cause? Is honor tastier than life?"

"Is freedom not life, Elaine?" John parried. "Are not freedom, liberty and life all one? Are not chains, bondage and death all one? Must we all not choose one side or the other for the good of all mankind? . . . I have said what I feel, that no one can afford to be neutral in this war."

"And I say that *I can* afford to be neutral, for I hate all war!" Elaine exclaimed. "I see what it is doing, what it has done and I fear what it will do. Look at that boy, Edmund! I know much more than you think I know about him. I do not defend him. I am saddened by his change and by his weakness. Yet I blame the war, the army, not the boy that was within him."

John listened attentively, suddenly realizing that Elaine has very likely learned somehow of Edmund's attempt upon The Lieutenant's life at the Sneden's Landing post. He remembered that the young corporal was delirious and could have rambled out of his mind.

The Lieutenant and others had learned indirectly that Kearney, after being discharged and crossing the river, was for some unknown reason, taken into custody in New York and now lingers in a British prison. Gray had not told this to Elaine, believing it would unnecessarily worry her. So he listened carefully as she revealed more than he had thought she knew.

Aware of his wife's sister-like interest in Kearney, he had debated telling her what the all-knowing eyes and ears of Sergeant Abbott had reportedly discovered. Abbott had informed Craig and Craig the post's headquarters, that the discharged corporal was taken.

But, unknown to Gray, Elaine had asked Abbott to learn, if possible, whether Edmund was all right and if he needed anything. Then a few days later the Indian rebel scout told her not to worry, that Kearney was somewhere in York.

Andy had hoped she would not press him for more, but Elaine persisted, discovering from Abbott's reluctant lips that the youth was in the British gaol.

"The boy is in English prison," the Lenape Indian finally told her. "Betrayed by false friends."

Abbott always had referred to Kearney with the deprecatory term, "boy." It was about the only overt indication of dislike, if not distrust, he held for the river side-reared army corporal.

And with that information, which she believed others knew and were trying to shield from her, Elaine had opened the table discussion by saying she believed the army should help the youth if he needed it. She was prepared to disclose she knew Edmund was imprisoned when John's tabooed mention of the word "neutral" dropped a curtain of silence over the table.

Now, in the privacy of their bedroom, Elaine re-opened her argument that the army should offer some assistance to a former soldier now imprisoned.

"I have heard that Edmund is in prison in York. He is so weak and helpless alone," she said. "Is there not something the army can do for him? Is there not something, John, that we all could do for him?"

What Matters Now the Little Things?

"You know as much as I do, Elaine," John replied. "I had hoped you would be spared the needless worry. Otherwise I would have told you myself. Abbott, and all of us feel there is nothing we can do. We know not even why he was taken."

"Have you no heart, John?" Elaine asked bitterly. "Surely there must be something can be done for him! At least for his dear mother's sake. God rest her soul!"

"What, Elaine?" John perturbedly inquired. "He is not longer with the army."

"You could inquire!" irately charged the officer's wife. "Can you not forgive the boy? Does not the good Lord ask us to forgive others? Is that the way you would follow the word of God? I am sure that he intended to hurt you up the river. But I am also sure that he was sorry as indeed am I . . . and I fear it was all my fault."

It was at this precise moment that a night duty officer knocked on the Baummeister door and called up to the candle-lighted window, that Lieutenant Gray was wanted immediately at headquarters. The officer was no sooner dressed and downstairs than the American Commander-in-Chief and his party appeared coming down the gorge road at 9 P.M. An advance non-commissioned officer awakened Stephen Bourdette. Another called for Pete Baummeister. All the guards bustled. The raised voices and commotion brought night-capped heads to opened windows, straining through the darkness to see what was going on.

The frightening situation, the appearance of the American Chief that late at night combined to terrify Elaine, not for her own sake, not so much for that of her family, but for the safety of her soldier husband.

What mattered the little things that bothered her so much a few moments ago? What has she said in anger that now she repented? Why had she not held her husband close to her while she had him within her arms' reach?

"What a fool," she thought, "am I!"

It was several hours before The General's departure, the fastening of the Durham boats at their moorings and the return of the officers and aides to their pillows.

The sentinel's cry of "All's well!" signified the quiet resumption of interrupted night, and with it John Gray now re-ascends the stairs to the second floor of the Baummeister house. The candle-lighted room is still aglow and before him, in the center of the room, stands his bride.

Her arms outstretched, her eyes red from the tears shed repentingly over the past few hours, Elaine runs weeping into her husband's welcoming arms. On her toes, reaching up to smother his face with kisses as he bends far over to receive them, she pleads, "Forgive me, John!"

"I need not forgive, thee, Elaine. When there are two of us, then two must give and two must take and both be for the other," he says as Elaine, sitting him in the rocker, pulls off his boots. Her husband's philosophic remarks often puzzle her as does this one.

The tear-stained young face looks up at him quizzically. Her head cocked slightly to the side, reveals her bloodshot, watery eyes.

"I think," she says with a half-smile," that needs explaining. But I think I should first explain that if there is anything that I can do for Edmund, I should so do. You know what they say happens to so many of the people who are thrown into those prisons. It is just horrible to even think of them."

"True," Gray replies. "We may be able to do something, or at least find out more about it. Asher Levy's friend down there, Haym Salomon, released on parole by the British, may be the one who can do it. That is if we can get through to him. And if anyone can, I am sure Asher will find a way . . . But now, do you remember what Chief Perawae once told us up there on the ancient old castle grounds? I could not help but think of it as I came up the stairs."

"I remember many things he told us."

"Well," says John very seriously, looking over at the burning log in the fireplace, "there is one thing he told us which almost took place tonight and something we should never allow to happen. The Old Chief said, when he gave us that one and only piece of advice, 'Never let the smoldering embers of your fires gaze too long, nor through the night, upon your wrath, and let them always live and die looking brightly upon your smiles and joys.' It was good advice, My Love. Good advice."

"Ah, yes!" Elaine answers reminiscently, "I well remember that."

In their customary nightly routine and enrobed in their long woolen nightshirts, together they blow out the candles. Then, with their arms entwined around each other, they go over, as they always do, to look out their window upon the river, gently flowing under its dark-blue canopy of stars.

"Look across there, Elaine," John says, pointing. "That post, named for The General may soon be under siege . . . The north and east slopes may catch trouble for weeks . . ."

"I know." his wife glumly responds. "Though I want not to talk about it, I would know one thing. Are you to be over there?"

"No," Grays answers solemnly. "Those that are there may soon be brought over here. Likely they will evacuate the whole works, or certainly most of it before it blows. And then I think we may all be moving out of here into West Jersey."

"And I will go with thee, John Gray!"

Her husband laughs, saying, "Nay. You will stay here. What would you do in with all those camp wives and women? I can just see thee!"

"Ay, but I would be by thy side!"

"It is not to be. I say no, Elaine."

Elaine's eyes follow her husband's through the window. They look out over the darkened waters of the great river toward the silhouetted, mount-like rise of land, clothed only in dimly reflected starlight.

It is a dark, bleak scene once the eyes lift up from the star-sparkling, rippling river. On the mount and below it, in widely scattered areas, can be seen the flickering campfires, all seemingly quietly at rest on old Manna Hata's warring island, once the home of peace-loving people.

Elaine turns suddenly away and John moves with her. They face each other. The bride of seven weeks looks up and gazes intently deep into her husband's eyes and he, in turn, in hers. Their arms close tightly about each other as their lips press hungrily together.

Engulfed with each other's fullness of life, they press, as though into one, the warmth of their bodies. And she whispers as rapidly as her short, swift gasps for breath permit, "I love you . . . Oh, John, John . . . I love you so."

Suddenly her husband gently lifts her in his arms, carries her across the room and, with one hand, pulls back the covers of the downy quilt. Outside can be heard the changing of the guard. Their voices filter, tiptoeingly unheard in and out of the darkened room.

And soon now the blue petticoat scarf on the back of the Windsor rocker waves no longer in the breeze that came through the partly opened window. For the wind from the distant ocean, 20 miles southeast, has suddenly shifted westward.

And now, much later, when only a hooting owl and Papa Pete's rhythmic snoring disturb the quiet, Elaine taps her sleeping husband's shoulder. He responds finally with a grunt and then an excited, "What? What?"

Calmly and deliberately his wife of Dutch, French and English ancestry, says to her half-awakened spouse, "But I am still a neutral!"

Sullenly her husband retorts in full capitulation, "Yes, yes, I know, Elaine! Now may I please go to sleep?"

But silence, struggling to take back its dominion over night, waits again until the echoing voice of the watchman's words die away over the water:

"All's well 'nd two o'clock!"

26

Saturday, November 16. . .

The Battle for Fort Washington

All Eyes Concenter On the East Bank

At daybreak this morning the Barbette Battery was crowded with staff officers and their aides. All fixed their eyes upon Fort Washington's works across the river. A short time later inhabitants from all around had gathered in whispering groups.

No one is sure about anything. They have all heard that Mount Washington is to come under siege. Some have stolen behind the water front redoubts and guards who probably would not stop them anyway and clambered part way up the rocky slopes to see what may be a battle for the fort on the New York side.

There are a few of the region's natives who are Royalists. Though the patriots have their own suspicions, which are not always valid, there is almost no sure way of sometimes distinguishing between a taciturn Tory and a neutral. Regardless, all know that the Loyalists hope that Howe can put a quick end to the American Rebellion. Conquering Fort Washington would be a big step in that direction.

The patriot sympathizers generally tolerate known true neutrals. They do so with disdain, but it is the "Turncoat Tory" and the "Turncoat Whig" whom they despise.

It is those, they claim, who put their patriot coats on one day and turn them inside out the next, depending upon which side, rebel or redcoat, is nearest to their door. The staunch patriots charge that the "Turncoat Tory" swings along with whichever army is occupying the valley.

So Whig and Tory look across the river at the site of the impending siege against Manhattan's last American defense post. It is a good mile from fort to fort, west to east.

Unlike the giant rock walls of the west bank, across the river the shore resembles a miniature Palisades that shield the vast wooded areas, dales and the long plateau—the 100-foot high rise of land known now as Mount Washington. Owing to the terrain, Fort Lee's mountain-top observers are denied a full view of any Fort Washington movements, except in certain exposed areas. And no observation is possible of military operations occurring on the mount's northeast, east and west slopes.

Except by ascending the rough and treacherous Fort Washington inclines along the fort road and entering the main gate, which lies above and beyond the guarded passes and defiles, visitors, or attackers, are forced to use the other ascents to the summit, all of which are perilous, if not suicidal. That is, unless one knows in advance the detours, by-passes and openings through the abatis defenses, around the redoubts and between the entrenchments.

In some places the mount rises almost straight up from its river base. Except for a few areas on the east, the precipices similarly reach perpendicularly up from the water's edge of the Harlem River. There that circuitous waterway winds up north out of the East River to become eventually the "Harlem Creek."

Together the Harlem's river and creek encircle the upper end of the mount until they enter into Hudson's river at the Spuyten Duyvil. It is that "cut," or opening, of the Harlem into the Hudson at the Spuyten Duyvil that completes nature's geographical forming of Manhattan's island, thus preventing it from becoming a peninsula extension of Westchester.

This entire northern, mount-like extremity was said to have been the exclusive domain of the ancient Chief, Manna Hata. Its precipitous elevations extend four miles north to south and average no more than about two-thirds of a mile in width from the Hudson east across to the Harlem River.

At the mount's southern end, below the heights of Harlem, run the Harlem plains. A sudden drop off the plain's southwestern end is the Hollow Way.

It is the Hollow Way that the Continentals still proudly point out as the site of their victory. And the mount's defenders boldly claim they will put the redcoats to rout in the same way once again.

Below, or south of the Harlem plains, Lord Percy's British brigades stand poised for attack on the same grounds they have held since pushing the rebels out of New York. Here they have waited restlessly since September 15, for most have seen little action other than a occasional brush in their probes against the fort.

Only Percy's Fourth Brigade and two battalions of his Sixth have seen some minor skirmishing in Westchester. That was when they were ordered up to support Howe after the White Plains battle.

Since its prehistoric creation with the earth's genesis, the high forested rock-bound upper tip of Manhattan's island has never been in such demand. Over 100 years ago it was not considered of any value at all except by the Indian inhabitants. They had continued to occupy the mount even after they had unwittingly forfeited its ownership under the terms of their sale of the lower part of the island to the Dutch. In that sale, the Indian tribes understood, incorrectly, that they were retaining for their use the rights to the island's upper half.

To the Indian inhabitants, the tree-crowned heights and forests were the only valuable grounds on the island. Here they found shelter, fished, hunted and lived in peace except for some occasional feuding with tribes across the river or to the north. To the south of the high ground, paralleling the great waters of the Mahicanittuck, they planted their fields of corn.

It was not far north of here, in the inlet, that the white man and his *Half-Moon*, dropped anchor under the eyes of their astounded ancestors. And for years, long after most of the tribes had vanished from the island, were seen the overgrown, unattended fields of Indian maize, visible from afar. Their stalks waving spectral-like and neglected in the air, presented a haunting memory, anachronistically recalling the departed, forgotten original people, their past and their culture.

It was ground for which the practical and prosaic Dutch had little use and considered worthless. But they began to change their thoughts about the high mount when:

"Magistrate Van Oblimus obtained consent of his fellow townsmen for the occupation of a part, and seeking the relics of the aboriginal owners, purchased for his hardy son, Hendrik, the first settler, the equivocal right to squat with molestation on their half-cultivated oasis."[1]

After that, the desire for acquiring lands on the mount gradually increased. And in proportion to that desire the redmen were pushed farther and farther back into the wilderness and oblivion.

However, that was almost 100 years ago. And since then, settlers have seen it as a mount of great beauty, an attractive scenic spot upon the island and one richly clothed in nature's rarest garments. In 1712:

> "It had become desirable in the view of the British Governor, to allot the common lands, in strips which extended from river to river, among the freeholders of the Dutch village."[2]

Once "The Fairest Land On Which the Foot Of Man Had Ever Trod"

And so, within the century, the Indian encampments, one on the south side of Inwood Hill, another on Jeffery's Hook, have both disappeared. The "birch bark country,"[3] as it was called, that stretched far above and below, north and south of Jeffery's Hook, was called "Weckquaskeek" by the original natives and the earliest white settlers. Later the Dutch, French and English bestowed their own names on the various sections of the area.

Early arriving white men would say of the site:

> "It (is) no wonder that Hendrik Hudson here chose to drop the *Half-Moon's* anchor. It was no wonder that they declared it, way back there more than 200 years ago, the fairest land on which the foot of man had ever trod."[4]

And all these reminiscent thoughts and more flash through the minds of the American inhabitants who this morning stand along and under the Palisades watching the mount a mile away. Most stand in awed silence as the Saturday dawn begins brightening the water's edge. There underneath the towering monolithic guardians below the cliffs they look over at a peaceful scene and tensely await the thunder of cannons.

It is the morning of the day Andy Abbott has chosen to move Perawae and Minnie and all their earthly belongings downriver by two canoes into the Kill von Kull and then over to Perth Amboy's post.

It is a good day to make the trip, Abbott feels. All attention will be focused upriver on the mount. Since the Abbotts will be headed downstream, there is little fear of enemy interception. Besides, General Howe has been making every effort possible to befriend the Indians in the hope of inducing them to rise up against the American forces and the inhabitants of all the thirteen States, or "colonies," as Sir William insists they are. And Sergeant Abbott's wearing apparel is more buckskin than military. He has never worn much in the way of a uniform.

Before dawn Honest Sam had discovered the Abbotts making preparations to leave from the wharf in front of Ma Kearney's old house. He told Gray who was on his way up the gorge road to the Barbette. The Lieutenant immediately returned to the house, called Elaine, and together they hurried to bid the old couple goodbye.

Knowing she would never see either of them again, Elaine's eyes welled with tears as she embraced the pair while John helped Andy pack the old man's canoe. The Indian scout said nothing but simply with a gesture urged his parents to hurry.

On the tide, he pushed off, handling the forward canoe with his mother in the bow while Perawae paddled behind in the second bark. Both were connected by a stern to bow line. And thus the old couple departed.

Only Andy will be returning to the post from which he has been given an unlimited leave to escort his parents far south to the Brotherton Reservation at Edgepillock in West Jersey.

John and Elaine ran along the shore, returning to the ferry landing paralleling the birch canoes which stayed close to the river's bank. At the landing road, John left his wife to continue his ascent up the gorge road to the Barbette.

Elaine, hurrying to the end of the wharf, waved the wet linen handkerchief which she had pulled from her husband's pocket to dry her eyes. It was one of the pair she had given John for his birthday in August.

Minnie, from the bow, returned the farewell, as others of the hamlet joined Elaine in returning the Indian woman's sad and solemn, hand-waving good-bye. They had heard that Indian Abbott was taking his parents south to join the other Unami people, but they had not realized that this was their farewell departure until Elaine told them.

All that is now left of the once great culture belonging to the friendly, trusting, peace-loving Haqninsaq tribe of the Unamis from the Lenni Lenape Nation of the Algonkians, or "Delawares," as the white man called them, is the rapidly overgrowing castle grounds of Oratam.

There on The Mountain's west slope, several miles south, overlooking the valleys westward of the Palisades, are the deserted remnants of the tribe's last village. And down under the Bluff

Rock Barbette's heavy guns, tied lovingly and carefully to Ma Kearney's old wharf, as though someday its owner would come back and reclaim it, is Old Chief Perawae's beloved dug-out canoe.

These are the last relics of the old culture as now across the river begins another battle for the new.

Such are the thoughts that flash through Andy's mind as he paddles downstream—down the river he knew and loved so well as a boy.

He looks at Elaine waving from the ferry landing and remembers when he first saw her, and of her kindnesses to him and Andrea— his beautiful lost Mahtocheega—and the cold winter burial of Little Bear Princess in the white man's graveyard. And how Elaine regularly put flowers on the ground under which she lay.

And his eyes stretch across river as he paddles. Then for the moment, he ignores the white man's warring. Instead, the scene reminds him of the story that was told often by his maternal forebears. Surely now his mother must be thinking of it too, the tale of love between an Indian boy and girl.

Once, he now recalled, he had brought Mahtocheega in this very canoe here to the middle of the river under the moonlight shadows of the great flat rock. He did so especially to tell her the legendary story of the uniting lovers of the divided Unami and Munsee peoples, the oft-feuding peoples of his Lenni-Lenape Nation.

And, Like the Waters, So Pass the People And Their Legends Unto the Sea

Now once again the tale sweeps through his memory:

... *They had met by chance on the river when their birchen canoes nearly collided in fog. The girl, Paalochquew, or Little Red Wing,*[5] *came from the sunrising side of the river. The boy, Teedyuscung, from the sunsetting side.*

Meeting clandestinely, since both their tribes were in a constant state of feud, they soon drew their blood and sealed their troth, asking Mother Earth, Father Sky and the Sun God to be their witnesses.

And so at night when they would steal away from their people, they would call each other with the voice of the owl across the water and then meet in midstream. But one night the moon appeared suddenly from behind its heavy clouds and the Unami and Munsi warriors, guarding their fishing banks, let go their arrows.

Caught between the missiles of both their feuding families, Paalochquew and Teedyuscung were sure they would meet death together. However, the young brave thought quickly and as the moon again receded behind the clouds he pulled Little Red Wing into his craft and paddled swiftly upstream toward the west bank, saving himself and his beloved. Teedyuscung set his sweetheart's overturned canoe adrift, causing all eyes to focus upon it. Meanwhile the lovers escaped in the night.

For many hours they paddled upstream with the tide and made their way far distant from their warring families. Both tribes now realized that Teedyuscung and Paalochquew were lovers who had met nightly in violation of their tribal customs.

Putting down their weapons, the two families searched the Mahicanittuck's waters together in vain for the lovers' bodies. But the warriors' truce was short-lived. Soon the two tribes were again renewing their ancient feuding.

Neither Paalochquew or Teedyuscung was ever heard of again, for they moved ever farther north and westward. And it was said they joined others, building a tribe called, "The Peace People," and uniting at last the Unami and Munsee families of the Lenni Lenape Nation. . . .

All this passed through Abbott's mind as the army scout kept a sharp eye out to his left for a sign of battle activity on Mount Washington's grounds. And soon the two canoes were only specks in the distance as Elaine followed their course until they disappeared.

If the many frightened Fort Lee observers were able to look down on Mount Washington from above, they would see it sprawling with some 30 widely scattered American defense posts. All these redoubts and entrenchments are designed to protect the main fortification grounds and stockade, Fort Washington on the summit.

The main works sit high atop the precipice where, on the west, steep rock walls look precariously down upon Fort Washington Point and its battery towering over Jeffery's Hook. Other smaller works and redoubts surround the main fort at various distances from its center.

The northernmost posts are Forest Hill and its supporting redoubt, Cock Hill Fort, which sits high on the mount's northern end and overlooks the Spuyten Duyvil. And on the opposite side of the Harlem River, near the Spuyten Duyvil, are the redoubts known as Forts 1, 2 and 3.

These are a few of the northern outposts on the Westchester side. East of them at the bend of the Harlem-Hudson River junction, is the King's Bridge which the Americans destroyed and the Hessians took over and have now rebuilt.

On the Manhattan Island side of King's Bridge, well down the road from the bridge itself, is a strong American redoubt known as the King's Bridge Battery. And eastward of King's Bridge, on the Westchester side of the Harlem, is the Americans' Fort No. 4, or Fort Independence. It was a post of major importance until evacuated by Greene's forces under Colonel Lasher on October 28 when Knyphausen made his push toward King's Bridge.

The old King's Bridge road runs up the island from New York town. It crosses over the Harlem into Westchester on the King's Bridge. A branch of this road runs directly into Fort Independence.

It is at the King's Bridge where the Harlem, more creek than river, bends on its west to east line as though it were making certain of its task to bite the island away from Westchester. For here it sharply enters its southern course into the wider body of the Harlem.

Then, joining the East River around Manhattan's east side, the combined waters encircle the old American Grand Battery and empty into New York Bay. And with its increasing flow come the rushing Long Island Sound's waters, escaping through the Hell Gate to join the East River's march to the sea.

So at the foot of Manhattan takes place the handshaking confluence of the East River's waters with the lower Hudson—a confluence which, ages ago, made old Chief Manna Hata's lands an island.

All this General Howe knows and dislikes. His winter Manhattan encampment must be secure and not subject to nuisance raids from a fortress virtually mounted over his head all winter. It is one more reason, in Sir William's mind, why Fort Washington must be erased.

Not much more than a quarter of a mile below the King's Bridge is the Dyckman Bridge. Its highway from the west crossed the Harlem and ran into the King's Bridge road at the far northern end of the island until the Americans recently destroyed both bridges.

On the Westchester side of the Harlem, on both the north and south sides of the roadway, are a string of redoubts. These defense posts run north to south on a line from Fort Independence. They were evacuated by the Americans along with Fort Independence when Knyphausen advanced. The British have now garrisoned the southernmost of these posts with heavy artillery to cover their Harlem River crossing and assault.

These, then, were the main rebel fortifications on the mount's northern and northeastern outer defenses. All of them on the Westchester side of the river have now been abandoned.

General Knyphausen, in command of the Hessian troops and the entire northern attack sector of the British operation, has already sent a spearhead of his army across the recently rebuilt King's Bridge. It is these troops which have been camped "for some days within cannon shot of Fort Washington." Constantly drilling in preparation for the attack, Knyphausen's troops await orders on the island side of Manhattan to advance on the mount's northern approaches.

This morning, shortly after dawn, the Hessian commander received his order and in two columns the German mercenaries, joined by more of their forces from Westchester, head for the strongly defended American slopes.

The Strategy Unfolds

The Hessian right wing, facing the precipitous northern approach side closest to Hudson's river, is led by Colonel Johann Rall. The left, moving toward the mount's northeastern slopes and defenses which face the Harlem River, is under Major General Martin Schmidt.[6]

Still looking down from above upon the island, might be seen the 20-gun British frigate, *Pearl*.[7] She is anchored south of the Spuyten Duyvil and south also of Tubby Hook. Her larboard guns are trained on Forest Hill. But that redoubt is safely out of the frigate's range and no more in the man-of-war's reach than is the vessel in the rebel battery's sight.

The enemy ship disdainfully by-passed the outer redoubt to the north on Cock Hill. That small isolated garrison made immediate preparations to withdraw back into Forest Hill when the man-of-war menacingly came downriver from Haverstraw Bay with the tide yesterday.

The American defenders, studying all possibilities, are confident that Knyphausen's assault, without full knowledge of the terrain and the location of the works defending it, cannot succeed.

However, even if the Forest Hill outer works should be overrun,

the troops could still withdraw higher into Fort Washington's
formidable defenses on the summit. But without knowledge of the
mount's intricate defense system, such a perilous assault would be
exceptionally difficult and could prove extremely costly for any
attacking enemy force.

So, faced with this threat, Colonel Magaw has stationed himself
within the main fort itself in order to provide a central command
post for what appears may be a three-pronged infantry attack on
all sides, except on the west which is protected by sheer precipice
walls. For these walls, ascending from the North River's waters,
present a front of mostly steep cliffs which rise up perpendicularly
before the onlooker.

Magaw has assigned one division of his less than 2,800-man force
to defend the northern sector. This corps will hold the left flank
above the rocky northern ascents nearest the Hudson. His right
wing extends eastward and downward into the high rocky woods,
crags and treacherous declivities above the Harlem River where it
swings south along the Harlem and then west above the Hollow
Way confronting Percy's redcoats.

The stoutest rebel allies are the precipices. These towering,
glowering buttresses surround almost three-fourths of the mount's
circumference. They support the summit of the mount, a rugged
irregular plateau where are entrenched the fort's protecting earthworks, abatis and stockaded walls, main gate of which opens
westward. The plateau or plain, rises toward the center. It is an
eminence that stretches from the Hudson to the Harlem, sometimes 200 feet above both the waters, creating an ideal site for the
main fortification.

It is this insurmountable looking defense which makes a direct
assault upon the works suicidal. But in addition is the semi-
secretive layout of the fortifications that make up the mount's
skillfully camouflaged redoubts and earthworks. It is these that
give to the place a comfortable feeling of security and promote its
"unassailable" reputation.

Only from the air can these hidden defense posts be spotted.
Only the command staff and their aides, one of whom is missing,
know the exact positions of the earthworks in relation to the others.

On the east brow, below the Long Hill and its Long Hill Road
on which Fort Washington and its northern redoubt, Forest Hill,
are located, is the lengthy King's Bridge Road. It runs through a
hilly declivity before it bends northeastward around an inlet of the
Harlem River called Sherman's Creek.[8]

To the south of the Sherman Creek inlet, on a steep, well protected elevation known as Laurel Hill, is the single-gun, Laurel Hill battery. Almost directly under the main fort's eastern sector, this fieldpiece and redoubt defend Fort Washington's eastern slope and its ascents where the perpendicular precipice dissolves into rugged slopes.

Towering over the north-south Long Hill Road, Fort Washington and part of Forest Hill look down and over the Laurel Hill battery on the Harlem River and eastward toward the enemy.

On its south side, Fort Washington looks down upon the Harlem plain and its defenses. On its west, it overlooks the Hudson's waters and across at Fort Lee. It is to the south of the fort where run the three main lines of American entrenchments from west to east across the island. Each of the three lines bisects the main highway up from New York town, the so-called King's Bridge Road. It is the postriders' and stagecoach route north to New England.

Nearest to the fort is the first of the three cross-island American defense lines laid out. But now it is the American defenders' third line of defense. The second line is the center of the south sector's defense system while the forward line, the last to be laid out but the first of the three completed, is considered "the first line," the forward entrenchments.

All three lines stand now fully manned on the plateau above the Hollow Way facing Lord Percy.

The forward, or first line, looks down on the Hollow Way pass just before the roadway veers south toward the city. The second line is a mile north of the first. The third a mile north of the second, and the fort itself is a mile and a half north of the third line.

Strong entrenchments and abatis barricades surmount the rocky heights of the first line and defend the approaches to the plains. Though not quite as strong, the second and third lines are similarly fortified. From Fort Lee's Bluff Rock much of the southern sector can be seen clearly through field glasses, where forest patches do not obstruct the view.

A string of unconnected batteries in front of the first line's earthworks, the outguard posts, look down and guard the entrance road to the Hollow Way. The southernmost outworks of these advance guard posts are at the Point of Rocks, a good mile and a half south of the forward line of entrenchments.

Here the outpost defenses run more westerly toward the Hudson

River. This, the least precipitous section, is the most vulnerable. On the opposite side of the Point of Rocks, the outposts run in a northeastwardly direction along the southeastern bank of the Harlem River.

Some of the rebel infantrymen still give their own accounts of the Battle of Harlem Heights which occurred a little to the southwest of the Point of Rocks exactly two months ago today.

On the right flank of the Point, close to the Hudson, is an advance picket post. On the far left flank of the Point is the Snake Hill battery and post. And north of this, looking down over the Harlem from their high vantage post are two batteries on a hillock. All are far forward of the first defense line.

On the extreme left flank of the American third line, standing high above the Harlem River, is the home of Colonel Roger Morris. Located on the east side of the King's Bridge highway, the house sits on the summit of Break-Neck Hill.

Homesteads, Inns and Inhabitants Stand In the Path of War

Built in 1756 by the wealthy British officer, Roger Morris, the home was taken over by the American Commander-in-Chief prior to the Battle of the White Plains. It was occupied by The General at a time when the Morrises were visiting in the highlands.

So stand the defenses south of the mount's fortress. Colonel Magaw must use part of his force to repel an attack from the south. Another division will be required to face an assault that may come simultaneously from the east and possibly from the north. All this the colonel prepares for, except he doubts his enemy will attempt to scale the north walls.

Still looking down on the mount from the air, if that were possible, one would see three inns spotted along the King's Bridge highway as it runs northward from out of the pass at the Hollow Way on its way toward the bridge. One of these is the Widow Day's Tavern at the southern extremity of the heights. A second is the famous Blue Bell Tavern, located at the east side of the road at the top of the long, steep rise up the Inwood Hill. The third inn and tavern is Cox's place at the King's Bridge.

The farmland deeds for all these lands run from west to east, river to river across the island. Through the area are scattered some 30 or more homesteads. Among the land-holding families are such names as Dyckman, Vermilte, Nagle, Post, Van Oblimus, Moore, Bowers, Aitken and Maunsell.[9]

All now, come together in huddles, the Loyalist-leaning ones criticizing the patriots among them, and the Whigs and patriot supporters of the cause condemning the Tories. But, like the neutrals, now few among the patriots are as vociferously outspoken as in the past. The outcome of the impending battle could well deprive them of their homes, properties and possibly their lives.

On the mount's west side along the Hudson no elaborate works were ever deemed necessary other than the heavy gun batteries to prevent enemy shipping from passing upriver. Here the sheer cliffs and steep, rocky precipices with their densely thick areas of boulder-strewn forests, rise almost straight up from the river's bottom.

Only Fort Washington Point's heavy artillery lies defiantly guarding the mount's west side. The large redoubt is located high above, but slightly to the north of Jeffery's Hook. The batteries act like overlords of the river's east bank, protecting the eastern terminus of Bourdette's and the army's ferry routes as well as the eastern end of the Chevaux de Frise.

Since these overlording batteries work in conjunction with Fort Lee's artillery, they make the possession of one or both of the twin forts imperative to an enemy seeking river control.

Until recently the British high command's plans had not called for an assault. They favored by-passing the fort and surrounding it under a long siege, hoping to starve out the defenders while the main British force linked with its northern army and drove toward Philadelphia. The Westchester campaign was a part of that strategy.

For most of those watching from Fort Lee's side of the river, the west facade of Mount Washington is about all that they can easily see in addition to the frigate, *Pearl*, anchored north of Jeffery's Hook. Even though this November, Saturday morning has dawned bright and clear, any view of action on Fort Washington's northern approaches is limited for the trembling inhabitants even from the high Bluff Rock. The sight of the beautiful Mount Washington eminence clothed in nature's fall array is lost before their eyes and smothered in their fears.

General Howe's Plan: A Four-Pronged Attack

General Howe's plans call for four simultaneous attacks. The first under General Knyphausen with detachments from Rall's brigade and the Waldeck Regiment.

The second attack will be launched by General Lord Cornwallis with the First and Second Battalions of the Light Infantry regiments and two battalions of guards under Brigadier General Matthews. All of these are to be supported by the First and Second Grenadiers and Lord Cornwallis's 33rd Regiment.

The third attack is to be a feint. It will be an amphibious crossing from the Westchester side of the Harlem. It will appear to be a drive directed at the rear of the third American cross-island defense line.

The feint is to draw attention and American strength toward the amphibious crossing, thus weakening the third line and its guarding of the main fort and works on the summit. This maneuver will be commanded by Colonel Lord Sterling. It will employ his 42nd Regiment and be supported by two battalions of the Second Brigade.

If successful it should distract the rebels facing Lord Percy as he drives from the south at the defenders' Harlem plains lines, thus enabling an outflanking of the American defenders along the mount's southern bastion.

The fourth attack[10] will be Lord Percy's drive from the south with one British and one Hessian brigade. The initial drive will be executed against the mount's forward or first line of entrenchments in order to bring Percy's forces up on the plains. Their objective is to overrun the mount's southern escarpments, outposts, the three entrenched cross-island defense lines and then be prepared to assist in storming the summit.

Howe's first attack, under Knyphausen and his 4,500 troops,[11] is considered the main drive. Knyphausen personally requested that he and his Hessian corps have the honor of executing the major assault. This, the key of the entire operation, will be against the so-called "insurmountable" north precipice and escarpments.

Far below the mount and well to the north, the two-column Hessian movement comes to a halt. Colonel Rall's troops form the right wing, Major General Schmidt's, the left. The two columns pause in the woody lowland swamp areas about two miles below the fort's accesses.

General Knyphausen himself joins the forces, choosing to stay with Schmidt's wing as he runs over the strategy of the operation. It is now a little before 7 A.M.

The second assault operation under Lord Cornwallis is the one for which the 30 transports were daringly towed through the American blockade by Captains Wilkinson and Malloy. Cornwallis's troops will be carried across the Harlem from the Westchester side, east of the King's Bridge. Some will embark at the Dyckman Bridge landing wharfs, be carried down with the tide about a mile and land under the American redoubt at Laurel Hill.

The little Laurel Hill redoubt commands the Sherman Creek landing area and its eastern approaches to the fort. Its battery is located on a precipice which gives it control over the area.

Units of the Cornwallis force will come directly across the river at this point and land under, and in range of, this battery.

The feint under Lord Sterling will be made with a landing midway between Fort Washington's southern escarpments and the Americans' third cross-island defense lines—the last southern defense before the fort itself.

If Sterling's ruse works, the Americans will be drawn from their entrenchments and forced to swing their left around east and face the Harlem River. All three of the American cross-island lines would then be diverted from their front which faces south and Percy's troops.

General Howe has planned meticulously. In that diversion, a hole in the American cross-island lines will enable Percy's troops to pierce through in a surprise attack upon the defender's forward entrenchments.

If all goes well, Percy will then move swiftly in to overrun the second and the third rebel lines. With Knyphausen attacking on the north and Cornwallis on the east, there will be no supporting American forces available to throw against Percy.

Once the three cross-island lines are overrun, Percy will unite with Sterling's forces and together join Cornwallis's attack on the east and then Knyphausen's forces as needed.

If Howe's plan works, the Juggernaut will crush the Americans' vital stronghold on Hudson's river. It will open up the waterway to British shipping, enabling unity with the British forces north under Sir Guy Carleton.

It will also simplify any crossings of the Hudson for an invasion of New Jersey, unless a surrender is negotiated beforehand. And it will deprive the rebels of their last remaining defense post on Manhattan. This should certainly, Howe thinks, further disillusion and dishearten the American cause, its rebel army and their Congressional leaders in Philadelphia.

Fort Washington proper is located on the brow of the Long Hill. Five bastions protrude out from its center. Three of these face the north, the center one of the three being the largest and strongest. Two bastions project out the south side, one at the southwest

corner and the other at the southeast. They overlook the three
cross-island entrenchments on the plateau beneath the fort.

Only one of the three northern bastions, the center structure,
has supporting breastworks but no intrenched lines. For below it,
down the north side, is the steep, wooded, rocky area which it
commands, making an assault ascent virtually impossible without
full knowledge of the terrain, its by-passes and safety zones.

On the Long Hill's northern brow is the so-called "Forest Hill
Redoubt." It is similar to, but larger than, the one on Mount
Laurel. Manned by a three-gun battery, the Forest Hill Redoubt
assists in defending the Hudson River Chevaux de Frise. From its
high prominence it has successfully hurled an enfilading fire down
upon the enemy's ships that have attempted to run the blockade.

North of Forest Hill can be seen Spuyten Duyvil, a mile and a
half distant. The Duyvil is about the same distance from Forest
Hill as the hill post is from the main fort on the summit.

Farther upriver, also overlooking the Hudson, is the previously
mentioned Cock Hill Redoubt. It sits on a round wooded knoll
crowning the hill just above Spuyten Duyvil and south of the
river's entrance into the Hudson. Cock Hill mounts two guns.

The main King's Bridge highway, winding northward out of the
city through the plains of Harlem, makes its way under the Long
Hill and Fort Washington's works, over the Laurel Hill Redoubt
site and around under Forest Hill's three guns. There the road
bends eastward and works down to the north side of Sherman's
Creek.

The highway there is along the bed of the deep gorge. Where the
gorge ends and the road bends again northward, there is still
another redoubt. It is a small guard post. Beyond it, the road
continues toward the Dyckman bridge and beyond that to the
King's Bridge.

As a further deterrent to an attack from the north, several lines
of abatis barricades stretch from Forest Hill down to and across
the gorge highway. These rows of felled trees with their branches
pointed and facing any oncoming enemy, are made even more
formidable by the steep inclines. Above them glower the guardian
fieldpieces commanding the highway on both its sides.

Any enemy attacking from the north—the King's Bridge area—
will catch the enfilading fire from the overhead artillery pieces.
These can pour down mercilessly on the assaulters' right and left
wings, forcing the attackers to hesitate before attempting a frontal
maneuver.

To the west of the fort's bastions, commanding the steep Hudson River slopes, the menacing-looking Fort Washington Point battery lies half-way down the cliff. It is about one eighth of a mile from the fort and sits about the same distance above Jeffery's Hook. It commands everything within range of its 32-pounder.

It is this weapon and another like it at Forest Hill which together with Fort Lee's Bluff Rock batteries and their fieldpieces along the shore at Bourdettes, have caused more damage to Admiral Howe's ships than the rebel commanders realize.

Two other 32-pounders are mounted on Fort Washington's bastions. One on the south. The other on the east. In addition, among the other pieces of heavy armament employed in the fort's defense system, there are: two 18-pounders; seven 12-pounders; five 9-pounders; fifteen 6-pounders; eight 3-pounders; and two 5 1/2-inch howitzers. All of these have long been in position at the many scattered outposts and redoubts described.

In spite of its natural defenses and their man-made improvements, the formidable Mount Washington works have their one unfortunate Achilles' heel—defection from within. Therefore the complement of less than 3,000 defenders is small in contrast to the more than 10,000 British and Hessian troops[12] about to make the assault. And particularly so with a defector, unknown to Magaw, turning the fort's key over to the enemy.

Its Secrets No Longer Are Secret

Were Howe not armed with the detailed knowledge of the entire mount's defense system, he would likely never risk an assault such as he plans.

A long siege—a surrounding of the garrison—would have been the alternative. For Fort Washington has no casement constructions, no barracks, no deep well for permanently supplying it with water, very little fuel, only limited stores and magazines and an inadequate supply of provisions to withstand a siege of any length. The fort and the mount have recently been almost entirely dependent for their sustenance upon their sister fortress across the river.

General Howe also is now aware that the fort inside is little more than an open earthworks with virtually no interior constructions outside of a few offices. He knows the location of the wooden magazine, the exact location of headquarters, of the camp wives and women's bivouac area, the wooden huts and tents housing the personnel and the exact location of all the ordnance, especially the four big 32-pounders.[13]

The British command is aware that most of the wives and camp followers have been evacuated. Some have crossed the river to New Jersey. Some have taken refuge in the homes of friendly inhabitants near and outside the perimeter of the American defenses. Some have been assisted in getting to the neutral grounds. And some have stayed on, determined to remain beside their husbands, kith and kin.

Margaret Molly Corbin,[14] wife of Pennsylvania regimental artilleryman, John Corbin, is one of these. A defiant woman and a devoted wife, Molly is highly respected by the men and officers of her husband's battery.

She cooks and bakes for them when she is not helping her husband with his duties, or attending to the sick and injured. There is very little that the stanchly patriotic young woman cannot do according to the stories told by the artillerymen assigned to Forest Hill.

Molly has been beside her husband ever since his enlistment with the Pennsylvanians months ago. Attached to Colonel Moses Rawlings' infantry regiment of Marylanders and Virginians, Corbin mans one of the Forest Hill battery's two 18-pounders overlooking the northern defense slopes.

This morning after two days of argument, Corbin succumbed to his wife's refusal to retire across the river with the other women. She has even declined to withdraw from Forest Hill and seek the protection offered at the main fort. The adamant, self-willed, Ireland-born girl with whom officers of the post dare not argue when her ire is high, has made up her mind to stay at her husband's side. And at her husband's side she will stay.

For five months the fort has stood atop the "Acropolis of New York."[15] Five months ago Chief Engineer Colonel Rufus Putnam began laying it out. Shortly after, the construction work began under the laborious efforts of the Pennsylvania regiments, commanded by Brigadier General Thomas Mifflin. At about the same time General Hugh Mercer and his troops were at work erecting the initial Bluff Rock defense system across the river.

Mifflin's fifth regiment was under the command of Colonel Magaw who, consequently, has been with the twin forts since their first stages of construction. Mifflin's third regiment on the Jersey side was under the command of Colonel John Shee who left for home in September on a furlough after bitterly complaining about the rattlers and copperheads. He never came back to rejoin his unit. Its command then fell to the regiment's lieutenant colonel, Lambert Cadwalader.[16]

All of these regiments arrived in New York at the end of June. "They are strong in numbers but not in arms," Mifflin had told the American Commander on July 5.[17]

The men worked hard on the constructions and drilled diligently in preparation for the coming of the enemy during the summer months, but a fourth of them were always on the sick list.[18] Yet back in Philadelphia these same units had been commended by The General himself for their healthy appearance and their drills which by summer had become a monotonous chore.

The infantry troops have participated in very few maneuvers and have seen very little military action. They were held as a supporting force during the Long Island battle and were never called up until the affair was all but over. However, on several occasions, they have made forced marches against Tory raiders in Westchester, but otherwise, have seen only limited military action.

They did share in the bustling movements, the transportation of equipment and supplies, and some have engaged in a few minor skirmishes with the enemy during the American army's encampment on Mount Washington in September and October. Now they are isolated on their mount.

Greene decided that the fort should be reinforced several weeks ago. He sent Colonel Rawlings' regiment of Maryland riflemen and some Pennsylvanians under Major Otho Williams across.[19] The additions, about 1,200 troops in all,[20] brought the fort's complement up to almost 3,000 men.

That addition has helped to reassure both Greene and Magaw. Still ringing in Greene's ears is the September 12 recommendation of the Council of War. The Council had concluded at that time that it would require 8,000 troops to man the defenses of Mount Washington and its dependencies.

The *Pearl's* Broadsides Open the Battle

Howe needs no balloon over Mount Washington to determine its strengths, weaknesses and areas of greatest vulnerability. Though he has the key unlocking its defenses he does not know the mount's actual manpower. He believes it to be greater than it is.

In deploying his small force of defenders, Colonel Magaw has assigned about 1,200 men to the north walls under Colonel Rawlings. About 700 on the east slopes face the Harlem under Colonel Baxter. On the cross-island's defense lines, across the plateau on the south, Magaw has stationed 800 riflemen under Colonel Cadwalader.

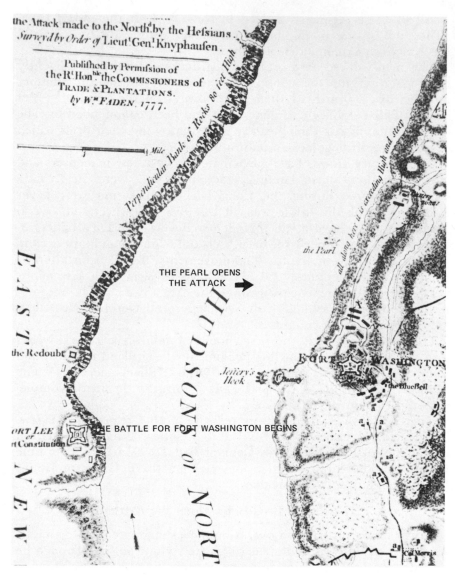

The *Pearl's* Broadsides Open the Attacks—British Faden map shows the Fort Washington battleground and the *Pearl*—Map 614A, From British Military Collections, Courtesy of former B. Altman, Company.

In the fort itself and manning the west slope defenses including the Washington Point redoubt, the post commander has retained 300 men under his personal direction. By a network of connecting paths and entrenchments, most of the commands can be swiftly shifted to any area under attack on comparatively short notice.

At 7 A.M. the frigate, *Pearl*, lying about a half mile north of Jeffery's Hook between Fort Washington and Forest Hill, discharges its cannon with a thundering barrage. It is the signal launching the attack.

The man-of-war's guns pound the north slope's defenses, thoroughly confusing the defenders. The ship's action could be the signal for an amphibious invasion from the Hudson's side, but no enemy transports appear in sight to support that conjecture. The barrage also could be a feint to distract the defenders' attention from the other slopes. And this is exactly what it is, in part, and what Magaw decides it is, for the barrage is also covering and preceding an enemy advance from the north.

The rocky walls on both sides of the river reverberate with the echoing cannonade. The warship's heavy guns shower the trees and crags that rise up from the river and the northern slopes approaching Forest Hill.

Along the water's edge the riverside hamlet's people around Bourdette's Landing cup their eyes against the rising morning sun to see the man of war in action. Fearful that it, or one of its kind, might next turn upon the Jersey shore, many of the women grab their children and run back into their homes as the thundering explosions slap back against the Palisadean walls.

On the Bluff Rock and its parapets the battery's artillerymen and headquarters staff officers gather, attempting to assess the distant action.

On the water-front a detachment of Glover's Massachusetts seamen have worked through the night rounding up all available river craft. Some 40 small vessels have been brought into the docks at Bourdette's and at Moor's Landing below it.

This assembling of boats on the Jersey side can mean one of two things in the opinion of the soldiers and inhabitants viewing the scene. Either there will be an attempt made by the Fort Lee garrison to reinforce Fort Washington, or a plan is under way to evacuate the troops under siege.

On the Barbette gun mount, not too far from the staff officers who stand looking across, some with field glasses they pass from one to another, is Captain Gooch. Gooch has a reputation for daring.

Known for his swiftness in executing a command and holding an enviable reputation for reliability and efficiency, the captain, like all the others, stands awaiting orders. The Bostonian, it is said, has never failed, when called upon in the past, to get a message through even under the most difficult of circumstances.

The General Arrives, Crosses and Surveys the Ramparts

Summoned from Hackensack, the American Commander joined Greene, Putnam, Mercer and Ewing on the Bluff parapet shortly after the cannonading began. All stand grouped on the ramparts. Their aides, nearby, watch from vantage points on gun mounts, mammoth rock boulders, or along the parapets which in some places line the cliff's edge.

Commands have gone out alerting the troops on the main mountain for whatever orders may come. All artillerymen manning the redoubts along the water front, as well as the Marbleheaders standing by their boats, await what they expect will be an order to reinforce Fort Washington.

The American General receiving no word from Magaw and unable to determine what is taking place on the sectors of the fort hidden from view, finally takes Generals Greene, Putnam and Mercer[21] and crosses the river in a Durham boat.

Manned by some the Marbleheaders' strongest oarsmen, the little vessel hugs close to the lee side of the Chevaux de Frise. Behind it two other craft convey the blindfolded horses of the commanders. Their steeds have long since been trained for, and accustomed to, boat traveling river crossings.

At Jeffery's Hook they land and mount, ascending the narrow path carved out of the slope and leading up to the Washington's Point redoubt and thence to the main fort. The heavy Washington Point pounder is still hot and smoking from sending out an annoying fire toward the cannonading frigate about half mile upstream.

After a quick survey of that post, The General and his party spur their animals up the rugged, narrow, wagon road to Fort Washington. There they confer briefly with Magaw who still oozes confidence. Magaw relieves The General and his party from some of their forebodings.

Joined by Magaw, the party gallops down to the third defense line closest to the fort where they dismount at the Chief's old observation site near his former Morris House headquarters.[22] Here he scans the Harlem's east bank and the assembling enemy forces southward under Percy in the wooded area on the other side of the Hollow Way.

Satisfied with Magaw's deployment of his troops and the formidability of the defenses, The General and his staff agree that Knyphausen's threatening attempt to scale the northern walls is a brazen feint. The entire mount's defense system seems one which the cautious General Howe will not risk frontally.

In fact it is not an objective that even a desperate enemy would think of attacking frontally. They conclude that Howe plans a long siege to starve out the garrison, and the most now to be expected are probes upon all lines for a test of strength.

Why would General Howe risk the lives of thousands of men, all easy targets, struggling up precipitous slopes and having no knowledge of the terrain and its complex defense system, with virtually no chance of overrunning the impregnable mount and its fortress?

So The General and his party return to the Bluff Rock site atop the Palisades at Fort Lee, confident of the ability of the fort to repel its invaders.

But, in anticipation of the worst the American Commander orders further construction works and preparation of alternative plans in case evacuation is necessary.

Seeing the handwriting imaginatively spread across the facade of the mount presaging what is to come, The General orders that Greene continue with his removal of stores from Fort Lee. There seems to be no question in the Virginian's mind that both forts must now be evacuated, and that the American forces must concentrate on the defense of Philadelphia from secluded retreats in the mountain ranges of West Jersey.

At present soldiers not on duty climb atop high trees, storage houses and magazines seeking a vantage view of the impending action. Little, however, can be seen outside of the *Pearl* and the Washington Point redoubt exchanging pointless fire. Nevertheless, most of the command, the off-duty men and visiting officers come over from The Mountain periodically to take a look and, seeing nothing, return to duty.

Among the officers now on the Bluff are Beall, Heard, Bedford, Biddle, Blodget, Irvine, Roberdeau, McAllister and Clotz. But outside of some puffs of smoke from cannon fire in the distance on both sides of the fort and from behind it to the east, little is visible. However the noise at times becomes thunderous. It is then that the severe cracking seems to come from all sides of the mount.

At about this time the Commander-in-Chief, Greene, Putnam, Mercer, returning from across the river to the Bluff heights, rejoin Ewing and the other officers. Steadily they keep their eyes on the scene, occasionally getting clear glimpses of some action and pointing it out to others.

Only The General looks constantly across, seldom taking his telescope away from his eyes. He speaks to no one, concentrating all his attention on the mount.

North of the mount, obscured from the view of Fort Lee's observers and from Fort Washington's lookouts as well, General Knyphausen's two columns come to a halt under the cover of the forest area. It is the first stop the Hessians have made in their march toward the fort's north defenses.

Covering Knyphausen's movement, the *Pearl* hammers at the north slope with her broadsides, hoping to throw the defenders into confusion. Colonel Rall, commanding the Hessian right, brings up a fieldpiece and forces the forward rebel Cock Hill garrison guards out of their nest.

With guns thundering behind them and Rall coming at them from the front, the Cock Hill defenders pull back on Forest Hill, allowing Rall to set up his heavy armament on their deserted site. In British hands, the forward post now turns its fire around on the Americans' Forest Hill works.

Knyphausen's halt also enabled the Hessian left column under Schmidt to catch up with the attack plan time schedule. Schmidt's column was slowed down owing to marshlands, rocky hillocks and thick clusters of overgrown forests. It is a terrain more difficult to maneuver than they had expected. And now to make things worse, they are rapidly coming under the range of the rebel artillery which showers them from the crests above their heads.

Howe is insistent that the operation be simultaneously executed. The halting of the Hessians' two columns comprising the British right wing gives all units an opportunity to synchronize their attacks in accord with the master plan.

The British commander-in-chief has set 8 o'clock for the second advance barrage and 10 o'clock for the main attack upon the American works.[2 3] Howe expects the entire garrison will surrender before noon.

The timing gives British Commodore Hotham's *Pearl* ample time to soften the slope's north defenses and at the same time to lay some broadsides into Fort Washington's outer works. The brunt of the bombardment is now directed at the Forest Hill redoubt. The redoubt answers with its two 18 and its heavy, blockade-guarding 32-pounder. Most of the hits on both sides fall short of their marks.

Colonel Rawlings with his Maryland, Virginia and Pennsylvania riflemen and artillerymen commands the three-gun Forest Hill works. The high, strategically well placed rebel post is the sharpest thorn in Colonel Rall's side as the Hessian officer surveys through his field glasses the American-held works above his head.

Creeping upwards through abatis after abatis as the man-of-war's barrage subsides, Rall cautiously leads his men from one ledge to the next under continuous fire. Only his advance knowledge of the location of the joining connecting paths and of the positions of the Forest Hill's earthworks, entrenchments and guard posts makes possible the exceptional progress up the steep inclines.

Again from the *Pearl* the man-of-war begins lobbing shot, shell and grape behind the American defense post. The besieged redoubt now is faced with two fronts, one the warship slightly behind it on its left, the other, a frontal attack by Rall's forces, preparing to dash up the treacherous terrain and overrun the Forest Hill defenses.

The withering rifle fire from Colonel Rawlings' infantrymen rains down continuously from the heights of the summit. Despite it, the undaunted Hessians keep coming on, moving under the cover of their protecting company's fire while each platoon alternatingly loads and fires as their comrades advance.

Assault Of the North Slopes

To the Forest Hill defenders' far right appears another threat, the Hessians' left wing. Though it is technically under Major General Martin Schmidt's direction, Lieutenant General Baron Wilhelm von Knyphausen is marching along with the lead officers of this column, often personally helping his men in hacking away at the obstructions.

They struggle through the almost impassable rows of abatis barriers. The felled trees add to the troops' hazards as they clamber up the rugged, rocky ridges, always under fire from the northeast outposts and constantly returning shot for shot while advancing by platoons.

The Americans guarding the pass as it comes through the gorge from the King's Bridge are Knyphausen's and Schmidt's first major obstacle. The Hessians seem uncannily aware of all the openings, tunnels and passes through the barricades. And uncannily they find them.

To Rawlings on Forest Hill, Knyphausen and Schmidt's wing appears to be driving east under Fort Washington toward the Laurel Hill post rather than toward the northern slope. The formation at first looked to be a flanking joint action with Colonel Rall's right wing.

Now when the 18-pounder on Laurel Hill lets go a murderous barrage on the heads of the struggling Hessians, already faced by the guards' rifle fire above the pass, the entire Knyphausen-Schmidt movement again stops.

Knyphausen knows that to come much closer under Colonel Baxter's Laurel Hill works will bring his troops within the range of the Pennsylvania riflemen waiting for the enemy's closer approach and the order to fire.

Meanwhile, Rawlings watches with a puzzled eye the Knyphausen-Schmidt advance to his right while his artillerymen and riflemen hammer away at the Rall column below him on the slopes. At the same time an occasional ball from the pounding broadsides of the frigate sends splinters of iron and wood ricochetting within the redoubt's area.

Men on both sides begin falling as the heated battle for the heights progresses. Wounded, dying and dead are carried to the rear behind both the American and British lines.

With the sudden unexpected halt of the Knyphausen-Schmidt left wing, Colonel Baxter on Laurel Hill, who came over from Fort Lee with his 200 Bucks County, Pennsylvania militiamen just six days ago (and whose gallantry so impressed Elaine Gray) shifts his eyes from the halted Hessian column to a new threat from the east where British General Matthews with his guards and light infantry are making an amphibious crossing of Sherman Creek beneath him. Now it is clear why the Hessians on his left have halted.

Northeastward Baxter sees the British boats loaded with troops, pouring over the Harlem Creek from King's Bridge. The American colonel counts 20 of the redcoat-loaded flatboats slowly making their way toward him down the creek. He counts another ten of the craft moving in a mass, some still being loaded on the Harlem's east bank.

His is a formidable post, Baxter thinks, made so by nature's precipice-like rock walls, but can it withstand such a threatened joint attack?

The colonel, who has a reputation for daring equal to his dislike for war, shifts his field glass from north to east and back again taking in the Knyphausen-Schmidt attacking arm on his far left and the assault troops coming in left of his front.

Realizing he cannot expect help from Rawlings, high on his left and far too busy attempting to fend off the Hessians' right wing, Baxter and his men steel themselves for the two-prong drive, a combined flanking-frontal attack.

This amphibious east slopes assault on Baxter's Laurel Hill defenses is Howe's second attack force. It may combine with the Knyphausen-Schmidt wing to run over Baxter's defenses, or it may execute the operation alone.

This would allow the Hessian left to go to Rall's aid with an outflanking maneuver against Rawlings' right. It is this vulnerability the Forest Hill commander feared as he watched the Hessians evident drive toward Laurel Hill in the unfolding drama.

Howe's clever strategy, aided by Demont's plans, puts both the Forest Hill and Luarel Hill works in a vise-like grip. Either redoubt is subject to a flanking attack which necessitates that both commanders draw off their frontal defenders to resist encirclement, thus weakening the lines holding out against the enemy before them.

General Matthews' command comprises four British regiments of light infantry and guards. They had formed at King's Bridge and are a supporting force for General Lord Cornwallis's corps. The British nobleman heads the First and Second Grenadiers and the Thirty-third Foot.

Cornwallis also is in command of the entire second attack force and its amphibious operation. His troops embarked directly opposite the Laurel Hill defenses but were held back until Matthews' crowded transports were visible on the way down the Harlem from King's Bridge.

As Matthews' transports head for their landing on Sherman Creek northward of Laurel Hill's defenses, Cornwallis moves his men across the Harlem directly under the slopes fronting Laurel.

Baxter now has Cornwallis at his front, Matthews on his lower left and the Knyphausen-Schmidt columns farther to his north but higher on the slopes and prepared to come around and pounce upon his rear.

British and Hessian fieldpieces open up simultaneously. The barrage is ineffective owing to the difficult trajectory. The 700-man garrison stands firm and defiant. Baxter's single cannon and his men's musket and rifle weaponry return the fire as the battle for the eastern slopes begins.

There is little hope that the colonel and his Laurel Hill post defenders can hold out very long against Cornwallis, Matthews and very likely Knyphausen and Schmidt. Even though the latter should go to Rall's aid against Rawlings, hope for Baxter's success grows dimmer by the minute.

Thus far General Howe's first and second attack forces are on schedule, and proceeding according to plan.

The third attack force, the feint under Colonel Sterling and his Scottish Highlanders, is to land south of Cornwallis's crossing. The Sterling division is poised on the Harlem's east bank awaiting the signal. In support of it are two British battalions of the Second Brigade. The British colonel's planned crossing point will land him behind, or north of, the third American cross-island lines that guard the southern bastions of Fort Washington.

From the high parapet of those bastions Commander Magaw and his worried staff look down nervously upon the steep, southeast sides of the fortress' ramparts, for in the distance Sterling's Highlanders, loading into the flatboats, are now moving across the river behind the Americans' third line.

The feinting Highlanders will give every indication of outflanking the American left with an assault upon their rear. This would cut off any American retreat up from the first and second lines in the event Percy's south forces break through. Magaw sends word warning Cadwalader of the enemy threat.

Through Magaw's Eyes High On the Ramparts

Magaw shifts his glass away from the southeast scope where the disembarking Scots run for the embankments to escape the rebels' artillery fire. He focuses his telescope south and sees Percy's regiments beyond the American lines, marching in continuous columns out of the forest groves across the highway and the Hollow Way. It is an overwhelming force.

Their bands beat, but the sound of the drums and bagpipes is drowned out by the heavy British fieldpieces covering their advance. The barrage is answered by all the American cannon along the forward redoubts fronting the rebels' first cross-island defense line. It is the follow-up reply to the cannon shot fired from the Harlem's east bank—the signal opening the main push simultaneously all around the mount.

Southwest, a good two and a half miles away, Magaw can see the Point of Rocks. It lies about a mile beyond, or south of, the Americans' forward line. Between the Point and the line is a heavily wooded forest on the plateau above the road. Here begin the plains of Harlem.

The Point of Rocks redoubt commands the road to Kings Bridge which winds below it. Owing to the rising precipice here, the highway bends eastward and then turns up north along the hilly banks of the Harlem River, following the river and creek north.

Under the severe British bombardment, answered in kind by the American defenses, Magaw sees Hessian General Johann Stirn's forces joining with General Lord Percy's. Uniting they move up under their barrage to assault the American lines dug in above the plains.

Eastward, to his left, the worried American colonel notices that Cadwalader is turning his left wing to meet the Highlanders' threat.

Too late, Magaw finally realizes that Sterling's small body was a feint to divert Cadwalader from the Percy-Stirn's frontal drive upon the rebels' forward line.

Sweeping his telescope around northeast, Magaw can see Baxter's Laurel Hill defenders leveling their fire on Cornwallis's charging attackers and on Matthews' regiments struggling up the slopes. Farther north and higher on the ridge the Colonel catches sight of the Knyphausen-Schmidt columns ready to move either toward Laurel Hill, or northwestward around the mount to Rall's aid.

Puzzled by the astounding progress of his enemy's four-pronged attack and his adversary's uncanny knowledge of the terrain and its works, Magaw is sure that Howe is not planning a long siege against Mount Washington.

Howe himself stands with Lord Percy at the head of the fourth attack force. The British commander-in-chief has found everything in his favor thus far. He is determined now that nothing must go wrong. Sir William has sized up his battlefield opponent and is chagrined that he is matching wits with only a rebel colonel.

It is not only a blow to his pride, but Howe had counted on bagging the rebel Chief personally in his own lair, not a mere colonel field commander.

Facing Howe, Percy and Stirn on the southern front is Colonel John Cadwalader. Under Cadwalader are Magaw's and Shee's Pennsylvanians, part of Miles' regiments, the Rangers and a few broken companies. Cadwalader has the advantage of well dug-in defenses protected by a difficult, steeply inclined terrain that ordinarily would present an almost insurmountable hazard for an enemy. But the problem is eased considerably when the attacking forces have full knowledge of the defense system's details and secret constructions.

Such knowledge is an unknown factor in Cadwalader's reckoning. As it is, his sector of 800 men faces around 2,000 enemy. And he has only one fieldpiece, a six-pounder.[24] However, on all sectors the situation for the defenders hourly grows more serious without adding the tragic news that their adjutant has betrayed them.

So, despite the vast power that the King's Juggernaut is bringing in upon them, each of the scattered garrisons and its outposts valiantly fights on.

Magaw's deployment of his less than 3,000 troops seems to be militarily the wisest strategic disposition possible in view of the unusual course of events. Now it waits to be seen whether the advantages of courage and terrain can outweigh those of courage and number.

From his central command post above the four-pronged, encircling attack forces, the mount's commandant knows that he is facing a world-renowned military commander, recognized for his careful, cautious, and sometimes overly cautious, stratagems.

Magaw can now see the British commander's carefully designed attack plan unfolding. Howe intends to come at him from all points of the compass. All but one, the west. But even there the *Pearl* stands firing as if it, too, is preparing the way for an amphibious attack up from the banks of the Hudson's shore.

At the appointed hour the British single cannon shot from across the Harlem had launched the offensive, and all the attacking forces went into action.

When the barrage lifted and the swarms of troop-carrying flat-boats and bateaux had unloaded men and equipment under the Americans' heaviest artillery, the dead and wounded lay strewn along the Harlem's west bank. The drive then shifted into a gallop, and vengeance was in the saddle.

Despite Baxter's savage enfilading fire and shelling from Laurel, Cornwallis's troops forge ahead up the slopes. The American batteries play on anything that moves within range. Cries of pain ring out above the holocaust from both sides as ball and grape pierce through flesh, leaving behind writhing bodies, or stilled corpses that moments ago were youth in the prime of life.

The last of the British troops arriving on the peppered Harlem's west shore pick up their dead and wounded as their comrades push on and upward, row following row. Cornwallis's men before Laurel Hill and Matthews' troops on Sherman Creek under the hill's left flank, perilously pick their way up the inclines. Dodging as best they can the rebel fusillades, they return the fire at repeated intervals.

Meanwhile, at the southern outskirts, below the three American lines, the rebel pickets at the Point of Rocks' outpost keep up a steady fire on the approaching Hessian forces under Stirn. Driving ahead, despite their constantly falling comrades, the mercenaries force the 20-man rebel picket post to withdraw under the impact. The overrun defenders pull back behind the American first line, thankful they are still alive.

One by one the outer works fall before Percy's men on Stirn's right. The British fieldpieces and a howitzer are brought into action. Their barrages lift, and in charge rows of redcoats. Firing, loading, advancing and firing in regiments, they empty the rebel outposts, sending any escaping forward defenders back behind their lines.

Gaining a foothold on the high plain, Percy sends a column of his light infantry through the woods toward the Americans' first line. Cadwalader's men turn their six-pounder on the redcoat advance and then combine it with a raking cross-fire from the rifle regiments.

Many of the daring, charging light infantrymen are felled by Cadwalader's expert marksmen. So many drop under the Pennsylvania riflemen's fire before gaining their objective, a defile in the terrain, that the entire column veers around to its left taking cover within a heavily wooded area.

From behind their entrenchments, the American riflemen can hear the pitiful cries of the enemy wounded and the death agonies of others.

For a brief time now the action ceases, not only along the southern front but also on the east slopes. The defenders, weighing the sudden pause and silence, for awhile believe they have successfully repulsed the south and east attackers.

But the heat of battle is still severe on the north precipice, while on the southeast General Sterling and his Highlanders are, in accordance with orders, holding still. For Sterling has succeeded with his feint in bringing Cadwalader's third line around to meet the threat of a flank. And this is what Howe and Percy had wanted.

As planned, it has weakened the cross-island lines and prepared them for the run-through. That drive will sadly dispel the optimistic hopes of some of the defenders who believe Howe has changed his mind, finding the cost of continuing too great.

For almost an hour and a half the British slow down their attack on the south and east owing to a tidal water problem that has set back some of the Cornwallis and Matthews transports. The long pause, though cooling the guns on the south and east and buoying the hopes of American optimists, does not stop the fighting on the northern slopes.

There, Rawlings has his hands full trying to keep Rall and his Hessians from gaining ground up the precipice slopes. At the same time the Forest Hill commander realizes that Knyphausen plans to outflank the American hill from the post's right while Rall continues his frontal assault.

Struggle For Forest Hill

Unabated, the battle for the north slope soon becomes a blood-spilling deluge of horror wherever one looks. Obstinately persistent the Hessians, despite their numerous losses, drive up the slopes, constantly gaining ground. Advance knowledge of the works makes their task easy. Even so, every step is perilous.

Nevertheless, Rall and his men have advanced with remarkable valor for mercenaries, gradually crawling up closer upon Rawlings high post on the summit of the steep cliffs. But it has cost, and the Hessian colonel's losses have mounted.

View from the Northeast of the Attacks Against Fort Washington b Thomas Davies—Courtesy of The New York Public Library, The I. N. Phelps Stokes Collection of American Historical Prints.

Some of his young countrymen have clung for their lives to the limbs of trees where the cliff's face is steep and rugged. And while waiting for help, a few have been shot loose by the defending riflemen above their heads.

The American marksmen are strategically placed on all the ledges of the precipitous slopes, but the Hessians, mysteriously successful in locating equally advantageous positions, pick off the rebel riflemen and open the ascents for their comrades.

Rebel fire takes a heavy toll of the young Hessians. As they fall, their heavy muskets with fixed bayonets drop down the slopes. Weapons, knapsacks and gear fall ahead and beside the German mercenaries. Their torn, crumbled uniforms, meticulously clean a few hours ago, now enshroud their hurtling forms.

Some of the youths tumble and roll a hundred feet and more, leaving a trail of blood over the jagged rocks before coming to their lifeless end on the crags below. For some, their bones and bodies broken, the end is quick and merciful. Others must moan in agony for hours before death or rescue.

To the Americans manning the Forest Hill works there seems to be no end to the oncoming Hessians. Always from behind the forward ranks reinforcements appear when it is believed there could not possilby be any more. Undaunted by enemy fire over their heads, unnerved by their comrades who fall beside them, and cooly unperturbed by the frightening climb before them, the fearless German youths struggle upward.

At intervals the assault halts while Rall brings up his fieldpieces, sending rounds from his ten heavy weapons pounding into the American redoubt. Always in the forefront Rall leads his troops on. He asks nothing of them that he would not do himself.

The 59-year-old officer is a handsome, well preserved product of European nobility's manhood. A successful military life has always been his ambition. And ambition is his prime motivator. Courteous, pleasant and gracious in social circles back in the Vaterland, the highly respected and admired militarist was often the toast of associates and has always been a favorite of the ladies.

The Hessian regimental commander is almost like a brother to his stern, Prussian, superior officer, General Baron Wilhelm von Knyphausen. Knyphausen is only one year the colonel's senior, but the Baron has frequently gone out of his way to help promote the career of his friend and junior officer. However, General Knyphausen has frowned upon his subordinate commander and frequently reprimanded him for his recklessness and disregard for caution.

Rall, principally a military machine, is a man fired with extraordinary determination. Obstacles are, for him, invitations to be conquered. For the colonel is one who must win and who must be first. And this has, paradoxically, nursed his weakness—overconfidence bordering on conceit.

While the battles for Forest Hill on the north and Laurel Hill on the east continue with ever mounting costs on both sides, Howe reveals his surprising knowledge of and acquaintance with the camouflaged works. In those concealed defenses, the unsuspecting American command have stored much of their confidence that Fort Washington cannot be taken by storm.

Hidden fleches, redoubts and access ways to the varied brush-covered works, gun mounts and magazines have been the post's well kept secrets. Even some of the defenders are not aware of the many concealed artillery and musket-line posts. It is from these that devastating surprise fire was to have been poured upon the unsuspecting heads of those attempting to scale the precipices.

It is true that the attackers have had phenomenal success in discovering a few of the outer-post concealments. But this has been generally considered chance. Even those breakthroughs along the north walls under Forest Hill and on the east slopes under Laurel must be attributed to the enemy's good fortune, or their scouts' good eyesight. But certainly not to the enemy's precognition. Such a thing is not believed possible.

But Rall's knowledge of the north post's defenses, enabling him now to seek out the strategic areas and often take the rebel guards by surprise, is not chance. However, aiding him, in addition to the detailed north slope plans is the colonel's extreme self assuredness.

That, his ego and his disregard for caution give him those attributes which adventurous youth seek in their leaders. Though some are the ingredients that eventually will cause his undoing, they are, nevertheless, the magic elements that inspire his men to follow him magnetically over the highest walls.

. . . And Some Disappear Into the Quieter Water of Oblivion

So, forcing themselves perilously, foot by foot up the heights, often straining on in agonizing pain always under fear of instant death, the struggling Hessians cling to the branches of trees momentarily to catch their breath. Then on and upward they plod with musket balls, grape and round shot whistling around their heads. Some pierce the trees above them splintering the tall growth that rise out from some of the almost perpendicular rock walls where no man can stand upright.

Up with the van of his troops, Rall shouts encouragingly to his men, distracting their attention from some of their less fortunate comrades who fall, casualties to the opposing wills of nations that mock the big hopes of little men.

Some fall, screaming in horror to the foot of the cliffs. Their terrified, shrieking, hopeless outcrys end abruptly before their final breath is drawn. For them, it is their last taste of the air that showers down the invigorating sparks of life upon the growing forests, totally oblivious to the clowning mortals with their raining death of shot and shell.

More than one of those who fall is heard to shout, "Gott in Himmel!" And then often the last audible words, "Mutter! Mutter! . . . O, Mein Gott! . . ."

They are the last of all earthly resorts. And the pitiful pleas ring out hopelessly unanswered, calling for their first and last spiritual and physical allies to rescue them from the unknowns of eternity, as they have so often rescued them before.

Then suddenly their tortured, childlike screams cease quickly in a thudding sound that sets the vibrant boyish life within loose to vanish swiftly, as though over some great falls, disappearing momentarily to rise anew again somewhere beyond in the distant, quietly flowing waters of oblivion.

Unable to see their hidden foe showering death upon them from over the crest of the slopes, the perservering Hessians press upward through the raining hail of deadly fire. It is as though every one of them has been temporarily hypnotized by the indomitable will fanning the flames of ambition that burn hot within the breast of Colonel Johann Gottlieb Rall.

Pressing rapidly up upon Rawlings and his men, swarms of blue coats in their yellow breeches, black boots and brass-mounted high hats steadily creep closer. Despite the rebels' bitter fighting and firing, the Hessian troops forge ahead and up toward the cliff tops. Their buckles and brass sparkle in the sunlight filtering down through the dropping multi-colored fall leaves.

Then up and over the cliff's ramparts, like hordes of giant ants, the German mercenaries pour in upon the forward American defenses, forcing them into a withdrawal.

First only a few scale the heights. Then behind them countless more force their way up and over. Some fall on both sides. But soon the Hessians gain their front along the cliff's edge.

Immediately Rall orders the 32-pounder on its swiveling gun mount be taken, and in short order his men have the cannon that has commanded the high northwest rampart.

Under the overwhelming drive, the rebel artillerymen, joining the forward infantry line, retreat to the second ridge. By companies the American Forest Hill defenders repeatedly fire, withdraw, load and fire, finally relinquishing control of the cliff-top crest and its precipice edges to the massing hordes of bayonet-wielding enemy.

Staying close to the ground the Hessians lay down a heavy fire upon the slope-defending rebels while their comrades by the hundreds climb up and over the crest, shouting at the tops of their lungs as they attain the hill's first and most formidable rise. In regimental order the mercenaries line up, repeatedly loading, firing and reloading.

And now, to the Americans' dismay, their hot, overworked muskets and rifles begin fouling. The overheated, clogged barrels become useless sticks in their hands, merely clicking and spitting in the face of the charging enemy.

Frustrated by useless firearms and with few bayonets to defend themselves in hand-to-hand combat, the weakened and undermanned garrison, its "insurmountable" defenses conquered, begins to disorganize.

Despite Rawlings' appeal for the men to withdraw orderly, some break and run toward the rear. A few are now half way to the mount's fort. But the main body sullenly pulls back. Shunning a rout, they reorganize under Rawlings and his officers.

The amazed Hessians cannot understand what is happening. Only scattered and sparse rifle fire answers their fusillades. But they are still much pinned down by the Americans' two 18-pounders which are far from fouled. The Continental artillerymen continue blasting away from their location on a knoll well up from the crest where Rawlings now has reformed his forces along his secondary line.

Astounded by the Hessians' remarkable feat in overcoming the defenses under such relentless rebel fire, the puzzled American officers concede that "the impossible" has happened. Only the most rigidly disciplined troops and an exceptional command could have accomplished what Rall, his officers and troops have done, is the thinking of the rebel officers.

One Hessian company commander, Captain Hohenstein, who is now urging his men up and over the rocky edges under the periodic but accurate American firing and the pounding of the defenders' 18-pounders, will say later "The Hessians made impossibilities possible."[2][5]

Hohenstein will also have to credit the adjutant betrayer from the American command for a major part of the success. For the advanced knowledge of the post's defenses which Howe earlier distributed to his staff officers gave the attackers the exact locations of the well-defended, carefully concealed, tree-covered fleches and hidden earthworks.

All through the American defenses in all sectors of the mount the unaccountable breakthroughs of the secret defenses become the American field commanders' major concern. Nevertheless, the Hessians pay heavily for their gains.

Among those reaching the Forest Hill crest after having fought for every foot in their battle against countless obstacles, many fall at the very end of their climb. They are the victims of the accuracy, not the volume, of the receding rebel rifle fire.

The angry and confounded Pennsylvanians, Marylanders, Virginians and Carolinians, cursing their fouling weapons, are thankful for their 18-pounders that blast away at the Hessians attempting to re-form for attack on the crest. The two fieldpieces delay Rall's bayonet-charging attack upon the Americans' secondary line, thus giving Rawlings time to reorganize.

At the side of his gun, Artilleryman John Corbin has long since given up his attempt to force his wife to take cover within the fort about a mile to the rear. Instead, exposed to death, she has loyally remained by his side, giving him and his gunners water, mopping his brow and helping with the wounded.

When Corbin's swabber falls with a ball in his side and retires to the rear with the wounded, "Molly" Corbin, who on Tuesday celebrated her 25th birthday, picks up the swabber's long, heavy bore-wiper.

Without hesitation she takes over as her husband's swabber. Joining in like a trained cannoneer, she swabs while another, a young boy, assists in loading. Both stand back covering their ears as Corbin and his first assistant gunner take aim and fire. Untiring, she keeps up the terrific pace beside her husband and his two remaining gun crew.

The constant firing of this 18-pounder and the other on the left present a deadly threat to Rall who encounters difficulty enough swiveling around the captured 32-pounder. Trajectory, know-how and an ammunition shortage for the big weapon pose more problems.

Through his field glasses the German colonel sees the unbelievable sight of a woman apparently fighting along with the rebel gunners on the knoll. Having never before seen a skirted female in a Quaker cap on a battlefield, Rall and his staff repeatedly look to make sure of what they see. The colonel hands his telescope to Captain Walther, standing nearest to him, asking him to confirm the oddity.

Walther does so and agrees jocularly but with amazement. As he is about to lift the scope once more to his eyes, the young Hessian captain falls dead[26] at Rall's feet, a ball through his skull between the eyes.

Death for the youthful officer is instantaneous. But for the others, men and officers on both sides, it is less merciful as the casualties, dead and wounded, mount.

Rawlings' right wing has kept its eye on Knyphausen's "demonstration"[27] to the southeast. It had appeared the Hessian left was aiming at Laurel Hill. Then suddenly it swung right just as Rall's troops reached the hill's cliff tops.

The turn of Knyphausen's force away from Laurel and up toward the Americans' right flank on Forest was activated by a prearranged signal. I was timed perfectly, for Rawlings, as the Hessians had hoped, sent the last of his reserves and a company of the Forest Hill defenders out to support the hill's east arm.

Swiftly the assigned Carolina and Virginia riflemen moved off down the hill toward the east slope to counter Knyphausen's maneuver. Though they reinforced the American right wing, they greatly depleted the American hilltop strength, consequently weakening it.

Rawlings' lines are over-extended in view of the strength his enemy is pouring in upon him. There is nothing he can do about it. There are no more reserves.

In comand of the right wing is Major Otho Williams.[28] Williams disperses his men and with cooled weapons by platoons they begin laying down a curtain of fire on the Knyphausen-Schmidt forces that have hacked their way through a labyrinth of obstacles under continuous fire from Laurel Hill's left and concealed fleches along the way.

Schmidt's advance knowledge of the location of the works eliminates their surprise effect and enables him to dispense with the annoyances. Often he does the surprising, taking the entire rebel guard and outpost before they have a chance to fire or escape.

Knyphausen and Schmidt, in swinging around to aid Rall, come under Williams' fusillades raining down on their heads. Despite this the Hessian force persistently drives ahead. Again Knyphausen[29] helps personally in breaking down obstructions to give his troops firm footing through the hidden easier ascents.

Nevertheless, the way is strewn with fallen men. Few look up except to exchange fire as a murderous rain of grape and round shower upon them. Occasionally the sides of the steep slopes break apart and avalanche down to compound their difficulties.

Seemingly oblivious to the dead and dying around them, both sides periodically resume bitter exchanges of cannon and small arms fire knowing that soon, and last, will come the final hand-to-hand combat ending the contest.

Phenomenally disciplined, the Knyphausen-Schmidt mercenaries are inspired by no high and noble cause, motivated by no great moral and spiritual incentive, yet they press on in an almost blind determination to execute their orders.

Rall is resolved that his regiment will be the first to victoriously enter the Fort Washington grounds. So, following their leader up and over the cliff and into the Americans' evacuated forward lines, the yelling, cheering Hessians scramble and begin reorganizing for the inevitable bayonet charge.

Meanwhile the Knyphausen-Schmidt columns press harder upon Williams. Once again the rebels are troubled by fouling firearms.

When Rall decides that the moment is right throughout his lines, the Hessian colonel raises his hand. The signal passes down through the officers. Each of Rall's companies check their arms, prepare to fire, load and charge.

Angrily they seek revenge for their wounded, dead and for the obstacles and trials they have encountered. The caldron of hate is now boiling over. The driving force behind them is not simply the execution of an order. It is vengeance.

Rall opens his attack with a rolling blanket of fire. It sweeps across the Americans' secondary defense lines. When it lifts and the smoke has cleared, many rebels lie, dropped by the fusillade. Slowly the Americans pull farther back. The wounded are taken to the rear and up into the interior defenses of Fort Washington.

Suddenly Corbin's gun sends a ball into the center of the Hessian lines creating momentary havoc. Then another falls among the confused troops.

The successful strikes cause the Continentals to let go with loud "Hurrahs!" The shouts echo up and down the lines as confidence, like a bouncing ball, jumps from one side to the other of the battlegrounds.

Rall conceals his anger, smarting from the accuracy of his enemy's gun blasts. He orders his marksmen to concentrate fire on the cannon to the left. They do.

A minute later John Corbin and his matross beside him fall dead, slumping alongside of the weapon's carriage. Molly Corbin, dropping her swabbing pole, rushes to her husband's side. Frantically she attempts to stop the ebbing flow of life gushing furiously from his mangled throat. Both Corbin and his assistant, a ball through his eye, have died almost instantly.

Despite his widow's hopeless, hysterical efforts to bring life back into his body, the fearless John Corbin of a few seconds ago is forever motionless. His glazed eyes stare vacantly upward at the blue, cloud-spattered heavens breezing indifferently under the last of the morning's bright sunshine.

Blood Stains and Gunpowder Dye a Gingham Dress

Molly Corbin's eyes turn suddenly from frantic hope and compassion into burning hate. Her mind, stricken by shock, becomes swiftly inflamed with uncontrollable rage. Abandoning all precaution, she strikes out for revenge.

Calling upon all her strength, she aims and fires the big 18-pounder with only the help of the young boy loader. Up until today the youth had been a drummer. Never before had he seen a cannon fired in battle, or faced men, masked with death, seeking his life.

The boy swabs. The woman, her flowing wide skirts often caught by the breeze, loads, aims and fires. Each time the discharge strikes close to Rall. Each time it takes a toll.

The unheard of sight of a woman firing a cannon, and with astounding accuracy, quickly animates the dispirited defenders. Throughout the hill, the inspiring appearance of a female almost singlehandedly manning an artillery piece, spreads an exhilarating breath of vigor temporarily though the rebel lines.

Rall, ever a gallant gentleman when it comes to womanhood, forbids his marksmen to fire upon her. Instead, he orders an encirclement to take the cannon and its crew on the left and another to take the other 18-pounder on a knoll to his right.

But Rall's right wing cross-fire rakes into the artillery positions. The woman gunner stumbles. Her arm, blood-reddened from her shoulder, drops limply as she crumples upon the ground only a few feet from her husband's stilled form.

Molly Corbin, November 16, 1776—From a Painting by Frank
Reilly in "Collier's Magazine," July 1, 1950.

Struck by three grape shot, her left side and upper arm bleed
profusely from the severe lacerations. But Molly Corbin has had
her revenge. Severely wounded and in doubly inflicted shock, she
lies stilled, and the battle rages around her.

Her right hand reaches over and grasps the limp, lifeless,
powder-blackened hand of her fallen man. She stares blankly into
space as the young drummer boy calls for help and holds her dirty,
blood-stained gingham dress against her gushing wounds.

In answer to the boy's calls, a Maryland rifleman tears off his
shirt and throws it to the youth as he, along with his regiment pull
back, firing, stopping to load, prime and then again firing and
withdrawing before the oncoming Hessian forces. Another hurls the
youngster his water canteen.

The wounded woman remains conscious. She is vaguely aware of
the retreat and the close combat fighting going on around her.
Then as the mercenaries press in upon the withdrawing American

forces, she insists the boy "make a run for it" back into the fort's
outer works. The youth refuses and stays by her side, tearing off
his own shirt to further bind the wounded arm.

Shouting encouragements to his men, Rall, at the head of his
troops, cries out, "All that are my grenadiers, march forward!"[30]

The Hessians advance in regimental order behind the forward
van that has safely picked its way through the stubbornly fighting
Americans. The withdrawing rebels wield their rifle butts against
the Hessian bayonets when firing is no longer possible. They
retreat reluctantly before the increasing waves of mercenaries, pulling back up the gentle slope to the fort's outer works.

Shouts of "Hurra! Hurra!" rise from the Germans' regimental
ranks. Their drummers strike up a march behind their advancing
troops, and the notes from the hautboys ring out with the confidence of conquerors.[31] Disdainfully ignoring the scattering rebel
fire from the few arms that are not yet fouled, the Rall men with
bayonets fixed push in from all directions.

Where groups of Continentals refuse to give ground and attempt
to stand and fight, the Hessians charge through with bayonets at
belly-level, exactly as they have been taught. Over the wounded
and dead, their own and their enemies, they move steadily
forward. Some of the defenders who take flight are caught
between enemy ranks and forced into combat until they can turn,
escape and make a run for the distant fort . . . unless it is too late.

In hopeless desperation Rawlings' rear guard attempts to fight
back, always against overwhelming odds. The Hessians, shouting
German oaths, drive on and hard. Finally Rawlings gives in and
orders a retreat, a full but orderly withdrawal behind the rampart
walls of Fort Washington.

There is no alternative. To his right Knyphausen and Schmidt
are overrunning Ortho Williams' right wing. If successful,
Knyphausen will close behind Rawlings' right in an outflanking
movement with Rall's forces.

Rawlings, though limping and bleeding from a ball that has
pierced his thigh, slows down the withdrawal pace in order to help
his men take the wounded with them. He orders a covering and
repulse fire on the advancing Hessians with every working rifle and
musket available.

Despite appeals from his men, he realizes it is now too late to
get a rescue party over to the Corbin battery. Reluctantly he
resigns himself to Molly's capture and the hope that the enemy will
properly attend her wounds.

Rawlings blames himself for his failure to save the girl. He watches through his field glasses when Rall's men encircle and take the two gun batteries. The woman and the boy drummer at her side are among the few who do not get away.

Major Williams who has brought his remaining right wing troops up alongside of the commanding colonel's men after having taken a hard pommeling from the swiftly advancing columns under Knyphausen and Schmidt, urges Rawlings to make rapidly for the fort.

Noting the enemy's increasing cannonading, Williams assures his superior that nothing more can safely be done for the wounded girl. The American Forest Hill defense commander regretfully agrees and sends word to all his officers to speed the withdrawal behind the fort's north and west bastions.

Help Comes to the Side of the Wounded Woman Gunner

What Rawlings and Williams do not see and cannot know is the considerate attention Rall pays to the wounded gunner's widow and the boy drummer who would not leave her.

The Hessian colonel takes her husband's coat, which the dead man had pushed between the spokes of one of the gun carriage wheels hours ago, and carefully drapes it around her. He gives her parched lips a drink from his own flask of rum and issues an order for a Hessian surgeon to give her immediate aid.

The German-speaking colonel orders that after her wounds are treated the boy and two prisoners escort her up to the American fort. Under a parole and a white flag, the command is soon obeyed.

Unmolested, the three carry her safely through the outer pass into Fort Washington. The scene provides a lull in the heated battle which resumes immediately after with intensity.

The ever-advancing Hessian forces, combined now with the Knyphausen-Schmidt columns, pursue the withdrawing rebels, some of whom reluctantly give in and fight viciously on until they are dropped.

Bayonets flash against gun butts and pikes in the hand-to-hand encounters. Some valiantly hold off their pursuers until their comrades are safe behind the battlements.

Within 100 yards of the fort's entrenchments,[32] the attackers come to a halt. There the Hessian colonel and his men take a position behind a large stone house[33] to await Knyphausen and

Schmidt to come up beside them. The Howe plan calls for a united storming of the fort's northwest bastions under Knyphausen unless the rebel commander capitulates.

Major Williams, moving back beside Colonel Rawlings into the fort's defenses is among the last to pull out from before the crashing Hessian advance and their range of fire and into the protection of the outer entrenchments. But as he guides the last of his men safely through the pass and is about to follow, he is struck down[34] and bayoneted in a final Hessian skirmish only a few hundred feet from the cover of the works.

To the credit of Rall and his men, Knyphausen and his 4,500 troops have gained the first major objective in Howe's four-pronged attack against the most formidable works of the mount that was thought to have been impregnable. So the Hessians stand at the northwest doors of the fortress ready to knock them in when the command is given.

The second, third and fourth attack forces were all synchronized with Knyphausen's operation, and all, except for minor hitches, have proceeded well for Howe. The unfavorable tide change that delayed some of the transport crossings and caused the drive to come to a long halt was the principal annoyance. It was at that point that the American Commander-in-Chief, after having observed the tight and seemingly stout defenses all along the mount, returned to Fort Lee. It seemed apparent then that Howe was jockeying for a long siege and nothing more.

Shortly after came the single crack of the British fieldpiece from the Harlem's east bank that sent all divisions driving against the American defenses.

The second attack force sent Matthews, under Cornwallis's command, heading his transports for the shore under the hot fire from the Laurel Hill redoubt where Colonel William Baxter's 700 defenders poured a merciless barrage down on the invading force.

Attack Force Number Two Battles Baxter's Defiant Defenders

Supported by a cannonade from the British guns on the east bank, Matthews landed almost under Laurel Hill. Cornwallis with his Grenadiers and 33rd Regiment came up behind to bolster Matthews' left. Despite the constant fire that Baxter held on his enemy below him and despite the barrage his two guns laid down, Cornwallis and Matthews made the shore, suffering only light casualties.

Their location gave them good coverage under the lee of the

Harlem's west embankments, better than was offered downstream
for Colonel Sterling. Sterling met much difficulty coming ashore in
his feint against Cadwalader's lines.

Baxter's high Laurel Hill position behind a number of concealed
fleches along the mount's eastern slopes gave him a decided
advantage, and he made the most of it. But Baxter faced two
skilled military tacticians in Cornwallis and Matthews.

Cornwallis alone is a dangerous opponent on the battlefield. He
is cautious, patient and an extremely clever strategist. In addition
this morning he had numbers on his side. The British lord allowed
Baxter to think his post secure and thus caused him to expend his
ammunition and waste his energy until the right moment. The
British general, certain that he would not need Knyphausen's help,
thus enabled the Hessian general, far to Baxter's left, to swing
away and north to aid Rall. The shift of the Knyphausen-Schmidt
corps away from Laurel Hill greatly relieved Baxter's anxiety.

While Cornwallis and Matthews battled with constant exchanges
against Baxter's stubbornly defiant redoubt, farther downstream
the American colonel saw a third landing operation.

Baxter's post is a mainstay in the mount's defense plan. Its
location makes it a protecting redoubt against an attack on the
southern cross-island third defense line under Fort Washington. So
the amphibious enemy invasion to his right grasps the colonel's
attention just as he gets the news that Knyphausen and Rall are
storming the northwest gates of the fort.

The redcoat landings south worry Baxter as much as does the
bad news from the summit. Howe is attempting to outflank
Cadwalader's left by wedging in behind the third line and the fort's
southern slopes above the Harlem plains. However, Baxter cannot
spare a man, and Captains Lennox, Tudor and Edwards, who were
called up with about 250 riflemen to man the redoubts along the
embankment, badly need help.

Baxter's own hands are filled keeping a galling fire pouring down
on the infiltrating invaders from the shore below him. Gradually
the redcoats move up, seek cover, fire in companies, move up
farther and seek cover again, while on Baxter's right and left
additional enemy columns slowly ascend in what is certain to
become an encirclement attempt of the rebels' Laurel garrison.

The redoubt's two heavy guns burn hot from the incessant
firing. The post counts a few dead and a number of its men
wounded, but not as many, Baxter is sure, as are certainly being
counted now among the attacking forces below him.

The Pennsylvanian Laurel Hill commander, moving rapidly beside his fighting Continentals, 200 of whom are his own Penn's State riflemen, brandishes his sword that sparkles brilliantly in the late morning sun. He hurries from company to company among his troops encouraging them and cheering them in every way possible, and then points out to officers the enemy's probable intentions. The hard fighting colonel, despite his dislike for war, has placed his troops carefully and strategically behind rocks, trees and at the well-concealed fleches throughout his breastworks.

Much to his surprise, it is the hidden earthworks which his enemy seems to locate with uncanny ease. Often they are wiped out before the camouflaged nests have begun to function. Through volleys of fire the redcoats doggedly drive up the difficult slope. It has been made more treacherous owing to last night's rain. In some sections they slip and fall, tumbling down the high, wooded, precipitous inclines when wet leaves under their feet slide and throw them off balance.

Some of the redcoat light infantry and guards balance themselves precariously on rocky ledges in order to load and shoot, covering for their companions as successive platoons slowly make their way up toward the Laurel Hill crest. A few provide excellent targets for the crack Pennsylvania riflemen and so never get off their shots. Instead they fall back down the inclines, many to their death.

Baxter and his 700 now face 3,500 enemy, crawling and clambering up the sharp slopes like swarms of bees before a beehive. Behind the four British light infantry and guards regiments come the First and Second Grenadiers and to their left, preparing for a pincer and left flank maneuver, follow Cornwallis's Thirty-third Foot.

One by one the outer rebel works of the Laurel Hill post fall, overrun by the onslaught of British redcoats. Before the advancing columns of bayonet-fixed muskets, the Americans give ground. Slowly at first, and then gradually picking up momentum as the shouting King's men increase in numbers, the spirited defenders reluctantly pull back. Some of the few Continentals owning bayonets contest the ground with squads of redcoats until, outnumbered in hand-to-hand fighting, they withdraw breathlessly back up the wooded slopes.

Attempting to keep the retreat from turning into a wild rout, Baxter struggles desperately with the help of his officers to maintain his troops' morale. He shouts encouragements, directing his men to take the uphill passes to the rear into the Fort Washington east gate. And now the British Tommies pour over the crest.

A climbing rifleman, perched on a high rock near the center of the redcoats' forward line, with his weapon primed seeks a target. The sparkling steel sword which Baxter brandishes to guide his men, catches the marksman's eye.

Attack Force Two Takes Its Objective

Certain that he has high rank in his sights, the soldier lines up the bright, glittering steel flashes of Baxter's sword through a line of vision aimed at the officer's head. Slowly he squeezes the trigger. William Baxter, the war-hating colonel drops dead. The marksman's ball sailed a straight course, crashed through the skull and lodged in the officer's brain.

Their leader fallen, the Laurel Hill defenders look to the leadership of the subaltern officers. They too are thrown into confusion but quickly recover and direct the badly mauled remaining troops and the ambulatory wounded up to Fort Washington's inner works. Weakened and exhausted, the whipped but valiant little garrison struggles to reach an entrance under the eastern abatis. Forced to leave their dead and dying behind, they stumble breathlessly under the safety of the eastern ravelin.

So, at great cost, yet less than that paid by Knyphausen and Rall's Hessians, the second attack force reaches its goal. And now that body, under Cornwallis, stands at the fort's east gates ready to storm inside when the command is given.

Baxter and his men had held out the longest. Their stubborn fight delayed Cornwallis from swinging some of his troops over to Sterling's and Percy's aid, thus hampering the British encirclement operation on the south sector. While that assistance would not have altered the outcome for the doomed American garrison, it would have resulted in heavier casualties on both sides, particularly among the rebels.

Sterling's attack, the intended feint, soon blossomed into a full scale affair. As Howe had foreseen, it had worried the late Colonel Baxter and caused Cadwalader to turn his left away from Percy's front.

When the cannon signal for the main push sounded, Sterling's transports made for the Harlem's west bank under a protective barrage from the Westchester side of the river. As the British colonel's 42nd Highlanders approached the shore, a mile south of

Laurel Hill, the Americans manning the breastworks above the river rained their fire on the Scots who had no place to seek cover.

The landing, observed by the Cadwalader cross-island lines, facing south and Lord Percy's threat, were also seriously troubling Magaw, plagued from the north by Rall, Knyphausen and Schmidt. And Magaw has no more reinforcements to stem Sterling's apparent flanking maneuver as he tremulously watches and fears the worst at his post on the Fort Washington ramparts. Magaw had earlier sent a hundred men and an 18-pounder, but begrudgingly so, since Rall and Knyphausen were even then pressing him hard from the north and west.

Dissatisfied with such a token force, Caldwalader reluctantly spared fifty of his own men, under Captain Lenox from the cross-island defenses, to help stop Sterling's rising tide.[35] In all the American defenders totaled 250 rifleman and a gun battery. But from that force a murderous fire poured out and down on the 800 invading Highlanders.

A few of the bateaux now flounder leaving the still targets easy victims for the rebel marksmen. On top of the fusillades the artillerymen and their 18-pounder add havoc to the landing Scottish soldiers of the King.

Unable to return the fire from within the small, crowded, floundering transports, many Scotsmen drop under the American raking. Some in panic jump into the water. Others wounded, crumple into the bottom of the little boats as the oarsmen frantically try to pole the vessels off mud banks and on to the shore.

Many jump overboard in the confusion and swim or wade their way through the mucky waters of the creek. The deeper depths take their toll of the Highlanders who cry for help, struggle and drown under the weight of their heavy knapsacks, muskets and gear.

Many of the vessels make it safely over the river's shoals and reefs which at high tide would offer no obstacle. If the Scots escape unharmed from the rain of fire over their heads, they spill out of the flatboats onto the beach and acurry for cover like hundreds of suddenly hatched caterpillars emerging as though on a signal from the gossamer-like webbing of their egg casings. They dash madly up from the water, seeking the security offered under the lee of the embankments. The Sterling operation seems to be bordering perilously close to failure.

For awhile even Sterling doubts his Highlanders' ability to get a foothold on the shore. But the Scotsmen do not panic. Courageously persevering they re-form and begin returning the fire from the edge of the river embankments.

Others, in larger numbers, come up from behind, reinforcing the gradually strengthening lines. Despite the incessant, accurate fire raining havoc down from concealed positions above their heads, the continuous line of transports makes its way to the shore's west bank not far from the Morris House. Sometimes the overloaded bateaux have to thread their way through struggling, drowning men, or around overturned vessels. Eventually numbers and courage succeed.

To the Brave, Fat, British Major Goes Some Credit

Much of the credit for the 42nd Highlanders' valor in Howe's third attack force operation goes to Major Murray of the Scottish regiment.

Murray[36] is a rotund little man. Very much overweight, his five-foot, six-inch frame has more than it can humanly do to carry his 230 pounds. For most of that bulk is concentrated in his forefront and primarily in his abdominal pouch. Therefore, when en route with his marching troops, his usual mode of locomotion is, of necessity via conveyance. So generally he is carried alongside of his men by his horse and carriage.

Consequently an amphibious movement is for him, a particularly beastly piece of business that he distastefully must up with put. And without his horse and carriage, which cannot be transferred across the river until later, the major's pedestrian military participation is severely limited. Both his avoirdupois affliction and his gout, neither of which he allows to interfere with his insistence on being in the heat of battle, have restricted him to sedentary, non-ambulatory battlefield activities.

Known in his earlier days as a resourceful, brave, daring man of action, Major Murray detests the illness and overweight curse that have overtaken him. His urgent request that he be allowed to go along with his Highlanders, who have the highest regard for him, was not denied. But it did pose problems.

Sitting in the rear of the bateau with many a shot popping close by, Murray kept up a constant line of encouragement to his men, even jesting at the inaccuracy of the enemy's fire and loudly challenging the rebels, and with choice expletives, their ability to "hit an elephant a rod in front of ye blasted noses."

The major's remarkable composure is largely responsible for the success of the first wave of boats to reach the shore. The troops, on orders to run for cover under the embankments immediately upon landing, do exactly what they're told. In their frenzy none realize they have abandoned Major Murray, left sitting in the boat's stern.

Unable to get up and out of any chair without assistance, the irate officer shouts out after his men. His booming voice gives even Baxter's cannon, a mile north, competition.

"One of ye bloomin' blasted, bastard kilters git back here!" he yells at the top of his lungs. "Git back here and gee me a hand 'ut of this goddamned boat!"

Four of his Highlanders turn around, rush back to the bateau, lift their beloved 230-pounder out of his seat. Sitting him upon their crossed, clasped hands they carry him, wading through the shallow water, up the muddy bank to the joyous hurrahs from his Scots.

Even the bewildered American defenders, believing the Highlanders were carrying a wounded man to shore, humanely aimed their fire elsewhere. Many of those same "humane" rebels will, a short time later, be lining up before the fat Scottish major whom they had spared, as prisoners of the British regiment. However, the major's fearlessness contagiously spreads throughout the invasion force.

Once well established on the shore, Sterling has little trouble preparing his Highlanders for the feint. The attack upon those small American redoubts which has taken such a heavy British toll—many dead and wounded Scots lie behind the angry and chagrined regiment—is all that is now on the Highlanders' minds. Fired with anger and revenge they impatiently await the signal to charge.

Eight hundred redcoats[37] soon stand ready to charge the American redoubts. Then by companies they load, fire and advance in waves, closing in upon the 250-man garrison under the commands of Captains Lenox, Tudor and Edwards.

The intensity of the fire momentarily threatens to break down the defenders' morale, but the Continentals recover and hold, returning a raking fire in a lengthy exchange. Despite it, the King's men move in still closer.

A charge is imminent. Lenox, Tudor and Edwards know it. They give the order to withdraw into the American second and third cross-island lines. Most of the retreating garrison, fighting as they withdraw, are driven back above the third lines and up the slopes toward the fort as the Highlanders charge in upon them.

By sheer numbers the enemy attackers pour in to overwhelm the rebel redoubts, capturing the cannon that had given the invaders so much trouble. In hot pursuit the Highlanders stay close on the heels of the Americans who turn and fight, then run, turn, and fight some more as they struggle toward the southern abatis under Fort Washington. There, through the passes up to the fort, the battered surviving forces scramble into the fortress's inner defenses.

The spearing columns under Sterling, driving up from the shore, over the rebel redoubts and up by the Morris House, demand Magaw's and Cadwalader's worried attention, for the movement puts the Highlanders in a perfect position to maneuver into the rear of the southern cross-island American defense lines.

Thus Howe's third attack force has done more than feint. It has driven in Cadwalader's left wing outpost, sending it back into the mount's summit defenses. Just as Howe intended, Sterling has distracted Cadwalader from Howe's fourth attack force now coming up at him from the south under Lord Percy and Hessian General Johann Stirn.

So, at a cost of 90[38] dead, wounded or drowned, the Sterling Highlanders have attained their objective.

Cadwalader, as commander of the southern defenses, sent Magaw's regiment and a number of broken companies from Miles' and other units into the first lines, during the enemy's lull earlier in the morning. It was thought then that Howe had siege, not assault, on his mind.

So when the British single cannon shot sounded, Percy's brigades began to move up under a heavy cannonade from twelve British fieldpieces, with the British commander-in-chief personally participating in his fourth attack force.

Though synchronized with the first, second and third, the fourth attack moved more rapidly than Rall and Knyphausen on the north and Cornwallis and Matthews on the east. Mostly under Howe's observation, Percy carried out his superior's command to move leftward, as though toward the Hudson and the Americans' weaker right wing. But that wing was well protected by the high rise of the land and the Point of Rocks promontory.

A heavily wooded area there provides excellent cover for any attacking force. Deceived by the apparent British move, Cadwalader moved some of his forces to his right and weakened his left to counter Percy's threat against his right. Meanwhile both sides kept up a constant exchange of weaponry.

Then, following a severe covering barrage, Howe's right drove in through Cadwalader's weakened left and seized the Americans' far left forward redoubt. Percy's heavy artillery and a howitzer raking, followed by a rush from his redcoat light infantry, sent the redoubt's defenders back into the forward lines. Thereafter, all became silent at that sector as Stirn seemed to be again shifting toward Cadwalader's right.

It was at this point that the rebel field commander, after he had sent reinforcements against Sterling at his back, discovered that the British colonel's amphibious assaulters had overrun Lenox, Tudor and Edwards.

Since the American colonel, in attempting to muster all his undermanned division's might against Percy, has depleted his secondary line, he cannot further weaken his small remaining garrison by drawing off more reinforcements to send Lenox, Tudor and Edwards. And with Percy pressing him frontally, and then suddenly Stirn's Hessians appearing from out of the woods, hammering at his right defenses along the Point of Rock, Cadwalader sees withdrawal his only solution.

Running through his mind is the fear it is too late. Stirn, swinging west and north may already be at his rear, overrunning the secondary lines and waiting to seal him in between with Howe's and Percy's help.

To swing his entire line backward and westward is, he knows, now impossible. An orderly withdrawal, with an attempt to keep the enemy in his front in check, and with the hope Sterling is not waiting for him at his rear, is Cadwalader's only recourse.

The American colonel's main objective is to prevent his troops from getting caught between the two fires that now threaten him.[39] The pounding from Percy and Stirn at Cadwalader's front increases with intensity.

Fortunately for the Cadwalader men, the American secondary line, stretching across the island, runs a little below Morris's place. There some soldiers' huts have been left standing and the area enclosed, giving it the appearance of formidable looking bastions at the lines' eastern terminus.[40] Though virtually impotent after it was almost entirely evacuated to replenish the forward lines, Sterling, with orders now to carry through the feint if he can and push into the American rear, does not know the area is vacated.

The sight of the works which he presumes are filled with rebels whose marksmanship is well known, brings the British officer to a dead stop. This hesitation reaches Cadwalader's ears just as Percy and Stirn drive harder against his retreating maneuver.

As the King's men close in, skirmishing increases. In some close quarter fighting, clashes occur with pikes and gun butts crashing against bayonets and sabers in scattered noisy melees amidst wild howling and cursing. And, above the din, always awesomely present, are heard pitiful screams of pain and agony. But the rear guard, keeping up an obstinate fighting front give their comrades the badly needed time to seek the heights where they in turn cover the retiring rear.

Cadwalader, amazed that Sterling is not at his behind, backs up his men into the secondary lines with the redcoats and Hessians close behind him. The Highlanders' commander, meanwhile, had been trying to figure out how he could outflank the "empty" bastions. As the Americans pour in from the south he realizes too late that they had been virtually untenanted. Sterling has missed a rare opportunity for glory.

Growing more bold now, the retreating American force slowly pulls out of the secondary defenses and heads for the third cross-island lines and then, beyond it, the southern ramparts of Fort Washington. In a small wood Cadwalader and his defiant corps stop, turn and deliver a heavy devastating fire down upon their pursuers.

Howe's Fourth Force Completes the Strategic Operations

Surprised by the sudden and unexpected turnabout, Percy orders a halt under the terrific fusillade. Frantically the British forward lines scatter, fanning out in all directions seeking shelter. Sterling and his Highlanders, who have come to life after discovering the empty bastions, have also joined in the purusit of the Cadwalader forces.

North of Percy, they push in on Cadwalader's left flank, forcing him out of the woods and on and up under the abatis passes when Howe, Percy and Stirn resume their push. Cadwalader leads his badly mauled southern sector defenders into the overcrowded inner works behind the fort's southern escarpments. With them they carry a number of their wounded. The dead are left behind on slopes red with blood.

Entering Fort Washington's south ravelin behind the abatis-surrounded outer grounds of the four-acre fortress, Cadwalader's troops add over 700 more to the rapidly increasing number inside. The stenching mass of sweating, fatigued bodies, milling aimlessly in shocked confusion within the bastions until they fall exhausted, often beside some hungry post dog that ever begs for food, now overflow the compound. Ordinarily 400 men within Fort Washington's walls result in overcrowded conditions.

And so Howe's fourth attack operation has achieved the first part of its objective. But it has taken a force of over 2,000 men to drive the 800 southern slope defenders out of their lines and back up into the fortress grounds on the summit. And there were more than that, for some of Sterling's 800 Highlanders joined Howe, Percy and Stirn at the close of the assault drive. As though that were not enough, soon behind them came part of Cornwallis's division. And it included a few of Matthew's men who had succeeded in pushing the remainder of Baxter's east slope defenders up behind the fort's eastern ravelins.

Now clustered behind the ramparts of Fort Washington, Magaw counts almost 2,800 badly whipped and exhausted Continentals including many wounded, some dying. Only their extreme fatigue prevents a pandemonium in a compound intended to accommodate but a seventh of its now expanding number.

Under a flag a British officer arrives and hands the shocked, dejected Magaw the second summons he has received in 24 hours, this one from General Knyphausen. Meanwhile, Howe orders Sterling, Cornwallis and Matthews to join Percy and Stirn in surrounding Fort Washington on the east, south and west. They link up with the Knyphausen, Rall and Schmidt forces on the north.

From the Harlem River across the plains to the Hudson and up its precipice slopes, the British lines reach out and extend their noose. Matthews' light infantry and guards[41] spread out around the Hudson's steep ascents until they join with Knyphausen's men.

Fort Washington is surrounded. That encirclement is one of the British commander's long-sought objectives.

It is a big moment for Howe, and it will be his one and only outstanding victory in the long 1776 campaign. For Mount Washington is soon to be his.

The fort, once called "The Citadel," has all but fallen. The surviving defenders from Howe's four-pronged attack stand huddled hopelessly together within the walls' confines, unable to offer further resistance.

Throughout the long battle which on the north slope, lasted two and a half hours, Fort Washington has not fired a single cannon shot. With his small complement of defending troops scattered all around the fortification's outer ten-mile circuit of defense, Magaw could not bring into play any of his heavy armament without endangering his own troops.

Silence Settles Ominously Over "The Citadel"

Ironically, now when Magaw could use his artillery to repel the enemy outside his gates and massed beyond the surrounding abatis walls below him, he dare not. The enemy's response, mercifully being withheld at present, would become a raining bombardment[42] delivering mass death uselessly into the fort's over-crowded interior upon the heads of almost 3,000 helpless men.

Nevertheless, Magaw makes a last-minute attempt to rally his troops. Placing a last hope in the occurrence of some miracle, as does a drowning man certain that rescue will come before death, the commanding colonel tries in vain to convince his staff officers to resist until help comes over from Fort Lee. His arguments are futile. The hopes, the bones, the bellies and the spirits of the officers and men can be drained no more.

Rall, in Knyphausen's name, gives Magaw two hours to reply. Since the Hessian colonel and his grenadiers succeeded in storming the difficult north precipices, it will be they, Howe and Knyphausen decide, who will lead the final attack if Magaw fails to capitulate.

In issuing Knyphausen's summons, Rall required that Magaw answer by raising a white flag after lowering the American standard to signify surrender.

The flagpole's tip is the highest thing over all Manhattan Island. It is clearly visible from across the river on the high rocky bluff at Fort Lee.

A death-like silence pervades within and outside the fortress as Magaw and his officers study the summons. Their words are inaudible. Only the post chaplains's voice is clearly heard raised in prayer. His lips tremble as though presaging the horrors of the tragic days to come for the rebel survivors of the battle for Fort Washington.

Slowly and solemnly he reads from his prayer book, "We dwell in the shelter of the Almighty for He is our refuge and our fortress."

No one speaks. Only the cries and the agonizing moans of the wounded break the stillness of the huddled men lying exhausted before the chaplain as he tries to comfort them.

Resigned, with no alternative, in less than the stipulated two hours, Magaw answers the summons. However, though he orders the white flag raised, he does not strike his colors, replying to Rall that he will negotiate.

Rall, representing Knyphausen and Colonel Patterson, Howe's adjutant, meets with the post commander only after insisting that Magaw strike his colors. In no position to parley,[43] the American colonel faces the two officers, equal with him in rank, but emissaries of the King's generals who have him encircled and at their mercy. He realizes that Howe has set the conditions and directed his subordinates to demand them.

Sir William's military stature does not permit him to negotiate with a rebel colonel and neither does Knyphausen's. So the conference has its predetermined outcome with enemy officers bound to demand unconditional surrender.

The King's representatives concede only to: guaranteeing safety for Magaw's men and baggage; permission for the troops to keep their personal baggage; and the concession that the American officers retain their swords.[44] This, in the view of the British officers, is a most generous grant, particularly since the entire rebel force faces capture or annihilation.

And so Magaw, with no other recourse signs the agreement of surrender.

Helpless Observers On the Great Bluff Rock

Fort Washington has been Howe's most coveted prize since he launched his New York campaign. His regret now is that he has not bagged the rebel "Fox" in the conquest. In that delightful event he would have happily personally participated.

From across the river on a high ledge of the Bluff Rock, The General, surrounded by his shock-stricken officers, has watched the unexpected surprise storming of the mount's works. The American officers have been speechless since it was first realized by the distant signal cannon shot and the ensuing barrages, that an all-out enemy attack was in progress. Even so, for an hour or more none believed an assault could be maintained or succeed.

When it was clear that the defenders were rapidly being overrun, few words were spoken on the Fort Lee promontory. Only the American Chief's occasional brisk questions and exchanges with his generals broke the long, silent observation.

Standing near their worried leader are Putnam, Mercer and, most crestfallen of all, Greene. All have trained their glasses almost

Helpless Observers on the Bluff Rock—A Painting by H. Willard Ortlip entitled "Washington at Fort Lee," published in "The Literary Digest", November 13, 1926.

constantly upon the largely obscured scenes going on behind the high woods across the river.

Intermittently their field glasses pick up some action occurring along the steep ravines. Each notes it and advises the other, seldom commenting but often damning some action with a few oaths and curses directed at the enemy, or the defenders if a tactical error is seemingly committed.

They watch every detail of whatever maneuvers are glimpsed in the scope of their sights. Then laboriously they attempt to put together the pieces of action in an effort to determine all the attacks and repulses in the massive operation since all communications with the sister fort have been cut off.

No messenger or dispatch has arrived since The General and his party returned to Fort Lee from their survey of the mount earlier this morning. One officer has been sent across, Captain Gooch, from whom nothing has as yet been heard. And two orders have been issued by The General. One has put all troops on alert and under arms. The other has set the engineers to collecting all river craft available.

To the Bluff Rock observers it was soon evident that Howe had set in motion a masterful lightning stroke of exceptional, overwhelming proportions aimed at the immediate overrunning of the works. They knew then that the British commander had no intention of undertaking a painfully prolonged siege, regardless of his usual cautious efforts to avoid unnecessary casualties among his troops.

Like a merciful curtain shielding their eyes from most of the tragic drama, the intervening hills and forests on Mount Washington's northwest, west and southern sectors hide much of the battling from Fort Lee's view. The terrain's scattered forest screenings have spared the west bank's observers the disheartening sights of numbers versus courage, of gun butts meeting bayonets, of pikes against pikes.

And the forests' veils have also prevented the American staff and other observers from noting how easily the enemy troops with uncanny ability pierce the concealed defenses with, seemingly, a knowledge superior to that of the defenders themselves.

One of the first to notice the enemy's unusual sense of precognition in the location of the hidden defenses was Captain Alexander Graydon of Colonel Cadwalader's regiment. Graydon, who is now a prisoner within the fortress is mentally noting for inclusion in his *Memoirs* some far distant day that:

> "Howe must have had a perfect knowledge of the ground we occupied."[45]

It will be a long time before the well-kept secret of the British commander-in-chief's success in the attacks against Fort Washington will be known. In fact it will be a long time before any details of the battle reach the American Commander-in-Chief's ears. However, now he watches, deeply grieved over the little he is able to see and greatly distressed over what he knows is happening.

Though the terrain's curtain may obstruct vision generally, there is nothing blocking out the constant roar of the cannonry. The bursting barking guns echo repeatedly through the Harlem River valley, bouncing from there back west across the island to strike thunderously against the Palisades' walls. Back and forth they thunder, sounding like giant barrels of cannon balls rolling from beam to beam with crashing thuds in the hull of a storm-tossed ship.

The awesome pounding of the air reverberates up and down Hudson's river. And frequently clouds of smoke rise above the tree-tops, spattered occasionally by flames that leap skyward as barns, buildings and woodlands catch fire. Red hot missiles fall on and ignite hay mounds and cornstalks in fields alive with firing, dodging, retreating Continentals. The distant action gives the Bluff Rock observers only glimpses of the macabre happenings. But enough to cause imaginations to soar. And the soaring imaginations are not too far from the gruesome reality.

The Daring Captain Gooch Flirts With Death

At the outset when The General's telescope assured him of the intensity of the action on the north slopes and convinced him of the serious danger that threatened Magaw, he spoke hurriedly to Greene and the generals around him. All members of his war council, they agreed that the defense could be in danger.

Tom Paine, at Greene's request, summoned Captain Gooch who was taken into The General's huddled conference with Putnam, Mercer and Greene. A minute later the young captain was running swiftly past all bystanders. He raced for his horse at the Barbette's sentry post, mounted and disappeared down the gorge road bound for the Bourdette ferry landing.

Every eye on the Bluff Rock as well as the many watching from the river's edge was directed on the captain as two powerful Marblehead oarsmen rowed him across. There was tenseness among the observers as the little rowboat worked up along the lee side of the Chevaux de Frise and then around into the cove at Jeffery's Hook. There the American messenger jumped out and dashed up the river's east bank into the Americans' ascent road to the fort.

The higher he ascended toward the summit and Fort Washington's inner works and headquarters, the heavier became the rain of missiles over his head. Then, suddenly, all firing ceased. And all that Gooch could hear as he stealthily made his way upward, but always staying off to the left of the path were shouts interspersed with loud "Hurrahs!" However they came only from the guttural-sounding throats of the Hessians.

Clothed in his easily identifiable buckskins and hunting shirt, the hatless, unarmed captain reached the summit and saw the fort's outer works before him and a pass he recognized through the exterior abatis. To get through he must dash by the milling enemy soldiers gathered wearily along the fort's outer lines but rejoicing over their success.

Then to his disgust he saw the white flag waving on the high mast while the fort's standard was slowly being lowered. From out the post's exterior perimeter a party of Hessian officers under a truce banner were seen returning to their lines.

Gooch waited no longer. He sprinted across the open field between the outskirts and the enemy-held lines along the slopes. From there he made it safely under the pass through the abatis.

The astonished Hessians, previously ordered to hold their fire, were more amused than concerned at the sight of a single soldier rushing to join his comrades' retreat into the fort. Most would have let him go even though they had not been ordered to hold their fire.

Inside, Gooch gave the downcast Colonel Magaw his Commander-in-Chief's message, assuring the fort commander that:

"if he could hold out until evening and the place could not be maintained, he (The Commander-in-Chief) would endeavor to bring off the garrison in the night."[46]

In light of what the Chief had accomplished in the crossing of the East River on the night of August 29, a clandestine movement of the Fort Washington garrison would have been comparatively simple.

But The General's message arrived too late. Magaw, already agreed to surrender, was preparing to negotiate. Furthermore he had ordered, in accordance with Rall's demands, the striking of the American standard.

When the rebels' flag came down, a clamourous uproar echoed through the forests and above the enemy troops as British and Hessians loudly cheered the striking of the yellow, blue and white Continental colors.[47] To them it was confirmation of victory.

Gooch then had to make his way through the victorious enemy lines and back to his Chief. Threading his way over the exhausted bodies standing, sitting and lying on the grounds, their faces reflecting fright, fatigue, hunger and the despair of beaten men, Gooch reached the American forward defenses where the Continentals' first line, still at alert beside their loaded muskets, rifles and heavy weapons, pass him through to a back path under the abatis. It is now the least dangerous route to the Hudson's shore.

Many of the Continentals who know the captain realize or correctly surmise the purpose of his mission. And with the white flag over their heads and their colors struck, they know the futility of their Fort Lee comrades' efforts and of Gooch's attempt to save them. And so, with the vacant, hopeless look of doomed men, they wished him well and directed him down the slopes. A few raised tired hands in a last farewell.

Gooch's message from Magaw to the American General declared

that the enemy was in possession of all the redoubts and defenses surrounding the fort and had almost entirely encircled the garrison's survivors who stand dangerously overcrowded in the post's small compound. He closed his message, stating that under those conditions capitulation or annihilation faced the remaining American troops, and that he trusted His Excellency would agree with his decision to capitulate.

The drawn and haggard face of the defeated fort commander made an indelibile impression on Gooch he cannot easily erase. The painful vision persists of the men, and the colonel as he scribbled the note, his features wan and contorted in agony after two sleepless nights . . . and Magaw's sickly looking smile as he handed the message over in a futile attempt to conceal his deep despair, then courteously wishing the captain a safe return over the river.

All these things, and particularly the silently imploring faces of the whipped and hopeless defenders, flash through Gooch's mind as now he cautiously picks his way down through the Hessian-held upper ridges of the slopes. Upon him rests the responsibility of bringing back some account of the brave attempts of the defenders to repel the jaws of the Juggernaut. He is determined he will do so.

Fortunately for Gooch the exhilarated, victory-happy enemy have dropped their guard. They had earlier thwarted several attempted breakthrough escapes with their bayonets. But there are few Hessian sentries yet posted on the comparatively unknown steep path down the west side of the slope which the Continentals had directed Gooch to take.

However, he does come across a few noisy celebrators while stealing his way down the rugged cliffs. But now the Hessians do not want to see, or even care about any occasional escapee, assured that one could not get very far anyway.

Gooch has more than one narrow escape. In one instance a Hessian, loaded with grog, sticks out his right arm from behind a tree as the fleeing captain passes. Taken by surprise, the officer runs still faster, diplomatically refusing to shake hands with the drunk whose left hand is busily engaged against the big tree trunk attending to the relief of his heavily brandied bladder.

Even the wily Gooch at times discounts his chances of getting through. Dodging, evading and outwitting the sprinkled enemy force on the west side, the captain finally reaches his boatsmen who also have narrowly escaped detection. Concealed close to the

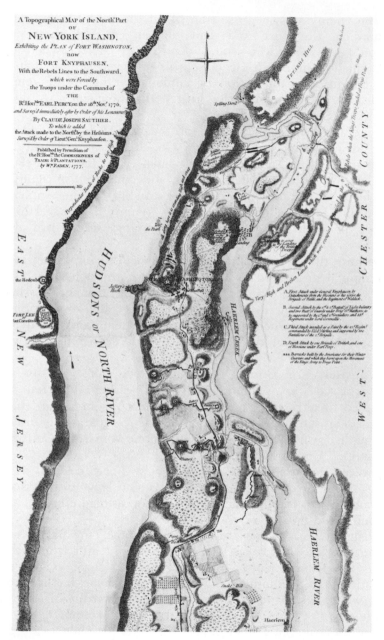

The Encirclement of Mount Washington Creates Fort Knyphausen—British Sauthier-Faden Map depicting the attacks on Fort Washington—(#614A) Courtesy of former B. Altman Co., original I. N. Phelps Stokes Collection of American Historical Prints, The New York Public Library.

bank under the cover of a dense thicket at the high end of the cove, they are difficult even for Gooch to locate.

The return crossing is without incident. And on reaching Bourdette's dock, the shore's observers give the three men a "Bravo! Bravo!" welcome.

Up on the Bluff Rock, the American Army's Continental Commander and his officers have seen the white flag raised. And then, shortly after, the striking of their colors.

His clothing torn and dirty, his face scratched by brushes, his body stenched with sweat, Gooch dismounts from his horse at the Bluff Rock sentry post and hurries toward The General and his staff, their eyes glaring at the unbelievable sight of the British colors flying over Mount Washington.

Gooch's message is anticlimactical, but The General takes the note from Magaw, reads it, takes off his tricorn, wipes his brow and hands the paper to Greene, directing him to read it aloud to the officers, all of whom have gathered waiting to hear everything Gooch can tell them.

At the Chief's request food and drink are handed to the captain who is commended by the Continental Commander. Then, after taking a long gulp of water, the officer recounts all that he has seen.

When he is finished and all questions are answered, the exhausted hero withdraws.

The American General looks once more across the river. His face is a grievous composition of sorrow and anger. He turns away, and addressing Greene calls for an immediate Council of War.

A few hours later in the Long House south of Fort Lee's parade grounds, Greene, Mercer, Putnam and others gather. Their faces are drawn. It is now 5 o'clock. Darkness is settling rapidly over the shocked silence pervading through the Fort Lee post.

The General had repaired to Greene's quarters shortly after calling for a council. And now, at the Long House, the conference he calls is brief. One matter only is on his mind to be resolved:

Fort Lee is to be abandoned.[48] The transfer of supplies and ordnance to West Jersey is to be accelerated. All preparations must proceed with priority over other routine matters.

And with that the conference is adjourned.

On Fort Washington the brief surrender papers were signed by Magaw in the name of the Continental Army post and by Rall and Patterson in the name of Knyphausen and Howe for His Majesty's armed forces. It was then 4 o'clock.[49]

The long dark shadows of the Palisades grow with the rapidly setting sun that now drops fast behind the mountains in the west. And those shadows almost spill over the river on the captured Manhattan Island mount as the white flag comes down and the British colors rise briefly in their place.

They fly until twilight, proclaiming the power of King George III through the arms of his military might in North America. And they remind all of His Majesty's subjects of the Crown's determination to crush the American rebellion.

Under the flag of their enemy flying over the post that so many have known so long as "home," the 2,800 American prisoners wait dejectedly for their captors' next move. They all know the fate that is in store.

And so an aura of gloom now hangs over the heads of the garrison's soldiery. It contrasts with the joyous, shouting enemy troops outside who have completely encircled the fort's perimeter.

Fear for what will happen next becomes uppermost on their minds. Every American rebel knows about and holds in dread the British goals of New York town.

Notorious for their filth, the countless numbers who starve to death and the rat-infested chambers, the British prisons' reputations do much to promote American defections. And they are one of the British army's strongest inducements for getting the populace to sign the Oath Of Allegiance To The Crown.

The prison system's infamous name has spread widely throughout the colonial states since August. The gaols provoke more terror among Americans, soldiers and civilians alike, than does any other confrontation with death itself. And the hopeless faces of the prisoners, their eyes stoically attempting to conceal the terror they feel, are proof of that.

Among the Living and the Dead

There is something fortunate to be said in behalf of the American dead whose battlefield sacrifices today have mercifully spared them the agonies of the living, wounded or not.

Fifty-nine American defenders are counted among the dead. Ninety-six of the garrison lie wounded, some mortally and some destined to be maimed for what little time remains in their lives.

Among the British dead are 20 redcoats and 58 Hessians, a total of 78 against the rebels' 59. Thus, 137 from both sides lie dead at the end of the day, their bodies scattered. Some rest at the base of slopes, in the river's bottom, on the fields or in the various redoubts and earthworks.

Among the British wounded are 102 redcoats and 272 Hessians, a total of 374 against the rebels' 96. So, 470 from both sides lie in pain. Some may never walk, and some may never see again. And many will succumb to their wounds and injuries even before tomorrow's dawn.

In all, the day-long battle has cost the American and British armies 607 casualties.[50] The 137 deaths and the 470 torn bodies have embittered both sides. And added to the rebels' costs will be the more than 2,800 prisoners and their fate. All in all, for both armies it becomes an extremely costly price to pay for a post that was on the verge of being abandoned anyway.

Among the dead American officers, in addition to Major Williams and Colonel Baxter, are Colonel Miller, Captain McCarter, Lieutenant Harrison and Lieutenant Tannihill.[51]

Among the enemy officers who paid the full price, in addition to Captain Walther, are Captain Medern of the Wutgenau Regiment and his Lieutenant von Lowenfeld, Colonel von Bork, Captain Barkhausen and Lieutenant Briede. Both of the latter were on Knyphausen's staff.[52]

Immediately after the enemy's flag is raised, Hessian Captain von Malsburg and his infantrymen march in and take possession of the fort. As he enters the crowded compound of aimlessly milling, confused men, a combination of hate and defiance written over their sullen faces, the Hessian officer can see through their expressions the haunting fears they nurse for the imprisonment they face.

The scene is worse than horrible even for the eyes of the hardened Prussian militarist. Owing to the scarcity of American surgeons some of the men attempt to bandage their own or comrades' gaping wounds and injuries. In shock some watch their own blood draining from their bodies. Dazed, they no longer attempt to stem the bleeding. Some, brought in alive a few hours ago from the battlefield, now mercifully lie dead. Others wrench in agonizing pain, begging for water from the long-emptied water kegs, for there is no well, no water source on the summit.

Located as it is, high on the rocky mount, the fort has never had its own water source, a fact, which if known by the enemy, would have made it more vulnerable than its appearance implies. For its supply of water, the fort has had to rely upon water kegs, filled daily from below. Rain water, when the rains come, has supplemented the daily barrel-filling.

And now every water keg and bucket has been drained dry by the severe demands of the last few prostrating hours of the post's short, five-month existence.

Hessian Captain von Malsburg is no sooner inside the compound than he is immediately surrounded by a few of the more frightened subaltern officers who press in upon him, using all the wiles they can think of in an effort to ingratiate themselves. Some invite him to their barracks for a touch of their special brandy, wine, or with the hope of bestowing gifts upon him in order to receive favors in return.

Fear and anxiety cloak their faces. They press punch, grog and cold cakes upon him and his staff. They praise him and his troops for their outstanding valor, showering upon them complimentary remarks and lauding the captain for his affability.[53]

But von Malsburg, whose knowledge of English is limited, listens, frowns and goes about his business, contemptuously ignoring his would-be bribers. It is not long before he and his men realize that the ingratiating attempts are motivated purely out of self-preservation.

So von Malsburg is not taken in by the flattering comments and the enticing offers from the few who give to the whole a bad name. The Hessian captain brushes away the ingratiatory attempts with a disdainful look. He follows strict military protocol in the task before him and in his broken English directs Magaw to lead his garrison out on the camp grounds for the surrendering of their arms.

Carrying out Colonel Rall's specific order regarding the seriously wounded Molly Corbin, von Malsburg courteously speaks with her, then quietly orders special arrangements be made for transporting her off the mount. Carried into Magaw's quarters upon being brought in from the battlefield, the gunner's widow lies in critical condition on the officer's cot.

She had been taken there on Colonel Magaw's order after Rall had made sure she was escorted safely into the fort. The Hessian colonel's considerate directive to his regimental surgeon to do what he could to attend her wounds may have saved her from bleeding to death.

In the fort the post's surgeon saw that she got special attention. He carefully dressed and bound the wounded arm and placed it in a sling after finally succeeeding in removing three grape shot and cauterizing the torn, lacerated flesh.

The unflinching, uncommunicating young woman, her lips

quivering in pain, never shed a tear. She nods her head but says no words to anyone.

Attempting to hide their fears under the false veil of bravado by empty jests and disparaging remarks behind the backs of their German-speaking Hessian captors, the garrison's defeated, bearing their arms for the last time, march out of the fort. Downcast though they are inside, the Continentals, as a whole, refuse to be humiliated.

Magaw, in his last minutes together with his men, highly lauded each regiment for the courageous efforts it had made. He talked with the wounded and the dying, attempting to comfort them.

There was not one among them, he proudly told his troops, who did not earn and greatly deserve his country's praise for so nobly upholding The Cause and the new nation's honor on the battlefield.

And so the able-bodied of the mount's garrison—almost to a man—moved out with their heads held high. Among them are many nursing bitterness. Some angrily blame the colonel. Others charge the defeat to Greene and the American Commander-in-Chief himself, while a few, presuming more knowledge than others of the political machinations in Philadelphia between the States, trace the fault directly to the Congress.

They all march down the trail that leads to the fort from the post road. Then on still farther they move, their muskets and rifles pointed down toward the ground. They pass through some of their own abandoned breastworks into a wide open space near the main road.

It is here in the open meadow lands southeast of the fort, the scene of furious fighting only a few hours ago, that they are to be mustered out and marched to captivity in New York town. The wounded, some on make-shift stretchers, are to be conveyed in wagons. Those who can walk must do so.

The Long March to Prison Begins

In the fields of the lands belonging to Blazius Moore of the city are now arrayed two Hessian regiments, one under Colonel Rall and the other under Colonel Alt von Lossberg. Both are under arms.

Between these two regimental columns the sullen American troops must march. By companies they pass through, laying down their weapons and giving up their yellow, blue and white banners

while the stern, immobile-faced Hessian officers and British commanders, escaping the stench of the dirty, battle-scarred men,
look on from a respectable distance.

As the Americans move out, a number of the Hessian guards
who are supposedly in charge of the prisoner detachments, begin
robbing them of clothing, personal belongings[54] and trinket
keepsakes. Fights break out with increasing violence that threaten
to disrupt the whole assemblage.

British officers immediately take over, stop the Hessians'
plundering and divert the defenseless captives to the opposite side
of the meadows.

It is after 5 o'clock in the afternoon. The long shadows of the
pre-sunset hour are solemnly and morbidly cast over the fields. The
humiliating laying down of arms is over for the 2,837 prisoners,[55]
of whom there are 230 officers and 2,607 privates.

All are formed into detachments, placed between lines of British
armed guards and marched off to begin their long trek, without
food and very little water. Their destination is, as each one of
them knows, the British prison confines in the city.

Before them are eleven miles of hard marching. It will be dawn
and later before they reach the captured port city. It is the city
which will recall to many both pleasant memories of the days
before the Battle of Long Island and horrible ones in the tragic
times that followed. And now for them it forebodes no good.

One English officer's diary will later read:

> "Many of the Rebels who were killed in the late affairs, were without
> shoes and stockings and several were observed to have only linen drawers
> on, with a Rifle or Hunting shirt without any proper shirt or waistcoat.
> They are also in great want of blankets . . . in less than a month they must
> suffer extremely."[56]

There is no question about the fact that the downfall of the fort
and the severe losses in personnel are a disastrous blow to the
military, the Congress and the country. But the losses in supplies,
ammunition, ordnance and materiel are so great as to weaken the
American army to the point that its continuation as a fighting
force is now dangerously jeopardized.

Partly illustrating this are the amounts of iron ordnance and
small arms captured by the British today alone. Included are:

> 4 32-pounders; 2 18-pounders; 7 12-pounders; 5 9-pounders; 15
> 6-pounders; 8 3-pounders; 2 5½ inch brass howitzers;[57] 200 iron fraise
> of 400-weight (used in the blockade construction work); 2,800 muskets;
> 400,000 cartridges; 15 barrels of powder; over 2,000 shot and shell.[58]

In addition are to be added the ordnance and supplies taken during the last few weeks when Fort Independence and Fort Valentine were overrun. In the loss of those posts, Knyphausen acquired:

4 12-pounders; 10 9-pounders; 10 6-pounders; 37 4-pounders.[59]

For the struggling thirteen united colonial states the day, November 16, will become one of the Continental Army's most disastrous in the war for independence. In the harried hours of the month ahead, the fall of Fort Washington and its significance will be the principal topic of discussion behind the American lines, behind the British front, in Boston, in Philadelphia, in England, in Europe, among Tories and among the disheartened patriots. For with a few lightning blows the Juggernaut has destroyed the equivalent of over one-half the Continentals' main army insofar as its fighting strength is concerned.

The news will restore faith in Great Britain that a quick end to the tragic war may soon come. It will put Sir William Howe once again back firmly in the good graces of His Majesty, his cousin the King, Lord North, Parliament and Lord Germaine. So it is not Howe's intention now to stop with so much going in his favor.

Sir William has unleashed his hound dogs and they are eager for more game. So he casts his eyes and directs the wheels of his Juggernaut toward the Jerseys. There, or across the river Delaware in Penn's colony, he will stage the final fox hunt. Of that Sir William is now more certain than ever. It is only a question of time.

On the Bluff Rock The Long Vigil Ends

On the Bluff Rock the American officers slowly turned away from their scattered observation posts along the precipice rocks. All day they had waited for the order that might attempt a rescue of their comrades. Now the long vigil is over.

All follow the earlier footsteps of their Chief, Greene, Mercer and Putnam down the Bluff Rock trail to the gorge road and up to the main camp on The Mountain's summit. But of all the sorrowful, crestfallen faces in the procession of the Continental Army chieftains, none is more dejected than that of the slightly limping General Greene.

In his sleepless, pre-dawn hours of tomorrow's morning, Greene will write his close friend, General Henry Knox:

"I feel mad, vexed, sick, and sorry. Happy should I be to see you. This is a most terrible event; its consequences are justly to be dreaded."[60]

Greene, like the Commander-in-Chief, had spent an almost day-long vigil observing from the cliffs, consulting frequently with The General, others of the war council and his staff, waiting and hoping that the American Leader would order him to direct a rescue operation. The order never came.

But Greene was not alone in waiting in vain for that command. Also glumly, hopefully waiting for that order on the Bluff Rock batteries' ramparts, in addition to The General's council and many of the troops, were: Generals Ewing, Irvine, Roberdeau, Fellows, Wadsworth, Stevens, Beall, Heard; Colonels Hand, Durkee, Small-wood, Bedford, Biddle, Snarl, Swope, Cunningham, Montgomery, Watt; Assistant Commissary of Stores Jonathan Gostelowe, Adjutant General Thomas Paine, who is almost always seen standing close beside Greene, and many subaltern officers.

But among the American cause's optimists who have watched the distant battling from The Rock are Lieutenant Colonel Pelissiere, the French military engineer, and Polish Army Captain Taeusz Andrezey Bonaventare Kosciusko. Both men are two of the vanguard of European volunteers from France, Poland, Germany and other countries, offering their services to the American Continental Army and the new nation in its fight for independence.

Critically analyzing Howe's strategy from their observations, Pelissiere and Kosciusko, speaking to each other in French, remain behind discussing the operation from its tactical aspects. Using long sticks, they sketch in the soft soil the strategies each believes one or the other of the two opposing military forces should have used.

Both officers have gained wide reputations in professional military circles. Both are providing the Continental Army the skilled engineering assistance sorely needed.

Pelissiere's services have been of great assistance to the rebel army. His October 21 report[61] of the Fort Lee defense system is still under much discussion.

Kosciusko, who arrived last summer, has been at work in Philadelphia preparing the fortification system for that city's defenses. Now on his way to serve the northern army department at Ticonderoga, Kosciusko has stopped en route to meet The General. But the day he has picked could not have been more inauspicious, especially for any discussion of Fort Washington's defenses.

The Polish officer speaks both French and English, in addition to his own language. And, owing to the single language limitations of the American officers, the pointed sticks' tactical explanations in the soft earth are a linguistic foreign puzzle for the Yankee observers attempting to listen in.

However, the Continentals do gather that both strategists believe Fort Washington could have been held against the enemy's ten or twelve thousand troops by a well-supplied and equipped force of 9,000 men. But neither of the two military engineers suspects betrayal or takes it into account.

While the air of optimism Kosciusko and Pelissiere bring to the American fort is invigorating, it does not spill over upon the rebel rank and file in this, the army's most depressing hour. Instead, gloom enshrouds the entire area, military and civilian.

Among the inhabitants, the patriots and neutrals are the most concerned about the future. During the past few days they have watched with growing trepidation the movement of men and supplies out of Fort Lee.

It has not been possible to conceal the exodus of wagons. Periodically they have rolled out of the fort, down the west slope into the valley, across the river Hackensack into Hackensack town, then on to Acquackanonk, Newark, New Brunswick, thence toward the mountains behind Morris Town or else west toward Princeton.

The sight brings joy to the Tories and Loyalist sympathizers. For them, it is the forerunner of the rebels' end. For them, it is proof that His Majesty's troops will shortly be invading the Jerseys and bring the insurrection its close.

One such strongly suspected Tory sympathizer is Jeffery Gartleck. It is said that he uses his black bonded servants, Immanuel, Isaiah and their children, Ben and Katie May, to gather information from The Mountain, its soldiers and the inhabitants. And it is believed that he peddles the information to the enemy across the river.

Only for this reason, generally, does Gartleck allow Ben and Katie May to visit the hamlet people. It was for this reason that he has permitted them occasionally to attend Elaine's "school" for the neighborhood children.

Each time they return Gartleck pumps all the information possible from the boy and his sister, becoming angry at times when they do not tell him what he wants to know. And this he also does with their parents whenever they leave the place to fish, pick up supplies at the stage stop and the little store that Bourdette runs under the fort's Bluff Rock, or visit Black Jennie, the Bourdettes and Baummeisters.

Much of what the black, bonded servants, Ben and Katie May see that they think might be damaging to The Gen'l and his army, the black family, all four of them agreeing, guardedly keep to themselves. For they know Gartleck's activities are prompted by British sympathies. So his bonded servants have proved to be poor spies for the Tory's nefarious purposes.

It was Jocko, who has lately taken a more than friendly interest in Katie May, that learned about Gartleck's "pumping" of his servants from the pretty little black girl. The youth immediately told Gray who passed on the information to his superiors. Neither Colonel Bedford nor Major Blodget felt that the children's meager information could give the enemy much assistance even were the young blacks forced to reveal what they might have seen.

Though Bedford and Blodget discounted the possibility of Gartleck, or others, gaining any valuable intelligence by such methods, they were glad to get Jocko's report. Commending the Barbette Battery's "adopted soldier," they all agreed it was wise to be alerted to Gartleck's tactics.

There Are the Bound and the Unbound

Jeff Gartleck had been willed Immanuel, Isaiah, Ben and Katie May Gartleck by his father, a New York landowner upon his death in the senile years of his life. Old man Gartleck had been a kind master to his black servants, treating them more as members of his household, having been made a widower by the early death of his wife.

However, the old man had lost track of his wandering son until shortly before he died at a time when he failed to recognize his returned offspring. But the Gartleck servants never had good relations with Jeffery, even before he ran away from home, an event, it was believed, that hastened the death of his mother.

Unlike Bourdette, who had granted Jennie and her son, Caesar, their freedom, Gartleck had held the black family in tight bondage. Since the majority of the river and mountain people despise bondage and slavery of any kind, Gartleck has never been "accepted" by the hamlet since taking up residence south of Bourdette's some years ago.

Most of the river and mountain people find bondage so despicable that they secretly engineer the escape of black slave runaways and bonded servants, as well as the indentured who have not been honorably released from contracts they have properly fulfilled.

Stephen Bourdette has been one of the principals in aiding runaways up through the mountain passes into the Ramapos from where many make their way still farther north. Always assisting in these nocturnal enterprises is his colleague in all matters, Pete Baummeister.

It is this attitude and the constant re-telling of Bourdette's treatment of Jennie and her son around the mountain and along the river that irritates Gartleck. He has heard the story recounted so often that sometimes he is sure it is done purposely to prod him into giving his servants their freedom.

And Gartleck is right. The story of Jennie and Caesar is almost always repeated within his earshot: How Bourdette had offered the mother and her son assistance in escaping after he had rescued the woman and child from the mast and spar raft on the river.

It was over 20 years ago when Jennie, her husband, Ebenezer, with their only child, a boy of five, accompanying their white family owners in a pettiauger, were caught in a fierce squall on the Tappan Zee.

When the mast broke and the little vessel capsized, their white owners, man and wife, went under with the sloop. Jennie's husband, Ebenezer, somehow managed to put his wife and son on the mast and spar which still dragged part of its canvas, but Ebenezer was carried away in the rough seas and swift current to drown before their eyes.

Bourdette, who had been caught in the same storm but safely rode it out, rescued both mother and child. He brought them back to the ferry dock where he and Rachel carried them into their home and nursed them through their shock and injuries.

The ferry owner gave the black woman her choice of returning to her former owner's New York family if there were any to be found, escaping if she wished up through the mountain passes toward a colony of formerly bonded people located beyond the distant Ramapo Mountains, or staying with the Bourdettes as long as she chose.

Jennie asked to stay, at least for awhile. That was over 20 years ago. She and Caesar, now almost 26 years old, though free to do so, have never left the Bourdette household.

It is that story of "Bourdette and his humanity!" that Gartleck dislikes to hear retold so often.

So, it was today, when the people from all around the river side of The Mountain, after straining their eyes on Mount Washington most of the day, sadly returned home, that Katie May and Ben watched a merchant at the stagecoach-stop beckon Asher Levy up from the boat dock. Their voices were low but audible enough for the boy and his sister to hear every word as they listened and patted the horses.

Feeling that they could safely reveal to "Mars'a Jeff" what they had overheard without endangering "The Gen'l's" army, since what they heard had nothing to do with the military, Ben and Katie May replied freely to Gartleck's expected questioning.

It had been a privilege for them to go off the place, a privilege that Gartleck had surprisingly granted them unhesitatingly when the cannonading began. And since what they overheard dealt entirely with Edmund Kearney, it seemed a good way to repay their white owner without telling something that might hurt the rebel soldiers.

Therefore they reported innocently enough that the merchant had told Lieutenant Levy that Kearney had been imprisoned in New York town but escaped and was killed.

Gartleck seemed not at all interested in the fate of the former American army corporal whom everyone along the river and on The Mountain had known. He wanted to learn from Katie May, who is more communicative than her brother less about Kearney and more about the traveling merchant, a likely rebel spy.

The young girl, bent on telling all she heard, went on to disclose that Levy had called "The Lootenan' " out of the Baummeister house, followed by Elaine, and told them all that the merchant had told him: ... That some unknown defector befriended Corporal Eddie; that Kearney and the traitor haggled over money Kearney was to get; that the traitor had Eddie thrown in jail and that the former army corporal was drowned in the river while trying to escape.

What Gartleck wanted to know was: Who was the merchant that talked with Levy? What did he look like? What was he selling, if anything?

At this point Ben walked over to the pile of hay his father was throwing up back into the loft from which it had fallen. Picking up a pitchfork the young boy began assisting Immanuel who asked his son what news he'd heard about the battle on the mount.

There was much to tell his father about the battle as seen from the cliffs, about the captain who dashed up the mount just when the white flag was raised and what he and Katie May had heard about young Kearney. In recounting his story and throwing the hay up on the loft at the same time, Ben left Katie May alone answering Gartleck's questions.

To "Mars'a Jeff's" insistent queries regarding the merchant, Katie May simply said that Lieutenant Levy talked to the stranger through the coach door, and so, she insisted, she could not see the man inside.

And that exactly was the important information Gartleck wanted. If he could identify and show some proof that someone is a rebel informer, carrying information out of the city to the American forces, the Tory spy would get a fat bonus. And that bonus is now within his hungry reach. All he has to know is who that merchant traveler is. He is sure that Katie May and Ben have seen more than they tell him.

Gartleck has a reputation for cruelty. Animals and people have often felt the violence of his wrath. His wife, who had lain for months a crippled imbecile from a fall downstairs which, it was learned, he had caused in an argument over the couple's failure to have children, died less than a year ago.

The boat builder and fisherman is also known to have killed animals merely for the sake of seeing them die, uninterested even in their hides. He has been known to have beaten a horse close to death because it had stumbled and thrown him. He has often struck Immanuel and Ben, but he has always been afraid to lift his hand against Isaiah or Katie May.

Reddening with anger and determined to discover the identity of the rebel informer in the coach, he grasps Katie May's arm, squeezing it much harder than he realizes, demanding, "Who was it? You damned well know who it was! Who was it?"

Wrenching in pain, Katie May cries out, "Ise doan know! Ise doan know! Stop dat! Youse hurtin' me! Ise tell ya Ise doan know!"

The young girl's screams startle her father and Ben. Both drop their pitchforks and run toward Gartleck. Immanuel's brown eyes are blazing as he comes almost flying at his white owner, striking away Gartleck's arm from his daughter's and throwing the boat builder off balance and back on his heels.

The stocky, heavy-set Tory, shorter in stature by seven inches than the tall, six-foot, wiry, 50-year-old Negro, does not need to hear Immanuel's angry order, "Let 'er go!" He does so from surprise but with anger in his eyes at being threatened.

Enraged, Gartleck picks up his birch branch riding whip and begins beating his black servant, five years his senior. As Immanuel holds his head between his arms and cringes from the whip lashes, Ben picks up one of the pitchforks from the floor and rushing toward Gartleck, shouts, furiously, "Leave him be! Leave him be!"

Gartleck, seeing Ben angrily charging in upon him, a pitchfork in his hands, flees up the loft ladder, still holding his riding whip.

Ben has no intention of pursuing the Tory informer, choosing instead to go to his injured father's side. As he helps the bleeding man up and walks with him toward the barn door through which Katie May had run toward the house, they hear Gartleck's piercing scream behind them. They turn in time to see their owner fall from the broken ladder into the upended points of the pitchfork that Gartleck had earlier left standing up against the rungs.

Violence Falls When Reason Rises

Both Immanuel and Ben run swiftly to the fallen man. The sharp prongs of the fork pierced his heart and chest when the rickety, temporary, makeshift ladder gave way and broke, sending Gartleck plummeting onto the fork's upraised blades.

One blade in his heart protrudes from his back. Ben and Immanuel can see at a glance that Gartleck, his heart pierced and his skull bleeding badly from the fall, is dead.

Seeing his father whipped and bleeding on the ground had so enraged the youth that hate seethed in his hot veins. Now as he looks down upon the man to whose will he had been forced to bend so long and who had made him learn to hate, there is no sympathy, but rather great relief in what he sees.

One thing makes him content, even proud of himself. He recalls that within that horrible brief moment when every hateful thought he had ever nursed against Gartleck surged though his mind, he had decided to help his father on the ground instead of pursuing the despised object of his wrath.

Ben has long harbored thoughts of violence against Gartleck, and his conscience has worried him for it. He has often felt a pitchfork in his hands piercing through Gartleck's deserving body while the man screamed and crumbled on the ground. He has felt death in his hands . . . but now, strangely, he had tonight instead turned back to help his father . . . He was glad.

Through Ben's frightened but relieved mind suddenly flowed the full meaning of all his mother's teachings. It was they, he believed, that had withheld his hand from murder. For it was she and her teachings, which had ever emphasized that men sow what they reap and that the Lord's vengeance is as swift and terrible in its justice as any that mortals can inflict.

Immanuel and Ben know that regardless of providential justice they will likely be blamed for Gartleck's death when his Tory friends and conspirators find him. For most of the neighbors to the south of the house are as strong Loyalists as was the boat builder. And many are Gartleck's friends, though not admirers of his tactics.

So the black man and his son realize they must immediately escape and leave the body just as it is if they are to save their own lives.

Informing the trembling Isaiah and Katie May of the accident, Immanuel orders them to pack only enough for their bare needs so as not to be weighed down.

In the darkness, for it is now close to nine in the night, they set out for the Bourdette house along the shore road. They must get to Stephen Bourdette's place. And there they will tell "Mars'a Stevin" the truth about everything. Immanuel warns his family that they must hurry quietly and not be seen.

Passing near the whitewashed frame house, they stop short as they very nearly walk directly into the Baummeisters, Stephen Bourdette, John Gray and Asher Levy, sitting and standing around on the ferry-master's veranda, all talking concernedly about the battle. Fearing to interrupt, Immanuel backs his family quietly behind the bushes, expecting to contact the ferry owner alone when he leaves.

Bourdette, Baummeister and his wife have assembled to hear from Gray what the loss of the fort across the river will now mean, and from Levy what he has learned about Kearney.

At the moment the second lietuenant is recounting everything the merchant has told him about the corporal's death. He repeats what he had told Elaine and John earlier. All listen unbelievingly. Elaine sobs quietly as her husband's arm extends comfortingly around her shoulders.

Levy's account is almost verbatim what the merchant told him. It is the report which Haym Salomon had pieced together at Levy's request for information regarding Kearney and which Salomon directed his merchant to give secretly to the Bluff Rock lieutenant.

Much is what Katie Mae and Ben had heard and reported to Gartleck except for the additional fact that Kearney had made friends with an American traitor. A traitor who was paid money by a high ranking British officer for some Continental Army plans that were in his possession.

Then the former corporal, having aided the defector in some unknown ways, demanded a portion of the money whereupon the two men broke up. Shortly after that, the stranger, who acquired sudden influence owing to his services to the Crown, feared the young corporal's threats and demands and on false charges, had the youth imprisoned.

Accused as a rebel soldier turned spy to report on British activities in New York, Kearney had no defense except the American traitor, who it is said, was an officer at Fort Washington, and who now betrayed his young befriender.

Worst of all was that the youth's cunning accomplice plotted with Kearney's gaolers to have him done away with before any hearing or trial could take place. As prearranged, Kearney was allowed to escape from one of Provost Marshal William Cunningham's gaolers.

As expected, the escaping Kearney, unaware that he was being followed, headed for Hudson's river. There he took the first rowboat he came upon and breathlessly set out for the Jersey shore only to be shot at and followed by a gaoler in a whaleboat. The shots pierced Kearney's boat which soon went down from under him, forcing him to swim for his life across the wide river.

In no time the gaoler and his assistant in the whaleboat were upon him. Coming alongside of the youth, struggling against gaoler and the tide, the deputy demoniacally pushed the frantic escapee under the water with his oar. He did so repeatedly as Kearney fought hopelessly for breath and life.

At last the youth's head went under for the last time. The gaoler and his oarsman, having passed a line around the leg of their victim, then held the hapless corporal's head down under water until they were sure all life had left him. They then hauled the body back into the whaleboat as though it were a lifeless man-eating shark and returned to shore.

An unobserved witness watched the deliberate murder from the river's bank. In fear of his life he reported it only to Salomon and other patriot sympathizers.

Then the deputy and his assistant brought Kearney's body back to Cunningham, for all three were in on the plot to share in the blood money offered by the now influential American defector, said to be under protection by General Howe's order.

In arresting the former rebel militiaman under trumped charges, his name had been either misunderstood, or purposely mispronounced, and recorded as "Carnay." The French-sounding pronuciation had assured his gaolers that the youth was one of those Frenchmen who had come over to help the rebel army. The present anti-French attitude among the British, stemming from the two nations' constant entanglements, had not in the least helped Kearney, under the name of "Carnay."

Before Cunningham the dead youth's pockets were turned inside out for any valuables that might be added to the provost marshal's coffers. A soaking wet paper gave evidence of the corporal's army discharge. It revealed his correct name as "Edmund Kearney." To the three gaolers' astonishment, the name was identical with that of the deputy who had drowned the youth.

The suddenly alarmed gaoler looked at the paper, then down at the drowned youth's bloated form. Around the corpse's neck, the frantic, 40-year-old deputy spied a chain and locket. Becoming strangely excited, he grabbed the neckpiece from around the boy's throat and nervously opened the small, hinged, silver case.

The shocked, chalk-faced man, who 18 years ago had left his wife and infant son to fare for themselves on the river's banks, saw within his hands a lock of his own hair, just as Carrie and he had once inserted them—strands from both their heads, still in the locket on the beaded chain of Job's tears.

"Me God! Me own son!" he screamed. "Oi've moided me own child! Oh, me God! Forgee me!"

He rose and in a wild frenzy ran outside of the gaol's outer hall. Prisoners who had silently witnessed the scene behind their bars watched him disappear out through the large heavy iron grated door. It clanged tight shut behind him as he vanished, clutching his throat with his hand and screaming as though someone were choking him to death. In his clenched right fist he tightly grasped the silver locket. Its chain of beads dangled mockingly behind him.

He fell, stumbling to the courtyard ground, yelling incoherently until he was at last carried away, kicking, screaming and cursing, soon ending up a raving maniac in one of Cunningham's cells.

Edmund Kearney Senior was no longer the gaoler holding the keys to the rat-infested prison. A prisoner of himself and his twisted mind, for him there is no escape but one.

Elaine has muffled her sobs in her handkerchief as she hears Levy recount the story the second time. It is the way Salomon had unraveled it through his many contacts in and out of Cunningham's gaols. And it is the way he gave it to his merchant to pass on to Levy.

Horrified by the cruel turn of events and the disastrous fate of her childhood playmate, and recalling the occasion of Edmund's leaving just a fortnight ago, Elaine pulls away from her husband's encircling arm and moves to the darkened end of the veranda. Just then Katie May, unable longer to hold back her cough, gives the black family away.

Asher and John immediately run over to the brush to investigate. As they do the four frightened runaways come out into the open yard fronting the Baummeister home. The light from the whale oil lamps within the house, reflecting on the grounds through the 12-pane glass window, barely reveals the huddled Gartleck servants.

No breeze blows. It is a rare night for the middle of November, warm, almost hot outside, as the last of the katydids send out their shrill call, while in the distance two owls hoot their way through the trees on the precipice in their nocturnal hunt for survival.

It could be the last of the Indian Summer nights, Stephen tells Baummeister, and the ferry-master agrees. For all is seriousness this night on The Mountain and along the water's edge.

Tragedy has struck the hamlet's people almost as hard as if the fall of the mount had been Fort Lee. And there are not many among the inhabitants who doubt that Fort Lee also has fallen.

So the black family, coming out of the dark shadows and asking to talk only to "Mars'a Stevin," suddenly bring more tragic news to the mournful gathering.

The ferry owner quickly responds to Immanuel's request. Meanwhile Katie May runs crying into Elaine's arms. Then Isaiah is joined by Marie Louise, and the black woman is soon sobbing out the story to her and her husband.

Realizing that the rest of his family are telling everyone and not only Bourdette, Ben tells John and Asher. There is no doubt in any of the Gartleck family's minds that their affairs are as safe with the Baummeisters as they are with the Bourdettes. It is soon promised that they will be safe and everything arranged for.

Bourdette informs Immanuel that they all must get away tomorrow at dusk and make for the Ramapos' mountain colony and go on north from there if they wish. The stopping over places are all safe, he assures them. They will be given plenty of supplies which Jennie, Rachel and Marie Louise will prepare.

In the meantime, they are to spend the night in the old Kearney cottage which Perawae and Minnie left in order. Food will be supplied and they are told to rest and prepare for tomorrow night. Their guide, Bourdette tells them, will be Honest Sam, who knows every foot of the trial and many paths that are unknown to anyone else.

In this way, Bourdette assures them, they will have their freedom. And even though they are not at all at fault and cannot be blamed for Gartleck's death, their escape to a new life is wise.

Marie Louise and Elaine take all four into the kitchen and feed them. Then Honest Sam leads them along the river to the deserted Kearney house.

Before they all part it is agreed that no word of the Gartleck tragedy will be spoken.

Finally Katie May asks Elaine and John to tell Jocko so that she may say goodbye to him. The married couple promise the sad eyed girl that they will if necessary drag Jocko away from his horses to say goodbye tomorrow. She smiles thankfully and parts.

What Bourdette and Baummeister do not tell anyone, is their plan to follow Nicausie Klep to Gartleck's house tomorrow morning and come upon him in the barn of his Tory friend. Both regularly fish together each Sunday morning. So Nicausie is bound to be the one to find the body.

Walking in upon Klep they will, it is decided, discover him bending over the corpse of his co-conspirator. They will then allow matters to take their own course.

By hurling incriminating questions at Nicausie and asking him if he knew whether Gartleck sent his black servants over to New York town early yesterday with a friend and why, they will confuse his guilty, spying mind. And then they will throw suspicion upon Klep implying that he and Gartleck had engaged in a death struggle. Then they hope to convince the always heavily imbibing Nicausie that possibly he is guilty of something he doesn't remember.

In this way Bourdette and Baummeister hope to have the baffled man so vigorously protesting his innocence that Gartleck's Tory partner will gladly help with the quick burial of his kinless friend. In fact he may be induced to do the honors all by himself.

And so tomorrow morning that is exactly what the ferry owner and ferry-master will do. This will account for the many strange stories which in the years to come will be told about the unexplained disappearance of Jeffery Gartleck and his four black bonded servants the day Fort Washington was lost.

Thus there are few people who sleep without nightmares at or near Fort Lee this Indian Summer night. Above the Baummeister house which now darkens as the whale oil lights go out one at a time, the picket guard on the high rampart of the massive Bluff Rock looks across at the British campfires slowly burning down and fading out on what is no longer the American-held Manhattan Island.

Forever in the Past

All of the captured troops who only last night held Fort Washington, are at this midnight hour marching toward the horrendous chambers of the British prisons in the city. And the picket guard's thoughts go farther. For he recalls that here at Fort Lee was to have been Fort Washington's escape hatch on this, the day of storming—the *day* if ever the mount should fall.

Here was to have been the funnel that would have emptied the twin fort of its garrison, rescuing the troops from the jaws of the Juggernaut. But Fort Lee has failed to execute that mission, not because of its own inadequacies, but because of the most imponderable of imponderables—human error by human judgment.

It is judgment, the lonely sentinel remembers once having been told, that is God's most generous gift and man's most ignored and neglected talent, yet all things, animate and inanimate, are dependent upon it wherever, whenever, man holds the reins.

Eight miles away in Hackensack, the candles still burn in The General's quarters in the Zabriskie house. And there he writes, bringing to an end his and his army's most tragic day. For the wearied man must get off his report to Congress while the horrible catastrophe is still burning deeply into his mind. And in summing up his letter, he concludes:

> "The loss of such a number of officers and men, many of whom have been trained with more than common attention, will I fear be severely felt. But when that of the arms and accoutrements is added, much more so, and [there now] must be a farther incentive to procure as considerable a supply as possible for the new troops, as soon as it can be done."[62]

As he puts the quill back into the inkwell, he sees the hour hand at midnight. November 16, 1776, is forever behind him yet will be forever on his mind.

And below from The Green he hears the sentinel ring out, "All's well!"

27

Monday, November 18. . .

March of the Dead,
the Dying and the Doomed

Two "Escapees"

Of almost 3,000 Americans who two days ago manned Mount Washington's defenses, only the young drummer boy and the severely wounded Margaret Corbin remain this morning on the once supposedly invincible citadel. Only they and the Continentals who were killed in the action and who now lie together in the hurriedly dug, trenched graves, are left behind by the captives in their long march down into the King's prisons.

Hessian and British troops, having counted and buried their dead and assessed their costs, attend their wounded and take over their conquered mount, sorting the extensive arms, ammunition and materiel of all kinds acquired in the conquest. Much bedding, some huts and barracks are burned wherever the pox and contagion are suspected.

Southward, under a special order and strict security, the armed guards of the British reserves are escorting the last of the 2,836 prisoners through Manhattan Island into the custody of Commissary of Prisons William Cunningham. So horrible have been the stories told of the notorious gaols, and so unbelievable that many are certain the accounts are highly exaggerated and basically untrue.

However, just as the city itself is rapidly becoming known as the Tory capital of America, its prison system is gaining a notorious reputation for Loyalists' infamy. And into those ill reputed "holes of hell" Cunningham angrily prepares to herd and feed almost 3,000 unwelcome prisoners.

Impelled by the eroding traces of knighthood, the British and Hessian officers this morning spare Margaret Corbin and the drummer boy who stood by her. On order of the British high command the two were not sent with the others to New York town.

Largely through the gentility side of the warrior Rall, Knyphausen and the British commander the "escape" of the artillery woman and the youth is secretly permitted. More than that, it is "engineered." And the plan is simple. Its execution simpler.

Three subaltern officers assist the woman, her brain still somewhat confused and wandering, down the slope to the Hudson's shore. The young drummer boy, carrying her few salvaged possessions as well as his own, stays close to her side as she is carried between the crossed hands of two husky Hessian officers. Though weak, she is capable of standing and walking shakily, but not, certainly, down the slopes of the rugged mount.

Previously arranged, a flat boat equipped with oars is tied up at the cove just south of Jeffery's Hook. In consideration of the pain and suffering she is undergoing, the two Hessians exert extreme care in placing the wounded girl gently in a low, make-shift, blanket-surrounded seat.

Though the widowed woman is still in shock, dazed and incoherent at times, she is gradually regaining her senses following periodic lapses in her thinking. She does exactly as she is told. The drummer boy is ordered to get in beside her.

The youth, who is knowledgeable about rivers and experienced in boat handling, hopes, to himself, that all three Hessians will not add their weights to the little vessel. He was told that he and Madam Corbin are to be conveyed downstream to New York through some very choppy waters.

Since he has been told little else and cannot understand their German, he responds only to their sign language and gathers—as he looks longingly across at Fort Lee—that they are to be boated down to the British prison. He notices wistfully that only a single line holds the craft to the shore.

Were it not for the enemy's guns, he would be almost tempted to row the craft across to Fort Lee. But that he knows would endanger both their lives, and so he rules out any attempt to escape.

Then in accordance with the plot two of the officers higher up on the river's bank begin to argue in their native language. The third, who speaks some English, moves away from them and steals down to the raft,[1] hands the boy the unfastened end of the mooring line and whispers excitedly to him to row.

"Quick! Schnell! Schnell! Za boad row ober za wasser zu Foad Lee! Schnell! Schnell!" he insists, giving the raft a mighty push out into the stream.

There is nothing else for the frightened drummer boy to do. And he does it swiftly, fearing that at any moment shooting will break out. Since nothing he has ever heard about the Hessians has been good, he suspects it is a trick to drown him and his charge, thus saving the trouble of escorting two prisoners downriver. He rows furiously toward the Chevaux de Frise. Fortunately a favorable tide is on his side.

Once beside the blockade of partly sunken ships' hulks he is out of danger, and the river crossing is simplified. To his amazement he and his wounded companion have safely escaped. No shots are fired. No boat sets out from shore to chase them.

Then, exhausted from the strain of hard rowing without let-up, the boy slackens and treads water with his oars. He looks toward the shore expecting to discover at least two angry Hessian officers. Instead, unbelievingly, he sees the three calmly watching him, and all apparently in a jovial mood. The one who told him to go, now waves his hand in a pleasant goodbye.

Many years later when the boy is a farmer with a family in Pennsylvania, he will come across the unforgettable face of the Hessian officer. He will come across him, finding him plowing his fields—a farmer and head of a family like himself.

Until then, the former Hessian-hating young drummer boy will wonder why their escape was made so easy. And so too will Molly Corbin who has come out of her half-stupor and is swiftly becoming aware of what is going on around her.

She now fully recognizes the youngster who helped her load the fieldpiece Saturday. Quickly grasping what has happened, she attempts to help her gallant rescuer and oarsman by pointing out any obstructions in the river and by indicating the course to the landing below Fort Lee. And so under no pressure by pursuers, across the river they row close to the south side of the Chevaux de Frise.

The pair of escapees are now the only American participants who were in the battle and are now free on the Continental

Army's side of the river. Their surprising arrival brings soldiers, officers and the hamlet's inhabitants hurrying to the Bourdette landing after their espial by the Bluff Rock sentinels who spread the news.

Soldiers and civilians on the dock overwhelmingly greet the pair with questions. General Greene, receiving the news, hurries down from the fort's summit.[2] He orders the young woman taken to the special hospital tent where Dr. Shippen personally attends her. He takes the drummer with him up to his own headquarters.

From the youth's lips, and later from "Captain Molly Corbin," as she is soon to become known, the American Fort Lee commandant and his staff officers will learn all that will be found out about the November 16 tragedy for many days to come. The information, though meager, is hastily relayed to the Commander-in-Chief in Hackensack.

There the youth will be sent and further questioned by The General and his aides. A little later he will be sent home a hero and conducted to his farmer father's homestead outside of Philadelphia by a recruiting officer.

However, tomorrow he and Molly Corbin will become a special part of a sick and wounded train from the Fort Lee and Hackensack posts who will leave, some for the Newark and some for the Philadelphia hospitals.

Meanwhile, the over-crowded British prisons in New York cannot accommodate the larger part of the exhausted, unfed, bedraggled captives moving in upon them today. Many, shoeless, in dirty summer-weight garments, in torn and badly ripped trousers and coats now possess no other properties.

All have been standing under heavy guard today, some from dusk last night in the open without food and very little water. A number of them are now lined up in the outer prison yard, or marching toward it to be mustered in.

For them it has been a wearying 48 hours. Fortunately, Saturday night on the mount's carefully guarded grounds was not severely cold as some of the fall nights have been. But many of the captives were marched out Sunday and began pouring into the prison yards Sunday night. A few of the wounded and the dying arrived earlier in wagon trains under close guard.

"The Gaol"

Old Debtors' Prison, now called "The Gaol" by the British military, is filled to more than its capacity with American prisoners taken on Long Island, Kip's Bay, Harlem Heights and in the clashes in Westchester, Jersey and elsewhere. The 20-year-old, massive stone structure formerly housed mostly short-term occupants who could not meet their financial obligations. Now it is a stench-hole smelling of death.

Constructed when the city had only 10,530 inhabitants and 2,000 buildings which were clustered largely at the island's southern tip, it was known in 1756 as "The New Gaol." It had been built on the northeastern corner of The Commons, or "The Fields," as they were called, that lay along the high road to Boston.

The imposing, three-story, rough rock-constructed building with its underground vaults and dungeons, is topped by a cupola housing the alarm and fire bell. Straddling the outskirts of the city's residential and commercial development, the frighteningly impressive prison has stood as an admonition to all visitors to pay their debts.[3] And generally all visitors and residents have been sufficiently impressed to do so.

Now, marching into the crowded compounds by the hundreds, the Mount Washington prisoners bring the total number of Americans under British captivity to more than 4,000. The tremendous influx sends British officers frantically searching throughout the city for additional gaols into which to pack their rebel victims.

Captain Cunningham, the Provost Marshal and Commissary of His Majesty's Forces in America, who had demoniacally enjoyed presiding over the execution of Captain Nathan Hale in September, has not counted on providing for almost 3,000 more rebel prisoners. To Cunningham it becomes another aggravating duty taking up his time. Annoyed, he requires Howe's city occupation officers to commandeer more buildings for additional prison space. Added responsibilities do not improve the commissary's bad humor but do add to his irascible disposition which eventually reflects itself in his inhumane treatment of rebel prisoners.

Therefore, Cunningham, who is particularly irritable this morning following one of his weekend drunken orgies, is in an ugly mood. The necessity of having to put one of his own well trained, Tory American deputies into a cell reserved for raving maniacs when the gaoler went berserk after slaying his own son, has added to his troubles.

" 'Good' gaolers like old 'Ed The Whip' Kearney are hard to come by!"

In order to gain time in the search for additional prison space, the provost marshal orders all prisoners to be paraded for public exhibition near the Jewish Burial Grounds. Much to the commissary's disappointment, "no insult is offered them, nor any public huzzaing or rejoicing as is usual on similar and less important occasions."[4]

After that, the unfortunates, still unfed for over 48 hours, are marched away in different directions. Some have been siphoned off toward the large stone gaol. Another massive batch is led off to the new Bridewell Prison.

Others are escorted off to the two sugar houses, the Brick Presbyterian Church, the Middle Dutch Church, the French Church, the King's College buildings and into the underground chambers of the City Hall. Still others are parceled off to be placed in the dungeons of the old fort at Bowling Green.

Were it not that many high British officials and many of the military attend the services at 12-year-old St. Paul's Chapel on the west side of Broadway, it too would have been commandeered as an emergency prison today. The stately inspiring edifice with its beautiful English, Gothic-like steeple, is the Sunday gathering place for all the British and Tory elite among the loyal subjects of the Crown.

St. Paul's fortunately survived the city's great fire two months ago. And now it is surviving the "stigma" of being converted into a military prison, a fate that has befallen many of the city's other places of worship.

Churches, homes and other buildings, taken over by the King's army, have been clearly marked with the symbols, "G.R." The big initialed "George Rex" letters are intended to make it clear that all such marked structures are reserved specifically for His Majesty's armed forces.

St. Paul's Chapel has escaped such seizure and by order of the British command is not to be impounded for any military purposes. For the Sunday after-church gatherings at St. Paul's have become the edifice's chief contribution to the Loyalists' upper class and its influence within the city.

It is not too dissimilar from the social community services provided by Trinity Church until the Continental Army moved into the city. Those services ended in the fiery destruction of the church.

A Preacher And His Parishioners Protest A Prison In The Church

An Englishman who recently attended Sunday services at St. Paul's wrote home the other day, saying:

> This (St. Paul's Chapel) is a very neat church and attending it are some of the handsomest and best-dressed ladies I have ever seen in America. I believe most of them are whores.[5]

Unfortunately for the American captured heroes of Fort Washington, neither St. Paul's nor the Moravian Church was permitted to be used to help house the rebel prisoners. Had they also been taken over by the military for the purpose, it would not have been necessary to send many of the suffering captives into the overcrowded sugar houses and the dismal dungeons of the old forts.

But the Reverend Shewkirk of the Moravian Church and the members of his congregation protested to the British officers so vehemently that the order to use it was countermanded. Few of the officers had been given any idea of how much political influence the preacher and the church members exert in the port city's government.

It was 4 o'clock this afternoon when the military inspectors came to look over the church for its use as an adjunct jail. While the inspection was in progress, with the Moravian preacher loudly protesting the commandeering of his church for such a purpose, 400 of the starved, weakened, totally exhausted,[6] barefooted American Continentals—all in tattered filthy rags that pass as garments—were forced to stand outside shivering in the cold November wind. For them any refuge was a welcome one.

However, the preacher, joined by the bombastic voices of his influential Tory merchant parishioners and their threats, for they are instrumental in supplying the British army with its essentials, wins his argument. The unlucky rebels are then led away and into the freezing vaults under the old fort at Bowling Green.

In order to make sure that he is credited with having preserved the sanctity of the church by preventing its use as a prison, Preacher Shewkirk, who still blames the rebels for starting the city's fire, writes a self-exonerating explanation for the church records, stating:

> If these prisoners had come in, how much would our place have been ruined, as one may see by the North Church, not to mention the painful thought of seeing a place dedicated to our Saviour's praise made a habitation of darkness and uncleanliness.[7]

Since food shortages are severe and the military needs come first, the inhabitants of New York city run a poor second. Manhattan Island's British army is hard pressed for food supplies to meet its own use without having to feed the prisoners taken during a rebellion. So the prisoners' needs rate a very low third place.

However, out of pity and through the kindnesses of some of the prison guards and the humanity of some of the more sympathetic housewives among the inhabitants, some food and drink are finally slipped through to those at Bridewell and at The Gaol who will not be receiving their first prison meal until Thursday, three days from now.[8] It will then be over 100 hours since most of the Fort Washington captives had their last meal, Saturday morning before the battle.

Cunningham and his principal deputy, O'Keefe, have no patience with those under them who show any sympathy for rebel captives in their care. They only tolerate the outsiders who bring food for the prisoners because they can confiscate the choice morsels for themselves. And seldom do the prisoners get any of it.

The outsiders who come to the Bridewell Prison or to The Gaol nearby are subjected to close scrutiny by Cunningham and O'Keefe. Both men have their quarters in the latter. Nothing comes in or goes out of either place without one or the other approving it. Cunningham's quarters are to the right of the main entrance, O'Keefe's apartment behind the first barricade.

Beyond the prison grounds to the east are the gallows on the hill. Both prison compounds and gallows are located on the farthermost outskirts of the city. They adjoin the rapidly expanding "Canvas Town," a growing community by itself.

As the name implies, this section on the city's rim is a "town" of tents, some huts and a few dilapidated ramshackle buildings. It is the haven for the port's growing number of poor and destitute, some abandoned families from the half burned out part of the city, recluses, drifters and prostitutes.

The Canvas Town people, particularly the harlots, are the most generous in their frequent treks to the prisons. They carry food which some of them cannot afford to give away, but they seem to find a deep rewarding pleasure in sharing their own suffering with that of others worse off than they.

Though it is not quite in accord with the Reverend Shewkirk's philosophy relative to man's inhumanity to man, the Canvas Town people nurse a deep hatred for all kinds of oppression. They see in Cunningham and O'Keefe cruel men who symbolize hatred and oppression. And bitterly resenting all forms of tyranny inwardly, though not daring to express it outwardly in British-held New York, they attempt through kindness to counteract Cunningham's criminally tyrannical behavior.

Many of these outcasts of society, the jetsam and the flotsam of mankind's world, are themselves prisoners, prisoners of war's codes. For many of the women are the kidnaped victims of an unscrupulous dealer in human flesh named Trader Jackson.

Jackson is under contract to supply the King's troops in America with 3,500 women to meet the needs of the army's demands for the companionship of the opposite sex. In doing so, Jackson has shanghaied the innocents, blacks and whites, along with the doxies from London's streets. Though his acts are construed by society as criminal, he is automatically exculpated since the successful attainment of the end result for the invading forces is all that counts.

Therefore into the holds of his ships are thrown women from all walks of life who have been unfortunate enough to come within reach of his pirating crew of kidnaping vagabond seamen. In with the doxies go innocent young women who have fallen into the kidnaper's clutches. Then, stopping in the West Indies, the crews add more females to their cargoes after wild roundups to meet Jackson's quotas.

Enforced into prostitution in order to exist at all, these women soon lose all hope. They exist on a level hardly a step up from the city's poor, weak and the usual run of derelicts that whirl aimlessly around in the overcrowded dregs within the barrel bottoms of every city's steaming masses of congested humanity.

But since all are a part of society's spin-offs, they mix and exist with each other, some pulling the others down and others lifting the minds and hearts of still others upward. And so the "prisoners" under Jackson feel they somehow have a common denominator with the prisoners under Cunningham.

For under any rule, any government, or any segment of societal authority, when the governed can no longer control their destiny, even in some small way, disinterest, apathy and indolence join with corruption in dissolving the governed and destroying the government. Thus, when man discovers that he is unable to rise above the depths of degradation, futility fills his being.

And from out it all there then spreads infectious decay, bringing suicidal ruination and death to the governed and the self-destructing society.

And so, in their overwhelming sympathy the Canvas Town people seek to share their mutual misery. The fate of all persecuted mankind becomes their burden. Thus the Canvas Town people strive the hardest to feed the starving prisoners.

In years to come these outcasts of society will find a way to band with American, British and Hessian soldiers, escaped prisoners, runaway slaves, indentured escapees and some dislocated Indians forced from their lands. They will in time make their way into the western distant Ramapo Mountains across the river. There and northward, seeking independence, dignity and respect, they will form colonies, one of which will erroneously acquire the name, "Jackson Whites."

Defiant outcasts, they will rise to depict the indomitable will of man to exist. And rebels of a kind all their own, they will spring, almost entirely unknown, as one people and one culture from out the Eighteenth Century into the Twentieth, still bound together with a unique American identity.

They will be proud of the heritage of their differences, their singular culture, their will to succeed over every obstacle, every kind of adversity. And in those traits and in their background of heterogeniety they will, though alone, see themselves as pure Americans, as the true symbols of mixed cultures. And they will be known as "The Mountain People of the Ramapos."

Cunningham: Model For Iniquity

As Commissary of His Majesty's New York Prisons, Cunningham intends to prosper. As though striving to set the lowest possible standards of debased behavior in order that all of the ilk succeeding him for centuries to come, might have difficulty surpassing his depraved greed, bestiality and corruption, he and O'Keefe have worked out an elaborate system for swindling the prisoners out of everything—little though that is—which the poor wretches are supposed to get.

By slighting the prisoners a little at a time of all the provisions and supplies they are entitled to, the commissary and his deputy can the more swell their pockets and bellies. For the more the prisoners, the more will be the profits for their coffers. The more prisoners, the more food will there be to be embezzled. And the more "good" food and provisions that can be embezzled, the more there will be available for exchanging at a profit, for poorer quality food to give the prisoners.

As for the fate of his captives, Cunningham is heartlessly unconcerned. The tyrannical provost marshal is reputed to stop at nothing that will add to the miseries of his helpless victims. And neither will he hesitate to do everything that will add to his own wealth and comfort.

His bitter hatred for Americans finds vent in torturing his charges not only with searing-irons but by exposing them to bitter cold or extreme heat, if starving them does not bring the results he seeks. Whenever he is displeased with answers, or whenever an inmate has broken one of his innumerable rules, torturous punishment begins.

He forbids prisoners to see relatives or friends. Though some come long distances at great risks and much expense, pleading merely to see if their friend or kin is still alive, Cunningham concedes only to take whatever packages are brought and deliver them.

Very seldom do the unfortunates behind the bars ever know they have had visitors, no less that they had brought them packages. Packages, in Cunningham's opinion, are for him, not for incarcerated rebels.

Though beautifully clear spring water is close by and plentiful, the provost marshal orders that all inmates of the gaols be given only the muddy water to drink. This is the barreled rain water or that which has been collected from brackish, stagnant pools.

And when any of the captives are ill, or close to death, they are attended only by their fellow prisoners. It is rare that any surgeon visits the sick or dying. Generally the only time a doctor calls is when he arrives to declare the dead ready for burial.

So crowded together are the men that many are overcome by partial asphyxiation in their sleep one upon the other. This causes their bodies to weaken their resistance to disease, resulting in numerous cases of pleurisy. In short order the victim contracts other infections, unless he has been blessed by an exceptionally strong constitution.

And then with every illness comes the plaguing, debilitating dysentery attacks. When the thoroughly weakened human system

can take no more, death comes to end the useless struggle to hold
longer to a fleeting life.

No fires of any kind are allowed. No light, oil lamps or candles,
are permitted except those torches carried by the guards, regardless
of how dark the chambers or passageways may be. Always in the
prisons' dismal recesses, particularly in the darkness, are heard the
bat-like squeals of the ever-gnawing every-hungry rats.

Their beady little shining, white eyes eerily gleam out from
imaginary specters in the blackness like the hollow glowing sockets
of diabolically dancing demon dwarfs. They look like gargoyle
guardians, haunting the satanic outer chambers of the earth's
infernal place.

Occasionally the death-dealing pox-carriers will run over a man's
body or under his foot. If he nips too hard or too often, the
sleeking scavenger may find itself kicked up against the stone walls
of the prison.

Often an inmate in reckless fury will grab the biting, fighting
rodent and hurl it against the floor or wall with such force that
the mini-beast's entrails are splattered in all directions. And in
short time his cannibalistic cousins, brothers and sisters tear the
remaining carcass apart, devouring it down to the last drop of
blood.

Barred slits in the walls of the gaol cells are the only openings
to the outside world. Only a few of these have shutters on the
glassless window openings. Those with such shields offer some
protection from the weather. But the slits without them can soon
let in the blustery winds and weather, inundating the cells with
rain, ice and snow.

Though the two gaol buildings could not be much worse were
they used for cattle, the conditions in the sugar house prisons are
even more horrible. These old, dilapidated, rat-infested warehouse
structures have still narrower slits in the stone walls. So narrow are
the openings that no bars or iron grates are necessary.

One observer will write later from New York next summer
saying:

> I saw every narrow aperture of those stone walls filled with human
> heads, face above face, seeking (to get) a portion of the external air.[9]

Cunningham's weekly food rations per prisoner are two pounds
of hard tack and two pounds of raw salt pork. No means for
cooking the meat is provided. And it is very seldom that the
maximum amount of the rations reach each man. Purposely the

portions are measured out fraudulently short, and always the amount is decreased for any and all minor infractions of the prison commissary's ruthless rules. The accumulated savings, in one way or another, end up in Cunningham's bulging pockets with the deputy always receiving his "fair" share.

In the drunken orgies that terminate the Provost Marshal's frequent banquets, he invariably orders some of the prisoners to parade before his guests. Pointing to one or the other, he will say, "This is a damned rebel captain!" or "This is a damned rebel Whig!" Then, from that point on he will carry on a humiliating monologue, denouncing each man and the cause for which he fought.

Many American notables are often marched out for his amusement and for that of his banquet guests. One of these whom the prison captain took great delight in persecuting was the defiant Colonel Ethan Allen who, until his exchange last month, snapped back boldly at the furious provost marshal, refusing to allow the enemy "captain" to intimidate him.

As a result, Cunningham, knowing military protocol's recognition of rank, feared the colonel and possible reprisals. He soon drew in his horns and discontinued his harassment of the Vermont leader of the daring Green Mountain Boys.

Allan, who was captured at Ticonderoga, imprisoned for awhile in Boston, taken to England and brought back to New York for incarceration, had steadfastly repulsed every effort of the British to get him to defect. Cunningham's ridicule followed the unsuccessful British attempts to convert the Vermonter.

Others, equally devoted to the American cause, will be similarly tormented by the provost marshal as they are brought into custody. Among them will be such figures as: Judge John Fell of Bergen County in Jersey; Captain Travis of Virginia; William Miller of Westchester County in New York; and such officers as Major Brinton Payne, Major Levi Wells, Captain Van Zandt, Captain Randolph and Captain Flahaven.

Thirty Sleep Where Eight Were Crowded

It is physically easy for Cunningham to get the prisoners of high military rank, or those with notable political reputations down to The Gaol's main prison hall and banquet room. For the rough brown rock and stone building has three floors, and it is on the second floor, on the northeast side of the structure, where the high ranking officers and political prisoners are crammed into cells. These second floor "pens" are almost directly over the banquet hall.

Into one of these cells in which six or eight men overcrowd it, the prison's administrator now assigns 20 to 30 depending upon the size of the cell block. They are all so jammed together on the oak floors that they must turn on their sides at once in unison owing to the cramped conditions.

The highest ranking officer among them decides upon the moment to turn. He calls out either, "Left!" or "Right!" His command is followed by all the men at once rolling over on their sides in the direction called.

Far worse are the conditions in the cellar dungeons of these prison buildings, but since the second floor's largest cell block is the luxury area, reserved for only the highest ranking army captives and political prisoners, it has become known as "Congress Hall." Cunningham so called it in order to heap further derision upon the rebellion and the Continental Congress.

The large cell block, or "Congress Hall," is at the head of the stairway leading down into the first floor's main room. So when the commissary wants to entertain his guests, his guards have only to march a few selected inmates down the stairs into the main hall.

Cunningham has not bothered to give names to the dungeon rooms in the "bastille's" underground caverns. There the prisoners are hemmed in by windowless walls two feet thick. And there, under The Gaol's first floor, are three massive arched vaults nine feet high in their centers. These are enclosed by heavy iron grated doors, locked with giant bolts and reinforced by heavy chains.

There are no exterior openings. The only daylight that trickles into the subterranean dungeons filters down from the first floor above by way of the wide stone-block stairs. It spreads mistily through the blackened chambers, barely reaching some of the gaunt and grim, tear-stained, sallow-faced martyrs. Some, whose minds are going, try to cup it in their hands and foolishly attempt to hold tightly to each precious ray of the long and arduously reflected speck from the sun they seldom see.

Occasionally a gray rat can be seen scurrying across the stone floors, or down the stairs with a morsel of food gripped tightly in its jaws. Determined to survive at others' expense and prey upon the weakness, stupidity, kindness or gullibility of man, the smart rodent snatches his meal from out the hands of a sleeping prisoner or from off the plate of a gaoler who has let down his guard.

Sometimes the rays of light fall behind the slinking varmint, its long, scaly, slithery tail waving behind it. Then suddenly on the wall the rodent's shadow becomes a dark replica of itself, doubling even tripling its actual size.

And the overly enlarged morsel of food it carries becomes grossly enlarged in the silhouetted reflection, taking on imaginary shapes of anything the mind may fancy. The brazen among the prisoners then make guesses as to what it most resembles.

Some declare, with hopeful futility, it is some part of either Cunningham's or O'Keefe's detested anatomy. Another sees it as the whole body of a man. And still another declares it is an eaglet or the wing of the eagle mother herself.

Filth, famine, stench and death are everywhere throughout the prison except in the great hall and banquet room. It is here every new arrival must come as though before an emperor to receive his penal sentence.

The entire guard stands at parade rest, their arms bristling as the provost marshal sits before his table flanked by his deputy. One by one the new prisoners are marched before him. Each man gives his rank, his size, age and whatever other information Cunningham and O'Keefe can get out of him.

It is there the unfortunates first hear the dragging, terrifying sounds of chains and bolts, of bars being banged by empty drinking cups and of locks struck open and then shut. It is there the deputy writes down in the record book what has been taken from the prisoner, information that will never see the light of day. It is here the victim first hears the clanking of enormous iron chains and watches as the captive preceding him enters the dark vestibule and totally disappears as though swallowed up and devoured by the great gray stones of the prison building.

It is here Freedom bows her head and turns away, and, grieving, flees the site.

For many of the young men, the scenes about them will recall their long past school days. For, to some, there will come to mind the Homeric account of the Greek hero, Odysseus, entering the Stygian gates of Erebus. And for many of them it will become far worse than that.

It is the horrible hunger and thirst of their bodies that make the Mount Washington captives realize the unbelievable accounts they have heard of the enemy's prisons were not exaggerated. They could excuse not being fed during the long march into the city they had so valiantly defended just 60 days ago. They could even excuse being given brackish muddy water on their long march in. But now, days later, there is little food for them and few signs for providing any sustenance at all.

One of the last prisoner detachments en route from the fort stopped tonight at a farm house south of Mount Washington. Among the prisoners is Continental Army Colonel Thomas Bull. Bull will eventually reveal that his comrades were not fed at all through Saturday's battle, received nothing at all to eat Sunday and have gone throughout this entire day again without any kind of victuals. Their first meal of hardtack will be given them tomorrow morning after spending the night in the Methodist Meeting House.[10]

Another contingent arrived this afternoon and was marched directly into the Bridewell Prison. There conditions are said to be worse than in The Gaol itself.

With them is Private Oliver Woodruff who will live to tell that his party of captives survived on only muddy water from the day of the battle on the 16th to Thursday, the 21st. He will declare that it was not until the sixth day that they received their first meager rations of hardtack and pork.

For all of these 2,837 prisoners of war it is the beginning of one of the most tragic accounts in the American Rebellion. Few are destined to survive the destructive forces that will be exerted upon them by one man's depraved mentality, a mentality that will bring about the useless deaths of thousands of his helpless fellow beings owing to his position of autocracy with a mind twisted by prejudices in the body of a predaceous animal.

Counteracting Malevolence, Benevolence Eternally Rises

But, as always, there is ever a counteracting force that rises within the breast of civilized man to fight iniquity. Most often it rises too late and too slow for immediate help but in time for some future prevention. Such are the efforts of the American, Elias Boudinot.

Boudinot will be so moved by the horror stories he hears about the New York British prisons and the terrible prices being paid by his imprisoned countrymen, that he will act in an effort to do something about it. On his own credit, and at the risk of losing everything he owns in an attempt to help feed and clothe the Continental army's captured rebels, Boudinot will raise $40,000.

Like nature striving ever to counteract the destructive forces of man, the benevolent of man's species strive ever to counteract the malevolence within his kind. And among these are such patriots as Haym Salomon and Boudinot. They are not alone. But they are among the doers up in front.

A lawyer, statesman, churchman and ardent patriot, who puts his country and his fellow man foremost, Boudinot is one of the principal founders of the First Continental Congress. But soon he will become angrily aroused over what the colonists in the states will hear about Cunningham and his prisons. And from his home in Elizabeth, the fiery Jerseyan will spread his appeal throughout the new nation. His efforts will bring attention and relief to the suffering American captives when the British high command is accused of inhumane treatment of its prisoners.

However, the British leadership is concentrating upon winning the war, and the care of the captured will remain very much the same under Cunningham's continued administration. Though Boudinot's untiring efforts will bring some help for the incarcerated Americans, the New York prisons will remain abodes of horror.

And so now, with the war going in favor of the King's army and only a few of His Majesty's troops captives in the hands of the rebels—and they mostly Hessians—there are not many rays of hope for the captured Yankees and Buckskins. Only those officers and men who can be exchanged with the enemy for persons of comparable standing, have any chance of escape from the loathsome walls and Cunningham's clutches, unless they defect.

Except for those few fortunate ones who are exchanged, manage to escape, or the handful whose friends are able to buy their way out, most are destined to die, helplessly caught under the supreme rule of a maniac.

And yet the only sin for which they stand committed is that they defended a cause for a renewed birth of freedom and independence in an era spawned out of Great Britain's own Magna Charta which, they rationalize, supposedly extended man the right to do exactly what they have done.

Yet such thoughts as these and others that fill their perplexed minds, asking of themselves and of their god, "Why me?" bring no comfort to those arriving at their last breath.

But relief in death seldom comes mercifully. Some will starve. Some will succumb to asphyxiation and to heat prostration. Some will die of scourgings. Some of frostbite. Many of the dreaded jail fever, "The Plague," as smallpox and typhus spread from one to another. And some will be hanged by the provost marshal on false accusations for alleged crimes of which they are innocent.

As horrifying as those last hours may be for the dying, they will often be even more horrendous for their surviving fellow inmates. It will be the strong and the "untouched" who will watch through the long nights, listening to the moaning of the last ebbing sounds of life from the mouths of those they knew and the impatience of the rats, gnawing away beneath the oaken floors will be the only accompaniment. It will be the living who will hope and pray to die less miserably.

Only on the prison ships which are now being prepared to house more captives, will conditions likely be worse. For these will likely include many of the sick and diseased prisoners whose illnesses are considered contagious.

One of these abandoned old hulks is the former British ship, *New Jersey*. Since it is no longer considered seaworthy, it stands in the harbor ready as an adjunct to Cunningham's prison system. It will soon acquire a reputation as a tomb for the living and the dead unequaled to any of Cunningham's other gaols.

In this one gruesome grisly sepulcher alone, now lying grimly with its deserted sisters isolated in New York's bay, it will be recorded that 11,000 Americans perished.[11] But the gaols on shore will also count their victims by the thousands. Even though their crowded conditions are to be occasionally alleviated by the use of the British navy's unrepairable hulks, when jail fever reaches its peak, as it will in the coming year, the death carts will be rolling through the streets day and night.

It will be worse at the Middle Dutch Church prison than anywhere else for it is there the dying incurables will be sent. From eight to ten bodies will be carted away from this church prison almost every morning.

All the corpses will be dumped into ditches on the far outskirts of the city.[12] There is where old Gaoler Kearney's son was buried after his father drowned him. But it was a burial the brutal deputy did not attend, for after he discovered what he had done and lost his mind as its consequence, he was dumped into the cell from which he will never emerge alive.

Under such intolerable prison conditions and under such sufferings, it is inconceivable to the Crown's army command that the adamant prisoners consistently refuse opportunities to defect and enlist in the King's armed forces. This, to Cunningham, is a reflection upon his system indicating he is not severe enough in his methods.

Despite constant proddings and enticing inducements, only a few of the American rebels defect. And among these few "the idea of an opportunity to eventually desert (is) probably the moving cause."[13]

Conjectures as to their fate, the injustices of King George, rationalization as to their right to fight for liberties as extracted from King John at Runnymede, hunger, food and death—all are bits of conversation that Private Oliver Woodruff hears, vehemently expressed by his cell mates. Woodruff, along with 19 others, is crowded into the northwest cell block on the second floor of Bridewell Prison.

From Woodruff's Window In the Northwest Cell Block

The cramped pen boasts one barred opening, or window slit, without shutters. It looks out upon the distant Hudson flowing down from the north. And directly under the window is Woodruff's place on the hard, wooden floor.

He pays little attention to his fellow inmates and their complaints, their concern about "rights" and their fate. Instead he is wondering how he can devise a method for keeping out the wind and water when the cold storms of winter begin to blow. For Private Oliver Woodruff is bent upon only one thing, survival.

Fortunately, he tells himself, he is not among those poor souls who have been assigned to the dark, windowless dungeon chambers in Bridewell's damp underground cellars two floors below. He is thankful for what he has and resigned to make the most of it. A practical, ingenious youth, who has learned to overcome difficulties, he will eventually design something to keep out the severe weather.

Right now he is more interested in looking out through the window opening and beyond it northward. There he can barely discern the jutting rock bluff on the Palisades. There he can see in the evening's softly settling twilight the flickering lights of campfires. And right now he becomes more interested in looking out northwards and remembering.

Two weeks ago young Woodruff was one of the gunner's helpers on The Bluff Rock Battery. And now, he sadly reminds himself, he would still be there had he not asked to be transferred to Rawlings' regiment in order to be with his Pennsylvania friends on Mount Washington.

His transfer went through too easily. How much he wanted it then! But now, how much he regrets that he was given it!

As he looks at the slowly setting sun and the peaceful Palisades across the river, then up toward the battery on The Rock, he bemoans the fate he made for himself and to which he is now resigned. He wonders why the Creator did not give man the great range in foresight he gave him in his hindsight?

Woodruff is destined to be one of the 800 fortunates out of over 2,800 Fort Washington captives arriving in New York today who will live to be free again. He will live to become ninety years old,[14] ever respectfully remembering the lives and the deaths of so many of his comrades through and after the Battle for Fort Washington.

But 2,000 of those men captured Saturday will pay in full the price that Liberty's name exacts from many. For that lady, too, is a tyrant of a kind, requiring as she does that the maimed, the taken, and the dead pay disproportionately for the rights, the privileges and the daily pleasures of the living who cavort freely at her feet.

The long rolls of the dead that are to be carted out of Cunningham's prisons will eventually lie heavily upon the provost marshal's head. For the troubled conscience of malevolent men seldom escapes the hunt-down by the two slowly pursuing huntsmen, Retribution and Justice. So it will be for Cunningham.

Despite the long list of atrocities for which the prison captain could be charged, fifteen years from now he will find himself convicted of merely forgery in England. For that comparatively minor offense, in light of the long list of heinous crimes that stain his name, the former Provost Marshal and Commissary of Prisons for His Majesty's Army in North America will be sentenced to death and hanged on the gallows August 10, 1791.

To Private Woodruff and other survivors of Cunningham's odious reign over American prisoners in New York, the commissary's execution will exemplify delayed justice and the amazing, circuitously winding course which Justice may have to sometimes take in order to exact avengingly the bitter price for retribution.

So the survivors will shake their heads in wonder and think only of the atrocious, capital crimes that the sealed mouths of their comrades could bring before the indicted villainous murderer of prisoners in the imaginary Tribunal of the murdered dead.

According to accounts that will be passed on from mouth to mouth, but for which there will be found no official confirmation, it will be said of Cunningham that, upon his condemnation to death by hanging, he made a dying confession stating:

"I was appointed Provost Marshal to the Royal Army, which placed me in a situation to wreak vengeance on the Americans. I shudder to think of the murders I have been accessory to, both with and without orders from the Government, especially while we were in New York, during which time there were more than 2,000 prisoners starved in the churches by stopping their rations which I sold.

"There were also 275 American prisoners and obnoxious persons executed, which were thus conducted.

"A guard was dispatched from the Provost about half-past 12 o'clock at night to the Barrack street and the neighborhood of the upper barracks, to order the people to shut their window shutters and put out their lights, forbidding them at the same time to look out of their windows and doors on pain of death.

"After (this) the unfortunate prisoners were conducted, gagged, just behind the upper barracks, and hung without ceremony, and there buried by the black pioneer of the Provost."[15]

Howe Plans His "Final" Stroke

General Howe's great victory has brought him glowing praise and accolades from his officers who are citing it as a brilliant stroke of genius. But it will be some time before news of the achievement reaches England and his accomplishment properly acclaimed.

Though Sir William was able today to at last see Mrs. Loring and relax with his "Sultana" at his Beekman House headquarters, he is determined that this time he is not going to lose his present, hard-earned strategic advantages over his ever-elusive, rebel opponent by dilatory actions and pleasureful procrastinations. Now is the time to follow-up. Now is the time for business.

At his headquarters at Delancey's Mill's in Westchester, he, General Lord Cornwallis and his staff have earlier today put the finishing touches on a surprise plan to invade the Jerseys. It is to be a swift and mighty assault upon the remnants of the Continental Army under the rebel Leader. Some of the King's officers believe that finally a stroke has been devised that will end the aggravating American uprising.

Howe's plan calls for crossing the Hudson, thus slicing the Americans' northward communications. Then, with a possible surprise maneuver, he will surround and besiege the American Commander and his troops at Fort Lee. With the help of Admiral Howe's men-of-war and the transports on the Hudson, he will move in on the mountain fortress in a wipe-up action.

The massive sweep will, it is proposed, drive through East and then West Jersey into Pennsylvania. Once the British forces cross the Delaware and march triumphantly into Philadelphia, the redcoats, supported by the Hessian forces, should be able to capture the Continental Congress.

Utmost secrecy surrounds every detail of the plan and the many operations attending it. All along the river's east shore there is a bustling of activity that always foreshadows something big about to happen. But all movements are skillfully concealed from the rebel observers across the Hudson. And only a few rank and file redcoats know exactly what is in the wind, though many guess correctly.

In the minds of the British army's top command is the hope that the operation will become the long-awaited coup de grace. There is a strong spirit of confidence that at last the remainder of the rebel army is about to be destroyed.

The selection of a commander to head the amphibious invasion and lead the British forces over the northern end of the Palisadean range, then eight miles down south through the valley to come up and around for the encirclement of Fort Lee, is therefore, an important decision. It is a much coveted assignment, the outcome of which could be momentous. In the event all goes well, His Majesty, King George III, will heap high honors upon the head of the victorious commander of such an expedition.

Logically, General Knyphausen should be given this prized command in view of his corps' outstanding success last Saturday. However, politically, if a Hessian-led operation should indeed bring down the curtain and spell the finale of the two-year rebellion, it would not sit too well back in London.

The embarrassment it would cause is not difficult to imagine. No Britisher would want to hear that it took a Hessian general and his troops to put a stop to one of Great Britain's family quarrels.

So the decision requires some tactful diplomacy on Howe's part. He therefore renames Fort Washington, "Fort Knyphausen," in honor of the Prussian general and, except for a token force of German jagers and grenadiers, orders Knyphausen and his corps to take over the former rebel fort and its mount.

Again the Bag Is Set To Catch the Wily Fox

This gives credit to the Prussian general and accords his troops their earned honors while, at the same time, it opens the way for Howe to hand the invasion operation and its potential, particularly in prestige, over to a member of the British nobility. Made almost to order in fitting that assignment is the 38-year-old British Earl of

Cornwallis who so commendably stormed Fort Washington's eastern slope.

Nine years younger than Sir William, Major General Earl Charles Cornwallis, now in the 20th year of his service in His Majesty's army, is reaching an enviable peak in his career. He has served in both the House of Commons and the House of Lords, but he has yet to attain wide recognition as a military strategist despite his commendable record in Germany during the Seven Years' War.

And so Howe names him to direct the invasion of the Jerseys. Opposing the Earl is an older man, for the American Commander-in-Chief is six years up on the rather heavy, somewhat awkward Cornwallis who, nevertheless, ranks among the elite officers of the British army.

There is a slight cast in Cornwallis's right eye. And it is that eyelid that flutters for just a fraction of a second, revealing the nobleman's elation as Howe hands him the orders and the plans, Cornwallis's part in the entrapping operation.

It is a command he had expected. Except for the brief flutter of his eyelid there was no other display of emotion. The Earl now has the much sought after opportunity of outwitting the ever-escaping Fox who, after Fort Washington, certainly must be badly limping and lying extremely vulnerable on the Hudson's west bank.

Cautiously Cornwallis now devotes all his thoughts and summons all his accumulated knowledges of military strategy to encompass just one thing: the bagging of his quarry.

Early tomorrow morning Lord Cornwallis will have completed the assembling of his British and some few Hessian troops inland above King's Bridge. None of them will be informed until they are on the Jersey shore of what is in store. Only a handful of highly trusted officers on Cornwallis's staff know the objective behind the preparations, but all the troops have their suspicions.

Under this pressure neither Sir William, nor any members of his command, are concerned over American prisoners and their state under Cunningham. In fact, it is expected that soon more captives will be coming in by the thousands. So Howe leaves the problems of the prisoners and their confinement to his subordinates.

And out of the northwest window slit in the cell block on the Bridewell's second floor, Prisoner Woodruff looks longingly on the encroaching darkness over the cold fall November night. He watches the black shadows of the Palisades creeping eastward over the river and gazes up toward the Palisadean rock bluff.

Then he focuses his eyes across from there at the former

American citadel, now in enemy hands. Suddenly the sinking sun's dark tentacles plunge him and the fading sight before his eyes under night's mantle.

Obscured from Woodruff's hungry, longing vision northward, far off on the Bluff Rock Barbette's ramparts, a sentry tries to show Second Lieutenant Levy what appears to be a number of flatboats some distance upriver strung along the east bank.

Surveillance Upriver

Owing to the Hudson's bend northwestward just beyond the Bluff Rock, it is difficult even in broad daylight to observe river movements very far north. The zig-zag projections of the cliffs obliterate what little can be seen along either bank of the river beyond the Spuyten Duyvil. So the stream's slight bend north-westward prevents a clear view of the eastern shore beyond that point.

It is for this reason that the northern, or left flank outpost for Fort Lee is located so far upriver at Sneden's Landing. It has always served as a very valuable observatory post for any enemy movements taking place north of the Spuyten Duyvil, upriver as far as the Tappan Zee. Thus Fort Lee Bluff and its outpost garrison at Sneden's Landing give the Americans more than 16 miles of northward surveillance of the enemy's side of the river, from Fort Lee to beyond Tarrytown. This surveillance has been doubled since the fall of Fort Washington.

But the settling darkness destroys any possibility for the sentinel to point out to Levy what he thought he had noticed in the distance. All that can be seen now are countless enemy campfires on and along old Mount Washington. Like a sparkling necklace around the earth's collar as it rises up from the water, they dance like enchained fireflies up and down the river's eastern shores.

Levy does notice that there appear to be far more fires than were noticed last night, especially in the area between the Duyvil and Phillips's at Wepperham,[16] south of Dobb's Ferry on the east bank.

Asher reports this and the sentinel's observations to John Gray. He in turn passes it on to Major Blodget. Blodget mentions it to Colonel Bedford and Bedford reports it routinely on to General Irvine's staff adjutant.

But since no exact observations were noticed and the sentinel was not sure of what he saw, no one seems very much concerned.

Particularly since Howe does not follow-up his pursuits, or gains, closely one upon the other.

Once again there is spreading throughout the Fort Lee encampment the belief that Howe will settle down now for the winter. The increasingly colder days and still colder nights give much credence to the likelihood, especially since the chilling north winds have occasionally dumped down a few light snow showers.

Thus, some officers and most of the enlisted men have tried to convince themselves the campaign is over for the winter. And some contend this time Howe is surely retiring with his Sultana into winter quarters on Manhattan's tip. The General and his staff are taking no chances. The evacuation of the fort and the withdrawal of the army into West Jersey is ordered to proceed at an even more rapid pace.

Supplies and some materiels, but very little armament, have been moved out and more go daily. Much is quietly being transferred over toward Lord Stirling's country in a place carefully chosen by The General among the hills west of Morris's Town. It is believed by some that Lord Stirling may have suggested the place.

The continuing difficult task has been carried out again throughout this long hard day on The Mountain but not without much grumbling and complaining. Some of the officers agree with their troops that the evacuation is not necessary and that the well-protected Fort Lee encampment and its guardian batteries on the Bluff Rock are the safest places for wintering through until the spring. But despite the grumbling the evacuation continues.

For soldiers and inhabitants it has been one more very depressing day at Fort Lee. The depression, rooted in fear and uncertainty, has spread down among the valley people. All have still to come out of the trough of despond resulting from Saturday's great losses. And now, with the certainty that the fort will be abandoned, the inhabitants are fearful of what might soon befall them.

It is not only the Hudson River people who quake now. Word of the tragedy on Manhattan has reached the Congress and all the thirteen states. Gloom spreads more rapidly than sunshine among the Americans who have seldom enjoyed the thrill of experiencing good news.

Since the battle on the mount the Tories are finding converts and recruits more plentiful than ever before. Even the most optimistic of the patriots are beginning to believe that the end of the rebellion is near at hand.

Only the American Chief, his staff and his Council of War, reflect hope and confidence. Seemingly, taking a cue from their Leader, they now appear stern, tight-lipped and unemotional.

There are no raised voices in behind the whale oil lighted windows of the Baummeister house under the cliff and the lonely sentinel by his fire on the high Bluff Rock. But a lengthy talk is coming to an end as Gray, Marie Louise, and Papa Pete finally give up their argument with Elaine.

It began like a crash of thunder when Elaine, in her usual calm, decisive manner, told her husband and her parents at the dinner table that she was going to leave with the camp women for West Jersey, and that she had made up her mind to stay with her husband wherever the war carried him.

Despite an hour of heated argument, John, her father and mother have not been able to change her mind. For it is a course of action she has been contemplating for some time. Tonight she made her decision clear.

Even the horse and wagon she will drive are settled. She will take her own mare which Bourdette uses only rarely anymore for replace-lending any lame horse on the light stage passing through. And she will take the light covered wagon that Ma Kearney gave her and the Baummeisters when the fish-woman acquired her fish cart. Furthermore, for she had it all planned before she spoke her mind tonight, since some of the camp women with wagons are carting some of the sick and wounded, she will take a few with her to the Newark hospital, or farther.

John angrily tries to talk her out of the whole idea, pointing out that her place is with her parents until the war is over, while Paul thinks it a great idea and asks if he can go along. Marie Louise, knowing her daughter, has given up any further attempts to dissuade her. As for·Papa Pete, he too knows his daughter. Reluctantly he gives up arguing, sits back, scowls and puffs his pipe furiously. In no time he succeeds in driving everyone, coughing and choking, away from the table.

Shaking his head, he mumbles to himself, "Dot Molly Korban! Dots vot it ist! Ellie vas torkeeng mit her! Dot's vot! Dot Ellie' ist got humbug ideas! Dot's vot!"

There will be much talk, some useless arguing and little sleep in the Baummeister house tonight. But there is not very much hope that Elaine will change her mind.

. . . Or Westward Into the Country

The sentinel, relieved from duty on the Bluff Rock ramparts, has just completed his supper of salt pork and Indian mash stew heated over the cooking fire on the rock's edge. Since the fire is high, he uses its light to scribble a letter home despite a slightly chilling north wind at his back.

Under the dateline, "Fort Lee, November 17, 1776," he writes in part:

"The enemy have been busy all day, in removing the stores at Fort Washington, and have burnt several houses, for what reason we cannot conjecture. As this post, which was intended to keep the communication open, has now become useless it will probably be abandoned as soon as the stores can be removed. Whether the army will move higher up the river or westward into the country, I imagine is not yet agreed on."[17]

28

Tuesday, November 19. . .

Soon Comes the Hour for Departure

The Wounded Widow Heroine Passes Through

Yesterday Elaine took over the task of assisting the wounded Molly Corbin. She helped her out of her blood-soaked clothing and saw to it that the woman had a complete wardrobe for the long ride. She will go by army wagon to Hackensack's hospital, via private stage to Newark's hospital and then on to the Philadelphia one.

The General has ordered a special stage and officer detail for the journey. And so Elaine, who attended her needs, prepared her for the trip.

The post's surgeon gave the hamlet's lately shunned wife of John Gray a free hand, saying he himself could do no more than Madam Gray. And besides, the army physician admits he is used to doctoring men, not women.

So in their short time together yesterday, Elaine and Molly Corbin, who are only five years apart in age, had learned much about each other.

Several of the hospital helping housewives came in when Greene and his aides were not visiting the eyewitness participant of the battle and asking countless questions. And, from Molly's little observation of the other women, she realized they looked upon Elaine with a feeling of contempt, for some unaccountable reason.

It was not long before the garrulous fraus made it clear to the wounded widow that, "Elaine Gray is a neutral!"

It was little Hans Onderdonk's mother, whose brother-in-law's White Plains death has made her dislike neutrals, who is the self-acclaimed spokeswoman for the women patriots of The Mountain. Polly was the first to slight Elaine after her defiantly open declaration of neutrality on the Bluff Rock. And Polly continued speaking her mind before the heroine. But she always waited until Elaine was out of earshot.

When Elaine left the special hospital tent assigned to the wounded widow, the women hurled their little darts for the benefit of the heroine's ears. But the female artillery fighter, though in pain and suffering agonizing mental grief for the lost man she had loved and followed into battle, still had the keen power of woman's intuition.

Though she has been long part of an army camp and a man's military world, the sharp-eyed, sharp-eared Irish girl quickly discerns anew the eternal interplay of women against woman. Regardless, she had been Elaine's ally from the start, neutral or not.

Polly and the Widow Clara Edsall and their obviously planned dialogue exchange, were easily discerned. Particularly amusing to the suffering woman gunner were their words on Elaine's independent attitude.

"How zat Ellie Gray kin stan' up 'afore peoples 'nd tell zem she's a nootrell 'un, I kin fer za life ov' me not see," says Polly, shaking her head negatively from side to side. And, answering her, also obviously for Molly's benefit, the Widow Clara declared, "Nor I! Why, right before her eyes, she can see here men, and even women agivin' of their lives for liberty, just as done this poor soul! Neutral! Bah!"

It was Polly's naive assumption that this kind of thinking was exactly what would please the ears of the states' first war heroine. But the "war heroine," her eyes closed, gave no sign of having heard anything. In silence, she had listened until the ferry-master's daughter returned after emptying the washbowl water and the chamber pot, jobs that neither Polly or Clara ever volunteer to perform.

Elaine, tight-lipped, her petite resolute chin poked slightly outward under her firmed mouth, had resolved to ignore the taunts of the older women. She had known them both all of her life, and, she told herself, she still loved them dearly.

Would not she, she pondered, feel the same were she in their place?

The bride of less than four fortnights, who learned from her Indian friends to cast her eyes through the eyes of others, tries to understand the housewives' feelings of hostility. In fact, Elaine believes she is better able to understand their attitude than her own outburst which was not against The Cause so much as it was out of love for her husband.

But Elaine has Dutch blood. And Dutch blood seldom changes its flow of direction even when it knows it is going the wrong way.

As soon as she re-entered the tent, the ferry-master's daughter knew that words regarding her had passed. The sudden stillness under the canvas made it evident.

Molly broke the silence. Clothed and sitting up on the hospital cot, she was obviously somewhat tired by her visitors and their questions despite their kindnesses. Word of her deed brought the curious and the well-meaning as well as the high ranking officers, but only a select few with passes could get through the guards. The parades in and out of the tent had been courteously conducted but were not restful.

Other than answering questions, Molly Corbin, except with Elaine, had not been very communicative. However, now the Erin-born woman addressed her remarks, particularly, it seemed, to Polly and Clara while Elaine courteously looked up occasionally as she listened. Though paying attention, The Lieutenant's wife continued making some extra bandages for the wounded woman to take with her. The four were alone in the tent as she spoke.

" 'Tis nigh toime ta go," she began with her undeniable Irish accent, and speaking with obvious pain. " 'Tis griteful Oi am fer ye many kindnesses . . . frem ahll of ye. When the redkoots kom—'n ye may be shor they'll be a'komin' soon—ye best had be neither fer, or a'gin 'em . . . Else ye 'n yer 'omes 'n yer larnds will be a'sufferin'.

" 'Tis not another whye for ye wimmen if yer marn be awhye frem ye, ceptin' ta be nootrell. 'N even be he wee ye, 'tis barter ye both be nootrell thon ta be tarn frem each other ahwye. 'Tis the arnly whye nowwa fer ye wimmen weeout yer marn, or wee 'im.

"Ay, 'tis different when ye air by thar side! Shor 'n Oim not tarkin' 'bout thot! When ye air wee 'im, ye mus' help protect and defend 'im as best ye karn. When ye air not, it farls upon ye ta protect 'n defend, as best ye karn, what is 'is and yarrs by yeself.

" 'Tis the men, God love 'em, who air alwhyse the weakest of us. Shor, 'n Oi know mine was. 'N 'tis ye wimmen air the strongest. 'Tis ye who air 'is unseen drivers fer roight or wrong.

"Think well on't. 'Tis wimmen alone who steers the whye the world is 'n the whye it goes. 'Tis wimmen who could 'ave stopped ahll this warrin' . . . 'n mybe 'tis wimmen somewhere who started it by not a'steppin' on't when they should . . . 'N 'tis ahll Oi 'ave ta sigh, ceptin' may the good Lord bless 'n keep ye, 'n ahll yer own, sife through these ahfull bard toimes."

Polly looked at Clara. Clara back at Polly. Elaine finished her bandage wrapping, wondering if Molly might have also heard the dead Colonel Baxter's same reasoning. No one spoke in reply. There was no time.

Jocko's voice from outside the tent flap called out, "Missy E! Missy E, wese ready now foah da lady to go."

Polly and Clara went out first, carrying the bandages, a basket of victuals and Molly's old clothes, washed and wrapped in a linen cloth. Purposely, Molly Corbin had held back in order to go out with Elaine and alone express her thanks to The Lieutenant's wife.

It was sometime later before Elaine came out, supporting Molly's good arm until the escort officers took over. All three women helped in placing her in the wagon seat alongside of Jocko.

Several sick soldiers were lifted into the back of the vehicle. These were to be treated at the Hackensack hospital.

One officer then climbed up front on the outside of the seat beside the wounded girl after wrapping several blankets around his charge and tethering his horse to the rear of the vehicle.

Three wagons were in the train, the rear two carrying more of the sick who were destined for either the Hackensack or Newark hospitals. Accompanied by the two cavalry officers and a detail of riflemen, the three-wagon caravan and its escorts moved off as Greene and members of his staff joined the ring of soldiers who collected to cheer and wave a goodbye to the sad heroine of the battle for Fort Washington.

As always for special parties, Captain Charles Craig who is hoping day to day for the return of his Indian Sergeant Abbott, leads the train down the fort road accompanied by two of his scouts.

When the cheers died down and the wagon was out of sight, a depressingly ominous silence fell over the group of well-wishers. Both Polly and Clara were in tears as they returned to their voluntary chores with the sick.

The Continental Army's first woman cannoneer, now an erect,

silhouetted, blanket-wrapped figure in the wagon seat, flanked by the black boy and the officer, disappeared down into the valley.

But Margaret Corbin had left behind two women, each of them far more tolerant of a third, the self-declared "nootrell." And the "nootrell" one had been left with many things to think over, but now, more than ever, intolerant of war.

From this experience and her talks with "Captain Molly," as General Greene calls her, Elaine was determined that she would join the camp women in order to stay with her husband when the army moved out. She would tell the whole family. If Molly Corbin could do it, why couldn't Elaine Gray?

But John Gray's wife abruptly reminds herself that Molly Corbin was not with child. Elaine Gray is. Yet why should that make so much difference? What the wounded widow had said about happiness flashed through her mind.

"Me Goil," Molly had told her sadly, " 'appiness ye cannot bouy like as a passage on yer ferry. Ye 'ave ta dream 'n plan 'n mold it whilst ye got it in ye 'ands . . . iffin once ye 'ave the makin's of it. Oi 'ad the makin's of it jest like ye 'n Oi kept it by me 'slong as God was willin'. 'N now Oim glad Oi did. So, Goil, once ye 'ave them ingred'ents, ye pour thom 'n, like as ye make a col'erd candle, or knead the dough of the bread, ye makes yer 'appiness wee whut ye got 'slong as ye ken . . . 'n 'slong as God is willin'."

So Elaine was sure in her mind that Molly had pointed her the right way. War, or no war, her place was by her husband. While certainly, in war, running constantly from the enemy, could not bring them much happiness, they would be near one another and grasping what little pleasures life offered.

Helping, serving and giving of each other, this, too, should be a pleasure even amidst horror, death and the worst of all possible situations, she told herself, for happiness and love are like crumbs, thrown behind in the wake of hell raging over the earth. And, unless quickly grabbed up and devoured, those crumbs, like the bread, the staff, the spring of life, as the Domine Remlin puts it, are swiftly lost, ground under the trampling heels of man's perpetual reach for the ever-elusive, better temporal world.

She would make it known to John and the family. She would go westward with the camp women when the army went. She would remain as near as possible always to the man she loved. She would tell them, possibly tomorrow after thinking well upon it. And she did.

With the transfer out of many of the sick, Elaine, despite the opposition, prepares to go along with the army. She even arranges the closing of her little school with its few remaining pupils.

Only Paul, Joseph and Jocko are left, and Jocko no longer attends. He is kept busy driving the wagons with his father, but since Katie May and Ben went into the Ramapos with their parents, Big Tom's son has become sad and unusually serious, although the Baummeisters have kept him informed, assuring him the Gartleck blacks are well and safe.

Hans Onderdonk is still suffering from shock after having learned of his uncle's death. The boy had worshiped his Uncle Abe who had become the youth's hero and principal subject of conversation. Besides, Hans' mother, Polly, had not looked favorably upon Elaine as a teacher following the "neutrality outburst," as Polly calls it. Consequently, Mother Onderdonk has used some poor excuses to keep Hans home.

The scarcity of horses and wagons is a serious problem for the military. It is one more reason why Elaine feels she should turn over her old mare to the army but only under her own supervision. The horse's partial blindness has caused her to withhold offering the animal to the wagon masters, fearing it would suffer misuse.

So great are the demands upon the wagons and teams that Wagon Master Graves and his son have had their hands full for the past few weeks transferring supplies to the little ferry for loading on boats which from there take their cargoes by water to Newark.

In the Highlands and the Valleys the People Tremble

Greene has made three appeals to Newark for more boats. These were to have been sent up the Passaic and Hackensack Rivers.[1] Impatiently the post commander has awaited them in order to ship his supplies out by water and keep his ammunition on dry land. Chancing valuable, irreplaceable arms and ammunition by water is too risky.

So, much materiel piles up, lying along the boat docks on the Overpeck Creek and the Hackensack River and causing the curious and the gossipers to make all kinds of speculations.

There will be much more to talk about when the valley inhabitants hear that The General today ordered all the enemy prisoners now held in Maryland be transferred to Fort Lee.[2] This will cause speculation that Fort Lee is to become a base for prisoners in an effort to promote exchanges with the enemy and to prevent it from being bombarded by the men-of-war. But the inhabitants, who dislike the thought of having Hessian prisoners in their county, have no ground for fear—at least from that source—since the order will be revoked in another two days.

It is the strange distribution of the remaining American army forces up the Hackensack valley and into the Hudson Highlands on both the west and east sides of the upper Hudson River northward beyond the British lines that gives additional cause for speculation.

From the Three Pidgeons Tavern, located six miles south of English Neighborhood on the edge of the Bergen Woods east of Secaucus, all the way up the valley north through Tappan Town and westward to Sidman's Bridge, which guards the Ramapo Pass, the countryside has been buzzing with rumors. Fear of the area's Tory inhabitants and the retaliations they will commit if the Continentals move out is far greater among the populace than their fear of the redcoats themselves.

Other than the perplexing movement of supplies, there seems to be no other indication that the army will withdraw its forces from the valleys and the Highlands. Holding all these posts from North Castle westward to the vital Ramapo Pass are about 12,500 men, at least on paper, for not all are with their regiments, and many are not fit and able for duty.

These lines and posts north of Fort Lee, stretching across the river up to North Castle, maintain the principal supply and communications routes down from New England. The main linking route, north to south, passes under the hills of North Castle through the White Plains. It then runs to the upper Hudson, crossing by ferriage at Peekskill, Verplanck's Landing, or King's Ferry at Parson's Point. But below those ferries, the next crossing is Dobbs Ferry, now in enemy territory.

In addition to their military value, these army lines and garrisons bolster the morale of the trembling patriot inhabitants by their very presence. For many home owners still quake from having felt the stings of Tory raiders.

This line of troop concentrations and posts, beginning with the Ramapo Pass area and Sidman's Bridge at the south end of Smith's Cove,[3] forms a wide arc that extends northeast and then eastward and south eastward into the North Castle Hills.

From his Peekskill headquarters Major General Heath commands all forces from Peekskill west to the Ramapo Pass on the west side of the river. On paper Heath can show a force of 5,000 men. Actually there are only about 3,000 fit for duty.

Of these, about 400 guard the Ramapo Pass. This mountain cut opens into the westernmost Dutch farm lands and leads into the interior through mountainous iron mine roads, passing various settlements as it winds south through the Jerseys. It then wanders through the Jersey Watchung Mountains on its way to the Delaware. Several connecting roads link it to the more commonly traveled New York to Philadelphia highways. The pass itself is about 21 miles inland and south of Peekskill. Its 400 Ramapo Pass guards are under Colonel Jedediah Huntington, headquartered at Sidman's Bridge.

What has seemingly put the people in Huntington's territory at ease lately is the news that all of his troops have been ordered to build huts for winter quarters. And Huntington proudly has reported that his men's log huts are "homey, very warm habitations."[4]

For 25 Miles the Defense Arc Curves
From Ramapo To North Castle

Geographically, the Ramapo Pass lies about 14 miles in or west, from Nyack on the river, and Nyack is about 17 miles north of Fort Lee. About six miles below or south of Nyack is Greene's northernmost outpost for Fort Lee. Under Colonel Durkee and his Major Clarke, it looks down on Sneden's and Slauter's Landings and across the river at Dobbs Ferry which now are under British control.

About seven miles north of Nyack lie the Haverstraw Bay docks, and about eight miles north of them is Peekskill. All of this ground has been placed under Heath's command. It extends from Peekskill south along the west bank of the river to Sneden's outpost. Then from Peekskill his picket lines stretch east southeast several miles to link with Lee's troops 13 miles away at North Castle above the town of White Plains. Lee, on paper can show a force of 7,500, but this count boils down to less than 6,000 fit and able for duty.

This then is the American military "arc" line that ties up, on paper, some 12,500 men of which less than 10,000 are fit for duty. Its purpose and its orders are to guard the supply lines from the north. But this Continental Army show of strength also keeps the New York Committee of Safety happy, for the wealthy, but frightened, land owners have exerted much influence upon the Congress in the past.

Also helping to appease the region's influential voices is a recently completed chain barricade of 1,800 feet stretched across the river just north of Peekskill. The heavy cast iron links reach from the Fort Montgomery garrison post on the west bank to Anthony's Nose on the east shore.

Twice it has been separated after holding only a few hours. This has so angered the frantic Committee of Safety which had expected the barrier would ward off British attempts to ascend the Hudson, that the Continental Army's Chief Engineer, Colonel Rufus Putnam, has been ordered to study its strength and value in his survey of the defenses of the county.[5]

South of this arc, downriver at Fort Lee, Greene is in command now of only 2,667[6] troops after having lost 2,800 of his men on Mount Washington. The Fort Lee post commander's diminished forces include Generals Hand and Beal's regiments and what is left of General Ewing's brigade.[7]

On the "front" lines facing the enemy are between twelve to thirteen thousand Americans fit for duty, if not equipped for fighting. Behind this frontal line on the river's west bank and around to upper Westchester are: The General's personal command, in Hackensack and Acquackanonk, which he estimates at 5,000[8] but about half that number are "fit for duty"; Stirling's 1,200 near new Brunswick;[9] and small posts, mostly militia, at Newark, Amboy and at the way stations along the route south.

In all, the entire army now opposing Howe cannot muster more than 15,000 troops "fit and able," all poorly equipped. But the dwindling strength of this main Continental Army defending the communications to New England, the Jersey mainland, and Philadelphia is so scattered that it invites trouble. So far apart are the army's units that, in the event of a major enemy push, the results could be tragic.

In addition, morale is falling. Many more each day are reporting sick. Hundreds are on leave or furlough. But even worse are the prospects for further recruiting. And, on top of all this, the American staff officers have become suddenly aware that 2,060 enlistments are to expire on November 30, ten days from tomorrow.[10] Still more will expire a month later on the first of the new year.

The most dreaded fear now haunting the American command is that, with expiring enlistments, increasing illnesses, lowering of morale and the oncoming of winter, there is a strong possibility that the entire army will dissolve within forty days.

There is one major advantage that the Americans hold over their enemy, the nature of the terrain they occupy. Particularly Greene on The Mountain at Fort Lee. For the Rhode Islander commands what is said to be the strongest natural defensive post along the entire coast.

The sheer walls of the precipitous Palisades look over the almost mile-wide river the enemy must cross before coming under a rain of death from the precipice's summit.

Certainly in medieval days the tall menacing Bluff Rock site, with a natural fortress wall and moat, would have provided absolute impregnability from an eastern assault. And now its forbidding appearance and the positions of the two armies, make many American and British soldier with an interest in military strategy wonder if General Howe does not regret his initial attack on Long Island.

What, they query, would have been the results had Howe jumped from Staten Island directly into Jersey? Could he not then have cut the rebels off from the mainland as now he is? And could he have not then taken control of the Hudson and severed the Americans' communications lines with New England? What then, would have stopped him from sending his brigades across the Jerseys and dislodging the seat of all the trouble in Philadelphia?

To Nathanael Greene, who has come to believe too strongly in the formidability of natural fortresses, the Commander-in-Chief's order to evacuate seems to be a bit premature. There are, in his opinion, a few things that can be said in favor of holding.

One is today's wet, cold weather which is now at last ushering in the end of an exceptionally mild fall. Even the farmers are convinced that winter is about to set in. And there on The Mountain, Greene believes, would be the best encampment quarters for the winter months. For here the enemy's moves could be constantly kept under observation.

But the now much more cautious Nathanael Greene has been severely burned by one poor decision. He had unwisely once failed to heed the advice of his older and more prudent mentor. And by overriding that counsel he had brought about one of the greatest catastrophes of the war.

Three nights of nightmarish dreams have followed. He would never again make a decision without placing tremendous weight upon all its possible outcomes. For the former commander of the lost fortress has developed a sudden new-found respect for those valuable experiences that may often hang freely, waiting to be plucked from some older and wiser heads.

And so the evacuation goes on as decided, unquestioned. Despite the activities centering around the abandoning of the post, Greene

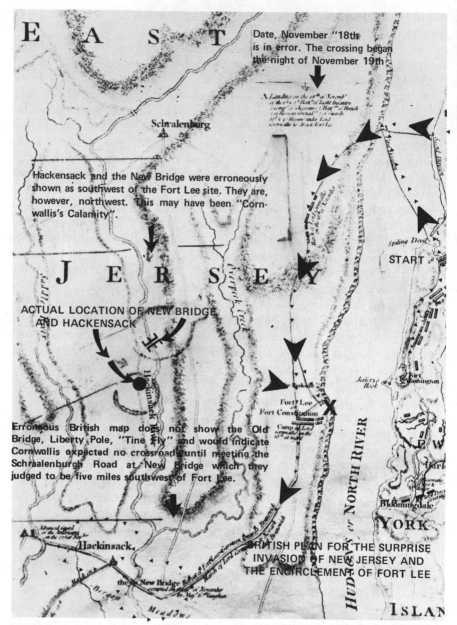

Overlaid on this British Map (#600 LLFTC), Sauthier-Faden, February 25, 1777, are the glaring errors indicating the paucity of knowledge regarding the Jersey terrain available to Lord Cornwallis on November 20. — Original Map in Clinton Collection, Clements Library.

has ordered increased picketing and surveillance of the enemy's movements.

Howe Seeks and Finds the "Blind Spot"

Unaware of Fort Lee's evacuation plans, Howe and Cornwallis had carefully ascertained the positions of the rebel troops in their defense "arc" line from Fort Lee to North Castle. Somewhere north upriver there had to be an unprotected invasion site out of the Americans' observation field. And there was.

Between Fort Lee's Bluff Rock and near the fort's northernmost left flank outpost at Sneden's Landing, the Palisades stand up as precipitously insurmountable as the Bluff Rock, 300 feet and higher almost from out of the water's edge. There are some 13 miles of rock wall that rise out of the river until it finally tapers down northward and disappears under the slot where the Tappan Zee waters flow into the valley.

Between Greene at Fort Lee and Durkee at Sneden's outpost, the curvatures of the Palisadean wall prevent one post from seeing anything of the other over the 12-mile span. But together they are able to observe some 30 miles of the opposite shore north of Mount Washington.

However, there is one dangerous "blind spot" area on the rebels' shore unobservable by either lookout post. It is a stretch under the Palisades about half way between the two lookouts. It is the area of the Closter docks, the old dock at upper Closter and a newer one downriver at so-called "Lower Closter."

These are two docks, or landing areas, long used by the river's fishermen and boatmen. At each there is a small house, seasonally used by fishermen. Both are now deserted. It is said that Tom Kearney, a boat builder, no relation to the Fort Lee Kearneys, built the one at the old dock before defecting to the British. A fisherman is said to have built the house at the other which is about seven miles north of Fort Lee.

At the old dock a perilous, rough, narrow trail zig-zags its dangerous way under occasional avalanches of small rocks up the steep sides of the precipice that makes many wonder how such a road or trail, could ever have been built. Over the crest it becomes wider as it leads straight down into the little village of Closter.

Since farmers have long brought their wares and produce out of the valley and down the steep trail to the river in team-drawn wagon sleds for transporting by pettiauger to New York town, the long thoroughfare, an extension of the valley's Old Hook highway, has acquired the name, "Closter Dock Road." So the place is called simply the "Closter Dock."

The other newer dock, about a mile south of the older landing, has also been used by farmers, travelers and fishermen.

In ancient times the Indians brought their clams and oysters all along here, cracked and ate them, leaving large deposits of shells on the banks.

Here also a narrow, zig-zag, old Indian trail similarly ascends the cliffs which are somewhat less precipitous and not as high, but are, nevertheless, dangerous and circuitous.

Rising one foot every five feet, the trail winds its way to the summit. There it widens somewhat before it descends over the mountain, taking a southwesterly course down into the valley.

Like the Closter Dock Road, the trail road intersects the north to south King's Highway running up and down the valley. And it too has been used by farmers—berry-growing farmers particularly—who sent their produce downriver. The site is sometimes called "the Lower Closter Dock." It is not mapped.

Under the Noses Of the Lookouts

On the British Headquarters' plans Howe and Cornwallis have made it clear to the regimental commanders by the map's penciled markings that the old dock at the upper Closter site is to be the main invasion point. Since it lies about eight miles north of Fort Lee and approximately three miles south of the outpost at Sneden's, a carefully conducted night maneuver could place the redcoats over the precipice, in the valley and in a position to intercept any alarm from the Sneden's Landing post while they march down on Fort Lee before the rebels there are fully awake. The carefully worked out plan appears sound.

Colonel Durkee and his Major Clarke, commanding 508 men[11] at the Sneden's Landing outpost, have maintained a constant vigil of enemy movements across the river, or at least those which come within their view.

And Howe and Cornwallis have done their best to keep their operation out of their enemy's view. Durkee's lookouts must not observe the preparations taking place below Phillips's place[12] near Yonker's Mill[13] at Wepperham or the operation's surprise effect would be lost.

This location is about seven miles north of the Spuyten Duyvil

Diorama made of crossing, possibly at Lower Closter area, built to scale by W. Fred Winterhoff, Westwood, New Jersey, 1972, shows British boats and troops crossing the Hudson River under the Palisades about dawn November 20, 1776.

where the river widens to almost a mile. Owing to the protrusion, or jutting out of the Palisadean wall a little north of the Bluff Rock, it is a spot obscured from Fort Lee's vision. Also contributing to its invisibility from the fort is the fact that at Spuyten Duyvil the river begins to bend very slightly northwestward.

In addition to primary observation posts, Durkee's surveillance includes strung-out picket patrols which venture along the cliffs' summit trails and along the river's shores. For it is Durkee's job to be the eyes and ears of Greene's guardian Fort Lee left wing.

Sunday night, his way having been reported clear by Bergen County Tories, Lord Cornwallis prepared to cross with a small exploratory staff of officers and guards in an armed sloop. The secret nocturnal landing was to be made at upper Closter's old dock where he could temporarily occupy the deserted old house for his field headquarters. The sloop was to be secluded in a cove out of sight.

While Cornwallis was slipping through under the American surveillance in the darkness of yesterday's pre-dawn hours to check the terrain and map his strategy in the old fisherman's hut, the worried Fox in Hackensack was reviewing in his mind the deplorable state of affairs and eagerly waiting word from Congress. His problems, without the annoyance of a procrastinating and dilatory Congress, are enough to strain any man's patience.

The shortage of men, arms, clothing, supplies, ammunition and weapons is one thing, but the army's enforced acceptance of politically appointed officers, rather than militarily trained leaders, wears down his endurance.

His long-standing complaints and warnings sent off to the Philadelphia body have borne no fruit. The General had hoped for positive Congressional action that might have prevented the loss of Manhattan and its principal citadel. It had not come.

Now, perhaps, with the army's near collapse, the States' representatives will be forced to act. All kinds of stories come from Philadelphia reporting on the Congress's bickerings among themselves. Some are saying that many of the statesmen spend more hours haranguing in attempts to outdo one another in oratory for home consumption, than they do in proposing ways to save the nation from destruction.

Some wonder when the Philadelphia gentlemen in the so-called "Cradle Of Liberty" intend to do something about the nation's survival. Especially now that Howe is pointing himself in their direction and intends to ring them all in as his prize.

So the American General will very likely be buoyed by a letter from the august body in which John Hancock, penning him tonight, states:

"Sir:
"I have the honour to transmit the enclosed resolves in obedience to the commands of Congress . . . You will perceive from the vote of Congress the sense of that body with regard to the necessity of furnishing the troops for the new army as soon as possible, a copy of which I have forwarded to the respective States agreeably to the orders of Congress. I have also written to the States southward of Pennsylvania, inclusively, urging them to lay up magazines of military stores and salt provision, for the use of the Army and militia, in case it should be necessary to call them into the field the approaching winter.

"As our enemies will doubtless open the campaign early in the spring, it is absolutely necessary we should prepare for them, and exert ourselves to fill up the Army agreeably to the new establishment.

"The Congress, to remove every objection, and in hopes of forwarding the recruiting service, have resolved that the troops may be engaged for three years, without presenting inlisting rolls, both for that term, and during the continuance of the war, as ordered by a former resolution . . ."[14]

Needed: That "Higher Type Of Patriotism"

Though the enlistment period of three years is needed, overdue and now welcomed by the American generals, the Congress still has not given The General his long-requested "articles of war." As one historian someday will say of the statesmen:

> "It (the Congress) hesitated to adopt the much needed articles of war so vital for military discipline. The army could fall apart at its basted seams since it was not bound by the severe articles of war which held the enemy force rigidly together.
> "It required, however, a higher type of patriotism than most politicians possessed to uphold The General's hand at the hazard of their precious popularity."[15]

The Congress's somewhat encouraging news, late though it is in coming, will not get to the chief until Friday. That will be two days after the Continental Army's narrowest escape yet from the ever-widening Juggernaut.

Today The General and his aides have been busily handling a backlog of correspondence and principally his report to Congress. It will include all he knows about the fall of Fort Washington. It will be disheartening, but it will make the august body wish they had taken earlier steps toward united action.

Working in the big living room of the mansion house which Peter Zabriskie and his family have turned over for the Hackensack-based headquarters, the American Commander and his aides have had little time to eat, but Tavern-keeper Archibald Campbell, who with his family, prepares all the meals for the headquarters staff, insists they do.

A patriot who guards his tongue as he guards his property, Campbell takes particular care in preparing and serving The General's food, even though he must at times submit to the embarrassing questions and surveillance of the Chief's bodyguards.

Both he and Zabriskie, who is a bold leader among the Dutch patriots, know how torn is the Hackensack countryside by the religious and political antagonisms generated by whigs, Tories, and the opposing Conferentie and Coetus sectarian parties.

The nose-snubbing church-goers of the two religious groups are in many cases mortal enemies whose allegiances have been cast into either the American or the British camp. And Campbell often finds himself in between.

Particularly among the usually peace-loving Dutch settlers, there are few who know, or care, how far back go the ideological traces of their religious and social philosophies and bigotries. They are bigotries carried over from their forebears, Anglicans and non-Anglicans as well. With both, there came across the seeds of prejudices cultivated in the trenches between the Cromwellians and the Royalists a century ago. Now those seeds are giant forces.

The Whigs and Tories, like the coetus and conferenties, see only the procedures of religious worship, only the methods of governing, only the interpretation of rights and property in their search for an allegiance upon which to hang their hats. Therefore they cannot see rising around them the great wave of enlightenment and reformation sweeping over the ocean onto their continent, cresting in the American Revolution. They do not and cannot see the bursting human tide, held in abeyance throughout centuries of repression. They do not see the individual finally ascending to dignity and status any more than they see the centuries-old origins for their religious and social philosophies and bigotries. Before their eyes only are their allegiances, their devotions, their hates, their prejudices and their leaders carrying their immediate hopes.

Though unaware of all the confluent forces and philosophies erupting in the breasts of their fellow men, former peace-loving neighbors and friends, Campbell and Zabriskie are concerned about the nefarious plotting that goes on around them. It is for this reason that the tavern owner carefully superintends the food which his help prepares for The General's table. Campbell and his family take no chances and the American Commander's bodyguards endorse his precautionary measures.

Both men know that a Tory plot[16] to take the rebel Chief's life is more than just a rumor. They know also that the plotters are possibly not far away. So the American Commander's two admirers have warned the army personnel, but the officers place little credence in hearsay.

As things now stand there is enough to worry about without paying mind to rumors, particularly "Tory Tales." Such stories strike fear among the inhabitants but little if any among the soldiery. Bigger problems face the military without having to worry about Tory rumors.

So, after finishing supper, The General reads over the report to Congress, handed to him by Colonel Harrison, and signs it. In his accountings The General has noted the paucity of information available on the fall of Fort Washington. He then informs the Congress why he is evacuating Fort Lee, stating in part:

In the Report To Congress Goes A Warning

"As Fort Lee was considered as only necessary in conjunction with that on the east side of the river to protect the communication across and to prevent the enemy from free navigation, it has become of no importance . . ."[17]

Then, disclosing the removal of the fort's supplies to Acquackanonk, Boundbrook, Brunswick, Princeton and Springfield, The General adds that:

. . . Those places will not be subject to sudden danger in case the enemy should pass the river, and which have been thought proper as repositories for some of our stores of provisions and forage."

Pointing directly to the problem of enlistment expirations, the General's letter, which is addressed to President of the Congress, John Hancock, notes that Hand's and Beal's Flying Camp troops at Fort Lee will soon be free to leave with their terms of service completed. He adds:

"If the enemy should make a push in this quarter (Fort Lee) the only troops to oppose them would be Hand's, Haslet's and what is left of Smallwood's regulars."

Then, devoting a lengthy section of his report to the pathetic letter he has recently received from Colonels Miles and Atlee, two of the imprisoned officers in New York who wrote of the "distressed situation of our prisoners,"[18] The General urges Congress to seek ways to alleviate the American sufferings. He suggests expedients be adopted in order to furnish them with blankets, clothing and other necessities.

After signing the report and completing some further correspondence and routine military matters, the Virginian upon whom heavily weighs the failure or success of the American rebellion, dismisses his aides and bids them good night. His boots, burdened by the heavy weight they carry, step solidly with a strong rhythmical cadence up the creaking oak stair treads, passing the guard at the door of his room on the second floor of the three-story home. They have carried him miles and miles and again to rest as they have through so many wearisome nights before.

Under the light of the oil lamp in the hall, he says a brief, almost abrupt thank you and good night to the second floor sentry. The guard had lighted the candlestick atop the Winthrop cherry desk in the far corner of his room. The door closes and the rain patters down on the roof's hand-hewn cedar shingles.

Through the windowpanes on the east wall the army's Chief peers out until his eyes become adjusted to the darkness. He can see the night watch exchanging a lighted torch with another sentry down by the Hackensack River dock. For a brief moment his mind is carried 250 miles away to the river Potomac.

But there is no time for that. He quickly closes the shutters, removes his coat and sits down to write his brother, John Augustine Washington.

In the long outpouring the American Leader recounts the engagement with the enemy at White Plains and the fall of Fort Washington, mentioning his disappointment in not being able to save the Manhattan fortress from its humiliating, tragic capitulation. He writes:

> "And what adds to my mortification is that this post (Fort Washington), after the last ships went past it, was held contrary to my wishes and Opinion, as I conceived it to be a hazardous one; but it having been determined on by a full council of General Officers, and a resolution of Congress having been received strongly expressive of their desire that the channel of the river, which we had been labouring to stop for a long time at that place, might be obstructed, if possible, and knowing that this could not be done unless there were batteries to protect the obstruction, I did not care to give an absolute order for withdrawing the garrison, till I could get around and see the situation of things, and then it became too late, as the fort was invested.
>
> "Upon the passing of the last ships, I had given it as my opinion to General Greene, under whose care it was, that it would be best to evacuate the place; but, as the order was discretionary and his opinion differed from mine, it unhappily was delayed too long, to my great grief; as I think General Howe, considering his army and ours, would have found it difficult, unless some southern expedition may prove successful, to reconcile the people of England to the conquest of a few pitiful islands, none of which were defensible, considering the great number of their ships, and the power they have by sea to surround and render them unapproachable."

However, regardless of the American Commander-in-Chief's belittling of General Howe's success, back in London Sir William's capture of Staten Island, part of Long Island, and all of Manhattan Island will become a proud feather in the Viscount's hat, but, realistically, the rebels' Chief is right. Howe and his army are still a long way from Philadelphia.

In another part of his letter to his brother, The General, regretting that the "different States are so slow and inattentive to that essential business of levying their quotas of men," writes:

"In ten days from this date, there will not be above two thousand men, if that number, of the fixed established regiments on this side of Hudson's river to oppose Howe's whole army, and very little more on the other to secure the Eastern Colonies and the important passes leading through the Highlands to Albany and the country about the lakes."

And then, explaining the handicap of "short inlistments," he says:

"In short, it is impossible for me in the compass of a letter to give you any idea of our situation, of my difficulties, and of the constant perplexities and mortifications I meet with, derived from the unhappy policy of short inlistments and delaying them too long."[19]

Not For "Twenty Thousand Pounds A Year"

Finally, near the closing of the lengthy unburdening of his mind, the rebel Chieftain confides to his brother:

"I am wearied almost to death with the retrograde motion of things, and I solemnly protest that a pecuniary reward of twenty thousand pounds a year would not induce me to undergo what I do; and after all, perhaps, to lose my character, as it is impossible, under such a variety of distressing circumstances, to conduct matters agreeably to publick expectation, or even to the expectation of those who employ me, as they will not make proper allowances for the difficulties their own errors have occasioned."[20]

Besides those problems he has with the Congress, The General has, in addition to his countless other military headaches, a growing number of internal dissensions among his officers. They have spread to involve even his closest staff members.

The Continental Army Commander has found that the slender threads of confidence in him and in the war's outcome, stretch thin and often to the breaking point when retreats and defeats on the battlefields far outweigh success. And now he experiences the sickening feeling of reverses mounting ever higher as army morale and his troops' confidence in him begin sinking ever lower.

Particularly undermining morale is the enemy's widely heralded assurance that the war is about over. This alone spreads poisonous pessimism throughout the rank and file.

The American Commander-in-Chief has sensed the growing decline in confidence in the changing attitude of his own adjutant, Colonel Joseph Reed. Few who know, suspect that The General knows.

But the Chief has felt the extent of the divisive effect that Lee has had upon, not only Reed's thinking, but the Commander-in-Chief's staff as well. However, he refuses to allow such things to affect him, or to turn his mind away from his single, his determined, his avowed objective.

Inwardly he is comforted by the extreme loyalty and devotion which the majority of his officers give him. Outwardly he shows no awareness of the heated arguments and closed-door discussions that take place over his leadership and ability to command as contrasted with the army's second in command, General Charles Lee. He is as cognizant of Reed's new-found admiration for Lee as he is of Greene's deep dislike for the so-called "Hero of Charleston," though it is generally assumed that he is oblivious to all such intra-staff bickerings.

It is only recently that Colonel Reed has seemingly shifted his support to Charles Lee. Others are doing the same thing, or considering it. For coming up in the near future is the grand prize, the command of the new "Continental Army" which the Congress is soon expected to form.

Many foresee a battle brewing for this post. And some consider it good politics to be alined with the right man when the time comes.

But Joseph Reed and Greene are not of that ilk. Reed is motivated by a soldier's admiration for a general's battlefield victory. He would very likely take violent umbrage were it even implied he is not loyal to his General and Chief. And Greene is motivated by a dislike for Lee and his pompous attitude.

In the room directly above the Commander's the adjutant general tries to sleep, but his mind revolves around the state of the army, the correspondence and the work of the day. He wonders what would be the state of affairs were Charles Lee in full command of the Continentals. His mind then jumps to Greene's recommendations regarding some Rhode Island officers under Lee's command.

Why, he wonders, did the Chief order that those recommendations be forwarded directly to Lee? Why had not Greene, a Rhode Islander, made the recommendations directly to Lee? Or, most proper of all, why had not the Chief made the recommendations himself, instead of Greene?

And surely the recommendation that Lee's forces should be moved out of North Castle and across to the west side of the river was not a recommendation for Greene to make. But he had, and The General promptly forwarded it to Lee, trusting Lee would decide to do so on his own and not wait for a direct order from the army's Chief.

For the Commander highly respects Lee's military acumen and fully recognizes his reputation with the Congress and his popularity with the people. However, for the Virginian to have to "order" the Continental Army's second in command around would not be the wisest, nor the most politic approach, especially at this time.

It is no wonder, Reed tells himself as he tosses restlessly on the spool bed, that Lee's dispatch which arrived late this afternoon for the Commander, was so irate. Reed was inclined to sympathize with Lee.

Is it any wonder that Lee, the victor over Clinton in Charleston, wrote angrily that his officers accused Greene of "partiality to his connexions and townsmen, to the prejudices of men of manifestly superior merit."[21]

It is no wonder, the adjutant thinks, that Lee said of Greene's list of recommendations that "some of the subjects he recommended were wretched."[22]

And it is a good thing, Reed assures himself, that the army's second ranking commander, listed his objections to moving from his post at North Castle. The pondering, tossing adjutant general tries to put his mind at rest by promising himself he will write Charles Lee personally at the earliest opportunity and give him support.

In a house not many doors away from the Zabriskie home, Abraham Van Buskirk,[23] former stagedriver, farmer and doctor, who has surreptitiously transferred his allegiance from the American cause to the British, is meeting in the dim candlelight of an old warehouse by the river. With him is Daniel Isaac Brown, lawyer, court clerk and surrogate. Both are members of the Provincial Congress.

Van Buskirk and Brown, unknown to their neighbors, have just received secret commissions in the British territorial army. Van Buskirk is a lieutenant colonel in the King's Volunteers. Brown has been secretly commissioned a major in the same regiment.

In their clandestine warehouse meeting, they are joined by Edward Earl and William Van Allen.[24] All four are believed to be good Whigs by the valley's many patriots. But all four are part of the first British-sponsored and well organized Tory troop company in the territory.

Campbell and Zabriskie are not making idle gossip when they warn The General's staff of possible mischief afoot.

Up from the Hackensack Green the voice of the night watch calls out his "Nine o'clock, 'nd all's well!" Even the Tory plotters repair to their homes. Reed, too, has done with his contemplations and has fallen asleep. Only The General's candles still burn. Their dim light is barely reflected through the closed shutters out upon the chilling, rain-swept night that gloomily enshrouds the army's encampment on the Green and the little village up from the river's bank.

At Fort Lee, eight miles southeast of Hackensack by the Little Ferry and about ten miles by the New Bridge, the blanket of rain and darkness clothes the mountain top and closes out other things from its vision.

Greene, late in the day, briefed his officers on the plans for the evacuation of the troops from the post. It is no secret now that the fort is to be completely abandoned. But it may be days before the evacuation operation is completed. Seemingly there is no great immediacy.

The confirming news has made the night a harrowing one for the members of the Baummeister and Bourdette households and some of the people of the hamlet. It is as though the very foundations they have learned to live upon for so long are to be torn out from under them. Though most everyone expected this was sooner or later to be, the certainty now of being without the garrison of soldiers always around them and always over their heads like a protecting cover, suddenly strikes them with a blow they had hoped would never come.

All of the members of the two households and their close neighbors had gathered early in the evening at the Baummeister home at Gray's request. A few tears in Marie Louise's eyes were warning enough for the assemblage gathering in her parlor that something portentous was in the offing.

When they were all seated after the Bourdettes and others had dried off from the rain before the big fireplace, John Gray came directly to the topic, advising them that as soon as all supplies and materiel have been moved out of the post, the works are to be abandoned.

He was not sure, nor was anyone else, The Lieutenant told them, where the army was to be quartered for the winter. But he felt that they should all be informed of what to expect in order to take whatever precautions wisdom dictated.

A Question Drowns A Room In Silence

Looking forward to all possibilities, frightening though they might be, Gray suggested that they bury anything of great value in the event of enemy, or Tory raids by Loyalist partisans from the valley. But "of most importance," he said, "it is The Gen'l's advice that ye stay neutral to best protect your homes and property."

It took "Old Granny" Bourdette to ask the one question that had been preying on everyone's mind. And she asked it of Elaine in her rarely used, extremely serious and concerned tone of voice which all know will brook no quibbling.

"Air ye agoin' with 'em, Elaine?" inquired Rachel.

The answer was unhesitating.

"I am, Granny," adamantly replied the younger woman who had always paid close attention to Rachel Bourdette's sound advice. For, like most of the wives, Elaine has revered and admired the older woman for her hardiness and her early pioneering of The Mountain area. It is that, her gruff bluntness, respect for truth and her sharp mind which have made Rachel Bourdette the sage and the seer of the little hamlet. And she is so recognized by the men as well as the women of the area.

"Then ye air not in yer right senses, Elaine," came back the older woman's sharp retort. "Do ye thinks ye ken rear chull'en on a battlefield?"

Elaine made no answer. The room suddenly was drowned in stillness. Gray, who has been worried over his wife's insistence that she will go wherever the army takes her husband, became happily buoyed by Rachel's outspokenness.

It had taken him as well as everyone else by surprise. Even Jennie, a past master at firing poignant statements or questions behind a facade of big, brown innocent eyes and impishly smiling gleaming white teeth, had not ventured to ask that question.

Gray, hoping that Old Granny's wisdom would make a deeper impression upon Elaine's set mind than all the fruitless arguments he, her father and her mother had advanced, spoke up and relieved the room's tension. He assured everyone that the local militia would be around to offset any mischievous enemy activities.

And So To Bed

Amidst incoherent mumblings spilling out from under long solemn faces, a few of the guests moved out of the room while others filled their cups with Marie Louise's peach punch from her big china bowl. There were traces of tears in more eyes than just Marie Louise's but none in Granny Bourdette's nor in Jennie's. Their lives had gone over many rugged mountains and through too many stormy days to be upset by simply one more of life's trials.

In a few minutes the hardiness of the river people reasserted itself as it always seems to do in hurdling difficulties. Then jests and half-jests followed, though they fell on sickly smiling faces reflecting weak attempts to hide the fears their eyes expressed.

Some crunched mechanically upon Jennie's sugar cookes, stacked high in a serving plate on the buffet sideboard. Soon all bid each other good night and left through the lightly falling rain.

John and Elaine were the first to go upstairs to bed, looking in on the soundly sleeping Paul with a poke of their candlestick through his door as they passed his room.

For the first time since she married John Gray over two months ago, Elaine seems suddenly and strangely reminded of the preachers's hesitating, deep-throated vows he had asked them to repeat, particulary, "until death do us part." For the first time in her life she suddenly felt the dreaded fear of love's impermanence parasitically trying to attach itself to escaping life and happiness.

In their room the couple silently undressed. No words were passed. No mention made of what he had said in the living room below, nor of Old Granny's remarks.

Despite her desire to go along with the army, Elaine intuitively knew before and definitely knows now that it cannot come to pass. Old Granny had told her what she had not wanted to tell herself.

There is a life she carries within her womb. And to that life she owes all the protection she can offer for having, with her husband, summoned it into being.

Elaine, somewhat in a stupor from the thoughts that raced around within her mind, stepped up to the dresser, blew out the candle and stared out of the east window through the dark, cold rainy night. In the far distance across the water she could see a few of the enemy's flickering campfires on the mount near the newly named Fort Knyphausen.

After banking the ashes of the dying embers of the fire and smothering the large logs within the fireplace, John slowly stole up behind his wife, placed his arms gently around her waist, enrobed in her best flannel nightgown, and softly kissed away her tears that now rolled steadily down her cheeks. He folded her close to him, lifted her easily in his arms and dumped her gently on the feather mattress.

Off in the direction of the ferry landing dock they could hear the night watch call out, "Nine o'clock, 'nd all's well!"

There is no night watch some seven miles upstream in the weather-beaten old house by the old dock landing in upper Closter, nor opposite it, on the Hudson's eastern shore. There flatboats and barges loaded with British and Hessian soldiers have been coming down from just above the Spuyten Duyvil ever since sunset. Some move diagonally across from their loading stations, some from near Phillips's place almost directly opposite Closter's dock.

It is there on the west bank that Cornwallis and his staff make their final plans for assaulting the high precipice that rises darkly above the old house by the water. Despite the rain and the cold, a thing Cornwallis had not counted on even though it is working to his great advantage, the six to eight thousand troops[25] are eager to get on with it. The regiments have been especially trained and prepared for the hardships the enterprise holds in store.

All of the men are well fed, clothed and equipped. And with a veneer of bravado that cloaks the trepidation each man feels as he stares up at the perpendicularly rising precipices, silhouetted against the blackness of the night before them, the redcoats and Hessians jump, chilled and wet, from the boats to the shore.

They accept the cold wet night as another test of their rugged endurance. Quietly and orderly they strike out in hushed but excited spirits, feeling their way in the darkness toward their regimental stations at the cliffs' base. Under the tapering rain they await their officers' orders.

The invasion of the Jerseys has begun. But in Hackensack and Fort Lee the night watch call out their familiar "Nine o'clock, 'nd all's well!"

29

Wednesday, November 20. . .

Lord Cornwallis Leads
the Amphibious Invasion of the Jerseys

Before Them Lies A Sleeping Monolith

In last night's darkness the rain-drenched troops emptied out on the Hudson's west shore under towering rock walls. Hundreds of boats carried them from the New York side across the unusually calm river. Overloaded flatboats conveyed men, horses, supplies, baggage and armament.

In crossing they squatted uncomfortably on the wet decks of the sloops and barges, frequently getting in the way of the seamen. They could see, grimly outlined in the night's blackness, the high, ominous face of the Palisades. It was those awesome cliffs that they would be scaling before dawn. To some the sight reminded them of a huge sleeping prehistoric monster such as those recounted by old mariners' sea tales.

South of Phillips's place and north of the Spuyten Duyvil the small craft loaded up at various embarkation points along the New York side. Under arms, with full packs, prepared to march and battle, by companies in continuous regiments, they lined up, waiting their turn to scramble for places on the transports' unceasing cross flow.

Quietly marching down from the heights of Fordham through the black forests, some could hardly see their comrades in front of them. All formed dark silhouettes, blurred, indistinguishable images before the landscape's horizon. The figures became larger and sharper as they passed the scattered, flickering-out campfires along the way. They boarded with amazing order and calmness.

Burning sulkily the occasional flames spurted momentarily, then retreated leaving short shadowy glimpses of the vast amphibious movement taking place on the river and its shores. They were the last fires the men would see or feel until after today's dawn.

In the midstream almost on a line with one another are three men-of-war. They assisted in guarding and guiding the little vessels in their hazardous crossings. These were the frigates that stole through the Chevaux de Frise before the Mount Washington battle.

Admiral Howe had an added assignment to carry out below Fort Lee in support of the invasion. Off Bull's Ferry one of his transports was prepared to unload a raiding party of jagers against the small garrison based above the ferry landing. At a signal these Hessian infantrymen were to launch a surprise attack upon the Bull's Ferry post. The exchange of fire[1] would, it was planned, cause Fort Lee to concentrate on the attacking force to its right, thus helping to conceal the invasion operation in progress upriver on its left under the Closter Dock. But this feint at Bull's was not destined to materialize.

It is now past midnight Wednesday, November 20. For over three hours Cornwallis's astounding expedition has proceeded with amazing efficiency despite the adverse weather that has turned the narrow precipice trail into a slippery, rock-strewn mountain-side of small gullies, racing down the treacherous path to the river. The leaves underfoot slide as though on sheets of ice bringing down many a face smudged in the earth, as the soldiers climb one foot closer to the summit for every three or four steps they take.

Owing to the weather, the time and the place, the rebels thus far are unaware of the maneuver.

Under Commodore Hotham the seamen handle the river crossings with remarkable skill. Though faced with difficult conditions, they successfully prevent upsets. However, a few of the heavily loaded lead boats, whose soldiers jump out too soon in waist-deep water, have narrow escapes, but there is no loss of life.

On the Jersey shore Cornwallis's fisherman hut headquarters is flooded with candlelight. Never in its 25 years of existence has the deserted stone and timber, sand-floored, one- room, low ceilinged riverside dwelling been the center of such attention.[2]

Sentinels are posted everywhere. High ranking commanders continuously move in and out through the busy door while outside the strings of regiments file two abreast and follow in each other's footsteps up the rugged, zigzagging trail which begins some distance north of the homestead. They form what seems to be an unending line of men, horses, gun carriages, baggage and supplies. Slowly and ponderously through the dismal night they struggle up the long, treacherous ascent toward the distant summit.

Lord Cornwallis's maps, sketched by Tory partisans, are not accurate. What lies over the summit will be an entirely new world for the British forces who must rely entirely upon Tory guides recruited from Bergen for the expedition to lead them onto and into America's mainland.

And so all through the night the boats keep up their constant ferriage. For many a British and Hessian soldier, despite masks of bravado, the dark, Palisadean ridge—a seemingly insurmountable wall—becomes a giant obstacle. It causes even the bravest to tremble at times with fear and uncertainty for the unexpected that lies before them. Some wish they had been among the small body of advance scouts assigned to the shorter, less perilous old Indian trail a mile south at the new dock.

Over the Great Rock Wall A Continent Sleeps

Many of the King's men, ever since they arrived in New York's harbor, have looked across at the great wall along the Hudson's west bank wondering what lay behind it. Each man in his own way has been moved by the strange, lengthy, volcanic hump of mountainous landscape. Some have admired its wonderous beauty. Some have looked upon it with awe. All, moved by normal curiosity, have made guesses as to what is on the other side.

However, most of the invading foreign troops are aware that over the rock wall and westward lies the continent of America. And it is that about which many have heard so much. It is that land around which their childhood dreams often have been spun, fanned by countless, fascinating stories of adventure. It was the lure of seeing that bounteous, beautiful country which induced many a soldier and sailor to enlist in His Majesty's army and navy.

Like the unscalable walls of an ancient castle, surrounded by its deep moat, the America beyond lies obscured, and hence, inviting.

The British nobleman and leader of the expedition moves in and out of the stone house. He is keeping a firm personal hand on the tremendous task placed on his shoulders. For he sees it as the main maneuver in what may be the climax of the campaign. It could be the greatest military service he will ever be called upon to perform for his King.

The Earl oversees the assembly locations of the rapidly accumulating troops one minute and the next he is briefing his command officers inside the house. In formation the troops empty out of the small transport vessels and then up to assembly points before starting up the dangerous spirally trail.

The two docks at lower and upper Closter, a mile apart, have given the British high command two entrances over the cliffs into the valley. Since Cornwallis's Tory advisors have shown great concern over Fort Lee's northernmost outpost under Durkee at the Sneden's Landing site, an advance scouting party, supported by a battalion made up of guards, grenadiers and light infantry have ascended the cliffs on both the old dock's trail and the new dock's narrow path.[3]

Both advances are to intercept any riders or forces that might come down from Sneden's Landing garrison three miles north of Closter village. They are to clear the way to the King's Highway in the valley and cut off any rebel alarmers before they can alert the militia or ride on down to warn Fort Lee. These two advance guards will form the right and left wings for the main body as it comes down over the Palisades' west slope into Closter village.

So the main army pushes its way up the slopes on the old Closter Dock trail. Stumbling, falling, struggling they run into the constant problem of congestion. Only a few torches are carried.

After disembarking they feel their way in the darkness. The men stay close with their units, marching for a distance, halting, standing at ease and waiting until the companies ahead of them thin out as they move up to attack the hazardous incline's narrow rocky trial.

Plodding ever upwards upon the heels of the men in front, the invaders follow in the footsteps of the vanguard—handpicked light infantrymen, chasseurs and engineers who are well ahead. Their forward scouts have already conquered the mountain trail.

The van, led by the Tory guides who supposedly know the terrain, has cleared away major obstacles for the main body of troops, horses, supplies, and armament. Some now wait at the summit, sending out picket forces to probe the way into the valley.

Twenty-four hours ago Cornwallis and his staff toasted the success of the enterprise in the name of King Goerge III. That was shortly before leaving his comfortable Westchester quarters and shortly after Howe handed him his orders at 9 P.M. in the British commander-in-chief's De Lancey Mill headquarters.[4]

And now the expedition's commander stands wet and cold in deep conference with Major General Vaughan, Brigadier General Matthews and the Hessian commander, Colonel Donop. The eyes of all four men occasionally lift skyward in a vain attempt to focus upon the long winding lines of red and blue coats challenging a precipice. All they can make out are dark, towering stone shapes, glowering down upon them as though they were the angry outpost sentinels guarding the edge of a new-found world.

Far behind the van on the summit and its advance scouts the long lines reach back through the hundreds of vessels across to the river's New York shores. The crossings gradually roughen as the waters, spanked by an increasing southeast wind and troubled by the shifting tide, toss the boats around more perilously on choppy waters.

Throughout the black night and into the break of dawn, the armada of river-boats carries its countless loads in a steady stream onto the Jersey coast. Each boat more easily now swiftly and quietly deposits its load under the bleak monoliths rising up from the river's banks.

Under sail, oars and often propelled by the poling seamen at bow and stern, the ships maneuver into assigned beachheads. Occasionally one is swamped, but British sailors, especially assigned to take care of such emergencies, promptly go to the aid of vessels and men. Sometimes it is a single awkward soldier, encumbered with knapsack, bed-roll, canteens, bayonet, powder pouch and musket who upscts the order of things by falling into the water after losing his balance while disembarking.

Upon setting foot ashore and after breaking ranks before reassembling for marching orders, some of the soldiers make a dash into the bushes. The fear of treading on snakes in the darkness does not deter them from answering urgent beckonings, induced by fear, excitement and seasickness.

This night and morning have been enough to give the most stalwart among the brave, severe cases of the American "green apple quick-step." But this time it is not green apples.

So even the redcoats' dread of meeting wild animals, curling rattlers or copperheads does not lessen the lightning speed at which some strike out for the bushes. Besides, the men have been told that reptiles have gone into hibernation for the winter. But all nature has not, including the periodically terrifying rock-falls—small avalanches that pour down from the perpendicular heights above the soldiers' heads at the foot. They are set off by the tramping of men and horses and the movement of heavy equipment high on the unseen rock-covered corkscrew trail near the summit.

Such rock-falls are common during rains, but now the increasing pounding from the feet of the guards, engineers and chasseurs, who ascend most of the time two abreast over the treacherous, infrequently traveled trial, sets off the slightly embedded rocks. A single slip of the foot sometimes does it, causing one stone to start a cascading performance which swiftly gathers others, large and small, for a furious race down into the mountain's thickets on the river's bank.

And the perilous job of dragging the army's few heavy pounders on their carriages nearly a half mile up the steep, circuitous incline multiplies the rock-slide dangers.

At times the fury of the avalanching cascades makes the invaders wonder if the angry earth at the very eastern edge of America is not itself fighting to reject unwelcome visitors. And some of the soldiers with imaginations even begin to think it might be so. Particularly when a few point out the 100-foot menacing looking profile of an angry Indian's head, overlooking the river on the cliffs' face northward.

A Thoroughly Organized Expedition

So when one of these slides occurs, it is not uncommon for a few white or yellow breeches, still drooping almost to the boot-tops, to be seen hurriedly wiggling an escape from out rock-bombarded bushes. The booted feet under the sagging pants shuffle jerkily to keep barely out of reach from the tumbling stones and boulders.

Above the fallen colorful breeches, the surprised soldier carries his inseparable musket in one hand, attempting vainly to hold up his trousers with the other while angrily making his ludicrous wobbling exit from the brush and his flight out from under the showering stones.

After awhile they will be too busy struggling up the trial to think of fear, or other things. The preservation of their lives temporarily becomes their only thought and the sole reason for existence. Those at the base, waiting to ascend, hope the sky will bless them with light before it is their turn to move upon the mountain. However, most are disappointed and go forward without a touch of sunrise to light the path.

In the distance Indian Head Rock

Soon after dawn the river-crossing phase of the expedition is completed, and the bulk of the army is atop the defile. As they look down upon it in the light of day they see places over which they labored no wider than five feet across to a crag's precipitous edge and a sheer drop hundreds of feet to the shore below.

Behind the advance of scouts, guards, engineers and chasseurs have struggled the first and second battalions of grenadiers, two battalions of guards, the Thirty-third Regiment, the Forty-seventh Highland Regiment of the reserves, three battalions of Hessian grenadiers, 100 of Rogers' Rangers without arms, carpenters, auxiliaries and reserves. Behind this invasion of New Jersey is a most thoroughly organized expedition.[5]

It is 9:45 o'clock in the morning before the last of the troops, horses and impedimenta are on the summit.[6] The drizzling rain has not slackened. On the heights over 5,000 troops hurriedly breakfast while the advance guards cautiously proceed two miles down the west slope into Closter town.

By companies the troops are temporarily halted and widely spaced in carefully assigned stations along the mountain-top. Some try to dry out their wet clothes while others attempt to heat rations over countless hastily lighted fires that struggle to stay lit against wet wood.

The troops' rest is brief. Once the entire corps is fully reorganized and the advance has probed the trail into the valley highway's north and south arteries, the march again resumes. The road down the mountain's slope takes the main body to a point north of "Demaree's" or Demarest's mill and "Vesterfelt's," or Westervelt's place.[7]

The left van, proceeding south after scaling the lower Closter mountain, is about three miles south of Closter when it is halted by volleys of rifle fire. The wing's advance guards have accidentally stumbled upon an American militia post. However, the musketry exchange, though holding up the entire march, is brief.

The surprised rebel militiamen disperse quickly at the sight of the enemy's strength. And again the British vanguard moves on.

The rain has stopped, but the resulting mist hangs heavily over the valley. It makes progress tediously slow even for Howe's two hand-picked Tory guides. One leader of the left wing van, took that British arm up from the lower Closter over and down into the valley. He is Tory Major John Aldington of Hackensack,[8] a close friend of his superior in rank, Tory Colonel Abraham Van Buskirk. Van Buskirk leads the right van into Closter.

Into the Hidden Valley With Dreams Of Glory

Aldington was reared in the English Neighborhood and farmed 20 acres there until recently. Earlier this year his brewery building, constructed on his land, was seized by the Continental Army when his Loyalist leanings were made known. His affection for the King immediately flamed into a belligerent animosity for the rebels.

Then the Tory offered his services to the Guides and Pioneers' Battalion of the British army and was given a commission as a major under Colonel Van Buskirk. Aldington looks forward to being in on "The Kill" when the King's men surround and capture the rebels and their Commander-in-Chief at Fort Lee. For there, they will take over control of the surrounding country and the valley where his own rebel-seized lands stand. A seven-mile march south and the King's men will give him his revenge.

Traveling in the van of the troops is another one who General Howe has personally recommended as a knowledgeable guide for Cornwallis's corps, one who is familiar with the works at Fort Lee. He is the corps' newest, taciturn enigma, William Demont, a defector about whom little else is known except by the British commander-in-chief.[9]

Walking up over the precipice crest and winding their way through the groups of soldiers as they wait for the order to advance in their march into the valley, Cornwallis and his aides go over to the far brow of the mountain. The nobleman has of late been worried following word of his wife's illness back in England. And now, there below him over the gentle west slope through the gray mist lies the Hidden Valley.[10] It offers him, he hopes, success and an early return to London and his ailing marchioness.

Beyond the King's emissary, widely stretched before his eyes, lies the eastern terminus of Britain's North American colony. Up until this date he has seldom set foot on anything but the continent's fringe islands.

To the south, seven miles away is his day's objective, Fort Lee. And about six miles to its west lies Hackensack. Through it, he can see on Aldington's roughly marked map, the highway to Aquackanonk and Newark and thence the stage road to Philadelphia.

Cornwallis is a man of single purpose. He focuses his field glasses on the road below him to Fort Lee. For there today lies his battleground and in it possibly a destiny that could bring the colonies back under the Crown where they belong.

The expedition's commander has many advantages. He has completed a remarkable, surprise amphibious invasion of the main continent without—from all appearances—having been detected until the van of his force came upon the militia quarters in the valley's Tinefly lowlands. And the operation, the river crossing and then the scaling of a precipice mountain wall with thousands of men in darkness, under the most trying conditions, is a mammoth accomplishment.

What is more, it was executed at a difficult point along the river and one that his rebel enemy never suspected the British could pierce. So the surprise element, Lord Cornwallis believes, is still working in his behalf.

Also in his favor is some valuable intelligence he has received in Continental Army correspondence which emboldened Tory parties have intercepted. The confiscated papers include dispatches directly out of the Americans' main headquarters.[11]

From them the British command has learned of Greene's frustrated efforts to get his boats up from Newark into Overpeck Creek for use in transporting supplies by water to and from Fort Lee. Secondly he learns much from the captured dispatches of what the American Commander-in-Chief has disclosed to the Philadelphia Congress.

Unfortunately these documents reveal the Continental Army's desperate state of affairs. They disclose the distressing enlistment problems, particularly the dangers incumbent within the army's short-term recruitment plan imposed by the Congress and the weakening effect it has upon the strength and morale of the army. The revelation that many rebel enlistments soon expire brightens the picture from the enemy's point of view.

In addition, thanks to the increasing boldness of the Jersey Loyalists, the British command has acquired some of the American Leader's personal letters. Most enlightening of these is one to Ned Rutledge.

The Rutledge letter reveals the unfortunate situation in which the rebel General finds himself owing to "cursed short enlistments." He had further revealed to Rutledge dates of the expiring enlistments. Some on December 1, others on January 1, when, he said, "the whole army will leave him, as they have undergone great fatigue during the whole campaign, have suffered amazingly by sickness and the approach of winter." The letter further notes that the army gives the appearance of starving and that all are in want of clothes.[12]

Military accomplishment is Cornwallis's primary ambition. The captured dispatches now further fan his hopes. One piece of news—the plan to evacuate Fort Lee—especially concerns him.

General Cornwallis, at 38, is in the peak of his career. He recognizes the limitations age imposes upon military achievement and he has heard it said and argued countless times that "a soldier is no longer at his best when the sap has ceased to mount."

And so, at this high point in his military life, the expedition's commander is in a hurry. He is now within easy grasp, he feels, of one of those major tactical accomplishments which all military leaders dream about.

These thoughts flash briefly through his lordship's mind. His pleasant gentle smile and wide open big blue eyes that light up his long nose on its convex profile, but never flinch or shift, radiate sincerity and dedication. It is in direct conversation with Cornwallis that his conversants acquire the feeling he is penetrating their innermost thoughts.

This, and a heavy bearing, carried under that somewhat awkward gait, give him a distinction from which his associates gather a surprising surge of confidence. His lordship's mien, his reserved, quiet, contemplative manner, even under the severest of strains, tend to mark him as one of the finer personalities within the gentry of the English aristocracy.

The Plan

The Marquis often is somewhat conscience-stricken by the realization that he is carrying out disagreeable orders against many of his own countrymen in a distasteful rebellion. However, like the Howe brothers, he never lets these thoughts deter him from his duties and his loyalty, nor does he allow such thinking a voice.

To bring the revolting colonies to their senses and back under allegiance to the Crown, Cornwallis believes, justifies the British military mission in America. And there, in that valley, lies the possibility of doing so without the letting of too much further bloodshed.

It could be accomplished by encirclement and a siege of Fort Lee in the event the fortress, like Mount Washington, refused to capitulate. Under a long siege, staged around the English Neighborhood area, supported by Admiral Howe's troop landings at Bull's Ferry and the admiral's pounding of Fort Lee by the river's armed vessels, the place could be isolated and starved into surrender if the storming of it from the west were overruled.

He would leave Major General Vaughan commanding the besieged fort on the north and west. Howe's crossed troops from Bull's Ferry would block the south and the Admiral's men-of-war would hammer broadsides from the east. Cornwallis could see himself then conducting his troops through Hackensack in a drive through the Jerseys.

Though his orders now restrict him to go no farther than Brunswick,[13] their necessary alteration might enable him to cross the Delaware and take the Continental Congress. However, Cornwallis is sure that the capture of the Congress would be an honor Howe might wish to reserve for himself unless he succeeds in forcing the American Commander's surrender at Fort Lee.

As Cornwallis surveys the terrain and envisions success within his grasp from the west slope above Closter, Aldington sends up word of the valley's clearance. However, it was but a short time after this that the march abruptly halted, stopped by the brief exchange of fire at the Tinefly militia headquarters. Aldington was blamed.

The invasion's leader does not hold the same respect for Aldington as does Howe. The Earl disdains all defectors. Unlike Howe, Cornwallis finds them, regardless of what cause they espouse, obnoxious, but his orders are to make full use of them.

Down into the lowlands and south along the King's Highway, the marchers make their way two abreast. It is now 10 A.M. The surprising appearance of over 5,000 redcoats marching through their valley alerts the frightened inhabitants for miles around.

Throughout the entire area the Tory partisans spread word that the war is about to end. That the rebellious colonies will be restored to the Crown before sunset. The patriots, seeing the almost endless lines of enemy soldiers tramping past them, wonder if perhaps the Tories are this time right.

The sight of thousands of redcoats and Hessian bluecoats, the flashing steel of glistening bayonets, brass buckles and buttons, pieces of heavy artillery and all the necessary war equipment is enough to convince even the most ardent patriot that the conflict must be drawing to a close. For all know the poor condition, the inadequately equipped and trained status of the sickly American army at Fort Lee, particuarly since the loss of Fort Washington.

As one recorder will someday write:

"To sensible, practical men it was obvious that the rebellion was over in the Hackensack valley and that it would soon be over everywhere."[14]

With this state of mind predominating, Howe's recent offers of amnesty and unconditional pardon to all who wish to reaffirm allegiance to the King are widely circulated by the Tories. Increasing numbers of inhabitants, in order to safeguard their lives and their properties, will soon eagerly be accepting the Crown's offers. Even among the militia there is a growing feeling that further resistance is no longer possible.

So, as though adding tinder to the flaming fire, into this vale that extends northward into the Hudson valley above Tappan town and south down to the Three Pidgeons east of "Sacacus," the enemy marches on to the beat of drum, bagpipe and fife. Their mission no longer is a secret.

They will meet cheering Loyalists, silent Whigs and apathetic neutrals. The strange, old-world names of Dutch, German, Swiss and English inter-married families will challenge their pronunciations as well as their orthography.

They will meet the families of rebel soldiers, of those loyal to the Crown and those whose members are divided in their allegiance, brother against brother, father against son. One such family is the upriver Snedens. Ma Sneden is a Loyalist, but one of her sons, John, is a rabid rebel who enlisted in the Continental Army. So also is it similarly true of the Van Buskirk family, the Demarests, Westervelts, Paulsons, Van Horns and the Zabriskies.

The odd mixtures of foreign names which the British soldiers have never heard before will puzzle them: Goetschius, Wortendyke, Duryee, Demaree, Vesterfeldt, Banta, Blanch, Blauvelt, Bogert, De Graw, Roelefson, Terhune, Tallman, Talma, Naugle, Lozier, Lydecker, Demott, or an occasional Ackermann and Schoonmaker, among whom some Hessian soldiers believe they may surely find a distant relative.

What the Hessians will find pleasing is that here is not the wilderness they have been told about. Here are not the wild lands where the cannibal Americans would slit their throats, cut them up, cook and eat them.

Here, instead, they find a valley whose widely spaced rich farmlands are dotted with beautiful, substantially built homes of quarried brownstone—stone lifted from beneath the sub-soil and cut to size with a saw to create "Dutch houses," indigenous only to the area. Here they find well-kept farms and gardens, barns and grounds.

But it is the attractive and strikingly unusual brownstone homes that surprise both the Hessian and the British soldiery, awed by the bindings of pig's hair, mud and straw that hold the solid cuts of sedimentary rock firmly together.

And it is the wide overhangs of the houses, most all facing south to ward off winter's snows and screen off summer's sun, as well as the gable and gambrel roofs and the half-open Dutch doors, that spellbind the invading army.

Under Van Buskirk's guidance some of the army's right wing scouts, guards and chasseurs who led the descent down the Closter Dock road, swerved south on the highway, staying about two miles behind the Aldington-led left wing, thus giving the main army a double forward van. Before that they paused briefly at the cross-roads to probe the intersecting highways in all directions, bringing the astounded Closter proprietor of the Lone Star Inn[15] out in his nightshirt to see what was happening.

Under questioning the frightened innkeeper, joined by the proprietor of the Albany stage coach stop and blacksmith's shop next-door, corroborates Van Buskirk's estimate that the road up to Fort Lee from the valley is a good eight miles due south.

Since no rebels are reported anywhere in the vicinity, half of the Van Buskirk-led wing remains behind to guard the intersection. It will later fall behind Cornwallis's main force and bring up the army's rear guard.

Fait Accompli

Cornwallis, proud of the crossing and cliff-scaling feats his men have performed, hesitates to drive them too hard toward an objective that cannot move away. Momentarily he reflects upon the good fortune he is having. He is sure his enterprise will become a topic that will be widely discussed in America, in England and by military leaders throughout the world.

Ordinarily, militarists would contend that the chances of success for such a maneuver were very slim. It was a brilliant stroke of Howe's, he thinks, to select this opening from the river into the valley through a cut that was left totally unguarded by Greene.

Of the feat, Sir William will write in his report to Lord George Germaine, Colonial Secretary of State of King George III, this tribute to the naval personnel's performance:

> "... and the unwearied spirit of the seamen, from the transports as well as ships-of-war, in dragging the artillery up the difficult heights for sustaining the infantry on their landings can never be exceeded..."[16]

Pressing onward, the corps moves somewhat faster down the old King's Highway. For Cornwallis, the first stage of his operation is over. Now comes Part Two, the attack upon the fort. And thus far there is no indication that his enemy is yet aware of his coming, else certainly a brush with the rebels' forward pickets should have taken place.

Aldington has more than once reminded Cornwallis of the bridge across the Hackensack river although the Earl had been well briefed at Howe's headquarters regarding its strategic significance. Consequently, the British commander ordered Vaughan to send a strong picket force of light infantry off westward in the direction of the structure earlier this morning.

The picket captain's orders were to seal off any possible escape of the enemy force over the crossing into Hackensack and to keep the main body informed of their actions. Couriers have come back reporting no signs of any of the rebel troops at or near the span.

Cornwallis is therefore convinced that word of his invasion has not yet reached his enemy's ears. He marvels at his good fortune.

The British Earl knows that in General Howe's over-all plan the crossing of the Hudson and the assaulting of the fort are major objectives in the grand pincer movement. But he also knows that they are only pieces in the main design.

For, in the event that the King's men cannot put an end to the whole business in Jersey before winter closes in, Howe is counting on Carleton in the north to destroy the rebel army there and sweep into Albany. Sir Guy will then march down the Hudson valley, severing American communications, and assist Howe's forces in the destruction of their enemy, whether in Jersey or Pennsylvania.

Encouraging Prospects But Terrain Ignorance

All of this will have to be accomplished in the spring if the assault on Fort Lee does not meet with a major success and the rebels are not brought to their knees within the next few weeks. However, in light of the recent victory on the mount, the lately acquired intelligence revealing the Continental Army's collapsing status and now the invasion's astounding progress, British prospects appear highly encouraging.

In the British chief's haste in launching the Jersey invasion, he has had to plan with an inadequate knowledge of the Jersey terrain, particularly the region encompassing the peninsula upon which the Palisadean wall rests. Against his better judgment, he must rely almost entirely upon Jersey's Bergen County Tories for the locations of the roads, rivers and the outlying picket posts that extend from out Fort Lee, guarding it and its communications.

His own surveyors have little knowledge of the area's geography and have few sources from which to acquire it, except through the Tory adjunct to the Crown's forces, the Guides and Pioneers' Battalion.

In great haste the British command has gathered up all available information about the country on the west side of the mountain wall from all available sources. And much of it is inaccurate.

Even the Bergen County Tory guides do not seem to have good knowledge of the terrain. Each is acquainted with his own area and, generally, only vaguely familiar with all the characteristics of adjacent ones.

Except for a traveler's knowledge of the main highways and byroads such as Van Buskirk has acquired from his experiences in driving the stagecoaches, the guides do not have a surveyor's, map-maker's, or a geographer's knowledge of the peculiar Palisadean peninsula.

From a military surveyor's point of view, the Tories have not provided sufficient over-all knowledge of the terrain to be of much assistance in mapping the valley for the invasion forces.

The Lay Of the Land

Looking from the east bank of the Hudson at the Palisades and toward the invisible hidden valley behind it, presents an entirely different view and concept when the valley is exposed to observation from the west brow of the mountain range above the vale.

So the "unrecognized" peninsula is the American Commander's greatest asset, and he knows it. He knows the advantages as well as the disadvantages of being on a 25-mile long peninsula. And he has, therefore, recognized its creek and two rivers lying to the west, the Overpeck inlet, the Hackensack and Passaic Rivers as vital military assets in the event that a retreat from the fortress should be suddenly warranted. And now it is suddenly warranted.

So the British commander, from a position on the brow of the mountain overlooking the valley cannot be expected to realize he is on a peninsula, no less the strategic possibilities it offers his foe. He does not see it stretching up from Bergen Point, opposite Staten Island, northward to almost the village of Closter, carrying the Palisadean mountain range and the Hackensack valley. He does not see it set off from Hackensack village by the Hackensack River.

And neither can he realize the important fact that Hackensack village is in turn, set off, or separated, from Aquackanonk village by the Passaic River. Furthermore both the rivers are unfordable except far northward. But Cornwallis has been repeatedly reminded about the bridge over the Hackensack, and so he moves to block it off.

Far to the south and off to the west of the peninsula, lies the Newark Bay whose mouth empties into the Kill von Kull. The Kull partly encircles Staten Island at Bergen Point. It is into the Newark Bay and then the Kull that the Hackensack's southern end, westward of Bergen Woods, a tributary of the river, called Overpeck Creek, winds off through the tidal waters of the cedar swamps. It reaches north of Sacacus ("place of snakes") and west of the English Neighborhood, through swamps, salt marshes and meadows, much of which is impassable.

Of importance to Fort Lee is that the Overpeck Creek, mostly unnavigable marsh at this point, winds its way up toward the intersection of the road from the fort and the lengthy, north to south King's Highway intersection. It is on the upper end of the King's Highway, some seven miles north, where Cornwallis's van is now moving toward Liberty Pole.

Two miles south of the Fort Lee Road-King's Highway intersection, west off the highway, and through the old Indian village of Achenkesacky, is the Little Ferry to the village of Hackensack. Its passengers get off at the dock just east of the Village Green. Five miles southwest of Hackensack, by the Polifly Road, is the Passaic River bridge into Acquackanonk village.

The Passaic, like the Hackensack River, is unfordable except high up near its source. There it comes down from the highland mountains in the northwest where, after its descent from the Ramapo, it creates the great falls, about seven miles west of Hackensack village. Both rivers, therefore, can only be crossed by bridge or ferriage, a vital military factor.

While the Passaic River has only one main bridge at Acquackanonk, the Hackensack boasts two. One of these, the oldest and much used "Old Bridge," lies about four miles north of Hackensack's Village Green and its Little Ferry terminus.

The bridge adjoins the old Jacobus Demarest house which has stood since 1693 on the east bank of the river along the east shore's river road opposite Bogert's place in what is known as Steenrapie. Since the building of a second bridge, a mile and a half south, the span has acquired the name, "Old Bridge." It is about six miles northwest of the Lower Closter new dock.

Two Bridges Miles Apart Could Cost the Lord His Victory

The second bridge over the Hackensack is the newest bridge. It spans the river about two and a half miles north of the Hackensack Green at the village's north end. The bridge's western terminus almost empties into the house of John Zabriskie, the miller.

The grist mill owner, who built his home here in 1737 and became a respected colonial magistrate, is now one of those suspected of strong Loyalist leanings. Zabriskie is destined to be arrested within the year for his Tory activities. His home will be confiscated by the American army in the name of the Continental Congress.

Logically this span across the Hackensack River has become

known as the "New Bridge." As the crow flies, it is about seven miles northwest of the Fort Lee Bluff Rock. But by the circuitous roads from the fort to the New Bridge via Liberty Pole, Tee Neck and the New Bridge Road, it is over eight miles with another two and a half miles to the Green.

The Little Ferry, though time-consuming, is shorter by almost three miles, while in between the two routes is the seldom used, uninviting and dangerous, passage through the "Impossible Swamp" to Tee Neck and Terhune's mill south of the New Bridge. It cuts out the well traveled stagecoach highway through Liberty Pole.

From the Lower Closter new dock to the New Bridge is only seven miles straight flight but over ten miles after winding through the byroads to get there. The route to the old bridge is, on the other hand, the popularly used one in the upper valley and is almost straight across six miles and easy to follow. There are no American pickets posted there. It is too far upriver.

There are rebel pickets at the new Bridge which Major General Vaughan's captain and his scouting party do not find until it is too late. The likelihood is that, if Vaughan and Cornwallis received intelligence about a bridge uncovered by rebels, it has been the old bridge rather than the vital New Bridge.

Cornwallis and Howe have never seen the Hackensack River as the peninsula-maker it is. Unfortunately for their invasion operation, they have not viewed the entire region, its creek, rivers and swamplands in the same light as the American General.

While his eyes have perceived the region and Fort Lee from both the offensive and defensive angles, the British high command have seen them from across the Hudson, exclusively as standing objectives waiting to be seized without giving much regard to their escape hatches.

They have looked upon them only from an offensive angle, simply as objects next to be assaulted. They have set their thoughts upon "a precipice which bounds the shore for some miles on the west side of the river."[17] In doing so, and for want of accurate intelligence regarding the geography and the terrain problems, their minds are closed to their enemy's possible means for sliding out from under their grasp.

One British officer will recall the expedition's lack of infor- mation about the terrain, saying:

"If the situation of this ground had been perfectly known with regard to Overpeck Creek, the most of the rebels might have been intercepted in their retreat."[18]

If Howe and Cornwallis could look upon the surprise-filled hidden valley through the same eyes as the American Leader, they would now undoubtedly make many corrections in their strategy. For The General sees it as "a very narrow neck of land," according to his letter to Congress, written yesterday from Fort Lee. In it he added that the fort is no longer defensible since, he states:

> "(It has been) considered as only necessary in conjunction with that (Fort Washington) on the east side of the river to prevent communication across and the enemy from free navigation."[19]

The Peninsula

Another enlightening description of the peninsula's indefensible nature, as seen from its southern end at Bergen Point westward of Paulus Hook, was written just before the Hook's garrison was evacuated.

A member of the Paulus Hook garrison during its evacuation, the writer, as quoted in the *Pennsylvania Journal and Weekly Advertiser* of October 9, 1776, gives this description of Bergen:

> "... a narrow neck of land, accessible on three sides by water, and exposed to a variety of attacks in different places at one and the same time."

Then, referring to the peninsula's southernmost post which lay opposite British-held Staten Island at Bergen Point, the soldier added:

> "A large body of the enemy might infallibly take possession of the place whenever they pleased, unless we kept a stronger force than our numbers will allow."[20]

It is Greene's adjutant, Thomas Paine, who describes it as:

> "a peninsula, varying from one to two miles in width, bordered on the east by New York harbor and the North river, and on the west by the waters of Newark bay, Hackensack river, Overpeck creek and the adjacent marshes... the place (Fort Lee) being on a narrow neck of land."[21]

Paine's explanation of the army's position on this day will say:

> "Our force was inconsiderable, being not one-fourth so great as Howe could bring against us. We had no army on hand to have relieved the garrison had we shut ourselves up and stood on the defence. Our ammunition, light artillery, and the best part of our stores had been

removed from the apprehension that Howe would endeavor to penetrate the Jerseys, in which case Fort Lee could be of no great use to us; for it must occur to every thinking man, whether in the army or not, that these kind of field forts are only for temporary purposes, and last in use no longer than the enemy directs his force against the particular object which such forts are raised to defend."[22]

Conjecture

[What happens next will baffle future historians attempting to resolve: Whether Cornwallis's scouts did not know there were two bridges over the Hackensack; the reason for the British delay; the actual landing dock, whether at "Upper" or "Lower" Closter; and exactly who informed the Fort Lee garrison that Cornwallis was coming.

One theory here expounded, is that a sentry from Colonel Durkee's garrison, stationed on a promontory rock south of Sneden's Landing above Coates' river sloops, sent out the alarm. Certainly he could have sighted the British ships-of-war, moored several miles south midstream. Then, hardly believing his eyes, at daybreak he could have observed the hundreds of small boats returning empty to the New York shore.

Certainly the American post's officers then would be called upon to verify the observation. Durkee would likely have ordered his highest ranking and most responsible officer, Major Clarke, to ride at great speed some 12 miles to give Greene the alarming news.

Clarke might have stopped at Fordy Closter's store on the highway, verifying the news and possibly escaping just before the van of Cornwallis's right wing came down the Closter Dock Road. Or he, if indeed it were he, might have ridden through and seen the main body pouring down Closter Dock Road from the mountain-top. And on his way south to the fort he could have hurriedly alerted all picket posts and the militia headquarters at "Tinefly," or today's Tenafly.

Or, as it will be contended by some, a Closter farmer saw the marching troops, jumped on his plow horse, and galloped to Fort Lee to inform the garrison. And there will be other local historians who will present data purporting to show Cornwallis's troops disembarked at the lower Closter dock—the new dock—landing. The Upper Closter Dock, they will say, was not the invasion point. Today the Lower Dock, called Huyler's Landing, leads over the mountain into the Borough of Cresskill.

As for Cornwallis's so-called "delay," if such there was, many varied reasons will be advanced. However, regardless of all the enigmas—the landing site, the two bridges, the alleged "delay"—and regardless of who brought the alarming news, the noises through the night by a 5,000-man amphibious army must have disturbed fisherman and farmer. And logically they could have also disturbed a sentry somewhere along the river within sight of the invasion area.]

Dawn, Fort Lee, November 20, 1776

At sunrise, it is just another morning at Fort Lee, Wednesday, November 20. It is a damp, cold, somewhat hazy morning. The smoky smell of burning wet wood from the many cooking fires permeates the chilling air.

Pickets are coming in, wet and hungry from their pre-dawn duties. Others go about their various tasks. Grumbling at the night's cold rain, some of the troops throw their damp, torn, ragged coats over them and bind cloth wrappings around shoeless feet.

Outside a few of the log huts and tents, non-coms and commissioned officers struggle in vain to get some order and discipline from the heavy grog drinkers of the night before. Their attempts are almost humorous, for the job is a difficult one, especially early in the morning and in the middle of the week.

Rumbling empty wagons and teams, those scarce, badly needed commodities, roll squeakily out of the quartermaster's corral and wagon repository area up to the summit for their customary routine orders. For days now, from dawn to sunset, they have been continuously carrying out the arduous task of removing stores, ammunition, supplies and the light weaponry of the fort across the Hackensack.

Some carry the expendable supplies only down to the landing near the Little Ferry dock to await the boats coming up from Newark Bay. They will transport them to the quartermaster corps at Newark town en route to West Jersey.

Occasionally a loaded wagon becomes mired in the mud from standing all night in a rut. A team of horses is hitched and another pair is added to speed the task. Meanwhile, as always, soldiers' brawn is called upon to push the vehicles' big wheels up on solid ground.

Jocko and his father in their rig, pull around one of the mud-splattering scenes on their way over to the Barbette Battery. Along with other wagon masters, Graves has been especially assigned to help move out the supplies and equipment from the Barbette under Gray's and Levy's command. It will be the first time in many days that Jocko has had a chance to see and talk to his two friends.

Over on the main encampment's southern outskirts, coming up from the old Bourdette cow path and pasture behind the army's slaughterhouse, Elaine and Paul, their arms filled with freshly made bandages, hold their noses from the stench. Elaine winces and turns her head away as the last cry of a little calf splits the air. Paul watches curiously as the butcher slits the animal's throat and laughs at the girl's fright and the boy's awed interest.

At the hospital compound, not far beyond the burial grounds, they meet Polly and little Hans, both of whom also carry bandages, sugar cookies and other tasty victuals for the sick. The bandages are the work of many of the women inhabitants of The Mountain and the riverside, all folded last night by candlelight.

Polly has changed completely in her attitude toward Elaine since "Captain" Molly passed through. Then, too, she has heard of Elaine's intention to go with the camp women when the army leaves in order to be with her husband. But it is a touchy subject which she dares not mention. And there is always, among women, a feminine compulsion to sympathize with a departing soldier and his wife, particularly when rumor has it that the woman is with child. So Elaine is back in Polly's good graces.

In fact, Madam Onderdonk, convinced that Elaine's little neutrality outbreak over a week ago was just a womanly emotion of a sort, has become more attached to Elaine than before. But she has learned what topics are safest with her fiery young friend.

Polly, who has long admired the Abbotts, knows of Elaine's similarly strong attachment for the Indian family, and especially the understanding sympathy Elaine gave the widower Abbott through his grief.

Often Polly had spoken of how frequently she had noticed the army scout standing beside the grave of his lost Mahtocheega in the nearby burial grounds. Even now, upon his return from a scouting expedition, he is sometimes seen quietly meditating beside the stone slab Old Stephen and Papa Pete chiseled out and placed upon the mound, facing it carefully to the east.

And frequently, in silent respect some distance away, leaning against a soldier-hut and holding the reins of two horses, Captain Craig, waits for his sergeant. Then both men ride off down into the valley to carry out a headquarters order.

No word of Abbott has been heard since he paddled off downstream with his parents five days ago on their way to Brotherton in West Jersey. So Polly, reminding Elaine of Andy Abbott's moments of reverence at the grave of his young squaw, expresses curiosity as to whether the army scout will ever return to The Mountain.

"I would think not," Elaine tells Polly. "Though I am sure that he will rejoin the army wherever it goes, at least until his enlistment expires at year's end. I see no reason why he should return here."

"Ahl uf dem vee vill miss much," Polly replies. "Neva vill I shed zem from mine thoughts, yet, fer za life uf me, I neva dream vunce zat I would eva see 'n Injun in grief even fer zair own vuns."

"Polly, there are times you bewilder me," replies Elaine. "Think you they are not beings like us?"

"Yah, I know! I know, El'e!" retorts the older woman. "But I vus not brought up as ye. I vas taught zu fear zem, 'nd I'm supposin' zay us too, as vell. Ven I kom ober, zay vas ahl 'memberin' zer massakers 'ere 'bouts by 'undreds uf Injuns..."

"'Twas not they that started that!" Elaine irately interrupted. "'Twas the villain Governor Kieft who ordered his men in the night, to brutally murder and mutilate a thousand Indians, men, women and children who came to him for protection from the Mohawks. 'Twas at Ahasimus on Pauw's land Kieft first massacred the Indians. Had they no right on their own lands to fight back savagery with savagery?"

Polly's repeated, "Yah, I know! I know!" was a concession sufficient enough for Elaine to end the conversation as the two women and the boys walked on to the hospital tents.

From inside the extra large log hut that serves as part of the hospital unit and in which medical supplies are stored and food prepared for the sick, the first cook brings out an empty porridge kettle. He greets the two women but quietly pulls them both aside as he closes the door behind him to drown out the groaning agonizing cries of the men on the hospital cots, usually reserved for those judged seriously ill.

"Them's who hollers loudest is no sicker den me 'n you," he tells Elaine and Polly. "You knows why deys ahollerin' so now; 'Scause da soigen's in dare. Dat's why! Dem odders lyin' dare ableedin' 'n won't eat. Dem's da real sick uns. See dis pour'idge pan? Empty! ... Who ate it all? Dem's who's ahollerin' most. Dats who!"

Both women have long been aware of the truth the cook speaks. But hearing it every day as though he were telling it for the first time, has become tiresome. However, they have noticed how much improvement some of the men show when the surgeon moves out to one of the other hospital huts and tents.

At the north end of the drill grounds where the fort's head-quarters are located, the battalion majors congregate to receive their orders for the day. Often from scattered areas of the encampment can be heard the raised voices of non-commissioned, or young subaltern officers, angrily reprimanding their companies for various shortcomings. Some of the troops, though standing at attention, chuckle at each other's remarks through the slit sides of their partially closed mouths.

At the gun mount the men from the engineers' battalion get ready to begin their day's work, dismantling the heavy pieces of armament, many of which have never been fired. It is a task which is scheduled to begin in earnest this morning.

At the foot of the gorge road, some distance from the ferry landing, Bourdette and Baummeister, who have been lamenting the loss of what little was left of their ferriage business by the fall of Fort Washington, are watching the men who have started to dislodge the shore battery cannon.

The task of helping in rolling the heavy artillery carriages up the steep incline is one no man seeks. General Mifflin has come out early with his aides to supervise the operation while Marie Louise, Rachel, Jennie, Caesar and Honest Sam have all gathered to watch the dangerous undertaking.

In the fort's southwest area, the wearied night pickets drag themselves toward the cozy warmth of their log hut fireplaces and their beds after a long night of patrolling. The little cabins are no longer meticulously maintained. The street signs, washed by many rains, are illegible. Some have been knocked over and used for fire wood. Others, askew, have never been straightened.

The appearance of the huts, inside and out, as well as the entire grounds, all show the effects of neglect. For, even before the battle of Fort Washington only four days ago, much evacuation work had taken place. On top of that was the growing rumor weeks ago that both forts were to be abandoned and the garrisons moved out to winter quarters near Brunswick or Trenton. And so the interest in maintaining quarters to be occupied only temporarily waned.

But, to the tired, returning, night-watch sentries, the curling, white, billowing smoke from the chimney-tops and the sweet, sleep-inviting odor of burning apple wood, white pine and oak, become delightfully inviting on this cold, misty morning in mid November, particularly during disheartening times. Besides, it is far better to have a nice day of restful sleep than to have to drag cannon and haul stores, ammunition and supplies to the wagon-loaders.

And at this early hour, a good distance southwest of the camp grounds, where the tents of the camp women are pitched, can be heard chattering feminine voices, the yelling and shouting of children and the constant rattling of pans and banging of cauldrons, always in the center of the cooking process.

These isolated camp followers comprise a strange mixture of loyalty, love and loneliness. For they are not only the wives, children and sisters of soldiers, but also sweethearts, hangers-on and widows—soldiers' widows, who in some cases have turned prostitutes in order to survive.

However, the questionable, or so-called "shady women," keep discreetly to themselves in a little area off from the rest. They often pretend they are what they are not—wives, sole relatives, or problematical widows of missing soldiers displaying appealing, unfading hopes of becoming reunited.

Around them persists that questionable doubt, an aura of uncertainty, that vacillates between tolerance and condemnation, tempered by the nomadic wanderings of warriors' women in the harsh, abnormal settings of bitter warfare.

Here, trailing with the army, the camp women, some with offspring, may eke out an existence. They are willing to endure hardship, disease and danger in exchange for being near the side of loved ones. Here, for them is security, particularly for the homeless ones. Here, for them, is a hope for eating and living at whatever the cost. The alternative could be starvation.

The Post's Alarm Splits the Air.

The Post's Alarm Splits the Air

So, all throughout Fort Lee's extensive grounds, its works along the river's shore and on its Bluff Rock battery site, it has, up until this hour of ten o'clock in the morning, been just another day unfolding.

But at almost precisely upon the hour, a sweating horse and his excited rider[23] rush past the lower road sentries, pausing briefly before galloping up the western slope on the way to the fort road. Some know him. All pass him through to Greene's headquarters.

Almost immediately after he enters, a hurried summons is issued for all the post's regimental and staff officers. Even before they all arrive, assembling around the fort commandant, the alarm bells ring out with a boisterous clattering such as no one has ever heard before.

In all, Fort Lee along with its outposts, pickets and other personnel number 2,667.[24] And the unprecedented alarm brings every man running to his unit for emergency orders.

It is the first time that the general alarm, which calls every able bodied soldier to his station in the event of extreme necessity, attack fire, or disaster of any kind, has ever been sounded three times. And in rapid succession.

Most of the fort's complement do not remember whether the thrice-sounded signal means attack or fire, but they all know it means they are to drop everything and report to superiors without delay. It causes the off-duty personnel and the unassigned to scramble around in confusion. Men, singularly and in groups run, crisscrossing the fort's grounds in all directions.

Greene orders Captain Gooch to ride to the north outposts and bring in the guards on duty. Paine is to see to Gooch's baggage. Another officer rides to bring in the southern outposts as far down as Bull's Ferry.

Work parties, companies and their non-coms are hurriedly summoned and ordered to have all men gather only essential possessions, clothing, bedding and cooking utensils that can be put together in light rolls. Each man is to be fully armed and ready to move out prepared for battle. And within ten minutes most are.

In some sectors near Pandemonium breaks loose as the troops rush around the encampment carrying out the emergency orders. All wonder what now is about to happen. But it is not long before they hear the enemy has landed upriver and is marching through the valley.

Orders go out informing the artillerymen that only light armament is to be dragged off in the evaucation. Every gun carriage bearing the smaller, easily rolled pounders, is brought forward into the rapidly forming lines of march. From the Bluff Rock's artillerymen the soldiers on the main camp grounds learn there is no action on the river within view.

This news, spreading through the rank and file, relieves their minds that the enemy is not also coming across from Fort Washington. Some had expected Howe would try a pincer movement.

Greene advises all his officers of the serious state of things and acquaints them with the plan of escape by a forced withdrawal to Hackensack unless the enemy cuts them off. The word filters down to the troops.

On the Bluff Rock, Gray's men sight two enemy ships of war downstream. Both vessels haul anchor and unfurl sail in preparation to get under way. They are quickly identified as the *Renown* and the *Repulse*. Except for that, Gray reports no other activity under The Rock or within view on the water.

Word spreads that a post dispatch rider was seen taking off for Hackensack immediately after Greene was informed of the enemy crossing. This they know means that The Gen'l himself will be riding over from the encampment post on the Green to be with his troops. His presence always helps, but right now the natives need someone to allay their fears even more so than the soldiers.

Fright and confusion spread through the sparsely populated little hamlets of the northern valley and in short time will sweep throughout the Hackensack and Passaic River settlements. From house to house along the shore and over the western slope, the fort's resounding alarm gives the inhabitants the terrifying news that they have dreaded to hear and yet expected.

However, the loyal subjects of the King happily wait to welcome the peninsula's invaders.

Every available wagon is summoned into service including those scheduled for repairs. Every man ready to march, frantically assists in wagon-loading the long trains, already moving out and down the road into the valley.

Stores, magazines, provisions, baggage are literally thrown aboard. Some thirty Philadelphia wagon teams, all heavily loaded, work into the lines of marching men, gun carriages and farm wagons. They follow the swiftly moving van in beginning its dangerous, uncertain attempt to evade their approaching foe and escape across the Hackensack.

Recognizing what is happening, but unable to comprehend its full effects, the inhabitants come out to cheer the men on. They offer what services they can and try to get answers to their countless questions.

Fears for what lies ahead grip their minds. They have felt complacently secure under the shadow of the fort's garrison. All except the few Loyalist sympathizers among them who often pose as neutrals.

Roll calls ring out. As names are called, companies come together. Rapidly by twos, paying little heed to any orderly formation, they move into the steadily retreating columns. Abandoning everything that cannot be carried with ease, they cling only to their field packs, rifles and rations.

Word spreads swiftly that the enemy has been sighted advancing down the valley south from Closter. Officers are warned that a brush is expected before reaching Hackensack, but that "God willin' we hopes ta make it 'cross" [the 100-foot wide river into Hackensack town] "afore sundown 'less'n da'basards stops us."

Little effort is needed to speed the march. The Continentals know they will be hopelessly outclassed and outnumbered by the enemy's corps. They rush through every movement. Excitement fills the air. There is no panic. Some are even eagerly looking forward to a battle. But the militiamen largely prefer their fighting behind a fortress.

Order Comes From Chaos

In an amazing change from a scene of confused intermingling of wagons, horses, gun carriages and men, running helter-skelter, a remarkable state of order and discipline takes shape over the encampment grounds. It is order spurred out of confusion by the promise of assured strong leadership.

It is also that unity through comradery for which soldiers reach in their sudden, hurried need for shelter within the security of the firm guidance of the pack. It is that self-saving frightened grasp for discipline that drives the protection-seeking individual back into his family circle, society, nation—to his company, regiment or army— when the crucial hour threatening destruction strikes. For only then do most men unhesitatingly cast off their treasured but cumbersome garments of independence. Only then do they willingly submit to and look upon discipline and order as their saviors, in answer to the ringing cry for survival, the pristine instinct.

In this turmoil General Greene moves quietly astride his recently acquired former Tory-owned horse which he finally purchased from the New York Committee. The black stallion carries his master from one unit to another through the throngs of troops gathering on and moving out of the assembly grounds.

Amidst angry commands from irate non-coms and shouting, busy soldiers answering gruffly to their names, officers strain to give orders above the commotion.

His aides beside him, Greene calmly rides in and out of the bustling ranks speaking briefly to regimental and brigade commanders. His demeanor, radiating confidence and strength, has a soothing influence upon the whole assembly. With the post commander at the head of his troops, company by company, the corps follows its vanguard down The Mountain's west slope into the direction from which the enemy brigades are advancing.

Every man knows that it is a battle against time, and time is what the garrison needs. No tents are struck. Much equipment will be left behind. Everywhere kettles of porridge are left boiling over the dwindling flames of the cooking fires that spit angrily at the softly showering rains trying to quench them.

Many a hungry mouth will savor that food and yearn for a mouthful before the day ends.

But there is more than porridge left behind. Heavy ordnance, supplies of all kinds, and quantities of miscellaneous equipment are sacrificed in the hope of escape.

Issuing numerous orders to subordinate officers, Generals Ewing, Hand and Beal struggle to keep the withdrawal organized and moving behind Greene. Ewing's brigade is much reduced from its original complement. Hand and Beal have been left with the command of mixed brigades of Virginia, Delaware, Massachusetts and Connecticut troops as well as many Pennsylvanians.

And heard over the Delaware State Troops, that once extremely proud, special band of men under Colonel Haslet's strict command, is their leader's popular, unmistakable voice. It rings out over his regiment. These are the continentals which in appearance, discipline and loyalty, have often been cited by other regimental commanders as paragons of excellence.

At the eastern end of the grounds can be heard General Roberdeau's commands. There, the Barbette Battery from the Bluff Rock comes up behind Roberdeau's men when they pull sadly and reluctantly out from their promontory post and move down over the gorge and up on the main parade grounds.

Always all around are heard the constant rumbling of wagons and whinnying of horses. They outsound the shouts of soldiers answering orders and roll calls.

And the rain comes down lightly under a miserable, clammy cold blanket of air that threatens momentarily to turn into wet snow. The soggy ground spatters the already mud-covered, cloth-wrapped feet of the bootless ones with the leafy muck of the earth's pre-winter mantle.

The yelling of orders and directions resounding over the mountain-top's garrison, gives off a cacophony much like a colony of agitated monkeys. Even while the men are marching, the dedicated non-coms, determined to carry out their duties, sound out, calling off the rolls of their squadrons in a desperate effort to leave no one behind.

". . . Richard Swedland!" shouts one voice. If there is no reply, it is repeated. If he is missing, a corporal runs back to make a last-minute check. Then on goes the call, not just one or two groups simultaneously, but hundreds throughout the encampment. . . .

". . . James Ireland! . . Dannie Ireland! . . James Turk! . . William Spain! . . John China!,. . David Pollock! . . Peter Chinn! . . Adam Christ! . . John Baptist! . . Jacob Rosecranz! . . Thomas Levy! . . Nathan Solley! . . John Solomons! . . Aaron Isaacs! . . John Israel! . . Abner French! . . John English! . . David German! . . Shelly Holland! . . William Scott! . . Peter Welsh! . . Peter Danes! . . William Rome! . . [25] On and on they go.

Meanwhile, at the fort's headquarters, Colonel Bedford, Paine and a company of men from Bedford's command hurriedly clean out the most important documents, dispatches, and papers for carting to the wagons. Greene has ordered nothing be left behind that could give the enemy any military intelligence.

Paine, who has seen to the care of Gooch's baggage and that of the other captains assigned to round up the outposts, now hastily gathers up his own personal notes and writings which he had hoped soon to publish under the title, "The Crisis Number I."

Never did a title have a more appropriate ring. Some of his notes are carelessly dumped into the wagon and covered with a tent canvas to keep out the rain. A number of the printed pronouncements drop from a broken box and blow off in the wind.

The corpulent Major Blodget lends a hand until Colonel Biddle assigns him to see what can be done with Doctor Shippen's hospital charges. A number of the patients were extremely sick up until this morning when, with the news of the approaching enemy and the plans for a hurried retreat, in which the ill might be left behind, miraculous cures took place.

The thought of capture and the fear of the enemy's prisons were the two single prescriptions some needed to bring the pseudo-sick back on their feet. Others, along with several soldiers who have been held in the fort's jail pending court martials for desertion, theft and other offenses, decide to take off into the woods. And take-off they do. Into the deep thickets and forests on the western slope they make their way, gathering up whatever loot and liquor are in reach.

This is the exit they had thought of but did not know would come so easily. And far better it is than a long, cold march in freezing rain only to end up dead at the end of a Hessian's bayonet.

For them, The Cause, Liberty, Independence, Freedom, have lost all allure. For them, survival, living, loot and liquor, have immediate satisfactions, not found in chasing after vague ideals for others' benefit.

With the ringing of the alarm throughout The Mountain's summit, Elaine, leaving Polly with Hans in the hospital hut, chases Paul home and hurries toward the surgeon's tent to hear the news that the entire encampment is to be moved out without delay. Her immediate thought is John and a sudden desire to change her mind again.

On her way down the cow path in Paul's footsteps, she sees a body of soldiers who appear to have just consulted with Bourdette, joined now by Paul at the ferry owner's barn. The swiftly acting soldiers lead away all the horses, hers included, up the gorge road. She knows in a glance the animals are being requisitioned by the army for its rapid evacuation of the fort.

Tears well in her eyes as she sees her horse commandeered. Now, even were she to change her mind, there would be no way to go along. Besides she is not prepared, and now there is no way she could join the camp women. She knows only a few by name. Then, too, they are surely the first that will move out, probably by the safest route over the Little Ferry.

Perhaps, she tries to assure herself, there will be a way to join the army later on. Her concerns again focus on her husband.

The first thing she must do is get John's knapsack and marching things. They are kept by their bedroom washstand ready for such an emergency.

She must hurry them up to him, and her mother must prepare food, lots of food to take along. There is little time. She must hurry.

Both her mother and father are gratefully relieved that, regardless of the reason, Elaine has been forced to change her mind. Granny Rachel will later declare that it took the whole British army "ta make Ellie switch 'er mind once 'twas made-up." Not an accurate statement but close to it.

In a few minutes the young woman and her brother, carrying the knapsack and cloth-wrapped bags of victuals between them through the drizzle up the cow path to the parade grounds, find their way through the milling soldiers to the headquarters. There Elaine sees her husband and with her own especial signal for which she is noted, a trilling of her tongue against the roof of her mouth—the closest to a whistle she has ever been able to come— she quickly gets his attention.

With a few long strides he is beside her as Paul blurts out, "She ain't a'goin' withs ya, John!"

Gray had known when the gong sounded three times that the camp's evacuation would be rapid. He also realized that it put an end to Elaine's hopes for going out along with the army—a possibility he had never thought was very likely, despite Elaine's will.

"'Tis best this way, Elaine," he says, approaching her. "T'would never work out, Dear One. Never, I assure thee. 'Tis best this way."

Elaine holds back her tears. She does not speak, but nods her head in reluctant agreement.

Gray puts his arms through the harness of his knapsack after slipping the package of victuals under its flap, covering it from the rain. Placing his arm around her shoulders, his blue petticoat scarf waving wet around his neck, he presses her close to him, and the couple walk over to his battery assembling under Asher Levy's direction.

It is the moment both have long feared would someday come and which both silently dreaded, never allowing their lips to speak of it and trying in vain to prevent their minds from thinking on it. In both their dreams, nightmares have been frighteningly woven around this hour.

Neither one can find words. There is no time for long farewells. No time for tears. Only hope and memories flood their minds as they walk slowly toward the artillerymen of the old Bluff Rock

Barbette Battery. Both are oblivious to the shouting and commotion of the busy, rapidly emptying encampment.

Gray's concern for his wife and the Baummeisters in the event the area is overrun by the enemy was, he tells himself, fortunately made clear to all of the hamlet last night. He is glad now that he spoke to them as he did. He was right, he thinks, in guessing it would come today.

By now the Bourdettes, the Baummeisters, The Mountain's and the river's people have gathered at the fort's west gate alongside of the road which here begins its dip into the valley. Here the troops pause for their last minute reorganization and final regimental counts. And here they impatiently wait their turn to move out uncrowded and down the decline in order to keep the units properly spaced a safe distance apart.

It is there that Gray directs his wife and Paul to wait with the others for a last goodbye while he joins Levy, his men and the struggling crews assigned to hauling the gun carriages for the first leg of the march. In minutes they are before the west gate. There the unit halts and waits its signal to move out.

Gray had appealed to his superior officers to spike the big guns, but it was decided there was not sufficient time, and the risk was not worth the attempt.

All five 32-pounders being left on The Rock are comparatively good weapons though of an old vintage as also are the 24-pounders and lighter iron and brass ordnance. Leaving behind these and other heavy pieces including those along the shore, shakes the morale of the rank and file when it becomes known that the armament is to become their enemy's.

The abandonment of weaponry is not only in itself discouraging, but it convinces them that the approaching foe must be closer than they are led to believe.

There by the summit's west gate the worried inhabitants solemnly gather. Waiting and watching on the high ground, they overlook the valley that stretches far beyond the slope's high descending roadway, now streaming with marching men. They wait mainly to bid goodbye to the Barbette's artillerists. Like rain-drenched mourners, they line the roadway's edge. Foremost are the Baummeisters and the Bourdettes.

Paul and Hans climb a tree for a better view of the glum, mud-spattered troops, some of whom have had no breakfast. Polly stands beside her farmer husband and next to Elaine and Papa Pete. Old Stephen and Rachel with Jennie, Caesar and Honest Sam look on under the overhang of the old deserted Michael Smith house.

Greene Leads the Van Down the Fort Road

The saddened well-wishers with armfuls of fruits, vegetables and bread place the victuals in the passing wagons. Some hand out dried fish, apples, pears and peaches to the soldiers.

It is the artillerymen of the Bluff Rock Barbette Battery to whom the people of the hamlet have felt closest during the last four and a half months. So the artillerymen's wagon with Big Tom in the driver's seat and Jocko alongside, handling the wagon brake, seems to get the extra dividend of edibles.

Covered from the rain by their deer skin hides, Big Tom and Jocko are too seriously intent upon their responsibilities to notice the hamlet people's especial generosity.

In the train's brief pause, John leaves the battery and walks over to Papa Pete. The elderly man's pipe puffs out his rapid, short smoke rings of deep concern.

His breath and that of the others is heavy from the hurried hike up to the summit without the benefit of horses. Only one lame mare—Bourdette's oldest animal—has been left for the use of the river people until they are reimbursed by the army with the notes Greene has given them. That was one of the last-minute things the fort commandant ordered before personally leading the van of the troops down the mountain road when the marchers began.

In the lead, behind Greene, march the better appearing, well-equipped regulars, including Haslet's time-expiring men, some of whom have been lately talking about going home and very little else.

Well out in front of Greene's vanguard, Captain Craig and his scouts, badly in need of Indian Abbot and his knowledge of the terrain, undertake the difficult probing in search of the enemy's van and its exact location.

It is that unknown factor that seriously endangers the marching rebel force. And it is that which now slightly holds up the pace of the march, allowing John Gray a last few minutes with his wife and the family that had opened their hearts to him, a stranger, just one hundred days ago.

With one arm around Baummeister's shoulders, Gray withdraws a pistol, powder pouch and balls from inside his surcoat and quietly slips them into his father-in-law's longcoat pocket. Then grasping the ferry-master's large, rough hand, he says,

"It was my father's, Papa Pete. Take it and use it only if ye must. God only knows now what might happen. I have not fired it except for practice. Take care of her for me. God willin' I will be back with ye soon."

"Nein, Dzon! Vot vill ye do mitout it?" the older man asks protestingly. "I haff mine musket. No vun vill harm Ellie. You bat it. Vy vould dey?"

"I know not," Gray responds, turning from him to go over to Elaine and the others. "'Tis that I would make sure. Besides, I never will use it. I only fire the big ones, Papa. Know you not that?" he adds with a wry smile.

"Gott be mit you, mine son!" comes back Baummeister's reply. It is a meaningful farewell from the father-in-law who has grown to love Gray in the short time they have known each other. "Gott be mit you!"

Leaving his wife, whose eyes stoically repress her tears, until last, Gray, his scarf flapping from around his neck in the wind and the water dripping from the corners of his tricorn, plants a kiss on Marie Louise's tear-stained face. Walking over to the Bourdettes, he places his arm comfortingly around Old Granny, hugging her slightly, then Jennie whose sobs, intermingled with, "Lawdy! Lawdy! Oh, Lawdy!" audibly resound above the clamor around them.

He waves a goodbye to Paul and Hans up in the tree and affectionately taps the shoulders lightly of Old Stephen, Caesar, Honest Sam and others in parting gestures before drawing Elaine aside under the rain-sheltering eaves at the eastern end of the Smith house.

Elaine looks up pathetically into her husband's eyes. She strains successfully in withholding the emotions welling up within her being. Then, as though impelled by some occult prescience, declares coldly and with a fightening immobility of countenance, "I will never see thee again. Will I, John-G?"

"Rubbish, Elaine! Rubbish!" comes back his reply in a sharp, reprimanding tone. "The King's men cannot chase us to the wilderness outreaches of America. Soon they will tire and 'twill be over."

With that her eyes flush with tears she can no longer restrain. Trying to console her, John continues:

"We have had together a touch of Heaven. Some can ask no more. Some are given much less than we. Some more. Be not sad. We knew this day would come. And there will be more for us together. We should think 'o that.... But whatever happens, let us look happily on what we've had. If it should be that I do not return, and 'tis well we face the worst of possibilities, you must go on. Wiser ones than we have said there is ahead a better tomorrow. Let us then look to it."

He wipes the tears from her face with the end of his scarf, kisses her gently, and with his arm again about her shoulder returns her to the gathering, then turns quickly away and rejoins his men.

Asher Levy glances at the sad-eyed group of onlookers. He waves them a quick farewell as Gray comes up beside him at one of the gun carriages. Noticing their second lieutenant's gesture, the men of the battery do the same.

Then Elaine, as though she had forgotten something, rushes up to the wagon, reaches up and grasps Big Tom's hand, then Jocko's.

"Nev'va ya mind, Missy E. Nev'va ya mind," Jocko comfortingly tells Elaine. "We'se gonn' watch 'im careful like. I'se gonn' keeps mah eye on 'im. Nothin' a'needin' fer ta worryin' 'bout."

The distraught young woman says nothing, but hugs Jocko, who has come down from the wagon seat to pull a canvas tighter over the wagon's load.

Breaking away, he says, "Missy E, ah laks dat Katie May. Yall knows dat. So wills ya tell 'er I'se gonn' come back fer 'er caus'in she knows ah laks 'er 'n she laks me? So wills ya tell 'er fer me, Missy E? Wills ya?"

"You know I will, Jocko. You know I will," Elaine promises.

At this moment, The Leiutenant's celebrated scarf blows from his neck as he tugs at his knapsack, straightening it on his back. The sudden wind gust carries the blue petticoat stripping almost to Elaine's feet. She quickly retrieves it before it reaches a puddle of muddy water.

Returning it to her husband, she scoldingly tells him it is too wet to go back around his throat and forces it into his pocket. He reluctantly submits.

Then barely audible, she rapidly whispers in his ear, "If it is a boy, we will call him John. So you, John-G, hurry back to *us* safe."

Gray, taken by surprise, stares at her quizzically, then smiles happily and bestows a hurried kiss on her forehead, promising, "I'll be back!"

Suddenly the order comes up the lines and the lengthy train begins moving again, increasingly more rapid as it pulls away.

Several of the Barbette men shout orders. Over the commotion,

the Scot, Sergeant Lawrie Mac Namara, yells, "Down with Rex!"
And the Irish actor, Corporal Monahan, pulling one of the gun
carriages with others, calls out, "'Tis a play Ohim a'writin' next
with me the 'Ero and the King and 'Owe the vill'ins."

For Them No Beat of Drums

There are no sounds of fifes nor bagpipes. No beat of drums.
The cadence of the marchers is almost at a double time gait down
the mountain's slope. It is a pace that some will not be able to
hold very long through the muddy lowlands and up and down
through the scrawny, hilly ridges and the scraggly dales of the
valley to the river Hackensack.

For by the best trail, the Liberty Pole Tavern road, it is over ten
and a half miles to the New Bridge from the fort's grounds. It is
over nine miles to the bridge from the foot of the fort road in the
valley. However, the last two miles from the bridge to
Hackensack's courthouse on The Village Green should be easy
unless the enemy is in close pursuit and successfully makes the
crossing.

Word comes up the lines to the rear guard, bringing up the end
of the formation still assembled on the summit, that the American

For them no beat of drums

Commander has arrived. That he has joined Greene midway on the fort road. Both of the nation's top commanders are now leading the march into the valley. The news heightens the air of suspense that hangs as tremulously as the mist over every head.

Earlier in the morning The General had finished his breakfast of coffee, boiled fish, a slice of tongue, toast and butter, brought to him by Innkeeper Archibald Campbell whose hostelry soon is to become a center for the recruitment of British soldiers.[26]

It was shortly after breakfast that the express rider brought him word that "a great number of the enemy have landed between Dobbs's Ferry and Fort Lee."[27]

Accompanied by his aide, William Grayson,[28] a company of guards and his own bodyguards, The General reached Greene at the troops' van in forty minutes via the Little Ferry short route.

Following a quick council and having no word from Craig as to the exact location of the enemy vanguard, the two leaders, in accordance with their emergency withdrawal plan, decide to separate the withdrawing forces. They break the corps into three divisions, each to take a different route into Hackensack, thus assuring the escape of some in the event of a confrontation at the crucial Liberty pole intersection.

So the Chief and Greene, leading thier faithful Continentals, head the main body toward the Liberty Pole into the path of the oncoming enemy Juggernaut. This will save part of the almost 3,000-man garrison and prevent a total disaster in the fight, or brush, that is almost certain soon to occur.

The Escape Plan: Three Routes West

Following in the tracks of the camp women's wagon train which took the southernmost Little Ferry route, farthest from the enemy, some of the sick and many of the lighter wagons accompanied by about a fourth of the corps, move through the meadow trails to the ferriage way under General Hand.

Another division under General Beall, also about a fourth of the corps' force, takes the unpopular center route through the marshes of the upper Overpeck Creek. A dangerous, swampy trial, it is almost on a direct line west of the fort road where it intersects with the King's Highway.

The seldom used treacherous lowlands can save much time in crossing to the Tee Neck from Van Horn's Mill through the Impassable Swamp. But in weather such as today's a man could easily miss his step and be up to his waist in muck.

The main body, moving northward toward the Liberty Pole road, will veer west past Luguier's mill to the Pole at its intersection with Tinefly road. There, unless the enemy has been encountered, they will try to reach the heights of the Tee Neck ridge. From there they will make their way north along the ridge to the New Bridge road, down that artery about a mile and three quarters to the bridge, unless they are set upon.

It is the longest but the best roadway for it is the most traveled. And it is the only way that the big, overloaded wagons and gun carriages can be gotten off under such emergency conditions. However, it is the riskiest since Cornwallis is marching due south, the Continentals due north, and both heading for the point at which each plans a turn in opposite directions, the inter-section—unless the two armies meet and clash. But so far the enemy columns have not been reported by Craig and his scouts.

Once the American rear guard has cleared and passed the Liberty Pole, the way to the bridge should be unopposed unless Cornwallis sends a force to intercept the crossing. And that is one thing The General and Greene fear the astute British general has done. A brush at the bridge is sure to come, they feel, unless a battle materializes at the Liberty Pole crossroads, and both confrontations could occur simultaneously.

Certain that the Pole intersection is to be the day's critical spot and the key to his success or failure, the rebel General spurs his horse. With his aides and guards he rides ahead to the four corners, leaving Greene to continue with the breaking up of the army into its three divisions and their separate routes to the Hackensack. At the Pole's corners, with Grayson by his side, he and his battalion of guards keep watch over the crossroads while awaiting Greene and his troops and word from the scouts.

Bundled under the cold wet wind astride Old Magnolia, The General, flanked by his staff officers, watches almost motionless as the vanguard of the struggling columns of soldiers with their loaded wagons and gun carriages safely pass through the corners, then westward toward the Tee Neck heights.

Some men more than others seem to push themselves miraculously beyond their normal endurance. Bearing weighty packs and muskets, their sackcloth-wrapped feet, or boots if they have them, sink soggily into the red clay mud.

The frenzied innkeeper of the Liberty Pole Tavern opposite The General and his guards, who are widely strung out along the southern side of the road, watches with his wife and others from the tavern window. He has heard the British forces are moving down upon him through the northern valley. And now, seeing the American forces lined up across the road and all around his place, and an army of rebels moving westward over the intersection, the tavern owner suddenly visualizes his property might at any moment become the scene of a raging battle.

He is consoled by the fact that wet powder does not burn and rainy weather and musketry are not compatible. Perhaps the British are bogged down up Closter-way, the nervous innkeeper tells his wife in an attempt to bolster his own hopes.

"They will maybe not come in such weather," he comfortingly tells her. "Maybe they will wait and then these soldiers will be gone."

Battling Time and the Elements

From the innkeeper's tavern—to which the stage runs after curving from the King's Highway on its way northward up from Bergen village, the Three Pidgeons, Day's Tavern and the fort road—the Tinefly section of the highway begins its northern continuation through Vesterfeldt's lands toward Closter and Tappan towns. From there it winds its way up through New York's Highlands to King's Ferry into Westchester and New England.

So it is here at the Tory-despised Liberty Pole, where the American Commander oversees the march safely through the cross-roads without any sign of the enemy. It is a depressing parade of muddy men, horses, wagons and rolling armament, dragged out of ruts and ditches and always hurried faster from one perilous post to the next, ever reaching for the crest of the looming, distant Tee Neck ridge.

As the last half of the evacuees pour down the fort's turnpike road to the highway intersection, they divide. Some go the Little Ferry route behind the smaller wagons. Some are assigned to take the course through the Impassable Swamp.

There is little present fear for the forces taking the central and southern routes. It is the last of the contingent marching for the Liberty Pole that is now the staff's greatest concern. The Chief and Greene have dinned it into the ears of all their officers and the officers into the ears of all their non-coms that every man must reach the Tee Neck high ground before the enemy is aware of them, or all could be lost. Even there, they are told, there can be no letup of the pace.

So with bowed heads under heavy loads the men virtually plough through the miring ruts. Every step for the man behind is worsened by the sickening, sinking suction holes made by the man ahead.

It is a battle now. A battle against time and the elements. Paradoxically, however, the elements are mostly on their side.

Still waiting word from the probing scouts under Captain Craig, the American command is puzzled at the invader's failure to make an appearance. Not even an adventuresome forward picket has been sighted. The absence of any indication of the British army anywhere near the crossroads, while extremely comforting, confounds the rebel command. Why, if Fort Lee is their objective, has the enemy moved so slowly? Is it possible they have cut across to the Hackensack and now have command of the New Bridge?

If so it will soon be known. Once they have passed over the Tee Neck ridge and arrived at the Schraalenburgh and New Bridge roads' intersection,[29] they will have their answer, and they happily get it when the American vanguard hears from its forward scouts that the way to the river and across is all clear.

The General, realizing the perilous state of his army even though he may successfully lead them out of immediate danger, directs Grayson to return with a covering squad of light horse to Hackensack and send a dispatch to General Lee. He instructs Grayson to inform Lee that it would be *advisable* for him:

> "to remove the troops under his command at North Castle to the west side of the (Hudson) river and there await further orders."[30]

Grayson is about to leave when Craig at last rides up to Greene, who has now joined his Chief at the crossroads. The captain brings the news that a strong advance part of the enemy have proceeded to and are now halted on "a hill two miles above the Liberty Pole."[31]

Armed with this added knowledge and his instructions, Grayson and his party spur their horses off toward the New Bridge, reported clear by the scouts. On his way he passes General Ewing's advance pickets who confirm that the enemy has not as yet appeared and the bridge is safely posted.

The main line of march[32] now is a continuous one from the English Neighborhood intersection at the fort's turnpike road, past the Liberty Pole, up to the Tee Neck, along the Schraalenburgh and down the road to the New Bridge.

But under Generals Hand and Beal the two split-off divisions still are making their way over the central or swamp trail, and the

Little Ferry crossing. The hardest traveling of those divisions is encountered by the men battling through the swampy marshlands and over seldom-used footpaths up on the Tee Neck and then trying to cross the river at Jacob Terhune's mill.[33] The benumbing, near-feezing rains chill their bodies, cramping hands and feet.

All the troops are constantly prodded to make greater speed, forcing many to fall out, discard equipment and even weapons in order to lighten their loads. There are no rest breaks and those who take them, dropping out exhausted from the rapid pace, do so at their own risk. Along the roads and byways all kinds of discarded paraphernalia are dropped and scattered.

Captain Gooch, who rounded up the outposts, arrives at the Pole's crossroads leading the northern pickets and sentinels safely into the retreating columns. Drenched, they join their water-logged comrades. Bereft of all personal belongings and baggage, they hope, but futilely, that tent-mates will have carted their knapsacks for them, or that their gear is secure in one of the hastily loaded wagons. For some it will be so, but in the hasty exodus much has been left behind and few have had time to think of others. None are able to lug extra weight.

Through Ruts, In Rain, In Mud and Mire

Some of the wagons sink down in seas of red sandstone mud. To free them hurriedly, they are partly unloaded. Supplies, baggage and even ammunition are discarded along the sides of the rutted, boggy roadway.

Occasionally an exhausted soldier waits until he is unobserved, then swiftly hurls his musket into a thicket or down a ravine. He can say later that he left it behind in his haste or loaned it to an unknown duty picket.

Anything that can lighten his load he discards in order to save his hard-earned clothing, blankets, or his pair of priceless boots or shoes he values so highly that he carries rather than wears. Among the less hardy militiamen little thought is now given to what might happen if the enemy should suddenly confront them. Their course of action, they know, will be flight, entrusted solely to their legs and feet, bare or covered.

However, as for those with bare or barely covered feet, there are some who have seldom ever worn boots or shoes until recruited into the army. They are the "hard-feeted" ones. Even Indian Abbott's deerskin moccasins would for them be uncomfortable.

The Lieutenant's battery successfully passes the Liberty Pole crossroads. All of them breathe a sign of relief as they do so. Taking turns dragging their 12-pounder gun-carriage, one of several which the artillerymen have so far successfully taken off, the Barbette men proudly pull their piece southwest past the Pole through a dangerous stretch of lowland.

Gray and his men have carefully nursed the cumbersome weapon through and over one difficulty after the other. Only by stopping and pooling all of their battery's brawn with that of another did they in one instance prevent a carriage belonging to a sister battery from sinking helplessly into a mudhole that would have swamped it up to its hubs.

Now the same thing happens to Gray's carriage. All has gone well until they reach the bog lands and the forest area southwest of the Liberty Pole. The tree trunks over which the heavy 12-pounder must be rolled through the rain-fed lowland are in place when suddenly they separate under the increasing flow of the madly rushing stream.

In moments the water begins gushing around the sinking logs and the heavily weighted wheels of the carriage. Gradually at first, down into the sucking bed of the bog, the half-ton vehicle slowly submerges.

With it there seem to go the sinking hearts of the already over-taxed spirits of the old Barbette Battery's artillerymen. Other units also struggle with their carriages, four of which have already been abandoned, hopelessly mired, or turned over in the deep mud holes.

As the two logs on the left side begin to separate, allowing the wheel to slip deeper into the mire, the weight of the pounder carries it up on one side causing the carriage to totter perilously over to the left. Just before it loses its balance and topples into the rushing, mucky stream, Gray, Levy and five of the artillerists, giving no thought for the danger to themselves, leap into the ankle-deep current.

Without orders or direction they put their combined strength beneath the wheel. While others come quickly to the rescue and pull it forward, the seven men right it and safely push it back on solid ground.

It is a narrow escape for the now extremely valuable fieldpiece, but its rescue is credited to the Barbette men's long months of cooperatively working with one another. Like a team of well-disciplined ants, each man in an emergency knows what is expected of him and does it undirected.

In the lower southern column the camp women and their train cross over the Little Ferry between several companies of General Hand's troops. With previous permission, the husbands of many of them have left their own ranks to escort wives, and in some cases their families in the auxiliary train. For many of the men and women own their own wagons and teams. Faithfully these wives have followed their husbands no matter where the banner has taken their men.

Most of the troops along the central route have now safely passed through the Impassable Swamp and reached the northern outskirts of Hackensack town. In small boats, rafts and barges they cross the river near Terhune's mill when Beall gives the order. Some of Beall's men are led north along the east bank to the New Bridge.

At the New Bridge, General Ewing, much to his surprise, reaches and crosses the wooden span without sight of a single enemy. Then, as ordered, Ewing and his men begin collecting all the river craft afloat.

Helping first to carry over some of the riflemen under Beall at Jacob Terhune's landing, Ewing's troops maneuver the native's vessels high onto the west bank of the Hackensack, making sure the pursuing enemy has no means of crossing.

It was earlier decided that once every man is safely crossed to the west side of the river, the New Bridge is to be destroyed. All boats brought over to the west bank are immediately staved in.

Now—of all the days and hours of the month—the boats and men Greene ordered weeks ago from Newark, arrive. They have made their way since dawn through the tall, thick grasses rising in the salt marshes of the Overpeck Creek. Unaware of the fort's evacuation, the vessels unload several militia engineers intended to assist in the removal of the fort's stores. They land a good way south of the road up to the post.

No pickets, no sentries are visible. No one is on hand to greet and guide the force up to the highway and thence to the mountain encampment. The young Jersey militia officer in command finally decides there is nothing else to do but march northward along the highway toward the fort road, ascend it and report to Greene personally. Surely there will be sentinel posts and pickets en route.

By this time the retreating troops which have taken the southern routes across the meadows and marshes have cleared the area. Most are in Hackensack, or about to be shuttled across the river.

When the rear guard of the northern columns is finally moving past The General at the crossroads, the arriving militia on the Overpeck are landing and seeking the outpost guards in the meadowlands on the western outskirts of the English Neighborhood. Unwittingly they are walking into an evacuated encampment about to be overrun by an enemy still nowhere in sight.

One Last Precarious Look-Around

Meanwhile, Greene, hearing that all northern pickets are safe within the lines, discovers no word has been heard from those who manned the southern outposts at Bull's Ferry. Greene is advised these must have been safely rounded up and crossed by the Little Ferry.

He decides to make sure but at great risk to himself. The former twin-forts commander is determined to save every man he can.

Still indelibly impressed upon his mind are those he lost four days ago—losses for which he holds himself accountable. There could be stragglers, or some in need of help, and instead of assigning the task to a subordinate, he decides to gallop back alone two miles to the fort road and ascertain that all have been brought safely off The Mountain.[34]

On his way he passes the army's bewildered rear guard covering party who wonder why their commandant is galloping the wrong way.

Greene rounds up a few stragglers and orders them to catch up with the troops, impressing them with the consequences of capture. He is almost impelled to ride all the way to the fort itself but wisely decides against it.

Then, feeling confident that the other divisions have safely crossed by their assigned routes, he assures himself that the southern pickets have undoubtedly done likewise. He reins in his sweating stallion, shakes the rain from his tricorn and gallops back to the side of his Chief at the Liberty Pole.

The Baffling Mystery

Finally the American Chief, Greene, their staffs and guards, fall in with the end of the lines, backed only by the army's rear guard force. All scan the Tinefly road down which come Craig and his scouts, reconfirming that the enemy is moving again from the hilly ground two miles north.

The British commander's puzzling and inexplicable delay baffles the American officers in their attempts to decipher the invading army's strategy. Several of the staff members have listened to Paine who has strongly contended that there must be another force driving simultaneously out from Staten Island toward Brunswick.

It is Paine's belief that Howe is staging a giant pincer movement. One force will press down upon the Americans from the north. The other will come from behind to cut off the retreating army from the south, possibly at New Brunswick or even Newark. Paine fears the rebel army may become wedged between the two powerful jaws of Howe's Juggernaut.

It is at first conjectured in the rebel lines that Sir William may be leading the invasion forces. But soon Craig discovers and reports that Lord Cornwallis, not Sir William, is the rebels' antagonist in the operation.

Therefore the American officers are giving some concern to Tom Paine's thinking. If the adjutant general is right, part of the invasion corps may now be making its way across the upper Hackensack at the old bridge, a likely spot since there is no report of them over a mile south at the New Bridge.

All these thoughts vex the American military staff. But the enemy's present delaying tactics, if that's what they are, will always be a puzzle in Paine's mind. He does not hold too much respect for General Howe's talents as a military strategist, but now the British commander's strategy has him confused.

In time Paine will criticize the British strategy, saying:

> "Howe, in my little opinion, committed a great error in generalship in not throwing a body of forces off from Staten Island through Amboy, by which means he might have seized all our stores at Brunswick, and intercepted our march into Pennsylvania..."[35]

However, Cornwallis today has his enemy running and perplexed. The gentleman statesman and militarist is definitely heading for a victory. Though his 5,000-man army[36] is behind schedule, it now again begins moving steadily, if not speedily, onward.

Like Howe, Cornwallis is a precise man. And precise generalship is not always conducive to celerity. Also, it is possible that the Tory guides may have to shoulder some of the responsibility.

Aldington has advised the British command that the rebels might escape over "the bridge"—the only bridge to Hackensack. If he has left it at that and overlooked mentioning the Old Bridge upstream at Steenrapie, south of Kinneckimack, it is no wonder that Major

General Vaughan's captain and guards are sending back word that the rebels are nowhere near the *Old Bridge*.

However, it does not take long, even in the rain, for the British scouts and probing party to discover that they are in control of the wrong span. When the King's scouts locate the New Bridge, a mile and more below the old one, they find it fully in command of several rebel battalions.

To get this alarming news back to Cornwallis, who is temporarily halted on the Tinefly high ground over three and a half miles east, is a difficult task for the British rider. Not only is he unfamiliar with the unmarked roads, but rain, mud and the difficulty of the terrain are all against him. By the time he arrives and catches up with the command staff, the van of the King's men is headed into the vitally critical intersection.

At the same time, the American columns begin crossing the New Bridge by the hundreds, placing their feet gratefully on the west bank, north two miles from Hackensack's Village Green.

Unaware at first that their enemy has entirely evacuated the fort, the British advance scouts gradually move through the Liberty Pole, down the King's Highway to the fort road and up its turnpike.

Despite the news from the scouts that some Americans were moving on and over the New Bridge, Cornwallis proceeds to go ahead with his encirclement plans, convinced the main rebel force must be holding the fort. The bridge business can wait until later.

Over-cautious, the Earl is certain that the American "Fox" will defend Fort Lee as he did Fort Washington.[37] However, word from his van that the bewildered forward pickets are moving up into the fort unchallenged soon convinces him the garrison has escaped.

Inhabitants give British officers individual accounts of the exodus, pointing out the discarded baggage, supplies and armament off to the sides of the roadways, in ditches and ravines.

Forward pickets enter the post and take twelve stragglers found hiding in the woods, all in their cups.[38] Meanwhile the probers to the south along the King's Highway run into the rebel militiamen coming up from the creek. A skirmish ensues. The pickets' shots hit several Americans. All take flight. Some are captured and disclose they are "up from Newark."[39] The rest make their escape in the boats on which they came, or flee down the road to the Little Ferry.

Some of the rebels were part of the Newark militia detachment.

Some were part of the southern and Bulls Ferry outpost guards drawn off from their stations by Greene's officer who was sent to bring them up into the withdrawing columns.

All were then suddenly surprised by Cornwallis's probers on the highway and dispersed with several volleys. Those who knew of it, raced for the Little Ferry and made it. Others of the fort men stayed with the Newark militia who survived the brief skirmish and took to the boats, leaving behind on the shore brass fieldpieces, baggage and supplies which were to have been loaded on the vessels.

The British pickets made no effort to pursue the fleeing rebels. They were satisfied to count among their captives one lieutenant and one ensign.

It is one o'clock in the afternoon as General Lord Cornwallis stands on top of the most annoying, most celebrated, most feared and most desired British objective in the entire campaign.

The high table rock from which the Earl looks out east and down upon Manhattan Island, has been like a thorn imbedded deeply in the Howe Brothers' progress for almost five months.

The capture of the Palisadean fortress is another great victory for the King and the Empire. And Cornwallis thankfully muses that it has not cost the Crown a single casualty.

The accomplishment will overnight net the Earl fame, once the news reaches London. But, in addition to the victory itself, it has robbed the rebel forces of desperately needed arms, equipment and provisions. And, as an added bonus, the invaders are rounding up thousands of head of cattle[40] along the creek's meadows. These were to have amply fed the American army throughout the winter.

On the fort grounds, most of the American tents stand as they were left.[41] Cauldrons and kettles still simmer with porridge. Some with steaming soup.

Utensils lie exactly where left when the alarm sounded. Ovens are found smoking. Wafts of the inviting scent of baking bread attract the hungry Hessians and redcoats who lose no time in sampling rebel food.

Under the blacksmith's shed the forge fire burns low. It glows from the embers protected by the lean-to roof.

On the south end of the camp grounds a young calf cries out. Tethered to the side of the butcher shop, it was to have been the next in line to feel the quick shock of the butcher's cleaver. Unwittingly Lord Cornwallis had granted the creature a stay of execution.

Some of the heavy 32-pounders on the Barbette stand loaded, ready for firing along with a total of some 40 or 50 cannon waiting to be loaded.[42] Not a single weapon is spiked, giving the enemy further proof of the rapidity with which the fort was emptied.

Overlooking the river and the once impenetrable Chevaux de Frise across it, the big silent Barbette guns now must serve those at whom they have so long so effectively been aimed.

One British officer, commenting later on the victory, will reflect upon the scene in these words:

> "On the appearance of our troops, the rebels fled like scared rabbits... They have left some poor pork, a few greasy proclamations, and some of that scoundrel Common Sense man's letters, which we can read at our leisure, now that we have got one of the 'impregnable' redoubts'..."[43]

"His Lordship Cornwallis's face seems to be set towards Philadelphia," Francis Lord Rawdon will soon be writing Robert Auchmuty in London, reflecting that dangerous spirit of over-confidence which often infects the successful pursuer and heightens his vulnerability.

Lieutenant Colonel Rawdon, a trusted confidant of Cornwallis, despite Rawdon's age of 21 years, will tell his friend, Auchmuty, that at Philadelphia the British army "will meet with no kind of opposition."

As the young nobleman now stands beside his commanding officer on the Bluff Rock, the tall, dark youth, who has been described as "the ugliest man in England," thinks of many things he will say to friends when he gets a chance to write them. This is but one thought that comes to mind in his observations of his commander.

Rawdon, who has been in the American war from its beginnings at Lexington and who was cited by Burgoyne for distinguished service after, as a company lieutenant, he led his grenadiers into the battle of Bunker Hill when the battalion's captain fell, sees the war rapidly coming to a close. And he will make this known to Auchmuty on Monday when he will write:

> "I hope we will be at Amboy or Brunswick tomorrow (Tuesday, November 26) or next day, if it will leave off raining. You see, my dear sir, that I have not been mistaken in my judgement of this people.
> "The southern people (Rawdon considers Jersey part of the south, contrasting Jerseyans with the New Englanders whom he considers to be in the north) will no more fight than the Yankees. The fact is that their army

is broken all to pieces, and the spirits of their leaders and their abettors is also broken. However, I think one may venture to pronounce that it is well nigh over with them."[44]

The youthful nobleman and officer, of whom it is said that no man possesses a higher degree of that "happy but rare faculty of attracting to him all who come within his sphere of influence," is, however, wanting in an adequate knowledge of the terrain that lies to the west. But that is understandably true of the entire British command at this time.

Blinders Blur the Victors' Vision

In the minds of the British leaders the pursuit of the retreating Continental Army appears to be little more than a clean-up operation. Not fully aware of the fact that they are standing on a peninsula, and that they are not yet on the mainland, the invaders apparently do not realize the advantage that could be theirs were they to drive on. For were they knowledgeable of the terrain, they would. However, they seem not to realize that their "Fox" will next jump across a second river, the Passaic, taking that bridge—as his men are taking the Hackensack's—up with them.

The capture of what Rawdon describes as "the other famous fortification, called Fort Constitution or Fort Lee"[45] and so much materiel all without a fight builds a disastrous overconfidence in the victors that some will in the future say proved tragically costly for England.

Nevertheless, in defense of the alleged procrastinated strategy, it must be said that the fort had first to be possessed. And secondly the invaders were then not in ideal condition for further pursuit. These are now wearied, wet, footsore troops.

They crossed a river last night, scaled a giant precipice, marched 12 miles to climb the same mountain from the west and have had little to eat throughout the night and morning. Yet before the day is over some may be called upon to march west ten miles and bivouac on the Hackensack's east bank.

For any army just the accomplishment of scaling the steep slopes of the Palisades with all impedimenta in daylight would be considered a remarkable feat. Particularly is this so in the 18th Century under adverse weather and over rutted, mud-soaked roads on which no man among the overseas troops has ever before set foot.

The capture of so much armament and equipment at the post and along the roads in addition to thousands of head of beet is without precedent in the memories of the King's men. Previous victories have been at a great cost in lives. This one has not yet recorded a single casualty. And only a few rounds of ammunition have been fired in minor skirmishes.

All kinds of reports now reach Cornwallis's ears. From General Vaughan's rear regiments he learns that the British army's camp women, following behind the main columns, report personally capturing a few hungry footsore rebel stragglers[46] who dodged out of the woods begging them for food without realizing that the women's wagons were part of the British train.

On the western slopes where the rebels had their prison stockade adjoining an isolation hospital tent, three surgeons who reside in huts nearby were in attendance. All three and 99 privates have been rounded up.[47] They claim they were not informed of the evacuation, but upon hearing the alarm, two of the guards ran up on the camp grounds to find out what was going on. When they did not return, the others took off while the surgeons went back to sleep.

Cornwallis waits for Howe to come across the river and prescribe the strategy of pursuit. He will of course leave a force behind him before heading for Hackensack.

If Lord Rawdon is right, the Earl hopes—tomorrow—to bring the American Commander-in-Chief to battle and then get Howe's permission to push on to Philadelphia.

Rawdon in recalling the hour will write:

"His Lordship pressed forward as quick as he could toward Hackensack New Bridge, but the people belonging to the fort had the heels of him."[48]

No Longer An Obstacle In His Path

Howe, arriving in a longboat from a man-of-war off Bourdette's, takes over command of the so-called "impregnable" fortress. In ascending the gorge road and standing upon The Rock he momentarily glows with the exultation of the conqueror. For now, at last, he puts his foot heavily down upon the monolith as though he were stamping victoriously upon this, his enemy's demoralizing sentinel of resistance. The imposing, mammoth, overawing menace has all too long stood, a threatening symbol of defiance to His Majesty's will.

Sir William is sure that with the fall of Fort Lee, following as it does the capture of its twin across the river four days ago, the inhabitants will be convinced the rebellion is falling apart. And he is right.

The people of The Mountain area and along the river, however, keep their thoughts to themselves. They simulate neutrality and stay as far away as possible from the invaders, remaining indoors whenever they can. Nevertheless, astute British officers soon learn the political leanings of most residents.

In Howe's letter to Lord Germaine 13 days from now, the British commander-in-chief will detail his "return of ordnance and stores taken from the enemy since the landing at Frogs-Neck in West-Chester county, from the 12th of October to the 20th of November."

It will list the materiel taken at Fort Lee and, when published by the Tory-controlled New York press and embellished by exaggerations, will result in a wave of American criticism censuring General Greene.

Greene, in anger, will answer his critics in a letter to Governor Cooke on December 21. He will call the reports "malicious" and declare the enemy's listings "untrue" and "a grand falsehood," contending that not an article of military stores was left there worthy of mention.*

The Disputed Report

The Howe report which Greene will dispute will list as captured the following:

"... Fort Lee, the rock, redoubt and batteries, in the Jerseys. Iron ordnance: 5 thirty-two pounders, 3 twenty-four ditto, 2 six ditto, 2 three ditto, 1 thirteen inch brass mortar, 1 ten-inch ditto, 2 thirteen inch iron mortars, 2 ten-inch ditto, 2 eight-inch ditto.

"On the road leading to Hackensack, in the Jerseys. Iron ordnance: 2 twenty-four pounders, 2 eighteen ditto, 4 twelve ditto, mounted on travelling carriages, 4 six pounders.

"TOTAL. Iron Ordnance: 9 thirty-two pounders, 5 twenty-four pounders, 4 eighteen pounders, 49 four pounders, 10 three pounders, 2 five-and-half inch brass hoitzers, 1 thirteen-inch brass mortar, 1 ten-inch ditto, 2 thirteen-inch iron mortars, 1 ten-inch ditto, 1 eight-inch ditto.

"SHOT

"Round, loose. 1,087 thirty-two pounders, 272 eighteen pounders, 2,637 twelve pounders, 300 six pounders, 760 six pounders, 870 three pounders

---

*See "Greene Answers His Critics" under "Thursday, December 26 . . ."

"CASE. 30 thirty-two pounds, 40 eighteen pounders, 340 twelve pounders, 290 nine pounders, 71 six pounders, 39 three pounders, 1,159 double-headed of sorts, 42 boxes for grape.

"SHELLS

"156 thirteen-inch, 311 ten inch, 1,140 eight inch, 1,170 five-and-half inch, 1,200 four-two-fifths inch,

"Powder, Barrels . . .15; Musquets of sorts . . .2,800; Musquet cartridges near . . . 403,000; Iron—Toms . . . Bar 20, Rod 5; Intrenching tools of sorts . . 500; Armourers tools, sets . . .6; Hand barrows . . .200; Gyn, complete . . .1; Sling carts . . .2; Iron fraizes of 400 weight each, supposed to be intended to stop the navigation of Hudson's river . . .200;

"A large quantity of other species of stores not at present ascertained.

"(Signed) Sam. Cleaveland, B. Gen. Royal artillery

Admiralty"[49]

Sir William's comprehensive report of the army and navy's activities will include an item on the return of prisoners taken, which will read:

"November 20, Fort Lee: Commissioned officers. . . 1 lieutenant, 1 ensign; Staff. . . 1 Quarter-master, 3 surgeons; Privates. . . 99."

The assumption for these losses, some Americans later will conjecture is that the lieutenant was in charge of the body of men who came up from Newark as were also the ensign and quarter-master. As for the others, since all suspected contagion cases were placed in an isolation quarter down a path on the western slope in the same sector as the army's prison stockade, the surgeons, some of the sick and the stockade's prisoners were inexplicably left behind.

Some will say that Blodget's men were at fault for not rounding up all of the ill. They will charge that those who were assigned to the task of hurriedly gathering up the sick, believed "the sick never get well anyway."[50] And, furthermore, they were extremely fearful of going anywhere near the isolation area.

So when hard-pressed officers commandeered them and their badly needed wagons for baggage-loading they had to happily cancel their "mercy" mission and gladly join the train with a far better chance to escape. For in the mad scramble everywhere to transport materiel, baggage, supplies, ammunition boxes and muskets with only seconds to spare, little if any attention was paid to protocol.

However, all of this will be conjecture, except as unknown captives mentioned as "taken" in enemy accounts.[51]

Howe's December 3 report to Germaine in London will not

mention casualties. However, Admiral Lord Howe, in writing his account to the Admiralty Office in London, from his flagship, *Eagle*, on Saturday, November 23, will note that some Americans paid with their lives, saying:

". . . Some few of the enemy were killed, and about twenty-seven taken, with many pieces of artillery, and a large quantity of ammunition and stores. . ."[52]

However, the admiral will not indicate whether the "few" enemy killed were encountered by his seamen and marines, by Cornwallis's vanguard, or the southern-sent pickets in their encounter with the men coming up the road from the creek. But thus far neither side reports any casualties among its own troops.

Mobility: A Ray Of Hope Seeps Through Darkness

The rain has now turned into lightly dusting snowflakes under a cold wind and overcast sky. The November afternoon gloomily gives in to the dusk, and under it Howe and Cornwallis, jubilant over their victory, meet to plan tomorrow's chase.

Many of the occupying forces make use of their enemy's tents and fires and bivouac for the night on the rebels' deserted encampment grounds. Others settle down along the King's Highway.

A detachment of the 16th Dragoons and some companies of light infantry under Colonel Harcourt, moving in over the river from Fort Washington, are ordered to advance toward the Hackensack at dawn under Major General Vaughan. Harcourt sends a night company of dragoons to probe the way along the enemy's route to the Hackensack.

For the Continental Army, the costly losses in armament, tenting and materiel which Cornwallis and Howe consider a crowning blow to the rebels' cause, may have a bright side. Dejected though they now may be, the fleeing Americans—if they can be held together once again—can profit from a mobility which they are now learning to depend upon. And it is mobility which it must now fully employ if it is to survive.

On The Mountain and along the shore which the Fort Lee garrison held last night without the slightest suspicion of what was soon to come upon them, the British and Hessian soldiers, bloated with their overwhelming victory, and despite the cold, strut over their conquered grounds in high spirits. For tonight, those who are in charge of the occupation, will sleep in their enemy's log huts and tents, all waiting for them to fall into.

Their boisterous merrymaking tonight will become frightening for The Mountain and the river people even in the seclusion of homes behind closed shutters and barred doors.

Elaine has long since retired to her room after having stood on the road out of the fort beside her father and Bourdette for hours, joined by some of the frightened inhabitants of the western slope. In the cold rain they watched the last of the rapidly disappearing rear guard troops. Each of those left behind on the deserted fort grounds to meet the King's much heralded, vaunted and feared army, now silently sent up his own prayer of hope.

One of The Mountain's farmers, whose high barn roof commands a fairly good view of the valley, finally brought them the good news that every one of the marchers had passed the Liberty Pole without incident. Declaring that by this time the whole division must be up on the Tee-Neck, he added that, as far as he could see, there was no sign of the enemy coming from Closter.

That word brought a sigh of relief from all of the gathering and a "Thank, God!" from Elaine. But a few minutes later a farmer's hand from Garret Ledbecker of Liberty Pole came riding up with the warning that the redcoat army had reached "The Pole" and was swarming out in all directions.

Only yesterday Ledbecker told his patriot friends that Sir Henry Clinton had recently arrived from Charleston with 2,000 more troops after having been repulsed there by an operation for which Charles Lee is demanding full credit. Clinton's additions, he noted, disembarked from New York harbor.

Scorning the enemy forces, he reported hearing someone say that the King's men in America have all Europe wondering how it is possible the war of rebellion can still go on when "All told, the strongest military nation in the world (has) 32,000 soldiers in America and great quantities of guns and equipment."[5][3]

Ledbecker now fears he talked too soon.

It is the Hessians, the very mention of their name, that all seem to fear more than the British troops. The stories that have been circulated about their plundering in New York have brought their fearsome reputation riding on ahead of them.

Between them and the Tories, as Black Jennie puts it, "dere's allus plen'y ob stuffins' fer nightmares makin'."

So, back in her room, her reddened eyes and drawn features revealing the terrible strain of the day, Elaine despondently begins putting her husband's things neatly away in the big pine dresser drawers. She pays no attention to the excitement that is going around among the people of the hamlet as word passes that the redcoats and Hessians are all over the camp grounds and on the Bluff Rock.

Some are reported moving down cautiously through the gorge road headed for the ferry. A flag bearer on The Rock is seen signalling the frigates on the river and the twin fort on the east bank, now referred to by the British only as "Fort Knyphausen."

Paul excitedly comes upstairs to tell his sister what is happening, but she is oblivious to it all. Elaine's mind is with her husband and his battery struggling down the New Bridge road to the wooden span over which almost half of the withdrawing army are crossed and halted around Zabriskie's mill and homestead.

In the Baummeister kitchen Marie Louise, also in tears, and respecting Elaine's emotional upset, does not attempt to console her daughter.

At the kitchen window, Baummeister looks out at the approaching troops. Soon they will interrogate the entire household. The short blasts of his pipe indicate he is ready for them.

Which "George"?

On the Bourdette grounds a squad of Hessians stumble on Bourdette's precious keg of cider which he had thought was well hidden in the cold storage cave of the nearby cliff. He had hurriedly covered it with branches.

Upon seeing the plunderers and heedless of Jennie's shouting demand that he get back in the house "Quick!" the old man, pipe in hand, runs out on the grounds. Intending at first to try to stop them and make a complaint, Old Stephen suddenly substitutes conciliatory wisdom for impulsive imprudence and comes to a halt. Deciding he had better not do anything, he stands, pipe in mouth, belching out short quick puffs, and watches in misery as the Hessians down his cider. A few drink from their boots.

The young Hessians try to strike up a conversation but Bourdette is unable to understand their German and they his French and English.

Handing him a mug, one of them, apparently the leader, courteously invites Bourdette to have a taste of his own especially made, private stock of brew, gently demanding through motions and a mixed tongue, that he drink to the King's health.

After unsuccessfully trying to put them off and, fearing some possible reprisal, Stephen finally succumbs. Then, mischievously obliging, he holds up the mug, points it toward the west in the direction of the retreating army, rather than the east, saying loud and clear:

"Long live George, the rebel General and Chief!"

The soldiers, looking quizzically at one another and then at their leader, who hears the words, "George" and "rebel," believe that the ferry owner has toasted King George and condemned his enemies, the rebels.

They shout gleefully until they are spied by a stern-faced Prussian officer. Angrily he commands them in German to get back on the grounds with their company. Sheepishly they re-form and march stiffly off at double time. The officer then turns to Bourdette and, in good broken English, profusely apologizes to the amazed ferry owner. As he leaves the officer turns and says, smiling, "Dot vas verra goot!"

As plundering as both the British and Hessian troops will be in their sweep through Jersey, it will be the Tory pillaging and ravaging that will become hardest to endure. Already old neighbors are looting one another.

Long-smoldering prejudices will suddenly burst out, spewing vengeance and wrath over the countryside. Where once stood valleys of honesty, love, order, self-discipline and clean government, dishonesty, hatred, disorder and panic will soon threaten life and property. Thievery, incendiarism, rape and murder, like uncontrolled forest fires will spread wildly throughout the once quiet vales along the Hudson, Hackensack and the Passaic Rivers.

Adding to the tragic dilemmas of the confused patriots and neutrals, if not the Loyalists as well, are Howe's puzzling orders concerning plundering. The British commander has restricted the practice by redcoats but overlooks it by Hessians. This not only antagonizes the populace, but fans the mounting tensions rising between the British soldiers and the German mercenaries.

The boiling undercurrent of these dissensions festers within the separate army divisions. Knyphausen and Rall's military prowess on Mount Washington and the renaming of the fortress in honor of the Hessian general have not helped soothe the affronted redcoats who consider themselves second to none, and particularly not underdogs to the pompously strutting Hessians.

Tories Are Of Many Kinds

So while Hessian plundering is silently condoned and the red-coats are officially prohibited from enjoying these, "the fruits of war," the unrestricted Tories have no strings controlling them at all. The abundance of Tories in New York, in the valleys and throughout the Jerseys, generally, induces Paine to charge that it is the Tories who are responsible for bringing the British to the New York and New Jersey area for their campaign.

In censuring them later, he will say:

> "Why is it that the enemy have left the New England provinces, and made these middle ones the seat of war? The answer is easy:
> "New England is not infested with Tories, and we are. I have been tender in raising the cry against these men, and used numberless arguments to show them their danger, but it will not do to sacrifice a world to either their folly or their baseness. The period is now arrived, in which either they or we must change our sentiments, or one or both must fall.
> "And what is a Tory? Good God! what is he? I should not be afraid to go with a hundred Whigs against a thousand Tories, were they to attempt to get into arms. Every Tory is a coward; for servile, slavish, self-interested fear is the foundation of Toryism; and a man under such influence, though he may be cruel, never can be brave."[54]

Attempting to incite patriotism and draw unity from the mold, Paine is understandably harsh, drawing no lines of distinction around the various types of "Tories," "Royalists" and "Loyalists." All Tories are villains in the eyes of the adjutant general, and this assessment of them will add to his popularity.

For temperance and objectivity are not the ideal characteristics of the propagandist. And Paine is the country's Number One propagandist.

So, contrary to Paine's belief that all Tories are cut from the same piece of cloth, there are many classifications. There are a host of them, of course, who cannot stomach rebellion against the authority of the Crown. Many of these are law-abiding church people who follow the letter of the law as they do the tenets of their religion.

Yet these souls must listen to rebellion preached on one Sunday by one dominie and hear the Crown's views upheld on the following Sabbath by the alternate visiting preacher. If one were to examine all the varied classifications among the King's supporters, they would probably fall into six categories:[55]

(1) Those who have performed, or are still performing some service of one kind or another in behalf of the Crown; (2) Those who have taken up arms against the rebellion; (3) Those who maintain a uniform zeal for and loyalty to Mother England yet waver in that loyalty at times; (4) Those who still maintain their residence in Great Britain; (5) Those who have openly refused to support the American cause or to take up arms in behalf of independence; and (6) Those who have supported the cause, or who have taken up arms against the King "but afterwards joined the British forces as civilians or combatants."[56]

All of war's criminal tentacles are now at work in Jersey. British and American troops, Tories, Loyalists, Whigs and Patriots will feel the hateful sweep of vindictive punishment and destruction.

And in Jersey, Tory leader, Colonel Abraham Van Buskirk will soon become as hated and hunted as his counterpart, Major Robert Rogers over in Westchester.

In years to come, one writer will describe the countryside's panic-ridden state of things following this never-to-be-forgotten twentieth day of November, as follows:

"None was spared. Wives and daughters were ravished by drunken soldiers and sometimes before the eyes of husbands and fathers; homes were wantonly wrecked, fields were laid waste, barns and farm emplements were burned while murder of the inoffensive was of daily occurrence.

"Upon Whig and Tory alike, including those who had taken protective papers of Lord Howe, the sword of the vandals fell. Not only must the American Revolution be crushed, they said, but America itself must be blotted from the map."[56]

Only Minutes Lay Between Them

When Lord Cornwallis rode up into the abandoned fort at 1 P.M., the last of the American main corps were clearing the Tee-Neck ridge and beginning their last stretch, heading for the New Bridge Road. The two armies' personnel were then at times only about two miles or less apart, from van to rear, though earlier they had been closer.

Some of those who took the Little Ferry route were still on the east side but in the process of crossing by boat and ferry. The same was true of the mid-way marchers who, having cleared the Impassable Swamp, were slowly being transported over at Terhune's mill.

At the New Bridge the van of the main army, showing the effects of its long hard struggle, is at last stepping out of the deep muck on to the wooden bridge's thumping, creaking boards. Few of the soldiers will ever know how narrow was the gauge of their escape.

For it was after midday when the last of the Continentals passed The Pole, leaving the crucial crossroads to the oncoming Cornwallian corps. Pulling into the disappearing line of march behind Colonel Bedford's guards, the American Chief, his staff, aides and guards, were followed only by the division's rear guard troops. Rain, now mixed with snow and accompanied by a cutting, chilling wind, whipped down upon the lengthy strung-out procession.

Neither of the two armies was aware of how near they were to an encounter. The American Leader was almost certain a brush would occur. It was partly for that reason he ordered General Hand to direct one division through the mid-way swamp and General Beall the other by the Little Ferry.

No wagons or heavy equipment were moved under Hand along the marshy route to Terhune's place. Hand's men are crack riflemen. They would have served as a left wing flanking force in the event of a confrontation were the main army forced to turn about and fight with its back against the Hackensack.

Similarly, Beall's rifle regiment were to have become the army's right wing flank, throwing an enfilading fire upon the enemy's left if dire trouble came. Thus, the two crossing fires would have supported the main division and provided temporary cover. The enemy-delaying action was then to have enabled the bulk of the army to cross the river and establish a defense line along the river's west bank.

The splitting of the force into three divisions was not an impromptu decision. It was The General's approved emergency withdrawal plan. Had all the garrison crowded down upon the Liberty Pole route, the cross-peninsula maneuver would have ended in disaster. A large part of the rear, owing to its extended length in a train of almost 3,000 men, would have been splintered off and entrapped by the enemy vanguard.

Almost on the heels of the disappearing rebel rear guards, Cornwallis, preceded by his van, rode watchfully into the intersection. Under the clouded gloomy mist were silently occurring a few of the most pregnantly fateful moments in military history— moments that were to affect the world's continents for centuries to come.

To the British general only the objective mattered. The objective was Fort Lee. Why should he be concerned over a few frightened outposts who have escaped over toward Hackensack village? But that was before he realized it was the entire Continental army.

Opposite The Pole, at the wide door of the Liberty Pole Inn, the staunch patriot, Garret Leydecker, one of the most outspoken Whigs of the neighborhood, had stood with others watching the disappearing American division fade westward away.

Lydecker, whose farm and lands stand off to the west of the King's Highway in Liberty Pole's small hamlet, stands to lose much from the invaders. The Tory leaders in their reports to Cornwallis and Howe will lose little time in making Lydecker's strong anti-Loyalist views known to the enemy.

He will pay dearly for those sentiments in the days ahead as will many others of the area such as Garret Ledbecker and the Dominie Dereck Remlin. The British will take his cattle, make use of his lands for a part of their encampment, "tearing down and burning four thousand panels of four and five-rail fence,"[58] and then strip his home of everything movable.

This act will serve to arouse his anti-Royalist sentiments still more and induce him to enlist in the Continental Army. He will rise to the rank of captain and in later years will become a member of the Legislature.[59]

But at a few minutes after the half hour of noon, Leydecker and Ledbecker, who with others had gathered at the inn and tavern, felt their hearts beating almost in cadence with the pounding feet of the distantly vanishing symbols of a nation struggling out of crisis. And at the same time each kept one eye fearfully searching northward on the Tinefly road.

Then, first in small numbers, redcoats, Hessians and finally the British staff moved in. Never had a general in all war's horror-filled pages of history come quite so close to a crushing, earth-shaking victory.

And Ledbecker, in recounting it years later, would add that never would a victory—so close within his grasp—have more tremulously rocked the Eighteenth Century's foundations than that which Major General Charles, Second Earl Cornwallis, lost by minutes at half after noon that day.

So, unaware of his momentous hour, his Lordship set his mind upon one objective, Fort Lee, and rapidly he pushed on south to seize it.

Struggling Over the First Great Perilous Step

Meanwhile, the American Commander, unaware of his enemy's intentions and intelligence, drove his army ever harder west. At times pushed beyond endurance, yet enduring, they hungered for sight of the New Bridge Inn lying almost beside the wooden span that would carry them across.

The overloaded wagons and heavy gun carriages, a number of which lie abandoned, irretrievably lost in morasses, are now carefully trailed by especially assigned platoons. These men tug, push and often lift the loads when necessary.

There is no jesting. No laughter rises up from the throngs of footsore soldiers, artificers, bakers, blacksmiths, carpenters and cadre. Hungry and fatigued, the hard pressed, weakened army drives itself toward the Hackensack span.

Only the rugged regulars, the hard core, battle-scarred Continentals display the stamina that, seemingly, is the only thing that holds together the splitting and divisive forces that threaten to tear apart The Cause from its rebellious direction.

At a slightly slower pace the rear guard ploughs onward, remaining constantly alert for an ambush. At any time they expect the enemy's advance pickets will jump out and bark at their heels. Only the weather assures them that the invaders' firing pans are as wet as their own. This thought buoys their hopes that a volley of musketry will not momentarily rip into their backsides.

If that should happen, Bedford and his men know that they would be called upon to make the ultimate sacrifice, enabling The General and the army to re-form if possible. This would give the main body a chance for a running battle for the bridge. With such a weakened force as theirs and under such adverse weather conditions that deprive them of the use of weapons, there is, for them, no alternative but possible annihilation.

Grumbling Men, Rumbling Cannon, Wagons and Cattle

Some men struggle on in silence. Some, tiring under their loads, grumble even when their burdens are lightened by others. It is the "grumblers" who anger the hardened Continentals. Not when the grumbling is from anger, disgust or annoyance with the army but only when it stems from weakness—a condition they abhor wherever found.

Few of the generals have been out of their saddles all day. Among these are Greene and Mifflin who have munched on sea biscuits, occasionally handed up to them along the trek. Both have appeared everywhere up and down the lines, Greene watching his men, Mifflin his armament and supplies. Often they press the men

On right is the Liberty Pole Tavern site and left center is the Liberty Pole location and a later inn erected beside it. The smallest building on the right was part of the original tavern. The critical November 20, 1776, road junction is shown as it appeared about 1855. This is a painting by Maria L. Cass, who, in 1911, at the age of 80, painted the scene from memory as she recalled it 56 years before, and presented the canvas to Dr. Valentine Ruch, one of the last owners of the home. . . . Courtesy of Valentine Ruch IV, Southold, New York, owner of the original oil coloring.

unmercifully harder in order to speed the movement of wagons, cattle and cannon ever rumbling up behind.

They issue orders to officers, directing assistance to a wagonmaster mired in the mud, a stumbling youth bordering on exhaustion, or a horse gone lame. The strong bear the burdens of the weak.

A number of men place their weight behind the mired wagon and free it. Some strong arms lift the collapsing youth up on a wagon seat. The horse is unhitched and hobbles away, while its share in the team is replaced by a line from the pommel of Mifflin's steed until the bridge is crossed.

When some of the men see the Zabriskie mill, the inn or catch a glimpse of the bridge itself, they let go with a whoop, patting each other on the back as they point it out. There is little disorder of any kind. All hold their lines together in good form.

Arriving at the crossing, Greene, keeping an eye on the distant terrain to the north and east, supervises the long procession's last few hundred rods over the span. All along the river troops are seen poling boats across from the east to the west bank and there staving them in, often over the angry protests and tears of their owners.

"Victors" In A Different Way

Following Ewing's advance and the army's vanguard troops, the main body is soon followed across by the rear guard under Bedford. They pass between The General and his aides on the south side of the bridge's east terminus and Greene, his aides and Mifflin, on the north.

Some of the soldiers merely breathe easier as they step upon the boards. Some drop exhausted on the other side. A few, clowning happily at their good fortune and seldom perturbed by travail, throw kisses at the structure's uprights as though they were the doors of home.

They have sweated and panted their way, plodding over the little hills the Dutch called "bergs" and from which the peninsula derives its name. They have gone up and down over these risers, wallowing under heavy loads in the thick mud of the ravines that roll between the ridges into the glacially-made flatlands of the valley. All in the face of momentary disaster, they have trudged through bogs and over wildly running creeks in order to skirt marshlands and sunken, unkept, roads.

And the "victors," without a shot having been received or fired, place their feet on the temporary safety of the Hackensack's west bank. Two by two, squad by squad, they step on the cross-board planks, then over and off on Loyalist, the miller, Zabriskie's lands. The brazen ones, with the breath they have saved to do so, let go with a blast at King George before crumbling for a respite.

Thus the Continental Army completes the first and the most perilous step of what is to become an almost continuous march. A march to victory. A march of over 100 miles in 54 days along Jersey's roads and over its rivers, across the Delaware, and back again twice to Jersey. Some will call it the most momentously successful military maneuver in the history of all warfare.

The General, first seeing to the work of the engineers collecting and staving in the river craft, follows Greene across. Then, flanked by his staff and aides with the fort's former commander at his side, he dismounts and focuses his telescope upon the ridge rising up from the river. Puzzled that not a single British soldier has yet been sighted, the army's Chief shakes his head in disbelief.

Just before the order to destroy the structure is given, Craig, accompanied by one of his scouts, rides across and makes for the group of staff officers. He addresses Greene.

Criag, repeating his earlier intelligence that Cornwallis, not

Howe, leads the invaders, adds that the enemy is possessing the mountain's fort and is not in pursuit.

The American Commander-in-Chief, overhearing Craig's report, again shakes his head in puzzlement.

An aide, aside to Greene, says, "The Gen'l cannot make it out. First Durkee's major and now the scouts confirm 'tis Cornwallis. The 'Big Man' knows 'tis not like The Earl to miss his target by so much."

When the last of Craig's scouts is over, the bridge is torched. Under the fading twilight the fire throws an eerie light a mile around.

On Sunday the divided Conferentie and Coetus parties of the Dutch Church will not stare angrily at each other as they pass on the bridge road. At least not this coming Sunday, unless the span is repaired in time. The traveling church-goers will have to remain in the parish to which they belong, regardless of whether the visiting, preaching dominie is not an adherent of the sectarian party and tenets of their preference. The Hackensack parishioners will stay in Hackensack. The Schraalenburghers in Schraalenburgh. And both will blame the Continental Army for destroying their bridge and restricting their worship with a preacher not of their taste.

Far more leisurely now, with the tremendous pressure lifted from their shoulders, the main army corps slowly winds its way over the last two miles into the village of Hackensack. The sky's precipitation intermingles light dustings of snow. Near-freezing cold makes drudgery of the final stage. But rest, at last, is the reward. Only the lights of the scattered outlying farmhouse windows brighten the blackness periodically until, at last, the lamps of the village send out welcoming beams like beckoning streams of gold.

Riding behind one of the surviving gun carriages in the long columns of spent men, dragging their wheel-squeaking vehicles, go The General on Old Magnolia, members of his staff, the guards, and recently rejoining the Commander-in-Chief, his aide, William Grayson.

All are huddled under their surcoats. There are not many among them whose spirts are not as drenched as their bodies.

The deep, hundred-foot wide Hackensack River on their left is tonight their guardian. And the lengthy peninsula it creates with the Hudson and its menacing rock walls has, they believe, had a hand in miraculously helping them over the first hurdle to wherever "The Old Man" takes them.

Grayson informs his Chief that he has dispatched the message to Lee. Detailing the contents of the communication, the colonel lists the points, item by item, which he had been instructed to tell the North Castle commander.

Grayson states that he had made it clear to the Westchester commander that the enemy's objective was the possession of Fort Lee as a part of the design and that the foe "may have other and more capital views."[60]

Emphasizing the exactness of his wording and tone, the aide concluded that he had tactfully stated that "His Excellency *advises*" that the North Castle troops be brought over "on this side of the North River, and there wait further orders."[61]

Greene, remaining at the bridge with Mifflin and Bedford, lays out the defense plans for the night and stipulates the strength and location of the guard posts. He assigns Bedford to the north, Hand, center, and Beall on the river bank's south end.

During this pause on the Miller Zabriskie's grounds, the rear guard regiment warms itself beside small fires, started from the bridge's flaming timbers. They eat whatever victuals and biscuits they have saved, or whatever neighboring inhabitants sympathetically bring them.

A group of higher ranking officers among the subalterns, clustered around one of the fires and munching on bread from the miller's kitchen, excitedly discuss, debate and question the

Approach to the Bridge

maneuver and the state of affairs. None radiate much optimism. A few are more hopeful than the rest, expressing confidence that General Lee will save the army and The Cause.

They bandy around each other's bits of news, hearsay, or statements, reaching for confidence and hope, citing that:

... Durkee's men from Sneden's Landing have been ordered to abandon their post and join the march using the western Ramapo Pass route ... Mifflin has been ordered to set up the bivouac on The Green in Hackensack only for the night with the contingent stationed there, meaning that tomorrow the combined force will move across the Passaic River to Newark and into West Jersey.

A few of the officers want to place blame, hinting at Greene's loss of Fort Washington as the cause of the present disaster. Others quickly change the subject.

Some Look Hopefully For Lee

They declare:

... The General needs Lee and the North Castle men and armament to strike back... Lee should be with the army at the end of the week ... He will "play the deuce with Cornwallis" ... Only Providence saved the army this time!... Heath and Huntington will keep the watch over the Highlands and the upper valley while Lee comes to the army's rescue ... That is as long as the Canada-based British Army under Carleton does not break through Gates' and Arnold's Northern Department and sweep down through Albany to clasp hands with Howe in New York.

Those subalterns who have heard gossip of the high command's personnel "differences" with one another, ask wryly, "How will the 'Rhode Islander' (Greene) like the thought of a hostile fellow officer (Lee) rescuing him from an enemy that has possessed both his forts and captured half his forces?

The Greene-Lee "strained" relationship has been sensed by mostly upper echelon officers. And these have leaked it to those of lower rank. So there are many who believe it will be a humiliating, if not a degrading moment for Greene when he has to look to Charles Lee for succor. Some believe that "Nathanael" has held only contempt for "Charles" since the first time they met. And vice versa, for Lee cannot see a non-professional warrior—a Quaker smithy's son and "youngest general in the army"—holding equal rank with him.

One of the group, disliking the trend of the discussion and displaying more wisdom and knowledge than the rest about military tactics, points out that, while the army faces food, shelter, arms and spirit problems, it now has the makings of becoming a barking, biting hound on the hooves of the heavily pounding, lumbering enemy pack. Now, he argues, the rebels may learn the advantages of dodging and all those Indian tricks the Chief acquired from the native warriors. . . That is if the army can wiggle out and maneuver through this one last major escape.

It could now learn to strike quick effective blows and disappear silently into the shadows of the trees, he tells his fellow officers. For the army now must avoid the formal military open battlefield arrayals and the present military emphasis upon the entrenchment tool and the fortification system of defense—the only "approved" warfare strategy of world-wide "acceptance."

At that moment, the commanding officers call their subalterns together for instructions and the group breaks up.

Haven In Hackensack

All of the houses in the little Dutch village are bright with their whale-oil lamps and candle light as the troops drag themselves slowly onto the Village Green. In almost every window fronting the muddy road through the heart of town, faces are pressed against the glass as the wide-eyed villagers take in the unbelievable scene that passes by in the chilling duskiness of the night.

Everyone now realizes that the far-away war in New York town has at last come to his door. And most are equally convinced that the war is fast coming to an end, an end not to the liking of most Hackensack villagers.

In this atmosphere of invasion, overwhelming power and a climate replete with the heraldry of an enemy victory, the Tory wave will rise and crest in boldness. The invaders and their feats will spread delight among the Loyalists in inns, taverns, shops and homesteads throughout all the new nation.

The Hackensack church dominie, looking out upon the marching men will later describe the sight, saying:

> "It was about dusk when the head of the troops entered Hackensack. The night was dark, cold, and rainy, but I had a fair view of them from the light of the windows as they passed on our side of the street. They marched two abreast, looked ragged, some without a shoe to their feet, and most of them wrapped up in their blankets."[62]

At the northern end of the Village Green where the march

ends tonight, the American Commander and his staff are met by Peter Zabriskie and Archibald Campbell. In Campbell's tavern they sit down to hot stew, bread and wine. As usual, the host personally prepares and serves The General's plate. He first carefully tastes the food himself in front of the ever-hovering bodyguards. It is a brief meal dominated by awesome silence.

No time is lost over it, for the bivouacking problems are many. And of first importance are the preparations for tomorrow's second stage of the army's withdrawal. The accounting of losses, the feeding, clothing and re-equipping of the troops, bivouacking them without tenting shelters, planning and mapping the logistics of the protracted march across the Passaic to Acquackanonk, Newark, New Brunswick, Princeton, Trenton and the Delaware—all these matters must be properly directed before dawn. There will be little time for sleep.

Tomorrow's objective has already been determined. The combined rebel forces, comprising both the Hackensack garrison and the added Fort Lee army, will head for the Passaic River at sunrise and cross the bridge over the deep river into Acquackanonk.

Bivouacking on the Passaic's west bank tomorrow night, they will join the Acquackanonk post, picking up the large amount of stores previously stored there by Greene's order. They will gather up and stave in the river's boats along that stream, destroy the bridge and push on south into Newark, thus putting two river barriers between them and the enemy.

Of Grave Concern

One concern troubling the rebel command and the one feared by Paine and some of the officers is that Howe is sending off a second corps of his army from Staten Island to fall upon Mercer's post at Amboy. From there he could drive south into Newark and close his jaws on the Continentals.

The assurance that it is Cornwallis who leads the invading army at their backs gives credence to the argument. The likelihood is so logical it becomes hard to disbelieve.

However, no word of any such action has arrived from Mercer. It could be, some fear, that Howe surprised the post, preventing news of its fall from getting out.

The thought of this pincer closing around the rebel army in its weakened state makes it more imperative that Lee bring his division swiftly to The General's side.

Across the New Bridge—The First Great Perilous Step . . . Painting by B. Spencer Newman . . . The General and staff officers directing the movement of the train over the Hackensack in front of the Zabriskie House. Courtesy of Eugene Dinallo.

On the Village Green, under makeshift emergency shelters, in stables, warehouses, old buildings, sheds and lean-tos along the river front, and in a number of the village homes that have opened their doors to a few of the men, the rebels try to get a few miserable hours of sleep.

After being fed from the cauldrons of stew that are kept boiling through dawn, and by the generosity of many of the village people, they lie restlessly tossing, many remaining in wet clothing throughout the clammy night.

The fortunate ones are those welcomed into the warm, low-slung, sandstone homes built years ago by the Dutch and Huguenot settlers. Many sympathetic burghers and their fraus find lodging for some of the men, either in their homes or barns. They feed them well, dry their clothing and pack victuals in their knapsacks. Most fortunate of all are those who sleep the night on the warm kitchen floors before the open hearth.

It is Jocko who finds the long, open, empty horse and carriage shed by the church. A fully occupied lean-to on rainy Sundays, it now houses only an old broken, two-horse sleigh on which have been piled several bales of hay. The shed lies east of the Church On the Green. Young Graves remembered it from his trip to the Hackensack hospital a few days ago when he brought the wounded Molly Corbin over.

While others had been warming their hands and feet before the open campfires, Jocko and Big Tom took care of their sweating horses, unhitching them from the heavily loaded wagons and bringing them under the cover of the carriage shed lean-to.

After feeding the animals from a half empty barrel of oats and making use of some of the bales of hay, Big Tom and his son retrieve their own dry bedding from the bottom of the wagon.

In the rear of the rickety old vehicle, they find some of the bread, apples and Indian corn which the folks of The Mountain had dumped in the back. They had been overlooked by hungry foragers during the march.

Jocko will tell The Lieutenant about the cache. For there is enough to be shared with others after the stew, pork, bread and corn now cooking on the fires, have filled the belly.

Wagon-master Philip Reales and his son follow Graves' example, pulling in alongside of Big Tom's wagon under the shed. Graves and Reales exchange tales of the difficulties encountered. They leave young Joseph to unhitch, bait and bed down the horses. Jocko, meanwhile, has taken off after Gray to tell him about the comfortable accommodations available in the shed.

The youth has no trouble locating the two lieutenants, both aiding their men in getting settled for the night in a foundry they have taken over near the river. Impatient for their turn at the food being prepared on the cooking fires around The Green, the men of the artillery battery work the forge fires to roast some pork they have "acquired."

While their clothes dry from the rafters, they stand, sit and lie on the sand floor of the long building. All now wide awake, they vividly exchange stories detailing the harrowing experiences of their day. Their momentary burst of energy is a temporary outpouring released by the relaxing letup of tensions. It will disappear swiftly when they have eaten their fill, dispelled by physical submission to their true state of exhaustion which sleep will soon engulf.

A good many tents—far short of the vast number left

behind—had never been pitched and had never been removed from their carriers. They are now brought out of some of the wagons. Fortunately they had been left loaded, destined for New Brunswick.

When All Are Threatened, So Too Are All Their Walls

All over The Green and far beyond it, the encampment spreads out. Officers, rank and file, as do men of all classes in their mutual hour of distress, mix helpfully with each other. Suddenly, though only temporarily, the stone walls of differences and prejudices seem to have fallen away as a close, cooperative fellowship sweeps silently through the bivouac. Even the southern Buckskins speak almost cordially to the northern Yankees. Often some voluntarily help others.

And so arises a spirit of unity and harmony which only the threat of extinction is able sometimes to bring to the surface of human behavior.

Most commands are suddenly now given in a new tone of comradery. Even the manner of speaking seems to extend more respect and consideration. It soon causes Mike Monahan to break out with, "Begorra! 'Tis the new arh'me 'tis upon us!"

Far up the road to Essex near the Polifly highway, the camp women and their husbands also bed down for the night. They too cook and try to find sleep under hastily pitched tents and in barns not far from the Ackerman farmhouse.

Both Gray, his blue petticoat scarf making him easy to locate, and Levy, return with Jocko to look over the carriage shed situation. But they first assure the men of the company that whatever tidbits remain in the wagon will go into tomorrow morning's breakfast pot.

Jocko's description of the carriage house lean-to causes Gray and Levy to picture it a paradise in hay and straw. And to them it is. So there, much to Jocko's delight, they decide to make their bed for the night.

After getting a share of food proportioned out by the cooks at the campfires on The Green, Gray walks back to the carriage shed alone, carrying much of the night's meal to eat under the lean-to.

On his way, he casts his eyes eastward over the night's miserable darkness in the direction of The Mountain and Fort Lee. Only the river and the high hilly ridge's blackish silhouette beyond it meet his eyes. The distant view is obscured by the rising range and the thickness of the night.

Nevertheless, he looks there longingly, fearfully wondering. Softly under his breath he mumbles, "Elaine! My Elaine! ... God, please. ..."

Four and a half miles away by the straight flight of an eagle, Elaine has finally fallen asleep. Earlier she had found her husband's last note just as he had scribbled it on the writing desk before dawn this morning. He has often left her a note when leaving early in order to be on duty at the break of day. Now the little scrap of parchment has fallen from her hand on the empty pillow wet with tears beside her.

Though she had read it cursorily early this terrible morning, tonight, alone in her room, she virtually memorized the quill-scratched message. It did not make such a heavy impact this morning before things happened. But later she realized that he must have been obeying one of his oft-accurate premonitions. This one a feeling that he was to move out without time for goodbyes.

Before long the tears upon it had blurred some of the writing to the point of illegibility. Then mercifully she drifted to sleep, enwrapped only in the embrace of the feather-stuffed mattress her parents had given them as a wedding gift not two months ago. The few scribbled words on the parchment said all there was for him to say:

Terror In A Dream

"I cannot say, 'Good morning, for I do not feel 'twill be. I told you not that a trusted sentinel swore he saw small boats by the hundreds upriver, yet no one else could see a thing. 'Twas nigh dark, and wrongly it was jested he may have been too much in grog, or else was seeing something there that's been so all along. If 'tis mischief we could be marched today to challenge, and I must be up and ready. So, I cannot say, 'Good morning,' not until I hold you once again, and methinks and hopes 'twill be for always.

1, 2, 3. . . . .John-G

Restlessly tossing in nightmarish sleep, Elaine suddenly screamed, "No! Leave him alone! Go! Leave him be! ... Quick, John! This way! Come to me! .. to me! Quick, John. . ."

She awaked abruptly, still in the grip of her fearful vision. Trembling under the shock of the frightening dream, the eight-week bride rose, then sat back on the edge of the bed. Slowly she regained composure. Her heart stopped pounding as the alarming spectacle of horror slowly disintegrated, dissolved in the flood of consciousness.

Drawn to the window overlooking the black, misty outlines of the river, Elaine, seeking solace and escape from her mind's terrifying thoughts, wondered how often she and her husband had together gazed out upon that scene.

How often had they sent their dreams together rising up and passing miraculously through those 12-paned glass windows to be caught some day somewhere in the future! And how often here in reveries did they relive those few beautiful unforgettable hours of happiness on Oratam's ancient castle grounds!

Momentarily her thoughts shift to Andy Abbott and Mahtocheega and their rock-enchiseled symbols on the flat ledge. Their short-lived sign of happiness, their hopes and dreams, had suddenly become John's and hers, she thought. But, oh, for such a brief moment!

And so Elaine dejectedly looked out over the Hudson's blackness, repeating the numerical symbols which they had, in respectful reverence, adopted. She whispered softly, "*One* there was; *two* there are; *three* there will be, God willing. Oh, John! Where are you tonight! Where are you? You must come back! You must. . . to us! Please! Oh, God! Please!"

Midnight In the Mansion House

Back on the second floor east bedroom of Peter Zabriskie's big house the lighted desk candles still burn into the midnight hour. There the American Commander-in-Chief with difficulty keeps his eyes open as he pores over papers and maps, putting the last touches on his withdrawal strategy and its alternatives. All others in the household have fallen into bed and are long in slumber.

Getting up to stretch himself, The General looks longingly at the big canopied spindle bed and its inviting downy comforter. But resolutely he walks away and toward the window.

Throwing it open and pushing the shutters wide apart, he leans out and breathes deeply of the stilled, wet night air. Far to the northeast and scattered along the east bank of the river he sees, barely visible, the diminishing lights of the enemy's campfires. They are those of Colonel Harcourt's advance night probers. The redcoats, too, have at last quieted down after their long night and day pursuit of their elusive Fox.

. . . And Darkest Of All Dark Nights

His eyes turn eastward through the darkness and over the heads of the sentries guarding the ferry river road and the embankments. Every precaution has been taken to thwart any enemy attempts at pursuit until the Continentals are out of reach.

Far across the river, he, like Gray, sees the dark outline of the ridge that blocks a distant view of The Mountain fort.

Upon it and Mount Washington, he thinks in retrospect, he had once placed his hopes of repelling his enemy—an enemy too overwhelming in strength for any "fort" defenses. Both places are now his opponent's. A tragic loss for him, his army and for the hopes, upholding the Congress and the new nation. The constantly amassing British might had not been expected. Against it with his army there is little defense.

The General's mind jumps back 24 hours when he wrote his brother from this desk of his weariness and "the retrograde motion of things." How despondent, he thinks, was he then! How much more so now, this passing night!

His eyes move back from across the river and below upon the campfires of his army, bivouacking, exhausted, in uncomplaining misery on the Village Green. Over 3,000 men lie restlessly below him, their fate and their nation's in his hands. Most still have faith in him, he feels, though he knows many do not.

It is not just an empty rumor that the Congress and the States have lost confidence in their Commander-in-Chief. Though the talk of replacing him does not openly reach his ears, he knows it crosses thousands of lips.

The man's disciplined mind abruptly dismisses any lengthy dwelling upon the unalterable past. Only the immediate present and its partly moldable future possess his thinking. He closes the shutters, lowers the window and goes back to his desk. There is much to be done.

Acquackanonk is next. After that Newark. And, if Providence stays with him, he should have Lee's help in Newark before withdrawing west from there.

He sits at the desk, perusing the poor but only available sketch of the area, making notes with his quill of the map's inadequacies and inaccuracies. He then transfers his notes to the parchment paper by his side. Several times his eyelids close. Then at last the pen drops from his hand.

Soon his head droops. Slowly and gently it lowers, nestling comfortably upon his arms crossed on the desk-top. Now the candle burns low in the holder in front of him. It flickers almost in cadence with the beating pitter-pattering upon the cedar shingled roof.

The longest of all long days is over and the darkest of all dark nights is upon him.

Part IV

Hope

30

Thursday, November 21. . .

Retreat from the Peninsula

Rivers Fence the Juggernaut While the Rebels Wait For Lee

As Thursday, November 21 dawns, it lifts the hazy gray blanket from the peninsula's back and uncovers the valley and the Hackensack village lying safely on the river's west bank. With the first streaks of sunlight, the rebel bivouac of over 3,000 Continentals becomes exposed to the light of a brighter day.

Breakfasting on chunks of pork, sea biscuits and Indian corn, roasted to a crisp over the hot fires, some troops wait impatiently for the order to move out. Others strike their tents, while many throw part of the Hackensack garrison's supplies onto already overloaded wagons. An air of excitement generated by the pressing emergency and the precariousness of their position permeates the atmosphere and spreads throughout the village.

Few of the bedraggled army have found rest through the night. Many have only slightly dozed. They stand wearily in line, leaning half awake on their muskets. Others sit back on a rock or on the wet ground, knowing their clothing can be no colder and damper than it already is.

A few nostalgically strain their eyes eastward where the sun peeks over the summit of their evacuated encampment on The Mountain. Some of the troops look across the river and believe, at times, they see the enemy's advance scouts feeding their fires and making breakfast.

But it is the distant Palisadean ridge and their once formidable fortress above the Hudson that they now try in vain to glimpse.

Many chunks of meat, cut from the carcass of a calf or a lamb, still roast on some of the fires of the rearguard troops. Bread has been generously distributed by the villagers. Many of the women have stayed up all night baking for the army.

Husbands and children deliver the bushel baskets of oven-fresh loaves to the commissary along with fruit and corn. The commissary in turn distributes them to the regimental commissars.

Feeding the men and getting swiftly on with the march are the sole objectives now. Even before the sun appears over the western slopes of the distant Palisadean mountain, the wagons are hitched and the army's van moves up toward the Polifly Road.

No time is lost, for Cornwallis will certainly not be long deterred from spanning the narrow Hackensack after having so easily crossed his brigades over the wide Hudson.

The Continental officers all have their orders. The objective for the day is Acquackanonk, six miles southwest on the opposite bank of the Passaic River. There the army will annex the Acquackanonk garrison, now guarding some of the stores and arms which Gneral Greene transferred from Fort Lee. After that, the withdrawing forces will move down to Newark and pick up the militia and materiel garrisoned there.

In a "dead flat country," as The General describes the terrain, the loss of 500 entrenching tools at Fort Washington,[1] prevents the troops from digging in. The loss also greatly heightens the invaluable strategic contribution of the Hackensack and Passaic Rivers pending the hoped-for early arrival of General Lee.

It is common knowledge that Lee and his corps will arrive within days. Some are sure that the "Knight of the Flaming Sword" soon will be marching over the western Ramapo Pass route to the rescue of the army, joining them in Newark, possibly arriving there first. Much hope and talk now centers upon Charles Lee, the hero of Charleston.

The officers also know that The General has asked the Governor of New Jersey for more State militiamen. In addition they have heard the Commander has sent an urgent message to Congress asking for additional troops. This gives rise to the possibility the Americans will stand and fight either around Newark or to the west.

However, it is the "Flaming Sword" image of General Lee, arriving with his brigades in the nick of time to save America and

The Cause that makes up most of the conversation within the ranks of the down-hearted troops.

John Gray and Asher Levy have had little time to pause or think of other things than the heavy duties resting upon them. Nevertheless, the minds of both officers occasionally drift away from the campfire arguments of the soldiery.

Gray's thoughts speed off to his pregnant wife and his concerns for her and the Baummeister household under enemy hands. Levy's mind takes him to the side of his friend, Haym Salomon, whom he always fears may meet his death at the hands of the enemy in New York's prisons, lying far to the southeast across the Hudson.

Jocko, who is about to join his father and the wagon train, runs up to Gray with a small, leather-bound, red book in his hand. The officer instantly recognizes the youth's prize from Long Island. It has been one of the boy's most treasured possessions, an empty diary dropped by a fleeing Hessian and rescued by Jocko on the field at great risk.

Gray had often told Levy and others of the moment on the Brooklyn heights when a Hessian soldier advanced ahead of his party and almost bumped into the old Barbette Battery's defenses. The severely frightened young mercenary was caught between up-rights of a split-rail fence and ripped his surcoat and trousers in half in his haste to get away. He had made it safely back with most of his backside exposed to the enemy which could not shoot straight from the laughter that the scene provoked.

Jocko had seen the red book, a diary, and little else. The attractive, red-leather prize possessed his mind. And Big Tom's son was determined to possess the book, lying out in the no-man's-land between the troops, anyone's prize foolish enough to risk his life for it.

In the midst of the laughter, the older Graves saw his only offspring jump the parapet and, with lightning swiftness, dash for the Hessian's treasure, recover it and return safely through the light rain before the book was more than slightly moist or the enemy could get off a shot.

The battery's Major Blodget commended him, saying the book could have been important to the military, but scolded him, as did Gray, Big Tom and others for his impulsive, dangerous action. When it was found to be only an empty diary without any entries and no name within it, Blodget gave it to its rescuer. It then became his prized possession and one he intended to write in when Missy E taught him enough.

"Lootenan!" Jocko calls, hurriedly, running, shouting and smiling at the same time, and simultaneously handing Gray the red leather book, "We's goin' wid da wag'ns train 'n might on'ta New Ark, 'n might be youse ain't a'go'on dare too, Ise wan' youse ta have dis, caus'n Ise nevah goin' ta larn readin' and writin' now widout Missey E a'scoldin me. So youse keeps mah writin'-in book and youse fills it up foh me. Youse knows ahll 'bout writin' stuff."

Jocko does not wait for an answer. He leaves the stunned Gray standing, holding the boy's precious battle prize in his hand. In the next moment the agile youth jumps into the long seat beside his smiling father.

The older man holds the reins with one hand, throws a rough salute to the two officers and drives off, joining the wagon train as it winds its way up to the Polifly highway. Moments later the vehicles disappear far ahead of the army's van. They pull off toward the Passaic River.

"I dislike taking this from the boy," Gray says to Levy who stands beside his superior officer.

"If he wants that you have it, John, you had best keep it," Levy replies. "You have ability in penning the written word. Fill it up. Your friend, Jocko, wants you to do so. All you need is ink and quill. Elaine will value what you write and thank Jocko for't."

Hesitant for a moment, Gray looks at the book, thumbing through the empty pages that had long enraptured Jocko with hopeful visions of his own entries and accounts. Then, turning to Levy, he says, "Perhaps . . . Perhaps I shall."

The Lieutenant then briefly glances eastward and adds again, "Perhaps I shall."

Now, instead of the mountain fort on the Palisades acting as guardian-protector of the American forces, it is the flatlands and the rivers of the valleys to the west that take over the task. Westward of the Hackensack, which has temporarily stopped the Juggernaut, there are six miles to go before the army can span the quiet Passaic River, destory the Acquackanonk bridge, and put two streams between them and their pursuers.

The Passaic, named by the Lenni Lenape for its smooth, glistening, almost motionless deep waters, ranges from 150 to 200 feet across as it slowly winds its way under the bridge and past the village of Acquackanonk that was founded a hundred and three years ago. The river from here slowly ambles on south toward Newark after having come down many circuitous miles from the great falls about five and a half miles north.

There it plummets over a 70-foot chasm into the sparkling, churning waters at the base. In a thundering torrent the once gently flowing stream tumbles ton upon ton of silvery, crystal-like waters, suddenly released in a wild cascading crescendo, over the craggy rock cliffs. The falls roar an end to this amazing descent with an outpouring of swirling foam gushing into and around the rock-strewn basin.

High above this awe-inspiring, natural creation sits the inn and home of Captain Abraham Godwin. It is here that many of the post express riders stop and refresh themselves and their horses.

The great falls and the fordable waters and bridge below it are a long way north of Acquackanonk. So, thus the river provides a lengthy protective barrier for the Americans once they have safely made their crossing at Acquackanonk, destroyed the bridge and staved in all the river craft, or brought them up on the west bank.

Certainly Cornwallis will not go many miles north seeking to span the river below the falls. For in looking for an alternative crossing he would lose valuable time. He would be forced to backtrack many wasted miles along the west bank to Acquacka-nonk and Newark.

The Second Step: From the Valleys To the Unknown

From Acquackanonk to Newark will be the next trek, a long day's march of close to 12 miles along the river. At Newark the road divides with a northern spur running through Middle Brook and making its way westward to cross the Delaware at Coryell's Ferry.[2]

The Southern spur from Newark, running south and west of that village, goes through Elizabethtown, Spanktown, Woodbridge to the Raritan River ferry and the bridge across into New Brunswick.

From New Brunswick the road runs through heavy woodlands and thick forests into Princeton and then straight into Trent's town, or Trenton, on the Delaware's east shore.

And that last protective barrier, the river Delaware, lies 80 long, difficult miles southwest of the Bluff Rock on the Hudson. It is the last barrier before the seat of Congress in Philadelphia. It is the last barrier before the great wilderness mountains of Pennsylvania into whose sanctuary the army, if it is able to survive, might, if necessary, flee and hide indefinitely.

Now, up toward the Polifly Road, the American troops move in a slow procession. On the Essex street road, which eventually takes its travelers out of Hackensack into Essex County, the soldiers two abreast pass the 80-year-old home of Abraham Ackerman, now occupied by his descendants.

As they pass the big, sandstone, Dutch homestead with its architecturally perfect gambrel roof and wide over-hanging eaves, they can see the initials of the builder and his son, "AA" and "G. (Garret) A." with the date "1696"[3] carved into the heart-stones on the building's east end. Many of the soldiers had never known before the war that such a pleasant land and such sturdily built farmhouses existed in the valleys under the western slopes of the Palisades.

Some, however, have heard tales of the Hackensack valley and its Dutchmen and Frenchmen who quarry sandstone from out of the ground, saw it into blocks twelve to eighteen inches thick and so build homes with great permanence and comfortableness. They are the most substantial of dwellings, reputed to be easy to warm in winter and similarly easy to cool in summer.

To the soldiers, an officer's remark that the Ackerman house looks like a Dutchman standing with arms akimbo and pipe in mouth, seems like an accurate description. For, coming from the east upon it, the tall, brick chimney gives the appearance of a smoking tobacco pipe.

Distinctive in dignity, the homestead, like all of the sandstone constructed homes, reflects an air of study opulence and serenity that somehow lifts the spirits in crises hours. Since many of the rebel soldiers have never before seen any houses of stone, or brick, or such orderly farmers, the sandstone dwellings and their owners cause many a back-country Continental to stare wide-eyed and open-mouthed at them and their hospitality.

And from the Ackerman house and all the homes along the way, the residents now pour to give the soldiers water for their canteens, baked goods of all kinds, and countless ears of corn from their bins. For corn can be held and roasted Indian-style whenever the bivouac campfires are lighted.

Under the eaves at the side of the houses, on their grounds and both in front and behind the twelve-paned windows, peer the faces of children. Their parents, for the most part, look frightened and disheartened.

The loss of the American army around them spells trouble in the days ahead. All seem to know it but are resigned to accept it.

The women of the households look more wan and tired than the men. And well they should, for it is they who have stayed up most of the night cooking for the withdrawing army.

Until they are beyond Newark, the army will pass many similar sandstone houses but none so architecturally perfect as the Ackerman place on Essex street just below the Polifly Road. For farther south the red sandstone begins to disappear deeper and deeper below the earth's surface, dissolving itself within the glacial sediments. With no such soft red sandstone to quarry—sandstone that hardens the longer it is exposed to air and rain—the settlers built homes of wood, some importing bricks from England at great cost.

Thus the lines of marching men pass by the sturdy dwellings of the Brinkerhoffs, the Hoppers, Terhunes, Kingslands, Berdans, Vreelands, Bogerts, Demarees, Garritses, Yereances, Van Ripers, Kipps, Christies and others. Their French Huguenot, Dutch, English, Scotch, Swiss and Swedish bloods, slowly mixing with others, seem determined to continue their mingling and blending of fortunes, construction arts and labors into a neat, prosperous and beautiful valley, despite the war and the dissensions arising around and among them.

Back on the perimeters of the Hackensack camp, and in clustering groups under the towering spire of the Church On the Green, in Campbell's tavern, and around the headquarters at the Zabriskie mansion house, the worried people of the village gather and talk in hushed voices.

They watch officers, town officials and dispatch riders coming in from all directions. They see the figures in the early morning's light hurriedly enter and as swiftly leave the big house on some errand. The lines of soldiers move out and others form and follow with wagons of baggage and equipment.

The entire encampment area is like a beehive at the height of activity, for every man knows that across the river the enemy encampments are also buzzing with activity. And one thing only is on their mind.

The clustered groups are mainly the town's staunch Whig patriots, but among them are a number of suspected Loyalists. Like the unfortunate patriot inhabitants of Fort Lee, the Hackensack adherents of The Cause know that now there will be nothing to prevent the village from being overrun. British and Hessian troops, Tory Whig-haters and plunderers will surely soon be upon them. Every method of protection must be swiftly initiated.

Even under the pressures of a rapid withdrawal from the tentacular grasp of a powerful pursuer, the paper work of the army goes on. In the big living and dining rooms of the mansion house a few of the staff worked late last night. However, before midnight they had fallen asleep. Some on Madam Zabriskie's best horse-hair stuffed sofas. Others in the Windsor rockers.

A Noticeable Diminishing Regard

A few of The General's aides have noticed, and remarked among themselves, that Adjutant General Colonel Joseph Reed has recently displayed a diminishing regard for the American Commander-in-Chief. It is a reflection of a growing current feeling among many officers and men, but its appearance in Colonel Reed surprises the members of the headquarters staff. Reed, who formerly insisted upon personally carrying out The General's correspondence, now almost indifferently hands over many such responsibilities to subordinates.

The American Commander gives no indication that he senses any change in Reed's attitude. It is too busy a morning for that. So he perfunctorily asks his adjutant general to transcribe a message to Lee. It is one of several he had composed during the night.

The letter begins, expressing regrets for having "no news to send you but of a melancholy nature." He then recounts yesterday's events, mindful of his dispatch yesterday morning gently advising Lee to move his troops to "this side of the North River."

The Continental Army Commander now cloaks his order with utmost respect for the major general who is virtually second in command of all the army's forces. For the Virginian knows that Lee has the respect of Congress and the admiration of many of the officers. He does not know of all the hearsay and machinations that go on around him. But he knows the strength of Lee's popularity, since he himself is one of the North Castle commander's admirers.

However, he is unaware that yesterday Reed desired to alert Lee personally about the enemy's invasion and the retreat from Fort Lee. Without informing his Chief, Reed cornered an express rider about to leave with a dispatch for Heath at Peekskill. Asking the courier to take a message to Lee, Reed scrounged a piece of wrapping paper from the rider's pocket and with the broken end of a pencil, wrote:

"Dear General,

"We are flying before the British. I pray---"

Here the pencil broke and Reed gave the rest of the message verbally. The courier was to pass on word to the major general from Reed urging that Lee push on and join the American force in Jersey.

But when the message was orally delivered, it was jumbled causing Lee to describe it to Heath as "a short billet that I do not well understand."[4]

Reed, without mentioning his attempt to inform Lee, transcribes his Chief's letter to the North Castle commander in Westchester, stating, in part:

> "Upon the whole, I am of opinion, and the gentlemen about me agree on it that the publick interest requires your coming over on this side with the Continental troops, leaving Fellows' and Wadsworth's brigades to take care of the stores for the short stay, at the expiration of which I suppose they will set out home.

The General's letter then explains why the Westchester troops at North Castle should be moved out and across to the Hudson's west bank, hoping Lee can read between the lines and know—in case the letter is intercepted—the army's need of them. He states that the foe has shifted the seat of war to the west side of Hudson's river; the desire of the countryside in Jersey is to be supported by the army and, if not, they will cease to give support to The Cause; and that it is necessary to give "at least an appearance of force in order to keep this Province in connection with the others."

It is as tactful an "order" as he can give; it is as strong an appeal as he dare chance through enemy territory.

Then, giving his *order* more in the form of a strong suggestion than a command, The General adds:

> "Unless, therefore, some new event should occur, or some more cogent reason present itself, I would have you move over by the easiest and best passage. I am sensible your numbers will not be large, and that, perhaps, it may not be agreeable to the troops.
> "As to the first, report will exaggerate them, and preserve the appearance of an army, which will at least have an effect to encourage the desponding here; and, as to the other, you will doubtless represent to them, that in duty and gratitude, their service is due wherever the enemy make the greatest impression or seem to intend so to do."[5]

The General's Adjutant Decries "An Indecisive Mind"

He concludes his letter to Lee, ordering that the "North-Castle, Croton Bridge, and King's Ferry" stores be removed to Peekskill "under General Heath's eye. This, we hope, there will be time and means to do."

Colonel Reed then surreptitiously slips his own personal letter to Lee in with the courier's packet. In it Reed writes his newly acquired hero that he does not mean to flatter or praise him, but that the army and the liberties of America are entirely dependent upon him (Lee) to prevent the Continentals and their cause from being "totally cut off." He tells Lee:

"You have decision, a quality often wanting in minds otherwise valuable... and I have no doubt had you been here the garrison at Mount Washington would now have composed a part of this army."[6]

The adjutant general then briefly mentions the fall of Fort Washington. He informs Lee that Colonel Cadwalader who had been taken prisoner there was released without parole by his captors owing to "some civilities shewn by his (Cadwalader's) family to (British) Gen. Prescott."

Cadwalader, Reed writes Lee, is now saying that the enemy holds the Americans in contempt in consequence of their poor "plan of defence and execution" at Mount Washington.

The adjutant then discloses his own poor opinion of Greene as a commander, blaming Greene for the Fort Washington debacle. He writes that:

(The General's judgment) "seconded by representations from us, would I believe have saved the men and their arms, but unluckily General Greene's judgment was contrary; this kept the general's mind in a state of suspense until the stroke was struck."

Decrying what he calls the "indecisive mind," the adjutant general continues his lengthy letter, stating:

"Oh! General—an indecisive mind is one of the greatest misfortunes that can befall an army—how often have I lamented it this campaign.

"All circumstances considered we are in a very awful and alarming state, one that requires the utmost wisdom and firmness of mind. As soon as the season will admit I think yourself and some others should go to Congress and form the plan of the new army—point out their defects to them and if possible prevail on them to bend their whole attention to this great object—even to the exclusion of every other.

"If they will not or cannot do this, I fear all our exertions will be vain in this part of the world. Foreign assistance is soliciting but we cannot expect they will fight the whole battle—but artillery and artillerists must be had, if possible.

"I intended to have said more but the express is waiting—and I must conclude with my clear and explicit opinion that your presence is of the last importance."[7]

Meanwhile at North Castle Major General Lee is also busy with correspondence.

First he writes the President of the Council of Massachusetts, James Bowdoin, in an effort to arouse New England's fears should he and his troops be pulled out. He tells Bowdoin that he expects to look for assistance from Connecticut and Massachusetts "should the enemy attempt to open the passage of the Highlands, or enter New England."[8] Thus Lee plants in the mind of New Englanders the necessity that his division not only be reinforced but that the corps should be permanently maintained at North Castle, the door to New England, for the protection of all the northern provinces. The former British army officer appears to have his mind set against crossing his corps to Jersey in support of the American Chief.

The astute North Castle commander believes that Howe will soon point part of his army at New England. In that prediction, Lee is correct, but it will be some time before it occurs. And when it does General Clinton will direct the British operation which will bog down and become stalemated in Newport, Rhode Island.

Secondly, Lee, in an effort to get General Heath to carry out the call for help, writes the commander of the Peekskill troops, saying, "I have just received a recommendation, not a positive order, from the General to move the troops under my command to the other side of the river."[9]

Explaining his unwillingness to comply with the request, Lee orders Heath to execute the "recommendation." He directs Heath to send "two thousand of (your) corps" across the river to support the oppressed Jersey forces.

Heath refuses to carry out an order intended for Lee and advises his superior officer that he is declining to do so on the basis of his instructions from The General:

> "not to admit of moving any part of the troops assigned to me, unless it be by express orders from his Excellency or to support you (Lee) in case you are attacked."[10]

Before today is over, Lee will receive The General's second and slightly stronger request along with Reed's communication. And he will reply to Reed, giving several excuses for not executing the "request."

He will state that he has not the means for crossing; that he would not be able to arrive in time to be of service; and that crossing at King's Ferry would be such a delaying maneuver as to be useless at this time.

He will also inform Reed that he has ordered Heath:

> "to detach two thousand of his men to aid his Excellency." This, Lee writes Reed, would "answer better what I conceive to be the spirit of the orders."[11]

Lee's position, tottering on the edge of defiance is not unlike the present wavering spirit of the officers and men of the army and their faith in their Chief. The diminishing confidence of some of the men and officers in the American Leader, added to an almost outright defiance by his second in command, combine to cause a weakening of morale and a perilous "contagion of desertion which has been epidemic and now begins to rage after the manner of a plague."[12]

Charles Lee has been right about some things and wrong about many others. But the latter do not stand long in his memory. He has enjoyed a meteoric rise, thanks to Charleston and to the credit of subordinates in that siege.

And he was right about Fort Washington. That and his success in the South have in the opinion of many, made him the most admired commanding general in the American army. And no one knows it better than Charles Lee.

If the commander of the North Castle forces is lacking in pessimism and a genuine concern for the fleeing American troops in Jersey, the Commander-in-Chief of the harassed and broken army makes up for it. Like a calamitous, invisible shroud, gloom seems to hover over the mansion house on the edge of the Hackensack Green. Yet the work of running an army, even an army pressed and pursued, must go on. And it does, both inside and outside the big house.

By late afternoon almost all of the brigades have withdrawn from the town. Many are already safely across the Passaic and preparing to bivouac this night in Acquackanonk. Only The General, his suite, bodyguards, some of the headquarters personnel, a covering company of foot, a regiment of cavalry and the rear guard remain in the village encampment.

A Rift Breaks Through the Clouds of Darkness

When at last the remaining headquarters staff mount and leave, followed by the foot, cavalry and rear guard, the sun is low, hidden by a blanket of dark, threatening clouds.

The headquarters men put on a bold front. They, like the faithful, rugged Continental troops, try to keep up their unperturbed appearance. And in doing so they sprinkle jests into their conversations, jests that belie their feelings.

When the last of the scouts bring in word that the redcoats are searching the length of the river for lumber and boats and are already re-building the bridge, one of the American rear guard is heard to remark:

"'Tis with farst speed Howe moves! 'Hit takes old Sir Will'um all of twen'y-fer hours ta get chere frum da Lib'ty Pole. 'Hit mus' be 'causin' da Sultana's bizznez comes 'afor da King's."

A raucous laugh such as has not been heard among the troops since leaving Fort Lee, goes up as the soldier's remark is repeated and passed up the lines. The rolling laughter, gathering intensity when humorous embellishments are gracelessly added as the story progresses westward, breaks the tensions.

Despite the deplorable state of the army and the deadly gravity of its situation, the wave of laughter seems to be the first great step out from under the deadly closing jaws of the great Juggernaut by the small band of Continentals carrying the American cause farther and farther away from the final snap of death.

There will be many more steps to take, backwards and forwards. But the first and second of the most perilous crisis are slowly being left behind.

For a moment the great losses of the army are forgotten as the laughter briefly and incongruously frolics through the tattered, wearied and sullen lines of men like a breath of fresh air. But their losses keep hammering upon their minds—barrels of foodstuffs, pricelessly vital to an army, countless muskets, ammunition, artillery and armament both heavy and light, much baggage and equipment and personal properties, some 300 sorely needed tents very drastically in demand with winter on its way, tons of beef and pork left behind in pastures, 3,100 barrels of flour and 10,000 bushels of grain. These are a few of the catastrophic losses that plague, not only the minds of the high command but the rank and file as well.

For this disaster someone must be held responsible. And Greene is the one at whom his detractors within the service point the finger. It matters not that The General himself has assumed the blame.

Greene's deprecators, of whom both Colonel Reed and General Lee are two high on the list, begin sabotaging the name of the fort's former commander. Some are outspoken in their criticism. Some resort to innuendoes. And because of the seemingly strong bond between The General and Greene, the American Commander-in-Chief himself becomes a target for their anger and denunciations.

Thus, beside the visible foe, the army has its internal enmities adding to its increasing problems.

At times more destructive than the forces from without, the internal hostilities are mostly clandestine and so become difficult to locate, no less attack.

Crisis Totters On the Edge of Death

Greene's adjutant, Thomas Paine, watches with disgust and growing anger the insidiously corrosive undermining of the army's pillars. But the British-born supporter of the American cause serves in a semi-soldier, civilian capacity which makes him hesitant to enter into discussions which he knows would be useless.

Paine has witnessed the retreats that have followed catastrophes, the casualties and losses among young America's youth, the dead, wounded and imprisoned, the breakdown of civilian morale that infects recruitment and re-enlistments amid the fast approaching expiration of enlistment terms.

He has seen the figures on increasing desertions, the tragic lack of medical supplies and hospital facilities and the poor quality of so many politically appointed officers, many of whom are primarily concerned only with their personal ambitions.

He has seen the rebel army exactly as one British officer, writing home to London, sees them—"half-naked and hungry" and many close to starving.[14] He has felt the weakening pulse of some of the disheartened militiamen and some of the people throughout the thirteen states who now are rapidly losing faith in their Leader and in ultimate victory.

And he has lost patience with the Congress for its frequent delaying and vacillating actions on military matters and for its weaknesses and political intrigues which have often tied The General's hands.

And the former adjutant general of Fort Lee sees the enemy pointing itself directly toward Philadelphia. He sees Howe's plan which, if carried out, will give the enemy control of the Delaware.[15] This will be followed by the coup de grace, the capture of the Continental Congress itself.

But this the Congress also knows, and in desperation the august body is considering last resorts. One of these is a change in commanders.

To Thomas Paine there have not been many moments in the history of nations more trying than this. Not many nations have lived through such critical hours—hours fraught with peril, tragedy and chance, balancing on the scales of providence.

The adjutant gathers his precious personal notes and baggage, and he, too, heads out with the troops, catching a ride with one of the last wagons to pull away from the village. In the back of the vehicle he nestles down beside a broken drum-head.

Not many armies, he thinks, have staggered so long, so perilously on the edge of disaster and survived. Without a blank piece of paper on which to scribble his thought, he tears off the broken membrane from the top of the hollow cylinder and writes down the words upon the dried animal skin.

About to mount Old Magnolia, The General, having said his goodbyes and expressed his gratitude to Zabriskie and others, is approached by Archibald Campbell, the tavern owner. Campbell is choked and almost in tears as he hands the American Commander some wine and water for his canteen, saying, "Gen'l, what'll I do? I 'ave a fam'ly—lit'l ones—'n a lit'l prop'ty yonder. Should I take up 'n leave wee 'em?"

The Virginian calmly drinks the wine, thanks the tavern proprietor and says with little indication of the vast weights upon his mind, "Mister Campbell, stay by your family, Sir, and keep neutral."[16]

By nightfall British Major General Vaughan's forces have stretched their lines from the destroyed New Bridge south along the river's east bank with their left wing outposts almost opposite the Hackensack landing dock. There is nothing more they can do but bivouac for the second night and watch their prey disappear out of the village westward.

Much time was consumed in overrunning the deserted Fort Lee encampment and its environs. Too much time.

Vaughan's fruitless search for river craft and his orders for a swift rebuilding of the bridge generated noise and plenty of enemy activity until sunset. Frustrated by their close proximity to their quarry and eager for the catch, the redcoats gladly seek Tory assistance in preparing for their crossing tomorrow.

As ordered, Vaughan had moved in behind his dragoons upon the bridge at 9 A.M. this morning with his "2nd Battalion of Light

Infantry, the 2nd Battalion of Grenadiers and one company of Chasseurs."[17]

The major general's mission was to seize the span and "prevent its destruction by the enemy in their precipitate retreat"[18]—a rather belated concern and action by the British commanders, indicating a paucity of knowledge of the bridge, the area and the non-fordable stream. For the British officer's assignment is about 20 hours too late.

Yesterday, when Lord Cornwallis stood on the west slope of the Palisades trying to look through the misty rain for the so-called Hackensack River, he caught glimpses of the Hackensack valley and the town with its identifying church spire rising up from the Church On the Green. But no river. Owing to the Tee Neck ridge's height on the river's east bank, the Hackensack waters are not visible except farther northward.

To the Earl of Cornwall there appeared to be no river of consequence there in the distance. Certainly not one as wide as the Hudson. Certainly not one which could halt the Juggernaut.

For the Howe Brothers the day has been one of exultation ever since Sir William was rowed ashore at Bourdette's.[19] The occupation of the fort, the exchange of commendations and the bivouacking and feeding of the army came first. The chase was to be continued today. And then came the disappointing news that the bridge cannot be crossed until tomorrow.

Cornwallis last night, proud of his men and their accomplishment, ordered their rest and recuperation, directing use of their enemy's captured grounds, tents and supplies as needed. Some quartered on the grounds, some in the English Neighborhood, settling themselves around Van Horne's grist mill, on the Lydecker property and on the adjacent farms along the King's Highway north into Liberty Pole.

There was reason to be satisfied. The Juggernaut had now acquired control of the Hudson River. It had planted its feet on the mainland, albeit if only a peninsula attached to it. And it has sent the rebel army scurrying.

And so Howe, Cornwallis and their staffs, reviewing the work of the Crown's army during the past five days, have good reason to believe that they have broken the back of the rebel forces and likewise the American rebellion.

In less than a week the three lightning strokes, attack on Fort Washington, crossing of the Hudson and the invasion's triumphant march down the valley, and the seizure of Fort Lee, the rebels' central communications, intelligence and supply depot, have brought the Campaign of 1776 apparently into its conclusion. A conclusion that should soon return the rebellious colonies to the Empire.

Over on the west bank of the Hackensack no such thoughts are permitted in the American Commander-in-Chief's mind as he bids goodbye to Campbell. Then, turning his horse away from the westward line of march, he heads east toward the river landing, Greene at his side. Determined to ascertain for himself the progress of his opponents on the opposite bank, he focuses his field glasses on the scattered enemy picket outposts.

Though it is difficult to discern much in the overcast late afternoon light, the rebel Chief concludes his observations after studying the foe's movements for fifteen minutes. He is soon assured that his pursuers will be unable to make any sizeable crossing before morning.

But before they can, Greene tells his chief, they will have to do a pretty job of bridge building to carry such a caravan as theirs, or certainly some mighty extensive boat-repairing.

By dusk, after all have moved out except a few rear guards, thus returning the quiet little village temporarily to its former peaceful-ness, most of the American army have safely crossed the Passaic River at Acquackanonk. So now, six miles behind them, the Hackensack villagers see the lighted campfires of the stalled Jugger-naut. Their sparks fly high above the river's east shore as the townspeople brace themselves for tomorrow's unwelcome visitors. One townsman will write:

> "We could see their fires, about a hundred yards apart, gleaming brilliantly in the gloom of night, extending some distance below the town and more than a mile up towards New Bridge."[20]

Despite the aura of pessimism, the dangling calamitous cloud above their heads and the enemy's certainty that the end is only days away, the American Commander and the many who are loyally devoted to him, appear resigned to answer misfortune and defeat with the only weapon remaining in their possession: The re-doubling of every effort they can summon.

Out Of the Realm That Is Animal

It is this spirit that Paine grasps and about which he scribbles on the drum head. It is this "weapon," he believes, that the new nation and its army must adopt in the fight against adversities. It is this dedication to the beneficence of mankind, rather than to the self-centered disregard for others, so abundantly found in animals, that will build greatness in men and nations of tomorrow. It is this spirit, he thinks, that must in time spread from the army to the states, from the soldier to the civilian, from individual power to the power of the people.

On the high ground above the gently flowing Passaic, the business of war, logistics, retreat and strategy continues once again under candlelight. And once again the wicks burn down to their bottoms before they are snuffed out.

Among the many papers heaped before The General by his aides tonight at Acquackanonk, there are personal problem letters which are more important to the writers than the drastic state of the army and the country.

One of these is a letter from the imprisoned Colonels Atlee and Miles who jointly urge that they be exchanged for an American-held British officer.

Many such letters of appeal get the Commander's personal attention, but a reply to this at this crucial time can also serve a vital military purpose. Therefore he replies to the two officers, giving his approval willingly if they "can obtain General Howe's consent."[21]

Their letter also noted "the deplorable condition of our prisoners in New-York, for want of clothes and other necessities. . . and the scanty allowance of provisions." This information The General can also use.

Fraud Is An Art In War

In his shrewdly designed reply, courteously mentioning General Howe who will certainly be shown the carefully dated letter, The General pointedly informs the two men that he has "laid the matter before Congress" [22] with his personal recommendations for improving the conditions of the unfortunate prisoners. But this nip at Howe's prisons is not the letter's main purpose.

The communication from "Acquackanonk" is clearly dated, "Headquarters, November 21, 1776." It carries the Commander-in-Chief's signature at its close.

Thus, while revealing the rebel Leader's personal concern for his imprisoned men, it also conveys to the censoring scrutinizers of prisoners' mail in the British command offices in New York, as well as to Howe himself, that the American army surely cannot be "wildly fleeing before the enemy" if its Leader can take time out for such minor matters.

Yet that is what all New Yorkers and all the provinces are being told. Such "wild flight" descriptions undermine the states' morale and play into Howe's hands, causing many former patriots to sign Sir William's papers, promising allegiance to the Crown.

By The General's cunning little tactic, designed to get through to his enemy headquarters, he shows he can turn the tables on propagandists and make use of deceptive techniques when the stakes require it. And the stakes now do require it.

There is no reply yet among the headquarters' dispatches from The General's appeal to Governor William Livingston for troops. There is no word from Pennsylvania's committee nor from the Congress. But this is not surprising. It takes a fast express rider to make the trip to Philadelphia in a day.

Only General Lee has replied to his Commander's appeal for help. But Lee's reply is couched in excuses and an explanation of his effort to get Heath to send the reinforcements which The General has politely requested of Lee. The wily North Castle commander knows that in the absence of a "positive order" his actions cannot be construed as insubordination.

Without Lee's troops, without added Jersey and Pennsylvania reinforcements, the Juggernaut cannot be stopped. With them, the British army could be delayed, harassed and possibly forced to a standstill as was proved in White Plains.

The Grand Army, or what is now left of it, though badly broken is still in one piece. It has unbelievingly stepped safely across two river barriers, bringing itself temporarily out from between the jaws of the Juggernaut.

The problem now is to arouse the countryside, the Congress and the thirteen states. All must in unison throw their efforts into the army, their only defense. Rumors will take care of the countryside. Paine will make his outcry felt throughout the states. And General Mifflin, a Pennsylvanian, will try to drive the Congress into action.

Mifflin is to inform the nation's representatives in Philadelphia of their imminent danger and remain there directing the city's plan of defense. Writing to Robert Morris from Acquackanonk tonight, the Quaker Quartermaster General warns Morris that were the British to move against Philadelphia, the seat of the Congress would "a few hours after shake to her centre."[2 3]

Mifflin's letter should help in arousing swift support from Pennsylvania in behalf of the army. Similar letters soliciting military support are sent to other leaders including those in the Northern Department. All the state governors and their safety committees are apprised of the seriousness of the situation in urgent express dispatches. And so the alarm goes out, but any indication of desperation or hopelessness is tactfully avoided.

In order to keep New Jersey Governor Livingston abreast of the army's movements, The General writes the Governor from Acquackanonk tonight, stating:

> "... arrived at this place with General Beall's and General Heard's Brigades from Maryland and Jersey, and part of General Ewing's from Pennsylvania... Three other regiments, which were left to guard the passes upon Hackensack river and to serve as covering parties, are expected up this evening."[2 4]

Before noon tomorrow the few rear guard troops, keeping a surveillance over the Passaic's east bank and bivouacking on that side for the night, will destroy the bridge behind them after coming across and again taking up the rear in the march to Newark.

The river here is wide and deep and the bridge's span, stretching over 150 feet across, is longer by half than Hackensack's New Bridge. Again all river craft have been pulled up on the west shore and their hulls staved in.

The enemy's pursuit, already meeting unexpected hazards that are impeding its progress in the crossing of the Hackensack, now could be bogged down for days before getting across the Passaic.

The Bright Side Comes In View

It has proved to be time well bought for the Continentals. The march in the morning to Newark, nine miles south,[2 5] should be less hurried unless Howe has sent a force out from Staten Island through Amboy.

The militia troops from Newark and Elizabethtown are expected to reinforce the retreating army along with much needed supplies and materiel. And some among the marchers are wagering that the "Knight Of the Flaming Sword" will bring his corps to The General's side before the week is up. There is more sleep in Acquackanonk tonight than in Hackensack last night. The wagerers, who bet that "The Knight Of the Flaming Sword" is on his way, help to buoy spirits.

All kinds of credits for the army's success, thus far, are tossed about. Some say Cornwallis should be thanked for "taking his time." Some credit the rank and file of the army for enduring disaster as they did. Some say it was "The Bloke" who brought Greene the news just in time, and so they go on. However, Lee's supporters find a way through the maze of "Ifs" to credit their hero.

Had Lee complied with The General's request to come to his aid, they declare, the North Castle army might have met the enemy, been overwhelmed, forcing The General to send his forces into the fray, and all would have been lost. Lee's supporters may not be logical, but they are loyal.

General Lee Espouses "A Contrary Spirit"

Lee's followers can use the North Castle commander's own words to defend his disinclination to come to The General's side, as requested. They can quote him as saying:

> "There are times when we must commit treason against the laws of the State for the salvation of the State."[26]

Those will be the major general's words tomorrow when he writes to the President of the Massachusetts Council. In that communique, Lee, taking Colonel Reed's thoughts as his own, will say, in part, "Indecision bids fair for tumbling down the goodly fabrick of American freedom."

He will recommend that the Massachusetts body, "immediately (raise) an army to save us from perdition," pointing out that something must be done to counteract the failure of the Congress to "establish a noble army. . . on an excellent footing."

Taking a cue from Reed's letter, he will cite the present military situation, declaring that the Council should avoid the misfortunes caused by "an indecisive mind" and remedy the "indecision of Congress" and "the indecsion in our military councils which cost us the garrison of Fort Washington."

Then, in an attempt to define this "excusable" type of treason which can overcome poor decision-making, the scholarly-minded writer and soldier of fortune states that "indecision" should be counteracted "by a *contrary spirit*," which he is now putting into practice with The General.

"The present crisis demands this brave, virtuous kind of treason," Lee writes the Council. Rationalizing in this manner, the widely acclaimed hero of the Battle of Charleston suggests that the Massachusetts gentlemen commit a little treason "for the salvation" of The Cause.

And, in this manner, he seems to be attempting to justify his own refusal to cross over with his troops and aid his superior officer in an act which he believes would not be for the best interest of The Cause.

So Charles Lee, to whom many are transferring their hopes and faith, is now frequently mentioned in many conversations. His name will become a topic for the tongue, second only to the tragic stories of the army's status. On many lips and in many minds, military, civilian and political, Lee's virtues will now be extolled.

Though he finds writing difficult with only campfire light, Gray, before retiring, enters notes about the march in Jocko's diary. He is glad the youngster and his father moved on with the wagon train to Newark earlier in the day, but he admits there is a void around the bivouac without them.

Often throughout the day the officer has thought and worried about Elaine and the people of the hamlet under enemy occupation. At times it tortures his mind until he forces himself to think of other things. However, the patriot inhabitants have their own chain of intelligence. They pass on information from homestead to homestead.

It is said that everyone is to be given opportunity to sign the King's Oath. Thus far, Gray is told, most villagers say they will and little trouble is expected. Yet all know the enemy will confiscate everything they need.

Gray's mind is put at ease when Craig and his scouts confirm the patriots' reports. So at last he crawls in beside Levy under the lean-to. But sleep does not easily overtake him.

His mind tears through the past few days. . . his last few minutes with Elaine. . . the nightmarish march and the miraculous escape of the army.

Then again he is carried back to The Mountain. Elaine's eyes haunt him as he recalls her words, "I will never see thee again. Will I John-G?"

He shuts out the scene and the memories and thinks upon tomorrow. It will be another long hard day, and suddenly sleep takes him.

'N All's Welll

Two rivers eastward, Lord Cornwallis, unhappily assesses the failure of part of his objective, the most important part. Not only has his Fox gotten away, but he has gotten away too easily and too far. The Earl has just been informed that the Passaic is wider than the Hackensack and the enemy sleeps on its west bank. He does not have to be told that the bridge and the boats to cross it will be gone when he gets there.

But certainly, he thinks, the rebels cannot run forever.

Three rivers eastward, General Sir William and Admiral Lord Howe, reflecting upon a most successful six days, have little doubt that Lord Cornwallis will shortly close in upon his pursuers.

How possibly can such a beaten band and their Congress now expect to hold out against the power of the Empire and the will of the Crown?

As though disdainfully ignoring the question, the Americans' rear guard sentinel at the eastern terminus of the Acquackanonk bridge contemptuously sings out his, "All's well!"

Just as he does, the words of the distant night watch come up from over the quiet, motionless waters of the Passaic, and as though in answer, ring softly through the flickering campfires announcing, "Twelve o'clock 'n all's well!"

31

Thursday, November 28. . .

Newark: With Hope
They Wait for Lee in Vain

After Acquackanonk

Since leaving Acquackanonk last Friday, November 22, the Continental Army has spent five days in Newark after a nine-mile march. During that time it has regrouped, dug entrenchments, established picket posts and called in the area's militia.

It also was relieved to find that Howe, as yet, has not sent out a pincering force and come down on Mercer in Amboy. And today they still wait hopefully for General Lee, Governor Livingston's New Jersey militia units and the militia troops from Pennsylvania. But the long wait has so far been disappointing.

Only General Stirling and Colonel Hand have joined the force in Newark, having come up with their brigades from New Brunswick after receiving word from the Commander-in-Chief. And Mercer, upon The General's call, immediately began withdrawing his post from Amboy.

Howe has kept his left eye on Mercer, and belatedly ordered General von Murbach, whose brigade is under command of Colonel Johann Gottlieb Rall, to run over Mercer's garrison on the Kill von Kull opposite Staten Island.[1]

But von Murbach and Rall, too late, will find it deserted. The disappointed Rall will then move up to follow in rear guard position behind Cornwallis.[2]

Howe's right eye has been focused on Lee in the north. He has ordered General Clinton with a force of 6,000 troops to surround or by-pass the corps in North Castle in an attempt to support Rogers' Raiders and take the pass to Rhode Island and New England. However, unknown to Clinton, Lee will have at last made his belated, reluctant exodus from Westchester December 1.

So when Clinton arrives at North Castle, he will have just missed Lee and will move into Rhode Island, becoming harmlessly bogged down there for the winter.

The British commander, though convinced his campaign is coming to a successful end, is taking no chances. His left and right protected, Howe concentrates all his hopes on Cornwallis's front and its success. He orders Major General Grant and his 4th Brigade to come over from New York with his forces[3] to protect the Earl's lengthily extending lines and support his occupying troops in the villages.

Cornwallis has not had an easy time. Destroyed bridges and staved in boats have caused his lumbering, cumbersome 7,000-man corps to lose not hours but days in which the rebels have moved farther and farther away from the Earl's fast fading hopes.

It was Friday, the 22nd, six days ago, when the Americans withdrew from Acquackanonk. About that time the British engineers had managed to construct a bridge strong enough for the huge train. And that morning, while Lord Cornwallis, Major General Vaughan and Colonel Harcourt frustratedly stood on the Hackensack's east bank, urging the engineers to speed their work, the two rebel rear guard regiments under General Beall began tearing up the Passaic River span behind them.

For most of the rebels it had been a breakfast of wet rations. For some, whose fires were kept alive through a cold night of drizzling rain, there was roast corn and pork meat.

To the assistance of Beall's troops came a number of Acquackanonk's patriots led by John H. Post.[4] Taking over the job of dismantling the causeway, they made good use of their axes, horses and wagons, carting away the big heavy planks for concealment from the pursuing enemy.

Thus, though Cornwallis was only nine miles behind his fleeing Continentals, the distance might as well have been a hundred as the bedraggled Americans, almost leisurely, made their way to Newark.

There they have waited, certain that help will soon come. Not just from the local militia, Stirling's 1,200 up from New Brunswick and Mercer's force from Amboy—if the redcoats have not caught them—but especially they have hoped in Newark that surely there would arrive General Lee with his army of avengers.

Gray has developed a strong attachment for Jocko's red leather diary gift. Each night somehow, somewhere he records the events of the day. They are not entirely secretive, and both Jocko and Levy often give their own personal suggestions for entries that they think should be included. However that which is written as a continuous letter to Elaine is seldom exposed to others' eyes.

Levy is the only one who does occasionally read some of the contents aloud at Gray's suggestion. But Asher Levy never violates the blotter-covered sections, well aware that they are words meant only for Elaine.

Neither Jocko nor Levy have been able to understand why, at the end of every entry, The Lieutenant always writes the number, "123." Innocently they have asked but never get anything but a brusque reply that it is an old code symbol like "Your Obedient Servant," meaning "That Is All."

Levy, understanding, pursues it no further. But Jocko wants the exact words. Persistently he has struggled to discover their meaning, and persistently has the tight-lipped battery officer smilingly refused to reveal them.

One thing Gray will not do is read aloud any part of the diary to Jocko. When Gray's battery was settling down in the fields near the Newark school house and his men occupied the carriage lean-to barn and hayloft nearby, The Lieutenant attempted to return the youth his prized possession.

Big Tom, brushing down the sweating horses with his son's help, said, "Youse gotta keep dat writin' book, Lootenan', causin' da boy ain' gonna be 'appy lessin' ya doos. He'sa bin awantin' to gib ya dat writin' book fer a long spell, Lootenan. So now youse gotta keep it, n' pucha writin' words in't."

Jocko, brushing the nag's mud-splattered and gnarled mane, added, "Dat's right, Lootenan'! Dat's right!"

"All right, Jocko," Gray answered. "'Tis a thing I want and need to write in. But ye must know this! Missy E and I are not ever going to read one word of it to you. Ye have got to learn to read for yourself. So I'll take the book if ye will promise to learn reading and writing. I'll help you when I can... 'til we get back to Missy E. Do ye promise?"

"Yassuh, Lootenan' John, Ise promise," the boy replied laughingly.

The "Generous" Schoolmaster Has A Motive

Gray, like the rest of the army and The General himself, was over-optimistic. He had good reason to be. There was good reason to believe that Lee was on his way. And Gray's battery not only had the school grounds to itself, but even the school house and its "luxurious" outdoor latrine was turned over to him by the obliging schoolmaster.

The lanky, bespectacled tutor had dismissed his scholars the Friday afternoon of the army's arrival. Approaching The Lieutenant, he inquired, "I suppose, Soldier, that ye will all be on the run again tomorrow?"

"'Tis possible, Sir." Gray replied cautiously.

"We hear it is nigh over," the schoolmaster declared, hoping to get a choice bit of news in reply.

"Indeed?" questioningly exclaimed the officer, displaying a noticeable raise of his eyebrows to indicate the schoolmaster's information was, to him, "indeed" a surprising piece of hearsay.

"Indeed I trust so," declared the tutor. "It is a beastly business. The children are the victims of revolting war, if ye will forgive the pun. They are becoming as blind as their elders, I do believe. Ye must see, I am a neutral. I am neither Whig nor Tory-minded. And I believe this is as a schoolmaster should be in spells like this. I board with one who does not believe in rebellion, a Master Nutman, a neutral also, down yonder."

The schoolmaster pointed in the direction of the village, and Gray made a mental note of the approximate location—the location of a Tory very likely and one to be wary of. Then, explaining to Gray why he believed his profession required his neutrality, the tutor declared that he had no desire, nor intention, of becoming "a Nathan Hale," and introduced himself as Schoolmaster Nicodemus Grossbeck.

"My purpose in coming to you, Sir," said the loquacious pedagogue, his high chimney hat sitting shakily on his head, "is to ask that ye and your men not damage our schoolhouse."

Realizing that soldiers seldom have great respect for property in times of war, and that the military would make use of whatever they needed, regardless of appeals and requests, the schoolman, who is responsible for repairs and is not adept at making them, decided to beat the army to the starting line. He does so with a courteous offer of the building's use to The Lieutenant and his battery.

"Since the pupils are dismissed," continues Grossbeck, "until

next month in order to be with their own during this week of prayer
and the giving of thanks, I trust ye will use our school building
gently. We ask only that ye do not damage this place of learning,
that ye will replenish our firewood supply which ye use, and that
ye replace the red ink quill in the red inkwell and the black ink
quill in the black inkwell. This is of utmost necessity. And, Sir, the
lock key for the door is kept on the rafter these trying days, above
the door. Only one of our height," he notes, sizing up The
Leiutenant's tall stature, "can reach it."

Hopes Were High In Newark On Friday

Understanding Grossbeck's concerns, Gray thanked the schoolmaster, assured him they would make occasional use of the building, but observed that likely the battery would be billeted in the
long carriage lean-to and the barn. He promised it would be left in
good condition. The Lieutenant and his men had found the ideal
situation, thanks to Jocko's foresight in selecting the lean-to for his
wagon upon his early arrival in the town.

Of most importance were the ready-built outhouse latrines. What
more could an army on the march want? Particularly when the
green apple two-step calls—and all too often in the middle of the
cold night!

And where could the Blue Petticoat Scarf Lieutenant find a
better place than the unoccupied schoolmaster's desk to write in
his diary every night? And what better place than the schoolhouse
for a temporary headquarters where the men of the battery could
be assembled at one time?

There was much that had to be done that first night in Newark,
Friday, November 22. Defenses had to be set up, bivouacs
prepared and rolls had to be taken. The old 12-pounders the
battery dragged from Fort Lee had to be brought into position,
loaded and pointed toward the enemy's van on the road where it
intersects with the bridge. Levy handled this task with the
battery's cannoneers, all of whom came in for a commendation
from the major, colonel and the top staff command itself for
having successfully brought off the two fieldpieces.

Every man was close to exhaustion that night. In two days,
beginning Wednesday morning on the Fort Lee mountain, they had
covered 26 long, painful miles, many in torture. Twelve miles
Wednesday . . . six on Thursday . . . and another eight Friday.

Meanwhile, by Friday, the 22nd their enemy, after covering 18 miles from their landing in Closter, had only arrived in Hackensack.

But General Lee was coming. And that good news and word that General Mifflin and a party were preparing to go on to Philadelphia, where his express would carry mail for Philadelphia soldiers, gave the Pennsylvania men almost comfortable sleep.

Every Philadelphia soldier who could write scribbled a note home for the mail bags going out with General Mifflin's party. The Philadelphia-born Mifflin and Colonel Putnam will not only alert the Continental Congress but they will recommend what steps are to be taken for the defense of the city.[5] Mifflin is also to impress upon the law-makers the immediate need for both troops and materiel.

Gray and Levy both slipped letters into the packet. Gray wrote his father and sister, Marion, that there was a possibility he might get to see them if and when the army moved into the city or into winter encampment along the Delaware.

Courier Cornelius Cooper

Levy, who has often spoken to Gray about "Miriam," his childhood sweetheart, now of Philadelphia, added a letter to the bulging packet. Most of the correspondence carried the soldiers' optimistic belief that General Lee was soon to be "up with the army."

No express rider has been busier than the patriot volunteer courier, Cornelius Cooper of Kinderkermack[6] in Bergen County. Cooper has been traveling back and forth from The General to Lee at North Castle, carrying messages but no assurance that Lee is on his way.

The 52-year old tanner and farmer knows the countryside and the back roads to the river's still-standing bridges and the Hudson River ferry crossings probably as well as Indian Abbott. But Abbott's whereabouts is still unknown.

And so day after day, Cooper stays ready in the saddle. He is one of several very reliable couriers serving the army. In doing so the patriot willingly neglects his 70-acre farm and tanning operations on the west bank of the Hackensack in the Kinderkermack. Cooper's place overlooks the source waters of the frolicking, crystal clear tributaries of the upper Hackensack.

From Cornelius Cooper's lands the river can be seen dashing southward over the remnants of the glacial rocks and boulders which it has gently brushed aside throughout the unchanging centuries. The patriot was aware of the limitations of his abilities when he offered his services to headquarters during the critical hours of the campaign. Though too old for soldiering, he was not too old for service.

Cooper feels his efforts now have all been in vain. General Lee insists that there is no suitable means for crossing his corps. Next he argues that a crossing at King's Ferry would be too slow to be of any benefit to the retreating army. Then, finally, he insists that upper Westchester's people and their fine, fertile country should be protected at all costs. All this the courier gathers from the gossip and discussion by the aides about the dispatches he carries.

In Cooper's unexpressed opinion Lee has almost run out of excuses in trying to say that the American Commander's predicament is his own fault, and that he should extricate himself, if he can, by himself.

Almost 15,000 Strong . . . On Paper

As of Sunday, the 24th, General Lee's corps numbered 9,217 in his "Return of the Forces" report at North Castle,[7] but the count showed only about 5,580 "Present and fit for duty." The "Return of the Troops" at and around Newark on Saturday, the 23rd, showed a count of 5,589 "Present, fit for duty."[8] These figures exclude Heath's Peekskill-based forces and Mercer's men at Amboy.

Had Lee brought his army alongside of The General as requested, the combined 11,000-man force could have halted the British Juggernaut and probably severely crippled it, in the opinion of some of the American staff officers. Certainly, if nothing else, a show of force could deter Howe's machine. Therefore they answer their own inquiring "Why?," relative to Lee's delay, each with his own critical reasoning.

On Monday, the 25th, when Cornwallis completed his crossing of the Hackensack, Lee had not budged from his Westchester position. But the day before, Sunday, the American Commander, having no encouraging word from his second in command, wrote Lee twice. For when he heard that Tories had intercepted one dispatch rider, who substituted for Cooper, he immediately sent another message, relying this time on Cooper to get through.

And Cooper did get through. He carried Lee the news that The General's first communique of the day had been intercepted, but that it had said, "It was your division (Lee's, not Heath's) I want to have over."[9]

This was a mild rebuke to Lee in reference to the North Castle commander's attempt to have Heath send 2,000 of his men instead of any of his own. It was also a tactful "order" and no longer a gentle request.

The letter further noted that the enemy had successfully intercepted some of Lee's messages, stating, "Your letters to me have fallen with the mail into the enemy's hands."[10]

And, indeed, some have. Unfortunately these intercepted messages have provided the British with some intelligence they had not suspected. The contents of the Tory-seized dispatches clearly revealed that there was a developing rift in the American high command, a "tug-of-war" between its leaders.

The King's Men Stumble On A Touch of Eden

Here was another stroke of good fortune for the King's men. They make good use of it in kindling the fires proclaiming the coming of the end of the rebellion. It is fuel to help coerce the populace into signing Howe's allegiance oath in exchange for amnesty.

For despite the gentlemanly Lord Cornwallis's efforts to prevent vandalizing through exhortations to his men, the frightened people in the Juggernaut's path know that signing the oath is their only hope for saving themselves and their properties.

Cornwallis's appeal to his officers does have a controlling effect upon the British troops if not upon the Hessians and Tories. In it, the Earl states:

> "As the inhabitants . . . are in general well affected to government, Earl Cornwallis expects the commanding officers . . . will exert themselves to prevent plundering amongst the troops. A distribution of fresh provisions will be made as a gratuity to the fatigue they have undergone."[11]

Some say the unexpected beauty of the land and the countless years of work that have gone into its delightful appearance, even when viewed under miserable skies, have motivated Cornwallis's leniency. Certainly he and his English and German troops, held up by the destroyed bridges, discover, to their amazement, a surprising sight.

Before them they find a bountiful countryside, hidden behind the high walls of the Palisades. Instead of wild, uncivilized creatures, whom Hessian soldiers feared would eat them, they stumble instead upon a touch of Eden.

Here are a god-fearing, gentle, frightened people. Here are churches whose inspiring white steeples rise gracefully above their orderly, well-kept hamlets, their schoolhouses and brownstone-quarried homes. Here they see once-prosperous inhabitants.

And the eyes of the invaders widen in amazement at the style of life they discover. It is a life of rural beauty, great richness and abundance. It is a land surrounded by nature's affluence, the likes of which they had not dreamed existed over and beyond the western slopes of the Palisades.

One Hessian officer had written home, greatly surprised at what he had found in Long Island. He is even more surprised now at what he sees in the valleys of the rivers.

The largely Dutch and Huguenot landholders in Bergen and the valleys west of the peninsula have not reached, nor do they have the desire for, the state of opulence and elegance that has been characteristic of the predominantly English, Dutch and Huguenot Long Island and New York inhabitants. Instead the people of the valleys reflect a contagious cleanliness and sturdiness, built firmly upon a peace-loving respect for family, home and church.

They are more tactfully taciturn about their "wealth" in life than are their "cousins" across the Hudson. For they have a modest quietude all their own. It is a tranquility which only the catastrophe of war with its political and religious overtones now threaten to destroy.

To the Hessian officer, whose eyes are opened now to the other, the west side of the Hudson and the Palisades as he bridges the Hackensack and Passaic Rivers, the scene he remembered of Long Island is brought to mind. Months ago he had written home describing his impressions of New York, saying:

"Everywhere one sees real quality and abundance. One sees nothing useless or old, certainly nothing dilapidated. The houses are beautiful and are furnished in better taste than any we are accustomed to in Germany.

"At the same time everything is so clean and neat that no description can do it justice. The women are generally beautiful and delicately brought up. They dress becomingly according to the latest European fashions, wearing Indian calicoes, white cotton goods and silk crepes.

"There is not a single housewife who does not have an elegant coach and pair. They drive and ride with only a negro on horseback for an escort.

"Near the dwellings are the cabins of the negroes, their slaves, who cultivate the fertile land, herd the cattle, and do all the rough housework."[1][2]

But "Eden" Is Stripped Bare

While some of the invaders may be impressed with the valleys and their people, others of the enemy are stripping and pillaging. Among the plunderers are some of the inhabitants' own Tory-minded neighbors. They are often more busily engaged than the enemy in ravaging the countryside.

Weeping hysterically, the defenseless families can only watch as their homes and barns are looted and sometimes burned. Many have stripped themselves in compliance with earlier American military recommendations.[13] They thus deprive the enemy invaders of the opportunity.

Some of the most ardent patriots have obediently destroyed their forage, disposed of their cattle, grain and much of their foodstuffs. Others have taken their possessions to distant neighbors or friends for concealment. A few lose them to the invading army despite their loud protestations of loyalty.

Plundering and ravaging doubly increase as the invading army is augmented. Cornwallis' force has now been enlarged by General Harcourt's 15th Dragoons and Light Infantry. Harcourt came over last Thursday via Bourdette's Landing.[14]

As more redcoats pour down upon them in overwhelming numbers, many Jersey inhabitants, some from the Hackensack and Passaic valleys,[15] militiamen and even officers, come forward in answer to Howe's call and declare their loyalty to the Crown.

Hundreds of Jersey Dutchmen will join the State-wide march into British headquarters as the enemy Juggernaut, constantly gathering momentum, pursues the American army through West Jersey. However, the invaders will meet bitter opposition from the adamant Whigs, despite the patriots' certainty of facing a cold and hungry winter.

Many of the frightened signers of Howe's oath will include deserters, former "moderate Liberty men" and some who only professed to be Whigs. In Bergen hundreds, who secretly agreed to enlist in the King's army during the past few months, now walk into British headquarters, or up to Tory leaders, and proclaim their loyalty to the King.

Some enlist undoubtedly to save their homes and possessions. Some do so simply to get the five guineas bounty,[16] offered in British recruitment propaganda. A number of these have no taste for the Crown, its army, or its Tory leaders. Once the five guineas are in their pockets, they will disappear and be numbered among the British deserters.

Many Bergen County inhabitants who held off giving in to the British pressures for amnesty in exchange for allegiance, hold out no longer after hearing of the strippings received by the Preacher Romeyn, the Leydeckers and the Christies. All of these men and their families have been vandalized.[17] It was their sufferings from plunderers that induced Cornwallis to urge his officers to stop such actions.

These are the war's side shows, almost impossible to avert within the armies of either side. Such scenes will be repeated. Some worse than others. And lines will form of men and families eager to sign the oath during the next few weeks. For now it is difficult, if not impossible, to find defiant patriots "exposing their breasts to the sword of vengeance." It is no longer easy to find an optimistic Whig.

The American Commander, knowing that each hour makes it more hazardous for Lee to traverse some 75 miles in order to join the army, urged him in the second letter Sunday to come through "the western road by Kakiate" which The General points out "will be proper for you to take."

Though the army's Chief clearly indicated great concern over the route from North Castle, he expressly avoided what might be construed as another "order." He is aware of Lee's sensitivity in that respect. But urging Lee to "by all means keep between the enemy and the mountains," he added that he was leaving the selection of the route to him and closed with, "Hoping and trusting that your arrival will be safe and happy, I am, dear sir, your most obedient servant."

The Commander's carefully worded letter indicates how gingerly he handles the recalcitrant major general who has strained his patience and jeopardized the Continental Army by action bordering on insubordination.

The arrogant, yet highly esteemed professional militarist, has displayed vanity, jealousy and contempt, but he has, up until now, only teetered on the edge of disobedience, cunningly avoiding the pitfall of insubordination.

Charles Lee wants no part of that, regardless of how he detests being subordinate in rank to a "farmer" from Virginia. An act of proven insubordination would send his star tumbling. He is, he believes, too close to becoming the command-in-chief of Congress's "new army."

With Lee's forces are Generals Nixon's, McDougall's and Sullivan's brigades and Colonel Glover's regiment. Their combined trains, if brought to The General's aid, would reinforce him with much needed light and heavy armament, a number of howitzers, many skilled matrosses, fieldpieces on traveling carriages and Glover's versatile seamen-soldiers. Those Marbleheaders' unequaled accomplishments in river crossings soon will be vitally needed again.

The Impulsive Lee Writes Again

On Sunday, the 24th, Charles Lee also took his quill in hand. The pressure to move to his chief's side was slowly becoming too great for further resistance.

One of his letters was to the Commander-in-Chief. In this he said, in part, "I have received your orders, and shall endeavor to put them in execution."

This was the first time the major general had admitted that the previous dispatches carried the connotation of an "order." But his long-delayed compliance was followed with the disheartening statement that he would not be able to take "any considerable number" with him.

> "Not so much from a want of zeal in the men," Lee hastened to add, "as from their wretched condition with respect to shoes, stockings and blankets."[18]

His next communication was a personal one to Colonel Reed. It would not be in time for the same packet to Newark and would not be delivered until the 27th. Unopened it would move with headquarters on to New Brunswick today while the adjutant general, to whom it is addressed, will be on his way to see Governor Livingston in Burlington. In behalf of The General, Reed will ask Livingston for more Jersey militiamen.

In this correspondence to the adjutant general, Lee wrote Reed thanking him for his "most obliging, flattering letter," saying:

> "I lament with you that fatal indecision of mind which in war is a much greater disqualification than stupidity, or even want of personal courage."

Then, defending his failure to comply with The General's request for his aid, Lee wrote:

> "The General recommends in so pressing a manner as almost to amount to an order to bring over the Continental troops under my command—which recommendation or order throws me into the greatest dilemma from several considerations. . . ."

In lengthy detail, Lee enumerated the "several considerations," mentioning:

(1) The dire need of the troops; (2) The expiration of some of their enlistments today; (3) The possible lack of shelter on the west side of the river; and (4) The recently received intelligence that the enemy, including Rogers' corps, a brigade of Highlanders and Light Horse and a supporting British force, were all within his grasp.

Only the violent rain last night, Saturday, the 23rd, he wrote Reed, prevented him from attacking Rogers' men since they "Lye in so exposed a situation as to give the fairest opportunity of being carried off." Then, adding that he intended to try again "this night." the wordy, rationalizing Westchester post commander declared, "If we succeed we shall be well compensated for the delay."

Concluding the assumably confidential epistle which he had intended only for Reed's admiring eyes, Lee pompously admitted, as though with a side gesture of conciliation, that he would soon concede to The General's call for aid. Unabashedly he wrote:

> "I only wait myself for this business I mention of Rogers and Co. being over—(I) shall then fly to you—for to confess a truth I really think our Chief will do better with me than without me."[19]

Ominously Larger Looms the Spectre Of Final Defeat

Lee's letter arrived Monday, the 25th. For those who had believed he was half-way or more on the way to Newark, the word that he had not budged from North Castle sank their hopes farther in dejection.

On top of this, Craig's scouts brought the long-expected news that Cornwallis was fording the Passaic River one mile above Acquackanonk and was coming down upon the American encampment.

Without Lee's strength a stand at Newark was out of the question. Greene's army had only managed to come off from Fort Lee with two fieldpieces, 1,000 barrels of flour and 300 tents.[20] It had lost much equipment along the way.

The Newark militia and Lord Stirling's small force were inadquate to give the rebel army sufficient strength to make a stand, and Mercer's men had still not arrived from Amboy. Furthermore, supplies at Newark were inadeuqate for maintaining the defenders while those that Greene had sent ahead before the

20th to Acquackanonk, Springfield, Bound Brook, Brunswick and Princeton were now coming into great use.

So Brunswick, over the Raritan, is the army's next objective. The encampment was alerted yesterday and ordered ready to move out immediately after breakfast this morning. Even before dawn the scouts and the wagons were on their way.

Therefore this day has been a gloomy and an exhausting one. Lee was not in sight. The newly reinforced British army, carrying wartime luxuries as well as necessities,[21] thoroughly equipped with heavy and light armament and comprising fully trained and well-fed British and Hessian soldiers, was marching down upon Newark with precision-like efficiency. The remnants of the American troops, on the other hand, were not only bitter and bedraggled, hungry and sadly equipped, but their depleted ranks would soon be further decimated by expiring enlistments and more desertions. Though they have been miserably disheartened by similar distresses, now more than ever the spectre of final defeat looms ominously larger before them.

The King's men, their Tory compatriots and Loyalist supporters are as optimistic about the war's end as the Americans are pessimistic. One British officer, elated by the victorious sweep of the Crown's forces within the past ten days, writes in a letter home, saying:

"Cornwallis is carrying all before him. In short it is impossible but that peace must be the consequences of our success."[22]

Physically exhausted and mentally strained from their execution of hurried orders under the tense excitement of an overwhelming enemy threatening their rear, every rebel soldier in Newark sought a long sleep last night to fortify him for the 22 miles he must march today. There were only a few exceptions outside of the jittery sentinels and pickets.

But the wearied John Gray, his mind on Elaine and his thoughts always racing when night comes and sleep will not, was one of those exceptions. He went into the empty schoolhouse with his red leather diary just as he has done for the past five nights.

It is the closest he can get to the house under the Bluff Rock far to the northeast. Unconsciously, the diary into which he pours his thoughts and the day's events, has become as much her, or a link to her, as the blue petticoat scarf he invariably wears around his neck.

The whale oil lamp glowed faintly over the encampment field

and through the cornstalks from out the windows of the old frame structure, seat of learning for so many children past. Inside at the schoolmaster's desk the worn and tired figure of the young officer, slumping wearily in the hard Windsor-back chair, wrote lengthily under the heading, "New-ark, Wednesday, November 27, 1776."

He wrote of the advancing enemy ... that Mercer is to join the army at New Brunswick even though Lee has not been able to come across as yet ... that tomorrow's long 22-mile march is a dreaded one, but that it is believed the British army may bring its chase to an end at Newark.

He predicted correctly that Cornwallis's van may brush with the Continental Army's rear guard but that, owing to the enemy's clumsy and overburdened military train, The General will likely get his army to Brunswick without too much interference.

Suddenly the schoolhouse door opened. Through it, to The Lieutenant's amazement, walked Sergeant Abbott. Gray rose and hurried down the aisle between the rows of desks to greet the Indian who smiled rigidly as both men affectionately grasped each other by the shoulders.

In a brief, matter-of-fact account of his movements after leaving his parents with the remaining members of the Lenni Lenape tribe at Brotherton, Abbott disclosed that he had returned by water to Fort Lee, seen the Baummeisters, Bourdettes and Elaine and found them well and safe but stripped of many things by Tory plunderers.

He assured Gray that both the British and Hessian soldiers had proved to be more courteous and considerate than any of The Mountain and the riverside inhabitants had expected, causing many of them to sign the oath of allegiance to the Crown.

Since he wore no rebel soldier clothing and came up the river in his father's old canoe, and since Howe and the British soldiers are making a point of befriending all Indians, Gray knew that Abbott could get around and away without being suspected unless exposed by a Tory. And, fortunately, he was not.

The army scout informed Gray that he had turned over to Baummeister and Bourdette the location of his family's food cache on the castle grounds and guided Caesar and Sam to the exact spot. They were told to take the entire cache, or draw upon the extensive supplies for both families as their needs required during the coming winter.

With every sentence Abbott completed John Gray's face lit up with continuous expressions of happy relief and approval. Hungrily

he devoured the good news that all is well with Elaine, the
Baummeisters and the Bourdettes. He asked many questions to
which Abbott, saving words, patiently answered with a single
syllable or a shake of his head.

The sergeant climaxed his account with a letter for Gray from
Elaine. Casually, as though it were of least importance, Abbott
withdrew the sealed envelope from inside his deerskin coat and
again showing the traces of a smile, handed it to The Lieutenant.

Controlling an overwhelming desire to tear it open and absorb
each word of its priceless contents, Gray asked the Indian scout if
he had bedding for the night and if he had reported to headquarters.

Abbott assured him he had and that Craig had taken good care
of his horse, Chinqueka. The scouts, he told Gray, were to move
out ahead of the troops early in the morning and that he probably
would not see him again until Brunswick.

Gray inquired how Abbott had made his way to Newark. To
this the Indian pointed out the window to a brown stallion and
said, " 'Twas the persuaded kindness of an English Neighborhood
Tory. He will not need a horse for several suns to come. The
scouts will use it better."

Gray tore open Elaine's letter before Abbott had closed the
schoolhouse door behind him. In it the officer's wife wrote all
Abbott had told him. She said that they had not suffered under
the enemy as had others they had heard about. Papa Pete, she told
him, had been ill but was recovering, though still coughing badly.

Into the Blessed Pleasures Of Forgetfulness

"Andy surprised us," she continued. "We knew not where he
was. He intends somehow to make his way to the army and to
you, and somehow I know he will wherever ye are. He came
yesterday and leaves today. He has been of great help to us, all
Minnie's storage he has given us. It is just as well for I think we
will never see Minnie and Perawae again. I pray to God they are
well.

"Andy is waiting. By him I know this will reach you, Beloved. I
pray. I pray. Take my love ever, but stay ye safe and well for me,
John-G, and come ye back to me. May God be with you always.
Yes, 1, 2, 3 . 1, 2, 3. 1, 2, 3, forever and forever.

Ellie"

Over and over he read the letter and then began again to write.
"One, two, three! 1,2,3 . . ." he at last finally scribbled. And
there the quill fell from his fingers. His hand and arm, like the
pen, collapsed on Nicodemus's desk. The exhausted officer's body
drooped, eased at last into subconscious relief. Then gently his
head fell over his arms.

In a few moments the quill was shaking from the relaxed,
snoring snorts that belied the deep depth into which his dreams
had dropped him.

Suddenly, like a spore upon the wind, he was cast onto the high
ledge of rock above the great river. Now arm in arm he strolled
with the ferry-master's daughter. And then the two sat silently
until a little stranger mysteriously came and sat beside him. The
subconscious mind within the dreamer told him that it must be
Jocko. It must be Jocko! Still silently all three then sat and looked
down upon the deep waters and then out beyond the distant shore
below the rising sun in the far off horizon. It is some far off
distant era of imponderable time. It is the blessed pleasure of
forgetfulness.

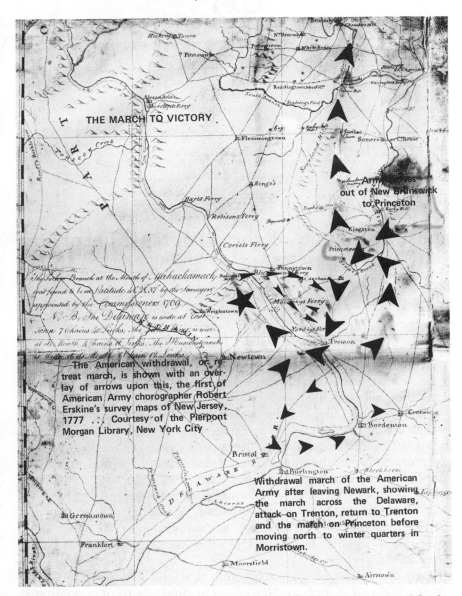

THE MARCH TO VICTORY.

Army moves
out of New Brunswick
to Princeton

The American withdrawal, or retreat march, is shown with an overlay of arrows upon this, the first of
American Army chorographer Robert
Erskine's survey maps of New Jersey,
1777 . . . Courtesy of the Pierpont
Morgan Library, New York City

Withdrawal march of the American
Army after leaving Newark, showing
the march across the Delaware,
attack on Trenton, return to Trenton
and the march on Princeton before
moving north to winter quarters in
Morristown.

Coming down from Hackensack, Acquackanonk, Newark, New Brunswick, the
Americans then withdrew into Princeton, Trenton, across the Delaware to
Newtown, settling all along the Delaware's west bank. They crossed the river
to attack Trenton December 26, returned to Pennsylvania and later recrossed
the river to march again on Trenton, withdrawing from the British there on
January 2 in order to make a surprise attack on Princeton on January 3.
They withdrew north to Morristown following the Battle of Trenton.

32

Friday, December 13. . .

End of the Great Retreat
and the Plunge of the Flaming Meteor

An Almost Costly Delay, Thursday, November 28

In the hurried exodus from Newark fifteen days ago, Charles Lee's letter to Adjutant General Joseph Reed was not separated from the mail packet.

Reed on the Chief's order was headed for Governor Livingston in Burlington in an effort to secure New Jersey militia reinforcements. Headquarters aides, therefore, placed the Lee-to-Reed communication in the post express rider's run-of-the-mill mail, now speedily outbound from Newark to Brunswick. In with the Chief's mail it was destined to be accidentally opened by him.

It was fortunate on that Thursday, November 28th, that the garrison, no less the mail, safely got away at all. The rebel army had waited almost too long for the recalcitrant North Castle commander.

Even the Congress had expected that the hero of Charleston would join his Chief in Newark and that there the combined troops would have slowed down, if not halted, the Juggernaut. For the rebels' Commander wrote the representatives in Philadelphia on the 23rd, three days before leaving Newark:

"I have wrote General Lee to come over with the Continental regiments immediately under his command."[1]

Neither The General nor the Continental Congress was aware that Lee was not even beginning to move at that time. It would be December 1st, eight days after that letter to Congress, before Lee would get as far as the east bank of the Hudson.[2]

The delayed wait in Newark was almost a costly one. The army's rear guard kept up a heavy exchange of fire on the enemy's van approaching the outskirts of the village while the main force made its way out of town on its way to New Brunswick.

This the Continental Army Commander knew would be the case when he ordered preparations Wednesday for moving out on Thursday. His adversary was closing in. Anger over Lee's failure to come to the army's aid overcame his patience Wednesday night, the 27th. With quill in hand, however, he controlled his emotions, stating:

> "My former letters were so full and explicit as to the necessity of your marching as early as possible that it is unnecessary to add more on that head. I confess I expected you would have been sooner in motion."[3]

The General and his troops survived another of the harried army's countless close calls the next morning in their flight from Newark. And so the imminent danger of being overrun began to effect a change in attitude toward the Charleston hero. The disappointed officers soon were attributing their predicament, at least in part, to Lee's procrastination.

In the Commander's next message to Westchester he would make it clear to Lee that his presence might have prevented the army's present predicament.

Meanwhile Lee's letter to Reed lay unopened. Were its contents known to the Chief the day before leaving Newark, Wednesday, the 27th, it is possible the irate American Leader would have shown considerably more exasperation, particularly under the strain of Cornwallis's rapid approach.

General Stirling and his Colonel Hand commanded the rear guard Thursday morning, the 28th. Since Stirling's troops had come up from New Brunswick fresh, well equipped and with a good knowledge of the highway west, they were in the best position to throw obstacles in the way of the pursuing army. They knew best what bridges to destroy and where felled trees would most delay the enemy. However, it was questionable whether Howe and Cornwallis would continue on to Brunswick, or call off the pursuit until spring.

Gradually the spire of Newark's Trinity Church faded from the

view of the disappearing Continental Army. Behind them Stirling's
men kept up a continuous fire, stopping the enemy van on the
northern outskirts of the village.

Not knowing what they were in for, the British columns halted
to reconnoiter the situation, thus giving Stirling ample time to
follow behind the main American force, now numbering less than
5,000 fit for duty.

The danger was again temporarily over. The escape from Newark
had been close. But since no losses were suffered the withdrawal
operation was judged a success.

It was another blow to Cornwallis. However, there was still
Brunswick on the Raritan before him. By Howe's order the Earl
can pursue his enemy no farther than Brunswick. It was an order
which Howe was later to regret.

Immediately after settling his train in Newark, the invading
general decided he must—with only one more chance before him—
take his enemy by surprise. He would march by night, swoop
down upon the rebel encampment at the first streak of dawn. And
this time they would not get away!

It was likely to be the Earl's last chance. Howe had drawn the
pursuit line at Brunswick not expecting he would have to extend
its lines that far to catch a disintegrating rebel army. Already
communication and supply lines were dangerously over-stretched.
Then, too, beyond the Raritan River at Brunswick lay the distant
Delaware.

Rivers! Rivers! Rivers! These, Cornwallis thinks to himself, have
been his enemy's constant ally. These have been his foe's greatest
advantage over the Crown's might. And the nights and days were
getting colder. Winter was fast approaching. His "Fox" must be
bagged at New Brunswick!

But if he should escape from there? What then?

General Howe would have to come to a major decision:
Continue the pursuit through Princeton, Trenton and across the
Delaware if necessary but at the risk of long supply lines; or go
into winter quarters until spring.

So, as the Continentals completed their 22-mile march to the
Raritan River, Lord Cornwallis planned to give them no rest and
possibly end the chase.

At sunset Friday, the 29th, the American rear guard crossed the
Raritan into the village of New Brunswick. The work of destroying
the bridge and beaching all the river's vessels began earlier in the day.
And once again the rebel army settled down and took stock of itself.

Saturday, November 30: March Through the Night

The three-day experience at Brunswick proved to be a harrowing one. In the night's early darkness Saturday, the 30th, Cornwallis and his invaders started their surprise 22-mile march to the Raritan through rain and mud and over the rebels' obstacles. They forded streams where bridges were destroyed.

It was another of the Earl's Herculean operations, principally aimed at closing the long dragged out New York Campaign, now spreading into the Jerseys. This time it was a last desperate maneuver. Brunswick was the ordered stopping point. Brunswick could be his last opportunity.

Unaware of its immediate danger on the southwest banks of the Raritan, the gloom-ridden American army was not only despondent over Lee's delinquency, but the strain of constantly being pursued, the decimated ranks by desertions and the expiration of thousands of enlistments coming on Sunday, the first day of December, gave the army little to be optimistic about. It was difficult to see any ray of hope militarily for themselves or for the new nation.

Most of the happy voices were those whose enlistments expired. They wanted no more of war. Only their joyous shouts rang out Saturday night in preparation for setting out for home Sunday morning. However, there were many, the faithfuls to the last, who were planning to re-enlist and remain with The General until the end.

The American command staff soon realized that a miracle of some kind was the only thing that would save the army and restore faith in The Cause throughout the country. Only a severe retaliatory blow could send the Juggernaut reeling back on its heels. General Lee's brigades could have provided the retreating force with the very ingredients for such a blow. And a strike at the British army's train and its flanks was imperative if the country's faith in the army was to be restored and the states reunited in continued resistance.

In this frame of mind the Continental Army's Leader wrote Lee once again. This time from his Brunswick headquarters Saturday, November 30.

The enemy, the Commander told Lee:

"has built up so much confidence through the advantages they have gained over us in the past (that it has) made them so proud and sure of success that they are determined to go to Philadelphia this winter.[4]

The letter went on, declaring that it had been anticipated the

British would take "Newark, Elizabeth Town and Amboy," possibly going into winter quarters before undertaking an attack on Philadelphia in the spring.

The General continued:

> "I have positive information that this is a fact and because of the term of service of the light troops of Jersey and Maryland are ended they anticipate the weakness of our army. Should they now really risk this undertaking then there is a great probability that they will pay dearly for it for I shall continue to retreat before them so as to lull them into security."

If anything could stir Lee into moving his forces rapidly southward, it would be the dream of gloriously charging, "flaming sword" in hand, to the rescue of the Continental Congress in Philadelphia. Unwittingly or not, The General opened an inviting door for Lee to charge through, but The General's letters have many subtleties to mislead the enemy who might intercept them. If this one were intercepted, his declaration of defiance and a promise to make his enemy pay dearly, were recorded mostly for General Howe's benefit.

Lee did not get a chance to react to The General's bait. For the letter was intercepted by some of the outlying enemy pickets who daily make a courier's dash to North Castle through the now enemy-held territory more perilous. Thus Lee would not hear of the Chief's concern for the Congress. And never would it be known whether the call of help for the representatives would prove stronger than that of the Commander-in-Chief's.

So Lee leisurely continued his preparations to cross the Hudson River December 1 via King's Ferry to Stony Point. He was still unhurried.

What the major general sought was an opportunity to perform some outstanding heroic feat, one he could individually execute with his brigades on his own initiative. Not one commanded by a ranking superior for whom he had little respect and whom he was likely to replace as chief of the American army.

It was that same Sunday at dawn in New Brunswick that the worried Continental Army Commander picked up some of the dispatches in the mail that had accumulated during the march to the Raritan. Some were letters opened for him by his aides. Some were letters still sealed.

Usually Colonel Reed, now in Burlington, took care of The General's correspondence. In Reed's absence the army's Chief took it upon himself to carry out the minor task.

One message was from Reed, happily informing his Chief that the New Jersey governor heard his appeal for militia troops and that Livingston had responded with a notice to all Jersey's militia colonels, ordering them to have their "battalions ready to march on the shortest notice."[5]   Here at last was an encouraging piece of news.

Then, without looking at the address, he sliced his letter opener through another envelope and began reading the contents until he suddenly realized the letter, though from General Lee, was not intended for his eyes. It was instead, a personal letter addressed to Reed.

A "decisive blunderer. . . cursed with indecision"

What was more distressing was that the contents were a reply to a confidential letter which Reed had undoubtedly written to Lee, criticizing the American Commander-in-Chief. It was soon evident that the adjutant had unburdened his thoughts on the 21st of November and Lee had answered on the 24th,[6] when The General read:

> "I received your most obliging, flattering letter. I lament with you that fatal indecision of mind which in war is a much greater disqualification than stupidity or even want of personal courage. Accident may put a decisive blunderer in the right—but eternal defeat and miscarriage must attend the man of the best parts if cursed with indecision . . ."

The General quickly realized that his adjutant general and secretary, in whom he had placed much trust, had condemned him for "indecision" in a letter to the Westchester commander which had flattered and extolled Lee's virtues. Now in The General's hands was incontrovertible evidence of what Lee and Reed thought of him—"a decisive blunderer. . . cursed with indecision."

The shocking communication fell like a bombshell upon the American Commander as he overcame his moral scruples in perusing a letter addressed to another. So he read on. Lee's rationalizing defense in having defied The General's call for his help, followed. He contended that it was concern for his troops, the protection of Westchester and Rogers' Tory activities there that dictated his decision to stand fast in Westchester while his Commander waited for him in Jersey. So Lee's closing of the astoundingly revealing letter was almost amusing, ". . . our Chief will do better with me than without me."

The American Commander is known to be one who seldom allows his ~ersonal feelings to prejudice him against those who carry arms in behalf of the American cause. Accordingly, he immediately forwarded the letter to Reed. In doing so, he explained that he had:

> "no idea of it being a private letter, much less suspecting the tendency of the correspondence. . ."[7]

The General's official relations with both Lee and Reed have not apparently changed. If there is hurt, it is deep and well concealed. Outwardly he maintains the same attitude toward both men as before. He gives no evidence of resentment. Spite is not in his make up. A tolerance and understanding of the reasoning and acts of others is a part of the man's code.

It is his country, the new nation and its preservation which he puts above all things personal. And that trait will, in part, help again to unify the splintering forces and continue the resistance far beyond the point of endurance. This is his avowed way in the execution of his military leadership, a leadership which, up until today, Friday, December 13, was about to be taken from him and handed over to his second in command.

It will be much later before the stinging impact of Reed's secret correspondence upon The General will be revealed to the adjutant. But months from now, when the Chief's trust in Reed is restored, and when both men are able to talk with less restraint as their former close friendship surfaces again, the American Leader will admit:

> "I was hurt . . . because I thought . . . myself . . . entitled . . . to your advice upon any point in which I appeared to be wanting."[8]

Will the Rebels Never Stand and Fight?

When Lord Cornwallis, in the midst of his night march on Brunswick, received a dispatch from Turkey Town, the former Indian "High Hills" country,[9] he acquired his opponent's intercepted letter. What most concerned Lord Cornwallis was what he most feared: that his quarry intended "to retreat before them so as to lull them into security."

Would the rebel never stand and fight?

There is no such "Stand and Fight" plan in the Continental Army Chief's plans. He had told Reed that he was prepared to:

"retreat to the back parts of Pennsylvania and to Augusta County in Virginia. (And there) we must try what we can do in carrying on a predatory war, and, if overpowered, we must cross the Allegheny Mountains."[10]

Though deeply offended, not so much by Lee's opinion of him as by Reed's, The General continued attending to his correspondence. His mind was more on the erosion of his army by expiring enlistments than on the growing disaffection within the top echelon of his army and his headquarters "family." The former problem he could do something about; the latter he could not.

Last night 2,060 of his troops completed their last day of military service, "and all the rest, not only of his contingent, but of the whole army, would be free by the 1st of January."[11] About three weeks ago, November 9, he had written Congress of the depletion of the Connecticut regiments, many of which, he reported, had been reduced "to little more than a large company."[12]

Then last night he informed Congress that:

"The Pennsylvania militia of General Ewing's brigade, though enlisted to January 1, were 'deserting in great numbers.' "[13]

Becoming greatly concerned, the Philadelphia body sent The General word that 2,000 Pennsylvania militia, a part of the Pennsylvania Associators, would join him within the coming week.

Bivouac At Brunswick

And this, the only good news that the Continentals have heard since the first day of their retreat when it was rumored Lee was coming to their rescue, spread through the cantonment last night. A glib tongued express rider confidentially whispered his bit of information to a friend. Before long there were few troops that had not learned of aid on its way. And this was before The General opened his dispatches this morning.

Of course the Pennsylvania Associators' additions cannot be compared with the strength behind Lee's corps. But this was help, even though it would only slightly compensate for:

"the contagion of desertions which (have) been epidemic and now rage after the manner of a plague."[14]

So it was that the little tidbit of uplifting news last night somewhat offset the depressing hollowness of the singing and shouting troops celebrating their last night in camp.

Clustered again around their several campfires adjoining a long wagon and carriage lean-to and an old barn stacked with hay, the Barbette Battery had made themselves comfortable. It was their third night in their Brunswick bivouac.

Abbott and Craig, whose scouts had settled themselves in the old, fire-destroyed, farmer's former home, had located the site and held it for Gray and his men.

And this night Abbott, leaving Captain Craig on a bed of hay snoring off a heavy indulgence of local grog, joined the only ones with whom he felt comfortable. Gray, Levy, Big Tom, Jocko and the men of the old Bluff Rock Barbette Battery are black and white men he knows and trusts. But Abbott remained in the fire's background glow, observing, listening and quietly stitching together a pair of winter buckskin trousers.

Sparked by the news that the Pennsylvania militia was coming, a relaxed, somewhat festive atmosphere overtook the company. It was partly to drown out the noise of the home-going merrymakers in the distance. Besides, the enemy was reported still in Newark, over 20 miles away, the farthest distance that has yet separated "Fox from Hound."

Gray, in accordance with his nightly custom, sat on a log writing in his diary. The book has become an outlet for his longing each sunset to see, or hear some word of, The Mountain on the Palisades.

Always after the sun went down and the night closed in, he would recount to her the events of the day. Now the diary is the closest he can come to the past. It is the closest he can come to the nights beside her at the window of their room. There, overviewing the glass-like waters of the river gently flowing beyond the Baummeister house, he would unravel all his day's worries. Understandingly she would listen, often seeing solutions and making suggestions far better than his own. That was Elaine, now another world away.

Except for the personal entries, Gray does not consider his diary recordings confidential. However, Levy, Kidd, MacNamara and Monahan are the only ones in the battery, outside of Gray, who can read at all. So generally no one shows any interest in The Lieutenant's "writin' in buk" with the exception of Levy and, of course, Jocko, who can only read a few words, and those thanks to Elaine's efforts.

Levy, at Gray's insistence, often writes an entry, makes changes and additions and reads excerpts aloud. His voice is exceptionally clear and resonant. It has that unique magnetic fiber that holds an audience's attention regardless of the subject matter. So, invariably, when Levy reads aloud from the diary, usually at Jocko's request, all campfire chatter stops and the men listen.

Gray's voice by contrast has no such merits. And he knows it as well as do the men of his command. But John Gray's other virtues, including his knack with the written word, make up for his slow drawl and oratorical deficiencies.

And, besides, The Lieutenant has told Jocko that he will not read to him until he makes progress by himself.

So Jocko relies on "Mista Secon' Lootenan' ", as he calls Levy, to read to him from the book while he looks on, trying to grasp the meaning of each word. For Jocko knows Gray will not break his vow. He knows he will not get a single line out of the lanky officer's mouth until he does what he promised.

The Coded Closing, 3

The Lieutenant's novel teaching method has worked better than he had thought. With Levy's, Gray's, Kidd's and Monahan's occasional promptings the "lesson" of words has become a game. Its interest on occasions has enticed some of the battery's illiterates to join in for their own edification. However, it is Jocko who has become the one most fascinated by letter symbols and the words they make.

One thing that no one of the listeners has been able to figure out is the closing of each day's entry with the numbers, "1, 2, 3," and the odd way Gray forms them at times. Since once before, at Newark, The Lieutenant did not obviously wish to discuss or explain the enigmatical numerals when questioned about the coded closing, his silence on the matter has been respected.

Thus, on the closing night of the army's month of tragedies, many of Gray's battery, who chose not yet to seek sleep in the hay of the deserted barn, sat with their backs under the long carriage shed. The three campfires, separately burning in front of the lean-to, threw their heat and light back to them under the overhang of the structure. A northeasterly breeze carried most of the smoke and flying embers southward and away from their position.

Some roasted and ate their Indian corn or chunks of pork. A

number, like Abbott, sewed upon their torn and tattered clothing, or repaired worn, dilapidated shoes. Others cleaned dirty, rusting muskets that had not been fired for days.

When Gray finally put the diary down, stood up and stretched, Levy, who had been sitting silently beside the blue petticoat scarfed officer, picked up the book. Holding it up before Gray, indicating a request for permission to read the latest entry, Levy quickly received the senior officer's affirmative nod. Jocko's sharp eyes caught the silent maneuver.

Big Tom and his son, sitting together before the fire at the carriage shed's far end, adjoining the stabled horses and wagon, were piecing together some broken leather harnesses. Dropping what he was doing, the youth got up and hurried over to Levy's side.

Asking the second lieutenant to, "Reads zit loud, Mista Lootenan, so'iz Ise kin goes 'long wid ya! Wills ya, Sir?," Jocko stole a furtive glance Gray's way. But The Lieutenant stared vacantly up in the air and stood as unmoved as the sturdy shed timber at his back.

Levy, always gracious, unhesitatingly obliged, while all those within hearing distance listened. Each man, however, kept on quietly about his task. It was a short entry, a brief account of the day, but at the end was the same inexplicable "123" closing, sketched in this enigmatical shape: ⟨

Corporal Monahan, who had never shown any interest in hearing about his or the army's daily events, had been sitting on one side of Levy. Jocko on the other.

The corporal, whittling on a snuffbox which he has long been carving from the root of a pear tree, had not been present on the occasion in Newark when The Lieutenant smilingly refused to divulge the meaning of his '1, 2, 3" closing. In doing so he left the impression that it was a kind of military secret.

Since Levy ignores and does not bother any longer to read the closing, Monahan, peering over the second lieutenant's shoulder, loudly asks Levy, " 'Tis curios Oi yam, ta know whut's zat funny lourkin' mark mean yonder at tha end? 'Tis it wan twenty-t'ree, Lieutenant?"

Before the officer can answer, Jocko responds, saying, "Das'sa secret code oney Lootenan John knows, 'nt taint no 'one hundred twen'y free'. Itsa 'one, two, free'."

Jocko takes a mischievous delight in displaying his knowledges. Then turning to Gray, hoping his own curiosity might be satisfied by a revelation of the meaning from The Lieutenant, Jocko asks the silent, motionless officer, "Ain't 'tit, Lootenan?"

Gray merely nods his head affirmatively. Others, unlike the black youth, had dismissed the enigma from their thoughts, concluding the sign probably represented some humorous symbol, or even a signal code which only first lieutenants knew anything about.

At the first mention of the numerical closing and the corporal's question concerning the "one hundred and twenty three," as Monahan read it, Abbott's eyes flashed in sudden interest. They raised from his stitching which now came abruptly to a stop.

Then when Jocko corrected the corporal's interpretation, explaining the numbers meant, "one, two, three," Abbott quietly rose from his squatting position, dropped his work and slowly stole over to Levy. Looking over the officer's shoulder, he unobtrusively examined the entry's closing.

Meanwhile, standing not far from where Abbott had been sitting and on the opposite side of the fire from Levy, Gray suddenly became uneasy. He watched Abbott rise. The Lootenant's eyes focused upon the Indian sergeant as he bent over slightly and perused the diary's closing of the entry.

It was not the book but the three numbers which aroused the army scout's attention. Those who watched quickly understood that.

No one of the battery's complement, excepting Gray, has ever seen the trace of a smile on Abbott's face. No one has ever heard him laugh. Most of the men who know the tall, powerful Lenni Lenape, though admiringly attached to him, believe he is incapable of laughter. And that is un-American, they believe, until the English playwright, Sergeant Kidd, reminds them that Abbott is the "only true American among you."

So the men of the battery tend to look up with respect to the Indian, despite his humorless demeanor. He has never hesitated to extend his help to them whether called upon or not. He has won their admiration for his silent sincerity of manner with which he carries a rare dignity seldom found among men.

Placing honesty and integrity alongside of his god, the "Young Eagle" frowns upon those few white men whom he sees as ones "lost" and wallowing in deception, dishonesty, greed and corruption. And it is this about Abbott that places him unconsciously above them in the minds of the Barbette Battery men and in their own self-assessment of their race at large.

Those who observed the Indian sergeant's almost unnoticeable action, watched his curiosity with only passing interest. A few presumed the numerals had a Lenni Lenape tribe significance of some kind. Yet they are all aware that Andy Abbott is a British-educated Indian. Most of the men know of his background with old Captain Nordstrom and his wife.

Some watched the Indian scout scan the contents of the diary page. Then, noticing him straighten up, they paid no further attention and returned to what they were doing. All except Jocko. His eyes remained fixed curiously upon Abbott, Levy and later, Gray.

Then, stoically erect, Andy glanced ever so briefly toward Gray whose eyes, reflecting a trace of guilt, returned the Indian's gaze. Gray's whole countenance expressed a strange mixture of sorrow and contrition as though appealing for understanding and forgiveness.

All of Abbott's, Perawae's and Minnie's kindnesses to him and to Elaine now flashed through The Lieutenant's mind... The castle grounds, Oratam's rock, the grave of Mahtocheega—the story of Young Eagle and Little Bear Princess—and the symbol of their union chiseled into stone. All these visions swiftly flew across Gray's thoughts as the eyes of the two men met.

John waited for his punishment, a hurt, disappointed look he would see on Andy's face—a blow more painful than a saber's slash. Then, for the second time in the span of their friendship, Gray saw the unquestionable trace of a smile streak swiftly and happily across the Indian's face. It instantaneously told Gray that Abbott had not only forgiven the intrusion into the Indian's revered memories, but that he approved of John and Elaine carrying on the symbol of devoted unity between two beings that once was his and Andrea's.

The fearful brief second was over. Pleased, rather than hurt, Abbott turned contentedly away. Gray drew a relieved breath, took the book Levy handed up to him and withdrew to his bed in the straw.

The bewildered Jocko was now not only confused, he was far more curious than ever.

Jocko Graves was not dubbed "Sir Sees All" by his father without good reason. The youth had not missed a split second of the eye exchange between Gray and Abbott.

He had caught The Lieutenant's grave expression as the officer's recently washed and straightened blue petticoat scarf gently blew in the soft breeze about his neck. And he saw, to his astonishment, what certainly appeared to be a bit of a smile flash across the face of the Indian scout. The smile and the eyes of the brown man were giving approval of some kind. Jocko was sure of that.

Now more than ever young Graves wanted to know the meaning behind the three enigmatical numerals. Somehow, sometime, somewhere he was determined to find out.

The main topic of conversation around the cantonment fires that Saturday night, November 30, also happened to be Gray's last entry in his book. It read, "We, of Penn's State born, were happy to hear that the Pennsylvania militia are coming soon beside us."

That optimistic news, which had been leaked by the courier and circulated through much of the camp all evening, did not officially reach The General until he opened the dispatch the following morning. When he did, it served little to solve the American Chief's mounting problems, topped now by prima facie evidence of growing intrigue among his top-ranking officers.

Nevertheless, the Sabbath church services had to go on, even though prayer could now not hold back the enlistment-ending men of General Reazin Beall's and General Nathaniel Heard's Maryland and New Jersey militia from their determined march out of the encampment, homeward bound.

It was to be said of the time-expired troops that all "being applied to . . . refused to continue longer in service" and could not be detained.[15] Many of these men, as described by Lieutenant Enoch Anderson of Haslet's Delawares, "arrived at Brunswick broken down and fatigued—some without shoes, some had no shirts."[16] And they were leaving the same way.

A Wish For A "Jersey Joan Of Arc"

Though the enlistment terms of most of The General's troops in Jersey will not expire for another month, many of the men in Brunswick, their spirits broken by the state of things, began deserting along with those discharged.

Lieutenant Gray was duty officer Sunday, December 1st. It was a busy morning for most of the officers who had to muster out and record the names of the term-ended soldiers, waiting impatiently to be discharged.

Much of the work, however, had been done the previous day. And so Gray and his diary found time together since the task for the charge-of-quarters was comparatively light.

Thomas Paine—From Daniel Edwin Wheeler's
Life and Writings of Thomas Paine. **Artist**
unidentified.

In the red leather book, just before noon, The Lieutenant wrote: *"Here at headquarters this morning I was one of the lucky few given a chance to read Mr. Paine's script called, 'The Crisis.' Though it begins cleverly saying, 'These are the times that try men's souls,' which indeed they do, I liked most his wish for a 'Jersey Joan of Arc to enspirit our country.' It made me think that it would be a great part for you, Beloved Ellie, were you not such an angry neutral most of the time. Forgive my jest! Methinks, though, Friend Paine has some good thoughts to say on Tories and peace. I trust he gets it all published soon. . ."*

Tories, amnesty and peace were constantly on the minds of the populace. As the army moved through the Jerseys with the Juggernaut breathing down its back, they were almost the only topics on the tongues and minds of every inhabitant. This was particularly so on that miserably depressing Sunday, December 1.

In addition to all else, neutrals, militiamen, Whigs and formerly staunch patriots were signing Howe's oath of allegiance in the wake of the British Juggernaut. By doing so, all who declared themselves were promised the protection of the King's men. Both Hessian and Tory were forbidden to molest anyone who had renounced the American cause.

After many inhabitants had signed the oath, they found, nevertheless, that the pieces of paper they held granting them full pardons, meant nothing at all to some raiding redcoat, Tory or Hessian party. The worst offenders were the Hessians since they could not read the King's English.

Perhaps the most humorous story about Loyalists, insofar as the fleeing American army is concerned, is one Gray inserted in his diary after leaving Newark. It is an account that makes Jocko howl with laughter, and one which he keeps repeatedly asking Levy to read to him.

Oddly enough, it was about James Nutman who was the landlord of the Newark schoolmaster, Nicodemus Grossbeck whom Gray had met. And Gray's diary entry tells it this way:

> "A gentleman traveling through us to Morris Town tells of a certain James Nutman, whose boarder was the same New-ark schoolmaster I told you of whom I met when we arrived there on the 22nd of this month.
>
> "Mr. Nutman had been captain of the militia in Newark but turncoated to the enemy. When the British troops landed on the Jersey shore, he was so exceedingly pleased, that he invited his friends and neighbours to keep *thanksgiving*, as he termed it, by taking dinner with him on the happy occasion. Often he would say with much seeming satisfaction that his dear brethren and protectors were come; and frequently he would repeat this question to his guests, 'An't you glad that they are come?'
>
> "The next day they arrived in Newark, and his 'dear friends and protectors' stripped him of all his moveable property, even to his shoes and stockings; and the poor wretch of a Tory was under the necessity of begging from his neighbours something to cover his nakedness."[17]

Patriots and Patriots In Part

It was not difficult for the massive British machine, thoroughly equipped for warfare with the most modern weapons, to convince farmers, shopkeepers, tanners, blacksmiths, millers, innkeepers, patriots and even many rebel soldiers that their American rebellion was about over.

Renouncing the American cause, many came from great distances to sign Howe's amnesty papers. By the hundreds they poured into Cornwallis's headquarters as the impressive army from Great Britian ground its way through villages and hamlets in close pursuit of the straggling remnants of the disintegrating rebel forces.

Yet most of those signing the oath one day would, on the very next, reverse themselves and swear allegiance to the American cause if the tide turned. For to most, life and property are tangible realistic things.

To most of the "summer patriots," ideologies do not have the same magnetism as do the visible and profit-making fields of growing corn. However, to the genuine patriots, ideologies, rooted deeply invisible in their land, have a magnetism drawn from out the past and the best of its legacies.

The American retreat march through the Jerseys consequently does not conjure up the same mental picture to the hundreds who signed the enemy's oath of allegiance as it does to the persistently defiant "patriots" among the inhabitants.

And many will never see the American escape in the same light as some of The Cause's European supporters, already on their way from Germany, France, Poland and other lands to back the rebellion.

For now, on their way from across the sea, are such men as Friedrich von Steuben and Count Casimir Pulaski. They are among many who will view the Continental Army withdrawal in its military light. They will be among those who will hail it as one of the world's most outstanding military achievements.

But not so in the eyes of many of the inhabitants on the scene. They dejectedly only see their army and The Cause it is trying to defend going the wrong way.

Rationalizing with their new nation's dream on one side and their own futures on the other, their consciences struggle, not only within their own bosoms but openly with their neighbors, in search for an answer to their dilemma: How much can one be asked to give of himself, of his own and of those dear to him for a dream, beautiful though that dream may be?

Into their lands, into their closely knit families, villages and
hamlets, they and their forebears have poured their energies and
their fortunes. Must they forfeit all, or sign the oath of allegiance
to the King?

In the triumphant march of Cornwallis's army with Howe's
forces behind him and more recruits daily added to the redcoat
and Hessian machine—all further supported by raiding Tory
parties— the King's oath becomes for many too threatening to
resist.

Nevertheless, the defiant ones in face of pressure become more
defiant. To them the dream is unnegotiable. Like pollen in the
wind, defiance spreads and from its seed now blooms supernatural
courage. Thus, imbued by the strength and inspiration of others,
increasing numbers, now doggedly determined, hold on to their
rebellion. Their fighting efforts to continue resistance will grow
through coercion, threats, promises and humiliation, absorbing in
their wake the neutrals and the oath-takers. But it will take a
turnabout, a blow, a strike, a hard one at the Juggernaut's
throat!—a miracle!

It was one of these angry defiant ones who wrote six days ago:

". . . We have not force enough to oppose their march by land. We look
to New-Jersey and Pennsylvania for their Militia, and on their spirit
depends the preservation of America."

"If in this hour of adversity they shrink from danger, they deserve to be
slaves indeed. If the freedom that success will insure us, if the misery that
awaits our subjection, will not rouse them, why let them sleep on till they
wake in bondage."[18]

The Earl's Last Chance

So the first day of December was a dismal Sunday. More than
just the coming of winter was in the wind. The General and his
aides under Colonel Harrison were completing the Chief's routine
report to the Congress. It was almost 1:30 in the afternoon.

Suddenly distant cannonading, followed by loud voices and great
commotion was heard coming up from the river road. In minutes,
shouting men were excitedly asking swiftly riding couriers and
sentinels what was happening. A rider darting toward headquarters
yelled out the alarming news that the British van in great numbers
was fast approaching the river's north bank.

The rebel Chief, his mouth firm as though he were clenching his

teeth in controlled anger, heard the rider give his aides the surprising news. He turned to Nathanael Greene.

How could it be? How could Cornwallis have gotten almost to
the Raritan's banks without detection by the pickets?

There was no time now to find out. Unquestionably the Earl
had moved all night and taken the unsuspecting American outposts
by surprise.

After all, it was Sunday, the most unlikely day of the week for
an attack. Except from General Howe! Sunday has always been
one of Howe's preferred days for making trouble. Surely Sir
William was behind this, or Cornwallis was learning from his
teacher.

Greene immediately conferred with The General who ordered
Harrison to hold the report for Congress for the next express and
to end it with an explanation. Greene sounded the alarm throughout the cantonment and commanded all regiments to fall out
under arms ready to move out. It was an easy order to carry out
for it was one which the army by now was always prepared to
execute.

Harrison, hurriedly complying with his Chief's order, added a
postscript to the report, stating:

> "1/2 after 1 o'clock P.M. The enemy are fast advancing, some of 'em in
> sight now."[19]

There was no outgoing express and would not be for some time.
Every man, horse and wagon was needed. Trenton and the
Delaware were 28 miles away. The rest of the report would have
to wait events. There was no time for anything now except to put
Cornwallis's cannonading and New Brunswick behind them, and
fast!

General Stirling and his brigade again took over the rear guard
with orders to delay the enemy until the depleted ranks of the
main army, now less than 4,000 strong,[20] cleared the town and
were safely beyond the reach of their pursuers.

Before Lord Cornwallis stood what might be his last chance to
bag his Fox. Before him and his hard pressed troops, anything but
fresh from their 22-mile all night battle through heavy brush, deep
marshes and over blockades of felled trees and destroyed bridges,
stood another cursed river rising up between them and their prey.
Across the Raritan he could see his elusive enemy and his enemy
him. His hard-fought-for element of surprise was lost.

A half-destroyed bridge and a number of small river craft along the bank were useless. He had a 5,000-man army to cross. Immediately he brought up his heavier weapons, and began pounding the river's southern bank where Stirling and his lone defenders weakly returned the barrage with small arms fire.

Meanwhile, redcoat engineers went rapidly to work repairing the span. Rounding up all available vessels they reopened John Inian's Ferry[21] which had long claimed the distinction of the first link of East and West Jersey right on the dividing line.

Presuming that the returning fire from Stirling's small arms and light pounders meant that the entire rebel force was planning to stand and fight, Cornwallis rushed his preparations for an amphibious attack. For 12 days and for over more than 50 torturous miles the Earl had chased his running quarry. Brunswick now had to be his Armageddon.

Furthermore, had not Howe ordered him to stop his train there regardless of whether or not he had overrun the rebels? Until Howe so ordered he could go no farther.

No man in all America was more frustrated late that Sunday afternoon when, in the midst of his preparations to cross the Raritan, the rebel fusillade became lighter, rather than stronger in intensity, and also more and more remote. It was not long before his forward scouts confirmed Cornwallis's worst fears. All that was left of the American encampment that had stood quietly peaceful there early that Sunday morning, except for the silent departure of the time-expired troops, was a big bonfire. On the flames now burned a great number of his enemy's tents.

In General Lord Stirling's haste to get away before the Earl's van fell on him, he sadly ordered his five Virginia and one Delaware regiment—all once the flower of the Continental Army— to heap one hundred of their tents upon the flames. For short of wagons and horses, the brigade was forced to leave much of their shelter and blanketing behind.[22]

Later Lieutenant Enoch Anderson of Haslet's Delaware Regiment would describe the long faces of his men as they saw the flames and billowing smoke consume their tents and bedding. Already the north wind and winter's touch were upon them. Of this disheartening disaster, Anderson would write:

> "When we saw them (the tents) reduced to ashes, it was night. We made a double quickstep and came up with the army about eight o'clock. We encamped in the woods with no victuals, no tents, no blankets. The night was cold and we all suffered much, especially those who had no shoes."[23]

Disappointment At Prince Town

With Greene at his side The General reached the rocky hill above Kingston and crossed the Millstone River before bivouacking by the little stream for the night. There the American Commander, discovering that Harrison had not as yet sent off his report to Philadelphia, completed the letter, stating:

> "We had a smart cannonade (across the Raritan) whilst we were parading (preparing to march out) our Men, but without any or but little loss on either side. It being impossible to oppose them with our present force with the least prospect of success we shall retreat to the West side of Delaware (River) and have advanced about Eight miles."[24]

Monday, December 2, was the American command's turn to be disappointed. Like Cornwallis at Brunswick, forced to await Howe's arrival, The General and his officers at Princeton were still awaiting Lee when word came that the North Castle commander had only yesteday, December 1, started to cross his corps over Hudson's river. Announced by The General at a brief council of war in the college town, the news was not only disappointing to the staff officers, it was antagonizing. A wave of resentment at Lee's procrastination swept over the gathering.

That step, ten days after the Commander had urgently requested and gently ordered it, now meant that Lee must risk moving his brigades on the edge of enemy-held territory. It also meant that Lee's army will not arrive beside The General in time to be of any use in combating the oncoming might of the British Juggernaut in Jersey.

Those loyal to Lee still believed he would come up in time to save the army. Surely, they contended, he had his reasons.

Who else was there in Westchester to oppose Rogers' Raiders? Who else could protect its passes from New England?

Others made no reply. But many of Lee's admirers among the officers were no longer his "blind followers."

Stalled in New Brunswick by orders of his superior officer, Cornwallis on Monday announced to the villagers that, under Howe's orders he was offering free pardons to all who took the oath of allegiance.[25]

As in Newark and elsewhere, those who came in and signed were soon to discover that the Hessians could not read and that the Tories did not bother to. Waving their pardon in front of Hessian or Tory noses helped in some cases. In others it mattered little.

For five days Lord Cornwallis remained bogged down in Brunswick, restricted by Howe's "Go no farther" orders. The most good he could do there was to accept the oaths of allegiance from American renouncers.

Impatiently he waited for General Howe and Major General Grant with his 4th Brigade. Monday, Tuesday, Wednesday and Thursday he spent tightening his lengthy supply lines, extending his scouting operations and assessing the growing undercurrent of hostility among the inhabitants.

Meanwhile the American army, which had withdrawn into Princeton on Monday, the 2nd, left Lord Stirling and his 1,200-man brigade in town to keep a surveillance on the enemy's movements southwestward out of Brunswick. From Princeton The General led his army to Trenton[26] to prepare for crossing into Pennsylvania. He needed time at Trenton for such a maneuver and for rounding up all the river craft as he has done so many times before. Since the Delaware here is wide and swift, he could use Glover and his Marbleheaders if only Lee would hurry them to his side.

At Princeton, Stirling's rear guard found a welcome but temporary relief from their hardships. For in the college town they occupied several buildings including Nassau Hall. And they enjoyed indoor lodgings for the first time in many nights.[27] Their comfortable quarters were provided at the expense and through the mixed reluctance and generosity of the trustees, administration, faculty and students.

Only the rear guard moved into the village. Most of the main army skirted the town, hurrying on to Trenton.

This was a disappointment to Gray. He now envied Stirling's men coming up behind. They would bivouac the night and remain in Prince Town. And that was something he had hoped to do. In fact he had looked forward eagerly to the possibility of seeing the men he knew and admired there. So the orders to march on by were hard on both Gray and Levy as they turned and saw Nassau Hall's tower diappearing behind them.

"I almost was tempted to desert for a day," Gray wrote later in his diary." Methinks Asher would have gone along with me, for we had counted so upon bivouacking there and seeing the old place again. There were memories that flew around me as we passed. So many pleasant ones did it provoke of that first day I arrived, of the many studious hours I spent, of the learned men who made me see and think of the vast dreams of civilization past, and flowing all around the present toward the unknown future. Though only *passing by, I was suddenly back again, and, Ah, Ellie! How I wished I could have been one of Stirling's lucky men!"*

After leaving Lord Stirling and his 1,200 Continentals behind at Princeton, the Americans trudged on through the gradually stiffening mud ruts toward Trent's town, 12 miles away.

For the past few days the skies have been gray and bleak. The nights have grown steadily colder. Hourly the snow-laden heavens have become more threatening. However, the firming ground, coated nightly by heavier blankets of frost, enabled the wheeled vehicles to roll more easily. It is the one blessing of the coming of winter the gun carriage haulers are thankful for.

A Fortnight and 84 Miles From Fort Lee: Trent's Town

Late Tuesday night, December 3, and throughout the early hours of the next morning,[28] the Continentals set up camp along the east bank of the Delaware. Here was the end of the Jerseys. And here almost was the end of their journey.

For two weeks, fourteen unforgettable days and nights, they had eluded the King's men across more than 80 miles of rough terrain. Through miserable weather and under some of the most trying of conditions, they had conquered rivers, forded streams, slept without shelter in fields and forests, shivered in tattered, summerweight clothing and gone hungry to bed with seldom a dream of hope.

So, in a fortnight, the American troops had covered some 84 miles, averaging six miles a day, to bring their backs to Pennsylvania for what might be a last ditch defense to save the seat of the new nation. They had still to cross the river, but regardless of what might be in store, the great march had brought all that was left of them to what should be the last step in the long campaign, the crossing of the army to the safety of the Delaware's west bank. For the likelihood was daily growing stronger that both armies would soon be forced to find their winter quarters and wait for spring.

There was much to do at Trenton. Forage and food had to be procured. The sick needed to be attended to. Nothing was to be left in the town that would aid the enemy if Howe and Cornwallis decided to continue their pursuit to the Delaware.

For miles up and down the river all vessels—many of them Durham boats, used by natives to transport produce—were commandeered and gathered for the mammoth task of ferrying supplies, armament, baggage equipment and finally the men across to the Newtown[29] encampment area on the west bank.

Inclement weather slowed the task which got under way sluggishly Thursday, December 5. There was no pressing haste. Stirling daily sent the encouraging news that Cornwallis had made no move out of New Brunswick. This intelligence fell happily upon The General's mind.

Then the very day the ferriage work began 2,000 Pennsylvania militia, all a part of the Pennsylvania Associators, marched as was promised, into the encampment grounds in Newtown.[30] They were part of Colonel Nicholas Haussegger's regiment comprising both Pennsylvania and Maryland Germans.[31] And this news also fell happily upon The General's mind.

Time To Face About

Was not this the time to turnabout and strike? What if Cornwallis, basking in comfort and confidence in Brunswick were surprised? A quick devastating attack could turn the tide of war.

Convinced by the downward state of things that he must do something to bring the disintegrating spirit of the country together again, the American Commander ordered some of the fresh Pennsylvania troops and a large corps from his ranks to prepare to march under arms at dawn Saturday morning, the 7th.

In reporting to the Congress later, he would say that he had decided to make "a face about with such Troops . . . and march back to Princeton and there govern myself by Circumstances and the movements of General Lee."[32]

However, unknown to the General, Lee and his army had only cleared the Ramapo Pass on Wednesday, the 4th. Heading for Chatham, 30 miles away, Lee's progress was slow owing to his troops' condition. Ill equipped, they lacked adequate clothing, blankets and food. It would take them four days to reach Chatham after clearing the Ramapo Pass. It would be Sunday, December 8th, before Lee would get to the little village and be welcomed by the numerous patriots in the rebel hotbed of Morris County.

Though only 2,000-strong, Colonel Haussegger's Pennsylvanians, now up beside the Chief, imbued new life and hope in the flickering morale of the rebel army on the Delaware's east bank. One of Gray's diary entries reflected the buoyed spirits. It stated:

"It was the most heartening thing that had happened to us for over a fortnight. We of Penn's State were filled with joy and bursting with pride when we saw those Associators coming in beside us. We knew that Philadelphia, the capital, certainly helped

to explain their arrival. Surely if help were to come to us at all, we expected it would be from the seat of the country. The joy of seeing them and that of stepping off the Durham boat on Pennsylvania soil Thursday, December 5, made my heart glad.

"Ah, it was good, Ellie! Of course I would have preferred to step out of a pettiauger under the Bluff Rock at Bourdette's Landing. Oh, how swiftly I would fly past Old Stephen's place, Granny, Jennie and to the Baummeister house! Dreams and reveries can be man's kindest and cruelest companions."

Again, on Friday, December 6, Stirling sent word, reassuring The General that the British were still encamped at Brunswick. But it was that day Howe arrived in Cornwallis' cantonment.

Accompanied by Grant and his 4th Brigade, Sir William was annoyed and disappointed. He had expected Cornwallis's efforts would have netted more profitable results. And in addition he now realized his error in ordering the Earl to stop at Brunswick.

Cornwallis, eager to renew the chase, assured his commander that the lengthy British lines, now extending circuitously some 58 miles from Fort Lee through Hackensack, Aquackanonk and Newark to the Brunswick cantonment, could be safely protected. Major General Grant and his 4th Brigade provided the reinforcements needed for that and the continuance of the pursuit.

Gravely concerned over the excessive extension of his lines and aware of General Lee's paralleling march, 12 miles northwest through Morris County's rebel land under the eastern slopes of the Watchung Mountains, Sir William hesitated. But not for long.

Taunted by his adversary's successful hairbreadth escapes and cleverly elusive tactics—tactics that have drawn the King's men deep into hostile territory—General Howe decided he must lift the ban and send the Earl on for one more chance at the Fox.

Gnawed almost to the point of anger at having been successively outwitted by the rebel Leader, Sir William ordered Cornwallis to continue his pursuit, but the British army commander mapped out a new strategy.

Bergen, Essex, Middlesex—And Now Hunterdon

With his change of mind about halting at Brunswick, the redcoats' commander-in-chief split his army into two divisions. The East-West dividing line of the Jerseys at John Inian's Ferry had seemed the likely limit for scattering the rebel forces when it was fixed over a fortnight ago. But not a single battlefield engagement had taken place. Therefore Howe was now convinced the game desperately needed a change in tactics.

Cornwallis's corps, the first division, was to comprise the right wing of a pincers movement. It would sweep down through Princeton, run over Stirling's guards and drive straight through to the Delaware, seek ferriage across for part of the force and march south along both banks of the river to crush the outlying enemy forces.

Meanwhile Howe's troops, the second division, would sweep in upon the main rebel force at Trenton. It was to be the left wing, or arm, in the pincers maneuver. It would circle around left of the rebels' Trenton encampment and simultaneously execute a frontal attack forcing the Continentals to fall back and up the east bank into Cornwallis's arms.

The Earl's troops which had crossed the stream somewhere around Coryell's Ferry would take care of the rebels' advance troops who had crossed to the west bank.

It was a sound plan with a good chance of success. And it justified Sir William's somewhat reluctant decision to change his mind about halting at Brunswick. It pleased Cornwallis, who had never wanted to recognize the demarcation line and was more than irked at the unnecessary and costly delay.

Aiding Howe in making the decision were the obvious advantages to be realized in "pushing on to the Delaware and the possibility of getting to Philadelphia"[33] plus the additional accomplishment of sweeping the rebel army out of Jersey.

His Majesty's commanding general had originally foreseen the campaign's end with the seizure of Bergen, Essex and Middlesex Counties.[34] Now it appeared he would have to add Hunterdon.

Naturally unaware of his opponent's plans, the American Commander began his march from Trenton toward Stirling at Princeton early Saturday morning, December 7. His last word from his close friend and compatriot, Brigadier General William Alexander, or "Earl of Stirling," though really not an earl at all,[35] was that the enemy had not moved out of Brunswick.

The General and his staff had agreed that very possibly Howe and Cornwallis planned to content themselves with their acquisition of East Jersey for the winter. And, since word had been received that Lee was either in or approaching Morris County, that intelligence could have a slowing effect upon the ever-cautious General Howe.

Therefore, governing himself "by circumstances and General

Lee," he left Ewing, Mercer and Mifflin in Trenton. He would pick up Stirling and his 1,200 troops in the college town and then spring a surprise on the enemy's New Brunswick garrison.

Suddenly, About-Face!

Now both the American Commander and General Lord Cornwallis were headed for the same place, Princeton. But Cornwallis, who had picked his way slowly and cautiously out of Brunswick, feared ambuscades. His Lordship had carefully studied the American "Fox" and his tactics.

And the precautious nobleman also knew he was gradually getting into territory which, like Morris County, was a nest for patriots. His flanks went out on both sides, while his van cleared away the felled trees and blockades, laid across the way by Stirling's rear guards.

When Stirling's pickets heard the distant familiar sound of bagpipes and drums, they knew the rolling, steady cadence accompanied a marching corps. It was not long before they discovered it was a force of some 5,000 troops.

Stirling with his twelve hundred had neither the desire nor the means of opposing the British and Hessian brigades plowing down upon him. He ordered an immediate double quickstep withdrawal to Trenton.

Despite their haste, Stirling's men destroyed the road and foot-bridges behind them. Even those over Stoney Brook, which is usually fordable anyway, were dropped into the stream. To cause their enemy as much trouble and delay as possible, the retreating rebel brigade strewed the highway with fallen trees, logs and brush.[36]

Just outside of the small village of Maidenhead, Stirling's van ran headlong into the American Commander and General Greene, leading their surprise attack corps to join the guards at Princeton. Alerted to the impending danger, The General ordered an about-face and put the combined forces into double-quick time back to Trenton with Stirling bringing up the rear.

Without Lee's brigades a confrontation with the King's men would be suicide in view of the enemy's strength and control over the province. Besides, Stirling's scouts and pickets had confirmed the news that two divisions had moved out of Brunswick, one veering right toward Princeton and Penny Town, the other left, heading directly for Trenton.

The disconcerting vision of an enemy pincers movement now in the making loomed large in the American Commander's mind. The army must complete its crossing of the river, and there was very little time left in which to do it.

Lieutenant Anderson of Haslet's Delawares, forming a part of the rear guard, later described the final about-face march back to Trenton village, stating:

> "We continued in our retreat—our Regiment in the rear and I, with thirty men in the rear of the Regiment and General Washington in my rear with pioneers—tearing up brdiges and cutting down trees to impede the march of the enemy. I was to go on no faster than General Washington and his pioneers. It was dusk before we got to Trenton. Here we stayed all night."[3 7]

The Sunday the Tables Turned, December 8

While Howe's division laboriously struggled on over obstacles in pursuit of the American Commander, Lord Cornwallis stormed through Princeton. Stirling's fires were still burning. But Nassau Hall and the other buildings which his quarry had occupied earlier that day, now stood empty of rebel soldiers.

Losing no time, the Earl pressed his right flank on toward the Delaware. Though Cornwallis refused to let himself become too confident, the chances never were so bright that he would soon be closing in upon his enemy. However, his men, wearied from the long, exausting march, could be driven no farther that day. He bivouacked for the night at Maidenhead.

Frantically searching for the river craft that was to have carried some of his force across, the British nobleman led his men on a 13-mile boat-hunting expedition the next day, Sunday, the 8th, in a futile attempt to locate vessels for ferriage. But the fruitless search ended hopelessly at Coryell's Ferry at 1 A.M. Monday morning, the 9th.

The American boat-gathering troops had done too good a job under Generals Ewing, Mifflin and Mercer. Mercer and his men had only recently joined The General after a forced march from Amboy.

Not a single seaworthy rowboat, bark or barge had been overlooked by the American scouting parties in their task. They had scoured the river banks for miles up and down the stream. Nothing navigable, nor even floatable, was left along the river's eastern shore.

Meanwhile the left wing maneuver under General Howe's

redcoats and Hessians had moved out of Brunswick even more cautiously than Cornwallis. Impeded by the obstacles placed in its path by the withdrawing American force, the British left did not get its van into Trenton until two o'clock the following afternoon, Sunday, December 8.

The jagers and light infantry sped to the river bank. They were just in time to see the last of the Americans' Durham boats disappearing before their eyes. The weary, poling crewmen carefully guided the big, sturdy old vessels that now carried the remaining loads of Continentals safely over to the Delaware's Pennsylvania shores.

Angry and disheartened after chasing their foe for 18 days over 80 miles of torturous terrain, the redcoat advance hurriedly called up their howitzers and gun carriages.

The British artillerymen swiftly brought a six-pounder down to the river's shore. Then another as the infantrymen and cannoneers began firing upon the last of the crossing rebels. But suddenly from concealed positions on the Pennsylvania side, the Continentals opened up with a heavy barrage from their emplacements in the woods. They had impatiently been waiting and expecting just such an action.

Jagers, light infantry and artillerymen were caught in the range and sent scattering up the river's banks. Put to flight by the severe American cannonading, the British troops drew back from the embankment after losing thirteen of their comrades.[38]

Lieutenant Anderson, writing later, said:

> "We were in the woods and bushes and none were wounded that I heard of... That night we lay amongst the leaves without tents or blankets, laying down with our feet to the fire. We had nothing to cook with, but our ramrods, which we run through a piece of meat and roasted it over the fire, and to hungry soldiers it tasted sweet."[39]

Since the British crossing of the river "being thus rendered impracticable,"[40] the bitterly disappointed Lord Cornwallis bivouacked his division in Penny Town. The first division encamped in Trenton. The giant pincer maneuver had failed. And once again "The Fox" had sprung the trap.

From all appearances the long campaign had now finally reached its end.

In these positions, the King's men would remain until today, Friday, December 13, when General Howe tonight will write in his report:

"The weather became too severe to keep the field and the winter cantonements being arranged, the troops marched from both places to their respective stations."[41]

A Long String of Vulnerable Posts

General Howe's "respective stations" now pose a problem, for they comprise a lengthy chain of vulnerable posts. Extending from Hudson's river across the Jerseys to the Delaware, they thread through large and small villages.

From New Brunswick southwest they reach into Princeton, Penny Town, Maidenhead and Trenton. And, to protect Trenton, Sir William is forced to extend his lines to Bordentown. Thus his guards are now strung out from Fort Lee and Paulus Hook across the Jerseys to Burlington County where a majority of the inhabitants are staunch patriots.

However, there is a strong Loyalist stronghold to the south of Howe's chain of posts in Burlington that vehemently supports the British occupation. The Tory faction there is led by the Crown's last royal governor of New Jersey, William Franklin, pro-British son of Benjamin, the Philadelphia patriot.

William Franklin's beautiful Burlington estate, "Green Bank," has been threatened by the former governor's refusal to side with the American cause. So General Howe, in extending his lines into Burlington and giving the deposed King's representative military support and protection, is not only pushing closer to Philadelphia, but he is, at the same time, bolstering the morale of the Loyalist inhabitants and the former governor in particular.

There is no similar strong pro-Crown faction on the north side of Howe's long chain. Instead, Morris, Somerset and Hunterdon County, the latter being the State's most densely populated, are contagiously infected with the rebellion. They pose a threatening problem that endangers the vulnerable British posts and which Cornwallis on the right, or north, must meet with extensive picketing and bold raiding parties. Some of these raids push deep into Morris County's interior.

Adding to Cornwallis's annoyance in the patriot hotbeds of Morris and Hunterdon Counties, is the movement of Lee's army into Morris County. His rebel corps, now bivouacking under the Watchung Hills, is more than an annoyance. It poses a threat that bears constant watching by the redcoats' surveillance.

Howe will admit his concern over the extensive length of his chain when, on December 20, he reports to Lord George Germaine, the Colonial Secretary of State for King George III, declaring:

"The chain is rather too extensive, but I was induced to occupy Burlington, to cover the county of Monmouth, in which there are many loyal inhabitants. . . "[42]

In winter quarters along the Delaware, Howe could, he believed rely on Burlington and William Franklin's loyal adherents to provide a buffer for his troops, when they are quartered through three cold months between Monmouth's patriots on the south and Hunterdon and Morris Counties' rebels to the north.

There had been some reports from Tory-minded Morris County informers that Stirling's men had cached much of Fort Lee's materiel somewhere outside of Morris's town, or Morristown. There were even rumors that an army encampment was under construction in the hills somewhere southwest of the village.

To some British intelligence officers this was of little concern. It could be a militia center, possibly preparing winter quarters for Lord Stirling's brigade since Stirling's own plantation home is only about eight miles away in Somerset County.

It also could be that Lee's brigades might winterize near Morristown if the conflict extended through to spring. Nestled in a chain of hills, the secluded post and Lee's forces are likely to become an annoyance but not a serious threat to the British push toward Philadelphia. However Lee has to be watched.

Despite his preparations to return to England owing to his wife's illness, General Cornwallis, from his Penny Town, or "Penningtown" headquarters, has kept his eye on Lee's movements along the British right. Yesterday, December 12, he ordered a surveillance party to ascertain Lee's "motions and situation."[43]

In Cornwallis's headquarters Monday night, the 11th, several British officers continued a long, and frequently heated, discussion over the impracticability of democracy in government. Especially in a government of diversified national backgrounds and interests. It is one of their continuing, friendly debates in which Plato's *Republic* and John Locke's tenets are pivoted around the principles of the Magna Charta and Parliament's Bill of Rights.

Always the rights and freedoms of mankind, the uncontrolled extension of liberties and privileges without a firm "driver" in the seat, center upon the expectations of the Americans and the futility of their cause.

Among the officers are those who guardedly express the belief that, under certain conditions, the American independence might possibly work. But the majority doubt it, both scorning and occasionally lauding the various aspects of a "free and independent united states of America." A better world, they contend, will come for all mankind through unity and not uncontrolled freedoms.

Among these British officers are Colonel William Harcourt, commander of the 16th Light Horse, and his captain, Banastre Tarleton, both of whom see eye to eye when anyone points out the senselessness of the American cause. Though they do not express their thoughts openly too often, both the colonel and the captain, listen to and generally agree with the argument that an American republic would eventually bring about its own destruction, were it ever to succeed in becoming established.

Like many of the King's officers, they too foresee a massive block of heterogeneous peoples of far-flung and countless differences, too unwieldly for self-control and too attached to Europe's roots and traditions, to develop a love of country—a spirit of unity and patriotism which they now only temporarily espouse.

With such uncontrollable freedoms, say some of the British officers, such a "republic" would eventually take its own life through self-indulgence, wanton self-interests and disastrous, unchecked exploitation of its resources and of each other.

In the middle of that conversation Harcourt received a messenger carrying his orders directing him to head an expedition into the Somerset and Morris County patriot hotbed territory.

Scouring the countryside all day yesteday, Thursday, December 12, the colonel, who is the younger brother of the Earl of Harcourt, and Captain Tarleton covered some 18 miles of ground with their 16th Light Horse before bedding down for the night. It was sunset when they took shelter in a Hillsborough barn close beside the Millstone River.

During the night embers from their fires ignited the dried out timbers of the old building which went up in flames, forcing them to sleep "in straw till 5 o'clock."[44] By 6 o'clock this morning the party was off and on its way again. It is a chilly, overcast December day. But worst of all it is Friday, the thirteenth, memorable in the Middle Ages for its "Black," or 'Bloody Friday," a day for executions, hangings, beheadings and all macabre events.

Some British seamen refuse to go to sea on such a day. Some ardently religious folks connect the number with the Last Supper and the "13" who were present at the event which was soon followed by the trial and crucifixion. But with the Harcourt and Tarleton raiders it is just another day. With them superstition is not a fetish.

Fearlessly riding deep into their rebel enemy's territory this morning, the 30 horsemen stopped and questioned every farmer, vendor and traveler along the way. At about 9 A.M. they halted and prepared to turn about and return to Penny Town with the accumulation of intelligence they had gathered.

Then one of them suddenly espied a number of armed rebel pickets, and all the horsemen made a dash for the frightened militia soldiers who swiftly scattered and disapperaed in the thickets.

One, however, was unable to get away. He was taken at the point of Tarleton's saber.

Friday, the Thirteenth, At Widow White's

About four miles away at the Widow White's inn and tavern, General Lee, still in his dressing robe after having spent the night in the Baskinridge, or "Basking Ridge," hostelry, has chosen to use the morning answering correspondence in his room. There are many things going around in his head, but he is particularly mindful now of his actions during the past 23 days. . .

. . . His delayed response to cross to Jersey. . . Congress's reaction. . . The argument he presented to defend Westchester. . . What if he did ignore his superior's advice for uniting forces?. . . It was not the best decision. . . It was not an order!

Then, he recalled, The General had insultingly written him in reply to his suggestion that he might attack the British flanks, "that although an army on the flanks of the enemy might well be effective, it would not be so if there were no army *before* the enemy"! . . .[45]

. . . And why, he wondered, had he not received a favorable reply from the Congress to "conduct a desultry war against the enemy" from Morris County. . . Perhaps he should have first given the Congress a better reason—or at least some reason—why he was not hurrying to the side of the Commander-in-Chief. . .[46] Why do they not see that he should have his own command, independent of the army's Chief?. . . That is the way he can best perform. . . Perhaps it will not now be long before the Congress will see the error of its ways and appoint him, as he should be, commander-in-chief.

Thirteen days ago Lee finally moved out of Westchester's North Castle just in time to escape the British under General Clinton who a short time later overran the village. He then made his way safely to Heath in Peekskill and there attempted to take two regiments of the highlands defense troops across with him.

Offended by Heath's earlier refusal to send 2,000 of his men to Jersey as a substitute for Lee's forces November 30, the American army's second in command now demanded the Peekskill commander turn two of his regiments over to him.

Heath, who had been directed by The General, to guard a wide semi-circle of the New York highlands from the Hudson west to the Ramapo Mountains, had been given a 5,000-man "paper" command of which only 3,500 were fit for duty. His brigades comprised both Connecticut and New York troops under Generals Parsons, James Clinton, George Clinton and John Morin Scott.[47] A 2,000-man withdrawal would seriously weaken Heath's command.

Despite the fearlessly arguing, protocol-defending, corpulent, bald-headed Major General William Heath, who, like Greene, had never been a Lee-admirer, the Charleston hero, as senior officer, declared he was taking advantage of his authority.

Heath responded that none of his men would go at his orders, and Lee must accept full responsibility.[48] There was nothing more the younger, 39 year-old, out-ranked officer could do to oppose his arrogant, imperious, 45 year-old senior officer's command. Lee is high echelon, a professional hero.

If Lee could strike a powerful blow at the enemy as he hopes to do, two of Heath's fighting regiments would be of invaluable aid in lifting high his torch over the land. All he needs is a single decisive stroke against the King's men. But it still could be executed without Heath's regiments.

So in view of Heath's strong objection, Lee on Monday morning, December 2, canceled the order, much to Heath's relief. And without the Peekskill post's 2,000, the former North Castle commander crossed Hudson's river Monday and Tuesday, December 2 and 3, from King's Ferry to Stony Point. It was then 13 days since the Continental Army Commander had first urgently appealed for Lee's aid.

On Wednesday, December 4, suffering from cold, lack of clothing, food and tenting, Lee's force passed through the Ramapo Pass into Jersey. It was the fourteenth day of the main army's retreat through the State and its fading hope that the North Castle division would come to its side.

Staying close to the foothills of the mountain range, the long hoped-for Lee reinforcements took the inland roads and passes to and through the Ramapos by way of Kakiat, Suffran's Tavern, then along the Ramapo River, passing the fort above the Pompton iron works. From there they skirted around the Horseneck River bend, east of Booneton's iron works into Chatham on Sunday, December 8, the same day the main American army ended its retreat on the west bank of the Delaware, a good 45 miles southwest.

Not apparently over-concerned about the critical state of affairs in Jersey and Pennsylvania which his own sluggish and egocentric actions had done nothing to help, Lee wrote the General and Chief Wednesday, December 11, from Morris's town about eight miles northwest of Chatham, that he had been obliged to halt his army for two days for want of shoes.[49]

The Continental Army's recalcitrant second in command appears to be almost oblivious, not only to the call of his superior but to the thousands of frightened Jerseyans and to reports of increased Tory raids throughout the Jerseys. And now he leisurely reads once again, with only passing interest, an urgent request from the Commander-in-Chief to "push on with every succor you can bring."[50]

Heedless of the undercurrent of dissatisfaction with his progress by some of his officers, the major general enjoys the reception the Morris and Somset County inhabitants extend to him and his army. Strengthened by his presence, they laud his past achievements and feed his ego.

Since Lee has not received The General's intercepted letter revealing the Congress's state of jeopardy, he is not yet inclined to rush his flaming sword to the Delaware any faster. However, the triumphant enemy march through the Jerseys has created havoc in all thirteen state legislative bodies, particularly New Jersey's assembly.

Despite the bold, untiring efforts of Governor Livingston and Attorney General William Paterson, the Jersey Legislature wobbles on the very brink of disbanding.[51] Reports that thousands of their constituents have signed the oath and received amnesty promises have almost completely dispirited the lawmakers.

Some describe the oath-signers' rush into General Howe's post at New Brunswick as like a pack of frenzied animals, stampeding before a forest fire lickety-split to reach the nearest river. It is as though the "British Protection Papers" were offering them some magic cover of security that would immunize them from all earthly harm.

In time they learn that waving the paper before potential pillagers has, in most cases, as little effect upon Tories as standing in a stream of water while a raging holocaust lowers its smothering pall on all things around it. The Continental Army's retreat, as one observer puts it, "has made thousands of Tories."[5][2]

Under these terrifying conditions, the Continental Congress, which had, up until lately, heralded General Lee as a military genius, is now more concerned with staying intact and saving the union than with replying to the Lee plan for carrying on a "desultry war" from Morris County.

Some Congressmen are also very much in a quandary as to why The General's possible successor is lagging in the Watchung hills. Why is he so dilatory in bringing the much-needed corps over? Why is it still some 50 miles away from where it should be and where it is demanded for the security of the nation?

Logistically, a 50-mile separation of the two divisions, they argue, is as bad as 300. They contend the North Castle men might just as well be in Canada, or up with Gates and Arnold in Albany.

Congress Flees

Today near-panic is sweeping Philadelphia. Word that Howe has reached the Delaware is on all lips. Certainly he will follow up his successes. The Continentals have not stopped the British from crossing the Hudson, Hackensack, Passaic and Raritan Rivers. So why should Sir William not continue his pursuit, cross the Delaware and take the Congress and the ragged army that tries hopelessly to defend it? And all in one stroke!

Of what good will Mifflin's Philadelphia defenses be against Howe's powerful military machine? Surely, whether the end comes there or not, the enemy will winter in Penn's city!

When, on the day before yesterday, the 11th, a British detachment took possession of Burlington, Philadelphians 20 miles away became convinced that Burlington was Howe's prelude to a march on the capital city. Both Generals Mifflin and Putnam, though having devised a defense plan for the Quaker city, immediately advised the Congress to adjourn and transfer the seat of government to Baltimore.

Today, with news that Trenton, the east bank of the Delaware and both East and West Jersey as far as Burlington, have been overrun by the giant British behemoth, the Continental Congress began a hurried 110-mile flight from Philadelphia. They will transfer the wobbling nation's business to Maryland. There the Congress might be assured temporary safety in its determination to hold the new nation together as long as a breath of hope remains.

GENERAL CHARLES LEE.

Major General Charles Lee, Second in Command of the Continental Army—From George H. Moore's *Treason of Major General Charles Lee, 1860.*

During the depressing journey many of General Lee's supporters now ask themselves what accounts for the major general's failure to bring his forces against the enemy in Jersey. Their explanations are numerous. Some are defensive. But most agree that their "knight" has something in mind. Surely the "flaming sword" will flash, and Sir William will be sent back staggering from the blow.

And that is exactly what Charles Lee has in mind.[53] A devastating blow at Howe's rear, or right flank, could indeed turn the drive, relieve the pressure on the main army and bring him honors.

To do so without Heath's 2,000 troops will necessitate the use of local militia and armaments. Such an accomplishment, if timed just right at The General's most precarious moment could earn him the American command.

Charles Lee, "Soldier's Soldier"

Though Lee is a vainglorious egotist in the eyes of those who dislike him, he is, nevertheless, a dedicated professional soldier, a soldier of fortune in a sense, but truly a so-called "soldier's soldier." Popular with his men, the commander is considerate of their needs.

Seeking a military career early in life, he became an ensign when he was 16 and a major at the age of 30. So it was that Charles Lee, who was born in England in January of 1731 of a family with good social standing, followed in the footsteps of his father, an army officer. His mother was the daughter of a baronet. Lee's military career is starred with testimonials of bravery and honors.

He first came to America with Braddock and survived Braddock's defeat unscathed. Shortly after that he was adopted by the Mohawk Indians and, for a brief time, took a Seneca Indian woman for his wife.[54]

On returning to England, Lee served under Burgoyne in Portugal, ending the campaign there on a colonel's half-pay. In recognition for his accomplishments in Portugal, he received commendations from his commander and from the King of Portugal.

Becoming a violent opponent of Toryism, the British colonel in 1773 wrote against the Tories of America. He called America, "Liberty's last and only asylum" some years before Paine began saying the same thing. His criticisms brought him much attention and numerous friends among the colonists in their initial dissensions with the Crown.

In America the British-born militarist and opponent of Toryism began consorting with the country's patriots in an effort to be named commander-in-chief of the rebel army. Though failing in that, he was appointed one of four of the Continental Army's major generals in June of 1775. However, he refused to accept the office until Congress resolved to indemnify him "for any loss of property he might sustain."[55]

Lee had ingratiated himself with the states' representatives when he excoriated King George III and the British ministry in a letter from Philadelphia to Burgoyne in Boston, saying:

"Of all courts I am persuaded that ours (England's) is the most corrupt and hostile to the rights of humanity."[56]

Lee's cleverness in repartee, coupled with his caustic tongue and his written and verbal attacks on His Majesty's government, endeared him to the new nation's political figures. Owing to the paucity of professional militarists in the colonial states, Charles Lee's services were widely heralded, and he encountered no difficulty in being appointed second in rank to the Virginian, a status he hoped to correct.

But Friday, the thirteenth, was lurking in the shadows to all but end Charles Lee's career.

Yesterday, Thursday, the 12th, General Lee left Morris's town and marched his corps to Vealtown,[57] about eight miles southwest. Here he was two miles away from General William Alexander Stirling's 700-acre plantation home.

All army officers have heard of the grand manner of living said to chracterize "the altogether affected style and splendor of this farm in the wilderness, probably unequalled in the colonies."[58]

Only six months ago the major general bought an estate in Berkeley County, Virginia.[59] And just two months ago the Congress, in appreciation of his victory in South Carolina, "advanced him $30,000 to repay the money he had borrowed to buy his plantation."[60] "Officers' Talk" had made Stirling's home sound like something almost lifted right out of "Merry Old England." Certainly it would be a place for the new Virginia property owner to look at on the morrow!

As Lee perceives the American rebellion, it appears to be one frowning upon the landed gentry yet not entirely divorced from its control. It appears to be a movement scowling upon manor life simply because of its associations with aristocracy, yet depending upon "aristocracy" to guide it to the freedoms it seeks.

Discussions along these lines are as vociferous at times as the voices of John Adams, Patrick Henry, Tom Jefferson and such officers as Hamilton and Burr. At other times this talk is guarded and considered premature.

For does not The General himself represent the landed gentry of Virginia? Is not a large plantation owner virtually in the same cupboard as General Howe? Lord Howe? Lord Cornwallis?

And, Lee asks himself, is not that part of the reason that he bought his estate in Berkeley? Did it not sit him well to be a "landowner"? Was it not a prerequisite to becoming "Commander-in-Chief of the Continental Army"?

Guns Blaze And A Courtyard Is In Panic

If Lee is to become the army's chief, it is only proper that he be acquainted with the style of living enjoyed by his officers. Therefore, in the morning a short ride over to the Stirling home, possibly in search of needed supplies, would be an interesting experience for the French officers in his party, as well as himself.

So, late yesterday afternoon, Lee and his party, leaving General Sullivan in charge at Vealtown, set out southeast for Basking Ridge. The Widow White's inn and tavern in the little village, about two miles from Vealtown, would provide a good place for temporary working quarters where both food and lodging could be supplied. And there the major general and his party spent the night.

With no reply from the Congress and a firm order now from The General to "push on," any hopes he had entertained of making a bold stroke against Howe now seemed dashed. Unless, of course, an opportunity presented itself along the way.

Despite his many faults, Charles Lee is a conscientious, hard working military commander who generally plans and thinks through his problems. At times, however, impulsiveness and his driving ambition rob him of good foresight, frequently nudging him into devious, scheming and embarrassing situations, particularly with pen and ink.

Not an officer who escapes camp routines, nor one who could be called a "ladies' man," readily succumbing to the allurements of the opposite sex, Lee's sojourn to the Widow White's tavern with his staff was probably partly regular army business and partly curiosity and surveillance, if looking over Stirling's manor house can be considered "surveillance."

So, after working late last night with his staff on the intelligence that his scouts have brought in preparatory to continuing his march toward Coryell's Ferry, Lee arose this morning to complete some personal correspondence. Appearing more unprepossessing than usual with his long nose, thin, slightly stooped figure of average height, the sleepy-eyed major general stirred the log embers in the fireplace and soon had a blazing fire throwing its heat toward his writing desk.

One colleague who always listens sympathetically to Lee's criticisms of the conduct of the war is the Northern Department commander, General Horatio Gates. And to Gates in Albany he writes:

"The ingenious maneuver of Fort Washington has completely unhinged the goodly fabric we had been building. There never was so d----d a stroke. Entre Nous a certain great man is damnably deficient. . . ."[61]

Just then shots and excited voices rang out in the yard below his window.

Half an hour earlier the militia soldier, with Tarleton's saber at his throat, had admitted that General Lee and a small party were in the vicinity. Then seizing two more sentries and a dispatch rider, carrying a message from Lee to Sullivan, Harcourt had the confirmation he wanted.

Cautiously the dragoons rode within sight of the tavern. A few of them tethered their horses in the woods. Under a surprising covering of musketry fire half of the British patrol then charge in upon the unalerted guards with sabers flashing. Lee, dropping his quill, rushes to the window and looks in unbelieving amazement upon the sickening scene below. An immediate quick escape is his only possible out.

A Humiliating End for A 29-Year Career

Rifle fire and screams now terrifyingly break the quiet air of the courtyard. Guards run into the inn and toward the barn and outhouses. Each man seeks the nearest cover as dragoons pour out from four sides upon them. The Widow White's excited hounds and Lee's spaniels add their barking to the melee.

Soon Captain Tarleton's stentorian voice shouts out a demand that all within and without the inn surrender on pain of setting the building afire. More rifle shots follow.

A horse, harnessed to a wagon in front of the tavern, whinnies pitifully as a ball creases its foreleg. Several of the guards, who had put up their muskets earlier in order to gather wood, now lie moaning in their death throes.

Several of the general's aides, Captain Wilkinson of Lee's staff, his guards and the Widow White all urge Lee, who has run downstairs in his nightshirt and robe, to hide until help arrives. Lee in disgust dismisses the thought in horror.

One horse, a courier's, without a rider stands saddled only fifty feet from the inn's back door. Lee, his sword in hand, decides to make a dash for it while his men keep up a covering fire.

Then one of the dragoons crashes through the front door followed by Tarleton and others. An older woman, the cook of the household, fearing for her life, falls down on her knees and begs for mercy.

The youthful Tarleton has no intention of doing her injury. He had been reared loving women, not harming them. In his barracks was a letter he had finished to his mother in England with the closing words:

"One who will always be proud to subscribe himself your affectionate son." [62]

All he wanted from the old woman was the whereabouts of the rebel general. She answered by pointing to the kitchen.

Led by Tarleton the dragoons swarm through the old hostelry, pressing their sabers against the throats of the gun-loading rebel troops before they have a chance to reel around and fire. Harcourt's remaining cavalrymen encircle the house.

Lee, taking the only open way out, rushes out of the rear door, brandishing his sword futilely as his enemy captors surround him.

Captain James Wilkinson, who has been with General Lee's staff throughout the campaign, witnessed the major general's capture and escaped upstairs into Lee's quarters, bolting the door behind him. Wilkinson later described the scene, stating:

"The unfortunate Lee, mounted on my horse which stood ready at the door, was hurried off in triumph, bareheaded, in his slippers and blanket coat, his collar open, and his shirt very much soiled from several days' use." [63]

Wilkinson rescued Lee's unfinished letter lying on the table-desk where its writer left it in his haste. And there by the table, Wilkinson later wrote that he stood waiting for a fight to ensue within the house. But, according to the captain, "the raiders had their objective and hurriedly sped off with him."

Escorted away in humiliation, the "Hero of Charleston," the once widely heralded "Knight of the Flaming Sword" and one of the strongest of America's British-born symbols of opposition to the Crown's colonial policy, is a prisoner. Not only is he a prisoner of the army and the empire he had once so gloriously served but he has been captured by the very army unit that he had commanded 14 years ago during the Spanish War in Portugal,[64] the Queen's Light Dragoons of the 16th Light-Horse Regiment.

In the eyes of these men Lee is a deserter. In the pages of history the irony of fate will seldom experience a more humbling moment.

In the clamor, in the brief rattling of sabers, in the death-dealing fire of pistols and muskets, all amidst the painful whinnying of horses, the barking of hounds, the shouting of men and the yelling of orders over the stench of powder and the cries of the wounded, Charles Lee's meteoric star crashes to earth.

That is the way it was in and around the Widow White's inn and tavern in the remote village of Basking Ridge at a little after 10 o'clock this morning, December, Friday, the thirteenth.

They will take the captured rebel general first to Penny Town. He will cover over 30 miles in less than seven hours, a distance which he and his army moved in about two weeks, counting all delays. However, Charles Lee will be closer to the American Commander-in-Chief than he has been for some time and closer than he will be for over a year. For from Penny Town the prisoner will be moved to New Brunswick and then to New York.

Addendum: Fall Of the Shooting Star

[Charles Lee will weather the desires of some British officers to see him tried as a deserter simply by proving he resigned from His Majesty's services before entering the American army. The imprisoned commander will finally be exchanged for British General Prescott in May 1778. He will then be welcomed back with open arms by the Congress, the army and the people of the states.

In the 17 months of his captivity, Lee will be treated well, enjoying large quarters of his own and guest-dining privileges.[65] It will be facetiously said of him in the years ahead that, deprived temporarily of the chance to tell the American Commander how to run his war, Lee "proceeded to tell William Howe how he should run his."[66]

The statement will not be far from the truth. For on March 29, he will draw up a plan "to be followed by the Howes if they desired an early triumph."[67]

When exchanged and returned to his American command, Lee will continue playing his devious, self-centered and, ultimately, self-destructive role. For he will tell both the Congress and the American army staff command that "he had discovered Howe's plan of campaign for the year 1777 and would have revealed it to the comittee (Congress), even though this meant violating the confidence Howe had hospitably placed in him."[68]

The "committee" Lee will refer to is the one he will, at General Howe's prompting, ask the Congress to send to him in his prison quarters to discuss important "proposals." The Congress, however, will see through this as another attempt by Howe to lower America's resistance with unacceptable peace proposals and will not asnwer their captured major general's letter.

Lee's chance of full redemption, in the opinion of his critics, will come about 18 months from now upon his exchange. Then, on June 28, 1778, he will err tragically on the battlefield near Monmouth Court House in Jersey.

There, to his detriment Lee will cling fatefully to a disastrous antipathy for executing the orders of his Commander—a Commander who the major general once said "was not fit to command a sergeant's guard." And there at Monmouth his defiance will lead to charges of treason, ending with a court martial that will terminate the ill-starred general's career in disgrace. This time for good.

For the summer of 1778 will see the humiliating trial, after those 90 days from the enemy's prison to a hero's festive return and reception at Valley Forge and in the Congress to a battlefield reprimand, a court martial and a verdict of guilty. Guilty of disobedience to orders, misbehaviour before the enemy and disrespect to the Commander-in-Chief will be the decision.

Though his sentence will be a disgraceful 12-month suspension from the army, Lee will not return to the service. He will die at the age of 51 in 1782 on his Virginia estate—the grounds of which he had once wanted to compare with William Alexander Stirling's plantation a few miles from Vealtown in the little village of Basking Ridge on a dark Friday in 1776.

History will say of him that he was arrogant, sarcastic, dogmatic, slovenly, vain, petulant, devious, profane, ambitious, "violently changeable in his opinions, excitable almost to the verge of madness," a brilliant military strategist, a commander thoughtful of his men, a "soldier's soldier," and early in 1776 and later, a militarist "almost universally thought to be a 'prodigious acquisition' owing to his adherence to the American Cause."[6 9]]

"I think the game will be pretty well up"

On the west bank of the Delaware this same day the American army has not been buoyed by the news that Lee and his division are stalled near Morris Town. And more disheartening is the word that the Congress is flying out of Philadelphia.

As the sun goes down behind a heavy gray sky hovering over the Pennsylvania banks of the Delaware, the American Commander at his temporary quarters in a farmhouse near the falls of Trenton ends another day of concern for his suffering troops. His face is drawn from worry and lack of sleep. He has spent long hours seeking some way to strike at the British machine.

Something must be done! Some surprise—a blow, yes a miracle—must be executed to prick the rising British balloon, save the Continental Army and restore confidence in the nation. But to do so he must have Lee and his division by his side.

Turning temporarily to his personal correspondence and unburdening some of his thoughts in a letter to his brother, The General writes:

> ". . . In short, your imagination can scarce extend to a situation more distressing than mine. Our only dependence now is upon the speedy enlistment of a new army. If this fails, I think the game will be pretty well up, as from disaffection and want of spirit and fortitude, the inhabitants, instead of resistance, are offering submission and taking protection from General Howe in Jersey."[70]

Interrupted by the excited, horror-stricken face of his adjutant, Colonel Reed, the rebel Chief puts his quill down to read a courier's dispatch from General Sullivan. The message is brief. Lee has been taken and Sullivan is assuming the division's command, pending further orders.

The capture of the rebel army's second in command coming in the wake of the mass retreat, the occupation of the Jerseys by the enemy and the flight of the Congress from Philadelphia, will fall down upon the colonial states, their people and their legislatures like the final closing clang of a coffin's lid.

Even far up with the Northern Department the effect will be demoralizing. Dr. James Thacher, who serves with Gates in the north, will reflect the attitude of the country mildly when he writes in his diary, a *Military Journal of the American Revolution*, that "Another disaster of much importance is the capture of Major-General Lee."[71]

Thacher will rank this latest casualty alongside that of the loss of Fort Washington. Most of Lee's supporters will agree. Some will go so far as to predict the general's capture is tantamount to returning the colonies to the Crown.

But in five days, on Wednesday, December 18, Major General John Sullivan will be leading over 2,000 troops, still fit for duty, into the American encampment along the west banks of the Delaware. The force will be all that is left of the almost 7,000 "on paper" North Castle division which, at its best, only could count 5,000 fit for duty. However, these are, though ragged, the rugged, battle-scarred Continentals, the mainstays of the division, as are most of those still standing loyally by The General, Greene, Stirling, Mercer and Ewing.

The sight of these troops, though less in number than he expects will be like a long-delayed and partial answer to The General's prayers. With them and his main division there may be a slim chance that the flickering dying spark of the American cause might be recaptured before the lid slams shut.

Where the Heart Is

"There seems nothing to do but pray," John Gray writes in his diary under the whale oil light of the sentry house by the Delaware's cold, ice-forming waters. *"The fear that the river may freeze over and the enemy's crossing simplified, is ever fearful in our minds, even though some inhabitants laugh at such thoughts this early."*

Gray, warming himself frequently in front of the log fire in the ramshackle old riverside cabin, serving as a sentinel's station, has filled in all the events he can recall since the first of the month. Continuing, he writes:

"It is now almost midnight and getting very cold as I look out from the window of this post on the dark waters. But instead of the occasional silvery sparkles as the waters flow with ice chunks over rocks to the falls, I see only the Hudson. I see it bathed in summer's moon-lit skies under The Rock. I am at old Fort Constitution, at Fort Lee. I am home. Who would have thought a year ago that I would forsake my life-long ties to my Philadelphia home for one so far away?

"Yes, there I am home with my arms wrapped about you. There I am home with you, looking out on the North River's silent passage through the night to the outstretched arms of its distant sea.

"So now 'tis Goodnight! Goodnight I must to the moonlit river, to the sea, to the Great Bluff Rock, to my country . . . Ah, but most of all, to my beloved. Now there seems nothing to do but to pray to God to preserve them all . . . 1,2,3. I do! Ah, yes, I do!"

It is a few minutes before midnight. Almost time for the changing of the guard. Gray carefully writes in his red leather book the entry's date, "Friday, December 13, 1776."

Now he buttons his surcoat, bundles it tightly around him, turns up the collar around his neck and walks out into the night. His blue petticoat scarf flows brisky behind his collar under the wind-blown snow.

It is a night as cold and dismal as the crisis and the darkness which now falls dolefully over the land and the thirteen colonial states which, like the shivering eaglet—now free and on its own—trembles in the high tree above the water. It must now struggle on alone for its survival.

33

Thursday, December 19. . .

Hour of Decision
Along the Arc of Gloom

Close To the Precipice of Panic

Winter's cold rains, sleet and snow have prematurely descended
with their icy winds upon the Delaware. It is a cold snap that has
suddenly dulled the Juggernaut's taste for pursuit. For the past five
days both armies have lain quietly opposite each other along the
banks of the Algonquians' river.

Some fear the waters will freeze and enable the enemy to cross
on ice to Pennsylvania and fall upon the American posts. But most
of the inhabitants believe it will take a long, intense cold spell in
the middle of winter to permit such a crossing.

Rumblings of fear are not found spreading only through Pennsylvania and Jersey's villages and along the Delaware valley, but
now the entire nation trembles. News of the successes of Howe's
army and the Continental Army's losses and rapid deterioration is
on all lips:

. . . The 80-mile retreat—"a wild flight of scared rabbits" say the
Tories. . . All Manhattan Island lost as well as Long Island and
most of Westchester. . . Fort Washington and Fort Lee taken and
all of East and West Jersey in the enemy's possession, returned to
the King by a disintegrating American army—an army plagued by
desertions, expiring enlistments and as infected by defections as
the people of the provinces. . . And exhausted people and

provinces, suffering from foraging enemy ravagers, all followed by Tory plunderers in the wake of a triumphant enemy Juggernaut.

Throughout the colonial states, never before pushed so close to the precipice of panic, tongues wag and ears listen, assured that it is the end of a campaign of chaos.

Now added to the wagging tongues is the news that New Jersey's Legislature is dissolved. Then, upon this discouraging word, there comes the staggering account detailing the capture of the American army's second highest ranking commander.

And so the imprisonment of Charles Lee and the enemy's extension of its lines into Bordentown, 20 miles from Philadelphia, ends a month of horrendous disasters for the American eaglet and leaves the new nation sinking rapidly into despair.

The tragic series of military disasters throughout the campaign's last five months has struck a devastating blow to the states' economy. Inflation costs have eroded the value of the currency. Already paper money is shunned as virtually worthless.

It takes forty Continental dollars to buy a dollar in specie.[1] The effect is almost as demoralizing as the military catastrophes. It has caused many to urge that the army surrender and the Congress sue for peace.

It is no wonder, some say, that the European countries are not interested in coming to America's aid. Do the starry-eyed dreamers not see that The Cause is lost?, they ask. Are "The Dreamers" not aware that this is not the age of miracles?

Paying no attention to the country's mounting pessimism, The General re-forms his army from Coryell's Ferry south along the Delaware's west bank to below the Trenton falls. The re-organization, conducted as secretly as possible, forms a rough 25-mile "V," or arc, pointed at the enemy. It comprises three divisions of the army.

The northernmost division has its headquarters at Coryell's Ferry. This 2,000-man corps is made up of brigades under Generals Stirling, Mercer, Stephen and Roche de Fermoy. They cover a seven and a half mile sector of the west river bank south from Coryell's, running six miles through McKonkey's 40-year old ferry house on the Jersey side to Yardley's, about a mile and a half south of McKonkey's.

The center division of the arc has its headquarters where the Trenton Ferry's west terminus was located. This 550-man corps is under General Ewing's command and covers the river south from Yardley's and four miles through the westerly terminus of the

Trenton Ferry, then down the river bank another six miles to Bordentown.

The southernmost division of the V-shaped defense line has its headquarters at Bristol. That 1,800 man force is under former Colonel Cadwalader, who has been given the temporary rank of brigadier general. Cadwalader's command extends south of Ewing's, six miles downriver opposite Bordentown, then six and a half miles farther down through Bristol to Dunk's ferry. The convex-shaped pocket, with the river forming a formidable defense barrier, places a semi-circular protective ring around Philadelphia, southwest to its rear.

Along the expansive arc are over nine ferry crossings. All have been closed or carefully guarded by the Continentals. Most of them are insignificant, but all must be carefully watched.

At each ferry landing men throw up earthworks. At some, guns are mounted. Owing to the great scarcity of tents, many of the men build rude huts, or locate old deserted buildings, expecting that the army will now settle down along the Delaware for the winter.[2] That is, whatever is left of it after the expiration of the January 1 enlistments in 12 more days.

What Is There To Be Concerned About?

General Howe has ordered his troops into winter quarters. However, the American camp is not yet aware of it. The British army's 80-mile chain[3] dare not be stretched any longer. Its southernmost point at Bordentown has its picket post at Mount Holly, less than 20 miles from Philadelphia, but the long thin string behind it now concerns the British staff.

The Juggernaut is strung out through Bergen, Essex, Middlesex, Huntington into Burlington Counties. Howe's accomplishments are earning him high commendations. His Majesty has much to be pleased about, for the reports are glowing. Sir William has driven the rebels out of New York town, Long Island, Westchester and now New Jersey. He has control of the lower Hudson and America's largest seaport.

Even though he has not crushed the Continental Army and captured its Congress, the British commander has established a string of connecting posts from Hackensack and Amboy, through Newark, Brunswick, Princeton, Maidenhead, Trenton, Bordentown and Mount Holly.

Howe has the stepping stones into Pennsylvania, a dispirited people and their ragged, weakened, starving disheartened army, hungry for home and peace, all silently working for him. Spring will be time enough to finish off the business.

As for the long chain of vulnerable posts with its left wing only 18 miles across the river from Philadelphia, this would ordinarily be something serious to worry about. The strung-out lines do pose an enticing enemy target. However, with winter coming on and the rebel army tottering on its last legs, what is there to be alarmed about?

So, leaving Knyphausen in New Brunswick, Grant in Princeton, Rall in Trenton and Donop in Bordentown, General Howe returns with Cornwallis to New York, arbitrarily deciding to bring the Campaign Of 1776 to a close. He would rest on his laurels until March. And in New York, Cornwallis prepares to return to England to see his ailing wife.

Uncertainty hovers over the American arc lines. The defenders are not sure what to expect next. This state of dubiety, the bitter cold weather, inadequate shelter, a scarcity of blankets, clothing, shoes and food, all have caused strain.

Within Lieutenant Gray's battery the men have always enjoyed a close comradeship even under stress, but with the recent addition of the quarrelsome Private Uriah Wright to the company, the former comradery has been smothered in the uneasinesss Wright's attitude and presence provokes. And the cantonment's prevailing tensions serve to heighten the men's jitters in their new home, an abandoned, fire-wracked old barn and stable they now occupy since moving up fron Trenton Ferry.

Along with the rest of Irvine's brigade, which is part of General Greene's and The General's command, the battery is located south of Robertson's mill and north of McKonkey's Ferry landing on the west shore.

It is the end of the sixth day of bivouacking on the Pennsylvania ground. It is the end of the battery's third day in their stable quarters, far more comfortable than rolling up close to a fire on the snow-covered ground outside, as those who have not built lean-tos and huts must do.

The two burning campfires, over which they have cooked their night meal of pork and toasted Indian corn with hardtack and rum, send their smoke and dying embers up through the gaping hole in the roof that had once before tasted fire until its rafters were charcoal black.

"Yud tink," speaks out the sullen, ever-complaining Uriah

Wright, "dat da Big Ole Man frum Va'ginny s'got hisself a way oud a'dis mess. Enny goddamned fool knws 'e ain't! Da damn game's up! Som'un ought tell 'im. Den we's all cud ga 'om now, 'stead a'waitin' til da foist."

Wright, An Unwelcomed Addition

Typical of many of the Continental Army units, the old Bluff Rock Battery is ardently loyal to the American Commander. To them The General is almost as much respectfully *their* "Old Man" as he is, in a different sort of way, "My Old Man," to Madam Martha Washington. For it is widely known that that is her admiring, if not her most endearing, term of reference used in mentioning him.

Wright's remarks about The General are not his first disparaging statements aimed at belittling the American Commander. Usually, however, they are ignored since Private Wright is intensely disliked by the men for various other reasons.

Through some of his Irish friends in other battalions, Corporal Mike Monahan had learned that the battery's recent addition was transferred from another regiment in the Delaware Continental line after a court martial which had sentenced him to 17 lashes. Theft had been the charge, and the sentence included the loss of his corporal's rating. But Monahan, with only hearsay evidence, has told only Gray and Levy about his "inside information."

Indignant at Wright's latest gibe, and no longer able to withhold answering the private's constantly demeaning remarks about The General, Monahan quickly and sarcastically replies, "So, 'tis 'ome ye would be a'goin, Wright. Shur' 'n whan ye would be gettin' thar, I supposin' ye would be a'doin' a wee bit a hoss stealing? Wouldn't ye now?"

Wright had been moved into the battery on Colonel Hitchcock's orders, passed down from Major Blodget. From the very beginning there was something about his bearing, his sneering manner and his disgruntled attitude that conveyed to the men of the battery the impression that Uriah Wright was not for them. But his assignment to the unit was an order about which they could do nothing except to show their dislike for the order and the man.

Never before in their long days of close, warm friendship for one another have so many of the battery's men reported losses of small things, or found their little secretly cached supply of nuts, biscuits and various food morsels missing—stolen! Never before have they cast so much suspicion upon each other. Even the field mice, or the occasionally surfacing rats, are exonerated suspects from such underhanded and contemptible pilferings.

Yet, though all signs eventually point toward Wright, there is no proof, no way of knowing for certain that he is the root of their growing dissensions. For Wright is cunning, too cunning to be easily snared.

He has been caught too many times before, and his experiences have made him adept. A professional thief, the demoted corporal has become skillful in avoiding mistakes and covering his tracks.

In this atmosphere the artillerymen, tense enough from the depression that besets them all, cling close to Gray and Levy for the guidance that strongly controlled reins have upon a team of horses. The knowledge that both officers, to whom they are all closely attached, have applied for leave and soon may be going to Philadelphia, has caused them much unexpressed unrest.

Among most of them there is the determination to re-enlist on the first of the coming month, yet each is disturbed by the gnawing fear that Wright is correct in saying that the game is almost up. But they despise him for saying so.

So, as Monahan's stinging reply to the unpopular soldier falls down upon the suddenly silenced men in the old barn, each stops what he is doing and looks up. The artillerymen's antagonism for the newcomer has flourished owing to Wright's goading, insulting, sly remarks, hurled at Jocko during the past few days. Always, however, Wright has craftily waited until Big Tom, Gray and Levy are not in earshot. In this way the former corporal could, if need be, deny any charges made against him.

Uriah Wright has no liking for anyone with pigment different from his own. It matters not what wealth of character, or how fine is the stature wrapped beneath the living tissue within the soul, Wright looks no deeper than the surface.

The men sitting and standing around the hot embers of the slow-burning, carefully guarded fire in the center of the barn, keep one eye on the tense moment while they stretch their hands out for the fire's warmth, or spear another piece of meat with ramrod or bayonet, appearing as though they had not heard or seen anything.

All are verging on ill temper following a hard day, drilling, felling trees, splitting logs and chopping fire wood, all under a cold wind and a gray, overcast sky, threatening more snow on top of the blanket that now whitens the countryside.

Those eating, crouched to the side of the barn beside their beds of hay, look up. Others are sound asleep, or pretend to be. Some repair torn garments or dry their clothes and clean the mud from wet boots. And many, uninterrupted, clean their muskets.

Few men ever physically challenge Monahan. And now he glares at Wright as though inviting him to dare reply. The two men, each with fire in his eyes, stare coldly at one another.

Wright, more inclined to be a bully than a fighter, loses his bristles in the face of the battery's Irish corporal and his angry stance. The private gradually lowers his glance. Furtively he looks around, then turns his back on Monahan, ignoring the intentionally stinging insinuation in fear that possibly Monahan does know about his secret—his previous actions and the court martial.

The Corporal's Target Is Much Bigger Than the Object

Monahan's flaming eyes do not waver. They burn their message through Wright's shifting gaze into his brain. It is not the despised, demoted corporal alone that is the target-image of Monahan's wrath. It is also what he represents—bigotry.

The Irishman had sensed the unwelcome private's poisoned mind before the others. He had, at the outset, perceived Wright's dislike for Negroes, especially freed slaves. Uriah considers all blacks, browns or colored men to be beneath him and unentitled to the freedoms and rights of white men.

Monahan knew it would be inevitable that this mentality would vent its hatred, not very likely on Big Tom, but surely eventually upon the kindly, gentle, all-trusting Jocko. The Erin-born corporal has known too many "Wrights" to believe it would be otherwise. Soon he was proved right.

So Monahan's target is not only the battery's newcomer. It is all that the unfortunate creature represents in Monahan's eyes. The God-fearing noncommissioned officer nurtures a hatred for evil as deeply seated as Wright's seeming antipathy for his fellow man.

Monahan puts self-interest, prejudices, theft, murder and unjustified war on the lowest rung of civilization's ladder. Wright, however, were he conscious of it, puts them on the ladderless rung, the only plateau he recognizes—self perpetuation and personal survival.

In arguments with his comrades the artillery corporal holds stubbornly to the belief that "maniacal degenerates among us" are as threatening to the "fabric of liberty" as the British and the

Hessians. The offensive enemy at war, Monahan argues, is one and the same as the criminal at large, whether he knows it or not. Both in his own way destroy man's attempts to be "civilized," except that the enemy in combat does so openly and honestly, face to face, the Irishman declares.

The severest penalty for the enemy in combat is death, Monahan argues in debate. Why should it not be death for offenders who hide within the ship they degenerately try to destroy? The severest penalty for the enemy of civilization, if it cannot be exile, must be death, the corporal argues.

Isolation and exile do not change the human mold, he will say, and then, to clinch his arguments, he will quote Edmund Burke's, "Among a people generally corrupt, liberty cannot long exist."

To this he adds, "Shorr, 'n whart batter way is thar fer ta destry orselves than fer ta allows ourr executioners to roam amongst us?"

Nothing riles the Bluff Rock Battery corporal more than to hear of bribery and deceit among civilians, government representatives and military personnel. His heroes are not military men.

Instead they are the orators who speak out for the American cause such as Burke, Henry, Jefferson, Ben Franklin, John Adams and others. He never loses an opportunity to hear anything he can about their oratory.

During the march across the Jerseys the big, robust, powerfully strong 24-year old Jerseyan, who soon is to be made a sergeant, lifted the 39-year old adjutant general, Tom Paine, on his shoulders and carried him across streams just to hear Paine talk. But Paine is not a loquacious conversationalist, particularly during strategic withdrawals.

So Monahan's attempts to get the writer to discuss religion, especially his views about the deity, were fruitless. The laughing corporal later jested that Paine did not want to take the chance of offending the Lord during *that* "crisis."

The Bluff Rock battery men think much along the same lines as Monahan. They have all lived closely knit to one another. And Jocko and his father are part of them. So the black youth's method of silence, totally ignoring Wright's remarks about skin, Negroes, slaves and sarcastic references to freedmen, is the only way the youngster has of coping with the court martialed soldier's anger. And those who have overheard Wright's slurs, though irate, agree with Jocko.

The artillery unit, therefore, had put Wright in a closed category all by himself within their circle. Monahan tonight had merely sealed him tighter within the estrangement.

It is a category which Big Tom and his son knew from experience. They also know, and Wright is aware of it, that the old Barbette Battery's men have a singular attachment for the Graves. All but Wright have come under the spell of working and living with Big Tom and Jocko. And so the battery's fellowship is strongly bonded and firmly respected.

Owing to their detestation of prejudice the men of the old Barbette often find themselves unpopular with some of the other companies, but it never bothers them. Theirs is a strange mixture of men and minds in which Gray, Levy and Abbott have, along with the Graves, inadvertently helped to cement the group's thinking and attitudes.

Unobtrusively the door to John Locke's essay on human understanding has been left ajar. And part of that "opening" could be credited to the effect and influence of Nathanael Greene.

At least some of Greene's Quaker background has made its impressions on them as well as on all his troops, even though the general has long been dropped as a Friend within the sect owing to his military role.

One of Greene's tenets is an abhorrence for violence. It is a principle which he has been forced to revise, arguing unhesitatingly that violence must be employed in order to overcome violence. With this Monahan and the artillerymen thoroughly agree.

So all of these various influences, a wide multiplicity of ingredients, have gone into the molding of the old Barbette Battery's artillerymen. All of these factors plus the days on the Palisadean Bluff Rock, exposed to the charms of the wholesome river people, and the long trek of sharing and suffering together, have bred in this small body of Continentals a new tolerance and the seeds for a new wave of thinking in a new nation struggling to live.

The Monahan-Wright confrontation has taken only a few minutes. Each man finds himself suddenly back where he was before Wright's dispiriting remark.

Only Abbott and Craig, who along with six of the scouts have taken shelter with their horses in the old badly burned cattle stalls of the big barn, have been unmoved by the incident. Craig, simply because he is sound asleep. The captain, who is staying unusually sober these days, is comfortably nested on a bed of hay only ten feet from his faithful horse.

And Abbott who has smartly taken advantage of rising heat has an over-view of the men. For, six feet over their heads, he squats beside a hayloft bed and stitches a winter trim of fox fur on his deerskin coat. But, except for a swift glance at the two angry men which told him all there was to know in seconds, the last descendant of the long line of Lenni Lenape chiefs shows no concern for white men's senseless bickerings.

Abbott is more concerned about Chinqueka, stalled beside Craig's mare, for there is still much of the barn left to catch fire. In the event of that, or any emergency, he must be ready to hurl himself on his mare's back to get her out. For precaution and prevention are part of his tribal heritage.

By the light of one of the fires, a whale oil lantern, and the help of candles set upon milking stools, Levy reads to Gray excerpts from a letter that came from his betrothed. Miriam's Philadelphia message arrived in today's packet of mail from the capital city. The same packet had brought one for Gray from his sister, Marion.

It is not the first time this evening that the two men have hungrily devoured the contents of their lengthy letters. But now they share them. Since the two families are unknown to one another in Penn's city, both Levy and Gray read aloud and compare parts of their treasured correspondence. Anyone caring to listen in is welcome to do so. And there are many interested ears that do, including Monahan's.

There are few secrets the men of the old Bluff Rock Barbette keep from one another. They have been too close and too near death together to hide most of their secrets even if they wanted to. They have shared battle wounds, injuries and pain as well as mail—little though it is—shoes, clothing, blankets and their lives. Therefore it is acknowledged that those who wish to do so are welcome to listen in to the officers' readings.

Among the men only Wright does not know that Gray's depression of late is largely owing to the fact that it is impossible to get messages through to his wife and for her to get word to him. He has heard nothing from her since Abbott three weeks ago brought him her letter and assurance that all was well at Bourdette's Landing.

No packets have gotten through from East Jersey other than couriers' dispatches from Huntington and Heath in the upper highlands. In view of the terrifying reports and rumors that pillaging, rape and murder are rampant throughout all of Jersey, every man of the battery feels for the Blue Petticoat Scarf Lieutenant.

Elaine, the riverside families and The Mountain people are close to the Barbette Battery's happiest memories. Therefore, without any secret agreement, no one mentions Fort Lee, the great Bluff Rock, or anything pertaining to The Mountain and Hudson's river in Gray's presence. All know how much suffering The Lieutenant undergoes as each day passes without news from the house under the Bluff Rock.

Levy's voice trembles slightly as he reads a part of Miriam's letter concerning the second lieutenant's friend, Haym Salomon. After briefly explaining his friendship for Salomon and the merchant's imprisonment by the British in New York, Asher reads on:

. . . and pray to God it is not Pandora's"

". . . No Sooner than your friend, Haym Salomon, was released from Cunningham's gaol did he make for the Congress here. He tells horrible tales about the York prisons. It is hard to believe them.

"His knowledge of languages was put to great use by the gaolers. Since he speaks so many languages and reads them all as well, his life was probably saved owing to their need for an interpreter. Everyone here listens to what he says. Even the Christian preachers speak highly of him. He asked me about you and I told him all I knew. Then he told me the story of the bolt of cloth he sent you for your Officer Gray's lady. We do not know any of the Gray family in Penn's City, but I trust that he and his lady will honor us at our wedding when that distant day comes.

"Here are some of the things Haym said to the committee. I noted them for I knew you would want to hear them: 'We are not getting freedom and liberty from this war. We are only opening the box for them so that little by little they will be acquired. . . We must remember that they have been locked up by tyrants; they have been trampled upon by dynasties; they have been choked by monarchs. . . Slavery and bondage are as old as man himself. Few civilizations have not enslaved others. We are but a short step away from Egypt, Greece and Rome. . . We here are only making liberty and the freedom of man possible. . . That is all we can do at first; we can only open the door and pray to God it is not Pandora's.'

"Oh, Asser Dear, I wish you had heard him! He then read the talk which the Bishop of St. Asaph gave on the Massachusetts Government Act in May, two years ago.[4] It was the one that the Bishop made to the House of Lords, warning the King and saying,

'By Enslaving your Colonies you extinguish the fairest hopes of Mankind.'[5]

"Things are very frightening here about us. We do not know what to expect next. I do hope you and Officer Gray get your leaves and visit us before Lord William and his men. . ."

A number of the men listened attentively as Levy read Miriam's letter. The only comment came roaring up from Monahan, exclaiming, "Begorra! Thar's a foine fella for ye, thot Zollamon! Thar's a real Yank a'doodle dandy fer ye! Oi cud lissen ta 'im fer a fartnight, Lootenan."

Continuing addressing Levy, Monahan says, "Iffin ye see 'im in Penn city, you tell 'im so."

Then, turning to Gray, Monahan asks, "Lootenan, reckin ye cud read us a bit 'ere 'n dare frum yer sister's letter? Narthin' perseenel in't, mind 'ja, Lootenan. Jus whud eev'a ye theenk is roight 'n pro'pa."

A Surprise Package

Gray graciously agrees and reads excerpts from Marion Gray's communication in which she, too, reflects the entire city's fear of a possible British siege. She expresses concern over her brother's possible visit, saying that as much as she and her father desire to see him, it might not be the right time owing to the frightening state of things in the city.

Marion tells of the great shortage of food and the efforts of the women to supply the army with clothing, blankets and tenting. She tells how the women—excluding the Quakers—are busy melting down everything made of lead that they can find to make bullets. She closes with a prayer for Gray's safety and repeats her fears for him should he visit the city if it is attacked.

The postscript, which Gray does not read aloud, explains the package that had come with the mail. It reads, "Father has made these boots for your friend, Jocko. They were the best Papa says he could do with the poor measurements you sent him."

No one had seen Gray pick up the package earlier at headquarters and place it under his knapsack. And now, after Jocko, who has helped his father bed down the wagon horses, returns to Gray's side before the fire, The Lieutenant quietly helps him read Marion's afterthought.

With much syllabic prodding by the officer, the youth, his eyes slowly becoming larger in astonished delight, finishes reading the postscript. As he does so, Gray hands him the package.

The excited youngster quickly unwraps the paper while the men nearby inquisitively look on. Then, almost in unison, they gasp in amazement as the new shining leather boots, exactly Jocko's size, emerge.

Thrilled with bursting pride, the boy nervously scuffs off the old, over-sized summer moccasins he has worn since Long Island. Beneath them he unwraps layers of rags and paper, spiraled around his feet in accordance with the soldiers' custom when shoes, moccasins, or boots, become too worn. Most of the wrappings are damp, the outside almost soaking wet, explaining Jocko's constant sniffles.

The boots are a perfect fit. The youth's face beams with delight as Gray and Big Tom smile happily at the lad's joy. Tom's eyes water. It is as though he, too, had been handed a valuable, pre-Christmas gift.

Before long the whole company has heard about Jocko's new boots. Only one man among them, Uriah Wright, does not show any interest in the youngster's acquisition. Wright does not move from his remote corner at the side of the barn where he continues the cleaning of his musket.

Though many of the men have footwear far worse than Jocko's, they appear as happily elated as he. A number of the company go over to take a closer look at the priceless boots and to congratulate the broadly smiling youth. But Wright only looks up from what he is doing, sneers slightly and then continues his gun-cleaning.

News of any kind travels fast between companies within the regiment. And the privy between the barn and the deserted cider mill nearby, is the communications center. When Philip Reales there hears about the popular Jocko's new boots, he takes the tidbit of information back to his son at their quarters in the mill. Joseph loses no time in rushing over to see the newest in footgear.

The Caribbean-born son of the wagoner also has an acquisition he has wanted to show Jocko. So, under his arm, he tucks the box containing his new-found friend, a pet chipmonk. The fat, friendly, fearless little animal which Joseph calls "Terry," since he is uncertain whether it is a "Theresa," or a "Terrence," answers to the call of anyone with a nut to offer.

Pinching himself to make sure he isn't dreaming, a stunt he says he learned from Missy E, Jocko stands in disbelief, staring down at his feet and the brilliantly shining brown leather boots covering

them, and then up at Gray as Joseph comes through the half
burned out barn doors.

"You gave me something to write on, Jocko," Gray says. "Now
I give you something to walk on. But you still have to learn to
read and write because my father wants to hear from you how you
like them. Ye hear?"

"Yass, Siree! Yass . . .ss, Sir . . rr . . ee!" the youth promises, and
then turns to show Joseph his new finery.

Engrossed with the footwear such as he has never seen or held
in his hands before, Joseph puts the box containing Terry on the
floor beside him when Jocko insists his friend try on the boots.
Young Reales becomes so enrapt with his unique sartorial experience that he is unaware that his little pet has poked its nose out
from under the cover of its box and started out on an exploring
mission.

Some of the men still roast pieces of meat and corn over the
hot coals of the fire while others carry out little personal chores,
repairing clothing or cleaning weapons. A few play at cards and
some at gambling games with pay-money they have not yet received.

Wright cleans his gun near the wall. Abbott sews his deerskin
above their heads in the hayloft.

And Joseph's furry pet runs up near any man who is eating and
waits for a morsel to be thrown his way. It then dashes back into
its box behind Joseph and Jocko to devour the scrap. Suddenly it
darts toward the far wall and across Wright's sight.

"Damned varmit!" yells the irascible Wright, throwing a stone
that barely misses the little animal.

Immediately all eyes focus on the scene. Joseph, fearing for his
escaped pet, shouts, "Don't! Don't! Please don't! He won't hurt
nothin'!"

But the angry private responds by picking up and hurling
another stone at the uncomprehending little beast.

The boy finally struggles out of the single boot he had been
trying on but not before Jocko, bare-footed, races toward Wright
who, in stature, is not much taller than the diminutive young
Graves himself.

When his second stone misses its mark, Wright grabs the ramrod
and draws back his arm to throw it at the puzzled ground squirrel.
The animal now sits up on its haunches, wondering what strange
action this fool being, ranting before him, will perform next. It
cocks its head questioningly to the side. A perfect target!

Shouting, "Stop! Stop it! He ain't gonna hurt'cha!", Jocko throws Wright's arm up over the man's head, ruining his throw and sending the amazed private back on his heels and tumbling him down on the floor, the ramrod still clutched in his hand. Losing his balance in the impact, Jocko staggers backward.

Swift As the Cobra's Tongue

Enraged by what he considers to be an attack upon him by a black, the violent, quick-tempered court martialed soldier, believes that Jocko, a youngster, and a Negro at that, has not only bested him and made him out to be a fool in the eyes of the battery, but has humbled and humiliated him as well.

Furiously he raises the ramrod over his head and with renewed madness in his greenish blue eyes, exclaims, "Goddamed you, Boy! I'll teach you not to. . . ."

All those whose attention has been drawn to the scene, rush toward Wright and Jocko, who, too, has stumbled and fallen to the floor. But none of them, including Gray and Levy in the forefront, are anywhere near close enough to prevent the maniacal private from falling down upon the youth prone on the ground.

Then, like a plunging hawk from over their heads, a long, spear-like human figure drops down upon Wright. With a deafening thud the two bodies crash to the earthen floor.

From the overhead loft, Andy Abbott had watched, then acted. In the nick of time he had plummeted down to save Jocko and put an end to the white man's idiotic tantrum. Then the Indian scout seizes the ramrod, tearing it out of Wright's hand as the stunned private sits up in a dazed stupor, not knowing what hit him. Holding his aching head and with his glazed eyes vacantly staring off into space, the subdued soldier is motionless as Abbott hurls the rod far against the barn wall.

Andy Abbott looks at the flabbergasted Wright sitting almost semiconsciously at his feet, and, assured that the ramrod-wielder has completely quieted down, returns slowly to the loft without ever uttering a word.

Meanwhile, the men, almost as dazed by Abbott's swift action as is Wright, crowd around Jocko and help him back on his feet.

Joseph, whose one thought was the rescue of his pet, catches the little animal and returns him safely to its box. The frightened boy wastes no time in hurrying Terry back to the peaceful quiet of their cider mill quarters.

Gray, Big Tom, Monahan and Levy, making certain Jocko is all right, ignore the dazed Wright. Slowly they walk with the shaking youngster back to their places beside the fire, but not until Monahan, aching for an excuse to go on where Abbott left off, is restrained by Levy.

In describing the scene in a letter to his brother, Sergeant Benson Kidd will write that he had never seen a human move so speedily as did Sergeant Abbott. It was as "swift as the spitting of a cobra's tongue" the sergeant will say.

Again, as with all violent outbreaks, suddenly there is silence. The fury of a moment subsides almost as quickly as it explodes.

Tom places his good arm around his son's shoulders and hands him his boots. Jocko, whose patience with Wright had reached the breaking point, has cooled the anger that flashed from his eyes at the antagonistic soldier. It was the same frustrated, fiery anger that had once flashed from Ben's eyes at Jeffery Gartleck.

But now Jocko's eyes lift toward the hayloft at Abbott clamly resuming his stitching.

The Indian scout intuitively senses the youth's gaze attempting to catch his. Abbott, his features as immobile as a statue, turns his glance briefly toward Jocko's thank-you nod. The brown man's head slowly, almost imperceptibly, moves up and down in taciturn acknowledgement.

Getting up off the ground, Wright grumbles that he had no intention of hitting the animal nor of injuring the boy. Very loudly he insists that he was only trying to scare "the varmint" and make it run away. And, making sure that all hear him, he exclaims that he only intended to frighten the Graves boy.

Wright says no more when Monahan loudly proclaims that, "Whut thees baht'rey needs most 'tis a little hangin' or a noice fi'rin' line aht sunrise."

No one of the company believes Wright's protestations, but since no one has been hurt, Gray and Levy—both of whom along with Monahan, had pounced to Abbott's side fearing a fight was in the making—decide to keep the unpopular Wright as segregated from the rest of the battery as possible. Monahan and Wright definitely must be separated.

Gray orders that the obnoxious private be given only privy duties and isolation chores until further notice.

The General Has A Plan

The tensions throughout the army's jittery bivouac areas are severe enough without the need for interior squabblings. All regiments are under orders to be ready for action on short notice and all troops are on constant alert.

Ever since the army arrived on the Delaware's west bank, company commanders have been under orders to be ready for the King's men at all times. The fear of a surprise enemy crossing hovers over the army like Dionysius' sword.

Colonel Daniel Hitchcock, who had once objected to his transfer to the Bluff Rock owing to his dislike for rattlesnakes, tonight confidentially asked Gray and Levy to withdraw their requests for leaves.

Quartered with the old couple, whose burned out barn and deserted cider mill some of the regiment are using, Hitchcok, on orders invited Gray and Levy to his upstairs room in the 40-year old Bucks County fieldstone dwelling.

The two artillery officers early in the week had declined an invitation to stay in the spacious home, choosing instead, like Craig, to be with their men. But after the trying evening in the barn the warmth and quiet of the farmhouse, plus a drink of the colonel's wine were a pleasant relief for John and Asher late tonight.

When, in confidence, Hitchcock informs them that The General has a plan "to bring the army and the country out of the 'slough of despond' and that every man's services will be needed to execute it," both Gray and Levy unhesitatingly withdraw their requests for leave.

The colonel points out that neither he nor any of the regimental or brigade commanders knows what is afoot, and that the Council of War will not make any announcement until the plan is put into operation.

Hitchcock reluctantly admits that the high command of the army is seriously concerned, far more so than appears on the surface. He smiles weakly as he tells the two younger officers that everything could fall apart any day. He adds with a sickly half-smile that he wishes he knew which will bear down on the American army first, Howe or the first of January—the day that thousands more enlistment terms expire.

Back in the barn by the fire after most of the men are asleep, Gray writes in his diary. In doing so he finds a closeness to Elaine that gives him comfort and peace of mind.

In the night's entry, the Lieutenant contrasts the Commander's "wearied appearance these days" with the vibrant way he looked back on the Bluff Rock. One top-ranking officer, Gray writes, says that The General seems very tired and that, "He is always grave and thoughtful. He appears pensive and solemn in the extreme."[6]

After explaining the three positions of the army in his diary, the officer adds that Colonel Hitchcock is leaving the post above McKonkey's tomorrow to bring 900 of his Rhode Island Continentals down under Cadwalader's command at Bristol to help reinforce the American right wing. This, Gray notes, will give Cadwalader 2,000 troops to block a possible Hessian crossing in that sector, 18 miles from Philadelphia. And so he writes:

"It is no wonder that I hear from my sister in Philadelphia how frightened are the people of the capital. At least they will find no military stores there, for I am sure that all supplies have been transferred.

"Marion writes me that The General has asked Mr. Robert Morris to raise cash to pay the soldiers so that the army will not dissolve, and that Morris is assuring The General of fifty thousand dollars on his own credit. But more than that, it is said that, through his help, soldiers' relief associations are now being organized, and that the gentleman is raising three million food rations for the men."[7]

Before The Blue Petticoat Scarf Lieutenant finally affixes his "1, 2, 3" at the close of his entry, he re-examines some of the items he has recorded. He attempts to analyze the whole situation in an effort to discover what now will really happen to the American army.

The challenging thought lifts him out of the drowsy stupor into which Hitchcock's wine had dropped him and which very nearly dropped Asher's lids before the second lieutenant reached his straw bed.

Gray's thoughts first center on the Congress and its move to Baltimore. Was their move out of the city premature? Especially since it is now known that a British order, signed by Howe and brought to the American side by a patriot spy, reads:

"Headquarters, December 14, 1776 (Trenton). The Campaign having closed with the Pursuit of the Enemies Army near ninety miles by Lieut. Gen. Cornwallis' Corps, much to the honor of his Lordship and the Officers and Soldiers under his command, the Approach of winter putting a Stop to any further Progress, the Troops will immediately march into Quarters and hold themselves in readiness to assemble on the shortest notice."[8]

Surely this means Howe is calling off the "Fox" hunt until spring.

If that is the case, Gray thinks, Philadelphia is safe for a while, and this makes it more than likely The General has "something in mind". . . But why is Hitchcock reinforcing Cadwalader below Trenton? . . . And this northern sector of the arc, headed by Greene? It already includes General Stephen's Virginia Continentals, General Mercer's forces of Connecticut, Maryland and Massachusetts men— Continentals and militia—General Stirling's two Virginia Continentals, Haslet's Delawares and a regiment of Pennsylvania riflemen. . ."

Tomorrow they will be reinforced with the remainder of General Lee's army, now under General Sullivan[9] who has already reached the cantonment after crossing at Coryell's ferry. However, the long expected troops from Westchester are said to be in very bad shape. . .

But Roche de Fermoy's German regiment and one of Pennsylvanians will in turn be reinforcing Sullivan's men. Sullivan's present corps comprises General St. Clair's brigade, Colonel Glover's Marbleheaders and Colonel Sargent's New Hampshire, Connecticut and New York contingents. . . Here indeed are concentrated enough troops to at least snap at the heels of the British machine.

. . . Hitchcock may or may not know more than he told us, Gray thinks, but from the looks of the arc line with its southern, central and northern divisions of the army, whatever is going to take place will mostly involve General Greene's large division here around McKonkey's Ferry. For here is where the strength is surely concentrated. . . Then, too, Greene needs to do something to answer his critics.

. . . Also there are some encouraging bits of news. One is that Tom Paine's *Crisis* is going through the Philadelphia presses today. . . And the same courier from the capital city brought word that Benjamin Franklin is about now arriving in France on the 16-gun sloop, *Reprisal*, under command of Captain Wickes of Maryland. Gray and other Philadelphians believe that if anyone can get the French to support the American cause, Ben Franklin is the one to do it. . .

. . . Then there is a story going around that The General has assigned some engineers to work with Morris County militiamen in preparing a large bivouac area outside of Morristown for winter quarters. If so, what is the army doing down here as long as Howe has hibernated unless The General is planning something very big indeed?. . .

Into Gray's mind now drift thoughts of Elaine as he pokes the fire, thus taking him back to the hearthside in their bedroom on the east end of the Baummeister house eighty miles away. But Pennsylvania's cold night air drops down through the large gaping hole in the burned out barn roof. Through the aperture a cloud covered moon casts a yellowish glow into the spacious stables.

The tired officer deeply yearning for the distant object of his affections, conjures up her face and figure in the embers of the campfire.

Now, for brief seconds that traverse days of memories, he and Elaine are together strolling along the ledge path under the Bluff Rock, then on the shore road beside the river and finally they stand embraced before Abbott's cottage on Oratam's castle grounds. . .

His reveries break when his mind suddenly shifts to his fears, allowing his imaginations to take over. He tries but cannot erase from his mind the horrendous reports he has heard of pillaging, rapine and murder in the wake of the armies.

His own inserted diary accounts of the enemy's depredations— reported and sometimes exaggerated stories of the violence, vengeance and retaliations—come back to mind, fresh from his recent entries. They cause him to abruptly stir the fire angrily, then turn away.

One letter in a copy of the *Pennsylvania Evening Post* which he had saved, now worries him. He had also read similar reports, one in the *Pennsylvania Journal and Weekly Advertiser*, but the *Post's* account he withdrew from his coat and read again:

"Since I wrote you this morning, I have had an opportunity of hearing of the particulars of the horrid depredations committed by that part of the British army, which was stationed at and near Pennytown, under the command of Lord Cornwallis.

"Besides the sixteen young women who had fled to the woods to avoid their brutality and were there seized and carried off, one man had the cruel mortification to have his wife and only daughter (a child of ten years of age) ravished; this he himself, almost choked with grief, uttered in lamentations to his friend, who told me of it, and also informed me that another girl of thirteen years of age was taken from her father's house, carried to a barn about a mile, there ravished, and afterwards made use of by five more of

these brutes. . . but wanton mischief was seen in every part of the country; everything portable they plunder and carry off, neither age nor sex, Whig or Tory, is spared.

"Indiscriminate ruin attends every person they meet with, infants, children, old men and women, are left in their shirts without a blanket to cover them. . . furniture of every kind destroyed or burnt, windows and doors broke to pieces; in short the houses left unhabitable, and the people left without provisions.

"For such is war!"

"They yesterday burnt the elegant house of Daniel Cox, Esq. at Trenton ferry, who has been their constant advocate and supporter of Toryism in that part of the country.

"Another instance of their brutality happened near Woodbridge; one of the most respectable gentlemen in that part of the country was alarmed by the cries and shrieks of a most lovely daughter; he found an officer, a British officer, in the act of ravishing her and he instantly put him to death. Two other officers rushed in with fuses, and fired two balls into the father, who is now languishing under his wounds . . ."[10]

Though his mind is troubled and concerned for his wife and the people left behind, Gray is comforted by recalling Abbott's report and Elaine's letter. To further allay his fears he reminds himself that Howe and Cornwallis have issued orders restricting wanton violence and pillaging. Some American officers have seen those directives.

Most comforting to Gray, however, are his personal experiences with army headquarters' use of atrocity stories, true, imagined or concocted. They serve a valuable purpose in arousing public anger. And public anger always helps to light the fires of hatred for the enemy. Since he sees no author mentioned in the news reports, and since the patriot papers' editors can write what they wish, there is, he believes, good reason to expect exaggerations. It is a poorly kept secret that the enemy does the same, attributing similar nefarious acts to the American army. Consequently, it is difficult to determine which side is the more deceptive. Nevertheless, Gray is convinced there is guilt of varying degrees on both sides.

The American army, The Lieutenant reminds himself, is not without its predaceous "animals." Court martials are not the only testimony to that! Besides, war gives man unrestricted license and issues rewards for death, maiming and destruction. Thus, to "maniacs" and "animals" war is an invitatin to make unlicensed use of one's aberrations.

So Gray consoles himself with the assurance that, while much may be true, much also may be exaggerated. There is little anyone can do to control the "maniac" and the "animal" in time of war. No military *"gentleman's* code," beyond which the supposedly *civilized* soldier, carrying his principles of battlefield conduct is not allowed to go, will stop the aberrational mentality. Thus the military prefers to look the other way when the bloodthirstiest of all creatures, the aberrant being, runs amuck and on *its* own.

"For such is war!" they will say. "For such is war!"

Somewhat relieved from his fears by considering all factors, Gray turns back to his diary. He writes now directly to Elaine, recounting the story of Jocko's boots and then gives some excerpts form Marion's letter. He states:

"One pair of shoes cost 600 dollars in Philadelphia, Marion wrote. So Jocko really wears a gold mine on his feet. And the way he pranced on them tonight you would think so.

"The prices in the city go up constantly, Marion says. The British sympathizers who flood the country with counterfeits are said to be the fault in part. One month of a soldier's pay will hardly buy the poor fellow a dinner in the city."[1][1]

The Owl Made No Mistake

In closing his entries, Gray writes as though it were a direct letter to Elaine: *"I must add this little note, Ellie, for I know that you do enjoy your superstitions. I had told Jocko your old wives tale that an owl lighting on a house chimney foretells the arrival of a newborn child.*

"Since leaving Fort Lee, he has sighted 12 owls predicting as many population increases (on your say-so). In one house where he had seen your owl's sign in the distance and coming up to the place, stopped to water his horses, he found the farmhouse occupied by only an 88-year old man and his 85-year old wife.

"My good young friend would not concede that you could possibly be in error. He was certain though, that the owl was, or that the bird had mixed his chimneys up until the old man tried to give 'Mister Oracle' one of his newly born hound pups from the barn. Jocko blames me for not telling him that animals and humans are all the same to an owl.

"But, much to Jocko's confusion, Mike Monahan, whose Irish forebears think not the same as yours, tells our friend that he has been misled, and that an owl on a chimney is a sure sign that death is visiting in the vicintiy. Now he does not know which omen to believe, fearing that if Monahan is right, we are all in danger.

"I think I shall tell him that in Ireland, Monahan's owls have their own ways for predicting which direction things are going, but that here all American owls are bewitched by you into forecasting happy events.

"Since I am quite sure, from his little sly remarks, that he saw an owl on Papa Pete's chimney somewhere in the past, I intend to tell him soon that he's right. There was.

"This I know will relieve the 'Sturm und Drang' from his mind. . . He is very eager to know what my numerals mean at the end of these diary entries. I have the feeling that somehow someway he is going to find out. So, until then, they are still known only to us, Abbott and Andrea.

"Regardless, sleep is now overtaking me. I must to 'hay'. . .

1, 2, 3, or as first we saw it, ζ *"*

In Desperate Need Of An Amazing Miracle

A few miles outside of Newtown in his upper bedroom quarters of the comfortable well preserved, sentinel-surrounded Bucks County home of William Keith on Knowles Creek, the American army Leader is also awake. He, too, is writing and deep in thought. Only the crackling of the logs on the hearth and the steps of guards outside the door disturb the quiet of The General's room. Out from his window, over the darkness of the night, two miles east, most of his ragged army sleeps at Beaumont,[12] overlooking McKonkey's Ferry.

For hours he has poured over his maps and papers contemplating the proposal he will bring before his Council of War. He looks for flaws in the plan that calls for a sudden powerful blow at Trenton, the cutting off of van Donop's forces at Mount Holly from the British string, the turn-about-face and a crushing blow upon Grant in Princeton. And then will come the climax, a swift march upon New Brunswick, the seizure of a £70,000 British pay roll known to be cached there and finally the withdrawal of the army to Morristown.

It will be carried out in defiance of the winter's treacherous weather. All to be done in sweeping surprise attacks executed with swiftness upon a Christmas-celebrating army directly under the closed jaws beneath the enemy's snoring nostrils.

And all three divisions are to act in concert. That will be hard to achieve since the army's communication system is poor. Now could be used the Long Island farmers and their plow horses which were offered as army messenegers in the Battle of Long Island.

Over and over again he ponders the pros and cons of the plan—his 5,000-man army against the powerful 10,000 troops in the enemy machine, but all so strung out on the opposite side of the river that any opponent would be tempted to snip at it piecemeal.

The American General knows that each passing day reduces his chances of holding his disintegrating army together. For each day sees it more depleted by "sickness and other causes."[13]

The long campaign has left the army with too many raw recruits and a force, half of which comprises weak, poorly trained, home-hungering militiamen. The American Commander describes them in these words:

"Most of them clad like scarecrows in worn and ragged garments, shod like tramps, if shod at all. . . many of 'em being entirely naked, and most so thinly clad as to be unfit for service."[14]

Congress's fears had increased daily in direct proportion to the army's decreasing hopes as Howe pushed toward the Delaware. The representatives had regularly prodded The General for assurance of their safety in the capital city.

Then, when he told them that he could not see any means of preventing the enemy from falling down upon them and upon Philadelphia,[15] they became annoyed and angry but far more realistic about the importance of a strong military force and far less philosophically oratorical.

Right alone no longer seemed to provide them might and security. And mottoes, threats and ringing phrases, hurled at the Empire and the King, were not evidently sufficient in stopping the advancing power of the King's men.

The army they had tended to neglect, whose hands they had virtually weakened and tied, and whose strength and staves they had sapped with restrictions and inadequacies, was suddenly their only hope. And now they ran to get behind it.

After December 13, The General became the lawmakers' scapegoat, and there was no Charles Lee to supplant him. There was nothing to do but blame him, yet take his advice. And his advice, which he issued to them through Generals Mifflin and Putnam, was to get out of Philadelphia and move to Baltimore. And they did. For before, on, and immediately after Friday, the thirteenth, the American Commander saw little hope of staging a successful about-face. He could see then that there would be no way of stopping Cornwallis and Howe once they crossed the river.

Now, as he gambles everything on hope for an amazing miracle, one of his main problems is the uncertain, ever-wavering sentiment of the Jerseyans. His secret operation could be quickly defeated by their leaks and Tory informers.

Unable to put themselves in the perilous position confronting the Jersey inhabitants, the rebel high command has become irritated by the thousands of Jerseyans who have signed Howe's oath. The General himself has felt so strongly that he angrily writes of them:

"The conduct of the Jerseys has been most Infamous. Instead of turning out to defend the country and affording aid to our army, they are making their submission as fast as they can."[16]

Eventually it will be realized that most of the oath-takers do so out of fear for their lives and property. Most pay no attention to the commitments they swear to uphold once the enemy is out of their sight.

However, a number are peace-hungry renouncers. They are the ones, who along with the Tories, the Continental commanders most fear and whom Thomas Paine now strikes at with his pen in the *Crisis* which is soon to inflame the country's patriots.

Among the wealthy and respected former adherents to The Cause who fall into the turncoat category and rankle the true patriots, are the brothers, John, Andrew and William Allen of Philadelphia. John was a member of the Committee On Observation. Andrew was a member of Congress and William was a lieutenant colonel in the 2nd Pennsylvania Regiment.

Then, in addition, there is Joseph Galloway. A talented man, he was a representative in the First Continental Congress. Another, who has become more discouraged than disloyal, is John Dickinson, an elected delegate to the Congress from Delaware.[17]

Though The General bemoans the intimidated oath-taking renouncers, their effect is not as damaging to the morale as is the abandonment of The Cause by some of the country's former, staunch, outspoken pillars of resistance. Counteracting such setbacks is difficult. However, occasionally cheery pieces of news brighten the horizon such as this report on some of those who signed General Howe's oath:

> "We are informed, from good authority, that many of the inhabitants of Monmouth county in New Jersey, who received written protection are *now* determined to return them to his Britannic Majesty's Commissioners in cartridges."[18]

Weighing all the problems that beset his army and which he must now consider in arriving at the most important decision of the campaign, and certainly of the war to date, the rebel Commander visualizes the tragic effects that will come of failure. The lives of so many of his devoted Continentals, those who have stood loyally by his side through two long and tiring years, would be sacrificed for nothing. For in failure nothing will be gained, but all will be lost. What is to be gained then by not gambling?

As it is the country teeters on the edge of its precipice. The newborn eaglet is only a river's breadth away from the British Lion's crushing jaws. When they close on the infant all will be lost anyway.

Philadelphia, though Marion and Miriam have not said so to Gray and Levy, knowing how it would upset them, is dangerously close to the breaking point. Panic is in every patriot's eyes if not yet in his feet. The flight of the Congress saw to that!

On the desk before the American Chief is a report on the capital city's inhabitants which he will send on to the Congress in Baltimore. It reads:

> "Numbers of families loading wagons with their furniture & c., taking them out of town... Great numbers of people moving... All shops ordered to be shut... Our people in confusion, of all ranks, sending their goods out of town... (The city)... amazingly depopulated."[19]

The Virginian gets up, pokes the fire slightly and stares into the glowing embers. A new rebirth of hope must be caught and held whatever the cost. And so for ten days The General has done little else but think about and plan the stroke that *must* be taken.

And now one thing has changed the outlook and improved the prospects. General Howe has arbitrarily decided to end the 1776 campaign and take himself back to New York. This is a most encouraging factor.

He places his forearm on the mantel shelf above the decorative blue tiles over the hearth. What day, what hour could possibly be more propitious than a week from this very day?

His head drops, as though in prayer upon his arms, the hands of which now clasp upon the mantel. It must not be on Christ's Day. This could not be . . . This must not be! . . . The 26th? Today, a week! . . Revelry and grog will have most of them in their cups. . . The 26th—a proper and fitting day "for't"! . . .

. . . Certainly the Hessians who hold Trenton will make the most of Christmas this year . . . They will have much to celebrate on the eve before. . . It is their night of merrymaking and one to which they all look forward. . . And most will extend their festive hours into Christmas Day. Few will even be awake for battle on the 26th. . .

. . . Ah, but how great the risk! 'Tis indeed a dangerous gamble. If it goes 'twill be all or nothing. That is certain!

Once having crossed his army under the Juggernaut's snoring nostrils, no retreat will be possible. 'Twill be a desperate venture! Tomorrow he must think more on't. Perhaps tomorrow he will hear from Honeyman the lay of things. But now to prayers and bed.

Trent's Town: Village On the River's Convex Nose

It is a good ten miles into the edge of Trent's Town, or Trenton, from McKonkey's Ferry and about eleven from Beaumont's along the best roads by the river. Located almost at the convex nose of the waterway and likewise at the convex arc of the American defense line protecting Philadelphia, the little Trenton village, boasting about 100 homes, is located at the highest most navigable point along the river.

The village was first settled by Mahlon Stacy who sold Colonel William Trent 800 acres of its farmland in 1714.[20] By donating some of his land to the Hunterdon County government, he induced the officials to make it their county seat. And thereafter the village became known as Trent's Town.

It has no natural defenses other than the Delaware River and Assunpink Creek which borders the village on the south and empties into the Delaware.

The friendly villagers have never had to think in terms of

defenses. They have had no fears of enemy attacks. The river on their western border is seldom thought of as a natural military barrier. The creek, in their minds, is not a watery moat protecting them from an enemy attack from the south.

The river gives them easy access to the city. It links them with the roads west and south. It, as well as the Assunpink Creek, provides them with a main source of food and contributes to their livelihood. And, at the same time, the lower Delaware River gives them access to all of the country beyond. It provides them communication with the south and a passageway to Europe.

The town of Trenton has two almost parallel main streets running north to south in a converging "V" shape. The two roads come together at the northern end of town where the "V", or wedge's apex, meets the main highways coming from the north.

The one main road on the west side of town, nearest the river is King Street. The other, to its east, is Queen. East of Queen, also running parallel with it, is an old back trail that extends from the Orchard at the southernmost part of town on the banks of the Assunpink Creek, north toward the convergence point of King and Queen.

All three of these north-south village "avenues" lead into the main highway coming from Princeton to the northeast, and the road from Penny Town, or Pennington, to the northwest.

At the southern end of Queen is the bridge across the Assunpink that continues Queen Street into Bordentown along the Bordentown Road. Four cross streets, running west to east from the river road, bisect parts of King and Queen Streets in the heart of the village.

They are, beginning at the southern end: Front Street, nearest the river; Second Street which runs through the back trail road and the orchard; Third Street which runs from King to the trail road; and Fourth Street which only runs from Queen into the trail road where it continues as a path into the forest.

When the American army withdrew across the river into Pennsylvania and the Hessian troops took over the village, many inhabitants and shopkeepers fled the town, frightened by the stories of depredations allegedly committed by the invaders. However, many refused to be intimidated.

Those who stayed went about their business as the Hessian troops moved in to take over old militia barracks, houses, shops and warehouses for their quarters. They confiscated most all foodstuffs within sight.

Residents, who at first feared the burning of their village, gathered in excited groups before the court house and its gaol, at the inn and taverns, within the church and in the shops as the enemy columns marched in upon them.

Those who had relatives in the outlying farms hurriedly abandoned their homes and sought refuge with kith and kin. Some crossed the river with the rebel army, taking what few possessions and valuables they could quickly scoop up. Most of these sought lodging with friends and relatives in Pennsylvania.

Among those American patriots who refuse to budge from their village homes is Stacy Potts, the tanner. His large, comfortable home stands on the west side of King Street[21] at the western foot of Third. It is his home that the commander of the Hessian garrison in Trenton has chosen for his headquarters.

Respectfully observing military protocol and exercising courtesy with and consideration of the inhabitants in his commandeering, Colonel Johann Gottlieb Rall has made himself a "guest" in the Stacy Potts' household.

The Hessian colonel looks with disdain upon the rebel troops. He has not the slightest fear of an attack. On the contrary, he would welcome one in order to teach "the rebel farmers" a lesson.

That he and Colonel Carl von Donop at Mount Holly are in command of the most forward spearhead of the British chain, an honor position, feeds the Hessians' ego. Rall's accomplishments during the campaign have earned him and his troops the prestige position which General Howe has assigned to them.

Rall's reputation had preceded him to Trenton. His exploits have been subjects of conversation in and out of both armies. The daring, fearless deeds of Rall's Hessian regiments, with the nail-chewing, red faced colonel always in the lead of his troops, have given Rall and his men a colorful reputation cloaked under an aura of invincibility.

It was Rall who had led the attack upon the Americans at Chatterton Hill in the Battle of the White Plains. And it was Rall who led his men up the perilous, deathly north face of Mount Washington to drive the Fort Washington defenders back behind their inner defenses. It was Rall who had summoned the fort's garrison to surrender just 33 days ago. And not more than a fortnight ago he came down on the post at Amboy only to find that the astute General Hugh Mercer had evacuated the garrison in time.

So the patriots in Trenton were not overjoyed when they

learned that it was the illustrious Rall and his regiments that were moving into town. Meanwhile Colonel von Donop pushed his forces six miles beyond Trenton to take over control of Borden-town and Mount Holly with picket posts extending as far south as Burlington.

It is a long way back to the British army's main supply bases and headquarters in Princeton and New Brunswick for both Rall and von Donop. So since von Donop is the superior officer in charge of the Hessian contingent which comprises about 3,000 men including grenadiers, jagers and the 42nd Highlanders,[22] half of which are under Rall, he is less flippant about "rebel farmers" and more cautious about defenses.

In command of all the British forces in New Jersey is the boastful General James Grant at Princeton. Grant and Rall share the same low opinion of the American army. To Rall's suggestion that more troops could keep the communications open, Grant told the messenger to "Tell the Colonel he is safe; I will undertake to keep the peace in New Jersey with a corporal's guard."[23]

Before the war, Lord Stirling, it will be remembered, overheard Grant boast to Parliament that if given 5,000 troops he could march triumphantly through all the colonies in short time. So Rall's disdain for his enemy's competence is buoyed by the mutually-shared spirit of the British army's field commander himself, leaving only von Donop doing the worrying.

The state of near-chaos that has enveloped the Jerseys quickly spread along the banks of the Delaware when the enemy poured into Trenton and then down upon Bordentown six days ago. However the extreme tension has somewhat subsided, but fear and panic still hang heavily overhead, now compounded by the dissolution of the New Jersey Legislature and the flight of the Continental Congress. In addition, marauding bands of Hessians, redcoats, Tory renegades and American deserters have roamed wildly over the countryside.

Their early ravaging and plundering so infuriated the outlying inhabitants and the soldiers of the Continental Army that retaliations came down upon the depredators with a vengeance. Bitter clashes of picket guards, strike-and-run attacks upon marching Hessian and British units, and the ambushing of strolling redcoats and Hessians by angry farmers and aroused Whigs has encouraged the patriots and greatly restricted the roving, foraging bands.

In Trenton, Rall has kept his troops under tight control. Some of their search parties, seeking foodstuffs in preparation for the forthcoming Christmas celebration, have been overlooked, but Rall does not overlook any infractions of his orders against villainy.

For this considerate attitude the colonel has won much admiration and respect from the Trenton inhabitants. One of those impressed by the Hessian commander's gentlemanly conduct and regard for the villagers under his control, is the American patriot, Abraham Hunt, who, like Stacy Potts, refused to budge when the enemy moved in.

Hunt, the town's principal merchant and its postmaster, lives in a large more pretentious home than Potts, just a block south at the corner of King and Second Streets.[24] He is a prudent man who knows when to be neutral.

All Is Not Calm Within the Juggernaut's Veins

Abraham Hunt's home is noted for its hospitality. His doors are always open. It is not unusual to find supper guests at the Hunt House any day of the week, any time of the year and especially around the Christmas season.

So, for Christmas Day, with a number of the town's people having deserted the occupied village, Hunt extends an invitation to Johann Gottlieb von Rall to be his dinner guest and the colonel accepts, despite his limited ability to speak, read or write English.

In his headquarters at the Potts' home tonight Rall and his adjutant, Lieutenant Jacob Piel, have been busy preparing new orders and regulations in an attempt to solve the growing animosities springing up between the English-speaking Highlanders, chasseurs, the light dragoons of the 16th British regiment and the non-English speaking Germans of Rall's three regiments, namely, "The Knyphausens," "Lossbergs," and "Ralls."

But also of greater concern to Piel than to Rall are the frequent rebel harassments of the outer guards. These minor annoyances require constant surveillance to prevent surprise enemy ambuscades. In these disturbances the English troops reluctantly assist, thus antagonizing the Hessians.

The increasing bitterness between the English and German soldiery stems from an incident at Princeton when a Lossberg officer was struck on the head with a punch bowl thrown by an English officer in an argument over military discipline.

Discord, once seeded, swiftly swept from the ranks of the officers into the lower echelons resulting in individual and group

encounters that have not helped a diminishing morale, already
weakened by long forced marches and no military action.

Piel brings to Rall the complaints of the troops which, in
addition to the friction between the two forces, includes: wretched
quarters in small, barren houses cleared out by the occupants; only
Madeira and no other wines and Madeira selling "at three shillings
and sixpence sterling a bottle,"[25] and all their "baggage is left in
New York."[26]

Rall, listening to his adjutant's reports, hears that one officer,
occupying a "fine house belonging to a merchant" and with rooms
to spare, found that all the servants remained behind to take care
of the premises. Then, when the officer bid one of the servants
bring him a candle, the servant replied, "If you wanted candles,
you should have brought them with you."[27]

The officer, Piel informs the half-smiling colonel, boxed the
servant on the ears for his sauciness and finally was "furnished
with *one* candle, but nothing else."

A courier's dispatch interrupts the session. Among the reports
Rall gets is word of the death of a close friend. It reads:

> "Captain Weitershausen of the grenadiers, was shot at Brunswick bridge
> by a rebel, who had concealed himself under the bridge. The Capt. had
> wrote by the last packet to his wife, desiring her to follow him to
> America."[28]

The same rider brought news that the rebels' General Lee has
been captured. But of most concern to Piel is that the enemy
across the river has all the boats at its command, and that all those
craft which the local Tories sank in an effort to hide them for use
in the British crossing, were discovered, raised and taken by the
rebels' secret agents. Those agents much later will be identified as
Joshua and John Mersereau.[29]

The Mersereaus are only a few of the American Chief's lately
organized ring of spies now wandering through the British encampments under the noses of Generals Leslie, Howard, Rall and
von Donop, in Princeton, Maidenhead, Trenton and Bordentown.
They are patriot horsemen disguised as farmers, merchants,
travelers and artisans, always professing to be strong Tories loyal to
the King. Some peddle tobacco since that product sells well in the
Hessian cantonments.

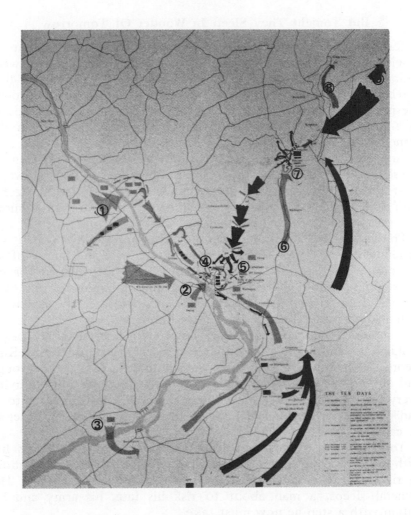

The Trenton-Princeton Battles . . . The above map and the two others of the Trenton and Princeton engagements are provided here through the courtesy of Dr. Kemble Widmer, adjunct professor, United States Military Academy at West Point. They are from his illustrated lecture, "The Ten Days That Changed the World." An authority on these battles, Dr. Widmer has carefully scaled these illustrations one inch to the mile. The author has over-layed the Widmer maps with numbers identified as follows:

(1) The first crossing site, December 25; (2) Where Ewing was scheduled to cross and did not, December 25; (3) Where Cadwalader was scheduled to cross and did not, December 25; (4) The First Battle Of Trenton, December 26; (5) The Second Battle Of Trenton, showing heavy black arrows coming down from upper right through Princeton indicating Cornwallis's army, January 2, 1777; (6) Nocturnal withdrawal of Continentals from Trenton to attack Princeton, night of January 2; (7) Battle of Princeton, January 3; (8) Americans withdraw to Pluckemin on way to Morristown after battle; (9) Cornwallis heads rapidly for Brunswick to protect his supplies and money chest.

But Tonight They Sleep In Wonder Of Tomorrow

Rall would be much more interested in Piel's report that 70 rebels came across yesterday and "carried off a family who went willingly, with three cows and some furniture,"[30] if he knew that a rebel spy had engineered the operation. Roving freely through the post selling tobacco, the secret agent had enabled the escape to take place before the hastily summoned pickets arrived on the scene.

Another one of those agents, known only by The General himself to be a loyal patriot, is John Honeyman of Griggstown in West Jersey. A weaver and a butcher, he recently secretly agreed with The General to pose as a traitor and enact the ignominious role of a staunch Tory.

Pretending that he was aiding the British army, Honeyman was denounced as a traitor. Then, convincing his wife and family of his defection, he fled to Trenton. Orders were then issued for his arrest on sight, but it is The General's especial command that "the rascal," John Honeyman, be brought in alive since the American Commander particularly desires to see him hang.

Monday Honeyman arrived in Trenton. He immediately began building a reputation as a butcher and a loyal supporter of King George III. During the past three days he has moved freely through and around the enemy-held village, quietly watching and observing everything that has taken place. Tomorrow he will steal out of town and gradually work himself back to the American lines in order to be captured and imprisoned.

Tonight John Honeyman sleeps, a man about to risk his life with every step he takes. Tonight Johann Rall sleeps, a man about to risk his life with every step he scoffs at taking. Tonight The General sleeps, a man about to risk his fate, his army and his nation with a step he now must take.

Tonight John Gray sleeps, wondering if there ever was an owl who perched of late on Baummeister's chimney. And if one did, what matter? How can sensible people put faith in such forebodings?

It is indeed the hour for decision along the arc of gloom.

34

Thursday, December 26. . .

"All Is Over"

Through the Bird's Eye

If General Howe could, like a great bird high over the river Delaware, have looked down upon the wintry scene below him over Bristol, over Trenton, Newtown, Beaumont and the ferry crossing up to Coryell's anytime during the past five days, he would likely leave "The Sultana" in New York and rush to warn General Grant at Princeton of what is happening. Cornwallis, getting ready to embark for England, would be behind him.

All three would speed reinforcements to Rall, order von Donop to withdraw from Mount Holly and Bordentown and cancel all Christmas celebrations. Then they would settle down and wait, this time to bring the ax down for a quick end to the American Rebellion. For Howe would see the concentration of a main body of rebels around Beaumont, another brigade up opposite Trenton, and a third massed around Bristol.

He would see them all hard at training and carrying out mysterious preparations, despite the bitter weather that has unexpectedly frozen the far distant upper Delaware. And all this would give Sir William and his command indisputable evidence that the last remnants of the rebel army are not hibernating until spring. In addition the rounding up and repairing of the river craft, especially the large Durham boats, under Colonel Glover and his

Marbleheaders who had come in with Sullivan as part of Lee's force, would certainly have given the King's men something to wonder about.

As seen from the low hanging, snow-laden clouds, the point of the Delaware's convex arc aims at Trenton. The village, from a military view, such as Rall has scoffed at taking, is isolated. Princeton's British post is about eleven miles northeast. Bordentown's Hessian post is about six miles south. So Trenton forms a sort of lonely spearhead into the convex nose of the Delaware along the river's lengthy dividing line between Jersey and Pennsylvania.

In the bird's-eye view, Trenton, at the western end of the narrow 40-mile waistline of New Jersey's midriff, resembles the State's belt buckle. For it lies in the State's center, marking the west end of the waistband, indented by the river's convex point that pushes wedge-like into Jersey's middle.

It is at Trenton that the river is divided into two parts, separated by the Trenton Falls. So the river's two divisions have become known as "above" and "below" the falls.

Below the falls the stream becomes wider, deeper and navigable but subject to treacherous currents. And it is below the Trenton Falls where lie the villages of Bordentown on the Jersey side and Bristol on the Pennsylvania bank, eight miles south. About 14 miles south of Bristol is Philadelphia.

For 25 years Robert Durham's[1] Durham-designed, Durham-built Durham sail, oars and pole-sweep boats have been the most popular transport vessels both above and below the falls. Besides people and animals they carry supplies and produce of all kinds including iron, flour, whiskey and corn. It is these Durham boats, along with other river craft, which Glover and his Marbleheaders helped to assemble during the past few days, though no one seemed to know why. But the busy preparations went on at McKonkey's, Trenton's and Bristol's west bank ferry terminals.

At each one of these three widely separated points along the 25-mile arc of defense, the tempo of the activities increased each day. Despite the bitter arctic weather that had set in, periodically depositing layers of snow and crusts of ice over the land, the troops drilled and worked. Freezing and grumbling, they carried out their orders.

However, none of the sectors was aware of what the other two were doing. Each assumed from past experience that it was strengthening its own defenses in preparation for an enemy attack that was sure to occur once the river froze over.

Though there was talk among the officers and men of a possible American counterblow, no one expected it would be anything more than a stepping up of the hit and run raids lately carried out against Howe's heels.

"Victory or Death"

The gathering of almost every floatable vessel on the west bank before the enemy reached the river's east shore two weeks ago was a mammoth task largely engineered by Captain Daniel Bray of Kingwood in Hunterdon County. Bray and his men performed a deed that would have done credit to Glover and his seamen. Now all week he has assisted the Marbleheaders, in the handling of the boats during the huge enterprise that began late yesterday and which is dramatically closing tonight.

So, from the ground view along the river, as observed by the troops participating in the three sectors, there seemed to be no synchronized plan of offense under way. But from the air the little pieces of the plan could have been seen falling into a curious operational pattern.

Though the seemingly disconnected activities began several days ago, it was not until Tuesday night, the 24th, that The General's council of War agreed upon all the ramifications of the highly secret attack-strategy and approved the plan that bears the password, "Victory or Death."

Originally The General planned a four-pronged attack on Trenton.[2] This was to have been immediately followed up with the surprise assault on Grant and Knyphausen. It was far from a simple operation. Its principal objectives were the same—to stagger the British army and acquire its £70,000 cash pay roll at Brunswick.

The southernmost prong was to have been under General Putnam at Philadelphia. Putnam was to have pushed a corps of Pennsylvania militia across the river and, supported by the Egg Harbor guards, was to run through von Donop's Mount Holly, Burlington and Bordentown posts. By successfully doing so Putnam would prevent von Donop from rushing to Rall's rescue in Trenton.

Acting as military governor of Philadelphia, Old Put begged off from the enterprise, contending he and his militia were needed in the defense of the city. But he agreed to lead his men across if weather and crossing conditions were perfect.

However, in view of his hesitation, if not reluctance, the fourth prong, forty miles south of Coryell's Ferry, was consequently eliminated from the operation.

This left the attack-plan relying solely upon a three-pronged drive with Trenton the initial primary target. But some aid was to be given by the river fleet and its marines.

Since General Horatio Gates was in Philadelphia, having left his winterizing Northern Department in command of subordinates at Albany in order to bring 500 of his troops to Jersey as The General had requested, the American Commander urged Gates to take over the third prong at Bristol and execute its crossing.

This force was to cross at Bristol and strike at Bordentown, diverting von Donop and keeping him busy while Trenton was under attack. Originally the fourth, or Philadelphia prong, and the Bristol prong were to have provided a united front in over-whelming von Donop. The changed plan placed this responsibility fully in the hands of the Bristol crossers.

However, Gates, still reeling from the news of the capture of his close friend, Charles Lee, who, like Gates, is a British-born professional soldier and a Virginia estate holder, declined The General's request on the grounds that he had important business to undertake with the Congress in Baltimore.

To those who know the 48-year old officer and especially to those who know of his warm friendship for Lee, a trip to Baltimore could only have political implications. And rumors do abound that Gates, with Lee out of the way, is an active contender for the post of Commander-in-Chief.

Holding many of each other's "Dear Friend" letters, castigating The General for alleged inefficiencies, Lee and Gates share similar uncomplimentary opinions of The General's ability to command the Continental Army.

The General had counted strongly on Gates' command of the Bristol prong in the attack strategy. The polite refusal, owing to Congressional "business," was accepted and the assignment was handed to Colonel Cadwalader.

The rebel Leader was aware that Cadwalader's Pennsylvania Associators would have responded more confidently to a general when he asked Gates to take over the operation's right flank. To solve this problem the Chief gave Cadwalader the rank of temporary brigadier general.

If the American Commander harbored any resentment for either Putnam's or Gates' disinclinations to assist in the Trenton attack plan, he did not show it. Both men had legitimate reasons to decline. In the case of Gates, The General knows of the friendship between the Northern commander and the Charleston hero. And he is not ignorant of Gates' opinion of him, an opinion which will someday draw the Northern Department commander into the infamous Conway Cabal effort to supplant the American Chief.

As he has with Reed and Lee, he accepts without malice Putnam's, Gates', or any of his officers' personal biases. No amount of hearsay, criticisms or malicious mouthings visibly affect him. Military competence of those around him is his primary concern and his sole criterion for the measurement of their worth to his army. It is this characteristic which will cause Thomas Jefferson to say of him that he never allowed hatred nor friends to bias his decisions.

So he settled on Cadwalader to command the right wing attack prong with about 2,000 troops. These comprise 1,000 Philadelphia Associators, 900 of Hitchcock's Rhode Island Continentals, a small Delaware militia company from Dover under Captain Thomas Rodney and two artillery batteries, each of which hauls a six-pounder.[3]

Looking northward, or upstream from Bristol, the second prong or central division in the three-pronged crossing maneuver, was assigned to Brigadier General James Ewing. This corps chiefly consists of Pennsylvania militiamen and some New Jersey troops, totaling 700 in all.

Its orders called for spearing across to the Blazing Star Ferry terminal site southwest of Trenton and blocking the bridge over the Assunpink Creek to prevent the Hessians from escaping southward toward von Donop. At the same time the main force was to drive into the village from the north and east in the massive encirclement operation.

The northernmost division, the left wing contingents—the uppermost or first prong— was designated the main body. McKonkey's Ferry site was selected as its crossing point. These were carefully picked troops, 2,400-strong, whose task was to march nine miles south to surprise the Hessian garrison and attack in concert with Cadwalader's and Ewing's forces.

Hope Rests Upon Six Legs

This first prong was the principal attack force. It comprised the brigades commanded by Generals Stirling, Mercer, Stephen, St.

Clair, Sargent, de Fermoy and Colonel Glover, who within the coming year will become a brigadier general. The 2,400-man division, with each of its seven above-mentioned commanders directing his own contingent, was split into two corps in the attack-plan. One was assigned to General Greene, the other to General Sullivan. In charge of the division's artillery—18 fieldpieces in all—was Colonel Henry Knox.[4]

The main body, or left wing of the expedition, was to hit Trenton from the north and northeast simultaneously with Ewing's 700 Trenton Ferry crossing troops coming up from the Blazing Star Ferry on Ferry Street southwest of town.

Meanwhile, Cadwalader and his 2,000 Bristol crossers were to drive through Bordentown at von Donop and his southernmost cantonments.

Then, after overcoming both Rall and von Donop, all three American divisions were to assemble in Trenton and reorganize before pushing on northward to surprise Grant at Princeton and after that Knyphausen at New Brunswick.

It was a brilliant stroke if it could be accomplished. But its successful execution rested on, among other things, how well its six dependent legs could stand up:

(1) the maintenance of the element of surprise;

(2) the information The General could acquire from his secret agents, particularly Honeyman in Trenton;

(3) the ability of his troops to stand up under the strain, the grueling march and the ordeal of battle against a powerful and efficient foe;

(4) the success of Glover's Marbleheaders and the Delaware river men in crossing all three divisions, miles apart from each other, at the proper hours;

(5) the weather; and

(6), as the Reverend Doctor Alexander MacWhorter put it, on divine guidance and the will of Providence.

Each man was to carry one blanket, cooked rations to last him three days, and each was issued forty rounds of ammunition. So provided and so equipped, the main, or left wing division, was to parade in the valley behind the hill at McKonkey's Ferry, but out of sight from the opposite shore, on the afternoon of December 25, Christmas Day,[5] and then move down into the boats.

First, the surprise element was guarded by the tightest of secrecy. Only the generals of the war council were aware of the plan, and no others would know of the crossing or the march until the hour it would take place.

Secondly, the necessary intelligence concerning the status of the Hessian garrison in Trenton was acquired in a unique, devious manner by Honeyman, the American Chief's own private spy. The General's especial small chest, which at one time was said to have contained as many as 1,800 gold guineas, allocated by Congress to pay his agents,[6] made it possible to enlist the services of such men as Honeyman.

The Jerseyman was a veteran of the French and Indian War and a member of Wolfe's bodyguard at Quebec. He had helped carry the mortally wounded commander off the field. Therefore, his interest in Trenton's, Princeton's and New Brunswick's garrisons, as a British veteran with a fine record of previous service made it easy for him to pose as a butcher and a horse trader. In this role he could tag along behind the Hessian pickets close along the Delaware and carelessly wander astray when it was time for him to be taken prisoner by the rebels.[7]

With the information the American Chief wanted in his head, Honeyman, leading a cow he had come across in a farmer's field, purposely walked into an American Ranger patrol. Taking their valuable spy proudly back to the American encampment after their prize had feigned an attempt to escape, the Rangers were congratulated by The General who demanded to speak privately with "the Tory rogue" to discover what he could before the man was tried and hanged.

The General's private one hour interview over, Honeyman was returned to his cell. But the spy had first divulged all details of the enemy's position to his Chief, whom he had first met in Philadelphia several years ago before the Congress selected its Continental Army leader.

Then someone forgot to lock the prisoner's cell door, and when a strange fire broke out near the log gaol during the night distracting the sentinel, Honeyman fled back to Rall. He then assured the Hessian commander there was nothing to fear from the rebels.

Until the war's end only the American General would know the true character and allegiance of John Honeyman. Only then, en route to Philadelphia, will the Continental Army Commander stop at the John Honeyman home, disclosing to the rebel spy's family, neighbors and friends, as well as the country at large, the invaluable secret agent services performed by the Griggstown man.

The Jersey weaver, butcher, British army veteran and horse trader will then suddenly become a hero instead of a traitor to his family, friends and the villagers. The significant part he played in saving The Cause through his espionage at Trenton in the crisis moments of December 1776 will then become nation-wide talk.

In The General's accounts of expenses which he will summarize for the Congress at the first of the year under the date, January 1, 1777, he will show an outlay of many thousands of pounds, reading:

"To Secret Service since the Army left Cambridge in April... while it lay at New York and during its retreat march through the Jerseys."[8]

1776's Sad, Solemn and Final Council of War

Armed with the information he needed, The General called the final Council of War for Christmas Eve.[9] It was one of many highly secret conferences held at General Stirling's headquarters in the old John Pidcock house.

Pidcock built the riverside home in 1702. It is now owned by the Robert Thompsons, their daughter, Elizabeth, and son-in-law, William Neely.

Both the Thompsons and Neelys moved out in order to give quarters to Stirling who shared the two-story one-room deep, stone homestead and its large so-called "Great Room" with several other officers.

The other tenants were Captains William Washington, a distant relative of The General's, and James Moore of the New York artillery who died yesterday morning in one of the bedrooms over the conference room, a victim of camp fever.

Also sharing quarters with Stirling and the two captains was the young, 18-year old Lieutenant James Monroe who is destined to become the fifth president of the United States.

The Christmas Eve conference was a solemn occasion. A young officer, dying in agony in the room above made it more so. The council was attended by Generals Greene, Sullivan, Mercer, Stirling, Roche de Fermoy, St. Clair and several colonels including John Glover. And so there the last details of the plan were ironed out and the complete strategy was finally adopted.[10]

Sitting behind Colonels Knox, Stark and Glover was the Reverend Doctor Alexander Mac Whorter, a Presbyterian minister from Newark.

The status of the soldiers, the preparation and operation of the transports, the condition of the troops, their inadequacies and low morale—brightened for many by the expiration of their enlistments in seven days—the maintenance of secrecy in carrying out the surprise attacks, were carefully considered.

All the council were impressed with the absolute necessity for success. It was clearly understood by each commander that failure, or any turn of the tide to the enemy's favor, was certain to end in disaster for the Americans with their backs against the river. In such an event, which was a recognized possibility, the end of the American Rebellion was almost a certainty.

The tenseness of the meeting was heightened for the American Chief by a communication from, and his reply to, Colonel Reed, stationed downriver under Cadwalader. And more than average strain was likewise weighing heavily upon Greene owing to his critics' recent attacks upon him over the loss of Fort Washington and Fort Lee. Of concern to all officers present were the absences of Generals Putnam and Gates.

Putnam explained his absence was due to his preoccupation with responsibilities as military governor of Philadelphia. Gates gave illness and business with the Congress in Baltimore as his excuses. Both men were in Philadelphia.

The question that could not be erased from any of the officers' minds was: Did the absence of two such reputable commanders from such a momentous conference imply that they questioned the advisability and seriously doubted the success of The General's plan?

Griffin's Good Intentions Jeopardize "The Plan"

Three days ago American intelligence agents intercepted a letter to a merchant in Philadelphia assuring the businessman that the British army was planning to be in Philadelphia, possibly between December 16 and 21.[11] This was reason enough to convince Putnam that defense, not offense, should be the army's mood.

He was certain of this when he heard that on Sunday, the 22nd, Flying Camp Colonel Griffin, in an action unauthorized by the American Commander and one which jeopardized his secret plans, crossed the river and raided the Hessian posts "betwixt Slab Town and the Black Horse."[12] Griffin had gathered a good force of Jersey militia on the Jersey side.

In the skirmish the Hessians retreated after some of their number were killed. But in the morning von Donop pursued the Flying Camp company with a force of 2,000 men and seven or eight fieldpieces, chasing the Americans back along the Mount Holly-Bordentown road to their boats and some into the deep brush on the Jersey side.

The act caused von Donop to alert all the lines and take extra precautionary measures, just the sort of thing the American command staff did not now want.

When, on Monday, the 23rd, the river showed signs of freezing over, but with only a thin layer of ice over which no one would dare walk, Old Put was sure defenses were of primary concern. So on Christmas Eve, when Colonel Reed, attached to Cadwalader's division at Bristol, rode to Philadelphia to urge Putnam to reinforce Griffin's Jersey command in the secret operation that Reed had just learned about from The General, the Indian fighter and Massachusetts-born, major general was wary.

Putnam contended that since Griffin was reportedly ill and that time was short and the militia in an "unprepared" state, a diversion was impractical.[13] In fact Putnam gave Reed the impression that he believed the entire operation was impractical.

It was on the day before this fruitless attempt to get Putnam's help that the now conscientious and penitent Joseph Reed wrote his Chief, ignorant of the plan that was under way. Reed, the former Charles Lee admirer who not so long ago had written Lee about a certain "indecisive" mind—a thing he would now like to forget wrote The General Sunday.

Evidence of the tight secrecy that surrounded the American Commander's Trenton plan is seen in Reed's Sunday, the 22nd, letter which the Thirteenth Regiment, Continental Infantry of Massachusetts Colonel sent from Bristol, urging the Chief to undertake "some enterprise." For Reed was not only a former confidant on The General's staff, he was also the army's adjutant general while simultaneously serving as the commander of the Thirteenth Regiment.[14]

Yet, as a part of Cadwalader's division, the former Charles Lee disciple indicates in his letter ignorance of the operation to take place in three days. And, curiously, he proposes a plan identical with that under way. Wrote Reed:

"We are all of opinion, my dear General, that something must be attempted to revive our expiring credit, give our cause some degree of reputation, and prevent a total depreciation of the Continental money, which is coming on very fast; that even a failure cannot be more fatal than to remain in our present situation; in short some enterprise must be undertaken in our present circumstances or we must give up the cause.

"In a little time the continental Army will be dissolved. The militia must be taken before their spirits and patience are exhausted; and the scattered, divided state of the enemy affords us a fair opportunity to trying what our men will do when called to an offensive attack."

Whether Reed had gotten word of "something under way," or whether he was clairvoyant is unknown, but he reveals one or the other in his question:

"Will it not be possible, my dear General, for your troops, or such part of them as can act with advantage, to make a diversion, or something more, at or about Trenton?"

Then, continuing with his uncannily perceptive advice, he wrote:

"The greater the alarm, the more likely the success will attend the attacks. If we could possess ourselves again of New Jersey, or any considerable part of it, the effects would be greater than if we had never left it."

Expressing hope that The General would consult his "own good judgment and spirit, and not let the goodness of your heart subject you to the influence of opinions from men in every respect your inferiors," Reed declared:

"I will not disguise my own sentiments, that our cause is desperate and hopeless if we do not take the opportunity of the collection of troops at present to strike some stroke. Our affairs are hastening fast to ruin if we do not retrieve them by some happy event. Delay with us is now equal to a total defeat. Be not deceived, my dear General, with small, flattering appearances; we must not suffer ourselves to be lulled into security and inaction because the enemy does not cross the river. It is but a reprieve; the execution is the more certain, for I am very clear that they can and will cross the river in spite of any opposition we can give them."[15]

On the following day, Monday, the 23rd, The General dispatched a prompt reply to Reed without so much as acknowleging the colonel's oracular military advice. Instead, attentive to protocol, he addressed his communication to: "Joseph Reed, or in his absence, to John Cadwalader, Esq., only, at Bristol." For the American Commander did not intend to have his letter run the risk of being intercepted by the enemy.

In his reply, The General stated:

"Christmas-day at night, one hour before day is the time fixed upon for our attempt on Trenton. For Heaven's sake keep this to yourself, as the discovery of it may prove fatal to us; our numbers, sorry am I to say, being less than I had any conception of: but necessity, dire necessity, will, nay must, justify an attempt.

"Prepare, and in concert with Griffin, attack as many of their posts as you possibly can with a prospect of success: the more we can attack at the same instant, the more confusion we shall spread and greater good will result from it. If I had not been fully convinced before of the enemy's designs, I have now ample testimony of their intentions to attack Phila-delphia, so soon as the ice will afford the means of conveyance. . .

"We could not ripen matters for our attack before the time mentioned in the first part of this letter: so much out of sorts and so much in want of everything are the troops under Sullivan, etc. Let me know by a careful express the plan you are to pursue. . . I am, dear Sir, Your obedient servant. . .

"P.S.—I have ordered our men to be provided with three days' provisions ready cooked, with which and their blankets they are to march; for if we are successful, which Heaven grant and the circumstances favor, we may push on. I shall direct every ferry and ford to be well guarded, and not a soul suffered to pass without an officer's going down with the permit. Do the same with you."[16]

The General's reply, if it was a reply to Reed's letter, now gave Cadwalader and Reed knowledge of the operation and their orders for participating in it. Only the army's war council had been aware of the plan by the 22nd. Now all division commanders were informed and, in addition, Colonel Reed.

The colonel, had he been omitted from The General's con-fidence, in view of his adjutancy would have been piqued by such an affront. Certainly Reed's letter to The General, whether subtle or not, seemed to indicate it.

Greene Answers His Critics

Regardless, it appears that either upon The General's or Cadwalader's instructions, Reed, on the same day, Monday, rode to Philadelphia to enlist the reluctant Putnam in the enterprise. When this failed, and a diversionary force of militiamen across the river at Philadelphia was no longer possible, a smaller diversionary strike had to be the council's decision. Consequently the final details of the three-pronged attack were ironed out and adopted Christmas Eve.

At the momentously grave conference session, Greene has tried to conceal the disturbance his critics have stirred up within his mind.

The dark clouds that hovered over the country just a month ago following the loss of the twin forts now sought someone upon whom to cast their shadows. So naturally, Greene, their former commander, has become the object of his countrymen's mounting anger.

The ire of his critics has increased proportionately as the losses suffered reach the ears of the populace. Most damaging are the Tory accounts and those appearing in New York's British-controlled press. In addition to these stories are the Tory-exaggerated tales of the Americans' wild, undisciplined flight—the rebel army, streaking through the Jerseys, heading for the Pennsylvania wilderness and rapidly disbanding in hopelessness.

Deeply hurt and sorely irritated by his critics, Greene angrily wrote Governor Cooke of his home State, Rhode Island. In reply to the charges made against him, he declared:

> "I am told some malicious reports propagated industriously about me respecting the loss of the baggage and stores at Fort Lee. They are as malicious as they are untrue. I can bring very good vouchers for my conduct in every instance and have the satisfaction to have it approved by The General under whom I serve.
>
> "Everything was got off from that place that could be with the roads and wagons we had to move the stores with. The evacuation of Fort Lee was determined upon several days before the enemy landed above us, and happily all the most valuable stores were away. The enemy's publication of the cannon and stores then taken is a grand falsehood; not an article of military stores was left there, or none worth mentioning."[17]

Sunday, the 22nd: Paine's *Crisis* Arrives

The strains and tensions of his officers weighed as heavily upon The General's mind as the worrisome condition of his troops. Sullivan's men, Lee's long-wandering corps from North Castle, had arrived in worse condition than some of the corps from Fort Lee. Their state and appearance were a disappointment but not disappointing enough to call off the expedition.

The American Chief was not to be swayed. Instead he took every possible step to give his army all possible support.

On the 22nd,[18] Sunday night, the express from Philadelphia brought in copies of Thomas Paine's *The Crisis, Number 1* bearing the next day's publication date.[19] Paine had seen to it that The General was among the first to read it. The citizen-soldier's *Common Sense*, written a year ago had reached the American Commander-in-Chief at Cambridge and had caused him then to praise the author in a letter to Joseph Reed, saying, "*Common Sense* will not leave many at a loss to decide."

Now the Continental Army Chief ordered Paine's latest inspiring treatise be read to the men in every regiment.

Having failed to get Putnam to commit himself except to promise to send militia if weather conditions permitted, and opposed to giving the acting military governor of the city a direct command, The General advised "Old Put" to prepare for any emergency. But he again urged him to support the Jersey militia at Mount Holly.

He recommended that those citizens having "any regard for the town" not lose "a moment's time... in putting it in the best posture of defense possible."

In addition, he wrote Putnam:

"I would have the public stores of every kind removed, except such as may be necessary for immediate use and except provisions."[20]

Then, on the very launching day of the attack operation, the 25th, The General dispatched an express to Cadwalader. He evinced alarm over word from Reed which the American Chief called, "discouraging accounts" from the colonel as to "what might be expected from operations below (at Bristol)." So in the Chief's final express to Cadwalader, he wrote:

"Notwithstanding the discouraging accounts... I am determined, as the night is favorable, to cross the River and make the attack on Trenton in the morning. If you can do nothing real, at least create as great a diversion as possible."[21]

It was The General's and the command staff's first inkling that something might go awry in the three-pronged maneuver. Nevertheless, the plans proceeded with a concentration upon the northernmost prong, the main division, to bring success to the expedition.

Aside from the stamina of the troops, the attack operation was dependent principally upon weaponry, muskets, rifles, cannon, transports, will and weather. To these the Reverend Doctor Mac Worter added as foremost, Providence. At the close of the Christmas Eve Council of War the preacher "called for divine guidance of the venture."[22]

The Boats

Thus, the factors of surprise, espionage, soldiery-stamina, will and armament, added to weather and overall Providence—all intricate parts of the perilous plan—were considered and shaped for Christmas Day.

The transports were to be brought down from upstream hiding to the west bank at McKonkey's Ferry. Among the river craft to be assembled were all 40 of the big Durham boats from the upper river.

The larger of these vessels can carry as much as 15 tons. From 40 to 60 feet long and eight feet wide, they are two feet deep and pointed at both ends, enabling them to be propelled in either direction. Durham designed them for operation by oars, poling, or sail.[23]

A steering sweep at both ends can be locked into the vessel's keel, giving the helmsman control of the craft at one end or the other. In sailing, the boat can make use of canvas on its two masts, but, when poled, a Durham vessel requires a crew of four in addition to a helmsman. The four poling crewmen run along a running rail on both sides of the vessel from bow to stern, using their setting poles to drive the craft forward.

It is these vessels that helped to carry the army safely across and out of the enemy's reach two weeks ago. Aided by flatboats, smaller craft and local patriots, they easily and quickly conveyed artillery, horses and men across.[24]

But yesterday, Christmas, the stream had begun to choke with the upriver's ice cakes, making ferriage under the cold arctic night especially difficult. So yesterday's orders, Christmas, December 25, included these directions for the enterprise:

The Orders

(1) Each brigade to be furnished with two good guides.

(2) General Stephen's brigade to form the advance party, taking a detachment of the artillery without cannon, but provided with spikes and hammers to spike up the enemy's cannon in case of necessity, or to bring it off it it can be effected.

(3) General Stephen is to attack and force the enemy's guards and seize such posts as may prevent them from forming in the streets, and in case they are annoyed from the houses to set them afire.

(4) Under Major General Greene's command, the brigades of Mercer and Lord Stirling to support General Stephen. (This is the 2nd Division of the main army, or its left wing, and is to march by way of Penington Road.)

(5)   Under Major General Sullivan's command, the brigades of St. Clair's, Glover's and Sargent's are to march by the River Road. (This is the 1st Division of the main army, or its right wing.)

(6)   Lord Stirling's Brigade is to form the reserve of the Left Wing, and General St. Clair's Brigade the reserve to the Right Wing. (These reserves are to form a second line in conjunction, or a second line to each division as circumstances may require.)

(7)   Each brigadier is to make the colonels acquainted with the posts of their respective regiments in the brigade, and the major-generals will inform them of the posts of the brigades in the line.

(8)   Four pieces of artillery are to march at the head of each column; three pieces at the head of the second brigade of each division; and two pieces with each of the reserves.

(9)   The troops are to be assembled one mile back of McKonkey's Ferry, and as soon as it begins to grow dark the troops to be marched to the ferry and embark on board the boats in the following order, under the direction of Colonel Knox:

    (a)   General Stephen's Brigade, with the detachment of artillerymen to embark first;

    (b)   General Mercer's next;

    (c)   Lord Stirling's next;

    (d)   General Fermoy's next—who will march into the rear of the 2nd Division and file off from the Pennington to the Princeton road in such direction that he can with the greatest ease and safety secure the passes between Princeton and Trenton. The guides will be the best judges of this. He is to take two pieces of artillery with him.

    (e)   St. Clair's, Glover's and Sargent's Brigades to embark in order. Immediately upon their debarkation, the whole to form and march in subdivisions from the right.

(10)   The commanding officers of regiments to observe that the divisions be equal and that proper officers be appointed to each.

(11)   A profound silence to be enjoined, and no man to quit his ranks, on pain of death.

(12)   Each brigadier to appoint flanking parties; the reserve brigades to appoint the rear-guards of the columns; the head of the columns to be appointed to arrive at Trenton at five o'clock.

(13)   Captains Washington and Flahaven, with a party of 40 men each, to march before the divisions and post themselves on the road about three miles from Trenton, and make prisoners of all going in or coming out of town.

(14)   General Stephen will appoint a guard to form a chain of sentries around the landing place at sufficient distance from the river to permit the troops to form, this guard not to suffer any person to go in or come out, but to detain all persons who attempt either. This guard to join their brigade when the troops are all over.

(15)   The countersign is "Victory or Death."[2 5]

The Plan Is Kept A Secret

In his report to Congress the day before Christmas The General made no mention of the Trenton attack plan. The routine communication dealt with the appointment of officers, problems involved in raising the new army, complaints that few militia had gone to Philadelphia and an appeal for funds.

The funds were for the "Military Chest," as he calls the account he uses for espionage payments. It needed replenishing, he declared, owing to "the necessity of a large and immediate supply of cash"[26] and in view of his expenditure of almost $8,414 during the past eight months from this coffer.[27]

By the same express, the American Commander, replying to a letter from Robert Morris in Philadelphia, made no mention of the event that was about to take place. To the patriot and financial backer of the Revolution, he wrote philosophically on the 24th:

> ". . . I agree with you that it is in vain to ruminate upon, or even reflect upon the Authors or Causes of our present misfortunes—we should rather exert ourselves, and look forward with Hopes that some lucky chance may yet turn in our favor.
>
> "Bad as our prospects are, I should not have the least doubt of Success in the end, did not the late treachery and defection of those who stood foremost in the opposition, while Fortune smiled upon us, make me fearful that many more will follow their example— who by using their influence with some, and working upon the fears of others, may extend the circle so as to take in whole towns, counties, nay provinces. . . .
>
> "I hope the next Christmas will prove happier than the present to you. . ."[28]

In this state of mind, under this canopy of gloom, Christmas morning dawned cold and blustery along the west bank of the Delaware under its unusually early winter blanket.

On the east bank the spirit of Christmas was in its second day of celebration. Only a few jitters occasionally dampened the British and Hessian soldiers in their merrymaking. But these "jitters," caused by surprise rebel raids, did not affect the Yankee-belittling commandant of the Hessian garrison in Trenton. Rall was unmoved by warnings.

Never had the Fates of Greek mythology given a warrior of old so many warnings as now they were issuing to Colonel Johann Gottlieb Rall in an effort to offset his destiny. Never had the Goddesses, Clotho and Lachesis, whom the ancient Romans and Greeks all knew measured out the span of each mortal's life, become more frustrated in what appeared to be the Fate's valiant effort to prolong the Hessian colonel's thread.

Griffin's unauthorized skirmish with von Donop's men on the Mount Holly-Bordentown road Sunday, the 22nd, was the first. It alerted von Donop, but it failed to impress Rall in Trenton.

Rall Heeds No Warnings

Then, on Monday, the 23rd, two American deserters, caught by British pickets, were brought into Trenton's Hessian headquarters. The American army, they informed Rall, was preparing an attack upon his Trenton post.[29] Rall laughed at the very thought of the idea.

A third warning came from Rall's superior officer, von Donop, who, alarmed by the Griffin raiders, inspected Rall's defenses in Tenton and reminded the Trenton commander that he had no natural defenses in the village with the exception of the Delaware on the west.

The area's commander noted that the rebels had every transport under their control for miles up and down the river and discounted the defensive value of the Assunpink Creek since it was easily fordable above, or east of the bridge. The villlage, von Donop reminded Rall, could be assaulted from every other direction over the flat surrounding country with its many back roads and byways.[30]

Colonel von Donop, annoyed by Rall's overconfidence, ordered the erection of redoubts. Rall accepted the order and approved the locations for two such defenses. However, he postponed following through with their constructions, scoffing at the rebels' potential to move against the British-Hessian might, except in a pin-pricking nuisance sort of way.

Ridiculing the possibility of an attack in sufficient force to endanger his superior troops, Rall, calling the American army "nothing but a lot of farmers," seemed to want an encounter.

After all, had not the British General Grant, commander of the entire British defense line, advised him by courier not to worry since he, Grant, could keep the peace with a corporal's guard?

So, to his own Major Friedrich von Dechow, who gave him a fourth warning, urging that Rall order the digging of trenches as outworks, the Hessian Trenton commander replied:

"Let them come! We want no trenches. We"ll at them with the bayonet!"[31]

On Christmas Eve, when British informers learned of the

American plans to attack the British lines, Generals Grant and Leslie, despite Grant's haughty attitude and his "corporal's guard" boast for handling the rebel army, notified all officers to be on the alert.

General Leslie, more concerned than Grant, got up out of his bed to scribble a personal note to Rall, stating:

"Be upon your guard against an unexpected attack on Trenton."[32]

Within the Hessian-held lines only von Donop and Rall's Major von Dechow were fidgeting. Rall was not.

If Lachesis and her allies were ever amazed at a mortal's pompous refusal to heed sound advice, they were now. It was their fifth warning. Not to be easily discouraged, however, they would try again and again, for there still was time.

So, when Grant's formal notice to all commanding officers along the line reached Trenton's headquarters Christmas morning, Major von Dechow, as commander of the Knyphausen Regiment, again advised Rall to take some immediate precautionary steps. He urged his post commander to send away the garrison's baggage and have the men dig in for a possible attack despite the holiday season.

But Christmas was the turn for "The Ralls," the colonel's own unit to be "Regiment of the Day." This required them to be on the alert, sleep in battle dress uniform and have their muskets within easy reach at all times. This in itself, was, in the opinion of the post commander, sufficient precaution.

Therefore, in answer to von Dechow's appeal, Rall declared that he did not believe the rebel Commander would attempt an assault.[33] Instead the advice-resisting colonel calmly went about preparing to dine under the comfort of the Hunt House and its hospitality. So Rall, unresponsive to Lachesis' efforts was Abraham Hunt's guest last night, the closing hours of Christmas Day.

It was the post commander's sixth warning, but the determined Lachesis and her "sisters" still had time for one or two more notices. Surely, one would prove to be the colonel's saving.

This was the general state of things late Christmas Day in the Hessian-occupied village of Trenton. Toward evening the plummeting temperature caused Rall to bundle his surcoat about his neck as he made his way through the biting cold wind that froze his moistened lips. The iron nail he constantly chews began to stick icily to the corners of his moistened mouth. He quickly removed it and put it in his pocket.

The Abraham Hunt house was only two blocks away, but they were a long, cold two blocks. A hot toddy at Hunt's will feel good tonight!

For a few moments the thought swept him backward many years and thousands of miles across the sea to Germany, to other Christmas Days. It is always such a big day in Der Vaterland. The Americans hardly celebrate it at all.

In a few moments the present caught up with him, and Hunt's black servant ushered him through the front door as the snow began to fall. Rall forgot all business and all memories as he entered the warm parlor and stood with his host before the blazing logs of the fireplace, sipping the hot toddy that he knew always awaited winter guests in the Hunt House.

Nine Miles North

Nine miles north the picked troops of the American army finished their parading behind the hill near the creek on Knowle's land. Parading was about the only way to keep warm while awaiting the crossing hour. Every man now knew a long march and a surprise attack were before them.

In contrast with previous meals, all had been well fed, but that big meal was wearing off and the cold night was blowing in. Now they almost looked forward to the crossing and the trek before them. Movement of the body, arms and hands was now imperative if circulation was to be kept going.

With nightfall the vanguard would be the first to move down to the boats. They would be ferried across to McKonkey's place, joining the horses already transported and shivering under a sleeting snow in the open hillside corral south on the river road.

Through the Night's Bleak Blackness

According to the calendar, the 25th was to be a full moon. But during the afternoon the rapidly accumulating gray clouds assured the high command it would be anything but a moonlit night.

It promised to be a particularly rough one for Glover's hardy Marbleheaders. Though they were accustomed to handling large boats and small craft in all kinds of weather, the task now before them offered an obstacle more difficult than any they had ever encountered.

The Durham boats were new to most of them, yet, in them,

they must carry out the operation in total darkness, hauling an army and its equipment across a river swirling with ice flows in a rapid current on a waterway with which they have had little time to become familiar.

And all signs were indicating much more than snow in the air. More than likely an early winter blizzard was hovering over their heads.

Twilight, dusk and darkness dropped down all at once. The winter solstice was in its fourth day and seemed to want to show the worst side of its bleakness.

Weather conditions were not a factor in the choice of date and hour. The full moon was thought of as both a possible hindrance and a help. The Christmas-celebration period was, however, an important element in the choice of day, for the after-observance hour was the most inviting for surprise. Also, the night's selection was the earliest possible time for the plan's execution. Fortunately, all of the factors, even the arctic storm, could contribute some advantages.

The severity of the weather increased the fears among the high command that the flowing ice could gather and firm itself and then freeze solid under a prolonged cold spell. With 48 hours of intense cold the Hessian and British army would not need boats to cross the Delaware, declared some gloom predictors. The enemy, they said, could march across the river, smash their way through the American defenses and walk unmolested into Philadelphia.

Two of the big problems that faced Glover's seamen were the crossing of the horses and artillery. Once crossed, the animals had to be corralled until most of the artillery carriages, men and supplies were safely over.

Guards were posted both north and south of the Ferry House and inn on Hunterdon County's Jersey shore. Pickets, taking turns in the bitter cold, patrolled the Jersey assembling area, but the corral, above the bank on a barren hillside, was directly exposed to the blistery north wind. The assembling area, in contrast with the corral, was on the lee side of the enbankment and protected from the weather's severity.

The McKonkey's Ferry crossing location was chosen with careful consideration of the politics of the Hunterdon County inhabitants on the Jersey side. Most are staunchly dedicated to the American cause. Even so only a few of the most tried patriots in the vicinity, including the innkeeper and ferry-master himself, had little more than an inkling of "something big" taking place.

Keeping what little they knew to themselves, they eagerly helped to fill the innkeeper's larder with hot wassail, cider, cakes and bread, soliciting the aid of other neighbors with sympathies similar to their own. They asked no questions, though some whispered that a surprise attack on Princeton must be in the making.

Corralling and tethering the horses was a small task, it was thought, until it was discovered the fencing enclosure was ripped open at the south end and had never been repaired. Seeking a volunteer to go over and remain with the horses, Colonel Bedford asked Gray to get him someone or assign the task to a reliable man in his battery.

Eager to have an important role in the massive, secret expedition under way, Jocko urged his father and Gray to let him volunteer for the small task. The open section of the enclosure would have to be roped in. It would be necessary for at least one man to oversee the animals until the dragoons and generals picked up their steeds.

Big Tom, somewhat reluctantly gave his consent, proud of his son's desire to do his bit for The General's mysterious enterprise, but Gray hesitated. To Jocko, Gray's hesitation was a sure indication of a negative answer. The youth's face, flushed with exuberance, fell as The Lieutenant, his blue petticoat scarf waving in the wind, replied:

"Methinks ye best stay with your father 'nd the animals on this side, Jocko. 'Tis ye both who know best how to get the horses aboard. 'Tis by itself a big job. Besides 'tis bitter cold 'nd over there 'tis worse. It may be hours before all are crossed 'nd the riders take their carriers. Yes, hours the way things are a'goin' now. Ye are not dressed for it, Jocko. I would yet stay beside Tom 'nd help him take charge the horses here 'til we come back."

Jocko's face dropped, but he argued back, "Ise as warm as a ear of roast'it corn, Lootenan. Ise knows dem 'orses betta den enie uv 'em. Sez yas, Lootenan. See, look, Ise got Pappy's old coat. See! It's warm. Pappy sez yas . . . Now you sez it!"

Gray, torn between denying the youth his chance to contribute to the venture and what he knew was to be a cold, lonely task, possibly without shelter for hours, looked at Levy alongside of him for guidance. Levy shook his head, clearly indicating he wanted no part in the decision-making.

"Stay you on this side, Jocko," Gray replied, almost pleadingly. The youth said nothing for a brief few seconds of silent staring.

Suddenly his usual happy, beaming brown eyes lost their smile. A pained expression clouded over his face as Gray's glance met his.

As though suffering in questioning desbelief—his voice lowered almost to a whisper— Jocko looked intently into The Lieutenant's steel blue eyes and said solemnly, "Lootenan, it's causin' Ise black. Ain't 'tit, Lootenan? It's causin' wese wuz oncet slaves, Lootenan! Ain't 'tit?"

It was Gray's face that now changed almost instantly. The officer's eyes and face now flushed with anger. Never in his long friendship with the youth had pigment seemed to matter. Never had its roots for prejudice ever surfaced between them.

Furious at his young friend's unexpected accusation, Gray, his pock-marks seeming to redden under his wind-blown scarf, angrily retorted, as his seldom-lost composure flew out of control, "Damn it, Jocko! You know that ain't so! . . . All right! Go then! Damn it! Tell the colonel you'll do it! . . But you take along a blanket! . . 'Nd here! Take this fer 'round your neck!"

From his inside pocket, The Lieutenant took the new, unused, blue petticoat scarf which Elaine had made for him to replace the old. He had never worn it preferring to stay with the original, old and stained reminder of Ellie and the more pleasant memories of the past.

Tossing it to the victoriously smiling Jocko, Gray said, "Wear ye that 'round your throat. And damn it! Ye keep warm! You hear, Jocko?"

Jocko's face reignited with unexpected success. He caught the folded cloth and tried to return it, saying, "No! No! No, Lootenan, Missy E made dat specials fer youse."

"Keep it and go!" demanded Gray, his anger still glowing.

Slowly and reluctantly, the youth, realizing that he had offended his friend and ally more than he had intended, turned away. Then he stopped and swung around on his heels, shouting to Gray from over his shoulder, "Thanks youse, Lootenan! Ah'll takes good care ob dis 'n brings it back careful. . . 'N, Lootenan, Ise pow'afull sorry fer whud Ise sezed. . . Youse forgibs me, doncha, Lootenan?"

The officer nodded his head and with a wave of his arm swiftly thrown out from his waist, watched his clever young friend dash excitedly over to Colonel Bedford's aide.

In his oversized coat and Elaine's extra scarf tucked under his big tricorn hat and around his neck, Jocko appeared like a midget alongside of the six-foot-four aide to the artillery battery's colonel. Snow now covered hat, scarf and coat.

Big Tom, who had been the first to give in to his son's request,
had stood behind Jocko and Gray during their verbal bout, shaking
his head at his son's persistence. Now Gray turned to the older
man, saying, "Tom, you should have stopped him! Why did you
tell him he could go if I approved?"

" 'Causin', Looten'nt, 'eed be da misery to be 'round iffen Ise
did'en," Big Tom replied. "Youse knows dat! 'Sides, 'e doan trusts
no'uns takin' care ob horses, 'ceptin' hisself. Iffin' youse sezed no
ta 'im, 'eed git ober dare som'ow."

A few minutes later Jocko went across in one of the big boats
alongside of the first horse to cross. With Big Tom's skill and the
blindfolded animal led carefully aboard, the steed, now accustomed
to being ferried across rivers, accepted the rocking boat with only
an occasional whinny. Huddled under his blanket on his seat beside
the horse, Jocko held the reins, stroking and comforting the
shivering creature.

Even before darkness set in Glover's men had begun floating the
Durhams, flatboats and other river craft downstream from the
marshland hiding place at Malta Island south of Coryell's Ferry.
Thanks to Daniel Bray and his Hunterdon County compatriots,
who had rounded up the river craft and tediously towed them
upstream out of sight from Cornwallis's searching scouts, the
Durham boats were now to perform one of the most successful,
strategic missions in military history.

However, the approximate 1,000 feet of icy river crossing took
much longer than expected. The accumulation of ice chunks, not
so much in the midstream's rapid current as along the shores, and
the difficulty of poling and rowing the heavily loaded vessels,
slowed down the expedition's timing.

Poling was a new art for the Marbleheaders and one they were
fast learning. But last night they were facing more than a new art.
It was an arctic blizzard.

The previously sodden, cold, threatening weather had gradually
acquired blasts of bitterly cold snow, sleet and wind. As the night's
darkness fell, the freezing gusts from the north increased with
intensity.

Leading two horses at a time from the landing, Jocko guided the
confused animals up the road to the fenced enclosure. He carefully tied each to the rails, having earlier roped in the unrepaired
section. His new boots kept his feet warm only as long as he was
moving and able to constantly wiggle his toes. He drew up his
gloveless hands into the long sleeves of his father's lengthy surcoat.

The high knoll and its enclosure are several hundred rods from the Ferry House and landing. Soon the snow again gave way to sleet, icing the road bed, making it more difficult to guide the horses up the slippery slope in the face of the blasting northeast wind.

Only the army's whale oil lantern, hanging from a branch on the lee side of the tree and marking the entrance gate to the enclosure, served as the youth's guide on the long trek from landing to corral. Trip after trip he made until all the horses were over.

"It will be a terrible night for the soldiers. . . "

On the opposite bank, the loading of men, artillery and the remaining horses proceeded all too slowly. Each unit had been given its position in the crossing. As ordered, every man carried a blanket. Most of them threw it over their heads and shoulders to keep out the combining and alternating deluges of rain, hail and snow.

It was a perfect night for a secret mission but not for the soldiers marching into it. One of The General's staff while waiting his turn for embarking wrote in his diary:

"Christmas, 6 P.M. . . It is fearfully cold and raw and a snow-storm setting in. The wind is northeast and beats in the faces of the men. It will be a terrible night for the soldiers who have no shoes. Some of them have tied old rags around their feet, but I have not heard a man complain.

"I have never seen Washington so determined as he is now. He stands on the bank of the stream, wrapped in his cloak, superintending the landing of his troops. He is calm and collected, but very determined. The storm is changing to sleet and cuts like a knife."[34]

By 11 P.M., the hail and sleet, driven by a high wind, doubled the difficulties of the boatmen and increased the soldiers' misery as they awaited their turn to embark. Captain Thomas Rodney wrote later in his dairy:

"It was as severe a night as ever I saw. . . (with this) storm of wind, hail, rain and snow."[35]

The General had crossed with Knox and staff members in one of the first transports that moved out. Suffering from a severe head cold,[36] the American Commander-in-Chief hid from others the miserable agony of the congestion that pounded in his head. His throat sore and his breathing difficult through his running nose, he nevertheless tried his best to conceal his condition from Knox and those around him.

During the crossing, the Continental Army's Chief perceived that the oarsmen and polers were having difficulty maneuvering the craft in the darkness through the swift current and its annoying ice floes. At the same time he noticed that Henry Knox, the big, strapping giant among the Chief's trusted advisers now sitting to his left, was unintentionally crowding him toward the starboard side of the vessel. Close to his commander, Knox's weight and The General's together put almost 500 pounds on the starboard side.

"Shift your weight, Knox," jokingly remarked the American Commander, "and trim the boat."[37]

With a hearty laugh, the boisterous former colonel, who only nine days ago was made a brigadier general, shifted his seat portside. The big Durham boat noticeably righted itself, causing every man aboard to burst out with laughter along with the army's commander of artillery himself.

The General's humorous jibe soon traveled up and down the ranks. Provoking laughter, it boosted morale all through the long solemn lines. Few men had ever connected their Chief with any act or remark even approaching humor.

Suddenly, to many of them, their Leader rose in stature to become a soldier, real and just as lifelike as themselves. In such a man they now more contentedly placed their trust.

In addition to his blanket, each man carried food rations for three days, 400 rounds of ammunition and extra flints in addition to his musket or rifle. All had been warned to keep their flintlocks wrapped up in cloth. However, many of the men had used whatever rags were at hand for tying around their shoes, or their feet, if they were shoeless.

There was good military order in both embarking and disembarking considering the intensity of the storm. But it was order which miraculously unfolded from the tensions and confusion created by adverse weather and almost total darkness.

To make up for the threadbare army's shortcomings, The General and his staff radically departed from standard military practices which call for two to three fieldpieces for evevery 1,000 infantrymen. Instead, nine cannons were assigned to each of the three divisions in the tri-pronged attack plan.

Therefore, Greene and Sullivan, commanding the two wings of the main northern division, had to cross three 6-pounders, three 3-pounders, one 4-pounder and two 5.5-inch howitzers.[38] A difficult operation even under normal crossing conditions.

Chief of artillery, Henry Knox, standing beside The General in the blowing gale on the lee side of the Ferry House, superintended the landing of the invaluable weaponry.

At times, like two tall ghostly silhouettes, the two men stood in awesome silence on the river's bank, blocked figures in the darkness of the wintry night. Born opposites, but bound in comradery, the statue-like close friends were caught only by the eerie glow from the lantern lights inside the busy bustling Ferry House.

Their occasional movements, brief exchanges and hurried orders, dispatched by waiting messengers to officers on both sides the river, constantly reflected their fears. Heightening everyone's concern, frequently a cannon-loaded vessel, or heavily laden troop transport, would lose its bearings and drift downstream in the storm's blinding fury.

Greene and Sullivan supervised the loading and embarking from the west shore. The former commandant of Forts Washington and Lee had at last found surcease of mind from his harassing critics through his angry reply to them, sent through Governor Cooke.

At his quarters in Bogart's Tavern in Buckingham, Greene left a copy of his letter with his personal papers on the desk in his room. It was a precaution characteristic of the Rhode Islander. Now, if the letter were intercepted, or went astray, a copy would be found in the event he did not return. So Greene's mind was free for the business of battle now very close at hand.

North from McKonkey's, the watch on Bowman's Hill, five miles upstream and atop a rise 310 feet above the river, had for days reported no observance of any enemy action opposite, along the Jersey shore southward of Coryell's Ferry. But observations throughout the day were reported obscured by the weather.

Weapons, Men and Diversities

Scouts sent northward along the Jersey bank corroborated the watch at Bowman's Hill. So it was assured that a march south was at least safe from any possible enemy movements coming southwestward from British Generals Grant and Leslie's post at Princeton. Such a maneuver could have put the rebels in a vice between Grant and Rall.

Thus the tedious crossing work continued, relieved from one frightening possibility. But the operation's slow progress soon found the expedition far behind its schedule. This, it was now feared, seriously endangered the vital and necessary ingredient for the mission's success: surprise.

With surprise and heavy weaponry, the war council was confident the Americans would hold the upper hand. The General and Knox had both emphasized the advantages of artillery over musket and rifle fire at the council sessions.

The army's chief artillerist has repeatedly contended that the cannon's credits are unsurpassable, pointing out that not only does artillery have power and distance but, in addition, it provides deadly accuracy at 500 yards with balls and over 250 yards with canister and grape.

Muskets, according to the Boston-born bookstore owner, who has made an extensive study of weaponry, are effective for only a maximum of 100 yards and are not as reliable, or as accurate, as the rifled barrels which the Pennsylvania Germans are turning out for the army. Rifles, Knox reminds his officers and men, have a range three times that of muskets but, unfortunately, cannot be fitted with bayonets.

Another advantage of cannonry, which The General noted at the war council in supporting his chief of artillery, is that these heavy weapons are not as temperamental under adverse weather conditions as are muskets and rifles. For small arms cannot be fired if the locks or the priming powder are even slightly damp.

On the other hand, cannons can be plugged against dampness. Oiled silk, waterproof bags keep their powder dry. And since such weapons are not discharged by a sparking mechanism, but by the live fire of a well-covered burning wick, or "match," they can be loaded and fired repeatedly in the wettest kind of weather. In addition there is the morale effect. For the cannon is a frightfully feared weapon on the battlefield.

When Knox, who, like Greene, supports The General almost without question on nearly every military issue, makes his point about artillery, few doubt his word. His knowledge, though based upon all the reading matter he could acquire on the subject, is not without experience.

As he speaks of weaponry with fellow officers, the eyes of his listeners are drawn to the two missing fingers of his left hand. The result of a hunting accident, those stubs are nevertheless part of the reason Henry Knox long ago determined he would master the art.

To those who know the American Commander and the officers of his council, particularly Greene, Stirling, Mercer, Sullivan, Knox and Glover, there is a strange, inexplicable bond that holds them loyally together. Yet their differences are marked.

Greene, the Rhode Island merchant; Stirling of New Jersey, son of a British nobleman; Mercer of Virginia, a Scotland-born physician; Sullivan, New Hampshire lawyer; Knox, the Boston, Massachusetts, book salesman, a contrast with the American Commander, a Virginia farmer; and Glover, whom the British officers take delight in calling "a fish dealer."

But in this diversified admixture of leadership, in this aggregate of men and minds from varied walks of life and from the farthest corners of the country, together with so many others of their kind who yesterday marched on Trenton, there rested the frightened American eaglet's life. The few among them who did not know it, later would.

A Near Calamity Is Rall's Seventh Warning

Stephen's Virginia Continentals made up the first brigade to cross since they, as the advance scouts and vanguard, had been ordered to proceed immediately without waiting for the main body. This they did, moving out with the snow and wind on their backs before darkness had set in. But a detachment of Stephen's van under Captain Richard Anderson of the 5th Virginia Regiment[39] soon very nearly ruined the high command's carefully planned enterprise.

Anderson's overenthusiastic van was destined to spearhead beyond James Slack, one of the local guides assisting the Continentals on the march. Slack had been assigned to lead Stephen and his men to a pre-selected point and there await the main body. However, in the growing darkness, Captain Anderson and his advance wandered too deep into Rall's northern outposts.

In the swirling blackness they inadvertently stumbled upon a lone Hessian sentinel who challenged them through a wind that gusted the ground snow into their faces. One of them, unnerved by the appearance of a Hessian enemy before him in the night, shot the guard.

The firing brought the alarmed picket post down upon them in a body. A brisk exchange followed.

Leaving six of their number dead behind them, the Hessian pickets rapidly retreated into town. Anderson's confused and nervous men, guilt-stricken, also took to their heels but in the opposite direction. They took time, however, to carry off six enemy muskets as trophies.[40]

Without a guide and unable to find their way back to Stephen and the brigade, the captain's Virginians, now lost, spent the rest of the night in a pine forest clearing near a storm-blown field of sleet-covered cornstalks.

The brush sent an alarm throughout the Hessian colonel's entire garrison. All five barracks were ordered under arms.

However the swift withdrawal of the attackers convinced Rall and his officers that the rebels were nothing more than a foraging mission that had wandered too far astray in the blizzard-blown countryside. So the alarm was lifted and the troops returned to quarters.

To the Fates, still trying to warn Johann Gottlieb Rall of things to come, it was, according to Lachesis's count, Rall's seventh warning.

Marbleheader William Blackler, helmsman of the boat that carried The General and Knox across hours earlier, was sensitive to the depressed spirits of the cold, shivering wet troops when, at Christmas's midnight, the massive ferrying task had hardly gotten under way.

In an effort to cheer the glum, frozen-looking soldiers, Blackler told and retold the story of General Knox's shifting seat to trim the boat. But by midnight it barely helped to lighten any hearts.

The entire crossing task was to have been completed by that hour. Yet there were still countless trips and hours to go before all the men were crossed. The long delay, the disruption of the schedule, could prove disastrous. The dawn-rising Hessian garrison could not likely be surprised in daylight.

Cold rain, mixed with snow and sleet, whipped by the intensifying northeaster greeted the below-freezing morning hours. The seamen now were hampered worse than before in their wind-blown craft as broken ice floes, accumulating near the shore, cracked against the poles and boat hulls.

Soon the freezing rain again turned to snow and, alternatingly with sleet, combined to strike and sting the exposed faces and flesh of the soldiers. In the darkness, visibility lessened, making most objects indistinguishable beyond a few rods.

Each helmsman fought his individual battle, attempting to keep his vessel pointed toward the port shore. Since all the arriving, heavily overloaded craft could not be docked simultaneously owing to the limitations of the ferry landing, many were partly beached.

Men jumping off frequently landed ankle and sometimes knee-deep, in the freezing water, wading their way through ice chunks to the shore. A few of the boats, unable to remain on course, ended up downstream hundreds of yards from the disembarking area. It was a night which no man having had a part in it would ever forget.

Shore Of Shadows, Statues and Silhouettes

Henry Knox's deep roaring, unmistakable voice, shouting his location like a clamoring buoy from the New Jersey side, saved many of the pilots from similarly ending up downstream. Among all the noises and sounds of the night rising above the frequent screams of the wind, few will be remembered by the helmsmen as more comforting to them in those hours than Knox's foghorn-like bellowing that guided them shoreward.

And among all the vignettes, the scenes of men and shadows, standing, moving, huddling, running, outlined through the falling snow in the gusting blackness, few will forget the American Commander-in-Chief, his cloak wrapped about him, sitting for long hours at a time on a discarded beehive overseeing the disembarking of his troops.[41] Though the movement was dropping precariously behind schedule and its timing was to have been a major weapon, he remained calm and seemingly unperturbed despite the strains upon him and the cursed continuing storm on his head and over his expedition. For by 3 A.M. this morning the boats were still coming across and the sleet was still driving down and piercing into open flesh like saber points.

Patiently waiting her master in the shelter of the ferry owner's carriage lean-to, Old Magnolia, the climate and environs above and beneath her cruelly sneering at her name—so reminiscent of peace and happiness—stomped occasionally. Then she would twist her head as she continued chewing on a mouthful of hay.

Swishing the snow and ice particles from her back with her long gray tail, the animal often turned her eyes to look for him whom she had carried so long so far. As always, the faithful mare knew he would draw from his pocket a tasty morsel—a piece of apple or a sweet—just for her.

Beside Old Magnolia, and less concerned, stood Blueskin, Billy's gelding, also saddled and waiting to go on. The General's black valet had put in a long 24 hours and, exhausted, fell asleep with his blanket around him in an old broken wagon seat next to Blueskin.

Under the carriage shed's partial shelter there was some warmth and comfort from the direct force of the sleeting, biting winds.

And Billy, like the cold, shivering soldiers in the long lines waiting for the order to push on, used American rebel ingenuity to make the best out of the worst of situations.

Eighteen years younger than his Chief, Brigadier General Henry Knox, cognizant of The General's heavy weight of responsibilities as well as the attempted concealment of his cold, took over much of the shore command work in order to lighten the Commander's task. He was not alone among the loyal staff to take initiative beyond orders after sensing and sizing up his Chief's worried, wearied state. Others did the same.

However, like The General, Knox's very presence inspires confidence. The American General, though sitting stoically at times on the overturned beehive, his sword between his legs, convinced his troops that their Leader was not only beside them but also of them.

Few boats reached shore that did not get his careful scrutiny. Few officers and enlisted men, struggling up the bank in the face of the night's buffeting winds, failed to escape his notice.

His mental notes of those without blankets and rations, with uncovered firing pans, or those with feet poorly shod, were quickly channeled into orders upbraiding regimental commanders. Busy couriers carried verbal messages ordering immediate rectifications. This attention to his men and their welfare inspired faith and with it a determination to succeed.

Knox's long and fond attachment for his Chief is distinctive. However, it has not changed the artillerist's similar, yet dissimilar, manner of leadership. For the Boston bookman is an extrovert who inspires confidence with an ebullient jocularity. He is a perpetual optimist. And he is not a reserved man among men.

Knox's effervescent, magnetic personality, trumpeted by his booming voice, gives him leadership ability without effort but makes the elite among his fellow officers raise their eyebrows. In almost every respect he is his Chief's opposite.

Yet it is these opposites in Knox that The General likes and admires, for he sees in the younger man, the city youth, those qualities and personality traits he lacks and finds so attractive in others.

And, as is so often true in the inexplicable phenomenon of self-assessment, Henry Knox sees in his idol, the wealthy country farmer, that striking reserve and magnetism seldom found among men. He sees the man as one whose moral strength is coupled with brilliance in foresight and judgment, cold equanimity under pressure and an enviable, sternly aloof taciturnity which remarkably sparks confidence in associates and inspires men to want to carry out his bidding successfully.

To Knox, this unique combination of disciplined qualities is what the artillerist admires. They are qualities he admires, and admires only. He has no intention of emulating his Chief, for strong personalities do not tolerate imitancy any more than they tolerate intimacy, very long or very well.

One Man's Gamble

It was no secret that The General was gambling all on a single shuffle of the deck. Despite weather, rain, snow, wind, hail and sleet, there was no turning back.

Despite whatever catastrophies might come—suffering, illness, or the reaper's sythe itself—there was to be no swerving from The Plan until Trenton was resolved by "Victory" or by "Death." That—the marching orders and the countersign said it—was no secret.

Knox, often looking solicitously concerned over at his Chief, was overwhelmed by the man's seemingly unruffled composure. The head cold and congestion he was suffering, thought Knox, would put another man to bed with grog and leeches. And yet the strong facial features, centered by those piercing cold blue eyes, reflected only the blazing fire of indefatigable determination. As the chief of artillery stole a glance in his Commander's direction, Knox watched The General roughly brush the snow from his pockmarked face.

There, thought the Bostonian, was the only telltale evidence of the many sufferings and illnesses the Continental Commander was said to have battled: smallpox, pleurisy, influenza, dysentery, possible typhoid[42] and even now, it is said, painful dental problems.

It is 4 A.M., and the belated time for moving out at last has come. All the troops which had assembled in secrecy so many long hours ago in the heavy forested area of Malta Island near the mouth of Knowles Creek[43] have ended the longest mile. Finally they stand upon the Jersey shore. Their long wait is almost over.

Four Hours Late Can Spell Disaster

Most of the troops are hardened Continentals, but now, wet, cold, shivering and half-blinded by the wind-blown sleet and snow, they are not much moved by Knox's encouragement.

The stalwart foot soldiers of the Grand Army are freezing and gloom-ridden.[44] To these veterans of Long Island, Kip's Bay, Harlem Heights, White Plains and the march across the Jerseys, it is another step. They want now only to get on with it.

It is five hours since Mercer's Continentals and militia from Connecticut, Massachusetts and Maryland came ashore. These are mostly crack troops of the campaign. Behind them were Lord Stirling and his Virginia Continentals, the reserves. Haslet's battle-tried, fighting Delaware men and a Pennsylvania rifle regiment were next. All of these troops, under Major General Greene, will make up the left wing of The General's main army division.

Next crossed the right wing of the division. Under Major General Sullivan, this flanking force came over with General Roche de Fermoy's command in the van. The Frenchman, the first of many from his country to be given a lead role in the American Rebellion, heads a regiment of Pennsylvania Germans and a number from a mixed Pennsylvania brigade.

Following deFermoy's men to the landing area was Sullivan's own division. It includes the brigades from St. Clair's, Glover's and Sargent's regiments, comprising men from New Hampshire, Massachusetts, Connecticut and New York.[45] Under Sullivan's leadership this right wing will drive into Trenton on the west side of town.

The timetable had called for the entire northern corps, all 2,400 men and their equipment to be crossed four hours ago.[46] That midnight-scheduled beginning of the march would have given the troops five hours to march the nine miles to Trenton, enabling a pre-dawn strike.

Now, at best, the village objective cannot be reached much before 9 A.M. It is not the first disappointing factor, nor the last. But The Plan *must* be carried through.

Each artilleryman, dragoon and general's aide-de-camp sought out his own horse from among those shivering, stomping and whinnying in the darkness of the wind-swept, snow-blinding corral. And angrily, each man, upon returning to his assembling area, reported there was no sign of anyone overseeing the corral. But the horses, they said, had been carefully tethered and blanketed, with belly straps tightened and secured. The commanding officers' animals, they pointed out, were orderly and separately tethered as far as they could make out in the darkness.

The First Casualty

When Tony Talo, the Barbette Battery's old veteran of the siege of Boston, returned with the battery's gun carriage horse, he excitedly reported to Gray and Levy that Jocko was nowhere in sight. It was then half after three in the morning.

Gray, Levy and Big Tom immediately set out toward the high knoll at the far distant point of the troops, damning themselves for having been too busy with the disembarking that they had not done so earlier. Surely Jocko had found good shelter somewhere. He was skilled at that. They would find him snug and warm, comfortably sound asleep.

The three men plodded up the hill beside the river road, trudging through the accumulating drifts of snow. In almost total darkness they reached the corral's west gate.

Then, to The Lieutenant's right, between a fence post and under the large oak beside it, partially covered by a heavy drift of snow and sleet, Jocko's crouched, blanket-covered form, slowly came into Gray's vision. The youth's big tricorn hat, covering the scarf around his ears, appeared from under the ice-stiffened blanket. His bent head rested on knees pulled up close to his chest.

Seemingly he was fast asleep, except that his outstretched hand, frozen, inflexibly gripped the handle of the burned-out whale oil lamp upright in the snow before him.

Without hesitating, Gray swiftly scooped up Jocko's half-frozen body in his arms. He shouted Levy's and Tom's name once above the howling wind, and the three men hurriedly made their way back to the landing dock. Gray carried the youth, the blankets of all three men wrapped around the crumpled form.

Blackler and his exhausted crew, their last trip completed, were about to pull back empty to the west shore when Gray spotted the Marbleheader's vessel about to take off. Ever ready for an emergency, or a mission of mercy, Blackler and his men, all of whom knew Jocko, crowded around Tom, Gray and Levy.

Putting the boy into the boat and tucking the blankets around and under him, Gray struck the youth's face and rubbed his body while Tom and Levy vigorously worked on his hands, arms and legs after removing his treasured boots. Then, as the artillery officer briskly shook the youngster's head and plied his face with his warm hands, Jocko's eyes opened.

The thin crusts of ice broke away from his slowly opening eyelids. He tried to smile, appearing almost comfortable, unharmed and warm. Elaine's handmade scarf which Gray had given him came down around his ears and was knotted under his chin. It had been pulled up around his head from around his neck and tied in exactly the same way The Lieutenant tied and wore his own favorite inseparable neckerchief.

"You are all right, Jocko! Ye will be well, Jocko!" Gray kept repeating, almost shouting. "Ye will be back in the barracks right soon."

Then all laughed, momentarily relieved, when the boy's lips moved gradually, saying "Ise . . . warm as a . . . roast'it . . .ear'a corn, Loo . . ten . . an. Tell Missy E . . . nothin' a'need . . . in' . . . fer . . . ta worry . . . in' . . . 'bout . . . Tell 'er nothin' . . . fer . . . worryin' . . . needin' . . ."

His eyes closed again. But there was life. There was breath. The damaged cells of his usually quick brain were fighting the melting disintegration of tissues. To his frantically worried father and to Gray and Levy the words from his lips, however slow, were all they wanted to hear.

Quickly they covered him over in the bottom of the Durham boat. Tom, kneeling beside his son, would stay with him. Gray did not need to urge the kindly Blackler and his Marbleheaders to hurry the youth across and to the Newtown Hospital.

Reluctantly Gray began backing away when Jocko suddenly opened his eyes again and addressed his father, saying, now with even more hesitation between words, "Pappy, youse aksk . . da . . . Loo . . ten . . an . . ."

"E's right chere, Son," Big Tom tells him, interrupting. "Youse kin aksk 'im yo'selv."

Bending over close to the youth's face, Gray said, "I'm here, Jocko. What 'tis ye would say?"

"Loo. .ten. .an, youse. . . ken tells me now. Whud dem. . . numbas . . . one . . . two . . . threes means 'n dat sign youse. . . allus. . . izza. . . rytin' en dat. . . buk Ise gibt ta youse?" the youth asks, adding, "Ise woon tells nobody, not ebin Missy E."

Amazed at his young friend's persistently inquisitive mind, Gray, worried but half smiling, replied, slowly whispering: "They mean—those numbers mean, Jocko— 'I am one with you! . . between Missy E and me. . . and now you, too. . . One, two three!. . Now you must go and get warm and better by the time I come back."

The cold brown lips widened in an effort to smile. And the big brown eyes smilingly closed.

At almost the same moment that Blackler and his men poled off with Jocko and his father, the signal on the shore spread up and down the long lines of soldiers. The first division troops began heading southward on to Trenton. The slightly slackening cold wind and sleet were now on their backs.

On To Trent's Town

Some inhabitants along the McKonkey's Ferry road, which begins forking toward the north, south and east settlements about a mile east of the ferry, have gotten word of the mysterious midnight crossing. Even at 4 o'clock in the morning the scattered farmers soon learn of big things that take place within miles of them.

Many of the Hunterdon County residents of the district are now elated to hear that a major American activity is under way. They welcome anything aimed at the constantly pillaging Hessian and Troy raiders. So some get out of their beds and appear on the dark wintry road to offer food and cider to the plodding, freezing, wind-blown soldiers. The silent troops march on, seldom partaking of anything.

Generally among the staunchest patriots there are secluded some few Tories and Loyalists faithful to the King who pretend a devotion to The Cause. These "pretenders" are the ones the Whigs and patriots know to be at large. It is constantly feared that one of them, or some alerted Tory, will ride posthaste and inform the enemy garrisons at Maidenhead, Princeton or Trenton. And actually one British informer has already done so.

At the fork in the road, a mile from McKonkey's, the division passed by Bear Tavern, taking the southern prong there toward Birmingham, a little northeast of Yardley's Ferry and about three miles south of McKonkey's.

At Benjamin Moore's house about four miles from McKonkey's, the procession halted, and the troops ate their rations.[47] They were now five miles from Trenton.

Here the road forks again, the left branch swinging eastward toward the upper northeastern section of Trent's town. The right continues along the river around the southwestern section leading through Front Street and then up into the orchard on the Assunpink Creek.

Unknown to the Continental Army, a Pennsylvania Tory who had come across the Yardley's Ferry Christmas Eve to spend the day with his New Jersey friends, learned early yesterday afternoon of the rebels' plan to march into Jersey. Determined to be of service to his king, the guest, excusing himself, hurriedly left his host and spurred his horse through the gathering storm to the Hessian post.

It was after nine o'clock in the evening when he finally was able to locate Colonel Rall. He had been passed from sentry to sentry and finally into headquarters. Desiring to give his alarming message only to the post commander personally in the hope of some reward, or recognition, the Bucks County informer rode up to Abraham Hunt's door as the cold ice and sleet blew against the back of his snow-covered surcoat.

Inside Rall was enjoying a game of cards but, at the same time, engaging in a serious discussion with his host. A threat had been made some days ago against Rall's garrison by Commodore Thomas Seymour, commander of the Delaware River's fighting seamen and their so-called "American Fleet," mostly gondolas, row-galleys, small schooners and sloops, gathered south of the falls all the way down to Billingsport. Seymour had boldly proclaimed, loud enough through the countryside for von Donop and Rall to hear, that he intended to prevent a Hessian drive into Philadelphia with all the strength and ships he could muster.

Seymour is not only a brave and bold man, known for his daring, adventuresome spirit, but he is, in addition, brazen. He has openly threatened the British high command with the promise that he would burn Trenton down with fiery hot projectiles if he saw a single British redcoat or a Hessian soldier pointing himself toward the capital city.

The American naval commander has erected a blockade across the river at Billingsport similar to the Chevaux de Frise across the Hudson at Fort Lee. He has defied Admiral Howe to attempt a breakthrough from the east by way of Delaware Bay. But no such thoughts have as yet entered the Howe brothers' minds.

It was this threatening Seymour proclamation that Abraham Hunt indelicately injected into the after-dinner conversation. Hunt wants his village to be spared from fire and has feared the commodore's threat might very likely be carried out. With his limited English vocabulary and in a broken dialect, sprinkled with German phrases and expressions, Colonel Rall angrily assured Hunt what he, Rall, would do if Seymour tried anything at all. It helped to relieve Hunt's mind, but he knew that Rall would have difficulty preventing Seymour from torching Trenton if Seymour so decided.

It was at this point that Hunt's servant answered the door and told the excited Tory informer that it was the colonel's instructions that he was not to be disturbed all evening. The frustrated alarm-carrier then wrote a note, saying it was urgent for the post's commandant to be given it immediately.

He handed it to the black servant and reluctantly left. Deciding he had done all he could possibly do for his King, the informer made his way back toward Yardley's Ferry.

After all, he thought, perhaps he was in error. Possibly the rebels were headed elsewhere. Maybe toward Maidenhead, or Princeton.

There was one way to find out. If he passed them on his way back, he would know for sure. He did. Self-satisfied, he mused contentedly that, thanks to him, Rall and his men would be ready and waiting for them.

Hunt's servant gave Rall the folded piece of paper which briefly stated that the rebel army was marching outside of Trenton on its way to attack the village. The colonel opened it, looked at the scribbled English penmanship, and thrust it into his jacket pocket.

To the Fates of ancient mythology, who take delight in juggling and pawning the stupidities and frailties of mortals, there now were gathering the demoniacally delightful sprites—humor, pathos, irony, and tragedy—all waiting to perform in a travesty of man. A travesty ridiculously resting on a scribbled piece of paper that will shape the destiny of nations. For that little piece of paper is Lachesis's eighth and final warning.

Johann Gottlieb Rall is a proud man. He has not encountered too much difficulty in learning to speak some broken English, but he has not gotten very far with its reading and writing. Colonel von Donop, however, has. And this, at times, singes Rall's pride. Consequently, he leaves this branch of his military duties to his adjutant, Jacob Piel. Piel will read the note later. And of what importance could a piece of paper, scribbled in English and, therefore, not from one of his officers, be on Christmas night?

Besides, Rall had no intention of letting his American host know that he, a Hessian colonel, could not read many English words, no less script sentences. So he stuffed the piece of paper into his pocket and, in his badly broken English, resumed the discussion about Seymour . . .

. . . *Lachesis and her friendly partner, Clotho, shake their heads in grief, throw up their hands and walk away, out of the life of Johann Rall. Sadly they hand him over to Atropos . . .*

A little later the Hessian commandant left the Hunt house. Bundling his coat around him, Rall took the nail he chews out of his mouth and put it into his pocket with the unread folded note. Then the valiant British hero of Fort Washington slowly made his way through the storm back to his quarters. He undressed, crawled into bed, concluding that it had been "eine sehr gut Weihnachten."

At that hour the rebels' first and main division was struggling with the Delaware. Now, hours later, despite the hardiness of these hand-picked troops, the earlier enthusiasm is fast waning. Partly it is owing to the growing intensity of the storm against threadbare summer clothing, poorly wrapped cloth-bound shoes, or— in many cases—shoeless feet with wrap-arounds.

More than the physical discomfort, however, is the depressing agony of conviction that the lost hours have robbed the carefully planned, secret expedition of the one major element it had primarily counted upon—surprise. Yet, though buffeted by rain, hail and snow, they stoically withstand the prolonged and continuous torture through the first four miles.

Then, when forced to remain standing to eat their rations at Birmingham's since officers fear sleep will surely overcome them if they drop upon the ground, some of the troops, prohibited from breaking ranks and under "profound silence" orders, doze off, squatting and leaning on their muskets. Some do so, electing sleep in preference to food. It is with difficulty that many of the men are aroused when time comes to continue. Dozing could mean death.

Encirclement Strategy

The upper or left fork at Birmingham runs eastward into the Pennytown to Trenton road. Greene's corps, splitting off from Sullivan's forces, now takes this route. They head for Trenton's north end where the village's King and Queen Streets wedge into the apex that leads to Princeton.

The lower or right fork at Birmingham runs into the southern end of the village by way of the river road. Sullivan's corps takes this route to encircle the town from the south. The distance each corps must travel is approximately the same.

The General elects to go with the larger body under Greene and keep his eye on the Pennytown and Princeton roads. Both of these highways are to be blocked to prevent any enemy escape to the British posts under Leslie and Grant.

It is planned that General Ewing's crossing at Trenton and General Cadwalader's at Bristol, coming into the village's rear doors, will link with Sullivan's corps. These forces are to block the Hessians' escape over the Assunpink Creek Bridge and hold off von Donop.

Ewing, with some of Sullivan's troops, is to prevent Rall's men from reaching the bridge and fleeing along the Bordentown Road to join von Donop. The plan calls for Temporary Brigade General Cadwalader to come up south behind Bordentown's Hessian commander and prevent him from rushing to Trenton in support of Rall. But, if nothing else, Cadwalader is to keep von Donop annoyed and busy while the first division attacks the Hessians' Trenton garrison.

However, much to the disappointment of the American staff there is no report that Ewing or Cadwalader have come across. One unconfirmed report, supposedly from forward scouts, has it that heavy ice and bad weather prevented Ewing from crossing and that these same conditions plagued Cadwalader's men, some of whom reached the Jersey shore and reluctantly had to go back when ordered to return.

With this disheartening information, the first division, both Greene's left prong and Sullivan's right, move on. It will be up to them to carry off the attack alone if Ewing and Cadwalader fail to cross.

And neither of them will get across in time to be of help. For the ice and storm will force both Ewing and Cadwalader to call off their expeditions, leaving the operation's fate solely up to the first division.

Every step now becomes physical torture as the two splintered forces of the main army trudge over the long miles through the freezing night. But at least one thing has turned to favor them. The wind is now on their backs instead of in their faces.

Only the torches of the fieldpieces, stuck in the exhalters, can be seen at times sparkling and blazing throughout the wintry night's long march. They give off an eerie glow that dances in the blown snow as the wearied procession silently moves through the darkness.

The American Commander, ever watchful for any glaring weaknesses or faltering within the lines, occasionally sees some of the men, exhausted under the strain, lagging behind the others. He rides up beside them speaking words of encouragement, or often repeating in a deep, hoarse, throat-sore voice:

"Soldiers, keep by your officers! For God's sake! Keep by your officers!"[48]

On one occasion he rides back to inspirit some stragglers and urges Old Magnolia close along the slippery embankment. Suddenly the mare loses her footing, stumbles and very nearly throws her master down the gully into a rocky declivity. However, The General holds on to Old Magnolia's mane and draws hard upon her reins while the horse struggles to regain her footing on the crest of the bank.

Both rider and animal recover themselves almost as quickly as they lose their balance.[49] It is a narrow escape for both man and horse, but it is safely over in seconds.

Needless to say the men who were falling behind were swiftly jolted out of their stupor by the near-accident. They needed no prodding into wakefulness for the rest of the journey.

When, during the long march, Sullivan sent word to the Commander that the storm was wetting the muskets, making them unfit for service, The General sent back a reply, terse, but pointedly pregnant with determination, saying:

"Tell General Sullivan to use the bayonet. I am resolved to take Trenton."[50]

If Sullivan, and the troops in general, did not realize before that nothing was going to stop their Chief from taking Trenton, they did now. And they knew he meant that with or without Ewing's and Cadwalader's second and third divisions, the objective was to be theirs, if necessary at bayonet point.

Another Jolt For The General

Lieutenant Gray and his Barbette Battery, a part of Captain Gooch's command under Major Blodget and Colonel Bedford, stay close to one another as they have always done, looking out for their own—also as they have always done. They have observed the ordered silence without a single violation, though they slow their steps as a body when one of them falters or pauses to rebind the wrappings around his feet and legs.

Always uniting their efforts, they quickly join together in aiding one of their struggling comrades. When their horse-drawn gun carriage needs an extra push up steep and slippery slopes, through deep ruts and over felled trees and other obstacles, not a man among the old Barbette Battery needs to be told what to do.

That is one reason Private Uriah Wright, with the concurrence of all members of the battery, has been assigned to remain behind on barracks and latrine duty.

Wright could never be one of them. Forced upon them, the private was like a nomad, wanting no part of the army except its pay and shelter. And the Barbette men, not of his ilk, wanted no part of him.

General Stephen's advance, which had tried in vain last night to locate their lost Captain Anderson and his Virginia riflemen, began resuming their hunt before dawn. They soon met with success, stumbling on the captain and his company, all of whom had found warmth and sleep in the pine forest. It is then that Stephen learns with horror about the brush with the Hessian post and the alarm it set off.

At about the same time Stephen is getting the bad news, the main body of the division comes up behind the brigadier general and his van. In the lead are the American Commander and Nathanael Greene.

Dutifully Stephen reports on Anderson's accidental brush with the enemy outpost. Turning red with anger as he hears the shocking account of the action which surely has now alerted Rall's garrison and probably Leslie's, Grant's and von Donop's as well, The General holds his brigadier commander of the Virginia regiment, who was one of the Continental Army Leader's political opponents back in Virginia, responsible. Angrily he excoriates the brigadier, declaring:

> "You, Sir, may have ruined all my plans by having put them (the enemy) on their guard!"[51]

However, the American Leader quickly regains his composure. He sees no reason to punish further the contrite officers and men, particularly the much embarassed Captain Anderson. Nevertheless, he orders that Anderson and his command stay with the brigade.

Without further delay, the General gives the signal for the shivering, snow-covered troops to push on through the pre-dawn darkness. The snow and sleet now have abated, but a driving cold wind still sends its icy blasts cutting cruelly through the ranks of the plodding, struggling Grand Army's first division.

Though now the Continentals cannot be sure that Rall's post is not poised and waiting for them, or that the awakened enemy Juggernaut is about to come in from all sides to devour them, the sleeping Hessian garrison, with the exception of its quiet outposts, is oblivious to all but the pleasures of a long post-Christmas sleep.

A few find dreams that take them home across the sea to their beloved "Vaterland." Their British comrades, the light dragoons and chasseurs, assigned to Rall, also likely dream but of Christmas bells in "Merry Old England." And, among them both, surely are some consciences disturbed by guilt.

It is the guilt that often overtakes the sympathetic giant, forced to destroy his brave but weakened foe. But for what reason he does not know. Such consciences are moved to wonder—more than usual now at Christmas time—what truly are the causes of these hates all harbor? Hates they harbor in a war they are forced to conduct against men no different from themselves. And so they dream.

A Hessian officer, who on Christmas day brought his journal up to date, has left it lying unclosed on the table by the cot on which he sleeps and snores. Its open pages display his entries of the 19th, 23rd and 24th—all in German script:

> "... The 19th one of the English lighthorse was twice badly wounded by a troop of rebels near Maidenhead. The 21st a horseman was shot dead.
>
> "The 23d Count Donop wrote to us from Bordentown, desiring us to be on our guard, for that he was certain of being attacked.
>
> "The 24th (Christmas Eve) the enemy actually attacked our grenadiers last night but without success, two Highlanders and a grenadier were wounded. We have not slept one night in peace since we came to this place. The troops have lain on their arms every night, but they can endure it no longer. We give ourselves more trouble and uneasiness than is necessary.
>
> "That men who will not fight without some defence before them, who have neither coat, shoe nor stocking, nor scarce any thing else to cover their bodies, and who for a long time past have not received one farthing of pay, should dare to attack regular troops in the open country, which they could not withstand when they were posted amongst rocks and in the strongest intrenchments, is not to be supposed."[52]

It is here the diary's entries ended. It is there that the young unknown Hessian officer's last earthly words of worry were left behind him.

Streaks of dawn would soon be in the east. Greene's corps, headed now by Stephen's, then followed by Mercer's brigades and behind them Stirling's reserves, has Roche de Fermoy's regiments bringing up the rear.

Fermoy is to drop behind when the division reaches the northeast outskirts of Trenton where the Pennytown, or Pennington Road, converges toward the Brunswick-Princeton-Trenton road. Fermoy is to place his troops across this vital junction, preventing any possible Hessian escapees from getting through to the British posts at Pennington, Maidenhead, Princeton, Kingston and Brunswick.

Fermoy's task of blocking any enemy retreat from out of the village will become extremely perilous if those northern enemy garrisons should suddenly appear, pouring down the road to aid Rall in Trenton and von Donop below him. Without Ewing and Cadwalader's forces for support Fermoy and the Continental Army's main division could end up within a deadly enemy vice. Leslie, Grant and possibly Knyphausen on the north; Rall and von Donop from below.

The division's right wing under Sullivan also now begins to see the first streaks of dawn as it approaches the town's back door along the river road. St. Clair's, Glover's and Sargent's troops move cautiously along the river toward the village's outposts, hopefully expecting to meet some of Ewing's division coming up to join them from the Blazing Star Ferry crossing.

Though they have been informed by scouts that no crossings have been made at or below Trenton, Sullivan's forces still cling to their hopes. However, Ewing will not make it across, and Sullivan alone will be expected to close Rall's back door.

On the Pennington Road of Trenton's outskirts in the cold early pre-dawn, Lieutenant Andreas Wiederhold stands guard with a corporal and 24 men from the Rall Regiment. It is the regiment which has been given the dubious honor of "Regiment of the Day."[53] Despite the honorary title, it means simply, 24-hour guard duty.

Halfway between that guardhouse and the town, Captain von Altenbockum's company from the Hessian Lossberg Regiment has established its quarters in the house of the prominent American patriot, General Philemon Dickinson. The Dickinson family abandoned their dwelling to the enemy troops when the Americans fled. Leaving their beautiful big river-view home behind them, the family took flight with the Continental Army across the Delaware to Pennsylvania.

To stand guard over his company and its quarters outside the big house, only a half a mile from town, von Altenbockum has posted a detail of 50 jagers. Cold and impatient, they await dawn and the end of their watch.

Almost directly opposite them, standing poised, frustrated and angry on the river's west bank, is General Philemon Dickinson. He commands some of Ewing's militia troops. But Ewing last night took one look at the river, another at the ice and still another at the blizzard overhead. Surely under such conditions, thought Ewing, The General has called off the enterprise and will await a more auspicious day and hour. No doubt Cadwalader, below at Bristol, will find it worse there and do the same.

So, much to Dickinson's regret, Ewing decided not to attempt it, convinced that neither a crossing nor an attack was possible on such a night. Dickinson's eagerness for action is not only inspired by patriotism, he is itching to drive out those who dispossessed him and his family.

Other posts, though of secondary importance, which, fortunately John Honeyman has informed The General he must prepare to take, are located as follows: (1) at the end of Queen Street on the Assunpink Creek bridge; (2) on the road to Maidenhead leading into Princeton; (3) on the road to the Trenton Ferry landing; and (4) on the road to Crosswicks which lies about three miles northeast along the road to Bordentown.

Of these, all but the Maidenhead post are below, or south of the main American division's left wing. So, in mapping out the march and planning the attack strategy, Honeyman's espionage information has been invaluable in this and many other ways.

The Battle

In an excellent example of timing and cooperative communications by dispatch riders, especially in light of the miserable weather, Greene and Sullivan withhold moving in on the two main outposts until they can do so simultaneously. Shortly after dawn upon an agreed signal, Stephen drives through Wiederhold's Pennington Road pickets and puts them to flight.

It is 7:10 A.M. The Battle of Trenton has begun.

At the same time, in pre-planned synchronization with Stephen's stroke, Sullivan sweeps down upon von Altenbockum's fifty jagers, entrapping the Hessian company just waking up inside the Dickinson house.

About a half-mile northeast the corporal's guard of twenty-four men under Hessian Lieutenant Wiederhold flee down the Pennington Road into the town before Stephen's advance.

Shouting, "Der Feind! Der Fiend!"[54] (The enemy! The enemy!) at the top of their lungs in an effort to arouse their drowsy comrades, quartered in homes and in the five military barracks in the village, the guards dash through the streets and spread the alarm.

Stephen's men, followed by Mercer's troops and the artillery, swiftly move into the apex of the King and Queen Streets' wedge in the village's northeast corner.

To the south of the town can be heard Sullivan's musketry followed by a heavy cannonade. Now Greene's artillery opens up on the northern fringe. The British post, Hessian and Englishman alike, suddenly realizes the shocking truth. The ragged rebels are storming in upon them through both their front and back doors.

Pouring out of homes and barracks, the bewildered defenders frantically try to respond to the hastily barked orders from officers who are not sure what to do. In the bitterly cold wind and in the face of the cutting sleet the Hessians fall into their ranks with no walls or entrenchments to shield them.

Now are lamented the unconstructed barricades and defense works which von Donop had ordered at the north apex of the King and Queen Streets wedge. The skeletal outline of the site clearly displays the markings of the planned layout Rall ordered at von Donop's insistence. But that was as far as the works ever got.

Without those defenses, pickets alone had to cover every approach to the town. The overwhelming pouncing upon the outposts by howling rebels, now charging down upon them like enraged demons from out the night's wicked storm, sends the frightened guards running. They stumble and hastily pick themselves up in their beeline back to the village.

Lieutenant Piel, whose quarters are next to Rall's on King Street was awake and dressed when distant shooting and the fleeing, shouting pickets alerted him to what some of the officers had feared might happen. Piel aroused Rall[55] and both men, along with Major von Dechow, sped to the street into which their troops were still outpouring from the barracks.

In near-hysteria at first, the men seek out their officers who, struggling against time, swiftly try to get their battalions into battle formations. Rall, quick of mind, rapidly decides upon a defense strategy.

Fortunately the Hessian regiments' identifying colors make the task of assembling easier in the frenzy of confusion as both musketry and cannonry now distantly blast away in front and behind them. By the colors of their uniforms the regiments, each of which is named for a Hessian commander, are easy to locate.

The Ralls' in blue, form under the colonel himself, while the Knyphausen fusiliers in black, have been ordered by their commander to fall back to King and Second Streets, north of the orchard, as reserves. A part of the scarlet-uniformed Lossbergs belonging to Dechow's battalions are ordered into a cross street. Their mission is to clear Queen Street while the main Lossberg body brings up the rear at right angles to the cross street sector.

Rall's Error

Calling out his commands in German and spinning around on his horse, his sword brandishing the air about him like a knight of old, Rall forms his regiment at the foot of King Street. He is determined to lead a bayonet attack against the American infantrymen and artillery battery brought into position against him at King Street's northern end.

A daring charge will disperse the rebels and restore the confidence of his men. This, in the mind of the Hessian colonel, will teach the rebels a lesson.

Blinded by overconfidence and carelessly underestimating his enemy's strength, Rall chooses an offensive strategy in preference to withdrawal. Before the Americans could get to the bridge over the Assunpink, Rall could now safely lead his troops out of Trenton over the creek and unite with von Donop's 1,600-man corps in Bordentown. There is still time. But Rall wants no such word as "retreat" to mar the records of his Hessian regiments. He erroneously decides to take the offensive and fight it out.

The General and Knox had previously decided to set up their artillery at the King and Queen Streets' apex. For, from this point, they can direct their six fieldpieces down both the main streets.

So now, four of the big weapons under Captain Thomas Forrest are trained on lower Queen Streets' right-angled formation of the Lossberg battalions. Two, under the battling Chatterton Hill of White Plains artillerist, Captain Alexander Hamilton, have their sights set on Rall's regiment that stands poised and ready for its charge up King Street.

The youthful Captain Hamilton, diminutive in stature, is pale and sickly looking, having raised himself from a sick bed. Determined to take part in the expedition, the generally neat and carefully dressed officer is not like his usual self. Only his tricorn hat, cocked forward and to the side of his head, is reminiscent of the soldier for whom, it is said, The General has expressed much admiration.

Like all the others, his snow-covered clothes are torn and his hands and toes are on the verge of freezing. But like every man that has endured the march and the night, personal pain and feeling are suddenly forgotten in the gnawing hunger for a badly needed victory.

At the apex, where the American weapons are now in place, Stephen's brigade, joins with Fermoy's troops. Then, while the main army moves up to the junction, Stephen and Fermoy leave Greene's division and swing to the left. They will circle around the upper outskirts of the village and help form the upper net from the Maidenhead-Princeton-Brunswick road all the way around to the Assunpink Creek on the village's south side.

Also swinging away from Greene's division at the same point, Mercer leads his men to the right, moving down into the west side of the town toward the Delaware in order to join with Sullivan's forces on the river road. Mercer's line will encircle the village's northwest outskirts to form a tightening string that almost closes off all escape routes for the beleaguered post. Mercer will also pierce the village center into the Hessian's left flank.

The one opening, the one unplugged hole in the encircling net, is the Assunpink Creek bridge west of the orchard. Toward this, Sullivan warily makes his way. He hopes the scouts are wrong and that at anytime he will run into some of Cadwalader's men coming up from their expected Bristol crossing to seal off the bridge and prevent any escapes south.

Sullivan sets his cannon up west of Front Street on the backs of Rall's and Dechow's Regiments, while New Hampshire Colonel John Stark of Sullivan's division leads his battalions distantly behind Rall and Dechow gradually hemming them in. Rall's chances of saving his garrison are now rapidly waning.

Stark pushes his right wing point of crack riflemen up to the Assunpink Creek bridge with orders to hold it. This van is to watch for and join Stephen's and Fermoy's corps coming westward down the creek from the apex and road junction in the village's encirclement operation.

As the Stark men close in upon the bridge, cutting off the Hessians' escape to Bordentown, Rall believes the main rebel force is at his front, concentrated at the apex of the main streets. He believes the rebels at his back are a feint, probably only a probing unit, and that the entire attack force is more sound than fury.

Were he better informed, he would have given a "sober second thought" to joining Donop. With the 3,000-man force the Hessians could have driven the rebels northward into the arms of the British at Pennytown, Maidenhead and Princeton.

At stake are Colonel Rall's 1,400 troops, 50 chasseurs, 20 light dragoons, six fieldpieces, much arms and ammunition and, of course, his outstanding reputation for intrepidity earned on Mount Washington.

The costly decision will cause General Howe to place the full blame of Trenton's loss upon Rall's head when the British army commander reports to Lord Germaine from New York, December 29. In his account to London, Sir William will say:

> ". . . This misfortune (The Trenton attack) seems to have proceeded from Col. Rall's quitting his post, and advancing to the attack, instead of defending the village. . ."[56]

However, just how Rall could have defended the village with an ever-tightening rebel ring enclosing him under heavy cannon fire from both directions, General Howe will not bother to explain.

Rall, spurring his horse along the front line of his troops in preparation for the charge up King Street, periodically makes an excellent target for the American sharpshooters when they dry their flints and priming pans. For, between the blowing sheets of sleet and snow, the horseman and his saber stand out even through the grayish morning light of the tapering blizzard.

Bent upon clearing King and Queen Streets with simultaneous bayonet attacks, the Hessian colonel is oblivious to the increasingly closer strikes of shell and grape from Hamilton's battery. His men are not. They cower out in the open street as the rebels' artillery barrage increases in intensity. The two guns Rall has ordered up for a cover barrage now are in place.

Until this point little rifle or musket firing has been heard. Stirling's brigade changes this.

Bringing up the rear of the American column, Stirling and his Continentals march straight through the road junction and its artillery base. They proceed down King and Queen street, entering the homes on both sides, but staying under the cover of Forrest's and Hamilton's artillery barrage.

Inside the long-emptied houses, they dry their pans and flints. From basement windows and from behind blinds and doors they begin laying down a fusillade upon the forming Rall and Lossberg ranks.

Urging his cannoneers to return the rebels' fire, the post's commandant suddenly winces in his saddle as a musket ball tears through the skin of his left hand. Still brandishing his sword with the other, he brings the wound to his mouth and spits the flowing blood onto the white ground.

Then taking a handkerchief from his pocket, he bandages the jagged laceration and gives it no further thought. The bayonet charge is the only thing that is on his mind. In the eyes of the ancient Greeks, the third Fate, Atropos, who closes man's threads is now closing in upon Johann Rall.

Dechow and his Lossbergs move out from a field between Third and Fourth Streets behind the English church. They are to synchronize their charge up Queen and King with Rall's men.

The Rall's regiment and a part of the Lossberg's steadily move up King Street toward Hamilton's battery immediately after their own two fieldpieces have lifted their barrage. Behind the two bayonet-charging regiments, the Knyphausens, near the orchard, stand in readiness, jittery and annoyed by the sporadic firing behind them from Sullivan's artillery.

Closer still on their backs are the approaching riflemen from Stark's battalions. Under this threat, the Knyphausens' rear guards about-face and prepare for Stark's assault.

Meanwhile, north of the orchard, on King Street, Hamilton's canister shots tear into the ranks of the oncoming Rall regiment. Forrest's do the same to Dechow's Lossbergs on Queen Street. But now, in addition, Mercer's corps pierces through at the village center and comes in on the Hessians' left. Mercer distinguishes himself leading his men in their drive through the Hessians' scattering lines.

At the same time Stirling's men keep up a constant fire from the house and basement windows of buildings they have infiltrated on both sides of the street.

The two Hessian regiments blindly try to return the fire with two volleys. Their charge brings them nowhere near the rebel batteries.

Caught between cross fires, half blinded by the sleet and unable to see their enemy, most of whom are concealed, Indian fashion, as The General learned it, in houses and behind fencings, the Hessians no longer respond to Rall's and Dechow's appeals for valor. They fall back in disorder as officers and close comrades, picked off by unseen riflemen or canister charges, drop dead, or fall beside them writhing in pain on the snow.

In the distance to the southeast, moaning, shrieking crowds of camp followers, men and women, scream and run about in helpless terror.[57]

The Battle Spreads With Savage Intensity

Now at its height, the two-hour battle for the strategic little village on the convex nose of the normally quiet Delaware, has become:

> "the noisiest, wildest, murkiest, most savage struggle that anybody on either side (has) ever known—and the most decisive. . ."[58]

Most of the Hessians' heavy weapons are in such fixed positions that they cannot be easily moved or quickly brought into play. The two that are fire only a few rounds. Then their gunners drop, picked off by rebel sharpshooters.

When the Hessians begin to waver, the Continentals charge. Under Stirling's command they cautiously make their way down both streets. Then when a charge spurts forth from within the battalions, the riflemen from the van companies pour out from the houses and from behind barns and fences. Whooping and running they join their comrades.

Weedon's Virginians drive down King Street under Captain William Washington and Lieutenant James Monroe. In the fore of their battalion, the two officers lead their men against the Hessian battery. They fall upon it in hand-to-hand combat and quickly take it.

Washington and Monroe are wounded in the melee. The captain suffers bullet wounds in both his hands.[59]

Under the unexpected rebel offensive, Rall and Dechow fall back with their regiments to Fourth and Third Streets toward the southern edge of town on the village's side of the Assunpink Creek. There they begin to re-form their depleted ranks.

Their dead and wounded lie motionless on the two streets, or struggle hopelessly to get out from under the continuous rain of canister shot and shell from the rebel batteries above them at the apex.

Some of the retiring Hessians, wiser than their colonel, continue their withdrawal, crossing through fire over the Assunpink bridge, or fording the creek. Some flee along the left fork toward Crosswicks six miles away, and span the drawbridge across that Creek. The Hessian post there is three miles east of Bordentown where the distant cannonading has alerted the worried von Donop.

There is still a slight chance of success for Rall if he were now to abandon his attack plans and, fighting off the rebels, lead his three regiments over the Assunpink. Sullivan has not yet come up to the Knyphausen Regiment reserves. Stark has not yet brought his main force to the bridge. A withdrawal now could be the Hessian garrison's salvation.

Rall's twenty British dragoons, like the Hessians running toward Crosswicks, also have abandoned the colonel to his folly. They, too, have taken off, spurring their horses along the Bordentown road to warn von Donop.

Pride and stubbornness are now the masters of the Hessian commandant. He cannot stomach the thought of retreat before an army, part of which he so gloriously conquered not quite six weeks ago and the rest of which he has openly ridiculed and contemptuously tried to ignore.

He will re-form and attack with the bayonet, for the colonel vividly recalls how the American rebels ran, scattering in fear, before his fierce bayonet attack on Fort Washington. Rall, unwilling to admit error, refusing to face realities, is convinced that he and his troops can do it again.

Unquestioningly obeying their commander, the Hessian officers reform their wavering troops. But the spirit of the men is fast flickering.

Second in command, Major Dechow reluctantly re-forms the Lossbergs in preparation for the charge. Like his men, Dechow sees the Americans closing in on all sides, their cannon fire constant and their rifle volleys sporadic but deadly.

Dechow turns and takes a quick glance toward the lightly guarded bridge, the last escape route, unless Rall can drive through the American circle at the rebels' hilltop apex batteries and storm the rebel position in a break-out toward Maidenhead and Princeton. Very shortly Sullivan, whose hammering in the rear is getting closer, will be up on top of the Knyphausen Regiment reserves. There will be no way out then except through the apex. The bridge will be sealed behind them.

However, Dechow is conditioned as are all of the Hessian officers. He will obey without question his superior's command. Now Rall's order comes: "Charge with bayonets fixed!"

In charge formation, bayonets glittering through the falling snow and the Hessian drums and hautboys striking up a marching cadence intended to incite the young German soldiers to conquer great heights along the path to military glory, Rall leads his regiment and some Lossbergs in a sprinting charge up King Street.

The Americans shower the oncoming waves with all the fire they can bring to bear. Canister, grape, rifle and musket shot intermingle with the wind-blown sleet and snow raining down upon the advancing forces.

At the same time Dechow leads his Lossbergs up Queen Street. The American fire is intense. Again the two streets are reddened by the fallen defenders.

Rall, in the lead, his blood-stained wrappings around his hand dripping a scarlet ribbon down the left side of his clothing onto his saddle and the horse's flank, is a determined man. Before him is the valorous way. He must drive through and overrun the rebels in their artillery nest. Once he forces an opening his battalions will sweep their way onto the Princeton road.

By alerting the Pennington, Maidenhead and Princeton posts, he will set the British forces in motion on a drive down from the north. Count von Donop will meanwhile push up from the south. With the river at their backs the American rebels will be driven in. Such was the colonel's hopeful vision.

But the Hessian troops are no longer sprinting. Some begin to fall back under the heavy American barrage. Others are stopped aghast by the splash of blood and the sight of a fallen comrade.

On Queen Street Dechow's troops suffer heavy casualties. They, too, begin to fall back. A retreat is now a military expediency if panic is to be prevented in the ranks. However, a courier brings Piel and Rall word that the Americans have closed in behind the Knyphausen reserves, closed off the bridge and launched an attack upon the Knyphausens' rear.

Belatedly, Rall now orders both his and Dechow's troops to withdraw to the orchard in support of the Knyphausen Regiment. All three corps in unity might still be able to crash through the bridge's defenders and escape down the Bordentown road to von Donop. It is a last and desperate resort.

The Hessian colonel has just given the order when he is struck and knocked from his horse by two musket balls. Both tear through his abdomen, leaving him prostrate in the snow. Two rebel sharpshooters had the same target in their sights at precisely the same second.

Rall is carried by aides, first into the church at Queen and Fourth Streets and later to his quarters in Potts' house.

His post command now falls to Dechow. Even before Rall called for it, the major had ordered his Queen Street battalions to withdraw, for the senseless last charge had cost the major's unit several officers and 30 of his enlisted men.

Dechow pulls back to the orchard and joins the beleaguered

Knyphausens trying to fight off an attack by Stark's New Hampshire men while attempting to break across the Assunpink bridge. Sullivan's forces, charging in droves up from around Trenton's back door on the river road, now move behind in support of Stark. Rall's regiment, leaderless, except for subaltern officers, withdraws in poor order up behind Dechow at the orchard.

Fighting is severe. Dechow makes a valiant effort to take the bridge, but the spirited New Hampshire Colonel Stark, taking the initiative out of his enemy's hands, leads his men against the Hessian major. In the encounter Dechow drops to the ground, critically wounded. He is taken prisoner by the advancing right wing of the American army division, his brief tenure as post commander at an end.

Uncertain as to what has happened to their two leaders, most of the bewildered troops cannot believe that both Rall and Dechow have fallen—and, as some say, are dead. Their sudden absence from the field seems to confirm rumors.

Confused company and battalion officers attempt to rescue order from out of Pandemonium. They issue contradictory orders that only compound the confusion, already heightened by the compressing of all the defenders into the orchard area east of the bridge.

Under almost constant shelling, the leaderless, panic-stricken regiments, once the pride of the King's mercenary forces in America, begin breaking. Fearing for their lives, they think now only of survival, be it flight or surrender.

In a mad dash for safety, some run through the fields east of the orchard where the terror-stricken camp followers wildly mill around weeping and shouting epithets at the rebels. The fleeing Hessians frantically search for a fording place. Some succeed. Some do not.

Those fleeing northeast in the hope of reaching the Princeton road run into the arms of St. Clair's and Fermoy's troops. Some escape by fording, or swimming the bitterly cold Assunpink above the bridge.[60] Freezing but living, they scamper away toward the Crosswicks drawbridge, now deserted by the guard of 100 men and three officers who long since have headed for Bordentown.

A large number of Dechow's men, fighting against capture, try to break across the Assunpink span. Most are repulsed by Stark's New Englanders. In this confusion, many mercenaries successfully make a wild dash with their pointed bayonets before them. In the midst of the bridge chaos, these mixed squads and platoons mass and pour over in spurts behind any leader. It is their last chance for freedom.

Frantically they rush through any gap they find in Stark's line and disappear in the woods along the Bordentown road. Others give up, grounding their weapons. They stand still. Sobbing with anger and frustration, they wait to be captured, offering no further resistance.

There is no top commander now to surrender for them. Many of their officers lie dead or wounded. Others are among the captured.

Over squads, platoons, companies and battalions, white handkerchiefs are raised in piecemeal capitulations all throughout the encircled village. Some attach white cloths ripped from under-garments to pikes and bayonets. Others tie them to their hats hung on poles. They wave them wildly over their heads.

A Crisis and A Fable End In Trent's Town

Scattered surrender signals now rapidly begin popping up over the battle area following many separate hastily called field con-ferences. There is no alternative. The entire garrison is surrounded and its remaining defenders about to be overrun.

Whooping with joy as the white flags rise above their enemy's heads and the Hessian muskets go slamming to the ground, the Continentals' raucous voices fill the bitter cold and sleeting air with excited chatter.

It is the first unconditional surrender for the American Grand Army, not only in the long, six-month old campaign, but since the war's beginning. More than that, it is an overwhelming and decisive victory. To the Continentals, flushed with a long-endured thirst for revenge, the enemy's silenced guns signal the end of the eaglet nation's most terrifying crisis.

The rebels throw their hats high in the blanketing snowstorm, impervious to the freezing weather that chills their limbs in icy stiffness. Their exulting voices suddenly seem to call back and at last revive that hope which so many of them—and so many within the new nation—had very nearly forever lost.

To them Trenton is not merely a victory. It also marks for them the end of a myth, a fable—the mistaken belief that their enemy army and its giant Juggernaut jaws are invincible.

The Toll

Now the sabers and the bayonets are sheathed, the guns stilled and the muskets put at rest. It is nine o'clock, the morning after Christmas. The battle is over, and its toll is taken.

Twenty-two young Hessians, no longer made up in their facade of ferocity, lie dead in the count. Most were draftees from the Dukedom of Hesse-Cassel and Hesse-Hanau lands, yanked like serfs from their families and farms to be trained in warfare and sold by German princes and dukes to nations paying the local ruler a set price for each man.

Unlike professional mercenaries, these draftees from Hesse, Brunswick, Waldeck, Anspach-Bayreuth and Anhalt-Zerbst had no choice. They were not volunteer soldiers of fortune.

Predominantly the offspring of a pious, agrarian German people, the conscripted Hessians are not all military-minded. Many of the Englishmen, volunteering in the King's own British army are petty criminals and heavy drinkers. Some of these redcoats, when contrasted with most of the drafted young Hessian farmers, are far more warlike than their German counterparts.

But the King must pay with added pounds for each of his mercenaries killed or wounded, while the British soldier who falls on the field is not so expensive.

One of the German rulers who supplies mercenaries to warring monarchs at a price, is the Duke of Brunswick. The Duke has a profitable contract with the British Crown. For example, he is to be paid over 11,517 pounds for simply being one of the King's suppliers.[61]

In addition, the Brunswick ruler receives seven pounds a head for each man he furnishes the British army. And for those killed he gets seven additional pounds. Thus, for the 22 Hessians lying dead in Trenton today, King George must pay the German potentate an additional 154 pounds. And, under the contract, three men wounded count as one man dead.

This adds, thus far, another 210 pounds that Britain must pay out in cash for this already expensive battlefield defeat. For 92 boyish-looking wounded Hessians—sans their tall hats, high-heeled boots and padded clothes—are being carried off the field, some mortally wounded.

Among the prisoners taken, 32 of the 948 are commissioned officers.

The spoils the Americans capture include:

six brass fieldpieces; six wagons; 40 horses; 1,000 muskets and rifles with bayonets and accouterments; 15 regimental and company colors; 14 drums; all the trumpets, clarionets and hautboys of two bands; and 40 hogsheads of rum.[62]

To the utter disgust of some of the hardy old Continentals, the American Commander, who wants no drunken soldiers on his hands, orders the hogsheads of rum staved in and spilled on the ground. The order is executed with extreme care and protracted delay, particularly that part which calls for rum spilling.

Retaliation: War's Ceaseless Cycle

Twenty-eight of the severely wounded prisoners are to be paroled and left in the town on order of the American Commander. Among these are Colonel Rall and Major Dechow.

Formalizing the surrender of the garrison, General Stirling accepts the swords of the regimental subaltern officers in the absence of any one designated post commandant. With both the garrison's leader and his second in command on death beds, the Hessian regimental officers order the laying down of arms. They surrender themselves, their swords and their commands to the American officer who four months ago surrendered his sword and command to the British on Long Island.

The American Chief now vividly recalls that day. That is one reason why he delegates Stirling for the honor. He now purposely remains quietly in the background.

Many of the men who have heard stories of Colonel Magaw's surrender of the Fort Washington post to Colonel Rall almost six weeks ago know why. They have heard how the British commander and his staff of generals disdainfully stood back on that dark day while subordinate British and Hessian officers and men humiliatingly struck the colors of the fort that was named in honor of the Number One American Rebel.

Nevertheless, The General, accompanied by Greene and aides, pays his respects to the mortally wounded Rall in the Stacy Potts house. He personally hands the dying man his parole.

The Hessian commander in preparing for his visitor, had asked to be dressed in his uniform. With the Potts family and the surgeon beside him, the colonel sat up in bed to receive his conqueror and accept the conditions of his short-lived earthly freedom.

When the visitors leave, the surgeon and Potts help to remove the colonel's blue coat. From out the pocket Rall withdraws the crumpled piece of paper, stuffed there last night when Hunt's servant gave it to him. He tries to read it and cannot. Potts obligingly does so for him.

"Hatte ich dies zu Herrn Hunt gelesen," Rall pathetically says to Potts, his wife and the Hessian surgeon, "so ware ich zest nicht hier."[63]

The surgeon, recognizing that the American hosts have little knowledge of the German language, translates it for them, saying, "He says that if he had read that last night at Mr. Hunt's house, he would not be where he is today."

To this the Fate, Atropos, in the wings, and possibly Lachesis, watching from some mount so oft enjoyed by Greek goddesses, might very well step out of character to say, "Jawohl!" For Colonel Johann Gottlieb Rall will die tomorrow.

On the American side, the toll is surprisingly light. Only the two officers, Captain Washington and Lieutenant Monroe, and two privates are wounded.[64]

However, for the Continental Army Commander, the victory is not as complete as was hoped. It is a plan unfinished. The failure of General Ewing to cross at Trenton Ferry and General Cadwalader below at Bristol enabled almost a third of the enemy garrison to escape and alert von Donop. And by now possibly Leslie and Grant have heard the news, for it is believed that about 500 have slipped through the American net.[65]

Had Ewing and Cadwalader been able to cross, Count von Donop and his post would likely now be bagged. But the extra strain upon his men without the Ewing and Cadwalader forces, and the cold miserable weather, in addition to the certainy that von Donop, Leslie and Grant are now alerted, make it necessary to call off the proposed second part of The Plan, the march on Princeton—at least for the present.

"What happened to Ewing and Cadwalader?" is the question that puzzles the American command. It is answered in part by the scouts.

Eventually The General and his staff will hear how Ewing, much to the regret of some of his officers, called the whole thing off believing the other divisions would do the same.

The high command will also hear how Cadwalader went a few steps farther than Ewing. Cadwalader attempted a crossing at Dunk's Ferry and succeeded in getting only a part of his corps over. This included four companies of Philadelphia militia and Captain Thomas Rodney's Dover company.

In five large bateaux and three scows, some could only get within 100 yards of the shore. These men then walked over the ice to reach the enbankment. There, at 8 P.M., they sought shelter and huddled under the cover of a pine tree forest, waiting for the others. Colonel Reed and one other officer got their horses across safely. This was all the assurance many others needed to convince them the job could be done if the will was there.

It was an hour later that the first and third battalions of the Philadelphia Associators came within 200 yards of the shore where solid ice jammed their vessels. They were conveying two field-pieces.

All 600 of the men scrambled over the ice but had to abandon the scows and their cannon. The men on shore were certain they could be landed and unloaded, but now came the disheartening command to return to the Pennsylvania side.

Cadwalader, on the Pennsylvania shore, decided that the operation must be called off. Like Ewing, he believed the other divisions would do the same. He dispatched a courier, ordering all those crossed to return. That was after 10 P.M.

Some of the men, angered at their commander's change of mind, very nearly decided to go on alone through the miserable darkness. They would execute their part of The Plan as best they could.

In a letter to his brother, Caesar, describing the cold Christmas night on the lonely Jersey bank along the freezing Delaware, Captain Rodney will later write:

The March Back

"... We had to stand six hours under arms, first, to cover the landing and till all the rest had retreated again; and by this time, the storm of wind, hail, rain and snow was so bad that some of the infantry could not get back until the next day."

Informing his brother that Cadwalader's order to come back across the river was disappointing to the men, Rodney will write:

"(The order) greatly irritated the troops that had crossed ... and they proposed making an attack without both the generals and the artillery."

Here Rodney will point out that the argument that dissuaded the troops was that if both the American Commander and they were unsuccessful, the American cause could be lost. But if the

Chief were unsuccessful, then it would be left solely up to the Pennsylvania-based forces and the Northern army above Albany to try to "keep up the spirit of America." So some began recrossing. The Maryland captain will conclude by saying:

> "if our generals (Cadwalader and Ewing) had been in earnest, we could have taken Burlington with the light troops alone."[66]

So, at the close of the battle, in which only a third of the planned attack force was able to participate, wisdom dictates a prompt recrossing of the Continental forces to the river's west bank and the safety offered on the Pennsylvania shores. The attack upon Princeton is canceled, at least for the time being.

It is a far from easy march back. However, all have eaten heartily, thanks to the Hessian commissary's ample stores and provisions. And many are also well fortified with a little of the "unspilled" confiscated rum.

Though success has made them unconscious of their own exhaustion following 24 ceaselessly grueling hours without sleep, physical collapse is close upon many of the men as they plough wearily back into the storm's north wind.

Fortunately—and with another thanks to their enemy—fewer Americans now are bootless, hatless or coatless. In fact, some of the rebels now look more like Hessian soldiers than the some 900 prisoners marching under guard back to McKonkey's Ferry in the rear of Stirling's corps.

General Stirling, who is in charge of the prisoners, tomorrow will write from "Newtown, Bucks county. . . December 27, 1776," saying:

> ". . . I was immediately sent off with the prisoners to M'Conkey's ferry, and have got about seven hundred and fifty safe in town and a few miles from here, on this side the ferry, viz. one Lieutenant Colonel, two Majors, four Captains, seven Lieutenants, and eight Ensigns. We left Col. Rohl, the Commandant, wounded on his parole, and several other officers and wounded men at Trenton."

Then, hearing rumors of the reported deaths of two Americans, Lord Stirling will add:

> "We lost but two of our men that I can hear of, a few wounded, and one brave officer, Capt. Washington, shot in both hands."[67]

Those "lost two," whom the general from New Jersey will

mention, are among the three, who, it will be said, "were frozen to death in the boats."[68] For exhaustion and sleep can now very easily overtake a man and quietly, icily hug him to death.

So, again in the literate, dreamy minds of the scholars of ancient Greece and its rapturous myths, the gods—always solicitous for warriors who have earned their peace and rest—surely are sending down one of their own from Mount Olympus. And he, with his son, Morpheus, will carry off the badly wounded to some far distant Valhalla. It matters not which hat the heroes wear. And it matters not the way their threads of life are knotted at the end.

The re-crossing of the Delaware is treacherous, slow and, even in the late afternoon's daylight, extremely difficult. It becomes worse as darkness approaches. The waning blizzard bequeaths its blistery cold winds to night. Now they sweep relentlessly over the ice and snow-covered earth.

Not a man nor cannon was lost in the nine-hour river crossing 24 hours ago. Now, however, although under the same wretched blanket of weather, they face more troublesome crossing conditions. And besides, there are more men to be transported. There also are the weak, the wounded, much captured armament and almost a thousand prisoners to compound the problems of a hazardous return. And they now must cross against, rather than with the wind.

Many of the troops, extremely weakened by the long, arduous, sleepless ordeal, have to be helped by the strong. Some are conveyed on the top of caissons or in the wagons. Laboriously they are helped, or carried, and huddled into the bottom of the Durham boats which cannot always be brought close into the landing dock. Many of the men assisting in the loading are soaked and ice-covered up to their knees in the river, some up to their waists.

In this operation, the vigorous, lively spirited Delawarean, Colonel John Haslet,[69] is outstandingly active in the exhausting work of loading men, prisoners, horses, the weak and the wounded into the vessels.

In the cold, slippery operation, Haslet, after safely getting his own horse aboard one boat, goes to the aid of a stumbling, sick, half-frozen soldier and assists him into the bottom of his boat.

The colonel's right foot rests perilously on one of the landing dock's sheared and shaking, ice-crusted pilings. His left spreads out on the rocking vessel's slippery stern gunnel for a brief few moments until the debilitated young soldier is comfortably placed alongside of others.

Suddenly a violent gust of wind strikes full force against the vessel on the dock's lee, or south side. At the same time, another Durham on its way out from the shore, alongside and to the south of Haslet's boat, is struck hard at the bow by the same driving wind-burst. It happens just as the outbound boat's stern is clearing the loading craft's bow.

The departing Durham's rear pivots back toward the dock. Its bow sharply swings out, downstream. The stern strikes forcibly against the loading vessel's bow.

This blow, coupled with the fierce wind against the docked boat's stern end, snaps the holding line. Released from its fastenings, the vessel's shore-end swings out violently from the dock under the extreme pressures of wind and current. Haslet's spread eagle legs stretch with the widening gap until, within seconds, he loses his balance and topples.

The colonel falls backward, tumbling through the ice chunks into the deep and freezing water. Momentarily he disappears beneath the churning icy surface.

Alarmed by the commotion, almost every man on or near the landing rushes to the scene. The congenial, popular and widely respected colonel, whose fighting reputation and daring on the battlefield have often brought him into the gun sights of enemy marksmen, is helped out of the water and back on the dock.

Someone hands him his wringing wet tricorn. He squeezes out the water. Almost before he has replaced it on his head, it has stiffened in the below freezing temperature.

Emptying the river from his boots and discarding his wet and stiffening surcoat, the commander of the once so-called "Flower" regiments of the Continental Army, the Delaware and Maryland troops who were the pride of Stirling's corps on Long Island, shakes himself and goes on about his task. However, he conceals his shivering and chattering of teeth under the dry blanket thrown over his head.

Fortunately, Stirling, who witnesses the accident from his horse on the enbankment, orders his subordinate to take shelter and dry out in the ferry-master's house without further delay. Haslet does so.

There are many others who get wet feet in the return but none as wet as Haslet's.

Whether from the joy of liberation or from a desire to ingratiate themselves with their rebel captors, the Hessian prisoners prove to be more than cooperative. Those who do understand some English make it their business to see that all the others carry out whatever commands are given them throughout the march and at the landing.

Seeing their enemy trying to get the coating of ice off the long-idled boats, the prisoners voluntarily help out in the task. They jump up and down in the Durhams, shaking the ice off the hulls. Their long black pigtails bob capriciously on their backs as they hop around on the boat bottoms.

Their amusing antics in an effort to be of service promote raucous laughter from their rebel conquerors. To some of the officers they resemble schoolboys enjoying their first recess.

". . . the dreadful effects of arbitrary power . . ."

The Hessian prisoners will be marched first to Newtown and then on to Philadelphia where "by an authentic account"[70] the returns will show a total prisoner catch of 930. Of these will be listed:

1 colonel; 2 lieutenant colonels; 3 majors; 4 captains; 8 lieutenants; 12 ensigns; 2 surgeon mates; 99 sergeants; 25 drummers; 9 musicians; 25 servants; 740 privates.

The returns will not show the number of wounded left behind in Trenton and paroled by the American Commander owing to the severity of their condition. The published account will, however, say of the prisoners marched into the capital city:

> "The wretched condition of these unhappy men, most of whom, if not all, were dragged from their wives and families by a despotic and avaricious prince, must sensibly affect every generous mind with the dreadful effects of arbitrary power."[71]

When the colorfully uniformed Hessian regiments, the blue Ralls, the scarlet Lossbergs and the black Knyphausens in dark blue coats, followed by their artillerymen with crimson lapels, are paraded through Philadelphia's streets after arriving there Monday next, the 30th, the sight of captured Hessians will help to relieve the frightened populace. For many of the inhabitants, fearing imminent enemy invasion, have wondered whether they should have flown the city along with the Congress and a number of the city's residents.

Remembering their fears and recalling all the atrocity stories they have heard, many of the townspeople will look upon the paraded prisoners with little sympathy. One eyewitness will describe the scene by saying:

"They made a long line—all fine, hearty looking men and well clad, with knapsacks, spatterdashes on legs, their looks were *satisfied*. On each side, in single file, were their guards, mostly in light, summer dress and some without shoes, but stepping light and cheerful."[72]

From Philadelphia they will be sent through Lancaster to western Pennsylvania and into Virginia. Generally, they will acquire the reputation for being model prisoners, obedient and docile. In the post-war years ahead, many of them will become part of more than 5,000 Hessian soldiers who will choose to remain forever in America.

The Ultimate Blame

It will be only a matter of hours before General Howe in New York will be jolted with the news that his army's Hessian vanguard at Trenton has been wiped out. Militarily he has made another blunder. And Sir William's critics will lose no time in placing the blame upon his head. They will contend he was in error in entrusting the van and left wing of his over-extended lines to the Hessian troops rather than to the British regulars.

The assignment of the honorary lead position to the mercenaries rather than to the redcoats has caused rumbling objections up through the string of posts that make up the enemy line from Bordentown to Brunswick. However, the British commander-in-chief's mistake has a plausible explanation.

Throughout the campaign the Hessians have generally been assigned the army's left wing position. So in the extended line of march toward Philadelphia, von Donop and Rall were the left wing but also the army's van, becoming at the same time, closest to the rebels' front.

The British high command recognized that inasmuch as the Trenton to Bordentown area lay closest to the Continentals, it was the most perilous position of the long invading chain. From the prestige point of view, militarily speaking, the position should have been assigned to the King's own men.

However, if Howe and his staff had replaced the left wing and vanguard with their redcoat regulars, the Hessian commanders were sure to have looked upon the act as one impugning "their military 'honor'."[73] And "military honor" is a touchy subject about which German officers are extremely sensitive. Consequently, Howe, unwittingly committing another costly mistake, erroneously curtsied to military tactfulness while prudent military judgment stepped aside.

All through the night, the pre-dawn hours and late into tomorrow's morning, the difficult troop recrossing task will continue. It will be late tomorrow afternoon before the last man will reach his cot, or crawl exhausted into his bedroll on the ground.

By that time some of them will have marched and fought continuously for almost 50 hours. They will by then have ploughed through bitterly cold arctic weather for 40 miles, most every step of which will have been arduously lifted in the face of a raging storm.

And in all that time they will have found no more than three or four hours of rest and cessation from one of the most grueling and most unparalled military operations in warfare's history.

Of it, one historian will some day say:

"This was a long and a severe ordeal, and yet it may be doubted whether so small a number of men ever employed so short a space of time with greater or more lasting results upon the history of the world."[74]

The Stroke Explodes With Vast Effects

In still later years another historian, after analyzing the momentous effects of this day upon the enemy, the war, the world and its future, will say that the American Commander-in-Chief and his army's attack virtually ended foreign rule in America. He will write:

"(The General's) one stroke, pitifully small by any standard, changed the whole course of the war... it saved the American cause... (it) made the rest of the war a foolish British impertinence, for it can be said, and not without reason, that at Trenton the British dropped forever the gage of final victory in the Revolution."[75]

The effects will indeed begin falling after this day and its tomorrow are over. Certainly with only five more days left before the new year arrives, and with it the expiration of so many more enlistments in the American camp, the New York Campaign of 1776 is chronologically supposed to end. And chronologically it will end the calendar year with these 12 outcomes swelling hope for the American Cause:

●*An end, at least temporarily, to the threat against Philadelphia;*
●*The forced withdrawal of Count von Donop from Burlington to Allentown;*

●*The eventual evacuation of every British post along the Delaware;*

●*An horrendous jolt and setback to the British command, Parliament and the Crown;*

●*Lord Cornwallis canceling his plans to return to England and joining Howe in a swift return to take over the army's command in Jersey;*

●*Providing Benjamin Franklin with arguments for involving France in the war against England;*

●*Assurance for the American army and the new states that The Cause is alive and that the enemy is not invincible, thus restoring waning confidence in the American Leader, its Congress and the nation's hopes for independence;*

●*The dropping of efforts in the Congress to replace the Continental Army's Commander-in-Chief and appoint another in his place;*

●*Renewed Congressional efforts to give the Commander-in-Chief greater support and more extensive military powers, passing a resolution vesting in him the following powers:*

> " 'full, ample and complete powers' to raise more battalions, infantry, light horse, artillery and engineers and to appoint all officers under the rank of brigadier general and to replace them at will, to fix their pay, to commandeer 'whatever he may want for the use of the army,' and to arrest the disaffected.";[76]

●*A stiffening of resistance by the country's patriots to the recently increased harassments from loyalists, particularly Tory raiders, and, conversely, a retrenchment by these pro-British harassers, who will become suddenly stunned and frightened by the unexpected turn of events;*

●*An end of the greatest of all the crises that will beset the Americans throughout the war, for none of all the many that will arise to threaten the newly formed nation will come so close to bringing about the complete destruction of the young eaglet;*

●*An increased respect and admiration for the united colonial states that will spread throughout Europe, bringing world nations and their peoples to support—and later bask under—the brightening torch of American liberty and independence and all the lifted restrictions on human freedoms which, in time, it is destined to espouse.*

By the end of the coming week, the diary-writing young Englishman, Nicholas Cresswell, will sum up the effects of Trenton and the Americans' further actions which will be taking place next Thursday and Friday. He will write in his journal:

"A few days ago they (the rebels) had given up the cause for lost. Their late successes have turned the scale and now they are all liberty mad again. . . They have recovered [from] their panic and it will not be an easy matter to throw them into confusion again."[77]

However, all these effects, though exacting a remarkably light toll upon the Continentals' Grand Army thus far, are yet to demand a much greater price. Though the costs to the King's Juggernaut will continue mounting, the American rebels will also pay a staggering stipend in blood before the campaign's curtains are drawn across history.

Trail Back To the Hudson

It was in the midst of the battle this morning that Lieutenant John Gray was grazed by a flying rock. Thrown up by a bursting ground shell, it struck the officer's flying petticoat scarf at the back of his neck, slightly tearing the cloth and the collar of his jacket. Having given his surcoat to Jocko last night, Gray had wrapped a blanket around him to keep out the cold until the battle opened.

One glance at the rock convinced him that he was surely looking at the same type of igneous crust that was volcanically oozed from the earth when the Palisades were born. Underneath the light summer jacket he had worn all through the march, The Lieutenant had packed in old cloth rags, papers, leaves and straw to keep out the cold. These had absorbed the stone's blow.

Gray quickly picked up the jagged, four-inch missile, thinking at first it was a shell fragment. Very briefly his mind flashed back to his Princeton class. The jovial, scholarly Professor Ezra, he recalled, had proposed the theory that the Palisades of the Hudson reached deep into a canyon in the ocean and probably stretched a finger into West Jersey, possibly as far west as the Delaware. Had he now found the clue?

Without giving it any more thought, The Lieutenant stuffed the stone into his jacket pocket and returned to the grim business of war. But in those brief seconds he remembered how he had told Jocko and Elaine of the professor's proposition. Along with Asser on the high Bluff Rock of The Mountain, all four had discussed the strange theory. Asser had been one of the doubters. And now here was the evidence. Or so Gray thought.

The brief incident caused Gray's mind to think of Jocko and wonder, as he has often done throughout the night, how he fares. The inquisitive youth had asked many questions about the professor's theory and the earth's beginnings. The rock would mean much to young Graves.

Gray's mind flashed to frightening thoughts, but the officer had convinced himself that the boy's ordeal in the cold corral would have no after effects. And he was glad that the youth and his father had not made the long trek to Trenton.

And then, as only the human mind can do in brief seconds, The Lieutenant's thoughts flashed between memories and fears to the Baummeister house and his Ellie.

"When? Oh, God, when would they get mail through?" he asked himself as he and his battery pulled west around Trenton with Mercer's corps to support Sullivan.

He suddenly waked himself from out of the hypnotic web of memories and fears and mused over how ridiculous the mind is to dwell on such things in the midst of battle. Again he returned to the business of death.

Though Gray does not know it, the post from Philadelphia will have a letter waiting for him tomorrow. Elaine had wisely written to her in-laws whom she has never seen. She enclosed a letter to be sent on to her husband if possible. It was written after she had learned from Abbott that the army was headed for Pennsylvania.

Elaine's letter carries good news. It notes just as she had said before in the one Abbott brought that the British were considerate and that they have evacuated the area except for patrols and foraging parties. Its main contents, the officer will find, are Elaine's concern for him, for Jocko and his father, for the battery and the army.

It will be late tomrrow night before the officer gets the long-awaited communication. Unfortunately, however, there will be a pall of gloom hanging over the men of the old Barbette Battery tomorrow that will turn Elaine's letter into sadness for her husband.

But today in Trenton there was no way for Gray to know that at the far northern end of what the learned professor believed was a strain of volcanic rock that reached into the Hudson's Palisades, Elaine on the Bluff Rock was tormented by a strong presentiment, one foreboding tragedy. Nothing like it had ever so disturbed her before.

For the young bride of "The Blue Petticoat Scarf Lieutenant,"

Christmas day had been one of sadness, just another in the day-in, day-out weeks of constant worry. Not only has it been so for Elaine, but also for all of the inhabitants of the water's edge and The Mountain. For they, too, have shared in the hopeful, lonesome vigil.

For over a month The Mountain's people have heard nothing but hearsay and false and frightful rumors about Greene and his men whom they had hosted so long. Yet the Fort Lee garrison had become an unforgettable part of their lives, lives which had been previously unexciting and uneventful.

Now they hungrily look for word, particularly some news about Colonels Bedford and Hitchcock's artillerymen, and John Gray especially. For the Baummeister-Gray marriage had tightly cemented the friendly alliance, not only between the Barbette Bluff Rock Battery and the people of the water's edge, but also between the fort's troops and The Mountain people.

Though the blizzard left its wind-blown white cloak lying coldly over the valley, The Mountain and Hudson's river Christmas night and has continued casting its sleeting veneer over the land into this, the following day, Elaine and her brother have, nevertheless, made a lonesome pilgrimage up to the deserted Barbette Battery site on the great Bluff Rock.

While Paul played around her husband's long-silent, spiked and ice-coated cannon on the old Barbette, Elaine walked through the snow down on the under-cliff footpath below the great table rock's overhang to the ledge rock. The artillerymen, who had often looked down and seen The Lieutenant and his betrothed sitting together on the wide projecting piece of precipice high over the river, had, consequently, named it, "Lovers' Ledge." And by no other name would they or others call it.

Now she stood there alone. Memories of the summer and fall raced across her mind. She trembled as she looked out across the river's mist at British-held Manhattan Island, for she sensed that something was wrong. It had to do with the enemy. It had to do with John.

It was intuitive fear, unlike the constant worry that had daily plagued her since her husband marched off westward. This was fear, haunting not only her waking hours but also the dreams within her subconscious mind.

It was fear more real than imaginary. It was perception and vision into the future. It was a strange hurdling of the mind over reasoning and understanding into an inexplicable dimension of reality that opens out through the window of what is to be and never can be altered.

Elaine, frightened by her own senses, yearned to see—just to see him. She wanted only to make sure her dream was just that and nothing more.

Her eyes dropped down to the waters far below. Memories persisted in rushing through her brain. Then her thoughts brought Jocko forcibly knocking at her mind. "Dear Jocko" she heard herself say aloud . . . "Big Tom! . . . All of them!"

"Oh, God!" she prayed. "Take care of them! . . . Take care of him!"

Gray's bride of just over two months is almost that long pregnant. She has borne her problems well, but for the first time since her husband and his battery marched away, Elaine is more than deeply troubled.

Struggling within her breast is the strong Dutch Baummeister strain holding the mind to only pragmatic explanations. It temporarily wins. The ferry-master's daughter dismisses her "unfounded" fears. She tries to attribute her depression to maternity's mysterious machinations.

Nevertheless, despite practicality, Elaine could not forget her nightmarish dream, not a bit of which she can remember since it awakened her with horror last night. All that it left behind was the frightful certainty that something terrible was occurring or about to occur, in some far distant place. Then terrified and perspiring, her heart beating rapidly, she awakened startled by the darkness of her room.

She groped her way to the window. Only a few live embers still glowed eerily across the hearth's andirons. Outside the blizzard still raged. The snow and ice-covered multi-paned windows stood like an opaque curtain between her and the dark, bleak, howling winter, raging furiously over the river below.

How often, she thought, how many times had she and John looked through this very window upon the moonlighted Hudson and, in pleasant reverie, dreamed hopefully of happier tomorrows! How long ago those joyous hours now seemed to be!

The cold night, the darkness and the blank white space beyond the twelve small window panes, together with the shock of her awakening, had filled Elaine with a terror such as she had never felt before. It was hours before she again closed her eyes in sleep, but throughout the day the tormenting nightmare preyed upon her mind.

All this and the strange inner foreboding had urged her to seek the solace of the ledge rock.

She slowly walked back, returning to Paul at the old Barbette. The worried girl took her brother's hand and the two made their way down the deserted gorge road to the peaceful quiet of the concerned hearts around the Baummeister fireside.

Back Into the Arms Of the Earth Mother

Exhausted, cold but at ease in the realization that their enemy's jaw has been temporarily broken, Gray and his battery slowly make their way back to quarters. The Petticoat Scarf Lieutenant and his men were in the van of the returning army and so were among the first to recross. It is not yet midnight, but for the troops coming in and yet to come across it is the ending of an unforgettable Thursday, December 26.

In a far corner of the old barn that has been the battery's home for the past week, Big Tom Graves sits crouched, silently staring into the ground. His head is buried in his huge hands. As though dazed with shock, he looks into space as he sits immovable beside a straw bed on which rests a covered form, the outline of which clearly marks it as a human corpse.

Gray's frightened eyes take in the scene. Fearfully they sweep up from the ground, drawn by the noisy hammering on the other side of the stable. By the light of the two lanterns at either end of the building, The Lieutenant can see that it is Andy Abbott putting the last few nails into the sides of a coffin, a coffin of pine boards ripped from an empty grain bin.

Praying that it is a mistake and not what he imagines, Gray, followed by Levy, moves swiftly toward the blanket-covered mound-like bed. He lifts the covering and to his horror looks down upon a smiling, lifeless face. Before him lies the boy who had slipped into his life and hugged his heart more firmly to his breast than if the black youth had been his younger brother. Distantly he hears someone tell him that the battery's mascot died without uttering another word after The Lieutenant had whispered in his ear on the boat last night.

Now those last moments in the boat flash through Gray's mind—telling Missy E not to worry... asking the meaning of the numerical symbols... the promise that he would not tell "not ebin Missy E...."

No more, Gray tells himself, will he answer the youth's countless questions about the thrilling world of people and things he found so fascinating all around him. Surely, Gray thinks, in an effort to convince himself his young friend could never die, surely he has just quietly stepped into that other world—into that other world enrobed with overwhelming answers to Jocko's insatiable quest to solve all the riddles of Creation. There will now be time for him, Gray thinks. But not in this world. For, in this world, Jocko Graves is dead.

Gray gently pulls the blanket over the same happy smile the youth had left him with last night. How could he have known then that it was the smile of death?

Overcome with emotion, Gray, his eyes moist, turns and walks outside alone.

In the morning, in a shallow grave not far from their quarters, the men of the old Barbette will solemnly watch as the sixteen-year old freedman returns to the fickle, all-encompassing arms of the Earth Mother. Trying desperately to control his grief, Gray will stand beside Jocko's distraught father.

The Lieutenant's pockmarked face will twitch in anguish. That and the watery beads dropping from his cheeks will be the only evidence of Gray's affliction. His arm will encircle Tom's shoulders, steadying the older man in the grim loneliness that can sink men's soul into despairing depths of unconsolable suffering.

Earlier tomorrow morning when Levy seeks volunteers for the hard, cold grave digging job, the men of the battery will be astounded when Uriah Wright steps forward, the first to do so. Stranger still will be his willingness to carry out the task alone if no one else volunteers. But there will be many offers. However, Wright will do much of the hard digging in the frozen ground. He will make no remarks. He will speak to no one.

Only Mike Monahan, who will hardly believe it, will have an aside comment to make. He will declare Wright must be terribly afraid of his god to be repenting his sins by punishing himself for his inexcusable attack on the Graves boy a few days ago. Nevertheless, Wright will labor throughout the cold morning, helped by others in the digging of Jocko's grave.

Oddly, however, he will not bow his head or enter into prayer with all the others as the regimental chaplain conducts the short service, saying in closing: "Many will die along far different paths of glory but none with such singular and modest greatness as Jocko Graves, the 'Youngest Soldier In the Continental Army' and this battery's first mortality. Into your hands, Oh, Lord, we commit his young soul. . . ."

Sadly the Barbette men will return to their tasks, a deep scar left in their ranks—the first and the hardest for them to accept.

But in the division's cantonment tomorrow, there will be much late sleeping, for the excitement of victory—despite weariness bordering on exhaustion—will not allow sleep to overtake all of them as easily as they thought it would tonight. So, throughout the next 48 hours over a thousand men will report "unfit for duty."[78]

All of that will be tomorrow. Tonight, from high above the bivouac, a day closes on a world-shaking event almost unnoticed. The hidden moon looks through the dark, cold night upon a village torn by battle. It looks down upon death and northward upon the last of the river-crossing troops, struggling against the arctic blow in boats that fight as hard as the marching men to stay on course.

The 1776 Christmas march on Trenton is fast fading into history some 32 hours from its beginning. Along the now coldly quiet shores of the river Delaware, and far and wide over the land, a great change is gradually about to take place.

Gruesome Is the Wake Of Battle

Eyes looking downriver from just about the Delaware's convex nose would be drawn to the dimly lighted homes of the few villagers who have remained in Trenton through the frightening battle. For them also sleep tonight is difficult.

Snow, ice, sleet and the wintry darkness do not hide the shattering destruction suffered by the riverside town. Dramatically telling the story of the violent, two-hour street battle are the trampled grounds, wrecked homes, the charred ruins, the damaged shops, smashed windows and bloody streets.

Nor do the blustery gusts of wind and their trailing white gowns conceal the gaping holes, torn open by shot and shell that have left splintered walls, broken chimneys and mangled roofs.

And where men dropped, there, gruesomely outlined, are the telltale artistries of war, etched in a frozen frieze with the erstwhile scarlet sap of human life.

Only horses, dogs and cats, the innocents of battle, lie still and unclaimed upon the earth's flattened, ermine-like easel. Stiff, silent and ice-covered, they will remain for days where they were dropped, comfortably at rest and free from the fear of man and all his horrors.

Now in the night's desolate stillness, brushed only by the wind's weakening breaths, no sign of life is seen outside the tightly shuttered homes. The bullet-riddled streets, which a few hours ago were ablaze with flashing, fusillading fire, bursting cannon shot, grenades and canister, are, but for the occasional, waning, howling wind-bursts, deathly stilled.

Those brief, wild melees and their saber wielding, bayonet slashing, shouting, charging men, all performing well their grotesque dance of death, are, like flashes of lightning, striking with deadly suddenness, then vanishing in stillness.

Inside the homes and barracks, the yellowish streaks of light from candles, lanterns and whale oil lamps, stream through ice-coated window panes. They tell of the midnight aftermath of battle, the struggle of surgeons to save the wounded, or ease the pain and soften the death of the dying.

Only yesterday those now somber, silent barracks and many of the homes which had quartered the Hessian soldiers, were ringing with the merry voices, the Christmastide songs and the rollicking tunes of German youth. Thousands of miles from their Vaterland, they sought to bring the celebrating spirit of their homeland and their loved ones into their isolated, enforced circle on a distant foreign soil.

For many it was the first Christmas away from home and kith and kin. There were prayers. And the chaplain led some in hymns. Music, laughter, toasts and drinking songs filled the air. Food and drink were plentiful.

The celebrating closed, and then came sleep—a sleep that violently ended amid cannon bursts, rifle fire. War! Only the pitiful shrieks of "Gott in Himmel!" rose above the uproar.

For the long, hotly pursued and struggling eaglet, for the rising new nation, it was the beginning of the end of the great depression which had brushed her feathers on the teeth of destruction. And the Christmas-celebrating Hessian garrison in Trenton was simply the victim—the way out and to recovery.

A Lion Dies

The yellowish streams of light from two houses on King Street will continue casting their ghastly, spectral glow upon the dark, snow-covered grounds like a vigil, all through the night. So likewise will the burning wicks in the five barracks. Some of the strong lamplight beams piercing the outside night, catch the shadowed pieces of destruction that are part of the aftermath of battle, caved-in doors, broken fences, extinguished black ashes where once stood an outhouse or carriage shed, splintered pieces of furniture, broken glass and, among other things, emptied, staved-in kegs of grog.

The light in one of the upstairs windows on King Street is from the bedroom where lies Colonel Johann Gottlieb Rall, once heralded for his skill and daring as "The Hessian Lion." In another house nearby lies his second in command, Major von Dechow. Both men are dying.

Many of the critically wounded lying now in the barracks will not survive. A few will die tonight. Their commander will die tomorrow, and the major will shortly follow the colonel to the grave.

Death is not felt lightly when it swoops down suddenly upon comrades who have shared hardship and danger. Even among the enemy there is often paradoxically to be found a prevailing repressed sympathy for the unknown fallen foe, except among the fanatics. Commonly a battlefield casualty is mourned silently in the breast of the enemy who brought him down.

So there frequently is a strange, masked affinity—a respect for one another—among opposing warriors. But it is an affinity that shrinks proportionately as the arena becomes less personal by its massive expansion. For with expansion comes the inpouring of staggering hordes of mortals, each without a separate face. Then it is that life, impersonal, remote, is lightly looked upon and the more easily erased.

Therefore, "The Hessian Lion's" rebel enemies will show a courteous respect for the Hessian dead, Rall and von Dechow in particular. For they had faces, personalities. They were enemies whom their foe had come to know and even respect. And valor and its fearless horsemen are the toast of warriors no matter where these dauntless riders gallop.

The colonel will be buried in the graveyard of the Presbyterian Church. But upon him, even in death, will be laid the responsibility for the loss of Trenton and all its reverberations. And in death he will be court martialed, tried and convicted by his Hessian peers for the careless military conduct of his command.

A young Hessian lieutenant of Colonel Rall's command will write the late commandant's epitaph, forever releasing Johann Rall from the concerns of the present. It will say simply:

"Hier liegt der Oberst Rall. Mit ihm ist alles all!"[79]

The inscription indeed will be correct in saying, "Here lies Colonel Rall. With him all is over." But much will be the repercussion above his head.

"That war is just. . . ."

On his writing desk in his room in the Stacy Potts house were many papers and most were taken by the American forces in overrunning the town. One, a small draft of a speech, or letter, that was intercepted in a dispatch, purportedly from Governor Livingston, was overlooked.

Stacy Potts, after checking on Rall's deteriorating condition with the surgeon in the dying officer's room, picks up the paper along with others on the floor beside a chair. Downstairs in his parlor he is about to throw the scribbled sheets into the fireplace when he decides to read whatever he can of the matter.

He peruses parts of it with difficulty since some pages are missing and make no sense. Potts comes to what is evidently the conclusion, reading the last few lines in Latin aloud to himself:

"'.. Bellum justum guibus necessarium, et quibus nisi in armis justitia non sit. . .'"

The well-to-do Trentonian, proud of his ability to translate Latin, smiles with self-satisfaction as he slowly interprets the quotation

"... That war is just which is founded in necessity, and without which justice cannot be obtained. . ."[80]

35

Friday, January 3. . .

The Long Campaign Closes
on a Crimson Path in Prince Town

The Juggernaut Staggers

In the wake of his Trenton catastrophe exactly one week ago yesterday, the war's status has grown steadily worse for General Howe and his leadership over the most powerful military machine of the Eighteenth Century World.

Lord Cornwallis, canceling his voyage back to England where his wife lies ill, has hurriedly returned to the British army's front lines in Jersey. There he has resumed command in an effort to restore confidence and order to the badly battered van of his forces. The Earl and General Grant immediately began preparing for both defensive and offensive action, assembling an 8,000-man force at Princeton.

The shocking news of the Trenton debacle will soon be reaching England. Its rapid spread throughout Europe will hold the Crown's all-powerful army up before royal ridicule in the closed circle of ruling monarchs. Now, to aggravate the disgrace, the Americans have followed up their success with annoying, flashing raids by their lighthorsemen almost under Grant's nose on the outskirts of Princeton.

On Monday, December 30, *The Pennsylvania Evening Post* reported,

". . . seven of the lighthorse belonging to this city (Philadelphia), took nine of the lighthorsemen from the enemy near Princeton without firing a shot."[1]

Most humiliating to the Crown's supreme military command, and particularly to the Hessian officers, is the report that over 900 British soldiers, mostly Hessians, have been taken and disgracefully paraded through the streets of Philadelphia. The mortifying account is a bitter and embarrassing retaliatory jab into Howe's pride, countering his New York parade of the Fort Washington prisoners a month ago. It was through Philadelphia that Sir William had hoped by now to be parading his troops in a victory celebration.

The revived spirit of the new nation is reflected in the brightened eyes of the patriots of the capital city where, almost overnight, the outlook has suddenly changed from extreme pessimism to high optimism.

Typical of this exuberance, the city's *Evening Post* describes the Continentals' success in Jersey with such words as:

"The enemy are every where flying before our army who frequently take small parties of them. Since the affair at Trenton, it is said we have taken four hundred, among whom are several officers."[2]

At the same time, stories abound telling of the atrocities committed by Cornwallis's army, especially during his absence. Many are founded upon fact, and many are, in accordance with approvable wartime military practices, extremely exaggerated in order to stoke the stoves that fire public hatred of the enemy.

Stirring up the Continentals and militia in Bucks County, Pennsylvania, are news accounts depicting the ravishing of young women, the plundering of homes and the killing of fathers rushing to the aid of their daughters.

The scenes described are of William Smith's home and farm near Woodbridge, Samuel Stout's house and farm in Hopewell and of other ravagings in the village of Maidenhead. The news accounts hit directly at the British cantonments in Maidenhead and Princeton.

A December 14 news account read:

"The progress of the British and Hessian Troops through New Jersey has been attended with such scenes of Desolation and Outrage, as would disgrace the most barbarous nations."[3]

After giving accounts of rape, plundering, property destruction and the driving off of farmers' cattle and sheep, leaving hundreds of inhabitants "reduced. . . to poverty and ruin," the writer appeals to the reader's "spirit to revenge," stating:

> "If these scenes of desolation, ruin and distress, do not rouse and animate every man of spirit to revenge their much injured countrymen and countrywomen, all Virtue, honour and Courage must have left this Country, and we deserve all that we shall meet with, as there can be no doubt the same scene will be acted in this Province (Pennsylvania) upon our own property, and our beloved wives and Daughters."[4]

So, as the diary-writing Englishman, Nicholas Cresswell, is saying and writing, the rebels, in the alarmed eyes of the British, have truly recovered from their "panic" and all the King's men will have trouble in once again confusing and staggering them.

While Howe's star begins its descent, the American Commander's once again begins its rise. With such exceptions as King George III, even the crown heads of Europe will begin to respect and favor the newly formed states, their military Commander and his "band of ragamuffin rebels" passing for an army.

But the rebel army, despite its victory in Trenton, is shortly to be reduced by the expiration of thousands of enlistments on January 1. Therefore an effort must be made to induce the troops to stay on whatever may be the costs involved. For a follow-up of the Trenton attack must be executed in order to hold the strategic and morale advantage now on the Americans' side.

Unfortunately, that follow-up—the move on Princeton and possibly New Brunswick—had to be canceled Thursday, largely owing to the failure of Cadwalader and Ewing to cross. Also to blame was the weather and the exhausted state of the first division troops.

Therefore, immediately after the recrossing and return to Pennsylvania, The General began re-designing his original plan's second phase, the Princeton-Brunswick operation. Without it the Trenton victory would become little more than a minor wound in the Juggernaut's side.

The Stroke Is Incomplete

One factor favoring a prompt execution of the follow-up attack was the advantage The General learned he had on the day after the army returned to Pennsylvania. Cadwalader and his troops were across and waiting for action.

The acting brigadier had heard Thursday's shooting, realized his Chief had crossed and sent word he would bring over his division at sunrise, the 27th. However, it was 10 A.M. Friday when finally the brigadier general succeeded in crossing his 1,800 men at the ferry above Bristol, intending, at last, to carry out his delayed mission. Cadwalader was unaware that the first division, after completing its stroke, returned to the west bank of the Delaware.

So the Philadelphia Associators and their commander found themselves on the Jersey side when the acting brigadier received his Chief's polite message. It expressed regret that the two supporting divisions had failed to cross on the night of the 25th.

The rebel Commander's note made it clear that Ewing's force was missed at the Assunpink Creek bridge. Pointing out how Cadwalader's troops were needed, he said that with them:

"The whole of the Enemy must have fallen into our hands."[5]

When Ewing earlier had heard of the first division's successful attack across from him, he rushed the news to Cadwalader. Chagrined, the brigadier general hurriedly wrote his Chief, explaining why he had not been able to cross.

Although the biggest obstacle in both Ewing's and Cadwalader's minds was the transporting of the artillery—and most everyone saw no reason why the crossing could not have been made without the heavy armament—this was not mentioned as a reason in the brigadier's explanation. But in that same message the apologetic division commander contritely replied that he would come across at sunrise and carry out his mission.

So it was that Cadwalader, on the morning of the 27th, found himself isolated and alone with his 1,800-man force on the Jersey side when The General's startling reply informed him that the first division had returned to Pennsylvania. This shocking news almost caused Cadwalader and his staff to order a speedy about-face back to the safety of the Delaware's west bank. Most of the command believed they were about to come face to face with a sorely wounded British lion.

Cadwalader and his staff believed that von Donop was still holding the Mount Holly, Burlington and Bordentown posts and that Rall had probably retreated in force, joining von Donop. The brigadier was faced with a dilemma.[6] What to do?

They were almost on top of Burlington. On their right, less than six miles away lay Mount Holly. To their left, six miles north lay Bordentown. And the river was on Cadwalader's back.

What the division's commander did not know was that the frightened Hessians who flew to von Donop in Bordentown and the dragoons who escaped northward to Princeton in the heat of battle, told hair-raising stories of the rebels' ferocity. They carried exaggerated tales of the size and vicious character behind their enemy in order better to justify their own flight. Some estimated the American attack force at 20,000-strong, well armed and superior to anything they had ever seen on a battlefield.

Consequently, von Donop immediately drew in his pickets, abandoning the van of the long British chain and retired his entire force to Allentown, about eight miles east of Bordentown. This enabled him to withdraw on the Kingston road into Princeton if pressed to do so, or await further orders in the wake of the Trenton disaster.

Reed Prevents Another Recrossing

Arguing vehemently against any thought of recrossing without getting into some action, Colonel Joseph Reed contended the division should pursue whatever gains The General had made in Trenton. His men, he angrily declared, would all go home if they had to cross back over that damned river once again! Especially without seeing action!

It was evident, he told the staff, there were no Hessians in Burlington. Therefore, would the staff compromise and at least go on to that town? Reluctantly Cadwalader and his staff agreed.[7]

There was good reason for Cadwalader and his other staff officers to listen to Reed. He had been The General's aide, adjutant general and confidant.

They knew nothing about the former brief, blind spell of hero-worship cast over him, among others, by Charles Lee. They knew nothing of Reed's one impulsive blunder with the pen and his "indecisive mind" description of his Chief.

Besides, though a Philadelphian, Joseph Reed was born in Trenton and attended the college in Princeton. He knew the area, its roads and its geography. There was sound reason to go along with the colonel's thinking, and so they did.

At 9 o'clock Friday night, after moving with extreme caution, Cadwalader's division moved into Burlington and found no foe. Reed and his men scouted ahead, reporting back that the enemy had also evacuated Bordentown. The village, however, was found sacked of all its supplies by the fleeing Hessians.

Encouraged by the apparent hasty flight of their enemy, Reed led his men on to Crosswicks. There the Trenton-born colonel and his band overtook a fleeing party of Hessians. Frightened by their enemy's approach so close upon their heels, the German mercenaries left behind a large quantity of stores which the Americans promptly seized.[8]

At Crosswicks the division encamped and remained until Wednesday, January 1. But during that encampment, Reed, pursuing his scouting expeditions, led his men into Trenton, Sunday, December 29.

The colonel and his troops found the battle-scarred village much the way it was left three days before. They saw no signs of the enemy with the exception of a few wounded Hessians and surgeons in "a dirty hospital."[9]

Meanwhile, the American Leader was unfortunately commanding an army that was about to be reduced to a skeleton force by Wednesday, the first day of the new year when thousands of his troops were scheduled to be discharged. Nevertheless, The General had set his mind upon a recrossing and follow-up attack. That must be done. And it had to be done soon.

On Sunday, the 29th, he had two days left before his success-celebrating troops—gloating over their proud accomplishment in taking a Hessian garrison during the closing hours of the campaign, thus honoring the end of their enlistments—would be following in the footsteps of those who left for home on the first of December. The task of convincing them to stay on a little longer would not be easy.

Yet this, too, had to be done. The troops must be persuaded to stay on. Cadwalader was not only now across the river and waiting, but the acting brigadier was also trying to make amends for his Christmas night shortcomings. For while waiting he had carried out The General's request of the 28th for intelligence concerning the enemy's positions. And in this espionage activity, Reed played a major role.

All a part of the new, blossoming "intelligence service," Cadwalader, early in the planning stage of the Trenton operation, had been asked by his Commander to:

> "spare no pains or expence to get Intelligence of the Enemy's motions and intentions."[10]

It would cost money, but that too, would be taken care of somehow. The "somehow" would be through the help of the patriot, Robert Morris. So The General assured Cadwalader that:

"Any promises made or Sums advanced, (would be) fully complied with and discharged."[11]

The Philadelphia Patriot and Financier Rescues The Cause

General Cadwalader and his staff worked hard for three days—from Saturday, the 28th through Monday, the 30th—rounding up the information The General needed. They employed whatever spies and sources within their reach.

On Tuesday, the 31st, Cadwalader sent the American Commander "a sketch map" on which he had plotted:

"all the approaches to Princeton, British artillery locations, British defenses, and the exact spots where the redcoats were quartered, as of Monday, the 30th."[12]

Therefore, while high-ranking officers, led by such orators as Generals Knox and Mifflin, pleaded with the troops Saturday and Sunday, the 28th and 29th, to stay on for six more weeks beyond their periods of enlistment, The General—never one oratoriously inclined—wrote an appeal for funds to the British-born, 42-year-old, Philadelphian, America's foremost financial supporter of the American cause, Robert Morris, stating:

"If it be possible to give us Assistance, do it; borrow Money where it can be done, we are doing it on our private Credit; every man of Interest and every Lover of his Country must strain his Credit upon such an Occasion. No Time, my dear Sir, is to be lost."[13]

And the following day, Monday, the 30th, The General again wrote Morris for cash to pay off his obligations to the spies in his rapidly expanding intelligence service. Not only was there no money to pay off the soldiers' wages and none to offer as a bounty for staying on, but the especial "military chest" of ready cash for paying spies was still empty.

The Commander wrote Morris:

"We have the greatest occasion at present for hard money to pay a certain set of people, who are of particular use to us. If you could possibly collect a sum, if it were but one hundred or one hundred and fifty pounds, it would be of great service."[14]

Morris immediately concentrated all his efforts upon raising the monies in the midst of the nation's crisis and its dearth of available cash and credit. The staunch patriot, Continental Congress member and signer of the Declaration of Independence, will draw from his own purse and credit in order to rush The General the desperately needed funds for carrying out his operations. This, Robert Morris has loyally done before, and this he will faithfully continue to do throughout the conflict.

In reply to the army Chief's appeal to the Philadelphia financier, Morris will shortly send him $50,000 in paper money, raised largely on the patriot's own credit. Indicative of the deplorable financial condition facing the hard fighting "free and independent united colonial states" on the eve of the new year, are the two nation-saving canvas bags soon to be on their way to the Continental Army Commander's depleted military chest.

Coming under guard directly from Mr. Robert Morris in Philadelphia, the two bags will roll out all the monetary scrapings the partner in the capital city's counting-house could raise. Coins of all kinds will be included. Among them:

> "410 Spanish milled dollars @ 7s. 6d., 2 English Crowns, 72 French crowns, 1,072 English shillings."[15]

When the long war finally does end, The General is destined in 1783 to remember this money so swiftly and so opportunely raised by the Liverpool-born financier under great difficulty. Of the incident, the Commander will say:

> ". . . the time and circumstances of it being too remarkable ever to be forgotten by me."[16]

Much Is Asked In Exchange For A $10 Bounty

As for the eventual destiny of one of the foremost behind-the-scenes patriots of the American cause, Robert Morris will be appointed the superintendent of finance toward the end of the war. He will be the founder of the Bank of North America but will refuse the office of secretary of the treasury. Later his speculations will bring him ruin. He will be imprisoned for debt, and the great patriot and financial supporter of The Cause in America's quest for independence will die, a broken man in 1806.

However, on the eve of the possible dissolution of the rebel army when a follow-up stroke is an absolute necessity for the further crippling of the King's Juggernaut, Morris enables the American Commander-in-Chief to promise each man a ten dollar bounty. And in addition the financier makes it possible for The

General to keep his word in the promised reimbursement of his spies.

And so the work of convincing the troops to remain three fortnights beyond their enlistment periods was launched with much oratory. The General personally addressed the men. Though not an eloquent speechmaker as are some of his officers, he nevertheless spoke forthright to his soldiers and assured them of the ten dollar bounty.

If they would stay with him, they had his word, he declared, that he would stand by his promise, putting up his own name, credit and wherewithal to make sure that the bounty money would be paid.

The men, who one officer described later as looking like "a flock of animated scarecrows," listened in anguish.[17] Of all the troops in the varied assembly areas, only the newly recruited militia still appeared well-dressed and fed. A ten dollar bounty was not an enticing inducement. It was a lot that The General and his officers were asking. Life, death or maiming were balancing on a seesaw in their minds.

Even some of Glover's Marblehead fishermen could not be lured. They could earn more money privateering.

What was a ten dollar Continental note alongside of the possibility of the valuable booty and profits to be made from looting enemy shipping?

Others of the Massachusetts regiment of fishermen and sailors preferred to join Commodore Seymour's Delaware River men.[18] However, the rest finally decided to remain with Glover and The General.

Most of the troops, listening to the appeals of their officers and finally to the "Old Man," were but a few days from discharge. Long the backbone of the Continental forces and the mainstays of their country's ragged military machine, the torn, tired, sick and hungry remnants of "The Grand Army," looked up pitifully with self-commiseration written over their drawn features.

The deep sense of loyalty they held for the Chief whom they had followed through the past six months was now, with great pains, weighed against their own physical exhaustion. They had literally reached the end of their amazing endurance, yet, thankfully, they were still all in one piece.

For most, the bounty in itself was not a factor. There was something far more than that, something beyond loyalty to a gallant and respected Leader, something intrinsic and indefinable that just could not be registered upon any scale. And each man knew, though none could very well explain, what it was.

And so the officers asked those who would forego their discharge for six weeks and be guaranteed a bonus to their pay, to step forward fron the ranks. Only silence filled the air.

Not a single man moved. Knox's head shook from one side to the other. Mifflin breathed heavily. The General on Old Magnolia was immobile. Had all their oratory, all their pleading, been in vain?

For A Better Society Of Man

Home, it appeared was too inviting. The thoughts of at last rejoining their loved ones rather than an army, cursed with payless paydays and bound to a Congress seemingly unmindful of their needs, were uppermost in their minds.

After all, had they not done their share for their country? Was it not time for others to do likewise? Why must they, who have given so much and risked their lives, be asked to give still more?

They were ragged, gaunt and fatigued. Many could not go on. Others would not. It was too much to ask.

Then suddenly, one man, then another, and another and still another stepped out from the ranks. In increasing numbers their feet moved forward. Knox shouted words of praise to each swelling company as the rows grew thinner and the number of re-enlistments soared.

The General wheeled Old Magnolia around and followed by his happily chatting aides, returned to headquarters. He had his ragged, tattered army back again.

Some will say it was the spirit of victory in the air since Trenton, the fighting instinct of men, fired with hate and seeking revenge. Others will argue that it was the natural act of the common man of 1776.

Biblically reared, they will contend, this was the inexplicable desire unselfishly to serve mankind, a course dictated by a devotion to his god, his family and his country, enabling him to put the lives and future lives of others before his own.

This, they will say, was the common man's way of stepping humbly and unheralded into a sealed and sacred place under the pillars of human rights that will forever hold up the new world's temple of dreams for a better society of man.

And still others will declare it was nothing else but the ten dollar bounty.

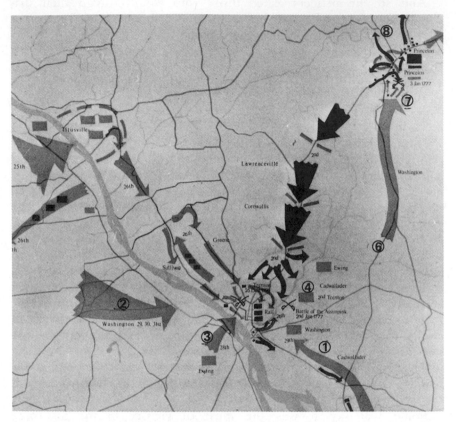

Overlayed on this Widmer map are the present author's numbers identifying the movements of January 2 and 3, as follows: (1) With Cadwalader across and waiting on the Assunpink the 29th for the main army, (2) The General crosses along with Ewing, (3) and assembles on the south side of the Assunpink Creek (4) drawing down Cornwallis's main army into Trenton (5) in the so-called "Second Battle of Trenton," or "Battle of the Assunpink." In a successful deception, the Continentals (6) make a night march, January 2-3, into the Battle of Princeton (7) and withdraw north before Cornwallis's main body can turnabout and overtake them. [Courtesy Dr. Kemble Widmer Collection, "The Ten Days That Changed the World."]

The Grand Prize Still In the Offing

Most of those Continentals who stepped forward Sunday morning, whether they sensed it or not, had chosen death. For some would die in battle. Others from disease or the ravages of the plague. Some within a few days. Others within a few months. Almost all within a few years. But almost all would die firmly believing that the foundations of the new nation and the causes it espoused were laying down a better world for those advancing in their wake.

So, on Sunday, December 29, The General's plan to return to Jersey, strike at Princeton and then, if possible, at New Brunswick and its vast military stores, began moving forward.

One of the American Commander's most tempting motives, and one confirmed by his spies, is that same British military chest of thousands of pounds cached in New Brunswick. It is the British army's pay roll monies just waiting to be seized. Few beside the American Commander and his war council know of this, for a leakage of such intelligence would cause the enemy to tighten its security. But those who do, know that the seizure of this coffer could bring the Juggernaut down on its knees.

Therefore there is a grand prize objective behind the follow-up stroke in Jersey. And, taking second place are such aims and objectives as acquiring control of the province, the securing of Philadelphia and the further restoration of the now rapidly rising American morale.

Determined to lose no time, The General ordered the moving over of some men and equipment Saturday. And on Sunday the fourth crossing of the Delaware was under way.

Reed, completing his survey of Trenton on Sunday, the 29th, was unaware that his Chief was preparing his second crossing into Jersey and his fourth over the Delaware.

The colonel, ever mindful of his impulsive "indecisive mind" letter to Lee, has since acquired a new and much more favorable opinion of The General's abilities. Reed's desire now is to atone for past errors with extra loyal service. He therefore sent word to the American Commander Sunday, the 29th, assuring him that Trenton was cleared and urging that he bring his division across "for the purpose of attempting a recovery of that country from the enemy."[19]

Although this crossing was in daylight, it took the army two days to get over. The ice-cluttered river conditions were even worse than on Christmas night. It was Wednesday, the first day of the new year before the contingent marched into Trenton and united with Cadwalader's forces.[20]

The first division comprised about 1,500. Cadwalader's force numbered about 2,100. To this 3,600, Mifflin raised and sent across another 1,600, mostly raw recruits from Philadelphia. The American Commander now led a 5,200-man army. Most of them were still poorly equipped. Most were still in ragged summer clothes and many were still not shod at all.

Only those assigned to a separate mission were missing. They included some of the sick and weak, declared not fit and able for duty. With them went a number of the wagons carrying baggage and supplies to a secretly designated place. All were escorted by a company of guards.

The General and Greene issued the secret sealed orders to the captain in charge. When opened as directed, he discovered his destination was north to Morristown. There in the Watchungs the party is to aid the local militia in preparing the winter encampment already under way.

The Rebels Bait the Hook For the Second Battle Of Trenton

Upon arriving in Trenton, The General heard that a large body of enemy troops were moving out of Princeton on their way to the Delaware River village. It was soon confirmed that Cornwallis had joined Grant in the college town and was leading a force of 8,000 men and a lengthy train of artillery. The advance was reported making rapid progress along the Trenton road after dawn yesterday, Thursday, January 2.

Anticipating this, the rebel Leader ordered General Roche de Fermoy's brigade, Colonel Hand's Pennsylvania riflemen, Colonel Haussegger's German battalion, Colonel Charles Scott's Virginia Continentals and a part of Captain Forrest's artillery battery to delay the enemy advance.

This division was ordered to take a position a short distance south of Maidenhead. There, halfway between Princeton and Trenton, they were to hold back the enemy vanguard until sunset if possible.

Howe and Cornwallis had estimated the rebel army strength two weeks before at 8,000 men along the Delaware and in Philadelphia, 500 militia troops in Morris County and a 3,000-man force still at Peekskill, North Castle and the surrounding area guarding the passes to New England.[21]

The exaggerated number of Americans reported to have taken part in the Trenton raid six days ago has caused Cornwallis to increase his striking power.

On Wednesday, upon entering Trent's town for the second time in a week, the Americans took a position on a ridge along the south bank of the Assunpink Creek. There they dug in and extended their lines three miles in length north and south of the creek's bridge. In town, on the north side of the Assunpink and its span, they stationed a strong force which occupied the houses along King and Queen Streets, much as they did a week ago. But now the objective was to draw the enemy into the town in order to take The General's bait.

In a house commandeered for his headquarters, The General and his staff began plotting a defense strategy that would draw his enemy into the northwestern half of the village, enabling a main striking force to pull out, circle northeast, and fall upon Princeton.

After a lightning stroke at the enemy-held college town, the army would immediately head for Brunswick, overcome the garrison and seize its stores, particularly the valuable military chest. Then, with all they could take with them, they would retreat into the Jersey Highlands, vanishing within the Watchung Mountains of Morris County.

The enemy, meanwhile, encumbered by their customary long and burdensome military train with all its usual, and frequently superfluous, impedimenta, might hardly be recovering from surprise and clambering out of Trenton, before the Americans' stroke is completed. "The Plan" looked especially good this time, for now Cadwalader's gathered intelligence of the enemy's strength and positions would prove extremely valuable.

Wednesday, January 1, was a warming, cloudy, threatening day. At sunset the rains came, and the previously ice and snow-covered roads, fields and frozen earth were, overnight, turned into seas of mud. Though the American corps under Fermoy found their bivouac night south of Maidenhead one of the most uncomfortable in their careers, they were, nevertheless, ready for Cornwallis' lumbering army, wallowing through ruts and fording flooded creeks up to their knees.

That was shortly after sunrise yesterday morning, Thursday, January 2. The rains had stopped.

In some places, after leaving Princeton, the immaculately dressed King's men sank up to their calves in the miry slush of melting snow mixed in with reddish clay. Horses, gun carriages and wagons bogged down as well as the foot soldiers. Some sank up to their knees in their struggle to guide the 28 guns of various calibers. And some of these were heavy 12-pounders.[22]

In the absence of General Fermoy, who was suddenly found mysteriously missing, Colonel Edward Hand took over the command[23] of the outguard division.

Adding to the Cornwallis army difficulties, now upon their heads came an ambush rain of fire which brought the van of the British force to a dead halt. Behind it the entire train stopped.

General Fermoy, who is often found in his cups, had left his troops to fend for themselves when the drenching rains urged him to seek a comfortable tavern in Trenton. There, much later, he was found and awakened from a severe case of inebriation.

The thin, balding, brilliant Colonel Hand stepped into the command position without difficulty. Hand has fashioned his Pennsylvania riflemen into a regiment known for their crack marksmanship.

So the colonel's men set the example with their rapid, deadly cross fire. The rest of the corps joined in, bringing the enemy train to a standstill, but not for long. Lord Cornwallis had quantity and power on his side.

It was now 10 o'clock in the morning, and the defensive action on the outskirts of Trenton by such a formidable body of troops convinced the British commander that the rebel Leader intended to defend the town whatever the cost.

And that was just what the nobleman had wanted—an open battle! He now launched a sweeping drive against Hand's men, forcing the Continentals to pull back.

Hand ordered a slow and protesting withdrawal, enabling him to place barricades across the path of the oncoming redcoats. Then, choosing a favorable position for pouring down enfilading fire each time he retreated, the rebel colonel and his corps disputed every yard the enemy advanced.

The American officer's orders were to delay the enemy until dark if he could manage it, and this he was almost able to do. With two guns from Captain Forrest's battery, Hand and his men made a strong and defiant stand at Five Mile Run.

The Earl Takes The General's Bait

Holding the high ground in the deep woods near the Shabbakonk Creek, the rebel corps faced the Earl of Cornwall's van, now reinforced by its supporting battalions. The Americans kept up a heavy and continuous fire from under their own barrage directed by Forrest's guns.

It showered the British with such a continuous rain of canister, grape and shell, that the redcoats, caught between rifle fires and under cannon bursts, began to break in confusion. To prevent a possible panic and rout, the forward command ordered a withdrawal.

Cornwallis hurriedly called his officers into a field conference. The British lord was certain that behind Hand's corps, a larger force, perhaps the main divisions of the rebels' army, was preparing for a major engagement, possibly a final show-down. At any moment they might pounce.

The British commander wanted nothing more. But he wanted to be ready for it. Ever since he crossed the Hudson November 19, forty-four days ago, he had hopefully looked forward to that day and hour when he would force the rebel Fox into open combat. Now, it would appear, that moment was about to be his.

If the rebel Leader wants it to be in Trenton, the grand guardian of the doors to Philadelphia and the damned rebel Congress, well and good! There it will be!

If the supposedly "Wise Old Fox" wants to put his back against the freezing cold Delaware River, so it will be! The easier then to drive him into it!

But now the hour was getting late, the American van and outguard must be wiped away. The staff conference ends with the decision to call up two battalions of Hessians from the rear.

For the past week the German troops have been fired with a desire to revenge their Trenton comrades and erase the dishonor from their escutcheon. Now let them have their chance!

But it was too late. When the field conference ended, the rebels had quietly stolen away.

During the British council of war the quick-witted Hand quietly led his corps out of the woods that covered them along the Shabbakonk Creek and back toward the American forward lines in Trenton. There Reed and his men occupied King and Queen Streets and were waiting behind buildings and fences to pick off the redcoat vedettes.

But Hand had cleverly cost the enemy another expensive three hour delay, if not more. The night's darkness The General wanted would soon be closing in.

Since the winter solstice was but ten days old yesterday, the day's light was short. General Cornwallis was impatient with his progress. His marching speed had been little more than one mile an hour. Before and after the British vanguard's brush with Hand's men, the redcoats, marching three abreast, had to halt at periodic intervals to flush out detached parties from the colonel's harassing and disappearing pickets. The Earl's advance was not only tedious, but it also was openly exposed to constant ambushing.

In hot pursuit of their elusive enemy, the British and Hessian jagers followed Hand's withdrawing forces into Reed's house-to-house defense in the northern end of the village. Here again the colonel's men and Reed's van made a strong stand and again brought the redcoat vedettes to a halt.

Once more the King's men stood on their rifles while a battery of artillery came up to dislodge the persistent American rebels. The delay cost Cornwallis another hour.

Meanwhile, Hand leisurely ordered his men into the houses with those already occupying the buildings under Reed and prepared for leveling enfilading fire on the enemy when they moved down into King and Queen Streets.

Disputing every step the redcoats' advance made into town, the Pennsylvania colonel, together with Reed and his corps, poured a withering fire down upon the steadily moving British column. From inside the houses and from behind fence posts, rifles and musketry crackled.

Returning shot for shot, the redcoats and Hessians advanced, repeatedly firing, loading, kneeling and firing. On both sides men dropped.

Blood began spilling after the first outburst emptied upon the heads of the King's men. Rifle fire poured in from all directions.

The dimming twilight, settling over Trenton's battle-scarred village, obscured vision and hampered marksmanship. The firing became wild and scattered.

But by five o'clock, as daylight faded rapidly into dusk, the British troops succeeded in driving the American defenders over the bridge and behind their defense works along the south bank of the Assunpink Creek.

The General's plan was on schedule and working with perfection.

Repulse At the Bridge

In hot pursuit, despite the twilight hour, the British van charged the bridge. Ready and waiting, the Americans easily turned the redcoats back. The forward command ordered a second charge and again the rebels repulsed their pursuers. The British tried still a third time, but the American defenders had constructed their defenses at the Assunpink expressly for hurling back their enemy at this point and at this particular hour. Everything was working exactly as planned. Never was the American staff so proud of itself.

Faced with the approach of nightfall the British vanguard commander was undecided about risking another attempt until Cornwallis came up with the main army.

The fast-loading jagers had not proved very successful in their day-long conflict with the slower loading, but far more accurate, Pennsylvanians and their rifled-barrel guns. The plain bore barrels of the muskets are no match in accuracy with the Pennsylvania Germans' new rifles. Besides, the redcoats and Hessians had had a trying day. It was up to the field commander to decide.

Nevertheless, one Hessian regiment meanwhile had tried a desperate flanking maneuver, in an effort to break through the Americans' three-mile line in the eastern sector. Ordered to make a hole in the Continentals' stringy defenses and separate the rebels' right, the regiment was nearly entrapped trying to ford the creek at its upper end. The Hessians, caught under a cross fire from Hitchcock's Rhode Island Continentals, were sent scurrying and wet back behind the British defenses.

After that, the redcoat van pulled back, allowing the artillery batteries to exchange a series of volleys with the American gunners. This ineffectual cannonading kept up for awhile and then died down. The Juggernaut's vanguard sat back and awaited Cornwallis and reinforcements from the main army.

Many of the King's officers strongly favored pushing over the bridge and scattering the rebel forces. Then in the morning they would finish up the task.

However, since the break of dawn the earl had pushed his troops over obstacles and miserably thawing roads, all under enemy harassment, and now night was fast closing in. The hastening long shadows of Thursday, January 2, were sulking into darkness. Cornwallis saw no wisdom in, or any reason for, a night attack.

The Earl's opponent had successfully delayed him,[24] but

Cornwallis saw the delaying tactics as merely a postponement of the pending open field conflict and showdown. He had his enemy with their backs upon the Delaware and not a boat behind them to effect their escape. This time "The Fox" would not get away. Morning would be time enough and, if necessary, His Majesty's forces would drive the rebel army down into Delaware Bay.

Cornwallis's staff was divided in opinion. Many of them were opposed to waiting until dawn. Fired with a desire for revenge and hungry for retaliation, they believed the irate British army's mood was enough to offset the disadvantages of fighting on through dusk.

Leading spokesman for those wishing to push on was Sir William Erskine, Cornwallis's quartermaster. Erskine had heard too many stories about the clever, military tactics employed by the Americans' "Fox." After all, why had he and his rebel army not escaped north and crossed back the way they had come earlier?

There was something that just did not seem right, Erskine contended. But when his commander pressed him for a valid reason for his qualms, Erskine could give none. No one, except possibly Erskine, could imagine the Continental Army withdrawing in the night. And not even Erskine envisioned them circling east and northeast for a strike at Princeton or Brunswick. This never entered Cornwallis's thoughts and only reached a tinkling alarm bell of some kind in Erskine's subconsciousness.

To Cornwallis's confident assurance that, "We'll bag him in the morning!," the quartermaster made one more effort to convince his commanding officer that an immediate attack was advisable. He declared:

> "My Lord, if you trust those people tonight, you will see nothing of them in the morning."[25]

Cornwallis was convinced that his enemy was as desirous for a showdown battle as was he. The British nobleman was certain that the American Commander wanted another victory to seal his recent success, and that Trenton's taste had made him overconfident enough to entice the British forces into a match on strong patriot territory, Hunterdon County.

A victory, or even a draw, would inspirit the Americans and their rebellion throughout the coming winter months. Erskine's imaginative conjectures were ridiculous and not worth further thought.

Why would the American Leader run away after going to all the trouble of inviting his lordship to a duel?

So General Cornwallis ordered his troops to bivouac for the night on the north side of the Assunpink facing his enemy's campfires on the south side of the creek. In a sense, the Earl felt that he had already been victorious. For his army had driven Hand and Reed and their combined forces out of the village and across the Assunpink Creek behind the American lines. His foe was entrapped in the King's snare. All now to be done was to spring the trigger.

The 2nd Earl of Cornwall now, as midnight, Thursday, January 2, approached, reminded himself that had it not been for the Trenton disaster, he would be on his way to England and the bedside of his sick wife. The past week had been an exhausting one.

The aggravations have mounted daily since he was forced to cancel his voyage home last Friday, December 27. Both he and Howe and the entire British staff had thought the campaign was over until the spring. The sickening news of the Hessian garrison's downfall, the return to his troops, and the preparations for settling the score have left their marks on the British lord's drawn features.

However, he was stimulated by the thought that the morrow, Friday, January 3, 1777, could prove to be a most eventful day, a victorious day that well might please His Majesty.

Since the British commander had left General Grant and Lieutenant Colonel Charles Mawhood in Princeton with orders that Mawhood was to proceed to Trenton in support of the main army this morning, Friday, January 3, Cornwallis was satisfied last night that his force would then be more than enough to overwhelm his foe in the morning.

Under Grant in Princeton would be a 1,200 garrison, large enough to deal with any possible detached rebel raiding parties. At the Maidenhead post the Earl had ordered General Leslie with another 1,200 troops to remain there on guard as reserves. This is the half-way point between Princeton and Trenton. Leslie was to await further orders.

With the arrival of Mawhood's force tomorrow, Friday morning, Cornwallis reminded his staff they would have a fighting force of over 5,500 men in Trenton to settle the score with the Americans' insurrectionary army. So, until late last night, General Cornwallis and his staff officers plotted the strategy for his attack operations at dawn today.

On it the British general and his officers slept soundly. They slept to the distant clanking and clinking of the rebels' entrenching tools, striking into the stones of the once again freezing earth.

It was a comforting sound to the King's men. Hearing those thumping noises and looking across the creek to see the occasional shadowy silhouettes of rebel soldiers, busily throwing up earthworks, were assurances that, at last, the Continentals were preparing to stand and fight. It would be an easy task for the well equipped and powerful British machine to run through the works with the bayonet and outflank their enemy's positions to the east and west simultaneously. Therefore the Juggernaut slept, anticipating today's dawn.

Twelve Miles Away

Twelve miles away in Prince Town's college where British General Grant's forces had taken over the village, a few of the King's officers last night found some amusement in baiting several of the ardent patriots of the hamlet who were attempting to rescue some of their things from Nassau Hall. The college president's home next door had already been sacked by the invaders.

The British staff now looks the other way when their redcoats indulge in looting and plundering, providing it is kept within moderation. Howe had to lift the ban when the English soldiers complained that if the Hessians were allowed to do so, then so should they.

Besides, many officers point out that pillaging in hostile territory is a good way to teach rebellious inhabitants a lesson. And Hunterdon County, like Morris, is another hotbed of rabid, rebel patriots who, some members of the British staff say, "need to be set straight."

Defying the invaders, the two elderly and highly respected community leaders, Preacher Walter MacMurphy and Miller Charles Kuederly, both staunch patriots and devotees of the college, had managed to save many of the valuable books and, through the help of townsmen, had rescued a number of the college's priceless possessions.

They had slipped away before and during the enemy occupation with much in their carriages, often with the aid of some of the sympathetic British officers. Last night the two had returned to 20-year old Nassau Hall, "the largest stone building in the colonies."[2][6]

With them came a faculty member, one of the few who had not flown with the trustees and the students to Cooper's Ferry in Camden County.[27] He is Professor Ezra Godfrey Clynes, an aging, philosophizing, liberty-loving, fearless defender of the American cause.

The learned scholar was determined to rescue his rare collection of stones, minerals and his records from his lecture room in Nassau Hall, by himself if necessary. However, Pastor MacMurphy and the miller, known as "Papa" Kuederly, insisted upon accompanying the cane-carrying professor through the British cordon surrounding the encampment and into Nassau Hall. The harmless appearance of the three men and the apparent legitimacy of their mission earned them not only the commanding officer's permission, but the courtesy and assistance of several of the British officers.

It was on their way out, lugging the professor's chest, that the three men were addressed and stopped by a young British lieutenant slightly in his cups. Clynes politely listened to the inebriate, around whom now other officers began to gather.

In A Search For Truth

The young Britisher was in a garrulous mood and the professor, always interested in picking up any information he could pass on to the patriot militia, was in a listening one. The amused "Doctor Ezra," as his students and the villagers affectionately call him, was not to be hurried away, despite the urgings of the preacher and the miller. The old man was in the lion's den and was happily ready to beard the beast in his lair, regardless of the state of its sobriety.

Standing in the corridor outside the prayer hall, through the open doors of which could be seen a large portrait of George II, young officer Drummond, in a lachrymose spirit of pedantry, questioned Clynes, asking

"Profeshair, why, Shirr, 'ave you inshructed all the chappies of this plice in revolt 'gainst 'is Majesty? Rawlley, Shirr, do you fellosh not ... not know what your free ... freedom ann'd innapen'ance... ann'd your'rr gotdamned lib. .lib'a'tee madness will bring you?.. Ruin!.. Ruin!..

"I say, Fellow, you will all be flo'ting in a sea without a rudder on your boat... Your'rr... your'rr freedoms and your lib'a'tees... will capsize your'rr... your'rr sh'ship when every free'freedom loving damned idiot begins running amuck upon the ... the deck ... ann'd ... ann'd pulling for themselves alone, upon the helm ...

"Thi. .think   you,   Shirr,   a   deck. . .deck'lar'a'shun   for
innapen'ance ish going to set you upon a magic course ovar a
glassy sea? No, Shirr!. . T'will only pull the cork ann'd let the
dirty, lil'il, gree. . . greedy bas. . .bastard in us all free. . . free,
unleashed to romp around as bloody well he will. . .

"Profeshair, you will shee blood now. . . bbb. . .but if you get
your deck'lar'a'shun there will be rivers of it spilled to pay for
it . . . You and your like, Profeshair, would take the halter from
around the head of your'rr. . . your'rr people and turn it into a
noose 'round their neck."

Though MacMurphy and Kuederly attempted to nudge Doctor
Ezra out through the central main door and down the stone steps,
the old scholar and patriot was determined to have the last say.
And he did.

Clynes was not prompted to answer Drummond personally. For
the officer's garbled thoughts, coming out as though through a
mouth full of pebbles, were, in the opinion of the educator, not
worthy of answering. However, the audience of officers had
listened in partial amusement but were generally respectful of the
septuagenarian, and it was to them, rather than to Drummond, the
elderly scholar addressed his reply.

Astutely avoiding being goaded into remarks which could be
construed as seditious, the doctor Socratically steered the minds of
the young British officers into their own House of Lords and
Commons. After all he was in the enemy's camp.

Were he baited into stirring up discontent with the outspoken
frankness of his nature, he could endanger not only himself but his
town companions. He therefore side-stepped the intoxicated
lieutenant's lengthy monologue and its implications of treasonable
teachings, asking with a broad, innocently smiling countenance:

"Gentlemen, does this human shell before you look like some-
one who seeks recklessly to spill the blood of his fellow man? Am I
that horrible to your eyes?

"I and my colleagues choose only to teach truth. For does not
learning become rewarding through its search for truth? Is this a
sin?

"If so we must condemn the great minds of the past for their
issues upon grave matters. If so we must disagree with Sir Francis
Bacon who, you remember, said, 'No pleasure is comparable to the
standing upon the vantage ground of truth,'[28] whereupon he
confessed to his venality as a judge. A strange kind of pleasure, you
may say, but ah! Who is the judge of pleasure?

"Each of us, small or great, must with our own conscience struggle. Pascal has taught us that, 'We know the truth not only by the reason, but also by the heart.'[29] And does not the Bible teach us that 'The truth shall make you free.'

"Therefore, Gentlemen, in seeking truth, are we not also seeking freedom? It cannot then be a sin for man to seek his freedom, and with his freedom, liberties. And through his liberties the independence of the mind, the soul, not for one man alone but for all his brethren.

"If this is wrong, if this is sinful, then do not stop with pointing the finger at one old man like me. Go you to the House of Lords, and Commons! Seek you there the men who take issue with His Majesty, King George, and are not hanged for doing so.

"I am merely one of many who agree with some of England's statesmen, yet not with all they say for I am in a quest for truth to feed my students, or guide them in the finding of it for themselves.

"Did not Edmund Burke argue against this war? Did he not declare in Commons that two million European Americans on this continent could bring 90,000 men into the field? Did he not say that they were multiplying at an incredible rate? Did he not say that while England spent time on the mode of governing, there would be two millions more to manage?

" 'Your children,' Burke told the Commons, 'do not grow faster from infancy to manhood than they spread from families to communities, and from villages to nations.'[30] And did he not say that your trade with America alone was nearly equal to what England carried on at the beginning of this century with the whole world?"

The professor kept up his unchallenged argument before an attentive and awed audience. The officers' smiles left their faces. The old lecture hall artist caught his listeners immediately after their dinner meal. It was their recreation hour. This was more than entertainment.

He noted, not knowing, nor caring whether any of them knew it or not, that Charles Fox in Commons, the marquess of Rockingham, the Duke of Richmond and Lord Camden in the House of Lords had taken issue with Lord North and the King's hard and unswerving policy.

He continued, declaring:

"Had not Lord Camden said, 'It is obvious that you cannot

furnish armies or treasure competent to the mighty purpose of subduing America'?[3][1]

"And did not John Wilkes, lord mayor of London, ask 'Who can tell, should success attend them (the rebels) whether in a few years the independent Americans may not celebrate the glorious era of the Revolution of 1775 as we do that of 1688?'[3][2]

"Certainly, Gentlemen, it is well known that the Earl of Chatham, William Pitt, submitted a peace plan similar to that of the Howes and the Franklin proposal, urging the dropping of taxation measures, the removal of the occupying troops and the repeal of the punitive acts.[33] *And it is the truth that this was rejected. All this, Gentlemen, is what the Bard of Avon would simply call 'The naked truth.'*

"Yes, the lieutenant is quite right. Freedoms and liberties could well wreck a ship of state uncontrolled, or over-controlled, at the helm. The human frailties of emperors and the 'Divine Right of Kings' are no less to be feared on board the vessel of government in the open sea than the immoralities of the common man at its tiller.

"When licensed by unchecked liberties and freedoms, the sordid side of man can prey like the jackal in the night upon the moral fibers of his fellow human beings. And, true, it then can eat away the beautiful, the noble and the spiritual contentment, ever lying potent and mostly latent within the human race.

"Was the venality of the great and honored Sir Francis Bacon any the less corruptibly corrosive upon the finer aspirations of man than was the greed and avarice of King Midas? Each, as every man must, stumbled haltingly to the truth.

"Are we all wrong, and wrong we all might be, to seek and teach the search for truth? Did not Voltaire say, 'Love truth, but pardon error'?

"Are we wrong to listen to the great minds within the House of Lords and Commons? Do some there not say that the course toward truth is not war but conciliation?

"There are those on this continent who are your blood relatives and whom you, in your guided vision toward truth, are legitimately convinced must be subdued. They, on the other hand, in their vision toward it, are just as legitimately convinced independence must be granted.

"So in this struggle over the rights of government, of nations, of people, of man, a struggle as old as man himself, the pursuit goes on and will go on, ever straining, bleeding, dying in the unending

search for the junction where right, reason and validity meet frank-
ness, fidelity and accuracy and together take the path called 'truth.'

"In this land to which you have come there are those who have
sought that junction along the road of freedoms and liberties
through the preservation of the natural rights of man, through an
informed and educated citizenry, through a popular form of
government, which the lieutenant says will bring it ruin. And all of
this within that circle would be woven into a free society, founded
upon the best of the moral fibers that exist in man.

"Is this wrong, Gentlemen, this search for truth along the road
of human rights? Will not an informed and educated citizenry,
through the individual liberties and freedoms which erudition will
bring to the common man, dissolve the cupidity of men in power?
Will it not destroy the venal bargainers who, in their self-seeking
contempt for mankind's betterment, gnaw away at the moral fibers
built, once firmly, block upon block, by men of honor and
integrity?"

Wavering back and forth through the old scholar's long oration,
Lieutenant Drummond tried unsuccessfully on several occasions to
answer the professor's numerous questions. However, each time he
would open his mouth, his eyes closed and only a lethargic mumble
passed his lips. But old Doctor Ezra, rising into his element as a
lecturer before a group of young men, went on.

To the tutor's implication that an informed citizenry was the
cure-all control for the unbridling of human rights, Drummond surprisingly came to life. This time he made sure his interruption stuck
and burst out with:

"Profeshair, you. . . you are, Shirr, verra drunk! . . Or you are a
bloom. . .bloom'in dreamer! . . Profeshair, you know what 'tis you
are doing? . . I'll tell you. . . you, Prof. . .eshair, what 'tis you—all
of you reb. . .reb. . .rebel clowns. . . are. . . are doing! . . Your'rr. . .
opening up Pandora's Box! . . That's what your'rr. . . doing! . . 'nd
out's going. . . going to come troub. . .trouble 'nd fighting such. . .
such as you. . . you never saw, 'nd varm. . .varmits such as you. . .
you never 'magined, 'nd more bloomin blood than's in your
damned Delaware! . . 'nd, Profeshair, as a. . .frr. . .friend, I am
going to. . . to ta. . . to tell you. . . you something. . . Profeshair!
You talk too much!"

With this the group broke out laughing. The pastor and the miller,
both extremely uneasy all through Clynes's lecture, again
tugged on him to come along. However, the old scholar was
determined to get the last word. Laughing along with the young

British officers, he nodded his head, agreeing with the wobbling, grog-filled, glass-carrying Drummond, saying:

"The lieutenant is right again, Gentlemen. He convinces me that I should be reminded of one, Arabella Young. For on her tomb-stone reads this epitaph, the like of which, I must admit, fits me:
" 'Beneath this stone, a lump of clay,
Lies Arabella Young,
Who on the 24th of May
Began to hold her tongue.' "

In the raucous laughter that rose from in front of the entrance to the candle-lit prayer hall where King George II still looked on, sternly unmoved in the background, MacMurphy and Kuederly escorted Clynes away. Carrying his little chest of stones out the front entrance, they pass the guard without being stopped.

In a few minutes Papa Kuederly and the clergyman breathed much easier with Doctor Ezra sandwiched between them in the Kuederly carriage. Hurriedly the miller sped his horse on to the MacMurphy home where the college sage is a boarder.

And so safely was rescued the professor's precious box of rocks from under the enemy's nose. But its deliverance had given the preacher and the miller some extremely anxious moments while the brazen old tutor was bearding the lion in his den. A box of rocks was not worth all that trouble in their opinion.

Seventy Miles Northeast

Some seventy miles to the northeast there was a different kind of fear tormenting Elaine Gray as she tossed in her sleep in the quiet of the Baummeister house. It was the second night of the new year.

The warming trend of the day had melted some of the ice that had formed on the eaves above her bedroom window. It was easier now, even in the night to see the Hudson's bleak river carrying the upper waters' ice floes down toward the bay and the ocean. However, with the night's return to freezing weather the long icicles again began dropping their tapering shadows down from the eaves in front of the glass panes.

Startled out of her restless sleep by a new and horrifying nightmare, the details of which she could not recall but which vaguely seemed to revolve about her husband, the ferry-master's daughter jolted herself up in bed. For brief seconds the long, dark shadowy icicles appeared to be swords and knives pushing against the glass panes as though attempting to drive their way into her room. With full consciousness came realization of her whereabouts, her sanity and safety, but a return to sleep was now impossible.

Throwing a blanket around herself, Elaine stirred the fire's sleeping embers until their flames enveloped the log of apple wood. Then, curling herself up in the large Windsor rocker, the trembling young bride of not four months stared vacantly out the window into the night's blackened shadows reflected into varied silhouettes by the white covering of snow over the land. Her mind, perplexed by the garbled vagaries of her ambiguous and cryptic dream, Elaine stretched her eyes across the river to the darkened hulk of rocky, rolling island, rising up from the eastern banks of the river.

In the gloom and stillness of the night, the young bride's mind wandered back to the tales of the ancient Chief Manna-hata and the peace and quiet that once was his upon the now much disputed island of constant contention. And so she remained with her reveries and fears until the night's curtain gradually rose up from the horizon, releasing the reddening draperies of the momentous morning of Friday, January 3, 1777.

This morning did indeed dawn momentously for General Lord Cornwallis. Last night he had heard Erskine warn him not to trust the rebels, or he was sure not to see anything of them in the morning. Never had Sir William Erskine made a more accurate prediction. By trusting "those people," as the quartermaster called the enemy, Lord Cornwallis woke up this morning to find his trap sprung and his "Fox" gone.

So, for the British Earl and his army, ready and prepared for "the big kill," the Second Battle of Trenton ended at midnight in a disgusting piece of trickery—a miserable fiasco! The nobleman's quarry had fled in the night, leaving him with an empty net.

For almost two days the Americans had been busy throwing up earthworks along the three-mile ridge on the south side of the Assunpink Creek. Their backs were indeed against the ice floes of the Delaware to the southwest. But this was planned. And von Donop and his remaining Hessians were to the southeast at Allentown.

It was a precarious position the American rebels held last night. Mercer's brigade held the left wing. Cadwalader's the center, and St. Clair's, Hitchcock's and Hand's men lengthened the Continentals' defense line which bent around to the northeast, pointing into the seldom used back road to Princeton. Behind the front line troops were the Americans' reserve forces. Among these are the

Egg Harbor guards whose ability to move rapidly in this area they know so well will earn them the ticklish task of helping to deceive the enemy through the night.

Only the Assunpink Creek and its well defended bridge separated Cornwallis from his long-hunted foe. The length and weakness of the American defense lines, with a bridge before them that could easily be overrun and a creek that had ample fording areas to the east, all under the defense of a tattered, torn and tired "army of rebel farmers," were an open invitation to a powerful military foe such as Cornwallis commands to come and take them. The invitation lured the British commander up to the very door of victory.

But to the discerning Brigadier General Sir William Erskine it was all just too good to be true and trusted. However, insofar as trust goes, Erskine will later be accused by the Trenton family with whom he lodged of taking their mahogany chairs and table in his train.

Not many Continentals outside of The General's war council could understand why their Commander had put them in such a dangerous defense position.

Why had he allowed his army to be pushed to the southernmost part of the village, farthest away from their crossing point and its vessels when it was generally assumed they were going to raid the Maidenhead and Princeton garrisons? Did The Gen'l not realize he was enticing Cornwallis to take him?

Before midnight they were to be awakened and would soon learn the reason. Orders were quietly relayed up and down the American lines.

All fires were to be kept burning and heaped high with logs. From one company to the next throughout every regiment went orders to prepare to march under arms and ready for action. Silence was impressed upon every man. No one knew what was to happen, but most were more favorably resigned to marching into action rather than attempting to find restless cold sleep on the ground.

A reinforced rear guard detachment of 400 troops[34] was assigned to keep up a constant appearance. Many of them were to maintain guard duty before the bridge. Others were assigned to keep up a continuous noise of shoveling and pickaxing with their entrenchment tools as though strengthening their earthwork entrenchments in preparation for the morning's attack. And this the unsuspecting enemy heard and comfortably enjoyed.

All men were ordered to pass before the burning fires at intervals, casting shadows of activity for the enemy sentinels to see and report to their duty officers. Guards especially were to keep up this deception all along the American lines. They were not to stop until daybreak in order to cover the secret movement of the marching force out of their defense lines and up along the road northeast toward Princeton.

This entire cover-up task was assigned to fast-moving light infantrymen who were to follow in the tracks of the rear guard behind the main army when dawn broke.

At one o'clock this morning the brigades, company by company, the men two abreast, began moving out. Gun carriage wheels were covered with cloth wrappings to dull the noise as they rolled over the ice-hardened earth.

No man was to speak unless absolutely necessary. Officers barely whispered. Orders were mostly relayed with hand signals. Sword-carrying commanders tied their sheathed blades securely to their legs to prevent rattling.

On Through the Cold Night's Obstacles

The plan called for skirting east, then north around the British left flank and next by-passing the redcoats at Maidenhead under Leslie. If they could steal by that post without alerting its perimeter's guards, the drive through the British post in Princeton would be made easier. Only the high command were informed of the plan, its operation and the army's destination.[35]

However, most of the troops soon figured out the maneuver. The objective was Princeton and possibly New Brunswick. This was, reportedly, The General's original intention. This certainly must now be his present one.

On the advice of local patriots, it was decided to take a new short route, recently cut through the forest, but a difficult one to traverse. Its tree stumps have been left protruding above the ground following the initial clearing and hacking through the brush. Over these the men tripped, fell, bruised themselves and cursed in the darkness. The projecting stumps presented major difficulties for the gun carriages and caissons. Under these obstacles rapid maneuvering was impossible.

However, in the army's favor was the cold northwest wind that had arisen earlier and sent the temperature down. For the marchers, this was a bonus. Causing the ground to freeze again, it enabled smoother traveling than the British encountered yesterday through slush holes and muddy ruts. It was the stretch of stump-cluttered north road that gave the procession the most trouble. Its irregular-sized spikes rising out of the darkened earth, dangerously tripping men and horses, seriously impeded progress.

The whole plan was a good one and a daring one. But the problem of the stumps on the new road had not been expected. The resultant unforeseen delay almost turned the entire operation into a disaster.

On through the cold night the troops trudged. Most of them are inured to forced marches, night or day in any kind of weather. It is almost a matter of habit with the old veterans now. Slowly, and silently, they made their way, wearied, bruised and hungry, most without sleep for over 24 hours. Into the little hamlet of Sand-town[36] they trudged.

In the van of the army General Greene on his black stallion led his brigade including the Dover light infantrymen and the Red Feather Company of Philadelphia. Behind them followed Mercer's brigade. The Scotland-born former physician was mounted on his own gray mare.

Alongside of Mercer, marching on foot, strode Colonel Haslet whose Delaware regiment of time-expired men have gone home. Haslet still limps from swollen legs, the aftermath of his fall into the icy waters of the Delaware a week ago.

Next came St. Clair's brigade followed by the Commander-in-Chief and his staff. General Sullivan and his brigade, who are to take over the army's right wing at Princeton were next. Behind them plowed the rest of the army. Captain Henry brought up the rear with the remaining three companies of the Philadelphia light infantry militia.

In all, the American force numbers about 5,000 men as it moves out of the night into the pre-dawn hours of the day.

Deathly business is before them and every man knows it. Yet few complain. For after all, except for the new recruits and some recently added militia battalions, a great number of them have asked for it. Most are the time-expired troops who volunteered to go on.

Never in their young lives have some of Henry's militia boys, bringing up the rear, been so close to any military action. Never have they been so close to the much talked about and terribly feared British and Hessian army.

The youngsters have been filled with stories of:

> *"the inhuman treatment of those who were so unhappy as to become prisoners"; [the British army's] "whole tract. . . of desolation and wanton destruction. . . of instances of rage and vengeance against particular persons"; [of] "Places and things, which from their public nature and general utility should have been spared by a civilized people, have been destroyed or plundered or both"; [of] "places of worship, ministers. . . treated with the most rancorous hatred, and at the same time with the highest contempt"; [of an enemy] "determined to give no quarter"; [of captured] "wounded and disabled,,, barbarously mangled or put to death"; [of a] "minister of the gospel at Trenton, who neither was, nor had been in arms. . . massacred in cold blood, though humbly supplicating for mercy"; [of the] "indecent treatment, and actual ravishment of married and single women, but such is the nature of that most irreparable injury, that the persons suffering it, and their relations, though perfectly innocent, look upon it as a kind of reproach to have the facts related, and their names known"; [and they are bloated with tales of unprovoked civilian murders, of women, old and young, some] "near seventy years of age", [one] "considerably advanced in her pregnancy" [and young girls] "horribly ravished" [or] "abused in a manner beyond description."*[37]

Now the young militia rear guardsmen, though thoroughly saturated with a bitter hatred for the enemy they were to fight, were also thoroughly saturated with fear of the horrendous Juggernaut only a creek's distance away from them in the night. They had reason to be jittery and nervous.

Into the Dawn Of January 3

Last to move out along the lines, leaving only the 400 light infantry decoys behind to tend the fires and the pickaxing, Henry's frightened rear guardsmen began seeing things as they steal out of the deserted earthworks and up on the road. For awhile their nerves held up.

Then something alarmed them, and, mistaking each other's gun-carrying shadowy figures for the enemy, fear and confusion took over. In panic they began running south along the road to Borden-town.[38]

It took Captain Henry and his officers some time to restore order. But the noise and commotion created, gave the militia captain some very trying moments.

However, it was the only nearly calamitous incident encountered in the nocturnal maneuver. Yet nothing more pointedly illustrated the intense nervousness and the terrific strain that enveloped the silently moving, cautiously groping and stumbling army through the cold night's dire blackness.

At Sandtown, about three miles east from their evacuated Trenton earthworks, they moved out of the stump-covered newly hacked-out short cut to the old, well-established Quaker Road. This they followed north about two miles over the Quaker Bridge across the Assunpink tributary. There they continued north again toward the two bridges. Two miles from each other, the bridges cross the winding Stony Brook outside of Princeton.

By taking this circuitous route instead of the main highway, the army can by-pass Leslie, two miles to the west off the main Princeton-Trenton artery at Maidenhead. For the Quaker Road runs almost parallel at times with the Princeton-Trenton highway.

At Sandtown the two roads run three and four miles apart but beyond Stony Brook and the Quaker Meeting House north of it, Quaker Road feeds into the main thoroughfare at the second Stony Brook Bridge. This is about two miles south of Princeton and a good four miles north of Maidenhead.

It is daylight. A clear, frosty morning is breaking out of the Friday morning, January 3, dawn as the American army comes out of the long night into Stony Brook hamlet.[39]

Yesterday Cornwallis left instructions for Lieutenant Colonel Mawhood at Princton to start for Trenton at dawn this morning, leaving behind his 40th Regiment and two troops of the 16th Light Dragoons to guard the post and stores in the college town.

The brilliant and audacious young colonel was to bring his remaining force, comprising the 17th Regiment, a part of the 55th Regiment and a troop of light dragoons to support the British commander in the riverside village on the Delaware. Mawhood ordered the rest of his 55th Regiment to follow as a rear guard detachment, keeping at a considerable distance.

So this morning at dawn, astride a brown horse, the lieutenant colonel, his two pet spaniels running at his steed's heels, led his troops out of Princeton in accordance with his commander's instructions. The British colonel's first stop along the main highway was to have been at Maidenhead, the half-way mark to Trenton. At Maidenhead he would pay his respects to General Leslie, bivouacking there with his 2nd brigade of about 1,000 men.

It was that enemy encampment which the rebel army had successfully skirted during the night. But by taking the painful, circuitous route through Sandtown the Continentals were now stealing out of the night onto the main highway into Princeton just south of the second Stony Brook bridge.

General Mercer's immediate aim is to destroy the bridge, thus preventing the Princeton garrison from escaping across it and alerting Generals Leslie at Maidenhead and Cornwallis at Trenton when the rebel army storms into Prince Town. So, shortly after dawn Mercer's vedettes and forward pickets come out of the back road and up on the highway. Now before them in the early morning light they see their objective, the bridge.

The Battle For Princeton Opens

At the same time, Mawhood's van, heading toward the American pickets, turns and crosses the bridge the rebels had planned to destroy. Mawhood's men reach a small hilltop on the road just south of the span, and both of the opposing forward pickets, espying each other almost simultaneously, come to a dead halt.

The British colonel's field glasses pick up the glint of metal in the sun's early morning rays. As he scans the wooded area from a hilltop perch he sees a motley group of rebels approaching from the side road.

The sight of such wretched looking soldiers emerging from a back-country, forest-covered bypath convinces Mawhood that Milord Cornwallis has scored his victory and that these unfortunates are a broken group of escaping stragglers from the beaten army.[40]

However, the astute redcoat commander, taking no chances, sends out a reconnoitering party to determine the strength of his foe and ascertain that it is not an American attack force planning to strike at Princeton. Meanwhile he orders his advance guards to withdraw from their hilltop and return to him across the bridge.

Owing to his uncertainty, Mawhood, seeking a strong strategic position in the event of serious trouble, sets his eyes on a rolling piece of high terrain covered by an orchard and dotted with several farm buildings. But the American vanguard has also seen that spot and its advantages. Both forces are on the north side of the bridge, but the Americans are the nearer to the orchard's high terrain.

On Mercer's order, led by his van, the brigade's spearhead comes dashing out of the woods to possess it. Mawhood's men, their colonel in the lead, also rush to take the hillock. The Americans gain it first and take positions behind a hedge facing Mawhood's men in the open field below them.

The British colonel deploys his troops in battle formation. Each side hauls up two fieldpieces and both open fire with small arms and artillery barrages.

The battle for Princeton opens.

Without word from his scouts, Mawhood concludes that Mercer's spearhead is the bulk of an enemy raiding party intended to divert British attention away from Trenton and on Princeton. He is unaware that it is Mercer's brigade supported by Cadwalader's division and their Pennsylvania Associators, a force of over a thousand men equal in strength to his own. And behind them, moving northward on the back road to Princeton, is the entire American army.

However, when Mercer and Cadwalader earlier cut left to block the bridge, Greene and the American Commander-in-Chief followed on behind General Sullivan, continuing along the back Quaker Road spur leading into Princeton. They were still paralleling the main highway.

Sullivan, forming the right encircling wing of the American attack force, was to have prevented the British garrison from escaping north to Brunswick while Mercer was to have blocked any flight south at the Stony Brook bridge.

At the same time, The General and Greene were to have driven the army's center from the southeast directly into the heart of the college town, splitting the surprised defenders, south into Mercer's hands and north into Sullivan's bag.

But the far-off sound of heavy gun fire from Mercer's left wing sector, south of Princeton, changes things. It causes the American Chief to swing Old Magnolia around.

Following a brief council with his staff, a dispatch rider from Mercer informs him that Mawhood has been encountered. This is an upset to the plan. The General heads for the trouble spot, directing Greene to pursue his frontal and right wing attack as planned. He instructs Sullivan to hold back some reserves pending a determination of the action below. Then with his guards and staff the Commander heads back to assist Mercer and Cadwalader.

Unobserved by Mawhood, Cadwalader forms his division behind the rolling hillocks and ridges some 300 yards to the rear of Mercer's position among the barren trees on the hilltop orchard. Mawhood's artillery trajectory directed at Mercer's lines, is too high. The rebels', on the other hand, is accurate.

After the American cannoneers get off two telling rounds, Mawhood, annoyed, orders a bayonet charge. He precedes it with a cavalry attack of 50 light horse dragoons who lead the dash up the slope.

Observing the field from behind Mercer's positions, Cadwalader first orders Captain Henry's light infantry to sweep in upon Mawhood's left, flanking the British light infantrymen as they charge toward Mercer's center, 100 yards away. Under the American cannonade and the continuous volleys pouring down from the hilltop and on their left flank from behind a fence 300 feet away, the British infantrymen and cavalry begin dropping.

Their lines waver under the heavy fusillade. In the wild confusion, over the cries and shouting of men and the painful whinnying of horses in fright and agony, Mawhood pulls back to re-form. Among his badly wounded is Captain Philips of the 35th.

Left lying on the field, the British dead and wounded present a macabre sight before the unbelieving eyes of the young American raw recruits. In horror they see the savagery of war and the beast-like inhumanity of man in the gaping wounds of some of their own. For now they stare in fright at the shocked, terror-filled eyes of their stricken comrades, looking hopelessly down upon the blood-gushing bullet holes through their own bodies, or at the dangling arms and legs from which a hand or foot has been severed and now sits grotesquely in a pool of deepening red death before them. Overhead gather clouds of gun smoke, acrid with the smell of powder.

Crying out for help, some of the wounded redcoats try to crawl back to their lines. A few make it. Others drop to the ground unconscious. Some dying. Some dead.

Beneath a mud-splattered, blood-stained scarlet officer's uniform lies the crumpled, lifeless body of one of the first to fall, the daring Captain Robert Mostyn of the 40th Foot Regiment. Mostyn fell with a piece of canister through his throat as he led his men near the bridge.

Undismayed by the failure of his first attempt to dislodge the rebels from their hilltop position, the British colonel now leads his 17th Regiment in a shoulder-to-shoulder bayonet charge up the ridge at the American-held position.

Shouting and slashing their way up the hillside, the bayonet-wielding British infantrymen pass over their own dead and through their own wounded toward the rebels' lines. Arriving on the crest, the redcoats drive in upon Mercer's brigade.

The brigadier urges his staff and their commands to stand their ground and step up their firing. He spurs his horse along the American line, encouraging his men to use their rifle butts if necessary. His officers do likewise as the British swarm in upon them.

Unhorsed, Mercer Falls

Few of Mercer's men have bayonets. Faced with the sight of glittering steel blades driving into them in waves of hundreds at a time, the orchard defenders falter under their enemy's covering artillery barrage.

When the cannon fire lifts and they see long rows of steel bearing down upon them, some of the jittery militia panic. They waver, break and pull back. But most hold their ground and level a withering fire that drops one after the other of the charging redcoats before they can pour in and over the slowly withdrawing Continentals.

Along with others Captain William Shippen falls, writhing in pain. In a few moments the Philadelphian's body is stilled.

Suddenly Mercer's horse whinnies, stumbles and falls in an agonizing shriek, her foreleg broken by a cannon ball. Thrown to the ground as the animal crumbles beneath him, Mercer quickly recovers himself and is up on his feet. Then, brandishing his sword, he turns and recklessly faces the enemy pressing down upon him.

Some of the Continentals with bayonets and others using musket and rifle butts, give ground slowly before the rigid line of methodically advancing King's men.

Minutes after getting to his feet, the Scotland-born physician from Virginia gives the order to retreat.[41] It is swiftly speeded down the lines to his officers and men as the wild melee opens in vicious hand-to-hand combat. The fighting spreads beyond the orchard, around the hilltop, the farmhouse and its adjacent buildings.

Riflemen on both sides carefully select their targets away from close combatants in order not to pick off their own men.

The piercing shrieks of the stricken, the excited shouting of orders, the blood-thirsty yelling of hate-crazed men on both sides, all are mixed with the cries of the wounded and the death throes of the dying.

For many long minutes the battlefield is like an inferno of enraged wild men, burning with retaliation, asking and giving no quarter. At last Mercer's men give ground. Carrying out Mercer's retreat order the brigade rapidly pulls back.

Led by the intrepid Mawhood, the emboldened British press on after their withdrawing foe, unchecked by the comrades dropping beside them.

Now a redcoat squad overtakes and surrounds the unhorsed American brigadier general. Refusing to surrender, Mercer is struck down by a rifle butt and left behind by the British squad who push on after the fleeing rebels.

Holding on to his rapier, Mercer regains his feet and violently wields the weapon, slashing out at his attackers. Left alone in the rear of his troops, the physician—his brigade now swiftly pulling back to the opposite ridge—is again surrounded and ordered to give up his sword.

To both the rebels and the redcoats this is the final culmination of months of pent-up angers and frustrations. Not since Long Island have the Americans been in such close combat with the enemy invaders whom they have learned to hate with increasing bitterness throughout the long expedition.

In a like manner, the King's men have chased the defiant rebel "insurrectionists," who have "disloyally renounced the Crown," through New York, Westchester and Jersey, building up with each passing month an insatiable desire to track down and annihilate the foe that keeps them from returning home.

Here then, for rebel and redcoat alike, is the cruel, culminating crescendo, the final, unrelenting stroke for retribution as the long, and now decisively prophetic campaign reaches its crisis and its furious climax.

The reasons, the politics, the causes matter not. No thought now is given to the Acts of '63, or the Navigation, Sugar, Quartering, Stamp, Declaratory, Townshend, Tea, Intolerable and Restraining Acts of the past thirteen years. No thought is given to the Boston Massacre. Only hate fills each man's mind.

With his refusal to surrender his sword, the fighting stubborn

Hugh Mercer seals his own fate. He is bayoneted seven times and collapses on the ground. His attackers push on over him in their pursuit of his retreating men. Then not far away Captain Leslie of the 17th Regiment drops with a rebel ball through the abdomen.

Gripping his sword tightly in his hand, Mercer feigns death while the enemy infantrymen push over and around his prostrate form. He will lie there until the Americans counterattack. Leslie now is being carried off the field.

Colonel John Haslet, still limping badly, sees the Virginia physician fall and attempts to rally Mercer's troops. Now, if ever, the former Delaware physician wishes he had his brave and scrappy Delawareans behind him as he valiantly tries to restore order to the dispersing Mercer troops.

Haslet Drops

Haslet, who practiced medicine in Dover, Delaware, before the war, ascends a mound and from it urges his subaltern officers to hold their companies together and keep raining volleys of fire on the advancing redcoats. He shouts out orders to load, fire and then withdraw in an effort to stem the enemy's advance.

Disregarding his own safety, the colonel exposes himself to enemy marksmen. One of them catches him in his sights. A few seconds later the fighting patriot colonel from Delaware drops with a ball through his head. He will not regain consciousness. Death will mercifully take him before the sun goes down.

Dead and wounded of both armies lie scattered over the battlefield as Mawhood's forces slowly push the Americans farther and farther back.

Tragedy follows upon tragedy in the bitter and slaughterous contest. The shocking effect of each catastrophe will have its own sad repercussions throughout the country and across the sea for years to come.

One rebel account will record the alleged murderous treatment of the 18-year old American lieutenant Bartholomew Yeates, son of the Reverend Robert Yeates of Gloucester County, Virginia, a relative of the Randolphs of Virginia. According to the report, Yeates, his ankle broken, crawled under a wagon for refuge.

Pursuing him, his enemy clubbed, shot and bayoneted the crippled lieutenant three times until he was dead, the report will state. The youth was attached to Colonel Reed's Virginia regiment.

And it was one of Reed's men who later declared that as the young officer was being struck he was "all the while crying for mercy."[42]

Mawhood Boldly Charges and Stops

Mawhood's charge is now unchecked. He pursues the withdrawing rebel troops to the top of the second ridge. There he stops short and pulls back his forces along the crest of the rise.

For now out of the same woods and back road bypath from which Mercer had appeared, Cadwalader's division emerges. Cadwalader leads his men down upon the bewildered Mawhood. The British colonel had not expected to see such rebel strength.

Mawhood orders a withdrawal. Pulling back toward Princeton, he takes a position behind a long rail fence and a deep ditch between two lengthy ground ridges. Extending his line so that all his troops may fire at once, he orders his artillery in his rear to keep up a continuous barrage of grape and round shot on the field between his resting riflemen and Cadwalader's slowly advancing Pennsylvanians.

Cadwalader Moves In Rashly

Without carefully analyzing all aspects of the situation, Cadwalader recklessly pushes his largely untried militia too close and too soon under the enemy's artillery barrage. The acting brigadier general orders his troops into positions only 150 feet from the enemy's fence barricade.[43]

Breaking his corps into divisions, Cadwalader alternately strings them out right and left in supporting lines, one behind the other. By platoons they are expected to file off and fire, pull out and reload in order to lay down an almost continous downpour upon the British lines.[44]

They had done this well on the drill grounds,[45] but not under a constant artillery barrage from Mawhood's eight fieldpieces laying canister and shot all over the field. Besides, on the drill grounds they had not been menaced by a bloodthirsty enemy's steel bayonets, 50 yards away and eagerly waiting for the command to charge in upon them.

In the background the British fifers and drummers keep up a steady roll that offers little consolation to the nervous rebel militiamen.

In Fright, Panic and Flight

The Pennsylvania Associators hesitate, falter and then begin dropping behind one another. They fall back in fairly good order until others start to scatter in fright under the enemy's pounding artillery and the British grenadiers' musketry and canister. These bursts and the cries of the stricken and wounded dropping to the ground beside them, send Cadwalader's forward lines into confusion.

To avoid panic and a rout the brigadier commander orders a withdrawal. In the melee, Captain Daniel Neil tries to rally his company. A few of his men drop, wounded. Neil is bayoneted and takes a gun butt full on the throat at the same time. He drops dead.

In their haste to carry out the order to retreat, the Associators abandon one of their fieldpieces and its battery to the charging redcoat bayonets.[46] The King's men then fall upon Cadwalader's artillerists. Dispersing them, they capture the rebel cannon. In a few minutes they turn the weapon around and begin firing it at its former owners.

Galloping up to the scene with his guards and staff, the American Commander, his breath steaming into the cold air along with that from Old Magnolia's snorting nostrils, sees in a glance Cadwalader's frantic efforts to prevent a mass flight along the wavering rebel lines. Only a few battalions valiantly try to hold together under the pressure as officers excitedly shout encouraging words of praise.

But most of the fear-crazed militia companies border on the edge of panic. Like a contagion their battle-shocked, terror-stricken faces spread from unit to unit throughout the ranks.

Instead of withdrawing in orderly fashion and returning their enemy's fire as they pull back slowly, some companies split up and run when a burst breaks near them. A wild rout of Cadwalader's entire brigade now seems inevitable. Wounded, dying and dead from both sides lie strewn over the field.

Then, to the amazement of his staff and guards, the American General throws caution aside. Alone he weaves old Magnolia in through the retreating men.

His head bare, his hat in hand, he waves the tricorn with wide, rapid, forward sweeping movements, calling to his officers and troops to stand and hold. His very appearance on the field lifts some out of their momentary fright. They stop, turn around and look up at him fully exposed to the enemy.

Leadership's Recovery

Guiding Old Magnolia up through the surprised, scattering militiamen, he hurls curses and mixed invectives at them for not staying with their officers. Angrily he attempts to shame them for not holding their ground.

Shouting that they can still achieve victory and that only a "handful of the enemy face them," The General urges his men to keep up their fire and hold their ranks.

The American Chief then fearlessly spurs his sturdy old white mare directly into the front lines' hottest fire.[47]

There, only sixty feet from a poised and ready redcoat, bayonet-fixed formation, awaiting the command to charge when their barrage is lifted, the American Commander-in-Chief, in close view to the enemy lines behind the rail fence, sits brazenly astride his mare.

Fiercely the big man waves his hat in that sweeping forward motion to his troops behind him, shouting that one good charge will send the enemy back flying.[48] He is determined that the lines of Americans on both sides will see him. And they do, as also do the astonished British troops.

It is their first sight of the ever-elusive rebel "Fox." And now, at last, he rises big in the saddle before them, face to face.

Standing upright in the stirrups, he continuously flourishes the tricorn in a forward motion, roaring at the hesitating militia to get back into ranks for a slow and orderly withdrawal to the rear. With renewed spirits the officers re-form their lines as the men under their commands gradually respond.

Reaction at first is slow, but the contagion of fear is now reversed. Hope and the unbeatable will to succeed now strangely spread a mysterious aura of courage and faith, at least temporarily, down through the long lines of fighting men. The vacuum of leadership is suddenly filled.

All of this happens rapidly. Even The General's own staff and guards are left behind in the swiftness of the episode. They follow in the distance. Then suddenly all bring their horses abruptly to a halt. Up in the front line's heat of battle near where they had seen him a few minutes before waving his hat right and left, a pounder strikes, sending up a billowing ball of fire and smoke. It envelopes man and horse in a white cloud of gunpowder.

Every man's eyes, rebel and redcoat alike, turn in awe at the sight. A rumbling of horrified voices in gasps of fear rise up all along the rebels' lines.

One of the Commander's aides, Lieutenant Fitzgerald, seeing horse and rider swallowed up in the cloud of gunsmoke, clenches his teeth, cries out, "Gad! He's fallen!" and covers his eyes with his hands.[49]

Staff and guards look on, stunned in disbelief. Then, as they spur their horses forward to the spot, the smoke clears. And there in the saddle, unharmed, and as big and as impressive as ever, the American Leader again waves his hat in a forward motion to the troops in his rear.

The burst had struck a tree trunk well enough away from horse and rider, but not far enough to avoid a showering of chunks of frozen earth, ice and snow, some concussion and a throat full of acrid gunsmoke. Old Magnolia snorts violently to rid her nostrils of the stench.

Now the British troops, awe-struck by their first sight of the big rebel army Chief of whom they had heard so many conflicting tales, stood amazed by the man's astoundingly good luck. But they were even more astonished at their own fortune in seeing the "villainous chap" they had heard so much ill about, dodging the King's barrage.

There before them he had dashed high in the saddle of his white mare exposing himself to their fire. It was something to tell if ever they wrote home again.

Even the British soldiers admit that their marksmanship is not as accurate as that of the American woodsmen with their rifled barreled weapons, but they had never thought that their comrades' aim was that bad! For when the smoke cleared there he was as calm, cool and as unruffled as the Giza Sphinx after a blinding sandstorm.

But he was not in that or any other place long. Seconds later he was seen somewhere else along the lines. So he was, after all not an easy target. The "Blasted rebel bloke just won't stand still!"

Mawhood Regains the Upper Hand

It is not reckless, foolish courage that has sent the American army Commander rashly to the head of his faltering troops and through the enemy's hottest fire. The General's whole objective is tottering along with the wavering and breaking Cadwalader front lines. Here the entire American dream could go down in a crashing, catastrophic end to the campaign, The Cause and the rebellion.

In the minds of the military strategists on the field, only precious seconds separated the objective's success from its collapse. And the rebel Chief had grasped that realization in one glance and with one swift and risky action. There was no time for lengthy consultations—no time for many minds in slow deliberations to decide on what to do. It was the time, fast escaping, to act and hopefully rally the spooked militia brigade, no matter what the risk. Much more than anyone then could imagine rested upon it.

Mawhood, who has sent dispatch riders north to warn the Princeton garrison with orders for them to support his rear, has also sent couriers south to inform Leslie at Maidenhead and Cornwallis in Trenton. However, Cornwallis, chagrined, has discovered his "Fox" has fled and is already angrily heading a forced march north to Princeton.

So, north of the Stony Brook, Colonel Mawhood is now sure he has victory within his grasp. And the observation of the rebels' Chief on the battlefield sparks his enthusiasm.

To take the "American Fox" is every British officer's dream. There is not an English or Hessian general in His Majesty's services, the young colonel knows, who would not like to be in Lieutenant Colonel Charles Mawhood's shoes right now.

But Mawhood cannot know that the American Commander sent word to Greene and Sullivan, ordering part of Sullivan's division— the reserves—to return on the double and reinforce Mercer's and Cadwalader's troops.

In fact, Mawhood is unaware that there is such a force as Sullivan's and Greene's circling behind him at Princeton. His scouts have brought no word of that. So the redcoat field commander only knows that he has scattered Mercer's force and holds its wounded commander and, more important, that the Cadwalader corps is about to be overrun with the American General likely to be bagged along with it.

Hand-to-Hand Combat To the Death

Advancing with precision the British lines move methodically in upon the retreating American ranks. Isolated pockets of men, furiously fighting in hand-to-hand combat, leave trails of blood and crumpled, prostrated forms in their wake.

One after the other of the American fieldpieces is taken. Around each battery, the rebel artillerists battle the oncoming bayonets with pikes and gun butts until they are forced to pull back. Like demons in a fiery dance of death, the contestants charge, chase and strike wildly out at one another.

Now the field is a riotous holocaust of enraged and frightened men in unloosed hate and fear. Riflemen and sharpshooters in the confusion abandon all efforts at aiming, firing, loading. As the fighting closes in upon them they resort to rifle butts.

Some turn on their heels and run. A few all along the lines attempt to fight off their assailants with long pikes taken from a fallen foe.

Under the fierce enemy drive the Americans give ground. Though a disastrous rout of Cadwalader's men, with companies of Mercer's reorganized regiments on the flanks and in the rear, had been temporarily averted by The General's rally, the front line rebel militia troops still waver dangerously.

Now the fronts of both opposing forces clash from one end of the battlefield to the other. The stricken stumble and fall. Wounded and dying lie scattered over the field. Their hopeless screams for help go unheeded under the trampling feet of the surging waves of redcoats who try to step over them. Over fallen, whinnying horses the British scramble on after their rebel enemies, inadvertently stepping on the prostrate forms under their feet.

Gradually the Cadwalader and remaining Mercer brigades are driven back until they again border on panic. Only the fighting will of the few prevents it.

As the temporary effect of the American Commander's bold rallying attempt begins to wear off, the pressing rows of sharp, glittering steel blades, driving in against their rifle butts and pikes, overcome the militia. Once more they tremble and relapse into "bayonet fever."

And so again the ranks fall back with increasing disorder, opening up deep gaps in the American lines as the militiamen break and run. This time for good.

One of the Continentals bravest young captains, John Fleming, struggles to hold the militia from breaking. Suddenly he wheels around, falling to the ground, clutching the mortal wound the ball has made above his heart.

To the Rescue Come The General's "Old Faithfuls"

Then, just as Mawhood is convinced a major victory is in his lap, an excited aide directs the colonel's fieldglasses to that same old mysterious back road out of the woods. To the British officer's dismay—his own troops badly battered, tired and suffering from heavy casualties—he sees regiment after regiment of his Yankee rebel, tatterdemalion enemy, fresh and eager for battle, emerging out of the woods from which the others had poured.

The puzzled redcoat commander now wonders if the distant forest harbors an endless reserve of Americans. And he had thought the first of them were merely a few stragglers, escaping from Cornwallis in Trenton!

Like avenging angels from out of the blue, the old standbys— veteran Continentals from Sullivan's command—move in rapidly toward Mawhood's flanks. They stop and stand poised. Those with bayonets take positions facing the center of the now halted and bewildered redcoats.

The Continentals pile up to their line, passing and ignoring the fleeing Cadwalader militiamen who, in stupefied amazement, stop running, catch their breath, and breathe easier under their new cover of security.

The Sullivan reserves include Hitchcock's Rhode Island Continentals, Hand's Pennsylvania riflemen, and the 7th Virginia Regiment. The sight of the old rough, tough veteran reinforcements, suddenly appearing on the field as though to rescue them, is more heartening to the new recruits than was even The General's daring and surprising presence among them.

In the rear of the Sullivan-sent reserves, on a farmyard ridge, Captain Joseph Moulder and his two-gun battery from Mercer's brigade, provide a cover for the new arrivals. Moulder's artillery opens up with a heavy shower of grape and canister that rains havoc upon the heads of Mawhood's stalled troops.

Fortunately Moulder has been able to hold his strategic ridge position securely during the seesawing skirmishing. However, some of his protecting militia took to their heels during the enemy advance. So Moulder sends a rider to The General's command post asking for replacements.

Counterattack

Establishing their threat to Mawhood's center and flanks, the Sullivan reserves pull back, letting Moulder's withering barrage send the redcoats in reverse behind their rail fence lines. Meanwhile, Cadwalader's and Mercer's brigades, recovering from their rout, reorganize and form under the Commander-in-Chief's orders while Moulder lays down his barrage.

In reply to the artillery officer's request, Captain Thomas Rodney and his Dover, Delaware, militiamen and some of the reorganized Philadelphia Associators ascend Moulder's ridge to support his cannonade with small arms.

Rodney works out a firing pattern enabling a continuous fusillade to pour down upon the enemy lines. The rapid frequency of the volleys, firing by platoons,[50] deceives Mawhood and his staff officers into over-estimating the Americans' strength.

Consequently, the redcoat commander goes on the defensive. At the same time he sends a rider, ordering that the rest of his 55th Regiment, his nearest hope of reinforcements, already on their way from Princeton, speed their march to his support.

Mawhood now stalls for time. Certainly Leslie's 2nd brigade should soon come up from Maidenhead on top of the rebels' rear. And hopefully Cornwallis with the main army should not be far behind.

All this is no secret to the Continental Army Chief. He knows how little time he has left. He lifts Moulder's barrage and orders the Virginians to lead the counterattack. With all his units reformed The General gives the order.

Yelling, firing, loading and firing, the 7th Virginia Regiment, the Rhode Island Continentals and the Pennsylvania riflemen under Hitchcock and Hand, drive into the British center and their right and left flanks. Behind them pile up the exhausted but revenge-seeking Cadwalader and Mercer troops.

The crack riflemen from Hand's regiment go against Mawhood's right. Hitchcock's best marksmen strike at the enemy's left. Driving and shouting, the Virginians crash in close hand-to-hand combat with the British center. Young Ensign Anthony Morris is among those giving his life in this drive.

Though fighting bravely to prevent it, the redcoats are forced to give ground. Gradually the spirited Virginians drive in the bulging British center and viciously follow through as their foe valiantly fight back. Mortally wounded, Morris and others of the Continentals' force are carried back. The young ensign's head gushes from the gaping wound. A few militia vomit at the sight.

The opposing forces struggle almost on top of each other. Mawhood's muskets now face the most intense American rifle fire of the battle on the east and west sectors where volley answers volley and where the combatants are not almost eye to eye. There on the flanks the American marksmanship is so accurate that the cries of the wounded cause one rebel soldier observer later to write that "they (the enemy) screamed as if so many devils had got hold of them."[51]

Though almost completely surrounded, Mawhood and his well

disciplined King's men fight on with extreme bravery. To their rear where they had looked for help from part of their 55th Regiment, hurrying on its way to Mawhood's side, General St. Clair and his brigade run head-on into the arriving British reinforcements on the main highway.

The brigadier's men attack the enemy battalions with such ferocity that the King's troops turn and retreat over the fields and along the road northeast to New Brunswick. St. Clair then sends a detachment hot on their heels for three miles. Near Kingston, the rebels will give up the chase.[52]

In pursuing the fleeing part of Mawhood's 55th Regiment, St. Clair orders two regiments of his brigade off the Princeton-Brunswick Road into the college town, severing Mawhood's connection with his 40th British Regiment which the colonel had left in Princeton to guard the stores.

Overwhelmed by the Americans' drive in upon them in the town, some of the British defenders withdraw into Nassau Hall. The rest flee north toward Brunswick. Surrounding the college buildings, St. Clair lays siege to the beleaguered isolated remnants of the enemy's 40th infantry.

Mawhood Breaks Through the Rebel Ring

Mawhood, now encircled by his foe, and with no word from his other half of the 55th Regiment, or the 40th in Princeotn, and still seeing no sign of either Leslie or Cornwallis to the south, decides upon a last desperate stroke. It is his alternative to surrender.

Rather than be taken prisoner by his rebel enemies, the astute young commanding officer chooses to make a daring break and cut a hole through his opponent's lines.

With his officers he swiftly plans a bayonet charge at the Americans' weakest sector. Once through, a mad dash across the bridge and on to the main highway should do it. And then on to join Leslie in Maidenhead.

At Mawhood's command the entire British corps comes suddenly and violently to life. With fixed bayonets, they charge madly into the sparsely defended southeast sector of the Americans' encircling ring. The lightning-like action takes the unsuspecting guards by surprise.

Cadwalader rapidly pours as many of his troops as possible into the gap in an effort to block the breakthrough. Most are too far scattered to get there on time.

Short of blades to fight the bayonet-charging redcoats, the Americans are forced to give ground to the driving enemy wedge. Giving way reluctantly, the rebels finally break apart, failing to muster sufficient strength to close the hole.

Through it, in swarming numbers, Mawhood's fiercely fighting and slashing troops crash their way out of The General's net. The redcoat-charging wedge bursts open like a giant gate.

Having discarded their knapsacks before the action, Mawhood and his men are unencumbered by blankets and packs. Striking out with deadly strokes right and left, the redcoat bayonets and sabers sparkle in the bright morning sun.

Along with the foot troops the mounted dragoons slash a clear path out toward the bridge and highway. However, their course now is sprinkled by increasing small arms fire from the pursuing American riflemen.

Sprinting as fast as they can with only one purpose in mind, the escaping King's men are guarded and aided by the saber-wielding horsemen. One cavalry troop brings up the rear and fans out on either side, opening still farther the wide-spreading wedge in the punctured American encirclement.

Swiftly chasing on the heels of the fleeing British troops, the Philadelphia light horse close in behind the escaping infantrymen. Their orders are to prevent Mawhood's forces from reaching Maidenhood to join with Leslie and Cornwallis. This, however, is now too much to expect.

Pressed by the American horsemen, who now tangle with the British dragoons, the Mawhood forces scatter in a rout after clearing the bridge. The excellent orderliness of their beginning dissolves into a mad race against capture.

Some are shot. Some are taken. Others disperse on either side of the main highway to Maidenhead, throwing their muskets in the woods, or dropping them in their tracks as the rebel light horsemen ride down upon them.

The field and the redcoats' pathway over the bridge and on to the highway are littered with discarded weapons and accouterments of every kind.

Finally the British dragoons angrily wheel about. They come to a halt and form a line in the rear of their escaping comrades as though warning the Philadelphia horsemen to come no farther.

Valiantly they wield their sabers in rider-to-rider duels in an effort to ward off the rebel cavalry until all of their comrades get safely away. The rebel horsemen, swinging their sabers, charge several times. Slashing back, the dragoons accept the challenge. The blood-spilling melee is short but vicious.

A few are unhorsed on both sides, but the dragoons bravely hold their ground until the captain of the Philadelphia light horse calls off the pursuit and returns with his troop to the main body.

Now parts of Colonel Mawhood's Princeton defense force are escaping at both ends, north to New Brunswick and south to Maidenhead and Trenton. Only a small number of the British colonel's 40th Regiment is trapped inside Princeton. These few, their escape route to Brunswick blocked by St. Clair's men, are now bottled up inside Nassau Hall.

"Victory"?

For the Continental Army Commander the planned attack on New Brunswick is ruined. The Mawhood encounter has seen to that. All the elements of surprise which he had counted upon so strongly have seeped out of the expedition.

Regretting the turn of events that now forces him to abandon the third and final step of his original plan, The General decides on taking whatever fruits he can out of the Princeton operation. They are far less than he had hoped for. There is more disappointment and sadness than there is satisfaction and joy in today's victory, if "victory" it is!

After gathering up their wounded and dead and marching on to Princeton proper with their prisoners, armament and booty, the main American army comes up behind St. Clair, his men lined before Nassau Hall. From out of the old stone building now are emerging the last of Colonel Mawhood's 40th Regiment. Filing out one by one, the 194 redcoats, some in tears, carry their wounded and their dead.

Each man drops his weapons on the ground. Officers surrender their swords. Many of them retain a haughty air. Some are furious with their officers and themselves for being captured. Their surrender also brings the release of 20 American prisoners who were held captive in the hall.

It took only one cannon ball to convince the last of the Princeton garrison to capitulate. Ordered by a party of Jerseyans to "Surrender or die!", their leader declined.[53]

When the hall's occupants refused St. Clair's ultimatum, the field commander ordered Captain Alexander Hamilton to bring up his artillery battery.

Hamilton fired one shot. It went through the building's entrance and decapitated the serious-faced George II hanging in the prayer hall.

No further inducement was necessary. The besieged defenders displayed a white flag. A few minutes later they began filing out of the college's main hall. The battle for Princeton was over.

From start to end the violent contest for Princeton, bringing the long, six-month campaign of 1776 to its gruesome and savage climax, has lasted less than an hour.

However, the Trenton and Princeton battles, linked with the strategic retreat which produced them will become the major topics of conversation on two continents for years to come.

Their costs, though heavy in dead, wounded and maimed on both sides, will be considered light in view of their tremendous significance. For the impact of these events upon the world society of man will be immeasurable in the recording of history for all time to come.

Nevertheless, the episodes, along with the crises-ridden campaign itself, will gradually lose their recognition among the foremost designers of mankind's past. For the pages of history will swiftly turn to other things. They will bury the military annal of 1776 and the first three days of 1777 beneath archives—archives which the Grand Army of 1776 made possible.

But now the buoyant uplift from the successes of a ragged, underfed army of speedily recruited civilians, sunken in despair by their continuous defeats at the hands of the most powerful military power in Europe, will be the nation's long-sought elixir.

Similarly, throughout all Europe, the humbling defeats, upsetting Great Britain's certainty that the rebellion is virtually crushed, will within weeks produce incalculable diplomatic repercussions in the courts of Europe.

Estimates of the Princeton casualties will vary on both sides. The Americans will report 400 of their enemy killed in the conflict, 100 of whom were counted on the field. Contradicting this, General Howe will declare 18 of his men killed, excluding ten artillerymen whom he will omit from his returns. He will add that 58 were wounded and 187 reported missing.

The Americans will count 40 dead. Among these are some of the best officers in the Continental Army. Many of the rebel wounded are in extremely bad condition, suffering from severe lacerations, deep puncture wounds and bayonet slashes sustained in the extensive close, hand-to-hand fighting.

Never have the army's surgeons been so busy and found themselves so shorthanded. The most severely wounded are loaded into the wagons along with assorted loot, supplies and the customary spoils of war. Among these are some good fieldpieces and many much-needed blankets.

Under guard behind the wagons are lined 300 British prisoners. Included are 14 officers.[54] They perk up with false hopes when they overhear the American subalterns passing on word that the enemy's main force is rapidly approaching along the road from Trenton.

Owing now to the pressing expediency of haste, the dead are left behind unburied. The decision to cancel the Brunswick attack was hurriedly presented to the war council on the field. The approach of Cornwallis, the serious condition of the wounded, the large number of prisoners[55] to be guarded, the mass of captured supplies, arms and accouterments and the exhausted condition of the troops who have had no sleep for two nights, all make it expedient to head for the safety of the Watchung Hills with as little delay as possible.

No one is more disappointed with the unavoidable decision than is The General himself. His staff unanimously supports him, yet all are aware that a successful New Brunswick attack and the capture of its reported payroll chest there, would undoubtedly crush the already staggering enemy Juggernaut.

The War's End, Just 700 Troops Away

That £70,000 chest in Brunswick alone might have provided sufficient inducement and the needed second breath necessary to refuel the spirit and the bodies of men who are almost now too weak to push on to the distant mountains. It is, however, The General's secret. And he keeps it to himself, though some have heard stories of a payroll there. So he adjourns his war council session on the bank of the Milstone[56] River near Rocky Hill this cold, tragic and momentous January morning.

On the day after tomorrow, Sunday, January 5, the Continental Army Commander will write the Congress from Morristown, reporting the events of the past few days. He will inform the country's fathers of his disappointment in not executing the planned Brunswick attack. And he will state that had he been able to make a forced march with six or seven hundred fresh troops to New Brunswick, he would have:

"destroyed all their stores and magazines, taken their military chest, containing seventy thousand pounds, and put an end to the war."[5][7]

The General's great disappointment will cause many of the Congress to do some hard soul-searching. And in that soul-searching the lawmakers will hasten to give virtually dictatorial powers to the Continental Army Commander-in-Chief. Furthermore, they will lsten to, and submit to, the growing demand that the Congress delimit its controls over the military.

Understandably, when Cornwallis waked at dawn this morning and discovered to his embarrassment and anger that the "Fox" he thought he had bagged was tearing his rear apart in Princeton and likely headed for the valuable stores at New Brunswick, his lordship moved!

In his unprecedented speed the British Earl has driven his troops breast-deep through the Stony Brook where the Americans destroyed the bridge behind them. He has added General Leslie and his 2nd Brigade at Maidenhead and picked up Lieutenant Colonel Mawhood for a full report of the catastrophic battle.

So rapid has been his lordship's pace out of Trenton that his van will report that they observed the American rear guard leaving the grounds of the military-sacked college town before the morning is over.

Within 24 hours, Lord Cornwallis's corps has met repeated disappointments in forced marches from Princeton to Trenton and now back from Trenton to Princeton. They have had little more than a fleeting glance at their enemy's ever-disappearing rear each time until they came up to and began firing upon the rebel detachment completing their destruction of the Stony Brook bridge.

Freezing in their wet clothing from fording the deep stream, hungry from having little more than a grab of hardtack for breakfast—their bowels bloated and unattended in their haste to move out—and wearied by the difficult, full pack-25-mile fruitless chase through bridgeless streams and over ice-covered roads, the British troops restrain their emotions with the constitutions of automatons.

So, withholding their logical irritability and concealing their understandable exhaustion, the Crown's soldiers press on behind their commander without an audible grumble. These are the men of the army of the king of the empire that rules the globe.

Primarily trained and prepared for meeting their enemy in conventional Eighteenth Century battlefield formations, they do not easily adjust to the American "Fox's" tactics. The American General's surprise, strike and run Indian techniques are not to the redcoats' liking.

Unlike the Trenton fray, Princeton's battle has cost the Americans heavily in casualties. In the severe fighting throughout the conflict the losses of commanders and subaltern officers mounted from the very beginning along with those sustained by the troops under them. Among the badly wounded is Brigadier General Mercer.

The former surgeon, who was carried off the field by his own men during the counterattack and placed temporarily under an oak tree, has examined his own wounds with a sad shake of his head. Carried later to the Thomas Clark farmhouse, Mercer is now under the care of Miss Sarah Clark and a black servant maid in the Clark household.[63]

Since he cannot be moved again, it was decided that the wounded commander, who led the right flanking attack on the Hessians in Trenton and was said to have advised the night march on Princeton, must be left behind by the army. Consequently he will be placed at the enemy's mercy.

Mercer was the American Commander-in-Chief's close companion in the French and Indian War. The General, deeply affected by the plight of his friend and comrade, will immediately intercede with General Cornwallis in behalf of his fellow Virginian and one of his most beloved officers.

The General will request Cornwallis to provide Mercer with every courtesy possible. Then sending his own nephew, Major George Lewis, with a flag to the British commander, the American Leader will ask that Lewis be allowed to remain with Mercer until his recovery.

Without hesitation the Earl will promptly grant the request. In addition the British commander will send his own staff surgeon to attend the stricken brigadier.

Mercer, who was an army surgeon in Europe, will watch attentively as Cornwallis' physician examines his wounds. Carefully the British doctor will observe the nature of each bayonet puncture, declaring that, though they are many and serious, none should endanger his life.

Then the fallen commanding officer will say to young Major Lewis:

Brigadier General Hugh Mercer

"Raise my right arm, George, and this gentleman will then discover the smallest of my wounds, which will prove the most fatal."

Doing as Mercer instructs, Lewis will raise the brigadier general's right arm, exposing a small, blade-width incision that appears to have struck deep into the general's right lung.

Mercer then will prophetically assure the surgeon:

"Yes, Sir, there is the fellow that will soon do my business."[64]

In the next few days, General Mercer will exonerate the British soldiers, charged with bayoneting a general officer who had allegedly surrendered his sword and was therefore a prisoner of war. Mercer will affirm that he did not surrender his sword, and that he only relinquished it when his arm wound prevented him from holding it.

The Toll

True to the warrior physician's self-prognosis, Hugh Mercer will be dead within nine days. The deep chest wound that pierced his lungs will bring about his end. He will die gasping for breath in the arms of Major Lewis Sunday, January 12.

Left on the field to be buried by the enemy are many Americans. One among these is another former physcian, John Haslet. A bullet through his brain spared him a lingering death.

There is a sad commentary to the Delaware colonel's tragedy. His aide, who saw that his body was placed respectfully alongside of the others, cleared his pockets of papers and personal belongings as are The General's standing instructions.

In his coat the aide found an order directing Haslet to go home to Dover on recruiting service since all his troops had left him on the expiration of their enlistments. Haslet, however, had not divulged the contents of the order to anyone, choosing instead to disobey it, at least, he thought, temporarily.

Among his long and depressing list of casualties, the American Commander counts many of his finest troops and some of the best officers in the Continental Army. The dead Colonel Haslet and the mortally wounded General Mercer lead the list. But in addition are, among others:

Twenty-seven year-old Captain William Shippen, the Philadelphian merchant who leaves a widow and three small children; the dead Captain Daniel Neil of New Jersey; twenty-one year-old Captain John Fleming of the Virginia Continentals' First Infantry Regiment whose record of brave and daring accomplishments won him an enviable reputation within the services; the dead Ensign Anthony Morris Jr. of Philadelphia and Lieutenant Bartholomew Yeates of Virginia.

General Lord Cornwallis has likewise lost heavily in the battle. Among the casualties within the British rank and file are some of Mawhood's best young officers. One of these is Captain William Leslie of the British 17th Regiment. He is the nephew of General Leslie and the second son to the Earl of Leven.

Young Leslie, attended by a rebel surgeon, was carried off with the Americans among their prisoners and wounded. He will be taken as far as Pluckemin. There he will succumb to his wounds on Sunday, January 5. Like John Fleming, the 22-year old redcoat also established an enviable record for bravery but in the King's army.

At Pluckemin the warm, friendly likeable young British officer who despite the serious nature of his wound, will joke with his rebel captors while being treated by the eminent American surgeon, Dr. Benjamin Rush of Philadelphia. When efforts to save his life end in vain, the enemy officer will be given a burial with full military honors by his captors.[65]

Eventually Dr. Rush will erect a monument over the captain's grave in Pluckemin which will attempt to show the sympathetic understanding of the individual American for the individual British soldier. The gesture will symbolize almost every enemy's compassion for the fallen foe.

Also among the King's men left dead on the field is another of the British army's popular and daring young officers, Captain

Robert Mostyn, "heir to an estate of twenty-five thousand pounds per annum in England."[66] The 25-year old officer fell leading his men of the 40th Regiment. He was caught with others of his command by a blast from an American battery. His face almost torn away, Mostyn fortunately died instantly.

One redcoat account will detail the alleged murderous treatment of the youthful Captain Philips of the 35th grenadiers. The captain, according to reports, was attempting to escape to New Brunswick to join his unit when he was overtaken on the Princeton-New Brunswick highway by a party of American horsemen from St. Clair's pursuing detachment.

The British version General Howe received declared that Philips was:

> "beset between Brunswick and Princetown by some lurking villains, who murdered him in a most barbarous manner; which is a mode of war the enemy (the Americans) seem from several late instances to have adopted, with a degree of barbarity that savages could not exceed."[67]

Two days hence, Howe will report his Princeton battle casualties to London, officially declaring:

> "loss upon this occasion to his Majesty's troops is 17 killed, and nearly 200 wounded and missing... Return of the Killed, wounded, and missing, of the following corps of his Majesty's forces, in the Jerseys, Friday January 3, 1777 to wit:
>
> "17th Regiment. — 1 captain, 12 rank and file, Killed; 1 captain, 1 lieutenant, 1 ensign, 4 serjeants, 46 rank and file, wounded; 1 serjeant, 1 drummer, 33 rank and file missing.
>
> "40th Regiment — 1 lieutenant wounded; 1 ensign, 3 serjeants, 1 drummer, 88 rank and file missing.
>
> "55th Regiment — 1 sergeant, 4 rank and file, killed; 1 ensign, 1 serjeant, 2 rank and file, wounded; 1 captain, 1 lieutenant, 1 ensign, 1 serjeant, 2 drummers, 66 rank and file, missing.
>
> "Total — 1 captain, 1 serjeant, 16 rank and file, killed; 1 captain, 2 lieutenants, 2 ensigns, 5 serjeants, 48 rank and file, wounded; 1 captain, 1 lieutenant, 2 ensigns, 5 serjeants, 4 drummers, 187 rank and file, missing.
>
> "Hon. Captain Leslie, of the 17th regiment of foot, killed.
>
> "Captain Philips, of the 35th grenadiers, killed on his way to join the battalion.
>
> "N.B. Since the above return many of the men missing have joined their corps.
>
> "It appears by the muster master general Sir George Osborn's return of the Hessian troops, after the affair of the 26th of December at Trenton, that the prisoners and missing amounted to about 700."[68]

Spectacle Of Horrors

Over the battlefield and around the open grounds before Nassau Hall and throughout the little hamlet, still called Prince Town by many, there hangs the acrid smell of gunpowder. Beneath the rising smoke from fires, cannon and musketry are heard the moaning cries of the wounded and the death rattles of the dying. Bitter enemies an hour ago, the stricken lie prone, side by side, friend and foe alike.

Sickened vomiting youngsters of the militia are patted consolingly on the back by the older, understanding, hardened veterans of more than one campaign. Carcasses of horses lie scattered over the bloody, snow-covered grounds of the Americans' well known seat of learning.

For youth who have never seen and experienced war, the spectacle of horrors and its revolting inhumanity now turn their stomachs.

Nevertheless they go on about the grim business of attending the wounded, urged by officers to make haste. A few of the young militiamen, their breaths steaming from the freezing, winter morning air, stop short their breathing like the hesitated puffs from a tobacco pipe, as the bodies of the dead are placed in rows upon the crimson-stained snow along the paths to the college.

In one nearby house to which a number of the wounded are carried, some screaming in agony, some silent in shock, the woman inhabitant has sent for other ladies of the village to help bind the wounds and ease many of the suffering along the way to certain death. The gruesome task has brought most of the townspeople out from their hiding places and from behind closed shutters where they had secluded themselves at the first sound of battle.

The housewife who turned her home into a temporary field hospital will later describe the scene, saying:

"Almost as soon as the firing was over, our house was filled and surrounded with them (The General's men) and himself on horseback at the door.

"They brought in with them on their shoulders two wounded Regulars; one of them shot at his hip and the bullet lodged in his groin, and the other was shot through his body just below his short ribs. He was in very great pain and bled much out of both sides, and often desired to be moved from one place to another, which was done accordingly, and he dyed about three o'clock in the afternoon. . ."[69]

On the field, no longer in the turmoil of battle, officers now bustle along with the troops in cleaning up, reorganizing and readying themselves for the long march north out of Cornwallis's grip.

The privilege of plundering is as strong a desire among the rebel troops as it is among the Hessian and British soldiers. Each army of men feels as justly entitled to the spoils of war as the other, despite the restrictions which both high commands may impose.

So The General's strict order two days ago forbidding his forces from plundering "anyone" has not set too well with some of his troops. They can comprehend, though complaining and in anger, the order's application to "Tories or others," but they do not like the phrasing, "any person."[70] This restricts them from enjoying the justly entitled spoils of war on the battlefield. These, they quietly insist among themselves, are theirs to taste, the earned desserts of war.

When the American Commander, overseeing the battlefield's dead and wounded and urging speed in preparations for the march, sees a wounded British youth, lying distraught in the snow, he draws in Old Magnolia's reins. The soldier weakly looks up, his face contorted with pain.

Attempting to console the young English boy, The General assures him that his wound will be attended and that he will be given every possible consideration, at the same time commending him for his gallant behavior. With his aides The General rides on.

A few minutes later the Continental Army Commander turns in his saddle to look at something to the rear.

He sees an American soldier beginning to strip the wounded British soldier, believing the youth to be dead.

Swiftly the Virginian swings Old Magnolia and rides in upon the surprised rebel. He scolds him severely and orders him back to his company. Then he directs a sentry stand over the wounded prisoner until he is carried to a convenient house where his wound may be dressed. He further orders an aide to see that the British youth is comfortably and properly assisted.[71]

In the distance The General, Greene and their staff officers notice part of Greene's old Bluff Rock Barbette Battery men, who were recently attached to Hitchcock's regiment. It appears that the procession is carrying one of their own wounded toward the temporary hospital quarters in Nassau Hall.

However, the American Leader and his officers are in search of General Mercer's whereabouts and think no more about it as they are guided to the Thomas Clark house. Upon seeing the condition of the Brigadier General, the Chief arranges for the care of his friend and former comrade in arms.

A close look at the solemn procession of the old Barbette Battery artillerymen on their way to the beautiful, but badly damaged college building, is enough to assure one of Greene's aides, sent to look into it, that they are carrying one of their own.

Second lieutenant Asher Levy heads the small detachment. Behind him march Sergeant Lawrie MacNamara, Corporal Mike Monahan, Private Orlof Swenson and Private Carmen Luciano. Each holds a part of the blanket in which rests the lifeless body of Lieutenant John Gray.

Covering the face and the deadly hole in the temple of the former Princeton scholar is his bloodstained blue petticoat neckerchief by which so many of Greene's men had come to know him. The musket ball, still imbedded in his brain, quickly delivered the Philadelphia tanner's son, bridegroom of "The Lady of the River," a merciful instant death.

Astride his horse, Chinqueka, Sergeant Andrew Abbott carries the dead officer's knapsack and belongings. Abbott rides behind the ragged, sad and speechless contingent. The sorrowful procession is hardly noticed in the confusion of the milling men, amid the agonizing cries of the wounded and the almost hopeless efforts of some of the rank and file to locate their units.

Noncommissioned officers shout orders and yell out the names of many who will no longer respond to roll calls. In this turmoil the remains of the former lieutenant of the Bluff Rock Battery are carried back to Nassau Hall.

Part Of the Game Of Chess Called "War"

Those of Greene's men, particularly the old "Flying Camp" troops, who knew John Gray and his blue petticoat scarf, stop and look. Many had known the officer only under the name Jocko Graves bestowed upon him, "Da Lootenan."

These now look on, regretfully accepting another death, almost resignedly. They stop with a respectful, brief, silent pause and hurriedly move on. For this they know is part of the game of chess called "war."

The Lieutenant had come to within less than a mile of his old college building where he had hoped to see the two men whom he had learned to admire the more as time went by. They were the college's president, Doctor John Wetherspoon and "Doctor Ezra," or as some had liked to call him, "Professor Stones." This appellation he had earned over the years owing to his intense interest in rock formations and the science of geology.

It was from Doctor Ezra Godfrey Clynes that Gray had learned much about the Hudson's Palisades whose mysterious origin both scholar and student had so often and so long discussed. It was for the professor that Gray had carried a rock specimen from the Palisades in his pocket and to which he had added another in Trenton.

As he has always done before with passing American troops, Clynes asked the first Continental soldiers he met after the battle if they had heard of the officer, John Gray. Told by someone he was with Hitchcock's regiment, the elated "Professor Stones" looked eagerly forward to seeing his former student.

The elderly educator's interest in locating one of his old scholars traveled down through the lines. It had reached Asher Levy as he and Abbott put the limp body into a blanket. Levy decided then to carry Gray to the old man and prevail upon him to see that The Lieutenant received a proper burial. For the whole army was now hurriedly moving on.

Thus the silent procession carried Gray back again to his alma mater. The army's recent military successes are darkened now for the Bluff Rock men, first with the death of Jocko and today with that of The Lieutenant. These have been the only two casualties they have suffered. Most grieved by the losses, particularly that of The Lieutenant who saved him from capture in New York, is Asher Levy.

As the small cortege moves toward the college building, Levy's thoughts carry him to the fort on The Mountain and the ferry-master's daughter. Both the second lieutenant and Abbott know how much Elaine feared her husband's death. And Levy now fears what the shocking news will do to her.

It will be up to the battery's next in rank to tell Gray's father and sister. It will be up to Abbott to give a full accounting to Elaine when he returns to his deserted home on Oratam's ancient castle grounds for the winter.

So now Levy's sad reveries momentarily take him back to Jocko's death and burial. The second lieutenant had known better than anyone how closely attached Gray was to the black youth. But he did not know until the boy's death how very deep was the strange, inexplicable bond of friendship that had grown up so firmly free of prejudices between the two, youth and man—years apart in age, worlds apart in differences.

Asher's mind then spins back to the chipmonk episode in the barn. Then to Wright's volunteer grave digging. . . Gray, along with others, had been astounded that anyone like Wright could make such a complete turn-about. And even to the point of becoming angry when others began helping in the excavation work. . .

"What," Levy asked himself, "could cause the inner emotions of a man's apparent violence to swing over in an entirely opposite direction like a pendulum?"

If Wright had that day expected some earthly reward, he gave no sign of it. And yet he got it!

On Jocko's frozen feet were the new boots that the cold-footed, court martialed corporal had envied. And these boots, it was known and agreed, were to have been buried with the youth. All knew that, and all believed that was as it should be. However, Big Tom had expressed no opinion. He had barely spoken since his son died.

Levy recalled how hushed the barn was that moment when Big Tom went up to the coffin—the box Abbott had made—and, at the last moment, gently removed the boots from Jocko's feet. The big, softly sobbing Negro held them tightly in his arms during the burial service.

Standing by the grave, the last to leave after the mound was pressed down by Wright and others, Big Tom watched the mourners depart. The half frozen Uriah walked behind the others. No one ever walked by his side.

The anger of the past events was gone. Small of frame, almost Jocko's size, the 40-year old Uriah Wright looked, and was, tired and cold. Only light Indian moccasins, wrapped with cloth bindings, covered his feet and ankles.

His self-imposed task was done. He wanted nothing for his action. In his mind he owed a penance, and he had paid it. He had committed a sin, and in his own peculiar way he had atoned for it. It was purely self-repentance. Never had anyone in the battery believed that the smelly, unkempt Wright could have looked so extremely contrite as he genuinely appeared.

Back in the artillery battery's stable quarters, Big Tom returned from the burial site, still clasping Jocko's boots to his breast. Then, to the amazement of those present, he walked directly up to Wright in a corner of the barn which the unpopular, small, wiry taciturn man has entirely to himself.

Speaking so softly that few heard him, even in the hushed silence of the quarters, Big Tom held out his son's boots to Wright, saying:

"Ah knows mah son. Ah knows dat boad him 'n 'is Mammy would wants youse ta hab dese boots. So, here! Youse take 'em!"

Tom forced the once shining leather footwear into the arms of the overwhelmed Uriah. He then turned on his heels and walked outside to be alone with his sorrow, leaving the generally irritable Wright stunned and speechless. Big Tom had carried out what he was sure was Jocko's last will and testament.

And Levy, now recalling the scene, remembers having noticed a faint smile sadly cross Gray's firm lips for the first time since Jocko's death.

Wright, who had seldom experienced kindness from others and therefore never gave it, stood aghast at Tom's unexpected action. He looked at the boots in his hands in humbled disbelief and then dropped down heavily on the wood milk stool by the straw of his bed.

He said nothing. However, when the men, following Gray's example, quietly chimed in with their chorus of "Here! Here!", Wright knew at last that he had been "accepted." And he knew also, in that one, rare, exalting moment of his life, that every man in the barn sincerely wanted him to wear Jocko's boots.

Perhaps it was true, Levy and Gray had thought in unison, that what Big Tom said was right. Perhaps the youth, whose lovable personality Wright had envied in life just as he had envied the black, shining boots, really would have wanted the unfortunate recluse who had once so contemptuously tried to hurt him, to acquire his proud and most precious possession. For Jocko had been taught—and believed in—the powerful effect of returning good for evil.

Certainly, as Levy recalled the event and remembered watching Wright closely, the man was shedding a tear. It certainly looked like one that fell upon the leather boots.

Hurrying now, the second lieutenant led the cortege to the stairs of the college hall. In Levy's hand is the red leather diary which had fallen out of Gray's surcoat. It brings a rush of memories to the officer's mind, particularly the last entry Gray had shown to him reading:

"December 27, 1776 — Elaine, Jocko is no more. He died on duty. We buried him in a quiet place a mile from the ferry near where we stay. Methinks there is no death to the soul of life. Yea, decay to the body; not to the spark of life it holds for a short time in one place for a brief time upon a piece of earth.

"Jocko I feel is with us. Not in the same way, but everywhere around us I feel he is looking on, nosing in, even on this as I write and he asks,

" 'Whuts dat means, Lootenan? . . Dat one, two three? . . Whuts dat means?' "

Two Rocks For "Professor Stones"

The book must go to Elaine. Levy hands it up to Abbott who understands. His face immobile, the Indian scout puts it carefully in the dead man's knapsack.

As the battery's artillerymen gently place the blanketed body on the ground before the steps of Nassau Hall, two neatly tagged rocks drop out of the coat pocket. Levy knew about them. Both were intended for Doctor Ezra's collection.

It was Gray's opinion, Levy recalled that the two rocks, one from the Palisades by the Hudson and the other from the Trenton battlefield, might confirm the old professor's pet theory. It was Doctor Ezra's contention that the long, volcanic Palisadean ridge, not only reached down into the Atlantic Ocean but that it extended west as well, perhaps to the Delaware.

Someone finally located the old scholar who had been helping with the British wounded in the large lecture hall, used as quarters by some of the King's officers. On one desk was an unfinished letter to an officer's father in London. Seeing no harm in reading anything the enemy left behind, the inquisitive scholar devours the contents. It reads in part:

". . . Some day this break of peoples between the seas, if the insurgents should succeed, will be remembered sadly. Nay! It will be regretted and may in time be restored.

"The new world needs England and England the new world if man's future civilization is to be assured, no less his survival. Rampant with Independence, Liberty and Freedom fever, they can, alone, drown themselves with the sweet taste of molasses. Without the mother country's moderation they can end up bloated in the bottom of the keg.

"Freedoms can bleed them of their liberties, and their liberties can turn them into packs of hungry wolves, multiplying until they lose all controls. Then in their unrestricted independence they may end up devouring, not only everything around them with their smothering freedoms, but, in the inevitable end, themselves.

"This war, I feel, Father, is only the trickling beginning of the

bloody flow of human life which liberty, unlicensed, must and will exact as man, unchecked, breeds greed, poverty and corruption, multiplying himself abnormally to doom all life and its posterity on the planet that cradled him. . ."

Clynes and MacMurphy both have read the unfinished letter on the desk and inquire from a wounded British sergeant who was quartered there. They learn, to their surprise, it was Lieutenant Drummond's desk.

Clynes has not forgotten the inebriate of the night before and inquires of the wounded sergeant of the officer's whereabouts. The sergeant points out the window to one of the lifeless bodies near the entrance, saying, "There 'e is. Next to the chappie with the blue scarf over 'is fice."

At that moment the miller calls his scholarly friend, saying that an officer of the Continental Army wants to see him. Thinking it must surely be his former student, the professor hurries outside where Levy approaches him.

It is a brief conversation. The old man's face drops as he lifts the scarf and sees his former student still in death.

By this time others stop even in the rush of moving on, believing the dead officer must be one of great importance. There are other dead to be left there, British and Amrican. Gray lies next to the British Lieutenant Robert Drummond.

Pastor MacMurphy and the miller, Papa Kuederly, come down the steps together as Ezra Clynes carefully places the neckerchief over The Lieutenant's face, saying very solemnly and with choked words, "He was right. He kept his word. He always said that he would be back. . . My poor John Gray! . . Poor lad!"

Levy, pointing out to Doctor Ezra the need for haste, asks the learned man to see that the officer's grave is marked properly with his officer's ranking. This and more the Professor assures him will be done, whereupon Levy hands the educator the two, tagged rock specimens. Each reads: "For Doctor Ezra."

Holding them as though they were precious gems, the scholar, adjusting his spectacles over his tear-filled eyes, reads each notation as though it were a personal letter. He then looks up at Levy, Abbott and the others and says slowly:

"He was a scholar to the last, never a warrior. In death he has struggled to prove a thesis that entranced him. I think, Sirs, he should be returned some day to the Palisades he loved and to the loved ones he left there. I shall hope so. Until then, I shall see that all that is right is done as I know you and your men would have it."

A tear drips down from Asher's cheek as he stands over the lifeless form for a last moment of meditation. He recalls Gray's comforting pat on his shoulder on Harlem Heights. His hand now makes the same gesture on the stilled form as though sealing friendship on through death. Then he turns quickly and joins his crestfallen artillerymen.

Not long after Gray's body is left behind with the other battle dead, returned at last to his former college grounds, Cornwallis's speedily moving van comes into sight. At the same time the American rear disappears from view.

His Lordship, now pushing his train to the point of exhaustion, makes for New Brunswick to unite with Major General Vaughan's command.[72] The Earl is certain that Brunswick is the rebels' next objective.

However, the American command heads instead for Somerset Courthouse and Pluckemin. From there they will set out for the hills behind Morristown. The pitifully fatigued Continental Army now at last marches toward its long-awaited winter encampment.

Like a tidal wave of countelss ships, of men and weapons, the Empire's Jagannath has extended its arms and chased its quarry across the Jerseys from the Hudson to the Delaware. And there, with its nostrils stretched too far from its tail, the indestructible giant became vulnerable.

It was there and then that the wry "Fox" turned and broke the weakened jaws which never again will be quite so feared, quite so formidable.

Again in London the words of Caron de Beaumarchais, talented author and writer of the century, will echo loudly. He had said in 1775, and others have repeatedly quoted him,

"All sensible people in England are convinced that the English colonies are lost to the mother country and this is my opinion too."[73]

On the great Bluff Rock of The Mountain of the Palisades only a lonely eagle looks east out upon Manhattan where the envoys of the world's mightiest nation now taste the painful miseries of a calamitous defeat. For to the west of the massive volcanic wall, 70 miles away, the infant nation has survived its first baptism under the terrifying crises of war.

So, on this day, three days late, the Campaign of 1776 comes to its cruelly bitter end on the bloodstained grounds leading to the very doors of the house of learning. There, an aging professor of the college at Prince Town looks out upon a campus, now a horrible panorama of passing war.

His eyes flushed in tears, the learned old tutor looks down on the bodies of the two officers. One in the Continental Army's blue, the other in the Empire army's red, they lie prostrate before him.

Mumbling in lament to his two friends, Kuederly and MacMurphy, as all three notice a single drop of blood oozing through the blue petticoat neckerchief over the American lieutenant's face, Clynes says slowly, almost inaudibly:

"Tis but a minute bloody drop of much that yet will pave the costly crimson path of man's fanatical quest for freedom. Yet 'tis a sight, unfortunately, which its blind world of benefactors, and the disenchanted of 'em, will, with cringing conscience, care not to see and less to remember."

And the preacher and the miller, comprehending and agreeing, shake their heads in acquiescence.

Epilogue

No longer are heard the thundering of cannon, the din of battle and the pitiful cries of the maimed and dying. All now is quiet. Peace once again rests over the valley of the Delaware.

Though Trenton and Princeton will save The Cause and at last end the nearly fatal chaos of the '76 campaign, there will be other perilous moments in the five years ahead. During those long, trying days there will be many beside the American Commander-in-Chief who will look back, convinced that those added sixty months of hardship and bitter struggle could have been avoided by Congressional foresight.

They will argue strongly that the campaign should have closed and the war ended victoriously for "The Grand Army" in New Brunswick.

If The General with fresh troops had driven on to his enemy's principal supply base, they will contend, the British chest of £70,000 would have been seized, the back of the King's army broken and the conflict ended.

However, despite the despair and disillusionment that will come to both armies and both nations before Yorktown in 1781, to Trenton and to Princeton will be credited the amazing turnabout. From that remarkable maneuver, history will say, there sprang a national unity of spirit—a spirit that will sweep away the chaos and the crisis that was 75 and 76. Like a tidal wave, a flood of hope will spread over the new colonial states, cementing their indivisable bond as never before. There will be other crises in the war but never again one so tottering on the precipice edge.

The overwhelming American compulsion for strength through unity which will last for almost a century, will rise from the determination, faith and hope of the army. And from the army it will be infused into the veins of the people.

Then into the forge fires at Philadelphia these and other of man's countless ingredients for good, will, like molten steel, release their flaming sparks—sparks that will someday torch the anvils of all nations. For now will be ignited and freed that long latent fire within the human breast—man's compassion for his fellow man.

And so from the great campaign and its terrifying crises of disillusionment and retreat, and out of the Trenton and Princeton turnabout, soon will spring a surging humane interest for over-populating man.

Partly born of the Americans' own suffering this zeal will become a passionate fight for the liberty of the world's teeming millions. And often unappreciated, the new nation will extend its "costly crimson path" to all peoples of the globe. The price will be higher than most nations will want to pay.

Therefore the newborn nation, thrilling with a renewed fervor for unity lifting out of the valley of the Delaware, will unwittingly be launching upon her unprecedented experiment in a new national ideology as the army's almost calamitous campaign comes to its close.

For now the eaglet will feel the power of her wings. For now, six months after conception on the forge in the foundry of differences at Philadelphia, the fledgling, stronger than before, will struggle on in her determined flight to carry a free and heterogeneous society of socially differing ethnic groups in geographically differing provinces into a hazardous journey toward an unpredictable destiny.

So years will pass in the wake of the horrendous hours and the grueling marches through the chaos that led to Trenton and Princeton. And in those passing years Dr. Ezra will spend many contemplative hours looking off into space from the steps of Nassau Hall.

Never again, following that fateful third day of January in 1777, will the spacious grounds appear to "Professor Stones" as the peaceful walks they were before the roll of drums.

Instead his eyes will again and again envision that same, grim, horribly pathetic sight. Always it will be that same bitterly cold morning. Always the same cortege of soldiers, pitifully carrying one of their own fallen comrades and gently depositing the crumpled, covered corpse on the steps before him.

Then, each time Dr. Ezra's mind will relive that frightfully shocking moment, there will always reappear before him the same ghastly spectacle. For there at the old man's feet his mind will ever see an especially loved student, killed in war. And there beside him another lifeless form, a British soldier, no longer of the enemy.

The British youth was John Gray's age. And Ezra Clynes was to remember him as the drunken enemy officer who only the night before had baited him in Nassau Hall... and then had to listen to one of his lectures!

Clynes had excused the British officer's conduct, charging it to frustration and bewilderment in the compulsory services of his king. The redcoat lieutenant, thought Ezra, had no other outlet for the turmoil and confusion pounding in his head. The understanding educator had comprehended this, and this he had forgiven.

Then, and the vision will always be clear but awesome, the cortege will move slowly away. Each time it will gently meld into the army. And the army will always disappear over the distant hills.

Trudging off through the light snow, the men of the little detachment—their worn bodies torn and drooping—will always reflect the deep traumatic pain within their mourning as they slowly fade out of the professor's vision.

Only one in the ceremonial-like procession, Ezra remembers and always notices, will hold his head high, firm, unbowed. He was the mounted one, the Indian scout. And always the brown man's torso remains upright in the saddle.

All this the sadly reflecting professor will see in his frequent, silent contemplations after those crises days of 1776 until his death. Were he given the powers of prophesy, the professor would be even more shocked at the sights which the future's curtain mercifully blots from his vision. For a number of those in that cortege are destined soon to sacrifice their lives along what the scholar himself had called "the costly crimson path to freedom."

However, in June of 1781, four months before Yorktown, the solemn tolling of the cemetery bell will again echo its dirge for the departed. This time for the old man of words and wisdom whose only deathbed request will be that he be placed in the burial ground between his "students," Gray and Drummond.

Seeing astonishment and curiosity in the eyes of those at his bedside, Doctor Ezra will answer their question before they ask, declaring abruptly, "Well! Someone must take care of them!"

As he and his visions will fade off in tranquil silence, so also will the individual members of the Barbette Battery, the cortege. A few will escape a total sacrifice on the professor's so-called "crimson path" for others' freedom.

Some will get through unscathed. Others, with little thought of any reward and without ever knowing the magnitude of their contribution, will give their lives to unborn millions, many of whom will be descendants of the enemy they tried to hate.

Asher Levy, who will break the news of John Gray's death to The Lieutenant's father and sister, will see his own betrothed, Miriam, sob in sympathy for Gray, but also in fear for Asher. In less than a year and a half, Miriam's nightmarish dreams of her betrothed will tragically end in reality on the battlefield at Monmouth Court House. For there the recently promoted first lieutenant will die, his legs shot out from beneath him.

In one way or another, the war and its side effects will slowly thin out the ranks of the old Bluff Rock Barbette Battery. Accidents, wounds, epidemics and a sudden, fatal strike on the battlefields, will, for some bring death. Among these will be Lawrie MacNamara, Benson Kidd, Tony Talo, Phillip Reales, Carman Lucius Luciano and Mike Monahan.

Young Joseph Reales will move west and become a farmer. Orlof Swenson will make his home in the south and through his knowledge of carpentry will acquire a wide reputation as a skillful builder. Uriah Wright, choosing the sea as a career, will take over a gun on a privateer. Still wearing Jocko's boots, Uriah will go down with his ship in a storm off Cape Hatteras.

Big Tom Graves, the use of his arm never fully restored after the Battle of Long Island, will settle down in Philadelphia employed by John Gray's father, the tanner. And there he will marry a second wife who will bear him two children.

One of these will be named John, the nearest Tom Graves will come to naming another child, "Jocko." For always uppermost in the old soldier's heart, and there bonded in lifelong affection, are the unforgettable memories of his first born, buried on the banks of the Delaware.

The biggest surprise in Graves's Philadelphia life will be the arrival there in 1781 of Ben Gartleck and his sister. With Katie May will be her four-year old son, Jocko, whom his deceased war-hero father never knew he had sired.

It will be Elaine who, equally surprised when the brother and sister turn up at the Baummeister house with Jocko's son, will help Katie May and Ben get to Philadelphia under the care of the happily astonished Grandfather Graves.

Elaine will ask Katie May to tell the Grays that someday she will take young Johnny to see them.

Andrew Abbott, whose parents will lie side by side in the burial ground at Brotherton when winter comes in 1779, will go back with the snows to the ancient castle lands of Oratam on The Mountain. And every spring he will return to the army. Abbott will command a troop of scouts when Captain Craig dies during a deeply inebriated sleep.

One of the Indian's most difficult tasks will be informing the pregnant widow of her husband's death long before the army will notify her. From then on Andy Abbott will do everything he can through the harsh winters to ease the path in the Baummeister household.

At the beginning of each of those winters the son of Old Chief will cut wood, hunt and fish, helping the struggling and aging Bourdettes and Baummeisters through the hardships encountered in the war loss of so much of their ferriage business.

Abbott will get his first look at Elaine's son, John, born July 12, 1777, when the Indian scout returns from camp to the deserted grounds of Fort Lee in December of that year. That winter he will redouble his efforts to aid the Baummeister family, their widowed daughter and her child.

In the middle of February, "Mama" Marie Louise will die from the plague, and Abbott will be on hand in the hamlet to help during her illness and through her burial on The Mountain. But the scout will have returned to the army when, four months later, Papa Pete is placed beside his wife, his deep grieving over her loss at last ended.

Then, making his home alone in the deserted Kearney house each winter, the Indian will be awakened one night in the winter of 1779 to help fight the fire that will engulf the Bourdette home. With his mare, Chinqueka, and Elaine in the Baummeister carriage he will assist the ferry owner and his household in their move down into the valley to join the household of his farmer son.

Often, entirely too often in the eyes of some of the rumor-loving housewives of the area, the winterizing Continental Army soldier will be seen helping Madame Gray in her efforts to manage the ferry business. She will carry on the work with 70-year old Honest Sam and share the meager profits with the Bourdettes. The struggle will not be easy, and so Abbott's help through the winter of 1781 will ease her burden.

During those winter days the army sergeant will take Paul, and the now almost four-year old Johnny, fishing, netting and trapping. And some of the tongues around old Fort Lee, The Mountain and in the little hamlet along the river's edge will wag. Talk will become gossip and gossip, hearsay.

In December of 1781, Abbott will return from the battle at Yorktown by way of Brotherton. There he will leave Chinqueka with the few remaining, struggling old people of his tribe. At Amboy he will borrow a canoe to make the trip up the Hudson to the Bourdette Landing.

And there Elaine will rush to him, revealing with tear-filled eyes that Paul has left to become a cabin boy on an ocean sailing vessel. The war's end and Abbott's safe return will soon take precedence in her thoughts as Andy consoles her. And the people of The Mountain, the hamlet and down in the valley will talk in whispers. Once more the tongues will begin to wag.

On Christmas day, Andy and Elaine, with Johnny between them in the Baummesiter's dilapidated old buggy, will drive over The Mountain to the church. There the Domine, Dereck Remlin, will join their hands in marriage. Now the gossipy wives of the villages and hamlets will become more unkind than ever.

Though neither Elaine nor her husband will show concern for the cutting tongues that will not tolerate "mixed marriages," they will both agree that it will be Johnny who will suffer in the end if the three remain in the riverside hamlet.

On the last April evening sunset of 1782, the couple, with Johnny tagging behind, will ascend the gorge road that was the Grand Army's beginning trek to victory six years before. They will stand silently on the great Bluff Rock site for the last time, looking down at the setting shadows of the cliffs on the smooth blue waters of the river, then out and over at Chief Mannahatta's ancient island to the bays and seas beyond.

Beside them, Johnny will climb around the rusting weapons of the long-stilled Barbette Battery, overgrown with foliage and covered at their base with the rotted leaves of six autumns.

They will not speak, but turning they will walk across the gorge, hand in hand, to the burial grounds. There, as she has so often done, Elaine will place forsythia buds upon the graves, one of which will be Andrea's resting place for more than eight years.

Again the couple will hold their silence, each with his own

thoughts, while John Gray's young son chatters away, talking to real and imaginary objects around him.

The woman will merely slide her arm gently through that of the man and all three will descend to the river home, for tomorrow they will leave it forever behind them.

On the bright and beautiful morning of May 1, 1782, Abbott will finish packing and stowing his wife's and stepson's possessions in the old pettiauger, *Hope*. As the pinkish dawn begins brightening in the eastern sky, he will carefully check over the little vessel, waiting for Elaine and her son to close her home and the past.

Abbott will have reason to be proud of the new looking sloop. It will have lain almost five years, half submerged in river mud at high tides when Andy salvaged and restored it. It had been badly rammed and partly sunk by the heavier British vessels when Fort Lee was overrun. Joined by Johnny, a toy he could not leave behind in his hands, the two will complete the vessel's final inspection.

Elaine alone will wander through the house before leaving. She will ascend the stairs. The past will begin pounding upon her brain. She will walk slowly into the big bedroom she and John had shared. A brief flood of painful memories will overcome her as she looks at the empty fireplace.

And then, for she must one last time, she will glance out the window before which so much so long ago had passed. Her eyes will be drawn to the dock, to Andy and her son, hand in hand on the landing beside the packed and waiting pettiauger. Old Chief's proud dugout canoe will lie tied to the vessel's stern.

Now 23 years old, once widowed and a mother, Dame Abbott will remind herself that she is again a married woman and getting old. She will turn swiftly on her heels, slam the Dutch doors behind her and run again toward her boy, her husband and *Hope* that lies waiting beside the dock.

Moments later the sloop, with its loaded canoe in tow, will put out into the stream and set its bow upriver with the tide.

With the south wind blossoming her canvas, the pettiauger will glide noiselessly through the sparkling blue waters under the Palisades. The young woman will try hard now to steel her thoughts away from all that once was. But the sun will strike the old Barbette Battery's Bluff Rock guns, spiked in silence and towering now harmlessly overhead in the thunder of their quiet reveries, and her thoughts will flash back to '76.

Avoiding another look upward, Elaine will look back downstream and her mind will return her to the *Hope's* stormy adventure on that hot day in July almost six years ago—her brother's fears, her father's faith. And she will wonder how Paul, afraid of water as he was, could ever become a cabin boy and take to the sea.

She will recall the crowds of people who live in the terrible congestion of New York town and the milling of the trembling inhabitants at Powles Hook when the cannon-blasting men-of-war came up the bay.

It was that day she first met John Gray and his new-found friend, Jocko Graves and his father, Big Tom. That thought will come upon her suddenly and just as suddenly she will try to dismiss it from her mind.

But as her eyes pass over the old landing dock and across the water, she will think she can hear Jocko's voice on the bow of the arriving transport waving a letter in his hand.

"Missy E! Missy E!" he will seem to call.

She will shudder and close her eyes. Then as they open, she will look up directly on "Lovers Ledge" and again memories will flood her mind—memories she had hoped to put behind her a few days ago when she burned the red leather diary, Jocko's gift to John, and all John's books and things, reminders of the past, particularly Locke's essay on Human Understanding.

Then, abruptly, she will turn her head away and again look upstream at the ever- widening silver river and the distant Tappan Zee, remembering how once it bristled with cannon-barking frigates.

At the tiller, her husband will suddenly lift his head skyward, There, high above the *Hope,* a seven-year old eagle will soar loftily. Behind the wide, gracefully floating wings of the king of birds, his mate and their struggling young offspring will hover briefly.

"Look, Muvver! Look!" Johnny will cry out excitedly to Elaine, sitting beside him in the bow. "Frwee uv 'vem!.. Ones...toos...frwees! Jes likes us is."

And as he points separately and in order to his stepfather, mother and finally to himself, he counts again, "Ones...toos... 'nd me, Johnny, frwees!"

Elaine, complying will raise her eyes and watch as the eagles dive down, swallowed up by the sprouting life of the trees and foliage on the crescent of the verdant Palisades. She will say nothing but her son's counting will cause her to wince. She will tightly close her fist and turn away as tears come to her eyes.

Her husband, too, will watch the feathered beauties disappear.

And, as the boy counts three a sad faint trace of a smile will cross the man's lips as he imagines he hears Mahtocheega's three sharp notes in the distant song of a bird above him on the cliffs. His eyes will drift backward to The Mountain as though sending a last momentary farewell to the quiet resting place, and he will then look at Elaine and she at him.

Moving rapidly away from the towering walls under which Admiral Howe's plans were dashed and from which heights many, many moons before, the Lenni Lenape watched the arriving white men, the pettiauger will leave her wake.

Through the war-stilled waters of Hudson's river, the little sloop and its three occupants will glide onward. Their destination will be the open, untamed last refuge in the crowded, over-populated world of antagonism, strife and fear.

The sole surviving descendant of the Great Chief Oratam and the once all-powerful "Original People," will guide the sloop to the distant new land and drop its anchor into another world.

All three will no longer turn their heads to look behind. For before them will softly beckon the promise of another life and hopefully a kinder and more resplendent tomorrow.

So it will be that onward to that unknown and its promises, disappearing slowly from the Bluff Rock's guns and The Mountain's lonely sentinels, will courageously and defiantly sail the little vessel, *Hope*.

Key For Locating Reference Notes
With Explanation and Partial Bibliography

(The reference notes for each of the 35 historical dates, or chapters, are listed and numbered separately according to chapters. Each numbered source note in the context has a coded numerical symbol, fully explained and identified under the "Key."

For example, in the opening chapter, Note #1 is found, under the notes listed for that date, or chapter, to be, "1. *32* SPNYS, p. 289." The numerical symbol, *32*, before the simplified abbreviated main letters of the work (SPNYS), is a random-chosen figure, that had been assigned to the source work during research. Those numbers are not sequential since many intervening works, so numbered and abbreviated, were most likely discarded, or unused in the references. However, under the 'Key," those numbers preceding a source work's initials are listed in ranking order beginning with the lowest coded numbers.

Thus "1. *32* SPNYS" will be found under *32* in the "Key" to be: "Dixon, Edward H., M.D., *Scenes In the Practice of A New York Surgeon*. New York: De Witt L. Davenport, Publishers (160-162 Nassau Street), 1855." Of course, the page cited under the note is the page on which the reference will be found.

The listed works under the "Key," therefore, comprise a partial bibliography. They will not, of course, be found arranged in an alphabetical classification.)

The Key

(Includes Partial Bibliography Unalphabetized)

2 SHAR = Van Doren, Carl, *Secret History of the American Revolution*. New York: The Viking Press, 1941.

3 MJAR = Thacher, James, M.D., *Military Journal of the American Revolution*. Hartford, Connecticut: Hurlbut, Williams & Company, 1862.

4 TCMAG = Reports by the army and navy commanders, Hon. General William Howe and the Hon. Admiral Richard Howe to Lord George Germaine and to the British Admiralty, *The Town and Country Magazine; or Universal Repository of Knowledge Instruction, and Entertainment*, Vol. VIII for the year 1776. London, England: Printed for A. Hamilton near St. John's Gate.

5 WOR = Ward, Christopher, *The War Of The Revolution*, ed. John Richard Alden. Vol. I of two-volume series; New York: The Macmillan Company, 1952.

6 RHSNJ V-I = Stryker, William S., Documents Relating To The *Revolutionary History of the State Of New Jersey*, Vol. I, Extracts From American Newspapers, Vol. I, 1776-1777. Trenton, New Jersey; The John L. Murphy Publishing Co., Printers, 1901.

7 AR = Alden, John Richard, *The American Revolution, 1775-1783*. Harper & Brothers, Publishers: New York, 1954.

8 SSS V-I = Commager, Henry Steele and Morris, Richard B., *The Spirit of 'Seventy-Six*. Vol. I of two-volume series; Indianapolis: The Bobbs-Merrill Company, Inc. 1958.

9 PYD = Martin, Joseph Plumb, *Private Yankee Doodle*, ed. George F. Scheer. Boston, Massachusetts: Little, Brown and Company, 1962.

10 TT = Chidsey, Donald Barr, *The Tide Turns.* New York: Crown Publishers, Inc., 1966.

11 RW = McDowell, Bart, *The Revolutionary War*. Washington, D.C.: National Geographic Society, 1967.

13 RWHV = Leiby, Adrian C., *The Revolutionary War In the Hackensack Valley*. New Brunswick, New Jersey: Rutgers University Press, 1962.

14 BHUS = Steele, Joel Dorman and Steele, Esther Baker, *A Brief History of the United States* (Barne's Historical Series). New York: American Book Company, 1871.

15 EAPH = Richardson, William H. and Gardner, Walter P., *Washington and the Enterprise Against Powles Hook*. Jersey City, New Jersey: The New Jersey Title Guarantee and Trust Company, 1938.

16 MWC = De Lancey, E. F., "Mount Washington and Its Capture On The 16th of November, 1776," *Magazine of American History*, Vol. I, No. 2. New York: February 1877.

19 ENYC = Ellis, Edward Robb, *Epic of New York City*. New York: Coward-McCann, Inc., 1966.

20 TTH = Bakeless, John, *Turncoats, Traitors and Heroes.* Philadelphia, Pa.: J. B. Lippincott Company, 1959.

21 SFT = Drowne, Henry Russell, *A Sketch of Fraunces Tavern.* New York: Fraunces Tavern, 1939.

23 LWTP = Wheeler, Daniel Edwin (ed.). *Life and Writings of Thomas Paine* 10 vols. New York: Vincent Parke and Company, 1908.

24 ISPUH = Mahan, (Captain) A. T., *The Influence of Sea Power Upon History,* 1660-1783. Cambridge: University Press, John Wilson and Son, 1890.

25 AR = Willcox, William B. (ed.) *The American Rebellion*, "Sir Henry Clinton's Narrative of His Campaigns, 1775-1782, With an Appendix of Original Documents." New Haven: Yale University Press, 1954.

26 JAM V-II-1 = Miller, Francis Trevelyn (ed.). *The Journal of American History*, Vol. II, No. 2. New Haven, Conn.: Associated Publishers of American Records, 1908. (Note: Pages 349-356, contain General Washington's Order Book, extracts of General Orders.)

28 GW = Thayer, William Roscoe, *George Washington.* Cambridge, Mass.: Houghton Mifflin Company, The Riverside Press, 1922.

29 BO76 = Coffin, Charles Carleton, *The Boys of '76*— A History of the Battles of the Revolution. New York: Harper & Brothers, Publishers, 1876.

32 SPNYS = Dixon, Edward H., M.D., *Scenes In the Practice of A New York Surgeon.* New York: De Witt L. Davenport, Publishers (160-162 Nassau Street), 1855.

33 WNJC = Richardson, William H., "Washington and the New Jersey Campaign," *Proceedings of the New Jersey Historical Society*, Vol. 50, No. 2, Newark, New Jersey: New Jersey Historical Society, April 1932.

36 CCNJ = Flynn, Joseph M., *The Catholic Church In New Jersey.* New York: The Publisher's Printing Co., 1904.

37 SINJ = Keasbey, A. Q., "Slavery In New Jersey," *Proceedings Of the New Jersey Historical Society*, Vol. 5, No. 2, April 1908. Newark: Library of the Society, 1908.

41 WOGW = Ford, W. C., *Writings of George Washington.* Boston: Small Co., 1910.

42 MCL = Lee, Charles, *Memoirs of the Late Charles Lee, Esq.* London, England, 1792.

44 GWEA = Kitman, Marvin (By General George Washington and Marvin Kitman), *George Washington's Expense Account.* New York, Simon and Schuster, 1970.

46 GW = Sears, Louis Martin, *George Washington.* New York: Thomas Y. Crowell Co., 1932.

49 WPA-SNJ = Works Projects Administration, "George Washington In New Jersey," *Stories of New Jersey*, Bulletin No. 5 Series. Newark, New Jersey: New Jersey Writers' Project, Work Projects Administration, 1942.

50 BCHS-RTP = Bogert, Frederick W., "Loyalists of Bergen County," *Bergen County Historical Society Revolutionary War Round Table*

Papers, 1960. Steuben House, North Hackensack, New Jersey: Bowne & Co. for the Bergen County Historical Society, 1961.

51 NJCS = Lee, Francis Bazley, *New Jersey As A Colony and A State,* Vol. II. New York: The Publishing Society of New Jersey, 1902.

53 NJA-TE = Kennedy, Mabon Steele, Cunningham, John T., Boucher, Bertrand P., Merlo, Patricia S., (Editors) *The New Jersey Almanac,* Tercentenary Edition. Trenton, New Jersey: The New Jersey Almanac, Inc. and Co-sponsor Trenton Evening Times, 1963.

54 JCHS = Eaton, Harriet Phillips, *Jersey City and Its Historic Sites.* Jersey City, New Jersey: The Woman's Club Of Jersey City, 1899.

55 GO = American Continental Army, "General Orders," Records of the American Army, *General Orders of the American Army.* Washington, D.C.: Army Archives [Also see 26 JAM V-II-1, pp. 349-356.]

56 OVB = Trust Company of New Jersey, *The Old Village of Bergen,* A History of the First Settlement in New Jersey. New York: Bartlett Orr Press, 1921.

57 GWAR = Flexner, James Thomas, *George Washington In the American Revolution, 1775-1783.* Boston: Little, Brown and Company, 1967.

60 SOR = Henderson, Peter, "Shadow On the River." Paper supporting historical military contribution of the Palisadean Bluff Rock to the War For Independence, prepared for the Palisades Nature Association of the Interstate Park Commission and read before the Bergen County (N.J.) Revolutionary War Round Table. Haworth, New Jersey: 1959. (Mimeographed.)

61 WS = Ketchum, Richard M., *The Winter Soldiers.* (The Crossroads of World History Series, edited by Orville Prescott.) Garden City, New York: Doubleday & Company, Inc., 1973.

62 DAB = Malone, Dumas (ed.), Dictionary of American Biography. *New York: Charles Scribner's Sons, 1933.*

63 AHAR = Ketchum, Richard M. (ed.) *The American Heritage Book of the American Revolution.* New York: American Heritage Publishing Co., Inc., 1971.

64 DNB = Masquer - Myles, *Dictionary of National Biography,* Vol. XIII. London, England: Oxford University Press, Ely House, 1968.

200 ROMNJ = Stryker, William S., *Official Register of the Officers and Men of New Jersey in the Revolutionary War.* Baltimore, Maryland: Genealogical Publishing Co., 1967.

201 JEA = Karp, Abraham J., *The Jewish Experience In America,* Vol. I, "The Colonial Period." New York: American Jewish Historical Society of Waltham, Massachusetts, KTAV Publishing Company, Inc., 1969.

202 NYIR = Office of the State Comptroller, *New York In the Revolution,* Vols. I and II. A compilation of documents and records of the State Comptroller, Albany, New York. New York: J. B. Lyon Company, Printers, 1904.

203 MSSRW = Massachusetts Records, *Massachusetts Soldiers and Sailors of Revolutionary War.* Boston: Wright and Potter Publishing Co., 1907.

204 RSNCAR = Daughters of the American Revolution, *Roster of Soldiers From North Carolina In the American Revolution.* Raleigh, North Carolina: The Daughters of the American Revolution, Raleigh, N.C., 1932.

207 AMH = U.S. Department of Army, *American Military History,* 1607-1953. Washington, D.C.: U.S. Government Printing Office, 1956.

209 HBC = Van Valen, J.M., *History of Bergen County, New Jersey.* New York: Publishing and Engraving Company, 1900.

213 HWP = Rösch, John, *Historic White Plains.* [Limited Edition] White Plains, New York: Balletto-Sweetman, Inc., 1939.

217 ABH = Ellis, Edward S. and Snyder, Henry, *A Brief History of New Jersey.* New York: American Book Company, 1910.

300 HDFW = Bolton, Reginald Pelham, "A History of the Defence and Reduction of Fort Washington" (New York: The Empire State Society of the Sons of the American Revolution, 1902), [Bound Pamphlet, 123 pages.]

301 HBCNJ = Westervelt, Francis A. (ed.), *History of Bergen County, New Jersey, 1630-1923,* Vol. I. New York: Lewis Historical Publishing Company, Inc., 1923.

302 MC = Hall, Edward Hagaman, "Margaret Corbin, Heroine of the Battle of Fort Washington" (New York: American Scenic and Historical Preservation Society, 1932), [Bound Pamphlet, 45 pages.]

303 FLNJ = Hall, Edward Hagaman, "Fort Lee, New Jersey," *Fourteenth Annual Report of the American Scenic and Historic Preservation Society,* pp. 169-244. Paper read before the New York State Legislature, Albany, New York, April 2, 1908. Albany, New York: L. B. Lyon Co., State Printers, 1908.

304 OMP = Hall, Edward Hagaman, "The Old Martyr's Prison." Paper presented to the Board of Aldermen of the City of New York by the American Scenic and Historic Preservation Society as "An Historical Sketch of the Oldest Municipal Building In New York City: Used During the War For American Independence: Built About 1756 and Known At Different Times As 'The New Gaol,' 'The Debtors' Prison,' 'The Provost,' 'The Hall of Records' and 'The Register's Office,' " New York, 1902. [Reprinted from "The City Record," New York, October 23, 1902.]

305 WAP = Thompson, Ray, *Washington Along the Delaware.* Trenton: Bicentennial Press, 1970.

306 SNJTC = State of New Jersey Tercentenary Commission, *The Monitor.* Tercentenary Tales. Trenton, New Jersey: The Commission, December 28, 1962.

307 TDR = Pearson, Michael, *Those Damned Rebels.* The American Revolution As Seen Through British Eyes. New York: G. P. Putnam's Sons, 1972.

312 GWAE = Fitzpatrick, John C.., *General George Washington's Accounts of Expenses.* New York: Houghton Mifflin Co., 1917.

313 GWW = Fitzpatrick, John C. (ed.), *Writings of George Washington,* Vol. 6. Prepared by the George Washington Bicentennial Commission. Washington, D.C.: U.S. Government Printing Office, 1932.

500 AA5-V-I & II = Force, Peter, (ed.) *American Archives (Fifth Series)*, Vols. I & II. Washington, D.C.: Prepared and Published Under Authority of An Act Of Congress by M. St. Clair Clarke and Peter Force, 1848.

501 ARII = Trevelyan, Sir George Otto, *The American Revolution*, Part II, 1776. London: Longmans, Green, and Co., 1903.

600 SFMP = Sauthier, Claude Joseph and Faden, William, (Map), "A Plan of the Operations of the King's Army under the command of General Sir William Howe. K.B. in New York and East New Jersey against the American Forces Commanded By General Washington, from the 12th of October, to the 18th of November 1776." Charing Crofs, England: W. Faden, February 25, 1777.

603 MAP-EWP = (See *600* SFMP above.)

604 MAPLI = Faden, William, (Map), "A Plan of New York Island with part of Long Island, Staten Island & East New Jersey, with a particular Description of the Engagement on the Woody Heights of Long Island, between Flatbush and Brooklyn, on the 27th of August 1776, between His Majesty's Forces Commanded by General Howe and the Americans under Major General Putnam with the subsequent Disposition of both Armies... An Account of the Proceedings of His Majesty's Forces at the Attack of the Rebels Works on Long Island, on the 27th of August 1776." (Engraved and Published according to Act of Parliament Oct. 19th, 1776.) Charing Crofs, London: William Faden, 1776.

605 ERSKMP = Erskine, Robert, F.R.S. Geographer to the Army, (Map), "Surveys Done for His Exc'y General Washington." Headquarters: 1777 with "Ajustants 1778-1779." [Original is in possession of the New York Historical Society.]

607 BRWKS = (An undated, unfinished military map delineating the layout of the Bluff Rock artillery works on the New Jersey Palisades above the Bourdet, or Bourdette, ferry landing in 1776; chorographer is unknown.) This map, believed to be the basis of Edward Hagaman Hall's "Fort Lee, New Jersey" data, provided the substantiating proof of the site's historical significance in 1955 (seee *60* SOR, pp. 7, 9, 10, 24) leading to its preservation and permanent protection from encroachment by developers.

608 MAP-ERS-M and
608 NDKMP = Right upper half of the Erskine-DeWitt Map 26, New York Historical Society Collection, credited to Captain John Watkins, between 1777 and 1780 and questionably correct. [Shows Survey Lines Map, Fort Lee and Northern Bergen County area, giving instrument readings.] Since a brief inscription purports to indicate the 1776 Cornwallis crossing and names the "New Dock" without showing, or naming, the Closter (Old) Dock, a dispute over the actual Cornwallis landing arose in 1974. Local historians in Cresskill, New Jersey, contended the invaders, therefore, marched through Cresskill rather than Closter, New Jersey.

609 MAP-ERSK-1-4 = Erskine, Robert, F.R.S., (Map), "A Map of Part of the States of New - York and New - Jersey: Laid down, chiefly from Actual Surveys, received from the Right Honorable Lord Stirling & others, and Delineated for the use of His Excellency General Washington." Headquarters, New Jersey: 1777. [National Archives and Records Service, General Services Administration, Washington, D.C.]

613 MAP-PHKF = Hills, John, Assistant Engineer to General Sir Henry Clinton, (Map), "Plan from Paulus Hook Ferry in the Province of New York and Parts adjacent from Actual Surveys 1781." This Clinton Collection map delineates the Palisades area west of the Hudson River from New York Bay north beyond Stony Point, locating roads and villages in the Hackensack and Hudson River valleys, according to information acquired by the British chorographers. It is inscribed, "To His Excellency Sir Henry Clinton, K.B., General and Commander in Chief of His Majesty's Forces of & in North America. . ." This map identifies the Bluff Rock artillery works as "Fort Constitution" and the main fort and works on the crest of the Palisades to the west of the Bluff Rock as "Fort Lee." [Original is in The William L. Clements Library, Ann Arbor, Michigan.]

614 MAP-AFW = Sauthier, Claude Joseph, (Map), "A Topographical Map of the Northern Part of New York Island, Exhibiting the Plan of Fort Washington, now Fort Knyphausen, with the Rebels Lines to the Southward, which were Forced by the Troops under the Command of The Right Honorable Earl Percy on the 16th November, 1776. . . To which is added the Attack made to the North by the Hessians." London, England: William Faden, 1777.

615 MAP-AFW2 = Sauthier, Claude Joseph, (Map), "Attacks of Fort Washington by His Majestys Forces under the Command of General Sir William Howe K:B., 16 November 1776," New York: Lith. For D. T. Valentine's Manual for 1861 by George Hayward, 171 Pearl St., New York.

Reference Notes

1

Friday, July 12 . . . The Invading Fleet Bares Its Fangs

1. *32* SPNYS, p. 289 (Note: Edward Dixon, M.D., was a great nephew of Stephen Etienne Bourdette. Dixon records that Stephen Etienne Bourdette purchased about 400 acres of what is now the Fort Lee - Edgewater cliffside and water-front property along the New Jersey Palisades. This was purchased from a freed black man who had been willed it by his former owner. The Bourdette purchase occurred about 20 years before the American Revolution. There are various spellings of the "Bourdette" name and consequently of the ferry site area which acquired it. Some references identify it as "Burdet Ferry," "Bourdette's," "Bourdett Landing" and "Moor's Landing." The land above the ferry first was called "The Mountain." Later, when the fortifications were begun, as "The Works On The Mountain," then as "Fort Constitution," and finally as "Fort Lee." Years later the water-front community acquired the name of Edgewater, and under the Bluff Rock a little 20th Century hamlet of some 40 homes developed under the name "Edgewater Colonists.")

2. *15* EAPH, p. 3

3. *6* RHSNJ, p. 224 (Note: Colonel Durkee of Connecticut was wounded in the Battle of Monmouth, June 28, 1778.)

4. *54* JCHS, p. 48

5. *Ibid.*

6. *15, op. cit.*, p. 5

7. *6, op. cit.*, p. 48, FN #2 (Note: Dr. John Wetherspoon was the sixth president of Princeton College. A staunch patriot, he served as a member of the Continental Congress and was a signer of the Declaraton of Independence.)

8. *8* SSS V-I, p. 423; and *6, op. cit.*, p. 145

9. *500* AA 5th V-I & II, pp. 258, 330, 374, 452 (Note: A replica of the frigate, *Rose*, was constructed in Canada, July 1970. It was docked in Newport, R.I., where it was later converted into a museum.)

10. *8, op. cit.*, p. 422
11. *13* RWHV, p. 44
12. *54, op. cit.*, p. 49
13. *19* ENYC, p. 161; and *55* GO, July 14, 1776
14. *15, op. cit.*, p. 63
15. *Ibid.*

2

Sunday, July 14... "To Conquer or Die"

1. *8* SSS V-I, p. 421
2. *10* TT, p. 19
3. *21* FT, p. 9
4. *13* RWHV, pp. 42-43
5. *303* FLNJ, p. 169
6. *21, op. cit.*, p. 12
7. *312* GWAE, p. 34
8. *55* GO, July 14, 1776
9. *21, op. cit.*, p. 14
10. *8, op. cit.*, p. 427
11. *Ibid.*
12. *8, loc. cit.*, citing "Brooks, *Henry Knox*, p. 58"
13. *2* SHAR, p. 230
14. *303, op. cit.*, p. 171

3

Monday, August 12... Soft As the Eaglet's Shell

1. *55* GO, August 6, 1776
2. *3* MJAR, p. 45
3. *Ibid.*, p. 52
4. *Ibid.*, p. 53
5. *303* FLNJ, p. 184
6. *Ibid.*, p. 196 (Hall, quoting Putnam - Gates Correspondence)
7. *3, op. cit.*, p. 48
8. *303, op. cit.*, p. 176

4

Sunday, August 18... Battling For the Hudson

1. *13* RWHV, p. 44
2. *9* PYD, p. 19
3. *4* TCMAG, p. 541
4. *303* FLNJ, p. 17 (Citing Putnam - Gates Correspondence)
5. *4, loc. cit.*

6. *303, op. cit.,* p. 192

7. *Ibid.,* p. 177

8. *Ibid.* (Note: Hall places Colonel Ward of Connecticut in command of the ferry at least until September 11, and states that Hardenbrook's body was recovered three days later and buried near the ferry. According to Hall, "his money and effects were placed in the hands of Colonel Ward."

9. *5* WOR, p. 210, quoting Fitzpatrick's George Washington correspondence, V. p. 44

10. *7* AR, p. 96

11. *5 op. cit.,* p. 205, quoting George Washington correspondence with Lord Stirling

12. *6* RHSNJ, p. 160

13. *500* AA 5th, V.3, pp. 815-818 (Also see "Headquarters Papers of the British Army In America, 1775-1783," MS., 4811, V. 42)

14. *303, op. cit.,* p. 176

15. *Ibid.*

5

Thursday, August 22. . . Defiance Meets the Threat Of Force

1. (Note: The "Three Pidgeons," a stage-stop and inn, was located several miles south of the Fort Lee intersection with the King's highway road, now Grand Avenue and Tonnele Avenue, Leonia, New Jersey. The inn was a favorite wayfarer's tavern along the lengthy north to south highway which passed through the eastern section of the Hackensack Valley.) Also see *13* RWHV, p. 42

2. *10* TT, p. 20

3. *Ibid., p. 11*

4. *Ibid., p. 17*

5. *501* AR, V. 2, 261n (Trevelyan states that it is difficult to believe that "these vessels were not specifically re-christened for the voyage, and that Admiral Lord Howe had nothing to do with it.")

6. *5* WOR, p. 209; and *10, op. cit.,* p. 29

7. *10, op. cit.,* p. 19

8. *Ibid.*

9. *Ibid.*

6

Tuesday, August 27. . . Battle Of Long Island

1. *4* TCMAG, p. 541

2. *5* WOR, pp. 213-14

3. *Ibid.,* p. 215

4. *7* AR, p. 96 (Note: In his *Battle of Long Island,* T. W. Fields is among others who quote the American Commander as saying: "Good god! What brave fellows I must this day lose!" Ward also notes this in *5, op. cit.,* p. 226.)

5. *10* TT, p. 31

6. *4, op. cit.,* p. 539

7. *5, op. cit.,* p. 226

8. *Ibid.,* p. 221, crediting Henry P. Johnston's *The Campaign of 1776* and T. W. Field's *The Battle of Long Island.*

7

Thursday, August 29. . . The Cul-de-sac

1. *4* TCMAG, p. 538
2. *9* PYD, p. 22
3. *5* WOR, p. 232
4. *Ibid.*, p. 233
5. (Note: The "Flying Camp" idea was intended to develop a fast-moving, easily transportable corps to be called upon for any emergency. It started out with great promise but never came up to expectations. Some of its recruits swore they would never cross the river to defend New Yorkers. The unit lost momentum rapidly after the fall of Paulus Hook and its personnel were absorbed by other regimental brigades.)
6. *5, loc. cit.*; and *7* AR, p. 100
7. *7, Ibid.*
8. *20* TTH, p. 103
9. *5* p. 235, citing Reed, Johnston, and Graydon
10. *Ibid.*, quoting Heath
11. *6* RHSNJ, pp. 173-74

8

Thursday, September 3. . . In the Womb Of Little Hope

1. *303* FLNJ, p. 177 (Note: Hall places Colonel Ward in command of the post, or at least in command of the shore batteries, at this time. He may have been relieved entirely from the post when Greene was appointed to take over the command.)
2. *13* RWHV, pp. 19-20
3 *Ibid.*, p. 12, citing L. H. Gipson, *Coming of the Revolution*, p. 134
4. (Note: The original name is believed to have been "Paw's Hook.")
5. *4* TCMAG, p. 541
6. *15* EAPH, p. 7
7. *Ibid.*
8. *Ibid.* p. 8
9. *Ibid.* p. 7
10. *4, op. cit.*, p. 539
11. *7* AR, p. 100, FN #11
12. *8* SSS V-I, p. 446, quoting Tallmadge, *Memoirs*
13. *5* WOR, p. 205 (Note: Christopher Ward's documentations, based upon well selected primary sources, have been found extremely valuable in validating many of the events covered in this treatment of the year, 1776.)
14. *Ibid.*, p. 230, quoting Fitzpatrick, VI., 4-7
15. *Ibid., p. 205, quoting Fitzpatrick, IV, 395, 397, 399, 414*
16. *Ibid.*
17. *Ibid.*, p. 204, quoting *Journals*, III, 322
18. *9* PYD, p. 23
19. *19* ENYC, p. 159
20. *3* MJAR, p. 60
21. *19, loc. cit.*
22. *5, op. cit.* p. 230 (Note: Ward censures the American Commander for not acting independent of the Congress, exercising his power of command and abandoning New York in accord with wise military strategy. He cites Claude H. Van Tyne and Sir John

Fortescue. Both were extremely harsh critics of the Continental Army's Leader, contending he lacked an "aptitude for war" and his "inadequacies as a really great commander in the field." Ward holds that "it seems impossible to avoid placing the bulk of the responsibility for the mismanagement of affairs on Long Island upon the shoulders of the commander-in-chief, George Washington." Ward adds that Thomas G. Frothingham was also of a similar opinion. However, within all this censure of the American general, Ward quotes the above historians' acknowledgements of the Continental Army commander as being "brave," "skilfull," "courageous," "noble" (in character), and grants that he had "the gift of inspiring confidence," rather than of having "military genius," and that he displayed "constancy" and "inexhaustible patience." Ward quotes Van Tyne, stating: "Even in the midst of his worst errors, his greatness and his magnanimity surmounts everything.")

23. *5, op. cit.,* quoting Rodney, C, 112
24. *4* TCMAG, pp. 537-539
25. *19, op. cit.,* p. 166
26. *5, op. cit.,* p. 241; and *9, op. cit.,* pp. 30-33
27. *313* WGW, V-6, p. 10
28. *33* WNJC, V-50 NJHSP, No. 2, p. 123
29. *Ibid.*
30. *13, op. cit.,* p. 27

9

Saturday, September 7... Secret Weapon: *The Turtle* Submarine

1. *303* FLNJ, p. 181
2. *5* WOR, p. 240
3. *8* SSS V-I, pp. 456-458
4. *Ibid.*
5. *5, op. cit.,* citing *Journals,* V, p. 749
6. *Ibid.,* p. 240, quoting Fitzpatrick, VI, pp. 28-29
7. *Ibid.*
8. (Note: Kip's Bay on the East River was located at approximately the east end of present-day 34th Street, New York City.)
9. *3* MJAR, pp. 62 and 122
10. *8, op. cit.,* p. 461, citing Fitzpatrick, WW, VI, pp. 27-32 (Note: In this letter, dated, "New York, Head Quarters, September 8, 1776," the American Commander explained to the Congress his decision to abandon New York. He presented the arguments for and against, noting:

"On every side there is a choice of difficulties.... I am sensible a retreating army is incircled with difficulties, that the declining an Engagement subjects a General to reproach and that the common Cause may be in some measure affected by the discouragements which it throws over the minds of many.")

11. *19* ENYC, pp. 164-166
12. *21* FT, p. 6
13. *8, op. cit.,* p. 458

10

Wednesday, September 11 . . . Down Goes the Olive Branch

1. (Note: Bull's Ferry was the next ferry crossing south of Bourdette's. It was about three miles downriver from the fort. Today the Bull's Ferry Road still leads down the Palisades at Weehawken to the area where the old ferry landing existed. It was the southern, or left flank, outpost for Fort Lee. The northernmost flank or outpost for Fort Lee was located above Sneden's Landing on its heights. However, secondary picket posts were undoubtedly located along the water front between the fort and its outer flanks.)
2. *10* TT, pp. 46-47
3. *3* MJAR, p. 56
4. *Ibid.*
5. *Ibid.*
6. *10, op. cit.,* p. 47
7. (Note: The term "chair" was used to refer to the gig, or a two-wheel carriage, drawn by one horse, a so-called one-horse shay.)
8. *10, op. cit.,* p. 48
9. *8* SSS V-I, p. 462
10. *500* AA, 5th, V-I, p. 237; and *16* MWC, p. 72

11

Sunday, September 15. . . Kip's Bay: Flight From the City

1. *6* RHSNJ V-I, p. 225
2. (Note: Hobuck and its varied spellings was later changed to Hoboken. An Indian name it is said to mean "The place from which comes the pipe for tobacco.")
3. *8* SSS V-I, p. 422, citing "Gr. Brit. Hist. Mss. Comm., *Hastings Manuscripts,* III, pp. 179-180"
4. (Note: In Leiby, *13* pp. 124, n72; 196, n31, a family by the name of Garlick lived one mile south of Bourdette's ferry. Leiby's account indicates that a John Garlick was counted among the Tory inhabitants of the area. However, the characters and family drawn here are, of course, fictional.)
5. *13* RWHV, p. 53, n41; (Leiby mentions an "Abraham Onderdonk" of Orange County, New York. However, the Hans and Abe and other Onderdonks in this work are fictional characters drawn in part from those mentioned in existing records.)
6. (Note: The American Commander-in-Chief visited the Barbados in the West Indies in 1751 and makes mention of it in his diary.)
7. *23* LWTP V-I, p. xxiii
8. *5* WOR, p. 242, quoting "Evelyn, 84"
9. *8, op. cit.,* pp. 459; 461-462
10. *Ibid.*
11. *Ibid.*
12. *500* AA 5th V-II, pp. 325, 328, 330; also see *16* p. 72
13. *8, op. cit.,* p. 460
14. *Ibid.*
15. *Ibid.*
16. *Ibid.*
17. *11* RW, p. 52
18. *8* pp. 459-60
19. *24* ISPUH, p. 342

20. *Ibid.*, p. 342-43

21. *Ibid.*, (Note: Mahan's analysis of what he calls Howe's "disastrous step" in August 1777 is pursued. Mahan notes that in October, Burgoyne was isolated and hemmed in, necessitating his surrender. Mahan states:

"In the following May the English evacuated Philadelphia, and after a painful and perilous march through New Jersey with Washington's army in close pursuit returned to New York." The Howes would be censured upon their return to England and would be accused by some of favoring and benefiting the American cause by their negligences, all of which they, of course, vigorously denied.)

22. *5, op. cit.*, p. 241, quoting "Fitzpatrick, VI, 53"

23. *6, op. cit.*, p. 224 (Note: Account is based upon the journal of the post's chaplain in Colonel Durkee's command. Item is also carried in the *Pennsylvania Evening Post*, November 19, 1776.)

24. *Ibid.*

25. *Ibid.*

26. *Ibid.*, pp. 185-86; 225

27. *5, op. cit.*, p. 241, citing Heath, Force, etc.

28. (Note: *The Pennsylvania Evening Post* of October 1, 1776 reported:

"The *Asia* and two other ships of war proceeded up the North River but were roughly handled by our battery at Powles Hook; and the next morning by daylight, the *Asia* came down much faster than she went up, three ships of war being nearly all destroyed by four of our fire ships that run in among them, and nothing prevented their total destruction but a gale of wind, that sprung up at that instant.")

29. *6, op. cit.*, p. 225; also see *56* OVB, p. 32 wherein is recorded the story of Paulus Hook and its pre-Revolutionary War race track. One of the horses used for racing and fox hunting in 18th century Jersey City was named "Old Mug."

30. *6, loc. cit.*,

31. *8, op. cit.*, p. 459, citing Cresswell Journal

32. *9* PYD, p. 32

33. *5 loc. cit.* citing "Heath, 50. . . Force 5, I, 443" etc.

34. *Ibid.*, p. 242

35. *9, op. cit.*, p. 32, n15

36. *Ibid.*, pp. 32-33 (Note: The area described is located today around the foot of 23rd Street near the small park on FDR Drive just south of the Williamsburg Bridge in New York City.)

37. *5. op. cit.*, p. 240, citing Evelyn and Serle

38. *9, loc. cit.*

39. *Ibid.*, p. 34

40. *Ibid.*, p. 40, n19 (Note: Private Martin's superior officer was Major Phineas Porter, Regimental Commander who was captured in this engagement.)

41. *19* ENYC, p. 166

42. *9, op. cit.*, p. 35, n18

43. *5, op. cit.*, p. 243

44. *Ibid.*, citing "Stephenson, I, 365"

45. *Ibid.*

46. *5, loc. cit.*

47. *Ibid.*, n30, citing Heath, Gordon, Graydon, Rodney, Force, Johnston

48. *8, op. cit.*, pp. 466-67, citing Journal of Benjamin Trumbull, a chaplain in First Connecticut Regiment, September 1776, Connecticut Historical Society Collection, VII, pp. 193-195

49. (Note: This location is in the vicinity of City College campus, Amsterdam Avenue, from about 136th to 140th Streets.)

50. *5, Ibid.*, citing "Stephenson, I, 365. . . Mackenzie, I, 50." (Note: In Ward's account, p. 457, n34, Mackenzie is quoted as saying: "The Rebels left a great quantity of Cannon, Ammunition, Stores, provisions, tents &c. &c. behind them.")

51. (Note: The area known as Incleberg lay between 4th and 6th Avenues. During the war it was a high piece of land between present day 34th and 40th Streets.)

52. *5, loc. cit.,* citing "Johnston, I, 237-39."

53. (Note: According to some legends Mrs. Murray purposely detained the British officers and is pictured as a young, attractive siren bent upon saving the Continentals from an encounter with a superior enemy force.)

54. *5, op. cit.,* p. 457, n35, quoting Colonel Humphrey, "Johnston, I, 238-39"

55. *6, op. cit.,* p. 225

56. *Ibid.,* p. 226

57. *Ibid.,* p. 224-25

58. *11* RW, p. 98 (Note: The Haym Salomon - Asher Levy friendship, as well as the Gray - Levy comradery, is fictional. However, Salomon was an important and devoted patriot during the Revolution. Levy, also a fictional character in this work, is drawn from another non-fictional figure, Asher Levy, an officer in the 12th New Jersey Regiment of the Continental Army. In confirming this, the author is indebted to Dr. Joseph Brandes' *Immigrants To Freedom,* and to the article "Asser Levy, A Noted Jewish Burgher of New Amsterdam" in *The Jewish Experience In America,* Vol I, New York, 1969, p. 65.)

59. *6, op. cit.,* p. 199

60. *Ibid.,* p. 225

12

Monday, September 16. . . Harlem Heights: The Turnabout

1. *6* RHSNJ V-I, p. 146 (Re: Wounded moved to N.J.)

2. *26* JAM V-II, No. 2, p. 350 (Note: Hitchcock was assigned at this time to the post on the Palisades under the command of Brigadier General Mifflin.)

3. *5* WOR, p. 247, citing "H. Johnston, 44-47" (Note: See map facing p. 50)

4. *Ibid.,* p. 244

5. *Ibid.*

6. *6, op. cit.,* p. 226

7. *Ibid.,* citing *"Pennsylvania Evening Post,* October 1, 1776"

8. *Ibid.*

9. *Ibid.*

10. *5, op. cit.,* p. 226

11. *Ibid.,* citing "Fitzpatrick, VI, 59"

12. *28* GW, pp. 80-81, citing "Ford, IV, 440"

13. *5, op. cit.,* pp. 237, 254, citing *"Journals,* V, 762"

14. *Ibid.*

15. *10* TT, p. 63

16. *5, op. cit.,* p. 248, citing "H. Johnston, 61-62"

17. *8* SSS V-I, p. 468

18. *Ibid.*

19. *5, op. cit.,* pp. 246-52; *6, op. cit.,* pp. 468-71; *10, op. cit.,* pp. 62-68, among others for this account.

20. *5, op. cit.,* p. 250

21. *8, op. cit.,* p. 469

22. *Ibid.* p. 470

23. *5, loc. cit.*

24. *Ibid.*

13

Friday, September 20... City On Fire

1. *55* GO, September 20, 1776

2. (Note: Washington Irving in his *Life of Washington*, Vol. II, Page 367, states that the American Commander-in-Chief "often made inspection trips as far as Powles Hook." It is understandable that such visits would also include stops at Bergen Point opposite Staten Island and possibly extended inspections as far as Perth Amboy. All were vitally important garrisons during this period.)

3. *55, Ibid.*

4. *16* MWC, p. 70 (Note: Source places Ewing at Fort Constitution at this time on basis of James Allen letter.)

5. *303* FLNJ, p. 169

6. *13* RWHV, p. 47

7. *6* RHSNJ V-I, p. 226, citing *Pennsylvania Evening Post*, November 18, 1776, report of discovery of a cache of arms in a deserted house near "Powles-Hook."

8. *10* TT, p. 67

9. (Note: The American Chief of Staff apparently had an especial place on the Bluff Rock where he made his personal observations. Paintings have depicted him on the site. The H. Willard Ortlip painting [circa 1923] shows him observing the Battle of Fort Washington from the precipice on November 16, 1776. However, in later years of the war during which Fort Lee had no strategic military value except for observing enemy movements, he was frequently seen by British officers across the river. It can be safely presumed he found the Palisades' high, natural observation towers of great military advantage in gathering intelligence of the enemy on Manhattan.)

10. *13, op. cit.*, pp. 6, 42, n124, 146, mentioning "Three Pidgeons Tavern"

11. *56* OVB, p. 31, noting that Paulus Hook was more than a ferry landing before The Revolutionary War and that it was "the terminus of the stage routes from Philadelphia." A sketch of the Parks' homestead is found on Page 43, Prior's Mill on Page 9. Leiby's work, cited above, has a sketch of the Van Vorst homestead on Page 6, crediting Winfield's *History of Hudson County*. Some good sketches of the Hook's fort are found in Richardson and Gardiner's account of the "Battle of Paulus Hook."

12. *13, op. cit.*, p. 51, citing *This Glorious Cause* by H. T. Wade and R. A. Lively, p. 223

13. (Note: An historical marker was erected some years ago at the foot of the Palisades where the ferry road led down to the water. It is in the present Borough of Edgewater, New Jersey. It reads: "South of the brook stood the Burdett homestead, Washington's local headquarters." Its identification is credited to the research work of the late Dr. William F. Conway of Edgewater, New Jersey.)

14. (McDowell, previously cited, mentions Haym Salomon's contributions to the American cause on Pages 98, 148, 174, 193. Salomon is said to be buried in the old church cemetery grounds near 8th Street, New York City.)

15. *8* SSS V-I, p. 476, citing Campbell's *General William Hull*, pp. 37-39, noting that Alexander Hamilton was then serving as a captain of artillery.

16. *Ibid.*, pp. 472-473, citing "Mackenzie *Diary*, I, 58-61"

17. *Ibid.*, pp. 473-474

18. *Ibid.*, p. 472

19. *3* MJAR, p. 57; *500* 5th V-II, p. 462, citing Sir William Howe's report to Lord Germaine, "York Island, September 23, 1776"

20. *8, op. cit.*, p. 471

21. *15* EAPH, p. 10

22. *500, op. cit.*, p. 462

23. *11* RW, p. 52

24. *8, loc. cit.*

25. *4* TCMAG, p. 612

14

Sunday, September 22 . . . "Apprehended last night . . . this day Executed"

1. (Note: In this account, some of the historical sources found helpful include: Commager, SSS V-I, *8*; Bakeless, TTH, *20*; Willcox, AR, *25*; Coffin, BO1776, *29*; and Force, AA, 5th, V-II, *500* among others.)
2. *20* TTH, p. 119
3. *29* BO76, p. 112
4. *20, op. cit.,* p. 120, noting, "Cunningham himself was hanged for forgery in London in 1791."
5. *6* RHSNJ V-I, p. 204, noting that a planned attack was called off for this date
6. *25* AR, pp. xxiii, 47, n16
7. *20, op. cit.,* p. 114
8. (Note: This site is located today in the approximate vicinity of the old New York City Grand Central Station.)
9. *20, op. cit.,* p. 118
10. *8* SSS V-I, pp. 475-76
11. *Ibid.*
12. *20, op. cit.,* p. 121

15

Monday, September 23. . . Avenging Broadsides Take the Hook

1. (Note: Under "General Orders," September 17, 1776, Greene was given the command of the post at Fort Constitution, later renamed, Fort Lee.)
2. (Note: Many scouting expeditions were periodically ordered. This one, however, is not substantiated.)
3. (Note: British war maps identified Spuyten Duyvil which is located north of today's George Washington Bridge and under the New York expressway, as "Spilling Devil.")
4. *6* RHSNJ V-I, p. 228
5. *Ibid.,* p. 227
6. *Ibid.,* p. 204
7. *Ibid.,* p. 228
8. *15* EAPH, p. 10
9. *6, op. cit.,* pp. 227-28
10. *Ibid.*
11. *Ibid.,* p. 204
12. *15, loc. cit.*
13. *8* SSS V-I, p. 479, quoting Drake's *Henry Knox*
14. *Ibid.,* pp. 480-84, citing Fitzpatrick, *Writings of George Washington,* V-VI, pp. 106-115
15. (Note: Richardson and Gardner in *Washington and the Enterprise Against Powles Hook,* p. 10, state: "The fact is that neither fort (Bergen Neck and Powles Hook) was a very safe place in which to be: 'Death Traps' was the soldier parlance for these hastily built earthworks.")
16. *6, op. cit.,* p. 204
17. *Ibid.,* pp. 228-29
18. *15, op. cit.,* p. 8

19. *56* OVB, p. 15
20. *Ibid.*, p. 32
21. *15, op. cit.*, p. 7
22. *Ibid.*
23. *Ibid.*, Title Page

16

Sunday, October 6. . . In the Interlude Comes Love

1. *500* AA 5th V-II, p. 498
2. *13* RWHV, p. 50
3. *500, op. cit.*, pp. 1066-67; and *13, loc. cit.*
4. *500, loc. cit.*
5. *Ibid.*, p. 523
6. (Note: Oratam, who was born in 1577 and died in either 1666 or 1667, was the Senior Sagamore and Sachem of the so-called Hackensack Indians, a tribe of the Unami Division of the Lenni Lenape Nation. Oratam, translated, is said to have meant "The Good and Affable One." In his lifetime he aided the white settlers who soon threatened and later destroyed his society. In his years of both pleasant and tragic associations with the white settlers, he became widely known as the Indians' "Peace Chief," for he had dedicated himself to the employment of only peaceful methods in the solution of controversial issues between the Indians and the encroaching settlers. His principal philosophy and manner of operation were based upon the concept that all problems could be resolved through kindness, attentive listening, extreme patience, sound reasoning and friendly exhortation. He early adopted and employed the policy never to command, compel or punish in the search for solutions. Through this policy and philosophy he had hoped to insure the survival of his people and to avoid war which he knew would destroy them. However, his practices, policies and procedures failed to achieve survival for his people).
7. (Note: An early Twentieth Century New Jersey historian, the late Francis C. Koehler, contended that the name, "Hackensack" was derived from the name of an early Indian chief who preceded Oratam and was known by the appellation, "Haqninsaq.")
8. (Note; The signature, symbol and sign used by Oratam was a horizontal, convex curve, underneath which—and indented about one-third of the way along the curve—was a check-mark coming off left of center of the convex curve which faced upward. It is not known what the symbol meant. Oratam's so-called "castle" is identified as "Indian Castle" in a copy of the Edsall Deed which was in the possession of Dr. Lewis M. Haggerty of Hackensack, New Jersey, an authority on the life and culture of the Indians of New Jersey. The castle's location is believed to have been in the neighborhood of Broad Avenue and Harwood Terrace is present-day Palisades Park, New Jersey. The site is a high rise of land, identified variously as both "Castle Hill" and "Indian Hill." It is very likely that Oratam's mark was very much in evidence in that area as well as in the valley below it as late as the Eighteenth Century. The high grounds on the western slope of the Palisades looked down on what is today Ridgefield Park, New Jersey. Ridgefield Park was the location, approximately, of the ancient Indian village of "Achenkesacky." It is from this site and name that the present city of Hackensack, New Jersey, derived its name.)
9. (Note: Roughly translated, "Pachgandhatteu" could mean, "The food is ready to be eaten. Come and get it.")
10. (Note: "Lenni Lenape" is said to be translatable into "The Original People.")
11. *7* AM, p. 102
12. *6* RHSNJ V-I, p. 193
13. *SOR, p. 22, n34,* citing Hall, pp. 188-89 and Force p. 1092 (Also see Correspon-

dence of General Hugh Mercer and President John Hancock of the Continental Congress, September 26, 1776.)

14. *303* FLNJ, p. 185
15. *57* GWAR, p. 94
16. *500* AA 5th V-III, p. 839
17. *303, op. cit.,* p. 182
18. *Ibid.,* p. 189
19. Taken from *Elisabeth* an encomium to Elisabeth Murphy Henderson, ©, August 28, 1966.

17

Wednesday, October 9. . . The Piercing Of the Chevaux de Frise

1. *10* TT, p. 79, citing Putnam - Gates correspondence
2. *303* FLNJ, p. 174
3. *Ibid.,* p. 175
4. *500* AA 5th V-II, p. 962
5. *303, op. cit.,* p. 187
6. *Ibid.*
7. (Note: These "rules" were posted in the old Black Horse Tavern and inn on the Old Black Horse Pike in Flourtown, Pennsylvania. Most taverns and inns of the Eighteenth Century era posted their own tavern rules. Prices were similar to those in "Rules Of This Tavern.")
8. *303, op. cit.,* p. 190
9. *500, op. cit.,* p. 869 (Note: Substantiating this, also may be cited the following sources of correspondence, likewise found in Force's work: Washington to Hancock, p. 869; Reed to Heath, *Ibid.*; Greene to Congress regarding embezzlement by surgeons, p. 974; Court of Inquiry letter regarding an officer, p. 992; Greene to Cooke, *Ibid.*; Washington to Cooke, p. 1009; Schuyler to Yates, p. 1016; Long to Washington, p. 1033; The General Orders, p. 1120; and Washington to Cook, p. 1095.)
10. *Ibid.,* p. 872
11. *Ibid.,* p. 870
12. *Ibid.,* p. 974
13. *Ibid.,* p. 973
14. *6* RHSNJ V-I, p. 207
15. *Ibid.,* p. 214
16. *500, op. cit.,* p. 979
17. *Ibid.*
18. *Ibid.,* p. 973
19. *13* RWHV, p. 220
20. *Ibid.,* p. 53
21. *500, op. cit.,* p. 961, citing Tilghman's letter to the New York Committee, October 9, 1776, from the Harlem Heights headquarters
22. *Ibid.,* p. 1041, citing Trumbull - Washington letter, October 14, 1776
23. *Ibid.,* p. 961
24. *Ibid.,* p. 990, citing Washington - Congress correspondence, October 11, 1776
25. *Ibid.,* p. 961
26. *Ibid.,* p. 1024, citing General Ewing's letter to the Maryland Council of Safety from "Camp near Harlem, October 12, 1776"
27. *Ibid.,* p. 973
28. *Ibid.,* p. 990
29. *Ibid.,* p. 961

30. (Note: Greene's reputed military acumen is detected here. This was an accurate prediction displaying good foresight in light of the events destined to take place. But his subsequent prediction of "little more to fear this campaign" was an error as was his later erroneous assessment of the formidability of Fort Washington. There is of course the possibility that Greene spoke with tongue in cheek in his morale-boosting correspondence with Cooke in order to keep New England's spirits as high as possible during the crises days.)

31. *500, op. cit.,* p. 997
32. *4* TCMAG, p. 687
33. *Ibid.,* p. 688
34. *32,* SPNYS, p. 295
35. *48* LWTP, pp. 94-95

18

Saturday, October 12 . .,. Circumvention via Westchester

1. WOR, p. 255 (Ward notes that the original name was "Throckmorton's Neck," later shortened to "Throck's," then "Throg's" and finally "Frog's Neck" or "Frog's Neck Point.")

2. *4* TCMAG, p. 681, quoting General William Howe's report to George Germaine, dated "New York, November 30, 1776" and published in the *London Gazette,* Whitehall, December 30, 1776

3. *Ibid.*
4. *8* SSS V-I, p. 485
5. *4, loc. cit.*
6. *Ibid.*
7. *6* RHSNJ V-I, p. 204
8. *8, op. cit.,* p. 484
9. *500* AA 5th V-II, p. 991
10. *Ibid.,* p. 920
11. *Ibid.,* p. 1009
12. *10* TT. p. 76 (Note: "The Sultana" as Howe's mistress was called, was Mrs. Joshua Loring, nee Lloyd; her cuckold husband was given the office of Commissary of Prisoners by Howe.)
13. *500, op. cit.,* p. 1025
14. *Ibid.,* p. 991
15. *213* HWP, p. 90
16. *5, op. cit.,* p. 255
17. *Ibid.*
18. *500, loc. cit.*
19. *5, op. cit.,* p. 256
20. *500, loc. cit.*
21. *Ibid.*
22. *500, op. cit.,* p. 1016
23. *Ibid.,* p. 957
24. *Ibid.,* p. 990
25. *Ibid.*
26. Ibid., *p. 1008*
27. 10, op. cit., p. 76 n27

19

Friday, October 18 . . . "Knight Of the Flaming Sword" To the Rescue

1. *8* SSS V-I, p. 476
2. *7* AR, p. 100
3. *29* B076, p. 84
4. *Ibid.*, p. 82
5. *Ibid.* p. 89
6. *303* FLNJ, p. 195
7. *Ibid.*, p. 196
8. *500* AA 5th V-II, p.1016
9. *Ibid.*, p. 920
10. *Ibid.*, p. 1095
11. *303, loc. cit.*
12. *500, op. cit.*, p. 1093
13. *Ibid.*, p. 1034
14. *Ibid.*
15. *Ibid.*, p. 1169
16. *Ibid.*p. 1034
17. *313* WGW, p. 229
18. *500, op. cit.*, pp. 1077, 1117, 1118
19. *Ibid.*, p. 1117
20. *6* RHSNJ V-I, p. 208
21. *500, op. cit.*, p. 1034
22. *5* WOR, p. 256
23. *Ibid.*, quoting *Journals,* VI, p. 866
24. *500, op. cit.*, pp. 990, 1117-18, 1035
25. *55* GO, October 13, 1776
26. *500, loc. cit.*
27. *Ibid.*
28. *Ibid.*
29. *Ibid.*
30. *Ibid.*, p. 1119
31. *Ibid.*
32. (Note: General Howe's perspective is visualized best in the British Claude Joseph Sauthier and William Faden map entitled, "Plan of the Operations of the King's Army under the command of General Sir William Howe, K.B., in New York and East New Jersey, Against the American Forces Commanded By General Washington, From the 12th of October, to the 28th of November 1776 Wherein Is Particularly Distinguished the Engagement on the White Plains, the 28th of October, By Claude Joseph Sauthier; Engraved by Wm. Faden, 1777."—Clinton Collection, William L. Clements Library, Ann Arbor, Michigan)
33. *500, op. cit.*, p. 1117
34. *Ibid.*
35. *Ibid.*, p. 1130
36. *Ibid.*, p. 1120; and *55* GO, October 18, 1776
37. (Note: See Sauthier-Faden Map, n32, above.)
38. *5, op. cit.*, p. 257
39. *8, op. cit.*, p. 487
40. *5, op. cit., p. 458*
41. *8, loc. cit.,*
42. *4* TCMAG, p. 681

43. *8, Ibid.*
44. *500, op. cit.*, pp. 188-89; and *8, op. cit.*, p. 488
45. *Ibid.*, p. 1130
46. *4, loc. cit.*; and *500, op. cit.*, p. 1203
47. *5, op. cit.*, p. 258, quoting Hufeland on the disputed casualty figures as reported by both sides
48. *10* TT, p. 72
49. *8, op. cit.*, p. 486; and *500, op. cit.*, pp. 1188-89
50. *500, Ibid.*, quoting letter from Glover, dated October 22, 1776, giving Glover's after-thoughts and reflections on the engagement
51. *Ibid.*; and *8, op. cit.*, p. 487
52. *500, op. cit.*, p. 1130
53. *4, loc. cit.*
54. *Ibid.*
55. *5, loc. cit.*
56. *4, op. cit.*, p. 682
57. *Ibid.*
58. *500, loc. cit.*
59. *Ibid.*
60. *62* DAB V-VI, pp. 98-101
61. *500, op. cit.*, p. 1096
62. *Ibid.*, p. 1130
63. *Ibid.*

20

Sunday, October 27 . . . Revised Objective: White Plains, Then the Hudson

1. *301* HBCNJ, p. 105
2. *13* RWHV, pp. 29, 61
3. *209* HBC, p. 58
4. *5* WOR, p. 258
5. *6* RHSNJ V-I, p. 208
6. *500* AA 5th V-II, p. 996
7. *19* ENYC, p. 172
8. *6, op. cit.*, p. 242
9. *500, loc. cit.*
10. *8* SSS V-I, p. 479
11. *13, op. cit.*, p. 123 (Note: See Leiby's illustration, "Certificate of Oath of Allegiance of Dirck Brinkerhoff, 1777"; also see *Sir Henry Clinton Collection,* William L. Clements Library, Ann Arbor, Michigan)
12. *500, op. cit.*, p. 1136
13. *Ibid.*
14. *61* WS, p. 37
15. *5, loc. cit.*
16. *500, op. cit.*, p. 1203
17. *4* TCMAG, p. 681
18. *5, loc. cit.*
19. *Ibid.*
20. *500, op. cit.* p. 1030
21. *Ibid.*
22. *Ibid.*, p. 1205

23. *Ibid.*, p. 1239
24. *4, loc. cit.*
25. *Ibid.*
26. *500, op. cit.* p. 1203
27. *4, loc. cit.*
28. *500, op. cit.* p. 1205
29. *4, op. cit.*, pp. 681-85
30. *500, op. cit.*, p. 1239
31. *13, op. cit.*, p. 57, n15 (Leiby, citing "2 Greene, Greene 266; Force (5) 629, 630:
'In Jersey, across the river from Dobbs Ferry,' a Hessian officer wrote, 'the enemy had a small camp, which high shrubs prevented us from seeing entirely, and in front of which, behind an embankment, they had posted an 18 pounder, which fired on a frigate and two transports that lay at anchor close to our shore.' Baurmeister 67")
32. *500, loc. cit.*
33. *Ibid.*
34. *Ibid.*, p. 1095
35. *Ibid.*, p. 1266 (Also see: *13*, p. 53 and *6*, p. 223)
36. *6, op. cit.*, p. 217
37. *Ibid.*, p. 223
38. *Ibid.*
39. *4, op. cit.*, p. 683
40. *500, op. cit.*, p. 958
41. *Ibid.*, p. 961
42. *Ibid.*, p. 990

21

Monday, October 28. . . Battle Of the White Plains

1. *600* S-Fmp
2. *4* TCMAG, p. 683
3. *600, loc. cit.*
4. *5* WOR, p. 397
5. *Ibid.*, p. 261, citing Trevelyan
6. *Ibid.*, p. 271 (Note: This site is in present day Scarsdale.)
7. *500* 5th V-III, pp. 473, 725-26 (Force quotes an officer's description of the flight as follows:
". . . like leaves in a whirlwind; and they ran off so far that some of the Americans ran out to the ground where they were and brought off their arms and accoutrements and rum that the men who had fell had with them which we had time to drink rounds with before they came on again.")
8. *5, op. cit.*, p. 262
9. *500, op. cit.*, p. 1283 (Note: Force quotes an "Extract Of A Letter From An Officer Of the Sixty-fourth Regiment, In New-York-Island, To His Friend In London, Dated New-York, October 30, 1776." In it the officer, assumably John Andre, is believed to be the first one to use the expression, "tatterdemalions" in reference to the poor appearance and condition of the American soldiers.)
10. *500, op. cit.*, p. 1241
11. *500*, p. 1271 n-1272
12. *Ibid.*
13. *Ibid.*, p. 1272
14. *213* HWP, p. 90 (Note: Rosch states "These were the flower of the British

Army."; Ward, *5*, WOR, p. 261, contends Howe's forces, including the reinforcements that arrived October 18, numbered about 15,000 men.)

15. *5, op. cit.*, p. 262, citing "Hufeland, fn # 9" ,Ibid.,

16. *Ibid.* p. 264, citing "Rodney, C, 143" quoting Haslet as saying, "It was so poorly appointed that myself was forced to assist in dragging it along in the rear of the regiment . . ."

17. (Note: This quotation is attributed to the American Commander-in-Chief.)

18. *5, op. cit.*, p. 264, citing "Rodney, C, 143 in fn # 17"

19. *213, op. cit.*, p. 92 (Note: Tompkins, in this work under "After the Battle Of White Plains," says of Hamilton's action: "Never did officers or men do better execution." He adds that Hamilton, in visiting the spot in after years, described the scene to a youthful friend stating, "For three successive discharges, the advancing column of British was swept from hilltop to river.")

20. *15* EAPH, p. 265

21. *29* BO76, p. 116

22. *5, op. cit.*, p. 265, citing "Trevelyan, Pt. II, Vol. I, 314-315"

23. *(Note: This road later became known as "Battle Avenue.")*

24. *5, op. cit.*, p. 260, quoting Trevelyan, stating:
"The Delaware regiment, which had learned at Long Island that prisoners are not easily made, unless they make themselves, brought up the rear and fought sullenly and composedly while many of the assailants followed them within shooting range."

25. (Note: The Americans retreated down what is known as Battle Avenue. They crossed the wooden bridge over the Bronx River on a road that later became Main Street. The road was later partly absorbed by the present day Bronx River Parkway. From the bridge the troops made their way to Purdy's Hill.)

26. *5, op. cit.*, p. 266, citing (fn 24-25) "Bancroft, V, 74; Irving, II, 393; Whitton, 149; Hufeland, 144; Greene, FV, 53"

27. *213, op. cit.*, p. 87

28. (Note: Letter on display in the William Clements Library, Ann Arbor, Michigan; original was transferred from the Library of Congress to the National Archives.–Information, courtesy of William Clements Library and Don Luce of U. of Michigan and Cresskill, N.J.)

22

Friday, November 1 . . . Duels In the Hills North Of White Plains: Operation Two

1. *4* TCMAG, p. 682
2. *213* HWP, pp. 4-9
3. *4, loc. cit.*
4. *213, op. cit.*, p. 11
5. (Note: Later named Lake Street.)
6. *213, op. cit.*, pp. 76-77
7. *Ibid.*, p. 78
8. *213, op. cit.*, p. 6, quoting Heath Memoirs
9. *Ibid.*, p. 7
10. *Ibid.*
11. *Ibid.*
12. *Ibid.*
13. *Ibid.*, p. 72 (Note: In his letter of November 2, 1776, *Journal Of the Provincial Congress,* Vo.. II, p. 317, George Clinton mentions the Queen's Light Dragoons and deserters who "come daily over to us.")

14. *213, op. cit.,* p. 81 (Note: The site today is where Broadway intersects Virginia Road at the foot of Miller Hill. The old tree was located in this area. It was mentioned in the Indians' deed of sale to the white men.)

15. *Ibid.,* p. 89

16. *Ibid.*

17. *4, op. cit.,* p. 683

18. *Ibid.*

19. *213, op. cit.,* p. 5

20. *5* WOR, p. 261; and *500* AA 5th V-III, p. 1271

21. *213, op. cit.,* p. 2

22. *500, op. cit.,* p. 1240 (Note: Aide Robert H. Harrison, in this citation, carries out his superior's correspondence orders and writes the President of Congress:

"Head-Quarters, White-Plains, October 25, 1776. . . I am charged by his Excellency to mention it to Congress as a matter that employed much of his thought and that seems worthy of their most serious attention. He has communicated it to several of the Generals and other officers, and to many gentlemen of sense and discernment, who all agree with him not only upon the propriety, but the absolute necessity that two distinct armies should be formed, one to act particularly in the states which lay on the east, the other in those that are on the south of the river. . .")

23. *Ibid.,* p. 1221

24. *Ibid.,* pp. 1280-81

25. *Ibid.,* p. 1284

23

Saturday, November 2. . . The Army Has Its Disillusioned

1. *36* CCNJ, p. 34 (Note: Father Bulger was "de-rided" in the snow, but its occurrence is recorded as of 1820.)

2. *37* "SINNJ" PNJHS V-v (2), p. 80 (Note: Keasbey, in his "Slavery In New Jersey" cites the 1797 State Supreme Court ruling which upheld the enslavement of Indians in New Jersey. He cited the case of Rose, an Indian woman, claimed as a slave. Keasby wrote that "Mr. McWhorter and Richard Stockton claimed that our laws had placed Indians on the same footing as Africans. . . citing that Indians had been so long recognized as slaves in our law that it would be as great a violation of the rights of property to establish a contrary doctrine as it would be in the case of Africans, and as useless to investigate the manner in which they originally lost their freedom."—pp. 79-80)

3. *50* BCHS (RWRTP), p. 77 (Note: Dr. Lewis M. Haggerty gives a detailed account of the difficulties encountered by the Jersey Indians and the trials which beset the Brainerds in the founding of the Brotherton Reservation, or as the Indians called it, "Edge Pillock" in Burlington County.)

4. (Note: The ancient Indian love tragedy surrounding the tale of Chinqueka and her love for the visiting prince is unlike the world's literary lover affairs, such as *Romeo and Juliet, Tristram and Isolde,* and *Hero and Leander,* in that it is founded only in American Indian lore and is, consequently, purely an American love tragedy. The story of Chinqueka, which is the Indian name for "goldfinch," often appears in the legends of the Lenni Lenape. It is very well told in Emogene Van Sickle's "The Old York Road and Its Stage Coach Days." The author locates the clan in the vicinity of Somerville and Bound Brook, New Jersey, and not far from the well known "Chimney Rock" site.)

24

Saturday, November 9 . . . The Great Juggernaut Grinds
To An Ominous Halt

1. *16* MAH-(mwc), pp. 78-79
2. *Ibid.*, p. 78, citing "Force 5th Series, 1294"
3. *Ibid.*
4. *Ibid.*
5. *Ibid.*
6. *Ibid.*, pp. 80-81 (See also *8* SSS V-I, p. 492 quoting part from *Magazine of American History.*)
7. *13* RWHV, p. 56, citing "3 Force (5)556; 2 Greene, Greene 261"
8. *Ibid.*
9. *6* RHSNJ V-I, pp. 230-31
10. *Ibid.*
11. *303* FLNJ, p. 196 quoting from Greene's correspondence, "Fort Lee, October 24, 1776"
12. (Note: General Greene's use of the term "Dobbs Ferry" to indicate the name of the landing place, ferry terminal and outlying American post on the west bank of the Hudson became synonymous with "Sneden's Landing" or "Sneden's Ferry" which was the generally accepted name for the place. There were few settlers in the area outside of the Snedens, the Corbett family and the Herrins who lived somewhat inland. The travelers frequently referred to it as "Dobbs Ferry" which was its east bank terminus. Since one dock was on the Corbett's property, it was also called Corbett's Landing. But the military post established here in the summer of 1776 was more often than not called the "Dobbs Ferry Blockhouse" (See *13* RWHV, p. 267). It was probably "built under the supervision of the French engineer, Colonel Jean Baptiste Gouvion, who had designed and constructed many of the works at West Point and Verplanck's Point," as Leiby points out in citing Heath, *McDougall Papers,* September 22, 1781, the New York Historical Society collections.)
13. *13, op. cit.,* pp. 56-57, citing "2 Greene, Greene 266; 3 Force (5) 629-30"
14. *313*, WGW, p. 258; and *500* AA 5th V-III, p. 557
15. *16, op. cit.,* p. 83, citing "Force 5th series, vol. iii, p. 519"
16. *303, op. cit.,* p. 205
17. *16, loc. cit.,* citing "Force, 5th Series, Vol. iii, p. 602"; also *5* WOR, p. 269, citing "Fitzpatrick, VI, 257-258"
18. *Ibid.*
19. *Ibid.,* citing "Force, 5th Series, Vol. iii, p. 619"
20. *6, op. cit.,* p. 223
21. *303, op. cit.,* p. 191
22. *Ibid.*
23. *Ibid.,* p. 193
24. *20* TTH, p. 165
25. *303, op. cit.,* p. 197
26. (Note: The popular pamphlet, "Common Sense," was published by Paine in January 1776. Proposing independence, it became widely read almost immediately and became a unique, singular accomplishment in the history of the American press. It is not known whether Greene, or anyone else addred Paine as "Common Sense," or is it known whether the Fort Lee commandant so referred to him in discussions with other officers. However, Greene did refer to Paine as "Common Sense" in a letter to his wife on November 2, 1776. — See *303, op. cit.,* p. 204)
27. *5* WOR, p. 275
28. Written especially for *Campaign Of Chaos—1776*
29. Version of old Irish folk song.

30. Version of a popular marching song of the Continental Army.

31. "The Liberty Song" was one of the many hastily composed pieces connected with flag raising ceremonies attending the erection of the country's many liberty poles.

32. Written especially for *Campaign Of Chaos—1776*

33. *48* LWTP V-I, p. xiv

34. *615* MAP-AFW (See D. T. Valentine's Manual for 1861 by George Hayward, 171 Pearl Street, New York, entitled: "East New Jersey Attacks of Fort Washington by His Majesty's Forces under the command of GenL. Sir. Willm Howe K: B. 16 Novr 1776"

35. Written especially for *Campaign of Chaos—1776*

36. *5, op. cit.,* p. 270

37. *16, op. cit.,* p. 82

25

Friday, November 15. . . Hour Of the Ultimatum

1. *5* WOR, p. 276, citing "Force, 5, III, 634, 639"

2. (Note: Housewives who kept a bottle of spirits handy in the house would rush to put such liquors into a secret cupboard when the parson was seen coming to call. Such "secret closets," therefore, acquired the name, "Parson's Cupboards." Home builders took great pride in constructing these well camouflaged cupboards, craftily designed so as to be difficult to detect.)

3. *609* MAP-ERSK-1

4. *500* AA 5th V-I, p. 663; and *303* FLNJ, p. 208

5. *6* RHSNJ V-I, p. 223

6. *13* RWHV, p. 56, citing "Kemble, 101"

7. *Ibid.,* citing, "2 Greene, Greene 266; 3 Force (5) 629"

8. *16* MWC, p. 84, citing, "Force 5th series, vol. iii, p. 653"

9. (Note: See *Memoirs Of Rufus Putnam*, R. Putnam, p. 65)

10. *603* MAP-EWP

11. *16, op. cit.,* p. 84, citing, "British return of ordnance and stores taken 12th October to 20th of November, 1776, Force, 5th Series, vol. iii, pp. 1058-9"

12. *500, op. cit.,* p. 557

13. *6, op. cit.,* p. 223, citing letter from *Pennsylvania Journal and Weekly Advertiser,* November 13, 1776

14. *600* MAP-KAP

15. *13, op. cit.,* p. 57, citing, "6 GW 244"

16. *613* MAP-PHKF

17. *16, loc. cit.,* citing "Force 5th series, vol. iii, p. 653"

18. *32* SPNYS, p. 406

19. *Ibid.,* p. 405

20. *Ibid.*

21. *Ibid.,* p. 407

22. *Ibid.,* p. 406

23. *Ibid.*

24. *Ibid.,* p. 294

25. *16, op. cit.,* p. 82 (Note: Fort George, honoring George III, was named by the British forces after the occupation of the fort by Howe's troops.)

26. *Ibid.,* pp. 66-67

27. *303* FLNJ, p. 210

28. *16, op. cit.,* p. 84

29. (Note: Clinton Point is also mentioned by Leiby; see *13* RWHV, fn 21, p. 58.)

30. *6, op. cit.,* p. 232

31. *Ibid.*
32. *13, op. cit.,* p. 89, citing "6 GW 275; 3 Force (5) 833. Heath Papers MHS."
33. *42* MCL, pp. 277-78; and *41* WOGW V-v, p. 47
34. *16, op. cit.* p. 82
35. *303, op. cit.,* p. 210; and *301* HBCNJ, p. 106; (Note: Known as the "Mansion House," this beautiful old, 18th Century home which was built in 1751, was razed in the mid-Twentieth Century to make room for commercial expansions.)
36. *13, op. cit.,* p. 57, citing "6 GW 244"
37. *5, op. cit.,* p. 269, citing "Bancroft V, 74"
38. *Ibid.*
39. *5, op. cit.,* p. 280
40. *4* TCMAG, p. 684; and *5, op. cit.,* p. 271, citing "Force (5)III, 330"
41. *5, op. cit.,* p. 275
42. *Ibid.,* citing "Force (5) III, 831"
43. *13, op. cit.,* p. 58, fn 21, citing "Greene Papers Transcripts H.L."
44. *Ibid.,* citing "6GW 287"
45. *Ibid.*
46. *5, op. cit.,* p. 459, citing *"Memoirs* of Captain Graydon, p. 186"
47. *4, op. cit.,* p. 683
48. *Ibid.*
49. *Ibid.*
50. *16, op. cit.,* p. 85
51. *Ibid.*
52. *Ibid.*
53. *Ibid.*
54. *13, op. cit.,* p. 7, citing "28 NJA 456"
55. *16, op. cit.,* p. 83
56. *Ibid.,* p. 86; and *13, op. cit.,* p. 59, citing "6 GW 286"
57. *313* WGW V-6, p. 286
58. *5, op. cit.,* p. 270, citing "Fitzpatrick XVI 150-152"

26

Saturday, November 16. . . The Battle For Fort Washington

1. *300* HDFW, p. 51
2. *Ibid.*
3. *Ibid.,* p. 50
4. *Ibid.*
5. (Note: In this Indian legend, recounted in the New Jersey Bell Telephone Company's *Tales of New Jersey* pamphlet, 1963, p. 25, the translation for "Paalochquew" is given as "Little Red Wing" meaning "flirt.")
6. *4* TCMAG, p. 682; and *5* WOR, p. 272, citing "Robertson, III"
7. *8* SSS V-I, p. 490
8. *16* MWC, p. 67
9. *300, op. cit.,* pp. 52-53
10. *4, op. cit.,* p. 683; and *614 A* MAP-AFW
11. *302* MC; and *300, op. cit.,* p. 30
12. *16, op. cit.,* p. 89; and *5* WOR, p. 271
13. *4, op. cit.,* p. 686

14. (Note: Margaret "Molly" Corbin was born in Pennsylvania November 12, 1751, the daughter of Robert Cochran who was killed in an Indian fight in 1756 during which her mother was taken prisoner by the Indian tribe. Shortly after Margaret was married the war broke out and she accompanied her husband, John Corbin, a Pennsylvania regimental artilleryman, to his station at Fort Washington. There, during the battle of Fort Washington, she helped swab and load the cannon to which her husband was assigned.

When he was mortally wounded, she took over its operation until she herself fell severely wounded with three grape shot through her arm. She lived to recover from her wounds but lost the use of one arm and was physically incapacitated for the remainder of her life. Her act brought her recognition as the first American woman to take a soldier's part in the war, and it served to inspire womanhood in greater active participation in the cause of the States.

A year and a half later another "Molly," Mollie Pitcher (Mrs. McCauly), was to take up her gunner husband's sponge when he fell in the Battle of Monmouth. She was to be widely acclaimed for her bravery.

Throughout the highlands of the Hudson where Margaret Corbin spent the remainder of her life and died at the age of 49 in 1800, she was known as "Captain Molly."

The enrollment in the American army's post-war Invalid Regiment for those "rendered by wounds incapable of doing field duty" is attested by "Pennsylvania Archives, 5th Series, iv, 65" as well as in other Revolutionary War Records. The first rations allowed her were inadequate in her handicapped situation and in 1779 the Supreme Council of Pennsylvania voted her a grant of $30, recommending the Congress also lend her its aid.

By a Congressional act in 1779, it was voted to give her "a pension of half the pay of a soldier for the rest of her life and to give her also one complete suit of clothes, or its equivalent in money."

Many years after her death, the childless woman who was buried near her river bank home not far from Cragston Brook in the High Lands, was exhumed. Her remains were transferred to the West Point Military Academy Cemetery. A monument there stands over her grave to her memory. A marker on the Military Cemetery Road indicates the location of the site.

Since there are no authentic records indicating how she was removed from Fort Washington after the battle, most of what happened to her until the year 1779 is a matter of conjecture—Source: "Margaret Corbin, Heroine of the Battle of Fort Washington, 16 November 1776," Edward Hagaman Hall, The American Scenic and Historic Preservation Society, New York, (Pamphlet) 1932.

It should be further noted that a tablet in memory of the Fort Washington heroine was dedicated in the Patriot's Corner of the Church of the Holy Innocents at Highland Falls, designed by Kerr Rainsford, on April 14, 1926.)

15. *300, op. cit.,* p. 26
16. *16, op. cit.,* p. 69, citing "Graydon Memoirs 181"
17. *Ibid.*; also *500* AA 5th V-I, p. 27
18. *Ibid.*
19. *16, op. cit.,* p. 86
20. *13* RWHV, p. 58
21. *8* SSS V-I, p. 492
22. *Ibid.*, p. 493
23. *5, op. cit.,* p. 272
24. *Ibid.*
25. *302, op. cit.,* p. 7
26. *Ibid.* p. 6
27. *5, loc. cit.,* citing "Robertson lll"
28. *16, loc. cit.*
29. *303* FLNJ, p . 87
30. *8, op. cit.,* p. 404
31. *Ibid.*

32. *300, op. cit.,* p. 30
33. *Ibid.,* p. 31
34. *302, loc. cit.,*
35. *8, op. cit.,* p. 493
36. *16, op. cit.,* p. 88
37. *8, loc. cit.,*
38. *Ibid.*
39. *5, op. cit.,* p. 273
40. *8, loc. cit.,*
41. *Ibid.,* p. 494
42. *5, op. cit.,* p. 274
43. *16, loc. cit., 16, loc. cit.*
44. *Ibid.;* and *300, op. cit.,* p. 31
45. *16, op. cit.,* p. 79
46. *300, loc. cit.; 16, op. cit.,* p. 88; *13* RWHV, pp. 59-60, citing "6 GW, 286-287"
47. *300, op. cit.,* p. 119
48. *303, op. cit.,* p. 214; *300, op. cit.,* p. 32
49. *Ibid.* p. 119
50. *16, op. cit.,* p. 89, citing "Force, 5th, iii, 925"; *300, op. cit.,* pp. 31, 119; and *5, loc. cit.,* citing "Force, 5, iii, 1058"
51. *300, op. cit.,* p. 120; *302, op. cit.,* p. 6
52. *Ibid.*
53. *300, op. cit.,* p. 119
54. *Ibid.*
55. *5, op. cit.,* p. 274, citing "Force (5) III, 1058" (Note: Ward, in citing Force, accounts for 2,837 officers and men. Reginald Pelham Bolton in Part IV of "A History of the Defence And Reduction of Fort Washington," *300* on Page 119, cites Commissary Department lists, giving 2,858 as the corrected figure after an original "official" account gave the number as 2,818.)
56. *Ibid.* p. 276, citing "Mackenzie I, 114"
57. *4, loc. cit.*
58. *16, loc. cit.*
59. *4, loc. cit.*
60. *8, op. cit.,* p. 495
61. *500* AA 5th V-II, p. 1170
62. *8, loc. cit.*

27

Monday, November 18 . . . March of the Dead, the Dying and the Doomed

1. *500* AA 5th V-III, p. 763; *302* MC, p. 11 (Note: Hall, citing Force, "5th iii, 751" in Greene to Washington correspondence, states that one American who reportedly escaped on a raft, and came across to Fort Lee on the 17th, was an artilleryman with Rawlings' forces. It has been assumed that someone such as he, who knew the Corbins, assisted her across the river.)
2. *302, op. cit.,* p. 12 (Note: Hall's footnote here states: "Mr. Arthur P. Abbott of Highland Falls, in a statement quoted on Page 143 of the *Annual Report of the American Scenic and Historic Preservation Scoeity,* 1915, says that Margaret Corbin was paroled to Greene across the river at Fort Lee and was carried with other sick and wounded to Philadelphia. The present writer has not found documentary evidence to confirm this statement.")

3. *304* OMP, p. 7
4. *300* HDFW, pp. 120-21
5. *19* ENYC, p. 171
6. *300, loc. cit.*
7. *Ibid.*
8. *Ibid.*
9. *Ibid., p. 122*
10. *Ibid.*
11. *304, op. cit.*, p. 10
12. *Ibid.*, p. 11
13. *300, loc. cit.*
14. *Ibid.*
15. *304, op. cit.*, pp. 13-14
16. *609* MAP - ERSK
17. *6* RHSNJ V-I, p. 236

28

Tuesday, November 19... Soon Comes the Hour For Departure

1. *303* FLNJ, p. 214
2. *500* AA 5th V-III, p. 763
3. *13* RWHV, p. 58
4. *500, op. cit.*, p. 794
5. *Ibid., p. 782*
6. *13, loc. cit.*, citing "Greene papers transcripts H.L." (Note: Hall, in his *Fort Lee, New Jersey,* estimated Greene's forces on the 15th of November, the day before the Fort Washington battle, to be about 2,500 officers and men (See *303* FLNJ, p. 207). However, Leiby, in his *The Revolutionary War In the Hackensack Valley,* quotes Colonel Samuel B. Webb as estimating, "Our whole body (at Fort Lee) did not amount to 2,000 at the time the enemy landed in the Jerseys..." (See *13* RWHV, p. 75, n#74 citing "4 Freeman 261.")
7. *500, op. cit.*, p. 763
8. *13, loc. cit.*, citing "4 Freeman 24"
9. *Ibid.*, p. 57, citing "3 Force (5) 634"
10. *11* RW, p. 98
11. *13, loc. cit.*
12. *609* MAP - ERSK - 1
13. *603* MAP - EWP
14. *500, op. cit.*, p. 787
15. *46* GW, p. 145
16. *13, op. cit.*, p. 61
17. *500, op. cit.*, p. 763
18. *Ibid.*
19. *Ibid.*
20. *Ibid.*, p. 767
21. *Ibid.*
22. *Ibid.*
23. *13, loc. cit.*
24. *Ibid.*
25. *303, op. cit.*, p. 216

29

Wednesday, November 20 . . . Lord Cornwallis Leads the Amphibious Invasion of the Jerseys

1. *500* AA 5th V-III, pp. 779-782, quoting Colonel Harrison - General Schuyler correspondence, dated November 20, 1776

2. (Note: There is little extant evidence outside of the allegedly erroneous historical marker and an old house at the old Closter Dock landing area, called "The Cornwallis House," that there were two riverside homes, or buildings, one at each of the so-called "Closter Docks." But there are sound arguments supporting the authenticity of the site and that stone or frame buildings existed there in 1776.

The Cornwallis invasion historical markers at this so-called "Upper Closter" or "Old Dock," mention the Kearney fisherman as the owner of the old house, located in today's Borough of Alpine.

Under control of the Palisades Interstate Park Commission, it is about a mile north of the so-called "Lower Closter Dock," or "New Dock" landing, which later became known as Huyler's Landing. This latter site, also under jurisdiction of the P.I.P.C., is an extension of the Borough of Cresskill's borders, and Cresskill claims its road and the "New Dock" site were the ones used by the British general and his army.

Nevertheless, in Closter, several miles north, at the foot of the Alpine to Closter road and former trail over the Palisades, a stone marker and plaque commemorate the Closter road and cite an unknown Closter farmer as the "Paul Revere" of the area who informed the Fort Lee garrison.

Meanwhile the town of Cresskill has a county historical marker identifying the Cresskill road as the authentic one. However, Closter retains its marker, claiming the singular honor in the unsolved and unresolved Lord Cornwallis Closter Dock and Farmer Controversy.)

3. (Note: See Note #2 above.)

4. *303* FLNJ, pp. 214-15

5. *Ibid.*; and *4* TCMAG, p. 684

6. *303, op. cit.* p. 216

7. *608* MAP-ERSK-M

8. (Note: Professor Richard McCormick, Rutgers University, contended in 1960 that it was Major John Aldington, a Tory, who led Cornwallis's expedition. See Microfilms, British Records, 1960, filed in New Jersey State Library, Trenton, N.J. There is no record nor proof that Colonel Van Buskirk was with the invasion forces at this time; his presence on the scene is the author's conjecture.)

9. (Note: There is no known record nor proof that William Demont was accompanying Cornwallis. It is the author's conjecture that he was. Since Demont eventually became the British Commissary of Prisoners in Philadelphia and was well acquainted with Fort Lee's defenses, it is a logical assumption that the invasion enterprise would have benefited considerably from his knowledges, particularly in view of the intelligence he provided Howe in the latter's successful assault on Mount Washington. See *16* MWC, pp. 80-81.)

10. (Note: The author's "Hidden Valley" appellation seems appropriate in view of the valley's total concealment from the eyes of those all along the east bank of the Hudson owing to the lofty Palisades which present a veritable wall, screening out New York's view of the valley.)

11. *303, op. cit.,* pp. 214-15

12. *Ibid.,* citing Robert Morris - Silas Deane correspondence

13. *6* RHSNJ-V-I, p. 367

14. *13* RWHV, p. 87

15. (Note: It is alleged by local historians that the so-called "Lone Star Inn" was located north of the Closter Dock Road's intersection with the highway in present-day Closter. It is believed to be the old Blauvelt, Vanderbeck and Parsons homestead.)

16. *500, op. cit.,* pp. 815-18
17. *4, loc. cit.,*
18. *500, op. cit.,* p. 764
19. *Ibid.,* p. 763
20. *6, op. cit.,* pp. 207-8
21. *303, op. cit.,* p. 218
22. *Ibid.*
23. (Note: Revolutionary War historians have searched unsuccessfully through American and British archives in an effort to discover the identity of the rider who notified the Fort Lee garrison November 20. While the town of Closter, N.J., has erected a statue to the "unknown Closter farmer," said to have brought the news, the adjoining community of Cresskill to the south dampens the legend with its contention the invading army came down through Cresskill, not up into Alpine and down into Closter, as some historians claim.

Thus the "farmer" story rests largely on poorly supported evidence. It is this author's opinion that the unknown legendary character is the product of misconstrued semantics.

This belief is based upon the following: (1) The only extant eyewitness account of the event at Fort Lee that day is found in Thomas Paine's "The Crisis" in which Paine states that "an *officer* arrived with information that the enemy with two hundred boats had landed about seven or eight miles above."; (2) In the British army records, General Howe, repeating Cornwallis, (*500, op. cit.,* p. 925), wrote Lord George Germaine on November 30, 1776 stating, "Had not the forces at Fort Lee been warned by a *countryman,* the Continental Army would have been taken." Since the British considered the Americans, rebels, or insurrectionists, they had not as yet deigned to recognize their opponents on an army-to-army military footing and were not prone to use the term "officer" in referring to a rebel soldier. Logically, Howe, would have called him a "countryman." (3) In 1895 Benjamin J. Lossing in his *History Of the United States,* taking Howe's "countryman" to mean "a farmer" wrote loosely, referring to Greene at Fort Lee, "That officer (Greene) was told of his danger by a *farmer* who awoke him from slumber."

Consequently Paine cited him as an "officer." Lord Howe called him a "countryman." Lossing promoted him to a "farmer."

Therefore the author of this work regretfully and reluctantly believes that "the farmer" is possibly a legend concocted from misconstrued semantics, desperately in need of some sound research, as is also the Major Clarke theory.

24. *13, op. cit.,* p. 58, n21, citing Greene's official returns which figure, Hall (*303* FLNJ, p. 207), also uses, citing Greene's "Return of the Forces Camped on the Jersey Shore Commanded By Major-General Greene, November 13, 1776." However, the army, after reaching Newark had picked up the Hackensack and Acquakanonk garrisons and, according to Washington's report to Congress November 23 (See Force, *500* AA 5th V-III, p. 822) then totaled a complement of 5,410 men.

25. (Note: The names chosen by the author in this roll call are a random selection of Continental Army soldiers taken from the 1776 official rosters as found in the following works: *200* ROMNJ; *207* AMH; *201* JEA; *202* NYIR; *203* MMSRW; *204* RSNCAR. Since all of the General Orders of the Continental Army for the period of November 10, 1776 to January 12, 1777, are missing from the War Records Branch of the National Archives and Records Services of the General Services Administration in Washington, D.C., exact roll calls for Fort Lee on this date were not procurable.)

26. *13, op. cit.,* p. 108, n25
27. *500, op. cit.,* p. 779
28. *303, op. cit.,* p. 217
29. *Ibid.,* p. 218
30. *500, loc. cit.*
31. *Ibid.*
32. *13, op. cit.,* p. 67 (Map, "Attack On Fort Lee, November 20, 1776." E. Tone, 1962.)

33. *Ibid.* p. 71, citing "3 Force (5) 1291"; and *23* LWTP, p. 5
34. *500, op. cit.,* p. 1071
35. *23* LWTP, p. 6
36. *8* SSS V-I, p. 496
37. *13, op. cit.,* p. 67
38. *8, loc. cit.*
39. *13, op. cit.,* p. 69, n54, citing "Commager and Morris, p. 496"
40. *8, loc. cit.*
41. *13, op. cit.,* p. 68, n51, citing "Glyn Journal PUL.1 NJA (2) 314, 315"
42. *8, loc. cit.*
43. *Ibid.*
44. *Ibid.* p. 497, citing "Gr. Brit. Hist. Mss. Comm., *Hastings Manuscripts,* III, 190, 192"
45. *Ibid.*
46. *13, op. cit.,* p. 69, n53
47. *4, op. cit.,* p. 686
48. *8, loc. cit.*
49. *4, loc. cit.*
50. *49* WPA - SNJ, p. 2
51. (Note: Leiby (*13* RWHV, p. 68, n51) quotes "Glyn Journal PUL.1 NJA (2) 314, 315", as stating, ". . . but all their sick fell into our hands. . .")
52. *4, op. cit.,* p. 688
53. *49, loc. cit.*
54. *23, op. cit.,* p. 7
55. *50* BCHS-RTP, p. 34 (Note: Fred W. Bogert cites Jones'*The Loyalists of New Jersey,* for this categorical distinction.)
56. *Ibid.*
57. *51* NJCS, p. 137
58. *13, op. cit.,* p. 86, n32, citing "Damages by the British, NJSL, Hackensack Precinct; HBP 79"
59. *Ibid.*
60. *500, op. cit.,* p. 779
61. *Ibid.*
62. *13, op. cit.,* p. 72, citing "Romeyn, Hackensack Church, 26"

30

Thursday, November 21 . . . Retreat
From the Peninsula

1. *5* WOR, p. 28
2. *53* NJA-TE, p. 480
3. (Note: The earliest known wing section of the so-called "Abraham Ackerman House," which stood at 184 Essex Street, Hackensack, New Jersey, was built in 1696. The main section in 1704 bore the initials of the builder and his son and the date, "1704." This house was said by architectural authorities to have been the perfect example of the gambrel roof construction which the Dutch and Huguenot settlers of the valleys designed and perfected and which, owing to the brown sandstone quarried from the ground, their pig's hair, mud and straw mortar, their overhanging eaves, provided their occupants with somewhat of a built-in "air conditioning" system.)
4. *500* AA 5th V-III, p. 795
5. *Ibid.,* p. 790
6. *Ibid.* p. 795
7. *Ibid.* p. 794

8. *Ibid.*
9. *Ibid.*, p. 595
10. *Ibid.*
11. *Ibid.* p. 791
12. *501* AR-P-II, pp. 18-19
13. *301* HBCNJ, p. 106
14. *49* WPA-SNJ, p. 3
15. *8* SSS V-I, p. 496
16. *301, loc. cit.*
17. *13* RWHV, p. 81, n17, citing "Glyn Journal PUL"
18. *Ibid.*
19. *Ibid.* p. 70
20. *301, loc. cit.*
21. *500, op. cit.*, p. 791
22. *Ibid.*
23. *8, loc. cit.*
24. *500, op. cit.*, p. 790
25. *6* RHSNJ-V-I, p. 273
26. *500, op. cit.*, p. 811

31

Thursday, November 28 . . . Newark:
With Hope They Wait For Lee In Vain

1. *13* RWHV, p. 81, n18, citing "Glyn Journal PUL"
2. *5* WOR, p. 281
3. *6* RHSNJ V-I, p. 367
4. New Jersey Historical Commission's *Newsletter*, V II, No. 6 Feb. 1972
5. *500* AA 5th V-III, p. 822
6. *13, op. cit.*, p. 75, n70
7. *500, op. cit.*, p. 831
8. *Ibid.* p. 822
9. *Ibid.*, p. 830
10. *Ibid.*
11. *13, op. cit.*, p. 74, n79
12. *Ibid.*, p. 77, n21, citing "Romeyn, Hackensack Church, 27"
13. *Ibid.*, pp. 54-55
14. *49* WPA-SNJ, p. 3
15. *13, op. cit.*, p. 78, n3
16. *Ibid.*, p. 78
17. *Ibid.*, p. 83
18. *500, op. cit.*, p. 831
19. *Ibid.*; and *8* SSS V-I, pp. 498-99
20. (Note: As contended by William R. Ward, "Washington's Retreat through the Jerseys, 1776," address before the New Jersey Historical Society, Newark, New Jersey, October 27, 1926.)
21. *49, loc. cit.*
22. *500, op. cit.*, p. 839

32

Friday, December 13 . . . End Of the Great Retreat and the Plunge Of the Flaming Meteor

1. *500* AA 5th V-III, p. 822
2. *303* FLNJ, p. 227
3. *Ibid.*
4. *8* SSS V-I, p. 499
5. *6* RHSNJ, pp. 240-41
6. *49* WPA-SNJ, p. 3
7. *Ibid.*
8. *Ibid.*
9. (Note: It is said the Indians called much of present Union County, N.J., "The High Hills." What they and the early settlers called "Turkey Town" became New Providence in 1778.)
10. *5* WOR, p. 280, citing "Gordon, II, 354"
11. *Ibid.*, p. 276, citing "Force, 5, III, 822"
12. *Ibid.*
13. *Ibid.*, citing "Fitzpatrick, VI, 265"
14. *Ibid.*, citing "Trevelyan, Pt. II, Vol. II, 18-19"
15. *Ibid.*, p. 281, citing "Fitzpatrick, VI, 320"
16. *Ibid.*, p. 280
17. *6, op. cit.*, p. 308
18. *500, op. cit.*, p. 839
19. *5, op. cit.*, p. 281, citing "Fitzpatrick, VI, 320-22"
20. *49, loc. cit.*
21. *53* NJA-TE, p. 489
22. *5, op. cit.*, p. 282
23. *Ibid.*, citing "Anderson, 27"
24. *49, loc. cit.*
25. *13* RWHV, p. 82, citing "3 Force (5) 927, Lundin, 159"
26. *303, op. cit.*, p. 225; and *49, loc. cit.*
27. *5, loc. cit.*
28. *6, op. cit.*, p. 274
29. *14* BHUS, p. 120, map, "Campaigns In the North"
30. *5, op. cit.*, p. 283, citing "Fitzpatrick, VI, 333"
31. *Ibid.*
32. *Ibid.*
33. *6, op. cit.*, p. 367, citing Howe-Germaine report, December 20, 1776
34. *Ibid.*
35. *5, op. cit.*, pp. 206-07
36. *Ibid.*, p. 284
37. *Ibid.*, citing "Anderson, 28"
38. *Ibid.*, citing "Lundin, 147"
39. *Ibid.*, citing "Anderson, 28"
40. *6, op. cit.*, p. 368
41. *Ibid.*
42. *6, op. cit.*, p. 367
43. *8, op. cit.*, p. 501
44. *Ibid.*
45. *10* TT, p. 97
46. *303, op. cit.*, p. 227
47. *13, op. cit.*, p. 89, n54, citing "6 GW 275; 3 Force (5) 833, Heath Papers MHS"
48. *303, loc. cit.*

49. *Ibid.*
50. *Ibid.*
51. *10, op. cit.,* p. 94
52. *Ibid.*
53. *303, loc. cit.*
54. *2* SHAR, p. 29-30
55. *Ibid.*
56. *Ibid.*
57. (Note: Now known as Bernardsville, N.J.)
58. *53, op. cit.,* p. 526
59. (Note: Now a part of West Virginia.)
60. *2, loc. cit.*
61. *8, op. cit.,* p. 500, citing "Charles Lee 'Letter,' N.Y. Historical Society Collection, V 348"
62. *Ibid.,* p. 503
63. *Ibid.* citing "Wilkinson, *Memoirs Of My Own Times,* I, 105-06"
64. *6, op. cit.,* p. 368, n2
65. *2, op. cit.,* p. 30, citing "Lee Papers, II, 37"
66. *10, op. cit.,* p. 102
67. *2, op. cit.,* p. 31, citing "Moore, *Treason,* 84-90"
68. *Ibid.,* citing "Baker, W.S., *Exchange Of Major General Charles Lee,* PMHB, XV, 26-34"
69. *5, op. cit.,* p. 667, citing "Trevelyan, Pt. II, 41-49; Bancroft, IV, 232-234, and V, 66-67; Irving, I, 413-419"
70. *8, op. cit.,* p. 504, citing "Fitzpatrick, ed., *Writings Of Washington,* VI, 346-347"
71. *3* MJAR, p. 66

33

Thursday, December 19 . . . The Hour For Decision
Along the Arc of Gloom

1. *14* BHUS, p. 135
2. *5* WOR, p. 290, citing "Force, 5, III, 1201"
3. *Ibid.,* pp. 291-92
4. *500* AA 4th V-I, pp. 103-04
5. *8* SSS V-I, pp. 230-31
6. *5, op. cit.,* p. 292, citing "Irving, II, 469"
7. *14, loc. cit.*
8. *5, op. cit.,* p. 291, citing "Stryker, TP, 48n"
9. *8, op. cit.,* p. 508
10. *6* RHSNJ, pp. 245-47
11. *14, loc. cit.*
12. *8, loc. cit.;* also see *10* TT, p. 108
13. *5, op. cit.,* p. 285
14. *Ibid.,* p. 286
15. *Ibid.,* citing "Fitzpatrick, VI, 346, 355, 381"
16. *Ibid.,* citing "Dunbar, I, 282"
17. *Ibid.,* pp. 281-287
18. *6, op. cit.,* p. 277
19. *5, loc. cit.,* citing "Force (5) III, 1199, 1434; Marshall, C, 105-107"
20. *53,* NJA-TE, p. 483

21. (Note: King later was renamed Warren Street. The Potts' frame house was turned into a tavern and called Wilson's Tavern before the site was purchased for the construction of a church.)
22. *5, op. cit.,* p. 291
23. *Ibid.,* p. 297
24. (Note: The Hunt House was located on what is now Warren and State Streets.)
25. *6, op. cit.,* pp. 432-33
26. *Ibid.*
27. *Ibid.*
28. *Ibid.*
29. *20* TTH, p. 166
30. *6, loc. cit.*

34

Thursday, December 26. . . "All Is Over"

1. *5* WOR, p. 293
2. *10* TT, p. 109
3. *5, loc. cit.*
4. *Ibid.*
5. *Ibid.*
6. *10, op. cit.,* p. 107
7. *20* TTH, pp. 165-70
8. *312* GWAE, January 1, 1777
9. *5, op. cit.,* p. 292, citing "Force, 5, III, 1376. Fitzpatrick, VII, 427n"
10. *Ibid.,* p. 293
11. *10, op. cit.,* p. 109
12. *305* WAD, p. 20
13. *Ibid.,* p. 28
14. *6* RHSNJ V-I, p. 216 n1
15. *8* SSS V-I, pp. 510-11, citing "Fitzpatrick, 30d, 426n - 427n"
16. *Ibid.,* p. 511, citing "Stryker, *Battles Of Trenton and Princeton, pp. 342-43*"
17. *303* FLNJ, p. 222
18. *305, op. cit.,* p. 22
19. *23* LWTP V-III, pp. 1-16
20. *305, op. cit.,* p. 27
21. *Ibid.,* p. 28
22. *10, loc. cit.,*
23. *5, op. cit.,* p. 293-94, citing "Dunbar, I, 282"; *10, op. cit.,* pp. 113-14
24. *Ibid.*
25. *305, op. cit.,* p. 29
26. *Ibid.* p. 27
27. *44* GWEA, p. 210; *312* GWAE, "January 1, 1777"
28. *305, loc. cit.*
29. *306* SNJTC, "Monitor," December 28, 1962, p. 1
30. *5, op. cit.,* p. 296
31. *Ibid.,* p. 297
32. *306, op. cit.,* p. 2
33. *305, op. cit.,* p. 30
34. *5, op. cit.,* p. 295, citing "Stryker, T.P., 362"
35. *Ibid.,* p. 294, citing "Rodney, C, 150-151"
36. *305, op. cit.* p. 32

37. *Ibid.*, p. 31
38., *10, op. cit.*, p. 114
39. *Ibid.*, p. 122
40. *5, op. cit.*, p. 297
41. *Ibid.*, p. 295, citing "Stryker, T.P., 362"
42. *10, op. cit.*, p. 130, citing "article by Marx in *American Heritage*, August 1955. Also, Knollenberg, *George Washington: The Virginia Period*, 1732-1775, Appendix, Chapter II."
43. *Ibid.* p. 114
44. *5, op. cit.*, p. 295, citing "Stryker, T.P., 137"
45. *Ibid.*, p. 294
46. *Ibid.*, citing "Rodney, C, 150-151"
47. *10, op. cit.*, p. 119
48. *8, op. cit.*, p. 512, citing Lisha Bostwick of the 7th Connecticut Regiment in Bostwick, *Memoirs,* letter.
49. *Ibid.*
50. *5, op. cit.*, p. 295
51. *10, op. cit.*, p. 122
52. *6, op. cit.*, p. 433, citing, *"The Pennsylvania Evening Post,* July 26, 1777"
53. *10, op. cit.*, p. 124
54. *Ibid.*, p. 123
55. *5, op. cit.*, p. 298
56. *6, op. cit.*, p. 369
57. *5, op. cit.*, p. 301
58. *10, op. cit.*, p. 128
59. *6, op. cit.*, p. 248, citing "Extract of a letter from an officer of distinction at Newtown, Bucks county, dated December 27, 1776." (Note: The "officer of distinction" quoted by Stryker is very likely General William Alexander, Lord Stirling, since Ward, *5* WOR, p. 302, states along with others that the prisoners were under his care.)
60. *10, op. cit.*, p. 125
61. *63* AHAR, pp. 172-173
62. *5, op. cit.,,* p. 302, citing "Force, 5, III, 1443, 1445-1446"
63. *306, op. cit.*, *The Monitor,* December 28, 1962, "With Him All Is Over" by John T. Cunningham
64. *5, loc. cit.*
65. *Ibid.*
66. *Ibid.*, p. 303, citing "Rodney, C, 150"
67. *6, loc. cit.*
68. *5, op. cit.*, p. 302
69. *33* WNJC, p. 151 (Note: Richardson, citing a "letter to General Caesar Rodney" states that Haslet "fell into the Delaware at 3 o'clock in the morning, and he has had swelled legs ever since.")
70. *6, op. cit.*, p. 249, citing "The Pennsylvania Evening Post, December 31, 1776"
71. *Ibid.*
72. *5, op. cit.*, pp. 304-305, citing "Stryker, TP, 213"
73. *10, op. cit.*, p. 104
74. *5, op. cit.*, p. 303, citing "Trevelyan, Pt. II, Vol. II, 113"
75. *13* RWHV, p. 101
76. *5, op. cit.*, p. 305, citing *"Journals,* VI, 1045"
77. *7* AR, p. 111, n25, citing *The Journal Of Nicholas Cresswell,* 1774-1777 (New York, 1924), pp. 178-180
78. *5, op. cit.*, p. 303
79. *10, op. cit.*, p. 126; *8, op. cit.*, p. 516 (Note: Epitaph translation is, "Here lies Colonel Rall. With him all is over.")
80. *6, op. cit.*, p. 267, citing "a paper undoubtedly written by Governor Livingston" and signed, "An American Whig—*The Pennsylvania Evening Post*, January 21, 1777"

35

Friday, January 3 . . . The Long Campaign Closes On A Crimson Path in Prince Town

1. *6* RHSNJ, p. 249
2. *Ibid.*
3. *63* AHAR, p. 173
4. *Ibid.*
5. *5* WOR, p. 306, citing "Fitzpatrick, VI, 445, 446"
6. *Ibid.*, p. 307, citing Irving, II, 494"
7. *Ibid.*, citing "Reed, I, 278-280"
8. *Ibid.*, citing "Rodney, T, 25"
9. *10* TT, p. 132
10. *20* TTH, p. 170
11. *Ibid.*
12. *Ibid.* p. 171
13. *5, op. cit.*, p. 308, citing "Fitzpatrick, VI, 457-458"
14. *Ibid.*, p. 462. "Notes, Chapter 27", n9
15. *Ibid.*, and p. 308; *20, op. cit.*, p. 170, all citing "Force, 5, III, 1486"
16. *20, loc. cit.*
17. *5, loc. cit.*, citing "Stephenson, I, 386"
18. *10, op. cit.*, p. 137
19. *5, op. cit.*, p. 307, citing "Reed, I, 281; Fitzpatrick, VI, 447-450"
20. *Ibid.*
21. *6* RHSNJ V-I, pp. 368-69
22. *5, op. cit.*, p. 309
23. *Ibid.*, citing "Stryker, TP, 259"
24. *10, op. cit.*, p. 132
25. *8* SSS V-I, p. 518
26. *53* NJA-TE, p. 188
27. *Ibid.*, p. 445
28. (Note: Sir Francis Bacon's *Of Truth*)
29. (Note: Blaise Pascal's *Thoughts,* Chapter 10, 1)
30. *307* TDR, p. 56
31. *Ibid.*
32. *Ibid.*
33. *Ibid.*, pp. 56-57
34. *5, op. cit.*, p. 311
35. *Ibid.*, citing "Rodney, T, 32-33"
36. *Ibid.*, citing "Stryker, TP, 276"
37. *6, op. cit.*, pp. 347-350, citing "*The Pennsylvania Evening Post* report of the Congress's April **18**, 1777, 'Committee Appointed to inquire into the conduct of the enemy' "
38. *5, op. cit.*, p. 312, citing "Rodney, T, 32"
39. *Ibid.*
40. *10, op. cit.*, p. 141
41. *8, op. cit.*, p. 520
42. *6, op. cit.*, p. 332; and *10, op. cit.*, p. 142
43. *5, op. cit.*, p. 314, citing "Rodney T. 34"
44. *6, op. cit.*, p. 260
45. *10, op. cit.*, p. 142
46. *5, loc. cit.*,
47. *Ibid.*
48. *10, op. cit.*, p. 143

49. *Ibid.*
50. *5, op. cit.,* p. 315, citing "Rodney T, 36"
51. *Ibid.*
52. *Ibid.,* p. 316
53. *Ibid.,* p. 215; and *63* AHAR, p. 206
54. *6, op. cit.,* p. 269
55. *Ibid.,* p. 265
56. (Note: Spelling of "Milstone" is taken from Erskine's 18th Century survey maps, Map #612, Section 4, indicating that original name may have been derived from mile + stone, or "milestone," rather than as contemporary spelling of the river and town implies, mill + stone, or "millstone.")
57. *5, op. cit.,* p. 317, citing "Fitzpatrick, VI, 470"
[Notes 58 to 62 inclusive were deleted in revision and shortening·of Chapter 35]
63. *217* ABH, p. 98
64. *Ibid.,* p. 100
65. *6, op. cit.,* p. 252
66. *Ibid.*
67. *Ibid.,* p. 370, citing "Extract of a letter from General Sir William Howe to Lord George Germaine, dated New-York, January 5, 1777"
68. *Ibid.,* pp. 370-371, citing "New York Gazette and Weekly Mercury, May 12, 1777"
69. *8, op. cit.,* p. 521
70. *6, op. cit.,* p. 257
71. *Ibid.,* p. 268, citing *"The Pennsylvania Packet,* January 22, 1777"
72. *Ibid.,* p. 370
73. *63* AHAR, p. 141

Historical Index

1135

Acknowledgement

In addition to so many who have generously assisted in the backstage efforts of this work, particularly his wife, critic and editor, for her wise counsel, patience and encouragement, the author desires to acknowledge, in a special niche by herself, his mother,

. . . Jennie Louise Clynes Henderson, 1879–1924 . . .

from whom he learned so much in such a beautiful, inspiring, but such a very brief association.

The End